Higher education...

The glare of an unfamiliar street lamp shining through the window woke Sam out of a restless sleep. She rolled over with a little moan—her head was buzzing and her mouth felt dry as cotton. What time was it? she wondered. Turning her head slightly, she saw the fluorescent glow of a small clock on a bedside table. 3 A.M. Beside her, a warm body stirred slightly, and she could feel an arm under her neck.

Suddenly Sam was wide awake. The body next to her—it was Aaron! They were in Aaron's suite, together, and it was three o'clock in the morning. She lay there, not moving a muscle, for several minutes, several *long* minutes, while the memory of what had happened just a few hours earlier flooded over her. Oh, no! What had she done?

Roommates

ALL-NIGHTER
Susan Blake

IVY BOOKS • NEW YORK

Ivy Books
Published by Ballantine Books

Copyright © 1987 by Butterfield Press, Inc. & Susan Wittig

Produced by Butterfield Press, Inc.
133 Fifth Avenue
New York, New York 10003

Library of Congress Catalog Card Number: 86-91848

ISBN 0-8041-0022-5

Manufactured in the United States of America

First Edition: June 1987

ALL-NIGHTER

Chapter 1

"Hi—anybody home?"

Loaded down with the books she'd just bought at the Hawthorne College bookstore, Samantha Hill stood in the doorway of Rogers House suite 2C. The living room floor was buried under even more half-empty boxes, bags, and suitcases than when she had left. A pair of Roni Davies's purple leotards were draped over the back of the green plaid sofa, and someone had left a plate of limp-looking celery sticks and a can of onion dip on top of Terry Conklin's stack of high school notebooks. Sam couldn't help grinning. Suite 2C was beginning to look like home.

"Hi," said Terry, coming out of her bedroom. As usual, she was wearing a pair of dark pants and a white blouse—they even looked like a uniform. She was carrying a thick book. "Did you find it?"

"Yes, I found it," Sam said, dropping her purchases with a thud on the coffee table. To cool off, she lifted her long wheat-blond hair off her shoulders and pulled it back into a ponytail with a rubber band she picked up from the floor. "But I'm afraid that you're not going to like the price," she added. "It was thirty-seven dollars."

"Thirty-seven dollars?" Terry yelped. She ran her hand through her hair. "For a chemistry book?"

"That's a small enough price to pay for becoming a doctor, isn't it?" Roni drawled, coming into the suite behind Sam. "I mean, after you graduate from Harvard med school you'll be making a mint, won't you?"

Glancing at Roni, Sam stifled a grin. This afternoon, her new suitemate was wearing skintight black leggings cropped at the ankles, a loose metallic-gold top that just reached her thighs, and a green scarf draped around her neck. Her auburn hair tumbled over her shoulders, and her sparkling green eyes were circled with gold eyeliner. She was barefoot. But this costume was conservative, compared with the outrageously sexy sheer pink tank top Roni had worn the day before. Sam wondered sometimes how tiny, conservative Hawthorne College and outrageous Roni Davies were going to survive each other.

Terry shrugged in response to Roni's question. "I won't be making money until *years* from now. And right now, I've got exactly forty-one dollars in my bank account." She looked down at the book. "I *had* forty-one dollars," she said with a mournful expression. "Now I've only got four."

"You can wait to pay me," Sam said, opening a

copy of one of her own books and leafing through it. "I've got plenty—for a while, anyway." Sam was used to lending money. Back home in Lewisboro, Illinois, her four younger brothers and sisters frequently overspent their allowances, and Sam bailed them out. It came with the territory of being the number-one child, along with the privilege of playing peacemaker among your younger siblings.

"That's okay," Terry said. "My scholarship check should be here any day now. But thanks anyway. I—"

"Pardon me. Is this suite two C?" inquired a cool voice.

Sam turned. The girl who stood in the door was tall and willow thin, with smooth, shoulder-length ash-blond hair and a gorgeous face, flawlessly made up. She was wearing a beige linen suit with a large-shouldered jacket and beige snakeskin pumps. She carried an expensive-looking leather suitcase.

"Don't tell us," Roni said, "you're Stacy! The elusive, mysterious Anastasia Vaughn Swanson, from Boston, Mass. The last of the 'sweet two C's.'" The way she said it, "two C" rhymed with "juicy."

"I suppose I *am* a little late," Stacy conceded in a breathy voice with a sophisticated accent. She dropped her suitcase in the doorway. "But I just got back from three months in Europe, and there were one or two things I had to attend to in Boston." When Stacy spoke, the word "Boston" came out sounding like "Bah-stan."

Sam came forward. "Oh, it's no problem, really," she said reassuringly. "Some of the others haven't shown up yet, either." She held out her hand and Stacy took it. "I'm your roommate, Sam Hill. And this is Roni Davies and Terry Conklin."

Stacy smiled. "It's good to meet you," she said rather formally.

Roni bounced onto the sofa, lifting her arms like a cheerleader. "Now that we're all here," she said, "let's hear it for the sweet two c's and the start of a wild and woolly year. All together now! Rah! Rah! Rah!" Sam, Terry, and Stacy just watched her. "What's the matter, gang?" she demanded, dropping her hands to her hips. When no one replied, Roni made a face and jumped off the sofa. "Y'all have positively no spunk," she complained. "Well, never mind. Stace, can we help you carry things from your car?"

While Stacy was trying to find room for all her clothes in her closet, Sam wandered onto the living room balcony and propped her elbows on the rail, her chin on her hands. She gazed down at Hawthorne Lake, which marked the center of the campus. Velvety green lawns cut by shaded paths surrounded the lake. For the past three mornings Sam had jogged around the lake. At an early hour, the scene was almost like the countryside around Lewisboro. But now the paths were crowded with freshmen at Hawthorne for Orientation Week, headed for lunch in the central dining hall. People clustered in groups of two and three, shouting back and forth to friends they seemed to know well already, even though everyone had arrived only a couple of days earlier. All of a sudden, Lewisboro seemed very far away.

Sam had been planning for this feeling since winter,

when she had received her acceptance letter from Hawthorne. In fact, by March, after hours of poring over the catalog and consulting with Jon, she had organized her entire college career. She would take five courses each semester so that she could spend her summers at home, working in her father's farm equipment business just as she had done for the last three years. And she would major in English, so that when she graduated she could go back to Lewisboro, get her teaching certificate, and teach at Lewisboro Regional High. And—of course—marry Jon Mayer.

At the thought of Jon, Sam's mouth curved in a soft smile. Although she and Jon had been together for nearly four years, she could still remember the first time they had met, across the second-period study hall table back at Lewisboro High. He had accidentally knocked her books off the edge of the table. When she'd bent over to pick them up, he had stepped on her fingers. He had ridden home on her bus to apologize and ended up staying for supper. They were only sophomores, but they had known right away how right they were for one another. They liked the very same things: hiking through the woods, taking their bikes for long rides in the countryside, dancing to country and western music, watching old movies on television while they munched popcorn—extra butter. They agreed on just about everything from pizza to politics.

Their friends told them they even *looked* as if they were made for each other. Sam was taller than most girls, but Jon was tall enough that she fitted comfortably under the curve of his shoulder. Her long hair, the color of harvest wheat, was the very same shade as his, and they both had a generous sprinkling of freckles across their noses. They both even had blue eyes. Even if you were going just by looks, they had been the best-matched couple at Lewisboro High.

Since grade school, however, Jon had planned to study engineering at the University of Illinois. Sam had always wanted to go to Hawthorne, where her mother had gone twenty-five years before. But Sam was confident that it would work out. After all, they'd be home for Thanksgiving and Christmas and spring break, and they could write and telephone each other in the meantime. Distance couldn't hurt a relationship as secure as theirs.

"What would you think about buying a portable stereo just for our room?" Roni's southern drawl drifted through the open window next to the balcony. "I saw one in town yesterday that would be perfect. It's got dual cassette decks and super speakers, and we could take it out by the lake when we wanted to."

Sam listened thoughtfully. From their first meeting she had liked Roni, who came from Atlanta, which was only about sixty miles to the south of Hawthorne Springs, the town the college was in. Roni had a daredevil streak in her that fascinated Sam, who prided herself on getting to the top by following all the rules. Roni talked as if she *lived* to break the rules. Of course, it helped that her parents obviously were generous with their cash and credit cards. It no doubt made rule breaking a lot easier.

"But I don't understand," Terry was saying plaintively. "What's wrong with the stereo that Sam brought?"

"It's in the living room, that's what's wrong with it," replied Roni. "I thought it would be nice if we had one for *our* room."

"But I need to study in here," Terry pointed out. "I have to study pretty hard if I'm going to get into a good medical school."

"Well, I don't think a little rock music ever keeps anybody from studying," Roni observed. There was a bang, as if she had slammed a drawer.

"But I can't *afford* a new stereo," Terry protested. "Not even half of one. In fact, I'm running over my budget already, and school hasn't even started yet."

"I see," said Roni. There was a silence. "Well, maybe I'll go ahead and buy a stereo and we can share it. What do you think of that?"

"But I don't think . . ."

Sam didn't hear what Terry didn't think. There was a knock on the door and she went back into the living room to answer it.

"Hi! I'm going over to the Commons and see what LuAnn is dishing up for lunch. Anyone want to come along?"

It was Pam Mason, their resident adviser. As RA, Pam was a sort of combination adviser and monitor for the forty girls who lived on the second floor of Rogers House, which was Hawthorne's freshman women's dorm. She was a chubby, redheaded junior who seemed to take her job as den mother and confidante to the new freshmen—or "freshpersons," as she called them—very seriously.

"Let me check," Sam said. She went to the door of the bedroom she shared with Stacy. "Hey, Stacy," she said, poking her head through the door. "How about walking over to the Commons for lunch?"

Stacy was sitting on her now carefully made bed, wearing an ivory-colored camisole over lace panties and stroking a stuffed tiger. "Lunch?" she said, coming out of her reverie with a start. "No, I don't think so. I'm not hungry."

Sam stared at her roommate. Now that Stacy had stripped down, Sam could see that she was extremely thin. "How about if I bring you a sandwich?" she asked tentatively. "Or I could make a salad for you."

Stacy smiled at her. When she smiled, her face seemed softer and rounder. "Well, you could bring me something to drink, if you wanted to," she replied, rolling over on her stomach and pillowing her head on her hands. "Something diet." She shut her eyes, then opened them and smiled again. "Thanks, Sam."

Sam closed the door just as Roni and Terry came out of their bedroom. "Anyone for lunch?" she asked. "Pam and I are going to the Commons."

"Me," Terry said quickly.

Roni shook her head. There was a pouty look on her mouth like the one Sam's little sister always wore when she couldn't get her way.

"Are you sure?" Sam asked.

"Yeah," said Roni, slinging her leather purse over her shoulder. "I'm going to hitchhike to the mall and go shopping. I'll get something to eat while I'm there." The mall was about three miles away.

Sam frowned. "Hitchhike?" Back in Lewisboro, hitchhiking was something everybody told you *never* to do, even when your car broke down.

"Sure. I do it all the time. I hitched to school every morning back in Atlanta." She giggled. "I went to this classy prep school, and it was really a kick to see the teachers' faces when I got out of a different delivery truck every morning."

Pam spoke up. "Yeah, maybe it *was* a kick. But do you think it's smart?"

Roni tossed her auburn hair defiantly and hitched up the shoulder of her top. "I can take care of myself. I'm a big girl."

"Sure," Pam said, giving her an appraising glance. "Well, have fun at the mall." She turned to Sam and Terry as the three girls left the suite. "So, you two, what do you think of college now that you've been here three whole days? Have you learned anything yet?"

"Well," Terry said soberly, "I haven't really had time to start the reading for my classes. I've been reviewing for placement tests."

Sam couldn't help smiling at Terry's completely serious answer. She thought of Terry's argument with Roni. Would two such completely different girls ever manage to live peacefully in one small room? Then she thought of Stacy—Stacy, who came from "Bah-stan" and drove into Hawthorne Springs in a Mercedes and snakeskin pumps. What would she and Sam ever find they had in common?

"I've learned something already," she said to Terry and Pam. "I've learned I've got a lot to learn."

Chapter 2

At the dining hall, which was in the Student Union building called the Commons, most of the freshmen still didn't seem to know what they were doing. They milled around outside the double doors to the dining hall, searching in pockets and purses for missing meal tickets, looking for the handful of RAs and upper class orientation volunteers they could safely follow. With Pam leading, Sam and Terry made their way through the crowd and got into the lunch line.

When they had filled their plates and the checker had punched their meal tickets, they found a table beside a window overlooking the lake. A boy and girl, paddles in hand, skimmed past the window in a yellow canoe, headed for the small wooded island in the middle of the lake. Sam stared at them; she felt suddenly lonely for Jon. They had gone canoeing sometimes on the lake outside Lewisboro.

Pam picked up her fork and glanced at Terry. "So

tell me about yourself, Ms. Conklin," she said, smiling. "You're from Philadelphia, right?"

Sam pulled her gaze away from the couple on the lake and looked at Terry. While she and Roni had already spent their evenings sprawled in the living room, talking about things—their hometowns, guys, why they'd come to Hawthorne—Terry had mostly listened. It wasn't that she was shy, exactly, Sam thought. It was just that she didn't seem to want to reveal too much about herself.

"Yes, I'm from Philadelphia," Terry replied. She looked away.

"And?" Pam asked, forking up a bite of salad. "There's got to be more to the Terry Conklin story."

Terry shrugged. "Not much," she said. "My dad is a tool-and-die maker in a machine shop. My mother clerks in a drugstore. My brother is dead."

Sam looked up at her, surprised. "I'm sorry," she said. "Was it a long time ago?"

"Two years," Terry said. She poured milk out of her carton into her glass. "Let's not talk about it, okay?"

"Okay," Pam said sympathetically. She turned to Sam. "What about you, Sam?"

Sam picked up a piece of cauliflower and began to munch on it. "I'm from a small town in Illinois. My dad sells farm machinery and my mother teaches school, and I've got two brothers and two sisters younger than me and an orange cat named Bloomfield." She paused, thinking with unexpected wistfulness about Bloomfield, who nipped people's ankles at the table until somebody gave in and sneaked him a bit of food. He especially liked peanut butter.

"That's all?" Pam queried. "How about a boyfriend?" She looked at Sam and Terry expectantly.

Terry shrugged, looking vaguely discontented. "I never had a lot of time for boys back in high school," she said, "what with studying and working. And I don't think things are going to be much different here." She paused and looked at Sam. "But Sam's got Jon."

"Who's Jon?"

"Sam's boyfriend back home," Terry explained. "Except that he's not at home just now. He's at the University of Illinois, studying to be an engineer." She grinned at Sam. "Sam has already told us all about her and Jon. At least twice."

"I see." Pam nodded, wrinkling her freckled nose, "One of *those*."

"What do you mean, one of *those*?" Sam asked suspiciously.

Pam shrugged. "The hometown honey syndrome. One of the most common freshman-year complaints."

"But it's not a complaint for me," Sam protested. She finished her salad and pushed her plate away. "I mean, both of us know exactly what we want, and we're willing to wait for it."

"That's what they all say," Pam told her. "At least, for the first month or two."

"What happens after that?" Terry asked curiously.

"After that, one of them usually decides that studying alone is a drag, or falls in love with somebody else, or goes off on a wild weekend fling with someone else —which naturally makes the other one mad. In the end, of course, they break up."

"But that's not going to happen to Jon and me,"

Sam protested. She put down her fork and folded her arms on the table. "We've been together for too long. When we say we're not going to date anybody else, we really *mean* it." She frowned. "And as for a week-end fling, that kind of thing is out of the question. Definitely."

With a smile, Pam reached out and touched her hand. "I'm not saying it will happen to you," she replied mildly. "I'm just telling you what *usually* happens to other people. I know, it happened to me my fresh-man year."

"To you?" asked Terry.

"Yeah." Pam gazed reflectively out the window. "He was at Princeton. He wrote every week for the first month. And then every two weeks. And then he called to tell me he was getting engaged at Christmas. To somebody else."

Sam thought how awful it would be if Jon did some-thing like that. But of course he wouldn't. And the idea of doing anything like that herself was unimaginable. "I'm sorry," she said.

"Hey, don't be," Pam replied. "It was the best thing that could have happened to me. It made me really wake up and think about who I am and what I want out of life instead of just floating along, doing the easy thing."

"Well, maybe it was good for you," Sam said stiffly. She wasn't sure she wanted to hear this. "But what we have together is really special, and—"

"Of course it is," Pam interrupted. "And I'm not saying that it will happen to you and Jon. Who knows? Maybe you're the exception that proves the rule."

Sam looked out the window. On the island, the couple had reappeared and were pushing the yellow canoe into the water. The girl looked up at the boy and smiled. He touched her arm, then bent to kiss her quickly. Sam looked away. It was almost too private—and too painfully touching—to watch. Now that she thought about it, Thanksgiving seemed like an impossibly long time away.

"Aren't you going to get dressed, Stacy?" Sam asked. "It'll be time to go over to the dean's house in a few minutes, and Pam said she didn't want anybody from her floor to be late."

It was Friday afternoon, and the girls in suite 2C were getting ready to go to a tea at Dean Peters's house. It was the last major event of Orientation Week. The boys would be wearing jackets and ties, and the girls were supposed to wear something dressy.

"I want the girls on my floor to be the most elegant ones at the party," Pam had told them.

"How ridiculous," Roni had muttered, screwing up her face.

"Listen, be grateful for small favors," Pam had said, laughing at Roni. "At least we don't have to wear white gloves anymore, which was expected when I was a freshman. But we all still line up and parade past Dean and Mrs. Peters, and shake hands. Mrs. Peters wears white gloves," she'd added.

Roni had groaned. "It sounds just like the crummy deb teas I used to have to go to back in Atlanta. A real pain."

Pam had gotten more serious. "Yeah, well, Hawthorne prides itself on teaching us how to be civilized, not just educated wild animals."

Roni had groaned again—more loudly, this time. "God, that sounds so pompous," she'd protested. "What if we don't *want* to be civilized? What if we *want* to be a bunch of wild animals?" Everybody had laughed as the meeting had broken up.

Now, as the other girls dressed, Stacy glanced up at Sam and shrugged carelessly. She was sitting at the desk on her side of their room, thumbing idly through a fashion magazine. In contrast with Sam's desk, which was already piled high with books and notebooks, Stacy's was carefully organized, with books squarely stacked and pens and pencils in little jars. "I don't think I'm going," she replied. "It's bound to be boring."

"But Pam said we *had* to go," Sam reminded her. "It's a compulsory affair."

"Tell Pam I'm not feeling well or something." Stacy flipped a page. "The last affair I went to was given by one of my father's campaign backers. Actually, it was more like a cocktail party, not a tea." She turned another page and added casually, "A sheikh asked me to go out with him."

"A sheikh?"

"You know. As in Saudi Arabia, or some silly place like that. He was wearing an Arabian headdress and two diamond rings."

"Oh." Sam could see that if you had been to affairs that were really more like cocktail parties where sheikhs wearing diamond rings asked you for a date, you might be bored going to a tea where all you did was shake hands with the dean and his wife. Still, Stacy had cut most of the orientation activities. She seemed to be hanging around the suite a lot, reading magazines and watching television. "I understand how you feel," Sam said, "but it would really be nice if all four of us could go together."

"Oh?" Stacy asked, looking up. "Why?"

"Because, well . . . because we're suitemates, that's why," Sam said helplessly. She reached into her closet for her most elegant dress, the white crepe with the circle skirt and low V neck that she had worn to her high school graduation dance. She'd been living in jeans and shorts all summer; it felt a little funny putting on a real dress and high-heeled sandals.

Stacy sighed and closed the magazine. "Well, if you're going to insist," she said with an air of reluctance.

"I'm not insisting, exactly." Sam slipped the dress over her head and zipped it up. "I'm just saying that it would be nice to—"

"Hey, has anybody seen Roni?" Terry popped her head into the room. She was wearing a dark blue old-fashioned dress with a prim lace collar. The color didn't do very much for her olive skin and dark brown hair. She wore a pair of low, square-heeled pumps.

"Roni walked over to Grove Street this afternoon," Sam replied, starting to put in her pearl earrings. "She said something about getting an outfit to wear to the party. Isn't she back yet?"

"Well, maybe you're right," Stacy said. "Maybe it would be nice." She was looking at Sam. Suddenly she stood up and went to her jewelry box. "These might look nice with your dress," she said. She held out a long strand of shimmering pearls. "There are earrings to match."

"Oh, Stace, *could* I?" Sam whispered, reaching out to touch them. "They're beautiful!"

"Yeah, sure." Stacy came up behind Sam and fastened the pearls around her neck. Then she lifted Sam's straight, heavy blond hair. "Do you ever wear it up?" she asked.

"Only in a French braid or a ponytail," Sam replied. "Why?"

"Sit down," Stacy commanded. "There," she said a moment later. She patted Sam's shoulder and turned her to face the mirror. She had knotted Sam's long hair into a sleek twist at the back of her head and fastened it with a gold clip. "Do you like it?"

"Wow," Terry said admiringly. "Is that really *you* in there, Sam?"

Sam stared at herself. "It . . . it's beautiful," she said. The girl who gazed back at her from the mirror looked like her much more mature, older sister. Her sun-bronzed skin glowed against the white dress, and Stacy's fabulous pearls glistened in the curve of her throat and at her ears. Her wheat-blond hair, lifted high and twisted on the back of her head with an unaccustomed elegance, had transformed her. She felt a little like Cinderella must have after she'd been tapped by her godmother's wand.

Sam glanced up. A smile lit Stacy's eyes and softened her face. "Thank you, Stacy," she said. "Terry's right. I barely recognize myself."

"That's what parties are for," Stacy said lightly.

* * *

The tea was already crowded by the time Sam, Stacy, and Terry arrived at the dean's house, close to the center of campus. The house was a white-columned southern mansion that looked as if it had come to life right out of *Gone With the Wind*, and Sam half expected to see Scarlett O'Hara step out onto the veranda, wearing a hoop-skirted ball gown.

As the girls came in, they filled out stick-on name tags at a table just inside the door and joined the reception line. The dean wore a slight frown behind his gold-rimmed glasses. His slender, pretty wife beamed at each student and introduced herself with a refined southern accent. She *was* wearing white gloves.

"So glad to meet you," Sam murmured politely to Mrs. Peters, relieved now that *that* unfamiliar duty was behind her. She escaped from the reception line to the dining room, where a refreshment table was set up, and waiters in neat gray uniforms poured punch and handed out little plates of sandwiches cut into stars and circles.

For a few minutes Sam wandered around the house, carrying her sandwich plate and gazing wide-eyed at the heavy, elaborately carved furniture and the crystal chandeliers that glittered in every room. People stood throughout the house in small clusters, wearing their best clothes and speaking hesitantly in muted voices while they tried not to drop crumbs on the Oriental rugs. It was the *stiffest* party Sam had ever been to. She caught a glimpse of Stacy, wearing a simple blue silk dress, staring out across the roomful of people. Although she looked bored, she also looked very much at ease, as if she went to this sort of party every day.

Sam definitely did not feel at ease. Even though she knew she looked quite sophisticated, she still felt like a small-town hick who might at any moment knock over some priceless antique or spill punch on the rug. She was more used to hamburgers on the grill in the back-yard and parties where people played violent games of volleyball in shorts and sweaty T-shirts. All this sedate southern elegance just wasn't normal.

"Don't worry. They'll only subject you to this high-brow stuff once or twice a year," said a self-assured voice in a strong Brooklyn accent.

Sam turned. The boy who had spoken to her was tall and dark, with curly hair and brown eyes that snapped as he spoke. She couldn't say that he was good-looking, exactly, but he had an air of energetic curiosity, and his gaze was penetrating. "That is," he added, "unless you're a southern-belle type who hap-pens to *like* eating fancy finger sandwiches and drinking punch out of ridiculous little cups with your little finger hooked out. If so, you can probably find a party like this somewhere on campus at least once a week."

"I don't intend to go looking." Sam smiled.

The boy leaned forward and stared at her name tag. "Sam," he said thoughtfully. He grinned, and Sam saw that one front tooth was a little crooked. "Sam Hill. Too bad. Does anyone ever ask you, 'What the Sam Hill . . .'?"

Sam stiffened. She had thought college would be a place where she could get away from boring, juvenile jokes about her name. "Actually, no," she said in a chilly voice, stepping back. "Sam happens to be short for Samantha." She looked at his lapel. The boy wasn't wearing a name tag.

"Pardon *me*," he said, arching an eyebrow. "Samantha. I should have known." He looked over her shoulder. "I think I see someone I know. Have fun." And he brushed past her and was gone.

What a *rude* person, Sam thought, staring after him. What if all the other boys at Hawthorne were like that? But it didn't really matter. She hadn't come to Hawthorne to find a boyfriend.

She had barely finished the thought when another boy approached her, smiling confidently. This one was blond and good-looking.

"You're a freshman, too?" he asked, holding out his hand. "My name is Charlie." He glanced down at his name tag. "I guess you already knew that."

Sam put down her cup on a small table and shook the boy's hand, feeling slightly silly. Back home, nobody shook hands, except at weddings, and generally the people shaking hands were only uncles and aunts. "I'm Sam," she said. She looked down at her name tag. "I guess you knew that already, too," she said, and giggled.

"So what do you think about the party?" Charlie asked. "Are you enjoying yourself?"

Sam glanced up at the painting over the fireplace— a portrait of a stern-faced nineteenth-century matriarch. "I keep having this funny feeling," she said, "that someone's looking over my shoulder."

Charlie laughed. "Hey, don't knock Mrs. Eliza Louise Hawthorne," he said. "Didn't anybody clue you in on the identity of our noble benefactress?"

Sam gave the portrait a closer look. "Oh, you mean *she's* the Hawthorne that started the college? Forgive me, Eliza Louise," she added reverently. "I didn't know."

Charlie laughed. "Listen I'm running low on liquids. Can I get you another punch?"

Sam glanced down at her empty cup. "Sure. Thanks," she said, handing it to him.

As soon as Charlie went for a refill, two more boys approached her.

"Hi, I'm Stuart," said one of them. When his friend said nothing, Stuart gave him a jab in the ribs.

"Oh, uh, I'm, uh, Joe," the other guy said. Sam laughed. She never had so much attention in her life. She looked down hastily. Was it the low-necked dress? Or perhaps it was the way Stacy had fixed her hair. Whatever it was, Sam had to admit that she was enjoying her popularity.

When Charlie came back with the punch, he had to elbow his way to her side.

"So this is what happens when I leave you alone," he said with a teasing smile, handing her a cup.

"Charlie, this is Joe," Sam replied, blushing. "And this is Stuart."

Charlie nodded, then took her elbow and pulled her away from the others, steering her toward the French doors that led out onto a stone terrace banked with fragrant late-summer roses.

"You're obviously going to be very popular at Hawthorne," he said as they sat down on the cool stone wall.

Sam blushed. She couldn't imagine what had happened. Then she realized that back home in Lewisboro, *everybody* had known about Jon and her. Even if the other boys had wanted to, none of them would ever have paid her any extra attention.

"Well, look, I'd really like to be at the head of the line," Charlie was saying with a grin. He reached out and took her hand. "I want to be the first to take you out. How about going to the movie at the Commons with me tonight? We could go over to The Eatery for a pizza or something before. Or we could walk to Grove Street, if you'd rather, and get something to eat there."

Sam looked down at Charlie's fingers around hers, feeling the color deepening in her cheeks. "Thank you," she said, "but I can't. I mean, I'm already. . ." She pulled her hand back and swallowed, wishing she'd had more practice saying no. "That is, there's someone back home. I mean, he's not exactly back home right now, he's away at school, too, but we decided we wouldn't date anybody else."

Charlie sighed and shook his head. "Rats," he muttered. "Just my luck. The prettiest ones always turn out to be spoken for."

"Thanks anyway," Sam said hastily, her face getting hotter and hotter. "I—"

"Sam! There you are!" It was Terry, wearing a frantic look on her face. "I've been looking everywhere for you. It's Roni!"

"What about her?" asked Sam.

"Come and look," Terry urged, grabbing her by the hand. "And tell me that it's not really true. Tell me that I'm seeing things!"

Chapter 3

But Terry *wasn't* seeing things. Roni had just reached the head of the reception line and was greeting Dean Peters and his wife, smiling at them graciously, even dropping a little curtsy. She was wearing a lipstick-red suit, vintage World War II, stiletto heels, a red velvet hat with a veil on top of rolled-up hair—and a pair of white gloves.

"Yikes!" Sam swallowed an astonished gasp, and her hand flew to her mouth.

"Yikes is right," said Terry as Stacy came up to join them. Even Stacy seemed taken aback. "Roni Davies is definitely making a big impression at Hawthorne," Terry added caustically. "She looks exactly like one of the Andrews Sisters."

"The Andrews Sisters?" Sam asked, hardly able to tear her eyes off Roni.

"They were this big singing sensation back in the

forties," Terry told her. "During the Second World War."

Stacy gave a short laugh that Sam thought actually sounded a little envious. "Well, now she's a big *swinging* sensation. Just look at her. She looks like she's having a lot more fun than the rest of us at this stupid, boring party."

Roni *did* look as if she were having fun, tossing her head and smiling, waving her white-gloved hands in animated gestures. Even Dean Peters was wearing a twitchy smile at the corners of his stern mouth, while Mrs. Peters was oohing over the vintage suit. And when Roni turned away, somebody over in the corner started to applaud. Somebody else called out, "Bravo!" and then the whole roomful of people began to clap. Sam suspected that Hawthorne's welcoming teas would never be the same again.

As Roni approached, she looked at them with a twinkle in her eyes. "Well, Pam *said* we had to be elegant," she said with a careless toss of her head. "She just didn't say which *era* we had to choose."

"I don't see why you didn't accept what's-his-name's invitation," Stacy was saying as she and Sam stood side by side in their tiny bathroom, brushing their teeth. It was nearly midnight, and all four suitemates had just gotten back from the movies at the Commons, followed by pizza at The Eatery.

Roni and Terry seemed to have forgotten their differences and Stacy had loosened up and started talking. She *did* do more than her share of bragging, but Sam had to admit that she had lots of interesting things to brag *about*. One time, for example, she'd been marooned on a deserted Florida key with a handsome young fishing-boat captain and had to be rescued by a Coast Guard helicopter.

"Charlie sounded pretty neat to me," Stacy went on, her mouth full of foam. "And he was good-looking on top of that." She added more toothpaste and began to brush again. "Anyway, going to the movies is just going to the movies. It's very innocent. You weren't thinking of going to bed with him, were you?"

Sam looked at herself in the mirror as she put her toothbrush away. Her cheeks were stained bright red. She and her friends back in Lewisboro had talked a lot about sex, but not in quite so casual a tone. Stacy was obviously a lot more experienced.

"No, of *course* I wasn't thinking of going to bed with Charlie," she said, picking up her hairbrush. "But that's not the point. The point is that Jon and I promised each other we wouldn't date anybody else." She began to brush her hair with short, hard strokes. "It doesn't matter how innocent a date it is," she added after a minute. "It's all a matter of principle."

"Well, it's a pretty ridiculous principle, if you ask me," Stacy said as she stepped into the shower stall. After a minute she added, over the sound of the water, "It sounds like a promise that's just itching to be broken." She poked her head around the shower curtain, and reached for the soap. "*Nobody* keeps promises like that anymore," she added with a scornful look at Sam. "It's very old-fashioned." She pulled her head back into the shower. "The next thing you know, you'll be telling me you're a virgin."

"Well, it may be old-fashioned," Sam said indignantly, "but that's how it's going to be." She yanked on the top of her new white pajamas, the ones printed with little blue flowers. One of the buttons flew off and landed in the corner. "And just for your information, I *am* a virgin," she added, bending over to pick up the button. "So *there*." As she left the room she heard Stacy's cynical laugh, and her face grew even redder.

But by the time Sam tossed back her quilted red bedspread and climbed into bed, most of her anger had subsided. She reached for the writing tablet on the bedside table. From Stacy's point of view, living in Boston and rubbing elbows with all those big-city people, maybe it *was* old-fashioned to be faithful to the person you loved. Since Stacy's mother seemed to be in the habit of acquiring a new husband every other year or so, no wonder the idea of being with just one person for a long time—and being a virgin, on top of that— seemed a little Victorian. Stacy had been out with so many different kinds of guys, she'd probably done it a dozen times already.

She plumped up her pillow and leaned back. Not having sex was one of the things Sam and Jon had settled pretty soon after they'd first gotten together. No matter how much they were tempted—and they'd been tempted a *lot*—they'd told each other that it wasn't worth it. Sex was something really special, Sam figured, to be shared between people who had made a permanent commitment to each other, who were prepared to have children. It wasn't just a casual evening's entertainment. And even though their commitment *felt* permanent enough, they weren't ready for children. So they weren't ready for sex.

Sam tilted the lampshade to get better light and picked up her pen. She had started a letter to Jon that afternoon but had laid it aside so that she could add details about the party. Now that she was ready to write, she didn't quite know what to say. She wasn't sure she ought to tell him that she'd been the hit of the party, even though she knew he wouldn't actually *mind*. He would probably get a kick out of knowing what a sensation she'd been with the guys. Still . . .

Stacy came out of the bathroom wearing a sexy-looking red satin nightgown that clung to her slender hips. Tendrils of damp hair curled at her neck. She looked a lot younger without all the careful makeup she usually wore. She cleared her throat.

"Listen, Sam," she said. "I'm sorry." She began to unfold her white satin spread neatly across the foot of her bed.

"Sorry about what?"

"About what I said a few minutes ago. About you being a virgin, I mean. That wasn't fair." She crawled into bed and pulled the covers tight beneath her chin. "I didn't mean to get so personal. What you do—or don't do—is your own business."

Sam put down her pen and thought. "I guess you did make me mad for a few minutes. But then I decided, well, look at how Stacy's lived, and the places she's been to, and the guys she's dated. And then, from that point of view, I could see why being a virgin might seem a little . . . well, actually, a little *backward*." Sam bit her lip, feeling the tips of her ears burning. "I can see why it might seem sort of out of it to you."

Stacy sat up again and reached to the shelf over her bed, pulling down a stuffed white rabbit. The shelf was full of other stuffed animals. "It's not . . . backward, exactly," she said, stroking the rabbit's soft, furry ears. "It's just that . . . well, most of the girls I knew back in prep school *weren't* virgins, that's all." She tugged at the rabbit's pink bow. "At least they said they weren't. And the way most of them talked about the details, I don't think they could have been lying." She yawned. "Gosh, I had no idea I was so tired."

It was on the tip of Sam's tongue to ask Stacy whether *her* first time had been a big deal, and whether the guy was an Arabian sheikh or a fishing-boat captain or just an ordinary person. Then she heard the deep, steady breathing of sleep coming from Stacy's bed.

Even though Hawthorne was small, with only 2,500 students, the first week of classes was like a three-ring circus, with everyone adding and dropping classes like crazy, trying to get just the right combination of teachers and class hours. Adds and drops were done in Hawthorne Hall, the ivy-covered brick building where the registrar's office was located together with the college's other administrative departments. The halls of the old building were jammed for several days with people trying to change their schedules. In the dining hall, the chief topic of conversation was the length of the waiting list for the most popular teachers and the most popular hours, and whether there was a chance of getting into those classes. The whole thing seemed ridiculous to Sam, who had planned carefully what she wanted to take and couldn't imagine a reason for changing her schedule.

"Really, I don't believe this," Roni groaned, sitting on the sofa in the living room of suite 2C on Wednesday evening, staring at her marked-over class program. Roni was an "undeclared" major, which meant she was still shopping around to see what interested her.

Sam looked up. "What's the matter?" She was sitting on the floor in her jeans and a T-shirt, sewing a button back on her favorite blue blouse.

"No matter what I juggle, I can't seem to get rid of that stupid nine o'clock Monday-Wednesday-Friday class. I'm on three different waiting lists for eleven o'clocks, but it's beginning to look hopeless." Roni adjusted the black headband that held back her auburn hair. Tonight she was dressed all in black: black skintight knit pants and a black top with narrow straps. "Yuck," she said. "Phys. ed. at nine o'clock. Impossible."

"What's impossible about P.E. at nine o'clock?" Terry asked from the stuffed chair in the corner where she was buried in her biology book. "Seems perfectly reasonable to me."

"What's impossible about it?" Roni cried. "Why, my blood is barely circulating at nine o'clock, that's what's impossible. I couldn't even *see* a volleyball, much less hit one." She glanced at Sam. "I never see you around here in the mornings, Sam. What time do your classes start?"

"At eight," Sam admitted. Her eight o'clock political science class only had about twenty students. "I wish it was a little later, too. Then I wouldn't have to go jogging before breakfast," she added. "I'm going to start getting up at six-thirty, I guess." The Commons dining hall opened at seven, but it was seven-thirty before she could get there, and this morning she had gone to poli. sci. in her jogging shorts, feeling sweaty.

"Jogging." Roni shuddered, digging a tattered copy of her class schedule out of her notebook. "Lord deliver us from people who get up at six-thirty to jog."

"It's good for you," said Terry. "Good for your body."

Stacy came out of the bedroom. She looked her usual stylish self in an emerald silk blouse and an elegant pair of green pants that emphasized her slenderness. "Ready?" she asked Sam.

"Is it time to go already?" asked Sam. She and Stacy were in the same art history class and were going to a slide lecture that evening.

Stacy nodded, making a face. "Really, this is such a waste. I already know all that stuff on cave painting that Simpson's lecturing on tonight."

"Then how come you're going?" Terry asked.

Stacy's face became hard, and she left the suite without a word, slamming the door behind her.

"Now you've done it," Roni cried in an accusing tone. "Really, Terry, has anyone told you what an accomplished *nag* you are?"

"But I just asked her why she was going to the lecture," Terry objected. "I mean, if she knows the stuff, why go? She gets bent out of shape too easily, if you ask me."

Sam pulled on her blue blouse and buttoned it up. She sighed. With all her contradictions, Stacy was an interesting roommate. But Terry was right: she got bent out of shape way too easily. "Guess I'd better go," she said, picking up her red backpack. "Maybe I can catch up with her."

Terry looked at her watch. "I'll come with you. My organic chemistry reading is on reserve at the library."

"That's right," Roni quipped. "Leave me to face this crisis alone."

She picked up her class schedule and began to review the eleven o'clock listings again.

Terry tucked her book under her arm and searched under the sofa cushion for her notebook. "Just stay away from Hopkins in the science department, and you'll be fine. He's a glutton for assigning reserve reading."

Sam had hoped to catch up with her roommate, but when the two girls stepped outside Rogers House, Stacy was nowhere in sight. Leaving Terry, she took the path that led down to the bridge over the lake. The Fine Arts Complex, which housed art, music, and theater, wasn't far from the Commons. She walked slowly in the early-evening twilight, her hands in the pockets of her white corduroy jeans, her backpack snug against her shoulders.

Of the five courses she was taking—Freshman English, History of Western Art, Political Science 210, Biology 101, and Physical Education 201—it was already clear which was her favorite. Political science won hands down, mostly because of Dr. Lewis. He was young, with longish blond hair and rimless glasses, and his reputation for radical ideas was campuswide. For instance, he insisted that you didn't learn just by reading in a book about what somebody else had done. You learned by doing whatever it was for yourself, and he had promised the class that they would study political action by taking part in it. Sam wasn't quite sure just what they were going to do, but Dr. Lewis obviously knew, and that was enough for her.

She walked over the rustic wooden bridge that crossed Hawthorne Lake and paused for a moment in the middle to watch the reflections of the setting sun dance on the water. The lake, about the size of a football field, shimmered softly. Two brown wood ducks were paddling toward the shore, and an owl was hooting sleepily as it woke from its day-long nap.

The other reason she liked poli. sci., Sam thought as she began walking again, was because of the class itself, which was an intriguing mixture of advanced freshmen and upperclass students. She'd been surprised to discover that the guy she'd met at Dean Peters's party, the one she had thought was so rude, was also in the class. His name was Aaron Goldberg, and he was a junior, which accounted somewhat, she thought, for his self-confidence. What had come off as rudeness at the dean's party now seemed much more like penetrating, probing curiosity. Obviously, Aaron Goldberg wanted to understand things, and he wasn't shy about asking. His searching questions, as well as Dr. Lewis's precise answers, livened up the class and made it interesting.

But Aaron wasn't the only interesting student in the

class. Most of the others were lively and curious, too, and some of their ideas amazed Sam. She'd never even thought about the things they found to ask questions on, and although she'd always considered herself a motivated, curious student, she was beginning to wonder where she'd been all her life. By the time she had graduated from high school, she felt as if she'd learned just about everything Lewisboro High had to teach. Now, here it was only the first week of class, and she was already beginning to feel as if the number of dates and facts and statistics they expected her to absorb was overwhelming.

The three-wing Fine Arts Complex was built of brick and covered with ivy, like most of the other buildings on the Hawthorne campus. It was much newer than the others, however, with a modern-looking shed roof over the theater auditorium and a glass wall on the side that faced the lake. When Sam got to the lecture hall, she looked around for Stacy but couldn't find her. Her roommate still hadn't shown up by the time the lights dimmed and everyone settled down to watch slides on cave paintings and listen to Professor Simpson's lecture. Afterward, Sam and two of the girls from the class walked back to the Commons and stopped at The Eatery for hot chocolate.

At eleven, Sam excused herself and walked back across campus to Rogers. The bridge was lit at night by street lamps, which cast pools of golden light onto the rippling water. Just on the other side of the lake, a bench was half-hidden by a clump of willows. As Sam got closer to it, she saw the two dark shadows sitting on it draw apart slightly and heard a light laugh, followed by a heavier chuckle. Turning away, she thought about Jon. She missed him terribly, the comfort of talking to him, the weight of his arm across her shoulders.

When she got back to the suite, she discovered that Stacy was already in bed. The covers were pulled up to her chin, and her face was buried in the pillows. In the light from the hall, Sam could see that she was holding her favorite stuffed rabbit tightly against her. An empty bag of chocolate-chip cookies lay crumpled up on the floor beside the bed.

Sam got undressed in the dark and took out the book light Jon had given her right before she'd left Lewisboro; she wanted to read his last letter one more time. It was only the second one she'd gotten, although she had written to him four times already. She could tell by the sloppy handwriting that he had been in a hurry when he wrote it. "I love you," it said in large letters at the end, "and I definitely miss you."

It felt better to see the words in Jon's handwriting. It was almost like hearing his voice. Sam read the letter over and over until she finally fell asleep. That night, her dreams were a mystifying puzzle of Neolithic cave paintings, boys with curly hair and probing brown eyes, and weird girls who wore sexy nightgowns, cuddled stuffed rabbits, and ate only chocolate-chip cookies.

Chapter 4

If the first week of classes had been a hectic blur, Sam thought, the second week promised to be even worse. Two of her instructors had already scheduled quizzes, she had to read a 350-page novel by Monday's English class, and Rush Week was coming up.

It was late Sunday afternoon, and the four suitemates were lying on the grassy slope between Rogers and the lake, a spot Pam had called "Rogers Beach." Wearing their swimsuits, they were reading and working on their suntans—and talking about the sorority scene at Hawthorne. Sam and Stacy had already made up their minds to pledge, but Roni and Terry had decided against it.

"I'd *like* to pledge, but I just don't have the time. Or the money," Terry was saying. "The dues are pretty steep, and there are parties all the time, which means more clothes and stuff that I can't afford."

"I think you mean stuff-y," said Roni, her voice

37

muffled. She was supposed to be reading a chapter of history, but she'd probably spent more time napping than reading. "Sorority parties are a real drag." She rolled over and shaded her eyes. "The Atlanta Junior Assembly all over again. Yuck," she said, shaking her head. "It's definitely not fun."

Sam finished rubbing suntan oil on her legs. She looked at Roni and then looked away again, wondering whether it was just her own small-town upbringing or whether she really had reason to be embarrassed by Roni's nearly nonexistent string bikini. "How do you know so much about sororities?" she asked Roni. "Were you ever in one?"

"Look, I just know, that's all," Roni replied. "You don't have to be some kind of genius to figure it out."

"Oh," Sam said, giving in with a little laugh, "okay." She turned to Stacy, who was lying on the towel beside her. "Hey, Stace, would you like me to put more lotion on your back? You're getting sort of lobsterish."

"If you want to," Stacy replied in a sleepy voice. She didn't stir as Sam rubbed the oil onto her bare shoulders. She was wearing a bikini, too, and Sam could see the bony ridge of her backbone. An art history text lay on the grass beside her, but she hadn't opened it.

"Which sorority do you want to pledge, Sam?" asked Terry.

"Alpha Pi Alpha," Sam replied. "It's the one my mother belonged to when she went to college here."

"That makes you a legacy," Roni said. "I'll bet the APAs will go crazy over you."

"Meaning?" Sam asked, looking up.

Roni shrugged. "Meaning that sororities usually make a big deal over legacies. All in the family, so to speak."

Sam put the top back on the suntan lotion. "I guess that's what I like about sororities," she said. "The members are like real sisters." She paused. "I mean, it's really neat to belong to a group that's going to support you, no matter what." Sam and Jon had spent a lot of time the previous winter talking about the pros and cons of joining, and they'd both decided to pledge. In his last letter, Jon had written that Rush Week was already under way at Illinois, and he thought he was going to be able to pledge his first choice.

"What about you, Stacy?" asked Terry. "Which one are you going to pledge?"

"Uh-huh," Stacy murmured. Then she said, "Oh, which? I don't know. It doesn't really matter, I guess. Alpha Pi Alpha, probably." She waved a fly away. "They're all just as boring."

"If you feel that way about it, why are you bothering to join at all?" Roni challenged.

"I really don't know," Stacy said, turning her head away from Roni and pulling her straw hat over her eyes.

"My, isn't this girl an incredibly witty conversationalist?" Roni asked in an admiring tone. She picked up the bottle of suntan oil and held it in front of her mouth like a microphone. "Here, on the shady banks of Lake Hawthorne—"

"The sunny banks, Sam corrected, sitting up.

"The *sunny* banks of Lake Hawthorne," Roni amended, "we are interviewing the world-famous Beacon Hill jet-setter, Miss Stacy Vaughn Swanson, who is looking bronzed and bored upon her return from . . . her return from . . ."

"The slopes of Mt. Everest," Terry put in. "Where she climbed to the incredible height of fifteen thousand feet . . ."

Roni grinned. "And enjoyed a delightful lunch with the shah of Abinistan——"

"There's no such country," said Stacy, rolling over on her back. "You just made that up."

"——and the sharina," Roni continued, ignoring her, "at the luxurious mountainside resort of Parnassus Springs. They discussed Miss Swanson's fervent desire to pledge a sorority——any old boring sorority——at Hawthorne College, where she is entering her freshman year. Miss Swanson was wearing a daringly cut white ball gown, trimmed in——"

"Actually, it was a bikini," Stacy disagreed, sitting up and pushing her straw hat onto the back of her head. "I was wearing a bikini. A blue bikini."

"A blue, thermal bikini designed especially for diving into the hot springs in air temperatures of twenty degrees below zero," Roni reported.

"That's pretty cold," Sam objected, "unless she had a wetsuit on over her thermal bikini."

"Wearing a wet suit," Roni added. "A diamond-studded wet suit."

"In spite of which, she looked ravishing. Absolutely ravishing," Sam finished, taking the bottle microphone from Roni.

"You guys," Stacy said with what sounded like real affection in her voice, "are something else."

Roni looked at Sam and Terry. "Are we ready?" she asked, nodding pointedly toward the lake.

"Ready on the right," Sam said. She stood up.

"Ready on the left," Terry agreed, dusting off her hands.

The three of them leaned over, picked Stacy up by the arms and feet, and carried her kicking and screaming to the edge of the water, where they unceremoniously dumped her in. But as Stacy fell, she managed to grab Sam's ankle, who pulled Terry's arm, who grasped Roni's hand.

"At least *I've* got a wetsuit," Stacy announced as she emerged, laughing, from the lake.

The APA house was a large, impressive brick mansion surrounded by huge old oaks and maples. All four of the sorority houses were located within a four-block area about a quarter mile from campus, and only juniors and seniors could live in them. Freshmen and sophomores had to live in the dorms.

But even if all the members didn't live in the houses, the sororities played a major role in Hawthorne's social life. When Sam had indicated on her admission application that she was interested in sororities, all four of them had sent letters telling what they did during the year. She was glad to see that APA had more things going on than the other sororities—parties and shopping trips, out-of-town weekends, trips to away football games.

A large white banner that read "Welcome Rushees" had been stretched across the APA front porch, and on the front door there was a huge wreath of flowers with the APA insignia in big gold letters in the middle. Girls wearing dresses and heels were standing on the shaded veranda at the side of the house, talking and holding punch cups and little plates of cookies. Sam could tell which ones were the rushees because they all looked so nervous. She could tell by the butterflies in her stomach and her clammy palms that she did, too.

Sam and Stacy had come to the party together. Sam was wearing one of Stacy's outfits: a sleeveless blue dress with magenta-and-gold bands around the skirt and a boxy gold jacket that made her feel like a fashion model. On her feet were a pair of new blue heels she'd found at the mall. Stacy was wearing a rose-colored nubbed-silk dress, with darker rose pumps. As usual, she looked perfect.

As they walked through the front door and signed the guest register, Sam was given a blue name tag instead of the pink one Stacy got. Her mother had promised her that as a legacy she would get special treatment, and the blue name tag was obviously just the beginning. The APA sisters all seemed to make a point of coming up to welcome her to the party, and the sorority president herself, a dark-haired, vivacious senior named Nancy Greer, took her on a guided tour of the sorority house. Stacy trailed along, looking only vaguely interested.

"The residents' rooms are all upstairs," Nancy said, leading them up the graciously curving staircase. "About forty girls live here." She smiled warmly at Sam, her friendliness spilling over into another smile for Stacy. "We really have a *wonderful* time," she added enthusiastically. "It's almost like a continuous party.

The sorority houses set their own curfews, and you can pretty much come and go whenever you want here at APA. Nobody checks, because it's nobody's business. Our visitation rules are flexible, too, so your boyfriend can stay as late as you like, as long as your roommate doesn't object."

"Hmmm," Sam mumbled. She hadn't thought about that part of it. She wondered if she would have the guts to say no if her roommate decided to ask a boyfriend to spend the night. She looked into one of the rooms. They were clean and freshly painted, but they weren't that big. Not nearly so large as the bedroom she shared with Stacy in Rogers House. They held the same standard-issue furniture, however.

"We don't have a lot of rules here," Nancy was saying. "For instance, we don't have a rule against keeping alcohol in your room. So if you want to have beer or wine or whatever, you can, as long as you're over twenty-one." She giggled a little bit. "Panhellenic rules say that we have to tell everybody that."

"I suppose you check IDs at the door," Stacy commented dryly.

Nancy shot her an offended look. "No, actually we don't enforce the drinking age," she said. "We don't think it's any of our business. We trust our sisters as individuals to decide for themselves what they want to do." She gave them a knowing smile. "That's one of the cardinal rules of APA. Live and let live. It saves a lot of wear and tear on everyone."

Sam nodded. Live and let live. When Nancy put it that way, it sounded reasonable. The sorority supported its members and trusted them to make their own decisions.

Nancy opened the door of a large, nicely decorated room. "Of course," she said, "even though we party a lot, we also hope our sisters will keep up their grades. We set aside this lounge as a place where you can study if your roommate has her boyfriend over or whatever."

When they got back downstairs, Nancy led Sam and Stacy out onto the veranda and took them around, introducing them to several APA sisters they hadn't met yet. Sam wondered if she was expected to remember everyone's name. She also wondered if this special treatment meant that there was a better chance of getting pledged. Finally, two of the girls took them over to the refreshment table, where a black-uniformed maid handed them cups of lemonade and plates of fancy sandwiches and little crackers with curlicues of pâté on them. And when it was time to go, several APAs walked to the door with Sam and Stacy to say good-bye. The attention was all very flattering, Sam thought; almost as flattering as the attention she'd gotten from all the guys at Dean Peters's tea. But to be honest, not nearly so much fun.

"Well, I'd say you're a shoo-in," Stacy remarked as they walked along Francis Drive on their way back to Rogers House. It was nearly seven.

"I don't know," Sam said doubtfully. "I mean, I suppose they treat all legacies like that. It might not mean a thing."

"Maybe not," Stacy said with a shrug. "But I still think you're a shoo-in." Sam sighed. "What's the matter?" asked Stacy. "It's what you wanted, isn't it? I mean, you said that you've been planning for a long time to pledge APA, and now it's about to happen." Sam nodded. "So what are you sighing about?"

"Oh, nothing," Sam replied. "Actually," she continued with a giggle, "I guess I'm sighing at the idea of having to wear heels every night this week. My feet hurt."

"Then *don't* wear them," said a voice behind her.

Sam spun around. It was Aaron Goldberg. He was wearing red jogging shorts and a red headband, and his tanned shoulders and thighs glistened with perspiration. He was running in place on the sidewalk just behind them.

"You have just butted in," Sam retorted hotly, "on a private conversation." The minute she said it, she wished she hadn't. It was a jerky thing to say. Why was she embarrassed that Aaron had overheard her stupid remark about her feet hurting?

"A private conversation on a public sidewalk," Aaron corrected her. He grinned and wiped the sweat off his face with the bottom of his tank top. "If you don't want to be overheard, you shouldn't talk so loudly."

Sam laughed a little and felt her face flush. "Yeah, maybe," she conceded, "but maybe you shouldn't *listen* so loudly."

Aaron's grin got wider. "I'll take it under consideration," he said. He turned to Stacy. "Hi. I'm Aaron Goldberg."

"Hi," Stacy said in an odd voice. Sam looked at her. The pink was rising in her cheeks, and her eyes were bright. "I'm Stacy Swanson. Sam's roommate."

"Good to meet you." Aaron jogged around them. "Well," he said to Sam, "I'll see you in class tomorrow."

"Sure," Sam muttered. "See you in class."

"I hope your feet stop hurting," he called back cheerfully. "You know, you could always take off your shoes."

"My goodness," Stacy said, staring at Aaron's muscular back as he jogged away. She sounded slightly breathless. "Where have you been keeping *him*? He's really gorgeous."

"You think so?" Sam asked as they started to walk again. "But he has crooked teeth. And anyway, he's kind of pushy. He's always got an answer for everything."

"Maybe he's just pushy compared to the boys back in Lewisboro," said Stacy. "Maybe it's just a matter of what you're used to."

Sam suddenly wished that Jon were there. She tried to imagine his familiar face, but for some reason she couldn't. Aaron's face kept getting in the way, and his teasing voice echoed in her mind. What a nuisance, she thought. She stopped and leaned against a tree.

"What are you doing?" Stacy asked.

"What does it look like I'm doing?" Sam said wearily. "I'm taking my shoes off."

On Friday morning, Sam didn't go on her usual early-morning run around the lake. Instead, she stayed in the suite, waiting for the knock on the door.

"What time do they deliver the pledge bids?" Terry asked, pulling her red flannel robe around her and rubbing the sleep out of her eyes. She took a carton of milk out of the small refrigerator under the shelf that served as their kitchen and poured it over a bowl of granola.

"They said by seven-thirty," Sam replied, pacing up and down. "So kids can get to their eight o'clock classes." She looked at her watch, discovered she had put it on upside down, and took it off. "It's seven-thirty."

"You're nervous," Roni observed, pouring herself a cup of coffee from the hotplate on the kitchen shelf.

"I am *not* nervous," Sam said, fastening her watch. "I'm just . . . nervous." With a laugh, she looked at Roni. "Why are you up so early today?"

"I am up early today," Roni replied patiently, "because today is the day my suitemates find out which stupid sorority they're stuck with for the next four years." She grinned. "Just ignore me."

Moments later, there was a knock on the door. Before Sam could get there, Stacy had come out of the bedroom and opened it. The girl standing outside handed her two white envelopes. Through the open door, Sam could see that the girl was one of the Alpha Pi sisters, and a warm wave of relief flooded through her. She'd made it! And Stacy had, too. Not only were they roommates, they were sorority sisters, too!

"Hey, congratulations," Jon said when Stacy called and told him the news. To save money, they had agreed to talk only every two weeks, for fifteen minutes, and just write the rest of the time. It was Sunday night, and this was their first phone call. Sam had been looking forward to it for days. "Everything's happening just the way we planned, isn't it?" he asked.

"Yeah," Sam said. She was lying on her bed with the telephone cradled against her shoulder and Jon's graduation photo propped on her stomach. She liked looking at his picture when she talked to him on the phone. It made it feel more like he was there—almost. "It just goes to show you what good planners we are."

Jon chuckled. "I know. How're your courses? Did you drop anything?"

"Are you kidding?" she cried. "After we spent so much time figuring out what I should take? No way." She told him about Professor Lewis's course, and then about English, where they had zipped through *Moll Flanders* in only three class periods. "I can't believe it," she told him. "Back in high school, we would have spent three weeks on that book. And now *The French Lieutenant's Woman* is almost due. She groaned. "God, I've still got sixty pages to go, and I've been reading all afternoon."

Jon laughed. "How about *Cliff Notes*? They might help."

"Don't tempt me," Sam said. "I might give in, but not yet."

He changed the subject. "How's Stacy?" Sam had told him all about her suitemates in her letters, and because Stacy was the most puzzling, she'd probably written more about her than any of the others.

Sam glanced over at Stacy's empty bed. Her roommate had come in earlier and then left again, not telling anyone where she was going. "I'm not sure. Sometimes she seems really up," Sam said. "You know, really excited about what's going on. But other times she just acts bored."

"If she is bored, I wonder how come she decided to go to Hawthorne?" Jon asked. "I mean, Hawthorne's so small, and it's kind of out in the country. Wouldn't you think Stacy would want to go to college in a big city . . . someplace more—sophisticated?"

Sam laughed. "There's a great story behind how she decided to come to Hawthorne. She told me about it when we were walking home from one of the parties this week. Apparently, she came here to spite her mother. Her mom wanted her to go to Vassar, where *she* went, but some counselor or something told her about Hawthorne, and she decided to come here. To make her mom mad. But now I think she kind of wishes she'd gone to Vassar." Sam hesitated. "Sometimes I sort of wish I had a different roommate," she said. "Stacy's pretty moody. I never really know what to expect from her."

"Well, don't let her get you down," Jon advised. "Hey," he said in a quiet voice, the one he always used when he was about to say something serious, "you know I love you, don't you?"

"Yes, I know," Sam said, her insides turning soft and warm. She touched his picture where the dimple creased his cheek. The glass felt cold and smooth, and she pulled her fingers back. "Me, too. I mean, I love you, too."

"You seem so far away."

"That's because I *am* far away. So are you. I wish you weren't," she added after a moment.

"I do, too," Jon said. "Except that might present a

problem. I mean, we might be led to do something we'd regret. At least for now. I mean . . . oh, forget it."

She smiled. "I'm smiling," she told him.

"Yeah, so am I." There was another silence, and then the sound of a buzzer in the background. "Well, our fifteen minutes is up," he said. "Good night, Sam."

"Good night, Jon."

For a long time after they'd hung up, Sam stared at Jon's photograph. She had thought that when she heard his voice, she would be able to see his face again, in her imagination. But all she could see was the image in the photograph, frozen into a perpetual graduation smile.

Chapter 5

The delivery of the pledge bids on Friday morning didn't mean the *end* of a hectic string of parties, as Sam had thought. In fact, it was just the beginning. The first was the pledge party on Friday night, where the new Alpha Pi pledges were serenaded by the actives and lavished with loving attention. It took place in the garden behind the Alpha Pi house, and all the girls carried candles. The soft golden lights kindled in Sam a wonderful, almost mystical feeling of sisterhood. She hoped Stacy felt it, too.

The pledge party went on until after midnight, but Sam was still glowing with happiness when she fell into bed just before one o'clock. On Sunday evening, she and Stacy went to their first sorority meeting and then to a party over at the Pi Phi house. Pi Phi was the "brother" fraternity to Alpha Pi, and the party was

51

designed to introduce the two pledge groups. It wasn't as formal as the earlier parties, and Sam, for one, was glad. Sick of wearing dresses and her good shoes, she had slipped gratefully into her favorite khaki shorts and an oversize red shirt with three-quarter-length sleeves. Her blond hair was tied back in a ponytail with a matching red ribbon.

Almost as soon as Sam walked in the door to Pi Phi, she was greeted by several members of the fraternity—not only the freshman pledges, but the upperclassmen as well. They seemed nice enough, although not very interested in her as a person. She tried to ask one boy about his classes, but all he wanted to do was dance with her. During the evening, Sam turned down half a dozen requests to dance because she was already taken. It was all very flattering.

The party seemed to be getting very loud, and Sam didn't really care for loud parties. As the evening wore on, it got even more raucous, and everywhere she looked there were discarded plastic cups. Sam wondered nervously what would happen if a neighbor complained about the noise and the Hawthorne Springs police decided to raid the party. Half the people were under age, but they were all drinking anyway. Sam herself had let somebody fill a cup of beer for her out of the keg, and she nursed it through the evening. Sometimes back in Lewisboro there'd been beer at parties, and once one of Sam's friends had opened up her father's liquor cabinet and they'd all poured themselves some Scotch. But Sam was afraid that if she got drunk she'd get sick, and that was enough to keep her from having a second beer. When one of the Alpha Pi pledges *did* get sick in the kitchen, she decided it was probably time to go. She looked around for Stacy, but her roommate had disappeared, so she walked back to Rogers House by herself, glad to be out of the noise and away from the smell of stale beer. She didn't feel much like studying when she got back to the suite, but she had to anyway. With everything else that had been going on over the weekend, there hadn't been much time for studying, and she had a paper due in English on Wednesday.

In spite of the amount of time she had been spending going to parties and sorority functions, Sam's top priority was still her classes. She was feeling comfortable enough in most of them to speak up without waiting to be called on. She'd never had any trouble with English, and she liked her English professor, a young black woman with a Ph.D. from Berkeley. They'd finished reading *The French Lieutenant's Woman*, and now they were going to study the movie version.

Biology was Sam's hardest class. Even though she thought her teachers at Lewisboro High had given her a pretty good science background, she found herself spending more time in the laboratory than she'd bargained for. Art history wasn't exactly hard, but she was disappointed about one thing: when she'd found out that Stacy was taking the course, she'd thought they would be able to study together. But Stacy cut most of the lectures and then borrowed Sam's class notes. After the first couple of weeks, Sam gave up the idea of studying with her roommate.

Poli. Sci. 210 was still her favorite. The class met

in a seminar room in the Baines Social Science Center, one of the oldest redbrick campus buildings, next door to Hawthorne Hall. They were studying the politics of food, a concept that was new to Sam. It was hard to look at stacks of frozen dinners at the local IGA and think about countries fighting bloody battles over them. She had never thought about a culture making rules against certain kinds of food or a country going to war over food. Dr. Lewis had thought about those things, though, and his descriptions were graphic.

"Here in the West," Professor Lewis told the class at the end of his lecture the following Friday, "we've gotten so used to plentiful food that we have no idea how little food people in other countries manage to exist on." He pushed his glasses up on his forehead and looked around the room. "But you people are lucky," he added. "You have the opportunity to experience this situation, firsthand."

"Uh-oh," said a boy in the front row, his pencil poised in midair. "Here it comes." He turned to the girl sitting next to him. "I hope you're ready to go on a diet, Monica."

Dr. Lewis grinned. "You got it, Art," he replied. "We're not just going to talk about a food shortage, we're going to experience one. I want you all to participate in a week of 'poverty meals'—the kind you'd be eating if you lived in one of the Third World countries. We'll be eating together every day, at a special table I've reserved in the dining hall. The regular kitchen staff is going to be doing the cooking—"

Several people cheered, and somebody said, "Yea, LuAnn. If she's cooking, it can't be all bad."

"Don't expect too much, even from our famous LuAnn," Dr. Lewis cautioned. "She's not supposed to do anything to make our meals taste any better. I've given her strict instructions about the kind and amount of rice to cook—"

"Rice?" the group chorused. There was a "boo!" from the back row, and one girl asked, "Chopsticks, anyone?"

"—and how to fix the beans."

"Oh, no, not beans! Yuck!"

Dr. Lewis held up his hand for order, and the class quieted down. "LuAnn's under orders. No spices, no sauces. Just plain rice and beans and, once in a while, fish. It's going to be a pretty bland, pretty boring diet. The kind of diet that nine-tenths of the world lives on."

"Yeah," interjected one of the boys, "but it's just for one meal a day, right? I mean, the rest of the time we're free to pig out on pizzas, right?"

"That depends," Dr. Lewis said, looking piercingly at his students. "Maybe some of you would be interested in volunteering to fast for the week, except for the class-planned meals, of course."

"What, no pizzas?" somebody cried in a horrified voice. "No ice cream?"

"No popcorn?" added someone else. "No candy bars? No cherry Cokes?"

Dr. Lewis laughed ruefully. "I can see that this idea is going over like a lead balloon." He shook his head. "Maybe I haven't made you sufficiently aware of the *urgency* of the hunger problem in some of these countries."

Sam looked up. "I'm interested in fasting," she said

shyly. "I don't see how you could really experience hunger if you just keep on stuffing yourself the way we do most of the time." Guiltily, she thought about the previous night. Sam and and her suitemates had gorged themselves on cookies fresh from her mother's kitchen via a giant "care package."

Aaron, sitting in front of her, had half turned around in surprise, as if he hadn't expected her to speak up. "I'll fast, too," he said. He ran a hand through his brown hair, ruffling it up in the back. "Sam's right. We all eat too much."

Sam blushed. From around the room, several other kids chimed in, agreeing to fast for the entire week, except for the communal meals they would eat in the dining hall.

"Okay," said Dr. Lewis, looking pleased. "We're going to start this project with the first meal on Sunday evening, at my house. I've got some slides I want you to look at, and then we'll have a discussion of the sources of the food we'll be eating and the way food affects the national economies of Third World countries."

"Awesome," somebody muttered. "Awe-some."

"That's right," Dr. Lewis agreed cheerfully. "Really awesome." He looked around the class. "I'll see you all on Sunday night."

"You're going to do what?" Roni asked. She pulled up her knee-length T-shirt and scratched her leg. "Sam, that's *the most bizarre* idea I've ever heard."

Roni and Sam were in the basement of Rogers House, doing their laundry. "I mean, learning by experience is one thing," Roni went on. "But eating tiny portions of beans and rice and fish all week is something else."

Sam laughed and poured a cupful of soap into the washer. "I think it's going to be kind of interesting," she said.

"Do either of you have room in the washer for an extra pair of jeans?" asked Terry, coming into the laundry room.

"Did you hear about this crazy diet that Sam's going on?" Roni demanded, hoisting herself up onto the table by the dryers.

Terry scrutinized Sam. "You're going on a diet?" she asked incredulously.

Sam took Terry's dirty jeans and stuffed them into her washer. "It's just for the week," she replied, telling Terry about the poverty meals. "It's for my poli. sci. class. To help us understand about hunger and the world food crisis."

"Oh, you'll understand about hunger all right," said Roni, pulling up her bare feet and sitting cross-legged. She winked at Terry. "In fact, I'll bet you the new P-Cats tape that Sam will cave in by the middle of the week."

"You're on," Terry said after some thought. "Except that when I win, you can buy me a George Winston tape instead. Sam has a lot of willpower. I think she'll hang in there."

A smile crept over Roni's face. "Yeah, but I just remembered Sam's got a big sorority party on Sunday night, and her Alpha Pi sisters aren't going to like it if she doesn't stuff her face right along with the rest of them. And didn't you tell me that you were supposed to be a hostess or something?"

Sam bit her lip. "Nuts! I forgot about the party. And Dr. Lewis is having the class over for dinner that night."

"Maybe you can do both," Terry suggested practically.

"Maybe," Sam said in an "I doubt it" voice. Being a hostess meant getting there early to help with the food, as well as staying to help clean up. She closed the washer and looked at her watch. "Whoops, it's late." She looked at Roni and Terry. "When this stuff is done, will you throw it in the dryer with your clothes? I've got to run to the art library and look at slides. Simpson is doing Norse gods tomorrow, and I've got a bunch of carvings and stuff to look at."

"Yeah, sure," said Roni. She raised her voice as Sam went out the door. "You better stick a few chocolate bars in your pocket. No matter how you slice it, it's going to be a long week."

Sam decided that she'd better skip the Alpha Pi party. After all, getting off to a good start on Dr. Lewis's hunger project *was* pretty important, and there'd always be more sorority parties. But when she called Nancy Greer at the Alpha Pi house and told her why she couldn't come, the sorority president sounded a little upset.

"Well, we really count on *all* our pledges to be here," she told Sam. "I hope you understand how serious this is."

"Oh, I do," Sam assured her quickly, feeling more

than a little guilty. She thought of herself as the sort of person who always lived up to her promises. "It won't happen again."

"I hope not," Nancy said.

Everyone was gathered in Dr. Lewis's backyard, under a huge old oak tree when Sam arrived. The evening air was just slightly chilly, and Sam was glad she'd worn her cord jeans and layered two blouses, a blue-and-white-striped one over a blue one. She talked to Monica for a while, sort of half looking for Aaron. She had the feeling that when he got there the party would get livelier. As it turned out, Aaron was a little late, but Sam was right—once he arrived, the conversation seemed to perk up.

After a while, when it got dark, Dr. Lewis took them onto the back porch, where he showed some interesting slides of areas in Africa and India that had been hit by famine. Then he and his wife invited them all into the kitchen. On a table stood a steaming pot of rice, another pot of cooked black beans, and a tray of something that looked like dried fish with their heads still on. Dr. Lewis handed out small portions to each of them.

"Yes, it *is* dried fish," said a voice, startling Sam as she stood on the back porch peering uncertainly at what had been put on her plate. "And yes, those *are* dried fish heads." It was Aaron.

"Must you always sneak up on people?" she asked crossly. "You scared me."

"You scare easily," Aaron countered with a grin. He was wearing a red V-neck sweater over a red shirt.

"Are you always so preoccupied that you don't notice when someone is sneaking up on you?"

Sam couldn't help herself; Aaron's grin was infectious. "I didn't think we'd have to eat the *heads*," she confessed with a smile. "But I've been fasting today, and I guess I'm hungry enough to try anything." She shuddered.

"Good for you." Aaron took a bite of his fish and chewed for a minute. "Of course, it doesn't *taste* all that good," he admitted a moment later. "However, in the name of science . . ."

Following Aaron's example, Sam closed her eyes and tried her fish. "Yuck," she said. "*This* is what most of the world eats?"

"Yeah. We're just spoiled, that's all," Aaron replied. "My brother's in West Africa in the Peace Corps and he says *we're* the ones who are out of step. But it's not just food, it's everything. He was home over the summer, but he went back early. He said he'd gotten addicted to the simple life, and he couldn't stand seeing another TV commercial trying to sell floor wax. He thinks we have shiny kitchen floors just so people can sell us floor wax."

Sam thought for a minute. She could see the logic of it. "Yeah, I think I understand," she began thoughtfully. "From that point of view, maybe we have television just so that people can sell us kitchen floors *and* floor wax." She made a face. "What a depressing thought." His electricity seemed to charge her, too, generating ideas that she'd never had before.

Aaron put down his plate and pushed his brown hair back out of his eyes. "Well, look at it this way . . ."

Sam listened, fascinated. She was as captivated by the way he spoke as by what he said. When Aaron talked, he punctuated his fast-paced points with staccato gestures, and electrical energy crackled out of him.

After what seemed like only an hour or so, Aaron looked at his watch. Most of the others had gone, and the two of them were nearly alone, sitting on the floor in a corner of the porch, leaning against the wall. "Hey," he said, surprised, "it's nearly midnight. I've got to get back and do some reading for tomorrow."

"Midnight!" Sam exclaimed. "It can't be." She'd meant to write Jon a long letter about her week before she went to bed.

"Come on," Aaron said, reaching for her hand and pulling her up. "It's only two blocks. I'll race you. Last one back to the dorms is a pumpkin."

Aaron won the race, but Sam gave him a good run for his money. When they reached the stone steps of Rogers House, both of them were breathless. Aaron looked at his watch in the glow of the light that hung over the door. "Three minutes . . . until midnight," he puffed. "Nearly pumpkin time. That means I have to ask fast."

"Ask what?" Sam bent over, still gasping for breath.

"Ask you to go to the movies with me sometime this week. Without popcorn, of course. Or Cokes. I'd hate to disappoint Dr. Lewis."

Sam straightened up and stared at Aaron. Saying no to guys had been getting easier ever since she'd first practiced on Charlie at the dean's party. But this time, it wasn't easy at all. This time, she wanted to say *yes*.

"I . . . I'm . . . sorry," she managed at last. "I'd like to, but . . . this week is going to be really tough." She'd told Charlie about Jon and about not dating other people. Why was it so hard to tell Aaron? "I've got a couple of quizzes and a ton of reading," she added lamely.

Aaron grinned. "Yeah, I understand." He reached up and touched her cheek gently with his thumb, as if he were brushing something away. "I've got a couple of major tests, too. Listen, I'll ask you again later." He looked down at her for a moment, his eyes very intense. Then he grinned. "See you at lunch tomorrow. In the meantime, remember—no snacking."

"Right," Sam agreed as he turned and jogged away. "No snacking."

She pulled open the heavy door and went up the stairs to the second floor. Stacy was already asleep. For some reason, Sam didn't feel like writing to Jon. She crawled into bed and lay there, staring up into the dark, feeling guilty for not writing, even though she wasn't breaking any sort of promise just by skipping one letter. But she felt something else, too. She felt the crackle of the energy that had charged her conversation with Aaron. And the heat of his eyes as he'd stood looking down at her on the steps of Rogers House.

Chapter 6

"Hold it!" Sam looked up from her lunch plate just as the flash bulb went off in her face. "Put your name here, please," a boy said, thrusting a clipboard in front of her.

"What?"

"Write your name on the line," the boy said patiently, as if he were explaining it to a six-year-old, "so we can print it under your picture in the paper. You want everybody to know who you are, don't you?"

Uneasily, Sam wrote her name in the space the boy indicated. "Who was that?" she asked Meg Palmer, a girl from her poli. sci. class. Meg was sitting across from her at the dining hall table. There was a big pot of rice between them, and next to the rice was a smaller pot of beans. Another bowl held a mound of something that looked like cooked turnip tops.

63

Meg grinned. "It was the newspaper photographer," she said. "The guy from the Hawthorne *Herald*. He's kind of pushy sometimes, but he's really a good photographer."

"What was he doing taking a picture of me?" Sam was glad that she'd bothered to get a little dressed up. She was wearing a green plaid tunic over her green wool skirt and black turtleneck top, and she'd pulled her hair back with combs.

"He took your picture," Aaron said, sitting down beside Sam, "because you're eating rice when everybody else is eating steak." He helped himself to a spoonful of rice from the pot in the middle of the table. "We're big news this week," he said, brandishing the spoon.

"They're not eating steak, exactly," Meg corrected him, glancing around at the other tables with an expression of longing on her face. "More like meat loaf. With mashed potatoes. It looks like some people have green beans." She sighed. "And apple pie, even."

"There's no real difference," Aaron told her. "Steak and meat loaf come from the same animal. Did you know," he asked Sam, "that it takes twenty-five hundred gallons of water to produce just *one* pound of beef?"

"No," Sam said, spooning up some beans, "I didn't know that." She didn't look at Aaron. But even without looking, she could see the fiery expression in his eyes. He approached everything from politics to jogging with equal energy. Sam wondered if he remembered that he'd asked her for a date, and then she pushed the thought out of her mind. It would be better if he'd already forgotten about it.

"And did you know," he went on, "that combined, the beans and rice you're eating have just as much usable protein in them as the same amount of hamburger?"

"No, I didn't know that, either," Sam said.

"The real question," Meg remarked, sounding slightly bored, "is whether we care." She leaned forward. "Or whether we're just doing this assignment to get a decent grade in Lewis's class."

"Yeah," Aaron muttered. He dug into his rice. "The big question. Do we really care, or are we more concerned with grades?" He looked around. Several other kids from the class were sitting at the other end of the long table. They hurriedly finished their rice and beans and left. "I have the feeling that not all of us care a lot," he added.

"Is this a closed table, or can anybody sit here?"

Sam looked up in surprise. It was Stacy, wearing a beige cashmere skirt and a blue angora sweater that just matched the blue of her eyes. She looked very slim and very elegant.

"Sure, sit down," said Meg, sliding her chair over. "Anybody who's dumb enough to eat beans and rice with us is welcome to. As far as I'm concerned, the more the merrier."

"Hi, Stacy," Sam said. "Aaron, Meg, this is my roommate, Stacy Swanson."

"We've met," Aaron said, shooting a curious look at Stacy. "How come you want to eat here?" He gestured toward the pot of rice. "It's not exactly a gourmet meal."

Stacy sat down and put a small amount of rice on her plate. "Because I think what you guys are doing is important." She looked up at Aaron searchingly. "I mean, I've been cutting down on food for a long time," she explained. "I think we all eat too much. And we eat too much of the wrong things." She began to eat her rice, slowly and deliberately.

"That's right!" Aaron said, leaning forward. His voice was eager. "Did you know that it takes twenty-five hundred gallons of water to produce just one—"

"Excuse me," Sam murmured, standing up. "I have to hurry if I'm going to make it to English on time." Aaron didn't seem to notice that she was leaving, and Sam felt a tiny, irrational stab of disappointment.

"I'll walk as far as the snack bar with you," Meg said, getting up, too. She looked at Aaron, deep in conversation with Stacy. "Only *some* of us are fasting, you know," she told Sam loudly, as she picked up her empty plate. No reaction. "Some of us are still eating *junk food*—and loving it."

"Yes, I know," Sam said, laughing. She glanced at Aaron and Stacy one more time as she and Meg walked away. Stacy looked more involved than she had since Sam had met her. Sam wasn't sure why her roommate's sudden interest in Aaron should bother her. After all, *she* wasn't going out with him. Why shouldn't Stacy be interested in him?

* * *

It was floor-meeting time again, and on Tuesday evening all the girls from the second floor of Rogers House gathered in the lounge. Sam had been late leaving the library and didn't get there until after the meeting had begun. Roni and Terry had already found places on the green vinyl sofa, while Stacy was lying on the floor, looking half-asleep. Sam sat down beside her roommate, wondering whether Aaron had asked *her* for a date. And if he had, what had she said?

"There's lots going on around campus this week," Pam was saying, looking down at a long list of notes. Like most of the other other girls, Pam was sitting on the floor. She was wearing a pink sweatsuit that Sam thought clashed terribly with her red hair.

"But first, a couple of housekeeping announcements," Pam went on. "The maintenance people say that one of the dryers is out in the laundry room. Apparently one of us, whose identity fortunately remains undiscovered, put a padded bra into the dryer, and it melted." There were several muffled titters. "The moral of this story," Pam said, "is real simple: Do *not* dry your padded bras in the dryer. If they get wet, hang them out on the balcony to dry." Now there was a chorus of full-fledged laughter.

"Item two," Pam said. She put her list down on the floor in front of her. "This one comes from our pest control service." She paused dramatically.

"Ah-ha!" someone exclaimed. "They're finally going to exterminate those guys from Baxter Hall who keep trying to climb up the fire escape!"

"No such luck," Pam said regretfully. "However, they do request that you stop feeding the natives. Apparently there's been a sudden upsurge in the mouse population around here, and although the age of the building is partly responsible, so are we. So, if you have food in your room, close the honey jar, put away the sugar, and don't leave stale popcorn sitting around. Those critters *love* to munch on stale popcorn."

She looked down at her list. "Well, so much for housekeeping. Now for the parties."

"Parties!" There was a loud buzz of approval from the crowd, and Roni sat up, looking interested for the first time.

"Ah," Pam said with satisfaction, her green eyes twinkling, "I see some of you have woken up. Now, let's see. First on the list, as you already know, is our very own 'Country à la Carte' party. This is an annual affair, which takes place on the evening after the first home football game, which, as you also know, is this coming weekend. Now, each suite has already been assigned a country—suite two B is France, suite two C is Australia, and so on. You'll decorate accordingly, and plan a menu"—she held up her hand, stopping the groans—"a very *simple* menu of goodies. Rogers House residents and their guests are then invited to travel from country to country, sampling the cuisine." She looked around. "Finally, I've been told to tell you not to serve any liquids that might get us all in trouble."

"No booze?" one girl remarked.

"Exactly," Pam said, pushing up her pink sleeves. "And I mean *no booze*." She looked around. "We're almost all under age here, and I don't want to be called into the dean's office to explain how it was that Rogers House got raided by Security, or worse—the Hawthorne Springs Police."

She looked back at her list. "Now. There are more parties, and other assorted important events, so listen up."

Sam listened with half an ear as Pam went through the rest of the things that were happening on campus in the next few weeks. It was a long list, and it didn't even include the sorority and fraternity activities. Sam sighed. There were so many things she *had* to do— homework, for one—that they completely overshadowed the things she *wanted* to do. What she had learned so far about Hawthorne was that there was always some special event she wanted to attend—and sometimes three or four of them. If she didn't learn to budget her time, she was probably going to find herself in trouble.

On Friday night, the Alpha Pi's gave a semiformal party for the Pi Phi's. Sam, who wasn't exactly sure how dressed up she was supposed to be, had borrowed a sparkly knit dress from Roni—one of her suitemate's most conservative outfits. Sam and three other pledges were assigned to help man the refreshment table, which mostly meant running back and forth to the kitchen to refill empty trays of sandwiches and bowls of chips. Since the party was at the Alpha Pi house, it was fairly subdued. Even so, the stereo seemed to be screaming at top volume, both living rooms were dark and filled with dancers packed elbow to elbow, and there was a constant stream of kids flowing up and down the stairs.

"What's going on upstairs?" Sam asked one of the sorority sisters when they were in the kitchen refilling a punch bowl. Sam had tied a white tea towel around her waist to keep from splashing anything on Roni's dress.

The girl, looking sexy in a low-cut orange knit dress, poured in another can of lemonade concentrate and handed Sam a wooden spoon. "Upstairs?"

"I mean, is there a place to dance or something up there, too?" Sam mashed the frozen juice against the sides of the bowl with her spoon. "A lot of people keep going up there."

The girl gave Sam a strange look. "Are you for real? They're going upstairs to be alone, get it?"

"Oh." Sam felt her face flush deep red. The girl must have thought she was a real dope. "Yeah." She put down the spoon and began to pick up the bowl. "I just wondered, that's all."

"Hey, we're not done yet," said the girl. "Put that back down. We don't want to leave out the most important ingredient." She reached into a cupboard and pulled out a big bottle of something clear, then began to pour it into the punch. Sam wanted to know exactly what kind of booze it was, but she couldn't see the label and didn't ask. The question seemed about as dumb as the last one she'd asked. When the girl was through pouring, Sam carried the heavy bowl out and put it on the table.

"Hey, want to dance?" asked a boy in a black crew-neck sweater. He put his hand on Sam's arm.

"I'm sorry," Sam said politely, pulling her arm away. She gestured toward the kitchen. "I have to work."

"Oh, that's okay," Nancy said breezily, coming up beside her. She reached over and untied Sam's impromptu apron. "You've been working hard all evening. Why don't you take a break?" She grinned at the boy in the black sweater. "Sam, this is Carl. He'll show you a good time."

"Yeah," Carl said, and took her by the arm. "Come on. Let's have a good time."

Before Sam could protest, she found herself in the dark living room, mashed up against Carl's chest. Both his arms were around her, and his beery breath fanned her face. The music throbbed with such a heavy beat that Sam could feel it coming up through her shoes, and Carl seemed to think that he was part of the act. He was singing, or at least Sam *thought* he was singing. It might have been moaning. But he didn't seem sick or anything, and after a few minutes she decided it was singing after all.

Finally, the song came to an end, and Sam pulled away. "Well . . . I have to get back to the kitchen now," she began.

Carl pulled her back to him again. "Hey, not so fast. Nancy said it was okay, remember? You're off duty, so let's have a good time."

"Yes, but I . . ." Sam tugged free of his arms. She really didn't want to dance with the guy again, but the music was starting, and she didn't want to say so and make a big scene. Then she saw Stacy, standing by herself at the door to the living room, silhouetted by the light from the hall. "That's my roommate over there," she said. "I, uh, I have to talk to her—about something important." She turned around and pushed her way through the crowd before he could say anything else.

Coming up beside her roommate, she said, "Hi, Stace, having a good time?"

For a moment, Stacy didn't answer. "I suppose so," she said in a bored tone. "It's not exactly the most exciting party I've ever been to. The only boys I've met so far are freshmen. I'm more interested in upperclassmen myself."

"Oh." Sam wasn't sure what to say. She looked out at the couples, wondering how it would be if she were out there dancing with somebody she really cared about, not some stranger. Then she said, "Actually, I've been thinking about going back to the suite. Are you ready?"

"Hardly. It's only eleven." Stacy raised her eyebrows, looking slightly curious. "What's the matter? I thought you were so hot on pledging Alpha Pi." She swayed a little.

"I don't know," Sam admitted. "It's just that . . . oh, I don't know. Sometimes I'm not sure whether I really belong here. Some of those Pi Phi guys are really awful," she said, thinking of Carl.

"Speaking of guys," Stacy said casually, "I wonder what fraternity that guy in your political science class— Aaron What'shisname—belongs to."

"I don't know," Sam replied. "Why?"

Stacy shrugged. "No reason. Just curious, I guess."

* * *

"Well, did you have fun?" Jon asked. It was early Saturday morning, and they were having their regular telephone conversation. "I mean, you make it sound like the party wasn't a whole lot of fun."

"I guess it wasn't as much fun as I thought it would be," Sam confessed, keeping her voice low. She was lying on the floor beside her bed, her feet propped up on the wall and her head on the floor. Stacy was still asleep in the next bed, snoring slightly. Jon's picture grinned at Sam from the table beside her bed. "I wasn't bored, or anything like that. I guess I just don't feel very much at home with the Alpha Pi's yet. Sometimes I feel . . . well, I sort of feel like a small-town hick who doesn't know the score." With a giggle, she told Jon about the mistake she'd made the night before, asking why the kids were going upstairs.

"Anyway," she continued after they'd both stopped laughing, "I've got to tell you about last Sunday. We all went over to Dr. Lewis's as part of our class, and I got into this really interesting conversation with this guy who knows the most fascinating—"

"Isn't Lewis that teacher who's making you starve?"

"Yeah. The class is really fantastic—even considering we had to eat rice all week. Sometimes I feel like all my old ideas are getting turned upside down, and . . . Oh, I don't know."

She paused, thinking about Aaron Goldberg. Ever since he'd asked her out, she'd been wondering how it could hurt to go. After all, it would just be a couple of friends doing something together. But she wasn't sure how to bring it up with Jon. Maybe it would be best to get at it indirectly and find out how he felt. "Uh, Jon," she said, "how are things going with you? I mean, about our arrangement and everything?"

"Arrangement?"

"You know, about dating." She tried to sound light and casual. "Has some terrific femme fatale come along and swept you off your feet yet?"

"No," Jon said. He sounded worried. "How come you're asking me that now?"

"Oh, no reason," Sam said quickly. She bit a hangnail. If he was happy with things the way they were, she couldn't be the one to suggest anything different. "I guess . . . I guess I just wanted to hear you say it, that's all. Sometimes I get a little, well, lonely."

"You haven't changed *your* mind, have you?" he persisted. There was tension in his voice. "Have you found somebody you'd like to date?"

"No." It was true—she didn't really want to go out on a formal date with Aaron. She just wanted to have a chance to talk to him again, that was all.

"Well, I haven't, either." He paused. "I . . . haven't, either."

"Well, that's good," Sam said, twisting the phone cord around her finger. "How many more weeks is it until Thanksgiving?"

"A hundred and fifty," Jon answered promptly.

They both laughed, but not very much.

Chapter 7

"This was all I could find," Stacy told Sam, unrolling a large map of Australia and holding it up in front of herself. "I hope it's okay. Hawthorne Springs isn't exactly the shopping center of the South, you know."

"It's fine," Sam assured her. She turned to Roni, who had happily volunteered to take charge of suite 2C's decorating and food for the party that night. She seemed to have a sixth sense about things like that. "Where do you want to hang this map?" she asked.

"How about over the sofa?" Roni suggested. She was wearing a pair of red leotards with a floppy red-striped top and a red scarf wound around her auburn hair.

"That sounds good," Terry said, climbing up on the sofa and reaching for the map.

It was the first time Sam had seen Terry without a

book in her hand in several days. Even though midterms were still several weeks away, she spent most of her time hunched over her desk, frowning in concentration.

"It's too bad nobody thought of getting a little eucalyptus, isn't it?" Stacy asked.

"Oh, yeah," Terry said. "It would have looked great over the map."

"Violà!" With a flourish, Stacy produced a large bouquet of dried eucalyptus from one of her shopping bags.

"Stacy!" Terry cried, giving her a quick hug. "I can't believe you found some." She took the eucalyptus and arranged some of it like a garland over the map. Putting the rest in a wastebasket, she set it on the floor under the map. "It looks terrific," she pronounced with satisfaction. "In fact," she added, surveying the suite, "everything looks pretty terrific."

Since their late, lazy breakfast out on the balcony, the suitemates had been decorating for the "Country à la Carte" party all morning. Using a copy Sam had gotten out of a book in the library, Roni re-created an Australian flag in poster paints on the glass door to the balcony. Red, white, and blue crepe-paper streamers swung across the ceiling, and a poster of a kangaroo was taped on the outside of their door, with a sign over it that read "Welcome to Down Under—All Kangaroos Must Be Leashed." After a great deal of searching, Roni had finally found a tape of "Waltzing Mathilda" to play on the stereo, along with some more serious Australian rock. Borrowing phrases from the song, the girls had hung a cardboard sign reading

"Koolabob Tree" on the big philodendron in the corner, and another that said "Beware! Ferocious Jumbuck" on a stuffed reindeer from Stacy's shelf. Sam had even hung her backpack on the wall, with a card on it that read "Tuckerbag."

"Speaking of looking terrific," Roni said, turning to Sam, "that was a great picture of you in yesterday's *Herald*. I especially liked the rice falling out of your mouth."

"It wasn't exactly flattering, was it?" Sam agreed with a laugh. "I don't think I'll be sending it home." She was silent for a moment. "I thought the caption was misleading, though. Didn't you?" she added. "It made me sound like we were political activists or something." The caption under the picture had read, STUDENTS GO ON HUNGER STRIKE.

Roni shrugged. "Sensational journalism, that's all." She grinned teasingly. "Sam, the campus radical. Whatever will the folks back in Lewisboro think?"

Sam looked at her watch. "Not to change the subject," she said, "but it's nearly two. What time's kickoff? I'd like to get to the football field before the game starts so we can see the band."

"It starts at three," Roni told her, and turned to Terry. "Did you pick up the tickets? Where are we sitting?"

Terry nodded. "The guy said the fifty yard line," she said doubtfully. "Is that good?" Terry had already confessed that this would be her very first football game, so no one was surprised at her question.

"Is that good?" Roni asked, rolling her eyes. "Is the fifty yard line *good*? My dear Miss Conklin, is the pope Catholic?" She did a little war dance, chanting. "Let's go, Hawks! Let's go, Hawks!" Stopping, she looked up. "Maybe we'll win this game, and make it three in a row!" The Hawks had already won their first two games, which had been played away.

"What are you guys going to wear to the game?" Stacy asked the others.

"Jeans and sweatshirts," Sam replied tentatively. When Stacy raised an eyebrow, she amended, "Corduroys and sweaters?" Stacy still look disappointed, so she said in a resigned voice, "Skirts."

"I think it would be nice if we dressed up a little," Stacy agreed with a nod of her head. "After all, it *is* the first home football game." She grinned. "Wouldn't it be nice if we had big football mums with streamers to wear with our skirts and sweaters?"

"Yeah," Terry said, "but it's way too late to get those now." She looked around. "We *do* have eucalyptus."

Stacy's grin got wider. "Wait here," she told them mysteriously, and went out into the hall.

"I don't understand it," Roni said in a half whisper to Sam. "What's gotten into Stacy in the last day or so? She's not acting like herself."

"If you ask me, she's in love," Terry put in, with a knowing look. "I saw her sitting with this incredible-looking guy in the dining hall yesterday. They were having lunch together, and she was looking up at him like he was the answer to her prayers."

"I wonder if she was eating with Aaron," Sam said thoughtfully. When Terry shrugged helplessly, Sam felt her stomach lurch. But then, why wouldn't Aaron give her up for Stacy, especially after she'd turned him down?

"Let's go, Hawks!" Stacy cheered, coming into the room carrying a large white florist's box. "Try these on for size, everybody," she said, opening the box. It contained four giant yellow mums with green streamers, Hawthorne's colors.

"Wow," Terry cried, holding hers with both hands. "I can't wear this—I'll need a wagon just to *carry* it!"

"You didn't need to do this, Stacy," Sam said, glancing at her roommate in surprise.

"I know I didn't need to, but I wanted to," Stacy said. "I mean, I truly wanted to. After all, it's our first football game together. That's something to celebrate, isn't it?"

Sam looked at her. Whatever the reason, Stacy certainly *did* seem different. She looked excited—her normally pale cheeks were pink, and her eyes were bright. Maybe Terry was right. Purposefully, Sam pushed the idea out of her mind. It wasn't something she wanted to think about.

It was a perfect day for a football game, with a clear blue sky and a crisp breeze that stirred the red-and-gold leaves on the campus trees. The Hawthorne football field was overflowing with excited students waving banners and flags in the bright afternoon sunlight.

The girls wove their way through the crowded stands to their seats, which were halfway up in the student section. As Sam walked past a line of fraternity pledges who had roped off a section of seats and were guarding it zealously, Roni tugged at her arm.

"My God," she said, pointing up into the stands. "What's that?"

Sam looked to where Roni was pointing. Ten rows above them, a fat man dressed in yellow-and-green-checked pants, a bright green blazer, and a yellow cap was waving a Hawthorne pennant in front of two rows of middle-aged couples, all wearing the same colors. Two of the women in the front held a green blanket with "HC '63" written on it in huge yellow felt letters. The rising, slightly off-key strains of the alma mater floated down from where they sat.

Next to Sam, Stacy wrinkled her nose. "Alumni," she said. "Tasteless, aren't they?"

Terry giggled. "Do you think *we'll* ever look like that?" she asked.

Roni gave her a withering look. "Not on your life," she said darkly.

They managed to find their seats just as the cheerleaders danced onto the field, dressed in flared yellow-and-green skirts and green sweaters. Sam stood up along with everyone else and cheered. And when the team ran onto the field, holding up their hands in the victory sign, the stands erupted in a frenzy of shouted cheers and claps.

"Look! It's the Hawthorne mascot!" Roni said on one side of Sam as they sat back down. A student dressed up in a feathered hawk suit tumbled and squawked on the sidelines.

"Who are we playing today?" Stacy asked.

"The Moore College Bandits," Roni replied, opening the program the usher had given her when they got there. "'Moore College,'" she read aloud, "'is a long-standing Hawthorne rival. Located only a hundred miles apart, the two schools have played each other every year for the last forty years.'"

Sam looked up and noticed that in the stands behind one end zone, a fraternity had draped a banner that read "Moore Is Less." At the other end of the field hung one that read "Ban the Bandits." It showed a large cartoon of a Bandit football player inside a red circle that had a slash across it. Sam had to grin when she saw the banners. Hawthorne might be small and the team might not win every game, but there was plenty of school spirit.

The game turned out to be more exciting than anyone had imagined. At the end of the first quarter, the score was tied at 7—all, and by the end of the half each team had scored another touchdown, making it 14—14. By then, Sam's throat was sore from screaming, and she wondered whether she would be able to talk at all when the game was over.

At halftime, Roni stood up. "I'm going for hot dogs and soft drinks," she announced. "Who wants what?"

Everybody gave her their orders, and just as she was leaving, the visiting team's band came out on the field. When they were finished playing, the Hawthorne band came out. To her surprise, Sam saw that Hawthorne's band didn't have on uniforms. Instead, they just wore blue jeans and white shirts.

"Where are their uniforms?" Terry asked, noticing, too.

The boy next to her shrugged. "They don't have any," he said. "A couple of years ago, the band decided not to buy new ones. Instead, they put the money into the scholarship fund."

"Sounds like a good idea to me," Terry said as the band began to play. Sam thought they sounded great, and even Stacy admitted that she liked them.

In fact, Sam noticed that Stacy looked happier than ever before. Just then she seemed to look for someone in the stands, though, and it suddenly occurred to Sam that she might be looking for Aaron. She had almost decided to ask her when Roni came back, loaded down with food and drink, and she lost her chance. They munched on their hot dogs and popcorn as the second half started.

The game wasn't decided until the last thirty seconds, with the Hawks on the Bandits' twenty-five yard line. The center hiked the ball, the quarterback dropped back to pass, and then everybody went wild.

"What's happening?" Terry cried as everybody stood up and started to yell. "Who's got the ball?"

"The quarterback, don't you see him?" Roni shrieked, jumping up onto her seat so she could see better. "It's a touchdown!" she cheered. "We won!"

"But he didn't throw the ball," Terry protested. "I mean, I saw him . . . the, uh, quarterback. He was going to pass. What happened after that?"

"It's called a fake pass play," Sam said, remembering some of the things Jon had told her about football. "The quarterback just pretended that he was going to pass the ball to fool the defense. He ran it in for a touchdown himself."

"Oh," Terry said, her mouth dropping open. "Is that allowed?"

The boy next to her shook his head. "Is that allowed?" he repeated incredulously. "Listen, it's not only fair—it's brilliant! Now we've got a three-game winning streak going!"

Terry shook her head as the band ran back onto the field and began to play Hawthorne's "Victory March" with a great deal of noisy enthusiasm. "I can see that this game requires lots of study," she said.

The girls laughed and began to follow the crowd down the steps and out of the stadium.

"God, isn't it terrific?" Sam sighed happily as they made their way through clusters of cheering students. "Our very first football game, and we won! We actually won!"

Roni grabbed Sam's hands and twirled her in a little dance. "Actually," she said, "it's probably because of us. We brought the team good luck." From behind them, a couple of boys whistled, and Roni turned around with a flirty grin. Her idea of dressing up for the game had been putting on a green long-sleeved sweater, a shiny gold-leather miniskirt over a pair of bright green stockings, and brown suede boots.

"Right," agreed Terry as they walked down the path toward the lake. "I can just see this week's headline in the Hawthorne *Herald:* 'THE SWEET TWO C'S FIRST FOOTBALL GAME A STUNNING VICTORY.'"

They all laughed.

It was nearly six o'clock when the suitemates got back to Rogers House and began to get the refreshments ready for the party. All the other residence halls had been invited to the dorm-wide party, and they expected their guests to start arriving anytime after eight. They had decided to serve what they called "Down-Under Punch," made from Roni's secret recipe and ladled out of the pink plastic wastebasket from Sam's room—carefully scrubbed, of course. Sam's mother had sent an enormous box of "Kangaroo Kookies" (chocolate chip), and Sam and Terry had spent part of the morning making what they called "Sydney Sandwiches" (curried egg salad), "Wollongong Weiners," and "Melbourne Mush" (a bean dip to be served with chips). Stacy contributed a large bowl of apples and pears, which they labeled "Billabong Fruit" and put in the middle of the table. Stacy also tied a couple of apples to the philodendron in the corner.

By nine, the halls of Rogers House were jammed with noisy people, moving from room to room admiring the decorations and enjoying different kinds of food and music. Suite 2C was incredibly crowded, probably because everyone seemed to like the Australian music, particularly when Roni put on Men at Work.

Sam, wearing a pair of Roni's skinny black pants and her own favorite oversized sweater, was just finishing her third or fourth cup of Roni's terrific punch when she looked up to see Aaron lounging by the door, watching her with a smile. Without stopping to think about what she was doing, she strode over to say hello, her face breaking helplessly into a wide grin as she got closer to him. Until now, the whole party had been a blur of music and faces, but suddenly everything had moved into sharp focus.

"Hi!" she said a little too loudly. "I didn't know you were coming to the party."

"I didn't, either," he said, "until I got the phone call."

Sam frowned "Phone call?" She was about to ask him what he was talking about, but he didn't give her the chance.

"Hey, your party table looks good," he said, taking her empty cup from her. "How about another cup of punch for you and one for me? And some food. I'm ready to break that fast in a big way."

He refilled her cup, filled one for himself, and made up a plateful of food. Then they went out on the balcony and sat with their legs dangling through the railing, eating and drinking and talking. A few other people wandered out and went back in again, and once Stacy came out and stood for a few minutes, as if she were going to join them. But she went back inside without saying anything, and they were alone again.

For a while they talked about themselves, about their other classes, movies they enjoyed, music they liked to listen to. The conversation was slow and comfortable. That's how Sam was feeling, too—slow and comfortable. Mellowed out, she thought, to use one of Roni's expressions.

"How did you happen to come to Hawthorne?" Aaron asked curiously after a while. "Georgia's a long way from Illinois."

Sam sipped her punch. "Old family tradition." She giggled a little. "Actually, my mom graduated from here. How about you?"

"I'm a Yankee, and I guess I wanted to live in the South for a few years."

"Do you like it here?" she asked.

Aaron bent his head to look at her. "Yes . . . and no. I mean, I like being at a small school where everybody knows everybody else." He looked out across the lake, where the lights on the bridge created silver pools of reflected light on the dark surface. "I like being away from the city."

"But?"

He shrugged. "But it's not real, in a way. Don't you ever get that feeling?" Sam shook her head. "Sometimes I feel like we're insulated from the real world, where bad things happen all the time and people have to make tough choices between two impossible alternatives."

Sam looked at him in surprise, then turned around. In the dimly lit room, the party was going strong, the stereo booming, kids dancing and laughing. "That's not real?" she asked. "It seems pretty real to me."

Aaron hesitated. "Yes," he agreed, "but . . . Look, in New York right now, people are trying to scratch out a living even though they have seven kids and a three-room apartment. And on the other side of town, women in sequined dresses sit in their opera boxes, transformed by the music. And the cabdrivers weaving in and out of traffic, trying to get you someplace in a hurry without killing you. In comparison, Hawthorne Springs is pretty dull."

"Oh." The thing about talking to Aaron, Sam thought a little woozily, was that you couldn't just have an idle conversation with him. As far as he was concerned, everything was *significant*. But she didn't really feel like talking so seriously right now. She felt like having some more of Roni's punch. Her glass was empty, and she held it out to him.

"More?"

She hiccuped slightly. "Yes," she said. "Roni makes good punch, doesn't she?"

Aaron grinned. "Yes, she does." He touched her hand as he reached for her cup, and she stared at the place after he had left. Her fingers actually tingled where he had touched them. What was going on?

But she was too happily giddy right this minute to try to puzzle anything out. The football game had been great, the evening was wonderful, and her response to Aaron's touch seemed to be a natural part of the whole thing. Her head was tingling a little too, probably because Roni had turned up the volume on the stereo.

Sam looked out beyond the balcony. The lights on the bridge were ringed with iridescent rainbows, and the harvest moon cast mysterious shadows across the silvery lake. This had to be one of the most *glorious* nights of her life.

When Aaron came back with another cup of punch, she heard herself saying, "Would you like to go for a walk?" She hadn't planned to suggest anything like that, but it suddenly seemed like a terrific idea.

Aaron looked at her for a moment. "Yeah," he said. "That sounds like a great idea."

She gulped down the punch he had brought her, and they went back inside. Casually, he draped his arm across her shoulders as they walked through the crowded suite. Just as they got to the door, they met Stacy.

"Oh, hi, Stacy," Sam said gaily. She giggled. "We're going for a little-bitty walk. Be right back."

For a minute Stacy just stared at them. Then she

tossed her head, frowning. "Suit yourself," she said shortly, and turned and walked away.

"Is your roommate mad at you?" Aaron asked. He had his hand on her shoulder, guiding her as they threaded their way down the hallway, still jammed with partying kids, down the stairs, and out the front door.

"I don't know." Sam was too happy to care whether Stacy was upset or not. "Sometimes she just acts funny, that's all. She's a funny-acting person." She threw up her arms and turned a delighted circle. The stars and moon spun around her. "Isn't it a wonderful night? A wonderful, wonderful, wonderful night?" She bumped into Aaron. "Oops, sorry!"

With a laugh, Aaron steadied her. "Watch it, there. This sidewalk is a little uneven." He slipped his arm around her waist.

"Or my *feet* are uneven," she said, giggling at the idea of uneven feet. "Maybe I've shrunk an inch on one side," she said, giggling harder. "Maybe I'll go through life sort of listing to starboard."

But it was nothing to worry about, at least at the moment. Right now, Aaron's arm felt warm and secure around her waist, and even though she had the faintly troubling thought that she should pull away from him, she didn't. *What about Jon?* a nagging little voice inside her kept asking. *What about him?* Sam argued back. *I'm here in college to try new things, to experiment. There's nothing wrong with a little experimenting, is there?*

Aaron looked up. "By the way, that's my dorm— Shepherd Hall," he said, pointing to a three-story residence building in the shadows ahead of them. "My suite's at the end on the second floor."

"Hey," Sam said, getting an idea, "Have you got any records we could dance to up there? I suddenly feel like dancing."

Aaron stared at her. "You mean, you want to come upstairs?" His arm tightened around her, and he pulled her around to face him.

"Yeah, sure," she said, leaning back against his arms. It felt good to lean against such strong arms. "Sure. That is, if your roommate won't mind." She giggled again. "I wouldn't want us to disturb your roommate—I mean, if he's studying or sleeping or something."

"My roommate's gone for the weekend," Aaron said.

"All the better," Sam said, laughing. "We don't have to worry about bothering him."

"Well, if you're sure," Aaron said, reaching for her hand. "Come on, then."

Sam followed him up the stairs.

Chapter 8

The light of an unfamiliar street lamp shining through the window woke Sam out of a restless sleep. She rolled over with a little moan—her head was buzzing and her mouth felt dry as cotton. What time was it? She wondered. Turning her head slightly, she saw the fluorescent glow of a small clock on a bedside table. It read three A.M. Beside her a warm body stirred slightly, and she could feel an arm under her neck.

Suddenly Sam was wide awake. The body next to her—it was Aaron! They were in Aaron's suite, together, and it was three o'clock in the morning. She lay there, not moving a muscle, for several moments, several *long* moments, while the memory of what had happened just a few hours earlier flooded over her. Oh, no! What had she done?

The worst part was that she could remember what she had done—she remembered every detail, in spite of the buzzing in her head. She thought back to how she'd followed him upstairs, giddy and giggling from Roni's punch, how he had turned on a small light in the living room and put a tape on the stereo, and how he had opened his arms, wordlessly inviting her to dance. With his arms tight around her, his face buried in her neck, his body taut and hard against hers, her breath had come quicker, her pulses racing, the room turning and whirling in the half-light. When he had kissed her, kissed her long and deeply, she hadn't wanted to resist. She'd only wanted to press closer against him. She'd been excited in a way that she had never before experienced. And when he had pulled her into the bedroom, she'd followed him willingly, even eagerly, without an instant's hesitation.

She closed her eyes, remembering. Remembering his gentleness, her uncertainty.

But the hot flush of pleasure that swept through her at the memory of the eager way her body had responded to Aaron's was swamped by an even hotter wave of guilt. Yes, she could remember what she had done and how she had felt, even the mundane details. It had hurt, a little bit, but not enough to make her want to stop. And Aaron had been gentle, careful and— Sam shuddered a little as she thought about him reaching around in his desk drawer for the condom—prepared. But the romantic cloud that surrounded the evening had disappeared over the past two hours. In its place was a throbbing guilt. She had broken her promise to Jon, betrayed him. With a guy she barely knew.

God, they'd never even been on a date! How was she going to live with herself?

Next to her, Aaron pulled his arm back and rolled over, turning to face the wall. Trying not to make any noise, Sam slipped out of bed and combed her fingers through her tousled hair. She found her top on a chair, her pants draped over the foot of the bed. She leaned against the wall while she struggled into them. As she fought dizziness, she realized the throbbing was only partly caused by guilt. It was largely caused by the first hangover of her life. Her heart beat furiously when she bumped the little table and the clock fell over with a thud, but Aaron didn't stir. She stood still for a minute, holding her breath and looking down at him, fighting a nearly irresistible urge to touch the smooth skin on his shoulder and the brown hair that curled at the nape of his neck. The lines of his face looked relaxed. The intensity that charged him seemed to have drained away in his sleep. Then he sighed a little and rolled back over, flinging his arm across the side of the bed where she'd been lying just the moment before. Groping her way to the door, she ran out before he could wake up.

Outside, there was a light in the empty hallway and a bright red exit sign over the stairs. Light-headed and more than a little nauseated, Sam felt her way down the back stairs of Shepherd Hall in the eerie half-dark, anxiously clutching the railing. What would she do if she met a guy coming upstairs? What could she say? She knew that he would be able to tell from just *looking* at her exactly what she'd been doing. But she didn't meet anyone, and once outside the residence hall, she was able to breathe easier.

The streetlights cast silvery puddles across the dark, deserted sidewalks. The campus was mostly quiet. Somewhere a stereo was still playing, and a few dorm windows were still lit, but Sam didn't see a soul on her way back to Rogers. She walked with her head down, her hands thrust deep into her pockets, concentrating on the path in front of her. But when she came to Rogers House, she couldn't bring herself to go in. Instead, she walked farther down the path, to the wooden bench beside the lake, where she sat for a long time, looking out over the water. She tried not to remember how it had been with Aaron, but she remembered all the same.

She had to think about Jon, too, and how this was going to affect their relationship. For years, she had cherished the dream of their first time together—the first time for both of them. She had thought how it would be: tender and sweet and fired with the pent-up desire they had felt for each other ever since the very beginning. Now that dream was spoiled, utterly and irretrievably spoiled. Part of what was beautiful about her relationship with Jon was gone forever. She got up and went behind some bushes to be sick. She hoped that throwing up would make her feel better . . . but it didn't.

The reading light beside the sofa was still on when Sam unlocked the door and let herself into the suite. She wasn't sleepy, so she opened the small refrigerator and took out a can of ice-cold ginger ale. Her mother always made her drink ginger ale when she'd been sick to her stomach. She noticed that there was also a plastic pitcher half-full of Roni's punch still in the refrigerator, and she closed the door with a shudder, not wanting to look at it. Walking out onto the balcony, she sat down, her back to the wall. She could hear the soft slap-slap of the water on the lake, the slight breeze felt good on her face.

"I *thought* I heard you come in," Roni said quickly, opening the glass door and coming out on the balcony. She was wearing a fuzzy cardigan over silky pajamas, and her long auburn hair tumbled over her shoulders. She had a bowl of leftover dip in one hand, a jar of dill pickles in the other, and a bag of potato chips under her arm.

"You've never stayed out so late before," she remarked, sitting down cross-legged opposite Sam, her back to the railing.

"Yeah, I know," Sam muttered, looking up at the sky. The Big Dipper was directly overhead. She and Jon used to trace out the route to the North Star, and she never could remember where to look. He always had to show her, and then he would tease her about never remembering. "I don't know how you can get straight A's in science," he'd say, "and forget how to find the North Star."

Roni leaned back against the railing. She opened the jar of pickles and held one out. "Want one?"

Sam shuddered and put a hand over her mouth. "I'm not much into pickles right now. Especially *this* morning."

There was silence. "I would tell you that we were

worried about you being out so late," Roni offered, "but it would probably make you mad." She bit into the crunchy pickle. "And I'd ask where you've been, but it's probably none of my business."

"Probably," Sam agreed, trying not to listen to Roni eating the pickle. She wondered if she was going to be sick again.

Roni glanced at her. Even in the half-dark, Sam could read the concern in her eyes. "I guess I'll ask anyway," she said. "Even if it *is* none of my business. Where have you been? We've been so worried about you."

Sam sat still for a moment, remembering what Nancy had said about it being nobody's business but yours what you did. Somehow, it didn't seem to work that way. If you cared about your suitemates, it *was* your business when one of them got into trouble. In a very small voice, she said, "I was with Aaron Goldberg. In his room."

"Oh." There was a silence. "All night?"

"Yes."

The silence got longer. "Well, was it good?"

"No. Uh, yes." Sam leaned against the wall and closed her eyes. "I don't know."

"Don't you remember?"

"Yes." She paused, thinking about Aaron, and then about Jon, and then about Aaron again. "I remember. Maybe it would be better if I didn't, though."

"How come?" Roni dragged a potato chip through the leftover dip. Then she said, "Oh, I see. It was your first time, wasn't it."

Sam pressed the can of ginger ale to her cheek. It was very cool. "Yeah," she said, "it was."

"But I thought you said you and Jon have been going together for four years? I mean, four years is a very long time to date somebody and not have sex. Didn't you, uh, ever . . . ?"

"No, never," Sam said despairingly. She thought about all the times she and Jon had pulled apart. "We were waiting . . . until we were absolutely sure." She bit her thumbnail. "Until we got married, actually."

"Oh, gosh." Roni didn't seem to know quite what else to say. "Well, in that case, I guess—"

The door opened and closed again. "Why are you guys sitting out here?" Terry asked, pulling her red flannel robe tighter around her and shivering a little. "Why aren't you asleep? It's after four."

"I was asleep," Roni explained, nodding toward Sam. "She just got home. Want a pickle?" She held out the jar.

"Uh, no, thanks." Terry sat down and gave Sam a curious look. "Just now?" she asked. "You just now got home?"

Sam nodded.

Roni put the pickle jar on the floor in front of her. She looked up at Sam. "How many cups of that punch did you drink?" she asked.

"Too many." Sam sighed. "Now I know why you called it 'Down-Under Punch.' How come you guys didn't tell me it was spiked? I wouldn't have had so much if I'd known."

"She didn't tell *anybody*," Terry replied. "And you sure couldn't taste it. Stacy and I just guessed. We only drank a couple of cups anyway, because Stacy said she was worried about the calories and I was worried about getting sick."

"Yeah, well," Sam said, "I wish I'd guessed, too."

"Listen, I'm sorry," Roni apologized. "I guess it wasn't a very good idea. Some of the other suites were doing it, and I didn't want us to be left out, that's all."

"Even after what Pam said?" Sam asked, beginning to feel a little angry. "I mean, you know that drinking in the dorms is against the rules. You might have gotten us all kicked out of school or something."

Roni shook her head. "Oh, come on, Sam," she said with a scowl. "Don't be so old-fashioned. You're a big girl now. And besides, practically all the suites were doing it. I mean, if the administration really wanted to crack down on drinking, they'd have to expel the whole dorm."

"Maybe." Sam sighed. She unlaced her sneakers and took them off. "But I still think you were dumb for making it. Or *I* was dumb for drinking so much of it, or something."

Roni looked closely at Sam, munching on another pickle. "Aaron Goldberg, huh? Is he that absolutely gorgeous guy you left with?"

"Aaron Goldberg?" Terry asked, looking from one of her suitemates to the other. "Who's Aaron Goldberg?"

"Aaron Goldberg is the guy Sam slept with tonight," Roni explained matter-of-factly. "You know, the cute guy with the curly brown hair and brown eyes who came to the party. The one who talks with his hands."

"She slept with him tonight?" Terry blurted out in amazement. "But what about——?"

"Oh, don't," Sam whispered. She dropped her aching head into her hands and began to cry as an awful feeling of emptiness opened up inside her. "Please, don't say anything." She was having a very hard time holding things together, and if Terry asked her about Jon, it would all fall apart in an instant.

Terry got up and came over to Sam. "Don't cry, Sam," she begged, putting her arms around her friend. "Please don't cry. It'll be okay, honest it will."

But now that the tears had started, Sam couldn't turn them off. She leaned against Terry and sobbed hard for a long time, while Roni silently stroked her hair. After a long while she stopped, hiccuping a couple of times. She wanted to talk about Aaron, about Jon even, but she couldn't find the words.

"Can I . . . can I have a drink of water?" she asked, feeling like a little girl. "My head hurts so badly."

"Of course you can," Terry soothed. "In fact, I know something that will make you feel much better." She laughed a little. "My dad drinks too much a lot of times, and I've always mixed up this stuff for him." She got up. "Wait right here. I'll be back in a flash."

Sam and Roni sat in silence, Sam hiccuping softly every now and then. The sky was getting gray in the east, and a few birds were chirping tentatively. But Sam hardly noticed. She was trying to keep from crying again, trying not to think.

"Listen, Sam, I'm really sorry about the punch," Roni said, breaking the silence. "I know I should have told you, but . . ." Her voice trailed off.

at's okay," Sam said wearily. "I can't blame you. were right, I'm supposed to be a big girl." She closed her eyes. "Big enough to keep out of trouble, anyway."

"Uh, listen, Sam, there's something else you ought to know," Roni said, shifting her weight uneasily. "I mean, before you tell Stacy about any of this."

Sam opened her eyes. "What?"

"Well, Stacy and Aaron . . ."

"What about them?" Sam pressed.

Roni shifted her weight again. "Judging from what Stacy said last night after the two of you left, I'd say she's pretty mad at you."

"Mad at *me*?" Sam asked in surprise. "But why?"

"Because you went off with Aaron when she was the one who called and invited him to the party."

"Oh, God," Sam moaned, dropping her head into her hands again. "Oh, my God."

"You heard me, Sam," Stacy said in an icy voice. Dressed only in her bra and slip, she took a sip of black coffee, then set the mug down on the desk to finish putting on her makeup. "I don't want to talk about it. I just want to get out of here. Now go back to sleep and let me get dressed."

It was nine o'clock on Sunday morning, and Sam had just woken up. She had gone straight to bed after drinking Terry's obnoxious cure for hangovers, and she had the feeling that it must have worked. Even though her head was still throbbing slightly, her stomach felt more settled.

"But I really think we ought to talk about what happened." Sam insisted. "We need to straighten it out." She opened the drawer of her night table and took out a bottle of aspirin. "If we don't, things between us are just going to get worse."

Stacy's jaw tightened, and Sam could see a pink flush rising into her cheeks. "Oh, is that so?" she asked, drawing a careful line with her lip liner and filling it in with pale pink lipstick. "I don't see how they could get any worse."

"Oh, Stacy," Sam said desperately, "you've got to believe me. I didn't know that you'd called Aaron to tell him about the party. He said something about getting a phone call before he came over, and I meant to ask him about it, but I forgot. Honestly, if I'd known how you felt about him . . . "

She stopped. There probably wasn't any point in arguing about it. Stacy wasn't looking at the situation rationally. She was acting as if she *owned* Aaron, when they'd only had lunch together a couple of times.

"If you'd known, things wouldn't have been any different," Stacy snapped. Her voice was tight, as if she were about to lose her temper. She shoved her makeup bag into the drawer and slammed it shut, knocking over the little mirror on the top of the dresser. "You would have slept with him all the same, no matter how I felt about it."

"No, I wouldn't have," Sam argued. She hadn't actually told Stacy that she and Aaron had slept together. But then, she supposed that it wasn't hard for Stacy to figure out since she hadn't gotten to bed until nearly five. She sat up and gulped three aspirin, washing them down with a swallow of water.

Stacy took the top off a bottle of cologne and splashed some on. "Oh?" she said sarcastically. She looked at Sam with a hard expression. "Tell me just what you're going to do about your wonderful Jon now that you've slept with Aaron? You made this big deal about being so much in love with him—what's he going to say when he finds out that you spent the night with someone else?"

"I'm not going to tell him," Sam said, suddenly deciding. The night before, it had seemed that her relationship with Jon was ruined. But that was then. In the morning light, she could see that she didn't need to tell Jon. Since it wasn't going to happen again, she didn't need to tell him.

"You're not going to tell him?" Stacy's voice was full of scorn. "After you two have shared so much, for so long? And I thought you were the faithful type, the type who never broke her promises."

"That's not it. I just don't think he needs to—"

Stacy wheeled around to face her roommate. "Come off it, Sam. The truth is that you're afraid to tell Jon, aren't you?"

"No," Sam said, getting angry herself now. She swung her feet over the edge of the bed. "I'm not afraid of losing Jon, if that's what you mean. I just don't think it's necessary to tell him, that's all."

"And I don't think it's necessary for us to talk anymore," Stacy shot back furiously. She pulled a blue cashmere sweater over her head and stepped into a slim gray skirt. "There's nothing you could say, anyway. I'm going to Atlanta," she said, fastening a gold locket around her neck. "Don't worry about me if I don't come back tonight. I have friends who will let me stay with them." As she straightened up, her elbow hit the half-full coffee mug and knocked it over. The dark brown liquid spread over a pile of papers. "There! See what you've made me do? Does that make you happy?" With one movement she swept the papers off the desk and into the wastebasket.

"Look, Stacy," Sam began, wishing that she could go back to the previous afternoon and start all over again. "I didn't mean to . . ."

"You certainly did! You know damn well you did."

"Uh, would anybody like breakfast?" Terry asked timidly from the doorway. She was wearing jeans and a tattered pink sweater, and she had a bakery box in her hand. "I got some croissants and jam in town. There's more on the coffee table in the living room."

"Eat them yourself," Stacy said, sweeping past her. "I'm not hungry."

Quietly, without saying very much, Sam ate one of Terry's croissants, grateful for her friend's thoughtfulness. Terry sat beside her, not saying very much, either. When Sam was finished, she hugged Terry. Then she pulled on a pair of old cords and a sweatshirt, got her bike out of the rack in front of the dorm, and went for a long ride in the wooded hills that rose to the north of the college. Her political science class was supposed to meet at Dr. Lewis's house in the middle of the afternoon to talk about the experience of eating "poverty meals" during the week, but she couldn't go. She couldn't possibly face Aaron after what had happened. After all, she was the one who had suggested leaving the party and going for a walk. It had been her idea to go up to his room, and she had gone into his arms with such eagerness. How could she have done such a thing? Once he thought about it, he was sure to think the worst. Sure to think that she'd had sex on her mind all evening long—maybe even every time they had talked! What in the world could she say to him when she saw him again?

But figuring out what to say to Aaron wasn't the hardest part, she thought as she pumped up a long hill and then got off her bike at the crest to catch her breath. The worst part was trying to imagine how she was going to handle herself the next time she talked to Jon. She'd meant what she'd said to Stacy—she wasn't going to tell him. It wasn't necessary to tell him, especially since she didn't intend to be alone with Aaron again, ever. As far as she was concerned, there wasn't anything between the two of them, and their night together was nothing but a mistake. Just a simple error in judgment, that was all. She'd just drunk too much of Roni's punch and then given in to feelings that she had stored up for years. She had lost her virginity to the wrong guy, but she hadn't done it on purpose, no matter what Aaron might think. She hadn't been in control of what had happened; that's all.

But mistake or not, Jon was bound to sense a difference in her. She couldn't describe it herself, and she wasn't sure she understood it, but it was there. The night before had changed her somehow, in some indefinable way, and Jon knew her so well that he was sure to notice it, either when they talked on the telephone or when they were together at Thanksgiving. She tried to imagine what would happen then. In spite of her brave words to Stacy, she needed Jon, more than she had ever needed him before. Stacy was right—she didn't want to lose him, to lose the security and stability that he had always represented to her. No, she wasn't going to tell him that she and Aaron had made love. But if he asked her, what would she say?

She still hadn't come up with an answer when the breeze turned cold. The sky began to look rainy, so she decided it was time to turn back. But there was one good thing, anyway, she reminded herself. Since she and Jon had talked just the day before, she wouldn't have to speak to him for two more weeks. Surely by that time she would have figured out what to say.

Chapter 9

As it turned out, Sam didn't have any time to figure out what to say to Jon. In fact, the minute she'd locked up her bike and walked in the door of her suite, the telephone was ringing. Terry picked it up.

"It's for you," she said, covering the mouthpiece. She looked a little scared. "It's Jon. This is the second time he's called."

"Oh, God," Sam whispered. She closed her eyes. "Tell him . . . tell him I'm not . . . " She squared her shoulders and took a deep breath, changing her mind. She reached for the phone. "I'll take it in my room." She stopped. "Is Stacy in there?" She didn't want to talk to Jon with Stacy listening in.

"No, she hasn't come back yet," Terry told her. "Listen, Sam, before you talk to Jon you ought to know that Aaron called too—twice. He wants you to call him as soon as you can."

Without answering, Sam stretched the long phone cord into her room and flopped down on her bed. "Hi," she said. She heard the sound of Terry's bedroom door closing.

"Hi," said Jon.

"I didn't expect to hear from you so soon," she said. She looked up. His picture was staring at her from the bedside table, its grin accusing. She reached up and turned it facedown.

"Actually, I didn't expect to call so soon." His voice sounded quiet, subdued.

"Jon, is something the matter? Are you sick?"

"No, I'm not sick. And nothing's really the matter." He cleared his throat. "Well, maybe. I mean, it depends on how you look at it, I guess."

"Look at what?" she asked, biting her lip. "What are we talking about?"

"Listen, Sam, I started thinking about it after our conversation yesterday morning. You know, when you asked if our arrangement was still on." *Yesterday?* Sam wondered. Was it only yesterday that she'd asked Jon that question? So much had happened—the game, the party, Aaron—that their last conversation seemed like a hundred years ago.

"Well, you kind of caught me by surprise," Jon was saying. "I mean, I've had something on my mind, and I guess we'd better talk about it."

"What is it?" Sam asked fearfully. She rolled over on her side and propped her head on her hand.

"Well, last week our fraternity put on a party for the

pledges in our sister sorority." He cleared his throat, then continued in a rush. "Anyway, I met this girl at the party. Afterward, we went for a long walk around the campus, and we sat by the field house for a long time and talked." He stopped, and there was a long silence, broken only by the crackle of static on the line. "I didn't kiss her, Sam, but I . . . I wanted to." He sounded miserable, Sam thought. Miserable and guilty —just the way she felt. Except that he really had no reason to feel that way, and she did. "I really wanted to," he said again. "I've been thinking about it all day, and I decided that the only thing I could do was to be honest with you, Sam. I want to see her again."

Sam felt as if she'd been punched—hard—in the stomach. She struggled to get her breath, but her throat closed on a sob. Everything around her was changing, everything. She'd made a terrible mistake, but she'd taken for granted that everything would go back to normal—eventually. She'd counted on Jon's stability, his steadiness—and now she couldn't anymore. But there was nothing she could do to change things.

As soon as she could trust her voice again, she managed to say, "Well, I guess if you really want to, then you should."

"Is that what you think?" Jon sounded doubtful. "What you *really* think?"

Sam felt tired, vulnerable, and very unsure. "I guess I don't know what I think anymore, Jon." She traced the quilted circle of the bedspread with her finger. "Before, back in Lewisboro, when we were planning our lives, everything seemed so easy. So . . . so sort of regular and orderly. But now I feel like I'm upside down or something. It's like how I used to feel when I was a little kid and I'd bend over and look up at the room through my legs. Everything would be upside down." She closed her eyes, trying to imagine Jon with someone else, but couldn't. The only person she could imagine Jon with was *her*. "What's she like? That girl, I mean."

For a minute he didn't answer. Then he said, "Well, if you really want to know, she's short, a lot shorter than you. She's got real long dark hair and dark eyes..." His words ended in a quick little laugh. "Actually, she's not a whole lot like you, if you want to know the truth." He cleared his throat again. "She's Chinese, actually. From Shanghai. And really smart. I enjoy talking to her. She's into computers, see, and she knows an amazing amount about software applications. In fact, I think she's the smartest girl I've ever met." There was an embarrassed pause, and then he added quickly, "Present company excepted, of course," in an unconvincing way.

Sam thought of the incredible electricity she felt when she and Aaron talked. How could she deny Jon the privilege of having that kind of exchange, even if it was with some other girl—even if it did make her incredibly jealous? "I'm glad she's smart," Sam said quietly. "It's important to have someone to talk to that you really respect. Someone you can learn from."

"This doesn't mean that we're breaking up, you know," Jon replied eagerly. "At least, not as far as I'm concerned. It just means that we're... well, that we're seeing other people." He hesitated, then explained softly, "I figure that if I go out, you should be able to, too. After all, it's only fair."

Sam couldn't help laughing a little. The whole thing was so ironic. Here was Jon, feeling guilty over walking across campus with some girl he didn't even kiss, while she . . . She pushed the thought out of her mind. She had to be fair to him. "To tell you the truth," she said as casually as she could, "I went . . . for a walk with somebody last night, too." It *was* the truth. Part of the truth, anyway.

"Yeah?" Jon sounded half-surprised, half-relieved. "Well, I guess I don't need to feel like such a jerk, then."

"No. And anyway, you're not a jerk."

They were both silent for a moment.

"Is he . . . well . . . what's *he* like?"

Sam let out a little laugh. She couldn't believe that she and Jon were actually talking about other people in their lives. "He's a junior from New York, and he's sort of into politics, and economics, stuff like that. He says he wants to be a lawyer."

"Oh. He sounds nice." There was a longish pause. "Uh, Sam," Jon ventured, "we're still okay, aren't we? I mean, I'd hate to think that this would cause anything big to come between us."

Sam took a deep breath. "I think so," she said. "I think we're okay. To tell you the truth, I wasn't even planning to see this person again."

"Well, remember, Thanksgiving is only a few weeks away."

She managed a giggle. "I thought it was more like a hundred and fifty."

Jon laughed. He sounded relieved, even happy. "Two hundred, actually. You know, we don't need to change all our plans just because of this thing. We can be together at Thanksgiving and Christmas, just the way we said we would. And next summer, too."

"Maybe it's not a good idea to plan too far ahead," Sam said, closing her eyes. "Thanksgiving and Christmas are enough for right now."

Jon cleared his throat. "Are you just trying to make it easier?" he asked tentatively.

"Easier to what?"

Jon's voice was rough. "Oh, I don't know." There was another long pause. "I think maybe we'd better stop talking for tonight. We seem to be going in circles."

"Yeah," Sam said. She was suddenly so tired she could scarcely hold her head up. "I think you're right. Good night, Jon."

"Sam, I . . . I still feel the same way about you that I always have. I mean, this doesn't change my feelings for you."

"I know," Sam said quietly. "Good night."

"Yeah. Good night."

Sam put the receiver back on the hook, pulled her pillow over her head, and cried. Eventually she fell asleep on top of the bedspread. Sometime in the night she woke up, and there was a blanket over her. Stacy's bed was still empty.

"Aaron called again last night, but I told him you'd already gone to sleep," Terry said the next morning as she picked up her chemistry book. "Is . . . is everything okay between you and Jon?" she asked. She blushed. "I wasn't listening in on your conversation or anything, but when I went in to cover you up, I could tell you'd been crying."

"Yeah, it's okay." Sam opened the granola jar and poured some into a bowl. "More or less." Her eyes felt as if she'd gone to sleep in a sandstorm. "Are my eyes very red?" She poured milk onto the cereal. Outside, it was gray and gloomy, and water was dripping onto the balcony.

"A little. There's some Visine in the bathroom. That usually helps."

Sam sat down on the sofa with her bowl. "Thanks. Did Stacy call while I was gone yesterday?"

Terry shook her head, looking worried. "No. Do you think we should tell Pam that she hasn't come back? I mean, what if something's happened to her?"

"I don't think we ought to say anything yet. Let's wait a little longer."

Terry picked up her poncho and shrugged into it. "It's raining," she said.

"That figures," replied Sam.

Stacy didn't come home until Monday night. When she did, she went directly to her room, took off her clothes, and went to bed. Tentatively, Sam asked her whether she wanted to go to the dining hall for dinner with them, or whether she'd like them to get her a sandwich or something, but she didn't answer. She was still asleep at noon the next day when Sam came back to the suite to study. Stacy got up and went to her one o'clock class, but she came back right afterward and sat on her bed, reading a magazine. She was still there at five when Sam got back from the biology lab. She looked up when Sam came into the room.

"Hi," Sam said hesitantly.

"Hi," Stacy said in a cool voice.

"Can we talk?"

"No. Thanks anyway."

"Listen, Stacy . . ."

Stacy got up and began to put on her cardigan. "You can talk," she said. "But if you do, I'm going out."

"Okay," Sam said wearily. "You win. No talking."

Stacy pulled off her cardigan and sat back down on the bed, opening her magazine again. "Thanks," she said.

"I've been calling you all week. Didn't your roommates tell you?"

Sam stared straight at the blackboard, her neck rigid. It was Thursday morning. She'd cut political science on Tuesday in order to avoid seeing Aaron, but she knew she couldn't do it again. Midterms were coming up soon, and she wanted to get a decent grade in all her classes.

Aaron's voice was low and urgent. "Look, Sam, I think I know how you're feeling. Can't we at least talk about it?"

Sam blinked hard, trying to stop the tears. What could Aaron possibly say that would help? But then she thought of how mad she'd been at Stacy for not talking things out. "I guess so," she said.

"After class?"

"I've got biology right after this."

"How about lunch? At The Eatery."

Dr. Lewis walked into the room, and Sam picked

up her pen. No matter how much she dreaded talking to Aaron, she couldn't put it off. "Okay," she said, sighing.

Dr. Lewis went to the front of the class and leaned one elbow on the podium, adjusting his glasses. "Before I start today's lecture," he said, "I'd like to talk about your midterm."

The class let out a collective sigh, and half the students slumped lower in their seats.

"I know," Dr. Lewis said sympathetically. "It's a bad time to talk about this midterm, considering all the other midterms you're facing." There was a ripple of laughter.

"Actually," Dr. Lewis went on, "I think you're going to like what I have to say."

"No midterm?" one boy asked hopefully.

"Almost," Dr. Lewis replied. "No midterm *exam*."

This time the class erupted in a shout.

"I said no *exam*," the professor cautioned, holding up his finger. "Instead of an exam, I'm assigning a project."

"I knew it," muttered the dark-haired girl next to Sam. "More starvation diets."

"No diets," Dr. Lewis said cheerfully. "This time, the actual projects are up to you. As you know, we've been talking for the last few weeks about the nature of political action, and it's time for you to show me how much you've understood. I'm dividing the class into groups of five or six, and I want each group to work together to develop an action project that will demonstrate the principles of effective political action, the moral uses of power. I want you to show me what you know about the *values* that underlie political power, and how those values influence the political system."

"I'd rather have an exam," muttered the girl sitting next to Sam. "This sounds like too much work."

Sam nodded. It *did* sound like a lot of work, but it sounded like fun, too. More fun than cramming for an exam and scribbling like crazy in the blue book for an hour, anyway.

"After you've developed your project and carried it out, I want you to write a short paper about your experience," Dr. Lewis went on. "Explain to me how it was supposed to work, how it *really* worked, and why there was a difference. Oh, yes," he added, "and I want you to tell me what you've learned from the project. The projects themselves are to be completed by a week from Thursday, and the papers a week after that." After a short pause for questions from the class, he assigned the teams. To Sam's great relief, she and Aaron weren't assigned to the same team.

"Is this table okay?"

Sam nodded and put her tray down on the table, which was tucked away in a secluded corner of The Eatery. Unlike the Spartan-looking dining hall, The Eatery looked more like a restaurant. There was a large selection of snack items available at the counter, green wooden tables and chairs, and a forest of ferns and spider plants hanging overhead. The music from the jukebox and the clatter of balls and cues from the adjoining poolroom were loud enough to keep their conversation from being overheard, and Sam was grateful for the privacy.

"Your roommates did tell you that I've been calling, didn't they?" Aaron sat down, his chair scraping across the wooden floor as he pulled it closer to the table.

"Yes," Sam replied, brushing a lock of hair out of her eyes. "I wasn't ready to talk to you." She looked up, feeling the heat spreading across her face. She knew she had to be honest with him. "I'm not sure I'm ready now. I guess I don't know what to say."

Aaron nodded. "Yeah, I understand. Uh, Sam . . ." He leaned forward over his pizza, his brown eyes holding hers. She tried to look away but couldn't. "I want you to know that I'm sorry for what happened Saturday night. It was all my fault." He gave her a crooked grin. "I mean, in one way I'm sorry. In another way . . ."

Sam wrenched her gaze away and took a bite of her pizza. It tasted like cardboard. "No," she said slowly, "I've thought about it, Aaron, and it wasn't your fault. The problem was that I'd had too much to drink. If it hadn't been for that, I don't think I would have suggested the walk." Her cheeks burned. "And I'm sure I wouldn't have suggested going up to your room."

"Yeah, well, I knew damn well you'd been drinking. I shouldn't have . . . well, I should have been more responsible. I should have made sure that you knew what you were doing, instead of talking myself into believing you did."

Sam put her pizza down. "Thanks for saying that," she said softly. "That means a lot to me."

"I guess I didn't object," Aaron went on as though she hadn't spoken, "because I wanted to be with you. I didn't want to stop you."

Sam looked over Aaron's shoulder. In the next room, she could see a boy and a girl bent over the pool table. Their shoulders were touching, and the boy was showing the girl how to make a difficult shot. She looked away, but not at Aaron. "I understand what you're saying, but it doesn't really change anything," she said.

"Change anything?" Aaron laughed dryly. "The only thing I want to change right now is the way you seem to feel about me, the way you've been avoiding me." He looked at her directly, his eyes intense. "I'd like to see you again, Sam. I enjoy our talks very much, and I want us to be friends."

"I . . . I can't," Sam said painfully. The whole thing was such an enormous, complicated mess. She had been so sure about her feelings for Jon, but now their whole relationship was nothing but a big question mark. She still loved Jon, even if he was seeing someone else and even if they had agreed that she could, too. And if Sam started dating Aaron, how would Stacy feel? Would it completely destroy their fragile friendship? But even more important, how could she and Aaron manage if they did see each other again? Sam was sure that she didn't want to repeat what had happened on Saturday night—not with anybody, not for quite a while. She wasn't ready to deal with that kind of intimacy in her life just yet. But once you'd had sex with a boy, could you see him again and just pretend it hadn't happened? Could you enjoy talking and being together without always wanting more? She didn't think you could.

"I can't see you again," she repeated. "I'm sorry."

Aaron frowned, his eyes darkening. "Why not? Is there somebody else? Do you have a boyfriend or something?"

"Yes," Sam admitted, "but we're free to see other people."

"Then why can't you go out with me? Are you still upset?"

"No, I'm not upset." She looked across the table at him, remembering how he had looked when he was asleep, so young and innocent. Something inside her stirred dangerously. She pushed the feeling away and stood up to leave.

"You haven't finished your pizza," Aaron said.

Sam picked up her books. "You can have it. I've got to get to class."

"You haven't heard the end of this, you know."

"Thanks for the pizza," she said, and walked away. She was surprised at how hard it was to turn her back on him.

Chapter 10

"Okay, are we all here?" asked the boy at the head of the table.

It was a few days after Professor Lewis had assigned the political science teams, and the tall, sandy-haired boy with freckles seemed to have appointed himself the leader of Sam's team. She knew that his name was Alex and that he was a senior and an officer in the Student Government Association—vice-president, maybe.

"We're all here," a girl confirmed, checking a list.

"Then let's get this show on the road," Alex said. "The sooner we get started, the sooner we can all leave."

They were on the second floor of the library, in one of the large carrels that were sometimes used for study groups. Besides Alex and Sam, there was Donna, who kept flashing seductive glances at Alex; Mike, an engineering type with brown plastic glasses and lots of pens in his shirt pocket; blond, vivacious Amy; and Bernie, who played on the football team and looked as if he put in lots of overtime at the training table.

"I've been thinking," Donna said, "and I think I've got a perfect project for us. It wouldn't take too much time, either. See, my cousin is a Republican party organizer in Atlanta, and she could put us to work handing out leaflets in a shopping mall or going door to door. We could probably do it in just a couple of hours."

Amy and Mike agreed that working for Donna's cousin sounded like a good idea. But the others objected. "If I'm going to work for a political party," said Bernie, tipping his chair against the wall and propping his feet on the table, "I'm going to work for the Democrats."

"Anyway," Sam added a little tentatively, "I'm not sure we'd get much out of just handing out leaflets or ringing doorbells. I mean, aren't we supposed to learn something from this project?"

"Sam's right," Alex said with an approving glance. "Anyway, I've got a better idea. The board of trustees is having a meeting here next week, right?"

"You mean, all those businessmen and doctors who think they know so much about how to run a college?" Amy asked sarcastically. Sam looked at her. She wasn't sure what trustees actually did, but she had the idea that they must be more capable than Amy thought.

"Yeah, those are the guys," Alex agreed, grinning.

"The ones who never listen to students' concerns. Well, I've got an idea that just might force them to sit up and take notice. And it's a winner for Lewis's class—a guaranteed A for all of us."

"That's what I need," Bernie agreed happily. "A guaranteed A."

"I was reading the brochure the trustees send our parents every year," Alex went on. "It tells about the investments the college has made, stuff like that. Would you believe that Hawthorne still holds stock in a couple of companies that do business in South Africa?" He shook his head in disbelief. "I mean, we must be the last college in the country that has South African stock. After all the stuff we've been reading in class, I'm convinced that the trustees should get rid of those holdings. But the only way to get them to do it is to force them to really *think* about the problem."

"But how do we force them to think about it?" asked Bernie.

"We stage a protest," Alex replied.

"A protest?" Sam asked nervously.

"Yeah," Alex said. "Other colleges have them all the time. We'd make picket signs, and then walk around with them in front of the building where the trustees are meeting. Then we collect our A from Lewis."

"All right." Bernie grinned and rubbed his hands together.

"But sometimes when there are protests the police come," Sam pointed out, "and everybody gets arrested." She looked around the table. "I don't know about you guys, but I don't want to get arrested."

"You're worried about getting arrested by the Hawthorne security guards?" Amy hooted. "They'd never arrest anybody."

Alex looked almost sorry. "It sure would be more dramatic if we did, though," he said. "They'd really listen then."

"Forget it," said Mike. "I'm all for the project, but Sam's right—we can't let it get out of hand. I say we just show up with some signs, march around for ten minutes or so, and then write our papers."

Everybody agreed; but Sam still didn't feel very comfortable about the idea. What if someone did get arrested? she wondered. But everybody else seemed to agree with Amy, so she kept her fears to herself. Anyway, what did she know? She was only a freshman.

The campus post office was located in the basement of the Commons, and Sam went there to check her mailbox every morning after the biology lecture. That morning there was a letter from Jon, and she tore it open anxiously. It was only a few lines, she saw, scanning the handwritten page. She read it hurriedly.

Dear Sam,

Thanks for being so understanding. I want you to know that I think you're pretty wonderful. Anyway, Thanksgiving isn't 150 weeks away. I counted. It's only six weeks away. See you then.

Love,
Jon

With a smile, she tucked the letter into the pocket of her green-and-black plaid jumper. Things between Jon and her weren't the same as they had been, but their relationship was still intact. She knew Jon too well—he couldn't have written that letter otherwise. She turned away, and ran right into Aaron.

"You should look where you're going, you know," he said with a challenging grin. He was wearing a dark brown sweater and a pair of tan cords. "It's sort of standard practice when you're walking somewhere."

The sight of Aaron jolted Sam back to the present. "I was thinking about something important," she said.

"Oh, really," said Aaron. "Well, speaking of something important"—he fell into step beside her—"Alex told me last night about this demonstration you've got planned for Lewis's class. I was kind of surprised that your group would go for it."

"Demonstration?" Sam repeated, frowning. She pushed up the sleeves of her black sweater. "I wouldn't quite call it that. All we're going to do, actually, is stand in front of Hawthorne Hall with picket signs for a few minutes, just to get the attention of the trustees. It's not a big protest march or anything like that."

"Maybe not, but . . . just be careful of Alex, okay? He sees himself as sort of a campus leader." Aaron held the door open for her, and they went outside. "But he might just get a little carried away. He's got some good ideas, but sometimes he tends to go off the deep end."

Sam shook her head and shifted her books from one arm to the other. A bright red leaf fell lazily from the tree above them and landed on Aaron's shoulder. She wanted to brush it off, but she didn't. "It's just a little picketing," she protested. "And you can't deny that it's a good cause."

"Yeah, it's a great cause," Aaron agreed thoughtfully. "If you can get the trustees to change their position on divestiture, you'll really have accomplished something."

Sam stopped where the path branched. "I'm going this way," she said, "to the library." She slipped her hand into her pocket and touched Jon's letter. "Thanks for the advice."

"Sure." Aaron grinned. "Hey, how about a movie Friday night? I heard they're showing *Jaws* again. It's guaranteed not to stimulate meaningful conversation, but it should be fun anyway."

Sam shook her head. "Thanks," she said, closing her fingers around the letter, "but I can't."

Aaron shrugged. "I'll ask again." He turned away. "I'm a patient guy," he said over his shoulder.

"Okay, Sam, here's your sign." Alex handed her a large red placard. On it, in bold black letters, were the words DIVEST NOW! "All you have to do is carry this and follow along with the rest of us. And don't get lost in the crowd, okay?"

"Uh, okay." Sam mumbled uncertainly. Then she remembered what Aaron had said about Alex. Looking at him, he *did* seem to be wearing a rather self-important expression. "What crowd?" she asked.

"Just follow everyone else, that's all," Alex muttered busily.

The group assembled with their signs in front of

Hawthorne Hall, a tall, dignified-looking brick building with two stone lions guarding the broad steps. Like the other buildings, Hawthorne was overgrown with ivy. For a few minutes, they walked around in a tight circle. Then, on a signal from Alex, they marched up the steps and made a shoulder-to-shoulder line in front of the double doors. Sam was sandwiched between Bernie and Amy, and she noticed that Amy was wearing a T-shirt that read NO NUKES.

"Why are we standing in front of the doors?" Sam asked uneasily.

"To keep people from coming out or going in," Amy said impatiently. She sounded as if she'd done this sort of thing before.

"Gosh, look at all the people," Bernie said, shifting his sign, which read STOP APARTHEID, from one hand to the other. "Looks like we're drawing quite a crowd."

They were. Classes were changing, and it was lunchtime. People on their way to the Commons stopped and looked curiously at the group blocking the doors to Hawthorne Hall. They stood on the sidewalk between Hawthorne and the Commons, milling around, talking, and pointing. Sam suddenly felt very visible— and nervous. She caught sight of Aaron, and once she thought she also saw Terry and Roni. But they were quickly swallowed up by the shifting crowd, which seemed to keep growing larger and larger. Pretty soon, it began to spill over onto the grass.

After a while, Alex stepped forward and began to read a speech into a microphone that was plugged into a small, portable PA system, which seemed to have appeared from nowhere. Sam was confused. In their planning session, nothing had been said about reading speeches or PA systems or anything like that.

"We're here," Alex began, "to dramatize the—"

His next words were lost in a squawk from the PA system. Somebody shouted, "Step back from the mike," and he did.

"We're here to dramatize the terrible injustice going on in South Africa," he said, beginning again. His voice boomed out over the PA system, and a couple of curious heads popped out of windows in the Baines Social Science Center across the grass. Sam could also see people coming out onto the plaza in front of the Fine Arts Complex and hurrying toward them to find out what was going on. "We want the Hawthorne College trustees to divest all the stock the college currently holds in companies that do business with South Africa. We want the trustees to recognize . . ."

Sam swallowed hard. The PA system seemed to boom Alex's words across the grass. They really *were* attracting a great deal of attention. There were at least two hundred people gathered now out in front of Hawthorne, listening intently to Alex's speech. More were joining the crowd every moment.

"Colleges all over the country have already divested . . ."

A white truck pulled across the lawn and parked at the edge of the crowd. Sam saw a couple of men wearing blue uniforms get out.

"Hey, look," she whispered to Bernie, more nervous than ever, "isn't that Security?"

"Yeah," Bernie replied, looking at the white truck.

"They've probably come to find out what's going on." He laughed. "Those wimps."

On the other side of Bernie, Mike grinned. "Or maybe they came to hear Alex's speech," he said. "It's not like they have to deal with a lot of major crime."

At the edge of the steps, the photographer from the Hawthorne *Herald* stepped up, loaded down with cameras. He pushed close to Alex and took several shots. Alex even appeared to be posing. Then the photographer turned and took a few more pictures of the protesters. Sam tried to turn her face away, but she wasn't sure she succeeded.

". . . the trustees blind?" Alex went on. "Can't they see that it's only a matter of time before the entire South African government is violently overthrown and . . ."

As the guards shouldered their way through the crowd, Sam lowered her sign. She took a nervous step backward against the wall, but Amy jabbed her in the ribs with her elbow, and she held the sign back up again.

Alex's voice had reached fever pitch by now, and the PA system echoed his words across the quad. More windows opened, and cars were beginning to stop out on the street.

"You are breaking the law. Please disband immediately," warned one of the security guards.

Alex paused and then continued his speech. No one moved.

"You're under arrest," the guard announced in a loud voice. He glanced nervously down the picket line. "All of you."

Alex lowered the paper he was reading from. "So

arrest us," he said calmly. He sat down cross-legged on the cement step. In the front of the crowd, several people cheered and clapped. Sam stared at Alex and the security guards. She was stunned. Under arrest? It couldn't be! It just couldn't be happening!

The guard shifted uncomfortably from one foot to another. He looked down at Alex, who was sitting with his arms folded. "Come on," he said, "get up. Make this easier for yourself." He sounded almost as if he were begging.

"You mean, make it easier for *you*," Alex challenged. "No way." He folded his arms across his chest and lay down on his back.

In the front of the crowd, several people started to chant, "Out of South Africa! Out of South Africa *now!*" Next to Sam, Amy sat down, her face flushed, eyes shining. On the other side, Donna sat down, too, propping her sign in front of her. Mike hesitated for a minute, then he sat down as well. Only Sam and Bernie were left standing.

"Oh, no," Bernie muttered. "Coach is going to *kill* me." Under his tan, his face was pale. Sam closed her eyes and took a deep breath, then opened them again. It all seemed like a bad dream—a nightmare.

"Out of South Africa! Out of South Africa *now!*" More people had started chanting.

"What's going on here?" Behind Sam the door opened, and she stepped aside. Dean Peters, looking flustered, was standing in the doorway, flanked by two important-looking men in three-piece suits. All three of them were scowling.

The security guard came up the stairs, stepping over Alex's prone body. "We seem to have a demonstration under way here, sir," he told the dean. "But we've got everything under control. Reinforcements are on their way, in case the crowd gets out of hand, and we've just arrested the demonstrators. We'll be taking them off to the security office as soon as the other truck gets here."

The dean looked at the line of protesters. His eyes fell on Sam. "You're not sitting down," he observed.

"I . . . I didn't think it would turn out . . . like this . . ." Sam stammered. "Sir."

He looked at Bernie. "Bernie, I would have thought you'd have more sense," he said mildly. "The coach is going to kill you."

"I know," Bernie muttered, scuffing the toe of his sneakers against the cement.

From the crowd, somebody shouted, "Tell the trustees to get Hawthorne College out of South Africa!" Cheers of "Out of South Africa!" began once more to ripple across the quad, with more and more people joining in. Even the people in the windows on the other side of the quad appeared to be chanting.

Looking furious, the dean stepped over Alex to the microphone and stood there for a moment. When the crowd had fallen silent, he said, "I think you will be interested to learn that yesterday afternoon, in closed session, the trustees voted unanimously to divest the college of all its stock in South Africa."

There was a loud cheer. When it had quieted, the dean spoke again. "I want you students—and you demonstrators, too—to know that this divestiture has been under consideration for the last six months. It was prompted by the trustees' fervent desire to show their support for all black Africans and for the antiapartheid movement."

He looked down at Alex. "Would you like to get up now, Alex?" he asked quietly.

Alex got up.

Chapter 11

"Name, please." An open file lay on the gray metal desk in front of the officer. He was wearing a blue uniform and a badge that read *Hawthorne College Security Force*. There was a tired frown on his face.

"Samantha Hill," Sam said in a subdued voice. The security office was very quiet. She was the last of the demonstrators to be questioned, and the rest were already gone. It was nearly four o'clock.

"Student ID number?"

"Two two eight, two six, three five five."

"Residence?"

"Rogers House, suite two C."

"Parents' names?"

Sam swallowed. "You're not going to call my parents, are you?"

"No, Miss Hill," the officer said wearily. "I'm just

133

filling out this form, and it asks for your parents' names. Now, do you want to tell me, or do I have to call the registrar's office and have them look it up in your file?"

"Mr. and Mrs. Elliot Hill," she said with a sigh.

"Thank you." The officer made several more notes in the file, then stood up. I must tell you that you've been charged with demonstrating without a permit, unauthorized assembly, and the use of an unauthorized PA system on the Hawthorne campus."

"Oh, God," moaned Sam.

The officer looked at her. "You are not being charged with resisting detainment," he added.

"I'm not?" She supposed that was good, but at this point it hardly seemed to matter.

"You didn't sit down, did you?"

Sam shook her head.

"The kids who sat down were also charged with resisting detainment," the officer said. He looked at her file. "I think I've got all the facts from the other kids, but let's hear your story, for the record."

"It was a class project," Sam told him. She felt like crying, and she had to blink fast to stop the tears. "For Dr. Lewis's political science class. We were supposed to develop a political action project and then write a paper about it. Our group decided to picket the trustees' meeting. It wasn't supposed to be such a big deal, honestly."

The officer shook his head. "I don't know why some of those faculty members just can't stick to their textbooks and lectures."

"But it's a whole lot better to learn something by

actually doing it, not just reading about it," Sam protested, stung into a heated defense of Professor Lewis. "It's not *his* fault that things . . . got out of hand."

"Okay, okay. Go on," urged the officer.

"Well, we decided to do the protest—you know, carry signs and stand in front of Hawthorne Hall for a little while. That's all. We didn't plan for anyone to give a speech, at least as far as I know. I don't know anything about how the PA system got there, and I didn't know there were rules about demonstrations and PA systems and things like that."

"When you were planning this protest, did you think to read the *Student Handbook*?"

Sam shook her head. Somebody had given her a copy of the handbook at orientation, but she didn't know where it was.

The officer smiled tolerantly at Sam. "You're supposed to apply for permission to assemble from the dean of students. And if you want to use a PA system, you've got to get special approval from the chief security officer. And the only place on campus that you can assemble for political causes is in the area just in front of Commons, by the bridge. Otherwise, it's unlawful assembly."

"But I didn't read the handbook," Sam confessed. "I just assumed that the others knew what the rules were."

"I understand. But it was your responsibility to know the rules about demonstrations yourself."

"But this was just a class project, not a demonstration," Sam exclaimed. "I mean, we believe in what was on those signs and all that, but it wasn't a *real* demonstration. It was just——"

The officer looked at her harshly. "Young lady," he said, "would you please tell me how anybody's supposed to know the difference between what you were doing and a *real* demonstration?"

Sam stared at him for a moment, her mouth open. Then she closed her mouth.

"Okay." He closed the file on his desk. "Your disciplinary hearing is set for next Monday in Dean Peters's office."

Sam's heart leapt into her throat. "Disciplinary hearing?" she gasped. "What's that."

"At three o'clock," the officer added, ignoring her question. Please read section four, paragraphs one through ten, of the Hawthorne Student Disciplinary Code, to familiarize yourself with the penalties that may be charged against you. At the dean's discretion, these penalties may include one or more fines, denial of certain or all student privileges, and suspension. The dean's decision may only be appealed to the president of the college."

For a minute, Sam actually thought she was going to faint.

"Did you?" asked Terry.

"No, but I thought I was going to," Sam replied, blowing her nose. She'd been crying for what seemed like an hour while her roommates tried to console her. All four of them——even Stacy, to Sam's surprise—— were sitting on the floor in the living room. Stacy even looked concerned. "The officer must have thought I was going to faint, too," Sam went on, "because he made me put my head between my knees and then got me a glass of water."

"Suspension?" Roni asked in disbelief. "They've got to be kidding. You don't get suspended for carrying a sign. Not in this day and age. Haven't they ever heard of freedom of speech?"

Terry shook her head, a solemn look on her face. "I'm afraid they're *not* kidding," she said. She held up the *Student Handbook*. "It says here that—"

"Give me that book," Roni commanded, snatching it out of Terry's hands. She read silently for a minute, then muttered, "Uh-oh."

"Uh-oh?" asked Stacy.

"Yeah," Roni replied. "Listen to this—" She began to read aloud. "A student who has been charged with an infraction of campus regulations is required to appear before the dean of the college, who will determine whether the student should be fined, denied privileges, or suspended."

"That's exactly what the security guy told me," Sam said. "Oh, no, what am I going to do?"

"I hate it when they use the words like 'infraction,'" said Terry. "It sounds so scary."

"You think *you're* scared?" Sam asked. "I'm the one who could be suspended."

"My father's a lawyer," Stacy said unexpectedly. "Maybe I should phone him."

Sam looked at her. Stacy was so unpredictable. For the past two weeks she hadn't been speaking to Sam, but now she was offering to help. Living with her was like riding a seesaw. "Thanks," Sam said with a small, resigned smile. "But he's pretty far away to do any good."

"I guess you're right," Stacy said. "Anyway, he's probably very busy. He probably wouldn't even help *me* if I needed it."

Just then the phone rang, and Roni scrambled to answer it. "It's for you," she said to Sam a moment later. "It's Aaron," she mouthed silently behind Stacy's back.

Sam took the phone into her bedroom and shut the door. She was afraid Stacy would stop speaking to her again if she found out that Aaron was on the phone. But Sam wasn't exactly anxious to talk to him, either. She wished he would stop calling. It would make things easier.

"I'm really sorry, Sam. I can't believe that even Alex would pull such a stupid stunt," Aaron said angrily after Sam had said hello. "He's been in student government ever since he came to Hawthorne. He knows the rules."

"It wasn't totally Alex's fault," Sam said. "I mean, I didn't know about the speech or anything, but I do think things just sort of got out of hand. The crowd got excited and started chanting, and—"

"That's not true, Sam," Aaron said, disgusted. "One of the guys in my dorm told me that Alex seeded the crowd in order to get everybody excited."

"Huh? Seeded the crowd?"

"Yeah. He had some of his friends start chanting, and of course everybody else joined in. And there's even a rumor going around that he had somebody call and alert Security, just to make sure that they'd come. What a jerk."

"But why would he *want* us to get in trouble?" Sam asked, bewildered. "I don't understand." She took the phone to her desk and sat down.

"It's like I told you," Aaron explained. "Alex thinks he's a campus leader, but he doesn't use good judgment. I suppose he thought that this way, you would make a bigger impact on the campus, maybe put more pressure on the trustees to do something." He cleared his throat. "Anyway, Sam, none of this is your fault. You're okay, aren't you?"

"Pretty much," Sam said wearily, leaning her head on one hand and twisting the phone cord around her finger. "But I've decided it's like everything else: you have to look out for yourself. I should have found out whether there were any rules against what we were doing, and what the penalties were for breaking the rules."

"Yeah, but you're just a freshman," Aaron persisted. "You can't be expected to—"

"Please," Sam broke in. "There's no point in arguing about it."

"You're right," Aaron agreed. "So, when's your disciplinary hearing?"

"Monday afternoon, at three."

"I'll be there."

Sam shook her head vehemently as she spoke. "I don't want you there," she said. "There's nothing you can do. There's nothing *anyone* can do. The dean looked pretty mad today, especially when he had to step over Alex to get to the microphone. I'll bet he's going to suspend all of us." She let out a short, bitter laugh. "It was all so stupid and pointless, too. The trustees had already decided to sell the stock. We didn't accomplish *anything*."

"Hey, wait. Aren't your forgetting that the point of the project wasn't to *accomplish* something. It was to *learn* something."

"Yeah, I guess so." Sam stopped, remembering how she had felt while she was being questioned by the security guard. "I guess one of the important things I learned was what it's like to feel like a criminal."

"Sounds to me," Aaron observed, "like you've already got part of your paper written."

"I should probably wait until after my hearing to start writing," she replied. Sniffing back the tears, she said, "There's no point in doing a paper if I . . . if I'm going to get kicked out of school."

She put down the phone and dropped her head onto the desk. Since she had come to Hawthorne, nothing had happened the way she'd expected. All her plans had come apart: her relationship with Jon was shaky, Aaron presented one complication after another, and now she might be suspended. She closed her eyes and let the tears come.

The next day was Thursday, the day Dr. Lewis's class met. Sam didn't want to go, but she was more afraid *not* to. Surely Dr. Lewis would have something to say about what had happened. In fact, she was kind of surprised that he hadn't called the evening before. Surely he'd heard about the demonstration by now.

But when she got to class, she found out why she

hadn't heard from Dr. Lewis. The secretary for the political science department had come in and put a note on the blackboard saying that Dr. Lewis had been called out of town the day before because of a family emergency. Although she hoped it was nothing serious, Sam was just as glad he wasn't there. She wasn't exactly anxious to sit in class and wonder what everybody was thinking. And she didn't want to see the other kids who'd gotten arrested. Most of all, she didn't want to see Alex, especially if it was true that he'd had somebody call Security. The whole thing had been so dumb, she thought as she hurried out of the classroom without speaking to anyone, even Aaron. It would have been a whole lot better if they'd just gone to Atlanta and handed out leaflets for the Republicans.

Sam found it was just as tough to face her other morning classes. She had the feeling that word had already spread across campus that the students who'd been demonstrating were going to be suspended. Wherever she went, people seemed to look at her nervously, sort of hanging back, not talking to her. It was as if getting taken away by Security was catching and getting suspended was terminal.

After lunch, she pulled on an extra sweater, got her bike, and went for a long ride in the country. She meandered along back roads and sat for a long time at a scenic overlook, soaking up the late autumn sun. Still, not even the crisp, sunlit air and bright reds and golds of the leaves could cheer her up. She felt as if there were a black cloud hanging just over her shoulder, casting a dark shadow across everything that was good in her life. How had things gotten so messed up? Jon,

Aaron, Stacy, and now the possibility of suspension—
how could so much go so wrong, so quickly?

It was nearly dark when she got back to the dorm,
exhausted not so much from riding as from worrying.
So instead of going to the Commons for dinner, she
made a cheese-and-bologna sandwich and went to bed
at eight-thirty. She'd never been so tired in her life.

She was still tired when she woke up on Friday
morning. Getting up early to jog didn't really seem
worthwhile, so she turned off her alarm, rolled over,
and went back to sleep. When she woke up again it
was nearly ten o'clock, and even Stacy was dressed
and gone. Bleary-eyed and feeling grumpy from sleeping so long, she pulled on her old blue chenille robe and
wandered out into the living room, not even stopping to
comb her hair. Roni was there, heating up some water
for coffee. The door had just closed behind Terry.

"So. You're human after all," Roni said, looking up
from the hotplate. "Just like the rest of us."

"Huh?" Sam snapped groggily. "What are you talking about?" She got the milk out of the refrigerator.

"Well, I wasn't sure. I mean, you've been a real
superwoman. All that getting up at the crack of dawn
and being sure your hair's combed before you open
your bedroom door and jogging and always getting to
class before the bell." She grinned. "It's good to know
that Sam Hill can sleep late and cut class."

Sam grunted. She didn't see what was so funny.

Roni grinned again. "And be a grump in the morning."

"I've got something to be grumpy about, if you ask
me," Sam said, plopping down on the sofa and pulling

the collar of her robe up higher. Her usual healthy bowl of granola didn't sound very appetizing. "Is there enough coffee for me?" she asked.

Roni raised an eyebrow. "Coffee? I thought you never touched the stuff."

"I don't," Sam said grimly. "But this morning it seems like sort of a good idea."

Roni poured her a steaming cup, and Sam slopped milk and sugar into it. She took a sip and shuddered. "Yuck," she said. "How do you drink this awful stuff?"

"I don't exactly," Roni said calmly, sitting down on the edge of the coffee table. "It's better if you just sort of sip it for the first minute or two." She put her cup down as Terry came through the front door. "I thought you were on your way to class," she said.

"I was," Terry replied. She had a copy of the *Herald* in her hand. "But I stopped by the newspaper rack in front of Baxter, and I thought Sam ought to see this." She handed Sam the newspaper.

Sam sucked in a short breath, then let it out. "Oh, God."

"What is it?" asked Roni.

Sam held the paper up in front of her.

"'Oh, God' is right," Roni said in a low voice.

On the front page of the newspaper was a three-column picture of Sam and the others, standing in front of Hawthorne Hall holding up their placards. The caption under the picture read DEMONSTRATORS ARRESTED, CHARGED WITH UNLAWFUL ASSEMBLY! The subcaption read, "Students Face Fines, Suspension."

Chapter 12

"Actually, it's not a bad picture," Roni said, taking the paper from Sam and holding it under the light for a better look. "In fact, you look very pretty in that sweater. I like the way you've got that scarf tied, too —it adds style," she said, trying to cheer Sam up.

The door opened, and Stacy came in. She had a copy of the *Herald* under her arm, too. "Is Sam—" She stopped, seeing Sam slouched unhappily on the sofa and Roni looking at the front page. "I guess you've seen it," she said.

"We've seen it," Terry said with a glum look.

Stacy took off her sweater. "It gets worse. I ran into Nancy a few minutes ago," she said, her voice carefully expressionless. "She seemed sort of worried about how Alpha Pi was going to take this. Making the front page of the paper and all," she added in explanation.

145

Sam looked up. "Alpha Pi?" she asked, surprised. "What have they got to do with this?" *Live and let live*, Nancy said when she was describing the way the sorority sisters treated one another. Sam had figured that the sorority didn't much care *what* you did.

Stacy poured herself a cup of black coffee. "Well," she said slowly, "it seems that they worry about their members getting negative publicity." She sat down next to Sam and threw her a sympathetic glance. "Nancy said that she was going to convene the membership committee this afternoon. It's possible that they..." She put her hand on Sam's arm. "Nancy says it's possible that they might ask you to resign from Alpha Pi. It seems that all pledges are on probation or something for the first year. If they get into trouble, the sorority usually disciplines them pretty severely."

"I don't believe this!" Roni cried, throwing the paper on the floor and beginning to pace around the room. "The hearing hasn't even taken place yet, and already that stupid sorority is talking about disciplining you. You're being found guilty before the trial!"

Stacy took a gulp of coffee. "Listen, Sam," she said, "I know we haven't been getting along so well, but I want you to know that I'm really sorry about all this stuff. If there's anything I can do to help..." Her voice trailed off.

Sam threw Stacy a grateful look. "Thanks," she said. Would she ever be able to understand her roommate's ups and downs? she wondered. One minute she was angry, the next she was okay again. Still, Sam appreciated Stacy's sympathy. Maybe things would be more comfortable between them now. She stood up and stuck her hands deep into the pockets of her old robe. "I've got a headache. I think I'll go back to bed."

Terry came over to Sam and put an arm around her. "That's not the answer," she said. "Going back to bed won't make you feel any better. It's just hiding out."

"Yeah, well, the way things are going, hiding out seems like a pretty good idea to me," Sam said. Just then, her fingers touched something in one of the pockets of her robe, and she pulled it out. It was a small good-luck charm in the shape of a gold four-leaf clover. When she saw it, her eyes filled with tears. She turned it over. On the back was inscribed, "Love Always, Jon," and under that the date, St. Patrick's Day two years before. She stared at the charm. Back then, it had been easy to believe that love was for always, that you could count on love never changing. It had been easy, too, to believe that you could make plans, and things would happen just the way you expected them to happen. But now she knew you couldn't do that, and she felt as if she'd been set adrift in a wide, empty sea, out of sight of the familiar landmarks. Suddenly she felt lonely and desolate.

"Listen, everyone," Roni said brightly, breaking into the silence, "I have this great idea."

"Oh, yeah? Let's hear it." Terry's voice sounded artificially cheerful.

"Well, it looks to me like the day's pretty well shot, wouldn't you agree? It's already after eleven, and all of us seem to have blown off class for the day. And the weekend doesn't look too hot, either, does it?"

"Actually," Stacy said slowly, "there's a home game tomorrow, and the Alpha Pi's are having a—"

"I *know* there's a home game," Roni hissed, shooting an annoyed glance at Stacy. "But I have a feeling that nobody in this suite is quite in the mood for a football game. Don't you agree?"

"Oh, I agree," Terry said, catching on and nodding vehemently. "Nobody's in the mood for a football game this weekend." She turned to Roni. "What exactly did you have in mind?"

Roni grinned. "Well, it just so happens," she said, drawing out the words slowly and deliberately, "that I know these really great people who live in Atlanta. They have this really funky old house, and they *love* having company for the weekend. The more company they have, the happier they are."

Sam stared at Roni. What was she up to?

"Really?" Terry asked with a straight face. "Isn't that an incredible coincidence? I was just thinking about what an interesting sociological experiment it would be to go to Atlanta and stay for the weekend with some people who live in a funky old house in Atlanta."

"And I also have some other friends," Roni went on, "who live on a horse farm and rent horses so people can go riding. Like on Saturday afternoons."

"You know," Stacy said, making a visible effort to get into the act, "it's amazing. Just this morning it occurred to me that I haven't been on a horse since I left Elizabeth Deere, and all of a sudden I got this urge to go riding."

"Right," agreed Terry, "this absolutely overwhelming urge to go horseback riding. Isn't that funny? It must be contagious. I was thinking the same thing myself." She turned to Roni. "I don't suppose," she asked, "that you might also have a friend who owns the best Italian restaurant in Atlanta, do you? Ever since I left Philadelphia, I've been hungry for good Italian food, and just last night I was wondering—"

"No," Roni said regretfully. "I don't." She held up her hand. "But I know exactly where to go to *eat* the best Italian food in Atlanta."

"And shopping?" Stacy asked, beginning to look more than mildly interested.

"Sure," replied Roni. She stood up. "Well, how about it? How about a weekend trip to Atlanta? It would be good for all of us to get away for a little while."

"Great idea," Terry said with a grin. "Let's go!"

"Rather a nice idea," Stacy said in a haughty voice. She sighed. "Actually, it would be *wonderful* to see a city again."

Sam looked at the three of them. "You guys are doing this just for me, aren't you," she said, fingering the gold four-leaf clover she still held in her hand. A wave of affection washed over her, and suddenly she didn't feel so alone.

"Whatever gave you that ridiculous idea?" Roni asked with an innocent smile.

"Of course we're not going just for you!" Terry exclaimed. "We're going so that I can have linguine with clam sauce."

"Don't believe a word of it," Stacy said with a look of satisfaction. "We're going so that I can ride horses and charge up to my limit at Saks. What better reason for a trip to Atlanta?"

"Yeah," Sam said. She grinned and dropped the

charm back into her pocket. "Well, thanks, you guys. Even if you aren't going just for me."

"Don't mention it," Roni scoffed. "It's all part of the deal."

"Oh, I wish we didn't have to go back," Sam said from her place in the backseat of Stacy's car. It was Sunday night, and they were on their way back to campus. "It's like going to sleep and having one of those nightmares that keeps coming back over and over again."

But Sam had to admit that the weekend in Atlanta had really helped to keep her mind off her troubles. On Friday night they had gone to a tiny, out-of-the-way Italian restaurant for dinner, and afterward Roni's friends had welcomed them into their home. On Saturday morning, they'd gone shopping at one of Atlanta's nicest malls, where Stacy had bought half a dozen new outfits—all size six, Sam noticed with a trace of envy. Afterward Stacy had treated them all to lunch in a cafe so dense with ferns and philodendrons that they'd felt as though they were having lunch beside the Amazon River. The cafe served only fish and salads, so they'd all had elegant three-hundred-calorie lunches. Stacy was obviously on a diet again, although why she *should* be was a mystery to Sam. She was already more than stylishly slender. Then they'd spent Saturday afternoon riding horses, and on Saturday night they'd gone to a wonderful old roadhouse and listened to a rock band. Everyone had slept until noon on Sunday morning, had a long, lazy lunch, and now the suitemates were headed back to Hawthorne.

They were only a few miles from campus. Ever since they'd left Atlanta, Sam had been thinking about the hearing the next day, and about the sorority, and— even though she didn't want to—about Aaron. She couldn't help wishing she could talk to him about what was going on. The weekend had been great because for part of the time, at least, she'd been able to forget about her troubles and just enjoy herself. But every so often, she had remembered the hearing, and the thought of it had ruined whatever she was doing. Or she would think about Aaron and Jon, and her stomach would suddenly lurch inside her.

"Try not to worry," Terry said practically. "Soon it will all be over."

"Right," added Roni. "For better or worse, in twenty-four hours you'll know."

Stacy didn't say anything. In Atlanta, she had seemed to become looser and friendlier than ever before. But as they got closer to the campus, she became more and more distant. Her face tightened up, her shoulders became rigid and tense. Sam looked at her roommate. What was going on inside her head? She'd noticed during the weekend that Stacy had hardly eaten anything, even the low-calorie diet lunch. In fact, now that she thought about it, Stacy looked even thinner than she had when she'd first come to Hawthorne.

But Sam didn't have to wait a day to find out everything. The girls were carrying their luggage back into Rogers House when Nancy Greer walked up.

"I was just coming to leave a note for you," she told

Sam, looking very serious. "I've been calling your suite all weekend, but nobody answered the phone."

"We went away for the weekend," Sam explained, trying to smile. "Uh, would you like to come upstairs so we can talk?"

Nancy looked around. "Actually, I think it would be better if we went down by the lake," she said. "I'd like to talk in private."

"I'll take your stuff upstairs," Terry said, lifting Sam's backpack.

"Thanks," Sam said. Her hands in the pockets of her jeans, she followed Nancy down to the bench beside the lake, where they both sat down. It was nearly five o'clock, and the early-evening sun slanted across the still water. Sam could see the tops of the pine trees reflected in the water, and not far away, she could hear the splat-splat of tennis balls bouncing on the court.

"I guess Stacy told you that the APA membership committee met on Friday afternoon to discuss your case." A flock of small brown ducks were gathered in the reeds at the edge of the bank.

"Yes," Sam said, watching the ducks. "I mean, she told me they were going to." One of the ducks broke away from the others and waddled toward them through the grass, obviously looking for a handout of bread crumbs and popcorn.

"Well, we did," Nancy said. "I'm on the committee myself. In fact, I'm the chairperson. Anyway, they asked me to have a little talk with you and tell you what we decided." She paused. "But first, I'd like to hear from you just what happened last week. Why were you demonstrating in the first place?"

Sam thought for a minute. From deep inside of her, she could feel a slow anger beginning to burn. "Isn't . . . uh, isn't this sort of backward?" she asked.

"Backward? What do you mean?"

"I always thought that people who were on trial got a chance to tell their side of the story *before* sentence was passed."

"But you're not on trial, Samantha," Nancy protested in a hurt voice. "Really, it's not anything like that at all."

"You just said that the committee made their decision when they met on Friday. But nobody from the committee came to me and asked what happened." She frowned at the duck, which was pecking at her shoelace. "That seems backward to me."

"Let me tell you what we decided," Nancy said, "and maybe you'll understand." She cleared her throat. "We decided to wait until the dean made *his* decision tomorrow, and see what kind of punishment you get. After all, if you're suspended . . ." Her voice trailed off, but the implication was clear. If Sam was suspended, she would also be thrown out of the sorority. After a moment, Nancy went on, "So you see, we didn't really make a judgment."

Couldn't Nancy see that the only fair way would have been for the committee to talk to *her* in the very beginning, before they even had their meeting? "Yes, but—" Sam began.

Nancy didn't let her speak. "However," she went on, "the committee *did* think that I should talk to you and tell you that we're very concerned about the kind of reputation you're getting. After all, you've had your

picture in the paper twice recently for rather...
unusual activities."

"My reputation?" Now the anger felt like hot little
pinpricks inside her.

"The members of APA don't usually get involved in
radical politics, Sam," Nancy said gently. "It's just not
the sort of thing we do. So often it turns out to well,
be... messy. And it always attracts a lot of unpleasant
attention. Like the kind of attention the *Herald*'s been
giving you lately." She laughed nervously. "You know,
we even had a call from the president of our alumnae
support group. She knew that you were an APA
pledge, and when she saw your picture in the paper,
she called to say that we should have a rule against our
pledges getting involved in radical politics. I'm afraid I
agree with her."

"But I'm *not* involved in radical politics," Sam protested. At least not yet, she thought, her anger rising
now to the surface. If this went on much longer, she
might be tempted to *get* involved. Obviously, some
things needed changing badly!

"But you *were* demonstrating, Nancy insisted." The
way she said the word "demonstrating," it sounded like
something awful—robbing little old ladies or something.

"Well, maybe I *was* demonstrating," Sam said, staring at Nancy. The anger had suddenly drained away,
and she felt cold. Icy cold. "What's wrong with that?
It's a free country, isn't it?"

"Of course it's a free country," Nancy replied
calmly. "And of course you're free to do whatever you
choose to do. But as an Alpha Pi member, you have

an obligation to project a certain image. When you do something like what you did last week, you're projecting an image that the sorority doesn't think is appropriate. If you find it necessary to demonstrate and picket and make speeches, I think you should probably reconsider whether you really belong in APA."

"I see," Sam said quietly. She thought for a moment about all the plans she had made back in Lewisboro and the way those plans had been changed. "I guess I really don't have to think about it very long," she said. "I already know what I want to do."

"Well, good," Nancy said briskly. "I thought you'd see things our way." She stood up and smiled down at Sam. "In the long run, Sam, I'm sure this will help you to become a much better sorority member."

"But wait, you don't understand." Sam stood up, too, feeling a flush of determination. "I don't want to be a better sorority member. In fact, I don't want to be a sorority member at all. Please tell the committee that I've resigned."

She didn't wait to see the look on Nancy's face but instead just turned and walked back toward Rogers House. She felt good. For the first time in weeks, she felt as though she'd done the right thing.

Sam looked at the clock on the bedside table. It was nearly nine, and she was considering making an unscheduled telephone call to Jon. Ever since she'd talked to Nancy, she'd been thinking about all the things that had happened. Now she wanted to talk to Jon, to tell him everything that had happened during the last week—the demonstration, the arrests, the thing with the sorority. She needed his opinion, to hear his views. And to get his support. Whether or not he would approve of what she'd done, he cared for her and would support her, she was sure of that. Picking up the phone, she dialed the number of Jon's dorm.

The phone rang several times. Finally, an unfamiliar voice answered—Jon's roommate, she guessed. "Jon?" said the voice when she asked to speak to him. "No, he's not here right now."

Sam's heart sank. She *needed* to talk to him. "When will he be back?" she asked. "It's important."

"Why don't you try tomorrow?" the guy said. "He's gone out for the evening, and I don't expect him back until real late."

"Gone out?" A sharp disappointment knifed through her.

"Yeah," said the voice. "He and his girlfriend just left for the movies, so like I said, he'll probably be late." There was a pause. "If you want to leave your name, I'll give him a message."

"Tell him Sam called." She put the phone down, very quietly, and then sat there staring at it.

Chapter 13

"I don't know why he said she was my girlfriend," Jon said unhappily. His voice sounded metallic and remote, as if he were a million miles away. It sounded guilty, too, Sam thought. "It just isn't that way between Li and me," he added. "Honest, she's just . . . she's just a friend, that's all."

Sam couldn't help smiling a little at Jon's confusion, but it was a sad kind of smile, an "I wish things could be different" smile. She was sitting on the coffee table in the living room, with her gray crewneck sweater half-on and her books in the pack at her feet. It was early Monday morning, and Jon's phone call had caught her just as she was ready to leave for breakfast.

"Well, I guess in some people's view being a girl and being a friend qualifies her as a girlfriend," Sam said, trying to make a joke out of it. The minute she'd said

157

it, she wished she hadn't. Even to her, it didn't sound very much like a joke.

Apparently Jon didn't think so, either. He snapped angrily, "Come on, Sam. Don't be this way. All we did was go to the movies. I thought we agreed that that was okay."

Sam sighed. "Yeah, I know. I shouldn't have said that. And I'm not mad, honest." It wouldn't help matters to be angry with Jon for not being around last night when she'd needed him, and the way things were, it wasn't very realistic to *expect* him to be around. After all, he was busy with his new life, new friends.

She looked at her watch; it was nearly seven-fifteen. She had decided not to go jogging, but she was hungry, and she needed to get some breakfast. "Listen, could we talk tonight?" I've got an eight o'clock class, and I need to eat something first."

"Yeah, sure." Jon sounded rather relieved. "But my roommate said you said it was important. Is everything okay?"

Sam sighed unhappily. "Well, actually, no. In fact, I've got a disciplinary hearing with the dean this afternoon. There's a chance I'll be suspended."

"Suspended!" Jon gasped. "My God, Sam, what have you done?"

"The details will have to wait until tonight," Sam told him. "There's no time now. How about if I call at six o'clock?" Anyway, she thought, by six o'clock she would at least be able to tell him the most important thing of all—whether she was still a Hawthorne student.

"Uh, well, six o'clock's kind of a bad time," said

Jon. "I mean, I've already made plans." There was a silence, long enough for Sam to wonder whether his plans involved the friend who was a girl but not a girl-friend. "How about later. Eleven, maybe?"

"Yeah. Okay. Eleven's good."

Their good-byes were brief and a little awkward. Neither of them said "I love you," the way they usually did.

"Good morning," Terry said, coming out of the bed-room and closing the door quietly so she wouldn't wake Roni. "I'm on my way up to the dining hall. Want to come with me?" She gave Sam a close look. "You look like you didn't get much sleep last night. Your eyes are kind of puffy."

Sam looked at Terry. "Looks like you didn't, either," she said, standing up and pulling her sweater the rest of the way on. "Your eyes are bloodshot."

"Yeah," Terry said glumly. She got her jacket out of the closet. "Maybe going to Atlanta just before mid-terms wasn't such a great idea. I tried to get back into my chemistry last night, and it was nearly three in the morning before I finished." She shrugged into her jacket and zipped it up. "And I've still got a paper and some other stuff to do for English. Yuck."

Outside, the morning was overcast and chilly, and there was a crisp bite in the air that reminded Sam it really was late October. She looked at the empty bench where she and Nancy had sat the night before, and she found herself telling Terry what had happened.

"You actually quit?" Terry asked in surprise. There was a squeak in her voice, and she stopped still in the middle of the bridge to stare at Sam. "You dropped out of Alpha Pi?"

Sam nodded. "Yeah, I was really mad, I guess. But I didn't do it *because* I was mad," she added as an afterthought. "I did it because all of a sudden I decided I didn't believe in this image stuff that Nancy was talking about." She poked Terry's arm. "Come on. I don't want to be late to class."

They walked the rest of the way across the bridge in silence. On the other side of the lake, they fell in behind two guys carrying backpacks, also on their way to the dining hall.

"It *isn't* fair," Terry said. "A sorority can't expect to make people behave like puppets. They ought to let people do what they—"

"Shhh," Sam said, trying to listen to the guys in front of them. "What are they talking about?"

"Yeah, it was really terrible about Bernie," one of them was saying. "Especially since they didn't win."

"I wish the coach hadn't benched him," said the other boy. "I mean, he could have waited until *after* the game, couldn't he?"

Sam winced. The coach had suspended Bernie? Oh, no! It had to have been because of the protest.

"Yeah, but I guess I can see where the coach was coming from," the first one said, stepping aside to let a girl onto the path in front of him. "You've got to admit that team members can't go around getting in that kind of trouble all the time. The big question is whether he'll be eligible for the rest of the season, after what happens at the hearing today."

"And what effect it'll have on the team if he isn't," the second one added thoughtfully.

"Yeah," remarked the first one as they reached the door to the dining hall. "You know, it would be a real shame if the dean kicked Bernie out of school in his senior year, wouldn't it?"

Suddenly Sam didn't have much of an appetite for breakfast.

At two o'clock, Sam went back to the suite to get ready for her hearing. She wasn't sure what you were supposed to wear when you went to see the dean, but jeans didn't seem exactly appropriate. A nice skirt and blouse would probably be better, and they'd make her look more adult than she felt just then. It hadn't been an easy morning. With Bernie getting benched, the demonstration seemed to have attracted even more attention than it had the week before. Sam could feel the curious eyes boring into her as she sat in her classes.

She walked into the suite and dropped her books on the coffee table, then straightened up. She could hear voices raised in Roni's room. The door was slightly ajar, and she couldn't help overhearing.

". . . but I don't *feel* like going to the dean's office," Stacy was saying in a firm tone. "I gave up my whole weekend to try to make her feel better—wasn't that good enough?"

"Look, Stacy," Roni said, "Sam is your roommate. Doesn't that mean anything to you?" Roni sounded as if she were going to explode.

Stacy's laugh was brittle and sarcastic. "I don't

know, ask her. She's the one who went off with Aaron the other night, even when she knew——"

Terry sighed. "We don't need to go into *that* again, Stacy. All we're asking you to do is spend a little while waiting in the dean's office with us to see how this comes out. It's just moral support. You don't have to *do* anything——just sit and wait."

Stacy let out a grudging sigh. "Oh, I guess so," she said. "As long as I don't have to stay too long."

Her ears burning, Sam quickly left the suite and went into the hall, not wanting them to know she'd overheard. So Stacy *was* still angry with her. Sam had hoped that maybe she had gotten over it, but apparently not. Apparently she still blamed her for stealing Aaron.

"Hi, Sam." It was Pam, carrying a basketful of folded laundry on one hip. She'd obviously just climbed the stairs from the basement laundry room because she was out of breath. "Listen, I saw the article in the paper on Friday. I stopped by your suite several times, but you guys weren't there." She paused to get her breath. "I figured you'd gone away for the weekend."

"Yeah, we did. Thanks for stopping."

Pam pushed her red hair out of her eyes with the back of her hand. "Boy, will I be glad when they get that elevator fixed. I'm getting tired of lugging clothes up from the basement." She glanced at Sam. "Well, I just wanted you to know that if there's anything I can do, I'm here. You know, if you need a character reference, or anything like that."

"Pam," Sam asked, "do you think the dean will

really *suspend* us?" She thought about Bernie getting benched. "What do you think will happen?"

Pam shrugged and looked away. "I can't even guess," she said. "I don't think anything like this has happened at Hawthorne since the late sixties, when there was a lot of demonstrating about Vietnam. In my opinion, we could use a little more of this sort of thing." Her face grew more serious, and she shifted the basket to the other hip. "I think we're too complacent. People should demonstrate about things they think are wrong or unfair." She started down the hall. "Like I said, if there's anything I can do, be sure to call me."

"Yeah," Sam said. Thanks. I appreciate it." She opened the door to the suite, banging it against the wall. "Anybody home?" she called loudly.

"I'm Samantha Hill," Sam said to the prim-looking secretary behind the desk in the dean's outer office. "I have a three o'clock appointment with Dean Peters."

The secretary nodded and reached for the telephone. She wore her hair pulled back in a bun so tight that it seemed to pull the skin on her forehead taut. She raised an eyebrow at the three girls standing behind Sam.

"They're with me," Sam explained. "They're just going to wait," she added. She glanced behind her. Stacy and Terry were dressed, like Sam, in skirts and sweaters. Stacy was also wearing heels and pearls. Even Roni had changed her act. Instead of the red tights and miniskirt she had worn to class, she was wearing a blue shirtwaist dress with blue flats. Sam thought she looked unusually respectable.

"I see," said the woman. Her voice sounded slightly disapproving. "Would you girls please have a seat," she said with a frown, nodding toward the chairs along the wall. "I'll tell the dean you're here, Samantha."

"Uh..." Sam shifted from one foot to the other while her suitemates went to the chairs and sat down. "I guess you know about all this?"

The secretary nodded slightly.

"I...I wonder...can you tell me what the dean decided—about the other cases, I mean?"

"No, I can't," the woman replied. There was a silence. "I can't tell you because you're the first," she said, softening a little.

"The first?" Sam asked in surprise. "The first hearing?" She couldn't decide whether that was good or bad for her, but it did mean that no one had been suspended yet.

The woman frowned again. "Yes, that's right. The first. Now, sit down, please." She punched a few numbers on the phone.

Sam sat down, with Roni on one side and Terry on the other. Stacy was on the end, acting quiet and very distant, the way she had on the way to the dean's office. They were all uncomfortably silent for a minute, then Roni leaned forward and gestured with her eyes toward the secretary, who was talking into the telephone. "Dragon lady," she mouthed.

"I'll bet she's got nothing to do," Terry whispered back, "but frown at students. She was probably hired out of all the other applicants for the job because of her outstanding ability to frown."

"Right," Roni agreed, giggling. "Instead of passing

a typing test, she probably had to pass a frowning test. To see how long she could frown without blinking."

"Shh," Sam hissed, grinning in spite of herself. "She'll hear you."

"Not likely," Roni said, but she settled back into her chair anyway. "She just put those funny dictation headphones on."

Just then the door to the dean's office opened and closed again. Sam looked up. Dr. Lewis had just come out. He strode across the room and stood in front of her.

"Hello, Samantha," he said, and held out his hand.

Sam stood up, feeling shy, and shook his hand. "Hello, Dr. Lewis," she said. "I guess you've heard about . . . well, about what happened last week."

"Yes, I learned about it when I got back to campus this morning," he said. "Aaron Goldberg was waiting in my office at eight o'clock to tell me about it." He smiled a little. "I'm sorry it had to happen at all."

"Yeah, me too." Sam looked down. "I . . . I hope we didn't get you in trouble." She nodded toward the door. "With Dean Peters, I mean."

"What?" Dr. Lewis frowned, and then his face cleared. "Oh, no, I'm not in any trouble. I just wanted to see him before the hearings began, so that he'd understand the background."

"What do you think?" Terry asked worriedly, standing up beside Sam. "Do you think he'll suspend them?"

"I don't now what—" Dr. Lewis was interrupted by the secretary, who stood up and came over to them.

"Dean Peters will see you now," she said in an oddly formal voice.

Chapter 14

When Sam came back out into the waiting room, the first person she saw was Aaron. He was wearing a blue-and-white-striped sweater and standing with Roni and Terry and Dr. Lewis. They all turned to face her.

"What happened?" asked Roni. "What did the dean say?"

For a second Sam just stood still, feeling the relief still flooding over her in warm waves. "He said the whole thing would be taken off my record," she said. "He didn't do anything at all." She shook her head, a little dazed. She still didn't understand exactly how it had happened, but it had. The dean had said he'd realized from studying her file and talking to Dr. Lewis that Sam hadn't really been demonstrating. She'd been taking part in a class project, and her greatest offense was her failure to find out the rules. "No penalties at all."

"Whoopee!" Roni threw her arms around Sam's neck, nearly throwing her off balance. Then, remembering where she was, she stepped back.

"Oh, Sam," Terry cried, tears in her eyes. "That's wonderful!"

Aaron stepped forward and took her hand. His brown eyes were warm, and they held a look of deep affection. Sam looked away, but she couldn't ignore what she saw there. Suddenly she knew that she couldn't hide from him, that she was going to have to confront what had developed between them.

"Hey, I'm glad," he whispered, and leaned forward to kiss her gently on the cheek.

"Well, that's good news," said Dr. Lewis. He bent over and picked up his briefcase, which was standing beside a chair. "I'll see you in class tomorrow," he told Sam as he left. "And don't forget that you've got a paper due on Thursday."

Sam nodded. "I won't," she said. She looked around the office. "Where's Stacy?" she asked.

Roni looked slightly disgruntled. "She was here for a few minutes," she said. "But then she had to leave."

Sam looked at Terry, who glanced swiftly and tellingly at Aaron. Sam got the message. Stacy had left when Aaron arrived, obviously upset that he had come to offer Sam moral support. "Listen," Terry said, glancing again at Aaron, "I've got to get over to the chemistry lab. Tomorrow's the midterm, and I have to look some things up." She turned to go.

"Wait up and I'll go with you," Roni said hastily, running after her.

"Penny for your thoughts," Aaron said suddenly.

He and Sam were walking up the hill behind the lake. They hadn't spoken for a long time. Sam had been thinking about Jon and Jon's friend and wondering if they walked together like this across the Illinois campus, not saying anything, just enjoying being together. It surprised her a little that she could think about Jon that way, about him being with somebody else, without feeling sad. But she didn't feel sad—she just felt thoughtful.

"I was thinking about Jon," she answered. It seemed like a good time to tell Aaron about Jon—and talk to him about the confusion and uncertainty that had sprung up inside her since they . . . since they'd made love.

"He's the guy you were going out with back home?" Aaron asked.

"Yeah, back in high school. He's at the University of Illinois now, studying to be an engineer." The path wound through a grove of pine trees, their dense boughs overhead filtering out some of the gray, late-afternoon light so that it seemed dark and chilly, almost wintry.

"Did you go steady for a long time?" Aaron's question was gentle.

"For four years." Sam picked up a long, twiggy branch with a few pine needles on the end. "We were . . . we were always so sure how we felt about each other, what we wanted to do." She cleared her throat.

"We were planning to get married after we got out of college."

Aaron turned and looked at her. "Past tense." It wasn't a question.

"Uh-huh. Past tense."

Aaron stepped off the path and followed a fainter trail around a huge gray boulder. The trail wound through the trees and emerged above a rocky bluff. Thirty feet below, Sam could see the campus, its lights beginning to twinkle in the twilight. They sat down on a fallen pine tree, shoulders touching.

"Do you still love him?" Aaron asked quietly.

Sam thought for a moment. "Yes, I guess I do. I mean, I've cared about Jon for such a long time. You can't just turn it off the way you shut off a faucet." She paused, watching a gray squirrel scurrying in the ferns at the edge of the rocky bluff. "But I'm not as sure about our relationship—about everything, really—as I used to be before I came to Hawthorne." She hesitated. "Before I met you." She took a deep breath. "Before the other night."

He looked down at her, and she could feel the warmth of his arm through his sweater. She pulled the pine needles off the tip of the branch and turned them in her fingers. Talking with Aaron, the way they were doing just then, was almost like thinking out loud. But somehow it seemed to be okay, maybe because he didn't seem to expect anything, didn't make judgments about what she was saying, the way most people would.

After a minute she said, "I used to imagine that I had everything all figured out. You know, how I felt about Jon and what I was going to do in college and the way things ought to go after graduation. Everything seemed comfortable and sort of safe and solid." She laughed a little. "We . . . we wanted to make love lots of times but we never did. We thought we ought to wait."

The green, brittle pine needles began to come apart in her fingers. Aaron didn't say anything, and after a minute, she said, "Now, I guess I'm not really sure what the rules are." She looked up at him and took a deep breath. "I like you, very much. I . . . I have the feeling that you like me, too. I'm not quite sure what to do about it, I guess. But now I think it's okay not to be sure."

Aaron made a little trench in the leaves at his feet with the toe of his sneakers. "You know," he said, "I used to think that if you didn't have to work toward something, it wasn't worth having. But now I know that some of the best things that happen to you aren't things you can plan at all." He bent his head and smiled at her. "Like meeting you, for instance. I mean, how could I have guessed that a guy like me from Brooklyn was going to meet a girl from Lewisboro, Illinois?"

Sam laughed a little. "I know what you mean," she said.

Aaron turned to face her. He touched her cheek, and his fingers were very gentle. "I understand that you've stopped making plans for now," he said, "but I hope that doesn't include next Friday night." That tender look was in his eyes again, the same look she had seen in the dean's office. But this time, she didn't look away.

"I guess it depends," she teased, "on what you have in mind."

"Well, then, how about a movie? You and me, that is."

Sam nodded. "That sounds nice," she said shyly. And when Aaron stood up and held out his hand, she took it.

"Who wants another slice of pizza?" Roni asked, knife poised over the big cardboard box in the middle of the coffee table.

"Me," Terry cried from her place on the floor. She propped herself on her elbows and handed her paper plate to Roni. "Without mushrooms, please."

"I'll take a piece with sausage on it," Sam said, "when you get a chance." She reached for a can of soda from the six-pack on the table. "Terry? Want another?"

"Yeah," Terry replied. She tugged her gray sweatshirt down over her jeans. "Only I've got to keep an eye on the clock. I have to—"

"I know." Roni heaved a dramatic sigh as she handed Terry her plate. "Tonight you have to study chemistry." She looked at Sam. "Have you ever tried to sleep in the same room with someone who's memorizing formulas? All she does is mutter numbers and equations. It's enough to drive a girl right up a wall."

Terry took her plate. "Have you ever tried to study chemistry," she asked reflectively, "in the same room with somebody who listens to rock music all the time on her stereo? Even the earphones don't help because this particular girl bangs things in time to the music."

"Bangs things?" Sam asked, trying to keep a straight face.

"Yeah, you know. Like pencils and her feet and the hairbrush. Anything that will make a noise."

"The thing is, I always wanted to play drums," Roni explained, licking her fingers. She dished out Sam's slice. "But my parents made me take piano lessons and voice lessons instead."

"And dance lessons"—Terry took up the litany— "and swimming lessons and gymnastic lessons and—"

"You guys are making too much noise," Pam said, poking her head around the door. There was a mock frown on her face. "You didn't even hear me knock. Better watch it or I'll report you all to the dorm council."

"Big deal," Roni said with a grin and a shrug. "Go ahead and report all you want. Who's afraid of the dorm council? We have just survived a trip to the dean's office!" She waved her knife. "Come in and have some pizza. We're celebrating."

"I heard," said Pam. She came in and sat down on the floor beside Terry. "Congratulations," she told Sam. "I'm glad to see that you've come back alive." She gave her a scrutinizing look. "And you seem to have your scalp, too."

"Actually, it wasn't so bad," Sam said. "Pass the hot pepper, please," she asked Terry. She turned back to Pam. "I was expecting the worst, but I guess the dean must have been in a good mood or something."

"Maybe it seemed that way to you," Pam said, "but Alex sure didn't think so."

"Alex?" asked Sam.

"Yeah. His hearing was late this afternoon, after yours. I just ran into him at the library. He said that the dean put him on campus restrictions."

"Campus restrictions?" Terry asked curiously. "That sounds pretty scary."

"He can't go off campus for thirty days." Pam accepted a piece of pizza from Roni. "And he's got to put in forty hours of work in the school cafeteria. Apparently, the difference between him and Sam was that he resisted the security officers. And he also seemed to be the organizer of the thing."

"Ha!" Roni said. "Serves him right." She sat back and drained her soft drink can. "No wonder he got grounded."

Pam laughed. "Well, I guess he *was* behind a lot of what happened. He told me that he had some of his friends out in the crowd, leading the chanting."

"Is it true that he had somebody call Security?" Sam asked. "Aaron said he'd heard that rumor."

Pam shrugged. "He says he didn't, but who knows? Alex likes publicity. He likes to have people looking at him, listening to him. You never can tell what he's up to."

The door to the suite opened, and Stacy came in.

"Hi, Stacy," Roni said. "We're having pizza to celebrate Sam's deliverance from the jaws of . . . the jaws of . . ." Her voice trailed off, and she stared at Stacy, her eyes getting bigger and bigger. The knife fell out of her fingers.

"S-S-Stacy?" Terry stammered. She bent forward for a closer look. "Is that really *you*?"

"It's me," Stacy said defiantly. She came into the living room. She was wearing skintight black leather jeans and a white, sleeveless turtleneck. She had on a heavy, silver chain necklace. And her hair... Sam gasped. Stacy's blond hair had been cut very short on the sides and long on top and was dyed hot pink and violent purple, with a streak of yellow. She was wearing very long silver earrings that dangled almost to her shoulders, and a thick line of black ringed each eye.

"Stacy!" Roni whispered. "You've gone punk!"

Stacy looked around. "Do you like it?" she asked. Sam thought she heard a tremor of uncertainty beneath the bravado in her voice.

"Like it? asked Roni. "Like it? I *love* it! Now I won't be the only crazy-looking one around here!" She frowned. "Except that I'm not so sure about that streak of yellow down the middle."

"Oh, I like the yellow," Terry said. She blinked. "It... uh, it's very nice. It, uh, gives you quite a *different* look." She cast a desperate glance at Sam. "Doesn't it, Sam?"

"Oh, yes, different," Sam said hurriedly. Very unusual. What do you think, Pam?"

"Exotic," Pam said. She cleared her throat.

"Do you *really* like it?" asked Stacy.

There was a strained silence, followed by an unconvincing chorus of "Oh, yeah!"

"Well, *I* don't!" Stacy wailed. Her shoulders shook and the tears began to flow.

"Well, then, why did you get it?" Terry asked, confused. "I mean, did somebody sneak up on you from behind and throw you down and dip you in Easter-egg dye?"

Stacy shook her head, her earrings jingling. "I just . . . well, I just decided that I was tired of looking and being so . . ." She wiped her eyes with the back of her hand, smearing the liner, and Sam handed her a tissue. "I'm tired of being who I *am*, that's all. I want to be somebody different."

"Excuse me," Pam said diplomatically. She got up. "I think I hear my homework calling me."

The others hardly noticed her leave. They were all looking at Stacy. She had collapsed on the sofa, her shoulders heaving with sobs.

"Tired of who you are?" Terry asked. She put a hand on Stacy's arm. "But you're so lucky! I mean, you've got a terrific figure and clothes and a car and all the girls envy you and——"

Stacy sniffled. "Terrific. They envy me. Isn't that great? Isn't that just wonderful?"

"But I only meant——"

"I *know* what you meant, but look at Sam, for instance. Nobody *envies* her——they just naturally like her. And when she gets into a stupid jam, everybody gathers around and wants to know what they can do to help." A tear welled up in the corner of her eye and rolled down her cheek. "Nobody wants to help *me* when I get into trouble."

Sam leaned forward and put her arm around Stacy's shoulder. Stacy hunched forward, shaking it off. "We'd like to help," Sam said quietly, "if you'd let us. But it's kind of hard to help somebody who, well, who . . ."

"Who hangs out in her bedroom most of the time," Terry said in a very quiet voice, "and refuses to talk to anybody, even her suitemates."

Stacy stared at Terry for a long moment. "Is that what I do?" she asked in a small voice.

"Yeah," Roni said, cutting another piece of pizza, "that's what you do." She handed Stacy the pizza.

"No, thanks," Stacy said, shaking her head almost automatically. "I'm not hungry."

"We feel rejected sometimes," Roni said calmly. She began to eat the slice of pizza Stacy had refused. "I mean, you never come to our popcorn parties and fast-food orgies. You don't study with us, or watch TV with us."

Stacy winced. "I suppose I don't," she said. After a minute she stood up. "Excuse me."

"Where are you going?" Terry asked.

"To wash my hair. The color is supposed to wash out." She looked down at Roni. "Will you save me a piece of pizza?" she asked tentatively. "Maybe I'll be hungry later."

"Sure," Roni said. "Great." She stood up, too. "Listen, I've got this really outrageous herbal shampoo I'll lend you. It's got this stuff in it that's supposed to . . ." Her voice trailed away.

Terry watched as the two of them went into Roni's bedroom. "Do you think she'll ever come out of it?" she asked Sam in a low voice.

Sam shook her head. "I don't know," she said. "Sometimes I think she's really tough inside and everything will be okay, eventually. But then sometimes I think she's so vulnerable and insecure that she'll never be able to deal with anything."

The phone rang. Terry stretched across the table and picked it up. "It's for you," she said after a minute. "It's Jon."

Sam took the phone. "It's not eleven yet," she said, glancing at the clock.

"Yeah, I know, but I started worrying about what you told me. So, I decided to call you earlier. What's all this stuff about getting suspended?" He really sounded alarmed.

"It turns out I won't be suspended, after all," Sam said, wondering if his change in plans involved the girl. "It's a long story. . . ." She began to tell him.

"Well, I guess you must be pretty glad about the way things turned out," Jon said when he'd heard about the disciplinary hearing and everything else. "Except about Alpha Pi, that is."

"No, I guess I feel okay about that, too," Sam told him. She put her feet on the coffee table and lay on the floor on her back. "It was probably just a matter of time, anyway."

She closed her eyes and thought about dancing squashed up against the guy with the beery breath. What kind of image was he supposed to project? she wondered. And how did that fit in with the way the Pi Phis saw themselves?

Jon cleared his throat. "Listen, Sam, I've been thinking, you know, about our arrangement." He cleared his throat again. "I think . . . well, I think maybe we ought to go back to going steady. Not seeing anybody else." There was a silence. "What do you think?"

Sam opened her eyes and stared up at the ceiling. "I don't know. It's hard to know what to do." She thought about Aaron, about the firm way he had held her hand as they walked back down the hill together. "I guess not," she said. "I guess I'd like to leave it more open." She twisted the phone cord around her finger. "I still care about you, Jon. But I think maybe we ought to leave it the way it is now."

"Oh." There was a longer silence. "Well, I'm really looking forward to Thanksgiving. I mean that, Sam. I really mean it."

"I know," Sam said quietly. "I am too. I can't wait to see you." She hung up the phone. A couple of months ago, it would have seemed very strange for her to be looking forward to spending Thanksgiving with Jon and this Friday evening with somebody else. Now it didn't. She thought that must mean something important.

"Is everything okay?" Terry asked, looking up from her chemistry book. "With Jon, I mean?"

"Yeah," Sam said. "It is. Everything is really okay."

Here's a sneak preview of *Crash Course*, book number two in the continuing ROOMMATES series from Ivy Books.

Stacy Swanson held the magazine closer and studied the photo of the pencil-thin model in the cranberry cashmere sweater. Yes, it was exactly what she wanted. She had lost another pound this week, and the sweater's clingy silhouette would show off her slender figure. That color would be perfect with her blond hair, too. She picked up a pencil and began to sketch idly on the edge of the page. With a black belt draped at the hip and maybe a straight black skirt, the outfit would be just right for a dinner out in Boston when she went home for Thanksgiving.

She smiled at the sketch. Oh, it would be great to go

back to Boston, to escape from this provincial little college, stuck in the middle of nowhere. That was what she needed—to get back to civilization, where she could go to the theater if she felt like it, or to an art show. Hawthorne College might be okay for some people, but not for somebody as sophisticated as Stacy Swanson.

All of a sudden, Stacy's suitemate Terry Conklin burst into Suite 2C, waving an envelope. "I got it! I got it!" she cried. "Did you guys get yours?"

"Get my what?" Samantha Hill asked, coming out of the bedroom she and Stacy shared. Sam was wearing her usual preppy outfit: khaki cords, a turtleneck, and a black sweater. With her long, wheat-colored hair pulled into a ponytail, she looked like the all-American girl.

Terry flopped down on the sofa next to Stacy. "Why, your midterm grade report, that's what," she said. She pulled off her blue cardigan and tucked her white blouse into her gray skirt. Terry's outfits always reminded Stacy of the uniforms she'd worn in Swiss boarding school the year she'd been sent off to Europe while her mother was getting her second divorce. They were certainly not something *she'd* wear by choice.

Terry looked at Stacy. "How'd you do, Stacy? What did you get?"

Stacy turned the page. "Why do you want to know?" she asked nonchalantly.

Stacy *had* gotten her grade report, but she hadn't opened it. At least she assumed that was what she'd gotten in the mail this morning, along with a note from Sydney, her mother, inviting her to spend Thanksgiving Day with Sydney and her friend David in Vermont. The ski resort where they'd be staying would probably be crawling with guys from Cornell and Williams... maybe she'd meet somebody really exciting. At any rate, someone more exciting than the guys at Hawthorne—but then, it wouldn't take much for that to happen, Stacy thought.

"Terry's asking about *your* grades because she wants to tell us about *hers*," Roni Davies remarked. Roni, who shared the other bedroom in the suite with Terry, was sitting on the floor, pulling curlers out of her frizzy auburn hair and listening to a record. She was dressed in one of her more conservative outfits: a pair of black leotards and a bright orange jungle-print silk T-shirt. From head to toe, Roni wasn't what you'd expect of a Southern debutante.

"Okay," Stacy said with a sigh, turning to Terry. "Tell us how you did on your midterms." Really. Terry was *such* a grade-grubber sometimes.

Roni dropped her comb and began to snap her fingers and dance to the music. "Yeah, come on, Terry," she said. "What's your payoff for all that bookworming? Do you get a free pass to medical school?"

Terry made a face at Roni. "Well, if you really want to know," she said, propping her feet on the coffee table and taking off her tortoise-rimmed glasses, "I did okay."

"That means you aced everything." Roni stood up and went to the compact refrigerator in the corner. "Right?" She took out a diet soda and a half-empty jar of pickles.

Terry put her glasses back on. "Well, I didn't exactly get *all* As," she confessed. She smiled. "But I *am* pulling an A in organic chemistry."

Sam glanced in admiration at Terry. "Wow, Terry,"

she said, "I'm really impressed. I didn't even know it was *possible* to get an *A* in organic." She looked at Roni. "So how'd you do?"

Roni turned off the stereo and sat back down on the floor, soda in one hand, jar of pickles in the other. "Nothing to write home about," she admitted. "*B*s and *C*s. I got a *C* in English because I got an "incomplete" on the last paper. But Richards gave me a *B* in ecology, which I wasn't expecting, so I got off okay." She fished a pickle out of the jar with a ball-point pen and put it in her mouth. "I'll bet you aced everything, huh, Sam?"

Sam's ponytail bobbed as she shook her head. "Don't I wish. But Dr. Lewis gave me an *A* in political science."

"Well, he *ought* to," Stacy said, "after the way that demonstration turned out." She opened the magazine to her sketch and picked up her pencil again. Maybe a hat, a fedora, would complete the outfit. "I mean, you were lucky you didn't get suspended."

Sam blushed. "Let's not talk about that. I'm just glad the whole thing's over."

Stacy added a feather to the hat she'd sketched. The whole thing with Sam had been kind of odd, actually. Samantha Hill wasn't exactly the kind of girl you'd expect to get involved in radical politics. It must have been the influence of her political science professor, or maybe Aaron Goldberg.

At the thought of Aaron, Stacy's stomach muscles knotted with jealousy. She pushed him out of her mind. It wasn't a good idea for her to think about Aaron and Sam or the fact that she had liked him first. Anyway, there were plenty of guys in her life—like Mark, the boy she'd gone out with Friday, or that Beta brother who'd called her again tonight, or Alex, the guy she'd danced with at the Alpha party last week. But it was hard not to think about Aaron. It wasn't just that she happened to like him. She hated being upstaged—especially by her own roommate. Things like that *never* happened to Stacy.

"So what about you, Stacy?" Terry asked.

Stacy gave a careless shrug. "I don't know. I haven't opened my report yet. It's only midterms after all."

"Well, if you feel that way about it . . ." Roni picked up the grade report envelope sitting on the table at the end of the sofa.

Stacy grabbed for the envelope. "Hey," she said, "that's *mine*."

But Roni had already ripped open the envelope with a dramatic flourish, as if she were giving out an Oscar. She began to read aloud: "Miss Stacy Vaughn Swanson, Suite 2C, Rogers House. Art 101, *F*. Music 105, *F*." Her eyes widened and her voice slowed. "English 102, *D*. Art 106—" She gulped. "Art 106, *F*."

"Come on, Roni," Terry said. "*Nobody* fails music appreciation. And with Stacy's talent, there's no way she'd flunk art." She grabbed the grade report from Roni's hand. Then she stared up at Stacy, her brown eyes huge and unbelieving.

"Oh, my God, Stacy," she said slowly. "Roni wasn't kidding. You're flunking absolutely everything. How are you going to get out of this one, Stacy?"

'Why did you get engaged to him when you didn't love him?'

'I'm fond of Christos—it seemed a good idea.'

Max laughed harshly. 'A good idea? You mean your father pushed you into it, and Christos's father pushed him—they're using you, both of you, ruthlessly. Your marriage is the cement in the unholy alliance between my half-brother and your father. They don't trust each other, with good reason, so they've each offered up a child, as a hostage for good behaviour.' He looked into her eyes. 'That's the truth, isn't it, Olivia?'

Dear Reader

The Seven Deadly Sins are those sins which most of us are in danger of committing every day, very ordinary failings, very human weaknesses, but which can cause pain both to ourselves and others. Over the ages, they have been defined as: Anger, Covetousness, Envy, Greed, Lust, Pride and Sloth.

In this book I deal with the sin of **Covetousness**. To covet is to begrudge someone else's possessions, to hanker after things owned by someone else. At some time or another, don't we all wish we were millionaires or had a wardrobe full of designer clothes? But daydreams are harmless—it is very different when a plot is hatched to take something valuable away from its rightful owner.

Charlotte Lamb

This is the second story in Charlotte Lamb's gripping new series, *SINS*. Watch out every other month for five more romances—all complete stories in themselves—where this exceptionally talented writer proves that love can conquer the deadliest of sins!

Coming in two months' time: HAUNTED DREAMS ... the sin of Envy. Have you ever felt that the grass was greener on the other side?

Also by Charlotte Lamb:

SECRET OBSESSION... the *Sin* of Pride...

DEADLY RIVALS

BY

CHARLOTTE LAMB

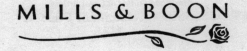

MILLS & BOON

MILLS & BOON and the Rose Device
are trademarks of the publisher.
Harlequin Mills & Boon Limited,
Eton House, 18-24 Paradise Road, Richmond, Surrey, TW9 1SR
This edition published by arrangement with Harlequin Enterprises B.V.

© Charlotte Lamb 1995

ISBN 0 263 79008 8

Set in Times Roman 10 on 12 pt
01-9506-55680 C1

Made and printed in Great Britain

CHAPTER ONE

THE little beach below her father's villa was private and lay at the end of a long, narrow, winding, rocky road which could only be reached through the villa gardens. In the early mornings, the beach was always empty, a stretch of white sand and rocks, with a thin belt of pine trees fringing it, and Olivia went down each day before breakfast to swim in the warm blue sea, feeling like Eve in the Garden of Eden, but without the serpent or Adam. She never had company. Her father didn't get up until much later, and any guests he had seemed to sleep late too.

Olivia loved the feel of the cool morning air on her skin as she wandered down the stony path, in her rope-soled sandals and sleek-fitting black swimsuit, hearing the murmur of the sea and the cry of gulls.

This morning a wave of such happiness broke over her that as she reached the beach she began cartwheeling over the sand, her smooth-skinned body supple in flowing movement.

A moment later she heard a harsh Greek voice shouting somewhere nearby, then the sound of running feet on the sand. Olivia was about to stand up when another body hit her violently.

The breath knocked out of her, she collapsed on the sand on her back with a man on top of her. A totally naked man.

Olivia screamed.

5

A hand hit her mouth, pressed down to silence her, muffling her cries. Olivia struggled against the bare male flesh, panic inside her.

Her golden-brown eyes huge, she threw a scared look up at him. He was big and powerful—that was her first impression. Wide, tanned shoulders, a muscled chest, flat stomach: it was an athlete's body. His colouring was Greek to match that deep voice: he had black hair, dusted with powdery sand at the moment, an olive-skinned face, glittering black eyes.

He stared back, those eyes narrowing, his winged black brows arching in sardonic comment.

'Blonde hair,' he said in English. 'A peaches-and-cream complexion...you have to be Faulton's daughter!'

Then his strong-featured face tightened in a grimace. 'Sorry if I startled you. Now don't scream again, there is no need to be alarmed. I'm not going to hurt you.' He took his hand away from her mouth and rolled off her at the same time, getting to his feet.

Olivia scrambled up too, sick with relief, shaking slightly, and beginning to get angry because she had been so frightened.

'Why did you do that?' she almost shouted at him.

He had his back to her. For all her anger, she couldn't help noticing how smooth and golden that back was: long, muscled, with a deep indentation running down the centre. He was winding a big white towel around his waist. Against the whiteness his skin was an even deeper tan, small dark hairs roughening his forearms and calves.

She looked away, swallowing on a sudden physical awareness, a pulse beginning to beat in her throat as she remembered that body lying on top of her, the forced intimacy of the brief contact.

He turned and looked at her coolly. 'You were about to crash into those rocks.'

Crossly she snapped, 'Nothing of the kind! I knew they were there! I was just going to change course to avoid them.'

His brows rose again. 'It didn't look to me as if you were.'

'Well, I was! I know every inch of this beach. If you hadn't interfered I would have veered to the right and gone on down into the sea.'

Just behind him she saw a pile of clothes on the rocks: crumpled, well-washed jeans, a cheap cotton T-shirt.

She looked back at him, frowning. 'Who are you? What are you doing on this beach anyway? It's private. Have you got permission to be here?'

'I'm staying at your father's villa. I arrived late last night, after you had gone to bed. Your father told me you were staying here too.'

She had gone to bed early; she always did, so that she could be up at first light. Olivia hated missing a moment of the morning here. It was the best time of day; each dawn was like the birth of the world—radiant, clear, breathtaking.

'My father didn't tell me anyone else was arriving,' she slowly said, running a still shaky hand through her short hair, which was cut in a bell shape, soft and silky like the petals of a yellow chrysanthemum, around her small, oval face. Olivia was only five feet four, and proportioned accordingly, with tiny hands and feet, a slender, fine-boned body. Her eyes were big, however, and wide-spaced, and her mouth was soft and generous, with something passionate in the warm curves of it.

The stranger's mouth was wide, too, but hard, the line of it uncompromising, forceful. 'I dropped in unex-

pectedly,' he said, and suddenly smiled, if you could call
the twist of that mouth a smile. Something was amusing
him, but that smile made a shiver run down her back.

'Where from? Do you live on Corfu?' Her father's
guests were usually rich businessmen and their wives—
people she tried to avoid as much as possible, and who
were often openly surprised, and curious, about her
presence, because few people knew that Gerald Faulton
had a child.

His marriage to her mother had ended in divorce when
Olivia was six and she had remained in her mother's
custody afterwards, growing up in a small town in
Cumbria, in the north-west of England. Gerald Faulton
had remarried once the divorce was final, only to divorce
again some years later, without having another child.
He had been married four times now, but Olivia was still
his only child, although they were hardly close; he didn't
keep in touch with her, except to send her a birthday
and Christmas present each year, usually some expensive yet impersonal gift she suspected was chosen by his
secretary. The only time they spent together was this
fortnight every year in his Corfu villa, and even then he
often had other guests to stay and saw very little of
Olivia.

The dark Greek eyes were watching her small mobile
face intently and she felt the skin on the back of her
neck prickle. Surely her thoughts didn't show in her face?
It always made her sad to think of her father; she did
not want this stranger guessing at her feelings.

But his voice was calm when he answered her. 'No, I
don't live here. I sailed here. My boat is down in the
harbour at Corfu Town.'

'You sail?' Olivia's golden eyes glowed with interest at that. 'I sail too. What size is your boat? Did you sail her single-handed, or do you have a crew?'

'I sailed single-handed—the boat's designed to be easy for one person to handle,' he said, giving her a shrewd look. 'Do you sail?'

'Not here, back home. I live in the Lake District, in England.'

He smiled, teeth very white against that deeply tanned skin. 'A lovely part of the country.'

'Oh, yes,' she said with fervour. 'Do you know it?'

He nodded, then, before she could ask him any more questions, he turned away, picked up his clothes and began to walk up the beach towards the pines behind which lay the white-walled villa.

Over his shoulder he said, 'Have your swim. See you later.'

Olivia watched him walk away, a tall, swift-moving man, the white towel flapping against his naked brown legs. Who was he? He hadn't told her his name or anything about himself, and she was consumed with curiosity, but it would have to wait until she met him again later back at the villa.

She turned and ran down into the sea, her body graceful as it dived through the blue water. Olivia swam like a fish. Her Cumbrian home was on the shores of one of the lakes which were the major tourist attraction in that part of England. She spent most of her leisure time on the water, sailing her small yacht, *White Bird*, and she had learned to swim at around the time she learned to walk. Her mother was a sports teacher at a local school and very keen on children learning to swim early, especially if they lived near water.

Olivia cut short her usual time on the beach that morning, but it was an hour later when she walked out on to the marble-tiled terrace where breakfast was eaten every morning in the shadow of the vines growing overhead. She had showered after her swim, her layered blonde hair was faintly damp, and she was wearing blue and white striped shorts which left most of her long, golden-brown legs bare, and a sleeveless yellow cotton top with a scalloped neckline.

Her father was at the table, reading yesterday's English newspapers, drinking coffee, having eaten his usual slice of toast and English marmalade, no doubt. Gerald Faulton was a man of ingrained habit, and disliked any changes to his routine.

He looked round the paper and gave her his abstracted smile, which always made her wonder if he really knew quite who she was and what she was doing in his house.

'Ah . . . good morning! Sleep well?' A well-preserved fifty-five-year-old, her father's once fair hair was now a silvery shade but his features were still as clear-cut and firm as ever because he dieted rigorously and exercised every day. His eyes were a piercing blue, a little cold, very sharp.

'Very well. Did you?'

'Yes. Been down to the beach, have you?' Gerald approved of his daughter's early rising and swimming, as he did of her glowing health and physical fitness.

'Yes. You should come down, Father. It's wonderful first thing in the morning.'

'I swam in the pool, as usual.' He didn't quite trust the sea. The water in his swimming pool was treated and 'safe'; there were no crashing waves to overwhelm you either.

Olivia never kissed her father; their relationship was far too distant for that. She smiled at him though, as she sat down opposite him, her golden eyes glowing with leonine warmth, but only got back that blank stare, as if Gerald Faulton found it hard to believe she was really his child.

Sighing a little, Olivia took one of the crisp, home-baked rolls put out in a silver basket in the centre of the table by the housekeeper, Anna Speralides, who looked after the villa whenever Gerald Faulton wasn't using it. Spreading the roll with home-made black cherry jam, she said casually, 'I met someone on the beach this morning. He said he was staying here, but he didn't tell me his name.'

Her father looked up, eyes alert. 'A Greek?'

'He spoke English fluently, but with a Greek accent.'

Gerald Faulton nodded. 'Max Agathios. Yes, he arrived late last night, unexpectedly.' He spoke in a clipped tone, his lips barely parting, and was frowning; she got the impression he was annoyed about the unannounced arrival.

Yet he had invited the man to stay. Olivia wondered why, but knew better than to ask. Her father did not like her to ask questions.

Max, she thought, remembering the hard, dark face. It suited him. She had wondered what his name would be, thought of all the Greek names she could remember...Achilles, Agamemnon, Odysseus...but had to giggle at the idea of him being called anything like that.

'Max doesn't sound Greek,' she thought aloud, tentatively watching her father.

For once Gerald Faulton seemed to be in a conversational mood. He shrugged. 'He was given his father's

name—Basil, I believe—one of the major Greek saints,
St Basil—but while old Agathios lived, to avoid confusion, they called the boy Max, which was his second
name. I think he got that from his mother's father.'
Gerald paused, frowning. 'I did once hear that his
mother's family were Austrian. I must ask him. Max's
mother was a second wife. The first one died. She was
Greek; she had a son, Constantine, then a few years later
I gather she died in childbirth and old Agathios married
again—a very beautiful woman, Maria Agathios—and
Max was born.'

Her father seemed to know a good deal about the
family. They must be wealthy, or important, or he
wouldn't be interested in them. The cynical little thought
made Olivia bite her lip. Her father wasn't that obsessed
with wealth. It was simply that his mind was one-track,
and business was what he lived for—if you weren't involved in his business he wasn't interested in you. Even
if you were his own daughter.

She looked down at her breakfast and suddenly didn't
want it; she pushed the plate away.

'Agathios,' she murmured, for something to say, and
the name suddenly rang a bell. 'Aren't they in shipping
too?' They would be, of course. What else had she
expected?

Gerald Faulton gave her an impatient look. 'They certainly are.' His voice had a snap. 'You should have
recognised the name at once. I thought you had.'

She had offended him again; she was expected to know
all about his company, and the other companies who
were his competitors and rivals, both in the United
Kingdom and worldwide.

He was frowning coldly. 'I thought you did business
studies at school? Don't they teach you the names of

the major shipping companies? Even if they don't, it would be the easiest matter in the world for you to find out for yourself, for heaven's sake! You might take an interest in my business. After all, one day you'll inherit my shares in the company! I don't have anyone else to leave them to!'

Angrily, he flapped his newspaper and went back behind it, instantly removed from her, absorbed once more into his normal world of business and finance.

Olivia wanted to shout at him that of course she knew all about his business! He had made sure of that, badgering her mother to put her through a business studies course at school and ever since sending her company brochures, talking to her endlessly about the company whenever she saw him, even though they spent so little time together. She had grown up with the subject permanently rammed down her throat.

Her father was the managing director of a British shipping line, Grey-Faulton, which had been built up after the Second World War by Gerald's father, Andrew, who had married the daughter of John Grey, who owned a rather run-down ferry business operating around Scotland. Andrew Faulton had built this into a thriving shipping business, expanding from ferries into freight, and in due course Gerald had inherited it all. Olivia had barely known her grandfather, who had died when she was ten, but she knew from what her mother had told her that Gerald had modelled himself on his father. 'I sometimes think that that ruthless old man was the only human being your father ever truly loved,' her mother had once said. Certainly the business was her father's driving obsession.

She should have guessed that the man she met on the
beach was somehow involved in shipping from the fact
that, for once, her father had talked so freely.

Sighing, Olivia felt the coffee-pot; it was lukewarm,
but before she could ring for more coffee, her father's
housekeeper brought it, smiling at the girl as she put
down the heavy silver pot.

'Oh, fresh coffee...thank you! A lovely morning
again, isn't it, Anna?' Olivia said, smiling back at her.

'Beautiful day,' agreed Anna. 'I heard you coming
downstairs, so I brought more coffee. Do you want
toast?'

Her English was very good, but her accent was
Corfiot; she had been born here. A woman of nearly
forty, she was faintly plump, with long, oiled black hair
which she wore wound on top of her head, warm olive
skin, big dark eyes and a full, glowing pink mouth. Anna
had the beauty of her island—fertile, sun-ripened, inviting. Olivia had met her every year for twelve years,
ever since Anna took over managing the villa. Anna's
husband had worked there too, part-time. They had lived
in a little annexe at the side of the villa, and Spiro had
also been a fisherman. A few winters ago he had died
in a storm, when his boat was lost, and there had been
sadness in Anna's big, dark eyes for some years, but
today it seemed to Olivia that Anna was more cheerful,
almost her old self again.

'No, no toast, thanks, Anna,' Olivia carefully said in
Greek; she only knew a few words but each year she
managed to add a little more to her vocabulary because
she liked to help Anna in the kitchen, learning Greek
cooking and the Greek language at the same time.

Anna laughed. 'You're getting a better accent, Olivia,'
she answered, in Greek.

The phone began to ring in the villa and Anna hurried off to answer it, returning a moment later to say to Gerald, 'It is for you. A Greek voice—he said to tell you Constantine. From London. Shall I put it through to your study?'

He got up, nodding, and followed Anna back into the house, leaving Olivia to finish her breakfast alone.

Constantine? she thought—hadn't her father mentioned that name just now? Oh, yes, Max Agathios had a brother called Constantine. Why was her father seeing so much of these Greek brothers? What was going on?

She had just finished her second cup of coffee when Max Agathios walked out on to the terrace. He was in his old jeans and T-shirt, but somehow they did not look shabby and disreputable on him. He managed to invest them with a sort of glamour, thought Olivia, staring at him.

He nodded to her. 'Where's your father?'

'On the phone to your brother,' she said, before she thought twice, and he gave her a quick, narrowed glance.

'My brother?'

Uncertainly, Olivia said, 'Well, I don't know that, I just assumed... It's someone called Constantine.'

'Ringing from Piraeus?'

'No, London.' Olivia was worried now. Would her father be angry if he found out that she had told Max Agathios about this phone call?

'Ah.' Max turned and stared out towards the misty blue mountains on the horizon, the heat haze between them and the villa making them shimmer as if they were a mirage. A moment later he turned, his face calm. 'Well, I'll see him later. I'm going down to Corfu Town to check up on my boat. I needed some work done on the radio and I want to make sure it has been done properly.'

'I'd love to see your boat!' Olivia said wistfully.

'Well, come with me,' he said, at once. 'If you don't mind riding pillion on my motorbike.'

She was taken aback. 'You ride a motorbike? Did you hire it here?'

'No, I always have it on my boat. It's more convenient to have your own transport, wherever you end up!'

'Yes, it must be.' Olivia flushed with excitement. 'I've never ridden on a motorbike—I've always wanted to though!' Yet she didn't dare leave without asking her father's permission. Gerald was unpredictable; he might not approve of her going off with Max Agathios, and she might return to find him icily angry with her. Olivia found her father far too alarming to risk that. She had never learned how to talk to him, or cope with his moods, except by keeping quiet and out of his way.

Anna came out to clear the table and Max Agathios turned to speak to her in Greek. Olivia watched them both, wondering what he was saying, what Anna was answering. Anna smiled at him and Olivia thought, She likes him! She had never seen Anna smile at her father like that. Anna's olive-dark eyes had a lustre and a gleam that Olivia recognised, instinctively, as sensual. Anna found Max Agathios attractive; she was responding to him as a woman to a man she wanted, and Max smiled back at her with an unhidden appreciation of Anna's ripe warmth.

Olivia looked down, feeling excluded, left out, like a child at a grown-up party.

'OK, we can go—Anna will explain where we've gone,' Max said, startling her by suddenly being closer than she had thought.

She looked up, her skin pink, her eyes bothered, and he gave her a mocking little smile, as if he knew what had disturbed her and was amused by her reaction.

Anna had gone. They were alone on the terrace. Olivia hesitated, biting her lower lip, but why should her father object? He took very little interest in what she did while she was staying here, and if he disapproved of Max surely he wouldn't let him stay at the villa?

'Will I be OK dressed like this?' she uncertainly asked, and Max ran his eyes down over her slender figure in the brief striped shorts, the thin yellow top. That look made her breathless suddenly.

His brows lifted.

'Don't wear much, do you?'

'I didn't notice you wearing much on the beach this morning, either!' retorted Olivia, and he grinned at her wickedly.

'I wasn't expecting company. Well, come on! My motorbike is in the garage.'

They walked round to the front of the villa and went into the spacious garage, which usually just contained the bright red sports car her father had hired at the start of his holiday, as he did every year. Today it held a motorbike too; Max wheeled out the gleaming black machine, which was obviously new, streamlined and light, for easy transport on the boat, no doubt. Max picked up the black and yellow crash helmet which had been left on the leather saddle and held it out to her.

'Put this on.'

She hesitated. 'What about you?'

'I'm borrowing a spare one from the gardener,' he said with amusement, shouldering into a black leather jacket.

She had seen the gardener coming to work on his old bike, wearing a scratched and battered helmet, and laughed at the idea of Max wearing it.

As she began fumbling with the straps of his helmet he pushed her hands aside and adjusted them for her, his long, deft fingers cool on her flushed skin. The black leather jacket made him look bigger, more formidable than ever.

'Now put on this jacket,' he commanded, helping her into a leather jacket which was much too big for her.

'I feel ridiculous in it!' she protested, the cuffs coming down over her hands.

'It will be some protection for you though, supposing that we had a crash—not that that is likely; I'm a very experienced rider, but I'd be happier if you wore this,' he said, zipping it up, and standing so close that she was reminded of that moment on the beach when he had lain on top of her, naked, his body pressing her down. The memory sent heated blood rushing round her body; she couldn't look at him.

It was a deep relief when he helped her on to the pillion and swung in front of her. 'Hold on to my waist!' he ordered over his shoulder, and she tentatively slid her arms round him as he kick-started the powerful machine. His waist was slim, in spite of the leather jacket. Her fingers met on the other side.

A moment later they were riding up the stony private road to the public road running past the villa. It was only when they were out on the highway that Max let the throttle out and the motorbike really put on speed.

The ride was exhilarating. Olivia clung to Max's strong body, feeling as if they were moulded together, letting herself move with him, leaning this way and then that as he took the corners, the wind blowing her short hair up into golden filaments, her thighs forced against his, his blue jeans rubbing against her bare skin.

They drove past the lush olive groves which grew all over the island, past whitewashed houses set back from the road among orange and lemon trees, the dark tongues of cypress trees curling up against the blue sky. The air was full of the scent of flowers. The heat of the day was beginning to intensify now that the sun was riding higher in the sky, and Olivia felt perspiration trickling down her back, her thin yellow top sticking to her hot skin under the over-large leather jacket.

Corfu was a fascinating town, the architecture an international muddle of styles: a Byzantine church here, an elegant French ironwork balcony there, a Venetian subtlety down near the harbour, and elsewhere neo-classical Greek columns to be glimpsed beside plain modern villas. They even passed a flat green space where you could see English cricket being played, with men in white clothes running between the two wickets and people in straw hats sitting in deckchairs to watch, lazily clapping.

Corfu's history was complex; many races had come here over the centuries and left their mark behind them without making much impression on the Corfiots themselves, who continued to live as they always had, in the sun, growing their olives, looking after their sheep and goats on the herb-scented hills, where thyme and rosemary and basil grew wild, fishing in the rich blue sea, cooking in the tavernas and hotels, cheerfully accepting the tourists who flocked there.

As they rode down towards the harbour they passed a horse-drawn carriage slowly plodding along, under the fluttering awning a dreamy couple gazing out at the shops and tavernas they passed. The noise of Max's motorbike made the horse start in alarm, tossing its head, and plunging sideways across the road. The driver swore in Greek and reined his horse back tightly, soothing it with clicking tongue and murmured reassurance, then, as Max roared past, shouted angrily at him in Greek.

Max shouted back in the same language, grinning at him.

The driver waved a fist at him, but was laughing now.

'What did you say to him?' Olivia asked.

'You don't want to know!' Max turned his head to look at her, his dark eyes teasing. 'You must learn to speak Greek.'

'I am learning,' she said, then admitted, smiling, 'Slowly.'

'Well, I shouldn't learn what he just said!' Max said and laughed, slowing as they arrived down at the harbour.

His yacht was bigger than she had expected, and very impressive: white, sleek, fast and amazingly compact both in the two cabins and in the engine-room. It had been designed to be sailed by one person, but obviously it could hold several comfortably. It had sails too, which meant that Max could choose the form of power he preferred in whatever weather he found.

'She's wonderful,' Olivia said after the short tour of the vessel. 'I envy you. I've only got a dinghy.'

'Have you ever sailed around here?'

She shook her head.

'Would you like to?'

Her golden eyes glowed eagerly. 'I'd love to!'

He smiled at her, charm in the curl of his mouth. 'OK, give me a chance to check my radio, then we'll get under sail. There's enough wind today. Why don't you go and buy some food? Just bread, some cheese, a little salad—

tomatoes and onions, a lettuce—and some fruit for a dessert. We'll fish on our way, catch our lunch and cook it in the frying-pan. How does that sound?'

'Blissful,' she breathed, and his dark eyes glimmered.

'I can see you and I have the same tastes. Do you know Paki? Why don't we head that way? Have you been there?'

She turned her head out to sea, remembering the little islet which wasn't far from the coast of Corfu. 'Once, some years ago, by motorboat from the harbour here. I have a vague memory of a very green place, very peaceful.'

'When I was a boy we spent our holidays on Corfu— we had relatives here—and we always sailed over to Paki, every time we came. There are underwater caves there— fascinating places. If we have time I'll show you. I stayed on Paki for weeks a few years back, did nothing but catch lobsters and fish for mullet and snapper all day. When I wasn't fishing, I sunbathed and slept.'

'It sounds wonderful.' It sounded like the perfect holiday—she could imagine how it must have been. Paki was a tiny island covered in olive trees and vines and the maquis, that tangle of grass, herbs and spiky shrubs which in the sun gave out such an astounding scent, a scent which travelled for miles and met you long before you reached the island and which was the very essence of the Mediterranean coasts.

He watched her sensitive, revealing face intently, then said in a gentle voice, 'Off you go and do the shopping— have you got any money on you?'

She shook her head anxiously.

He laughed and produced some notes from a pocket in the leather jacket. 'This should be enough. Don't go too far, and don't be long. I won't take more than ten

minutes to check out my radio. Oh, yes...wait a
second...' He dived out of sight and came back a
moment later with a red string bag. 'Take this, you'll
need it.'

Olivia set off along the busy harbour, watching gulls
chasing their shadows across the blue sky, fishermen
mending nets or loading lobster-pots on to their boats,
behind her the rattle of mast wires, the flap of the wind
through sails, the slap of the water against the harbour
walls. She felt almost light-headed with happiness and
excitement. She couldn't wait to set out for Paki.

She had been here on Corfu for ten days and nothing
had happened until today—she had relaxed in the sun,
swum, eaten delicious Greek food, read one of the
paperbacks she had brought with her. She had barely
spoken to her father, or he to her; there had not, this
year, been any other visitors. Olivia had enjoyed herself,
but it had not been an exciting experience, merely a
peaceful one.

Since she met Max on the beach this morning everything had changed. She felt as if she had been asleep for
years, and suddenly woken up. She felt so alive. She
could almost feel the blood rushing round her body, the
air pumping in and out of her lungs...

She had never felt like this before; she was scared of
making too much of it. Max was probably only being
pleasant to the daughter of a man he was doing business
with; or maybe he was just bored and wanted someone
to help him pass the time. It couldn't mean more than
that. Not with a man like Max Agathios. And a girl like
her.

She made a rueful face. They were miles apart. Why
try to deny it? He was a lot older, for one thing, and,
for another... well, she wasn't naïve; he was far too at-

tractive not to have had a lot of other women, beautiful women, much more exciting women.

In fact, it was surprising he wasn't married.

She stopped in her tracks, standing still in the middle of the bustling street. What made her think he wasn't?

She hadn't thought about it before, but, now that she did, of course it was possible—no, probable—that he was married, a man of his age.

'Beautiful peaches,' a voice murmured coaxingly in English at her elbow and she started, realising only then that she had stopped right outside a greengrocer's shop.

She pulled a polite smile on to her face, answered in Greek, and saw the man's lined face break into surprised smiles.

A few minutes later she walked back to the boat with her net bag full of food and saw Max waiting for her on deck, the sun glittering on his raven-black hair, striking blue lights out of the thick strands of it. He had taken off his leather jacket, and the wind blew his T-shirt up and showed the tanned, flat planes of his stomach. Olivia felt her own stomach cramp in overwhelming attraction and her legs begin to tremble oddly.

She had to stop this happening! She mustn't lose her head over him. What did she know about him, after all?

He leaned on the polished wood rail and grinned down at her as she came aboard. 'Did you get everything?'

She held out the string bag, and his change. 'Yes. That was the first time I've ever shopped for food here—it was fun. I even managed to make myself understood in my pathetic Greek some of the time.'

He looked surprised. 'You do speak some Greek, then?'

'Anna teaches me while I'm here, and I have a tape I listen to every night while I'm here. Just tourist

phrases—please, thank you, where is the bank? That sort
of thing.'

'Well, good for you—very few visitors bother to learn
Greek, but it makes a big difference to us to have people
trying to speak our language instead of expecting us to
speak English.' He smiled, handing back the string bag.
'Will you put all this away in the galley and come back
up to help me? We'll leave at once. We can't be away
too long or your father might get worried.'

The galley was tiny and very compact—a place for
everything and everything in its place—the fittings all in
golden pine. Olivia put away the domed Greek bread,
the salad and fruit and cheese, then hurried back up on
deck to help Max set sail.

Minutes later they were moving out of the harbour
with a stiffish breeze filling the sails, the water creaming
past the sides of the boat. Max watched Olivia moving
around, nodding approval of her deft handling of the
ropes as they met the stronger waters of the sea outside
the harbour.

They took a couple of hours to sail to Paki, and
anchored off the coast just around eleven-thirty. Max
fished over the side, rapidly catching a small squid, which
he threw back, then some sardines, which he kept, and
a couple of red mullet.

They filleted the mullet, left the sardines whole, un-
filleted, then fried them all together, and served them
with salad, which Olivia had tossed together while Max
was fishing. She had squeezed a fresh lemon over the
contents of the wooden salad bowl and sliced the crusty
Greek bread, which smelt so good that her stomach
clenched in sudden hunger at the scent of it.

They ate their lunch on deck, the boat riding underneath them. The fish was better than anything Olivia

had ever eaten—she had never realised how good sardines could taste. There was almost nothing left for the screaming gulls which had gathered around at the smell of cooking fish.

After their white Greek cheese they turned their attention to the peaches Olivia had bought—big, yellow-fleshed, spurting with juice. Max made coffee in his battered old coffee-pot—not the usual Greek coffee, tiny cups of muddy black liquid syrup with sugar, but French coffee, served black, without sugar.

Olivia drank hers, then leaned back against the cushions propping her up and closed her eyes in the shadow of a canvas canopy Max had run out to give them some protection from the fierce afternoon sun.

'You aren't going to sleep, are you?' Max murmured, and she smiled lazily.

'Sounds wonderful to me.'

He laughed softly, his fingertip tracing the outline of her profile, his fleeting touch cool on her sun-flushed cheek.

'We shall have to sail back in an hour or so, or we'll find your father has raised an alarm for us. If you take a siesta, we won't have time to land on Paki.'

She yawned, hardly able to take in what he was saying. 'What?'

'I suppose we can always come back tomorrow,' he murmured. 'We could make an earlier start, get here by ten, land and eat ashore at one of the tavernas on Paki.'

Her lashes gold against her cheeks, Olivia dreamily said, 'That would be fun.'

She drifted off into blissful sleep and woke up with a start at the cry of a gull to find herself lying with her head on Max's shoulder, his arm around her.

As she shifted he looked down at her, their eyes very close; she saw the dark glaze of his pupils, tiny, almost imperceptible flecks of gold around them.

'Time to go back, I'm afraid,' he said, and she couldn't hold back a sigh of reluctance.

'I suppose we have to...'

'I don't want this afternoon to end either,' Max said softly and her heart turned over.

He slowly bent his head and Olivia lifted her own to meet his; their mouths touched, clung, in a slow, sweet, gentle kiss that set off a chain reaction through her whole body. Then she felt Max's hand slide up from her waist to her breast and gasped, quivering.

His mouth lifted; he looked at her, smiled. 'Am I going too fast for you? Don't worry, we'll take it at your pace, as slow as you like.' He paused, then said in an odd, wry voice, 'Olivia, am I crazy, or would I be...? No, not in this day and age, I don't believe it...'

Bewildered, she asked, 'What?' and he watched her in that strange, almost incredulous way.

'You're very lovely, you know that, Olivia—and I can't be the first man to notice the way you look, yet I get the feeling you haven't actually slept with anyone yet... Tell me I'm crazy! Not that it would make any difference, but you're so different from most girls I meet... So, are you?'

Very flushed now, she said, 'Yes... No... I mean... I haven't...' She was so embarrassed that she jumped and started brushing down her hair, pulling down her top. 'Shall we start back now?'

He got to his feet and started clearing the deck, a push of an electronic button sending the canopy back inside the top of the wheelhouse, the cushions all put away below. The anchor lifted, they set sail again, the breeze even stiffer now and blowing inshore so that they made good time back to Corfu.

While they sailed Olivia did the washing up and put things away in their accustomed places, relieved to be out of sight and out of his presence for a while. She was still getting over what he had said . . . the question he had asked. Had he really expected her to have slept with someone already? Admittedly, some girls she knew had already begun experimenting with boyfriends, but these days most people of her age were less likely to jump into bed at the first opportunity. AIDS had made that much of a difference.

They moored at Corfu harbour again, with the Judas trees which grew alongside casting their black afternoon shadows on them as they walked underneath to collect the motorbike from a nearby garage where Max had left it to be serviced while they were sailing.

They drove back to the villa as the heat of the day was dying down. Over his shoulder, Max shouted to her, 'I'm afraid we're quite late. I hope your father won't be too annoyed.'

Her arms holding on to him tightly because he was driving fast, Olivia said huskily, 'I hope not too.' Her father didn't normally mind what she did during the days she spent here; she wasn't thinking much about him and his reactions. She was more disturbed by the pleasure it gave her to feel Max's thighs against her bare inner legs, to press against his slim back, feel the motion of his body with hers as they swerved and swooped round corners with all the grace of a swallow in flight.

Ten minutes later they walked from the garage to the villa terrace, and met Gerald Faulton. Olivia's nerves jumped at the icy expression on his face.

'Where have you been?' he bit out, looking at her wind-blown hair and flushed face with distaste.

It was Max who replied. 'We left a message with your housekeeper—didn't you get it?'

Gerald Faulton turned his bleak eyes on Max. 'You've been gone since breakfast time. Do you know what time it is now?'

'I told Anna we might take my boat out—didn't she tell you that? We thought we would go over to Paki, fish, have lunch there. We've had a wonderful day.'

Her father did not look any happier. He stared at Olivia again, frowning. 'You have been on his boat with him all day?' he asked with ice on every syllable.

Max frowned too. 'I'm a good sailor, Gerald, I know what I'm doing. She was perfectly safe with me.'

'I sincerely hope she has been,' her father said through tight lips. 'I know some men find schoolgirls irresistible, but I didn't think you were one of them.'

Max stiffened, staring at him. 'Schoolgirls?' He repeated the word in a terse, hard intonation that made a shiver run down Olivia's back. He slowly turned his head to look down at her. 'What does he mean, schoolgirls? How old are you?'

All the colour had left her face. She had thought he knew. It hadn't occurred to her that he didn't. She hadn't pretended to be older than her age, she didn't wear make-up, she hadn't tried to fool him. Why was he looking at her like that? She couldn't get a word out.

'She was seventeen a couple of weeks ago,' Gerald Faulton told him. 'She has another year of school ahead of her, and I don't want her distracted before her final exams. I want her to do well enough to go on to university. I deliberately sent her to a single-sex school—I don't believe girls do as well if there are boys around. They are afraid to compete in case boys think they're blue-stockings.'

Olivia turned and ran into the villa, straight up the stairs to her bedroom. She knew there would be no trip to Paki tomorrow, no more rides on the back of Max's bike.

She didn't go down to dinner; Anna without comment brought her a crab salad on a tray an hour later, but she didn't eat any of it. She went to bed early and didn't sleep much.

She got up at dawn and went down to the beach as usual in the first primrose light of day, half hoping that Max might be there, half nervous in case he came. If they could talk, surely he would see—realise—that the years between them didn't matter that much. He had thought she was older, hadn't he? The essential person she was hadn't changed just because he now knew she was only seventeen. How old was he? she wondered, as she had wondered all night, during her waking hours of darkness. Late twenties? Thirty? Not much more than that.

OK, it was a big gap, but when she was twenty-five he would still be in his thirties, so it wasn't so terrible, was it? Men often married girls who were much younger than themselves. A lot of the businessmen who visited her father here brought much younger wives along with them.

If she could only talk to Max—but time passed, and he didn't show up; the beach was as empty as usual. She sunbathed and swam, sat staring out to sea feeling depressed. It would have been such fun to sail that beautiful white bird of a boat again today, to feel the sea swell under their feet and the wind in their hair, the maquis scent drifting out to meet them from Paki, to go diving maybe, when they arrived, and investigate the under-water caves. Olivia was a trained diver; she loved to explore the depths of the lake she lived beside, or the clear blue seas around Corfu.

She sighed, remembering the feel of Max's waist in her arms, the feel of his thighs pressing against hers as they rode along on the bike.

She should have known it couldn't be real—that exciting feeling in the pit of her stomach, the quiver of awareness every time he looked at her. She had been kidding herself. She was crazy.

Or was she?

Hadn't Max felt something too? He wouldn't have been so angry otherwise, would he, if he hadn't been attracted to her? She thought of the way his eyes had smiled at her, the way he had watched her on the beach early that morning, the way he had kissed her, his hands lingering as they touched her cheek, her throat, that soft brush of his fingers over her breast.

Colour crept up her face at the mere memory. She had been so deeply aware of him as a man, how could he not have been aware of her in the same way? Maybe she had imagined it. After all, she had never had a real boyfriend—only danced with boys at discos and had the odd kiss in a dark corner at a party. But could she have imagined everything that happened? The looks, the smiles, the tone of his deep, inviting voice?

Oh, what was the use of fooling herself? He had probably been nice to her for her father's sake! And now he knew that, far from pleasing her father, he had annoyed him, he would probably be distantly polite to her for the rest of his stay.

She walked back up to the villa and showered and changed for breakfast. As she was coming downstairs again she met her father, who gave her a hard, frowning glance.

'I want a word with you. Come into my study.'

Like a schoolgirl in front of the headmaster she stood while her father leaned against his desk, his arms folded. His gaze flicked down over her in that cold distaste he had shown when she returned with Max the previous day.

In a remote voice Gerald Faulton said, 'You should not have gone off all day with Max Agathios. You know that, don't you? It was reckless and foolhardy. You know nothing about the man.'

Flushed and upset, she burst out, 'We sailed to Paki, he caught some fish and we cooked it and ate it on board, then sailed back. Nothing else happened.' That wasn't the truth, the whole truth and nothing but the truth, but she wasn't telling him about the tenderness of that kiss, the brief brush of Max's hand on her breast. Her father wouldn't understand; he would leap to all the wrong conclusions.

'I'm relieved to hear it,' her father said, still distantly, then added in a dry voice, 'But he has something of a reputation with women. I might trust him as a business-man, but not with a woman, and he knew very well that he shouldn't take you out without getting my permission first.' Gerald's mouth twisted sardonically. 'Believe me, if he were your father, Max Agathios would never trust you with a man like himself!'

Red-cheeked, Olivia muttered, 'You're making too much fuss about nothing. In this day and age it is ridiculous...'

'I assure you, most Greek men would be just as pro-tective towards their young daughters. They wouldn't allow them to go off sailing alone, especially with someone like Max Agathios. They have more sense, and they understand their own sex. Left alone with an attractive woman, any man is tempted and, believe me, Max would never try this on with the daughter of one of his Greek friends.'

That wounded her. She knew it was true; she had far more freedom than many of the daughters of her father's local business friends. It hurt to think that Max had treated her with less respect than he would treat a Greek girl.

'What am I to do when I see him, then?' she asked miserably. 'Ignore him? After all, he is your guest...'

'Not any more,' her father said curtly. 'He has left and he won't be coming back.'

Olivia had been nerving herself to see Max again; she had sat on the beach and tried to work out what to say to him, how to thaw that hard, angry face back into human warmth. Now she felt as if a trapdoor had opened under her feet and she had dropped through into black, empty space.

He had gone, without even saying goodbye. She would probably never see him again.

Her father watched her pale face. 'And I shall have to be leaving tomorrow too, I'm afraid. Urgent business in Athens. There is no point in coming back either, my holiday is more or less over. So I've booked you on a flight tomorrow too, back to England.'

CHAPTER TWO

MONTHS later, Olivia discovered why Max Agathios had paid that sudden, unexpected visit to her father. One of her friends at school showed her a newspaper whose business pages carried a story about Max's shipping company.

'Your father sold this Greek guy some old ships, Loll, and now he's been made a director of the Greek company, it says here. And just look at the photo of the Greek guy!' Julie sighed noisily, gazing at the rather fuzzy picture of Max at the centre of the newsprint. 'If you ever meet him, tell him I think he's dead sexy.'

Olivia took the paper and sat down on the grass beside the tennis court on which they would shortly be playing. Julie turned her attention to the game in progress.

'Come on, you two! Speed it up! We're booked in here in five minutes!' she shouted at the girls playing, who yelled back rudely.

Olivia was reading the story with intent concentration. Julie had given her the gist of it succinctly enough: Max had bought two freight ships and a car ferry from her father earlier this year, the story ran, and now her father had been appointed to the board of directors of Agathios Kera, the shipping line operated by Max.

The story also told her something else—that Max and his brother Constantine had quite separate companies, and were in direct competition with each other, running ferries and freight ships between the Greek islands and mainland. The report claimed that both brothers had bid for Gerald Faulton's ships, and that Constantine, the older brother, was furious at being outbid by his younger brother. So that explained her father's phone call from Constantine! And Max's odd smile when he heard about it.

Olivia gazed at the picture of Max, her breathing quick. Julie was right. Even in the grey newsprint he looked sexy. Julie should see him in real life! Then her eye caught something she had missed in her first hurried reading of the story. Right there in the first sentence, immediately after Max's name, they had his age in brackets. Twenty-nine. She had been close enough in her guesswork then. He wasn't yet thirty.

She was now two months short of her eighteenth birthday, which made her just eleven years younger. It wasn't that big a gap, was it? she thought uncertainly, biting her lip.

Julie came back and flung herself down beside Olivia on the grass, her white skirts flaring, showing long, tanned legs. 'Are you going to stay at your father's Greek villa again this year?'

'I expect so,' Olivia said, mentally crossing her fingers.

Julie groaned. 'You might meet this Greek guy—lucky you! Can I come too?'

'Hands off,' Olivia said. 'He's mine.'

They both laughed, but secretly Olivia was serious. She felt sure she would see Max again that summer; it was a wild, irrational belief but a fixed one. She couldn't wait to get to Corfu.

A fortnight later she got a letter from her father telling her that he had sold his Corfu villa and was in the process of buying an apartment in Monaco. He suggested that this year they should stay at a hotel in the West Indies for their usual holiday together. She would probably find that more fun, he said; there would be plenty of young people of her own age around.

'The West Indies!' Julie said dreamily, reading the letter over Olivia's shoulder. 'I wish my dad would take me there, but he always goes back to Spain every year. As soon as I can afford to pay for my own holiday I am heading for the West Indies.'

Olivia wasn't really listening to her. She was staring at her father's immaculate handwriting, her golden eyes fixed and over-bright. She was saying goodbye to a dream. She had been living all year long on the hope that next summer there would be a re-run of the day she had spent with Max, and that this time there would be no abrupt ending, this time they would spend the whole summer together.

Now she knew it wasn't going to happen. She even had the feeling that her father had sold his villa to make sure it never happened. He might do business with him, sit on Max's board of directors, but she had picked up antagonism in him towards the younger man.

Olivia didn't know why her father felt that way, yet somehow she had felt it from the beginning. She had seen the coldness in his eyes whenever he looked at Max. Gerald Faulton did not like him. Why? she wondered, frowning. Was it just one of those indefinable dislikes, a mere clash of personalities?

Or was it because Max was twenty years younger, and already running his own company, being very successful? Business was all her father had ever really cared about—she could easily believe that he would resent a younger man coming along and successfully building up a business which might one day out-perform Gerald Faulton's company.

Of course, she could be imagining all this! Her father might have forgotten all about the day she spent with Max. He might have sold his villa for personal reasons of his own. No doubt he was buying a place in Monaco because it was a tax haven, whereas Corfu wasn't.

None of that mattered. All she cared about was that she wouldn't now be seeing Max.

Julie gave her a sideways look, her face curious. 'Why are you looking as if your pet rabbit just died? Don't you want to go to the West Indies?'

'Not much,' Olivia said truthfully.

In fact she didn't go anyway, because her mother had an accident the day before Olivia was due to leave. Another car pulled out of a crossroads, crashing into the side of Ann Faulton's car. When Olivia rushed to the hospital she found that her mother had serious injuries and would be kept in hospital for weeks, possibly months.

Olivia cabled her father the news, adding that she would not now be joining him in the West Indies. He sent her mother flowers and wrote to Olivia saying she was quite right to stay with her mother, and as soon as he had moved into his apartment in Monaco she must come to stay with him there.

Ann Faulton's recovery was slow and painful, even after she left hospital. Instead of going to college that autumn, Olivia stayed at home to nurse her mother. It was another six months before Ann Faulton was well enough to resume a normal life.

After that, Olivia took a part-time job working as a receptionist in the casualty department of the local hospital. Her mother didn't need her so much any more and

Olivia would have been bored doing nothing all day while she waited to start her course in public relations and media studies at college in the following autumn.

Ann Faulton was fully recovered, although her accident and the months of pain that followed it had aged her. She looked ten years older than she had, and she could no longer manage her job as a sports mistress. She retired, but she too hated having nothing to do, so after a few months she decided to open a sports shop in the Lake District.

Olivia had chosen a college two hours away from home so that she could visit her mother quite often. During her first year there, she lived on the campus, in a narrow little room as bare as a monk's cell, made a lot of new friends and learnt to live on very little, worked hard and went to a lot of parties.

She spent a fortnight with her father that summer in his elegant Monaco apartment with a view of the palace gardens, dark with cypress and brilliant with bougainvillaea. Gerald Faulton never mentioned either of the Agathios brothers, so eventually Olivia very casually asked over breakfast one day, 'Are you still on the board of Max Agathios's company?'

'Yes, why?' he asked, as if she might be an industrial spy, and she shrugged, still trying to look and sound totally offhand.

'You always say you want me to be interested in your business affairs. I read in the newspapers that you had joined the board of Agathios Kera, that's all...' She paused, then asked, 'Why Kera, by the way? What does that mean?'

'Leon Kera is a sleeping partner who put up some of the money for the company—he's a financier,' her father said flatly. 'The rumour is that Max Agathios is going to marry his daughter, which will keep the company in the family.'

Olivia's skin turned cold. 'Oh?' She took a painful breath. 'What's her name?' She had to know; she needed to know to believe it, to accept that Max was out of reach for her, that it was time to forget him.

'Daphne,' her father clipped out. 'She's Greek, a beautiful girl, typical Greek colouring—black hair, olive skin, dark eyes. She's clever too, a good head on her shoulders. She works with Max. I usually see her at board meetings, sitting beside him. More coffee?'

She shook her head, too stunned to speak, and her father got up from the table, putting his newspaper under his arm.

'Well, I have work to do,' he said, walking away without looking at her, to her relief, because she hated to think he might read her expression and guess at her feelings.

The last remnants of her dream had just died. She hadn't admitted it to herself, but she did now; for the past year she had gone on hoping that one day she would meet Max again and...

She broke off, biting down on her lower lip angrily. How stupid! She met a man once, spent a day with him, got kissed, and that was that. Why had she made such a big thing of it? He had probably forgotten her within a week.

Well, there were plenty of attractive guys around at her college. She had been keeping them all at a distance, turning down dates, refusing to get involved—but not any more. When she got back to college, she was going to have fun and forget Max Agathios.

* * *

The following two years were busy and enjoyable ones for Olivia. She did well in her course, and managed to get a good final result, and she was the centre of a lively social circle at her college. She went out with some of the best-looking men, but didn't fall in love with any of them, although several claimed they had fallen in love with her.

One guy asked her to live with him; another asked her to marry him. She turned them both down. Kindly. But firmly.

From time to time she read about Max in the newspapers. His company seemed to be growing rapidly—he was now running a cruise line around the Mediterranean and Aegean seas. She saw advertisements for his cruises all the time. He still seemed to run ferries in the Aegean, and had ships carrying freight from island to island there too, she gathered, but cruise ships were now the major part of his business.

From the sound of it, Max's company was now bigger than his brother's, or her father's. How did they like that? she wondered. They were both so competitive, and neither of them had much love for Max. It must be burning them up to see him forging ahead like this!

The summer of the year she left college she was invited to America for the whole summer by a guy she had been dating for months, but who was now returning for good to his Florida home after a year spent working in Britain.

His family had a beach house on the Keys in Florida; Gerry talked lovingly about brown pelicans and giant sea turtles, conch chowder and Key lime pie, mangrove swamps and glass-bottomed boats.

'I want you to meet my folks,' he said. 'And they're dying to meet you, they've heard so much about you.

Oh, come on, Loll—if you don't visit with us this year
we may never see each other again!'

Her mother persuaded her to join her father though.
After all, she pointed out, it was the only time they saw
each other during a year.

'OK, he isn't a loving father, but by his own rather
weird standards he's always tried to act like a father,
kept in touch, remembered your birthday and so on. I
think you should go.' Ann Faulton gave her a wry look.
'And from what you've told me about this Gerry, he's
getting far too serious about you, but you're not that
way about him. If you spend the summer with him and
his family he'll be entitled to think you like him more
than you do, Olivia.'

It was true, and, not for the first time, Olivia took
her mother's advice, told Gerry she was sorry but she
couldn't come to Florida, and went to Monaco instead.

The year since she last saw him showed her that her
father was beginning to show his age. Gerald Faulton
was now in his mid-fifties, and his hair was entirely silver,
his skin lined from years of sun-worshipping. His
regimen of diet and exercise had kept time at bay for a
long time, and he was still very slim and upright, but
Olivia felt a real pang of sadness as she realised that he
was beginning to lose the battle. His neck was wrinkling,
his jawline was no longer taut and firm, his eyes were
set deeper in his tanned skin and he no longer moved
with the same spring in his step.

His nature hadn't softened with time either; he was
as remote and cold of heart as ever. Within a couple of
days, Olivia was wondering why on earth she had taken
her mother's advice and come. Why did her father go
on inviting her when they had nothing in common,

nothing to talk about, and there wasn't a shred of warmth or affection between them?

At least the weather was good though; she could swim and sunbathe, and her father's small apartment was comfortable, indeed elegant.

One night Gerald suggested that they visit the Casino at Monte Carlo, the old Palais Casino on the main square, with its baroque décor, ornate, gilded, elegant. Olivia felt no excitement around the tables. She didn't want to play cards herself, or gamble on roulette; she soon grew bored with watching her father play baccarat, and instead began to wander around, looking at the *salles privées*, the silken brocade upholstery of chairs, the long swagged curtains, the paintings on the walls. She drank a glass of chilled white wine, a cup of coffee, nibbled nuts and crisps, watched over the bare white shoulders of a woman in black who was losing heavily at roulette, wondering how she could bear to throw her money away without a change of expression, and kept looking at her watch, hoping her father would show signs of getting bored.

Suddenly she realised that her father was no longer at the baccarat table.

He was standing near the main door of the big salon, talking to some people Olivia had never seen before—two men and a woman.

The older man was broad-set, wearing what she recognised as expensively tailored evening dress, his rather bull-like head set on heavy shoulders, his hair black, with a flash of silver at the temples. Olivia was not attracted by the ruthless force she read in his face and body, but she had read somewhere that power was an aphrodisiac, and she could believe it; some women might find him exciting.

Looking from him to the other, younger, man, Olivia saw such a strong likeness that it was obvious they were related; possibly brothers? No, the age gap was too great. They must be father and son.

The woman with them looked the right age to be the wife of the older man, yet she was so lovely Olivia found it hard to believe that she was the mother of a son in his twenties.

A slender, graceful woman with hair like black silk and eyes like jet, she wore a white dress that was elegant and yet sensual, clinging to her body from her shoulders to her ankles, covering everything and yet hinting at what lay underneath so that every man who passed her turned to stare as if wondering exactly what she was hiding.

Olivia watched her smiling sleepily, sensually, at Gerald Faulton, saw the way her father looked back, not even trying to hide the fact that he coveted the wife of another man, and was startled. She hadn't seen her father look that way at any woman before. It was not in his rather chilly nature, not in his controlled temperament.

But there was no doubt about it. Her father had an almost tranced look on his face, a flush on his high cheekbones, a brightness in his eyes.

Quickly, Olivia looked at the man she had decided must be this woman's husband. How did he feel about the way her father was watching his wife?

Or was she his wife?

Oh, yes, she thought, seeing a glitter in the man's heavy-lidded eyes, a streak of angry red staining his cheeks. That was a possessive, angry look, the instinctive reaction of a man watching his wife with someone else, and then something odd happened—he deliberately lowered his rather heavy lids, veiling that expression, as if he didn't want Gerald to see it.

Olivia was struck by that. Why was he afraid to let her father see his angry reaction?

Who was he? Someone who worked for her father? Someone who wanted to do business with her father?

It was very odd; she felt a distinct sense of familiarity whenever she looked at him. Had they met before, after all? She didn't remember it. And yet there was something...

While she was struggling to pin down whatever memory was trying to surface, her father turned to stare in her direction, and all the others looked round too.

Gerald Faulton made a peremptory gesture, beckoning her.

Olivia sighed, but obeyed, walking across the hushed, crowded room towards them, edgily aware of being watched all the way.

She was wearing her only really good evening dress, a classic backless slipper satin, tawny-coloured, with a deep V-neck, which left her shoulders and arms bare, the long skirts clinging from her waist to her thighs and then flowing easily down to her feet. The colour gave depth and brightness to her blonde hair, matched the golden colour of her eyes.

Her father had bought it for her, after deciding that nothing Olivia had brought with her was good enough for a party they had been to the night after she arrived.

The lifestyle on Corfu had been very different—far more casual and relaxed, a real beach holiday in the sun with a party style to match. Here, Gerald Faulton moved in circles who loved any excuse for dressing up: putting on jewellery, clouds of perfume, expensive designer dresses, the women competing to look the most stunning, the men apparently wanting the best-looking woman on their arm each night.

Gerald had gone with Olivia to choose the dress. It was ready-made, but designed by a top French couturier, and luckily fitted her as if it had been made for her, but Olivia wasn't quite comfortable in it—it was so formal, and yet left so much of her bare.

'Ah, there you are, Olivia. I want you meet some friends of mine... You've heard me mention Constantine Agathios, haven't you?'

She stiffened, her hand already held out, her eyes on the man's heavy, olive-skinned face.

It was a shock, and yet it wasn't. No wonder he had looked familiar! No wonder she had been increasingly sure she had seen him somewhere before.

He and Max might only be half-brothers, but they shared a family resemblance which was very marked, in spite of the age gap between them. She should have guessed at once. She was sure she would have guessed, sooner or later, if she hadn't been told.

He took her hand and Olivia shivered involuntarily as those large, tanned fingers swallowed hers up. She almost wondered if he would let her hand go again; did he ever let anything go? Meeting those heavy-lidded eyes was even more unnerving. This was a difficult, complicated man, she thought, staring back at him.

There was something belligerent, choleric, in that face; he had a temper, from the look of him. Not an easy man to deal with, or maybe even like? A bull on the point of charging, she thought—that was the impression he left on her, and yet there was something else, a craftiness about the half-hidden eyes, the line of the selfish mouth. She remembered the angry glitter of his eyes when her father stared covetously at his wife, the way Constantine Agathios had swiftly veiled that look, hiding it away. This man was full of rage, but he was cunning enough to hide it, which made him disturbing.

'I am delighted to meet you, Olivia—may I call you Olivia? You are very like your father. I feel I know you already, and you must be the same age as my son here, Christos,' Constantine said, and smiled suddenly, full of charm which Olivia didn't quite trust, although she blinked in surprise as it focused on her. That was something else he had in common with Max—Max had that charm, too, only in him it was genuine, full of warmth. She was sure that Constantine's charm was skin-deep.

'Thank you,' she murmured, flickering a look at the younger man. So she had been right—it was his son!

'What a beautiful dress—that colour is perfect with your wonderful English complexion and hair,' said the woman beside Constantine, in a deeply accented voice.

'My wife, Helena,' Constantine introduced her, letting go of Olivia's hand at last so that she could shake hands with his wife, who smiled in that languid, sleepy way at Olivia, as she had at Gerald.

'I always envy English women. They don't have the problem of coping with too much sun, ruining their skins, giving them wrinkles and lines before they're middle-aged. In my country, the sun is a woman's enemy.'

'We just have to cope with rain,' Olivia said, smiling back.

'You English always complain about your weather, but rain is so good for the skin that I only wish it rained in Greece every day!'

'If it did, you wouldn't,' Olivia drily said, adding, 'Anyway, your skin is wonderful—I wish I had that tan!'

'Thank you.' Helena smiled, accepting the compliment gracefully, a woman used to compliments yet silently immune to them, Olivia felt. Not vain, simply knowing precisely how she looked.

With that skin which had the polished lustre of gold silk, a light tan overlaying the original olive complexion, very few lines around her mouth and eyes, she could have been any age from thirty to fifty.

'My mother never sunbathes,' said the young man beside Helena. 'She wears a hat whenever she goes out in the sun, and lots of sunblock, yet she always seems to have her tan! I think it is just the natural colour of her skin.'

Olivia looked at him and felt her heart skip a beat, because Christos Agathios looked the way she was sure Max must have done at that age.

His black hair was very curly, whereas Max's hair was straight, and his face wasn't so tough, so honed and taut, but the family likeness was unmistakable, and so was the family charm which shone out of his smile, in this case a charm which held warmth and light-hearted humour.

'I've heard a lot about you,' he said, and her eyes widened.

'Who from?' she asked, faintly breathless. Max? Had Max talked about her?

Christos laughed. 'Your father, of course! Who else?'

Disappointment seeped through her, but she managed a pretence of laughter. 'Of course, silly question.' Why on earth would Max have mentioned her to his nephew, anyway?

Christos looked past her into the glitter of the salon, the fixity of the gamblers around the table, the tension in the air. He made a face, his nose wrinkling.

'Dead boring, isn't it? Why don't we go on some-where a bit livelier? I know a great nightclub not far from here—we can dance to some terrific music and you can meet some of my friends. They're all going to be there tonight.'

Her eyes brightened. 'I'd love that.' Then she looked at her father, her smile fading. She could never remember her father going to a nightclub or anywhere like that; he didn't like noisy pop music and he wasn't a big nightclub fan. She couldn't see him agreeing to Christos's suggestion.

He did though, immediately, all smiles. 'Good idea, why don't we make a night of it?'

On the way, she asked Christos, 'Have your family got an apartment here too?' and he shook his head.

'We borrowed one from a friend for a month. Your father said you just left college—have you got a job set up?'

'Yes, in London, in the marketing and public relations department of my father's company. What do you do?'

'Work with my father too.'

They grinned at each other. 'Nepotism for both of us, then,' Olivia said, and they laughed.

'I'm in the accounts department at the moment,' Christos confided. 'I did an economics degree in the States. But I'll take over running the firm one day so I'll move around from one office to the other until I know how the whole operation works.'

'That seems a good idea. I hope I'll be doing something like that, although economics isn't my strong point.' She grimaced and Christos laughed.

'Nobody can be good at everything. I expect your father has enough accountants working for him, anyway. He only has one daughter.'

'Yes,' Olivia said, not for the first time wondering how her father really felt about that. He must have hoped for sons to inherit the firm. Did he resent the fact that she hadn't been a boy? Did that explain the coldness in his eyes whenever he looked at her?

The nightclub was ultra-modern, with a rainbow of laser lights criss-crossing the darkness and the very latest music played continuously. The DJ was lively, professional, speaking English and French alternately, both very fluently, telling jokes in both, playing music from both countries. The floor was underlit with a cloudy light which shone upwards, giving a glimmer to faces as people danced.

At some stage her father, Constantine and Helena all slipped away, but Olivia hardly noticed them leaving. Christos had introduced her to a crowd of young people he had met down there. They were an international lot—English, French, some Greek—lively and friendly, easy to get on with. They all sat around on leather couches, talking and laughing, drinking, eating the only food the club offered—faintly stale *sandwich au jambon*: chunks of dry French bread with thin slices of ham between them.

She danced with a few guys, but mostly with Christos, and time slid by without Olivia ever even looking at her watch.

She was stunned, when they left eventually, to realise that dawn was breaking. Where on earth had the night gone?

Christos stopped in the strangely still and silent main square, empty for once of traffic, the shutters up over every window, Monte Carlo sleeping all around them.

Looking down at her with bright, sleepless eyes, he said, 'I don't want to go home yet, do you? Let's eat breakfast at a terrace café. I know somewhere that does a great croissant and the best coffee you can drink.'

She didn't want the night to end either. They ran, with linked hands, like children, through the streets, getting attentive looks from one of Monaco's policemen because they were still in evening dress and laughing, and might be drunk and a possible problem. Monaco had more policemen to the square inch than anywhere else in the world; that was why so many very rich people lived there. They felt safe and protected.

Olivia and Christos sat at a table outside on the pavement for an hour, drinking strong coffee, eating crisp, flaky croissants, watching the sun rise and the traffic around them thicken as the rest of the world woke up and set off to work.

They were still laughing, talking about films and favourite pop stars and what they liked to read. Christos had a terrific sense of humour; he was funny, quick with his retorts, kept her giggling.

Reluctantly, she looked at her watch at last and said, 'I suppose I'd better get home before my father calls the police.'

Christos grinned. 'And I bet he would too. Your father scares the living daylights out of me!'

She knew he didn't mean it. Christos wasn't the easily scared type. Life didn't hold much that scared Christos; he had too much of his father's nature in him. He might laugh a lot, but there was bedrock somewhere, under his friendly charm.

'What shall we do tonight?' he asked. He was taking it for granted that she would see him again, but Olivia wasn't offended. She didn't pretend she had another date, just laughed at him.

'You're sure of yourself, aren't you!'

He smiled into her eyes. 'We had fun last night, didn't we? And we both want to go on having fun. I've got a car. Why don't we drive to Juan-les-Pins, have dinner, then cruise the cafés—go to the Pam-Pam, Le Crystal, Le Refuge? Juan-les-Pins is always good fun, isn't it? If you sit in the Pam-Pam long enough you see everyone you know sooner or later.'

'Everyone *you* know, maybe! My friends never go there. Nor do I. Never been there in my life.'

'I'm shocked. Then we certainly must go tonight. You'll love it. It's crazy and as brassy as a fairground, but never dull.'

'Sounds like you, then!' mocked Olivia, and he roared with laughter.

When she got back to the apartment on Boulevard St-Paul, Olivia was nervous as she quietly unlocked the front door. She hoped her father would be asleep, then he might never realise that she had been out all night.

She was in luck. The apartment was silent, the door of her father's room closed. Olivia tiptoed into her own bedroom, undressed, washed, and went to bed. She was asleep almost before her head touched the pillow.

When she woke up it was afternoon; the room was shadowy because she had not opened the shutters but through the slats she could see sunlight gleaming. She looked at the clock and got a shock when she saw that it was nearly three. In the afternoon, she realised, and for a moment couldn't understand why she was in bed at that hour of the day. Was she ill?

Then she remembered, and almost fell out of bed. What on earth would her father say? When she'd showered, she nerved herself, opened her bedroom door, went in search of him, only to discover that the apartment was empty. He must have gone out.

He got back an hour later and never asked Olivia a single question, but simply told her he had had a phone call from a friend, inviting him to dinner—did she want to come along? It was an informal meal, it wouldn't matter if she didn't want to go.

'Well, Christos did ask me out...' she began, and her father looked pleased.

'Fine, then I'll go alone tonight. I'm glad you like Christos—you'll enjoy your visit more, having young people to go around with.'

Olivia loved Juan-les-Pins from the first moment she saw it. They left quite early, to drive from Monaco along the Corniche to Nice, then along the motorway to Antibes, across Cap d'Antibes, the promontory which thrust out into the sea, an expensive and exclusive part of this coast, covered in gardens and trees, with narrow roads going up and down the hill in a criss-cross pattern. Hidden behind high walls and large gardens lay the whitewashed villas of the very rich, sleeping in the sun. The top of the hill was surmounted by an old lighthouse; from up there visitors could view the surrounding land-scape, Christos told Olivia when they too stopped there in the warm evening light and had a Coke under the plane trees.

'There's Juan-les-Pins, down there,' he said, gesturing.

As they drove off the Cap, Olivia realised how Juan-les-Pins had got its name—there were not many pines left, but you could imagine how pretty it must have been when there had been little here but pine trees and sand. There were still some pines around the Casino area, but everywhere else had been built on; the blocks of apartments and hotels and cafés were so close together that it was a bottleneck of traffic by day, but at night it glittered with lights and throbbed with pop music.

The tiny, winding streets were thick with traffic, the pavements crowded with tourists out to have a good time, the cafés and bars pounding with music and laughter and people talking.

Olivia and Christos met some of the people they had seen at the nightclub the night before, and she soon realised that that was no coincidence—Christos had known they would be in Juan-les- Pins. The group visited a different resort every night, drifting around from one bar to another, dancing, talking, drinking coffee or wine, watching everyone else walking past on the pavements.

They did not get back to Monaco until the early hours again, but now Olivia knew that her father wouldn't say a word, even raise an eyebrow. He was delighted that she was dating Christos.

For the next couple of weeks that was the pattern of their days and nights. Olivia slept every morning and spent the afternoon swimming and sunbathing, and in the evening Christos arrived to take her out. Looking back on these days, it all seemed to be a shimmer of sunlight and laughter, a heady sense of freedom now that her exams were over and she had not yet begun to work for her living. Christos was the perfect playmate— she enjoyed being with him, and she liked him more than anyone else she had ever dated.

She only wished these days didn't have to end. If only real life need never break in on them! That was how she felt about this holiday—that it wasn't quite real, a golden fantasy of sun and sea and glittering evenings together. She would miss Christos when they left here. She wished he lived in London and they could meet again—or wouldn't their relationship work back in grey, rainy, all too real old London?

It never entered her head that Christos might ask her to marry him.

Two days before she was due to leave Monaco Olivia was just about to walk into the sitting-room when she overheard her father talking on the phone. 'Kera died last night,' he said in a curt, clipped tone. 'I just got a call from Opie. As soon as the funeral is over... The next board meeting...'

Olivia halted, her hand on the door. Was he talking to Max? She was angry with herself for the immediate prickle of her nerves, the heat hitting her skin. What if he was? So what? Don't be so stupid! she told herself.

She heard her father hang up, heard the window on to the balcony being slid open. Olivia took a deep breath, walked in there, saw Gerald standing in the sunshine, staring down over the pink palace of the Grimaldi family, the hereditary princes of Monaco, but from his heavy frown, his abstracted air, not even seeing the beauty of the view.

As she walked out to join him he started and gave her a blank look. 'Oh, Olivia! There you are. Yes. I was just on the phone to Constantine...'

'Constantine?' she repeated, taken aback. Was he lying? But why on earth should he?

'Yes. I've invited him and Helena, and Christos, to dinner for your last evening here.' He pulled his wallet out of his inner jacket pocket, counted out some banknotes, handed them to her. 'I want you to look pretty for the occasion. Buy something new, something very special.'

Dazedly, she took the money, not really listening, her mind on Max. Was her father going to tell her that Max's partner had died? Had Max married Daphne Kera yet? And who on earth was Opie?

She could hardly ask her father. She knew she would only get that cold, remote stare, and be snubbed for her pains. Gerald had always been secretive.

Whenever Gerald had a dinner party he brought in a professional chef with his own staff so that neither he nor Olivia had to worry about the arrangements for the evening. They could concentrate on their guests.

The party went as smoothly as they always did, yet Olivia sensed tension in the room all evening. Her father and Constantine were in an odd mood: excited yet edgy. Helena was very quiet; she hardly said a word, watching her husband with what seemed to Olivia to be anxiety. Even Christos was not himself. He drank several glasses of wine with dinner, then went on to have a double brandy at the coffee stage, which made Constantine scowl at him.

'You've had enough to drink!'

Olivia saw Helena put her soft, tanned hand on her husband's dark sleeve, saw him turn his bull-like head to glare down at her. She didn't say anything, but her eyes must have pleaded, because he made a rumbling noise in his throat and fell silent.

'Christos, why don't you and Olivia get some fresh air, out on the balcony?' Gerald calmly suggested.

They stood together in the shadows of the balcony, looking at the glitter of Monte Carlo's lights around and below them. Far out to sea they could see a large boat moored, lit up like a Christmas tree, so that they could even see the people on deck dancing and standing about with drinks in their hands.

'One day I'm going to have a big yacht of my own,' said Christos, with a sort of desperate belligerence.

'Don't forget to invite me along on your cruises!' Olivia joked, and he turned to her suddenly, his face flushed, his breathing audible.

'If you married me, you'd always come along!' And then, before she quite took in what he'd said, he went on in a rush, 'Let's do it...let's get married, Olivia.'

She stared blankly for a second. 'Is this one of your jokes?' she asked, ready to laugh, but saw in disbelief that he wasn't being funny.

'Of course it isn't! Would I make a joke about something like that?' He sounded upset; he certainly wasn't laughing. There wasn't a flicker of humour in his eyes. He looked so serious, unsmiling, his voice husky, his face dark red.

She stared at him, too stunned to know what to say.

Christos grabbed her hand, lifted it to his mouth, kissed the palm, whispering, 'Please, Olivia...say yes...say you'll marry me... You've got to marry me...'

Nobody had ever looked at her with such helpless pleading eyes, sounded so much as if they really needed her. All Olivia's female instincts made her weak, warmth and compassion softening her.

'Oh...Christos...' she began in a quivering voice. She couldn't remember afterwards what she actually said, but it must have added up to yes, because Christos kissed her with such vehemence that she almost suffocated, then, holding her hand tightly, he pulled her back in to the sitting-room where the others were talking and drinking coffee, and burst out excitedly, 'Olivia and I are engaged!'

For one second there was a silence and Olivia saw the faces of Constantine and her father turned towards her.

They each had an identical expression—she didn't have time to be certain what it was before they were on their feet, smiling, exclaiming, kissing her cheek, shaking Christos by the hand.

Helena kissed her too, but seemed almost as surprised and taken aback as Olivia herself felt.

'Darling, Olivia is a lovely girl. I hope you're going to be really happy,' Helena told her son, hugging him, but her eyes were worried, and Olivia didn't blame her for looking so uncertain. Olivia was uncertain herself.

Gerald produced chilled champagne and fluted crystal glasses, they drank a toast, and Olivia looked up at Christos and couldn't help wondering if she was imagining all this. It had happened out of the blue; she hadn't expected it.

Engaged. She was engaged. She was going to marry Christos. She still couldn't believe it. But one thing was certain—her father and Constantine Agathios were very happy indeed, and Christos was euphoric, talking in an almost light-headed way, laughing at nothing, drinking far too much champagne.

Olivia watched him with warmth, smiling whenever their eyes met. It touched her that he should have been so nervous about proposing to her. He was a darling. No doubt about that. She did love him. She really did.

So why did she feel panic rising inside her every time she thought about marrying him?

CHAPTER THREE

'BUT you've only known him for a few weeks!' her mother said, stunned by the news which Olivia told her when she got back from Monaco on the following evening.

'That's why we've agreed to wait until next summer for the wedding. Oh, Mum, don't you think we realise we have a lot to learn about each other? We're not daft enough to rush into marriage yet.'

Olivia herself was still faintly bemused, couldn't quite believe it. Christos had driven her to Nice airport to catch her plane home that morning, and they had talked soberly in the car, and in the noisy terminal before she went through the departure gate.

Suddenly everything had seemed different. She was going back to real life, a raincoat over her arm because she knew it was raining in London and she would need it when she arrived there. The holiday was ending, the gaiety of beach life already receding into memory.

Except that she and Christos were engaged and she was wearing a ring he had given her that morning, a large sapphire set in a ring of diamonds, which they had stopped off in Nice to buy before driving to the airport. Olivia hadn't wanted a ring, had protested that it could wait—why didn't they buy one later? But Christos had insisted so fiercely that she had given way, especially as he had told her that it was his father who was paying for the ring. It was his engagement present to them.

Her mother looked at it now as it flashed on Olivia's finger, frowning. 'Your father didn't push you into this, did he? I mean, I can see he would be thrilled to get you married off to someone with such good shipping connections, but don't let him talk you into anything you don't want to do, Olivia.'

Olivia sighed. She didn't pretend not to understand what her mother was saying.

'I think Father did sort of... Well, he and Christos's father, Constantine Agathios, hoped... Oh, there was a touch of matchmaking going on!' She was sure about that now. She and Christos had been thrown together deliberately in the hope that they would be attracted to each other.

Ann Faulton looked angry. 'I don't like this, Olivia, I don't like the sound of it at all.'

'They can't force me to marry Christos if I don't want to, Mum, don't worry, and I don't believe they can make Christos do anything he doesn't want to do either. He's far too independent. Wait until you meet Christos— you'll like him, I know you will.'

Ann Faulton walked round the little sitting-room of her Lake District home, bristling like an angry cat. If she had had a tail, it would have been twitching from side to side.

'He was always cold-blooded and hard-headed, but I didn't think even Gerald would try to sell you off as part of a business deal! That's what he's up to, isn't it, he and Agathios?'

'I don't honestly know what they're up to, but at least Christos agreed with me that we should wait until next year; he thinks we need to get to know each other better too.' Olivia paused, choosing her words carefully. 'I don't think Christos is all that sure either. Oh, he likes me.

And it's mutual. Really, Mum, he's a darling, but I just don't know yet if it would work out between us. And anyway, we're both going to be busy for a while. I start work in the London office on Monday, and Christos is coming to London too, in November. At the moment he's working in Greece, but his father apparently plans to take over some new offices in the City, in St Mary Axe, which isn't far from where I'll be, so we'll be able to meet often once Christos arrives, and until then we're going to write to each other, and talk on the phone.'

Ann Faulton sighed. 'Well, as soon as Christos arrives you must bring him up here for a weekend, so that I can find out for myself what he's like.'

'I will, don't worry,' promised Olivia.

At the weekend she and her mother piled everything they could manage into the back of Ann Faulton's roomy estate car and drove down to London, so that Olivia could move into her new home, a one-room studio flat on the first floor of an Edwardian house in Gospel Oak, a northern suburb close to Camden Town.

Her mother drove back next day, and Olivia spent that Sunday arranging and rearranging her new territory, her stomach cramped with nerves whenever she thought of starting work in the morning.

The offices of Grey-Faulton were familiar to her, of course; she had often visited them in the past but only briefly, to meet her father before joining him for lunch nearby in his favourite restaurant, a lofty, gloomy room above an old public house a stone's throw from Liverpool Street Station.

The London office was not as large, or as busy, as the Aberdeen office, which had taken on new importance with the discovery of oil in the North Sea, requiring marine servicing of the oil-rigs, the delivery of freight to them, and the hire of merchant vessels by oil companies for a number of purposes. Gerald Faulton was more likely to be in Scotland than London for most of the year, since the bulk of the company business was done north of the border, but he kept a small London office because a portion of his trade was still done in the south.

Olivia's job would cover all aspects of the company's business. Once she had settled into the daily office routine, her father wanted her to travel, as he did, meet their employees at the various ports from which they operated, get to know as much as possible about what the firm did.

Pale and tense, she walked along St Mary Axe and into the narrow entrance of the building on that Monday morning. It was dead on the stroke of nine when she arrived; it was raining, a grey, drizzly rain, which made the roof tiles look black, dripped down the back of Olivia's neck and depressed her spirits even further.

In the reception lobby she found the chief clerk waiting, neat and grey-haired, with a clipped moustache and the air of a fussy terrier shepherding a lost lamb.

'Miss Faulton, welcome, punctual to the second, just like your father, and your grandfather before him,' he barked cheerfully, bustling forward to shake hands as soon as he saw her. 'Nowadays nobody bothers about a thing like that, but in my young days they taught us that punctuality was the courtesy of kings, and the men of your family never forgot that.'

'Hello, Mr Robner, thank you,' she managed, feeling the covert stares of the two girls working behind the counter.

They were there to deal with anyone who walked in off the street—the public wanting information or advice or someone calling to see an executive in the offices, or a crew member calling to see the personnel department.

Olivia wished that Mr Robner hadn't felt it necessary to come down to the front office to meet her on her first morning. She would rather have slipped in anonymously. She wanted to make friends with everyone who worked there, not put their backs up. Now they would all suppose that she expected to be treated like a princess, when what she really wanted was to be an ordinary member of the staff.

'Come along and I'll show you your office,' Mr Robner told her, guiding her towards the lift.

She followed him, sighing.

She spent the rest of the day alone in her recently redecorated office, waiting for the phone to ring, or someone to come in to see her. She sat at her desk and read the day's newspapers, shipping trade magazines, brochures. She watched the fax machine rattling out messages which never seemed to require answering, and didn't really apply to her. She read the letters on the most recent file, then ran out of things to do and stood by the window, listening to the rain splashing in the gutters, stared down into the street, watching people walk along the opposite pavement under bobbing umbrellas.

It was a relief to escape for an hour, for lunch. She ate a sandwich and did some shopping. Feeling slightly better, she tried a smile on the girls in the front office when she came back, and got blank, frosty looks in reply. It was a ghastly day. Olivia felt like running home. She felt like resigning there and then.

Back in her flat she sat down with a cup of strong black coffee, on the point of tears. It was all going to be so dreary, day after day of rain and hostile looks from the others who worked in the office. They hated her. She should never have taken this job.

The phone rang. She almost jumped out of her skin. She leaned over to pick it up. 'Hello?'

'Olivia?' a warm, confident, familiar voice said, and at once her heart lifted.

'Christos!' Her eyes brightened. 'Oh, Christos, thanks for ringing. I was dying to talk to you! Where are you?'

'London,' he said, and she took a surprised breath.

'But I thought you were going straight back to Greece!'

'Something urgent came up.'

She picked up an odd note in his voice and frowned. 'Is something wrong?'

'Nothing for you to bother about,' Christos said hurriedly. 'Just business. We're here for a couple of days—how about dinner tonight?'

'I'd love it,' she said.

'Pick you up in half an hour.'

She had to rush to get ready in time. She put on a dark brown and cream silk tunic, did her hair and face, used a perfume she had brought back from France. Christos arrived just as she was inspecting her reflection; he had come in a taxi which waited while he rang her doorbell.

She opened the door and for a second they were both unsure, surprised by the sight of each other in those unfamiliar surroundings, then Christos gave her his warm, loving smile and kissed her mouth, and she was so glad to see a smiling face that she clung, kissing him back eagerly. He lifted his head and she saw his eyes; she knew she had never kissed him quite that way before. He was startled. Was he even taken aback? Or was she imagining things?

He didn't say anything, just put an arm around her and ran her back to the taxi.

'So how was your first day at work?' he asked, as they drove off through the rain.

It was a safe, neutral subject and the atmosphere between them was not yet as casual and easy as it had been in Monaco until he proposed, so she plunged into talk about her job. 'Oh, it was ghastly, Christos. I didn't do a thing, there was simply nothing to do, I was so bored all day. The phone didn't ring, nobody came to see me except the chief clerk, and he was horribly obsequious because he's scared stiff of my father. I think I'm going to hate this job! It is going to be so dull.'

'Wait until there's a disaster...a ship goes down or there's an accident, a man is killed or a hold catches fire...' Christos said soberly. 'I haven't worked in PR but I know one thing—something is always happening on ships, something is always going wrong. Especially on merchant ships. Cargoes can be damn tricky. And when things go wrong the shipping company is always to blame. That's when the phone will ring and you'll be busy all day talking to the Press and trying to minimise the damage to the company. You'll wish for some peace and quiet then.'

'Is it really that bad?' she asked, surprised by his vehemence.

'It can be. We have a PR department which is kept pretty busy with one project or another, when it isn't fielding Press questions or thinking up ways of protecting our image. These days we're always being accused of discharging oil and causing environmental disasters, and it isn't some lazy, thoughtless fool of a sailor who gets the blame, it's the company who pays his salary, even if the company has a strict rule to cover discharge of oil.'

Olivia grimaced. 'Well, I must admit I feel pretty strongly about that too. Have you ever seen a seabird trying to fly with wings that are soaked in black crude oil? It's heart-rending. I just hope I never have to deal with that situation—I might not be very good at defending the company if we've caused that sort of nightmare.'

The taxi slowed and pulled up outside the hotel in Mayfair where Christos and his father were staying. Christos paid the driver, the hotel porter came out with an umbrella and they got in out of the rain and went straight in to dinner.

'Where is your father tonight?' she asked over their first course, a rich, creamy chicken soup which was just right for such a wet, cold evening.

'Oh, I don't know, he never tells me anything,' Christos said, making a face. 'Don't let's talk about him. Tell me what your mother said when she heard about us.'

She didn't tell him about her mother's suspicions. Did he guess at them anyway? 'She wants to meet you as soon as possible. When can you come up to the Lake District for a weekend?'

His expression was wry. 'I'll ask my father. I think we're going back to Greece on Wednesday or Thursday, but he might let me stay on to visit your mother. Especially if you ask him—he'll do it for you. He wants you to be happy.'

She laughed disbelievingly. 'Who are you trying to kid? I don't believe he cares whether I'm happy or not.'

Christos gave her an odd look that held either irony or cynicism. 'You're wrong. At the moment it's all he cares about.'

Olivia stared at him, wondering if she was imagining that look in his face, the dry tone of his voice, but at that second out of the corner of her eye she caught sight of someone walking rapidly through the lobby of the hotel, which she could see reflected in the mirrors on the wall of the dining-room.

'There's my father!' she exclaimed. 'I thought he was still in Monaco! What's he doing here? Maybe I'd better run after him and tell him I'm here?'

Christos caught hold of her wrist as she rose. 'No, don't. He is here to see my father. On urgent business.'

Olivia sat down again, and he let go of her.

'Business at this time of night?' she asked, and he shrugged.

'You know them. Day or night, business comes first with them. I told you, we're in London on urgent business.'

'And my father is involved in it somehow? I didn't realise he did any business with your father.'

Christos had that cynical look again. 'They're old friends. They've done plenty of deals in the past.'

'Is my father on your board, as well as on the board of your uncle's company?'

Christos grinned, amused. 'Of course not. Uncle Max wouldn't like that idea at all!'

A shiver ran down Olivia's back. She must have caught a chill, she thought.

'Don't you know anything about your father's business?' asked Christos, staring at her in that odd way, his mouth twisting.

'Not much, but I suppose I'll learn a lot more now I work there,' she said as the waiter brought their second course. She had chosen piperade, a Basque dish of peppers, tomatoes and onions, cooked until they were almost a purée, when eggs were added and scrambled into the vegetable mixture. It was light and delicious. Christos had a steak, very rare, with salad.

They finished their meal with coffee and then Christos wanted to go on to a nightclub, as they had in the South of France every night, but Olivia regretfully had to point out that she must get up in the morning and go to work.

'I'm a wage slave now, I'm not on holiday!' she said, and he pulled a face at her.

'How boring.' But he amicably took her home in another taxi at eleven o'clock and kissed her goodnight at her front door before leaving.

'How about dinner tomorrow? I'll pick you up here at seven.'

In bed that night she lay awake for a while thinking about Christos, wondering if he was really in love with her. Even more puzzling, was she really in love with him? When she was with him she always enjoyed herself. Look at tonight. When she heard his voice on the phone she had felt so much happier; he had entirely changed her mood simply by showing up out of the blue. He was such fun, so easy-going, so light-hearted.

But is it love? she thought, and couldn't make up her mind. She wasn't sure what love really was—would she know it if she felt it?

She suddenly remembered the odd shiver that had run down her back at the sound of Max's name. At the mere memory, she shivered again, turning pale, then flushing.

What was it she felt for Max? She had only seen him for one day, years ago, and yet when she heard his name she felt weak inside, as though she was falling apart.

Oh, don't be so stupid! she told herself. It was just a teenage crush, over years ago. It wasn't love. How could it have been? Love doesn't happen that fast! Stop thinking about the man. Think about Christos.

What were he and his father doing in London, for instance?

Something secretive, something important, that he couldn't talk about, but in which her father was clearly involved. Whatever it was, it made Christos excited, yet jumpy.

She had the feeling he'd been aching to talk to her about whatever was churning him up, but that he dared not risk it. Christos was very much in awe of his father, and she didn't blame him for that. Constantine Agathios was a very scary man. Christos might say that he cared about her and wanted her to be happy, but Olivia found that hard to credit. Constantine Agathios wasn't fond of her, didn't care about her; if she annoyed him she had the strong feeling he could turn very nasty indeed. There was black temper in that face. No wonder Christos was afraid of annoying him.

Next morning she had hardly walked into the office before the phone began ringing.

'Hello? Public Relations—this is Olivia speaking,' she said, half expecting it to be Christos again.

It was a breezy, assured voice, but not that of Christos. The accent was very much a London one, East End cockney. 'Hello, this is Rodney Fielding, *Daily Globe* newsroom. We've been trying to locate Mr Faulton, to talk to him about this ship going down off the coast of Turkey.'

'One of ours? We don't have any ships in that part of the world, I'm sure we don't,' Olivia said, startled.

'Not one of Faulton's own ships,' agreed the reporter. 'I'm talking about the Agathios Kera line—one of their ferries ran into fog between Greece and Turkey and collided with an oil tanker yesterday morning. Hadn't you heard about it?'

'No,' Olivia said slowly, horrified. 'Did you say the Agathios ship went down?'

'It finally sank this morning; it was crippled, couldn't be salvaged. They got most of the passengers off, but four people died and a dozen or so were injured, mostly burns—there was an explosion on the oil tanker.'

The brisk matter-of-factness of the voice appalled her. 'How terrible,' she said, paling. Only last night she and Christos had talked about oil spillage and an environmental disaster. It was almost as if they had conjured this up out of nowhere; she felt horribly guilty.

Oh, of course it was crazy to think like that! It wasn't her fault, and, thank God, she didn't have to fend off accusing questions, think up bland answers, explanations, apologies, because it was nothing to do with their company, yet she still had a superstitious feeling that somehow she and Christos had made this happen.

'Mr Faulton hasn't mention it to you?' asked the reporter.

'No, but why should he? It really has nothing to do with this company——' she began and the reporter interrupted.

'But he is on the board of Agathios Kera, isn't he?'

Olivia drew a sharp breath. She had forgotten that. 'Oh...yes,' she said slowly. 'But he's in London at the moment, not in Greece, which is the headquarters of the Agathios Kera line.'

'They have an office in London though, don't they? And I'm told they're having a board meeting this morning, to discuss the disaster.'

'Oh, are they?' Olivia was surprised into indiscretion. 'That's news to me. Look, I really can't help you, I'm afraid. I don't even know as much as you do, and I'm new here. I only started work yesterday.' She frowned, then said sharply, 'And anyway, why are you ringing here? Why not ring Agathios Kera's London offices?'

'I tried,' said the reporter cynically. 'It was busy.'

'Then try again!'

'I've been trying for the past hour. The line's engaged all the time. I think they've taken the phone off the hook. Not surprising really—they've had a bad month so far, what with the death of old Kera, and Max Agathios's financial problems . . .'

'What financial problems?' Olivia felt ice trickling down her spine. She was remembering that conversation she had overhead last week, the odd uneasiness she had felt as she listened.

'You really don't know much about the business, do you?' the reporter said pityingly. 'Look, Agathios borrowed heavily to finance his expansion into the cruise business. Cruise ships are expensive. He's had to invest a lot of money, and because of the recession people haven't been taking cruises.' He paused, laughed and added, 'Agathios has run into bad weather, in fact. What do you bet that that's our headline?'

'A bit obvious, isn't it?' Olivia muttered. She didn't share his sense of humour, but then she was personally involved in all this, and the reporter wasn't. To him this was just a story—he didn't give a damn about the consequences for everyone involved.

'Headlines have to be obvious,' he snapped. 'Anyway, Agathios's partner died at exactly the wrong moment.'

'Is there ever a right moment to die?' Olivia asked bitterly. 'I don't suppose the poor man wanted to die now.'

'Don't suppose he did,' the reporter said cheerfully. 'But he has made life very difficult for Max Agathios. Old Kera has always backed him financially, they've been a successful pair, and Max is going to miss him.'

Olivia was thinking, her face puzzled. 'But what about Mr Kera's daughter? Wasn't she an only child? Won't she inherit everything?'

'Oh, sure, but Opie won't want to put any more money into Agathios Kera.'

Olivia stiffened. 'Opie?' She recognised the name her father had said on the phone the other day. 'Who on earth is Opie?' Was it Daphne Kera's nickname, or something?

'That's the daughter's married name,' the reporter said, and Olivia almost dropped the phone. She sat staring at nothing while the man's voice chattered on in her ear. 'Daphne Kera married an Australian wool exporter. Simon Opie's not interested in shipping, and all his business interests are in Australia, so the rumour is that Daphne Opie will want to sell her share in Agathios Kera—the only question is, who would want to buy?' The reporter's voice had become brisk. 'Got to go. Look, darling, when Faulton gets back, could you give me a buzz, give me a shot at him before anyone else gets the chance? You owe me for all the information I've fed you. And take my advice—if you're going to hold down this new job of yours, you had better bone up on the shipping business fast!'

Olivia put the phone down as he hung up. Her mind was in chaos. What was going on? Her father had lied to her—by omission, at least, if not directly. He had said that Max was definitely going to marry Daphne. But Max hadn't. Daphne had married someone else, an Australian called Simon Opie. Why hadn't Gerald told her that? He must have known.

The phone rang again a few minutes later, and this time she was prepared to find herself talking to another reporter. She rapidly got rid of him, refusing to discuss the subject of Agathios Kera or the ship that had gone down off Turkey, but for the rest of the morning she was dealing with phone calls from various newspapers, all pursuing the same story.

She was relieved to escape to lunch, rather late, leaving the answerphone to take calls, and she didn't hurry back. After a leisurely lunch at a salad bar, she walked back in rather watery sunshine. It suddenly occurred to her that her father might well call in on her, as he was in London, to see how she was coping with her new job. She looked at her watch. Half-past two. The board meeting at Max's offices must surely be over by now? She began to walk faster.

There was no sign of her father though, and when she rang his secretary, Mrs Grange, she was told that Gerald Faulton hadn't yet returned.

'I'm snowed under with messages from newspapers, Mrs Grange,' Olivia said. 'I'm just refusing to comment, but when my father comes in would you ask him to let me know what he wants me to say to the Press about this Agathios Kera business?'

'Well, I'll leave him a message, Miss Faulton, but...well, I have a problem, you see. My little boy's school just rang—they think he has mumps. He's running a high temperature and his jaw has swollen right up. Normally my mother would deal with an emergency like this, but she's away. I'll have to go myself. I'm afraid your father's going to be very irritated.'

'No, of course he won't be, of course you must go,' Olivia said at once.

'Oh, thank you,' Mrs Grange said gratefully. 'I'll get one of the other girls to sit in here and man the phones.'

'I'll do that,' Olivia said at once. 'Switchboard can re-route any calls for me to my father's office. I don't have anything much to do here anyway.'

'Oh, would you? You wouldn't mind?' Mrs Grange's voice was startled. 'But what would your father say about you doing my job?'

'He won't mind, he likes me to take more interest in his business,' Olivia blithely said, yet thought: if he really does, why does he lie to me and keep so much from me? He never tells me anything, and if he does it isn't always the truth.

She collected her things, informed the switchboard that she would be in her father's office for the rest of the afternoon, and walked along the corridor to the large suite of offices Gerald Faulton occupied.

Mrs Grange was just leaving. She had been Gerald's secretary for only a few months, and seemed flustered, still nervous of his reaction to finding out that Olivia had taken over her job for the afternoon. A smartly dressed woman in her late thirties, with smooth dark hair and blue eyes, she was divorced from her husband but devoted to her only child, the boy, Andrew, who had just come down with mumps. Olivia suspected she would not be working there very long. Gerald expected his secretaries to be one-track-minded, to devote themselves to him and his business, not to husbands or children.

'If you could just write down any messages on this pad... and if you have to leave before five-thirty—even if you just pop out to the cloakroom—could you let the switchboard know?' Mrs Grange stammered out, watching Olivia uneasily.

Olivia nodded. 'Don't worry. Off you go, I'll cope here.'

When she was alone she walked out of Mrs Grange's little office into her father's much more spacious room. Olivia wandered around, stroking the panelled walls, pulling out a book here and there from the rows of tomes on shipping and the law in the polished oak bookcase, touching objects on her father's wide, leather-topped desk. She sat in his revolving leather chair, swung round in it, played with his intercom and tried the locked drawers in the desk.

She felt much as she had when she was a child and visited him here. Everything in this room was perfect, austere, placed precisely and always in its place. The room had its personal and particular smell: a mingling of leather and polish and the eau-de-Cologne her father used.

Olivia was almost in a trance, her hands on her father's desk, her head back against the deep leather upholstered chair, staring around her.

Suddenly a voice outside the door said sharply, 'You can't go in there! He isn't there, I tell you!'

Olivia jumped, looking at the door as it opened with a crash and someone came through it so abruptly that it was almost as if they had thrown themselves into the room.

Her golden eyes wide, she stared at Max Agathios.

He had stopped dead and was staring back at her.

The air between them seemed to her to shimmer, like the air in a desert, making Max's image come and go as if he were a mirage, and Olivia almost believed he was, almost thought she was fantasising. He wasn't really there, she had conjured him up because she had been thinking about him so much.

Behind him one of the office girls was babbling, 'I'm sorry, Miss Faulton, I told him Mr Faulton wasn't here, but he wouldn't listen, he forced his way in here. Shall I call the police?'

'No...it's OK...' Olivia managed huskily. 'There's nothing to worry about. I...I'll deal with it.'

The girl seemed uncertain. 'Well, I'll stay out here, in Mrs Grange's office, if you like, in case you need me——'

'Shut the door and get out!' Max snarled, and turned his black head to look at the girl in a way that sent her scurrying.

The door closed on her and Max looked back at Olivia. She had not taken her eyes off him since he erupted into the room. How many years? she was thinking. How many years since she had last seen him, on Corfu, in her father's villa? Not that many. She had been seventeen. Now she was twenty-two. Five years.

She had changed, she knew that; her father had called her a schoolgirl that summer on Corfu, and he had been quite right, she had to admit that now, however reluctantly. That was what she had been, an unawakened, wide-eyed schoolgirl completely out of her depth with a man like Max Agathios. Looking back, she was amazed he hadn't seen it, realised how young and inexperienced she was—surely he must have had some inkling?

Of course, she had been excited by him, trying to act very grown-up under the influence of her first strong sexual attraction, and in that lazy, casual beach atmosphere her true age might not have shown up, especially as neither she nor Max had been wearing very much. Clothes were often a good clue to age and background.

Max's clothes now were a million miles away from the old jeans and T-shirt he had been wearing that day in Corfu. Today his clothes were expensive, exclusive: he wore a smoothly tailored city suit in dark grey pinstripe, and with it a stiff white shirt and maroon tie. He looked formal, as remote as her father, and he had hardened, looked leaner, tougher, as if he had shed some weight, and with it the charm and warmth he had had five years ago, and which she had found irresistible.

She didn't think she liked this icy, hostile stranger.

Quietly, she asked him, 'Why do you want to see my father, Mr Agathios?'

'Why?' he repeated in a harsh, charged voice. Rage blazed out of him, the heat of it hitting her across the room. His black eyes glittered. 'I'm going to kill him!'

CHAPTER FOUR

OLIVIA sucked in air in a startled, incredulous, horrified reaction. Her golden eyes searched his face, looking for a trace of humour, for some evidence that the threat had been a joke, but his features were implacable, tight with anger and that deeply embedded hostility she had seen from the minute he forced his way into this office.

She swallowed, her face white, her eyes all pupil suddenly, a glassy, disturbed blackness eating up the golden glow of the iris.

'What are you talking about?' The whisper of her voice was only just audible in the room.

'You don't know?' The cold sneer in his voice hurt her, told her he despised her, hated her too.

'I wouldn't ask if I did!'

'You're sitting behind your father's desk, you're obviously running this office while he's not here—yet you don't have a clue what I'm talking about? Do you really expect me to believe that?' Max took a long stride and was suddenly on the other side of the desk, only inches away from her. He put both hands on the desk and bent towards her; Olivia flinched back in her chair. From the other side of the room he had been disturbing—this close he was a physical threat she found alarming. 'Don't forget, I remember you making a fool of me the first time we met! You're your father's daughter all right. Well, I don't fall for the same trick twice.'

'I didn't lie to you!' She had not got the chance to tell him that five years ago; she had been waiting ever since to put the record straight. 'I didn't realise you didn't know how old I was! It never occurred to me that you didn't know. You never asked and I didn't think of telling you.'

'I never asked because you looked older and...' He broke off, his face dark with smouldering rage. 'Oh, hell, never mind! I didn't come here to talk about old times. I'm not going to let you distract me from catching up with your father.'

His voice lashed her. To hide her fear, she began to talk far too fast, gabbling out the words. 'I wasn't trying to... I don't work here, I'm just taking over from my father's secretary for the day. Her little boy is ill, she had to go home, and I've just started to work here, in the public relations office...'

She broke off, seeing Max's eyes flash like black lightning.

'Public relations? Which means you deal with the Press.'

'Yes,' she whispered, biting her lip.

'And I've no doubt you've had plenty of calls from them today!' he bit out, and she couldn't deny it.

'Quite a few reporters have rung, yes, wanting to talk to my father, wanting quotes about the board meeting you held this morning, but I was no help to them—I didn't know as much as they did! They told me more than I could tell them!'

Max's mouth writhed bitterly. 'Did they tell you that my brother and your father covet my company, that the two of them conspired to buy up my late partner's shares so that they could get control, manipulate the board and get me kicked off it?'

Olivia felt sick. So that was what her father had been up to with Constantine Agathios?

'Kicked out of my own company!' Max ground out between his teeth. 'The company I built up from nothing, just a few battered old ships that should really have gone to the breaker's yard. Constantine inherited the lion's share of my father's fleet, and yet he resented the fact that my father left me anything at all. He hoped I'd go bankrupt, and I'm well aware that he secretly worked to steal my contracts, competed with me wherever he could, undercut me, lied about me. But I fought back; I worked like a slave to build up new routes, get new contracts, and I managed to find someone who believed in me and was prepared to back me.'

'Leon Kera,' she thought aloud, as he paused, and he gave her a cynical, icy look.

'Oh, you admit you know that much about my operation!'

She hated the contempt in his voice, and her skin tightened. 'I didn't say I knew nothing about you and your company. I said I knew nothing about my father's...plans...the board meeting...'

Her father had made sure she knew nothing, she realised. He had consistently lied to her, shut her out, ever since she had met Max in Corfu five years ago. Hadn't Gerald trusted her not to warn Max? She bit her lip. Well, if she had known, and had seen Max, wouldn't she have had a problem not warning him? How could her father do this? And Max's own brother, too! Cheating him, secretly trying to destroy him, to take his company away from him. Olivia was appalled.

'Leon Kera was the best friend I ever had,' Max said. 'I was lucky to know him; he was a great man. He invested in my company, bought a big block of shares when I went public, and he advised me. It was Leon's idea that we should go into the cruise business, but we weren't lucky with our timing.' He sighed, his mouth grim. 'Costs and interest rates went up steeply and because of the recession passengers cut back on holidays, especially expensive ones like cruises. We've had our problems, but I have no doubt that in another five years we'd have been as solid as a rock.' He stopped, his black brows meeting, his face tense and dark. After a brief pause he went on, 'But Leon died and the vultures moved in on me.'

'But how can they kick you out of your own company?'

He gave her an angry, impatient look. 'Still pretending you don't know a thing about it? I don't buy this innocence of yours. You're your father's daughter, and his only heir. Knowing him, he's been grooming you to take over from him one day. He won't have kept you in ignorance of what he's plotting with my brother!'

'My father never tells me anything.' There was bitterness in Olivia's eyes, in her voice, and Max watched her closely, frowning as though trying to decide whether or not to believe what he was seeing. 'My father doesn't even let his right hand know what his left hand is doing,' she told him, remembering the way her father and Constantine Agathios had thrown her and Christos together.

This summer when she flew in to Nice, she had felt adult, grown up at last, finished with her studies, about to enter the real world, become fully independent. She had thought she was making her own decisions, thought she was a free agent, and all the time she had been as powerless, as impotent, as governed, as a child.

I was their puppet—they pulled my strings, I danced and I didn't even know what was happening to me, she thought, humiliated and angry.

And what about Christos? Was he a puppet too, as hoodwinked as she had been, as manipulated? Or had Christos known what the two older men were up to? Had they ordered him to propose to her? Had he wanted to? Did he care anything about her? What did she really know about Christos?

Max was watching her fixedly, frowning.

'You expect me to believe that?'

Suddenly angry, Olivia met his eyes, her chin up, glaring. 'I don't care what you believe! It doesn't matter whether you believe me or not, but I tell you my father never takes me into his confidence, especially where business is concerned. Just tell me this . . . how can my father and your brother take your company away from you?'

Max bared his teeth angrily and ran a hand through his thick, black hair, ruffling it into confusion.

'OK!' he growled. 'OK, I'll play your little game, pretend you don't know. I suppose you're deliberately trying to slow me down, waste time, in the hope that one of those girls out there has called the police—but if that's your game plan, don't think it will save your father, because even if the police arrived they couldn't lock me up, only warn me not to breach the peace, because I haven't done anything. Yet. And sooner or later I would get to your father, even if he hides behind electronic devices and a whole mob of security people. One day I'll get him.'

Olivia believed him. There was such smouldering hatred in his jet eyes. Her hands began to shake and Max looked down at them. She snatched them out of sight, into her lap, trying to control the tremors running through her. She must try to stop him realising just how much he frightened her.

In a flat, clipped voice Max said, 'Leon Kera and I together owned sixty-five per cent of the company, and the rest was held by a lot of smaller shareholders. While Leon was alive I was safe, but the minute he died, my brother and your father got together to buy his shares from his daughter. I'd have bought them myself, if I had had the money, but every penny I have is tied up in the company, and no bank would lend me any more.'

The phone on the desk began to ring and Max broke off. Olivia automatically reached out, but Max got there first. He lifted the receiver, listened, then said tersely, 'Miss Faulton isn't taking any calls, and don't put any more through.'

He slammed the receiver down, the crash making Olivia jump. Max began prowling to and fro like a caged lion. 'Where was I? Oh, yes, I had no idea what was afoot until just before the board meeting. Of course, I knew Constantine coveted my company, but I couldn't believe Daphne would sell to him—she knew her father wouldn't have wanted her to do that.'

His face had an angry cynicism. He stopped in front of the window, staring out, his hands in his trouser pockets, his head back, his face darkly frowning. 'I should have guessed, I should have remembered...a woman scorned is a bad enemy.' He broke off, threw Olivia a swift, hard look and said grimly, 'Emotion is a dangerous ingredient if it gets mixed up in business affairs.'

'I'd heard that you and your partner's daughter were once... There were rumours you were going to marry her. But you didn't?' Olivia didn't like to ask directly what had happened between them, why Daphne Kera had married someone else, and was now deliberately setting out to ruin Max.

He ignored the tentative question, staring out of the window again, his back to her. His voice flat, he went on, 'At the board meeting this morning your father put down a motion calling me irresponsible and incompetent and demanding my resignation as managing director. I suddenly found myself without any friends around that table. They voted for my brother to take over running the company.'

Olivia watched the line of his back under that formal, elegant suit. He looked much better naked, she thought, remembering the first time she saw him, on the beach, that day in Corfu—and felt heat leap inside her. She mustn't think about that day. She must concentrate on what he had just said. Max was right. Emotion was a dangerous ingredient in business affairs.

Huskily, she asked, 'But...can they really do that? Take your company away from you? Couldn't you fight them? Can't your lawyers do something to stop them?'

He turned slowly, his brows lifted, giving her a long, incredulous look. 'I am almost tempted to believe you mean it—you really don't know anything!'

'I told you I didn't! Only what I've read or been told by the Press!'

He searched her face, then his mouth indented. 'I must be crazy, believing you! You're your father's daughter, one day you'll be running all this——' he gestured around the room '—and now you'll have my company too!'

'I don't want your company!'

He laughed bitterly. 'Well, you've got it. Or your father has, which will come to the same thing one day.'

'But...what about your shares in the company?'

He shrugged. 'Oh, they can't take my shares away. I still own more than thirty per cent, and if I can get a public shareholders' meeting I might still make them take me back on the board, but I can't make them give me back my job as managing director. Together, they own the majority of shares. That's why they're directors—I invited them all on to the board, that's the irony of it. Now they're kicking me out, and there is nothing I can do to stop it, nothing any lawyer can do either. I've lost my company and my brother has finally got what he has been coveting ever since our father died. Constantine has won.'

'For the moment,' Olivia softly said, wishing he wouldn't stand so close. She was more and more aware of him; the lean, powerful body was hard to ignore. Every time he moved, even breathed, her pulses reacted, shocking her because she hadn't expected him to have that effect on her, not now, not any more. Five years ago she had been easy to impress. She hadn't had a boyfriend, was a wide-eyed innocent. Max had had a walk-over with her. She'd grown up since then. She shouldn't be getting these waves of intense awareness.

Max leaned even closer, staring down into her golden eyes. 'Yes,' he slowly said. 'For the moment.'

'I'm sure you'll fight back.' He wasn't the type to give up a fight and just walk away. Max was a fighter; every tough bone in his body told you that, every pugnacious line in his face.

He half-smiled. 'I'm sure too, but if you're hoping to hear about any plans I might have, you can forget it. I'm not that stupid. I know that anything I say to you will go straight back to your father and my brother.'

Stung, she burst out, 'No! I won't even tell them I've seen you!'

There was a long silence while their eyes were locked. 'Won't you, Olivia?' he drawled. 'If I believed you, I might wonder why.'

She looked down, her lashes cloaking her eyes. 'They'd keep asking me endless questions. I...I don't want to be cross-examined; I don't want to get involved in any of this! I hate it, plots and back-stairs politics and——'

Max abruptly said, 'Is it true that you're going to marry my nephew?'

She had wondered if he knew. Huskily, she admitted, 'Yes, we got engaged last week.'

'Are you in love with him?' She hated the contemptuous twist of his mouth as he said that, and a dark flush crept up her face.

'I'm not discussing my personal life!'

'If you were in love with him, why would you mind admitting it?'

She tensed, realising how true that was, but defiantly threw back, 'If I wasn't, why would I get engaged to him?'

'Any number of reasons,' Max drily said. 'You might be ambitious, and there's no doubt Christos is a good catch—he's going to be very rich, one day. You could simply get married and think Christos would make a suitable husband, or you might have been badgered into it by your father——'

'No! He didn't!' Olivia might be angry with her father for the way he'd manipulated her and her life, but she couldn't discuss it with Max. That would be too disloyal, not to mention humiliating. 'My father would never badger me into anything!'

Max smiled cynically. 'No, I suppose not. He has other techniques for dealing with you, doesn't he? He freezes you into submission. If you disobey him he puts you in deep freeze until you're ready to do whatever he wants.'

He was far too shrewd; he saw too much, heard what you did not say; she almost began to think he could read minds, and Olivia found him even more worrying than her father, because she suddenly knew that Max Agathios could hurt her far more than her father ever had. 'I think you'd better go,' she broke out shakily. 'My father won't be back for hours; there's no point in your waiting.'

He considered her, his face cool and blank, then nodded. 'You mean it scares you even to talk about it? Isn't it time you found the courage to run your own life, Olivia? Make your own decisions, choose your own friends and lovers?'

She kept her eyes averted, didn't risk answering, but the stiff mask of her face was probably answer enough because Max laughed shortly.

'Well, give your father a message from me—tell him he may think he has got away with it, but I haven't given up; I'll get him if it's the last thing I do!'

He turned away and began to walk to the door. Olivia got up, intending to follow him and ask one of the junior secretaries to take over from her in her father's office, because she needed some time alone, she had to think. But just as his hand reached for the door-handle Max suddenly swung round again, making her nerves jump.

'That girl who tried to stop me coming in here will tell him I came,' he said tersely. 'So you'd better mention it first, or he'll wonder why you didn't say anything.'

She frowned, realised he was right, nodded without speaking, and that nod made them conspirators.

Max watched her, his eyes brilliant, searching hers as if looking for something in their golden depths. She tried to glance away and couldn't; she was trapped in the beam of his stare like a rabbit in headlights, her heart beating far too fast.

Max strode back towards her, took hold of her face with one hand, tilted her head back, while his other hand went round her waist, pulling her towards him.

It all happened too fast. She had no time to think, let alone stop him. His head came down and his mouth hit hers.

The kiss was fatal, a bullet to the heart. She felt her whole body jerk in shock, in a mixture of agony and intense pleasure. Her eyes stayed wide open, fixed, desperate, her skin was ice-cold, her mouth was burning. She was dying, shaking, her hands reaching out to hold on to him to stop herself falling down. She clutched his shirt and swayed, the only part of her that was still alive her mouth, kissing him back.

As suddenly as he had begun to kiss her he stopped, lifting his head, moving away.

She stood there, still wide-eyed, still white, still helpless in anguish.

Max stared at her, breathing fiercely, his skin dark red.

'Now at least you'll know what you missed,' he said between tight teeth. 'They coveted my company—even if you marry my nephew, you'll always remember I coveted you.'

Then he was gone, moving so fast she blinked as if at a lightning flash. The door slammed. Olivia felt her way around the desk like a blind man, sank back into the chair. Her ears were ringing. Her blood was roaring through her veins. She thought she was going to faint. She put her head down on the desk.

It seemed only a second later that the door crashed open again. She thought at first that Max had come back, and sat up in a hurry, flushed, distraught, her blonde hair tangled, her eyes wide.

'Olivia! My God, you look... What did he do to you?'

It was Christos, darkly flushed, anger in his eyes as he almost ran across the room.

Behind him she saw Constantine Agathios, glowering, heavy, his bull's head lowered as if he were going to charge, and her father, narrow-eyed, hard-faced, watching her as if he suspected, could guess, at what had happened, her emotional turmoil.

Christos came round the desk and bent down to look into her face. 'It's OK, Olivia, don't look like that... He's gone, and he'll never come anywhere near you again.'

She burst into tears and Christos put his arms around her, pulled her against him, held her like a child, stroking her hair, murmuring softly.

'Don't, darling, don't cry like that, you're safe now...'

She wasn't safe; she would never be safe again. That kiss had changed everything, her whole world was upside down and she couldn't tell Christos—how could she? What could she say? That she had realised she couldn't marry him because she could never love him? The fondness she felt for Christos would never turn into love—she had let herself think it might, had deceived herself, but she couldn't any more because that kiss had forced her to face the truth.

The intensity of her reaction had been a blinding shock, ripping away all her pretences, illusions, defences.

She clung to Christos, her face buried in his shirt, wondering desperately how she was going to get out of her engagement. Would it hurt his feelings when she told him? Did he really care?

'Pull yourself together, Olivia!' her father said in his cold, incisive voice. 'Let go of her, Christos! Here, take this, Olivia, wipe your face and blow your noise, snap out of it!'

He thrust a box of paper tissues into her hand, gestured to Christos to move away, then leaned on the edge of the desk, watching her as she shakily obeyed him, dried her damp face, wiped her eyes, blew her nose, dropped the used tissues into the wastepaper basket under the desk.

'Got a comb?' Gerald Faulton asked curtly. 'Use it, tidy yourself up, then you can tell us what Max was doing here, what he wanted, what he said.'

Olivia kept her eyes down, fumbled in her bag, found a compact, a comb, make-up, and did a repair job on her face. When her hair was smooth again, her lipstick renewed, her nose powdered, she sat up and felt able to meet her father's inimical eyes.

He had never loved her, she thought, staring back at him; all her life she had known that. Cold, bleak, rejecting, he had made it impossible for her to love him. It would be easier to bear if she knew why. What had she done to make her own father dislike her? Why, if he disliked her, did he keep in touch, make her spend those holidays with him every year? Duty, as her mother said?

'Now,' Gerald Faulton said, 'what happened?'

'You obviously know—he came here, he was looking for you, he was angry, very angry...' She tried to make her voice level and calm but it shook. 'He said...that he was going to kill you.' Max wanted him to know that. He wanted her to tell her father he had made that threat, or she wouldn't have told Gerald.

'Did he hurt you?' Christos asked, still looking anxious.

She glanced at him, her golden eyes sad, because she was fond of him, she liked him, Christos was a darling, but he was never going to be able to set her on fire. The way Max had, she thought, her pulses haywire. Oh, God, the way he had. That terrible power he had over her—the power of life and death. That kiss had unlocked the doors of heaven and hell. She had died under the touch of his mouth—and yet, too, she had been dead for years, and that kiss had brought her back to life.

'Hurt me?' she repeated, with wild irony. 'Oh, no, he didn't hurt me.' He just destroyed me, she thought.

'Then what was all the drama about?' bit out her father.

'Obviously, he frightened the life out of her,' protested Christos. 'Threatening to kill you ... shouting the place down, according to that girl out there, who heard his voice going on and on for ages, bullying Olivia. No wonder she was upset.'

Constantine Agathios interrupted, his heavy-lidded eyes intent on her. 'Did he tell you what he planned to do now?'

'I told you what he said ... he threatened to kill my father.'

Gerald impatiently said, 'Yes, yes, that's just a lot of hot air. He's far too clever to do anything of the sort and get locked up for life. Did he say anything else? Did you pick up any idea what he means to do now?'

She shook her head. 'No idea at all. I did ask him what he was going to do, and he said he wasn't going to tell me because I would only tell you.'

The two older men glanced at each other. Constantine brooded, his head down, his mouth a heavy line.

'What can he do?' asked Christos, shrugging. 'You have a majority on the board, you own more voting shares than he does... He's finished now, what can he do?'

'I wish I knew,' his father grunted. 'Max is as slippery as an eel. I still feel uneasy. I just wish I knew what he was up to!'

'Oh, come on,' said her father impatiently, 'he can't hurt us! We outgun him. While the two of us hold more shares, he's helpless.'

'Let's hope you're right,' Constantine said, but he did not look very reassured.

Olivia listened, her face blank but her mind very busy. Max might have lost control of his company, they might have out-manoeuvred him for the moment, but it was crystal-clear that he still worried his brother, who was uneasy, twitchy, afraid that Max still had an ace up his sleeve and could still beat them, somehow, some way. Logically, they had won, as her father had just said, but Constantine's own gut instincts, and his knowledge of his younger half-brother, warned him not to be too complacent, and Olivia was sure he was right to worry.

'You're superstitious about him!' Gerald Faulton muttered, frowning. 'You seem to think he has magical powers—but he doesn't, man! He isn't the devil incarnate. It's all in your own head! I tell you, he can't do anything about it. For one thing, he hasn't any money, unless he sells his own shares in the company.'

'He'd never do that!' Constantine grimaced. 'That would be admitting he had no hope of getting it back.'

'Well, there you are then!'

Christos had been listening to them, his face thoughtful. Suddenly he said, 'He could sell Hymnos!'

'What?' Gerald Faulton stared at Christos. 'Sell what?'

'I'd forgotten all about it,' Constantine said slowly, staring at his son. 'But you're right—he could raise money by selling Hymnos. Clever of you to think of it, Christos!'

'What are you both talking about?' Gerald asked, pale and frowning.

Constantine turned towards him. 'Along with his ships, my brother inherited an island from my father— it isn't very big, and it isn't inhabited, although Max has built himself a house on it, I gather, but these days, with Greek tourism growing by leaps and bounds, a small island in the Aegean could be very valuable. I've no doubt he could find a buyer, and he might raise a considerable sum by selling it.'

Gerald said shortly, 'Even so, there's nothing he can do. Oh, he could buy up a few of the smaller shareholders, but we'll still be in control because we have the majority shareholding.' He gave Constantine a cool, rueful look. 'Stop getting so worked up about him! We're as safe as houses.'

Constantine let out a long sigh. 'Yes, you're right, of course you are.'

Christos dreamily said, 'I've always envied him, owning Hymnos. I'd love an island of my own, wouldn't you, Olivia?'

His father gave him an indulgent smile. 'Well, if Max does put it on the market, I may buy it for you—if the price is right!'

A few weeks later Gerald walked into Olivia's office and threw down on her desk a folded copy of *The Times*.

'He did it! Look at that—I've ringed it. It seems you and Christos may be going to get a Greek island for a wedding present!'

Dazedly she picked up the newspaper and looked at the red-ringed property advertisement.

'FOR SALE: a floating Garden of Eden', the estate agency announced. 'The small island of Hymnos in the Aegean sea, with only one moderately sized house, with all modern conveniences, electricity generator supplying power to house, bathrooms, fully equipped kitchen, up-to-date radio equipment for emergencies, helicopter pad, boathouse, swimming-pool and well maintained paddocks—the perfect hideaway for the man who has everything except perfect privacy. Unmatched views, within two hours' sailing distance of nearest airport. To be sold at auction, all details supplied by agent.'

She slowly looked up. 'I don't imagine Christos's father really meant what he said. I can't see him buying some remote Greek island that is obviously going to cost a fortune, judging by all the expensive toys on it—helicopter pad, radio equipment, boathouse—heaven knows what price it will fetch at auction.'

Gerald's cold mouth twisted. 'If Max Agathios inherited it from their father, Constantine will want it. Surely you've realised how much Constantine hates Max? The two of them take sibling rivalry to a new height.'

Christos rang her at her flat that evening. 'My father's going to that auction!' he told her excitedly, and she drew a sharp breath.

'He was serious about buying it?'

'You bet he was! He's always resented the fact that Grandpapa left Hymnos to Max, not him, and nothing is going to stop him getting it at last. So he isn't going to leave it to intermediaries, he's going there himself, to make sure nothing goes wrong and someone outbids him ... and he suggests we go with him. The auction is to be held on the island itself—apparently the auctioneers plan to take people over by helicopter. There won't be a large group of bidders involved, at the starting price Max has set, but Dad plans to sail over there on his yacht, the *Agathios Athena*, so that we can see Hymnos for ourselves before the auction.'

Pale, reluctant, Olivia murmured, 'But ... I've only just started working here. I don't think my father would let me have the time off!'

'He's coming too,' said Christos. 'Dad talked to him a few minutes ago. We'll all fly over to Greece; *Agathios Athena* is tied up at Piraeus, we'll sail the day we arrive, spend one day at Hymnos, then sail back to Piraeus and fly to London again. It should only take three days—a long weekend, that's all. And your father has already said you could come, don't worry, so that's OK. It will be fun.'

Olivia rang off a few minutes later and looked at her own white face in the mirror.

She did not want to go to Hymnos, to watch Max's private paradise being sold to his brother. What if Max was there? She closed her eyes, biting her lip.

She wished she had the courage to tell Christos she didn't love him and she was sure he was not in love with her either, break off her engagement, face up to her father's rage.

But she didn't dare. Christos might not be heartbroken, but he was fond of her, he might be upset, and he would certainly be frightened of his father's reaction. So was she. Constantine terrified her. Almost as much as her father. When Gerald found out, he would be icy, implacable. He wanted her to marry Christos to cement his alliance with Constantine; if she didn't, he would never forgive her.

Oh, if only she weren't such a coward!

CHAPTER FIVE

OLIVIA hadn't been back to the Greek islands since that last holiday with her father on Corfu. As the plane began to descend to land at Athens airport, that October afternoon, she looked out of the window and saw the blue Aegean far below her, the autumnal colouring of the mountainous landscape behind Athens, and felt a sudden dart of *déjà vu*. Just over five years ago she had flown into Corfu, looked down on blue seas and green and brown mountains, felt a surge of excitement and anticipation. Greece had a light all its own; nowhere else had this immense clarity, a radiance like that of heaven. She felt the same surge again, and then just as suddenly sadness welled up inside her. That time she flew into Corfu she hadn't yet met Max, she was just looking forward to some weeks in the sun. Today she felt none of that eager excitement. Instead, she felt sick with guilt, with worry.

In front of her she saw Constantine's lowered, bull-like head, her father beside him reading a newspaper. Christos was sitting beside her. They had flown over here on Constantine's small private plane.

They had come to take another of Max's possessions away from him, something else he loved and they coveted—his private paradise, the advertisement in the newspaper had called it.

It must be agonising for Max to sell it. No wonder he was full of hate, for his brother, for her father. For her too? she wondered, and winced at the thought.

She shouldn't have come. She should have made some excuse, refused to go. It had been in her mind to do just that, but she had met her father's cold, level stare and the words had dried up in her throat.

Why am I such a coward? she silently accused herself, her eyes burning with unshed tears of self-contempt.

It was only as they began to come down through the clouds that they saw the smog hovering over the city; thick, yellow, damp, enveloping the Parthenon, the tree-crowned hills beside it, the Agora and the old houses of the Plaka, swirling around the tops of modern glass and concrete office blocks, making it impossible to see more than a few yards ahead.

'London used to get these fogs, years ago,' Olivia said to Christos, 'until they brought in the clean air laws and stopped people using coal, either in domestic fires or industry. Now smog is a thing of the past, thank heavens.'

Christos shrugged. 'Modern living has so many problems, and it has all happened so rapidly in Greece that we're still coping with the shock of the modern. At the moment, they're desperately trying to do something about the number of cars coming into the city—in the last twenty years the number of people living here has grown beyond belief, and they all have cars! Traffic is often jammed solid, especially in the centre. Whatever they try, people find a way round it though. They're determined to use their cars, although they're the first to complain about traffic-jams. By the end of this century I wouldn't be surprised to find private cars being banned from entering the centre of the city at all.'

Olivia nodded soberly. 'In London too. The car is becoming a nightmare, isn't it, if you live in a big city?'

Although it was October, it was still very hot, and as they made their way through the terminal sweat began to trickle down Olivia's back under her white shirt. It had been cold and windy in London, and the abrupt change in the weather was a shock, even though she had expected it to be warmer here, and had brought light clothes to wear on the yacht.

It took ages to drive to Piraeus in the yellowish smog. As she got out of the car on the dockside Olivia was stunned by the sheer size of Constantine Agathios's yacht. Remembering Max's boat, she had expected something much smaller, but this huge white yacht was like a small cruise ship—and had, she discovered as they went aboard, a crew of seven, including a chef and two stewards to serve food and drink and clean the cabins, who all lined up on the deck to welcome them to the *Agathios Athena*.

'Dad uses it to impress people,' Christos murmured, grinning at her. 'Politicians, clients, business partners. He calls it a legitimate business expense!'

It must cost a small fortune just to pay the mooring fees, thought Olivia, following him along a panelled corridor.

'This is your cabin,' Christos said, opening a door, and she looked into a small but well equipped room with a porthole window which was the only indication that they were on a ship. The furniture was elegant, even if kept to a minimum, leaving the middle of the room empty, to give the illusion of space. A narrow bed, with a low cabinet beside it holding a bedside lamp, a wardrobe, a dressing-table which could double as a table, were all set into the golden oak panelling on the walls, for stability when the boat hit bad weather, no doubt. Curtains and bedcovers matched, the material a light blue sprinkled with tiny flowers in pale pink and green, the same material also covering the small easy chair which was the only other piece of furniture in the room.

The impression was light, airy, charming. Christos stood in the doorway, watching her face, as Olivia looked around.

'Like it?'

She turned to smile at him. 'It's lovely. Amazing how so much was got into such a tiny room, and yet it looks quite spacious.'

'Dad had the best Greek yacht designer. If there is one thing we Greeks know about, it is ships. We were sailing the seven seas before the British stopped using coracles!' Christos was half joking, half serious.

'Chauvinist!' teased Olivia and he laughed, a little flushed but defiant.

'Well, why not? We all have our national pride, don't we? You can't say Britain doesn't!'

'True,' she said seriously. 'But we're all Europeans now. I can't wait for the day when we stop talking about our national pasts and start looking to our shared future.'

Christos grimaced at her. 'Maybe we should—but whether or not we ever will is anybody's guess. Old habits die hard. I think the tribal instinct in all of us is the real problem. It's in our genetic blueprint; we can't argue ourselves out of it.'

'Argue yourselves out of what?' a sharp voice asked from behind him.

They hadn't heard Gerald Faulton walking past. Christos swung round, startled, and Olivia tensed. Her father had always had that effect on her, she thought grimly. When had she ever felt at ease with him?

'Olivia and I were just talking politics,' said Christos cheerfully. 'I guess you could call it that. She's a strong

European—I'm not so sure it is going to work, politically.'

'Economics is what the common market is all about,' Gerald coldly informed him, his tone, his manner, leaving no room for discussion. 'And it has to work, for all our sakes. Are you coming up on deck to watch us sail?'

'I've done it a hundred times. I'll skip it this time; I have some phone calls to make,' Christos said, looking faintly sulky because Gerald had talked to him in a dictatorial way. He was used to that from his own father; he didn't see why he should put up with it from hers. 'What about you, Olivia?'

'I'd like to,' she admitted. 'I've never done it before.'

Christos grinned at her indulgently. 'OK. Mind you, in this fog, you won't be able to see much. I'll see you in the lounge for cocktails before dinner, in an hour, OK?'

Up on deck, Olivia leaned on the rail beside her father, watching as the port of Piraeus disappeared from view.

The big ships, the masts of shabby fishing boats, the harbour walls, and beyond that the rows of tavernas and little bars whose yellowish lights looked like the eyes of cats in the fog, vanished all at the same time as if eaten up, and suddenly the yacht was alone in rolling banks of soundless, clammy sea mist. Olivia shivered, and her father gave her a sideways frown.

'You should have put a sweater on. This mist isn't very pleasant, is it? Let's go inside. You had better change into something special for dinner—Constantine will expect it.'

She had known that—Christos had warned her to bring at least one dress suitable for a party. She went to her cabin, showered, put on the light green frothy chiffon, and an hour later joined her father in the elegantly furnished lounge where one of the stewards was mixing cocktails in a silver shaker. He turned, smiling, to ask what she would like to drink. Olivia asked for some lime and sparkling mineral water. Her father gave her a bleak look.

'Don't drink much, do you?'

'Not really. An occasional glass of wine, that's all.'

'Your mother didn't either,' grunted Gerald Faulton. 'She was a health fanatic before they invented the term.'

His drink arrived, a dry martini, which came stiff with ice which chinked as he lifted the glass to his mouth.

'Personally, I like a drink,' he muttered, skating a glance over her, taking in the well-brushed blonde hair, the low-cut green chiffon, around her throat the single string of good pearls which he had given her for her eighteenth birthday, in her ears the matching pearl studs he had given for another birthday and on her wrist a pearl and silver bracelet he had given her last year.

She had worn them all tonight, deliberately.

He didn't pay her any compliments, but he did nod approvingly, before taking another swallow of martini.

Olivia wasn't surprised. She would have been surprised if he had said something nice to her.

Her face wry, she sank with a swish of long skirts into one of the deeply upholstered sofas arranged around a low teak coffee-table.

'How long will it take us to reach Hymnos?'

'We should moor off the island tonight,' Gerald said. 'Within an hour or so, at this speed.'

'We are moving fast, aren't we? Yet the whole boat is really steady. Christos says his father had it designed by someone who is the top of the field.'

'No doubt he did,' Gerald said tersely. He did not own a yacht; obviously he didn't approve of Constantine having one, especially such a beautiful and expensive yacht. There was a puritanical streak in him that found it an affront to watch people enjoying themselves, especially if it meant spending large sums of money on their pleasure.

Olivia looked around the lounge, noticing that the table-top had a low rim around it to stop anything placed on it from rolling off, and the furniture had specially shaped feet at all four corners. The feet clicked into place in metal circles set in the woodblock floor.

In heavy seas that would help keep the furniture steady, stop it shifting with the roll of the yacht, yet it could be removed quickly and easily for cleaning purposes.

'Whoever he was, the designer was very ingenious,' she said.

Her father ignored the remark. In his cold, precise voice he said, 'We won't land until tomorrow morning, when everyone else who is interested will fly in by helicopter. There's to be a picnic lunch, which the agency is supplying, and then the auction in the afternoon, in the house itself. Apparently there's only a rough track up to the house from the small cove where we shall have to land, so we'll have to walk up there. I hope it isn't too far. I gather there is a four-wheel-drive vehicle on the island, which Max Agathios uses for driving around the whole place, but it is locked up in a garage and the agent said he didn't have permission to let anyone else use it.'

'Will he be there?'

'The agent? Of course.' Gerald gave her an impatient look.

'No...Max Agathios...' Flushed, Olivia kept her eyes down on her drink, knowing that her father was watching her closely.

She wished she knew what he was thinking, but she had always found that cold mask of his unreadable, except on the occasions when he meant her to realise he was angry with her.

'I've no idea,' Gerald said curtly, and although she didn't look at him she heard the angry undertone. Gerald did not want her to be interested in Max Agathios—there was suspicion and resentment in his voice.

Why did he hate Max? What had Max ever done to him? She couldn't ask, knew he wouldn't answer if she did; her father was intensely secretive about every aspect of his life.

Constantine arrived, heavy and glowering in evening dress, like an overweight penguin. He took the other corner of Gerald's sofa, told the steward to make him a Manhattan, then threw an assessing glance over Olivia, much as her father had done.

Unlike Gerald though, he commented on the way she looked. 'That's a very pretty dress, Olivia—it suits you, you should wear more clothes like that—glamorous, romantic. I like to see you in it.'

He accepted his glass from the steward and lifted it in a silent toast to her, adding, 'Women don't wear romantic clothes any more, I don't know why—all this feminism, I suppose. They want to look like men, which is ridiculous. A woman should look like a woman, not go around in jeans and T-shirts all day.'

Olivia felt irritation burn in her throat, but didn't say what she wanted to say. She knew she looked good in jeans and a T-shirt, and from the way men looked at her they usually thought so too. But she couldn't face an argument with Constantine Agathios, any more than she could with her own father. Coward! she thought. I'm such a coward—and despised herself.

Constantine frowned, glancing around. 'Why isn't Christos here? What's he doing? He knows what time I like dinner to be served.' He reached for the phone on a table beside him. 'In his cabin, I suppose, day-dreaming, instead of getting dressed. I'll give him a ring, tell him to get down here.' He dialled, took a sip of his drink with the phone in one hand, frowned even more as he listened. 'His line's engaged. Who is he ringing, at this hour?'

'He said he had to make a business call,' Olivia hurriedly said.

'Business call! Gossiping with his friends, that's what he means, and at my expense. He went to school in Athens, he still has a lot of friends there. I should have known that the minute he got back to Greece he would be on the phone to them all.'

Constantine swung his heavy head towards the steward discreetly standing at a distance, pretending not to be eavesdropping. 'Here . . . you! Go and find my son and tell him to get along here at once!'

'Yes, sir,' said the steward expressionlessly, moving away, but Olivia jumped up, putting her glass down on the coffee-table, her skirts swishing around her.

'I'll go!' She was dying to get away from the two older men—this was the perfect excuse.

She went out of the sliding glass doors on to the deck and walked towards the door which led to the gangway down to the cabins on the deck below, then halted as she realised that the weather conditions were quite different now.

They had sailed out of the mist. Around them lay blue sea, blue sky, a shimmering horizon with the pale wraith of the moon far out in the distance although it was still light enough to see for miles. There was no sign of land anywhere. The engines throbbed smoothly in the engine-room down below. The yacht was moving very fast, although the stabilisers with which it was fitted disguised its speed. Constantine wanted to reach Hymnos before nightfall. There were hazards under the waters around the island, he had said earlier, hidden rocks which could be very dangerous. The yacht's captain would prefer the chance to arrive in daylight and moor safely in the small natural bay.

Olivia leaned on the polished rail, watching the water churning alongside the hull of the yacht, white foam tossed like chiffon on the crest of the deep blue waves. While she gazed down, she saw Max's face form on the surface of the water, his black eyes staring at her, accusing her, angry, compelling.

Her heart clenched in pain.

She couldn't bear the idea of seeing him when they went ashore on Hymnos next day, feeling the lance of his bitter eyes. Oh, surely he wouldn't want to be there when they sold his island? Especially if he realised that his brother was planning to bid for it? Constantine had informed the auctioneers that he was arriving by sea and if they knew, Max would know.

She straightened and hurried off to find Christos, but met him on his way from his cabin.

'They sent me to find you,' she warned, and he grimaced.

'Dad getting nasty because I was late, was he? I forgot the time, I was so busy talking to my friends.'

'He said you would be—I told him you were making business calls!'

Christos grinned, put an arm around her, squeezed her warmly and kissed her hair. 'You're an angel! Well, come on—he can only kill me once!'

He was lucky that evening. When they reached the lounge Constantine was on the phone himself, talking in harsh, angry Greek to someone while Gerald silently listened. Olivia couldn't understand a word, but she didn't need to speak the language to understand the tone.

Constantine was furious about something! He slammed the phone down and turned to them with heavy black brows down over his glittering eyes.

'They've put the auction off until the day after tomorrow!'

'Can they do that?' bit out Gerald.

'You heard me trying to force them to change their minds, but it was no use, they had their heels dug in.'

'Why have they done it?' Gerald was narrow-eyed, hard with suspicion.

Constantine eyed him with sardonic irony. 'That was what I wanted to know. Illness, they said—the auctioneer went down with food poisoning today, but should be better within twenty-four hours.'

'Ridiculous. They could get someone else. Max is behind this—I wonder what he's really up to?'

Constantine looked grim. 'I wonder.'

They had dinner a few minutes later. Olivia wasn't hungry. After eating a little clear chicken consommé followed by a seafood salad, she skipped dessert. While the two older men sat over coffee in the lounge, Olivia and Christos went for a walk around the deck in the moonlight, but after a few minutes he looked at his watch with an exclamation.

'I forgot...there's another call I want to make... I won't be five minutes, Olivia, wait here...'

He vanished down the gangway to his cabin and Olivia leaned on the rail. The sea was no longer just an empty blue expanse—ahead of them loomed a dark shape which rapidly became a small island. It had a rocky headland, climbing hills behind it, the silvery grey-green of olive trees fluttering ghostlike in the moonlight, and here and there down the steep cliffs pines swaying gently in the breeze.

With a jab of shock, Olivia wondered, was this Hymnos? She hurried off to her own cabin to find a pair of binoculars she had brought with her, and came back on deck to focus on the island, get a clearer view.

The rocks were a strange colour, a terracotta red streaked with black, barbaric in colour and texture, the grain of the rock geometric, angular, jutting sharply in all directions, with rough grass and broom sprouting in crevices.

The binoculars up to her eyes, she searched the line of the cliffs but could see no sign of habitation. Max's house must be on the other side of the island.

On the rocky headland though, she saw movement. At first she thought it was a tree. Then she realised that it was a man. His arms were lifted, as if he was waving to her. She adjusted the focus of the binoculars, made his image sharper. She couldn't see his face, but she could see the way his thick hair blew backwards in the wind; hair as black as night, curling, rippling like seaweed against the sea-blue light of the moonlit sky. He was wearing black too; like his hair, his shirt blew back in the wind, loose of his black jeans, almost as if it were a cape. His arms were still lifted, the full sleeves of his shirt flapping around them.

Max? she thought, her body shuddering in shock.

Was it Max? Or did she just want it to be him? At this distance she couldn't be sure, but there was something intensely familiar about the black hair, the way he moved. It could be her imagination, though.

Behind him the sky was changing: clouds gathering, just one or two at first, drifting threads of smoky colour, black, grey, smouldering red, more and more of them, until the whole horizon turned dark with approaching storm.

The man on the headland let his arms drop, but stood there for a moment, staring down towards the yacht.

Could he see her? she wondered. He had no binoculars, but from that height he could no doubt see for miles.

Had he been waving to warn her about the coming storm? He must have seen that coming too, long before she did.

Behind her she heard hurrying footsteps and Christos appeared at her side, out of breath, flushed.

'Sorry about that, darling. Were you bored?'

'No, I've been watching the weather, it's changing again,' she said, and Christos threw a look at the sky, frowning.

'You're right—looks as if we might be in for a little rough weather.'

The man on the headland had vanished when Olivia looked back up there a moment later. The island looked empty again.

Within half an hour the storm hit them, buffeting the yacht violently. In spite of its stabilisers, the boat rolled and wallowed in the great black waves. Gerald Faulton looked a ghastly colour as he lurched to his feet and staggered off without a word to his cabin.

'Seasick, poor Gerald!' grinned Constantine, himself perfectly at ease with the mountainous seas. 'Never been seasick in my life, thank God. How about you, Olivia?' He scrutinised her, nodded approval of her colour. 'You look fine, good girl, but you'd better lie down in your cabin all the same. It's easier to cope with rough weather if you're lying down, and we've no idea when this storm will blow itself out. We're going to try to battle our way round into the shelter of Hymnos—inside the little bay we should be quite safe. Try and get to sleep. By the morning the weather should be fine again.'

Olivia found the storm exhilarating. Before she went down to her cabin she stopped to look up at the island. They were much closer now; she could see the sheer cliffs towering above them, the sea pounding the rocky beaches at their base. The yacht was turning, shifting, as the captain tried to bring it round the point of the island, into the calmer waters of the bay. Olivia held on tightly to the rail as the deck swayed and creaked under her feet.

Her fine green chiffon skirts whisked around her legs in the wind, then suddenly ballooned upwards, across her face, blinding her, the delicate gauzy material half suffocating her as it blew into her mouth. It was like walking into a spider's web. Olivia shuddered and let go of the rail to push the skirts down. At that instant the yacht plunged down into a great cleft between high waves; the sea washed over the rail and hit Olivia, making her gasp in shock.

The deck was awash with water. Becoming alarmed, Olivia turned to hurry down to her cabin, but her feet slid from under her, and she was flung sideways with such violence that although she grabbed for the rail as she fell against it her hands couldn't grip it, her body went on falling, toppling over.

As she fell overboard she screamed, but the gale caught her voice and tore it away soundlessly.

Nobody else had been on deck; the attention of the crew would all be focused in the wheelhouse. Nobody would know what had happened to her.

Olivia was too shocked to swim at first. She struggled crazily in the water, screaming, but the yacht had already moved on, was too far away for anyone to hear her.

The sea was strangely warm, after a long, hot summer, but the waves were as high as mountains. They rose and fell, crashing down on her relentlessly, dragging her backwards and forwards with them, like human flotsam, her skirts drifting on top of the water like seaweed for a moment, until they slowly filled with water and grew heavy.

A coldness invaded her brain, made her stop panicking, start to think.

When she fell the yacht had been turning into the lee of the island. She must be close to shore; there might be rocks nearby, or a strong tide which might carry her into shore.

She fought to stay calm, let herself float, lifting her head to look towards the island; it towered above her, rocky, inhospitable, yet the only hope she had.

She struck out towards it, fighting the waves which kept hitting her, forcing her backwards. Every time she lifted her head to check on the dark shape of the island she seemed no nearer. For every foot of progress she made, the sea forced her back again. She began to tire; her arms and legs aching, too heavy to lift, she was exhausted, weeping; she couldn't keep going. She couldn't swim another foot.

She was going to drown, here, off Max's island paradise, and nobody would ever know what had happened to her.

CHAPTER SIX

OLIVIA came back to life in agony, lying face down on sand, coughing and choking, her open mouth spewing water, her lungs heaving, her body shuddering violently.

When the convulsions stopped she lay weeping, not knowing where she was or what had happened to her, until strong hands turned her over on to her back.

Wet lashes curled back, shaking with sobs, she looked up at the face bending over her. She might have thought she had died and gone to heaven if it hadn't been for the sheer physical pain of coming back to life. Only living could hurt this much.

'You're going to be OK,' Max said quietly.

Her throat was raw; slowly, painfully, she managed to whisper, 'How did...? I was in the sea...how did I get here?'

'I saw you and swam out to tow you in.'

She was stunned. 'In that sea?' Behind her she could hear its roar, the thunder of the waves hitting rocks. The very sound of it made her shiver.

'I'm a strong swimmer.' His voice was curt, dismissive.

'You could have been drowned,' she said, eyes stinging with tears.

He shrugged. 'As I said, I'm a strong swimmer, and I know these waters. I often swim off this beach. If I hadn't gone in, you *would* have drowned—you were going down for the last time when I reached you. I was afraid I wouldn't reach you in time.'

She was seeing him through running curtains of water—at first she thought they were her tears, then she realised rain was pelting down.

'You saved my life. Thank you.' Every word cost her an effort, her throat was so swollen and sore.

She started violently as lightning tore down the sky. It seemed to be right overhead, the whole landscape lit up: boiling dark sea, banked clouds in the sky, a lone pine tree bending and swaying on the rocky cliffs above the beach.

Max got to his feet. 'We'd better get you indoors.' He bent and slid his hands underneath her, one under her knees, the other under her back, and lifted her as he straightened.

'I can walk,' she protested, too weak to struggle.

'Put your arms round my neck; it will make it easier for me,' was his only response to that.

Her arms felt heavy as lead as she lifted them; it was a relief to let them fall over his shoulders, clasping her trembling hands behind his nape.

Max began to walk quickly, with her held close to his body, her legs dangling, her wet, bedraggled skirts clinging against her sides. His clothes were saturated too, his shirt plastered to his chest.

'Where are we?' Olivia's voice was just a hoarse whisper, like the wind through dry, winter grass.

He looked down at her in obvious surprise. 'Hymnos—where else?'

'How far. . . to your house?' She remembered being told that there was a long walk up a steep track, and got out thickly, 'You can't carry me all that way.'

'I'm not going to. I drove down here. How else could I get here fast enough? I saw you from the cliff top, saw you fall off the yacht, and I got into my Land Rover and drove down here like a bat out of hell.'

He lifted his head and stared away into the night, and she watched his profile tense, tighten.

'I thought I wouldn't get here in time,' he muttered.

Olivia hadn't dared hope anyone would get to her in time. 'There was nobody on deck. I don't suppose anyone saw me fall in...' She frowned weakly, biting her lip. 'They won't know...until the morning when they find my cabin empty. Haven't you got radio equipment here? You could send a message to the yacht, let them know I'm safe.'

'I could,' Max said in a dry voice, and when she looked up at his profile it was set, unreadable. He wouldn't want to talk to his half-brother, of course, or her father, and who could blame him?

She sighed, and then felt her heavy lids closing. She couldn't force them up again. She drifted into semi-consciousness, too weary to fight the exhaustion taking her over.

Dimly, she was aware when Max put her into the back of his vehicle, laid her down full length, heaped blankets on her, got behind the wheel and began driving up the rutted track to the house.

Olivia was jolted and shaken every inch of the way, but she lay under her blankets, trembling, her teeth chattering with cold and shock. She didn't try to sit up or look out. She kept her eyes shut, even though she had recovered consciousness.

The vehicle stopped with a little bump, then Max got out and came round to get her out. First he wrapped her in one of the blankets, then lifted her bodily over his shoulder in a fireman's lift, her head hanging down behind him.

A door opened; yellow light shone round her, penetrating her closed lids. She opened her eyes then and blinked at the radiance, trying to see past it to catch a glimpse of the house, but Max had already begun to carry her inside.

He closed the door and the storm receded at once. Olivia stared around her and saw white walls, a greeny-white marble floor, a polished oak staircase leading upwards.

'First, a hot bath,' Max said, carrying her up the stairs.

She thought of it longingly; her very bones were aching with cold. She couldn't wait to slide into the warmth of a bath, wash the salt off her skin, out of her hair.

Max sat her on a wicker bathroom stool and turned to the large white bath; she heard the water gushing out. Her brain wasn't working very fast, but she suddenly stiffened.

'I can manage by myself now,' she hurriedly said, and Max straightened and looked round at her, his eyes ironic, his mouth wry.

'You can hardly move.'

It was true. She was half-dead from her long struggle with the sea, but she insisted, flustered at the very idea of him staying in the room while she took a bath.

'I can manage. Please, just...' She didn't like to finish the request. He had risked his life to save her, this was his home. She didn't like to say, Go, get out, I don't want you watching me take off my clothes.

'I don't want you drowning in my bath after I've pulled you out of the sea!' he said, sprinkling scented bath salts into the water. The bathroom filled with the fragrance of roses.

'I'm fine now,' she lied.

Max turned, surveyed her sardonically. 'OK, then, let's see you standing on your feet.'

She managed it, struggling up, gripping the edge of the bath to keep herself upright.

'There, you see?' she said, eyes defiant.

'Oh, yes, I see,' he drawled, walking towards her.

Alarmed, she backed, had to let go of the bath, and swayed dangerously. Max's arms went round her, stopping her from falling.

'Don't be so stupid,' he told her. 'You aren't even capable of unzipping your dress at the moment.' His hand moved up her back, she felt the long zip slide down, and thought, He's right, I couldn't have reached the zip, it's hard enough to do it when I'm feeling fit, but my arms are so heavy and tired. Every movement is an effort.

Max peeled the wet, clinging material off her body and the dress slithered to the floor. She felt him start to push the straps of her slip down over her arms.

Flushed and nervous, Olivia babbled, 'No, don't, that's enough...'

She tried to shift away but his arm was an iron bar across her back. His dark eyes held hers while he very slowly slid her slip down over her breasts, her waist, her hips, until it too fell to the floor.

Mesmerised, staring deep into his eyes, Olivia stopped trying to get away, gave herself up to the intense pleasure of feeling him look at her, touch her. She had had dreams like this—dreams she only dimly remembered—where Max touched her, naked, kissed her. In her waking moments she wouldn't let herself remember, but now the dream emerged into the light, was really happening, wasn't a fantasy, and she trembled and couldn't breathe.

He unclipped her bra, let it fall, and then she felt the slow, warm brush of his fingertips on her breast; her nipples hardened, rosy-pink and stinging with sensation.

'Max...don't...you mustn't,' she whispered.

He looked into her eyes. 'Tell me you don't want me to.... Tell me you don't like it...'

His hand travelled on, stroking over her midriff; he slid it inside her wet silky panties and she gave a little moan.

'I can't.'

'Can't tell me you don't like it?'

'Can't let you do it!'

'You can stop me if you tell me you don't like it,' he whispered.

The panties had gone; she was naked and he was looking down at her body in a way that made her skin hot, unbearably hot.

'Don't look at me like that!' She turned her face into Max's wet shirt, shuddering.

His hand covered the back of her head; he stroked her hair, lowered his cheek against it, murmuring inaudibly.

All she could hear was her own name. 'Olivia...Olivia...'

His other hand stroked down her body, her shoulders, her back, the soft swell of her buttocks; she felt pulses begin to beat everywhere he touched.

Suddenly he picked her up in his arms and she gasped, looking up at him. He was staring down at her body, the dark glitter of his eyes half veiled by their lids, his lips parted, his breathing audible, rapid. Suddenly he bent and kissed her breasts, his mouth opening over her nipples, sucking them in, his tongue caressing them.

Olivia felt a pleasure so sharp it was like a sword thrust into her. A groan forced its way out of her throat, even though she tried to keep quiet, not show him how he made her feel.

Max lifted his head, his skin dark red and burning hot. He looked into her eyes and his mouth went crooked as he tried to smile.

'I want you like hell, you know that, don't you?'

Olivia couldn't get a word out. She looked away, blushing, trembling.

A second later Max dropped her into the bath. She gave a choked cry; water went sloshing everywhere in a tidal wave. Max stood there laughing as it went over his legs and bare feet.

'Look what you've done... You're crazy!' she stammered. The marble bathroom floor was awash with water.

Max undid his shirt and flung it off. Olivia felt her nerves jump. 'What are you doing?'

He kicked his jeans off. 'What does it look as if I'm doing?'

'You aren't getting in here with me!'

'Yes, I am.'

She didn't know what to do. She couldn't get up again, try to get out of the bath; the cloudy, fragrant water was at least some sort of cover for her nakedness.

Out of the corner of her eye she saw that he was naked now, the strong, brown body moving towards the bath. Her heart almost stopped; she wanted to stare, to see all of him and at the same time she couldn't bear to look. She kept her head averted, but even so she saw one long, tanned leg stepping into the water, followed by another. Her eyes shot upwards, then down again, her face scarlet.

'I was in that sea too. I'm frozen to the marrow,' Max said, sinking into the water up to his chin. He closed his eyes and sighed deeply. 'Oh, that's better.'

His legs touched hers, one on either side of her. Olivia was stiff with awareness, feeling the muscled thighs moving against her. She stared at his face, so familiar yet so unknown, alien, puzzling.

With his lids down he looked like a blind statue: eyeless, formidable, carved stone features, a strong nose, tough cheekbones, jawline that threatened, a mouth which made her throat beat with a hot pulse.

His lids rose and he stared back at her. She didn't know what he was thinking. Worse, she was afraid of what he might be thinking.

Her colour rose higher. She wanted to look away but couldn't, wanted to ask him to go away, get out of the bath, leave her alone, but she couldn't say a word.

He shifted his position; his thighs moved in closer to her, enclosed her firmly, rubbing softly against her. She knew what she would see if she looked down into the bath: their flesh, clearly visible through the water, entangled together.

'You mustn't forget to wash your hair,' Max said, and got up, dripping, a golden-brown statue, very male. She thought he was getting out of the bath, but he reached for a shower attachment on the wall, and a moment later stood over her, directing it down on her head.

'I can do it!' Olivia sat up, water running down her face, and tried to grab the shower head from him, but he moved it away, turned it off, opened a cupboard above the bath and got out a bottle of shampoo.

'Let me do it!' said Olivia, but he ignored her. He tipped a creamy liquid into his palm, knelt down and began rubbing it into her hair, kneeling in front of her,

his strong fingers massaging her scalp. Olivia shut her
eyes, as much to stop herself seeing Max naked as to
protect her eyes from trickling soap bubbles. He rinsed
the shampoo off, then repeated the process.

'Dry your hair,' he ordered, tossing her a clean, dry
towel.

She obeyed, conscious of him watching the graceful
lift of her breasts as she towelled her hair. Max was
shampooing his own hair.

'Chuck me the towel if you've finished,' he said, and
Olivia leaned over to hand it to him. As he began to dry
his hair she stood up, intending to get out of the bath.

'Where do you think you're going?' Max asked,
dropping the towel on the floor. He caught her by the
waist and pulled her back into the water, this time lying
on top of him, her body between his parted legs.

All the air seemed to be driven out of her lungs.

'Don't, Max,' she whispered, feeling his hands sliding
over her bare flesh, his chest behind her back, his body
moving against hers.

'You didn't use any soap; there must still be salt on
your skin,' he huskily murmured, his chin on her
shoulder, his lips moving against her ear.

He picked up a bar of soap and began washing her
slowly, rhythmically, methodically: first her shoulders,
her arms, then softly over her breasts, while she trembled,
closing her eyes. The firm hand moved on down and
Olivia cried out.

'Oh . . .' It wasn't so much a protest as a response, an
instinctive, mindless response to unbearable pleasure.

She had never slept with anyone; no man had ever
touched her there before. It was the most secret, the most
guarded, the most sensitive part of her body, and as
Max's fingers invaded it she shook violently.

'No!' she muttered, very flushed, pushing his hand away.

Max didn't argue. Instead, he closed his hands on her waist, lifted her, spun her round, lowered her again, the breath catching in her throat as she found herself looking into his eyes.

He began soaping her back, her buttocks, her legs in that slow, exploratory fashion while he watched her face.

'You really turn me on, Olivia,' he whispered, then he lifted his sleek, dark, seal's head from the bathwater until their mouths met.

He turned *her* on; she couldn't deny it, even to herself. She kissed him back hungrily, her blood singing in her ears, giving in to the urge which had gripped her ever since she saw him taking off his clothes. She had never touched a man like this before; she and Christos weren't lovers—their kisses were affectionate rather than passionate, and there was no desire between them. She realised with a flash of understanding that there never would be, could be; she believed Christos was fond of her, and she was very fond of him, but he was more like a brother than a lover.

What hope had there ever been of her falling for any other man when she had belonged to Max, body and soul, ever since they met on that beach in Corfu? He had spoilt her for other men. None of them ever matched up. There was no one like him. She didn't want anyone else.

But she wanted him. She wanted him so badly she felt sick. She touched him with shaky hands, caressed his broad shoulders, the deep, muscled chest, ran her stroking fingers downwards and heard Max draw a long, sharp breath.

In their excitement they forgot where they were, their bodies tangled, shifting eagerly, coming closer, sliding down deeper into the water.

It was only when the bathwater came up over their faces that they broke apart, spluttering, laughing.

'The water's getting cold,' Max said, his voice thick, husky. 'Time to get out.'

He got out first and watched her rise from the water, her skin glistening, pink and wet. Max handed her a long, fluffy white towelling robe, shrugged into an identical one, and helped her tie the belt of hers around her waist.

'I'll go and find us a hot drink and something to eat,' he said. 'You get into bed.' He gestured out of the steamy bathroom, across the landing into a spacious, carpeted bedroom. A vast, four-poster bed took up the centre of the room; gauzy lace curtains hung around it.

'We don't have much trouble with mosquitoes indoors now, so long as you never open the shutters after dark, because these days we plug in electric insect killers every night,' Max said, as Olivia stared at the bed curtains. 'But when the house was first built, I did get pestered by mosquitoes, so I had these curtains installed round the bed, and slept behind them every night. I don't have to bother now.'

He pulled the curtains back. 'In you get. You need to keep warm. You're probably still suffering from shock.'

'I don't want to take your room—there must be others,' she protested, not meeting his eyes.

Max turned down the silky amber-coloured duvet cover. 'Get in my bed, Olivia.'

She knew then that he meant to share the bed with her.

'I can't sleep with you!' she wailed. 'I'm engaged to Christos, I gave him my word.'

Max took hold of her waist and almost threw her into the bed, pulled the duvet cover over her, and gave her a dark stare.

'You're not with him now. You're here, with me. I saved you from drowning—if it weren't for me you would be dead now. That makes you mine. I saved your life, so it belongs to me.'

She clutched the duvet, staring back wordlessly, her ears deafened by the sound of her beating blood.

Max turned and went out. For a minute she was frozen, then she rolled off the bed and almost fell over. Shaking, she made it to the door, to lock it and shut him out.

There was no lock or bolt on the door.

She quietly opened it and stood listening; she heard Max moving about downstairs, presumably in the kitchen. Olivia looked along the landing at the other doors. If any of those rooms had bolts or locks on the doors she could lock herself in and keep Max at bay until morning. She ran to the nearest door, opened it, saw at once that it had neither bolt nor lock, ran on to the next and found the same.

Why didn't he have locks on the doors?

Why bother on an uninhabited island? she realised. Who would he be locking doors against? But what if he had uninvited visitors? Criminals intending to burgle the house, or even kidnap or attack him? She was amazed that that shouldn't worry him.

She heard him then, coming up the stairs, and ran back to the main bedroom, climbed into the bed, clutching the white towelling robe around her, and pulled the duvet up to her chin and lay, waiting anxiously, her heart pounding right under her ribs.

Her eye caught something high up on the ceiling at the other side of the room. A little red light pulsed there, with a black box suspended on a pivot. What on earth...? Then it dawned on her.

A security system! So that was why Max didn't bother with locks or bolts. He had some sort of electronic security system installed here. If anyone broke in while he was here, an alarm would go off. What if he wasn't here, though? Ah, but then what use would locks and bolts be if there was nobody here, nobody to hear someone breaking down the door, smashing windows? No bolt or lock could keep out a criminal determined to break in. The only purpose of the alarm was to give Max warning, time to prepare his defences.

Then she looked at the camera again and blushed to her hairline, appalled. Was it on now? Had it been filming her? Was there a camera in the bathroom too?

Max came through the door at that moment, carrying a tray; the scent of coffee, of food, filled her nostrils and she suddenly felt hungry, which was ridiculous because she had had dinner not that long ago, but then so much had happened since then. Tension used up all your energy; her blood sugar was probably very low.

'Is that camera up there working?' she asked Max, who looked round over his shoulder at it, pausing mid-step.

'No, it isn't switched on.'

'There's a red light.'

'That is nothing to do with the camera—it means the security system has been switched on and nobody can get in or out of the house without setting off an alarm. The windows are alarmed, so are the exterior doors, and the stairs. I just set it before coming up here. It wasn't on five minutes ago.'

'But the camera isn't on?'

He shook his head. 'I only set that when the house is empty, to film any intruders.'

She watched him, hoping he was telling the truth. She thought he was; Max had a direct stare that made him very believable.

'Is there a camera in the bathroom?' she asked and Max gave her a dry, amused look.

'No.'

'Honestly?'

'Go and look, if you don't believe me! Now, are you hungry?'

'Well... I had dinner on board, at...' She lifted her arm to look at her watch.

She wasn't wearing a watch any more. It must have come off in the sea, she thought, the strap had been loose. Her father was going to be furious! That watch had been a Rolex, one of his birthday presents, and had no doubt cost a fortune.

She didn't look forward to telling Gerald. Her golden eyes darkened at the thought of her father.

'Have you been in touch with the yacht yet?' she asked Max as he set the tray down on one side of the bed.

He gave her one of his hard, narrowed stares. 'I'll do that later. If they think you're in your cabin they won't start worrying until morning, as you said.' He poured coffee from the silver Georgian coffee-pot which matched the silver tray it stood on, and offered her a cup.

Olivia reached for it and at that instant realised something else, staring at her left hand dumbly without taking the coffee.

'Oh! Oh, no...' she groaned. It was bare. Her engagement ring had gone. That, too, must be washing about in the sea. It must have come off, like her watch,

while she was fighting to swim ashore. She had noticed
only the other day that it was very slightly too big for
her and had meant to take it to a jeweller to have it
altered to fit better. She knew she had lost weight over
the last months, since her engagement began, in fact;
that was why both ring and watch no longer fitted the
way they once had.

'What's the matter now?' frowned Max.

'My ring... I've lost my engagement ring. It must have
come off in the sea.'

He stared at her in silence for a moment, then said,
'Do you believe in omens, Olivia?'

'No!' she denied, but she was lying. She did. It might
be a coincidence that she had lost her ring tonight. But
Olivia couldn't help feeling that it was a very odd
coincidence, happening at precisely this moment, when
she was about to find herself isolated on this island with
Max and faced with the temptation of his lovemaking.
A ring was only a symbol of an engagement; losing it
didn't mean she was free and yet she couldn't pretend
it made no difference. It was as if fate had intervened
to make it easier for her to forget about Christos and
her promise to marry him.

'I do,' said Max in a deep voice. 'Now, drink your
coffee, Olivia, and eat one of these.'

She took her cup of coffee and stared at the plate he
had laid on the cover in front of her. She recognised
pitta bread, the flat, mostly unleavened Greek bread
which could be toasted and split to hold food. The smell
of grilled lamb was delicious; she flapped back the split
pitta and saw salad with the pieces of lamb kebab it held,
rings of onion, chopped lettuce, tomato and cucumber.

'I shouldn't eat any more,' she told him, her mouth watering at the smell of the food, scented with thyme and rosemary and lemon.

'I've cooked it now; you might eat it,' Max said, sitting down on the end of the bed and taking a bite of his own pitta sandwich. 'Mmm . . . it's delicious!'

She ate some too. He was right, it was delicious.

'Did you grill it over charcoal?'

He nodded. 'Most of my cooking is done over charcoal, and I tossed the salad in lemon and a little natural yoghurt.' He grinned at her. 'I'm a good cook, if a little limited. I cook either fish or meat when I'm here—the lamb's my own. I run a few sheep here, and goats, keep some meat in deep freeze for when I'm here, but I mostly live on fish. I enjoy fishing off my yacht—the snapper is very good around here, so is the mullet, and I catch lobster, prawns, squid and sardines, clean them and gut them, sprinkle them with herbs and a little lemon juice, and chuck them on to the barbecue, serve them with some plain boiled rice or salad—a quick, simple meal and very healthy.'

Olivia had finished her sandwich. She thirstily drank some coffee; it was strong and very good. She was on edge, nerves prickling. How was she going to stop him getting into bed with her? He knew now that she wanted him, she hadn't been able to hide it. He wasn't going to be stopped by the fact that she had promised to marry another man, especially as the other man was his nephew. Christos might not be the man who had snatched Max's company away from him, but she had no doubt that in Max's eyes he shared his father's guilt.

Somehow she had to bring the temperature down, make this crackle of electricity between them die away.

Huskily, she asked, 'When you aren't here, who looks after your animals?'

Max answered casually enough, smiling at her. 'A fisherman and his wife come over several times a week, check that everything is OK. When I'm here, they sometimes stay to help out; it is a useful addition to his income, especially if the fish aren't running. A bad fishing trip can mean hard times for them. They're glad of a guaranteed second income. In weather like this they can't get over, of course. It takes them a couple of hours to sail here.'

'So it takes them all day to sail here and back again?'

'They usually stay overnight—there's a staff flat over the garage. Then they sail back next day, unless there are urgent jobs to be done, and then they stay longer.'

Max took her plate and cup, put them on to a table near the window, and came back, untying the belt of his white towelling robe.

Her heart racing, Olivia said hoarsely, 'Max, I'm not sleeping with you! I'm still engaged to Christos...'

'Tell me you love him,' Max said, letting his robe fall to the floor, and her golden eyes opened wide, pupils dilated with desire, riveted on him, her mouth going dry. He was so beautiful; she wanted him so fiercely.

She swallowed. She couldn't lie to him, with those jet eyes fixed on her, watching every expression passing through her face.

'I am engaged to him!' was all she could say.

'But you aren't in love with him and never have been.'

She bit her lip, colour coming and going.

Max pulled back the duvet and she shrank against the pillows. 'No, Max! Don't.'

'Why did you get engaged to him when you didn't love him?' he asked, his hand reaching for the belt of her own robe.

She grabbed his hand, pushing it away. 'I'm fond of Christos—it seemed a good idea.'

He laughed harshly. 'A good idea? You mean your father pushed you into it, and his father pushed him— they're using you, both of you, ruthlessly. Your marriage is the cement in the unholy alliance between my half-brother and your father. They don't trust each other, with good reason, so they've each offered up a child, as a hostage for good behaviour.' He looked into her eyes. 'That's the truth, isn't it, Olivia? And you know it.'

She sat there, her face white suddenly, stricken, nodding. She hadn't faced it before, but she knew, had always known, from the moment she met Christos and realised that her father wanted her to date him, that it had all been set up. She was being manipulated towards an arranged marriage.

'How could you let your father do that to you?' Max asked as though he despised her for it, and she couldn't answer; tears welled up into her eyes and trickled down her cheeks.

'Did you want his approval that badly?' Max asked, and she found her voice, even though it shook, answered that, wildly, tears running down her face now.

'Maybe I did... I suppose I did... I've always been scared of him, all my life, ever since I was little. He's always been there, like one of those Easter Island statues, on my horizon—never making sense, never human, staring over my head, stony, cold, faraway. He has never once shown me affection, do you know that? I suppose I wanted him to; I wanted him to be pleased with me, just for once. I wanted him to look at me and see me, really see me, smile at me. Don't we always want our parents' approval? Is that so odd? OK, I knew he and Constantine were pushing me and Christos at each other, and I'm sure Christos knew, although we never talked about it. One half of me knew it wasn't what I wanted, that I didn't love Christos and never could, but there was that other half which got in the way. I knew my father wanted me to marry Christos, and I wanted to please him, so I let it happen.' She was white, sobbing, she looked angrily at him. 'You have no right to despise me for it, anyway, it's none of your business!'

Max got into bed with her and pulled her, struggling, into his arms, gentling her as if she were a panic-stricken animal. 'Ssh . . . I'm sorry, don't cry like that, ssh . . .' He stroked her hair and Olivia lay against him, her crying slowly dying away until she was still, soothed into sleepy warmth.

'I'm so tired,' she whispered. 'I just want to go to sleep, Max.'

'Go to sleep, then,' he softly said, holding her, and she gave a long sigh, her body relaxing against him as sleep swallowed her up.

When she woke up again, the first thing she saw was light on the opposite wall—it was morning. The second thing to hit her was that she was now naked; at some time during the night Max had taken off her robe. She hadn't even been aware of it going, she had been sleeping too deeply.

Max lay behind her, breathing rhythmically in sleep, his warm, naked body touching hers from shoulder to knee. Olivia lay awake, listening to him, crazily happy to feel their close contact. They lay together like spoons in a drawer, fitting perfectly together, as if they belonged like that.

She wished she could see him, but dared not risk moving, for fear of waking him up. The physical effort of swimming against the currents to tow her in to shore must have been enormous; he must be as tired as she had been last night. Rested, she felt much better now, although her throat still ached; she was wryly afraid it would hurt for days. But at least she was alive, and so was Max. It could so easily have gone the other way; she could be washing around in the sea like her watch and her ring.

Involuntarily she was wrenched by a deep sigh, and Max shifted and yawned. Olivia froze. Was he waking up? She gave a gasp as his hands softly moved upward and touched her breasts.

'Good morning,' he whispered, his lips on her bare shoulder. 'You slept well—how do you feel?'

'Fine,' she muttered, pushing his exploring hands down, her breathing very audible. 'Don't, Max.'

A second later she was on her back and he was arching over her, looking down at her with smouldering, demanding eyes.

'I spent most of the night watching you and fighting with the urge to make love to you while you couldn't argue about it,' he bit out. 'But you were so tired I let you go on sleeping. We're both wide awake now though, and you aren't a schoolgirl any more, Olivia, you're an adult woman. It's time you started facing facts. We both know what we want and how we feel. You never loved Christos, your engagement doesn't mean a thing, does it?'

Her lips shakily parted; he put a fingertip on them, silencing her.

'Ssh...no more talking, Olivia. Let's just make love.'

CHAPTER SEVEN

OLIVIA felt hot tension coil inside her stomach; she wanted him, wanted him so much it hurt. But she turned her head away, talking fast, her voice shaking. 'No, I can't, Max, please understand—not while I'm engaged to Christos. I must tell him first, you've got to see that. OK, I'm not in love with him, any more than he's in love with me, but I am fond of him, and I did say I would marry him. Until I've broken off my engagement, I can't . . . just can't . . .'

'Don't be ridiculous!' he burst out, his voice thick with frustration. 'You admitted last night . . . your engagement doesn't mean anything.'

'It means I said I'd marry Christos, so I'm not free,' she muttered.

Max caught her head between his hands, forcing her to look at him, his black eyes fixed and fierce.

'You are going to break it off, though? You're going to tell Christos?'

His stare was hypnotic. 'As soon as I get him alone,' she whispered.

'Your father isn't going to like it,' he warned, and she almost laughed at the understatement.

'No, he isn't.' She didn't look forward to telling her father. She knew how he would look at her, how his cold eyes would make her feel.

Max watched her, his brows black and heavy. 'I'm afraid of his influence over you, Olivia. He isn't going

to accept it—and he and Constantine will try to make
you marry Christos.'

'They can't *make* me!' she said, whistling in the dark,
desperately hoping she was going to be strong enough
to stand against their anger.

Max's voice was harsh. 'Oh, I'm not talking about
actual bodily force. They won't make you go through a
marriage ceremony at gun-point, but there are other ways
of forcing someone to do what you want. You've admitted that you got engaged because your father wanted
you to.'

'Yes, but he didn't force me to get engaged! I just
knew he would be pleased if I agreed to marry Christos.'

Max's mouth twisted. 'Oh, come on, Olivia, we both
know your father scares you. You're so eager to placate
him you'll do whatever he wants.'

She flinched at the very idea of her father's fury when
he heard she wasn't going to marry Christos, but she
had made up her mind.

'Not this time,' she said, and Max watched her, his
face hard.

'All the same, I think it would be safer to present them
with a *fait accompli*. If you and I were lovers there'd be
no more talk of making you marry Christos. I know the
men of my family—he would never marry you once
you'd slept with me.' He smiled cynically. 'Oh, I'm not
saying he'd insist on you being a virgin, not these days,
but the idea of you sleeping with his own uncle... No,
he wouldn't stand for that.'

Olivia stiffened, ice trickling down her back. Was that
why he wanted to make love to her? To stop her marrying
his nephew? Did he really want her, or was she just a
weapon in his war against his brother and her father?
Was he using her to get revenge? After all, he hadn't

bothered to get in touch with her all these years—she might never have forgotten him after they met in Corfu, but Max had never tried to see her. No doubt he'd forgotten she existed—why kid herself? After all, why should he remember a schoolgirl he'd spent just one day with?

For her it had been different. That one brief meeting had made a deep, indelible impression on her. She had never forgotten him, even though she tried.

Had she betrayed herself, that day when he'd walked into her father's office in a black mood, the day they got control of his company? She had been so stunned to see him. Those vibrations of fierce attraction had begun again, and she hadn't been able to stop them. Had he picked them up? Had she somehow betrayed herself? Had he realised she was vulnerable to him?

Max read her changing expressions and frowned. 'What's wrong? What are you thinking? Say something, don't just look at me like that.'

He was doing it again, tuning into her mind, picking up what she was feeling and thinking, even when she tried to hide it from him.

Pain and then anger grew inside her. She put her hands flat on his shoulders and shoved, violently.

She caught him off guard. He sprawled backwards on the bed and Olivia quickly slid down from it to the floor, saw her white robe lying across a chair and grabbed it, hurriedly wrapping herself in it with trembling fingers as Max sat up and stared at her.

Once she was covered up again, she felt much safer. Of course, he was a powerful man, much bigger than she was, and much stronger, and they were quite alone here. If he chose to try force... But he wouldn't, she thought quickly. Not Max. She was certain of that, but still very edgy, because all her senses were so aware of him, naked on the bed, the golden skin gleaming in the morning sunlight. His body riveted her eyes—strong shoulders, a deep, powerful chest, his legs long and muscular.

She swallowed, desire hot inside her. She tied the belt of her robe tighter, one hand pulling the lapels of her robe across her breasts and throat.

'I'm not sleeping with you, Max!'

'We'll see about that,' he said in a soft voice that made her pulses beat fiercely.

'Are you threatening rape?' she angrily asked, and he frowned.

'That isn't funny, Olivia.'

'It wasn't meant to be. You'd have to use rape because I mean what I say. I will not sleep with you.'

'Listen——' he began, but she interrupted, a flush growing in her face.

'No, I won't listen! I'm sick of being pushed around, I'm sick of living my life to please other people. From now on, I'm going to please myself. I'm not giving in to anybody, not my father, not your brother, or Christos, or you!'

Max's eyes had narrowed, hard and watchful. For a moment he didn't move or answer her, then he said curtly, 'Keep thinking like that! Because you're going to be under a lot of pressure to go through with that marriage—have you got the backbone to stand up to your father and keep saying no, Olivia?'

'Yes,' she said, without a flicker of doubt this time. She couldn't say to him, I'm so angry with you that I'm no longer afraid of my father. I don't care what he thinks or how he talks to me. Her golden eyes said it though, glowing with the deep smouldering rage of the lioness.

'I wonder!' Max got off the bed and Olivia tensed, took several steps backwards.

'I meant what I said!' she warned again, and was given a long, dry, level look.

'I very much hope so.' He picked up his own robe, which lay on the floor, and slid into it, turning towards the fitted wardrobes which ran all along one wall of the room. 'Now what am I going to find you to wear? You can't put that chiffon dress back on, but none of my clothes is likely to fit you. I'm a head taller, for one thing, and built very differently.' He gave her a hard grin, then slid back one of the wardrobe doors, revealing neatly hung rows of clothes, most sheathed in covers. Max clicked through a line of jeans and cotton shorts, immaculately ironed shirts, then stopped and pulled down a large, baggy cotton sweater, which he threw to her. 'This is very long—could you wear it as a dress?'

She caught it and held it away from her to assess it. 'I think that would work. Thank you. I'd like to have a shower before I try it on though.' Her voice faltered. 'I...I suppose my...my other clothes are still wet?'

'Your bra and slip?' he said drily. 'No, they must be dry by now. While I was waiting for the coffee to percolate last night, I rinsed them out, to get the salt out of them, and hung them on the heated towel rail in the bathroom.'

Her face was startled. 'Thanks,' she said again. 'That was very thoughtful.' She wasn't used to being looked after by a man; most men she knew tried to get out of doing any household chores, and she would never have suspected Max of being the domesticated type. He was the most male man she had ever met, big and tough and with far too much machismo.

If she had thought about it though, she might have worked it out. After all, he lived here alone, sometimes for weeks on end, with only occasional help from the fisherman and his wife who looked after the property when Max wasn't here. She should have realised Max had to be very practical and quite self-sufficient, able to attempt any chore around the house, not needing other people's company, or he wouldn't choose an uninhabited island as his favourite retreat.

What did she really know about him though? She hardly knew him at all; yet she always felt she did. There had been an instant sense of familiarity, almost of recognition, the moment they'd met. Maybe she was kidding herself, maybe it was all illusion, but whenever they were together the same sensation returned: a sense of belonging, a warmth and security. She might not know everything about him—but a deep, inner conviction told her that the details of his character, his likes and dislikes, his hopes and fears, didn't matter as much as that instinctive, intuitive sense of belonging.

If she ever got the chance, she would be able to fit the pieces of the jigsaw which was Max Agathios together, finding out if they shared the same taste in films, music, books, places, food. If they didn't it wouldn't be important—they were two separate people; she didn't expect them to be mirror images of each other. All that truly mattered was the way he made her feel, and that was something she had known on sight the first time they met, even though she had been so young, even though she had never been in love before.

Because that was the truth, wasn't it? She was in love with Max, and she had been in love with him for five long years.

The sound of his voice, so familiar, so important to her, startled her out of her reverie. 'You can use the bathroom we used last night.'

She looked dazedly at him.

'Are you listening, Olivia?' he asked, coming closer, and her heart turned over inside her.

Somehow she nodded and said, 'Yes . . . of course . . .'

'Hmm . . .' he said on a doubtful note. 'Well, I'll have my shower in the bathroom across the landing, then we'll have breakfast. I'm expecting Spiro and his wife later today—the couple who look after the place while I'm away. They're coming over to get the house in shape before the auction. They were coming yesterday, but when the auction was postponed I sent them a message to come a day later.'

She remembered his brother's irritation on getting the news that the auction was postponed, and that in turn reminded her that she must let them know she was safe. Urgently she said, 'You won't forget to get in touch with the yacht after you've had your shower, will you?'

He looked at a clock on his bedside table. 'Ten past eight,' he said. 'I expect Constantine will be up by now; he always gets up early. He's such an obsessive character that he works long hours, even when he's supposed to be on holiday. The question is, when will they start wondering why you haven't appeared?'

'I don't know, not yet maybe, but I don't want them to think I've drowned—please get in touch at once.' Her golden eyes pleaded with him.

'After I've showered and dressed,' he said curtly. He collected clothes from the wardrobe and a chest of drawers, and went out without giving her another glance. He had not been pleased to be asked to contact his brother's yacht.

He would enjoy knowing that they all believed she was dead, thought Olivia with a pang of dismay. Max had called his half-brother obsessive—but what was he? They were driven, both of them, possessed by hatred of each other.

Sighing, she made her way to the bathroom they had used last night. It was spotless again—Max had tidied away the towels they had used, and the bath was gleaming. He was a very surprising man.

There was no lock on the door, so she moved a chair that was in the room into a position in front of the door, propped up below the handle. It wouldn't keep Max out if he was determined to get in, but it would at least delay him long enough to give her warning. She hung up the white robe, turned on the shower and stepped under it, hurriedly washing her hair and then herself. She wanted to get dressed as soon as possible. She would feel safer.

When she had towelled herself dry, she put on the bra, slip and panties she had found, as Max had promised, on the heated towel rail, and then lifted his white cotton sweater over her head.

The sleeves were too long; she had to roll them up or they would have hung down well below her hands. It could certainly pass for a dress, although it ended before knee level. It was baggy, but then that was quite fashionable, and the material was finely woven, soft thin cotton which clung where it touched, especially over her small, high breasts and the soft curve of her hips.

She eyed herself in the mirror doubtfully. Actually, it looked rather sexy, she realised, taken aback by her reflection. She hadn't expected that. She had thought she would simply look absurd, but the deep V of the neckline showed the plunge of pale, smooth breasts, and the hemline revealed far too much of her thighs. The effect of the dress was distinctly provocative, and Olivia wasn't happy about wearing it.

Max hadn't offered her any alternatives, though, and she certainly couldn't put her green chiffon evening dress on again, so it would have to do.

Sighing, she found a hairbrush among the toiletries on the bathroom shelves and slowly brushed her short blonde hair, wishing she had some make-up with her. Her face was pink and shiny from the shower. She looked schoolgirlish—until you noticed the way the sweater clung, she thought, mouth wry.

As she left the bathroom she walked straight into Max, who steadied her with both hands on her shoulders.

'Well, well,' he murmured, looking her over slowly. 'It suits you—you should always wear my clothes.'

Pink, she tried to change the subject. 'I'm starving—did you say something about breakfast?'

He laughed, his dark eyes glinting with mockery at her confusion. 'Yes, you can help me make it.'

She hadn't noticed much about the ground floor of the house last night, but now she looked around with curiosity at the hall they entered at the bottom of the stairs. She remembered the white walls, the marble floor which was streaked with green, but the pictures hadn't impinged on her last night. She took them in now: big seascapes and landscapes, blue and white and green, full of light and space. They covered the walls to the back of the house. On each side she saw doors leading into other rooms, caught glimpses of shining floors, light golden oak furniture, pale walls.

'When will you radio the yacht?' she asked, and got a sideways glance from Max.

'As soon as we've had breakfast.'

He pushed open a door and they walked into the kitchen, which was large and full of sunshine—the storm had blown itself out now, she saw, looking out of the window into a garden full of trees and shrubs. The grass was littered though, with leaves and branches, with torn flowers and a few tiles which must have been blown off the roof of the house.

'It was a really bad storm, wasn't it?' she murmured and Max nodded.

'I wouldn't have liked to be out at sea last night. I hope Constantine's captain rode out the storm in the bay. We'll be able to see the yacht from the headland— we'll drive up there later. There's a rough track. The four-wheel-drive takes it easily enough.'

He put on the coffee, asking her, 'What do you want for breakfast? How about scrambled eggs?' and when she nodded added, 'Will you scramble them while I lay the table?'

While she melted a small piece of butter on the hob, beat eggs and poured them into the pan, Max squeezed oranges, cut some slices from a loaf of domed Greek bread and laid the kitchen table. Just before the eggs were ready he produced a bowl of field mushrooms, cleaned and ready to cook, put a pan on the hob next to the one she was using and began to fry the mushrooms rapidly with some sliced tomato.

They ate breakfast side by side in front of the garden window. The coffee was as strong as it had been last night, and just as delicious, especially after the fresh, tangy orange juice and the food.

Max leaned back in his chair, eyes half closed, his expression contented.

'That was the best breakfast I've eaten for years.'

'Yes,' Olivia agreed, feeling far more alive now. 'Is your food brought over by your fisherman?'

'Some of it. Some I bring over in my boat, and the mushrooms I picked myself.'

She gave him a startled look, rather worried by that. 'You did? Picked them here?'

'Yes, some of them among the pines up there behind the house. A lot of mushrooms like the sandy soil in pine woods, did you know that? It's a good place to look for mushrooms—and they like birch trees too.'

'Are you an expert?' she nervously asked. 'I mean . . . you are sure those mushrooms were edible?'

He grinned at her. 'Don't worry. Of course, you have to be sure you know which are safe to eat and which aren't; it's easy to make a mistake and pick a poisonous mushroom which looks like an edible one. I have an illustrated book which shows the differences very clearly. I check any I'm not certain about.'

'I hope you were certain about all those we ate!' she said, laughing a little uneasily.

Max turned his dark head to smile at her lazily. 'Tell me if you start to feel ill, if you begin to throw up and everything goes black before your eyes!'

'Is that a symptom of mushroom poisoning?' she asked, worried.

'Well, it's certainly a symptom of something!' teased Max.

She made a face at him. 'Very funny. Will you get in touch with the yacht now? Christos may be banging on my cabin door at this very moment.'

He shrugged, untroubled by that. 'Knowing my nephew, I'd doubt that; he is not an early riser. I think they'll wait until nine to start banging on your door. So let's clear the table first, and load the dishwasher.' He got up and began collecting up the plates. 'I have every possible labour-saving device here—and the best available electric generator to keep them all working! I try to be self-sufficient.'

'So that you don't need anybody,' Olivia said quietly, getting up too, and he gave her a quick, penetrating glance.

'I told you, I do have people to come in and clean the house thoroughly every few days, and look after the livestock, especially if I'm not here.'

'But you don't need people,' said Olivia. 'You're self-sufficient; you prefer your own company. That's why you have a yacht you can sail single-handed, and a holiday home on an uninhabited island. You like being alone—you don't really like people enough to want them around much.'

He considered her, his black eyes hard and narrowed, his face unyielding. 'Amateur psychology, Olivia?'

She was putting the cups and plates into the dishwasher; straightening, she gave him a cool shrug.

'Just guesswork.'

'Hit-and-miss guesswork, Olivia,' he said drily. 'Oh, it's true, I like being alone—but it doesn't really follow that I don't like other people. I like some, I don't like others. I have plenty of friends, not to mention colleagues I like and trust. But if you're really talking about my half-brother, then no, I don't like or trust him, with good reason, as you know perfectly well. He has always hated me, from the day I was born. He resented my very existence. He wanted to be my father's only son. Of course, he hated my mother too, and made her life a misery. When he heard my father's will read out and discovered that I'd been left this island and some ships, he was so angry I thought he was going to kill me there and then. He coveted everything my father left me, and he was determined to get it all away from me. I knew that. I was always on my guard, but in business you have to take risks if you want to get anywhere. I had to borrow large sums of money to build up my company—how could I have guessed Leon would die so suddenly, and leave me wide open to attack? I had a run of bad luck—first a rise in interest rates, and a fall in business, then one of my ships sank, but none of that would have mattered if it hadn't been for Leon's death. That was my real blow.'

She watched his dark eyes, seeing the pain in them. 'You were really fond of him,' she realised, and Max gave her a bleak look.

'He was a close friend, a second father, he believed in me and I trusted him absolutely. You don't often meet someone like Leon. I'll never meet his like again, I'm sure of that. Losing my company isn't as heavy a blow as losing Leon.'

She bit her lip. 'How will you feel if Constantine buys the island at the auction?'

Max gave a mimicry of a smile, his teeth bared in a movement more like a snarl.

'How do you think I'll feel?'

Her nerves leapt. 'You won't like it,' she whispered, and he laughed then, angrily.

'You're so English, Olivia. Strong emotions terrify you, don't they? What you want is nice, bland, safe feelings; you're like a ship that never leaves harbour in case it meets strong winds or hits a rock. Doesn't it ever occur to you that, comfortable though your secure little harbour may seem, you're never going to experience any of the elation or excitement that comes with taking risks?'

'No, but I'm not going to drown either,' she said huskily.

'You're a coward,' he muttered, mouth crooked.

Olivia lifted her chin, defiance in her golden eyes. 'Not any more. I told you, I'm going to face up to my father.'

'And life? Will you face up to that? I wonder.' His mouth was crooked with angry mockery. 'I can't see you leaving your safe harbour and risking yourself on the high sea, can you?'

She thought of the great, greeny-black waves that she had had to fight her way through last night, the agony of trying to swim against overwhelming forces, the moment when she realised she was going to drown. Her face turned white.

Max was watching her intently, his eyes hypnotic, terrifying. She felt the force of his will, felt her body weaken, trembling, felt her senses drown in passion.

He took a step nearer and her pulses leapt. 'Don't touch me!' she cried out.

'Why not? It's what you want, what we both want,' he said huskily, and his hand reached for her, closing round her nape, his fingers strong and warm. 'The minute I first saw you, I knew I wanted you,' he said, and she wished she could deny that it had happened to her as instantly, but she knew he could feel the fierce racing of her pulse under his fingertips.

It made her angry to know she couldn't hide her reactions; she looked up at him, her golden eyes bitter.

'It couldn't have meant much—I never heard from you again, after that day! You forgot I existed.'

His eyes flashed, violence flaring in his face. 'That isn't true! I've never forgotten you—but I couldn't get in touch with you. I'd given your father my word.'

She froze, incredulity in her face. 'My father? What do you mean?'

'That night in Corfu, when we got back from sailing to Paki, he said you were much too young to know what you were doing. He didn't want you getting romantically involved with anyone yet, he didn't want you distracted from your studies, he wanted you to go on to university and get a degree. What he was afraid of was that you would throw up everything else to get married, and waste your brains. He told me he wouldn't give his permission for me to see you, and neither would your mother. She was even more determined to see you go to university, he told me. She believed in careers for women; she was against early marriages.'

'That's true, she is,' admitted Olivia. 'More than my father, in fact; I thought he just went along with the idea of further education for me because my mother insisted on it.'

'Well, he convinced me. I didn't want to be responsible for you giving up your chance at university; education is far too important. He made out a good case— said that we had only just met, one day wasn't enough for either of us to be sure it was going to mean anything, and it wouldn't be fair of me to try to grab you before you had had a chance to grow up, look around, find out about yourself.'

She looked at him tensely—what was he saying? That he had been as attracted to her as she had been to him?

'He asked me to give him my word I wouldn't try and see you again,' Max said flatly. 'At least, not until you left university.'

Olivia was stunned. 'He never told me!' Her face tightened with anger as she realised just what her father had done.

Max grimaced. 'He's quite a psychologist, your father. He knew me well enough to realise I'd listen to his plea to leave you alone until you were at least twenty-one. He pointed out that I was a lot older, and I'd met a lot of other women. He wanted you to be free to experiment, find out about yourself, meet other men. He asked me to wait. He said that as we often see each other at board meetings, he'd keep me in touch with what you were doing. I always asked after you—he told me you were working hard, and although he thought you often had dates, there was nobody special in your life.'

Flushed, she murmured, 'He was telling the truth—there wasn't.'

Max looked at her, his eyes hard, glittering. 'Not even Christos? He told me months ago that you were going to marry Christos.'

She looked at him sharply. 'Months ago?'

'Some time in May. I saw him at a board meeting and asked if you were going to spend your summer with him as usual, and that was when he told me you were going to marry Christos.'

Slowly, Olivia said, 'I only met Christos for the first time this summer, in Monaco. We didn't get engaged until just before the end of the holiday.'

They stared at each other. Max said something in Greek under his breath; she didn't understand the words but it sounded like swearing.

'He lied,' she said, almost incredulously because it was so outrageous a lie, so unbelievable.

'Yes,' Max said through his teeth. 'He was determined to keep us apart.'

'He knew I hadn't forgotten you,' she recognised, looking back over the last five years, and her eyes darkened. 'How could he do it?' Then, bewildered, 'Why did he do it? Deliberately, for his own ends, lying to stop you seeing me again, plotting to get me to marry Christos, when he knew I...' She broke off and Max looked down at her quickly.

'When he knew what, Olivia?' he whispered, and her colour deepened to wild rose. Max moved closer, brushed her hot cheeks with his fingertips as if to check that the colour was real.

'I wasn't deluding myself five years ago, was I? You felt it too, and I think your father picked it up at once.'

'How could he?' she broke out, her voice shaking with anger. 'How could he do that to me?'

'He hates me,' Max drily said. 'I'm not sure why. I've never done him an injury. I can't think of a single reason why he should dislike me so much that he'd lie and cheat to keep me away from his daughter.'

Uncertainly, Olivia said, 'He said you had a reputation, there had been a lot of women in your life, you were a playboy.'

Max laughed angrily. 'A playboy? He has an old-fashioned vocabulary, your father. That makes me sound like something in a 1950s B movie! I worked too damn hard for that—but I can't deny I like women. I'd dated quite a few over the years, but somehow it always fizzled out, it never turned serious. None of them was what I knew I wanted.'

Her whole body trembled with hope, with passion, with tenderness, then she remembered something else and her face tightened again.

'He also told me you were going to marry Leon Kera's daughter.'

Max shot her a frowning glance and grimaced. 'Yes...that wasn't actually a lie. We weren't formally engaged, but we had been seeing each other that year, quite a lot, and I was beginning to think Daphne might be the one...' He broke off, shrugging, and Olivia felt a sting of jealousy—had he and Daphne Kera been lovers? Was that why Daphne had been so bitter that she had sold her shares to Constantine?

'When I got back from Corfu I stopped seeing her,' Max said. 'I had to tell her why, of course.'

Olivia waited, breathless.

Max's face was grim. 'Daphne was bitter about it. I can't blame her. She knew as well as I did that I had been thinking of marrying her, even if nothing had been said. Her father wanted it, and I was very fond of Leon. If I hadn't met you, I would probably have married her, and we would both have been unhappy once it dawned on us that we'd made a mistake. I was very glad when Daphne met her big Australian because I could see she was going to be happy with him.'

'But she went ahead and sold her shares to your brother,' Olivia said quietly. 'If she's happy, why would she want to ruin your life?'

Max was silent for a minute, his dark face shuttered. In a bleak, flat voice, he said, 'I hurt her. I knew I had, I wished I hadn't, but I had to, once I'd met you. I couldn't marry Daphne then. But she took after her father in many ways—she had tunnel vision, she always went after what she wanted with unshakeable tenacity and she never forgot an injury. The fact that she was happily married to someone else didn't stop her being determined to have her revenge on me for the hurt I'd inflicted five years ago.'

Olivia couldn't help feeling sorry for Daphne, in spite of what she had done. Her bitterness was such a clear indication of how much Max had hurt her. Yet how could she go so far in her desire to hurt him back? She had wrecked his life.

'I wonder how she feels now,' she thought aloud. 'When she thinks about what she's done to you.'

Max laughed shortly. 'Pleased with herself, no doubt, for having got her own back. Daphne is a tough woman.' He gave Olivia a look which held laughter, tenderness. 'Unlike you.'

'I don't want to be that tough,' she retorted. 'I'd hate myself.'

'I wouldn't like you much either,' Max said, eyes amused, then he sobered. 'What I really can't fathom is why your father has always disliked me so much that he was determined to stop me seeing you.'

She sighed. 'I think he always wanted to be a big tycoon, get seriously rich, but he never quite made it, because he's far too cautious. He's like me, he doesn't take risks, and it seems to me that unless you take risks you don't make spectacular gains. He inherited a solid company, and he has run it well, but he has never really achieved all he dreamed of in the beginning. You've already made more of a name for yourself than he ever has—and my father can't forgive you for being what he wanted to be.'

Max's brows had risen as she talked soberly. 'You see him pretty clearly, don't you? I wonder if that's it. Maybe. I know he's full of seething envy and ambition. It doesn't seem much of a reason for trying to force his own daughter into marrying someone she doesn't love, does it?'

'I don't think he cares a damn what happens to me. I doubt if it ever occurred to him to think about my feelings. All he wanted was a chance to hurt you, in any way he could. That I might get hurt in the process was never important.'

Max put his arms round her and pulled her close, her face buried in his shirt. He stroked her hair and murmured huskily into her ear, 'He won't hurt you any more, I promise you that. He'll have me to deal with in future.'

She leaned on him, her eyes closed, feeling his warmth percolating through her, secure in his strength.

Somewhere in the house a clock chimed and her eyes flew open. 'It's nine o'clock! We were going to radio the yacht at nine...'

Max let go of her, his face wry. 'Yes, I suppose we have to let them know you're safe, although it would serve them right if we didn't bother.'

'I may be angry with my father, but he is still my father. I wouldn't want him to think I was dead,' she said gently. 'And then there's Christos... We aren't in love, but I'm fond of him. I'm sure he's fond of me, he'd be upset if he thought I'd drowned, and...'

'All right, all right,' Max said, winding his arm around her waist. 'You've made your point. We'll do it now.'

They walked back through the house and into a sunlit room furnished as an office with a leather-topped desk taking up the centre of the floor, one wall lined with locked filing cabinets and bookcases, against the opposite wall a fax machine and a photocopier, against another a desk occupied by expensive radio equipment.

Max sat down in front of the radio and began flicking switches while Olivia watched, fascinated. 'I'm putting out my call sign,' he said, and then stopped as an urgent voice came out of the speaker, talking in Greek.

Olivia didn't understand what was being said, and watched Max's face intently, anxiously, as he answered.

His expression had changed; he was frowning, she was sure his skin had paled, and his voice sounded harsh, disturbed. He spoke quickly, tersely, in muttered Greek.

After a very brief exchange, he switched off and sat there for a minute staring at nothing, his head bent.

'What is it?' Olivia burst out, tense with anxiety.

He looked around at her, his black eyes all pupil. For a minute she almost thought he wasn't seeing her, then his eyes focused and he gave a deep sigh.

'I'm sorry, I'm afraid I have bad news for you. There's no easy way of telling you this—the yacht has been trying to get in touch with me for some time, it seems. At eight o'clock this morning your father knocked on your door, and when he didn't get a reply he went in and discovered you weren't there and your bed hadn't been slept in. He raised the alarm, the yacht was searched, but of course there was no sign of you. Then they realised that you must have gone overboard during the storm. When the captain told your father, he had a heart attack.'

CHAPTER EIGHT

OLIVIA was still in shock when Max drove her down to the little stone-walled jetty where the yacht would tie up when it arrived. By then they could already see the yacht sailing towards them at full speed, the white prow cutting through the waves and sending a line of white foam curling back along the hull. The sea had calmed since last night; in fact it was like a millpond, vivid blue with the sunlight dancing over it and making a mosaic of little glittering facets; and the sky was so bright that the light blinded Olivia. She had to shield her eyes as she watched the yacht's approach.

'Where is that helicopter?' she fretted, looking up at the empty skies. 'Didn't you say it would arrive before the yacht got here? Why isn't it here yet? The sooner he gets to hospital, the better chance he's got. If there's any delay...' Her voice quivered and she broke off, then after a minute said, 'He never mentioned having a heart condition—I'm sure he's never had a heart attack before. I thought he was so healthy, and he isn't even sixty yet—that isn't very old.'

Max put an arm round her shoulders, his hand gripping her upper arm. 'Stop it! Don't work yourself up into another crying jag. You mustn't start worrying.'

'How can I help it? It's all my fault...'

'Olivia, for heaven's sake!'

'It is! If——'

'Don't start another of those sentences that begin with "if"! You didn't deliberately throw yourself overboard,

152

did you? You fell off the boat by accident—how can it be your fault your father had a heart attack when he heard you were missing?'

She obstinately finished the sentence he had interrupted. 'If we'd got in touch with the yacht earlier he wouldn't have thought I had drowned and he wouldn't have had a heart attack!'

'That was my decision,' he said curtly. 'If you want to blame somebody, blame me.'

There was a silence. She did, and they both knew it. Her golden eyes darkened with accusation and grief as she looked up into his watchful face.

Her voice was husky, low, angry. 'We should have let them know I was safe.'

His face tightened as if she had hit him. 'OK, I should have got in touch earlier than I did, but I had no idea he had a heart, let alone a heart condition!'

Her skin lost every touch of colour, so white that her lips looked almost red although she was wearing no make-up. 'How can you say such a cruel thing when he could be dy——?'

'He isn't going to die!' Max exploded and she felt the tension in his body, in the arm which held her close to him, in the hand biting into her upper arm. 'How many times do I have to tell you—I didn't get the impression this was a very serious heart attack.'

She wanted to believe him, but she was afraid to be too optimistic. 'You can't be certain about that!' she muttered, trying to pull out of his grip.

Max refused to let her go; his arm tightened even more, holding her closer, but when he answered his voice was gentle.

'Olivia, if I'd had any idea that this might happen I'd have got on to the yacht last night. I deliberately delayed getting in touch because I thought it would do your father good to have a shock. I thought…well, I suppose I hoped that if he believed you were dead he might realise how little he'd ever valued you. It might start him thinking about you, make him see how he'd been treating you, using you, pushing you into a marriage which was just one of convenience—his convenience, not yours!'

The yacht was very close now; they heard voices on deck, saw faces staring down at them, but Olivia was so stunned by what Max had just said that she didn't try to distinguish one face from another. She looked away, and angrily asked Max, 'Why didn't you tell me why you weren't in a hurry to get on the radio?'

'What would you have said if I had?' he asked in a dry tone, his mouth twisting.

'I'd have insisted you talk to them at once!'

Max laughed shortly. 'That's what I thought. I guessed you would be horrified by the idea of scaring him into taking a long, hard look at himself and his relationship with you, so I didn't bother to say anything to you.'

'You had no right to play God at my expense!'

'Maybe not, but I was only thinking of you. I had the best intentions.'

She gave him a bitter look. 'Are you sure you were thinking of me? Are you sure you weren't just getting your revenge because my father had helped your brother snatch your company away? Maybe you see his heart attack as karmic justice!'

His eyes flashed, his skin darkened with fierce blood. 'Is that what you think?' he harshly asked, letting go of her, his hand dropping to his side. His stare was hostile, piercing. 'Thanks very much.'

He strode angrily away from her to the end of the jetty as the yacht slowly backed into place, the engines almost at a standstill now, making very little sound, and at that instant the sky filled with the noise of a helicopter arriving.

Olivia fought with her tears, her throat salty with them, relieved to be able to concentrate on the helicopter, following its progress towards the helicopter pad near the house, on the high ground overlooking this bay. The olive and cypress trees stirred, whipped to and fro, bending almost to earth, the silvery-green leaves of the olive and the dark flames of the cypress agitated into a frenzy in the wind of the propellers as the machine settled down between them.

Even Olivia's blonde hair was wind-blown, tumbled about her pale face in light, ruffled waves.

Max swung round and walked rapidly back, his face rigid, jet eyes as sharp as knives.

He hates me! she thought, her stomach sinking as if she were in a lift which suddenly dropped like a stone. But her own anger was still fierce enough for her to stare back at him unsmilingly. If he had got on the radio last night, her father would never have had this heart attack.

Through clenched teeth Max bit out, 'I'll drive back up there at once, to pick up the doctor. You wait here—when they come ashore, tell them I won't be long, and they had better wait until the doctor gets here before moving your father.'

She nodded without speaking, unable to risk opening her mouth for fear she might break down altogether.

Max gave her another hard, angry look, and stalked away. She heard him start the vehicle, heard it roar away, but kept her eyes fixed on the yacht manoeuvring closer to the stone wall of the jetty. There was barely room for the large vessel to tie up—the jetty was very small and narrow, meant to take only small boats, like Max's own yacht, for which a special boathouse had been built nearby. From where Olivia stood she could see the white blur of the boat in the shadowy interior. No doubt Max had sailed here from Piraeus, like themselves.

Someone stared down at her from the deck of the *Agathios Athena*. She looked back, pale and tense, at Christos. She had never seen him look so serious; his tanned face was tight with control, his dark eyes searching her own face, as if looking for evidence of what had happened to her since they last saw each other.

The gangway was let down, locked into position and Christos walked to the head of it, but before he could descend his father had pushed past him and begun coming down towards her.

She felt her nerves leap as Constantine's bull head lowered, as if he were about to charge, his sullen eyes surveying her suspiciously, morosely, accusingly.

'How's my father?' she broke out huskily.

'Very ill,' he grated. 'Did you spend the night here?'

Her face burned. 'Didn't Max tell you? Yes, he rescued me, I was drowning and he swam out to save my life——'

'Who else is in the house?' demanded Constantine. 'Are those people who work for him here?'

She shook her head, aware of Christos coming up behind his father, watching her over his broad shoulder, his face shuttered and unreadable.

'You were alone here with him all night?' Constantine asked through lips that were tight with rage.

'I want to see my father,' she said. 'I'm going on board——'

'Not until you've answered me,' Constantine ground out, the whites of his eyes yellow with rage, little flecks of red around the pupil. 'Where did you sleep? Where did he sleep?'

She was trembling violently. 'Can I see my father, please?' she said again.

Christos said flatly, 'Let her go and see her father, Dad, stop hassling her—can't you see she's too upset to talk?'

Constantine turned to glare at him. 'I want the truth out of her, but she won't tell me anything. What do you think that means? It's obvious, isn't it? He's had her, and she doesn't want to admit it—she knows what will happen if she does. You aren't going to marry her after she's slept with him, are you?'

Olivia almost threw up, sickened and humiliated by his crudeness.

Christos looked uneasily at her white face and darkened eyes. 'I'm sorry, Olivia, but can't you set his mind at rest? Tell him nothing happened, and he'll leave you alone!'

She heard an intake of breath nearby, looked up and was appalled to see a row of faces on the deck of the yacht. The crew were all leaning on the rail, watching them and listening avidly.

In a low, shaking mutter, she said, 'I'll discuss it when we haven't got an audience!'

Both men looked round and up, frowning. Constantine's dark red colour deepened even more; he glared and bellowed, 'Get back to your work, all of you!' and his crew vanished hurriedly.

Olivia said quietly, 'On second thoughts, ask Max your questions, not me!'

Constantine glowered at her. 'Oh, I will, don't worry! If I get the chance! I notice he vanished as soon as I arrived!'

'He went to pick up the doctor from the helicopter,' she retorted. 'He'll be back. Oh, and he said you weren't to move my father until he got back.' Olivia paused, swallowed, and asked tersely, 'Now can I go and see my father? Was it a very bad heart attack?'

'It isn't so serious as we thought it might be at first,' Christos said in a gentler tone. 'We talked on the radio with the doctor who has flown out here—he's a heart specialist from the nearest mainland hospital, and he gave us advice on how to treat him. He's conscious and stable, but we must get him to a hospital as soon as possible.' He paused, frowned, and said slowly, 'You know, maybe you shouldn't see him, Olivia, not yet, not until the doctor is here. The shock of seeing you might bring on another attack.'

'Haven't you told him yet that I'm alive?' she broke out, appalled.

'Yes, of course, as soon as we heard it ourselves, but if you talk to him he might start asking questions, and the next you know he'll be working himself up into a state, the way my father just did.'

'He knows Max, he knows how far he'd go to hit back at us,' Constantine said heavily.

'Yes,' Christos said in grim tones, and they both stared at Olivia, who gave them a stricken look. She thought how close she had come to letting Max have sex with her last night, and felt a wave of nausea rise up inside her. What if Christos and his father were right? What if Max had taken an opportunistic chance of revenge on them? After all, she and Max had only met twice before—five years ago they had spent one whole day together, but then they hadn't met again until a few weeks ago, when he had come to her father's office and confronted her angrily.

What did she know about him? How had he got so close to her so quickly that she had been on the edge of giving in to him last night?

From the rough track leading up to Max's house came the sound of the four-wheel-drive vehicle bouncing over the ruts and stones towards them.

Olivia sighed with a strange sort of pain, and with relief. Max was coming; just knowing that she would see him again in a minute hurt and was a wild, sweet pleasure all at the same time. Her emotions were so confused, entangled, where he was concerned.

Thank God, though, he had the doctor with him. She could see other people in the vehicle—her father would get medical attention at last, and must soon be on his way to a hospital, for which she was deeply relieved and grateful.

Constantine glowered along the track, scowling. 'I'll get some answers now, if I have to smash the truth out of him! I intend to know exactly what happened here last night.'

'I almost died, that was what happened!' Olivia muttered angrily. 'And he saved my life. Not many people would have tried, in that sea—the waves were huge... I thought I had no chance... I was drowning, going down for the last time, but he swam out there and towed me in. I'd swallowed so much sea-water he had to pump it out of me.'

'God, you must have been scared stiff,' said Christos, looking and sounding as if he really cared. She had shaken him; his skin was almost as pale as hers. 'I don't know if I'd have had the nerve to swim out there in that storm. Oh, come on, Dad, whatever happened after that, it was very brave of him—and at least Olivia is alive! I don't know about you but I'm very grateful for that.'

Constantine gave him a contemptuous look, but didn't answer. Olivia couldn't stop a choked little giggle, which made him glare at her.

'Your father would rather I were dead!' she muttered, and Christos looked shocked.

'Of course he wouldn't, Olivia! He's just upset.'

A moment later, Max's vehicle screeched to a stop and a short, thin man wearing a white coat over a suit, followed by a nurse in a blue uniform, climbed out. 'Where's the patient?' the man demanded in a thick-accented English.

'Are you Dr Kariavis? The patient's still on the yacht—we were told not to move him until you came!' Constantine snapped, his heavy-lidded eyes glancing at his half-brother and away again as if he couldn't even bear to see Max.

'Well, I'm here, so let's get on board. There's no time to waste—the sooner I see him, the better,' the doctor said.

He walked towards the gangway, a large black case in one hand, and Constantine followed, talking to him in a rough, impatient mutter in Greek.

Olivia began to follow, but Christos caught her arm. 'Better wait until the doctor has seen your father, he'll advise us whether or not he's well enough to talk to you.'

Max watched them both, his body as taut as a bowstring, his face tense and grim.

Crew members came off the yacht and helped get a stretcher out of the back of Max's Land Rover. They carried the stretcher up the gangway, the nurse bringing up the rear with some other equipment which the medical team had obviously also brought with them in the helicopter. Max helped her carry the heavier items.

Christos touched her arm and she glanced up at him. 'Now that my father's not here, tell me what really happened?' he coaxed. 'Olivia, we're engaged. Don't you think I have the right to know what went on last night? I know Max has been interested in you for years——'

'What? What do you mean?' she asked sharply, eyes widening.

Christos looked sheepish, hesitated, muttered, 'Dad told me ages ago, before I even met you.'

'Told you what?' she repeated.

He shrugged. 'Oh…that Max had met you and fancied you, but that your father had warned him off because you were still at school.'

'My father told him.'

Christos nodded.

Rage mounted to her head. Her father had talked to Constantine, but he hadn't told her, had deliberately kept Max's interest in her a secret, as if she had no right to know something that important! Her father had treated her like a child! Then she thought, Well, at least he had some excuse—I was his child, he had known me all my life and was used to making decisions for me without consulting me. What about the way Max had behaved last night? He treated me like a child too; and he had no such excuse. I'm not his child, I'm a grown woman, yet he decided not to let my father know I was safe and deliberately didn't tell me what he was doing, or why. It's unforgivable.

How dare they treat me like this, both of them? She wanted to hit them, scream and yell at them, let her anger out.

But she didn't; she fought with it, refusing to let her mind cloud with all that red smoke of rage. She needed to be clear-headed, needed to think.

'How long ago did your father start plotting with mine?' she asked Christos, who looked wary.

'My father's never liked Max, you know that,' he hedged.

She looked into his eyes. 'They ordered you to propose to me, didn't they?'

Christos took on a faintly shifty look, and went red. 'They didn't order... Well, Dad did say something about it being a good idea, but... well, I knew I'd get married some time, have a family. I wanted children. And I had no one else in mind. I'm very fond of you... We get on, don't we? We had a lot of fun in Monaco. I wouldn't have proposed if I didn't like you.'

'Did they bribe or threaten?'

'Neither!'

'You know we aren't in love, Christos,' she said. 'You proposed because they told you to!'

He took on a sulky look; he began moving his foot, drawing circles on the sand which last night's storm had blown all over the jetty, staring down at what he was doing as though absorbed in nothing else.

'What's he been saying?' he muttered. 'You're different. I'm beginning to wonder if Dad's so far wrong. Something did happen last night, didn't it? He's been talking to you, putting ideas into your head.' He looked up, his lower lip sullen, his eyes accusing. 'For heaven's sake, Olivia, can't you see that he's using you to get his own back on us? He may fancy you, but he wants revenge too, and this way he could kill two birds with one stone—sleep with you and at the same time hit back at us for pushing him out of his company! He's a snaky bastard, you can't trust him an inch.'

She couldn't help laughing at that, but her eyes were angry. 'I certainly can't trust you, can I? Or your father? Or mine, come to that. You all plotted against me. You were only marrying me because it was a good business arrangement—it was my father's company you were marrying, not me, only you didn't bother to explain that. I was being sold a romantic deal, not a business contract, which was what it really was! It was all phoney, and you were in on the plan. I wasn't, was I? I was the only one who didn't know what was really going on!'

Christos burst out, 'That isn't fair, Olivia! I never plotted against you. I really thought we'd be happy together, I was serious about our marriage. OK, it wasn't exactly a love match...'

She laughed again, even angrier.

He gave her a furious look, even his ears red. 'Arranged marriages often work out better in the long run...'

'Who says so? Your father?'

'Yes, OK, he does, but I think he's right about that. You fall out of love. I know that. I've been in love several times—it never lasts, and then you get nasty squabbles and bad feelings left over. It was different with you and me. I thought we were friends. I was sure it would work between us.'

'Without love?' She shook her head, her eyes sombre. 'You know that isn't true. Liking isn't enough, Christos. I'm sorry, I do like you, and I thought we were friends too, but I got stampeded into our engagement, and I realised almost at once that I couldn't go through with it. Max didn't need to tell me anything I hadn't worked out for myself. I'm afraid I lost my ring last night in the storm. I can't give it back to you. It is insured, though, isn't it?'

'Yes,' he said curtly. 'I'll deal with the claim.' Then, 'He won't marry you, you know,' he muttered. 'Not after what your father did to him. He hates your family too much to marry into it.'

She was wrung by a spasm of fierce agony. He was right, of course. Max would not want to marry the daughter of a man who had tried to destroy him. There was no future for them.

She heard movements and looked round quickly. The crew were slowly, carefully, making their way down to the jetty again, carrying the stretcher, with her father strapped on to it.

Max was hurrying ahead. He passed her and Christos without so much as looking at either of them, and opened the back of his vehicle so that the stretcher could be slid inside without difficulty. The back seats had already been let down flat, leaving plenty of room.

Olivia met the crew as they reached the jetty. Her father's grey face was covered with an oxygen mask, but he was conscious; he looked at her, his hand stirring weakly on the blanket covering him.

She bent to kiss him on the cheek.

'You're going to be OK, Dad.'

Tears showed in his eyes and she saw his throat move, as if he was trying to speak to her. She read the wordless question in his face.

'I'm fine, I'm sorry you were worried. Don't try to talk, Dad, save your strength,' she said, horrified by the way he looked. He had aged ten years at least; all the life had been bled out of him overnight. Suddenly he looked old.

She held his hand tightly.

'Can I go with him in the helicopter?' she asked the doctor as he briskly came towards them, his white coat flapping in the wind blowing off the blue sea.

'I'm sorry, there won't be room.'

She turned pleading eyes to Max. 'Couldn't I squeeze in somewhere? I'm not very big.'

'It will be crowded as it is. The stretcher will take up a lot of room,' Max curtly said.

'We'll take you on the yacht,' Christos promised. 'But we can't leave until after the auction.'

Max's black brows jerked together. 'No need,' he said through his teeth. 'My helicopter will be back as soon as they've delivered him to the hospital.'

She looked down at her father. 'I'll follow as soon as I can,' she promised, kissed him again and stood back so that they could slide the stretcher into the back of Max's vehicle.

Max climbed behind the wheel and set off at a slow, steady pace. Olivia saw Constantine coming down the gangplank and looked up at Christos.

'I don't want to talk to your father, he'll only try to bully or browbeat me. I'll leave it to you to tell him that the engagement is over. I'm going to walk up to the house and wait for the helicopter to come back for me.'

She set off without waiting for Christos to reply. There was nothing else to be said now—she hoped she would never see either of them again.

Constantine called after her angrily, but she didn't look back. She kept going up the steep track, aware that Christos was talking to his father, and then that they were both following her, their feet scuffing in the dust, grating on the rocks underneath.

It was not an easy climb; she was soon out of breath and behind her she heard Constantine panting in thick gulps.

'Dad, do you want to have a heart attack too?' she heard Christos say anxiously. 'Take it easy! Why don't you sit down on that boulder...take a rest for a while...? Look, here comes Max again...he can give you a lift up to the house.'

Max's Land Rover drew up beside Olivia. He leaned over to open the door on the passenger side, looked at her grimly.

'Why didn't you wait on the jetty?'

'You'd better pick up Constantine, he'll never make it to the top by himself.'

'Get in,' he said through tight lips. 'I didn't invite him to my house—he can go back to his yacht.'

'He won't. He'll just have a heart attack trying to walk up to your house.'

'That's his problem, not mine. Get in!'

'You can't let your half-brother kill himself.'

'Why not? It would save me the trouble of doing it.'

She looked scathingly at him. 'You're as bad as he is! The two of you need your heads knocked together!'

Max switched off the engine, put on the brake, and got out. As he walked around the vehicle she began to hurry on upwards, but he caught her before she had gone half a dozen steps. He picked her up bodily, ignoring her squawk of protest, the muttered, 'Max, put me down!' walked back to the Land Rover and deposited her ungently into the passenger seat, then slammed the door on her before she could try to get out again.

Christos and Constantine caught up with them before Max had got back behind the steering-wheel.

'Go back to your yacht,' Max told them. 'The auction is off and I don't want either of you in my house.'

'Off?' roared Constantine.

'What do you mean, off?' Christos chimed in, his voice almost drowned by his father's.

'I've cancelled it; the island isn't for sale any more,' Max said brusquely. 'I'd like your yacht to leave immediately. This is private property, and you're trespassing.'

Olivia watched them in the driving mirror. Constantine was scarlet with exertion and heat, breathing thickly, glaring at his half-brother.

'When did you call it off?' he panted. 'Just now, after putting Faulton on to that helicopter? Oh, don't think you can pull the wool over my eyes! I know what you've been up to. You think you've been very clever, don't you? You've managed to break up my son's engagement, and Faulton's had a heart attack because you deliberately didn't let us know the girl was safe with you—if he dies, and she inherits, you'll marry her for her shares in your company, so that you can get me off the board of your company again.'

'If you don't cool down, it will be you having the heart attack, from the look of you!' Max drily said. 'Goodbye, Constantine. See you in the boardroom very soon.'

He climbed behind the wheel and started the engine again. Before he drove off, Christos materialised at the open window on Olivia's side.

'Remember, whatever he says, he's used you to get his company back, Olivia,' he said bleakly. 'You can't trust him.'

CHAPTER NINE

'COULD she trust *you*?' Max asked, and drove off with a grind of tyres on rock, a roar of the engine.

In spite of the mounting heat of the day Olivia felt cold and weary; she sank back in her seat, staring out of the window at the gleam of sunlight on olive trees, the dark shade of pines and cypress lying in pools beneath them. Beside her Max was silent, yet she felt his attention as she glanced sideways at his brown hands manipulating the wheel without effort.

The way he had manipulated her, she thought bitterly. Effortlessly, without even needing to try. Those hands had touched her and she had been lost. She despised herself. She had been a coward where her father was concerned, and a fool over Max.

'Do you think you're going to get your company back now?' she asked, and Max flicked his dark lashes towards her, his face guarded.

'Probably.'

Her mouth was bitter. 'Now that my father is a broken man and I'm not going to marry Christos any more, you mean?'

The lashes lifted; she caught a glimpse of those glittering, furious black eyes, then they were hidden again, but his face was clenched tight with rage.

'Be careful, Olivia!' he said through his teeth. 'Don't push your luck!'

'Luck!' she repeated, laughing scornfully. 'I haven't had any—not as far as men are concerned, at least. First

Christos proposing just because his father wanted him to—and then you...'

He pulled up outside the house with a grinding of gears and turned to confront her, his dark face tense and dangerous. Her pulses went out of control and panic made her tremble violently, but she put her chin up and defied him.

'Don't you come anywhere near me!'

'What will happen if I do?' he mocked angrily, sliding along the seat until he almost touched her. 'Going to beat me up, are you? My knees are knocking—can you hear them?'

'Oh, you think you're so funny!' she fumed, moving back even further until she was right up against the door and had nowhere else to go. 'I've got news for you. You aren't funny—I'm not laughing. Just because I'm a woman and not as strong as you are, you think I'm a pushover, don't you? You think you can make me do whatever you want. You, my father, Christos—you all treat me as if I was a halfwit, without a will of my own. Well, listen to this—I mean what I say! I don't want you touching me. Have you got that? I don't want you touching me, Max. I'm saying no, and I mean it. If you try to force me——'

'Did I try last night?' he bit out and she stiffened at the harsh tone. 'I had you naked in my bed, in my arms—and we were alone, miles from anyone else. I could have forced you then, Olivia, but I didn't, did I?'

She stared back at him, remembering the night before, biting her lip. It was true. He hadn't really argued that hard, he had accepted her refusal, even though she knew very well he hadn't wanted to—his frustration had been far too evident.

'I can't think straight,' she muttered. 'My mind's shot to pieces. I don't know what to believe. All I can think about is that my father may die...' She stopped short, gasped. 'My mother! I ought to have let her know he's been taken ill.'

'I thought they were divorced?'

'They are, but they were married; she'll be upset to hear about his heart attack. Can I phone her from here? I could have rung from the yacht; it never occurred to me.'

'You can phone from here.' Max opened his door and jumped down. Olivia got out too, before he came round to her side of the Land Rover.

She looked up at the empty blue sky. 'How long will it take the helicopter to fly to the mainland and come back for me?'

He looked at his watch. 'The pilot promised to turn right round at once—I'd say he'd be back here in around an hour.'

An hour alone with him! she thought, trying to control the rapid beat of her pulse, the hectic flow of colour in her face, aware of Max watching her intently, monitoring her reactions, his dark eyes narrowed and hard and dangerously bright. He was picking up too much, he was too clever; she was afraid of those sharp eyes of his, that even sharper mind.

She walked on ahead, too quickly, and pushed open the front door of the house, only to have it swing back on her as she was walking through it, the edge of the door striking her shoulder.

She gave a little squeak of pain and surprise, clutching her shoulder.

'What have you done to yourself now?' Max sounded furious and she resented it.

'Nothing! Can I ring my mother at once, please?'

'In a minute. Show me where that door hit you first.'

'I'll do nothing of the kind! I tell you, it was nothing, just a glancing blow, it doesn't hurt.'

Well, not much, she thought, aware of the throbbing pain on the soft pad of her shoulder.

'Then why is there blood on your sleeve?' asked Max, and she quickly looked down sideways, startled.

'I must have broken the skin—grazed it a little, it can't be anything much. I'll look at it later, after I've rung my mother.'

'You'll let me look at it now,' Max insisted again. 'If the skin is broken and you're bleeding that could be dangerous if it isn't dealt with at once, out here. You never know what you could pick up in an open wound. I'll wash it and put some disinfectant on it, put a plaster on it until you can get a doctor to look at it. When did you last have a tetanus shot?'

'Within the last six months.' She hesitated, then began rolling up her sleeve. Maybe he was right—she should let him put a plaster on the shoulder.

'No, that won't do—get the whole sweater off,' Max said.

Flushed and breathless, she opened her mouth to protest, and he gave her an impatient look.

'And don't turn coy on me! If you were on a beach you would think nothing of wearing a bikini in front of dozens of men. I've seen you naked and I've seen you in your bra and panties before, so just get my sweater off and stop arguing.'

'You're doing it again!' she indignantly said.

'Doing what?'

'Ordering me around as if I were a halfwit or a child.'

'Sometimes it's the only explanation!' Max took hold of her wrist and walked towards the kitchen, pulling her after him. 'Sit here, next to the table,' he commanded, pushing her down on to a chair. He pulled a clean white towel out of a drawer, and threw it to her. 'Get your sweater off and drape this around yourself for the moment.'

She dubiously eyed the towel; it didn't look very big. Max had found a clean plastic basin; he switched on the electric kettle, saying to her brusquely, 'This has boiled once already today, so I just have to reheat it a little.'

He put the basin on the table, switched off the kettle and poured the hot water into the basin, then went off to hunt through another cupboard for a bottle of disinfectant, a bag of cotton wool balls, a tin of medical plasters.

Olivia waited until his back was turned to take off her sweater, and hurriedly arranged the towel, tucking it under her arms to cover her from her breasts to her knees.

Squinting down at her shoulder, she saw the circle of bruising showing already, the smooth tanned skin puffing up, darkening, with a bleeding graze in the middle of the circle.

Max frowned at it, moistening cotton wool in the water cloudy with disinfectant now.

'Why did you say it didn't hurt? It must do.'

He gently began to clean the wound, and she tried not to wince, closing her eyes. He dried the skin again and then applied the largest plaster in his tin, a square which covered most of the bruise.

'Thank you,' she whispered as he dried his hands. She picked up the sweater to slip it back over her head. Max took it away from her.

'I'll do that.' But he didn't, not at once. He dropped it on the table and ran his long index finger down her naked arm. 'Your skin's as smooth as silk. A pity to be so rough with it—you should be more careful. Do you always walk into doors?'

Only when she no longer knew her own body space, she thought, only when her full attention was given to running away, instead of looking where she was going.

His finger was trailing on, caressing, tormenting. Her heart was in her throat; she couldn't swallow, or make a sound.

He waited a minute, then bent, very slowly; his lips touched her shoulder, kissing the bruised skin not covered by the plaster.

'So soft,' he muttered. 'Your skin is so soft and cool.'

A slow, sweet, sensual pleasure drowned her mind. She barely breathed, let alone thought. Her eyelids fell over her eyes; her lips quivered in an almost silent groan. His mouth invaded downwards, a conquering army on the march; her breasts were taken, the nipples hard and hot, her pale flesh full and aching.

Max suddenly picked her up from the chair, one hand under her legs, the other under her back.

Olivia's eyes flew open and she looked at him, shaking her head, but not able to speak because fever had possessed her.

Max looked at her quivering mouth. His eyes were hot black coals. Looking into those eyes, she was lost— they set fire to her; she was burning up.

A sound from the doorway startled them both. Max spun around, still holding her.

Christos was crimson, mouth open in a gasp, staring as if he didn't believe his eyes.

When he found his voice it was rough, disgusted. 'So my father was right! He had you last night, you lying little tramp!'

Max stiffened. He put her down into the chair again, moving between her and Christos.

'Get out!' he grated. 'Get out of my house before I lose my temper and knock your teeth down your throat!'

Olivia hurriedly pulled the sweater over her head, dragging it as far as it would go, to her knees, and stood up.

'Stop it, both of you!'

They ignored her. Christos was laughing furiously. 'I'm not afraid of you, damn you!' He came at Max like a whirlwind.

His first blow landed because Max hadn't quite expected him to move so fast. Olivia was sickened by the sound of bone hitting bone: a grinding scrunch, followed by a grunt of pain from Max as he fell backwards.

He stumbled into the wall, and Christos watched, grinning in satisfaction.

'You asked for that!'

Max straightened, face dangerous, and leapt at him across the room. This time it was Christos who was flung backwards. His head collided with the door-frame and he fell full-length like a tree brought down by an axe.

Appalled, Olivia waited for him to get up again, but he didn't. He lay there with his eyes closed, not moving.

'Oh, my God, you may have killed him!' Olivia said, running forward to kneel beside Christos.

As she looked at him his lashes fluttered, his eyes blinked and opened, he looked at her dazedly, then his eyes opened wider, recognising her, and he scowled.

'Are you all right?' she asked anxiously.

He put a hand to his jaw, explored inside his mouth with his tongue, and grimaced, his face sulky. 'I think one of my teeth is loose, otherwise I'm all in one piece.'

He glared at her and then at Max. 'Sorry to disappoint you, you didn't kill me.'

'Oh, stop it, Christos, don't be so childish!' Olivia burst out, getting up.

He got to his feet too, shakily, pulling away when she tried to help him. 'Leave me alone.'

'I thought I told you and your father to get off my island?' Max put a possessive arm around Olivia and jerked her against his side, keeping his arm around her.

Christos watched, brows heavy over his sullen eyes.

'We're going at once, don't worry. Before we sailed, I had the stupid idea that I ought to make quite sure Olivia wouldn't prefer to come with us, just in case the helicopter doesn't get back in time.' Christos laughed unpleasantly. 'Funny, really, isn't it? My chivalrous gestures always end up as jokes. Sorry I bothered you both when you were having such fun. Forget I interrupted.'

He turned on his heel and left, staggering slightly on his way to the front door.

'You didn't have to hit him so hard!' Olivia said, moving to follow him to make sure he was OK. Max refused to let go of her, his arm tightening.

'I didn't have to, no! I wanted to!' Max said, his eyes full of smouldering temper. 'He wasn't calling you a filthy name and getting away with it! Even if it had been true, he wouldn't have been justified in calling you that!'

'You can't blame him for thinking the worst of me, after what he saw just now!'

'Feeling guilty, Olivia?' Max asked drily, and she wished he wasn't so quick and shrewd.

'I was engaged to him——' she began, and Max cut her off with an impatient gesture.

'Don't start that again. We've been through that too many times already. You have no reason to feel guilty over Christos. It's only his pride that hurts, not his heart. Now, if you want to get in touch with your mother I suggest you do so now before the helicopter arrives. They shouldn't be much longer.'

He strode out of the kitchen and she followed him into the radio room again and watched him sit down and start operating the set.

'Sit here,' he commanded in that peremptory way of his a moment or two later. 'It's ringing.'

It was strange to hear her mother's voice, coming through a faint crackle of static electricity.

'Mum, it's Olivia,' she said, and her mother exclaimed in surprise.

'Where are you ringing from? You sound very far away.'

'I'm on Hymnos.'

'Where?'

'The island that was being auctioned, remember? I told you, that was why we came to Greece, to buy Hymnos.'

'I remember that, I just didn't remember the name. So, did they buy it?'

'No. Listen, Mum, something's happened—it isn't good news, I'm afraid. Dad's had a heart attack.'

She heard the inhalation of breath at the other end. 'Is it serious?'

'I don't know yet. They've flown him to hospital, and I'll be going there too shortly. I'll keep in touch and let you know how he is.'

'Yes, do that,' her mother said slowly. 'Are you OK, darling? You sound odd. It must have been a terrible shock for you too. Is Christos looking after you?'

'The engagement's off, Mum,' Olivia said huskily.

'What did you say? This line is so bad, I thought you said...'

'I'm not going to marry Christos,' Olivia repeated.

'That was what I thought you said! What on earth has been happening, Olivia? No, never mind—look, shall I come out there? Or don't you want me?'

'Oh, I'd love you to, Mum,' Olivia said gratefully. 'I didn't like to ask, but if you could... Could you get away?'

'I'll manage, leave it to me. Do I fly to Athens? Where is this hospital? How far is it from Athens? How would I get there?'

Olivia looked at Max who leaned forward and spoke into the microphone. 'Mrs Faulton...this is Max Agathios. I imagine you know who I am...'

'Yes,' her mother said, sounding even more startled. 'Of course, Mr Agathios.'

'I suggest that I book you on to a flight from Heathrow to Athens, and I'll meet your plane and take you to the hospital.'

'That's very thoughtful of you, Mr Agathios, and I'd be grateful if I could be met, but there's no need for you to book my flight for me too.'

'Mrs Faulton, I intend to be your son-in-law—please permit me to do this small service for you,' Max said formally.

Olivia stiffened, pale and then flushing angrily. How dared he?

Her mother audibly gasped. 'Oh. Oh, I see. At least, I don't, but... Well, it can wait until I see Olivia and find out exactly what's been going on over there!'

Max laughed shortly. 'Good. Now, I'll get my secretary to book your flight and get in touch to let you know the timings. I'll be waiting when you come out of the Customs area. I'll carry a board with your name written on it.'

Overhead they heard the sound of the helicopter whirring through the sky, and Max shot Olivia a glance, sat back and gestured for her to finish the call.

'Mum, I've got to go now, but I'll see you soon,' she said stiffly.

'I can't wait to see you and find out what on earth you've been up to!' her mother said in a dry voice.

Olivia's heart sank. Her mother was going to put her through a tough interrogation as soon as they were alone. Olivia didn't look forward to it.

Max ended the call as Olivia got up from her chair. She watched, glaring at him. When he got up too she snapped, 'How dare you tell my mother that?'

'Why shouldn't she know? She'll have to know sooner or later, or aren't you going to ask her to our wedding?'

'We aren't having a wedding!'

He pretended to be shocked, opening his dark eyes wide. 'No wedding? Olivia, I'm old-fashioned, I couldn't just live with you without marrying you.'

'You know perfectly well what I meant! You aren't marrying me just to get my father's shares in your company!'

'I don't need them,' he said, a glitter of excitement in his face. 'Events have moved on very fast today—while the medical people were loading your father on to the helicopter I came in here to check if there were any messages waiting for me, and found one, asking me to call an old friend.'

'Who?' she asked, his excited tone alerting her. Not Daphne Kera, surely? Jealousy niggled inside her chest. She watched him tensely, and Max grinned at her.

'He's a rival, actually, George Korsavo; his shipping company isn't as big as mine but it has some interesting contracts. It has been growing steadily for the last few years, and, most importantly, he owns it outright. He never went public; nobody else has any shares. He's older than me, in his late forties, and he only has two daughters and a son. Both girls are married, and have no interest in the firm, and his only son has never been interested in shipping. George heard I'd been forced off my board so he rang me to ask if I'd be interested in becoming managing director of his company. He's diversifying—he has bought into a private airfield and acquired a small private airline. His boy, Ioannis, is crazy about flying and works as a pilot; he persuaded his father to buy an airline for him but Ioannis isn't interested in the business side, just in the flying, at the moment. George can't give the same time and attention to both companies—he needs a partner, someone with money, someone he can trust, to take over the shipping side and run that for him. He asked me if I'd be interested, and I jumped at it.'

She frowned, 'But it won't be your own company!'

'I'll have a considerable share of it—I'm investing every penny I can raise.'

'But you aren't selling your island?'

'I have sold it,' he said, and her golden eyes opened even wider. 'Privately, to a Japanese buyer who wants to make it a holiday resort, build hotels and luxury holiday villas. The estate agent advised me to accept the offer, and cancel the auction. The new buyer refused to enter into an auction—if I didn't accept his offer he would withdraw, and his offer was so huge that I had to agree with the agent. I couldn't believe anyone else would pay that much. I was thinking it over when I got the call from George, so I told him yes, and then I rang the agent and told him to close the deal with the Japanese firm, then rang my stockbrokers and told them to start selling my shares in my own company. I'll need a lot of money to buy a partnership with George.'

'So you're pulling out of your own company altogether?' she slowly said and he shrugged.

'Constantine wants it—let him have it!'

'But...I'm confused,' she said. 'You told Constantine you'd see him in the boardroom very soon...and you told me you thought you would probably get your company back...'

'I don't want to give my brother any early warnings. If I'm to sell my shares at the top price I have to do it quickly, without anyone knowing what is going on.'

She saw the point of that. 'OK,' she conceded. 'But why let me think you were still hoping to get your company back?'

He shot her a dry look. 'You were so busy thinking the worst, I let you go ahead and do it. I was angry with you, I suppose, for being ready to listen to Christos and my brother, ready to believe their accusations. When are you going to start thinking for yourself, trusting your own judgement?'

He was right about that too, she couldn't deny it. Watching him uncertainly, she asked, 'But...won't you mind? I mean, your father left the company to you, and you built it up... Isn't it going to be hard to lose it?'

'What I did once I can do again,' Max said, his eyes bright. 'It's a challenge, and I love challenges! My father would approve, I'm sure of that. All he left me was a few old ships which won't last much longer anyway.' He laughed. 'They won't do Constantine much good. It wasn't them he was fixated on—he coveted them only because he was so jealous of me; he never forgave our father for having another son. You know, once I've sold my shares the share price will drop, and Constantine is going to have a problem. The shareholders, not to mention the other directors, are going to be furious, and they'll blame Constantine.'

She couldn't feel much pity for his half-brother. 'I'd like to be a fly on the wall when he discovers what you've done!' she said slowly.

Max laughed. 'So would I!'

They flew away ten minutes later into the glorious sunlight of an autumn morning. Staring down at the blue Aegean, Olivia found it hard to believe that so much had happened since she arrived in Athens.

It was only a couple of days ago, yet she felt as if she had experienced a whole lifetime, crowded with incident.

She spent hours in the hospital, waiting to see her father. Max made a number of phone calls, out of earshot, but he rarely took his eyes off her, and she couldn't deny she found his constant presence comforting.

He told her his secretary had only been able to book her mother on to the first flight next day. 'She will arrive around noon. I'll meet her, as I promised. Stop looking worried, Olivia, it is going to be OK—your father is in good hands.'

'I hope so,' she said fervently.

At last she was allowed to see her father, but alone, although Max walked with her to the door of the private room. Gerald Faulton lay on the bed, his chest bare but a cover pulled up over him. Its white weave made his skin look very grey, his lips were still blue, but she fancied he looked just a little better than he had; there was a trace of colour in his face and his eyes were clearer.

'I'm sorry to give you a scare, Dad, and cause all this trouble,' she said, holding his hand.

Weakly, he murmured, 'Don't be silly. I'm just glad you're alive.'

'Same here,' she said, pressing his fingers, and smiled waveringly.

He looked down at her hand. 'No ring,' he whispered, and she bit her lip.

'No.' She hadn't meant to tell him yet, in case it upset him.

'Did you end it?'

She nodded, watching him uneasily, but he didn't seem disturbed, or even surprised.

'It's Max, isn't it?' her father said in that dry, weak voice, and after a moment's hesitation she nodded. Gerald Faulton sighed, gave a pale smile. 'As long as you're happy.' He swallowed, and whispered, 'When I thought...you were dead...it hit me badly, Olivia. You're all I have in the world and I thought I'd lost you.'

Her eyes stung with tears.

Later, the specialist looking after him told her, 'It was a minor heart attack, but it was a warning. He must change his lifestyle if he wants to survive—he must take things easier, not work so hard...'

She laughed shakily. 'Shall I tell him, or will you? He isn't going to listen either way.'

'If he doesn't, I can't predict a future for him,' the man said grimly. 'He must stop drinking, stop smoking, take more exercise. And I'll tell him so, I assure you. Now, I suggest you get a good night's rest, Miss Faulton, you look very tired.'

Wearily she walked along the highly polished hospital corridor towards the exit, Max's hand under her elbow as if he was afraid to let go of her in case she fell over.

She felt as if she might, too; she had never been so tired in her life. It was only as they walked out into a soft dusk light that it dawned on her that her problems weren't over yet.

'Can you recommend a discreet hotel?' she asked Max. 'My luggage is all on the yacht, including my money, credit cards and passport. How am I going to get them back?'

'The yacht was heading for Piraeus. I'm sure Constantine will have someone pack up your things, and he'll bring them to the hospital tomorrow—he's bound to visit your father. As for a hotel, don't worry. I'll take you to the most sympathetic hotel I know.'

He had had a car waiting when they flew here earlier, which was parked in the hospital car park. She sank into the passenger seat and shut her eyes; Max started the engine and drove off. Olivia was so tired she almost fell asleep then. She woke with a start as they shot down into an underground car park.

'Where are we?' she asked, looking dazedly around.

'The hotel I told you about,' said Max, coming round to help her out of the car.

They went up in a lift from the car park; Olivia leaned on the steel wall, staring at her own reflection opposite: a blurred image with yellow hair and a white face, a ghostly wraith in a strange, very short dress.

'No hotel will let me in looking like this!' she wailed.

'This one will,' said Max, grinning at her as the lift stopped.

She walked out, looked around, expecting to see a hotel lobby, but found herself in a wide corridor with a polished floor.

'Where is this?'

Max steered her towards the end of the corridor. 'This way.' He produced a key and unlocked a door, and Olivia backed, shaking her head, angrily turning pink.

'I am not sharing your room! I want a room of my own!'

Max put an arm round her waist and lifted her off the ground, carried her inside the door and kicked it shut with one foot, leaving them in darkness.

'Let me out of here!' Olivia yelled, trying to break free of his grip. It was useless, of course. Max hoisted her up over his shoulder in a fireman's lift, and switched on the light. Her head hanging down, she found herself staring at a tiled floor; she twisted to get a view of walls papered in a pretty ivy-covered design.

Max opened a door on the left, switched on another light, and she had a disorientating glimpse of a bedroom, all cool colours: blue curtains, a blue and white carpet, a white bed. In spite of the stark simplicity there was an elegance and style which made it obvious that his décor had cost a great deal of money. She had never seen a hotel that looked like this.

'This isn't a hotel, is it?' she asked as Max dropped her unceremoniously on the bed. His face looked disturbingly grim, angular, set.

'It's my flat,' he said. 'This is my bed, and you are my woman.'

Her body jerked into fierce life, her pulses beating under her skin, her nerves jumping.

'No, Max, I won't, it wouldn't work out—after everything that's happened, we wouldn't be happy together,' she wailed, panic-stricken by the look in his eyes.

'I've waited for five years,' he said harshly. 'I hurt a man I admired very much, and owed an enormous debt to—I hurt his daughter, by jilting her for you. And eventually you cost me my company when Daphne sold her shares to Constantine and your father. I'm not complaining, Olivia—I'd do it all again tomorrow. You can't set a price tag on love. But don't tell me we wouldn't be happy together. Because I know I can't be happy without you. I don't want to live without you for even one more day.'

He pushed her down against the pillows and leaned over her, his face inches away, and she suddenly heard the wild racing of his heart. Or was it her own heart beating in that overheated way?

'I need you, Olivia,' he muttered, staring at her mouth. 'Tell me you need me too.'

She stared back, her mouth going dry, her body hot.

'Don't torment me,' he whispered. 'Say it—let me make love to you before I go out of my mind.'

'Can I stop you?' she asked, torn between wanting him and the fear that too much stood between them.

'You just have to say no,' Max said, his face even grimmer. 'You told me last night that you couldn't make love because you weren't free, you were still engaged to Christos, and I accepted that—in fact, I admired your principles. I find it hard to forgive my half-brother because he coveted my company—I had to be honest enough to admit I had no right to covet you while you were engaged to my nephew, even though I was certain you didn't love him, and he wasn't in love with you either. But you had given him your word—I respected that. But you aren't engaged any more. Forget your father, and my half-brother, and business. Forget everything that's happened lately. This is just you and me now.' He touched her cheek with one finger lingeringly, his eyes tender and passionate. 'I love you, Olivia. Will you marry me?'

She closed her eyes and stopped fighting the inevitable. She had known this would happen, ever since she saw him again, that day in her father's office when Max exploded into the room and blew her safe, carefully arranged life to pieces.

He was right: the only thing that mattered was the way he made her feel, the passion that she felt, now, vibrating between them. There were just the two of them in the world tonight, and Olivia wanted him more than she had ever wanted anything in her entire life; her body cried out for him, hungered for him, now. Now. And forever.

'Yes, Max,' she said.

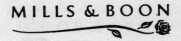

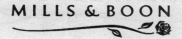

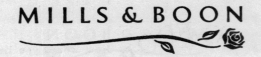

MILLS & BOON

Next Month's Romances

Each month you can choose from a wide variety of romance with Mills & Boon. Below are the new titles to look out for next month.

THE VELVET TIGER	Emma Darcy
FORGOTTEN HUSBAND	Helen Bianchin
READY FOR MARRIAGE	Debbie Macomber
THE ULTIMATE BETRAYAL	Michelle Reid
LEGALLY BINDING	Jessica Hart
NEVER A BRIDE	Diana Hamilton
SECOND-BEST BRIDE	Sara Wood
A RELUCTANT ATTRACTION	Valerie Parv
SIMPLY THE BEST	Catherine Spencer
EMERALD FIRE	Sandra Marton
VENGEFUL SEDUCTION	Cathy Williams
PASSION'S SLAVE	Rebecca King
A BUSINESS ARRANGEMENT	Kate Denton
BLIND TO LOVE	Rebecca Winters
A CAPTIVE HEART	Sally Carr
A STRANGER'S LOVE	Laura Martin

*Available from WH Smith, John Menzies, Volume One, Forbuoys,
Martins, Woolworths, Tesco, Asda, Safeway and other paperback stockists.*

SPRING FLOWERS COMPETITION

How would you like a years supply of Temptation books ABSOLUTELY FREE? Well, you can win them all! All you have to do is complete the word puzzle below and send it in to us by 31st December 1995. The first 5 correct entries picked out of the bag after that date will win a years supply of Temptation books (*four books every month - worth over £90*). What could be easier?

L	L	E	B	E	U	L	B	Q
P	R	I	M	R	O	S	E	A
I	D	O	D	Y	U	I	P	R
L	O	X	G	O	R	S	E	Y
S	T	H	R	I	F	T	M	S
W	P	I	L	U	T	F	K	I
O	E	N	O	M	E	N	A	A
C	H	O	N	E	S	T	Y	D

COWSLIP

BLUEBELL

PRIMROSE

DAFFODIL

ANEMONE

DAISY

GORSE

TULIP

HONESTY

THRIFT

PLEASE TURN OVER FOR DETAILS OF HOW TO ENTER

HOW TO ENTER

Hidden in the grid are various British flowers that bloom in the Spring. You'll find the list next to the word puzzle overleaf and they can be read backwards, forwards, up, down, or diagonally. When you find a word, circle it or put a line through it.

After you have completed your word search, don't forget to fill in your name and address in the space provided and pop this page in an envelope (you don't need a stamp) and post it today. Hurry - competition ends 31st December 1995.

Mills & Boon Spring Flower Competition,
FREEPOST,
P.O. Box 344,
Croydon,
Surrey. CR9 9EL

Are you a Reader Service Subscriber?　　Yes ❑　　No ❑

Ms/Mrs/Miss/Mr _____

Address _____

_____

_____ Postcode _____

One application per household.　　　　　　　　　　　　　　**F**

You may be mailed with other offers from other reputable companies as a result of this application. If you would prefer not to receive such offers, please tick box. ❑

DMA　　mps MAILING PREFERENCE SERVICE　　COMP395

L'ATTRAPE-CŒURS

Paru dans *Le Livre de Poche* :
NOUVELLES.

Aux Éditions Robert Laffont :
UN JOUR RÊVÉ POUR LE POISSON BANANE
nouvelles

FRANNY ET ZOOEY
roman

DRESSEZ HAUT LA POUTRE MAÎTRESSE,
CHARPENTIERS
suivi de
SEYMOUR, UNE INTRODUCTION
roman

J.D. SALINGER

L'attrape-cœurs

ROMAN

traduit de l'américain
par Annie Saumont

ÉDITIONS ROBERT LAFFONT

Titre original : THE CATCHER IN THE RYE

A ma mère

CHAPITRE 1

Sɪ vous voulez vraiment que je vous dise, alors
sûrement la première chose que vous allez demander c'est où je suis né, et à quoi ça a ressemblé, ma
saloperie d'enfance, et ce que faisaient mes parents
avant de m'avoir, et toutes ces conneries à la David
Copperfield, mais j'ai pas envie de raconter ça et
tout. Primo, ce genre de trucs ça me rase et secundo
mes parents ils auraient chacun une attaque, ou
même deux chacun, si je me mettais à baratiner sur
leur compte quelque chose d'un peu personnel.
Pour ça ils sont susceptibles, spécialement mon
père. Autrement ils seraient plutôt sympa et tout —
d'accord — mais ils sont aussi fichument susceptibles. Et puis je ne vais pas vous défiler ma complète
autobiographie. Je veux juste vous raconter ce truc
dingue qui m'est arrivé l'année dernière vers la
Noël avant que je sois pas mal esquinté et obligé de
venir ici pour me retaper. Même à D.B. j'en ai pas
dit plus, pourtant c'est mon frère et tout. Il est à
Hollywood. C'est pas trop loin de cette foutue
baraque et il vient me voir pratiquement chaque
dimanche. C'est lui qui va me ramener chez nous
quand je sortirai d'ici, peut-être le mois prochain.
Maintenant qu'il a une Jaguar. Une de ces petites

7

merveilles anglaises qui font du trois cents à l'heure. Et qui lui a sûrement coûté pas loin de trois briques. Il est plein aux as à présent. Ça le change. Avant, quand il était à la maison, c'était rien qu'un vrai écrivain. Il a écrit des nouvelles, ce bouquin terrible *La Vie cachée d'un poisson rouge*, au cas où vous sauriez pas. L'histoire la meilleure, justement, c'était *La Vie cachée d'un poisson rouge*, il était question d'un petit gosse qui voulait laisser personne regarder son poisson rouge parce qu'il l'avait acheté tout seul, avec ses sous. Ça m'a tué. Maintenant D.B. il est à Hollywood, il se prostitue. S'il y a une chose dont j'ai horreur c'est bien le cinéma. Surtout qu'on m'en parle jamais.

Là où je veux commencer c'est à mon dernier jour avant de quitter Pencey Prep. Pencey Prep est ce collège, à Agerstown, Pennsylvanie, vous devez connaître. En tout cas vous avez sûrement vu les placards publicitaires. Y en a dans un bon millier de magazines et toujours ça montre un type extra sur un pur-sang qui saute une haie. Comme si tout ce qu'on faisait à Pencey c'était de jouer au polo. Moi dans le secteur j'ai même jamais vu un canasson. Et en dessous de l'image du type à cheval y a toujours écrit : « Depuis 1888, nous travaillons à forger de splendides jeunes hommes à l'esprit ouvert. » Tu parles ! Ils forgent pas plus à Pencey que dans n'importe quelle autre école. Et j'y ai jamais connu personne qui soit splendide, l'esprit ouvert et tout. Peut-être deux gars. Et encore. C'est probable qu'ils étaient déjà comme ça en arrivant.

Bon. On est donc le samedi du match de foot contre Saxon Hall. Le match contre Saxon Hall c'était censé être un truc de première importance, le dernier match de l'année et on était aussi censé se suicider, ou quelque chose comme ça, si notre cher collège était battu. Je me souviens que vers trois heures, ce foutu après-midi, j'étais allé me percher en haut de Thomsen Hill, juste à côté du vieux canon pourri qu'avait fait la guerre d'Indépendance et tout. De là on voyait le terrain en entier et on voyait les deux équipes qui se bagarraient dans tous les sens. On voyait pas fameusement la tribune mais on pouvait entendre les hurlements ; côté Pencey un bruit énorme et terrible puisque, pratiquement, toute l'école y était sauf moi, et côté Saxon Hall rien qu'une rumeur faiblarde et asthmatique, parce que l'équipe visiteuse c'était pas l'habitude qu'elle trimbale avec elle des masses de supporters.

Au foot, les filles étaient plutôt rares. Seulement les Seniors avaient le droit d'en amener. Y a pas à dire, Pencey est une sale boîte. Moi j'aime bien être quelque part où on peut au moins voir de temps en temps deux ou trois filles, même si elles font que se gratter les bras ou se moucher ou juste ricaner bêtement ou quoi. La môme Selma, Selma Thurmer — c'est la fille du directeur —, elle venait souvent aux matchs, mais elle a pas exactement le genre à vous rendre fou de désir. Une brave fille, remarquez. Une fois, dans le bus d'Agerstown, je me suis assis à côté d'elle et on a comme qui dirait engagé la conversation. Je l'aime bien. Elle a un grand nez et les ongles rongés jusqu'au sang et elle se met un de ces foutus soutiens-gorge tellement rembourrés qu'on voit plus que ça qui pointe ; mais on aurait plutôt envie de la plaindre. Moi ce qui me bottait c'est qu'elle vous faisait pas tout un plat de son grand homme de père. Probable qu'elle savait qu'en vrai c'était un sacré plouc.

Si je me trouvais en haut de Thomsen Hill, au lieu d'être en bas à regarder le match c'est pour la raison que je venais de rentrer de New York avec l'équipe d'escrime. Le foutu manager de l'équipe d'escrime, ben c'était moi. M'en parlez pas. Le matin on était allés à New York pour la rencontre avec le collège McBurney. Mais y en avait pas eu, de rencontre ; j'avais laissé l'équipement, les fleurets et tout dans le métro. C'était pas totalement ma faute. J'étais toujours debout à regarder le plan pour savoir quand faudrait descendre. Donc on était rentrés à Pencey vers deux heures et demie alors qu'on devait rentrer pour le dîner. Et pendant tout le voyage du retour les autres de l'équipe m'avaient fait la gueule. En un sens, c'était plutôt marrant.

L'autre raison que j'avais de pas être au match c'est que je m'en allais dire au revoir au père Spencer, mon professeur d'histoire. Il avait la grippe et tout, alors je pensais bien qu'on se reverrait pas avant le début des vacances de Noël. Mais il m'avait écrit un petit mot pour me demander de passer chez lui avant de partir. Il savait que je reviendrais pas à Pencey.

J'ai oublié de vous dire que j'étais renvoyé. J'étais pas supposé revenir après les vacances de Noël pour la raison que j'avais foiré en quatre matières, et pour le manque d'application et tout. On m'avait souvent averti — en particulier chaque demi-trimestre, quand mes parents venaient voir le père Thurmer — qu'il était grand temps, qu'il fallait que je m'applique, mais j'en tenais pas compte. Alors on m'a flanqué dehors. A Pencey on met très souvent des types à la porte. Pencey a une fichue réputation question études. Sans rire.

Bref. On était en décembre et tout, un jour drôlement frisquet, à cailler sur place, spécialement en haut de cette foutue colline. J'avais seulement mon imper et pas de gants ni rien. La semaine d'avant quelqu'un m'avait piqué mon manteau en poil de chameau. Dans ma piaule. Avec mes gants fourrés qui étaient dans la poche. Pencey, c'est rempli de gangsters. Il y a un tas de types qui viennent de familles à fric mais quand même c'est rempli de gangsters. Plus une école coûte cher et plus y en a qui fauchent. Sans blague. Bon, j'étais toujours là-haut près de ce canon de malheur, à regarder le match et à me geler le cul. Sauf que le match m'intéressait pas trop. Ce qui m'intéressait, c'était plutôt de bien me pénétrer de l'idée que je faisais des adieux. Y a eu d'autres collèges, d'autres endroits, quand je les ai quittés je l'ai pas vraiment senti. Je déteste ça. L'adieu, je veux bien qu'il soit triste ou pas réussi mais au moins je veux *savoir* que je m'en vais. Sinon c'est encore pire.

J'ai eu de la chance. Tout d'un coup j'ai pensé à quelque chose qui m'a aidé à vraiment sentir que je m'en allais. D'un coup je me suis rappelé cette fois-là, vers octobre, lorsque Robert Tichener et moi et Paul Campbell on se faisait des passes de foot devant le bâtiment des profs. Sympa, les gars, surtout Tichener. C'était juste avant le dîner et la nuit tombait mais quand même on continuait. Ça devenait de plus en plus noir et on pouvait presque plus voir le ballon mais on voulait pas s'arrêter. Finalement on a été obligés. Ce prof, Mr. Zambesi, qui enseigne la biologie, il s'est pointé à la fenêtre et il nous a dit de rentrer au dortoir et de nous préparer pour le dîner. Bon, si je me mets à penser à des trucs de ce genre je peux me fabriquer un adieu quand j'en ai besoin — du moins la plupart du temps je peux ; alors cette fois, dès que je l'ai eu, mon adieu, j'ai tourné le dos au terrain de foot et j'ai descendu la colline en courant, de l'autre côté, vers la maison du père Spencer. Il habitait pas sur le campus. Il habitait dans Anthony Wayne Avenue.

J'ai couru tout le chemin jusqu'à la grille et là je me suis arrêté une seconde pour reprendre ma respiration. J'ai pas de souffle, si vous voulez savoir. Y a déjà que je fume trop — enfin, que je fumais trop, parce que maintenant on m'a interdit. Et puis que l'année dernière j'ai grandi de seize centimètres. C'est comme ça que j'ai attrapé des B.K. et qu'on m'a envoyé ici pour ces foutus contrôles et radios et tout. Mais je suis plutôt costaud, remarquez.

Bon. Lorsque j'ai eu retrouvé mon souffle j'ai traversé la route 204. C'était vachement gelé et j'ai bien failli me ramasser une gamelle. Je sais même pas pourquoi je courais — j'avais envie de courir, j'imagine. Une fois la route traversée ça m'a fait une drôle d'impression, comme si j'étais en train de disparaître. C'était un de ces après-midi vraiment dingues, avec un froid terrible et pas de soleil ni rien, qui vous donnent toujours l'impression qu'à chaque fois qu'on traverse une route on est en train de disparaître.

Ouah, quand je suis arrivé chez le père Spencer j'ai appuyé presto sur la sonnette. J'étais vraiment frigorifié. Mes oreilles me faisaient mal et je pouvais à peine remuer les doigts. Et je disais presque tout haut « Vite vite, ouvrez-la c'te porte ». Finalement Mrs. Spencer l'a ouverte, sa porte. Les Spencer, ils ont pas de domestique ni rien ; c'est toujours eux qui viennent ouvrir. Ils sont pas des rupins.

Mrs. Spencer a dit « Holden ! Quelle bonne surprise ! Entrez, mon petit, vous devez être complètement gelé ». Elle avait l'air contente de me voir. Elle m'aimait bien. Enfin je crois.

Ouah, j'ai pas traîné pour me mettre au chaud. J'ai dit « Comment allez-vous, Mrs. Spencer ? Comment va Mr. Spencer ? »

Elle a dit « Donnez-moi votre vêtement ». Elle m'avait pas entendu demander comment allait Mr. Spencer. Elle est un peu sourdingue.

Elle a accroché mon imper dans la penderie du vestibule et je me suis passé la main sur les cheveux. Le plus souvent mes cheveux je les fais couper en brosse, alors j'ai pas tellement besoin de me pei-

gner. J'ai répété « Comment ça va, Mrs. Spencer ? »
Mais plus fort, pour que cette fois elle m'entende.

« Moi ça va bien, Holden. » Elle a refermé la porte
de la penderie. « Et vous, mon petit, comment ça
va ? » A sa façon de poser la question j'ai su tout de
suite que le père Spencer lui avait dit que j'étais
renvoyé.

J'ai dit « Très bien. Comment va Mr. Spencer ?
C'est pas fini, sa grippe ?

— Fini ? Holden, il se comporte comme un
parfait... je ne sais quoi... Il est dans sa chambre.
Vous pouvez entrer. »

CHAPITRE 2

Ils avaient chacun leur chambre et tout. Des gens dans les soixante-dix ans ou même plus. Ce qui les empêchait pas de s'exciter encore pour une chose ou pour une autre — à leur façon un peu débile, tout de même. Je sais bien que c'est plutôt salaud de dire ça mais faudrait pas le prendre mal, c'est seulement que je pensais souvent au père Spencer et si on pensait trop à lui on en arrivait forcément à se demander à quoi ça lui servait encore d'être en vie. Vu qu'il était tout bossu, terriblement déglingué ; et en classe, chaque fois qu'il écrivait au tableau et qu'il laissait tomber sa craie, un des gars au premier rang devait se lever et la ramasser pour lui. A mon avis c'est vraiment moche. Mais si on pensait à lui juste un petit peu et pas trop on pouvait s'imaginer qu'au fond il se défendait pas si mal. Par exemple un dimanche, quand j'étais là avec d'autres gars à boire une tasse de chocolat, il nous a montré cette vieille couverture navajo assez esquintée que tous les deux, avec Mrs. Spencer, ils avaient achetée à un Indien de Yellowstone Park. On voyait bien que le père Spencer était sacrément fier de son achat. C'est ce que je veux dire. Prenez quelqu'un de vieux comme le monde, le père

Spencer par exemple, et rien que d'acheter une couverture le voilà tout frétillant.

Sa porte était ouverte mais j'ai quand même frappé, juste par politesse et tout. Je pouvais déjà le voir, assis dans un grand fauteuil de cuir, emmailloté dans cette couverture que je viens de vous dire. Quand j'ai frappé il a gueulé « Qu'est-ce que c'est ? » Et après m'avoir jeté un coup d'œil « Caulfield ? Entrez mon garçon ». En dehors des cours il parlait pas, il gueulait. Ça vous tapait sur les nerfs, quelquefois.

J'étais pas plus tôt entré que je regrettais d'être venu. Il lisait l'*Atlantic Monthly*, et y avait plein de médicaments et ça sentait les gouttes Vicks pour le nez. De quoi vous donner la déprime. Les gens malades j'aime pas tellement. Ce qui arrangeait pas les choses c'est qu'il avait son vieux peignoir minable qu'il devait déjà avoir en naissant. Et je peux pas dire non plus que j'adore quand les types de son âge se traînent en pyjama ou en peignoir. D'autant qu'ils se débrouillent si bien qu'on voit leur poitrine, toute en creux et bosses, et puis aussi leurs jambes. Leurs jambes, à la plage ou ailleurs, elles sont toujours blanches et sans poils. J'ai dit « Bonjour monsieur. J'ai eu votre petit mot. Merci beaucoup ». Il m'avait écrit ce mot pour me demander de passer lui dire au revoir avant de m'en aller en vacances, vu que je reviendrais pas après. « Fallait pas vous donner ce mal. De toute façon je serais pas parti sans vous dire au revoir.

— Asseyez-vous là, mon garçon. » Là, ça voulait dire sur le lit. Je me suis assis. « Comment ça va votre grippe, monsieur ?

— Mon garçon, quand j'irai mieux il sera bien temps d'appeler le médecin », a dit le père Spencer. Ça l'a plié en deux. Il s'est mis à glousser comme un dingue. Finalement il s'est calmé et il a demandé :

« Pourquoi n'êtes-vous pas au match ? Je croyais que c'était le jour du grand événement.

— Oui. J'y suis allé, j'ai dit. Mais je viens de rentrer de New York avec l'équipe d'escrime. » Ouah, son pageot était dur comme le roc.

Il est devenu plus sérieux qu'un juge. Et j'ai su que ça allait se gâter. Il a dit « Alors, vous nous quittez, hein ?

— Oui, monsieur. Je crois bien. »

Il s'est mis à branler du chef. Je suis sûr que dans toute votre vie vous avez jamais vu personne branler du chef autant que le père Spencer. On savait jamais s'il faisait ça quand il pensait profond et tout, ou bien s'il était seulement un vieux bonhomme qui commençait à perdre les pédales.

« Que vous a dit monsieur le Directeur, mon garçon ? Je crois que vous avez eu avec lui un petit entretien.

— Ah ! oui. Ah ! ça oui. J'ai dû rester pas loin de deux heures dans son bureau.

— Qu'est-ce qu'il vous a dit ?

— Ben... il a parlé de la Vie qui serait un jeu et tout. Et qu'il faut jouer selon des règles. Il a été plutôt gentil, je veux dire qu'il a pas sauté au plafond ni rien. Il répétait simplement des choses sur la Vie qui serait un jeu, vous voyez.

— La vie *est* un jeu, mon garçon. La vie *est* un jeu, mais on doit le jouer selon les règles.

— Oui, monsieur. Je le sais bien. Je sais. »

Un jeu, mon cul. Drôle de jeu. Si on est du côté où sont les cracks, alors oui, d'accord, je veux bien, c'est un jeu. Mais si on est dans l'autre camp, celui des pauvres types, alors en quoi c'est un jeu ? C'est plus rien. Y a plus de jeu.

« Monsieur le Directeur a-t-il prévenu vos parents ? m'a demandé le père Spencer.

— Il a dit qu'il le ferait lundi.

— Et vous, leur avez-vous écrit ?

— Non, monsieur. J'ai pas écrit. Parce que je les verrai probablement mercredi soir, en rentrant à la maison.

— Et comment pensez-vous qu'ils prendront la nouvelle ? »

J'ai dit « Ben... Ils vont être pas mal furieux. C'est sûr. Ça doit faire la quatrième fois que je change d'école ». J'ai hoché la tête. J'ai la manie de hocher la tête. J'ai dit « Ouah ». Parce que, aussi, je dis « Ouah ». En partie parce que j'ai un vocabulaire à la noix et en partie parce que souvent j'agis comme si j'étais plus jeune que mon âge, j'avais seize ans à l'époque et maintenant j'en ai dix-sept et quelquefois j'agis comme si j'en avais dans les treize. Et le plus marrant c'est que je mesure un mètre quatre-vingt-six et que j'ai des cheveux blancs. Sans blague. Sur un côté de ma tête — le côté droit — y a des millions de cheveux blancs. Je les ai depuis que je suis môme. Et pourtant j'agis quelquefois comme si j'avais dans les douze ans ; tout le monde le dit, spécialement mon père. C'est un peu vrai. Mais pas vrai cent pour cent. Les gens pensent toujours que ce qui est vrai est vrai cent pour cent. Je m'en balance, sauf que ça finit par m'assommer quand les gens me disent que tout de même, à ton âge... Ça m'arrive aussi d'agir comme si j'étais plus vieux que mon âge — oui, oui, ça m'arrive — mais les gens le remarquent jamais. Les gens remarquent jamais rien.

Le père Spencer a recommencé à branler du chef. Et aussi il s'est mis à se décrotter le nez. Il faisait comme s'il le pinçait seulement, son nez, mais en fait il y fourrait le pouce. Je suppose qu'il trouvait que c'était pas gênant puisque c'est seulement moi qui étais là. Et moi je m'en tape, dans l'ensemble, sauf qu'un type qui se décrotte le nez, quand on le regarde ça vous dégoûte.

Après, il a dit « J'ai eu le privilège de rencontrer

vos parents lorsqu'ils sont venus voir Mr. Thurmer il y a quelques semaines. Ce sont des gens très bien.

— Oh ! oui. C'est vrai. »

Des gens « bien ». Une expression que je déteste ; ça fait bidon ; quand je l'entends, ça me retourne l'estomac.

Et alors, d'un coup, le père Spencer a eu l'air d'avoir quelque chose d'extra à me dire, quelque chose de pénétrant comme un clou à m'enfoncer dans le crâne. Il s'est redressé un peu dans son fauteuil et il s'est mis à s'agiter ; mais c'était une fausse alerte. Tout ce qu'il a fait c'est prendre sur ses genoux l'*Atlantic Monthly* et il a essayé de le lancer sur le lit à côté de moi. Il a loupé son coup. C'était seulement à quelques centimètres ; il a loupé. Je me suis levé, j'ai ramassé le machin et je l'ai posé sur le lit. Et brusquement je pouvais plus me supporter dans cette pièce, je sentais que se préparait un sermon dans les règles, et le sermon tout seul d'accord, mais pas le sermon *et* l'odeur des gouttes Vicks pour le nez *et* le spectacle du père Spencer en pyjama et robe de chambre. Là, c'était trop.

Et ça a démarré. Il a dit, le père Spencer « Mais qu'est-ce qui vous prend, mon garçon ? » Et il l'a dit d'un ton vache, du moins pour lui. « Combien de matières présentiez-vous, ce trimestre ?

— Cinq, monsieur.

— Cinq. Combien d'échecs ?

— Quatre. » J'ai bougé un peu mes fesses sur le lit. Je m'étais jamais assis sur un lit aussi dur. « J'ai passé l'anglais impec, je lui ai dit, parce que *Beowulf* et *Lord Randal My Son,* on les a vus déjà, à Whooton. C'est-à-dire que j'avais pratiquement rien à faire en anglais, sauf de temps en temps écrire une dissert'. »

Il écoutait même pas. C'était rare qu'il écoute quand on lui parlait.

« Je vous ai saqué en histoire parce que vous ne saviez absolument rien.

— C'est vrai, monsieur. » Ouah, c'était vrai. « Vous aviez pas le choix. »

Il a répété « Absolument rien ». C'est un truc qui me rend dingue. Quand les gens disent deux fois la même chose alors que la première fois vous étiez déjà d'accord. Et voilà qu'il l'a dit une troisième fois. « Mais absolument rien. Je me demande même si vous avez jamais ouvert votre manuel de tout le trimestre. Alors ? Dites-moi la vérité, mon garçon.

— Ben... Ça m'est arrivé d'y jeter un coup d'œil », j'ai dit. Pour pas le vexer. Il adorait l'histoire.

« Ah ! vous y avez jeté un coup d'œil ? il a dit, très sarcastique. Votre... heu... votre copie d'examen est là-bas, sur la commode. En haut de la pile. Apportez-la-moi s'il vous plaît. »

C'était un rudement sale coup, mais je suis allé chercher la feuille et je la lui ai donnée — qu'est-ce que j'aurais pu faire d'autre ? Et j'ai repris place sur son paddock en béton. Ouah, vous pouvez pas vous figurer ce que j'étais fumasse d'être venu lui dire au revoir.

Il tenait ma copie comme si c'était de la merde. Il a dit : « Nous avons étudié les Égyptiens du 4 novembre au 2 décembre. Les Égyptiens, c'était votre sujet en option. Ça vous intéresserait d'entendre ce que vous avez trouvé à raconter ? »

J'ai dit « Non monsieur. Pas tellement ».

Il a lu quand même. Les profs on peut pas les arrêter quand ils ont décidé quelque chose. Ils font comme ils ont décidé, c'est tout.

Les Égyptiens étaient une ancienne race de Caucasiens résidant dans une des parties nord de l'Afrique. Cette dernière, comme nous le savons, est le plus large continent de l'hémisphère oriental.

Et il fallait que je reste assis là, à écouter ces conneries. On peut dire que c'était un sale coup.

Les Égyptiens sont pour nous aujourd'hui extrê-
mement intéressants et à cela il y a diverses raisons.
La science moderne cherche toujours quels ingré-
dients secrets les Égyptiens utilisaient quand ils
emmaillotaient les morts afin que leurs visages se
conservent sans pourrir pendant des siècles et des
siècles. Cette passionnante énigme est encore un défi
à la science moderne du vingtième siècle.

Il s'est arrêté, il a posé ma copie. Je commençais
à le détester ou tout comme. Il a dit, d'une voix
très sarcastique, « Votre composition — si on peut
dire — se termine là ». J'aurais jamais cru qu'un
vieux type pourrait être sarcastique et tout. Il a
ajouté « Toutefois, vous m'avez mis un petit mot au
bas de la page ».

J'ai dit « C'est vrai ». J'ai dit « c'est vrai » à toute
pompe parce que je voulais l'arrêter avant qu'il lise
ça à haute voix. Mais on pouvait plus l'arrêter. Il
pétait des flammes.

Alors il a lu : *Cher Mr. Spencer, je n'en sais pas*
plus sur les Égyptiens. Je n'arrive pas à m'y intéresser
vraiment quoique vos cours soient très intéressants.
Mais si vous me collez ça ne fait rien puisque je vais
être collé en tout sauf en anglais. Avec mes respects.
Holden Caulfield. Il a posé ma saloperie de copie et
il m'a regardé comme s'il venait de me flanquer
une dérouillée au ping-pong. Je crois que je lui
pardonnerai jamais d'avoir lu tout haut ces conneries. Moi, si c'était lui qui les avait écrites, je les lui
aurais pas lues. D'ailleurs, cette foutue bafouille, je
l'ai ajoutée simplement pour qu'il soit pas trop
emmerdé de me saquer.

« M'en voulez-vous, mon garçon, pour la mauvaise note ? »

J'ai dit « Oh ! non, monsieur. Sûrement pas ». J'en
pouvais plus de l'entendre m'appeler tout le temps
« mon garçon ».

Quand il a eu fini, il a voulu lancer ma copie sur

le lit. Seulement, bien sûr, il a raté son coup. A fallu que je me lève une fois de plus et que je la ramasse et la remette sur l'*Atlantic Monthly*. C'est chiant de recommencer ça toutes les deux minutes.

« Qu'auriez-vous fait à ma place ? il a dit. Dites-moi la vérité, mon garçon. »

C'était visible qu'il se sentait pas à l'aise de m'avoir saqué. Alors je l'ai baratiné. Je lui ai dit que j'étais un vrai cancre et tout. J'ai dit que si j'avais été à sa place j'aurais fait exactement pareil et que la plupart des gens se rendaient pas compte comme c'est dur d'être prof. Ce genre de laïus. La salade habituelle.

Ce qui est bizarre, c'est que je pensais à autre chose en lui servant mes commentaires. J'habite New York, et je pensais au lac de Central Park, en bas vers Central Park South. Je me demandais si l'eau serait gelée quand je rentrerais à la maison, et si elle l'était, où seraient allés les canards. Je me demandais où vont les canards quand l'eau se prend en glace, qu'il y a plus que de la glace. Je me demandais si un type vient pas avec un camion pour les emporter dans un zoo. Ou s'ils s'envolent on ne sait où.

Bon. J'ai de la veine. Je veux dire que je peux faire mon baratin au père Spencer et en même temps penser à ces canards. C'est curieux, on a pas besoin de réfléchir tellement quand on parle à un prof. Mais brusquement il m'a interrompu en plein discours. Lui, fallait toujours qu'il vous interrompe.

« Qu'est-ce que vous pensez de tout cela, vous, mon garçon ? Dites-moi. J'aimerais le savoir. »

J'ai dit « Vous parlez de mon renvoi ? » J'avais envie qu'il couvre sa poitrine toute en creux et bosses. C'était pas tellement beau à voir.

« Si je ne me trompe, vous avez déjà eu des ennuis à Whooton et à Elkton Hills. » C'était dit sur un ton non seulement sarcastique, mais aussi vraiment vache.

« J'ai pas eu trop d'ennuis à Elkton Hills. On m'a pas renvoyé. C'est moi qui suis parti.

— Pourrais-je savoir pourquoi ?

— Pourquoi ? Oh ! monsieur c'est une longue histoire. Je veux dire que c'est plutôt compliqué. » J'avais pas du tout envie de lui raconter. D'ailleurs il aurait pas compris. C'était pas du tout son rayon. Une des principales raisons qui m'ont fait quitter Elkton Hills c'est que j'étais entouré de faux jetons. Là-bas c'est tout pour l'apparence. Par exemple, y avait ce directeur, Mr. Haas, qu'était le plus vrai faux jeton que j'ai jamais rencontré. Dix fois pire que le Thurmer. Par exemple, le dimanche, quand les parents venaient au collège, il faisait sa tournée pour leur serrer la main. Super-aimable. Sauf si un gars avait des parents un peu vieux et un peu moches. Vous l'auriez vu avec les parents de mon copain de chambre. Je veux dire, si la mère d'un des gars était plutôt grosse et un peu ringarde ou quoi, et si le père était un de ces types qui portent des costumes très épaulés et des souliers en cuir noir et blanc tout ce qu'il y a de démodé, alors le sale bonhomme leur touchait à peine la main, d'un air compassé, et puis il s'en allait parler pendant peut-être une demi-heure avec les parents de quelqu'un d'autre. Je peux pas supporter. Ça me déprime tellement que j'en deviens dingue. Ce foutu collège, je le détestais.

Le vieux Spencer m'a demandé quelque chose, mais j'ai pas compris. Je pensais à ce Haas de malheur. J'ai dit « Quoi, monsieur ?

— N'êtes-vous pas un peu inquiet à la pensée de quitter Pencey ?

— Oh ! oui, ça m'inquiète un peu. Certainement. Mais pas trop. Pas encore, en tout cas. J'imagine que j'ai pas encore très bien saisi. Avec moi ça prend du temps. Pour le moment je pense qu'à rentrer à la maison mercredi. C'est plutôt débile, non ?

— Et vous ne vous faites aucun souci pour votre avenir ?

— Oh ! oui bien sûr. Bien sûr que je me fais du souci pour mon avenir. » J'ai réfléchi une minute. « Mais pas trop, quand même. Non, pas trop quand même.

— Ça viendra, a dit le père Spencer. Ça viendra un jour, mon garçon. Et alors il sera trop tard. »

J'ai pas aimé l'entendre dire ça. On aurait cru que j'étais mort ; ou tout comme. J'ai eu le cafard. J'ai dit « Je suppose que vous avez raison.

— J'aimerais vous mettre un peu de plomb dans la tête, mon garçon. Je cherche à vous aider. Oui, ce que je cherche, c'est à vous *aider*, dans la mesure du possible. »

Et c'était vrai. C'était visible. Mais l'ennui, c'est qu'entre nous y avait des années-lumière. J'ai dit « Je m'en rends compte, monsieur. Merci beaucoup. Sérieusement. J'apprécie drôlement. Je vous assure ». Et je me suis levé. Ouah, j'aurais pas pu rester assis sur ce pageot dix minutes de plus même si j'avais risqué ma vie en le quittant. « Ce qu'il y a, c'est que maintenant faut que je m'en aille. J'ai tout un équipement à prendre au gymnase. Pour le remmener chez moi. » Il m'a regardé et il s'est remis à branler du chef, avec un air rudement sérieux. Et tout d'un coup ça m'a fait de la peine pour lui. Mais je pouvais pas traîner plus longtemps, avec ces années-lumière entre nous et puis vu qu'il continuait à manquer le but chaque fois qu'il lançait quelque chose sur le lit, et tout le reste, son vieux peignoir minable qui lui couvrait pas bien la poitrine, et cette sale odeur des gouttes Vicks pour le nez — J'ai dit « Écoutez, monsieur, vous faites pas de souci pour moi. Je vous assure que ça ira. C'est seulement que je suis dans une mauvaise passe, en ce moment. Tout le monde a des mauvaises passes, vous savez.

— Non je n'en sais rien, mon garçon. Je n'en sais vraiment rien. »

Ce genre de réponse, je déteste. J'ai dit « Moi je sais. Moi j'en suis sûr. Vous faites pas de souci pour moi ». C'est comme si j'avais mis ma main sur son épaule. J'ai dit « Okay ? »

— Voulez-vous une tasse de chocolat avant de partir ? Mrs. Spencer serait...

— J'aimerais bien, mais l'ennui c'est que faut que je m'en aille. Faut que je fonce au gymnase. Merci quand même. Merci beaucoup, monsieur. »

Alors on s'est serré la main. Toutes ces conneries. Ça m'a quand même foutu le cafard.

« Je vous enverrai un petit mot, monsieur. Et soignez bien votre grippe.

— Au revoir, mon garçon. »

J'ai refermé la porte et j'étais dans la salle de séjour quand il m'a gueulé quelque chose, mais j'ai mal entendu. Je me demande si c'était pas « Bonne chance ! » J'espère que non. Merde, j'espère bien que non. Je crierais jamais « Bonne chance » à quelqu'un. C'est horrible, quand on y pense.

CHAPITRE 3

JE suis le plus fieffé menteur que vous ayez jamais rencontré. C'est affreux. Si je sors même simplement pour acheter un magazine et que quelqu'un me demande où je vais je suis capable de dire que je vais à l'Opéra. C'est terrible. Ainsi quand j'ai dit au père Spencer qu'il fallait que j'aille au gymnase chercher mon équipement et tout c'était un foutu mensonge. Parce que mon foutu équipement, je le laisse même pas au gymnase.

Quand j'étais à Pencey je logeais dans un des nouveaux dortoirs de l'aile Ossenburger. C'était réservé aux Juniors et Seniors. Moi j'étais encore Junior. Mon copain de chambre était Senior. Ossenburger, c'est le nom d'un ancien de Pencey. Il a fait ses études à Pencey et après, il a gagné des masses de fric dans les pompes funèbres. Son truc, c'est qu'il a créé partout dans le pays ces services d'inhumation qui vous enterrent les gens de votre famille pour cinq dollars l'unité. Vous auriez dû voir le père Ossenburger. Il faisait sans doute rien d'autre que les fourrer dans un sac et les balancer dans le fleuve. En tout cas il a donné plein de pognon à Pencey et Pencey a donné son nom à notre bâtiment. Il venait toujours au collège dans sa foutue Cadillac pour le premier match de l'année et fallait qu'on se lève tous dans la tribune et il avait droit à un ban et des hourras. Puis le lendemain matin à la chapelle il faisait un speech qui devait bien durer dix heures. Il commençait par au moins cinquante plaisanteries foireuses juste pour nous montrer quel vrai mec il était. Vrai mec mon cul. Puis il se mettait à nous dire qu'il avait jamais honte, quand il était dans les emmerdes, de s'agenouiller et de prier. Il disait qu'il fallait toujours prier Dieu — Lui parler et tout — n'importe où on se trouvait. Il disait qu'on devait penser à Jésus comme à un copain et tout. Il disait que lui il arrêtait pas de parler à Jésus. Même quand il conduisait sa voiture. Ça me tuait. Je vois bien ce gros salaud retors passant la première en demandant à Jésus de lui envoyer quelques macchabées de plus. La seule bonne partie de son discours ça a été en plein milieu. Il s'évertuait à nous montrer quel type sensas' on avait sous les yeux, un foutu mec et tout ; et alors, brusquement, ce gars assis dans la rangée devant moi, Edgar Marsalla, il a lâché un pet superbe. C'était vraiment grossier, spécialement dans la chapelle, mais c'était aussi très marrant. Super, le Marsalla. Il a presque fait sauter le toit. Y a pas eu grand monde qui a ri tout haut et Ossenburger a fait comme s'il avait pas entendu, mais le père Thurmer, le dirlo, était assis juste à côté, dans les stalles, et c'était clair que lui il avait entendu. Ouah, il était dingue. Sur le moment il a rien dit, mais le lendemain soir il a ordonné un rassemblement dans la salle d'étude du bâtiment des profs et il s'est amené avec un discours tout prêt. Il a dit que le garçon qu'avait fait son malin à la chapelle méritait pas d'être à Pencey. On essayait de décider Marsalla à en lâcher un autre, juste pendant le discours de Thurmer, mais il avait plus la forme. Bref c'était là que je logeais à Pencey. L'aile Ossenburger, dans les nouveaux dortoirs.

J'ai été content de me retrouver dans ma chambre, après la visite au père Spencer, parce que tout le monde était au match et on avait du chauffage, pour changer. Ça faisait intime. J'ai ôté mon imper et ma cravate et déboutonné le col de ma chemise et mis sur ma tête la casquette que j'avais achetée à New York le matin même. C'était une casquette de chasseur, rouge avec une très très longue visière. Je l'avais vue à l'étalage de ce magasin de sports, quand on était sortis du métro juste après avoir découvert que j'y avais laissé les foutus fleurets. Elle m'avait coûté seulement un dollar. La façon dont je la portais, c'était la visière à l'arrière — un genre plutôt ringard je dois dire, mais j'aimais bien. Et ça m'allait vraiment pas mal. Ensuite j'ai pris le bouquin que j'avais commencé à lire et je me suis assis dans mon fauteuil. Y avait deux fauteuils dans chaque box. J'en avais un et mon copain de chambre, Ward Stradlater, en avait un. Les bras étaient en triste état, parce que tout le monde s'asseyait dessus mais ça restait quand même des fauteuils pas mal confortables.

Le livre que je lisais, c'était un bouquin que j'avais eu par erreur à la bibliothèque. Ils avaient fait une erreur et je m'en étais aperçu qu'une fois de retour dans ma chambre. Il m'avaient donné *La Ferme africaine* par Karen Blixen. Je pensais que ça allait être dégueulasse mais pas du tout, c'était un bon livre. Moi je sais vraiment pas grand-chose mais je lis des masses. Mon auteur préféré c'est mon frère D.B., et celui qui vient après c'est Ring Lardner. Quand j'allais entrer à Pencey, mon frère m'a offert un livre de Ring Lardner, pour mon anniversaire. Dedans il y avait ces pièces de théâtre très marrantes, un peu dingues, et puis une nouvelle au sujet d'un agent de la circulation qui tombe amoureux de cette fille très dégourdie qu'est une fonceuse. Seulement le flic il est marié, donc il peut pas l'épouser ni rien. Et alors cette fille, à trop foncer elle finit par se bousiller. Ça m'a presque tué, cette histoire. Ce que je préfère c'est un livre qui soit au moins de temps en temps un brin marrant. J'ai lu un tas de classiques, *Le Retour au pays natal* et tout, et j'aime bien, et j'ai lu aussi des livres de guerre et des polars. Mon rêve, c'est un livre qu'on arrive pas à lâcher et quand on l'a fini on voudrait que l'auteur soit un copain, un super-copain et on lui téléphonerait chaque fois qu'on en aurait envie. Mais ça n'arrive pas souvent. J'aimerais assez téléphoner à Karen Blixen. Et à Ring Lardner, sauf que D.B. m'a dit qu'il était mort. Tout de même, prenez ce bouquin, *Servitude humaine* de Somerset Maugham. Je l'ai lu l'été dernier. C'est pas mal et tout, mais j'aurais pas envie de téléphoner à Somerset Maugham. Je sais pas, c'est le genre de mec que j'aurais jamais envie d'appeler. J'appellerais plutôt le petit père Thomas Hardy. Son Eustacia Vye, elle me plaît.

Bon. J'ai mis ma casquette neuve et je me suis installé à lire *La Ferme africaine*. Je l'ai lu déjà mais je voulais relire certaines parties. J'avais guère relu plus de trois pages quand j'ai entendu quelqu'un qui entrait à travers la douche, en écartant les rideaux. J'ai pas eu besoin de lever la tête pour savoir tout de suite que c'était Robert Ackley, le type qui occupait le box d'à côté. Dans le bâtiment où je logeais il y avait une douche tous les deux boxes, et quatre-vingt-cinq fois par jour environ le mec Ackley me tombait dessus. A part moi, c'était probablement le seul type de tout le dortoir à pas être au match. Il allait presque jamais nulle part. C'était un type très spécial. Un Senior, et il avait déjà passé quatre ans à Pencey mais jamais personne l'appelait autrement que "Ackley". Même Herb

Gale, son copain de chambre, il lui disait jamais "Bob", ou seulement "Ack". Si un jour il se marie, sûrement sa femme dira aussi "Ackley". C'était un de ces très très grands types au dos rond — il mesurait pas loin de deux mètres — et avec les dents pourries. Tout le temps qu'il a créché dans le box à côté je l'ai jamais vu se les brosser, les dents. Elles étaient toujours jaunâtres, dégueulasses, et quand on le voyait au réfectoire, la bouche pleine de purée ou de petits pois ça vous retournait l'estomac. En plus, il était couvert de boutons. Pas juste sur le front et le menton comme la plupart des types, mais partout sur la figure. Et puis il avait une personnalité rudement pénible. Même c'était plutôt un sale type. Bref, je l'avais pas à la bonne.

Je le sentais juste derrière ma chaise, perché sur le rebord de la douche, qui jetait un coup d'œil circulaire pour voir si Stradlater était là. Il pouvait pas souffrir Stradlater et il se pointait jamais quand Stradlater était là. Il pouvait pour ainsi dire souffrir personne.

Il est descendu de la douche et il est entré dans la piaule. Il a dit « Salut ». Il disait toujours ça comme s'il crevait d'ennui ou de fatigue. Il voulait surtout pas qu'on se figure qu'il venait vous faire une petite visite. Fallait qu'on croie qu'il était là par erreur et tout.

J'ai dit « Salut ». Mais sans lever les yeux de mon livre. Avec un type comme Ackley, si on levait les yeux du livre on était foutu. De toute façon on était foutu, mais peut-être pas aussi vite si on le regardait pas tout de suite.

Il s'est mis à tourner en rond tranquillos', comme à son habitude en tripotant mes affaires sur le bureau et la commode. Il était toujours en train de tripoter les affaires des autres et de les examiner. Y avait des moments où vraiment il me tapait sur les nerfs. Ouah. Il a dit « Ça a marché, l'escrime ? »

C'était seulement pour m'empêcher de lire en paix, parce que l'escrime il s'en foutait. Il a dit « On a gagné ou quoi ? »

J'ai dit « Personne a gagné ». Mais j'ai pas levé les yeux.

Il a dit « Hein ? » Il avait la manie de tout le temps vous faire répéter.

J'ai redit « Personne a gagné ». J'ai jeté un coup d'œil pour voir ce qu'il fabriquait avec les trucs sur ma commode. J'ai vu qu'il regardait la photo de ma copine de New York. Sally Hayes. Il avait bien dû la regarder au moins cinq mille fois depuis que je l'avais, cette photo. Et aussi, quand il avait fini, il la remettait jamais au bon endroit. Il le faisait exprès. C'était visible.

Il a dit « Personne a gagné ? Comment ça ?

— J'ai laissé les foutus fleurets et tout le barda dans le métro. » J'avais toujours pas levé les yeux.

« Bon Dieu ! Dans le métro ! Tu veux dire que tu les as *perdus* ?

— On s'est trompés de métro. Fallait sans arrêt que je me lève pour vérifier sur le foutu plan. »

Il est venu vers moi et il s'est mis juste dans ma lumière. « Hey, j'ai dit, depuis que t'es là ça fait vingt fois que je lis la même phrase. »

N'importe qui aurait compris l'allusion. Mais pas lui. Pas Ackley. Il a dit « Tu crois qu'ils vont te les faire payer ?

— Je sais pas, et je m'en fous. Pourquoi tu prendrais pas un siège, môme Ackley ? T'es juste dans ma lumière. » Il aimait pas ça quand on l'appelait « môme Ackley ». Il était toujours à me dire que j'étais un foutu môme, parce que j'avais seize ans et lui dix-huit. Quand je l'appelais « môme Ackley » ça le mettait en boule.

Et il restait là. C'était exactement le genre de gars qui se retirait pas de votre lumière quand on lui demandait. Il finirait par le faire, mais comme on

le lui demandait ça durait plus longtemps. Il a dit
« C'est quoi que tu lis ?

— Un foutu bouquin. »

Il a relevé le livre du dos de la main pour voir le
titre. Il a dit « C'est bon ?

— Cette phrase où j'en suis, elle est très chouette. »
Quand ça me prend, je peux être vraiment sarcastique. Il a même pas pigé. Il s'est remis à traîner
dans la chambre, en retripotant mes affaires, et les
affaires de Stradlater. Finalement j'ai posé le livre
par terre. On pouvait rien lire avec un type comme
Ackley sur le dos. Pas la peine d'essayer.

Je me suis laissé glisser au fond du fauteuil et j'ai
contemplé le père Ackley qui se croyait chez lui. Je
sentais la fatigue de ce voyage à New York et j'ai
bâillé deux ou trois fois. Puis j'ai commencé à faire
un peu l'idiot. Quelquefois je fais vraiment l'idiot,
juste pour pas trop m'emmerder. Ce que j'ai fait,
ben j'ai ramené en avant la visière de ma casquette,
puis je l'ai tirée sur mes yeux. Comme ça je voyais
plus rien. Et j'ai dit d'une voix tout enrouée « Je
crois que je suis aveugle ». Et puis « Mère bien-
aimée, tout devient tellement tellement sombre.

— T'es cintré, ma parole.

— Mère bien-aimée, donnez-moi la main. Pourquoi vous me donnez pas la main ?

— Putain, t'as quel âge ? »

Je me suis mis à tâtonner devant moi, comme un
type qui est aveugle, mais sans me lever ni rien.
J'arrêtais pas de répéter Mère bien-aimée pourquoi
vous me donnez pas la main. Bien sûr c'était pour
faire l'idiot. Le genre de truc que j'aime. En plus je
voyais bien que le gars Ackley enrageait. Ce mec il
réveille mes instincts sadiques. Souvent avec lui je
suis plutôt sadique. Mais j'abandonne assez vite. J'ai
remis la visière en arrière, et je me suis calmé.

Ackley a demandé « C'est à qui, ça ? »

Il tenait la genouillère de mon copain de chambre.

Ce mec, Ackley, faut toujours qu'il tripote quelque chose. Il tripoterait même votre suspensoir à l'occasion. Je lui ai dit que c'était la genouillère de Stradlater. Alors il l'a lancée sur le lit de Stradlater. Il l'avait prise sur la commode de Stradlater alors il l'a lancée sur le lit.

Il est venu s'asseoir sur le bras du fauteuil de Stradlater. Il s'asseyait jamais *dans* un fauteuil. Toujours sur le bras. Il a dit « Ousque t'as dégoté cette casquette ?

— A New York.

— Combien ?

— Un dollar.

— Tu t'es fait pigeonner. »

Il s'est mis à se curer les ongles avec le bout d'une allumette. Fallait toujours qu'il se cure les ongles. Ça valait le jus, il avait toujours les dents jaunes et des oreilles pleines de crasse mais il passait son temps à se curer les ongles. J'imagine qu'il se figurait que ça lui donnait le genre du type super-soigné. Tout en se curant les ongles il a encore jeté un coup d'œil à ma casquette. Il a dit « Chez nous, putain, quand on porte une casquette comme ça c'est pour chasser le daim. C'est une casquette de chasse au daim.

— Tu déconnes. » J'ai ôté la casquette et je l'ai examinée. J'ai fermé un œil comme si je voulais la prendre pour cible. J'ai dit « C'est une casquette de chasse à l'homme. Moi je la mets pour chasser l'homme.

— Tes vieux, ils savent qu'on t'a renvoyé ?

— Ben non.

— Ousqu'il est, Stradlater ?

— Au match. Il a une fille. » J'ai bâillé. Je bâillais tous azimuts. D'abord il faisait trop chaud dans la pièce. La chaleur ça endormait. A Pencey, ou bien on pèle de froid ou bien on crève de chaud.

« Stradlater le magnifique », a dit Ackley. Et puis

« Hey, prête-moi tes ciseaux une seconde, si tu les as sous la main.

— Non, ils sont dans ma valise. Tout en haut de la penderie.

— Tu me les passes une seconde ? J'ai une petite peau qui faut que je coupe. »

Ackley, il s'en foutait qu'on ait mis les affaires dans la valise et qu'elle soit en haut de la penderie. Je lui ai quand même ressorti les ciseaux. Et dans l'opération, un peu plus j'y passais. A l'instant où j'ai ouvert la porte du placard, la raquette de tennis de Stradlater — avec sa presse de bois et tout —, tout ce foutu bazar m'est tombé en plein sur le crâne. Ça a fait un énorme bang, et j'avais tellement mal que j'en aurais chialé. Ben, le gars Ackley, ça l'a tué ou presque. Il s'est mis à se bidonner. J'ai eu droit à son rire de fausset tout le temps que je descendais ma valise et que je lui sortais mes ciseaux. Un truc de ce genre — un type qui reçoit un rocher sur la tête — et voilà mon Ackley qui se gondole comme une baleine. J'ai dit « T'as un foutu sens de l'humour, môme Ackley. Tu savais pas ? » Je lui ai tendu les ciseaux. « Laisse-moi être ton manager. Je te ferai engager à la radio. » J'ai réintégré mon fauteuil et il s'est mis à couper ses grands ongles cornés. J'ai dit « Tu pourrais pas faire ça au-dessus de la table ou quoi ? Coupe-les au-dessus de la table, tu veux ? J'ai pas envie de marcher pieds nus sur tes saletés de rognures d'ongles ». Il en continuait pas moins à les laisser tomber par terre. Il est puant. Je vous jure.

« Qui c'est la fille qui sort avec Stradlater ? » Fallait toujours qu'il soit au courant des copines de Stradlater, quand même il pouvait pas le souffrir.

« Je sais pas. Pourquoi ?

— Comme ça. Bouh, je peux pas le voir ce couillon. C'est un vrai couillon que je peux vraiment pas voir.

— Mais lui il te trouve super. Il m'a dit que t'es un foutu prince. » Quand je fais l'idiot, j'appelle les mecs des princes. C'est une façon de pas m'emmerder ni rien.

« Il a toujours ses grands airs, a dit Ackley. Je crois même pas qu'il est intelligent, ce con. Il *se figure* qu'il l'est. Il se figure qu'il est le plus...

— Ackley ! Bordel ! Veux-tu *s'il te plaît* te couper les ongles au-dessus de la table ? Je te l'ai demandé cinquante fois déjà. »

Il s'est mis, pour changer, à se couper les ongles au-dessus de la table. Ce mec, la seule façon d'en obtenir quelque chose c'était de gueuler.

Un moment je l'ai regardé faire.

Et puis j'ai dit « T'es en pétard contre Stradlater à cause qu'il t'a bousculé pour que tu te laves les dents une fois de temps en temps. S'il a tellement crié c'était pas pour te vexer. D'accord il s'y est mal pris mais il voulait pas te vexer. Tout ce qu'il voulait c'est te dire que t'aurais meilleure allure et que tu te sentirais mieux si seulement tu te lavais les dents de temps en temps.

— Arrête. Les dents, je me les lave. »

J'ai dit « Pas vrai. C'est pas vrai, je t'aurais vu ».

Mais je l'ai pas dit méchamment. D'un sens ça m'embêtait pour lui. Parce qu'on aime pas si quelqu'un dit qu'on se lave pas les dents. J'ai ajouté « Stradlater, il est okay ». J'ai dit « Stradlater est un type pas mal. Tu le connais pas, voilà le problème.

— Je continue à penser que c'est un sale con. Un sale con et un crâneur.

— Il est crâneur mais il est très généreux pour certains trucs. Sans blague. Écoute, suppose par exemple qu'il porte une cravate ou autre chose, Stradlater, et que toi t'en aies envie. Disons qu'il a une cravate que t'aimes à la folie — je te donne juste un exemple. Tu sais ce qu'il va faire ? Probable qu'il va l'enlever et te la tendre. Sans blague. Ou

34

bien — tu sais ce qu'il va faire ? Il va la laisser sur ton lit. Ou ailleurs dans tes affaires mais en tout cas il va te la *donner*, la foutue cravate. Les autres types, pour la plupart...

— Merde, dit Ackley. Si j'avais son fric je ferais pareil.

— Pas vrai. »

J'ai secoué la tête. « Pas vrai, môme Ackley. Si t'avais son fric tu serais un des plus...

— Arrête de m'appeler "môme". Bon Dieu, je suis en âge d'être ton père.

— Et ta sœur. » Ouah. Par moments Ackley, il vous tapait sur le système. Il manquait jamais une occasion de signaler qu'on avait seize ans et lui dix-huit. J'ai dit « D'abord, je voudrais pas de toi dans ma famille.

— Eh bien arrête de m'appeler... »

Tout d'un coup la porte s'est ouverte et le gars Stradlater s'est pointé, en fonçant. Il arrêtait pas de foncer. Avec lui y avait toujours urgence. Il est venu près de moi et il m'a donné une claque sur chaque joue — des claques pour rire mais c'est plutôt rare qu'on trouve ça marrant. Il a dit : « Écoute. Tu vas quelque part ce soir ?

— Je sais pas. Ça se pourrait. Bon Dieu qu'est-ce qui se passe dehors — il neige ? » Il avait plein de neige sur son manteau.

« Ouais. Écoute. Si t'as rien de spécial, tu voudrais pas me prêter ta veste de tweed ? »

J'ai demandé « Qui a gagné ?

— Ils en sont seulement à la mi-temps. Nous on se barre. » Et puis il a dit « Sans blague, tu mets ta veste de tweed ce soir ? J'ai renversé des saloperies sur mon blazer gris ».

J'ai dit « Non, mais je tiens pas à ce que tu me la déformes avec tes foutues épaules et tout ».

Lui et moi on était pratiquement de la même

taille mais il pesait deux fois plus lourd. Il avait des épaules extralarges.

« Je vais te la déformer. » Il a foncé vers la penderie. Il a dit « Comment ça va, Ackley ? »

Au moins, Stradlater, voilà un gars qu'était plutôt sympa. Bon d'accord, c'était un peu bidon ses manières mais lui il manquait jamais de dire bonjour à Ackley et tout.

Quand il a dit « Comment ça va ? » Ackley s'est contenté de pousser un grognement. Il lui aurait bien pas répondu mais il avait pas le cran de pas pousser au moins un grognement. Puis à moi il a dit « Bon, moi je me taille. A tout à l'heure ».

J'ai dit « Okay ». Ackley, quand il retournait dans sa tanière ça vous brisait pas vraiment le cœur.

Le gars Stradlater s'est mis à enlever son manteau et sa cravate et tout. Il a dit « Je me donnerais bien un petit coup de rasoir ». Il avait une barbe plutôt drue. Je vous jure.

J'ai demandé « Et ta fille, elle est où ?

— Elle m'attend à l'Annexe. »

Il est sorti de la chambre avec sous le bras sa trousse de toilette et sa serviette. Sans chemise ni rien. Il circulait toujours torse nu parce qu'il se trouvait vachement bien bâti. Il l'était. Faut bien le reconnaître.

CHAPITRE 4

J'AVAIS rien de spécial au programme aussi je suis allé avec lui aux lavabos et pendant qu'il se rasait on a discuté le coup. On était seulement nous deux bicause le match. Il faisait une chaleur d'enfer et les vitres étaient couvertes de buée. Contre le mur du fond y avait une dizaine de lavabos en enfilade. Le sien, à Stradlater, c'était celui du milieu. Je me suis assis sur celui à sa droite et je me suis mis à ouvrir et fermer le robinet d'eau froide — une manie que j'ai, c'est les nerfs — Stradlater se rasait en sifflant *Song of India*. Il sifflait toujours très aigu, et pratiquement jamais dans le ton et en plus il choisissait des trucs difficiles, même pour quelqu'un qui sait très bien siffler, des trucs comme *Song of India* ou *Slaughter on Tenth Avenue*. Pour bousiller un air il avait pas son pareil.

Si vous vous souvenez, j'ai dit qu'Ackley était plutôt dégueulasse. Eh bien Stradlater c'était kif-kif mais dans un genre différent. Stradlater était dégueu en douce. A première vue on le trouvait impec, mais par exemple vous auriez vu son rasoir ! Toujours rouillé et plein de mousse séchée et de poils et de merde. Il le nettoyait jamais. Stradlater, il avait toujours *l'air* propre lorsqu'il avait fini de s'arranger mais quand on le connaissait bien, en douce il était dégueulasse. S'il voulait avoir l'air propre c'est qu'il était follement amoureux de sa personne. Il se croyait le plus beau gars de l'hémisphère occidental. Faut admettre qu'il était plutôt bien. Mais c'était le type de beau gars qui aurait fait dire à vos parents, en admettant qu'ils aient vu sa photo dans l'Annuaire de l'École : « Qui est donc ce garçon ? » Je veux dire qu'il était spécialement le genre de beau gars de l'Annuaire de l'École. J'ai connu à Pencey un tas de mecs que je trouvais beaucoup mieux que Stradlater mais si on avait vu leur photo dans l'Annuaire ils auraient pas fait le même effet. On leur aurait découvert un grand nez ou les oreilles décollées. Ce serait pas la première fois que ça arrive.

Bref. J'étais assis sur le lavabo près de celui où Stradlater se rasait et je tripotais le robinet. J'avais encore ma casquette rouge, avec la visière à l'arrière et tout. Vrai, elle me bottait, cette casquette.

« Hey, qu'il m'a dit, Stradlater, tu veux me rendre un grand service ? »

J'ai dit « Quoi ? » Avec pas trop d'enthousiasme. Il demandait tout le temps qu'on lui rende un grand service. Supposez un très beau gars ou un gars qui se prend pour quelqu'un d'extra, ce type-là il sera toujours à vous demander de lui rendre un grand service. Parce qu'il s'adore il se figure que vous aussi vous l'adorez, et que vous mourez d'envie de lui rendre service. En un sens c'est assez poilant.

Il a dit « Tu sors ce soir ?

— Ça se peut. Je sais pas. Pourquoi ?

— J'ai cent pages d'histoire à lire pour lundi. Et en plus j'ai une dissert'. Tu me la ferais pas, ma dissert' ? Si je ne la rends pas lundi, je vais avoir des emmerdes. Voilà pourquoi je te demande. Tu veux bien ? »

Ça m'a semblé un peu fort. Le comble de l'ironie.

« C'est à moi que tu demandes de faire ta dissert' ? A moi qu'on vient de flanquer à la porte ?

— Ouais, je sais. Ce qu'il y a c'est que j'aurai des emmerdes si je la rends pas. Tu serais un pote, un vrai pote. D'accord ? »

J'ai pas répondu tout de suite. Avec les salauds dans son genre, le suspense c'est pas mauvais.

J'ai dit « Sur quoi la dissert' ?

— N'importe quoi. Une description. Une pièce dans une maison. Ou bien une maison. Ou un endroit où t'as vécu — tu vois le truc. Du moment qu'on décrit. » Tout en disant ça il bâillait comme un four. Moi ça me la coupe. Je veux dire quand quelqu'un bâille juste au moment où il vous demande un service. Il a dit « Mais arrange-toi pour que ça soit pas trop bien. Ce con d'Hartzell, il trouve que t'es génial en dissert' et il sait qu'on crèche ensemble. Alors mets pas toutes les virgules au bon endroit ».

Encore quelque chose qui me la coupe. Quand on est bon en dissert' et qu'on vient vous parler de virgules. Stradlater il faisait toujours ça. Il voulait qu'on se figure qu'il était nul en dissert' pour la seule et unique raison qu'il mettait pas les virgules au bon endroit. Avec Ackley c'était un peu la même chanson. Une fois, à un match de basket j'étais assis près d'Ackley. Il y avait Howie Coyle dans l'équipe, un joueur terrible, capable de marquer un panier du milieu du terrain, sans même toucher le panneau ni rien. Ackley a pas arrêté de répéter tout au long de la partie que Howie Coyle avait exactement le *gabarit* d'un joueur de basket. Merde, je peux pas supporter.

Au bout d'un moment j'en ai eu mon compte d'être perché sur ce lavabo alors je me suis donné un peu d'espace et j'ai commencé à faire des claquettes, pour rigoler. Juste pour rigoler. J'y connais pas grand-chose, aux claquettes, mais par terre il y avait du carrelage, ça rendait plutôt bien. Je me suis mis à imiter un de ces types dans les films. Dans les comédies musicales. Pour moi les films c'est pire que la peste mais j'adore imiter les acteurs. Le gars Stradlater, il me regardait dans la glace tout en se rasant. Et moi j'ai besoin d'un public. Je suis un exhibitionniste. J'ai dit « C'est moi le fils du Gouverneur ». Je me défonçais. Claquettes tous azimuts. « Le Gouverneur, il veut pas que je devienne un danseur de claquettes. Il veut m'envoyer à Oxford. Mais les claquettes j'ai ça dans le sang. » Il a ri. Le Stradlater. Il avait pas mal le sens de l'humour. « C'est le soir de la première aux Ziegfield Follies. » J'étais hors d'haleine. J'ai pas beaucoup de souffle. « Le premier danseur en peut plus, il est saoul comme une vache. Alors qui est-ce qu'ils prennent à sa place ? Ben moi. Le gamin génial de ce vieux schnock de Gouverneur.

— Où t'as dégoté ça ? » a demandé Stradlater. Il parlait de ma casquette de chasse. Il l'avait pas encore remarquée.

De toute façon j'étais essoufflé. Aussi j'ai arrêté de déconner. J'ai ôté ma casquette et je l'ai contemplée pour la quatre-vingt-dixième fois environ.

« Je l'ai achetée à New York ce matin. Un dollar. Elle te plaît ? »

Stradlater a hoché la tête. Il a dit « Super ». Mais j'ai compris qu'il cherchait seulement à me flatter bicause immédiatement après il m'a dit « Écoute, tu me la fais, ma dissert' ? Faudrait que je sache.

— Je la fais si j'ai le temps. Si j'ai pas le temps je la fais pas. » Je me suis rapproché, j'ai repris ma place sur le lavabo à côté de lui. J'ai demandé « Qui c'est la fille que tu rencardes ? Fitzgerald ?

— Bon Dieu, non. Cette salope et moi c'est fini.

— Vrai ? Alors tu me la refiles ? C'est mon type.

— Prends-la. Mais elle est trop vieille pour toi. »

Subitement — et sans raison valable sauf que j'étais d'humeur à plaisanter — j'ai eu envie de dégringoler de mon lavabo et de lui faire une bonne prise de catch. Disons une cravate. Au cas où vous connaîtriez pas, on passe le bras autour du cou de l'adversaire et si on veut on l'étrangle. J'ai bondi comme une panthère sur Stradlater.

« Arrête Holden, sacré bordel », a dit Stradlater. Il avait pas envie de chahuter. Il était en train de se raser et tout. « Qu'est-ce que tu cherches ? Tu veux que je me la tranche ? »

Je l'ai quand même pas laissé aller. J'avais une prise plutôt bonne. J'ai dit « Allons, petit père, libère-toi du rude étau de mes biceps.

— Bor-del. » Il a lâché le rasoir et il a relevé brutalement les bras. C'était un gars très costaud. Moi je suis plutôt faiblard. « Maintenant arrête tes conneries. » Il s'est remis à se raser. Il se rasait toujours deux fois pour être vraiment biautifoul. Avec son vieux rasoir pourri.

J'ai demandé, en regagnant mon perchoir, « Si c'est pas Fitzgerald, c'est qui ? La môme Phyllis Smith ?

— Non. Ça devait mais ça a foiré. Maintenant, j'ai la copine de chambre de Bud Thaw. Tiens, j'oubliais, elle te connaît.

— Qui ?

— Cette fille.

— Quoi ? j'ai dit. Elle s'appelle comment ? » J'étais pas mal intéressé.

« Attends que je réfléchisse... Heu, Jane Galla-gher. »

Ouah. J'en suis presque tombé raide.

« *Jane* Gallagher. » Quand il a dit ça je suis même descendu du lavabo. Et un peu plus je tombais raide. « Tu parles si je la connais. Pas l'été dernier mais celui d'avant elle habitait pratiquement la maison à côté de la nôtre. Elle avait cet énorme doberman. C'est comme ça qu'on s'est parlé. Son chien venait tout le temps dans notre... »

Stradlater a crié « Bordel, tu me prends la lumière, Holden. Tu peux pas te mettre ailleurs ? »

J'étais terriblement surexcité. Ouah. Dans tous mes états.

J'ai demandé « Elle est où ? Faudrait bien que j'aille lui dire un petit bonjour. Elle est où ? A l'Annexe ?

— Exactos'.

— Comment ça se fait qu'elle a parlé de moi ? Est-ce qu'elle va à B.M. maintenant ? Elle disait qu'elle irait peut-être. Elle disait, ou bien à Shipley. Je croyais qu'elle allait à Shipley. Comment ça se fait qu'elle a parlé de moi ? » Vrai, j'étais dans tous mes états.

« Bordel, je sais pas. » Qu'il a dit, Stradlater. « Soulève-toi, veux-tu. T'as le cul sur ma serviette. » Je m'étais assis en plein sur sa foutue serviette.

J'ai redit « ... Jane Gallagher ». J'en revenais pas. Sacré bordel.

Le gars Stradlater se mettait du Vitalis sur les cheveux. Mon Vitalis.

J'ai dit « C'est une danseuse. La danse classique et tout. Elle s'entraînait deux heures par jour, même en pleine chaleur. Elle se faisait du mouron pour ses jambes, de peur qu'elles deviennent moches, trop épaisses et tout. Je jouais sans arrêt aux dames avec elle.

— Tu jouais à *quoi* ?

— Aux dames.

— Aux *dames* ! Putain.

— Ouais. Elle voulait jamais bouger ses dames. Chaque fois qu'elle avait une dame elle voulait pas la bouger. Elle la laissait au dernier rang. Quand ses pions étaient allés à dame, après elle y touchait plus. C'était juste que ses dames elle aimait les voir au dernier rang, bien alignées. »

Stradlater a pas bronché. Ce genre de truc, ça n'intéresse personne.

« Sa mère jouait au golf dans le même club que nous. J'y faisais le caddie de temps en temps pour ramasser un peu de fric. J'ai fait le caddie deux ou trois fois pour sa mère. Son score c'était à peu près cent soixante-dix pour neuf trous. »

Stradlater écoutait à peine. Il arrangeait ses crans et ses bouclettes.

J'ai dit « Faudrait tout de même que je descende lui dire un petit bonjour.

— Ben, vas-y.

— Tout à l'heure. »

Il a refait sa raie. Pour se coiffer ça lui prenait des heures.

J'ai dit « Ses parents ont divorcé. Sa mère s'est remariée à un alcoolo. Un type efflanqué avec des jambes poilues. Je me rappelle. Il était tout le temps en short. Jane disait qu'il était censé écrire pour le théâtre, mais moi je l'ai jamais vu rien faire d'autre que s'imbiber et puis écouter tous les foutus programmes policiers à la radio. Et se balader à poil dans la baraque. Avec Jane qu'était là et tout.

— Ah ouais ? » il a dit, Stradlater. Ça c'était quelque chose qui l'intéressait. L'alcoolo se baladant à poil dans la maison avec Jane qu'était là. Les trucs porno, Stradlater, ça le travaillait.

« Elle a eu une enfance pourrie. Sans blague. »

Mais il en avait rien à foutre. C'est seulement les trucs porno qui l'intéressaient.

« Jane Gallagher. Bon Dieu ! » Je pouvais plus penser qu'à ça. « Faudrait que j'aille lui dire un petit bonjour, tout de même.

— Ben vas-y. Au lieu de tout le temps le répéter. »

Je me suis approché de la fenêtre, mais on voyait rien dehors. Y avait trop de buée. J'ai dit « En ce moment j'ai pas la forme. » C'était vrai. Pour ce genre de choses, faut avoir la forme. « Je croyais qu'elle allait à Shipley. J'aurais juré qu'elle allait à Shipley. » J'ai tournicoté un peu dans la pièce. J'avais rien d'autre à faire. J'ai dit « Le match, ça lui a plu ?

— Ouais. Je suppose. Je sais pas.

— Est-ce qu'elle t'a raconté qu'on jouait tout le temps aux dames ?

— Je sais pas. Bordel, je viens seulement de la rencontrer », a dit Stradlater. Il avait fini de peigner sa biautifoul perruque. Il rangeait ses affaires de toilette dégoûtantes.

« Écoute, dis-lui bonjour pour moi. D'accord ?

— D'accord », a dit Stradlater, mais je savais qu'il le ferait pas. Prenez un type comme Stradlater. Jamais il a dit bonjour aux gens quand vous lui demandez.

Il a regagné la piaule, mais moi je suis resté un moment aux lavabos, je pensais à la môme Jane. Après, j'ai aussi réintégré la piaule.

Stradlater était devant la glace, occupé à nouer sa cravate. Il passait la moitié de sa vie devant la glace. Je me suis assis dans mon fauteuil et pendant un moment je l'ai observé.

Et puis j'ai dit « Hey, va pas lui raconter qu'on m'a foutu dehors.

— Okay. » L'avantage, avec Stradlater, c'est qu'on était pas obligé de lui donner des explications pour la moindre chose comme c'était le cas avec Ackley. Principalement, je suppose, parce que les histoires des copains il s'en foutait. Avec Ackley c'était différent. Ce salaud d'Ackley fourrait son nez partout.

Stradlater a enfilé ma veste de tweed.

« Dis donc, essaie de pas la déformer. » Je l'avais peut-être mise deux fois.

« D'accord, je ferai gaffe. Où sont mes foutues cigarettes ?

— Sur le bureau. » Il oubliait toujours où il avait mis ses affaires. « Sous ton écharpe. » Il les a fourrées dans la poche de sa veste — dans la poche de *ma* veste.

Tout d'un coup, pour changer, j'ai ramené en avant la visière de ma casquette. Je me sentais énervé. J'ai toujours tendance à m'énerver. J'ai dit « Et où tu vas avec elle. T'as décidé ?

— Je sais pas. New York. Si on a le temps. Elle a seulement demandé la permission de 9 h 30 ce soir, cette connasse. »

J'ai pas aimé sa façon de parler. Aussi j'ai dit « Elle l'a fait pour la raison que sans doute elle ignorait totalement quel charmant salaud tu es, quel salaud bien tourné. Si elle avait su elle aurait probablement demandé la permission de 9 h 30 *demain matin* ».

Stradlater a dit « T'as raison ». On pouvait pas facilement le mettre en boîte. Trop prétentieux, le mec. Il a dit « Bon, sans rire, tu penses à ma dissert' ? » Il était habillé, prêt à partir. « Te casse pas trop. Rappelle-toi simplement que ça doit être vachement descriptif. Okay ? »

J'ai pas répondu. J'avais pas envie. J'ai juste dit « Demande-lui si elle continue à garder toutes ses dames au dernier rang ».

Stradlater a redit « Okay », mais je savais bien qu'il demanderait pas. Il a filé à toute pompe. Après son départ j'ai passé une bonne demi-heure assis dans mon fauteuil, sans rien faire. J'arrêtais pas de penser à Jane et à Stradlater qui sortait avec elle et tout. Ça m'énervait tellement que j'en devenais dingue. Je vous ai déjà dit que Stradlater était sacrément porté sur le sexe.

Tout d'un coup Ackley s'est repointé, en traversant la douche comme d'habitude. Pour une fois dans ma putain de vie j'ai été vraiment content de le voir. Ça me changeait les idées.

Il m'a collé au cul jusqu'au dîner en parlant de tous ces types de Pencey qu'il pouvait pas souffrir et en se pressant un gros bouton qu'il avait sur le menton. Il se servait même pas d'un mouchoir. A vrai dire, je sais même pas si ce taré en avait un. En tout cas je l'ai jamais vu s'en servir.

CHAPITRE 5

LE samedi soir on bouffait toujours la même chose. On était censés s'en mettre plein la lampe parce qu'ils nous servaient des steaks. Je parierais mille dollars que si on avait droit au steak le samedi soir c'était pour l'unique raison que beaucoup de parents venaient au collège le dimanche et le Thurmer se figurait probablement que les mères demanderaient à leur petit chéri ce qu'il avait mangé la veille ; et alors il répondrait « un steak ». La bonne combine. Mais les steaks fallait les voir. Des petits machins tout durs et desséchés qu'on pouvait à peine couper. Le soir du steak on avait aussi cette purée à grumeaux, et pour dessert du pudding, du *Brown Betty*, un truc infect que personne mangeait sauf peut-être les mômes des petites classes qui n'y connaissaient rien et des types comme Ackley qui engouffraient n'importe quoi.

Mais quand on est sortis du réfectoire, c'était chouette. Y avait par terre dix centimètres de neige et ça tombait encore à la pelle. C'était vachement beau. On s'est mis à se jeter des boules de neige et à faire les cons tous azimuts. Des jeux de gamins, mais on rigolait bien.

J'avais pas de rencard. Alors avec mon copain

Mal Brossard — un type de l'équipe de lutte — on a décidé de prendre le bus pour Agerstown et de se taper un hamburger et peut-être voir une cochonnerie de film. On avait pas envie de passer la soirée au collège sans lever le cul de dessus nos sièges. J'ai demandé à Mal si ça l'embêtait qu'Ackley vienne avec nous. Je demandais pour la raison qu'Ackley faisait jamais rien le samedi soir sauf rester dans sa chambre à tripoter ses boutons ou quoi. Mal a dit que ça l'embêtait pas vraiment mais que ça l'emballait pas non plus. Il aimait pas trop Ackley. Bon, on est allés dans nos piaules pour s'habiller et tout en mettant mes bottes et mon fourbi j'ai braillé pour savoir si Ackley voulait venir au cinoche. Il m'a très bien entendu à travers les rideaux de la douche, mais il a pas répondu illico. C'était le genre de type qui détestait vous répondre illico. Finalement il s'est amené à travers les foutus rideaux et il était là sur le rebord de la douche à me demander qui est-ce qu'y aurait à part moi. Fallait toujours qu'il sache qui est-ce qu'y aurait. Ce type, je vous jure, s'il fait un jour naufrage et qu'on va le chercher avec un canot de sauvetage, avant de monter faudra d'abord qu'il se renseigne pour savoir qui tient les rames. Je lui ai dit « Mal Brossard ». Il a dit « Ce couillon... Bon, d'accord. Une seconde ». Il avait toujours l'air de vous faire une faveur.

Il a mis dans les cinq heures pour se préparer. En l'attendant j'ai ouvert la fenêtre et j'ai tassé de la neige dans mes mains et j'ai fait une boule. La neige était juste bien pour ça. J'ai pas lancé la boule. J'allais la lancer. Sur une auto garée de l'autre côté de la rue. Mais j'ai changé d'idée. L'auto était toute blanche et chouette. Puis j'allais la lancer contre une fontaine mais ça aussi c'était blanc et chouette. Finalement, cette boule je l'ai pas lancée. J'ai simplement fermé la fenêtre et j'ai déambulé dans la piaule en tassant la neige encore plus dur.

Et je l'avais toujours à la main quand on est montés dans le bus, moi et Brossard et Ackley. Le conducteur a rouvert les portières et il m'a dit de la jeter. J'ai dit que j'allais pas la lancer sur quelqu'un mais il m'a pas cru. Les gens veulent jamais vous croire.

Le film qui était à l'affiche, Brossard et Ackley l'avaient vu déjà, alors tout ce qu'on a fait, on s'est tapé deux hamburgers et après ça on s'est offert quelques parties de flipper, et puis on a repris le bus pour Pencey. Je m'en foutais de pas voir le film. C'était supposé être une comédie avec Cary Grant et toute cette merde de stars. J'étais allé d'autres fois au cinoche avec Brossard et Ackley et ils se fendaient la pipe pour des choses qu'étaient vraiment pas marrantes. Même d'être assis à côté d'eux c'était pas drôle.

Quand on est rentrés au dortoir il était seulement neuf heures moins le quart. Le gars Brossard, c'était un fana du bridge et il est allé faire un tour dans le couloir pour se chercher des partenaires. Le gars Ackley s'est établi dans ma chambre, pour changer. Mais au lieu de s'asseoir sur le bras du fauteuil de Stradlater il s'est vautré sur mon lit, la figure dans l'oreiller et tout. Il s'est mis à parler d'une voix ronronnante en pressant ses boutons. Je lui ai lancé au moins mille allusions plutôt transparentes mais sans réussir à m'en débarrasser. Il a continué à marmonner des choses sur une fille avec qui il était censé avoir fait l'amour l'été d'avant. Il m'avait déjà raconté ça mille fois. Et ça changeait à chaque fois. Ça s'était passé dans la Buick de son cousin et puis la minute suivante c'était sur la promenade d'une station balnéaire. Mais naturellement il frimait. Si quelqu'un était encore puceau c'était bien lui. Je suis même pas sûr qu'il ait jamais seulement tripoté un peu une fille. Pour finir en tout cas il a fallu que je me décide à lui dire que je devais faire la dissert' de Stradlater. S'il voulait bien vider les lieux je pourrais peut-être me concentrer. Ça a pris du temps comme d'habitude mais quand même il a fini par dégager. Alors je me suis mis en pyjama et robe de chambre, j'ai enfoncé ma casquette sur ma tête et j'ai attaqué la foutue dissert'.

L'ennui, c'est que j'arrivais pas à penser à une pièce ou une maison à décrire comme Stradlater avait dit. Je raffole pas de décrire les pièces ou les maisons. Donc voilà ce que j'ai fait, j'ai parlé du gant de base-ball de mon frère Allie. C'était un bon sujet de description. Vraiment bon. Mon frère Allie avait un gant de base-ball pour joueur gaucher. Parce qu'Allie était gaucher. Ce qui prêtait à description c'est qu'y avait des poèmes écrits sur les doigts et partout. A l'encre verte. Mon frère les copiait sur son gant pour avoir quelque chose à lire quand il était sur le terrain et qu'il attendait que ça redémarre. Maintenant il est mort, mon frère. Il a eu une leucémie, il est mort quand on était dans le Maine, le 18 juillet 1946. Vous l'auriez aimé. Il avait deux ans de moins que moi mais il était dans les cinquante fois plus intelligent. Il était super-intelligent. Ses professeurs écrivaient tout le temps à ma mère pour lui dire quel plaisir ça leur faisait d'avoir Allie dans leur classe. Et c'était pas du baratin. Ils le pensaient pour de vrai. Non seulement Allie était le plus intelligent de la famille mais en bien des façons il était le plus chouette. Il se mettait jamais en rogne. Les rouquins, on dit qu'ils se mettent en rogne facilement, mais Allie jamais. Je vais vous dire le genre de rouquin que c'était. J'ai commencé à jouer au golf quand j'avais à peine dix ans. Je me souviens d'une fois, l'année de mes douze ans, je plaçais la balle sur le tee et j'ai eu comme l'impression que si je me retournais je verrais Allie. Je me suis retourné. Et tout juste, il était là, assis sur son vélo, de l'autre côté de la clôture — y avait cette clôture qui entourait le terrain — et il était là, à cent cinquante mètres de moi environ qui me regardait faire. Voilà le genre de rouquin que c'était. Bon Dieu, on a jamais vu un môme aussi chouette. Pendant les repas ça lui arrivait de rire tellement en pensant à quelque chose qu'il en tombait presque de sa chaise. C'était l'année de mes treize ans et mes vieux allaient être forcés de me faire psychanalyser et tout parce que j'avais brisé toutes les vitres du garage. Je leur en veux pas. Je couchais dans le garage, la nuit où Allie est mort, et j'ai brisé toutes les foutues vitres à coups de poing, juste comme ça. J'ai même essayé de démolir aussi les vitres du break qu'on avait cet été-là, mais ma main était déjà cassée et tout, alors j'ai pas pu. Un truc idiot faut bien le dire, mais je savais plus trop ce que je faisais et vous, vous savez pas comment il était, Allie. J'ai encore quelquefois une douleur à la main par temps de pluie, et je peux pas serrer le poing — pas le serrer complètement — mais à part ça je m'en fiche. J'ai jamais eu l'intention d'être chirurgien, ou violoniste.

En tout cas c'est ce que j'ai décrit dans la dissert' pour Stradlater. Le gant de base-ball d'Allie. Justement je l'avais dans ma valise alors je l'ai sorti et j'ai recopié les poèmes qui étaient griffonnés dessus. Tout ce que j'ai eu à faire c'est de changer le nom d'Allie qu'aurait montré que c'était mon frère et pas le frère à Stradlater. Je peux pas dire que ça m'emballait mais j'étais incapable de penser à autre chose de descriptif. D'ailleurs j'aimais bien, comme sujet. Ça m'a pris à peu près une heure parce qu'il a fallu que je me serve de la machine à écrire pourrie de Stradlater et elle se bloquait sans arrêt. La mienne, je l'avais prêtée à un type qui logeait au bout du couloir.

J'ai fini vers les 10 h 30. Je me sentais pas fatigué, aussi j'ai regardé un moment par la fenêtre. Il neigeait plus mais de temps en temps on entendait une voiture qu'avait des problèmes de démarrage. On entendait aussi ronfler Ackley. A travers les rideaux de la douche. Il avait de la sinusite et quand il dormait il suffoquait un brin. Ce mec, il avait tout. Sinusite, boutons, dents gâtées, mauvaise haleine, ongles pourris. On pouvait pas s'empêcher de le plaindre un peu, le pauvre con.

CHAPITRE 6

Y a des choses, on n'arrive pas à s'en souvenir. En ce moment je pense à Stradlater quand il est revenu après son rencard avec Jane. Pas moyen de me rappeler exactement ce que je faisais quand j'ai reconnu son foutu pas dans le couloir. Probablement que j'étais encore en train de regarder par la fenêtre, mais je vous jure, je m'en souviens plus. J'étais trop tracassé, voilà tout. Quand je suis vraiment tracassé, je me contente pas d'attendre que ça passe. Souvent même ça me donne la colique ; mais je vais pas aux chiottes ; je suis trop tracassé pour y aller. Je veux pas arrêter de me tracasser pour y aller. Si vous connaissiez Stradlater vous seriez tout pareil. Cette espèce de salaud et moi il nous était déjà arrivé de sortir ensemble avec des filles, alors je sais de quoi je parle. C'est un mec qu'a pas de scrupules. Sans blague.

Bon. Y avait un lino tout le long du couloir et on entendait les pas qui se rapprochaient. Je me rappelle même pas où j'étais assis quand il est entré — à la fenêtre ou dans mon fauteuil ou dans le sien. Je me rappelle pas, je vous jure.

Il est arrivé en râlant à cause du froid au-dehors. Puis il a dit « Ousqu'ils sont, les autres ? C'est comme la morgue, ici ». J'ai même pas pris la peine de lui répondre. S'il manquait de jugeote au point de pas se rendre compte qu'on était samedi soir et que tout le monde était sorti, ou au plumard, ou at home pour le week-end, j'allais pas me casser à le lui dire. Il a commencé à se déshabiller. Et pas un foutu mot sur Jane. Pas un. Moi non plus j'en pipais pas un. Je me contentais de l'observer. Tout ce qu'il a dit c'est merci de lui avoir prêté ma veste. Il l'a mise sur un cintre et il l'a rangée dans la penderie.

Ensuite, il a dénoué sa cravate et il m'a demandé si j'avais écrit sa foutue dissert'. Je lui ai dit qu'elle était sur son pageot. Il l'a prise et il l'a lue, en déboutonnant sa chemise. Il était debout, torse nu, à lire et à se frotter les pectoraux et l'estomac avec cet air stupide que ça lui donne. Faut toujours qu'il se caresse l'estomac et la poitrine. Il s'adore, ce mec.

Tout d'un coup il a gueulé « Holden. Sacré bordel. T'as parlé d'un gant de base-ball.

— Et alors ? » Que j'ai dit. Vachement glacé.

« Quoi, Et alors ? Je t'ai pas expliqué que ça devait décrire une maison ?

— T'as dit que ça devait être descriptif. Si c'est un gant de base-ball je vois pas la différence.

— Bon Dieu de bon Dieu ! » Il était dans tous ses états. Vraiment furax. « Tu fais toujours tout de travers. » Il m'a regardé, il a crié « Pas étonnant si on te fout à la porte. Tu fais rien comme il faudrait. Je te jure. Jamais rien ».

J'ai dit « Bon. Eh bien, rends-moi ça ». Je me suis approché, je lui ai arraché la feuille des mains. Puis je l'ai déchirée en quatre.

« Qu'est-ce qui te prend, bordel ? »

Je lui ai même pas répondu. J'ai jeté les morceaux dans la corbeille à papiers. Puis je me suis allongé sur le lit et pendant très longtemps lui et moi on s'est plus rien dit. Il a ôté toutes ses fringues sauf le slip, et moi, étendu sur mon lit, j'ai allumé une cigarette. C'était interdit de fumer dans les dortoirs mais on pouvait le faire tard dans la soirée quand tout le monde dormait ou était sorti, donc que personne sentirait la fumée. D'ailleurs, je le faisais juste pour embêter Stradlater. Ça le rendait dingue quand on se foutait du règlement. Lui il fumait jamais au dortoir. Seulement moi.

Il avait toujours pas sorti le moindre mot sur Jane. Alors moi, j'ai fini par remettre ça. « Si elle avait que la permission de 9 h 30, tu t'es vraiment pas pressé pour rentrer. Tu l'as mise en retard ? »

Il était assis au bord de son lit, il se coupait les ongles des orteils. Il a dit « De trois-quatre minutes. Y a qu'elle pour pas demander plus que la permission de 9 h 30 un samedi soir ». Bon Dieu, ce que je le détestais.

« Vous êtes allés à New York ?

— T'es pas bien ? Comment on aurait pu aller à New York ? Fallait qu'elle soit rentrée à 9 h 30, je t'ai dit.

— Manque de pot. »

Il a levé les yeux. Il a dit « Écoute, plutôt que de fumer dans la chambre, pourquoi tu vas pas dans les chiottes ? Toi t'es déjà renvoyé, mais moi faut que je tienne jusqu'aux exams. »

J'ai fait comme si j'avais pas entendu. J'ai continué à fumer comme un dingue. Je me suis seulement tourné sur le côté et je l'ai regardé se couper les ongles des pieds. Pencey, quelle boîte ! On passait son temps à regarder un mec ou un autre se couper les ongles des pieds ou se tripoter les boutons.

« Tu lui as dit bonjour pour moi ?

— Ouais. »

Mon œil. Le salaud.

J'ai continué « Qu'est-ce qu'elle a dit ? Tu lui as

demandé si elle laisse toujours ses dames au dernier rang ?

— Non, je lui pas demandé. Putain. Qu'est-ce que tu crois qu'on a fait toute la soirée ? Joué aux dames ? »

J'ai même pas répondu. Bon Dieu, ce que je pouvais le détester.

Au bout d'un moment, j'ai dit « Si t'es pas allé à New York, où t'es allé avec elle ? » J'arrivais pas à empêcher ma voix de trembler tous azimuts. Ouah. Je commençais à vachement m'énerver. J'avais comme l'*impression* qu'il s'était passé quelque chose.

Il avait fini de se les couper, ses foutus ongles. Il s'est levé du lit, et il était juste en slip et il s'est mis à rouler des mécaniques. Il s'est approché de mon paddock et il s'est penché au-dessus de moi et il me flanquait des gnons dans l'épaule soi-disant pour rigoler. J'ai dit « Merde, arrête. Où t'es allé avec elle si t'es pas allé à New York ?

— Nulle part. On est resté dans l'auto. » Il m'a redonné une mandale — toujours pour rigoler.

J'ai dit « Arrête, *merde*. L'auto à qui ?

— A Ed Banky. »

Ed Banky, l'entraîneur de basket, à Pencey. Le gars Stradlater était un de ses chouchous parce qu'il jouait centre dans l'équipe, et Ed Banky lui prêtait sa voiture. C'était interdit aux élèves d'emprunter les voitures des profs mais les salauds de sportifs, ils se tenaient les coudes. Dans tous les collèges que j'ai fréquentés, les salauds de sportifs se tenaient les coudes.

Stradlater continuait à m'asticoter. Il avait sa brosse à dents à la main. Il l'a mise dans sa bouche. J'ai dit « Et alors ? Vous avez fait ça dans la putain de bagnole d'Ed Banky ? Dis-le ». Ma voix tremblait comme c'était pas possible.

« T'as pas fini ? Ta sale langue, tu veux que je te l'astique au savon noir ?

— *Dis.*

— Secret professionnel, mon pote. »

La suite, je m'en souviens pas très bien. Je sais que je me suis levé de mon lit, comme si j'allais aux chiottes ou quoi, et alors j'ai voulu le frapper, de toutes mes forces, en plein sur la brosse à dents pour qu'elle lui transperce la gorge. Mais j'ai raté. J'ai pas touché au bon endroit mais seulement sur le côté de la tête ou par là. Ça lui a probablement fait un peu mal mais pas autant que j'aurais voulu. Ça lui aurait sans doute fait bien plus mal mais je me suis servi de ma main droite et je peux pas serrer le poing, à cause de cette fracture que j'ai eue.

Et, sans trop savoir comment, je me suis retrouvé sur le foutu plancher et Stradlater installé sur ma poitrine avec la figure toute rouge. C'est-à-dire que ses foutus genoux m'écrasaient la poitrine et il pesait bien une tonne. Il me tenait les poignets alors je pouvais pas cogner. Je l'aurais tué.

Il a dit et répété « Mais qu'est-ce qui te prend, bon Dieu ? » et son imbécile de tronche devenait de plus en plus rouge.

J'ai dit « Ote de là tes genoux dégueulasses ». Je hurlais presque. Sans blague. « Allez, tire-toi de là, salopard. »

Il bougeait pas. Il a continué à me tenir les poignets et moi j'ai continué à l'appeler salopard pendant au moins dix heures. J'ai du mal à me rappeler tout ce que je lui ai dit. Je lui ai dit de pas se figurer qu'il pouvait faire ça avec n'importe quelle fille quand ça lui chantait. Je lui ai dit qu'il en avait rien à glander qu'une fille garde ou garde pas ses dames au dernier rang, pour la bonne raison qu'il était un crétin. Il avait horreur qu'on l'appelle un crétin. Tous les crétins ont horreur qu'on leur dise qu'ils sont des crétins.

« Maintenant tu la fermes, Holden, il a dit, avec toujours la tronche cramoisie. Tu la fermes. Point.

— Tu sais même pas si son prénom c'est Jane ou June, foutu crétin de mon cul.

— Maintenant, Holden, *ferme-la*, il a dit, bon Dieu, je t'aurai averti. Si tu la fermes pas je te fous une pêche. »

J'ai dit « Ote de là tes genoux de crétin puant.

— Si je te laisse aller, tu la fermes ? »

J'ai même pas répondu.

Il a redemandé « Holden, si je te laisse aller, tu la fermes, oui ou non ?

— Oui. »

Il s'est relevé et moi aussi je me suis relevé. J'avais la poitrine en compote à cause de ses saletés de genoux. J'ai dit « T'es rien qu'une saloperie de sinistre crétin ».

Ça l'a rendu totalement dingue. Il a secoué son doigt devant mon nez. « Holden, sacré bordel, maintenant je t'avertis. Pour la dernière fois. Si tu fermes pas ta gueule je vais... »

J'ai dit « Et pourquoi je la fermerais ? » Et là encore je hurlais littéralement. « C'est bien le problème avec les crétins de ton espèce. Vous voulez jamais discuter. De rien. C'est comme ça qu'on reconnaît un crétin. Il veut jamais rien discuter d'intell... »

Alors c'est parti et je me suis retrouvé au tapis. Je me souviens pas si j'étais complètement K.O. mais je crois pas. C'est plutôt dur de mettre quelqu'un complètement K.O. Sauf dans les films. Mais je saignais du nez tous azimuts. Quand j'ai rouvert les yeux le gars Stradlater se tenait juste au-dessus de moi. Il avait sous le bras sa foutue trousse de toilette. « Bon Dieu, pourquoi que tu fermes pas ta gueule quand on te le dit ? » Il avait l'air plutôt énervé. C'était probablement la trouille que je me sois fendu le crâne quand il avait cogné sur le plancher. J'avais rien de cassé. Dommage. Stradlater a dit encore « Putain, tu l'as bien cherché ». Ouah. Il avait l'air vachement mal à l'aise.

Je me suis même pas donné la peine de me relever. Je suis resté couché par terre en continuant à l'appeler sinistre crétin. J'étais furax, j'en pleurais presque.

Il a dit « Écoute, va te laver la tronche. Tu m'entends ? »

Je lui ai dit d'aller se laver la sienne, de tronche, sa saleté de tronche de crétin. C'était pas très malin mais j'étais tellement furax. Je lui ai dit de s'arrêter chez le concierge, Mr. Schmidt, en allant aux lavabos et de faire ça avec Mrs. Schmidt. Elle avait dans les soixante-cinq piges.

J'ai attendu que le gars Stradlater ferme la porte et s'éloigne vers les chiottes et alors seulement je me suis relevé. J'ai cherché partout ma foutue casquette. Finalement je l'ai retrouvée. Elle était sous le lit. Je l'ai enfoncée sur mon crâne, j'ai tourné la visière vers l'arrière parce que c'était plus à mon goût, puis je suis allé regarder ma tête de con dans la glace. Vous avez jamais rien vu d'aussi sanglant. Du sang, j'en avais partout, sur la bouche et le menton et même sur mon pyjama et ma robe de chambre. C'était un spectacle à faire peur et en même temps je trouvais ça fascinant. J'avais l'air d'un gros dur. Je m'étais battu à peu près deux fois dans ma vie et les deux fois j'avais dérouillé. Je suis pas un dur. Si vous voulez savoir, je suis un pacifiste.

J'avais bien l'impression que le gars Ackley avait entendu le chambard, que ça l'avait réveillé. Aussi j'ai écarté les rideaux de la douche pour aller voir chez lui ce qu'il faisait. C'était pas souvent que j'y entrais, dans sa piaule. Ça chlinguait toujours un peu, bicause il avait pas tellement des habitudes de propreté.

CHAPITRE 7

Y AVAIT un petit peu de lumière qui filtrait à travers les rideaux, venant de notre chambre et tout, alors je voyais vaguement Ackley dans son paddock. J'étais foutrement sûr qu'il dormait pas. J'ai dit « Tu dors, Ackley ?

— Nan. »

C'était pas mal sombre et j'ai trébuché sur un soulier et j'ai bien failli me ramasser. Ackley s'est assis dans son lit, appuyé sur un coude. Il avait plein de blanc sur la figure, du produit pour les boutons. Dans l'obscurité ça lui donnait un peu l'air d'un fantôme.

J'ai dit « Qu'est-ce que tu fabriques ?

— Ce que je fabrique ? Figure-toi que j'essayais de dormir quand vous deux les mecs vous avez commencé tout ce boucan. Pourquoi vous vous êtes bagarrés ?

— Où elle est, la lumière ? » J'arrivais pas à trouver l'interrupteur. Je passais la main partout sur le mur.

« Pourquoi que tu veux de la lumière ? C'est juste à côté de ta main. »

J'ai fini par trouver le bouton. J'ai appuyé. Ackley a replié son bras devant ses yeux.

« Bordel » il a dit, « qu'est-ce qui t'est arrivé ? » Il parlait du sang et tout.

« J'ai eu une petite discussion avec Stradlater. » Je me suis assis sur le plancher. Y avait jamais de sièges dans cette piaule. Ce qu'ils en foutaient je me le demande. J'ai dit « Écoute, t'as pas envie de jouer un peu à la canasta ? » C'était un fana de la canasta.

« Tu saignes encores. Putain. Tu ferais mieux de mettre quelque chose dessus.

— Ça va s'arrêter. Écoute. Qu'est-ce que tu penses d'une partie de canasta ?

— De canasta. Putain. Tu sais quelle heure il est, non ?

— Il est pas tard. Dans les onze heures, onze heures et demie. Pas plus.

— *Pas plus !* » Puis il a dit : « Écoute, moi demain matin je me lève pour aller à la messe, bordel. Vous deux, vous vous mettez à brailler et à vous battre en plein milieu de la nuit... et pourquoi vous vous êtes battus ? »

J'a dit « C'est une trop longue histoire. Je voudrais pas te les briser. C'est pour ton bien ». Je lui racontais jamais ma vie privée. D'abord, il était encore plus abruti que Stradlater. A côté d'Ackley, Stradlater c'était un génie. J'ai demandé « Hé, c'est okay si je dors dans le plumard d'Ely ? Il rentre pas avant demain soir, non ? » Je le savais qu'il rentrait pas. Ely allait chez lui pratiquement tous les week-ends.

« Moi j'ai pas la moindre idée de quand il rentre », a dit Ackley.

Ouah. C'était chiant. « Qu'est-ce que tu veux dire, bon Dieu ? Tu sais pas quand il rentre ? Il revient jamais avant le dimanche soir, non ?

— Non. Mais bordel je peux pas dire à n'importe qui de coucher dans son plume si l'envie lui prend. »

Ça m'a tué. Je me suis étiré un peu — j'étais

toujours assis par terre — et j'ai tapoté sa foutue épaule. J'ai dit « Môme Ackley, t'es un prince. Tu le savais ?

— Non. Mais c'est normal, je peux pas dire à n'importe qui de coucher dans son...

— T'es un vrai prince. Môme, t'es un gars cultivé et raffiné. » Et allez donc. « T'aurais pas des cigarettes, par hasard ? Si tu me dis que t'en as je tombe raide.

— Eh bien non, j'en ai pas. Écoute, pourquoi vous vous êtes bagarrés ? »

J'ai pas répondu. Tout ce que j'ai fait, c'est me lever et aller regarder par la fenêtre. Brusquement je me sentais très seul. J'avais presque envie d'être mort.

Ackley a demandé, pour la cinquantième fois « Pourquoi vous vous êtes bagarrés ? » Il commençait à m'emmerder.

J'ai dit « A cause de toi.

— De *moi* ? Putain.

— Ouais. Je défendais ton honneur. Stradlater disait que tu étais un pourri. Je pouvais pas laisser passer. »

Il s'est drôlement énervé. « Il a dit ça ? Sans blague ? »

J'ai admis que c'en était une, de blague, et je me suis couché sur le paddock d'Ely. Ouah, je me sentais si mal fichu. Je me sentais vachement seul.

J'ai dit « Ça chlingue ici. Tes chaussettes, on les sent de loin. Tu les donnes jamais à laver ?

— Si ça te plaît pas, tu sais ce qui te reste à faire, a dit Ackley, très spirituel. Et tu pourrais peut-être éteindre cette saloperie de lumière ? »

Mais j'ai pas éteint tout de suite. Je suis resté allongé sur le plumard d'Ely, et je pensais à Jane et tout. Quand je pensais à elle et Stradlater dans l'auto de ce gros cul d'Ed Banky, garée quelque part, je me sentais devenir complètement cinglé.

Chaque fois que j'y pensais l'envie me prenait de me jeter par la fenêtre. Ce qu'il y a, c'est que vous connaissez pas Stradlater. Moi je le connais. A Pencey, la plupart des gars comme Ackley, par exemple, ils *parlent* tout le temps de rapports sexuels avec les filles. Mais le gars Stradlater, lui, des rapports il en a pour de vrai. Personnellement je pourrais nommer au moins deux filles qui ont fait ça avec lui. Sans rire.

J'ai demandé « Môme Ackley, tu voudrais pas me dire l'histoire de ta vie aventureuse ?

— Toi tu voudrais pas éteindre la lumière. Demain matin je me lève pour la messe. »

Je l'ai éteinte, sa foutue lumière, si fallait que ça pour le rendre heureux. Et je me suis recouché sur le plumard à Ely.

« Qu'est-ce que tu veux faire ? dormir ici ? » a demandé Ackley. Ouah, c'était vraiment l'hôte parfait.

« Peut-être. Ou peut-être pas. Arrête de te tracasser.

— Ça me tracasse pas. Mais si Ely s'amène j'ai pas envie qu'il trouve un gars dans son pageot.

— Relaxe-toi. Je vais pas dormir là. Ça me ferait mal d'abuser de ton hospitalité. »

Deux minutes plus tard il ronflait à pleins tubes. Je suis resté étendu dans le noir, et j'essayais de pas penser à la môme Jane avec Stradlater dans la foutue bagnole à Ed Banky. Mais c'était presque impossible. L'ennui, c'est que je connaissais la technique du mec Stradlater. Ce qui n'arrangeait rien. Une fois, lui et moi on avait été ensemble dans l'auto d'Ed Banky, Stradlater à l'arrière avec sa fille, et moi à l'avant avec la mienne. Faut voir la technique qu'il avait, le salaud. Tout d'abord il commençait à baratiner la fille sur un ton tranquille, très *sincère* — comme s'il était pas seulement un très beau gars mais aussi un gars très gentil et *sincère*. Rien qu'à l'écouter, j'avais envie de vomir. La fille répétait « Non *je t'en prie*. Pas ça. *Je t'en prie*. » Mais le gars Stradlater continuait de la baratiner avec sa voix si sincère, à l'Abraham Lincoln, et finalement y a eu ce terrible silence à l'arrière de l'auto. C'était vachement embarrassant. Je pense pas qu'ils l'ont vraiment fait, ce soir-là, mais ils ont été vachement près de le faire. Vachement.

Comme j'étais couché là, m'efforçant de pas trop réfléchir, j'ai entendu Stradlater qui revenait des lavabos et rentrait dans la chambre. Je l'entendais qui rangeait ses affaires de toilette crasseuses et tout, et puis qui ouvrait la fenêtre. C'est un adepte de l'air frais. Puis, au bout d'un petit moment, il a éteint la lumière. Il avait même pas jeté un coup d'œil pour voir où j'étais passé.

Dehors aussi, dans la rue, c'était déprimant. Y avait même plus de bruit de voitures. Je me sentais tellement seul et mal foutu que j'ai voulu réveiller Ackley.

J'ai dit « Hey, Ackley ! », guère plus fort qu'un mumure pour que Stradlater entende pas à travers les rideaux de la douche.

Ackley non plus a pas entendu.

« Hey, Ackley ! »

Il a toujours pas entendu. Il dormait comme une souche.

« Hey, Ackley ! »

Cette fois il s'est réveillé.

Il a dit « Qu'est-ce qui te prend, bon Dieu ? Je dormais, bordel.

— Écoute. Comment on fait pour entrer dans un monastère ? » j'ai demandé. Une idée qui m'était venue. « Est-ce qu'y faut être catholique et tout ?

— Sûrement qu'y faut être catholique. Mon salaud, c'est pour me poser une question aussi idiote que tu m'as rév...

— Haha, rendors-toi. En fin de compte, j'entre pas au monastère. Avec ma chance habituelle, j'en choisirais probablement un avec dedans des moines tordus. Tous des foutus cons. Ou juste des cons. »

Quand j'ai dit ça, Ackley s'est dressé dans son lit. Il a braillé « Écoute, ce que tu dis de *moi* je m'en branle, mais si tu commences à raconter des vacheries au sujet de ma foutue religion, bordel...

— Doucement, j'ai dit. Personne raconte des vacheries sur ta foutue religion. » Je suis descendu du pageot à Ely et j'ai ramé vers la porte. Je m'en ressentais pas de rester plus longtemps dans cette atmosphère débile. Je me suis quand même arrêté en route pour prendre la main d'Ackley et la secouer avec une ardeur pas trop convaincante. Il a retiré sa main. Il a dit « Qu'est-ce qui te prend ?

— Rien. Je voulais seulement te remercier d'être un tel foutu prince, c'est tout. » J'ai dit ça d'une voix très sincère. Et puis « T'es un chef, môme Ackley. Tu le sais ?

— Gros malin. Un jour quelqu'un va te casser la... »

Je me suis même pas donné la peine de l'écouter. J'ai refermé la foutue porte et je me suis trouvé dans le couloir.

Tout le monde dormait, ou bien était sorti, ou à la maison pour le week-end, et dans le couloir c'était très très calme et déprimant. Devant la porte de Leahy et Hoffman il y avait le carton vide d'un tube de dentifrice et en me dirigeant vers l'escalier j'ai tapé dedans à coups de pied avec mes pantoufles fourrées de mouton. Ce que je pensais faire, je pensais que je pourrais descendre voir ce que fabriquait Mal Brossard. Et puis tout d'un coup j'ai décidé que ce que j'*allais* faire c'était foutre le camp — à l'instant même et tout. Pas attendre au mercredi ni rien. Je voulais plus continuer à traîner là. Je me sentais trop cafardeux, trop seul. Alors j'ai décidé que je prendrais une chambre dans un hôtel à New York — un petit hôtel pas cher et tout — et que je me laisserais vivre jusqu'à mercredi. Et puis, mercredi, j'irais à la maison, bien reposé, en pleine forme. Je supposais que mes parents auraient pas la lettre du père Thurmer disant que j'étais renvoyé avant peut-être mardi ou mercredi. Je voulais attendre qu'ils l'aient reçue pour rentrer à la maison, et qu'ils aient complètement digéré la nouvelle. Je voulais surtout pas être là quand la lettre arriverait. Ma mère ce genre de truc ça la rend hystérique. Mais une fois que c'est digéré elle prend pas trop mal les choses. En plus, j'avais comme qui dirait besoin d'un peu de congé. J'étais à bout de nerfs. Sans blague.

Bon. En tout cas, c'est ce que j'ai décidé. Aussi je suis retourné dans ma chambre et j'ai allumé la lumière pour faire mes bagages et tout. Y avait déjà pas mal de choses dans mes valoches. Le gars Stradlater s'est même pas réveillé. J'ai allumé une cigarette et je me suis rhabillé et puis j'ai fini de remplir mes deux valises. Ça m'a pas pris plus de deux minutes. Les bagages avec moi c'est toujours du rapide.

Y a une chose qui m'a fichu un coup. Fallait que je remballe mes patins à glace tout neufs que ma mère venait de m'envoyer deux jours plus tôt. Oui ça m'a fichu un coup. Je pouvais voir ma mère entrer chez Spaulding et poser au vendeur un million de questions idiotes — et voilà que j'étais encore flanqué dehors. Je me suis senti vraiment triste. Elle m'avait pas acheté les patins qu'il fallait — je voulais des patins de compétition et elle avait pris des patins de hockey — mais quand même je me sentais vraiment triste. Presque chaque fois qu'on me fait un cadeau, pour finir je me sens vraiment triste.

Lorsque mes bagages ont été bouclés j'ai fait le

compte de mon fric. Je me rappelle pas exactement combien j'avais mais j'étais à l'aise. La semaine d'avant, ma grand-mère m'avait sérieusement renfloué. J'ai une grand-mère qui s'en balance de dépenser son pognon. Elle perd un peu la tête — elle est vieille comme le monde — et elle m'envoie au moins quatre fois par an de l'argent pour mon anniversaire. En tout cas, même à l'aise, j'aurais pas craché sur quelques dollars de plus. On sait jamais. Alors ce que j'ai fait, je suis allé au bout du couloir réveiller ce type, Frederick Woodruff, qui m'avait emprunté ma machine à écrire. Je lui ai demandé combien il m'en donnerait. C'était un gars qu'avait du fric. Il a dit qu'il savait pas. Il a dit que ma machine il avait pas vraiment envie de l'acheter. Finalement il l'a quand même achetée. Elle coûte environ quatre-vingt-dix dollars et il m'en a donné seulement vingt dollars. Il était furax que je l'aie réveillé.

Quand j'ai été prêt à partir, avec mes valoches et tout, je me suis arrêté un petit moment près de l'escalier et j'ai jeté un dernier regard sur le couloir. J'avais les larmes aux yeux, je sais pas pourquoi. J'ai mis ma casquette sur ma tête et tourné la visière vers l'arrière comme j'aime et alors j'ai gueulé aussi fort que j'ai pu *Dormez bien, espèces de crétins*. Je parierais que j'ai réveillé tous ces salopards de l'étage. Et puis je suis parti. Un abruti avait jeté des épluchures de cacahuètes sur les marches de l'escalier ; un peu plus je me cassais la figure.

CHAPITRE 8

IL était trop tard pour appeler un taxi, aussi je suis allé à pied jusqu'à la gare. C'était pas très loin, mais il faisait un froid de loup et la neige rendait la marche pas commode et mes valoches me tapaient dans les jambes. Ça paraissait quand même bon de prendre l'air. Un seul ennui, le froid qui me piquait les narines et le bord de la lèvre supérieure là où Stradlater avait cogné. Il m'avait écrasé la lèvre contre les dents et c'était plutôt sensible. En tout cas pour mes oreilles j'avais vraiment du tout confort. Cette casquette que je m'étais offerte, elle avait des oreillettes repliées à l'intérieur et je les ai sorties — l'allure que ça me donnait je m'en foutais totalement. D'ailleurs y avait personne dehors. Les gens ils étaient tous au pieu.

J'ai eu de la chance. Quand je suis arrivé à la gare j'ai attendu le train pas plus de dix minutes. En l'attendant, j'ai ramassé de la neige pour me frotter la figure. Ça saignait encore un peu.

D'habitude, j'aime bien prendre le train, la nuit en particulier, avec la lumière allumée et les vitres tellement noires, et puis le type qui circule dans le couloir en vendant du café et des sandwichs et des magazines. Si je prends le train le soir, je peux même, d'habitude, lire une de ces histoires idiotes des magazines sans dégueuler. Vous voyez de quoi je parle. Une de ces histoires où il y a tous ces types à la con qui s'appellent David et toutes ces filles à la noix qui s'appellent Linda ou Marcia et qui passent leur temps à allumer les foutues pipes des susnommés David. Oui, d'habitude, je peux même lire une de ces histoires pourries quand je suis dans un train, le soir. Mais cette fois c'était différent. Ça me disait vraiment pas grand-chose. Je suis resté assis sans rien faire. Tout ce que j'ai fait, c'est ôter ma casquette et la mettre dans ma poche.

Et voilà qu'à Trenton, y a une dame qui est montée et qui s'est assise auprès de moi. Pratiquement le wagon était vide bicause ça commençait à être tard et tout, mais elle s'est assise auprès de moi plutôt que sur une banquette vide parce que j'étais sur la banquette près du couloir et elle avait un gros sac. Elle a posé le sac en plein milieu du couloir et le contrôleur ou n'importe qui aurait pu se prendre les pieds dedans. Elle portait une orchidée au revers de son tailleur, comme si elle venait d'une grande grande soirée ou quoi. Elle avait dans les quarante ou quarante-cinq ans, je suppose, mais elle était très bien. Les femmes, ça me tue. Sincèrement. Je ne veux pas dire que je suis un obsédé sexuel — oh ! non, quoique ça m'intéresse, le sexe. Mais les femmes, je les aime bien, voilà tout. Elles laissent toujours leurs foutus sacs en plein milieu du couloir.

Bon. On était assis là, et brusquement elle m'a dit « Excusez-moi, mais n'est-ce pas un autocollant de Pencey Prep ? » Elle regardait mes valises, dans le filet à bagages.

J'ai dit « Exact ». Oui, elle avait raison. J'avais un foutu autocollant de Pencey sur une des valoches. Pas malin de ma part, faut reconnaître.

Elle a dit « Oh ! vous êtes à Pencey ? » Elle avait

une voix agréable. Ou plus précisément comme une agréable voix de téléphone. Elle aurait dû transporter un téléphone avec elle.

J'ai dit oui.

« Oh ! c'est merveilleux. Peut-être que vous connaissez mon fils. Ernest Morrow ? Il est à Pencey.

— Oui bien sûr. On est dans la même classe. »

Son fils était sans aucun doute le plus sale con qui soit jamais allé à Pencey, dans toute l'histoire pourrie de ce collège. Son fils, quand il venait de prendre sa douche, il arrêtait pas de faire claquer sa vieille serviette mouillée sur le cul des gars qu'il rencontrait dans le couloir. Voilà le genre de mec que c'était.

Elle a dit encore « Oh ! c'est merveilleux ». Mais pas d'un ton ringard. Elle était seulement très sympa et tout. « Il faudra que je raconte à Ernest que nous nous sommes rencontrés. Pourriez-vous me dire votre nom ? »

J'ai répondu « Rudolf Schmidt ». Je m'en ressentais pas de lui raconter toute l'histoire de ma vie. Rudolf Schmidt, c'était le nom du gardien de notre bâtiment.

Elle a demandé « Vous aimez Pencey ?

— Pencey ? Ça va. C'est pas le paradis, mais c'est un collège pas plus mauvais que les autres avec certains des profs qui sont très consciencieux.

— Ernest s'y plaît tellement ! »

J'ai dit « Oui, bien sûr ». Puis je me suis mis à débiter des conneries. « Ernest, il s'adapte à tout et à tout le monde. Vraiment. Je veux dire, il sait vraiment comment s'y prendre pour s'adapter. »

Elle a dit « Vous trouvez ? » On voyait qu'elle était drôlement intéressée.

« Ernest ? Mais oui. » Je l'ai regardée ôter ses gants. Ouah, elle avait des diam's à tous les doigts.

Elle a dit « Je viens de me casser un ongle en

70

sortant du taxi ». Elle a levé les yeux et elle a eu comme un sourire. Elle avait un sourire extra. Sans blague. La plupart des gens ont à peine un sourire, ou bien un sourire dégueu. « Mon mari et moi, nous ne sommes pas sans inquiétude au sujet d'Ernest. Nous avons l'impression qu'il n'est pas très sociable.

— Pas sociable ? Comment ça ?

— Eh bien... C'est un garçon très sensible. Il a toujours eu du mal à se faire des amis. Peut-être prend-il les choses trop au sérieux pour son âge. »

Sensible. Ça m'a tué. Ce type, Morrow, il est à peu près aussi sensible qu'une lunette de W.-C.

Je l'ai bien regardée. Elle avait pas l'air d'une andouille. Elle avait l'air d'une personne très capable de se faire une idée claire du genre de petit con qu'elle a pour fils. Mais on peut jamais dire, avec les mères. Elles sont toutes légèrement fêlées. En tout cas celle-là me plaisait. La mère du gars Morrow. Elle était très chouette. Je lui ai demandé « Puis-je vous offrir une cigarette ? »

Elle a jeté un coup d'œil autour d'elle. « Je ne crois pas, Rudolf, que ce compartiment soit pour fumeurs. » Rudolf. Ça m'a tué.

« Aucune importance, j'ai dit. On peut toujours fumer jusqu'à ce que quelqu'un râle. » Elle a accepté la cigarette et je lui ai donné du feu.

Elle s'y prenait bien. Elle aspirait la fumée et tout mais elle l'avalait pas à toute pompe comme le font la plupart des femmes de son âge. Elle avait du charme. Elle avait aussi beaucoup de sex-appeal, si vous voulez savoir.

Elle me regardait d'un air bizarre. Elle a dit tout d'un coup « Je me trompe peut-être mais j'ai l'impression que vous saignez du nez, Rudolf. »

J'ai hoché la tête ; et sorti mon mouchoir. « J'ai reçu une boule de neige dans la figure. Une très serrée, très dure. » Je lui aurais probablement raconté ce qui m'était arrivé en vrai si ça n'avait pas demandé trop de temps. En tout cas je l'aimais bien. Je commençais à regretter de lui avoir dit que mon nom était Rudolf Schmidt. J'ai dit encore « Ce brave Ernie. C'est un des gars les plus populaires à Pencey. Vous le saviez ?

— Oh ! non. »

J'ai hoché la tête. « Ça nous a pris pas mal de temps pour le connaître. C'est un drôle de garçon. Un garçon *étrange*, de bien des manières. Vous voyez ce que je veux dire ? Par exemple, la première fois qu'on s'est vus, j'ai pensé qu'il était plutôt snob. C'est ce que j'ai pensé. Mais j'avais tort. C'est juste qu'il a une personnalité tout à fait originale et que ça prend un certain temps pour le connaître. »

Mrs. Morrow disait rien mais si vous aviez pu la voir. Ouah. Prenez la mère de n'importe qui et tout ce qu'elle veut entendre c'est que son fils est formidable.

Et alors je me suis lancé dans un super-baratin. J'ai demandé « Est-ce qu'il vous a parlé des élections ? Les élections de notre classe ? »

Elle a fait non de la tête. Je l'avais mise en transe. Sans blague.

« Eh bien, on était tout un tas à vouloir qu'Ernie soit président de la classe. C'est-à-dire, il était quasiment choisi à l'unanimité. C'est-à-dire qu'il était le seul gars capable de faire les choses comme il fallait. » Ouah. J'étais vachement lancé. « Mais qui a été élu ? Harry Fencer... Et pourquoi ? Pour la raison bien simple qu'Ernie a pas voulu nous laisser le présenter comme candidat. Parce qu'il est si modeste et timide et tout. Il a *refusé*. Ouah. Il est *vraiment* timide. Vous devriez l'encourager à surmonter sa timidité. » Je l'ai regardée. « Il vous a pas raconté ça ?

— Oh ! non. »

Encore une fois j'ai hoché la tête. « C'est bien Ernie. Tout à fait lui. Il a qu'un seul défaut, il est trop timide et modeste. Vous devriez l'aider à gagner un peu d'assurance. »

A ce moment précis, le contrôleur est venu réclamer le billet de Mrs. Morrow et ça m'a donné l'occasion d'arrêter mes salades. Mais j'étais content de les lui avoir servies. Prenez un type comme Morrow qu'est toujours à taper sur le cul des gens à coups de serviette — et en cherchant à leur faire mal —, les types comme lui ils sont pas seulement des emmerdeurs quand ils sont jeunes, ils restent des emmerdeurs toute leur vie. Mais après tout ce que j'avais inventé on pouvait parier que Mrs. Morrow continuerait à penser à lui comme à un gars très timide et modeste qu'avait pas voulu se porter candidat pour être président. C'est bien possible. On peut pas dire. Les mères, dans ces cas-là, elles sont plutôt bornées.

J'ai dit « Voulez-vous qu'on boive un verre ? » Moi ça me tentait. « Si on allait au wagon-bar. Oui ? »

Elle a demandé « Êtes-vous sûr d'avoir le droit de vous faire servir des boissons alcoolisées ? » Mais elle prenait pas ses grands airs. Elle était trop sympa pour prendre ses grands airs.

« Eh bien, non, exactement, mais en général ça passe, vu ma taille. » J'ai dit encore « Et puis j'ai pas mal de cheveux blancs ». Je me suis tourné de profil et je lui ai montré mes cheveux blancs. Ça l'a fascinée. J'ai dit « Bon, alors, on y va ? D'accord ? » J'aurais bien aimé qu'elle dise oui.

« Non, vraiment. Je crois qu'il vaut mieux pas. Mais je vous remercie beaucoup. » Elle a ajouté « D'ailleurs, le wagon-bar est probablement fermé. Il est très tard, vous savez ». Elle avait raison. J'avais oublié l'heure qu'il était.

Enfin elle m'a encore regardé et elle a fait la remarque que je redoutais. « Ernie m'a écrit qu'il rentre à la maison mercredi. Que les vacances de Noël commencent mercredi. J'espère que vous n'avez pas reçu de mauvaises nouvelles de votre famille. » Elle avait l'air de s'inquiéter pour de bon. C'était visible qu'elle cherchait pas simplement à se mêler de mes affaires.

J'ai dit « Non. A la maison tout le monde va bien. C'est moi qui dois subir une opération.

— Oh ! je suis vraiment désolée. » Et on voyait qu'elle bluffait pas. Immédiatement, j'ai été tout aussi désolé d'avoir dit ça ; mais c'était parti.

« Rien de bien grave. Juste une minuscule tumeur au cerveau.

— Oh ! non. » Elle a mis la main devant sa bouche et tout.

« Mais ça ira, je m'en tirerai. C'est tout à fait à l'extérieur. Et un tout petit machin. Il faudra pas plus de deux minutes pour l'enlever. »

Et alors je me suis mis à étudier cet horaire des trains que j'avais sorti de ma poche. Rien que pour m'arrêter de mentir. Une fois que j'ai commencé, je pourrais continuer pendant des heures. Sans blagues. *Des heures.*

Après, on a plus beaucoup parlé. Elle a feuilleté ce numéro de *Vogue* qu'elle avait, et moi j'ai regardé un petit moment par la fenêtre. Elle descendait à Newark. Elle m'a souhaité mille fois bonne chance pour l'opération et tout. Elle m'appelait toujours Rudolf. Finalement elle m'a invité à rendre visite à son Ernie durant l'été, à Gloucester, Massachusetts. Elle disait que la maison était en plein sur la plage, et ils avaient un court de tennis et tout, mais je l'ai remerciée en lui expliquant que je devais accompagner ma grand-mère en Amérique du Sud. Et là je poussais un peu vu que ma grand-mère sort presque jamais de sa maison sauf peut-être pour un petit truc comme une matinée théâtrale. Mais je serais pas allé voir ce con de Morrow pour tout l'or du monde, même si j'avais été totalement dans la dèche.

CHAPITRE 9

La première chose que j'ai faite en débarquant à Penn Station, ça a été d'entrer dans une cabine téléphonique. J'avais envie de donner un coup de bigo à quelqu'un. J'ai laissé mes bagages dehors, en m'arrangeant pour pouvoir les surveiller. Mais à peine j'étais à l'intérieur, je me suis demandé qui je pourrais bien appeler. Mon frère D.B. était à Hollywood. Ma petite sœur Phoebé va au lit à neuf heures — alors je pouvais pas l'appeler. Ça lui aurait rien fait que je la réveille, mais c'est pas elle qui aurait répondu ; les parents auraient décroché ; donc pas question. Ensuite j'ai voulu passer un coup de fil à la mère de Jane Gallagher, pour savoir quand Jane était en vacances, mais non, ça me disait rien. D'ailleurs il était vachement tard. Autrement il y avait bien cette fille, Sally Hayes, on sortait souvent ensemble, et elle je savais qu'elle était déjà en vacances — elle m'avait écrit une longue lettre à la con m'invitant à venir la veille de Noël l'aider à garnir le sapin et tout — mais j'avais peur que ce soit sa mère qui réponde. Sa mère connaissait ma mère et je pouvais me la représenter tirant illico ses conclusions et regalopant jusqu'au téléphone au risque de se casser une jambe pour annoncer à ma

mère que j'étais à New York. Et puis j'avais pas
follement envie de parler à la vieille Hayes. Une
fois elle avait dit à Sally que j'étais un excité. Elle
disait que j'étais un excité sans but dans la vie. Puis
j'ai eu l'idée d'appeler Carl Luce, qui avait été à
Whooton en même temps que moi. Mais je l'aimais
pas des masses. Alors, pour finir, j'ai appelé personne. Au bout de vingt minutes au moins je suis
ressorti de la cabine. J'ai repris mes valises et j'ai
marché vers ce tunnel où sont les taxis, et j'en ai
pris un.

Je suis tellement distrait que j'ai donné au chauffeur du taxi ma vraie adresse, comme ça, par
habitude. J'avais complètement oublié que je devais
me planquer deux ou trois jours dans un hôtel pour
pas rentrer à la maison avant le début des vacances.
Quand je m'en suis souvenu on en était déjà à la
moitié du chemin. Alors j'ai dit « Hey, ça vous
ennuierait de faire demi-tour quand ça sera possible ? Je vous ai pas donné la bonne adresse. Je
voudrais retourner d'où on vient ».

Le chauffeur était un petit malin. « Je peux pas
faire demi-tour ici, mon vieux, c'est un sens unique.
Maintenant faut que je continue tout le chemin
jusqu'à la Quatre-vingt-dixième rue. »

J'ai pas voulu me lancer dans une discussion. J'ai
dit « Okay ». Puis ça m'est revenu à l'esprit, tout
d'un coup, « Hey dites donc, vous avez vu les
canards près de Central Park South ? Le petit lac ?
Vous savez pas par hasard où ils vont ces canards,
quand le lac est complètement gelé ? Vous savez
pas ? » Je me rendais compte qu'il y avait guère
plus d'une chance sur un million qu'il sache.

Il s'est retourné et il m'a regardé comme si j'étais
vraiment fêlé. « A quoi tu joues ? A te foutre de ma
gueule ?

— *Non* — c'est seulement que ça m'intéresserait
de savoir. »

Il a rien répondu. Et moi j'ai plus rien dit. Jusqu'à ce qu'on sorte du parc dans la Quatre-vingt-dixième rue. Là il a dit « Bon. Alors p'tit gars ? Où ? »

— Eh bien, le problème c'est que je veux pas aller dans un hôtel de l'East Side où je pourrais rencontrer des connaissances. Je voyage incognito. » Je déteste employer des expressions à la con comme "voyager incognito". Mais quand je suis avec un mec ringard, forcément je lui parle ringard. « Est-ce que vous sauriez par hasard ce qu'il y a comme orchestre au Taft, ou au New Yorker ?

— Pas la moindre idée, p'tit gars.

— Bon — eh bien déposez-moi à l'Edmont. Si vous voulez on peut s'arrêter en route et prendre un verre. Je vous invite. Je suis en fonds.

— Impossible. Désolé. » Très cordial, le pépère. Très forte personnalité.

On est allés à l'Edmont et j'ai rempli la fiche. Quand j'étais dans le taxi j'avais mis ma casquette sur ma tête juste comme ça, mais je l'ai ôtée avant d'entrer à l'hôtel. Je voulais pas avoir l'air d'un tordu. Ce qui est plutôt ironique car après j'ai appris que ce foutu hôtel était plein de pervers et de crétins. Des tordus en tous genres.

On m'a donné une chambre pourrie, avec comme vue par la fenêtre l'autre côté de l'hôtel. De la vue ou pas de vue, je m'en tamponnais. J'étais trop déprimé pour que ça me touche. Le groom qui m'a conduit à ma piaule était un très vieux type, dans les soixante-cinq piges. Je l'ai trouvé encore plus déprimant que la chambre pourrie. C'était un de ces gars au crâne déplumé qui essaient de cacher leur calvitie en ramenant en travers les cheveux qui leur restent sur le côté. Moi, plutôt que de faire ça, j'aimerais mieux être chauve. Et tout cas, quel boulot exaltant pour un type dans les soixante-cinq piges. Trimbaler les valises des autres et attendre le pourboire. Je suppose qu'il était pas trop intelligent mais c'est quand même effroyable.

Après son départ, je suis resté un moment tout habillé à regarder par la fenêtre. Vous pourriez pas croire ce qui se trafiquait dans l'autre aile de l'hôtel. Et les gens se donnaient même pas la peine de descendre les stores. J'ai vu un mec avec des cheveux gris, un air très distingué, et il était en caleçon, et il faisait quelque chose que vous trouveriez à peine croyable si je vous le raconte. Primo il a posé sa valise sur le lit. Secundo il en a sorti un tas de vêtements de femme et s'est habillé avec. Des vrais vêtements de femme — bas de soie, souliers à hauts talons, soutien-gorge, et un de ces corsets avec les lacets qui pendaient et tout. Et puis il a enfilé cette robe du soir, noire et très étroite. J'invente pas, je vous jure. Enfin il s'est mis à marcher de long en large dans la chambre à petits pas comme font les femmes, en fumant une cigarette et en se regardant dans la glace. Et il était tout seul. A moins qu'il y ait eu quelqu'un dans la salle de bain — là je peux pas dire. Et puis, par la fenêtre juste au-dessus de la sienne ou presque j'ai vu un gars et une fille qui s'aspergeaient mutuellement avec l'eau qu'ils avaient dans la bouche. C'était probablement pas de l'eau mais du whisky et de l'eau, mais je voyais pas ce qu'il y avait dans leurs verres. En tout cas, d'abord le gars prenait une gorgée et la crachait sur la fille, et après elle faisait la même chose sur lui. Bon Dieu, chacun son tour. Vous auriez dû les voir. Ça les rendait hystériques, comme s'il leur était jamais rien arrivé d'aussi drôle. Sans blague, c'était un hôtel qui grouillait de pervers. J'étais probablement le seul mec normal — si on peut dire. J'ai été fichument tenté d'envoyer un télégramme à Stradlater lui suggérant de prendre le premier train pour New York. Dans cet hôtel il aurait été le roi.

L'ennui, c'est que les idioties de ce genre, même si on voudrait pas que ça existe, à les regarder on est comme fasciné. Par exemple, cette fille qui se faisait cracher sur la figure, elle était vraiment pas mal. C'est ça mon problème. Dans ma tête, je suis probablement le type le plus vicieux que vous ayez jamais rencontré. Quelquefois je pense à des choses vraiment dégoûtantes que ma foi je ferais bien si l'occasion s'en présentait. Même, je me rends compte que ça peut être marrant, dans le genre dégueulasse, si un gars et une fille ont trop bu tous les deux, de s'asperger mutuellement la figure avec de l'eau ou quoi. Mais c'est *l'idée* qui me plaît pas, elle est puante, si on l'analyse. Je me dis que si on n'aime pas trop une fille, on devrait pas chahuter du tout avec elle, et si on l'aime, alors on est censé aimer sa figure et si on aime sa figure on devrait pas lui faire des saletés comme l'asperger d'eau et tout. C'est pas bien que des trucs dégoûtants puissent être tellement marrants. Quand on essaie de pas être *trop* dégoûtant, quand on essaie de pas gâcher quelque chose de vraiment bon, les filles elles vous aident pas beaucoup. Y a deux ans, j'ai connu une fille qu'était encore plus dégoûtante que moi. Ouah, pour une dégoûtante, c'en était une. Mais pendant un moment on s'est bien marrés, dans le genre dégoûtant. Le sexe, j'y comprends vraiment rien. On sait jamais où on en est. Pour le sexe j'arrête pas de me donner des règles et aussitôt je les oublie. L'année dernière je me suis donné pour règle de plus tripoter les filles que je trouve emmerdeuses. Et pourtant, la même semaine — le jour même je crois bien — avec cette andouille d'Anne-Louise Shermann, on a passé toute la soirée à se papouiller. Le sexe, c'est vraiment quelque chose que j'arrive pas à comprendre. Je vous jure ça me dépasse.

Comme je restais planté là, il m'est venu à l'idée que la môme Jane, je pourrais lui bigophoner à son collège au lieu d'appeler sa mère pour m'informer de la date des vacances. Les élèves avaient pas le droit de recevoir des communications tard le soir mais j'avais arrangé ma petite histoire. J'allais dire à la personne qui répondrait au téléphone que j'étais l'oncle de Jane. J'allais dire que la tante de Jane venait de mourir dans un accident d'auto. J'allais dire qu'il fallait que je parle à Jane immédiatement. Ça aurait sûrement marché. Si je l'ai pas fait c'est pour la seule raison que j'étais pas en forme. Ces combines-là, si on est pas en forme ça marche pas.

Au bout d'un petit moment je me suis assis dans un fauteuil et j'ai fumé deux cigarettes. Je dois reconnaître que je me sentais plutôt excité, sexuellement parlant. Alors tout d'un coup j'ai eu une idée, j'ai sorti mon portefeuille et je me suis mis à chercher l'adresse que m'avait donnée ce type de Princeton que j'avais rencontré à une surprise-partie l'été dernier. J'ai fini par la trouver. Dans mon portefeuille le papier avait pris une drôle de couleur mais on pouvait encore lire. C'était l'adresse d'une fille qu'était pas vraiment une prostituée mais qui faisait ça à l'occasion une fois de temps en temps à ce que m'avait dit le type de Princeton. Un jour, il l'avait amenée à un bal à Princeton et il avait bien failli se faire renvoyer. Elle avait été strip-teaseuse de music-hall ou quelque chose dans le genre. Bon. Je suis allé au téléphone et je l'ai appelée. Son nom c'était Faith Cavendish, et elle vivait à Stanford Arms Hotel, à l'angle de la Soixante-cinquième avenue et de Broadway. Sûrement un endroit minable.

D'abord j'ai pensé qu'elle était pas chez elle. Pas de réponse. Finalement quelqu'un a décroché.

J'ai fait « Allô ? » d'une voix grave pour qu'elle puisse pas deviner mon âge ou quoi. D'ailleurs j'ai la voix plutôt grave de nature.

Une voix de femme a dit « Allô ». D'un ton pas

80

trop aimable. Moi j'ai dit « Je parle bien à Miss Faith Cavendish ? »

Elle a demandé « Qui c'est ? Bordel, qui c'est qui m'appelle à une heure pareille ? »

Ça m'a foutu les foies. J'ai pris un ton tout ce qu'il y a d'adulte « Bon, je sais qu'il est très tard. Je vous prie de m'excuser, mais j'avais hâte de vous joindre ». J'ai dit ça d'un ton vachement charmeur. Vachement.

Elle a encore demandé « Qui c'est ?

— Écoutez, vous me connaissez pas, mais je suis un ami d'Eddie Birdsell. Il m'a conseillé, si un jour je venais en ville, de vous inviter à prendre un verre.

— *Qui ça* ? Vous êtes un ami de *qui* ? » Ouah ! une vraie tigresse. Elle en était presque à m'engueuler.

J'ai dit « Edmund Birdsell. Eddie Birdsell ». Je me souvenais plus si son prénom était Edmund ou Edward. Je l'avais rencontré une fois seulement, à cette foutue surprise-partie.

« J'connais personne qui s'appelle comme ça mon petit père. Et allez pas vous figurer que ça m'amuse qu'on m'réveille en plein milieu... »

J'ai insisté « Eddie Birdsell ? De Princeton ».

Je me rendais compte qu'elle se creusait la tête.

« Birdsell, Birdsell... De Princeton... Princeton College ?

— C'est ça.

— Et vous, vous êtes aussi de Princeton ?

— Disons... plus ou moins.

— Oh... Comment va Eddie ? Mais bordel c'est tout de même un peu fort d'appeler quelqu'un à c't'heure-là.

— Il va bien. Il m'a demandé de vous faire ses amitiés.

— Ben, merci. Faites-lui les miennes. » Puis elle a dit « Il est extra. Qu'est-ce qu'il fabrique à pré-

sent ? » Elle devenait tout à coup drôlement ami-
cale.

« Oh ! toujours pareil. » Ce qu'il fabriquait, qu'est-
ce que j'en savais, moi. Ce type, je le connaissais à
peine. J'ignorais même s'il était encore à Princeton.
J'ai dit « Écoutez, ça vous conviendrait qu'on se
retrouve pour prendre un verre quelque part ?

— Dites donc, vous savez l'heure qu'il est ? C'est
quoi votre nom, sans indiscrétion ? » Subitement
voilà qu'elle prenait l'accent anglais. « A vous
entendre vous devez être plutôt jeunot. »

J'ai ri. « Merci pour le compliment. » J'étais tout
ce qu'il y a de plus aimable. « Je m'appelle Holden
Caulfield. » J'aurais dû lui donner un faux nom mais
j'y ai pas pensé.

« Ben écoutez, Mr. Cawffle, j'ai pas l'habitude
d'accepter des rendez-vous en plein milieu de la
nuit. Je travaille, moi. »

J'ai dit « Demain c'est dimanche.

— Ben quand même. Faut qu'je dorme pour être
fraîche demain. Vous savez ce que c'est.

— Je pensais qu'on pourrait juste prendre un
verre ensemble. Il est pas tellement tard. »

Elle a dit « Ben, c'est très gentil de votre part.
D'où est-ce que vous m'appelez ? Où vous êtes en
ce moment ?

— Moi ? Je suis dans une cabine téléphonique. »

Elle a dit « Oh ». Et puis il y a eu un long silence.
« Ben, j'aimerais beaucoup vous rencontrer un jour
ou l'autre, Mr. Cawffle. Vous avez l'air très gentil.
Vous avez l'air d'un très gentil garçon. Mais il est *si*
tard...

— Je pourrais venir jusque chez vous.

— En temps ordinaire je dirais "super". Je serais
ravie que vous passiez prendre un verre, mais je
loge avec une copine et en c'moment elle est
malade. Elle ferme pas l'œil de la nuit et voilà qu'à

la minute, d'un coup, le sommeil l'a prise. Alors, vous comprenez...

— Oh ! Quel dommage !

— Vous êtes descendu où ? On pourrait p't-être se voir demain ? »

J'ai dit « Demain je pourrai pas. Ce soir seulement c'était possible ». J'ai été con. J'aurais pas dû dire ça.

« Ah ! bon. Je regrette beaucoup.

— Je dirai bonjour à Eddie de votre part.

— C'est ça. Merci. J'espère que vous serez content de votre séjour à New York. C'est super, New York.

— Je sais. Merci. Bonne nuit. » J'ai raccroché.

Ouah. J'avais tout fichu en l'air. J'aurais quand même dû m'arranger pour aller boire un coup avec elle ou quoi.

CHAPITRE 10

IL était pas encore très tard. L'heure qu'il était j'en suis pas sûr mais je sais qu'il était pas très tard. S'il y a une chose que je déteste c'est me mettre au lit quand je suis même pas fatigué. Donc j'ai ouvert mes valises et j'ai sorti une chemise propre et je suis allé à la salle de bain pour me laver et me changer. Ce que je voulais faire, je voulais descendre au rez-de-chaussée et voir ce qui se passait dans la Lavender Room. La Lavender Room c'était une boîte de nuit qu'ils avaient dans l'hôtel même.

Comme j'étais en train de mettre une chemise propre j'ai presque décidé de passer un coup de fil à ma petite sœur Phoebé. J'avais vraiment envie de lui parler. Une gosse pleine de bon sens et tout. Mais je pouvais pas courir le risque de lui téléphoner parce que c'était seulement une gamine et à cette heure-là elle était sûrement plus debout, et encore moins près du téléphone. J'ai considéré la possibilité de raccrocher si mes parents répondaient, mais ça aurait foiré. Ils auraient deviné que c'était moi. Ma mère sait toujours quand c'est moi. Elle a le don de télépathie. Mais sûr que ça m'aurait pas déplu de bavarder un petit moment avec la môme Phoebé.

Vous devriez la voir. De toute votre vie vous avez jamais vu une gamine aussi mignonne et aussi futée. Elle est très intelligente. Depuis qu'elle va en classe, elle a eu que des A. En fait, je suis vraiment le seul idiot de la famille. Mon frère D.B. est un écrivain et tout, et mon frère Allie, celui qui est mort, celui dont je vous ai parlé, c'était un génie. Je suis vraiment le seul idiot. Mais la môme Phoebé, vous devriez la voir. Elle a ce genre de cheveux roux, un petit peu comme étaient ceux d'Allie, qu'elle porte très courts en été. En été, elle les aplatit derrière ses oreilles, elle a de chouettes petites oreilles. L'hiver ils sont plutôt longs. Quelquefois ma mère lui fait des nattes mais pas toujours. En tout cas, ça lui va bien. Phoebé n'a que dix ans. Elle est un peu maigrichonne comme moi, mais joliment maigrichonne. Une mignonne petite crevette. Je l'ai observée une fois de la fenêtre alors qu'elle traversait la Cinquième Avenue pour aller au parc et c'est ce qu'elle est, une mignonne petite crevette. Cette môme, si on lui dit des trucs, elle sait toujours exactement de quoi on parle. Je veux dire, vous pouvez l'emmener n'importe où. Par exemple, si vous l'emmenez voir un film dégueulasse elle saura que le film est dégueulasse. Si vous l'emmenez voir un film plutôt bon elle saura que le film est plutôt bon. D.B. et moi on l'a emmenée voir ce film français *La Femme du boulanger*, avec Raimu. Ça l'a tuée. Mais son film favori c'est *Les Trente-neuf Marches* avec Robert Donat. Ce foutu machin elle le connaît par cœur bicause je l'ai emmenée le voir au moins dix fois. Quand par exemple le gars Donat arrive à cette ferme écossaise, dans sa cavale pour échapper aux flics et tout, Phoebé dira très fort dans la salle du cinéma — juste en même temps que le type du film : « Tu manges du hareng ? » Elle connaît tout le dialogue par cœur. Et quand ce professeur dans le film, qui est en fait un espion allemand, lève le petit doigt avec une phalange en moins, pour désigner Robert Donat, la môme Phoebé le gagne de vitesse — elle lève *son* petit doigt vers moi dans le noir, juste sous mon nez. Elle est au poil. Vous la trouveriez au poil. Le seul ennui c'est qu'il lui arrive d'être un peu trop expansive. Pour son âge, elle est très émotive. Vraiment. Autre chose encore qu'elle fait, elle écrit tout le temps des livres. Seulement elle les finit jamais. Ça parle toujours d'une petite fille qui s'appelle Hazel Weatherfield — mais la môme Phoebé elle écrit ça « Hazle ». Hazle Weatherfield est une fille détective. Elle est censée être orpheline mais de temps en temps son paternel se pointe. Son paternel est toujours un gentleman, il est grand, il est séduisant, il a dans les vingt ans. Ça me tue. La môme Phoebé vous l'aimeriez, je vous jure. Quand elle était toute petite elle était déjà futée. Quand elle était toute petite, moi et Allie on l'emmenait au parc avec nous, spécialement le dimanche. Allie prenait son bateau à voiles, le dimanche il aimait bien s'amuser avec, et on emmenait la môme Phoebé. Elle avait mis ses gants blancs et elle marchait avec nous, comme une dame et tout. Lorsqu'on se lançait, Allie et moi, dans une conversation sur les choses en général, la môme Phoebé, elle écoutait. Comme c'était qu'une gamine, ça nous arrivait d'oublier qu'elle était là mais elle nous le rappelait. Elle arrêtait pas de nous interrompre. Elle bousculait un peu Allie ou bien elle me bousculait et elle demandait « *Qui* ? Qui a dit ça ? Bobby ou la dame ? » Et on lui disait qui avait dit ça, alors elle disait « Oh » et puis elle continuait bien vite à écouter et tout. Allie aussi, ça le tuait. Je veux dire que lui aussi il la trouvait au poil. Maintenant elle a dix ans et c'est plus un bébé mais elle a pas changé, les gens qui l'entendent ça les tue — du moins tous ceux qu'ont un brin de sens commun.

Bon. C'est quelqu'un à qui on a toujours envie de téléphoner. Mais j'avais trop peur que mes parents répondent et découvrent que j'étais à New York et foutu à la porte de Pencey et tout. Aussi j'ai simplement fini de boutonner ma chemise. Une fois prêt j'ai pris l'ascenseur et je suis descendu dans le hall pour voir ce qui se passait.

Dans le hall il y avait seulement quelques mecs du genre marlou et quelques blondes du genre putain. Mais on entendait jouer l'orchestre, ça venait de la Lavender Room. Lorsque je suis entré c'était pas la grande foule mais ils m'ont quand même salement placé, à une table tout au fond. J'aurais dû agiter un billet d'un dollar sous le nez du maître d'hôtel. A New York, l'argent a toujours son mot à dire — sans blague.

L'orchestre était infect. Buddy Singer. Ça y allait mais c'était plouc. En plus il y avait très peu de gens de mon âge. Personne de mon âge, en fait. On voyait que des vieux types qui paradaient avec leurs petites amies. Sauf à la table juste à côté. A la table juste à côté il y avait trois filles à peu près dans les trente piges. Trois filles plutôt moches et elles avaient sur le crâne la sorte de chapeaux qui tout de suite vous faisait dire qu'elles vivaient pas à New York. Quand même la blonde était pas trop mal. Elle était assez mignonne, la blonde, et j'ai commencé à lui faire un peu de l'œil mais juste à ce moment le garçon est venu prendre ma commande. J'ai demandé un scotch-and-soda et je lui ai dit de pas mélanger. J'ai demandé à toute pompe, parce que si vous hésitez ils pensent que vous avez pas vingt et un ans et ils refusent de vous servir des boissons alcoolisées. Ça n'a pas manqué, il a dit « Excusez-moi, mais auriez-vous quelque chose qui me permette de vérifier votre âge ? Votre permis de conduire, par exemple ? »

Je lui ai lancé un regard glacé, comme s'il m'avait

mortellement insulté et j'ai dit « Est-ce que j'ai l'air d'avoir moins de vingt et un ans ?

— Excusez-moi, monsieur, mais nous avons nos...

— Okay, okay. » Et puis merde, je me suis dit. « Donnez-moi un coca. » Déjà il s'en allait mais je l'ai rappelé. « Vous pouvez pas y mettre deux gouttes de rhum ? » J'ai demandé ça très poliment et tout. « Je me vois pas rester dans un endroit aussi ringard sans un petit remontant. Pouvez pas me mettre deux gouttes de rhum ?

— Excusez-moi, monsieur... » Il en démordait pas. Je lui en ai pas voulu, faut se mettre à sa place. S'ils se font prendre à servir de l'alcool à un mineur ils perdent leur boulot. Et mineur, je le suis foutrement.

J'ai recommencé à faire de l'œil aux trois sorcières de la table voisine. C'est-à-dire à la blonde. Pour les deux autres, aurait vraiment fallu être en manque. Je suis resté très discret. Je leur ai juste jeté à toutes les trois mon coup d'œil super-relaxe et tout. Ce qu'elles ont fait, elles, toutes les trois, c'est se bidonner comme des andouilles. Sans doute elles trouvaient que j'étais trop jeune pour juger quelqu'un d'un seul regard et tout. Ça m'a exaspéré. On aurait cru que je voulais les épouser, ma parole. Après ça j'aurais dû les ignorer mais l'ennui c'est que j'avais envie de danser. Par moments, le besoin de danser vous saisit aux tripes et j'étais dans un de ces moments-là. Alors subitos' je me suis penché et j'ai demandé « Est-ce qu'une de vous aurait envie de danser ? » J'ai demandé ça avec les formes. D'une voix tout ce qu'il y a de convenable. Mais bordel, ça aussi elles l'ont pris à la rigolade. Elles se sont remises à glousser. Trois vraies andouilles. Sans blague. J'ai dit « Allons-y, je vais danser avec vous chacune à son tour. D'accord ? Ça vous va ? Allons-y ». J'avais vraiment besoin de me dégourdir un peu.

Finalement, la blonde s'est levée pour danser avec moi parce que c'était visible que je m'adressais spécialement à elle et on s'est dirigés vers la piste. Quand elles ont vu ça les deux autres ont frôlé la crise d'hystérie. Fallait vraiment que je sois privé pour avoir eu l'idée de m'occuper de ces nénettes. Mais après tout ça valait la peine. La blonde était douée pour la danse, une des meilleures partenaires que j'aie jamais eues. Sans blague, il y a des crétines qui vous sidèrent complètement quand elles dansent. Prenez une fille vraiment intelligente et la moitié du temps quand vous dansez avec elle, elle cherche à *vous* conduire ou bien elle danse tellement mal que la seule solution c'est de rester assis et de s'imbiber en sa compagnie.

J'ai dit à la blonde « Vous dansez vachement bien. Vous devriez être professionnelle. Sérieusement. J'ai dansé une fois avec une pro et vous êtes deux fois meilleure. Avez-vous déjà entendu parler de Marco et Miranda ? »

Elle a dit « Quoi ? » Elle écoutait même pas. Elle regardait tout autour d'elle.

« Je disais avez-vous déjà entendu parler de Marco et Miranda ?

— J'vois pas. Non, j'vois pas.

— Eh bien, ce sont des danseurs. Elle est danseuse. Elle danse mais elle est pas terrible. Elle fait tout ce qu'elle est censée faire mais elle est pas tellement terrible. Savez-vous quand on peut dire qu'une fille est une danseuse vraiment terrible ? »

Elle a dit « Hein, quoi ? » Elle écoutait même pas. Elle avait la tête ailleurs.

« Je disais : savez-vous quand on peut dire qu'une fille est une danseuse vraiment terrible ?

— Euh...

— Eh bien... là où j'ai ma main dans votre dos. Si je pense qu'y a rien sous ma main — pas de fesses, pas de jambes, pas de pieds, *rien* — alors la fille est une danseuse vraiment terrible. »

Mais elle écoutait toujours pas. Aussi je l'ai ignorée un moment. On a seulement dansé. Et cette conne, bon Dieu, elle y allait. Buddy Singer et son orchestre infect jouaient *Just one of those things* et même eux ils arrivaient pas à bousiller ça complètement. C'est un machin super. En dansant je me suis pas lancé dans des trucs compliqués — je peux pas souffrir les mecs qui en dansant font ces trucs-là pour épater — mais je la faisais se remuer vachement et elle me suivait impec. Le plus drôle c'est que je pensais qu'elle aussi elle se donnait du bon temps et tout d'un coup elle m'a lancé cette réflexion stupide « Moi et mes copines, hier soir, on a vu Peter Lorre. L'acteur de cinéma. En chair et en os. Il achetait son journal. Il est *mignon* ».

J'ai dit « Vous avez de la chance. Vous avez vraiment de la chance, vous savez ». Quelle idiote ! Mais elle dansait impec. J'ai pas pu m'empêcher de poser un instant ma bouche sur sa conne de tête, dans la raie des cheveux. Elle a gueulé.

« Hé, qu'est-ce qui vous prend ?

— Rien. Rien me prend, j'ai dit. Vous dansez superbement. J'ai une petite sœur qu'est seulement en septième. Vous dansez aussi bien qu'elle et elle danse drôlement mieux que n'importe qui, vivant ou mort, bordel.

— Vous pouvez pas être poli ? »

Ouah. Une femme du monde. Putain, une *reine*.

J'ai demandé « D'où vous êtes ? »

Elle a pas répondu. Elle était trop occupée à regarder aux alentours pour le cas où Peter Lorre se serait encore pointé, je suppose.

J'ai répété « D'où vous êtes toutes les trois ? »

Elle a dit « Quoi ?

— D'où vous êtes ? Si ça vous coûte répondez pas. Faudrait surtout pas vous surmener.

— Seattle, Washington. » Elle a dit ça comme si elle me faisait vraiment une faveur.

J'ai dit « Vous avez beaucoup de conversation. On vous l'a déjà signalé ?

— Quoi ? »

J'ai pas insisté. Ça lui passait par-dessus la tête. « S'ils jouent quelque chose de rapide, on swingue un peu ? Pas le swing ringard, pas en sautant sur place, un swing en souplesse. Quand ça sera du rapide, les vieux types, les gros lards, tout le monde va s'asseoir, alors on aura de la place. D'accord ? »

Elle a dit « Ça m'est égal. Hé, quel âge que vous avez ? »

Ça m'a pas tellement plu. J'ai dit « Oh putain ! allez pas tout gâcher. J'ai douze ans, bordel. Je suis grand pour mon âge.

— *Écoutez*. J'vous l'ai déjà dit. J'aime pas cette façon de parler. Si vous continuez comme ça j're-tourne avec mes copines. »

Je me suis confondu en excuses parce que l'or-chestre se lançait dans du rapide. Elle s'est mise à danser un boogie-woogie avec moi mais pas ringard, tout en souplesse. Elle.était vraiment douée. Je la touchais et ça suffisait. Et quand elle tournait sur elle-même, elle tortillait du cul si joliment. J'en restais estomaqué. Sans blague. Quand on est allés se rasseoir j'étais à moitié amoureux d'elle. Les filles c'est comme ça, même si elles sont plutôt moches, même si elles sont plutôt connes, chaque fois qu'elles font quelque chose de chouette on tombe à moitié amoureux d'elles et alors on sait plus où on en est. Les filles. Bordel. Elles peuvent vous rendre dingue. Comme rien. Vraiment.

Elles m'ont pas invité à m'asseoir à leur table — principalement parce qu'elles étaient pas au cou-rant de ce qui se fait — mais moi je me suis installé avec elles. La blonde qui dansait si bien s'appelait

Bernice quelque chose — Crabs ou Krebs. Le nom des deux moches c'était Marty et Laverne. Je leur ai dit, juste comme ça, que je m'appelais Jim Steele. Puis je me suis efforcé d'avoir avec elles une petite convers' intelligente. Pratiquement impossible. Fallait tout leur souffler. On aurait pas pu dire laquelle des trois était la plus stupide. Et toutes les trois elles arrêtaient pas de jeter des coups d'œil autour d'elles comme si elles s'attendaient à voir débarquer à tout instant une troupe de vedettes du ciné. Elles devaient se figurer que les stars, quand il en venait à New York, ça fréquentait la Lavender Room, plutôt que le Stork Club ou l'El Morocco. Bon, il m'a bien fallu une demi-heure pour trouver où elles travaillaient et tout, à Seattle. Elles étaient dans le même bureau d'une compagnie d'assurances. J'ai voulu savoir si le travail leur plaisait mais pas possible d'obtenir une réponse sensée de ces trois idiotes. Je pensais que les deux moches, Marty et Laverne, étaient peut-être sœurs, mais quand je leur ai demandé elles se sont vexées. On voyait qu'aucune des deux avait envie de ressembler à l'autre et on pouvait pas le leur reprocher mais, bon, c'était tout de même marrant.

J'ai dansé avec elles — les trois — à tour de rôle. Une des moches, Laverne, dansait pas trop mal mais l'autre, la môme Marty, c'était la catastrophe. On aurait cru trimbaler la Statue de la Liberté autour de la piste. La seule façon de pas trop souffrir en la traînant c'était de lui dire des blagues. Alors je lui ai annoncé que je venais de voir Gary Cooper à l'autre bout de la salle.

« Où ça ? elle a demandé, vachement excitée. *Où* ?

— Oh ! vous l'avez loupé. Il vient de sortir. Pourquoi que vous avez pas regardé quand je vous l'ai dit ? »

Elle s'est pratiquement arrêtée de danser et elle

a essayé d'apercevoir la tête de Gary au-dessus des têtes des danseurs. Elle a dit « Oh, crotte ! » Je lui avais quasiment brisé le cœur. Sans rire. Je regrettais déjà de l'avoir charriée. Y a des gens, on devrait jamais les charrier, même s'ils l'ont pas volé.

En tout cas, voilà le plus drôle. Quand on est retournés s'asseoir, la Marty a dit aux deux autres que Gary Cooper venait de partir. Ouah, Laverne et Bernice, quand elles ont entendu ça j'ai bien cru qu'elles allaient se suicider. Elles étaient dingues et elles ont demandé à Marty si elle l'avait vu et tout. La Marty, elle a répondu qu'elle avait juste réussi à l'entrevoir une minute. Ça m'a tué.

Le bar fermait pour la nuit, aussi je leur ai vite payé à boire à chacune, deux fois de suite avant que ça ferme, et pour moi j'ai commandé deux autres cocas. Y avait des verres plein la table. Laverne la moche en finissait pas de se foutre de moi bicause je buvais du coca. Elle avait un sens de l'humour à toute épreuve. Elle et Marty sifflaient des Tom Collins — et ça en plein mois de décembre. Elles avaient rien trouvé de mieux, les connasses. La blonde Bernice, elle buvait du whisky à l'eau. Et elle aussi elle avait une bonne descente. Toutes les trois elles continuaient de chercher les vedettes de cinéma. C'est à peine si elles échangeaient quelques mots. La môme Marty parlait plus que les deux autres mais ce qu'elle disait, c'était barbant et vieux jeu comme d'appeler les chiottes le "petit coin" et elle trouvait que le malheureux joueur de clarinette tout avachi du Buddy Singer était vraiment terrible quand il se levait et jouait en solo. Elle appelait sa clarinette un "bâton de réglisse". Des trucs à l'eau de rose. L'autre moche, Laverne, elle se croyait du genre très spirituel. Elle arrêtait pas de me dire de téléphoner à mon père et de lui demander ce qu'il faisait ce soir. Elle voulait à tout prix savoir s'il avait une petite amie. *Quatre fois* elle m'a remis ça

— pour sûr qu'elle avait de l'esprit ! Bernice, la blonde, c'est à peine si elle ouvrait la bouche. Si je lui disais quelque chose elle faisait « Quoi ? » Au bout d'un moment ça vous tape sur les nerfs.

Subitement, quand elles ont eu vidé leurs verres, toutes les trois se sont agitées et elles ont dit qu'elles allaient au lit. Elles ont dit qu'elles voulaient se lever de bonne heure pour la première représentation au Radio City Music-Hall. J'ai essayé de les persuader de rester encore un peu mais elles ont refusé. Alors on s'est dit bonne nuit et tout. Je leur ai dit que j'irais les voir si je passais un jour à Seattle, mais ça m'étonnerait — que j'aille les voir je veux dire.

Avec les cigarettes et tout j'en ai eu pour à peu près treize dollars. Je trouve qu'elles auraient pu offrir de payer les consommations qu'elles avaient prises avant que j'arrive, bien sûr j'aurais pas accepté mais elles auraient pu au moins le proposer. Au fond, ça m'était plutôt égal. Elles avaient tellement peu d'éducation et elles s'étaient mis sur la tête des minables chapeaux de carnaval. Et aussi leur histoire de se lever de bonne heure pour la première représentation au Radio City Music-Hall, ça me donnait le cafard. Si quelqu'un, par exemple une fille sous un horrible chapeau fait tout ce chemin, de Seattle (Washington) à New York, bon Dieu — et en fin de compte se lève tôt le matin pour aller voir une saleté de première représentation au Radio City Music-Hall ça me fout un cafard monstre. Je leur aurais bien payé *cent* consommations pour qu'elles me racontent pas ça, ces trois connes.

J'ai quitté la Lavender Room pas longtemps après elles. D'ailleurs ça fermait et l'orchestre était parti depuis des siècles. Et surtout c'était un de ces endroits où on se sent vachement mal si on est pas avec quelqu'un qui sait danser et que le garçon vous laisse commander rien d'autre que du coca. Y a pas au monde une seule boîte de nuit où on puisse rester assis pendant des heures sans une goutte d'alcool pour se biturer. A moins d'être avec une fille qui vous tape vraiment dans l'œil.

CHAPITRE 11

D'un coup, comme j'étais encore dans le hall, Jane
Gallagher m'est revenue à l'esprit. Et une fois que
je l'ai eue à l'esprit je pouvais plus m'en débarrasser.
Je me suis assis dans le fauteuil cradoc du hall et
j'ai pensé à elle et Stradlater, ensemble dans la
foutue voiture d'Ed Banky, et même si j'étais à peu
près sûr que Stradlater l'avait pas fait avec elle —
parce que la môme Jane, je la lisais comme un livre
— j'avais quand même toujours ça à l'esprit. Oui je
la lisais comme un livre. Je veux dire qu'en plus du
jeu de dames elle aimait le sport et une fois que je
l'ai bien connue on a joué ensemble au tennis
presque tous les matins et au golf presque tous les
après-midi. J'en suis arrivé à la connaître intime-
ment. Je ne parle de rien de *physique* — non c'était
pas physique — mais on se voyait tout le temps. On
a pas besoin de trucs vraiment sexuels pour connaître
une fille.
   On s'est rencontré bicause ce doberman qu'elle
a, il avait pris l'habitude de venir pisser sur notre
pelouse et chaque fois ma mère ça la mettait en
rogne. Elle a bigophoné à la mère de Jane et elle
en a fait tout un plat. Ce genre de chose, ma mère
peut en faire tout un plat. Et voilà que le lendemain,

au club, j'ai vu Jane couchée sur le ventre près de la piscine, et je lui ai dit bonjour. Je savais qu'elle habitait la maison d'à côté mais je lui avais encore jamais parlé. Cette fois-là mon bonjour elle l'a reçu plutôt froidement. J'ai eu un mal de voleur à la convaincre que moi j'en avais rien à glander que son chien pisse ici ou là, et même dans notre salle de séjour. Bref. Après ça Jane et moi on est devenus copains et tout. Le même après-midi j'ai joué au golf avec elle. Elle a perdu huit balles. *Huit.* Pour lui apprendre à au moins ouvrir les yeux quand elle fait un swing ça a pas été de la tarte. J'ai tout de même énormément amélioré son jeu. Au golf je suis très fort. Si je vous disais mon score pour un parcours vous me croiriez probablement pas. Une fois j'ai failli être dans un court métrage. Mais à la dernière minute j'ai refusé. Quand on déteste autant le cinéma, je me suis dit, faudrait être gonflé pour les laisser vous mettre dans un court métrage.

Jane, c'est une drôle de fille. Je ne la décrirais pas comme une vraie beauté. Mais moi je la trouvais chouette. C'était comme si elle avait des tas de bouches. Je veux dire que lorsqu'elle parlait et qu'elle commençait à s'exciter sa bouche allait dans cinquante directions à la fois, ses lèvres et tout. Ça me tuait. Et sa bouche elle la fermait jamais complètement. Elle la gardait toujours un petit peu entrouverte, spécialement quand elle s'apprêtait à taper sur une balle de golf ou quand elle lisait un bouquin. Elle était toujours en train de lire et elle lisait de bons bouquins. Elle lisait aussi plein de poésie et tout. C'était la seule, à part ma famille, à qui j'ai montré le gant de base-ball d'Allie avec les poèmes écrits dessus. Elle avait pas connu Allie parce qu'elle venait dans le Maine pour la première fois cet été-là — avant ça elle allait à Cape Cod — mais je lui ai raconté plein de choses sur Allie. Ces choses-là, ça l'intéressait.

Ma mère l'aimait pas tellement. C'est-à-dire que ma mère se figurait toujours que Jane et sa mère faisaient exprès de prendre des airs et de pas lui dire bonjour. Ma mère les voyait souvent au village parce que Jane et sa mère allaient au marché dans leur Lasalle décapotable. Et même, ma mère trouvait que Jane était très ordinaire. Moi pas. Elle avait un genre qui me plaisait, voilà tout.

Je me souviens d'un après-midi. La seule fois où Jane et moi on a été pas loin de flirter. C'était un samedi et il pleuvait des cordes, et j'étais chez elle, sous le porche, ils avaient un de ces grands porches fermé sur trois côtés. On jouait aux dames. De temps en temps je me moquais d'elle parce qu'elle laissait ses reines sur la rangée du fond. Mais c'était pas méchant. Jane, on avait jamais envie de trop se moquer d'elle. Je crois bien que j'aime me moquer un petit peu des filles quand l'occasion s'en présente mais c'est curieux, les filles que je préfère j'ai jamais envie de m'en moquer vraiment. Parfois je me dis que ça leur plairait. Au fond, je *sais* que ça leur plairait. Mais c'est dur de commencer quand on les connaît depuis très longtemps et qu'on l'a jamais fait. Bon. J'en étais à vous parler de cet après-midi où Jane et moi on a presque flirté. Il pleuvait des hallebardes, on était sous le porche et tout d'un coup ce salopard d'ivrogne s'est pointé, le mec marié avec la mère de Jane, et il a demandé à Jane s'il y avait des clopes dans la baraque. Je le connaissais pas beaucoup ni rien mais il avait l'air d'un type qui vous adresserait pas la parole sauf pour vous demander de faire quelque chose pour lui. Un pourri. Bref, Jane lui a pas répondu quand il a voulu savoir s'il y avait des clopes dans la baraque. Alors il a répété la question. Et elle a toujours pas répondu. Elle a même pas levé les yeux du damier. Finalement le type est rentré dans la maison. Et j'ai demandé à Jane ce qui se passait. Même à moi elle a pas répondu. Elle faisait comme si elle se concentrait sur la façon de déplacer ses pions. Puis, subitement, une larme est tombée sur le damier. Sur un des carrés rouges, ouah, je la vois encore. Elle l'a simplement étalée avec son doigt. Ça m'a drôlement emmerdé, je sais pas pourquoi. Alors je me suis levé et je l'ai fait se pousser un peu sur la balancelle pour m'asseoir près d'elle. J'étais pratiquement sur ses genoux. Et là elle s'est mise à pleurer pour de bon et en un rien de temps j'étais en train de la couvrir de baisers — *partout* — sur le nez le front les sourcils et tout — sur les oreilles — partout sauf sur la bouche. Sur la bouche elle voulait pas. Bref, c'est cette fois-là qu'on a été le plus près de flirter. Au bout d'un moment elle s'est levée et elle est rentrée prendre son sweater rouge et blanc — et je l'ai trouvée très chouette, avec — et puis on est allés au cinoche. En route je lui ai demandé si le salopard d'ivrogne — le mec marié avec sa mère — l'avait jamais baratinée. Elle était plutôt jeune, mais vachement bien roulée et ça m'aurait pas étonné de ce salaud. Mais elle a dit non. Et j'ai jamais su ce qui tournait pas rond. Y a des filles, avec elles vous savez jamais ce qui tourne pas rond.

Faudrait pas vous figurer, parce qu'on évitait les papouilles, qu'elle était un vrai glaçon. Grave erreur. Par exemple, on se donnait toujours la main. Bon, d'accord, c'est pas grand-chose. Mais pour ce qui est de se donner la main elle était super. La plupart des filles, si on les tient par la main, c'est comme si leur main était morte dès l'instant qu'on la prend, ou bien au contraire elles s'empressent de remuer la main sans arrêt comme si elles pensaient que ça va vous distraire. Avec Jane c'était différent. On allait au cinéma ou quoi et immédiatement on se tenait par la main et on restait comme ça jusqu'à la fin du film. Sans changer la position et sans en faire toute une histoire. Avec Jane, même si on avait la main moite y avait pas à s'inquiéter. Tout ce qu'on peut dire c'est qu'on était heureux. Vraiment heureux.

Je viens de penser à un autre truc. Un truc que Jane a fait une fois, au ciné, et qui m'a renversé. Je crois qu'ils passaient les Actualités et subitement j'ai senti une main dans mon cou et c'était la main de Jane. Marrant, non ? Ce que je veux dire c'est qu'elle était très jeune et tout, et la plupart des filles que vous voyez mettre leur main sur la nuque de quelqu'un elles ont dans les ving-cinq - trente ans et elles font ça à leur mari ou à leur gosse. Par exemple je le fais de temps en temps à ma petite sœur Phoebé. Mais si une fille est très jeune et tout et qu'elle le fait, c'est un geste tellement chouette que ça vous tue.

Bon. C'est à ça que je pensais comme j'étais assis dans ce fauteuil cradoc du hall de l'hôtel. La môme Jane. Chaque fois que j'en arrivais à son rancard avec Stradlater dans cette foutue voiture à Eddie Banky, je me sentais devenir dingue. Je savais bien qu'elle l'arrêterait illico s'il essayait de lui faire ça mais quand même j'étais dingue. A vrai dire je veux même pas en parler.

Le hall était presque vide. Jusqu'aux blondes à l'air de putes qui avaient disparu et brusquement j'ai eu envie de mettre les voiles. C'était trop déprimant. Et j'étais pas du tout fatigué ni rien. Alors je suis monté dans ma chambre et j'ai enfilé mon manteau. J'ai aussi jeté un coup d'œil par la fenêtre pour voir si tous les pervers étaient encore en action mais y avait plus de lumière ni rien. J'ai pris l'ascenseur pour redescendre et j'ai trouvé un taxi et j'ai demandé au chauffeur de m'emmener chez Ernie. Ernie's c'est cette boîte de nuit dans Greenwich Village que fréquentait mon frère D.B. avant d'aller se prostituer à Hollywood. De temps en temps il m'emmenait avec lui. Ernie est un grand gros type qui joue du piano. Un snobinard de première qui vous dira pas un mot si vous êtes pas un ponte ou une célébrité ou quoi. Mais le piano il sait en jouer. Il joue si bien qu'il est un peu à la noix en quelque sorte. Je sais pas trop ce que je veux dire par là mais c'est pourtant bien ce que je veux dire. Sûr que j'aime l'entendre jouer, mais quelquefois, son piano, on a envie de le foutre en l'air. C'est sans doute parce que lorsqu'il joue, quelquefois, même ce qu'il joue ça vous montre qu'il est un gars qui parle seulement aux grands pontes.

CHAPITRE 12

Le taxi que j'ai pris était un vieux tacot qui sentait comme si on avait dégueulé dedans. Si je vais quelque part tard le soir c'est toujours dans un de ces trucs vomitifs. En plus, dehors, c'était tout calme et vide, spécialement pour un samedi soir. Je voyais à peu près personne dans les rues. Juste de temps en temps un mec et une fille qui traversaient au carrefour en se tenant par la taille et un petit groupe de loubards avec leurs copines, tous se marrant comme des baleines pour des trucs sans doute même pas drôles. New York c'est un endroit terrible. Quand quelqu'un se marre dans la rue ça s'entend à des kilomètres. On se sent tout seul et misérable. J'arrêtais pas de me dire que j'aurais tellement aimé rentrer à la maison et discuter le coup avec la môme Phoebé. Mais au bout d'un moment, finalement, le chauffeur et moi on s'est mis à se parler. Son nom c'était Horwitz. Un type bien mieux que celui de l'autre taxi. Alors j'ai pensé que peut-être il savait, lui. Pour les canards.

J'ai dit « Hé, Horwitz. Vous passez jamais près du petit lagon, dans Central Park ? Du côté de Central Park South ?

— Le *quoi* ?

— Le lagon. Une sorte de petit lac. Où sont les canards. Vous voyez ?

— Ouais, et alors ?

— Ben vous voyez les canards qui nagent dedans ? Au printemps et tout ? Est-ce que par hasard vous sauriez pas où ils vont en hiver ?

— Où ils vont *qui* ?

— Les canards. Si jamais par hasard vous saviez. Est-ce que quelqu'un vient avec un camion ou quoi et les emporte ou bien est-ce qu'ils s'envolent d'eux-mêmes — pour aller vers le Sud, par exemple ? »

Le gars Horwitz s'est retourné et il m'a regardé. C'était le genre de type pas très patient. Pas un mauvais type, remarquez. Il a dit « Putain, qu'est-ce que j'en sais, moi ? Un truc aussi idiot, putain, qu'est-ce que j'en sais ? »

J'ai dit « Bon, faut pas vous fâcher ». Parce qu'il se fâchait, j'avais bien l'impression.

« Qui est-ce qui se fâche ? Personne se fâche. »

S'il devenait tellement susceptible valait mieux arrêter les frais. Mais c'est lui qui a remis ça. Il s'est encore retourné et il a dit « Les poissons y vont nulle part. Ils restent là où y sont, les poissons. Juste où y sont dans le foutu lac.

— Les poissons... c'est pas pareil. Les poissons ils sont pas pareils. Je parle des *canards*. »

Il a dit, Horwitz, « Et en quoi c'est pas pareil ? » Il a dit « Pour moi c'est tout pareil ». Quand il parlait c'était comme s'il y avait vraiment quelque chose qui le fâchait. « C'est plus dur pour les poissons, l'hiver et tout, plus dur que pour les canards, merde. Réfléchissez un peu, merde. »

Ça m'a coupé le sifflet pour une minute. Et puis j'ai dit « D'accord. Et qu'est-ce qu'ils font les poissons et tout quand le petit lac est complètement gelé, un vrai bloc de glace avec dessus des gens qui patinent et tout ? »

Le gars Horwitz, il s'est encore retourné. Il a

gueulé « C'qu'y font ? Qu'est-ce que vous voulez dire, bon Dieu ? Y restent où y sont, bordel.

— Ils peuvent pas faire comme si la glace était pas là. Ils peuvent pas simplement faire comme si.

— Qui a dit qu'ils faisaient comme si ? Personne fait comme si », a dit Horwitz. Il s'excitait tellement et tout que j'avais peur qu'il rentre dans un lampadaire ou quoi. « La foutue glace, ils vivent *dedans*. C'est leur nature, bordel. Ils restent gelés raides sur place tout l'hiver.

— Tiens. Et alors qu'est-ce qu'ils mangent ? S'ils sont gelés *raides*, ils peuvent pas nager ici et là pour se chercher de quoi manger et tout.

— Leur *corps*, bordel. T'es bouché ? Leur corps aspire sa nutrition et tout dans les algues et les cochonneries qui sont dans la glace. Ils gardent leurs *pores* ouverts tout le temps. Putain, c'est leur nature. Tu vois ? » Il a encore fait un vrai demi-tour pour m'expliquer ça.

J'ai dit « Oh ». J'ai laissé tomber. J'avais peur qu'il finisse par bousiller son taxi ou quoi. En plus, il était tellement susceptible qu'y avait pas de plaisir à discuter avec lui. J'ai dit « Voulez-vous qu'on s'arrête pour prendre un verre quelque part ? »

Il a pas répondu. J'imagine qu'il continuait à réfléchir. J'ai répété mon invitation. C'était plutôt un bon type. Très amusant et tout.

« J'ai pas de temps à perdre, mon pote. Et d'ailleurs quel âge que t'as ? Pourquoi que t'es pas encore au lit ?

— J'ai pas sommeil. »

Quand je suis descendu devant Ernie's, le gars Horwitz il a remis ça, pour les poissons. Sûr que ça le travaillait. Il a dit « Écoute. Si t'étais un poisson, la bonne Nature prendrait soin de toi, pas vrai ? D'accord ? Tu crois quand même pas que les poissons ont plus qu'à crever quand l'hiver rapplique ?

— Non, mais...

— T'as foutrement raison », a dit Horwitz, et il a démarré comme un bolide. C'était bien le type le plus susceptible que j'aie jamais rencontré. Tout ce qu'on lui disait le contrariait.

Même à cette heure-là, Ernie's était encore plein à craquer. Principalement des ploucs des collèges et des ploucs de l'Université. Presque tous les bon Dieu de collèges du monde entier commencent les vacances de Noël plus tôt que ceux où je vais, moi. C'était tellement comble qu'il fallait drôlement se magner rien que pour mettre son manteau au vestiaire. Mais ça faisait assez tranquille parce qu'Ernie était en train de jouer. Quand il s'asseyait au piano, c'était comme si on assistait à quelque chose de *sacré*. Personne est bon à ce point-là. Avec moi il y avait trois couples qui attendaient qu'on leur donne une table et qui poussaient et se dressaient sur la pointe des pieds pour mieux regarder le gars Ernie à son piano. On avait dirigé sur lui un grand projecteur, et placé devant le piano un énorme miroir, comme ça tout le monde pouvait voir sa figure pendant qu'il jouait. On pouvait pas voir ses mains, juste sa vieille grosse figure. La belle affaire. Je suis pas trop sûr du titre de cette chanson qu'il jouait mais en tout cas il l'esquintait vachement avec des trilles à la manque dans les notes hautes et un tas d'autres astuces que je trouvais très emmerdantes. Mais après la dernière note vous auriez entendu la foule ! De quoi vomir. Déchaînés, les mecs. C'était exactement les mêmes crétins qui se fendent la pipe au cinéma pour des trucs chiants. Je vous jure, si j'étais un pianiste ou un acteur ou quoi et que tous ces abrutis me trouvent du tonnerre j'en serais malade. Je pourrais même pas supporter qu'ils m'applaudissent. Les gens applaudissent quand il faut pas. Si j'étais pianiste je jouerais enfermé dans un placard. Bref. Quand il a eu terminé, que tout le monde applaudissait à tour de bras, Ernie a pivoté sur son tabouret et il s'est fendu d'un très modeste petit salut bidon. Comme s'il était un type vachement *modeste* en plus d'être un pianiste du tonnerre. Ça faisait vraiment charlot, vu qu'il est tellement snob. Le plus bizarre, quand il a eu terminé, c'est que moi j'ai eu envie de le plaindre. Je crois qu'il sait même plus distinguer quand il joue bien ou mal. C'est pas totalement sa faute. C'est à cause de ces abrutis qui applaudissent à tour de bras. Si on les laissait faire, ils embrouilleraient n'importe qui. En tout cas ça m'a encore foutu le bourdon et j'ai été à deux doigts de reprendre mon manteau et de rentrer à l'hôtel. Mais il était trop tôt, et je tenais pas à me retrouver seul.

Finalement on m'a donné cette table puante juste contre le mur et derrière une saleté de pilier qui m'empêchait de voir. C'était une de ces tables minuscules, tellement coincées que si les gens se lèvent pas pour vous laisser passer — et ils le font jamais, les salauds — faut pratiquer l'escalade pour s'y asseoir. J'ai commandé un scotch-and-soda, c'est ce que je préfère après le daiquiri. Chez Ernie, même un gosse de six ans pourrait boire de l'alcool tellement c'est sombre et tout, et ne plus tout le monde s'en fout de votre âge. Et vous seriez un drogué, tout le monde s'en foutrait tout pareil.

Autour de moi c'était rien que des ploucs. Je vous jure. A cette autre table minuscule, juste à ma gauche, pratiquement sur moi, il y avait un type pas gâté avec une fille pas gâtée. Ils devaient avoir à peu près mon âge, ou peut-être un petit peu plus. C'était marrant, on voyait qu'ils se donnaient un mal de chien pour pas écluser trop vite le minimum qu'il fallait commander. J'avais rien à faire de mieux, alors j'ai écouté un moment leur convers'. Le type parlait à la fille d'un match de football qu'il avait vu l'après-midi. Il lui racontait l'action dans les moindres détails — sans blague. J'ai jamais entendu quelqu'un d'aussi barbant. Et ça se voyait que la fille était pas intéressée masi elle était encore moins gâtée que lui alors je suppose qu'elle pouvait pas faire autrement que l'écouter. Pour les filles vraiment moches, c'est pas drôle. Je les plains. Quelquefois j'ai même pas le courage de les regarder, spécialement quand elles sont avec un abruti qui leur raconte un match de football à la con. A ma droite, les discours, c'était plutôt pire. A ma droite il y avait un mec typiquement « Yale » en costume de flanelle grise avec un gilet à carreaux genre pédé. Ces salauds des facs snobinardes ils se ressemblent tous. Mon père voudrait que j'aille à Yale, ou peut-être à Princeton, mais bon Dieu je mettrai jamais les pieds dans une de ces universités pour poseurs de première, plutôt crever. En tout cas ce mec typiquement « Yale » était avec une fille extra. Ouah. Vraiment super. Mais fallait les entendre. D'abord ils étaient tous deux un peu partis. Lui, il la tripotait sous la table et en même temps il lui racontait qu'un gars de son dortoir s'était presque suicidé en avalant tout un tube d'aspirine. Et la nana disait « Oh ! c'est horrible... Non, darling. Je t'en prie. Pas ici ». Imaginez que vous papouillez une nana tout en lui racontant le suicide d'un copain. Ça m'a tué.

Sûr, je commençais à me sentir comme un veau primé au concours à rester là assis tout seul. Avec rien d'autre à faire que boire et fumer. Quand même, ce que j'ai fait, j'ai dit au garçon de demander à Ernie s'il voulait prendre un pot avec moi. Je lui ai dit de lui dire que j'étais le frère de D.B. Je crois qu'il a pas seulement pris la peine de transmettre le message. Ces salauds-là, ils font jamais ce qu'on leur demande.

Subitement, une fille s'est approchée en s'exclamant « Holden Caulfield ! » Elle s'appelait Lillian

Simmons. Mon frère était sorti un certain temps avec elle. Elle avait de très gros nichons.

J'ai dit « Salut ». J'ai essayé de me lever, bien sûr, mais c'était pas commode, là où je me trouvais. Elle était en compagnie d'un officier de marine qui avait tout l'air d'avoir avalé un manche à balai.

« Quel plaisir de vous rencontrer ! » a dit la môme Lillian Simmons. Du flan. « Et votre grand frère, qu'est-ce qu'il devient ? » C'était la seule chose qui l'intéressait.

« Il va bien. Il est à Hollywood.

— A Hollywood ? C'est merveilleux ! Qu'est-ce qu'il y fait ? »

J'ai dit « Je sais pas. Il écrit ». J'avais pas envie de parler de ça. Je voyais que pour elle c'était génial que D.B. soit à Hollywood. Tout le monde ou presque est du même avis. Et la plupart du temps des gens qu'ont pas même lu ses nouvelles. Moi ça me rend dingue.

Lillian a dit « C'est super ». Puis elle m'a présenté au type de la Navy. Il s'appelait le capitaine Blop ou quelque chose du genre. C'était un de ces gars qui se figurent qu'on va les prendre pour une tapette s'ils vous fracturent pas les os en quarante morceaux quand ils vous serrent la pince. Bon Dieu, je déteste cette faune. « Vous êtes seul, baby ? » m'a demandé la môme Lillian. Elle bloquait tout le passage. Ça se voyait qu'elle adorait bloquer le passage. Le serveur attendait qu'elle dégage mais elle faisait pas attention à lui. C'était marrant. Ça se voyait aussi que le serveur l'aimait pas trop, et jusqu'au type de la Navy qui l'aimait pas trop, même s'il la rancardait. Et moi non plus je l'aimais pas trop. Personne. Aurait plutôt fallu la plaindre. Elle m'a demandé « Vous n'avez pas de copine, baby ? » J'avais réussi à me mettre debout et elle m'aurait pas seulement dit de me rasseoir. Le genre à vous laisser pendant des heures sur vos cannes. Elle a

dit au type de la Navy « C'est pas un beau gars ? »,
et à moi « Holden, vous embellissez à vue d'œil ».
Le type lui a dit de pas rester dans le chemin, qu'ils
bloquaient le passage. Elle m'a dit « Venez vous
asseoir avec nous, Holden. Amenez-vous avec votre
verre. »

C'était clair qu'elle essayait de se mettre bien
avec moi pour que je raconte ça à D.B. J'ai dit que
je m'apprêtais à partir. « J'ai quelqu'un à voir.

— Tiens, tiens, ce petit bonhomme. Eh bien, tant
mieux. Le grand frère, quand vous le verrez, dites-
lui que je ne peux pas le souffrir. »

Et elle s'est barrée. Le type de la Navy et moi
on s'est servi de l'« Enchanté d'avoir fait votre
connaissance ». Un truc qui me tue. Je suis toujours
à dire « Enchanté d'avoir fait votre connaissance »
à des gens que j'avais pas le moindre désir de
connaître. C'est comme ça qu'il faut fonctionner si
on veut rester en vie.

Puisque j'avais dit que je devais rejoindre quelqu'un j'avais pas le choix, fallait que je parte. Même
pas moyen de traîner un peu pour entendre le père
Ernie jouer quelque chose d'à moitié convenable.
Comme j'allais sûrement pas m'asseoir à une table
avec la môme Lillian Simmons et son capitaine de
frégate et m'ennuyer à crever j'ai mis les voiles.
Mais quand je suis allé récupérer mon manteau
j'étais furax. Y a toujours des gens pour vous gâcher
le plaisir.

CHAPITRE 13

Je suis rentré à pied à l'hôtel. Quarante et un pâtés de maisons. Je l'ai pas fait parce que j'avais envie de marcher ni rien. C'était plutôt parce que j'en avais marre de prendre des taxis. Les taxis, on s'en fatigue comme on se fatigue des ascenseurs. Tout d'un coup on veut aller à pied, même si c'est loin ou même si c'est haut. Quand j'étais petit, ça m'arrivait souvent de monter par l'escalier jusqu'à notre appartement. Au douzième étage.

On voyait presque pas qu'il avait neigé. Y avait presque plus trace de neige sur les trottoirs. Mais il faisait un froid glacial et j'ai sorti ma casquette de ma poche pour me la mettre sur le crâne. Je me foutais pas mal de l'allure que j'avais. J'ai même rabattu les oreillettes. J'aurais bien voulu savoir qui m'avait fauché mes gants à Pencey, parce que mes mains étaient gelées. C'est pas que j'aurais fait grand-chose, si j'avais su. Je suis un type assez dégonflé. J'essaie de pas le montrer mais c'est pourtant vrai. Par exemple, si à Pencey j'avais découvert celui qui m'avait volé mes gants je serais probablement allé voir le salopard dans sa piaule et j'aurais dit « Okay. Maintenant, si tu me rendais mes gants ? » Et le salopard qui les avait piqués aurait

probablement répliqué, d'un air innocent et tout
« Tes gants ? Quels gants ? » Et alors ce que j'aurais
fait, j'aurais ouvert le placard et trouvé les gants
quelque part. Peut-être cachés dans ses foutues
godasses. Je les aurais sortis de là et montrés au
gars en disant « Je suppose que ce sont *tes* gants ? »
Alors le salopard m'aurait servi le regard trompeur
de l'agneau sans tache et il aurait répondu « C'est
bien la première fois que je vois ces gants-là. S'ils
sont à toi, prends-les. J'en veux pas de ces saletés ».
Et alors je serais probablement resté sans bouger
pendant cinq bonnes minutes, les foutus gants à la
main et tout, en me disant que ce type je devrais
bien lui balancer mon poing sur la gueule et lui
défoncer la mâchoire. La suite, c'est que je manque-
rais d'estomac. Je resterais là à m'efforcer d'avoir
l'air d'un dur. Ou alors peut-être je dirais quelque
chose de cinglant et vachard pour le vexer au lieu
de lui casser les dents. Bon. Mais si je lui disais
quelque chose de cinglant et vachard il réagirait en
venant vers moi pour me déclarer « Écoute, Caulfield. Est-ce que tu me prends pour un malhonnête ? » Alors, au lieu de répondre « Tout juste,
espèce de salaud » je dirais simplement, j'imagine,
« Ce que je sais c'est que mes foutus gants étaient
dans tes godasses ». Alors le gars saurait immédiatement que je cognerais pas et il dirait probablement « Écoute. Réglons ça tout de suite. Est-ce que
tu prétendrais que je suis un voleur ? » Et moi je
dirais probablement « Personne a dit que quelqu'un
était un voleur. Ce que je sais, c'est que j'ai retrouvé
mes gants dans tes foutues godasses ». Et ça pourrait
durer des heures. Finalement, je me tirerais sans
l'avoir effleuré. J'irais sans doute aux chiottes pour
fumer une sèche en douce et me regarder devenir
un gros dur dans la glace des lavabos. En tout cas
voilà ce que j'avais dans la tête tout le long du
chemin en rentrant à l'hôtel. C'est pas drôle d'être

un trouillard. Peut-être que je suis pas *totalement* un trouillard. Je sais pas. Je crois que je suis peut-être en partie un trouillard et en partie le genre de type qui se fout pas mal de perdre ses gants. Un de mes problèmes c'est que ça m'emmerde pas vraiment quand je perds mes affaires. Ma mère, quand j'étais gosse, ça la rendait folle. Y a des gars qui passent *des jours* à chercher quelque chose qu'ils ont perdu. Je possède vraiment rien que ça m'ennuierait vachement de perdre, il me semble. C'est peut-être pour ça que je suis en partie un trouillard. Mais c'est pas une excuse. Absolument pas. Ce qu'il faudrait c'est pas être du tout un trouillard. Si on est censé défoncer la mâchoire de quelqu'un, si on se sent l'envie de le faire, on devrait le faire. Mais pour ça je suis pas doué. J'expédierais plutôt un gars par la fenêtre ou bien je lui trancherais la tête à la hache plutôt que lui défoncer la mâchoire. Je déteste les batailles à coups de poing. Ça m'ennuie pas trop de recevoir les coups — bien sûr sans aller jusqu'à dire que j'en raffole — mais ce qui me fout les jetons dans un échange de coups de poing c'est la gueule du mec. Voilà le problème. Ça irait mieux si tous les deux on avait les yeux bandés. Quand on y réfléchit, c'est une trouille d'un genre spécial, mais c'est quand même la trouille. Faut bien l'admettre.

Plus je pensais à mes gants et à ma trouille et plus je me sentais à plat et donc j'ai décidé d'arrêter quelque part pour prendre encore un verre. J'en avais pris que trois chez Ernie et j'avais même pas fini le dernier. Ce qui est sûr, c'est que j'ai une fichue descente. Quand je suis lancé je peux boire toute la nuit sans seulement qu'il y paraisse. Une fois, à Whooton ; cet autre gars Raymond Goldfarb et moi, on a acheté une demi-bouteille de whisky et un samedi soir on est allés la siffler à la chapelle pour que personne nous surprenne. Lui il était schlass, mais moi ça se voyait presque pas. J'étais seulement très flegmatique. J'ai vomi avant d'aller me coucher mais y avait pas vraiment nécessité. Je me suis forcé.

Donc, avant d'arriver à l'hôtel j'ai voulu entrer dans ce bar puant mais deux gars en sont sortis, complètement défoncés, et ils m'ont demandé où était le métro. L'un d'eux était un mec d'un type très cubain, il arrêtait pas de me souffler à la figure son haleine empestée pendant que je lui indiquais la direction. Finalement, ce bar de malheur, j'y suis même pas allé. Je suis simplement rentré à l'hôtel.

Le hall était vide. Ça chlinguait comme cinquante millions de cigares refroidis. Je vous jure. J'avais toujours pas sommeil mais je me sentais mal foutu. Déprimé et tout. Je me disais que je serais presque mieux mort, tout compte fait.

Et voilà qu'en plus je me suis mis dans la merde. Comme j'entrais dans l'ascenseur, le liftier m'a dit brusquement « C'que ça vous intérese de passer un bon moment ? Ou bien c'est trop tard pour vous ? »

Je lui ai demandé de quoi il parlait. Je voyais pas où il voulait en venir.

« Qu'est-ce que tu dirais d'une pépée ? »

J'ai dit « Moi ? » Une réponse idiote mais c'est très embarrassant quand quelqu'un se met à vous poser une question comme celle-là.

« Quel âge que t'as, chef ? il a dit.

— Pourquoi ? j'ai dit. Vingt-deux.

— Humm. Alors ? C'que ça t'intéresse ? Cinq dollars la passe. Quinze dollars pour toute la nuit. » Il a jeté un coup d'œil à sa montre « Jusqu'à midi. Cinq dollars la passe, quinze dollars jusqu'à midi. »

J'ai dit « Okay ». C'était contre mes principes et tout, mais je me sentais si déprimé que j'ai même pas réfléchi.

113

« Okay quoi ? Une passe ou jusqu'à midi ? Faut que je sache.

— Juste une passe.

— Okay. C'est quelle chambre ? »

J'ai regardé le truc rouge sur la clef, avec le numéro. J'ai dit « Douze-vingt-deux ». Je regrettais déjà d'avoir mis ça en train mais maintenant c'était trop tard.

« Okay. J't'envoie une fille dans un petit quart d'heure. » Il a ouvert les portes. Je suis sorti. J'ai demandé « Hey, elle est jolie ? Je veux pas d'une vieille pouffiasse.

— Ce sera pas une vieille pouffiasse. T'inquiète pas.

— Je paie à qui ?

— A elle. Allons-y, chef. » Il m'a pratiquement fermé les portes au nez.

Je suis rentré dans ma chambre et j'ai passé un peu d'eau sur mes cheveux mais avec la coupe en brosse on peut pas vraiment les coiffer ni rien. Puis j'ai fait un test pour voir si mon haleine empestait pas trop, après toutes les cigarettes et puis les scotch-and-soda que j'avais bus chez Ernie. On met la main en dessous de la bouche et on envoie le souffle vers le haut en direction des narines. Ça semblait pas trop infect mais je me suis quand même lavé les dents. Puis j'ai encore changé de chemise. Je savais bien que j'avais pas à me pomponner ou quoi pour une prostituée mais ça me donnait au moins quelque chose à faire. J'étais sexuellement excité et tout mais j'étais aussi un petit peu inquiet. Si vous voulez savoir, eh bien, je suis puceau. Sans blague. J'ai pourtant eu plusieurs occasions de plus l'être mais je suis pas encore allé jusqu'au bout. Il arrive toujours quelque chose. Par exemple, si on est chez la fille, ses parents se rappliquent toujours au mauvais moment, ou bien on a peur qu'ils rappliquent. Ou si on est sur la banquette arrière d'une voiture y a toujours à l'avant le rencard de quelqu'un d'autre — une fille je veux dire — qui essaie toujours de savoir ce qui se passe dans tous les coins de la foutue bagnole. Je veux dire qu'une fille qu'est à l'avant en finit pas de se retourner pour voir ce qui se trafique à l'arrière. Quand même, au moins deux fois j'ai bien manqué faire ça. Une fois surtout, je me souviens. Mais quelque chose a foiré, je me rappelle plus quoi. Ce qu'il y a, c'est que lorsqu'on est tout près de le faire avec une fille — qu'est pas une prostituée ni rien — elle cesse pas de vous dire d'arrêter. Et moi l'ennui c'est que j'arrête. La plupart des types arrêtent pas. Moi je peux pas m'en empêcher. On sait jamais si les filles elles veulent *vraiment* qu'on arrête ou si elles ont juste une frousse terrible, ou si elles vous disent d'arrêter pour que, si vous continuez, ce soit *votre* faute et pas la leur. En tout cas, moi j'arrête. L'ennui c'est que j'en arrive toujours à les plaindre. Je veux dire que la plupart des filles sont tellement demeurées et tout. Quand ça fait un petit moment qu'on les tripote on les voit qui perdent la tête. Prenez une fille qui devient vraiment passionnée, eh bien elle a plus sa tête. Je sais pas. Elles me disent « Arrête », alors j'arrête. Quand je les reconduis chez elles je regrette toujours de les avoir écoutées, mais à chaque fois je recommence pareil. Bref.

Bref, tout en me changeant de chemise je me suis dit qu'en somme c'était le jour ou jamais. Je me figurais que si elle était une putain et tout ce serait un bon exercice préparatoire au cas où je me marierais un jour, par exemple ; quelque chose qui parfois me tracasse. A Whooton, j'ai lu ce bouquin où il y a un gars très sophistiqué, sensuel, aux super-bonnes manières. Son nom c'était monsieur Blanchard, je m'en souviens encore. Un livre pourri mais ce Blanchard était pas mal. Il avait un grand château et tout en Europe, sur la Riviera, et là il passait son temps à battre des femmes à coups de club de golf. C'était un vrai tombeur et tout ; les femmes lui résistaient pas. Dans un passage il disait que le corps d'une femme est comme un violon et tout, et qu'il faut un musicien super-doué pour en jouer convenablement. Un vrai bouquin à la gomme, je m'en rends compte — mais cette histoire de violon, quand même, ça m'est resté. Et c'était en partie pour ça que je voulais un peu de pratique au cas où un jour je me marierais. Caulfield et son Violon Magique, ouah. C'est à la gomme, je m'en rends compte, mais c'est pas *trop* à la gomme. Ça me plairait assez de devenir plutôt bon à jouer de cette musique-là. La moitié du temps, si vous voulez vraiment la vérité, quand je chahute avec une fille, bon Dieu, j'ai un mal fou à seulement savoir ce que je cherche. Prenez cette fille dont j'ai parlé, avec qui j'ai bien failli faire ça. M'a fallu pas loin d'une heure pour seulement lui enlever son soutien-gorge. Quand je l'ai eu enlevé, elle était prête à me cracher à la figure.

Bon. Je tournicotais dans la chambre, attendant que la putain se pointe. Je continuais à me dire « Espérons qu'elle est jolie ». Mais au fond je m'en foutais un peu. J'étais seulement pressé d'en avoir terminé. Finalement on a frappé et quand je suis allé ouvrir, ma valise était en plein dans le chemin et je suis tombé dessus et j'ai bien failli me casser les rotules. Je choisis toujours le bon moment pour trébucher contre une valise ou quoi.

Lorsque j'ai ouvert la porte, la putain se tenait là. Elle était en manteau et tête nue. Avec des cheveux blonds mais ça se voyait que c'était pas naturel. Toutefois, elle ressemblait pas à une vieille pouffiasse. J'ai dit « Comment allez-vous ? » Ouah. Les bonnes manières.

« C'est vous l'type que Maurice a dit ? » elle a demandé. D'un air pas trop sympa.

« Le garçon d'ascenseur ?

— Ouais.

— C'est moi. Entrez, je vous prie. » Je prenais comme de l'aisance. Je vous jure.

Elle est entrée aussitôt, elle a enlevé son manteau et elle l'a jeté sur le lit. Dessous, elle avait une robe verte. Puis elle s'est assise de côté sur la chaise devant le bureau et elle s'est mise à balancer le pied. Pour une prostituée, elle était très nerveuse. Je vous jure. Je pense que ça tenait à son jeune âge. Elle avait à peu près le même âge que moi. Je me suis assis dans le fauteuil, à côté d'elle, et je lui ai offert une cigarette. Elle a dit « Je fume pas ». Elle avait une toute petite voix haut perchée. On l'entendait à peine. Quand on lui offrait quelque chose elle disait pas merci. Elle avait vraiment pas d'éducation.

J'ai dit « Permettez-moi de me présenter. Mon nom est Jim Steele ». Elle a dit « Vous auriez pas une montre sur vous ? » Elle se foutait pas mal de mon nom, bien sûr. « Hey, vous avez quel âge ?

— Moi ? Vingt-deux.

— Tintin. »

C'était drôle qu'elle dise ça. C'était ce qu'aurait dit un mioche. On penserait qu'une pute et tout ça vous dirait « Mon cul » ou « Arrête tes conneries », et pas « Tintin ».

J'ai dit « Et vous ? »

Elle a dit « L'âge de pas m'en laisser conter ».

Elle avait de la repartie. Puis elle a encore demandé « T'as une montre sur toi, hey ? » Et en même temps elle s'est levée et a fait passer sa robe par-dessus sa tête.

Quand elle a fait ça je me suis senti tout chose. C'était tellement soudain et tout. Je sais qu'on est censé être très excité quand une fille se lève et fait passer sa robe par-dessus sa tête mais je l'étais pas le moins du monde. Ce qui me travaillait c'était pas le sexe, c'était plutôt la déprime.

« T'as une montre sur toi, hey ?

— Non, non, j'ai dit. J'en ai pas. » Ouah. Je me suis encore senti tout chose. J'ai dit « Comment vous vous appelez ? » Elle était en combinaison rose. C'était vraiment embarrassant. Vraiment.

Elle a dit « Sunny ». Et puis « Bon, on y va ?

— Vous auriez pas envie qu'on cause un peu ? » C'était une question plutôt débile, mais je me sentais vraiment tout chose. « Est-ce que vous êtes telle-ment pressée ? »

Elle m'a regardé comme si j'étais dingue. Elle a dit « De quoi qu'vous voulez causer ?

— Je sais pas. Rien de spécial. Je pensais simple-ment que vous aimeriez peut-être qu'on bavarde un peu. »

Elle s'est à nouveau assise sur la chaise près du bureau. Mais c'était visible que ça lui plaisait pas. Elle a recommencé à balancer son pied — ouah, elle avait la bougeotte.

« Voulez-vous une cigarette, à présent ? » J'avais oublié qu'elle fumait pas.

« J'fume pas. Écoutez, si vous voulez causer, allez-y. Moi j'ai à faire. »

Mais j'arrivais pas à trouver de sujet de conver-sation. Je lui aurais bien demandé comment elle était devenue une putain et tout mais j'osais pas. D'ailleurs elle aurait sans doute pas voulu le dire.

Finalement, j'ai demandé « Vous êtes pas de New York ? » C'est tout ce que j'avais trouvé.

Elle a dit « Hollywood ». Puis elle s'est levée et elle est allée vers le lit, là où elle avait posé sa robe. « Y a pas un cintre ? J'ai pas envie qu'ma robe soit comme un chiffon. Elle sort du nettoyage. »

Tout de suite j'ai dit « Bien sûr ». Trop content de me remuer un peu. J'ai emporté la robe jusqu'à la penderie et je l'ai mise sur un cintre. C'est bizarre, quand j'ai accroché le cintre ça m'a donné le cafard. Je la voyais qui entrait dans un magasin et achetait cette robe et personne dans le magasin savait qu'elle était une prostituée ni rien. Le vendeur pensait sûrement quand elle l'a achetée, sa robe, qu'elle était une fille comme les autres. Ça m'a redonné le cafard. Je sais pas trop pourquoi.

Je suis revenu m'asseoir et j'ai essayé de soutenir la convers'. Mais elle était pas douée pour l'échange de propos. J'ai demandé « Vous travaillez toutes les nuits ? » Et quand ça a été dit j'ai trouvé ça très déplacé.

« Ouais. » Elle se baladait dans la pièce. Elle a pris le menu sur le bureau et elle l'a lu.

« Dans la journée qu'est-ce que vous faites ? »

Elle a haussé les épaules. Elle était plutôt maigri-chonne. « Je dors. Je m'offre un ciné. » Elle a posé le menu et elle m'a regardé. « Bon, alors, on y va ? Faudrait pas croire que j'ai toute...

— Écoutez, j'ai dit. Ce soir, je me sens pas très en forme. J'ai pas dormi la nuit dernière. Sans blague. Je vais vous payer et tout. Mais si ça vous ennuie pas trop on le fera pas. D'accord ? »

La vraie raison, c'était que je voulais tout simple-ment pas le faire. A vous dire toute la vérité je me sentais plus déprimé qu'excité. C'était *elle* qui me déprimait. Sa robe verte pendue au cintre et tout. Et d'ailleurs je pense pas que je pourrais *jamais* faire ça avec quelqu'un qui passe la journée assise devant un film idiot. Réellement, je pense pas que je pourrais.

Elle s'est approchée de moi avec cette drôle d'expression comme si elle me croyait pas. Elle a dit « Qu'est-ce qu'y a ?

— Rien. Y a rien. » Ouah, je devenais nerveux à mon tour. « C'est seulement que j'ai eu récemment une opération.

— Où ça ?

— Au machin-truc. Mon clavicorde.

— Hein ? C'est quoi ?

— Le clavicorde ? j'ai dit. Eh bien en fait c'est dans le canal rachidien. Je veux dire très très profond dans le canal rachidien. »

Elle a dit « C'est vache ». Puis la voilà qui s'assoit sur mes genoux. « T'es mignon. »

Elle me rendait encore plus nerveux. Je continuais à pencher la tête en arrière. « Je suis pas encore complètement remis.

— T'as l'air d'un type du ciné. Qui c'est ? Voyons. Toi tu dois savoir. Bon Dieu, c'est comment, son nom ? »

J'ai dit « Je sais pas ». Elle était vissée sur mes genoux. « Mais si. Tu sais. Il était dans ce film avec Mel-vine Douglas. Ç'ui qui jouait le p'tit frère de Mel-vine Douglas. Qui tombe du bateau. Tu vois qui j'veux dire ?

— Non, je vois pas. Je vais le moins possible au cinéma. »

Et alors elle s'est mise à faire des choses. Osées et tout.

J'ai dit « Ça vous ennuierait de laisser tomber ? Je viens de vous expliquer que j'avais pas la forme. Je relève d'une opération. »

Elle a pas bougé de sur mes genoux ni rien mais elle m'a jeté un sale coup d'œil. Elle a dit « Écoute. Je dormais et c'taré de Maurice m'a réveillée et s'tu crois que je...

— J'ai *dit* que je vous paierais votre visite et tout. Je vais le faire. J'ai plein de fric. C'est juste que j'en suis encore à me remettre d'une très sérieuse...

— Bon Dieu, t'as dit à Maurice que tu voulais une fille, alors c'était pour quoi ? Si tu viens d'avoir c'te foutue opération de ton foutu machin-chose. Hein ?

— Je croyais que j'allais beaucoup mieux. J'ai

été un peu prématuré dans mes calculs. Sans blague. Excusez-moi. Si vous pouviez vous lever une minute, j'irais chercher mon portefeuille. »

Elle était furax, mais elle s'est levée et je suis allé chercher mon portefeuille dans la commode. J'ai sorti un billet de cinq dollars et je lui ai tendu. J'ai dit « Merci beaucoup. Un million de fois merci.

— Pas cinq. C'est dix. »

Elle cherchait à profiter de l'occase. Je m'étais douté que ça arriverait. Oui, je m'en étais douté.

J'ai protesté. « Maurice a dit cinq. Il a dit quinze jusqu'à midi et seulement cinq pour une passe.

— Dix pour une passe.

— Il a dit cinq. Je suis désolé. Vraiment désolé. Mais je casquerai pas plus. »

Elle a haussé les épaules, comme elle avait fait déjà, et puis elle a dit, très froidement, « Ça vous ennuierait d'me passer mes fringues ? Ou c'est-y trop demander ? » La môme, elle vous glaçait un peu. Même avec cette toute petite voix, elle pouvait encore vous donner les chocottes. Si elle avait été une grosse vieille pouffiasse avec plein de peinture sur la figure et tout elle vous aurait pas autant impressionné.

Je suis allé lui chercher sa robe. Elle l'a enfilée et tout, et après elle a pris son manteau sur le lit. « Salut, Couille molle. » Elle a dit.

J'ai dit « Salut ». Je l'ai pas remerciée ni rien. Je suis bien content de pas l'avoir fait.

CHAPITRE 14

QUAND la môme Sunny a été partie je suis resté un moment assis dans le fauteuil et j'ai fumé deux ou trois clopes. Ouah, je me sentais misérable. Je me sentais tellement vidé, vous pouvez pas vous imaginer. Ce que j'ai fait, je me suis mis à parler presque à voix haute, à parler à Allie. Je fais ça quelquefois quand j'ai le cafard. Je lui dis d'aller à la maison chercher son vélo et de venir me rejoindre devant la maison de Bobbie Fallon. Bobbie Fallon, il habitait tout près de chez nous dans le Maine — y a des années, c'est-à-dire. En tout cas ce qui est arrivé c'est qu'un jour Bobby et moi on allait au lac Sedebego à bicyclette. On emportait nos sandwichs du déjeuner et nos carabines à air comprimé — on était des gamins et tout qui se figuraient pouvoir attraper quelque chose avec leurs carabines. Bon. Allie nous a entendus en parler et il a voulu venir et je voulais pas l'emmener. Je lui ai dit qu'il était trop petit. Aussi, maintenant, de temps en temps, quand j'ai le cafard, je lui dis « Okay. Va à la maison et prends ton vélo et rejoins-moi devant la maison de Bobby. Grouille ». C'est pas que je voulais jamais l'emmener avec moi quand j'allais quelque part. Mais ce jour-là j'ai pas voulu. Il s'est pas fâché, Allie

— il se fâchait jamais — mais quand ça va mal j'y repense.

Finalement, je me suis déshabillé et je me suis mis au lit. Quand j'ai été au lit j'ai eu envie de prier, mais j'ai pas pu. J'arrive pas toujours à prier quand j'en ai envie. D'abord je suis en quelque sorte un athée. J'aime bien Jésus et tout mais je suis pas très intéressé par tout le reste qu'on trouve dans la Bible. Par exemple, prenez les Disciples. Ils m'énervent, si vous voulez savoir. Après la mort de Jésus ils se sont bien conduits mais pendant qu'il vivait ils lui ont été à peu près aussi utiles qu'un cataplasme sur une jambe de bois. Ils ont pas cessé de le laisser tomber. Dans la Bible, j'aime presque tout le monde mieux que les Disciples. En vrai, dans la Bible, le type que je préfère après Jésus c'est ce dingue qui vivait dans les tombes et arrêtait pas de se couper avec des pierres. Ce pauvre mec, je l'aime dix fois plus que les Disciples. Quand j'étais à Whooton, ça m'est souvent arrivé de me disputer là-dessus avec Arthur Childs, un garçon qui logeait au bout du couloir. Le gars Childs, c'était un quaker et il lisait tout le temps la Bible. Il était sympa, je l'aimais bien, mais j'étais pas d'accord avec lui sur un tas de trucs dans la Bible, spécialement les Disciples. Il prétendait que si j'aimais pas les Disciples alors j'aimais pas Jésus ni rien. Puisque Jésus avait *choisi* les Disciples, il disait, on était censés les aimer. J'ai dit que je savais qu'Il les avait choisis, mais Il l'avait fait *au hasard*. Je disais qu'Il avait pas le temps de se mettre à analyser les gens. Je disais que je reprochais rien à Jésus. C'était pas Sa faute s'Il avait pas le temps. Je me souviens avoir demandé au gars Childs si à son avis Judas, celui qui a trahi Jésus, était allé en enfer après son suicide. Childs a dit « Oh ! certainement ». C'est exactement là-dessus que j'étais pas d'accord. J'ai dir « Je parierais mille dollars que Jésus a jamais envoyé le Judas en enfer ». Je le parierais encore si j'avais les mille dollars. Je crois que n'importe lequel des disciples l'aurait expédié en enfer à toute pompe mais je parierais tout ce qu'on voudra que Jésus l'a pas fait. Le gars Childs il a dit que mon problème c'est que j'allais pas à l'église. En un sens il avait raison. J'y vais pas. D'abord parce que mes parents ont pas tous les deux la même religion, et dans la famille les enfants sont athées. Si vous voulez savoir, je peux même pas supporter les aumôniers. Ceux qu'on a eus dans chaque école où je suis allé, ils avaient tous ces voix de prédicateurs foireux quand ils se lançaient dans leurs sermons. Bon Dieu, je déteste ça. Je vois pas pourquoi ils peuvent pas parler d'un ton naturel. Quand ils parlent ça fait tellement bidon.

Bref. Quand j'ai été couché j'ai pas pu dire la moindre petite prière. Chaque fois que je commençais je revoyais la môme Sunny quand elle m'appelait Couille molle. Finalement, je me suis assis dans mon lit et j'ai fumé une autre sèche. Le goût m'a paru horrible. Je devais bien avoir grillé deux paquets de sèches depuis que j'avais quitté Pencey.

Subitement, pendant que je fumais au paddock quelqu'un a frappé à la porte. J'espérais que c'était pas à *ma* porte qu'on frappait mais déjà je savais. Je vois vraiment pas comment je pouvais savoir mais je savais. Et aussi je *savais* qui frappait. Comme ça, par intuition. J'ai dit « Qui est-ce ? » J'avais les foies. Dans ces situations-là je suis trouillard.

On a seulement frappé encore. Plus fort.

J'ai fini par sortir du lit, et en pyjama je suis allé ouvrir. J'ai même pas eu à allumer la lumière parce qu'il commençait à faire jour. Devant moi il y avait la môme Sunny et Maurice le garçon d'ascenseur marlou.

« Qu'est-ce que c'est ? Qu'est-ce que vous voulez ? » Ma voix tremblait pas possible.

« Presque rien, a dit le Maurice. Juste cinq dollars. » C'était lui qui blablatait. La môme Sunny, elle restait plantée là, bouche ouverte et tout.

« Je l'ai déjà payée. Je lui ai donné cinq dollars. Demandez-lui. » Ouah, cette voix que j'avais, qui jouait des castagnettes.

« C'est dix dollars, chef. J'te l'avais dit. Dix dollars pour une passe, quinze dollars jusqu'à midi. J'te l'avais dit.

— Vous m'avez pas dit ça. Vous avez dit *cinq* dollars pour une passe. Vous avez dit quinze dollars jusqu'à midi, d'accord, mais j'ai distinctement entendu...

— Sors-les.

— Et pourquoi ? » j'ai dit. Bon Dieu, mon vieux cœur battait la chamade à me faire foutre le camp. Si seulement j'avais eu mes fringues sur le dos. C'est terrible d'être en pyjama quand il vous arrive quelque chose comme ça.

« Allons, chef », a dit le Maurice. Puis il m'a poussé brutalement de sa main dégueulasse. Je suis presque tombé sur le cul — c'est qu'il était un sacré malabar. J'ai pas eu le temps de me rendre compte que déjà lui et sa Sunny étaient tous les deux dans ma chambre. Ils avaient même l'air de se croire chez eux. La môme s'est assise sur le bord de la fenêtre. Le Maurice a pris le fauteuil et il a desserré son col et tout — il avait son uniforme de liftier. Ouah, j'étais vachement mal à l'aise.

« Magne-toi, chef. Faut que je retourne bosser.

— Pour au moins la dixième fois je vous dis que je vous dois pas un *cent*. Je lui ai déjà donné ce que...

— Arrête ton baratin. Magne-toi.

— Pourquoi que je lui redonnerais cinq dollars ? » Ma voix s'en allait en morceaux tous azimuts. « Vous essayez de me rouler. »

Le gars Maurice a déboutonné sa veste d'uniforme. Tout ce qu'il avait dessous, c'était un col de chemise bidon, pas de chemise ni rien. Un large torse couvert de poils. « Personne essaie de rouler personne, il a dit. Magne-toi, chef.

— *Non.* »

Quand j'ai dit ça il s'est levé et il s'est avancé vers moi et tout. Il a pris un air très très fatigué ou très très excédé. Bon Dieu, j'en menais pas large. Il me semble que je croisais les bras. Si seulement j'avais pas été en pyjama, je me serais senti plus à l'aise.

« Magne-toi, chef. » Il était maintenant quasiment contre moi. C'était tout ce qu'il trouvait à dire « Magne-toi, chef ». Un vrai crétin.

« *Non.*

— Chef, tu vas m'forcer à t'bousculer un peu. J'y tiens pas mais ça m'a l'air nécessaire. Tu nous dois cinq dollars. »

J'ai dit « Je vous dois *rien.* Si vous me touchez, je gueule comme un sourd. Je réveille tout le monde dans l'hôtel. La police et tout. » Ma voix tremblait vous pouvez pas savoir.

« Vas-y, gueule si ça t'chante, il a dit. Tu veux sans doute que tes parents apprennent que t'as passé la nuit avec une pute. Un chiard de la haute comme toi ? » Il était futé dans son genre, le salopard. Faut bien l'admettre.

« Laissez-moi tranquille. Si c'était dix dollars fallait le dire. Mais j'ai distinctement...

— Tu vas t'décider ? » Il m'avait plaqué contre la porte. Il était presque sur moi, son torse pourri et tout velu et tout.

J'ai dit « Laissez-moi tranquille ». J'ai dit « Sortez de ma chambre ». J'avais gardé les bras croisés et tout. Bon Dieu, je me sentais minable.

Et alors Sunny, pour la première fois, a dit quelque chose. « Hé, Maurice, tu veux que j'prenne son portefeuille ? Il est sur le machin-truc.

— Ouais. Prends-le.

— Touchez pas à mon portefeuille.

— J'l'ai déjà », a dit Sunny. Elle a agité le billet de cinq dollars. « Vu ? Tout c'que je prends, c'est les cinq que tu m'dois. J'suis pas une voleuse. »

Subitement, je me suis mis à chialer. Je donnerais n'importe quoi pour pas avoir chialé mais j'ai chialé. J'ai dit « Non, vous êtes pas des voleurs. Vous êtes en train de me piquer...

— La ferme ! » a dit Maurice. Et il m'a donné une bourrade.

Sunny a dit « Fous-lui la paix. Viens. On a le fric qu'y nous d'vait. Allez, viens.

— Je viens », il a dit, le Maurice. Mais il démarrait toujours pas.

« Tu m'entends, Maurice ? Hey, fous-lui la paix.

— Mais personne veut du mal à personne », il a dit, avec un air angélique. Et puis il a claqué les doigts très dur sur mon pyjama, je vous dirai pas à quel endroit. Bon Dieu, ça m'a fait mal. J'ai gueulé qu'il était qu'un sale connard. « Un quoi ? » il a dit. Et mettant sa main derrière son oreille comme un type qu'est sourdingue « Un quoi ? J'suis un quoi ? »

Je chialais encore à moitié. J'étais dans une rogne noire et puis à bout de nerfs et tout. « T'es qu'un sale connard, j'ai répété. T'es qu'un crétin malhonnête et dans deux ou trois ans tu seras un de ces types avec juste la peau sur les os qui arrêtent les gens dans la rue pour leur demander une petite pièce et se payer un café. T'auras de la merde plein tes fringues et tu... »

Alors c'est parti. J'ai même pas essayé d'esquiver ni rien. Tout ce que j'ai senti ça a été un terrible coup de poing dans l'estomac.

Je suis sûrement pas tombé dans les pommes bicause je me souviens que de par terre où j'étais je les ai vus sortir et refermer la porte. Je suis resté un bon moment par terre, comme j'avais fait avec Stradlater. Seulement cette fois j'ai cru crever. Sans blague. J'avais l'impression d'être en train de me noyer. J'arrivais plus à respirer. Quand finalement je me suis relevé, je suis allé à la salle de bain plié en deux, les mains pressées sur l'estomac et tout.

Mais je suis dingue, bon Dieu c'est vrai que je suis dingue, je vous jure. A mi-chemin de la salle de bain voilà que j'ai commencé à prétendre que j'avais une balle dans le ventre. Le gars Maurice m'avait flingué. Maintenant je ramais vers la salle de bain où j'allais me taper un grand coup de whisky pour me calmer les nerfs et me donner l'énergie d'agir pour de bon. Je me voyais sortant de la foutue salle de bain tout habillé, mon revolver dans la poche, encore faiblard sur mes guibolles. Je descendrais par l'escalier au lieu de prendre l'ascenseur, je me cramponnerais à la rampe et tout, avec un filet de sang qui coulerait du coin de ma bouche. Ce que je ferais, je descendrais quelques étages — en me tenant les entrailles, le sang dégoulinant de partout — et là j'appuierais sur le bouton pour appeler l'ascenseur. Dès qu'il ouvrirait la porte, le gars Maurice me verrait le revolver à la main et il se mettrait à hurler de cette voix aiguë du mec qu'a la frousse, pour que je lui laisse la vie sauve. Mais je lui ferais la peau. Six balles en plein dans son gros bide poilu. Puis je jetterais le revolver dans la cage de l'ascenseur — après avoir essuyé mes empreintes et tout. Enfin je me traînerais jusqu'à ma piaule et je bigophonerais à Jane pour qu'elle vienne me panser les tripes. Je la voyais me glissant une cigarette entre les lèvres pour que je fume tandis que le sang arrêterait pas de couler.

Le cinoche. Ça vous démolit. Sans blague.

Je suis resté une heure environ dans la salle de bain à faire trempette. Puis je suis retourné me coucher. J'ai mis pas mal de temps à m'endormir. J'étais même pas fatigué. Mais finalement, le sommeil est venu. Ce qui m'aurait plutôt tenté c'était de me suicider. En sautant par la fenêtre. Je l'aurais probablement fait si j'avais été sûr que quelqu'un prendrait la peine de me recouvrir aussitôt que j'aurais touché terre. J'avais pas envie d'être entouré par une troupe de badauds stupides qui resteraient plantés à me reluquer quand moi je baignerais dans mon sang.

CHAPITRE 15

J'ai pas dormi trop longtemps, car lorsque je me suis réveillé je crois bien qu'il était seulement vers les dix heures. Aussitôt après avoir fumé un clope j'ai senti que j'avais plutôt faim. J'avais rien mangé depuis les deux hamburgers à Agerstown, avec Brossard et Ackley, quand on avait voulu aller au ciné. Ça faisait une paye. Dans les cinquante ans à ce qu'il me semblait. J'avais le téléphone à portée de la main et je l'ai décroché pour demander qu'on me monte le petit déjeuner mais brusquement j'ai pensé que c'était peut-être Maurice qui le servait. Faudrait être cinglé pour croire que je mourais d'envie de le revoir. Aussi je suis resté au lit encore un moment et j'ai fumé une autre cigarette. J'ai été tenté de donner un coup de fil à Jane pour voir si elle était rentrée chez elle et tout, mais j'avais pas vraiment le cœur à ça.

Ce que j'ai fait, j'ai appelé Sally Hayes. Elle va à Mary A. Woodruff et je savais qu'elle était à New York puisqu'elle m'avait écrit, il y avait quinze jours. Sally, elle me plaisait pas tellement mais on se connaissait depuis des années. Dans ma bêtise j'avais cru d'abord qu'elle était intelligente pour la raison qu'elle savait un tas de choses sur le théâtre et les pièces et la littérature et tout. Lorsqu'une personne en sait aussi long sur tout ça, il faut du temps pour décider si au fond elle est pas quand même idiote. Pour Sally il m'a fallu des années. Je pense que je l'aurais su bien plus vite si on avait pas tant flirté. Le problème c'est que je me figure toujours que la fille avec qui je flirte est intelligente. Ça n'a foutrement rien à voir mais malgré tout c'est ce que je pense.

Bref. Je l'ai appelée. D'abord c'est la bonne qui a répondu. Ensuite le père de Sally. Enfin je l'ai eue, elle. J'ai dit, « Sally ?

— Oui — qui est-ce ? » Une question plutôt conne. J'avais déjà dit à son père qui c'était.

« Holden Caulfield. Comment tu vas ?

— Holden ! Ça va. Et toi ?

— Super. Écoute. Bon, comment ça va ? Je veux dire, le collège ? »

Elle a dit « Bien. Enfin... tu sais...

— Super. Bon, écoute. Je me demandais si tu étais libre aujourd'hui. C'est dimanche mais il y a toujours un ou deux spectacles le dimanche. Des trucs de bienfaisance. Tu veux venir ?

— *Épatant.* » S'il y a un mot que je déteste c'est celui-là. Ça fait nouille. Un instant j'ai été tenté de lui dire de laisser tomber, qu'on sortait pas. Mais on était lancés dans le blabla. Ou plutôt, elle était lancée. Moi je pouvais pas placer un mot. D'abord elle a parlé d'un mec d'Harvard — sûrement un bizuth mais elle s'est bien gardée de le mentionner — qu'aurait fait n'importe quoi pour elle. Qui bigophonait *jour et nuit*. Jour et nuit — ça m'a tué. Puis elle a encore parlé d'un autre mec, un cadet de West Point qui lui courait après aussi. Youpee. Je lui ai donné rendez-vous sous l'horloge du Biltmore, à deux heures, et je lui ai dit de pas être en retard bicause la séance commençait sûrement à deux heures trente. Elle était toujours en retard. Et j'ai raccroché. Sally, elle m'énervait, mais physiquement elle était drôlement bien.

Après, je me suis levé et habillé et j'ai refait mes bagages. Avant de quitter la chambre j'ai quand même jeté un coup d'œil par la fenêtre pour voir ce que fabriquaient tous ces pervers mais les stores étaient baissés. Le matin ça jouait les pudiques. Puis je suis descendu par l'ascenseur et j'ai réglé ma note. J'ai pas vu le gars Maurice. Évidemment, je me suis pas trop cassé à le chercher, ce fumier.

J'ai pris un taxi devant l'hôtel mais j'avais pas la moindre idée de l'endroit où aller. J'avais nulle part où aller. C'était seulement dimanche et je pouvais pas rentrer à la maison avant le mercredi — ou au plus tôt le mardi. Et je m'en ressentais guère de chercher un autre hôtel pour m'y faire encore massacrer. Aussi ce que j'ai fait, j'ai dit au chauffeur de m'emmener à Grand Central Station. C'est tout près du Biltmore où j'avais donné rendez-vous à Sally et je me suis dit que je déposerais mes bagages à la consigne automatique, puis que j'irais prendre mon petit déjeuner. J'avais plutôt faim. Dans le taxi j'ai sorti mon portefeuille et j'ai compté mon argent. Je me rappelle plus exactement ce qui me restait mais c'était pas la gloire ni rien. Ces foutues deux dernières semaines j'avais dépensé une fortune. Sans rire. Je suis drôlement panier percé de nature. Ce que je dépense pas, je le perds. La moitié du temps j'oublie même de ramasser ma monnaie, au restaurant et dans les boîtes de nuit et tout. Mes parents ça les rend dingues. On peut pas leur en vouloir. Remarquez, mon père a du fric. Je sais pas combien il se fait — il discute jamais ce genre de choses avec moi — mais un bon paquet, j'imagine. Il est conseiller juridique. Ces gars-là ils s'en mettent plein les poches. Une autre raison que j'ai de me dire qu'il a du fric, c'est qu'il en investit dans des spectacles à Broadway. Ce sont toujours des fours, et ma mère ça la rend dingue. Elle est pas très costaud depuis que mon frère Allie est mort. Elle est toujours pas mal nerveuse. Voilà aussi pourquoi ça m'embêtait tellement qu'elle apprenne qu'on m'avait encore foutu dehors.

Quand mes valises ont été enfermées dans un casier de la consigne de la gare, je suis allé au buffet et j'ai commandé un petit déjeuner. Pour moi c'était un énorme petit déjeuner — du jus d'orange, des œufs au bacon, des toasts et du café. D'habitude, je bois seulement un peu de jus d'orange. Je suis pas un gros mangeur. Vraiment pas. C'est pourquoi je suis tellement maigre. On m'a mis à ce régime où on ingurgite plein de féculents et de cochonneries pour gagner du poids et tout, mais je l'ai même pas suivi. Quand je sors, généralement je mange un sandwich au fromage et je bois un verre de lait malté. C'est pas beaucoup, mais dans le lait malté y a plein de vitamines. H.V. Caulfield. Holden Vitamine Caulfield.

Tandis que je mangeais mes œufs, deux religieuses sont entrées avec leurs bagages et tout — j'imaginais qu'elles attendaient le train pour changer de couvent ou quoi — et elles se sont assises au comptoir à côté de moi. Elles avaient l'air de pas savoir quoi faire de leurs bagages, aussi je leur ai donné un coup de main. C'était ce genre de valises bon marché, qui sont pas en vrai cuir ni rien. Je sais que ça n'a aucune importance mais pourtant j'aime pas lorsque quelqu'un a des valises camelotes. C'est terrible à dire, mais je peux même détester quelqu'un rien qu'à regarder ses valises, si elles sont trop camelotes. Une fois, il m'est arrivé un drôle de truc. Quand j'étais à Elkton Hills, au début j'ai créché avec un gars, Dick Slage, qu'avait des valises vraiment purée. Au lieu de les poser sur l'étagère il les laissait sous le lit pour que personne les voie à côté des miennes. Ça me déprimait à

133

mort et j'avais envie de foutre les miennes en l'air ou même de les échanger avec les siennes. Les miennes venaient de chez Mark Cross et elles étaient garanties cuir de vache véritable et tout et je suppose qu'elles avaient coûté un joli paquet. Mais curieusement, voilà ce qui s'est passé. Ce que j'ai fait, j'ai fini par mettre *ma* valise sous *mon* lit au lieu de la mettre sur l'étagère parce que, comme ça, le gars Slage aurait plus son foutu complexe d'infériorité. Alors voilà ce qu'il a fait, lui. Le lendemain, il a ressorti ma valise de sous le lit et il l'a replacée sur l'étagère. J'ai mis un petit moment pour comprendre. Il voulait que les gens se figurent que ma valise c'était à lui. Tout simplement. Pour ça il était bizarre. Par exemple il me lançait toujours des plaisanteries désagréables au sujet de mes valises. Il arrêtait pas de déclarer qu'elles étaient trop neuves, ça faisait *bourgeois*. C'était son mot favori. Il l'avait lu quelque part ou entendu quelque part. Tout ce que je possédais était vachement *bourgeois*. Même mon stylo était *bourgeois*. Fallait toujours qu'il me l'emprunte mais ça restait quand même un stylo *bourgeois*. On a été ensemble seulement deux mois. Ensuite, l'un et l'autre, on a demandé à changer. Le plus drôle c'est qu'après il m'a plutôt manqué, parce qu'il avait un foutu sens de l'humour et quelquefois on se payait du bon temps. Ça me surprendrait pas tellement que je lui aie manqué aussi. D'abord, c'était seulement histoire de blaguer qu'il disait que mes affaires faisaient trop *bourgeois*, ça me gênait pas et même ça m'aurait plutôt amusé. Mais peu à peu ça a cessé d'être une blague. Au fond, c'est vraiment difficile de partager une chambre avec quelqu'un si vos valises sont nettement mieux que les siennes — quand elles sont de premier choix et pas les siennes. On pourrait se dire que si l'autre est intelligent et tout et qu'il a le sens de l'humour, il devrait s'en foutre de pas avoir les meilleures valises. Mais voilà, il s'en fout pas. Pas du tout. C'est une des raisons pourquoi j'ai fini par loger avec un crétin comme Stradlater. Au moins il avait rien à m'envier, question valises.

Bon. Les deux religieuses étaient assises à côté de moi et on a comme qui dirait engagé la conversation. Celle qui était la plus proche avait un de ces paniers dont se servent les religieuses et les nanas de l'Armée du Salut pour quêter, à Noël. On les voit au coin des rues, spécialement dans la Cinquième avenue, devant les grands magasins et tout. Bref, celle qui était près de moi a laissé tomber le sien par terre et je me suis baissé pour le ramasser. Je lui ai demandé si elle faisait la quête pour une œuvre charitable. Elle a dit non. Elle a dit qu'elle avait pas réussi à mettre le panier dans la valise, alors elle le portait à la main, c'était tout. Quand elle vous regardait, elle souriait gentiment. Elle avait un grand nez et dessus des lunettes avec une monture métallique ce qui est pas très joli, mais son visage était vraiment agréable. Je lui ai dit « Je pensais que si vous faisiez la quête je pourrais vous remettre ma petite contribution. Vous garderiez l'argent pour le jour où vous feriez vraiment la quête ».

Elle a dit « Oh ! vous êtes trop aimable ». Et l'autre, son amie, a levé la tête. L'autre, tout en buvant son café, lisait un petit livre noir qui ressemblait à la Bible mais en bien plus mince. Pourtant c'était un livre du même genre que la Bible. Toutes les deux, elles déjeunaient de toasts et de café. Ça me déprimait. Je déteste manger des œufs et du bacon ou quoi à côté de quelqu'un qui prend seulement du café et des toasts.

Elles m'ont laissé leur donner dix dollars pour leurs œuvres. Elles arrêtaient pas de me demander si j'étais sûr que je pouvais me le permettre et tout. Je leur ai dit que j'avais pas mal d'argent mais elles voulaient pas me croire. Finalement, elles ont pris mon billet. Et elles m'ont tellement remercié que ça devenait embarrassant. J'ai détourné la conversation vers des sujets d'ordre général et je leur ai demandé où elles allaient. Elles m'ont dit qu'elles étaient professeurs et qu'elles venaient de Chicago pour enseigner dans un couvent de la Cent soixante-dix-huitième Rue ou peut-être la Cent quatre-vingt-deuxième Rue, une de ces rues loin là-bas dans les quartiers chics. Celle qui était près de moi, avec les lunettes à monture métallique, m'a dit qu'elle enseignait la littérature et que sa compagne était prof d'histoire et d'instruction civique. Puis je me suis mis à me demander vraiment ce que pouvait bien penser — étant une religieuse et tout — celle qui était assise près de moi et qui enseignait la littérature, quand elle lisait certains livres au programme. Des livres où on parlait pas nécessairement de plein de choses sexuelles mais des livres avec des amants et tout. Prenez l'Eustacia Vye, dans *Le Retour au pays natal* de Thomas Hardy. Elle était pas tellement sexy ni rien mais quand même on se demande ce qu'une bonne sœur qui lit le bouquin peut bien en penser. Évidemment j'ai pas posé la question. Tout ce que j'ai dit c'est que la littérature était ma matière favorite.

« Oh ! vraiment ? Oh ! j'en suis ravie, a dit celle qui enseignait la littérature. Qu'avez-vous lu cette année ? Ça m'intéresserait de le savoir. » Elle était vraiment sympa.

« Eh bien, la plupart du temps on faisait les Anglo-Saxons. Beowulf et Grendel et Lord Randal My Son et tout ça. Mais quelquefois on devait lire en option des livres supplémentaires. J'ai lu *Le Retour au pays natal* de Thomas Hardy, et *Roméo et Juliette* et *Jules Cés...*

— Oh ! *Roméo et Juliette*. Très bien. Vous avez

aimé, je suppose ? » On aurait pas vraiment cru que c'était une religieuse qui parlait.

« Oui. Oui, j'ai beaucoup aimé. Il y avait quelques petites choses que j'aimais pas. Mais dans l'ensemble c'est très émouvant.

— Qu'est-ce que vous n'aimiez pas ? Vous en souvenez-vous ? »

Franchement, c'était gênant en un sens de parler de *Roméo et Juliette* avec elle. Parce qu'il y a du sexe ici et là dans la pièce et elle c'était une religieuse et tout. Mais elle me demandait, alors j'ai discuté un peu avec elle. « Ben, Roméo moi je l'adore pas, et Juliette pas tellement non plus. Non, je les adore pas. Je veux dire... je les aime bien mais... Par moments, ils sont pas mal énervants. En somme, la mort de Mercutio, j'ai trouvé ça beaucoup plus triste que celle de Roméo et Juliette. En fait, j'aimais plus tellement Roméo après que Mercutio a été poignardé par cet autre type — le cousin de Juliette — c'est quoi son nom ?

— Tybalt.

— Ah ! oui, Tybalt. Le nom de celui-là, je l'oublie toujours. C'était la faute de Roméo. Moi, celui que j'aime le mieux, dans la pièce, c'est Mercutio. Tous ces Montagu et Capulet ils sont pas mal — spécialement Juliette — mais Mercutio il était... c'est dur à expliquer. Il était très intelligent et amusant et tout. Ça me rend dingue si quelqu'un se fait tuer — spécialement quelqu'un de très intelligent et amusant et tout — et que c'est la faute de quelqu'un d'autre. Roméo et Juliette, au moins, c'était leur faute à eux. »

La religieuse m'a demandé « Dans quelle école êtes-vous ? » Elle voulait probablement qu'on en finisse avec Roméo et Juliette.

Je lui ai dit à Pencey, et elle en avait entendu parler. Elle a dit que c'était une très bonne école. J'ai laissé passer. Puis l'autre, celle qui enseignait l'histoire, elle a dit qu'il fallait qu'elles se sauvent. J'ai pris la note pour leur déjeuner, mais elles ont pas voulu me laisser payer. Celle avec les lunettes m'a obligé à lui rendre le papier.

Elle a dit « Vous avez été plus que généreux. Vous êtes un très gentil garçon ». Elle était vraiment sympa. Elle me rappelait un peu la mère du gars Ernest Morrow, que j'avais rencontrée dans le train. Principalement quand elle souriait. Elle a dit « Nous avons été si heureuses de bavarder avec vous. »

J'ai dit que moi aussi j'avais été heureux de bavarder avec elles. Et c'était la vérité. Je crois que j'aurais été encore plus heureux si j'avais pas eu peur, tout le temps où on parlait, qu'elles essaient subitement de savoir si j'étais catholique. Les catholiques essaient toujours de savoir si vous êtes catholique. A moi ça m'arrive surtout parce que mon nom de famille est irlandais et que la plupart des gens d'origine irlandaise sont catholiques. En fait, mon père était catholique. Il a renoncé quand il a épousé ma mère. Mais les catholiques essaient toujours de savoir si vous êtes catholique, même quand ils ignorent votre nom de famille. Lorsque j'étais à Whooton j'ai connu un gars, Louis Gorman, qui était catholique. Le premier gars que j'ai connu là-bas. Lui et moi, le jour de la rentrée, on était assis sur deux chaises voisines, dans le couloir de l'infirmerie, attendant de passer la visite médicale, et on s'est mis à parler tennis. Il était très intéressé par le tennis et moi aussi. Il m'a dit qu'il allait chaque été aux championnats nationaux, à Forest Hills ; je lui ai dit que moi aussi, et ensuite pendant un bon moment on a discuté des grands cracks du tennis. Il en connaissait un fichu rayon sur le tennis, pour un gars de son âge. Sans blague. Puis, subitement, en plein milieu de la conversation, il m'a demandé « Tu ne saurais pas par hasard où se trouve l'église catholique ? » Et à la façon dont il le demandait, c'était sûr qu'il essayait de savoir si j'étais catholique. Pas moyen de s'y tromper. Non qu'il ait eu des préjugés, mais il voulait savoir. Il était content de parler tennis et tout, mais ça se voyait qu'il aurait été encore *plus* content si j'avais été catholique et tout. Ces trucs-là, ça me rend dingue. Je dirais pas que ça a gâché toute notre convers' — pas vraiment — mais ça lui a quand même pas fait du bien. Voilà pourquoi j'étais content que les deux religieuses me demandent pas si j'étais catholique. Probable que la conversation aurait pas été complètement gâchée mais ça aurait pas été pareil. Je reproche rien aux catholiques. Certainement pas. Je m'y prendrais sans doute de la même façon si moi j'étais catholique. En un sens, c'est juste comme mon histoire de valises. Tout ce que je dis c'est une convers' sympa, ça l'esquinterait plutôt. Voilà tout ce que je dis.

Quand les deux religieuses se sont levées pour partir, j'ai fait quelque chose de très stupide et très gênant. Je fumais une cigarette et en me levant à mon tour pour leur dire au revoir je leur ai soufflé par mégarde de la fumée à la figure. C'était vraiment pas exprès, mais quand même. Je leur ai présenté mille excuses et elles ont été très polies et compréhensives et tout. Mais quand même, c'était gênant.

Après leur départ, j'ai regretté de leur avoir donné que dix dollars pour la quête. Mais j'avais pris ce rendez-vous avec Sally Hayes pour aller au théâtre et fallait bien que je garde un peu de fric pour les billets et tout. Ça m'empêchait pas de regretter. Saleté de pognon. Qui finit toujours par vous flanquer le cafard.

CHAPITRE 16

QUAND j'ai eu fini mon petit déjeuner il était guère plus de midi et je devais retrouver la môme Sally qu'à deux heures, aussi je suis parti en balade. J'arrêtais pas de penser aux deux bonnes sœurs. J'arrêtais pas de penser à ce vieux panier esquinté qui leur servait pour la quête quand elles étaient pas occupées à faire la classe. J'essayais de me représenter ma mère ou quelqu'un d'autre, ma tante, ou la mère plutôt barjot de Sally Hayes quêtant pour les pauvres à l'entrée d'un grand magasin en récoltant le fric dans un vieux panier esquinté. C'était difficile à imaginer. Pas tellement ma mère, mais les deux autres. Ma tante est pas mal charitable, elle se remue beaucoup pour la Croix-Rouge et tout, mais elle est très bien sapée avec du rouge à lèvres et autres cochonneries. J'ai peine à me la figurer prenant part à une œuvre de bienfaisance s'il fallait pour ça qu'elle porte des vêtements noirs et pas de rouge à lèvres. Et la mère de Sally, bordel. Celle-là, pour qu'elle fasse la quête avec un panier à la main, faudrait qu'elle soit fichument sûre que les gens en lui donnant leur obole seront baba d'admiration. S'ils se contentaient de laisser tomber leur fric dans le panier et puis s'en allaient sans rien lui dire, en l'ignorant et tout, elle en aurait très vite marre, elle resterait pas plus d'une heure, elle rendrait son panier et elle s'en irait déjeuner dans un endroit chic. C'est ce qui me plaisait avec ces religieuses. On pouvait dire immédiatement qu'elles allaient jamais déjeuner dans un endroit chic. Mais aussi ça me rendait vachement triste, la pensée qu'elles allaient jamais déjeuner dans un endroit chic. Je savais que c'était pas trop important, et quand même ça me rendait triste.

Je me suis mis à marcher vers Broadway, comme ça, parce que ça faisait des années que j'étais pas allé par là. Et puis j'espérais trouver un magasin de disques ouvert le dimanche. Il y avait ce disque que je voulais acheter pour Phoebé, qui s'appelait *Little Shirley Beans*. C'était difficile de se le procurer. Ça parlait d'une petite gamine qui voulait pas sortir de la maison parce que ses deux dents de devant étaient tombées et elle avait honte. J'avais entendu ce disque à Pencey. Un garçon d'un autre étage le faisait souvent passer et je lui avais demandé de me le vendre parce que je savais que ça plairait à la môme Phoebé mais il a refusé. C'était un très vieux disque, un disque super que cette chanteuse noire, Estelle Fletcher, a fait il y a vingt ans environ. Elle chante ça très Dixieland et provocant, pas le moins du monde à l'eau de rose. Une blanche, elle chanterait ça tout sucré, mais la môme Estelle Fletcher, elle connaissait son boulot et c'est un des meilleurs disques que j'aie jamais entendus. Je pensais l'acheter dans un des magasins ouverts le dimanche et puis l'emporter au parc. C'était dimanche, et le dimanche Phoebé va très souvent au parc pour faire du patin à roulettes. Et je savais quels endroits elle fréquente.

Il faisait pas aussi froid que la veille mais le soleil s'était pas encore montré, un temps pas terrible pour la balade. Quand même y avait quelque chose de bien. Une famille marchait devant moi, des gens qui sortaient de l'église, c'était visible, le père, la mère et un petit gosse dans les six ans. Ils avaient l'air plutôt pauvres. Le père portait un de ces chapeaux gris perle que portent les pauvres quand ils se mettent en frais. Lui et sa femme avançaient en bavardant, sans surveiller leur gosse. Le gosse était impec. Au lieu de marcher sur le trottoir il se baladait dans la rue mais tout près du bord du trottoir. Il faisait comme font les gosses, comme s'il marchait sur une ligne bien droite, et tout le temps il arrêtait pas de fredonner. Je l'ai rattrapé, et j'ai entendu ce qu'il chantait. C'était ce truc "Si un cœur attrape un cœur qui vient à travers les seigles". Il avait une jolie petite voix. Il chantait comme ça, pour lui tout seul. Les voitures passaient en vrombissant, les freins grinçaient tous azimuts, ses parents faisaient pas attention et il continuait à longer le trottoir, en chantant "Si un cœur attrape un cœur qui vient à travers les seigles". Alors je me suis senti mieux. Je me suis senti beaucoup moins déprimé.

À Broadway, y avait la grande foule et la pagaille. Dimanche, et seulement midi, et quand même partout du monde. Les gens allaient au ciné — le Paramount, ou l'Astor, ou le Strand ou le Capitol, ou un autre de ces endroits dingues. Ils étaient tous sur leur trente et un, parce que c'était dimanche, et ça n'arrangeait rien. Mais le pire c'est qu'on pouvait voir que tous ils *voulaient* aller au ciné. Je pouvais pas supporter. Je peux comprendre qu'on aille au ciné quand on a rien d'autre à faire, mais quelqu'un qui *veut* y aller, et même marche à toute pompe pour y arriver plus vite, ça me démolit. Spécialement quand je vois des millions de gens qui font la queue, une queue terrible qui va jusqu'au coin de la rue suivante, et les gens qui attendent avec une patience du tonnerre de prendre leurs billets et tout. Ouah, j'aurais voulu foutre le camp de Broadway sur-le-champ. J'ai eu de la veine. Dans le premier magasin de disques où je suis entré, ils avaient un exemplaire de *Little Shirley Beans*. Ils m'ont fait payer cinq dollars vu que c'était un disque si difficile à trouver, mais je m'en moquais pas mal. Ouah, qu'est-ce que j'étais heureux ! J'avais vachement hâte d'être au parc pour voir si Phoebé était là et lui remettre son cadeau.

En sortant du magasin de disques, je suis passé devant un drugstore et je suis entré. J'avais comme l'intention de donner un coup de bigo à la môme Jane pour savoir si elle était déjà en vacances. Donc je suis entré dans une cabine et je l'ai appelée. Par malheur, c'est sa mère qui a répondu, alors j'ai raccroché. Je m'en ressentais pas de me laisser entraîner dans un long discours et tout. J'adore pas parler au téléphone avec les mères des filles que je connais. J'aurais pu au moins lui demander si Jane était rentrée. Ça aurait pas été la mort. Mais j'avais pas envie. Faut être en forme pour faire ça.

Je devais encore me procurer ces foutues places de théâtre, aussi j'ai acheté un journal et regardé ce qui se jouait. Comme c'était dimanche il y avait seulement environ trois spectacles. Aussi ce que j'ai fait, je suis allé prendre deux places d'orchestre pour *I know my love*. C'était une séance de bienfaisance. J'avais pas tellement envie de voir ça mais je savais que la môme Sally, la reine des cruches, elle allait en faire tout un plat quand je lui dirais que j'avais des places, bicause y avait les Lunt et tout. Elle aime les spectacles qui sont censés être très sophistiqués et pleins d'humour et tout, avec les Lunt et tout. Pas moi. Si vous voulez savoir, j'aime pas beaucoup le théâtre. C'est pas aussi dégueulasse que le cinéma mais y a vraiment pas de quoi s'extasier. D'abord je déteste les acteurs. Ils agissent jamais comme des gens ordinaires. Ils *croient* qu'ils le font. Les bons le font parfois — disons, un peu — mais pas de telle façon que ce soit drôle à regarder, et si un acteur est vraiment bon, c'est tout de suite évident qu'il *sait* qu'il est bon, et ça gâche tout. Prenez par exemple Sir Laurence Olivier. Je l'ai vu dans *Hamlet*. D.B. nous a emmenés voir *Hamlet* l'année dernière, Phoebé et moi. Il nous a d'abord emmenés déjeuner au restaurant et après on est allés voir Sir Laurence Olivier dans *Hamlet*. Lui, il l'avait déjà vu, et à la façon dont il en parlait, pendant le déjeuner, j'avais une hâte folle de le voir moi aussi. Mais ça m'a pas tellement plu. J'arrive pas à comprendre ce que Sir Laurence Olivier a de si merveilleux, c'est tout. Il a une diction du tonnerre et il est vachement beau et il est agréable à regarder quand il marche ou qu'il se bat en duel ou quoi, mais d'après ce qu'avait dit D.B. c'était pas du tout comme ça qu'il était, Hamlet. Là on aurait dit un foutu général, au lieu d'un type du genre triste et coincé. Ce qu'il y avait de mieux c'était quand le frère d'Ophélie, celui qui à la fin se bat en duel avec Hamlet, était sur le point de s'en aller, et son père lui donnait un tas de conseils. Pendant que le père lui donnait ses conseils, la môme Ophélie chahutait avec son frère, le taquinant, s'amusant à tirer son épée du fourreau et quand même il s'efforçait d'avoir l'air intéressé par les salades de son père. Ça c'était chouette. Ça, j'ai vraiment aimé. Mais y a pas tellement de choses dans ce genre. La seule chose que la môme Phoebé a aimé, elle, c'est quand Hamlet tapote la tête de son chien. Elle a trouvé que c'était drôle et gentil. Ça l'était. Ce qu'il faut c'est que je lise cette pièce. Voilà l'ennui, faut toujours que je lise les trucs moi-même. Un acteur sur la scène, je l'écoute à peine. J'en finis pas de me tracasser de peur que d'une minute à l'autre il fasse quelque chose qui colle pas.

Quand j'ai eu les places pour le spectacle avec les Lunt, j'ai pris un taxi pour aller au parc. J'aurais dû prendre le métro ou quoi bicause je commençais à être à court de fric mais je voulais quitter cette saleté de Broadway le plus vite possible.

Dans le parc c'était infect. Il faisait pas trop froid mais le soleil se montrait toujours pas, et on avait l'impression qu'il y avait rien dans le parc que les crottes de chien et les mollards et les mégots des vieux et que si on voulait s'asseoir tous les bancs seraient mouillés. De quoi vous foutre le bourdon, et de temps en temps, en marchant, sans raison spéciale, on avait la chair de poule. On pouvait pas se figurer que Noël viendrait bientôt. On pouvait pas se figurer qu'il y aurait encore quelque chose qui viendrait. Mais j'ai continué à me diriger vers le Mall parce que c'est là qu'elle va, Phoebé, habituellement. Elle aime faire du patin près du kiosque à musique. C'est drôle. Moi aussi, quand j'étais petit, c'était ma place favorite.

Pourtant, quand je suis arrivé, je l'ai vue nulle part. Il y avait quelques gosses qui patinaient et tout, et deux garçons qui jouaient au volant, mais pas de Phoebé. J'ai vu une gamine de son âge, assise toute seule sur un banc, qui resserrait ses patins. J'ai pensé que peut-être elle connaissait Phoebé et pourrait me dire où elle était, aussi je me suis approché et puis je me suis assis près d'elle et j'ai dit « Tu connaîtrais pas Phoebé Caulfield, par hasard ? »

Elle a dit « Qui ? » Elle était habillée avec seulement des jeans et environ vingt pull-overs. On voyait que c'était sa mère qui les lui tricotait, ses pulls, ils étaient plutôt informes.

« Phoebé Caulfield. Elle habite dans la Soixante et Onzième Rue. Elle est en septième, à...

— Vous la connaissez, vous ?

— Ouais, je suis son frère. Tu sais où elle est ? »

La gamine a demandé « Elle est dans la classe de Miss Callon, non ?

— Euh... Je crois.

— Alors elle va probablement au musée, aujourd'hui. Nous, on y est allés samedi dernier. »

J'ai demandé « Quel musée ? »

Elle a comme qui dirait haussé les épaules. Elle a dit « Je sais pas. Le *musée*.

— Oui. Mais celui où il y a les tableaux ou bien celui où il y a les Indiens ?

— Celui des Indiens. »

J'ai dit « Merci beaucoup ». Je me suis levé et déjà je m'en allais. Mais subitement je me suis souvenu que c'était dimanche. J'ai dit à la gamine « C'est *dimanche* ».

Elle a levé la tête. « Oh ! alors, elle y est pas. »

Elle se donnait un mal fou pour resserrer son patin. Elle avait pas de gants et ses mains étaient toutes rouges et glacées. Je l'ai aidée. Ouah, ça faisait des années que j'avais pas eu en main une clef de patins à roulettes. Et pourtant ça m'a pas semblé bizarre. Supposez que dans cinquante ans d'ici on me mette en main une clef de patins, dans le noir absolu en plus, et je saurai encore ce que c'est. Quand son patin a été arrangé elle m'a remercié et tout. C'était une gamine très gentille, très jolie. Bon Dieu, j'aime quand une gamine est gentille et polie si on lui a arrangé ses patins ou quoi. La plupart des gamines le sont. Sans blague. Je lui ai demandé si elle voulait venir prendre avec moi un chocolat chaud ou quoi mais elle a dit non merci. Elle a dit que son amie l'attendait. Les gamines, elles ont toujours une amie qui les attend. Ça me tue.

C'était dimanche et donc Phoebé serait pas là avec sa classe et le temps était humide et pourri mais quand même j'ai traversé le parc jusqu'au musée d'Histoire naturelle. Je savais que c'était de ce musée-là qu'elle parlait, la gosse aux patins. Je connaissais par cœur la routine des visites au musée. Phoebé allait à la même école où j'allais quand j'étais petit et on se tapait tout le temps le musée. On avait ce prof, Miss Aigletinger, qui nous y emmenait presque tous les samedis. Parfois on observait les animaux et d'autres fois on regardait ce que les Indiens avaient fait dans les temps anciens. Poterie, et paniers tressés et tout ce fourbi. Quand j'y repense je suis tout content. Même à présent. Je me souviens qu'après avoir examiné les trucs des Indiens on se rendait généralement dans le grand auditorium pour voir un film. Christophe Colomb. Ils passaient tout le temps Christophe Colomb découvrant l'Amérique, ce mal qu'il avait eu à décider Frédéric et Isabelle à lui prêter le fric pour acheter des bateaux et puis les marins qui se mutinaient et tout. Le père Colomb on s'en foutait un peu mais on avait toujours plein de caramels et de chewing-gums et à l'intérieur de l'auditorium ça sentait vachement bon. Ça sentait comme s'il pleuvait dehors, même si en vrai il pleuvait pas, et qu'on aurait été dans le seul endroit au monde qui soit plaisant, sec, confortable. Je l'aimais, ce sacré musée. Je me souviens que pour aller à l'auditorium on traversait toute la salle des Indiens. C'était une longue longue salle et on pouvait parler qu'à voix basse. La maîtresse marchait en tête et la classe suivait en bon ordre. Une double rangée de mômes. Moi, en général, j'étais à côté d'une fille qui s'appelait Gertrude Levine. Il fallait tout le temps que je lui donne la main et sa main était tout le temps moite ou poisseuse. Le sol était en pierre et si on avait des billes et qu'on les laissait tomber elles rebondissaient comme des dingues dans un boucan de tous les diables, et la maîtresse arrêtait les rangs et revenait sur ses pas pour voir ce qui arrivait. Mais Miss Aigletinger, elle se fâchait jamais. Ensuite, on défilait devant cette longue longue pirogue, à peu près aussi longue que trois Cadillac mises bout à bout, avec dedans une vingtaine d'Indiens, quelques-uns qui pagayaient, d'autres qui se contentaient de prendre des airs de durs, et tous le visage barbouillé de peintures de guerre. Il y avait à l'arrière du canot un type très impressionnant qui portait un masque. C'était le sorcier. Il me donnait la chair de poule mais je l'aimais bien quand même. Et puis, si en passant quelqu'un touchait une pagaie ou quoi, un des gardes recommandait « On ne touche pas, les enfants » mais c'était dit d'une voix aimable, pas comme l'aurait dit un sale flic ni rien. Ensuite on longeait une grande vitrine avec dedans des Indiens qui frottaient des bâtons l'un contre l'autre pour faire du feu, et une squaw tissant une couverture. Cette squaw tissant la couverture était courbée sur son ouvrage et on voyait ses seins et tout. On s'en mettait plein les mirettes, même les filles qu'étaient que des gamines avec pas plus de seins que les garçons. Enfin, juste à l'entrée de l'auditorium, tout près de la porte, y avait l'esquimau. Il était assis au bord d'un trou dans un lac gelé et il pêchait. On voyait déjà au bord du trou deux poissons qu'il avait attrapés. Ouah, ce musée était plein de vitrines. Y en avait encore plus à l'étage avec dedans des cerfs qui buvaient l'eau d'une mare et des oiseaux qui gagnaient le sud pour y passer l'hiver. Les oiseaux les plus proches étaient empaillés et pendus à des fils, et ceux du fond étaient simplement peints sur les murs mais ils donnaient tous l'impression de voler vraiment vers le sud et si on penchait la tête, et si en quelque sorte on les regardait par en dessous ils semblaient encore plus pressés de voler vers le sud. Ce qui était extra dans ce musée c'est que tout restait toujours exactement pareil. Y avait jamais rien qui bougeait. Vous pouviez venir là cent mille fois et chaque fois cet esquimau aurait tout juste réussi à attraper ses deux poissons, les oiseaux seraient toujours en route vers le sud, les deux cerfs, avec toujours leurs beaux bois et leurs pattes fines, boiraient toujours dans la mare et cette squaw aux seins nus tisserait toujours la même couverture. Rien ne serait différent. Rien, excepté *vous*. *Vous* seriez différent. Certainement pas beaucoup plus vieux. Vous seriez juste différent, c'est tout. Cette fois-ci vous auriez un manteau. Ou bien le gosse qui vous donnait la main la fois précédente aurait la scarlatine et on vous aurait attribué un nouveau compagnon. Ou bien ce serait une suppléante qui serait en charge de la classe à la place de Miss Aigletinger. Ou vous auriez entendu vos parents se disputer très fort dans la salle de bain. Ou vous seriez juste passé dans la rue près d'une de ces flaques avec dedans des arcs-en-ciel de mazout. Je veux dire que d'une manière ou d'une autre vous seriez différent. Je peux pas expliquer. Et même si je pouvais, je suis pas sûr que j'en aurais envie.

Tout en marchant, j'ai sorti de ma poche ma vieille casquette de chasse et je l'ai mise sur ma tête. Je savais que je rencontrerais personne de connaissance et le temps était humide. J'ai marché, j'ai marché, et j'en finissais pas de penser à la môme Phoebé qui allait au musée le samedi comme j'avais fait. Je me disais qu'elle verrait les mêmes trucs que j'avais vus et que c'était *elle* à présent qui serait différente chaque fois qu'elle les verrait. En pensant à ça j'étais pas vraiment triste mais j'étais pas non plus follement gai. Y a des choses qui devraient rester comme elles sont. Faudrait pouvoir les planquer dans une de ces grandes vitrines et plus y toucher. Je sais que c'est impossible mais, bon, c'est bien dommage. Bref, je marchais je marchais et j'en finissais pas de penser à tout ça.

Je suis passé du côté du terrain de jeux et je me suis arrêté à regarder deux petits mômes qui faisaient de la balançoire. Y en avait un qu'était plutôt grassouillet et j'ai appuyé de la main sur la barre, du côté du plus maigre, pour équilibrer le poids en quelque sorte, mais c'était visible qu'ils voulaient pas que je m'occupe d'eux alors je les ai laissés tranquilles.

Puis il s'est produit quelque chose de bizarre. En arrivant devant le musée, subitement j'y serais pas entré pour un million de dollars. Ça me disait rien, voilà tout. Quand je pense que j'avais traversé ce maudit parc exprès pour ça. Je serais probablement entré si Phoebé avait été là, mais elle y était pas. Aussi, en arrivant devant le musée, j'ai simplement pris un taxi pour aller au Biltmore. Je mourais pas d'envie d'y aller, au Biltmore. Mais j'avais donné ce foutu rencard à Sally.

CHAPITRE 17

J'ÉTAIS vachement en avance au rendez-vous, aussi je me suis assis sur une de ces banquettes de cuir près de l'horloge dans le hall, et j'ai regardé les filles. Pour beaucoup de collèges les vacances avaient déjà commencé. Il y avait bien un million de filles, assises ou debout, ici et là, qui attendaient que leur copain se pointe. Filles croisant les jambes, filles croisant pas les jambes, filles avec des jambes du tonnerre, filles avec des jambes mochetingues, filles qui donnaient l'impression d'être extra, filles qui donnaient l'impression que si on les fréquentait ce seraient de vraies salopes. C'était comme un chouette lèche-vitrines, si vous voyez ce que je veux dire. En un sens c'était aussi un peu triste, parce qu'on pouvait pas s'empêcher de se demander ce qui leur arriverait, à toutes ces filles. Lorsqu'elles sortiraient du collège, je veux dire. On pouvait être sûr que la plupart se marieraient avec des mecs complètement abrutis. Des mecs qu'arrêtent pas de raconter combien leur foutue voiture fait de *miles* au gallon. Des mecs qui se vexent comme des mômes si on leur en met plein les narines au golf, ou même à un jeu stupide comme le ping-pong. Des mecs terriblement radins. Des mecs qui lisent jamais un bouquin. Des mecs super-casse-pieds. Mais là faut que je fasse attention. Je veux dire quand je parle de certains mecs qui sont casse-pieds. Je comprends pas les mecs casse-pieds. Non, vraiment pas. Quand j'étais à Elkton Hills j'ai partagé une piaule pendant deux mois avec un gars qui s'appelait Harris Macklin. Il était très intelligent et tout, mais c'était un des pires casse-pieds que j'aie jamais rencontrés. Il avait une de ces voix râpeuses, et pratiquement il arrêtait jamais de parler. Et le plus terrible c'est qu'il disait jamais rien qu'on aurait eu envie d'entendre. Mais y avait une chose qu'il pouvait faire. Il pouvait siffler mieux que n'importe qui, le salaud. Il était, disons, en train de retaper son lit, ou de ranger des trucs dans la penderie — il avait toujours des trucs à pendre, ça me rendait dingue — et alors il sifflait, du moins quand il parlait pas de sa drôle de voix râpeuse. Il pouvait même siffler du classique, mais la plupart du temps il sifflait du jazz. Il prenait quelque chose de très jazz, comme *Tin Roof Blues* et il le sifflait si bien, si tranquillement, tout en accrochant ses affaires, que franchement ça vous tuait. Naturellement, je lui ai jamais dit que je trouvais qu'il sifflait vraiment au poil. On va pas déclarer comme ça à quelqu'un « Tu siffles vraiment au poil ». Mais je suis resté avec lui pendant à peu près deux mois, quand même il était casse-pieds, juste parce qu'il sifflait vraiment au poil. Mieux que n'importe qui que j'aie jamais entendu. Donc, les casse-pieds, je peux pas en parler. Peut-être qu'on devrait pas tellement se tracasser si on voit une fille sensas' qu'en épouse un. La plupart font de mal à personne. Et peut-être que secrètement ils sifflent tous vraiment au poil ou quoi. Qui sait ? Pas moi.

Finalement, voilà que la môme Sally montait les marches, et je les ai descendues pour aller à sa rencontre. Elle était vachement chouette. Sans blague. Elle avait un manteau noir et une sorte de béret noir. Elle portait presque jamais de coiffure mais ce béret, c'était vraiment joli. Le plus drôle c'est que dès l'instant où je l'ai vue j'ai eu envie de me marier avec elle. Je suis dingue. Je la trouvais même pas tellement *sympa* et tout d'un coup je me sentais amoureux et je voulais qu'on se marie. Je vous jure, je suis dingue, faut le reconnaître.

« Holden. C'est merveilleux de te revoir. Y a si longtemps ! » Elle a une voix qui vous casse les oreilles et ça me gêne quand on est quelque part ensemble. Ça passe parce que c'est une tellement belle fille. Mais quand même ça m'emmerde toujours.

J'ai dit « C'est extra de te revoir ». Et je le pensais. « Alors, comment tu vas ?

— Absolument impec. Je suis en retard ? »

J'ai dit non. Pourtant elle était en retard d'à peu près dix minutes. Je m'en foutais. Toutes ces conneries dans les bandes dessinées du *Saturday Evening Post* et tout, montrant des types au coin des rues qui sont furax parce que leur copine les fait attendre — de la blague. Quand elle arrive au rendez-vous, si une fille a une allure folle qui va se plaindre qu'elle est en retard ? Personne. J'ai dit « Vaudrait mieux se dépêcher. Le spectacle commence à deux heures quarante ». On a descendu les marches vers l'endroit où sont les taxis.

Elle a demandé « Qu'est-ce qu'on va voir ?

— Je sais pas. Les Lunt. Y a que pour ça que j'ai pu avoir des places.

— Les Lunt ? Oh ! merveilleux. » Je vous le disais qu'elle serait ravie quand elle saurait qu'on allait voir les Lunt.

On a un peu flirté dans le taxi qui nous emmenait au théâtre. D'abord elle voulait pas bicause elle avait du rouge à lèvres et tout, mais je faisais ça vraiment au séducteur et elle avait pas le choix. Deux fois, quand le taxi a dû s'arrêter brusquement bicause la circulation je suis presque tombé de mon siège. Ces salopards de chauffeurs de taxi ils regardent jamais où ils vont, je vous jure. Puis, juste pour vous montrer que je suis vraiment barjot, comme on se remettait de la grande embrassade je lui ai dit que je l'aimais et tout. Naturellement, c'était un mensonge. Mais au moment où je l'ai dit j'étais sincère. Je suis dingue, je vous jure.

Elle a dit « Oh ! chéri, moi aussi je t'aime ». Et puis sans même reprendre son souffle « Promets-moi que tu laisseras repousser tes cheveux. Les coupes en brosse ça devient ringard. Et tu as de si jolis cheveux ». Jolis, mon cul.

Le spectacle était pas aussi mauvais que certains que j'ai vus. C'était quand même du genre merdique. Environ cinq cent mille ans dans la vie d'un vieux couple. Ça commence quand ils sont jeunes et tout, et puis les parents de la fille veulent pas qu'elle épouse le garçon mais elle l'épouse quand même. Ensuite ils vieillissent. De plus en plus. Le mari va à la guerre et la femme a un frère qui boit. J'arrivais pas trop à m'y intéresser. Je veux dire que ça me faisait trop rien quand quelqu'un mourait dans la famille ou quoi. C'était juste une poignée d'acteurs. Le mari et la femme étaient un vieux couple pas mal — avec de l'humour et tout — mais j'arrivais pas à m'y intéresser. D'abord, ils arrêtaient pas, tout le temps que durait la pièce, de boire du thé ou un truc du même métal. Chaque fois qu'on les voyait on voyait aussi un genre de maître d'hôtel qui leur fourguait du thé ou bien c'était elle, la femme, qui versait du thé à quelqu'un. Et y avait tout un peuple qui allait et venait sans cesse — on en était étourdi à voir les gens toujours s'asseoir et se lever. Alfred Lunt et Lynn Fontane jouaient le vieux couple et ils étaient très bons mais je les aimais pas tellement. Je dois dire pourtant qu'ils étaient particuliers. Ils jouaient pas comme des gens ordinaires, ils jouaient pas non plus comme des acteurs. C'est difficile à expliquer. Ils jouaient plutôt comme s'ils savaient qu'ils étaient des célébrités et tout. Ce que je veux dire c'est qu'ils étaient bons, mais qu'ils étaient *trop* bons. Quand l'un avait fini sa tirade, l'autre lui donnait la réplique à toute vitesse. C'était censé être la façon dont les gens parlent et s'interrompent et tout. L'ennui c'est que ça faisait *trop* comme les gens parlent et s'interrompent. Ils jouaient un peu à la manière du gars Ernie jouant du piano, au Village. Quand on est *trop* bon, alors, après un moment, si on n'y prend pas garde, on a tendance à se donner des airs. Et on n'est plus bon du tout. En tout cas ils étaient les seuls de la troupe — les Lunt — qui paraissaient avoir quelque chose dans la tête. Faut le reconnaître.

A la fin du premier acte, on est sortis avec tous les autres connards pour fumer une cigarette. Vous parlez d'un plaisir. Dans toute votre vie vous avez jamais vu autant de mecs à la gomme qui fumaient comme des locomotives en discourant sur la pièce et en s'arrangeant pour que tout le monde puisse entendre leurs remarques subtiles. Près de nous un abruti d'acteur de cinéma tirait sur sa sèche. Je sais pas comment il s'appelle, mais il joue toujours le rôle d'un gars qui dans un film de guerre est toujours saisi de trouille quand vient le moment de passer à l'attaque. Il était avec une superbe blonde, et tous les deux s'efforçaient de prendre un air blasé et tout, comme s'ils ignoraient que les gens les regardaient. Drôlement modestes. Je me marrais bien. Sally disait pas grand-chose (sauf pour s'extasier sur les Lunt) bicause elle était occupée à se montrer et faire du charme. Subitement, à l'autre bout du hall, elle a vu un type qu'elle connaissait. Un type qui portait un de ces costumes de flanelle gris foncé, et un gilet à carreaux. Très classe. Un peu bien. Il était debout contre le mur, à fumer comme une cheminée d'usine avec un air de se barber royalement. La môme Sally en finissait pas de répéter « J'ai déjà rencontré ce gars quelque part ». Quel que soit l'endroit où on l'emmenait, elle avait toujours déjà rencontré quelqu'un, ou du moins elle se le figurait. Elle a répété ça jusqu'à ce que j'en aie marre et que je lui dise « Si tu le connais, pourquoi tu vas pas lui faire la bise ? Il serait content ». Quand j'ai dit ça elle a râlé. Mais finalement le type l'a vue et il est venu vers nous et ils se sont dit bonjour. Si vous aviez pu être là quand ils se sont dit bonjour. Vous auriez eu l'impression qu'ils s'étaient pas vus depuis au moins vingt ans. Vous auriez eu l'impression qu'au temps où ils étaient mômes ils prenaient leur bain dans le même baquet. De vrais potes. J'en avais la nausée. Le plus drôle c'est qu'ils s'étaient probablement rencontrés juste une fois, à une de ces conneries de surprises-parties. Quand les mamours ont été terminés, la môme Sally a fait les présentations. Le nom du gars c'était George quelque chose — je me rappelle même pas — et il était à Andover. Tu parles. Vous auriez dû le voir quand Sally lui a demandé comment il trouvait la pièce. C'était le genre de mec bidon qui a besoin d'espace pour répondre quand on lui pose une question. Il a reculé, et il a marché en plein sur le panard de la dame qu'était derrière lui. Il lui a probablement cassé tous les orteils. Il a dit que la pièce elle-même était pas un chef-d'œuvre mais que les Lunt bien sûr étaient tout simplement des anges. Des anges. Putain. *Des anges.* Ça m'a tué. Puis lui et Sally se sont mis à parler d'un tas de gens qu'ils connaissaient tous les deux. C'était la convers' la plus débile que j'aie jamais entendue. Ils arrêtaient pas de penser à toute bringue à des endroits et puis de penser à des gens qui y vivaient et de mentionner leur nom. Quand le moment est venu de retourner s'asseoir j'étais sur le point de dégueuler. Et après, à l'entracte suivant, ils ont continué leur chiante conversation. Ils ont continué de penser à encore d'autres endroits et à encore d'autres gens qui y vivaient. Le pire c'est que le mec avait une de ces voix à la con, très Ivy League, une voix très fatiguée, snobinarde. On aurait cru entendre une fille. Le fumier, il se gênait pas pour me chouraver mon rancard. A la fin de la représentation, j'ai même cru un instant qu'il allait prendre un taxi avec nous. Il nous a accompagnés sur le trottoir un bout de chemin. Mais il devait retrouver d'autres abrutis, pour boire un verre il a dit. Je me les représentais installés tous ensemble dans un bar, avec leurs gilets à carreaux, critiquant les pièces et les livres et les femmes de leurs voix fatiguées, snobinardes. Ils me tuent, ces mecs.

Lorsqu'on en a été à prendre le taxi, après avoir écouté pendant dix heures ce sale faux jeton qui va à Andover, ben la Sally je la détestais. J'étais vraiment prêt à la ramener chez elle et tout — pas de problème — mais elle a dit « J'ai une idée sensas' ». Elle avait toujours des idées sensas'. Elle a dit « Écoute, à quelle heure dois-tu être chez toi pour dîner ? Je veux dire, es-tu terriblement pressé ou quoi ? Dois-tu rentrer pour une heure précise ? »

J'ai dit « Moi ? Non. N'importe quelle heure ». Ouah. Là, vraiment je baratinais pas. « Pourquoi ?

— Si on allait faire du patin à glace à Radio-City ? »

C'est le genre d'idée sensas' qu'elle avait toujours.

« Du patin à glace à Radio-City ? Tu veux dire maintenant ?

— Rien qu'une heure. Tu ne veux pas ? Si vraiment tu n'en as pas envie... »

J'ai dit « J'ai jamais dit que je voulais pas. Si *toi* tu en as envie, allons-y.

157

— Vraiment ? Ne dis pas oui si tu n'y tiens pas. Tu sais ça m'est égal qu'on y aille ou pas. »

Tu parles que ça lui était égal !

Elle a dit « On peut louer ces adorables petites jupes de patinage. Jeannette Cultz en a loué une la semaine dernière. »

Et voilà pourquoi elle était tellement emballée. Elle voulait se voir dans une de ces petites jupes qui descendent juste au ras des fesses et tout.

Alors on y est allé et ils nous ont donné des patins, et ils ont fourni à Sally cette petite jupe tortille-du-cul en toile bleue. Je dois reconnaître que là-dedans elle était vraiment chouette. Et faudrait pas croire qu'elle l'ignorait. Elle s'arrangeait pour marcher devant moi et me présenter son mignon petit cul en direct. Vrai, il était plutôt mignon.

Le plus drôle c'est qu'on était elle et moi les super-cloches de toute la patinoire. Je dis bien, les super-cloches. Parce que des cloches y en avait. Les chevilles de la môme Sally se pliaient en dedans, pratiquement jusqu'à toucher la glace. Ses chevilles, elles avaient l'air con et aussi elles devaient lui faire un mal de chien. Les miennes non plus étaient pas à la fête. Les miennes, c'était la torture. On devait avoir une fichue allure. Et le pire c'est qu'on s'exhibait devant au moins deux cents personnes qu'avaient rien de mieux à foutre que de rester plantées au bord et regarder les autres ramasser des gadins.

J'ai fini par dire « Veux-tu qu'on aille s'asseoir à l'intérieur et on boira quelque chose ? »

Elle a dit « Ça alors c'est une idée géniale ». Elle aussi elle souffrait le martyre. C'était inhumain. Elle me faisait pitié.

On a ôté les foutus patins et on est entrés dans le bar où on peut aller en chaussettes se rafraîchir l'intérieur en regardant les patineurs. Aussitôt assise la môme Sally a enlevé ses gants et je lui ai donné une cigarette. Elle avait l'air plutôt misérable. Le garçon est arrivé et j'ai commandé un coca pour elle — qui boit pas d'alcool — et pour moi un whisky mais il a pas voulu m'en servir, le salaud, alors j'ai pris aussi un coca. Puis je me suis mis à faire brûler des allumettes. Je m'amuse à ça quand je suis d'une humeur particulière. Je les fais brûler jusqu'à ce que je puisse plus les tenir, alors je les laisse tomber dans le cendrier. C'est à cause des nerfs.

Puis subitos' et sans prévenir, Sally a dit « Écoute, faut que je sache. Tu viens m'aider à décorer l'arbre, la veille de Noël ou tu viens pas ? Faut que je sache ». Elle était encore de mauvais poil à cause de ses chevilles.

« Je t'ai écrit que je viendrai. Tu me l'as demandé au moins vingt fois. Je viens, d'accord.

— C'est que, tu comprends, faut que je sache. » Elle s'est mise à observer tout ce qui se passait dans la salle.

Brusquement je me suis arrêté de frotter les allumettes. Et je me suis penché vers elle par-dessus la table. Y avait des trucs qui me trottaient dans la tête. J'ai dit « Hé, Sally.

— Quoi ? » Elle examinait une autre fille, au bout de la salle.

J'ai demandé « Dis, Sally, t'en as jamais marre ? Je veux dire, t'as jamais peur que tout devienne dégueulasse si tu fais pas quelque chose pour l'empêcher ? Je veux dire, tu aimes le collège et tout ça ?

— Je trouve qu'on s'y barbe vachement.

— Mais est-ce que tu détestes ça ? Je sais que c'est vachement barbant, mais est-ce que tu *détestes*, voilà ce que je veux dire.

— Ben, non, je *déteste* pas absolument. Faut que tu... »

J'ai dit « Ben, moi je *déteste*. Ouah, c'est fou ce que je déteste. Mais pas seulement ça. Je déteste vivre à New York et tout. Les taxis et les bus de Madison Avenue, avec les chauffeurs et tout qu'arrêtent pas de gueuler après vous pour qu'on sorte par l'arrière, et rencontrer des types à la con qui disent que les Lunt sont des anges, et se faire trimballer dans l'ascenseur vers le haut et vers le bas quand on voudrait seulement en sortir, et les types de Brook's qui passent leur temps à retoucher vos pantalons et les gens qui toujours...

— Je t'en prie, ne crie pas », a dit la môme Sally. Et c'était bizarre parce que je criais même pas.

J'ai dit « Prends les voitures, par exemple ». J'ai dit ça d'une voix très calme. « Prends la plupart des gens, ils sont fous de leur voiture. Si elle a une malheureuse petite égratignure ça les embête, et ils sont toujours à raconter combien de *miles* ils font au gallon, et ils ont pas plus tôt une voiture nouvelle qu'ils envisagent de la changer contre une encore plus récente. J'aime même pas les *vieilles* voitures. J'arrive pas non plus à m'y intéresser. J'aimerais mieux un cheval. Un cheval, au moins, c'est *humain*, bon Dieu. Un cheval, au moins on peut... »

Sally a ronchonné « Je vois pas de quoi tu parles. Tu sautes d'une chose à...

— Je vais te dire. Tu es sans doute la seule raison qui fait que je suis à New York, en ce moment. Si tu étais pas là je m'en irais très loin d'ici. Dans les bois ou autre part. T'es pratiquement la seule raison qui me fait rester. »

Elle a dit « Tu es gentil ». Mais on pouvait voir qu'elle avait envie de changer de sujet.

J'ai dit « Faudrait que tu ailles un jour dans un collège de garçons. Essaie pour voir. Y a que des types foireux, et tout ce qu'ils font c'est étudier afin d'en savoir assez pour arriver plus tard à s'acheter une saloperie de Cadillac, et faut prétendre que ça vous embête si l'équipe de foot a perdu, et on glande du matin au soir à baratiner sur les filles et sur l'alcool et le sexe, et on forme des petits groupes merdiques de soi-disant copains qui se serrent les coudes. Les gars de l'équipe de basket se lâchent pas. Les catholiques se lâchent pas, les cochons d'intellectuels se lâchent pas, les types qui jouent au bridge se lâchent pas. Même les mecs qui appartiennent au foutu Club du Livre du Mois se lâchent pas. Si on essaie d'avoir le moindre échange de vues...

— Écoute. Il y a un tas de gars qui trouvent quelques avantages à leur séjour au collège.

— D'accord, d'accord. Pour certains. Mais moi, voilà tout ce que j'en retire. Tu vois. C'est ce que je veux dire. C'est exactement ce que je veux dire. Je retire pratiquement rien de rien. Je suis coincé. Je suis vraiment coincé.

— En effet, ça paraît évident. »

Et subitement je l'ai eue, mon idée. J'ai dit « Écoute, la voilà mon idée. Je connais un type dans Greenwich Village, je peux lui emprunter sa bagnole pour une quinzaine. On est allés au même collège et il me doit encore dix dollars. Ce qu'on pourrait faire toi et moi c'est partir demain matin pour le Massachusetts et le Vermont et tout ce coin, tu vois. Là-bas, c'est vachement beau. Vachement ». Plus j'y pensais plus je m'emballais, je me suis penché et j'ai pris la main de Sally. Quel *crétin* j'étais ! J'ai dit « Sans blague, j'ai à peu près cent quatre-vingts dollars à la banque. Je les retire demain matin à l'ouverture. Ensuite je vais voir ce type et je lui emprunte sa bagnole. Sans rire. On vivra dans un village de bungalows jusqu'à ce qu'on ait plus de fric, et quand on en aura plus je chercherai du boulot quelque part et on vivra quelque part près d'un ruisseau et tout, et plus tard on se mariera ou quoi. Je casserai tout notre bois pour l'hiver et tout.

Sacré bon Dieu on pourrait avoir une vie du tonnerre. Qu'est-ce que t'en dis ? Hey. Qu'est-ce que t'en dis ? Tu viens ? Je t'en prie. »

La môme Sally avait pas l'air contente. « Ce genre de truc, c'est pas possible.

— Pourquoi ? Pourquoi, bordel ? »

Elle a dit « Arrête de râler comme ça ». Mais je râlais pas. Elle disait des conneries.

« Pourquoi pas possible ? Dis-le.

— C'est pas possible. Voilà tout. D'abord, on est encore pratiquement des enfants. Et as-tu seulement pensé comment on se débrouillerait si tu trouvais pas de travail quand on n'aura plus d'argent ? On mourrait de faim. C'est de la dernière extravagance, c'est même...

— Ça a rien d'extravagant. Du travail, j'en trouverai. T'en fais pas. T'as pas à t'en faire. Qu'est-ce qu'il y a ? Tu veux pas venir avec moi ? Dis-le si tu veux pas. Dis-le. »

Sally a dit « C'est pas ça. C'est pas du tout ça ». En un sens je commençais à la détester. « On aura tout le temps pour ces choses-là. Et d'autres choses. Je veux dire quand tu auras fini tes études et tout et si on se marie et tout. Y aura un tas d'endroits merveilleux où aller. Tu es simplement...

— Non, y en aura pas. Y aura pas un tas d'endroits où aller. » J'avais à nouveau un cafard monstre.

Elle a dit « Quoi ? Je t'entends pas. Ou bien tu brailles ou bien tu... »

J'ai dit « Non, y aura pas d'endroits merveilleux où aller quand j'aurai fini mes études et tout. Ouvre tes oreilles. Ce sera entièrement différent. Faudra qu'on descende par l'ascenseur avec des valises et tout. Faudra qu'on téléphone à tout le monde et qu'on dise au revoir et qu'on envoie des cartes postales des hôtels où on logera et tout. Et je travaillerai dans un bureau, je gagnerai plein de fric, j'irai au boulot en taxi ou bien en prenant le

162

bus dans Madison Avenue, et je lirai les journaux, et je jouerai tout le temps au bridge, et j'irai au ciné voir plein de courts métrages idiots et "Prochainement sur cet écran" et les "Actualités". Les Actualités. Putain. Il y a toujours une foutue course de chevaux, et une bonne femme qui casse une bouteille au-dessus d'un bateau, et un chimpanzé affublé d'un pantalon qui fait de la bicyclette. Ce sera pas du tout pareil. Tu vois pas du tout ce que je veux dire. »

Sally a dit « Peut-être. Mais peut-être toi non plus ». On en était à plus pouvoir se souffrir. Je m'en rendais compte que ça rimait à rien de s'efforcer d'avoir une discussion intelligente. Je m'en mordais les doigts d'avoir essayé.

J'ai dit « Allez, on se tire. Si tu veux savoir j'en ai plein le cul de toi et de tes manières. »

Ouah, qu'est-ce que j'avais dit là ! Ça l'a mise dans tous ses états. Je sais que j'aurais pas dû dire ça et en temps normal je l'aurais probablement pas dit. Mais elle me tapait sur les nerfs. Habituellement je suis jamais grossier avec les filles. Ouah, elle était vraiment dans tous ses états. Je lui ai fait mille excuses mais elle en avait rien à foutre. Même elle chialait. Ça m'a donné un peu les jetons parce que j'avais pas trop envie qu'elle rentre chez elle et raconte à son père que j'avais dit que j'en avais plein le cul, de sa fillette. Son père, c'était un de ces grands types qu'ouvrent à peine la bouche, et j'avais pas la cote avec lui. Une fois il s'était plaint à Sally que j'étais vraiment trop bruyant.

J'en finissais pas de répéter « Je suis désolé. Je te jure.

— Tu es désolé. Tu es désolé. C'est drôle. » Elle pleurnichait encore un peu et alors je me suis réellement senti désolé d'avoir dit ça.

« Viens, je vais te reconduire chez toi. Sans blague.

— Je peux rentrer chez moi toute seule. Merci.

Si tu crois que je vais te laisser me ramener à la maison tu es dingue. Dans toute ma vie jamais un gars m'avait dit ça. »

Si on y réfléchissait, c'était assez marrant, notre histoire et brusquement j'ai fait quelque chose que j'aurais pas dû faire. J'ai ri. Et j'ai un de ces rires très fort et pas malin. Au point que si jamais un jour j'étais celui qui serait assis derrière moi au cinoche je prendrais la peine de me pencher vers moi pour me dire de la fermer, please. La môme Sally, ça l'a exaspérée.

Je suis resté encore un moment à dire que je regrettais et à essayer de me faire pardonner mais j'ai pas réussi. Elle a continué à me répéter de m'en aller, de la laisser tranquille. Alors finalement je suis parti. D'abord j'ai récupéré mes chaussures et mes affaires et puis je suis parti sans elle. J'aurais pas dû, mais je commençais à en avoir vachement marre.

Si vous voulez savoir, je sais même pas pourquoi j'ai commencé à lui raconter tout ce blabla. Je veux dire qu'on s'en irait dans le Massachusetts et le Vermont et tout. Si elle avait voulu venir je l'aurais sans doute pas emmenée. C'est pas le genre de fille qu'on voudrait emmener. Le plus terrible c'est qu'au moment où je lui ai demandé j'en avais bien l'intention. Voilà le plus terrible. Bon Dieu, je vous jure, je suis complètement barjot.

CHAPITRE 18

QUAND j'ai quitté la patinoire j'avais un peu faim, aussi je suis entré dans un drugstore, j'ai mangé un sandwich au fromage et bu un lait malté, et puis je suis allé au téléphone. J'avais envie de donner un autre coup de fil à Jane, pour voir si elle était chez elle. C'est que ma soirée était libre et je voulais appeler Jane et si elle était là l'emmener danser quelque part ou quoi. Du temps où je la fréquentais j'ai jamais dansé avec elle ni rien. Mais une fois je l'ai vue danser. Elle avait l'air de drôlement se défendre. C'était au bal du Quatre Juillet, à notre club. Je la connaissais pas encore très bien ; elle avait un cavalier et j'ai pas voulu m'interposer. Son cavalier c'était ce terrible mec, Al Pike, qui allait à Choate. Lui non plus je le connaissais pas bien, il traînait toujours à la piscine. Il avait un slip de bain en latex blanc, et il arrêtait pas de sauter du grand plongeoir. Toute la journée il faisait la même saloperie de demi-vrille. Le seul plongeon qu'il savait faire ; mais il se croyait très calé. Rien que du muscle, pas de cervelle. En tout cas, ce soir-là, c'était avec lui qu'elle était, Jane. Je me demandais bien pourquoi ; je vous jure. Lorsqu'on a commencé à sortir ensemble je lui ai posé la question ; comment ça se faisait qu'elle avait eu rencard avec un foutu crâneur comme Al Pike. Jane a dit qu'il était pas crâneur. Elle a dit qu'il avait un complexe d'infériorité. C'était pas pour se donner un genre mais comme si elle le prenait en pitié. Avec les filles, c'est bizarre, chaque fois qu'on mentionne un type qu'est un salaud cent pour cent — mesquin, crâneur et tout — quand on dit ça à une fille elle vous répond qu'il a un complexe d'infériorité. Peut-être qu'il en a un mais à mon avis ça l'empêche pas d'être un salaud. Les filles, on sait jamais ce qu'elles vont penser. Une fois j'ai arrangé un rencard entre la copine de chambre de Roberta Walsh et un de mes amis. Mon ami s'appelait Bob Robinson et lui, le complexe d'infériorité, c'était pas de la rigolade. Il avait honte de ses parents et tout parce qu'ils se mélangeaient dans les temps des verbes et qu'ils roulaient pas sur l'or. Mais c'était pas un salaud. C'était un très brave type. Pourtant la copine de chambre de Roberta Walsh, elle l'a pas aimé du tout. Elle a dit à Roberta qu'elle le trouvait trop prétentieux — et ça pour la *seule raison* qu'il lui a raconté que dans sa classe c'était lui qui était responsable du groupe de "débats". Cette petite chose de rien du tout et elle le trouvait prétentieux. L'ennui avec les filles c'est que si un garçon leur plaît il peut être le plus horrible des salauds elles trouveront qu'il a un complexe d'infériorité et s'il leur plaît pas, il aura beau être un brave type et avoir un énorme complexe elles diront qu'il est prétentieux. Même les filles intelligentes sont comme ça.

Bref. J'ai donné un coup de bigo à Jane. Pas de réponse. Alors j'ai raccroché. Et puis j'ai ouvert mon carnet d'adresses pour chercher quelqu'un qui serait disponible. L'ennui c'est que dans mon carnet d'adresses il y avait seulement trois personnes. Jane, et cet homme, Mr. Antolini, qui avait été mon professeur à Elkton Hill et mon père — c'est-à-dire son numéro au bureau. J'oublie tout le temps de noter le nom des gens. Finalement, j'ai appelé Carl Luce. Il avait eu ses diplômes à Whooton, après mon départ. Il était de trois ans mon aîné et je l'aimais pas beaucoup, c'était un de ces types très intellectuels — il avait le plus haut Q.I. de l'école — et j'ai pensé qu'on pourrait peut-être dîner ensemble et échanger quelques idées. Par moments il vous faisait découvrir des choses. Alors je lui ai bigophoné. A présent il était à Columbia, mais il habitait la Soixante-cinquième Rue et tout, et je savais qu'il serait chez lui. Quand je l'ai eu il a dit que c'était pas possible qu'il se libère pour dîner mais qu'on prendrait un verre à dix heures au Wicker Bar, dans la Cinquante-quatrième Rue. J'ai eu l'impression qu'il était plutôt surpris de m'entendre. Une fois je l'avais traité de gros cul faux jeton.

Fallait que je tue le temps jusqu'à dix heures. Aussi ce que j'ai fait, je me suis payé un ciné à Radio-City. C'était probablement la pire chose à faire mais y avait pas loin à aller et je trouvais rien d'autre qui m'aurait tenté.

Quand je suis arrivé c'était la parade sur la scène. Les Rockettes secouaient la tête tant qu'elles pouvaient comme elles font quand elles sont en ligne et se tiennent par la taille. Les spectateurs applaudissaient comme des dingues, et derrière moi un type arrêtait pas de dire à sa femme « Tu sais à quoi c'est dû ? A la précision ». Ça m'a tué. Après les Rockettes un type est venu en smoking avec des patins à roulettes et il s'est mis à patiner sur une série de petites tables et en même temps à dire des plaisanteries. C'était un très bon patineur et tout, mais ça m'amusait pas tellement parce que je me le représentais *s'entraînant* pour devenir un type qui fait du patin à roulettes sur une scène. Ça semblait tellement idiot. Je suppose que c'est seulement que j'étais pas dans l'humeur qui convenait. Et après lui il y a eu ce truc de Noël qu'ils donnent chaque année à Radio-City. Tous ces anges partout qui sortent des coulisses, partout des mecs portant des crucifix et du bazar et toute la bande — des milliers — qui chantent à plein gosier « Come All Ye Faithful ». Vous parlez d'un show-biz ! C'est supposé être foutrement religieux, je sais, et très joli et tout, mais bordel je vois rien de religieux, rien de joli dans une troupe d'acteurs qui baladent des crucifix sur la scène. Quand tout a été fini et qu'ils ont vidé les lieux on sentait qu'ils avaient qu'une hâte c'était d'aller en griller une ou quoi. J'étais venu déjà l'année précédente avec Sally Hayes et elle en finissait pas de s'extasier sur les costumes et tout. J'ai dit que le petit père Jésus Il aurait probablement dégobillé s'Il avait vu ça, tous ces costumes à la gomme et tout. Sally a dit que j'étais un athée sacrilège. C'est peut-être vrai. Ce que Jésus aurait *sûrement* aimé c'est le gars dans l'orchestre qui joue des timbales. J'ai observé ce gars depuis l'âge de huit ans. Mon frère Allie et moi, si on était avec nos parents et tout, on se levait de nos sièges et on s'avançait pour mieux le voir. C'est le meilleur batteur que j'aie jamais vu. Il intervient seulement deux fois pendant tout le spectacle, mais on a pas l'impression qu'il s'ennuie quand il fait rien. Et puis quand il frappe c'est tellement bien, tellement chouette, et son visage prend un air si concentré. Une fois, quand on est allés à Washington avec mon père, Allie lui a envoyé une carte postale, mais je parierais qu'il l'a jamais eue. On était pas très sûrs comment mettre l'adresse.

Lorsque le machin de Noël a été terminé le foutu film a commencé. C'était tellement putride que je pouvais pas en détacher mes yeux. Ça parlait de cet Anglais, Alec quelque chose, qui une fois revenu de la guerre a perdu la mémoire à l'hôpital et tout. Il sort de l'hôpital appuyé sur une canne, boitant tous azimuts et il se balade dans Londres sans savoir qui il est. En fait c'est un duc, mais il s'en souvient plus. Alors en prenant le bus il rencontre cette fille sympa, cette fille sincère. Le bon Dieu de vent lui a arraché son chapeau et lui il le rattrape ; et ensuite ils montent dans le bus, à l'étage supérieur et ils s'assoient et se mettent à parler de Charles Dickens. C'est leur auteur favori à tous les deux et tout. Alec il a sur lui un exemplaire d'*Oliver Twist* et elle aussi. J'en aurais vomi. Bon, ils tombent aussitôt amoureux pour la raison que tous les deux raffolent de Charles Dickens et tout, et lui il aide la fille à faire marcher sa maison d'édition. Parce que la fille publie des livres. Seulement ça marche pas très bien bicause son frère boit comme un trou ce qui les met dans la dèche. Le frère est du genre très amer vu qu'il était médecin pendant la guerre et que maintenant il peut plus opérer à cause de ses nerfs démolis, aussi il pinte sans arrêt mais il est assez spirituel et tout. Bref. Le gars Alec écrit un livre et la fille le publie et tous les deux ils ramassent du flouze à la pelle. Ils sont sur le point de se marier quand cette autre fille, Marcia, entre en scène. Marcia était la fiancée d'Alec avant qu'il perde la mémoire et elle le reconnaît quand il est dans la boutique en train de donner des autographes. Elle dit à Alec qu'en vrai il est duc mais il la croit pas et il veut pas aller avec elle voir sa mère ni rien. Sa mère est aveugle comme une taupe. Mais l'autre fille, la fille sympa, elle le pousse à y aller. Elle est très généreuse et tout. Alors il y va. Pourtant la mémoire lui revient pas, même quand son danois saute autour de lui et que sa mère passe ses doigts sur son visage et lui apporte son ours en peluche qu'il traînait partout avec lui quand il était petit. Et puis un jour y a des mômes qui jouent au cricket sur la pelouse et il reçoit une balle de cricket sur la tête. Alors immédiatement la mémoire lui revient. Il entre dans la maison et il embrasse sa mère sur le front et tout. Il est de nouveau un vrai duc et il oublie la môme sympa qui a une maison d'édition. Je vous dirais bien le reste de l'histoire mais j'ai peur de vomir. C'est pas que je craigne de vous la *gâcher* ou quoi. Putain, y a rien à *gâcher*. En tout cas, à la fin, Alec et la fille sympa se marient et le frère qui est ivrogne reprend le contrôle de ses nerfs et il opère la mère d'Alec qui retrouve la vue et pan le frère alcoolique et la môme Marcia découvrent qu'ils s'aiment. Ça se termine quand ils sont tous assis autour d'une grande table de salle à manger à se boyauter parce que le danois entre avec un tas de chiots. Tout le monde croyait que c'était un mâle, je suppose, et ce serait ça qui les fait rire. En conclusion ce que je peux dire c'est n'allez pas voir ce film si vous voulez pas vous vomir dessus.

Ce qui m'a tué c'est qu'il y avait une dame assise à côté de moi qu'a pleuré tout le temps. Plus c'était bidon et plus elle pleurait. On aurait pu penser que ça voulait dire qu'elle avait le cœur tendre mais j'étais juste à côté d'elle et j'ai bien vu que c'était pas le cas. Elle avait avec elle ce petit gosse qui s'ennuyait à mourir et qui demandait à faire pipi mais il était pas question qu'elle l'emmène, elle arrêtait pas de lui chuchoter de se tenir tranquille. Pas plus de cœur qu'un loup affamé. Les gens qui pleurent à s'en fondre les yeux en regardant un film à la guimauve, neuf fois sur dix ils ont pas de cœur. Sans rire.

Quand le film a été fini je me suis rendu au Wicker Bar où j'étais censé rencontrer Carl Luce, et tout en marchant j'ai pensé à la guerre. Ces films de guerre ça me fait toujours cet effet-là. Si je devais aller à la guerre je crois pas que je pourrais le supporter. Sans blague. Si c'était seulement qu'on vous emmène et qu'on vous tire dessus ça irait encore, mais faut rester tellement longtemps dans l'armée. C'est ça l'ennui. Mon frère D.B. il y a passé quatre ans. Il a fait aussi la guerre — il a débarqué au jour J et tout — mais je crois qu'il détestait encore plus l'armée que la guerre. A l'époque j'étais pratiquement encore un môme mais je me souviens quand il venait à la maison en permission et tout, il faisait pratiquement que rester sur son plumard. On le voyait presque jamais dans la salle de séjour. Plus tard, quand il est allé en Europe et qu'il a fait la guerre et tout il a jamais été blessé ni rien et il a jamais eu à tirer sur quelqu'un. Tout ce qu'on lui demandait c'était de trimbaler toute la journée un général à la cow-boy dans une voiture d'état-major. Une fois il nous a dit, à Allie et à moi, que s'il avait dû tirer sur quelqu'un il aurait pas su de quel côté tirer. Il disait qu'il y avait dans l'armée autant de salauds que chez les nazis. Je me souviens qu'une fois Allie a voulu savoir si c'était tout de même pas trop mal qu'il aille à la guerre puisqu'il était écrivain et que ça lui donnait des choses à écrire et tout. Il a envoyé Allie chercher son gant de base-ball et puis il lui a demandé qui était le meilleur poète de guerre, Rupert Brooke ou Emily Dickinson. Allie a dit Emily Dickinson. Je m'y connais pas beaucoup vu que je lis pas souvent de poésie mais je *sais* que ça m'aurait rendu fou s'il avait fallu que j'aille à l'armée et être tout le temps avec ces types comme Ackley et Stradlater et le gars Maurice. En colonne avec eux et tout. Une fois j'ai été dans les Boy-Scouts, pendant à peu près une semaine, et je pouvais même pas supporter de regarder la nuque du gars qui marchait devant moi. On arrêtait pas de vous dire de regarder la nuque du gars qui marchait devant vous. Je le jure, s'il y a jamais une autre guerre ils feront mieux de me sortir tout de suite des rangs pour me coller en face du peloton d'exécution. J'aurais pas d'objections. Mais D.B., ce qui m'étonne c'est qu'il détestait tellement la guerre et pourtant qu'il m'a fait lire ce bouquin *L'Adieu aux armes*, l'été dernier. Il m'a dit que c'était du tonnerre. Ça m'étonne vachement. Dedans il y avait ce type, le lieutenant Henry, qu'était soi-disant un type sympa et tout. Je vois pas comment D.B. pouvait tellement détester l'armée et la guerre et tout et quand même trouver sensas' un livre aussi bidon. Je veux dire, par exemple, je vois pas comment il peut aimer un livre aussi bidon et aimer aussi celui de Ring Lardner, ou l'autre qu'il adore, *Gatsby le Magnifique*. D.B. s'est fâché quand j'ai dit ça, et il a dit que j'étais trop jeune et tout pour apprécier, mais je crois pas. Je lui ai dit que j'aimais Ring Lardner et *Gatsby le Magnifique* et tout. C'est vrai. J'ai adoré *Gatsby le Magnifique*. Ce vieux Gatsby. Un pote. Ça m'a tué. En tout cas je serais plutôt content qu'ils aient inventé la bombe atomique. S'il y a une autre guerre j'irai m'asseoir juste dessus. Je serai volontaire pour ça. Je vous jure. Vous verrez.

CHAPITRE 19

Au cas où vous connaîtriez pas New York, le Wicker Bar il est dans cette sorte d'hôtel grand luxe, le Seton. Pendant un moment j'y allais souvent, mais plus maintenant. Peu à peu j'ai cessé d'y aller. C'est un de ces endroits réputés très sophistiqués et tout, et on y voit parader tous les types à la flan. Y avait deux Françaises, Tina et Janine, qui venaient jouer du piano et chanter trois fois par soirée. L'une jouait du piano — d'une façon positivement dégueulasse — et l'autre chantait, et les paroles de ses chansons c'était des cochonneries ou bien c'était en français. Celle qui chantait, la môme Janine, elle commençait toujours par chuchoter des trucs dans le foutu micro. Elle disait « Et maintenant nous aimerions vous dire une love story à la française. C'est l'histoire d'une petite Française qui arrive dans une grande ville comme New York et qui tombe in love with un petit gars de Brooklyn. J'espère que vous aimerez very much ». Et alors quand elle avait fini de chuchoter et d'être drôlement futée elle se mettait à bramer un truc idiot, moitié en anglais moitié en français et ça rendait fous de joie tous les corniauds de l'endroit. Si on restait assis là un moment à écouter ces crêpes applaudir et tout, on en arrivait très vite à détester le monde entier, je vous jure. Le barman aussi il était infect. Un vrai snob. Il vous adressait pratiquement pas la parole sauf si vous étiez une huile ou une célébrité. Si vous étiez une huile ou une célébrité ou quelque chose comme ça alors il vous donnait encore plus la nausée. Il s'approchait de vous et il disait avec son grand sourire charmeur, comme s'il était un gars extra même si ça se voyait pas tellement « Eh bien, comment ça va dans le Connecticut ? » ou « Comment ça va en Floride ? » Ce bar était un endroit épouvantable. Sans blague. J'avais fini par plus y aller.

Quand je suis arrivé, il était pas tard. Je me suis assis au comptoir — y avait la grande foule — et j'ai commandé deux scotch-and-soda, avant même que le gars Luce soit là. Je me suis levé pour passer la commande afin qu'ils voient comme j'étais grand et me demandent pas si j'avais l'âge légal. Et puis j'ai regardé un moment tous les frimeurs. A côté de moi y en avait un qui faisait du gringue à la fille qui l'accompagnait. Il arrêtait pas de lui dire qu'elle avait des mains aristocratiques. Ça m'a tué. A l'autre bout du bar c'était plein de pédés qu'avaient pas trop l'air de pédés — je veux dire qu'étaient pas trop à manières ni rien — mais on voyait tout de même bien que c'étaient des pédés. Finalement le gars Luce s'est amené.

Le gars Luce. Quel drôle de zèbre ! Quand j'étais à Whooton on me l'avait attribué comme Conseiller d'Études. Le seul truc qu'il ait jamais fait ça a été ses petits cours sur le sexe tard le soir dans sa chambre pleine de types. Sur le sexe il en connaissait un rayon, spécialement sur les pervers et tout. Fallait toujours qu'il nous parle de ces mecs inquiétants qui ont des liaisons avec les moutons et de ceux qui se baladent avec des petites culottes de filles cousues dans la doublure de leur chapeau et tout. Et des pédés et des lesbiennes. Le gars Luce il connaissait tous les pédés et toutes les lesbiennes des États-Unis. Vous aviez juste à mentionner quelqu'un — n'importe qui — et aussitôt il vous disait si c'était un pédé. Quelquefois on avait peine à croire. Ces gens qu'il prétendait être homosexuels et tout, des acteurs de cinéma et tout. Parmi ceux qu'il mentionnait, bon Dieu y en avait même qui étaient mariés. On cessait pas de lui demander « Tu veux dire que Joe Blow est un pédé ? Joe *Blow* ? Ce grand dur qui joue les gangsters et les cow-boys? » Et le gars Luce disait « Certainement ». « Certainement », c'était un mot qu'il répétait tout le temps. Il disait que ça changeait rien qu'un type soit marié ou pas. Il disait que la moitié des gars dans le monde sont des pédés qui s'ignorent. Qu'on pouvait pratiquement le devenir en une nuit si on avait ça dans le tempérament. Il nous foutait drôlement la frousse. Je m'attendais à tout instant à être changé en pédé ou quoi. Le plus curieux, c'est que ce gars, j'avais l'impression qu'il était lui-même un peu pédé, en un sens. Il disait tout le temps « Tiens attrape ça, vieux » en vous pinçant les fesses quand on passait dans le couloir. Et chaque fois qu'il allait aux chiottes il laissait toujours la porte ouverte et vous tenait des discours impossibles pendant que vous vous brossiez les dents. Ce genre de truc c'est plutôt pédé. Sans blague. J'ai connu quelques vrais homos au collège et tout, et ils sont toujours à faire des trucs comme ça, et voilà pourquoi avec le gars Luce j'ai toujours eu des soupçons. Ça empêche pas qu'il soit intelligent. C'est vrai.

Quand on le voyait il disait jamais bonjour ni rien. La première chose qu'il a dite en s'asseyant c'est qu'il pouvait rester seulement deux minutes. Il a prétendu qu'il avait un rencard. Puis il a commandé un Martini sec. Il a dit au barman super sec et pas d'olives.

« Hey, j'ai un pédé pour toi, j'ai dit. A l'autre bout du bar. Attends, regarde pas. Je l'ai mis de côté pour toi. »

Il a dit « Très drôle. Toujours le même, Caulfield. Quand vas-tu cesser d'être un môme ? »

Mes plaisanteries ça l'emmerdait, c'est sûr. Mais lui il m'amusait. C'était un de ces types qui m'amusent pas mal.

J'ai demandé « Comment ça va, ta vie sexuelle ? » Il détestait qu'on lui demande des choses de ce genre.

Il a dit « Relaxe-toi. Prends un siège et relaxe-toi, sacré bordel ».

J'ai dit « Je suis très relaxe. Comment c'est, Columbia ? Tu aimes ? ».

Il a dit « Certainement. Si je n'aimais pas je n'y serais pas allé ». Par moments il était casse-burettes.

J'ai demandé « Et c'est quoi ton sujet principal ? Les pervers ? » Je faisais seulement un peu l'idiot.

« Tu te crois marrant ? »

J'ai dit « Bon, je plaisantais. Écoute, hey, Luce. Tu es un type intellectuel. J'ai besoin de tes conseils. Je suis dans un terrible... »

Il a gémi. « *Écoute*, Caulfield. Si tu voulais bien t'asseoir et qu'on boive un verre tranquillement, en ayant une tranquille petite convers'... »

J'ai dit « D'accord, d'accord. T'énerve pas ». Je voyais qu'il s'en ressentait pas du tout pour une discussion sérieuse. C'est l'ennui avec ces intellos. Ils veulent jamais rien discuter de sérieux à moins que ce soit *eux* qui l'aient décidé. Aussi, tout ce que j'ai fait c'est choisir un sujet plutôt général. J'ai demandé « Sans blague, comment ça va ta vie sexuelle ? Tu sors toujours avec la même fille, celle que tu avais déjà quand on était à Whooton ? Celle au fantastique...

— Bon Dieu, non.

— Et pourquoi ? Qu'est-ce qui lui est arrivé ?

— Je n'en ai pas la moindre idée. Autant que je sache, et puisque tu demandes, elle est probablement devenue la Putain du New Hampshire.

— C'est pas gentil. Si elle était assez chouette pour te laisser la tripoter tout le temps, au moins tu devrais pas parler d'elle en ces termes.

— Bon Dieu, a dit le gars Luce, ça va donc être une conversation typiquement à la Caulfield ? J'aimerais bien le savoir dès maintenant. »

J'ai dit « Ben non. Mais quand même c'est pas gentil. Si elle était assez chouette pour te laisser...

— Est-ce qu'on doit vraiment poursuivre sur un sujet aussi scabreux ? »

J'ai rien répondu. J'avais un peu peur, si je la fermais, qu'il se lève et me quitte. Aussi tout ce que j'ai fait, c'est de commander un autre whisky. J'avais envie de me soûler à mort.

« Avec qui tu sors maintenant ? Tu peux me le dire ?

— Personne que tu connaisses.

— Dis-moi qui. Je la connais peut-être.

— Une fille qui vit dans le Village. Elle est sculpteur. Si tu veux savoir.

— Ouais ? Sans rire ? Elle a quel âge ?

— Bon Dieu, je lui ai jamais demandé.

— Enfin, à peu près quel âge ?

— Pas loin des quarante piges, j'imagine », a dit Luce.

J'ai dit « Quarante ? Ouais ? T'aimes ça ? Tu les aimes aussi vieilles que ça ? » Si je posais la question, c'est pour la raison qu'il était plutôt bien informé sur le sexe. Un des rares types à l'être aussi bien parmi ceux que je fréquente. Il avait perdu son pucelage à quatorze ans. Sans rire.

« J'aime les femmes mûres, si c'est ce que tu veux dire. Certainement.

— Ah bon ? Pourquoi ? C'est mieux avec les vieilles ou quoi ?

— Écoute. Soyons clairs. Ce soir je refuse de répondre à un interrogatoire typiquement Caulfield. Quand vas-tu cesser d'être un gamin, bordel ? »

Pendant un moment j'ai plus rien dit. Pendant un moment j'ai laissé tomber. Puis le gars Luce a commandé un autre Martini et il a dit au barman qu'il le voulait encore plus sec.

J'ai demandé « Écoute, ça fait combien de temps que tu es avec elle ? Cette fille, qui est sculpteur ? » Ça m'intéressait vachement. « Tu la connaissais déjà quand tu étais à Whooton ?

— Sûrement pas. Elle vient d'arriver dans ce pays, il y a quelques mois.

— Vrai ? Elle vient d'où ?

— Elle vient de Shanghai.

— Sans blague ! Une Chinoise, bordel ?

— Certainement.

— Sans blague ! Tu aimes ça ? Qu'elle soit chinoise ?

— Certainement.

— Pourquoi ? J'aimerais bien que tu me dises.

— Il se trouve simplement que la philosophie orientale me paraît plus satisfaisante que celle de l'Occident. Puisque tu demandes.

— Ah oui ? Qu'est-ce que tu veux dire par ''philosophie'' ? Tu veux dire le sexe et tout ? Tu veux dire que c'est mieux en Chine ? C'est ce que tu veux dire ?

— Pas nécessairement en Chine, bon Dieu. En Orient. Allons-nous continuer longtemps cette conversation idiote ? »

J'ai dit « Écoute, soyons sérieux. Sans rire, pourquoi est-ce mieux en Orient ?

— C'est trop compliqué pour en parler comme ça, a dit le gars Luce. Simplement là-bas on considère le sexe comme une expérience à la fois physique et spirituelle. Si tu crois que je suis...

— Mais moi aussi ! Moi aussi je trouve que c'est

une ce-que-tu-dis — une expérience à la fois physique et spirituelle et tout. Bien sûr. Mais ça dépend
avec qui je le fais. Si c'est avec quelqu'un pour qui
j'ai...

— Caulfield, pas si fort, bon Dieu. Si tu ne peux
pas baisser la voix, laissons tomber. »

J'ai dit « Okay, mais écoute ». Je m'excitais, et
c'est vrai que je parlais un peu trop fort. Quelquefois
je parle un peu fort quand je m'excite. « Ce que je
veux dire, c'est que je sais que ça doit être physique
et spirituel et artistique et tout. Mais ce que je veux
dire c'est que ça peut pas l'être avec n'importe qui,
n'importe quelle fille avec qui on flirte. T'es d'accord ? »

Le gars Luce a dit « Laisse tomber. Tu veux ?

— Okay, mais attends, écoute. Disons, toi et cette
Chinoise. Pourquoi c'est si bien, vous deux ?

— Laisse tomber, je t'ai dit. »

Ça devenait un peu trop personnel mes questions,
je m'en rendais compte. C'est un des emmerde-
ments, avec Luce. Quand on était à Whooton, il
vous faisait raconter les choses les plus personnelles
qui vous arrivaient, à *vous*, mais *lui*, si vous lui
posiez des questions du même genre il était pas
content. Ces mecs intellectuels, ils aiment pas avoir
avec vous une conversation intellectuelle à moins
que vous les laissiez diriger l'opération. Toujours ils
veulent que vous la fermiez quand *ils* la ferment, et
que vous rentriez dans votre chambre quand ils
rentrent dans la leur. Quand j'étais à Whooton, ça
le rendait fou le gars Luce si à la fin d'un de ses
cours sur le sexe on quittait sa chambre pour aller
continuer la discussion entre nous — je veux dire
les copains et moi. Dans la chambre de quelqu'un
d'autre. Oui ça le rendait fou. Il voulait que chacun
regagne sa piaule et se taise quand il avait fini d'être
le grand leader. Il avait trop la trouille qu'il y en

ait un qui dise quelque chose de plus intelligent que ce qu'il avait dit, lui. Moi ça m'amusait.

J'ai dit « Peut-être que j'irai en Chine. Ma vie sexuelle est branquignole.

— Rien d'étonnant. Ton esprit manque de maturité. »

J'ai dit « C'est bien vrai, je le sais. Tu veux que je te dise mon problème ? Je peux pas arriver à être intéressé sexuellement — je veux dire *vraiment* intéressé — par une fille qui me plaît pas tout à fait. Je veux dire qu'il faut qu'elle me plaise totalement. Sinon, mon foutu désir d'elle, il fout le camp. Ouah, ça déglingue complètement ma vie sexuelle. Ma vie sexuelle est pourrie.

— Certainement. Bon Dieu, la dernière fois que je t'ai vu je t'ai dit de quoi tu avais besoin.

— Tu veux dire d'aller voir un psychanalyste et tout ? » C'est ce qu'il m'avait dit que je devrais faire. Son père était psychanalyste et tout.

« A toi de décider, bon Dieu. Ça me regarde pas comment tu mènes ta vie. »

Je suis resté un petit moment sans lui parler. Je réfléchissais.

Et puis j'ai dit « En supposant que j'aille voir ton père et que je lui demande de me psychanalyser et tout, qu'est-ce qu'il me ferait ? Je veux dire : qu'est-ce qu'il me ferait exactement ?

— Bon Dieu il ne te ferait rien. Simplement il te parlerait et tu lui parlerais. En premier lieu il t'aiderait à reconnaître les types de réactions inhérentes à ta forme d'esprit.

— Les quoi ?

— Les réactions. Ton esprit fonctionne suivant... Écoute, je ne vais pas te donner un cours élémentaire de psychanalyse. Si tu es intéressé appelle-le et prends rendez-vous. Si tu ne l'es pas, abstiens-toi. Franchement, moi je m'en moque. »

J'ai mis la main sur son épaule. Ouah, il m'amusait. J'ai dit « T'es un vrai salaud sympa. Tu savais ? »

Il a regardé sa montre. Il a dit « Faut que je me tire » et il s'est levé. « Bien content de t'avoir vu. » Il a appelé le barman pour savoir ce qu'il lui devait.

« Hey, j'ai dit juste avant qu'il se barre, est-ce que ton père t'a jamais psychanalysé ?

— Moi ? Pourquoi tu demandes ?

— Comme ça. Alors ?

— Pas exactement. Il m'a aidé à trouver un certain équilibre ; une analyse complète n'a pas été nécessaire. Pourquoi tu demandes ?

— Comme ça. Je me posais la question.

— Salut. Bonne continuation. » Il laissait un pourboire et il allait filer.

J'ai dit « Prenons encore un verre. Je t'en prie. Je me sens très seul. Sans blague ».

Il a dit qu'il pouvait pas. Il a dit qu'il était tard, et alors il est parti.

Le gars Luce. C'était un vrai emmerdeur, mais il avait certainement un excellent vocabulaire. Parmi tous les types de Whooton, c'est lui qui avait le vocabulaire le plus étendu. On nous avait fait passer un test.

CHAPITRE 20

JE suis resté assis à m'humecter les amygdales.
J'attendais que Tina et Janine viennent faire leur
numéro mais elles étaient pas là. Un type à l'allure
de pédé avec des cheveux ondulés s'est mis à jouer
du piano, et puis Valencia, une nouvelle minette, a
fait son tour de chant. Elle était pas douée mais
tout de même moins mauvaise que Tina et Janine
et elle chantait de bonnes chansons. Le piano était
juste auprès du comptoir où je me trouvais. Alors
Valencia était pratiquement à côté de moi et tout.
Je lui ai fait un peu de l'œil mais ça a pas eu l'air
de l'intéresser. Je l'aurais sans doute pas fait si
j'avais pas été plein comme une huître. Quand elle
a eu terminé, elle s'est barrée si vite que j'ai même
pas eu le temps de l'inviter à s'asseoir avec moi
pour prendre un verre. Alors j'ai appelé le garçon.
Je lui ai dit de demander à Valencia si elle voudrait
venir boire quelque chose. Il a dit qu'il ferait la
commission mais c'est probable qu'il m'a baratiné.
Vos commissions, les gens les font jamais.

Ouah, je suis resté assis à cette saleté de comptoir
jusqu'à environ une heure du mat', et j'étais de plus
en plus saoul. Je pouvais à peine y voir clair. Tout
de même j'ai fait rudement gaffe de pas chahuter ni

182

rien. Je tenais pas à ce qu'on me remarque et qu'on me demande mon âge. Mais... Ouah, je pouvais à peine voir clair. Quand j'ai été *vraiment* schlass j'ai recommencé à me raconter cette histoire idiote de la balle dans le ventre. J'étais le seul type du bar qui avait une balle dans le ventre. J'arrêtais pas de me passer la main sous la veste, sur mon estomac et tout, pour empêcher le sang de pisser tous azimuts. Je voulais que personne sache que j'étais blessé. Je cachais soigneusement mon état de fils de pute au ventre troué. Finalement, ce que j'ai eu envie de faire, j'ai eu envie de donner un coup de fil à la môme Jane pour voir si elle était rentrée chez elle. Alors j'ai payé ma note et tout, et puis j'ai quitté le bar et je suis allé là où sont les téléphones. Toujours la main sous ma veste pour empêcher le sang de dégouliner. Ouah, j'étais rond.

Mais quand je me suis retrouvé à l'intérieur de la cabine, et que j'ai voulu appeler Jane, eh bien j'avais plus la forme. J'étais trop soûl, j'imagine. Aussi ce que j'ai fait, j'ai appelé Sally Hayes.

C'est seulement après vingt faux numéros que j'ai eu le bon. Ouah, j'étais complètement défoncé.

Quand quelqu'un a répondu, j'ai braillé « Allô ». Je braillais parce que j'étais tellement soûl.

La voix d'une dame, une voix très froide a demandé « Qui est-ce ? »

— C'est moi. Holden Caulfield. Voudrais parler à Sally siou plaît.

— Sally dort. Je suis la grand-mère de Sally. Pourquoi appelez-vous aussi tard, Holden ? Vous savez quelle heure il est ?

— Ouais. Veux parler à Sally. Trrrès important. Passez-la-moi.

— Sally dort, jeune homme. Rappelez-la demain. Bonne nuit.

— Hey ! Faut la réveiller. Hey ! »

Alors une autre voix. « Holden, c'est moi. » C'était Sally. « Qu'est-ce qui te prend ?

— Sally ? C'est toi ?

— Oui, arrête de crier. Tu as bu ?

— Ouais. Écoute. Écoute, hey. Je viendrai la veille de Noël. Okay ? Décorer pour toi ce foutu sapin. Okay ? Hey, Sally, okay ?

— Oui. Tu es ivre. Va au lit maintenant. Où es-tu ? Avec qui es-tu ?

— Je viendrai décorer l'arbre pour toi. D'accord ? Hey, d'accord ?

— *Oui*. Va au lit maintenant. Où es-tu ? Avec qui ?

— Personne. Moi, moi-même et encore moi. » C'est fou ce que j'étais ivre. Je continuais à me tenir les entrailles. « Ils m'ont eu. La bande à Rocky. Ils m'ont eu. Tu savais ? Sally, tu savais ça ?

— Je t'entends mal. Va au lit maintenant. Il faut que je m'en aille. Rappelle-moi demain.

— Hey, Sally ? Tu veux bien que je décore l'arbre pour toi ? Tu veux bien, hey ?

— *Oui*. Bonne nuit. Rentre à la maison. Va te coucher. »

Elle a raccroché.

J'ai dit « Bou-nuit, bou-nuit p'tite Sally. Sally-en-sucre adorée ». Vous voyez à quel point j'étais ivre. Et moi aussi j'ai raccroché. Je pensais qu'elle rentrait juste chez elle après un rencard. Je me la suis imaginée quelque part avec les Lunt ou quoi, et ce taré qui est à Andover. Tous nageant tranquilles dans un foutu pot de thé et se disant des choses sophistiquées, et tous absolument charmants et totalement connards. Je regrettais vachement de lui avoir téléphoné. Quand j'ai bu je suis dingue.

J'ai encore traîné un moment dans la foutue cabine téléphonique. Je m'agrippais au téléphone pour pas m'évanouir. A dire vrai, j'avais pas la grande forme. Finalement, je suis quand même sorti de la cabine et je me suis réfugié dans les toilettes des hommes, en me mélangeant les cannes, et j'ai rempli d'eau froide un des lavabos. Puis j'ai plongé la tête dedans jusqu'aux oreilles. J'ai même pas pris la peine de la sécher ni rien. J'ai laissé l'eau dégouliner sur ma tronche. Puis je suis allé m'asseoir sur le radiateur près de la fenêtre. C'était chaud, c'était bon. Ça m'a fait du bien parce que je frissonnais comme un perdu. C'est bizarre, je frissonne vachement quand je suis ivre.

J'avais rien d'autre à faire aussi je suis resté assis sur le radiateur et j'ai compté les petits carrés blancs, par terre. J'étais trempé. Des litres d'eau me coulaient dans le cou, sur mon col et ma cravate et tout, mais je m'en foutais pas mal. J'étais trop ivre pour pas m'en foutre. Bientôt le type qui jouait du piano pour accompagner Valencia, ce mec très ondulé, genre pédé, est venu peigner ses boucles dorées. Pendant qu'il se coiffait on a échangé quelques mots, sauf que lui il était pas tellement aimable.

Je lui ai demandé « Hey, tu verras la môme Valencia quand tu vas retourner au bar ? »

Il a dit « C'est hautement probable ». Spirituel, le salaud. Faut toujours que je rencontre des salauds pleins d'esprit.

« Écoute. Fais-lui mes compliments. Demande-lui si le garçon lui a passé mon message, veux-tu ?

— Pourquoi que tu rentres pas chez toi, vieux ? Au fait, quel âge tu as ?

— Quatre-vingt-six ans. Écoute. Fais-lui mes compliments. Okay ?

— Pourquoi que tu rentres pas chez toi, vieux ?

— Arrête. » Et puis j'ai dit « Ouah, tu joues vachement bien du piano ». C'était pour le flatter. Si vous voulez savoir, il jouait comme un pied. « Tu devrais être à la radio, un type comme toi, avec l'allure que t'as. Toutes ces boucles d'or. T'as pas besoin d'un manager ?

— Rentre chez toi, vieux, comme un bon petit gars. Va à la maison et fourre-toi au pieu.

— Pas de maison où aller. Sans rire — t'as pas besoin d'un manager ? »

Il a rien répondu. Il est parti. Il avait fini de se peigner, de se tapoter les cheveux et tout, alors il est parti. Comme Stradlater. Ces beaux types, ils sont tous pareils. Quand ils ont fini de se peigner ils vous plaquent.

Finalement, lorsque je suis descendu de mon radiateur pour aller au vestiaire je chialais et tout, je sais pas pourquoi mais je chialais. Je suppose que ça voulait dire que je me sentais tellement seul et paumé. Et puis une fois au vestiaire je pouvais plus trouver mon foutu ticket. Mais la fille a été bien gentille, elle m'a donné mon manteau. Et mon disque de *Little Shirley Beans* que j'avais toujours et tout. J'ai voulu lui fourguer un dollar pour sa peine mais elle l'a pas pris. Elle arrêtait pas de me dire de rentrer chez moi et de me mettre au lit. J'ai un peu essayé de lui refiler un rencard pour quand elle aurait terminé son boulot mais elle a pas voulu. Elle disait qu'elle avait l'âge d'être ma mère et tout. Je lui ai montré mes cheveux blancs et j'ai dit que j'avais quarante-deux ans. Bien sûr je racontais des conneries, mais quand même elle était gentille. Je lui ai montré aussi ma casquette de chasse et ça lui a plu. Elle me l'a fait mettre sur la tête avant que je sorte parce que mes cheveux étaient encore pas mal mouillés. C'était une fille bien.

Une fois dehors je me sentais plus tellement ivre mais il faisait de nouveau très froid et mes dents se sont mises à claquer terrible. Je pouvais pas les empêcher. J'ai remonté Madison Avenue et j'ai attendu l'arrêt du bus parce que j'avais presque plus d'argent donc fallait que je commence à économiser sur les taxis et tout. Mais j'étais pas d'humeur à prendre le bus. D'ailleurs je savais même pas dans quelle direction je voulais me propulser. Alors je me suis dirigé vers le parc. Je pensais aller près du petit lac, pour voir ce que fabriquaient les canards, s'ils étaient encore là ou pas. J'ignorais toujours s'ils étaient là ou pas. Jusqu'au parc ça faisait pas très loin, et j'avais aucun endroit particulier où aller. Je savais même pas où dormir — donc j'ai marché. J'étais pas fatigué ni rien. Simplement, j'avais le cafard.

Et puis juste comme j'entrais dans le parc il m'est arrivé quelque chose d'horrible. J'ai laissé tomber le disque de Phoebé. Il s'est cassé en cinquante morceaux. Il était dans une grande pochette et tout mais il s'est quand même cassé. J'ai bien failli me remettre à pleurer tellement c'était un sale coup. J'ai seulement sorti les morceaux du carton et je les ai fourrés dans la poche de mon manteau. Ils étaient plus bons à rien mais je pouvais pas me décider à les jeter. J'ai continué à avancer. Dans la nuit noire.

J'ai passé toute ma vie à New York et je connais Central Park comme ma poche parce que j'y allais tout le temps faire du patin à roulettes quand j'étais môme et puis du vélo mais cette nuit-là j'ai eu un mal fou à trouver le lac. Je *savais* où il était — près de Central Park South et tout — mais j'arrivais pas à le trouver. Je devais être plus saoul que je pensais. J'ai marché marché et il faisait de plus en plus noir et c'était de plus en plus hallucinant. Tout le temps que j'ai été dans le parc j'ai pas vu un seul être humain. Et je m'en plains pas. Si j'avais rencontré quelqu'un j'aurais probablement bondi à plus d'un *mile* en arrière. Bon, quand même, le lac, je l'ai trouvé. Ce qu'y avait c'est qu'il était en partie gelé et en partie pas gelé. Mais j'ai pas vu les canards. J'ai fait tout le tour du foutu lac — à un moment j'ai même bien manqué tomber dedans — mais j'ai pas vu un seul canard. J'ai pensé que peut-être, s'il y en avait, ils dormaient dans l'herbe et tout, au bord de l'eau. C'est comme ça que je suis presque tombé dedans. Mais les canards je les ai pas trouvés.

Finalement, je me suis assis sur un banc, là où c'était pas trop sombre. Ouah, je tremblais toujours comme un dingue et mes cheveux sur ma nuque étaient pleins de petits glaçons, et ça malgré ma casquette. Je me faisais du souci, je pensais que j'allais probablement attraper une pneumonie et claquer. Je me suis mis à me représenter les millions de pedzouilles qui viendraient à mon enterrement. Mon grand-père de Detroit qui lit tout haut les numéros des rues quand on prend le bus ensemble, et mes tantes — j'en ai dans les cinquante — et ma ribambelle de cornichons de cousins. Ça ferait une foule. Quand Allie est mort ils sont tous venus, toute la troupe à la con. J'ai cette idiote de tante, celle qui a mauvais haleine, elle arrêtait pas de dire qu'Allie, il avait l'air si *paisible* étendu là, c'est D.B. qui me l'a raconté. Moi j'y étais pas. J'étais encore à l'hôpital. On m'avait mis à l'hôpital et tout, vu que je m'étais abîmé la main. Bon. Je me suis dit que j'allais sûrement avoir une pneumonie, avec ces glaçons dans les cheveux, et que je mourrais. Et ça m'embêtait vachement pour ma mère et mon père. Spécialement pour ma mère parce qu'elle est encore pas remise, à cause de mon frère Allie. Je l'imaginais qui saurait pas quoi faire de mes habits et de mon équipement sportif. La seule chose bien c'est que j'étais sûr qu'elle laisserait pas la môme Phoebé venir à mon enterrement parce qu'elle est encore trop petite. C'était la seule chose bien. Et puis j'ai pensé à toute la bande qui me foutrait au cimetière et tout, avec mon nom sur la tombe et tout. Au milieu de ces foutus trépassés. Ouah, quand on est mort, on y met les formes pour vous installer. J'espère que lorsque je mourrai quelqu'un aura le bon sens de me jeter dans une rivière. N'importe quoi plutôt que le cimetière. Avec des gens qui viennent le dimanche vous poser un bouquet de fleurs sur le ventre et toutes ces conneries. Est-ce qu'on a besoin de fleurs quand on est mort ?

Souvent, lorsqu'il fait beau, mes parents vont mettre des fleurs sur la tombe d'Allie. Je les ai accompagnés deux ou trois fois et puis j'ai arrêté. D'abord ça me plaît pas du tout de le voir dans ce putain de cimetière. Entouré par des types qui sont morts et sous des dalles de pierre et tout. Quand il y a du soleil ça peut encore aller, mais deux fois, oui *deux fois* on y était quand il s'est mis à pleuvoir. C'était horrible. Il pleuvait sur la saloperie de tombe d'Allie et il pleuvait sur l'herbe, sur son ventre. Il pleuvait tous azimuts. Les gens en visite au cimetière se sont mis à courir à toute pompe vers leurs voitures. Je me sentais devenir dingue. Ces gens, ils avaient qu'à monter dans les voitures et mettre la radio et tout et puis à s'en aller dîner dans un endroit agréable — tous, excepté Allie. Et ça je pouvais pas l'admettre. Je sais bien que c'est seulement son corps qu'est au cimetière et son âme est au Ciel et tout, le grand blabla, mais quand même je pouvais pas l'admettre. Je voudrais tellement pas qu'il soit là. Vous l'avez pas connu. Si vous l'aviez connu vous comprendriez. Passe encore quand y a du soleil mais le soleil il vient quand ça lui chante.

Au bout d'un moment, pour m'ôter de la tête l'idée d'attraper une pneumonie et tout, j'ai sorti mon fric et j'ai essayé de le compter dans la lumière pourrie d'un lampadaire. Il me restait que trois dollars et de la petite monnaie. Ouah. J'avais dépensé une fortune depuis mon départ de Pencey. Alors ce que j'ai fait, je suis allé près du lac, et j'ai lancé les pièces dedans, à l'endroit où c'était pas gelé. Je sais pas pourquoi j'ai fait ça mais je l'ai fait. J'imagine que je cherchais à m'ôter de la cervelle cette idée d'attraper une pneumonie et de mourir. Mais ça n'a pas réussi.

Je me suis mis à me demander ce que dirait la môme Phoebé si je mourais d'une pneumonie. C'était se tracasser bêtement mais je pouvais pas m'en empêcher. Ce serait moche pour elle si ça m'arrivait. Elle m'aime bien. Je peux dire qu'elle m'aime beaucoup. Vraiment. Bon, ça me trottait par la tête aussi j'ai fini par décider que je ferais mieux d'aller la voir à la maison en douce et je me suis dit que je me glisserais dans l'appartement sans bruit ni rien et qu'on aurait une petite convers' — elle et moi. Y avait bien la porte d'entrée qui m'embêtait. Cette saloperie de porte elle grince tellement. C'est un vieil immeuble et le gérant est flemmard, alors tout craque et grince. J'avais peur que mes parents m'entendent. Mais j'ai décidé de quand même tenter le coup.

Donc je suis ressorti du parc, et j'ai pris en direction de la maison. Je me suis tapé tout le chemin à pied. C'était pas tellement loin. J'étais pas fatigué. Je me sentais même plus ivre. Y avait juste qu'il faisait froid et qu'on voyait pas un chat.

CHAPITRE 21

ÇA a été mon coup de pot du siècle. Quand je suis arrivé à la maison, Pete, le liftier du service de nuit, était pas là. C'était un nouveau. Alors je me suis dit qu'à moins de me cogner en plein dans mes parents ou quoi, je pourrais dire un petit bonjour à Phoebé et me barrer après sans que personne sache que j'étais venu. C'était un coup de pot du tonnerre. Ce qui arrangeait encore la situation c'est que le garçon d'ascenseur était plutôt à classer dans les cloches. Je lui ai dit d'un air très détaché que j'allais chez les Dickstein. Les Dickstein ce sont les gens qui ont l'autre appartement au même étage. Puis j'ai ôté ma casquette pour pas faire mauvais genre et je suis entré dans l'ascenseur comme si j'étais terriblement pressé.

Il avait fermé les portes et il était prêt à mettre le truc en marche quand il s'est tourné vers moi et il a dit « Y sont pas là. Y sont à une soirée au quatorzième étage ».

J'ai dit « Aucune importance. C'est entendu que je les attendrai. Je suis leur neveu ».

Il m'a jeté un coup d'œil soupçonneux. « Tu ferais mieux de les attendre dans le hall, mon gars. »

J'ai dit « Je voudrais bien. Sincèrement. Mais j'ai une jambe esquintée. Faut que je la maintienne

191

dans une certaine position. Je crois qu'il est préférable que j'aille m'asseoir sur la banquette du palier ».

Il suivait pas ce que je racontais. Il a seulement dit « Oh », et on est montés. Bien joué, ouah. C'est marrant, suffit de s'arranger pour que quelqu'un pige rien à ce qu'on lui dit et on obtient pratiquement tout ce qu'on veut.

Je suis sorti à notre étage — en boitant comme un malheureux — et je me suis dirigé du côté des Dickstein. Quand j'ai entendu la porte de l'ascenseur se refermer j'ai fait demi-tour et je suis allé de notre côté. Tout se passait bien. J'étais dégivré. J'ai pris ma clef et j'ai ouvert. Doucement. Doucement. Puis encore plus doucement et tout je suis rentré et j'ai refermé la porte. Décidément, j'aurais dû être cambrioleur.

Bien sûr, dans le vestibule j'y voyais que dalle et je pouvais pas allumer. Il fallait que je prenne des précautions pour pas me cogner et faire du barouf. Mais en tout cas je pouvais dire sans hésiter que j'étais à la maison. On sent tout de suite une drôle d'odeur qu'on trouve nulle part ailleurs. Je sais pas ce que c'est. C'est pas du chou-fleur, c'est pas du parfum. Difficile de préciser mais on peut tout de suite dire qu'on est à la maison. J'ai voulu ôter mon manteau pour le mettre dans la penderie mais finalement je l'ai gardé parce que la penderie est pleine de cintres qui font un vrai tintamarre quand on ouvre la porte. Puis j'ai avancé doucement, doucement, en direction de la chambre de Phoebé. Je savais que la bonne m'entendrait bicause elle a qu'un seul tympan. Quand elle était gosse elle m'a dit, un jour son frère lui a enfoncé une paille dans l'oreille. Alors elle est pas mal sourde et tout. Mes parents, eux, ils ont les oreilles comme celles d'un chien limier. Ma mère, c'est-à-dire. Donc j'ai fait très attention en passant devant leur porte. Bon

Dieu, j'ai même retenu mon souffle. Mon père on lui casserait une chaise sur le crâne sans qu'il se réveille mais ma mère il suffit qu'un de nous se mette à tousser quelque part en Sibérie et elle entend. Elle est drôlement nerveuse. Ça lui arrive d'être debout toute la nuit à griller des cigarettes.

Finalement, au bout d'une heure ou presque, je suis arrivé dans la chambre de Phoebé. Et elle y était pas. J'avais oublié. Oui j'avais oublié qu'elle dort toujours dans la chambre de D.B. quand il est à Hollywood ou ailleurs. Elle aime, parce que c'est la plus grande chambre de la maison. Et aussi parce qu'il y a un grand vieux bureau dingue que D.B. a acheté à une dame de Philadelphie, une alcoolique, et puis un grand lit, un lit gigantesque, dix *miles* de long sur dix de large. Ce lit, je sais pas d'où il l'a ramené. En tout cas, la môme Phoebé elle aime dormir dans la chambre de D.B. quand il est là et lui il veut bien. Ça vaut le coup d'œil lorsqu'elle s'installe pour faire ses devoirs à ce bureau extravagant, presque aussi grand que le lit. Quand elle y est assise on la voit à peine. Mais c'est le genre de machin qu'elle aime. Sa chambre elle dit qu'elle lui plaît pas bicause elle est trop petite. Elle dit qu'elle aime s'étaler. Ça me tue. La môme Phoebé, qu'est-ce qu'elle a à étaler ? Rien.

Bon. J'ai filé tout en douceur jusqu'à la chambre de D.B. et j'ai allumé la lampe qui est sur le bureau. La môme Phoebé, elle s'est même pas réveillée. Je l'ai regardée un bout de temps, elle était endormie avec la figure sur le bord de l'oreiller et la bouche ouverte. C'est bizarre. Prenez les adultes, ils ont l'air tarés quand ils dorment la bouche ouverte, mais pas les gosses. Les gosses ils sont quand même chouettes. Ils peuvent avoir en plus bavé sur leur oreiller et ils sont quand même chouettes.

J'ai fait le tour de la chambre, sans bruit, en inspectant un peu les lieux. Pour changer, je me sentais en forme. J'avais plus du tout l'impression que j'allais avoir une pneumonie ni rien. Je me sentais juste en bonne forme, pour changer. Les vêtements de Phoebé étaient sur une chaise, près du lit. Pour une gamine elle est très ordonnée. Elle jette pas ses affaires n'importe où comme certains mômes. Elle bousille rien. La veste du costume brun que ma mère lui a rapporté du Canada était suspendue au dossier de la chaise. Son chemisier et le reste étaient sur le siège. Ses chaussures et ses chaussettes sur le plancher, bien alignées. Les chaussures, je les avais jamais vues. C'était des chaussures basses, marron, genre sport, un peu comme les miennes, et qui allaient bougrement bien avec le costume que ma mère lui avait acheté au Canada. Ma mère s'y connaît pour l'habiller. Sans blague. Ma mère a un goût du tonnerre pour certaines choses. Elle vaut rien pour acheter des patins à glace ou des trucs comme ça mais pour les vêtements elle est extra. Je veux dire que Phoebé a toujours des robes à vous époustoufler. Prenez la plupart des gosses, même si leurs parents sont à l'aise c'est dément les trucs qu'on leur met sur le dos. Phoebé, je voudrais que vous la voyiez dans le costume que ma mère lui a acheté au Canada. Je vous jure.

Je me suis assis au bureau du père D.B. et j'ai jeté un coup d'œil à ce qu'il y avait dessus. C'était principalement les affaires de Pheobé, ses affaires d'école. Surtout des livres. Le premier de la pile c'était *L'Arithmétique sans larmes*. Je l'ai ouvert à la première page et voilà ce qu'il y avait :

Phoebé Weatherfield Caulfield
7 B-I

Ça m'a tué. Son deuxième prénom c'est Joséphine, bon Dieu, pas Weatherfield. Mais Joséphine, elle aime pas. Chaque fois que je la vois, elle s'est trouvé un nouveau prénom. Le livre en dessous de l'arithmétique c'était une géographie et le livre encore en dessous un manuel d'orthographe. Elle est très bonne en orthographe. Elle est très bonne en tout mais elle est encore meilleure en orthographe. Et puis, sous le manuel, il y avait un tas de carnets. Des carnets, elle en a dans les cinq mille. On a jamais vu une môme avec autant de carnets. J'ai ouvert celui du dessus et j'ai regardé la première page. C'était écrit :

> *Bernice, on se voit à la récréation,*
> *j'ai quelque chose de très important à te dire.*

Sur cette page-là, c'était tout. Sur la suivante il y avait :

> *Pourquoi trouve-t-on tellement de fabriques de conserves dans le sud-est de l'Alaska ?*
> *Parce qu'il y a tellement de saumons.*
> *Pourquoi y a-t-il de riches forêts ?*
> *A cause du climat.*
> *Que fait notre gouvernement pour rendre la vie plus facile aux esquimaux de l'Alaska ?*
> *A chercher pour demain !!!*

> *Phoebé Weatherfield Caulfield*
> *Phoebé Weatherfield Caulfield*
> *Phoebé Weatherfield Caulfield*
> *Phoebé W. Caulfield*
> *P.W. Caulfield*
> *Faire passer à Shirley !!!*
> *Shirley, tu as dit que tu étais Sagittaire*
> mais t'es que Taureau apporte tes patins quand tu viens à la maison.

Je me suis assis au bureau de D.B. et j'ai lu le carnet tout entier. Ça m'a pas pris beaucoup de temps. Et je pourrais passer mes jours et mes nuits à lire ce genre de trucs, le carnet d'un môme, le carnet de Phoebé ou de n'importe quel môme. Les carnets de môme ça me tue. Puis j'ai allumé encore une cigarette — c'était ma dernière. Je devais bien en avoir fumé ce jour-là trois cartouches de dix paquets. Finalement j'ai réveillé Phoebé, j'allais pas rester assis à ce bureau jusqu'à la fin de mes jours. D'autant que j'avais peur que les parents me tombent dessus et avant je voulais au moins dire bonsoir à Phoebé. Aussi je l'ai réveillée.

Elle se réveille très facilement. Y a pas à crier ni rien. Pratiquement suffit de s'asseoir au bord de son lit, de dire « Réveille-toi, Phoebé » et toc, elle se réveille.

Elle a dit tout de suite « Holden ! » En jetant ses bras autour de mon cou. Elle est très affectueuse. Je veux dire, pour une gamine elle est très affectueuse. Parfois elle est même trop affectueuse. Je l'ai embrassée et elle a dit « Quand tu es arrivé ? » Elle était drôlement contente de me voir. C'est sûr.

« Pas si fort. J'arrive à l'instant. Comment tu vas ?

— Très bien. Tu as eu ma lettre ? Cinq pages je t'ai écrit.

— Ouais. Pas si fort. Merci. »

Elle m'avait écrit une lettre. J'avais pas pu lui répondre encore. C'était au sujet de cette pièce de théâtre où elle avait un rôle, à l'école. Elle me disait de pas prendre de rancards ni rien pour le vendredi parce qu'il fallait que je vienne la voir. J'ai demandé « Comment ça marche, la pièce ? Tu m'as dit que c'était quoi, le titre ?

— *A Christmas Pageant for Americans*. C'est moche, mais je suis Benedict Arnold. J'ai pratiquement le plus grand rôle. » Ouah, pour être réveillée elle l'était à présent. Elle s'excite beaucoup quand elle raconte des trucs. « Ça commence quand je suis en train de mourir. La veille de Noël y a un fantôme qui arrive et qui me demande si j'ai pas honte et tout ça. Tu sais. D'avoir trahi mon pays et tout ça. Tu viendras ? » Elle était assise toute droite dans son lit. « C'est ce que je t'ai mis dans ma lettre. Tu viens ?

— Bien sûr que je viens. Certainement que je viens. »

Elle a dit « Papa peut pas venir. Faut qu'il aille en Californie. Il prend l'avion ». Ouah, je vous le dis, sûr qu'elle était bien réveillée — pour se réveiller ça lui prend deux secondes. Elle était assise — ou plutôt comme agenouillée dans son lit et elle me tenait la main. « Écoute, maman a dit que tu arrivais *mercredi*. Oui, elle a dit *mercredi*.

— Je suis sorti un peu en avance. Pas si fort. Tu vas réveiller tout le monde.

— Quelle heure il est ? Ils vont rentrer très tard, maman a dit. Ils sont allés à une soirée à Norwalk, Connecticut. Devine ce que j'ai fait cet après-midi ? Le film que j'ai vu ? Devine ?

— Je sais pas. Écoute. Ils ont pas dit à quelle heure ils...

— *Le Docteur*, a dit la môme Phoebé. C'est un film spécial qu'ils passaient à la Fondation Lister. Ils le passaient uniquement aujourd'hui. Aujourd'hui c'était le seul jour. Ça parlait de ce médecin, au Kentucky et tout ça, celui qui a collé une couverture sur la figure d'une petite fille qu'est infirme et peut pas marcher. Alors ils l'ont mis en prison. C'était formidable.

— Écoute-moi une minute. Ils ont pas dit à quelle heure ils...

— Le docteur il a pitié. C'est pourquoi il lui fourre une couverture sur la figure et il l'étouffe. Alors on l'envoie en prison pour la vie mais cette petite fille qu'a eu la couverture sur la tête elle vient tout le temps lui rendre visite et le remercier pour ce qu'il a fait. C'était par charité. Mais il sait bien qu'il mérite d'aller en prison parce qu'un médecin a pas le droit de toucher à l'œuvre de Dieu. C'est la mère de cette fille de ma classe, Alice Holmborg, qui nous a emmenées. Alice est ma meilleure amie. La seule fille dans toute... »

J'ai dit « Attends une seconde, veux-tu ? Je t'ai posé une question. Ils ont pas dit à quelle heure ils rentraient ?

— Non, mais ils ont dit très tard. Papa a pris la voiture pour qu'ils aient pas à se casser la tête avec les trains. Maintenant il y a une radio dedans. Sauf que maman a dit que faut pas la faire marcher quand on circule. »

Je commençais à me détendre. C'est-à-dire j'en arrivais à m'en foutre qu'ils rentrent et me trouvent là. Je me suis dit merde, tant pis. S'ils me trouvent, ben ils me trouveront.

Phoebé, j'aurais voulu que vous la voyiez. Elle avait son pyjama bleu avec sur le col des éléphants rouges. Les éléphants, ça lui allait vachement bien.

J'ai dit « Donc c'était un bon film, hein ?

— Super. Sauf qu'Alice avait un rhume et sa mère arrêtait pas de lui demander si elle se sentait fiévreuse. En plein milieu du film. Toujours à un moment très important sa mère se penchait au-dessus de moi et demandait à Alice si elle se sentait pas fiévreuse. Ça me tapait sur les nerfs. »

Alors je lui ai dit, pour le disque. J'ai dit « Écoute, je t'avais acheté un disque. Seulement je l'ai cassé en route ». J'ai sorti les morceaux de la poche de mon manteau et je les ai montrés. J'ai dit « J'étais bourré ».

Elle a dit « Donne-les-moi ». Elle a pris les morceaux du disque et elle les a mis dans le tiroir de la table de nuit. Elle me tue.

J'ai demandé « Il vient D.B., pour Noël ?

— Maman a dit peut-être, ou peut-être pas. Ça dépend. Il sera peut-être obligé de rester à Hollywood et d'écrire un film sur Annapolis.

— Annapolis. Bon Dieu !

— C'est une histoire d'amour. Devine qui va être dedans. Quel acteur ? Devine. »

J'ai dit « Ça m'intéresse pas. Annapolis. Bordel. Qu'est-ce qu'il sait d'Annapolis, D.B., bordel ? Quel rapport avec le genre d'histoires qu'il écrit ? » Ouah. Son ciné ça me rend dingue. Ce foutu Hollywood. J'ai demandé « Qu'est-ce que tu t'es fait au bras ? » J'avais remarqué qu'elle avait un grand morceau de sparadrap. J'avais remarqué pour la raison que son pyjama a des manches courtes.

Elle a dit « C'est un garçon de ma classe qui m'a poussée, Curtis Weintraub, dans le parc, quand je descendais les marches. Tu veux voir ? » Elle commençait déjà à décoller la saleté de sparadrap.

« Laisse. Pourquoi il t'a poussée en bas des marches ?

— Je sais pas. Je crois qu'il me déteste, a dit la môme Phoebé. Cette autre fille et moi, Selma Atterbury, on a mis de l'encre et des saletés partout sur son anorak.

— C'est pas gentil. Qu'est-ce que tu es ? Encore un bébé ?

— Non, mais tout le temps dans le parc il me *suit*. Partout. Tout le temps. Il me suit. Ça m'agace.

— Sans doute qu'il t'aime bien. C'est pas une raison pour mettre de l'encre sur... »

Elle a dit « Je veux pas qu'il m'aime bien ». Puis elle a dit « Holden, pourquoi c'est pas *mercredi* que t'es rentré ?

— Quoi ? »

Avec la gamine, il faut toujours prendre garde. Ouah. Si vous trouvez pas qu'elle est futée c'est que vous êtes pas normal.

Elle a répété « Pourquoi c'est pas *mercredi* que t'es rentré ? hey, t'aurais pas été renvoyé ?

— Je t'ai dit. Ils nous ont libérés plus tôt. Ils ont...

— T'as été renvoyé. C'est bien ça ! » a crié Phoebé. Puis elle m'a frappé la jambe d'un coup de poing. Quand elle veut, elle s'y connaît pour serrer les poings. « T'es renvoyé. Oh ! Holden. » Elle avait sa main sur sa bouche et tout. Y a des moments où elle se met dans tous ses états. Je vous jure.

« Qui a dit que j'étais renvoyé ? Personne a dit que...

— T'es renvoyé. T'es renvoyé. » Et elle m'a encore frappé avec son poing. Et faudrait pas croire que c'était particulièrement doux. Elle a dit « Papa va te *tuer* ». Et puis elle s'est laissée retomber et elle s'est fourré l'oreiller sur la figure. Elle fait ça très souvent. Parfois elle est vraiment barjot.

J'ai dit « Arrête, veux-tu. Personne va me tuer. Personne va même... Allons, Phoeb', montre ta bouille. Personne va me tuer ».

Mais elle gardait l'oreiller sur sa figure. Quand elle s'obstine on peut rien en tirer. Tout ce qu'elle faisait c'était répéter « Papa va te *tuer* ». Et à cause de l'oreiller on la comprenait à peine.

J'ai dit « Personne va me tuer. Réfléchis un peu. Et d'abord, je m'en vais. Après, on verra bien. Je pourrais chercher un job dans un ranch ou quoi. Pour quelque temps. Je connais un type dont le grand-père a un ranch au Colorado. Peut-être que là-bas y aura un job pour moi ». J'ai dit « Je te donnerai de mes nouvelles et tout quand je serai parti si je pars. Allons. Enlève ça. Hey, Phoebé. Allons. S'il te plaît ». Mais elle gardait l'oreiller sur sa figure. J'ai tiré, mais elle est drôlement costaud. On se fatigue à lutter avec elle. Ouah, si elle veut garder l'oreiller sur sa figure qu'elle le *garde*. « Phoebé, je t'en prie. Allons. Montre-toi. » J'arrêtais pas de lui dire « Allons. Hey. Hey, Weatherfield. Montre-toi ».

Elle voulait pas. Parfois y a pas moyen de la raisonner. Finalement je me suis levé. Je suis allé dans la salle de séjour et j'ai pris quelques cigarettes dans la boîte sur la table. J'étais rétamé.

CHAPITRE 22

QUAND je suis revenu elle avait sorti la tête de l'oreiller, comme je m'y attendais, elle était couchée sur le dos mais quand même elle voulait toujours pas me regarder. J'ai longé le lit et je me suis à nouveau assis au bord, elle a tourné de l'autre côté sa petite bouille en colère. Elle me faisait la gueule. Juste comme l'équipe d'escrime à Pencey, quand j'avais laissé les foutus fleurets dans le métro.

J'ai demandé « Comment va la chère Hazel Weatherfield ? As-tu écrit d'autres histoires sur elle ? Celle que tu m'as envoyée est dans ma valise qui est restée à la gare. C'est très bien.

— Papa va te *tuer*. »

Ouah, quand elle a quelque chose dans la tête elle a pour de bon quelque chose dans la tête.

« Non. Pas vrai. Le pire qu'il me fera, il m'engueulera, et puis il m'enverra dans cette foutue école militaire. C'est le pire qu'il me fera. Et *d'abord* je serai même pas ici. Je serai parti. Je serai... je serai probablement au Colorado, dans ce ranch.

— Me fais pas rire. Tu sais même pas monter à cheval.

— Quoi ? Tu parles. On vous apprend ça en deux minutes. Arrête de tripoter ce machin. » Elle tiraillait sur le sparadrap de son bras. J'ai demandé « Qui est-ce qui t'a coupé les cheveux comme ça ? »

Je venais juste de remarquer qu'elle avait une coupe de cheveux très moche. C'était beaucoup trop court.

Elle a dit « Ça te regarde pas ». Quelquefois elle prend un air pimbêche. Elle peut être tout à fait pimbêche. « Je suppose que tu as encore loupé dans toutes les matières » elle a dit, très pimbêche. Quelquefois elle parle comme une saleté de prof et elle est seulement une petite fille.

J'ai dit « Non. J'ai pas loupé en Lettres ». Et puis, pour rire, je lui ai pincé le derrière. A la façon dont elle était couchée sur le côté, son derrière ressortait. C'était un tout petit derrière. J'ai pas pincé dur, quand même elle a voulu me donner une tape sur la main. Manqué.

Et puis subitement elle a dit « Mais pourquoi t'as fait ça ? » Elle voulait dire pourquoi tu t'es encore fait renvoyer. Et le ton qu'elle avait, c'était pas gai.

J'ai dit « Oh ! non, Phoebé, demande pas. J'en ai marre de toujours t'entendre demander la même chose. Y a un million de raisons. C'était un des pires collèges où je suis jamais allé. Plein de frimeurs. Et de sales types. Dans toute ta vie t'as jamais vu autant de sales types. Par exemple, si on discutait un coup dans une des piaules et que quelqu'un voulait entrer, personne aurait laissé entrer un type un peu charlot et boutonneux. Tout le monde lui fermait la porte au nez. Et il y avait cette foutue société secrète et j'étais trop trouillard pour pas m'en mettre. Un gars plutôt rasoir et boutonneux voulait s'en mettre aussi. Robert Ackley il s'appelait, il a essayé et il a jamais pu. Juste parce qu'il était rasoir et boutonneux. J'ai même pas envie de parler de ça. C'était une école puante. Crois-moi sur parole. »

La môme Phoebé, elle bronchait pas mais elle

écoutait. Je le voyais rien qu'à regarder sa nuque. Lorsqu'on lui dit quelque chose elle écoute toujours. Et le plus drôle c'est que la moitié du temps elle sait de quoi ça retourne. Sans rire.

J'ai continué à parler de Pencey. J'avais comme une envie d'en parler.

J'ai dit « Même les deux ou trois profs sympa, c'était quand même des tarés. Y avait ce vieux type, Mr. Spencer, sa femme arrêtait pas de nous offrir des tasses de chocolat et tous les deux ils étaient vraiment pas désagréables. Mais si tu l'avais vu, lui, quand le père Thurmer, le directeur, rappliquait en cours d'histoire et s'asseyait au fond de la classe. Parce que Thurmer il venait tout le temps passer une demi-heure au fond de la classe. Il était supposé venir incognito. Au bout d'un moment il se renversait sur sa chaise et se mettait à interrompre le père Spencer pour lancer des plaisanteries à la con. Et le père Spencer était là qui se tuait à sourire et à glousser et tout, comme si ce corniaud de Thurmer était un foutu prince en visite.

— Dis pas de gros mots.

— T'en aurais dégueulé, je te jure. Et puis la Journée des Anciens. Ils avaient ça, cette journée quand tous les tarés qui ont fait leurs études à Pencey vers les 1776 reviennent au collège et se baladent partout avec leurs femmes et leurs enfants. Si t'avais vu ce vieux type qu'avait dans les cinquante piges. Ce qu'il a fait, il est venu frapper à la porte de notre piaule et il a demandé si ça nous ennuyait qu'il aille aux lavabos. Les lavabos c'était au bout du couloir. Je vois pas pourquoi c'est à *nous* qu'il a demandé. Et tu sais ce qu'il a dit ? Il a dit qu'il voulait vérifier si ses initiales étaient encore sur une des portes des chiottes. Ce qu'il avait fait, y a dans les quatre-vingt-dix ans, il avait gravé ses vieilles connasses de saletés d'initiales sur une des portes des chiottes et il voulait vérifier si elles y étaient encore. Donc, mon copain de chambre et moi, on est allés avec lui aux lavabos, et on est restés là à attendre pendant qu'il cherchait ses initiales sur toutes les portes des chiottes. Et il a pas arrêté un instant de nous parler, nous racontant que ses années à Pencey c'étaient les plus heureuses de sa vie, et nous donnant un tas de conseils, pour notre avenir et tout. Ouah, il m'a flanqué un de ces cafards ! Je veux pas dire que c'était un mauvais type — sûrement pas. Mais y a pas que les mauvais types qui vous fichent le cafard. Même un *bon* type peut le faire. Pour ça y suffit qu'il donne un tas de conseils bidon tout en cherchant ses initiales sur la porte des chiottes — ça suffit. Je sais pas. Peut-être que ça aurait été moins pénible s'il avait pas été tout essoufflé. Il était tout essoufflé rien que d'avoir monté les escaliers et pendant qu'il en finissait pas de chercher ses initiales il respirait avec un bruit terrible et ses narines étaient bizarres et tristes tandis qu'il continuait à nous dire, à Stradlater et à moi, de bien profiter de Pencey. Bon Dieu, Phoebé ! Je peux pas expliquer. C'est juste que j'aimais rien de tout ce qui se passait à Pencey. Je peux pas expliquer. »

Le môme Phoebé a dit quelque chose, mais j'ai pas compris. Elle avait le coin de sa bouche contre l'oreiller et j'ai pas compris.

J'ai dit « Quoi ? Sors ta bouche de là. Je comprends pas quand t'ouvres pas bien la bouche.

— Tu aimes jamais rien de ce qui se passe. »

Qu'elle dise ça, j'en ai eu le cafard encore plus.

« Mais si. Mais si. Dis pas ça. Pourquoi tu dis ça, bon Dieu ?

— Parce que c'est vrai. T'aimes aucune école. T'aimes pas un million de choses. T'aimes *rien*.

— Mais si. C'est là où tu te trompes. C'est là où tu te trompes totalement. » J'ai dit « Pourquoi faut-il que tu dises ça, bon Dieu ? » Ouah. J'étais tout démoli.

Elle a dit « Parce que c'est vrai. Nomme une seule chose ».

J'ai dit « Une chose ? Une chose que j'aime ? Okay ».

L'ennui c'est que je pouvais pas me concentrer vraiment. Par moments c'est dur de se concentrer.

J'ai demandé « Une chose que j'aime beaucoup, tu veux dire ? »

Mais elle a pas répondu. Elle était couchée tout de travers, là-bas à l'autre bout du lit. Elle était bien à cinq cents *miles*. J'ai dit « Allons, réponds. Une chose que j'aime beaucoup ou simplement une chose que j'aime ?

— Que t'aimes beaucoup. »

J'ai dit « D'accord ». Mais l'ennui, c'est que j'arrivais pas à me concentrer. Tout ce qui me venait à l'idée c'était ces deux bonnes sœurs qui faisaient la quête avec leur vieux panier abîmé. Spécialement celle avec les lunettes à monture métallique. Et puis le garçon que j'avais connu à Elkton Hills. Il y avait un garçon, à Elkton Hills, il se nommait James Castle, qui voulait pas retirer quelque chose qu'il avait dit sur cet autre gars, très prétentieux, Phil Stabile. James Castle avait dit qu'il était crâneur, et un des salopards d'amis de Stabile est allé lui rapporter ça. Alors Stabile, avec six autres salopards, est entré dans la piaule de James Castle et ils ont fermé la porte à clef et essayé de lui faire retirer ce qu'il avait dit mais il a pas voulu. Et ils se sont mis au boulot. Je vous dirai pas ce qu'ils lui ont fait, c'est trop répugnant — mais James Castle a toujours pas voulu retirer ce qu'il avait dit. Et pourtant, si vous l'aviez vu. C'était un petit type maigre et l'air pas costaud, avec des poignets de la grosseur d'un crayon. Finalement, ce qu'il a fait, lui, plutôt que retirer ce qu'il avait dit, il a sauté par la fenêtre. J'étais sous la douche et tout, et même moi je l'ai entendu atterrir dehors. Mais j'ai cru que quelque chose était tombé par la fenêtre. Un poste de radio ou un bureau ou quoi, pas un *gars* ni rien. Puis j'ai entendu tout le monde qui courait dans le couloir et les escaliers, alors j'ai enfilé mon peignoir de bain et je suis descendu moi aussi à toute vitesse et il y avait James Castle étendu sur les marches de pierre et tout. Il était mort, avec ses dents et son sang projetés tous azimuts et personne voulait s'approcher de lui. Il portait mon pull à col roulé que je lui avais prêté. Et les types qui étaient avec lui dans la chambre ils ont simplement été renvoyés. Ils sont même pas allés en prison.

C'était à peu près tout ce qui me venait à l'idée. Les deux bonnes sœurs que j'avais vues en prenant mon petit déjeuner et ce gars, James Castle, que j'ai connu à Elkton Hills. Même pas vraiment connu, si vous voulez savoir, c'est ça le plus bizarre. C'était un type très tranquille. On suivait le même cours de maths, mais il était loin, à l'autre bout de la classe, et il se levait pas souvent pour réciter une leçon ou aller au tableau ni rien. En cours y a des gars qui se lèvent presque jamais pour réciter ou aller au tableau. Je crois bien que la seule fois où il m'a adressé la parole c'est lorsqu'il m'a demandé s'il pouvait m'emprunter mon pull à col roulé. J'en revenais pas qu'il me demande ça, c'était si surprenant et tout. Je me souviens que j'étais en train de me brosser les dents aux lavabos. Il m'a dit que son cousin venait le chercher pour l'emmener faire un tour en voiture. Je pensais même pas qu'il savait que j'avais un pull à col roulé. Moi, tout ce que je savais de lui, c'était que son nom se trouvait juste avant le mien, sur le cahier d'appel. Cabel R., Cabel W., Castle, Caulfield — je m'en souviens. Et en fait, je lui ai presque dit non, pour le pull. Juste parce que ce James Castle, je le connaissais pas bien.

« Quoi ? » Y avait la môme Phoebé qui me parlait, mais j'avais pas fait attention.

« Tu peux même pas trouver une seule chose.

— Mais si. Mais si.

— Alors, vas-y. »

J'ai dit « J'aime Allie. Et j'aime faire ce qu'on fait en ce moment. Être assis là avec toi à bavarder et réfléchir à des trucs et...

— Allie est *mort*. Tu dis toujours ça ! Si quelqu'un est mort et *au Ciel*, alors c'est pas vraiment...

— Je le sais qu'il est mort. Et comment que je le sais ! Mais je peux quand même l'aimer, non ? Juste parce que les morts sont morts on s'arrête pas comme ça de les aimer, bon Dieu — spécialement quand ils étaient mille fois plus gentils que ceux qu'on connaît qui sont *vivants* et tout. »

La môme Phoebé, elle a rien dit. Quand elle trouve rien à répondre elle dit rien. Pas un mot.

Moi j'ai dit « Et puis j'aime maintenant. Je veux dire, en ce moment. Être assis près de toi et faire la convers' et raconter des...

— C'est pas *vraiment* quelque chose.

— C'est absolument *vraiment* quelque chose. Pas le moindre doute. Pourquoi ça le serait pas, bordel ? Les gens veulent jamais admettre que quelque chose est vraiment quelque chose. Ça commence à me faire chier.

— Dis pas de gros mots. Bon, d'accord. Trouve encore une chose. Ben, ce que tu voudrais être plus tard. Par exemple, ingénieur. Ou conseiller juridique.

— Je pourrais pas être ingénieur. Je suis pas assez fort en sciences.

— Alors, conseiller juridique — comme papa.

— Les juristes sont des gens bien, je suppose, mais ça me tente pas. Je veux dire, ce seraient des gens très bien s'ils s'occupaient tout le temps de sauver la vie de pauvres types innocents et qu'ils aiment ça, mais c'est pas ça qu'on fait quand on est juriste. Tout ce qu'on fait c'est ramasser du flouze et jouer au golf et au bridge et acheter des bagnoles et boire des Martini et être un personnage. D'ailleurs, même s'ils s'occupaient tout le temps de sauver la vie des types innocents et tout, comment on pourrait savoir s'ils le font parce qu'ils *veulent* vraiment le faire ou parce que ce qu'ils veulent *vraiment* faire c'est être un avocat super, que tout le monde félicite en lui tapant dans le dos au tribunal quand le jugement est rendu, avec les reporters et tout, comme on voit dans les saletés de films. Comment ils peuvent dire que c'est pas de la frime ? Le problème c'est qu'ils peuvent pas. »

Je suis pas très sûr que Phoebé comprenait de quoi je parlais, après tout c'est qu'une petite fille. Mais au moins elle écoutait. Si au moins quelqu'un écoute c'est déjà pas mal.

Elle a dit « Papa va te tuer. Il va te *tuer*. »

Je faisais pas attention. Je pensais à quelque chose. Quelque chose de dingue. J'ai dit « Tu sais ce que je voudrais être ? Tu sais ce que je voudrais être si on me laissait choisir, bordel ?

— Quoi ? Dis pas de gros mots.

— Tu connais la chanson "Si un cœur attrape un cœur qui vient à travers les seigles ?" Je voudrais...

— C'est "Si un corps rencontre un corps qui vient à travers les seigles". C'est un poème. De Robert Burns.

— Je le sais bien que c'est un poème de Robert Burns. » Remarquez, elle avait raison, c'est "Si un corps rencontre un corps qui vient à travers les seigles". Depuis, j'ai vérifié.

Là j'ai dit « Je croyais que c'était "Si un cœur attrape un cœur". Bon. Je me représente tous ces petits mômes qui jouent à je ne sais quoi dans le grand champ de seigle et tout. Des milliers de petits mômes et personne avec eux — je veux dire pas de grandes personnes — rien que moi. Et moi je suis planté au bord d'une saleté de falaise. Ce que j'ai à faire c'est attraper les mômes s'ils approchent trop près du bord. Je veux dire s'il courent sans regarder où ils vont, moi je rapplique et je les *attrape*. C'est ce que je ferais toute la journée. Je serais juste l'attrape-cœurs et tout. D'accord, c'est dingue, mais c'est vraiment ce que je voudrais être. Seulement ça. D'accord, c'est dingue. »

La môme Phoebé, pendant longtemps elle a rien dit. Puis quand elle a dit quelque chose elle a dit « Papa va te tuer ».

J'ai dit « S'il le fait, je m'en fous pas mal ». Je me suis levé du lit parce que je voulais téléphoner à ce type qui avait été mon prof de lettres, à Elkton Hills. Mr. Antolini. Maintenant il vivait à New York. Il avait quitté Elkton Hills et il enseignait à New York University. J'ai dit à Phoebé « Faut que je téléphone. Je reviens tout de suite. T'endors pas ». Je voulais pas qu'elle s'endorme pendant que j'étais dans la salle de séjour. Je savais bien qu'elle allait pas s'endormir mais j'ai dit quand même « t'endors pas ». Pour être plus sûr.

Comme je me dirigeais vers la porte, la môme Phoebé a dit « Holden ! » et je me suis retourné.

Elle était assise dans son lit. Tellement mignonne et tout. Elle a dit « Cette fille, Phyllis Margulies, elle me donne des leçons de rot. Écoute ».

J'ai écouté, et j'ai entendu quelque chose mais pas grand-chose. J'ai dit « Bravo ». Puis je suis allé dans la salle de séjour et j'ai bigophoné à ce prof que j'avais eu, Mr. Antolini.

CHAPITRE 23

Au téléphone j'ai pas traîné, j'avais peur que mes parents me tombent dessus au milieu de mon discours. Ça s'est pas produit, remarquez. Mr. Antolini a été très aimable. Il a dit que je pouvais venir immédiatement. Je crois bien que je les ai réveillés, lui et sa femme, parce qu'avant de décrocher ils m'ont fait attendre des heures. La première chose qu'il m'a demandée ça a été si j'avais des ennuis et j'ai dit non. J'ai tout de même dit qu'on m'avait foutu à la porte de Pencey. J'avais pensé que je ferais aussi bien de lui dire. Et quand je l'ai dit il a lancé « Oh ! Seigneur ». Il avait le sens de l'humour et tout. Il m'a dit que si je voulais, je pouvais venir immédiatement.

Mr. Antolini, ça doit être le meilleur professeur que j'aie jamais eu. Il était assez jeune, pas beaucoup plus vieux que mon frère D.B. et on pouvait blaguer avec lui tout en continuant à le respecter. C'est lui qui finalement a ramassé ce gars dont je vous ai parlé, qui avait sauté par la fenêtre, James Castle. Le petit père Antolini a tâté son pouls et tout, et puis il a ôté son pardessus et en a enveloppé James Castle et il l'a porté à l'infirmerie. Même que son manteau soit plein de sang il s'en foutait.

Quand je suis retourné dans la chambre de D.B., Phoebé avait mis la radio. Il en sortait une musique de danse. Elle l'avait mise très bas, pour que la bonne entende pas. Si vous l'aviez vue... Assise en plein milieu du lit, en dehors des couvertures, les jambes croisées, comme un yogi. Elle écoutait la musique. Elle me tue.

J'ai dit « Allons. Tu veux danser ? » Je lui ai appris à danser quand elle était toute petite. Elle danse très bien. Moi je lui ai juste appris deux ou trois choses. Le reste, elle l'a découvert toute seule. On peut pas *vraiment* apprendre à danser à quelqu'un.

Elle a dit « T'as tes chaussures.

— Je les enlève. Viens. »

Elle a pour ainsi dire sauté du lit. Et puis elle a attendu que j'ôte mes chaussures et on a dansé un moment. Elle est vachement douée. J'aime pas les gens qui dansent avec des petits gosses. La plupart du temps c'est horrible. Je parle de quand on est au restaurant, quelque part, et qu'on voit un vieux type qui s'amène sur la piste de danse avec sa petite gamine. Généralement il arrête pas de tirailler dans le dos la robe de la gosse sans faire exprès et de toute manière la gosse sait pas mieux danser qu'un pingouin et c'est horrible, mais moi je danse pas avec Phoebé en public ni rien. On s'amuse à ça seulement quand on est à la maison. D'ailleurs avec elle c'est pas pareil bicause elle sait danser. Elle peut suivre n'importe quoi qu'on lui fait faire. Je veux dire si on la tient très serrée pour que ça gêne pas qu'on ait des jambes tellement plus longues. Tout le temps elle suit. Vous pouvez traverser ou faire toutes sortes de fantaisies, ou bien même un peu de boogie-woogie et elle suit. Vous pouvez même danser le tango, bordel.

On s'est offert quatre danses. Entre chacune elle est drôlement marrante. Elle reste en position. Elle dit pas un mot ni rien. Il faut rester tous les deux en position et attendre que la musique reprenne. Ça me tue. Et il est pas question de rire ou quoi.

Bon. Après ça j'ai arrêté la radio. La môme Phoebé a regagné son plumard et s'est fourrée sous les couvertures. Elle m'a demandé « Est-ce que j'ai fait des progrès ?

— Et comment ! » j'ai dit. Je me suis assis sur le lit auprès d'elle. J'étais pas mal essoufflé. Je fumais tellement, j'avais plus de souffle. Mais Phoebé était toute fraîche.

Subitement elle a dit « Touche mon front.

— Pourquoi ?

— Touche-le. Juste une fois. »

J'ai touché. J'ai rien senti.

Elle a dit « Il est pas plutôt chaud ?

— Non. Il devrait l'être ?

— Oui. Je fais monter la fièvre. Touche encore. »

J'ai encore touché, je ne sentais toujours rien ; mais j'ai dit « Je crois que ça commence ». Je voulais pas lui donner une saleté de complexe d'infériorité.

Elle a hoché la tête. « On peut faire monter la fièvre même au-dessus du thermonètre.

— Ther*mom*ètre. Qui t'a dit ça ?

— Alice Homberg m'a montré. On croise les jambes, on retient sa respiration et on pense à quelque chose de très très chaud. Un radiateur par exemple. Et alors le front devient si brûlant qu'il peut brûler la main qui le touche. »

Ça m'a tué. J'ai retiré ma main comme si je courais un danger terrible. J'ai dit « Merci de me prévenir.

— Oh ! j'aurais pas brûlé *ta* main. Je me serais arrêtée avant que ça devienne trop... *chuttt !* » En un éclair elle s'était assise toute droite dans son lit.

Elle m'a drôlement foutu les jetons. J'ai dit « Qu'est-ce qui se passe ?

— La porte d'entrée ! Les voilà ! »

J'ai bondi, je me suis précipité pour éteindre la lumière sur le bureau. J'ai écrasé ma cigarette sur mon soulier et je l'ai fourrée dans ma poche. J'ai agité l'air de la main pour dissiper la fumée — bon Dieu, j'aurais vraiment pas dû fumer. Puis j'ai attrapé mes godasses, j'ai plongé dans la penderie et j'ai fermé la porte. Ouah, mon cœur battait à toute biture.

J'ai entendu ma mère entrer dans la chambre. Elle a dit « Phoebé ? Allons, arrête ça. J'ai vu la lumière, mademoiselle. »

J'ai entendu Phoebé qui disait « Bonsoir ! J'arrivais pas à dormir. C'était bien ? »

Maman a dit « Superbe ». Mais j'ai tout de suite su que c'était pas vrai. Ça l'amuse pas de sortir. « Pourquoi ne dors-tu pas, je te prie ? As-tu assez chaud ?

— J'ai assez chaud. C'est juste que j'arrivais pas à dormir.

— Phoebé, as-tu fumé une cigarette dans ta chambre ? Dites-moi la vérité s'il vous plaît, mademoiselle.

— Quoi ? a dit Phoebé.

— Tu m'as entendue.

— J'en ai juste allumé une, juste pour une seconde. J'en ai juste tiré une bouffée. Et puis je l'ai jetée par la fenêtre.

— *Pourquoi ?* Peut-on savoir ?

— J'arrivais pas à dormir.

— Je n'aime pas ça, Phoebé. Je n'aime pas du tout ça, a dit ma mère. Veux-tu une autre couverture ?

— Non, merci. B'nuit, m'man. » C'était clair que Phoebé essayait de la larguer.

Mais ma mère a dit « Et ce film ?

— Super. A part la mère d'Alice. Elle a pas arrêté pendant tout le film de se pencher pour demander à Alice si elle se sentait pas grippée. On est rentrées en taxi.

— Laisse-moi toucher ton front.

— J'ai rien attrapé. Alice, elle avait rien. C'était seulement sa mère.

— Suffit. Dors, maintenant. Et ton dîner, il était bon ?

— Pourri.

— Tu sais que ton père en a assez de t'entendre dire ce mot. Qu'est-ce qui était pourri ? Tu avais une côtelette d'agneau premier choix. J'ai fait à pied tout Lexington Avenue rien que pour...

— La côtelette, ça allait. Mais Charlène, faut toujours qu'elle m'envoie son haleine, chaque fois qu'elle pose quelque chose sur la table. Elle envoie son haleine sur mon assiette. Elle l'envoie sur tout ce qui se trouve là.

— Eh bien, dors à présent. Donne un baiser à maman. As-tu dit tes prières ?

— Je les ai dites dans la salle de bain. B'nuit.

— Bonne nuit. Dépêche-toi de dormir. J'ai un mal de tête affreux. » Ma mère a très souvent mal à la tête. C'est sûr.

Phoebé a dit « Prends de l'aspirine ». Et puis « Holden revient mercredi, n'est-ce pas ?

— Autant que je sache. Maintenant rentre là-dessous. Enfonce-toi. »

J'ai entendu la porte se refermer. J'ai attendu quelques minutes. Puis je suis sorti de la penderie. J'y voyais rien. Je me suis cogné en plein dans Phoebé qui s'était levée pour venir me chercher. J'ai chuchoté « Je t'ai pas fait mal ? » Maintenant que les parents étaient là valait mieux parler tout bas. J'ai dit « Faut que je dégage ». J'ai trouvé à tâtons le bord du plumard et je m'y suis assis pour mettre mes chaussures. Je dois avouer que je me sentais mal à l'aise.

Phoebé a dit « T'en va pas maintenant. Attends qu'ils dorment. »

J'ai dit « Non. Maintenant. C'est le meilleur moment. Elle sea dans la salle de bain et papa mettra les Informations. Maintenant, c'est le moment ». Je pouvais à peine lacer mes souliers tellement mes mains tremblaient. Bien sûr s'ils m'avaient découvert ils m'auraient pas *tué* ni rien, mais ça aurait été plutôt désagréable. « Bon Dieu, où tu es ? » Je pouvais pas voir Phoebé tellement il faisait noir.

« Ici. » Elle était tout près de moi mais je la voyais pas.

J'ai dit « Mes valises sont à la gare. Écoute, aurais-tu un peu de fric, Phoebé ? Je suis pratiquement à sec.

— J'ai que mes sous de Noël. Pour les cadeaux. J'ai encore *rien* acheté.

— Oh ! » Non, j'allais pas lui prendre son fric de Noël. « T'en veux ?

— Je vais pas te prendre ton fric de Noël. »

Elle a dit « Je peux t'en prêter un peu ». Puis je l'ai entendue qui ouvrait le million de tiroirs du bureau de D.B. et qui cherchait avec la main. Il faisait tellement sombre, noir comme dans un four. « Si tu t'en vas, tu me verras pas dans la pièce. » Elle avait une drôle de voix pour me dire ça.

« Je te verrai. Je partirai pas avant. Tu te figures que je vais manquer ta pièce ? Ce que je vais faire, je vais rester chez Mr. Antolini. Jusqu'à mardi soir, sans doute. Et puis je rentrerai à la maison. Si je peux je te téléphone. »

Elle a dit « Tiens ». Elle essayait de me donner le fric mais elle trouvait pas ma main.

« Où ? »

Elle m'a mis l'argent dans la main.

« Hey, j'ai pas besoin de tout ça. Passe-moi deux

dollars, ça suffira. Sans rire. » J'ai cherché à lui redonner ses sous mais elle a pas voulu.

« Prends tout. Tu me les rendras plus tard. Rapporte-les en venant voir la pièce.

— Bon Dieu, y a combien ?

— Huit dollars quatre-vingt-cinq *cents*. Non, soixante-cinq *cents*. J'en ai dépensé un peu. »

Alors, brusquement, je me suis mis à chialer. Je pouvais pas m'en empêcher. Je me suis arrangé pour que personne m'entende mais j'ai chialé. La pauvre Phoebé, ça lui a foutu un coup et elle est venue près de moi et elle voulait que j'arrête mais quand on a commencé pas moyen de s'arrêter pile. J'étais toujours assis au bord du lit et elle a mis son bras autour de mon cou, et j'ai mis aussi mon bras autour d'elle mais je pouvais toujours pas m'arrêter. J'ai même eu l'impression que j'allais claquer à force de suffoquer. Ouah, la pauvre Phoebé, je lui ai foutu les jetons. La fenêtre était ouverte et tout, et je la sentais qui frissonnait parce qu'elle avait rien d'autre sur elle que son pyjama.

J'ai essayé de l'obliger à se remettre au lit, mais elle voulait pas. Finalement j'ai cessé de pleurer mais ça m'a pris très très longtemps. Alors j'ai fini de boutonner mon manteau et tout. Je lui ai dit que je lui donnerais des nouvelles. Elle m'a dit que si je voulais je pouvais dormir avec elle mais j'ai dit non, qu'y valait mieux que je me taille, que Mr. Antolini m'attendait et tout. Alors j'ai sorti ma casquette de la poche de mon manteau et je la lui ai donnée. Elle aime bien ces coiffures à la gomme. Elle voulait pas la prendre mais je l'ai forcée. Je parie qu'elle a dormi avec. Elle aime vraiment ces drôles de trucs. Puis je lui ai répété que je lui refilerais un coup de bigo si je pouvais, et alors je suis parti.

Ça a été vachement plus facile de sortir de la maison que ça avait été d'y entrer. D'abord, je m'en foutais un peu de me faire pincer. Vraiment. Je me disais que si on m'entendait on m'entendrait voilà tout. En un sens j'avais presque envie qu'on m'entende.

J'ai pas pris l'ascenseur, je suis descendu à pied. Par l'escalier de service. J'ai bien failli me rompre le cou sur dix millions de poubelles mais je m'en suis sorti. Le garçon d'ascenseur m'a même pas vu. Probable qu'il me croit encore chez les Dickstein.

CHAPITRE 24

MR. ET MRS. ANTOLINI avaient cet appartement grand luxe, à Sutton Place, avec deux marches à descendre pour entrer dans la salle de séjour et un bar et tout. J'y étais allé déjà plusieurs fois. Après mon départ d'Elkton Hills, Mr. Antolini était souvent venu dîner chez nous. Il voulait voir ce que je devenais. Il était pas encore marié. Puis, après son mariage, j'ai souvent joué avec lui et Mrs. Antolini, au West Side Tennis Club, à Forest Hills, Long Island. Mrs. Antolini s'y trouvait chez elle. Mrs. Antolini était pourrie de fric. Elle avait dans les soixante ans de plus que Mr. Antolini mais ils paraissaient bien s'entendre. D'abord ils étaient l'un et l'autre très intellectuels, spécialement Mr. Antolini, sauf qu'il était plus spirituel qu'intellectuel quand on discutait, un peu comme D.B. Mrs. Antolini parlait toujours sérieusement. Elle avait de l'asthme. Ils lisaient tous les deux les nouvelles de D.B. — Oui, Mrs. Antolini aussi — et quand D.B. est parti pour Hollywood Mr. Antolini lui a téléphoné pour lui dire qu'il avait tort. D.B. est quand même parti. Pourtant Mrs. Antolini lui avait dit que lorsqu'on écrivait comme lui qu'est-ce qu'on en avait à foutre d'Hollywood. C'est exactement ce que je disais. Pratiquement.

Je serais bien allé chez eux à pied pour pas commencer à dépenser le fric de Phoebé, ses sous de Noël, mais quand j'ai été dehors je me suis senti tout drôle. Comme étourdi. Alors j'ai pris un taxi. Je voulais pas mais j'en ai pris un. J'ai d'ailleurs eu un mal de chien à le trouver.

Quand j'ai sonné à la porte c'est Mr. Antolini qui a ouvert — après que le salaud de liftier se soit décidé à me laisser monter. Il était en robe de chambre et pantoufles et il avait un verre de whisky à la main. C'était un type plutôt sophistiqué et aussi il buvait pas mal. Il a dit « Holden, mon gars. Bon Dieu, il a encore grandi de vingt pouces. Bien content de te voir.

— Comment allez-vous, Mr. Antolini ? Comment va Mrs. Antolini ?

— On est tous les deux en pleine forme. Donnemoi ce vêtement. » Il a pris mon manteau et il l'a accroché à une patère. « Je m'attendais à te voir arriver tenant dans les bras un enfant nouveau-né. Nulle part où aller. Des flocons de neige sur les cils. » Quelquefois il a beaucoup d'humour. Il s'est retourné et il a hurlé en direction de la cuisine « Lillian, où en est le café ? » Lillian, c'est le prénom de Mrs. Antolini.

Elle a répondu en hurlant à son tour « Il est prêt. Est-ce Holden ? Salut, Holden !

— Bonsoir Mrs. Antolini. »

Chez eux fallait toujours crier. Parce qu'ils se trouvaient jamais tous les deux en même temps dans la même pièce. C'était plutôt rigolo.

« Assieds-toi, Holden », a dit Mr. Antolini. Il paraissait un brin éméché. A voir la pièce on se disait qu'ils venaient de recevoir des invités. Y avait des verres tous azimuts, des coupelles avec des cacahuètes. « Excuse-nous pour l'état des lieux. Nous avons eu des amis de Mrs. Antolini. »

J'ai entendu, venant de la cuisine, la voix de Mrs. Antolini mais j'ai pas compris. J'ai demandé « Qu'est-ce qu'elle a dit ?

— Elle a dit, quand elle va entrer, de ne pas la regarder. Elle sort de son pieu. Prends une cigarette. Tu fumes, en ce moment ? »

J'ai dit « Oui, merci » en prenant une cigarette dans le paquet qu'il me tendait. « De temps en temps. Je suis un fumeur modéré.

— Non, sans blague. » Il m'a donné du feu avec le gros briquet qu'il a pris sur la table. « Alors, toi et Pencey, ça n'est plus le grand amour ? » Il s'exprimait toujours comme ça. Quelquefois ça m'amusait et d'autres fois non. Il en faisait un peu trop. Je veux pas dire qu'il montrait pas de l'humour et tout, mais ça finit par être agaçant quelqu'un qui dit tout le temps des choses comme « Toi et Pencey ça n'est plus le grand amour ». D.B. aussi, souvent il en fait un peu trop.

« Qu'est-ce qui n'allait pas ? » m'a demandé Mr. Antolini. « Comment ça a marché en Lettres ? Je te montre la porte illico si tu me dis que toi, l'as de la dissert', tu as foiré en Lettres.

— Oh ! en Lettres ça s'est très bien passé. Quoique c'était plutôt de l'Histoire de la Littérature. Et de tout le trimestre j'ai fait que deux dissertations. Mais j'ai échoué en Expression Orale. Y a ce cours qu'on est obligé de suivre, un cours d'Expression Orale. Et là j'ai échoué.

— Pourquoi ?

— Oh ! je sais pas. » Je voulais pas trop me lancer dans les détails. Je me sentais encore pas mal étourdi et subitos' j'avais vachement mal à la tête. Je vous jure. Mais on voyait qu'il était intéressé, aussi je lui en ai dit un peu plus. « C'était ce cours où chaque élève doit se lever en pleine classe et faire un laïus. Et si le gars s'écarte du sujet on est censé gueuler immédiatement "Digression !" Ça me rendait dingue. J'ai eu un F.

— Pourquoi ?

— Oh ! je sais pas. Cette histoire de digression, ça me tapait sur les nerfs. L'ennui, c'est que moi j'aime bien quand on s'écarte du sujet. C'est plus intéressant et tout.

— Tu n'as pas envie, quand quelqu'un te raconte quelque chose, qu'il s'en tienne aux faits qu'il relate ?

— Oh ! sûr. J'aime qu'on s'en tienne aux faits. Mais j'aime pas qu'on s'en tienne *trop* aux faits. Je sais pas. Je suppose que j'aime pas quand quelqu'un s'en tient *tout le temps* aux faits. Mais y avait ce gars, Richard Kinsella. Il s'en tenait pas trop aux faits et les autres étaient toujours à brailler "Digression !" C'était horrible parce que d'abord il était très nerveux — et ses lèvres tremblaient chaque fois que c'était à lui de faire un laïus et du fond de la classe on l'entendait à peine. Mais quand ses lèvres s'arrêtaient de trembler un peu, ses laïus je les aimais mieux que ceux de n'importe quel autre gars. Il a pour ainsi dire échoué, remarquez. Il a eu qu'un D-plus parce qu'on lui criait tout le temps "Digression". Par exemple il a parlé d'une ferme que son père avait achetée dans le Vermont. Les types ont braillé "Digression" tout le temps qu'il a parlé et le prof, Mr. Vinson, lui a collé une sale note parce qu'il avait pas dit ce qu'y avait à la ferme comme animaux et légumes et tout. Ce qu'il faisait, Richard Kinsella, il commençait à vous parler de ça et puis tout d'un coup il se mettait à vous raconter que sa mère avait reçu une lettre de son oncle et que cet oncle avait eu la polio et tout à l'âge de quarante-deux ans, et qu'il laissait personne lui rendre visite à l'hôpital parce qu'il voulait pas se montrer avec une prothèse. Je reconnais que ça n'avait pas grand-chose à voir avec la ferme — mais c'était chouette. C'est chouette quand quelqu'un vous parle de son oncle. Spécialement quand il commence à vous parler de la ferme de son père et tout d'un coup il est plus intéressé par son oncle. Et c'est dégoûtant de pas arrêter de gueuler "Digression" quand il est sympa et tout excité. Je sais pas. C'est dur à expliquer. » Et puis j'avais pas trop envie d'essayer. Tout d'un coup j'avais cet horrible mal de tête. J'en pouvais plus d'attendre que Mrs. Antolini apporte le café. C'est un truc qui m'exaspère drôlement. Je veux dire quand quelqu'un *dit* que le café est prêt et qu'il l'est pas.

« Holden... Une brève question pédagogique un peu ringarde. Tu ne crois pas qu'il y a un temps pour tout ? Et un lieu ? Tu ne crois pas que si quelqu'un se met à te parler de la ferme de son père il devrait aller jusqu'au bout et *après* seulement te parler de la prothèse de son oncle ? Ou bien, si la prothèse de son oncle est un thème aussi intéressant, n'aurait-il pas dû le choisir comme sujet, et pas la ferme ? »

J'étais pas en grande forme pour réfléchir et lui répondre et tout. J'avais mal à la tête et je me sentais misérable. Si vous voulez savoir, j'avais même comme des crampes d'estomac.

« Oui. Je sais pas. Oui, je suppose. Je veux dire, je suppose qu'il aurait dû choisir son oncle comme sujet plutôt que la ferme si ça l'intéressait davantage. Mais ce que je veux dire aussi, c'est qu'il y a tellement de fois où on *sait* pas ce qui est le plus intéressant avant de se mettre à parler d'un truc qui *n'est pas* le plus intéressant. Je veux dire qu'on peut rien y faire. Mais je pense qu'il faut laisser un gars tranquille quand au moins il est intéressant, et puis tout emballé par quelque chose. J'aime bien lorsque quelqu'un est emballé par quelque chose. C'est chouette. Vous l'avez pas connu vous, ce prof,

Mr. Vinson. Lui et son foutu cours. Par moments y avait de quoi devenir maboul. Il arrêtait pas de dire d'unifier et puis de simplifier. Tout le temps. Y a des choses, c'est pas possible. Je veux dire, c'est pas possible de simplifier et unifier juste parce quelqu'un le décide. Vous avez pas connu ce prof, Mr. Vinson. Il était très intelligent et tout mais ça se voyait qu'il avait rien dans la tête.

— Messieurs, le café. » Mrs. Antolini entrait portant un plateau avec dessus du café et des gâteaux et des trucs. « Holden, ne t'avise pas de me regarder. Je suis affreuse. »

J'ai dit « Bonsoir Mrs. Antolini ». Je me levais et tout mais Mr. Antolini a saisi le bas de ma veste et a tiré pour me faire rasseoir. Mrs. Antolini avait plein la tête de bigoudis en métal. Elle était pas super. Elle avait l'air vachement vieille et tout.

« Je vous laisse ça là. Servez-vous. » Elle a posé le plateau sur la table aux cigarettes, en repoussant les verres. « Comment va votre mère, Holden ?

— Bien. Merci. Je l'ai pas vue très récemment mais la dernière...

— Chéri, si Holden a besoin de quelque chose, tout est dans l'armoire à linge. Sur le dernier rayonnage. Moi je vais me coucher. Je suis épuisée, a dit Mrs. Antolini, et elle avait vraiment l'air de l'être. Vous deux, les hommes, serez-vous capables de mettre des draps sur le divan ?

— Nous nous occuperons de tout. File vite au lit », a dit Mr. Antolini. Ils se sont embrassés, elle m'a dit bonsoir et elle est partie vers la chambre. Ils arrêtaient pas de s'embrasser en public.

J'ai bu une gorgée de café et mangé la moitié d'un cake qui était dur comme du caillou. Tout ce que Mr. Antolini a pris, c'est un autre whisky. Et avec très peu d'eau. S'il fait pas plus attention il deviendra alcoolique.

Brusquement, il a dit « J'ai déjeuné avec ton père il y a quinze jours. Tu savais ?

— Non.

— Tu te rends compte, bien sûr, qu'il s'inquiète beaucoup à ton sujet. »

J'ai dit « Je sais, je sais.

— Apparemment avant de me téléphoner, il avait reçu une longue lettre navrante de ton ex-directeur, qui se plaignait que tu ne faisais absolument aucun effort. Tu séchais les cours. Ou tu venais aux cours sans avoir rien préparé. Le comportement général d'un...

— Je séchais pas les cours. C'était interdit. Y en avait deux ou trois que je manquais une fois par-ci par-là, comme cette Expression Orale dont je vous ai parlé, mais je les séchais pas vraiment. »

Ce genre de discussion, ça me disait rien. Le café calmait les crampes d'estomac mais j'avais toujours un mal de tête épouvantable.

Mr. Antolini a allumé une autre cigarette. C'était un fumeur enragé. Puis il a soupiré « Finalement, je ne sais pas quoi te dire, Holden.

— Je reconnais que c'est pas facile de trouver quelque chose à me dire.

— J'ai l'impression que tu cours à un échec effroyable. Mais quel genre d'échec, je ne le sais pas encore. Honnêtement... Dis, tu m'écoutes ?

— Oui. »

On voyait qu'il s'efforçait de se concentrer et tout.

« Quel genre d'échec ? Comment tu t'en rendras compte ? et quand ? Eh bien, ce sera peut-être un jour — tu auras dans les trente ans — où, assis dans un bar, tu te mettras soudain à détester le type qui vient d'entrer simplement parce qu'il aura l'air d'avoir été autrefois sélectionné pour jouer dans l'équipe de football de son Université. Ou bien le jour où tu t'apercevras que de toutes tes études tu n'as retiré que juste ce qu'il faut pour pouvoir détester les gens qui disent "je m'en souviens" et pas "je m'en rappelle". Ou bien encore tu te retrouveras dans un bureau minable et tu découvriras que pour passer le temps tu en es à bombarder de trombones la dactylo de l'autre côté de la table. Ou n'importe quoi de ce genre. Je ne peux pas dire. Mais tu comprends où je veux en venir ? »

J'ai dit « Oui. Sûr ». Et c'était vrai. « Mais pour ce qui est de détester, vous vous trompez. Je veux dire, détester les joueurs de foot et tout. Vraiment. Je déteste pas trop de gens. Ce qui peut m'arriver, c'est de les détester *un petit moment*, comme ce type, Stradlater, que j'ai connu à Pencey, et l'autre, Robert Ackley. Parfois, je les détestais, mais ça durait pas, c'est ce que je veux dire. Au bout d'un certain temps, si je les voyais pas, s'ils venaient plus dans ma piaule ou si j'étais plus avec eux au réfectoire deux ou trois repas de suite, ils me manquaient en quelque sorte. C'est ce que je veux dire, ils me manquaient. »

Mr. Antolini est resté silencieux. Il s'est levé, il a pris un autre cube de glace et l'a mis dans son verre, puis il est revenu s'asseoir. On voyait qu'il réfléchissait. Tout de même, j'aurais bien voulu qu'il arrête la conversation, quitte à la reprendre le lendemain, mais il était lancé. C'est presque toujours quand vous êtes pas en forme pour discuter que les autres arrêtent pas.

« Bon. Écoute-moi une minute. Je ne vais sans doute pas trouver maintenant les paroles mémorables que je voudrais te dire mais dans un jour ou deux je t'écrirai une lettre. Tu pourras alors débrouiller tout ça. En tout cas, pour l'instant écoute. » Il s'est encore concentré. Puis il a dit « Cet échec vers lequel tu cours, c'est un genre d'échec particulier — et horrible. L'homme qui tombe, rien ne lui permet de sentir qu'il touche le fond. Il tombe et il ne cesse pas de tomber. C'est ce qui arrive aux hommes qui, à un moment ou à un autre durant leur vie, étaient à la recherche de quelque chose que leur environnement ne pouvait leur procurer. Du moins voilà ce qu'ils pensaient. Alors ils ont abandonné leurs recherches. Avant même d'avoir vraiment commencé. Tu me suis ?

— Oui monsieur.

— Sûr ?

— Oui. »

Il s'est levé et il a versé un peu plus de tord-boyaux dans son verre. Puis il est revenu s'asseoir. Pendant longtemps il a rien dit.

Et puis « Je ne voudrais pas t'effrayer. Mais je te vois très clairement mourant noblement, d'une manière ou d'une autre, pour une cause hautement méprisable. » Il m'a jeté un coup d'œil bizarre. « Si je note pour toi quelques lignes, les liras-tu attentivement ? Et les conserveras-tu ?

— Oui. Bien sûr », j'ai dit. Et je l'ai fait. J'ai toujours le bout de papier qu'il m'a donné.

Il est allé jusqu'à son bureau au fond de la pièce et sans même s'asseoir il a écrit sur une feuille de papier. Puis il est revenu, a repris son siège, le papier à la main. « Curieusement, ceci n'a pas été écrit par un poète, mais par un psychanalyste nommé Wilhelm Stekel. Voilà ce qu'il... Tu m'écoutes ?

— Oui. Bien sûr.

— Voilà ce qu'il a dit : L'homme qui manque de maturité veut mourir noblement pour une cause. L'homme qui a atteint la maturité veut vivre humblement pour une cause. »

Il s'est penché et m'a tendu le papier. Je l'ai lu aussitôt et puis j'ai dit merci et tout et je l'ai mis dans ma poche. Mr. Antolini, il était vraiment sympa de se donner tout ce mal. Sans blague. Quand même, j'avais de la peine à le suivre. Ouah, je me sentais tout d'un coup terriblement fatigué.

Mais lui, on voyait bien qu'il était pas du tout fatigué. Et puis il était pas mal éméché. Il a dit « Je pense qu'un de ces jours il va falloir que tu découvres où tu veux aller. Et alors, tu devras prendre cette direction. Immédiatement. Tu ne peux pas te permettre de perdre une minute. Pas toi. »

J'ai fait oui de la tête parce qu'il me regardait droit dans les yeux et tout, mais j'étais pas trop sûr de ce qu'il voulait dire. J'étais à moitié sûr, mais je l'aurais pas affirmé trop positivement. J'étais tellement vanné.

« Et j'ai le regret de te dire — il a dit — que lorsque tu auras une idée claire de là où tu veux aller, ton premier soin sera, je pense, de t'appliquer en classe. Il faudra bien. Tu es un étudiant — que l'idée te plaise ou non —, tu aspires à la connaissance. Et je sais que tu découvriras, une fois dépassés tous les Mr. Vines et leur Expression Orale... »

J'ai dit « Mr. Vinson ». Il voulait dire tous les Mr. Vinson, pas tous les Mr. Vines. Mais j'aurais pas dû l'interrompre.

« D'accord. Les Mr. Vinson. Une fois dépassés tous les Mr. Vinson, tu vas commencer à te rapprocher de plus en plus — c'est-à-dire si tu le *veux*, si tu le cherches et l'attends — du genre de savoir qui sera très très cher à ton cœur. Entre autres choses, tu découvriras que tu n'es pas le premier à être perturbé et même dégoûté par le comportement de l'être humain. A cet égard, tu n'es pas le seul, et de le savoir cela t'excitera, te *stimulera*. Bien des hommes ont été tout aussi troublés moralement et spirituellement que tu l'es en ce moment. Par chance, quelques-uns ont écrit le récit de leurs troubles. Si tu le veux, tu apprendras beaucoup en les lisant. De même que d'autres, un jour, si tu as quelque chose à offrir, d'autres apprendront en te lisant. C'est un merveilleux arrangement réciproque. Et ce n'est pas de l'éducation. C'est de

228

l'histoire. C'est de la poésie. » Il s'est tu un instant, il a bu une grosse gorgée de whisky. Puis il s'est remis à parler. Ouah, il était vraiment lancé. J'étais content d'avoir pas essayé de l'arrêter ni rien. « Je ne cherche pas à te faire croire — il a dit — que seuls les gens instruits, les érudits, apportent au monde une contribution valable. C'est faux. Mais ce que je dis c'est que les gens instruits, les érudits, s'ils sont aussi brillants et créatifs — ce qui malheureusement n'est pas souvent le cas — ont tendance à laisser des témoignages beaucoup plus intéressants que ceux qui sont *simplement* brillants et créatifs. Ils s'expriment plus clairement et en général ils cherchent passionnément à développer leur pensée jusqu'au bout. Et — plus important encore — neuf fois sur dix, ils ont plus d'humilité que le penseur peu instruit. Tu me suis ?

— Oui, monsieur. »

Pendant un moment il a plus rien dit. Je sais pas si ça vous est déjà arrivé, mais c'est plutôt dur d'être assis là à attendre que quelqu'un dise quelque chose pendant qu'il est en train de réfléchir et tout. Je vous jure. Je luttais pour pas bâiller. C'est pas que je le trouvais barbant — oh ! non — mais tout d'un coup j'avais tellement sommeil.

« Encore une chose que les études universitaires t'apporteront. Si tu les poursuis assez longtemps, ça commencera à te donner une idée de la forme de ton esprit. Ce qui lui convient et — peut-être — ce qui ne lui convient pas. Au bout d'un moment tu auras une idée du genre de pensées le plus accordé à ta forme d'esprit. Ça t'évitera de perdre un temps fou à essayer des façons de penser qui ne te vont pas, qui ne sont pas pour toi. Tu commenceras à bien connaître tes vraies mesures et à diriger ton esprit en conséquence. »

Et alors, tout d'un coup, j'ai bâillé. C'était franchement grossier mais j'ai pas pu m'en empêcher.

Mr. Antolini a ri, c'est tout. Il a dit « Viens » et il s'est levé. « On va te préparer le divan. »

Je l'ai suivi et il est allé vers le placard et il a essayé de prendre des draps et des couvertures qui étaient sur l'étagère du haut ; mais avec son verre de whisky à la main il y est pas arrivé. Aussi il l'a vidé et l'a posé sur le plancher, et après il a descendu la literie. Je l'ai aidé à la porter jusqu'au divan. On a fait le lit ensemble. Il s'y connaissait pas trop. Il bordait pas assez serré. Mais ça m'était bien égal. J'étais si fatigué que j'aurais pu dormir debout.

« Comment vont toutes tes femmes ?

— Ça va. » Pour la convers', y avait rien à me tirer, j'avais vraiment pas envie de parler.

« Et Sally ? » Il connaissait Sally Hayes. Une fois, je la lui avais présentée.

« Ça va. J'avais rendez-vous avec elle cet après-midi. » Ouah, ça semblait vieux de vingt ans. « On a plus grand-chose en commun.

— Une drôlement jolie fille. Et l'autre ? Dont tu m'avais parlé ? Dans le Maine ?

— Oh ! Jane Gallagher. Ça va. Je lui passerai sans doute un coup de fil demain. »

Mon lit était fait. « Tu peux t'installer, a dit Mr. Antolini. Mais je me demande où tu vas bien pouvoir fourrer tes jambes. »

J'ai dit « Ça ira. Je suis habitué aux lits trop courts. Merci beaucoup, monsieur. Vous et Mrs. Antolini, vous m'avez vraiment sauvé la vie, ce soir.

— Tu sais où est la salle de bain ? Si tu as besoin de quelque chose, hurle. Je reste un moment dans la cuisine — est-ce que la lumière te gêne ?

— Non. Oh ! non. Merci encore.

— De rien. Bonne nuit mon beau.

— B'nuit, m'sieur. Merci encore. »

Il est entré dans la cuisine et moi je suis allé à la

salle de bain et je me suis déshabillé et tout. Je pouvais pas me laver les dents parce que j'avais pas de brosse à dents. J'avais pas non plus de pyjama et Mr. Antolini avait oublié de m'en prêter un. Aussi je suis revenu dans la salle de séjour et j'ai éteint la petite lampe près du divan et je me suis mis au lit en slip. Le divan était beaucoup trop court pour ma taille mais j'aurais pu dormir debout sans problème. Je suis resté éveillé deux secondes à penser à tout ce que Mr. Antolini m'avait dit. Qu'on devait trouver la forme de son esprit et tout. C'était vraiment un type intelligent. Mais j'étais trop crevé, je me suis endormi.

Et alors quelque chose encore est arrivé. J'ai même pas envie d'en parler.

Je me suis réveillé brusquement. Je savais pas quelle heure il était ni rien mais j'étais réveillé. Je sentais un truc sur ma tête. Une main. La main d'un type. Ouah, ça m'a foutu une de ses frousses... Ce que c'était, c'était la main de Mr. Antolini. Ce qu'il faisait, il était assis sur le parquet, juste à côté du divan, dans le noir et tout, et il me tripotait ou tapotait la tête. Ouah, je parierais que j'ai bondi à mille pieds d'altitude.

J'ai demandé « Bon Dieu, qu'est-ce que vous faites ?

— Rien. J'étais simplement assis là, admirant... »

J'ai dit encore « Mais qu'est-ce que vous faites ? » Je savais vraiment pas quoi dire. J'étais vachement embarrassé.

« Tu pourrais baisser la voix ? J'étais simplement assis là... »

J'ai dit « De toute façon, faut que je m'en aille. » Ouah, j'avais les nerfs dans un état ! J'ai voulu enfiler mon pantalon. Dans le noir. Mais je m'embrouillais, à cause des nerfs. Je rencontre plus de foutus pervers dans les collèges et tout que n'importe qui de vos connaissances et ils se mettent toujours à leurs trucs de pervers quand *moi* je suis là.

« Il faut que tu ailles *où* ? » a dit Mr. Antolini. Il s'efforçait de se montrer très désinvolte et calme et tout, mais calme il l'était pas tellement. Croyez-moi.

« J'ai laissé mes bagages à la gare. Je pense que je ferais peut-être mieux d'aller les chercher. Y a toutes mes affaires dedans.

— Ils seront encore là demain matin. Allons, recouche-toi. Je vais au lit moi aussi. Qu'est-ce qui t'arrive ? »

J'ai dit « Rien. C'est juste que j'ai tout mon argent dans une des valises. Je reviens tout de suite. Je prends un taxi et je reviens ». Ouah. Dans le noir je me mélangeais les guibolles. « C'est pas à moi, l'argent. C'est à ma mère et je...

— Holden, ne sois pas ridicule. Recouche-toi. Je vais au lit moi aussi. L'argent sera encore là demain matin.

— Non, je vous assure, faut que j'y aille. Faut vraiment. » J'étais pratiquement tout habillé sauf que je trouvais pas ma cravate. Je me rappelais pas où je l'avais mise. J'ai enfilé quand même ma veste et tout. Mr. Antolini était maintenant assis dans le fauteuil, un peu en retrait, m'observant. Il faisait noir et tout et je le voyais pas très bien mais je savais qu'il m'observait. Il était encore en train de s'imbiber. Il avait son verre à la main, son compagnon fidèle.

« Tu es un garçon très très bizarre. »

J'ai dit « Je sais ». J'ai pas beaucoup cherché ma cravate. Pour finir je suis parti sans. J'ai dit « Au revoir, monsieur. Merci beaucoup. Sans blague ».

Il m'a suivi lorsque je me suis dirigé vers le palier, et quand j'ai appelé l'ascenseur il est resté planté sur le seuil de sa porte. Tout ce qu'il a fait, il a répété ce machin, que j'étais un garçon très très bizarre. Bizarre, mon cul. Puis il a attendu sur le seuil jusqu'à l'arrivée du foutu ascenseur.

Dans toute ma putain de vie j'ai jamais attendu un ascenseur aussi longtemps. Je vous jure.

Je savais pas de quoi parler en attendant l'ascenseur et lui il restait planté là, alors j'ai dit « Je vais me mettre à lire de bons livres ». Il fallait bien dire *quelque chose*. C'était très embarrassant.

« Tu récupères tes bagages et tu reviens ici dare-dare. Je ne mets pas le verrou. »

J'ai dit « Merci beaucoup ». J'ai dit « Au revoir ». L'ascenseur était enfin là. Je suis entré dedans et il est descendu. Ouah, je tremblais comme un dingue. Et aussi je transpirais. Chaque fois qu'il m'arrive comme ça quelque chose de pervers je fonds en eau. Et ce genre d'emmerde m'est arrivé au moins vingt fois depuis que je suis môme. Je peux pas m'y faire.

CHAPITRE 25

Quand je suis sorti de l'immeuble, le jour se levait. Il faisait plutôt froid mais ça m'a paru bon parce que je transpirais tellement.

Je savais vraiment pas où aller. Je voulais pas d'un hôtel pour pas dépenser le fric de Phoebé. Aussi finalement ce que j'ai fait, j'ai marché jusqu'à Lexington et là j'ai pris le métro pour Grand Central. Mes valises étaient là-bas et tout et je me disais que j'allais dormir dans cette connerie de salle d'attente où y a des bancs. C'est ce que j'ai fait. D'abord c'était pas trop mal parce qu'y avait pas beaucoup de monde et je pouvais mettre mes pieds sur un banc. Mais j'aime mieux pas parler de ça. C'était plutôt moche. Je vous conseille pas d'essayer. Sans blague. Ça vous flanquerait le cafard.

J'ai dormi seulement jusque vers les neuf heures parce qu'après un million de personnes se sont amenées dans la salle d'attente donc il a fallu que je remette les pieds par terre. Pas facile de dormir avec les pieds par terre. Alors je me suis redressé. J'avais toujours mal à la tête. C'était même pire. Et je crois bien que j'étais plus déprimé que je l'avais encore jamais été.

Je voulais pas, mais malgré moi je me suis mis à

penser au petit père Antolini et je me suis demandé ce qu'il dirait à Mrs. Antolini quand elle découvrirait que j'avais pas dormi là. Ça me tracassait pas trop parce que je savais que Mr. Antolini était très malin et qu'il trouverait bien une explication. Il pourrait lui dire que j'étais rentré à la maison. Bref, ça me tracassait pas trop. Mais ce qui me tracassait c'était ce truc de m'être réveillé quand il était en train de me tapoter la tête et tout. Je veux dire, je me posais la question de savoir si j'avais pas eu tort de croire qu'il me faisait des avances de pédé. Je me disais que peut-être c'était seulement qu'il aimait bien tapoter la tête des gars quand ils dorment. Ces choses-là, comment savoir ? On est jamais sûr. J'en étais à me demander si j'aurais pas dû reprendre mes bagages et retourner chez lui, comme j'avais dit.

Je commençais à réfléchir que même s'il était pédé il avait été drôlement chouette. Je me répétais qu'il avait pas râlé que je l'appelle si tard et qu'il m'avait dit de venir tout de suite chez lui, et qu'il avait pris la peine de me donner des conseils pour trouver la forme de mon esprit et tout, et qu'il était le seul type à seulement s'être approché du gars dont je vous ai parlé, James Castle, qui était mort. Je pensais à tout ça, et plus j'y pensais plus j'étais déprimé. Et j'en arrivais à me dire que peut-être j'aurais dû retourner chez lui. Peut-être qu'il me tapotait le crâne juste comme ça. Mais plus j'y pensais plus je me sentais cafardeux et paumé. Et puis, ce qui arrangeait pas les choses, j'avais vachement mal aux yeux. Ils me brûlaient et me piquaient, mes yeux, parce que je manquais de sommeil. Et aussi, je venais d'attraper une espèce de rhume et j'avais pas de mouchoir. J'en avais un dans ma valise mais je tenais pas à la sortir de la consigne et à l'ouvrir en public et tout.

Quelqu'un avait laissé un magazine sur le banc à

côté de moi, alors je me suis mis à le lire en me disant que ça m'empêcherait, au moins un petit bout de temps, de me poser des questions sur Mr. Antolini et sur un million d'autres trucs. Mais ce foutu article que je me suis mis à lire m'a presque fait me sentir encore plus mal. Ça parlait des hormones. Ça décrivait comment on devait être, la figure, les yeux et tout, si on allait bien question hormones. J'étais pas du tout comme ça. J'étais exactement comme le type dans l'article qu'avait des hormones dégueu. Alors je me suis rongé les sangs pour mes hormones. Et puis j'ai lu cet autre article sur la façon de voir si on a un cancer. Il disait que si on avait dans la bouches des écorchures qui mettaient du temps à guérir c'était probable qu'on avait un cancer. Ça faisait presque *deux semaines* que j'en avais une à l'intérieur de la lèvre. Aussi je me suis dit qu'il me venait un cancer. Ce magazine, rien de tel pour vous remonter le moral. Finalement, j'ai arrêté de lire et je suis allé me balader un peu. J'estimais qu'ayant un cancer je serais mort dans les deux ou trois mois. J'en étais positivement sûr. Ça n'avait vraiment rien pour me réjouir.

La pluie menaçait mais je suis quand même allé faire un tour. D'abord je trouvais que ce serait pas mal de prendre le petit déjeuner. J'avais pas faim mais je me disais qu'il fallait que je mange quelque chose. Que j'avale au moins quelques vitamines. Alors je me suis dirigé vers le quartier des troquets pas chers parce que je voulais pas dépenser beaucoup de fric.

Sur mon chemin je suis passé près de deux types qui déchargeaient d'un camion un énorme arbre de Noël. Un des deux arrêtait pas de dire à l'autre « Redresse-le, ce putain de bordel de merde de machin. Redresse-le, sacré nom ». C'était vraiment une façon super de parler d'un arbre de Noël. Et en même temps c'était marrant, tristement marrant, disons, et je me suis mis à rire. J'ai eu grand tort parce qu'à l'instant même j'ai bien cru que j'allais vomir. Sans blague. J'ai même commencé à vomir, et puis ça s'est arrangé. Je sais pas ce qui m'a pris. Je veux dire que j'avais rien mangé de pas sain et d'habitude j'ai l'estomac solide. Bon ça s'est arrangé et je me suis figuré que ça irait mieux si je mangeais un peu. Aussi je suis entré dans un troquet qui avait l'air bon marché et j'ai commandé du café et deux beignets. Mais j'ai pas mangé les beignets. Ça n'aurait pas passé. Ce qu'il y a, lorsque quelque chose vous tracasse, on peut plus rien avaler. Le garçon a été très sympa. Il a remporté les beignets sans me les faire payer. J'ai seulement bu mon café. Puis je suis reparti et j'ai parcouru la Cinquième Avenue.

C'était lundi et bientôt Noël, et tous les magasins étaient ouverts. Le bon moment pour se balader sur la Cinquième Avenue. Ça faisait très Noël. Tous ces Santa Claus rabougris agitaient leurs clochettes à chaque coin de rue et les filles de l'Armée du Salut, celles qu'ont pas de rouge à lèvres ni rien, agitaient aussi des clochettes. J'essayais vaguement de repérer dans la foule les deux religieuses que j'avais rencontrées la veille mais je les ai pas vues. J'aurais dû me douter que je les verrais pas puisqu'elles m'avaient dit qu'elles venaient à New York pour être profs mais je les cherchais un peu quand même. En tout cas, subitement, ça faisait Noël. Un million de petits moutards avec leurs mères avaient envahi les rues, montant dans les bus ou en descendant, entrant dans les magasins ou en ressortant. J'aurais bien voulu voir Phoebé. Elle est trop grande à présent pour que le rayon des jouets l'excite beaucoup mais elle aime flâner dans les rues et regarder les gens. Pas à Noël dernier mais celui d'avant je l'ai emmenée avec moi faire des achats. On s'est vachement bien amusés. Je crois que c'était à

Bloomingdale. On est allés au rayon des godasses et on a prétendu que Phoebé voulait une paire de ces bottines avec un million de trous où passent des lacets. Le malheureux vendeur, on l'a rendu fou. La môme Phoebé a essayé à peu près vingt paires et chaque fois le pauvre type devait lui lacer une des chaussures jusqu'en haut. C'était un sale tour mais Phoebé ça la tuait. Pour finir, on a acheté des mocassins qu'on a fait porter sur le compte des parents. Le vendeur a été très sympa. Je pense qu'il voyait bien qu'on se payait du bon temps parce que Phoebé peut jamais s'empêcher de rigoler.

Bon. J'ai marché, j'ai marché dans la Cinquième Avenue, sans cravate ni rien. Et puis tout d'un coup il m'est arrivé quelque chose de vachement effrayant. Chaque fois que j'arrivais à une rue transversale et que je descendais de la saleté de trottoir, j'avais l'impression que j'atteindrais jamais l'autre côté de la rue. Je sentais que j'allais m'enfoncer dans le sol, m'enfoncer encore et encore et personne me reverrait jamais. Ouah, ce que j'avais les foies. Vous imaginez. Je me suis mis à transpirer comme un dingue, j'ai trempé mon tricot de corps et ma chemise. Ensuite j'ai fait quelque chose d'autre. Chaque fois que j'arrivais à une nouvelle rue, je me mettais à parler à mon frère Allie. Je lui disais « Allie, me laisse pas disparaître. Allie, me laisse pas. S'il te plaît, Allie ». Et quand j'avais atteint le trottoir opposé sans disparaître je lui disais merci, à Allie. Et ça recommençait au coin de rue suivant. Mais je continuais mon chemin et tout. Je crois que j'avais peur de m'arrêter — à dire vrai je me souviens pas bien. Je sais que je me suis pas arrêté avant d'être vers la Soixantième Rue, passé le zoo et tout. Là je me suis assis sur un banc. J'avais peine à reprendre mon souffle et je transpirais toujours comme un dingue. Je suis resté assis là, une heure environ j'imagine. Finalement, ce que j'ai décidé, c'est de m'en aller. J'ai décidé de jamais rentrer à la maison, de jamais plus être en pension dans un autre collège. J'ai décidé que simplement je reverrais la môme Phoebé pour lui dire au revoir et tout et lui rendre son fric de Noël, et puis je partirais vers l'Ouest. En stop. Ce que je ferais, je descendrais à Holland Tunnel et là j'arrêterais une voiture, puis une autre et une autre et encore une autre, et dans quelques jours je serais dans l'Ouest, là où c'est si joli, où y a plein de soleil et où personne me connaîtrait et je me dégoterais du boulot. Je suppose que je pourrais bosser quelque part dans une station-service, je mettrais de l'essence et de l'huile dans les voitures. Mais n'importe quel travail conviendrait. Suffit que les gens me connaissent pas et que je connaisse personne. Je me disais que le mieux ce serait de me faire passer pour un sourd-muet. Et comme ça terminé d'avoir à parler avec les gens. Tout le monde penserait que je suis un pauvre couillon de sourd-muet et on me laisserait tranquille. Je serais censé mettre de l'essence et de l'huile dans ces bagnoles à la con et pour ça on me paierait un salaire et tout et avec le fric je me construirais quelque part une petite cabane et je passerais là le reste de ma vie. Je la construirais près des bois mais pas *dans* les bois parce que je veux qu'elle soit tout le temps en plein soleil. Je me ferais moi-même à manger et plus tard, si je voulais me marier, je rencontrerais cette fille merveilleuse qui serait aussi sourde-muette et je l'épouserais. Et elle viendrait vivre dans ma cabane et quand elle voudrait me dire quelque chose il faudrait qu'elle l'écrive sur un bout de papier comme tout le monde. Si on avait des enfants on les cacherait quelque part. On leur achèterait un tas de livres et on leur apprendrait nous-mêmes à lire et à écrire.

En pensant à ça je me suis vachement excité.

Vachement. Je savais que mon histoire de sourd-muet c'était débile mais je prenais plaisir à me la raconter. Et pour ce qui était de partir vers l'Ouest et tout, j'étais vraiment décidé. Ce que je voulais c'était d'abord dire au revoir à Phoebé. Alors, subitement, j'ai traversé la rue en courant comme un fou — et pour rien vous cacher j'ai manqué me faire écraser — et je suis entré à la papeterie et j'ai acheté un bloc-notes et un crayon. J'avais combiné d'écrire sur-le-champ un message pour Phoebé en lui expliquant où venir me rejoindre pour que je lui dise au revoir et lui rende son fric de Noël. J'irais à son école remettre le message à quelqu'un dans le bureau de la directrice en demandant qu'on le donne à Phoebé. Mais j'ai seulement enfoncé le bloc-notes et le crayon dans ma poche et je suis parti à toute bringue en direction de l'école. J'étais trop surexcité pour écrire mon mot dans la papeterie. Je marchais vite parce que je voulais le lui faire passer avant qu'elle rentre à la maison pour déjeuner et ça me laissait pas beaucoup de temps.

Bien sûr, je savais où était son école bicause c'est là que j'allais quand j'étais môme. Ça m'a paru drôle de m'y retrouver. Je m'étais demandé si je me souviendrais comment c'était à l'intérieur, eh bien oui je me souvenais. Ça n'avait pas du tout changé. Y avait toujours cette grande cour plutôt sombre avec les cages autour des ampoules électriques pour qu'elles soient pas cassées par un ballon. Y avait toujours les mêmes cercles blancs peints sur le sol pour les sports et tout. Et les mêmes vieux paniers de basket, juste un cercle, sans filet — rien que les panneaux et les cercles.

Je voyais personne, probablement parce que c'était pas la récréation et pas encore l'heure du déjeuner. Tout ce que j'ai vu c'est un mioche, un petit Noir, qui allait aux cabinets : sortant à moitié de la poche de son pantalon y avait un de ces laissez-passer en bois, le même que nous on avait, pour montrer qu'il était autorisé à aller aux cabinets et tout.

Je transpirais encore mais plus autant. Je me suis assis sur la première marche de l'escalier et j'ai pris le bloc-notes et le crayon que j'avais achetés. L'escalier, je lui trouvais la même odeur qu'il avait déjà quand moi j'allais à cette école. Comme si quelqu'un venait juste de pisser dessus. Les escaliers des écoles ont toujours cette odeur-là. Bon. Je me suis assis et j'ai écrit :

Chère Phoebé,

Je peux plus attendre jusqu'à mercredi. Je vais probablement partir en stop cet après-midi. Viens me rejoindre si tu peux au musée d'Art, à midi un quart près de la porte. Je te rendrai ton fric de Noël. J'en ai pas beaucoup dépensé.

Je t'embrasse.
Holden

Son école était pratiquement à côté du musée et elle devait passer par là pour rentrer déjeuner à la maison donc ça lui serait facile de venir.

Ensuite j'ai monté les marches jusqu'au bureau de la directrice afin de remettre le message à quelqu'un qui le porterait à Phoebé. J'ai bien dû plier le papier en dix pour qu'on lise pas. Dans une école on peut avoir confiance en personne. Mais je savais qu'on le donnerait à Phoebé si je disais que j'étais son frère et tout.

En montant l'escalier, subitement, j'ai cru que j'allais encore vomir. Mais ça a passé. Je me suis assis une seconde. Aussitôt je me suis senti mieux. Mais pendant que j'étais assis j'ai vu quelque chose qui m'a rendu cinglé. Quelqu'un avait écrit "je t'enc..." sur le mur. Ça m'a presque rendu cinglé. Je me suis dit que Phoebé et les autres petits mômes allaient voir ça et qu'ils se demanderaient ce que ça signifiait et alors un gosse taré leur dirait — et bien sûr tout de travers — et pendant deux ou trois jours ils y *penseraient* et même peut-être se tracasseraient. J'aurais bien tué celui qui avait écrit ça. Je supposais que c'était un clochard pervers qui se glissait dans l'école tard le soir pour pisser et puis écrire ça sur le mur. Je me voyais le prendre sur le fait et lui écraser la tête sur les marches de pierre jusqu'à ce qu'il soit mort et en sang. Mais en même temps, je savais que j'aurais pas le cran de le faire. Je le savais. Au vrai, j'avais à peine le cran d'effacer le mot avec la main. Je me disais qu'un prof allait me surprendre à le frotter et penserait que c'était *moi* qui l'avais écrit. Mais finalement je l'ai tout de même effacé. Puis je suis monté au bureau de la directrice.

La directrice était pas là, mais une vieille dame dans les cent ans était assise devant une machine à écrire. Je lui ai dit que j'étais le frère de Phoebé Caulfield, de 7B-1 et je lui ai demandé s'il vous plaît de donner le message à Phoebé. J'ai dit que c'était très important parce que ma mère était malade et qu'elle avait rien préparé pour le déjeuner alors il fallait que ma sœur me rejoigne et je la ferais déjeuner dans un drugstore. La vieille dame, elle a été très sympa. Elle a pris mon billet et elle a appelé une autre dame du bureau voisin qui est allée le porter à Phoebé. Puis la vieille dame dans les cent ans et moi on a parlé un peu. Elle était bien aimable et je lui ai raconté que j'avais été moi aussi dans cette école et mes frères tout pareil. Elle m'a demandé où j'étais maintenant et j'ai dit à Pencey, et elle a dit que Pencey était un très bon collège. Même si j'avais voulu j'aurais pas eu le courage de lui dire le contraire. D'ailleurs si elle trouvait que Pencey était un très bon collège fallait pas la décevoir. C'est pas génial de dire des choses nouvelles à des centenaires. Ils apprécient pas. Au bout d'un petit moment je suis parti. C'est bizarre, elle m'a hurlé « Bonne chance ! » tout juste comme le père Spencer l'avait fait lorsque j'ai quitté Pencey. Bon Dieu, comme je déteste quand quelqu'un me hurle « Bonne chance ! » quand je vais quelque part. Ça me fout le cafard.

Je suis descendu par un autre escalier, et j'ai vu un autre "Je t'enc..." sur le mur. Celui-là aussi j'ai essayé de l'effacer avec ma main mais il était gravé au couteau ou avec autre chose. Ça partait pas. De toute façon, c'est sans espoir. Même si on avait un million d'années pour le faire on pourrait encore pas effacer la moitié des "je t'enc..." du monde entier. Impossible.

J'ai regardé la pendule dans la cour de récréation, il était seulement midi moins vingt, donc j'avais du temps à tuer avant de voir arriver Phoebé. Mais j'ai quand même pris tout de suite la direction du musée. Je voyais pas d'autre endroit où aller. J'ai eu envie de m'arrêter à une cabine téléphonique et de donner un coup de fil à la môme Jane Gallagher avant de foutre le camp vers l'Ouest, mais j'avais pas le moral. D'abord j'étais même pas certain qu'elle soit déjà en vacances. Aussi je me suis rendu tout droit au musée et là j'ai traînassé.

Pendant que j'attendais Phoebé dans le musée, juste à côté de la porte et tout, deux petits gosses sont venus me demander si je savais où étaient les momies. L'un des deux, celui qui posait la question, avait oublié de fermer sa braguette. Je le lui ai dit. Et il s'est boutonné sans bouger de l'endroit où il était — il a même pas pris la peine d'aller derrière un pilier ni rien. Ça m'a tué. J'aurais ri si j'avais pas eu peur que ça me donne encore envie de vomir aussi je me suis retenu. Le gamin, il a encore demandé « Où qu'elles sont, les momies ? Vous savez ? »

J'ai un petit peu fait l'idiot. « Les momies ? Qu'est-ce que c'est ?

— Ben quoi. Des momies. Des types morts — et qu'on a enterrés dans leurs tombereaux et tout. »

Tombereaux. Ça m'a tué.

Moi j'ai dit « Pourquoi vous êtes pas à l'école tous les deux ?

— Aujourd'hui pas d'école », a dit le gosse qui menait la convers'. Il mentait, aussi sûr que je suis en vie, le petit cochon. Mais puisque j'avais rien à faire jusqu'à l'arrivée de Phoebé je les ai aidés à chercher l'endroit où sont les momies. Ouah, autrefois je connaissais exactement l'endroit mais y avait des années que j'étais pas venu au musée.

J'ai dit « Vous deux, les gars, ça vous intéresse les momies ?

— Ouais.

— Ton copain, il parle pas ?

— C'est pas mon copain. C'est mon frangin.

— Il parle pas ? » Je me suis tourné vers celui qu'avait pas ouvert la bouche. J'ai demandé « Tu sais pas parler ?

— Ouais, il a dit. Mais j'ai pas envie. »

Finalement on a trouvé l'endroit où étaient les momies et on est entrés.

J'ai encore demandé au gamin « Tu sais comment les Égyptiens enterraient leurs morts ?

— Nan.

— Eh bien, tu devrais. C'est très intéressant. Ils leur enveloppaient la figure dans ces étoffes traitées avec des produits chimiques secrets. Comme ça ils pouvaient rester enfermés dans leurs tombes des milliers d'années et leurs visages pourrissaient pas ni rien. Personne sait comment le faire. Même pas la science moderne. »

Pour arriver là où étaient les momies il fallait suivre une sorte de couloir très étroit avec des pierres sur le côté qui venaient des tombeaux des pharaons et tout. C'était plutôt impressionnant et les durs de durs que j'accompagnais ça leur plaisait pas tellement. Ils me lâchaient pas d'un poil et celui qui pratiquement avait pas ouvert la bouche se cramponnait à ma manche. Il a dit à son frère « On se taille. J'les ai vues déjà. Hé viens ». Il a fait le demi-tour et il s'est barré.

« C'est un foutu dégonflé, a dit l'autre. Salut ! » Lui aussi s'est barré.

Alors je suis resté tout seul dans la tombe. D'un sens j'aimais assez. C'était plutôt sympa et puis paisible. Mais tout d'un coup j'ai vu sur le mur — vous ne devineriez pas — j'ai vu un autre "Je t'enc...". Écrit à la craie rouge, juste au-dessous de la partie vitrée du mur, au-dessous des pierres.

C'est ça le problème. Vous pouvez jamais trouver un endroit qui soit sympa et paisible, parce qu'y en a pas. Ça peut vous arriver de croire qu'y en a un mais une fois que vous y êtes, pendant que vous regardez pas, quelqu'un s'amène en douce et écrit "Je t'enc..." juste sous votre nez. Essayez pour voir. Je pense que même si je meurs un jour, et qu'on me colle dans un cimetière et que j'ai une tombe et tout, y aura "Holden Caulfield" écrit dessus, avec l'année où je suis né et celle où je suis mort et puis juste en dessous y aura "Je t'enc...". J'en suis positivement certain.

Une fois ressorti de l'endroit où sont les momies j'ai dû aller aux toilettes. Si vous voulez savoir, j'avais comme la diarrhée. Bon, c'était pas trop méchant mais il m'est arrivé quelque chose d'autre. En sortant des chiottes, juste avant de franchir la porte, j'ai tourné de l'œil en quelque sorte. J'ai eu de la chance, j'aurais pu m'assommer par terre mais j'ai atterri sur le côté sans trop de mal. Et le plus curieux c'est qu'après m'être évanoui je me suis senti mieux. J'avais le bras tout meurtri de ma chute mais je me sentais plus si étourdi.

Il était à peu près midi dix aussi je suis retourné me mettre en faction à la porte pour y attendre la môme Phoebé. Je me disais que je la voyais peut-être pour la dernière fois. Pour la dernière fois quelqu'un de ma famille. Je pensais bien la revoir un jour mais pas avant des années. Je reviendrais peut-être à la maison quand j'aurais dans les trente-cinq ans, au cas où quelqu'un soit malade et veuille me revoir avant de mourir, mais ça serait la seule raison qui me ferait quitter ma cabane. J'ai même essayé de me représenter comment ça se passerait quand je reviendrais. Je savais que ma mère serait dans tous ses états et se mettrait à pleurer et à me supplier de pas retourner dans ma cabane, de rester à la maison mais je repartirais quand même. Je serais très flegmatique, je la calmerais, et puis j'irais à l'autre bout de la salle de séjour et je sortirais une cigarette de la boîte et l'allumerais. Froidement. Je suggérerais qu'on me rende visite mais j'insisterais pas ni rien. Ce que je ferais, je laisserais la môme Phoebé venir en vacances d'été et aux congés de Noël et de Pâques. Et je laisserais aussi D.B. venir passer un moment s'il voulait un coin tranquille et sympa pour écrire, mais il aurait pas le droit d'écrire des films dans ma cabane, seulement des nouvelles et des livres. Y aurait une règle, personne ne pourrait rien faire de bidon pendant son séjour dans ma cabane. Si quelqu'un essayait de faire quelque chose de bidon faudrait qu'il se tire.

J'ai jeté un coup d'œil à la pendule du vestiaire et il était une heure moins vingt-cinq. Je commençais à me demander si la vieille dame de l'école avait pas dit à l'autre de pas remettre mon message à Phoebé. Je commençais à me demander si elle lui avait pas dit de le brûler ou quoi. Ça me foutait les jetons. Je voulais vraiment revoir la môme Phoebé avant de prendre la route. J'avais son fric de Noël et tout.

Enfin je l'ai vue. Je l'ai vue à travers la partie en verre de la porte. Je l'ai reconnue tout de suite parce qu'elle avait ma dingue de casquette sur la tête — on l'aurait repérée à plus de dix *miles*.

J'ai franchi la porte et j'ai descendu les marches pour aller à sa rencontre. Ce que j'arrivais pas à comprendre c'est pourquoi elle portait une grosse valise. Elle pouvait à peine la traîner. Quand j'ai été plus près, j'ai vu que c'était ma vieille valise, celle que je prenais lorsque j'allais à Whooton. J'arrivais pas à comprendre ce qu'elle faisait avec ça. Quand elle m'a rejoint elle a dit « Salut ». Elle était tout essoufflée d'avoir porté cette dingue de valise.

J'ai dit « Je commençais à croire que t'allais pas venir. Qu'est-ce qu'il y a là-dedans, bon Dieu ? »

Elle a posé la valise. Elle a dit « Mes habits. Je vais avec toi. Je peux ? D'accord ?

— Quoi ? » j'ai dit. Et je suis presque tombé raide en le disant. Je vous jure. Je me suis à nouveau senti tout étourdi et j'ai cru que j'allais encore m'évanouir.

« J'ai pris l'ascenseur de service pour que Charlène me voie pas. C'est pas lourd. J'ai juste deux robes et mes mocassins et mes dessous et mes chaussettes et puis quelques autres petites choses. Tiens, soulève. C'est pas lourd. Soulève. Je peux venir avec toi ? Holden ? Je peux ? S'il te plaît ?

— Non. Et ferme-la. »

J'ai cru vraiment que j'allais tomber raide. Pourtant j'avais pas l'intention de lui dire de la fermer ou quoi, mais je me sentais comme si j'allais encore tourner de l'œil.

« Pourquoi pas, Holden ? Je ferai rien. Je viendrai juste avec toi, c'est tout. Je prendrai même pas mes habits si tu veux pas que je les prenne. Je prendrai seulement...

— Tu prends rien. Parce que tu viens pas. Je m'en vais tout seul. Alors boucle-la.

— *S'il te plaît*, Holden. *S'il te plaît*, emmène-moi. Je serai très très très... T'auras même pas à...

— Tu viens pas. Alors, suffit. Donne-moi cette valise. » Je la lui ai prise des mains. J'avais presque envie de la battre. Pendant une ou deux secondes j'ai cru que j'allais lui taper dessus. Sincèrement. Elle s'est mise à pleurer.

« Je croyais que tu devais jouer dans une pièce à l'école et tout. Je croyais que tu étais Benedict Arnold dans cette pièce et tout », j'ai dit. Et j'ai dit ça très méchamment. « Qu'est-ce que tu cherches ? A pas être dans la pièce ? » Elle a pleuré encore plus fort. J'étais content. Subitement je voulais qu'elle pleure à s'en fondre les yeux. Je la détestais presque. Je crois que je la détestais surtout parce que si elle venait avec moi elle jouerait pas dans la pièce.

J'ai dit « Allons-y ». J'ai remonté les marches du musée. Je pensais que le mieux c'était de déposer la foutue valise au vestiaire et Phoebé pourrait la reprendre à trois heures, après l'école. Parce qu'il était pas question qu'elle emporte la valoche à l'école. J'ai dit « Bon, allons-y ».

Mais elle a pas monté les marches. Elle voulait pas venir avec moi. Je suis quand même rentré dans le musée et j'ai mis la valise au vestiaire et puis je suis ressorti. Elle était toujours là sur le trottoir, mais quand je l'ai rejointe elle m'a tourné le dos. Elle fait ça quelquefois. Quand l'envie la prend elle vous tourne le dos.

J'ai dit « De toute façon je pars pas. J'ai changé d'avis. Alors arrête de pleurer et tais-toi ». Le plus drôle c'est qu'elle pleurait même pas lorsque je lui ai dit ça. En tout cas je le lui ai dit. Et puis « Viens maintenant. Je te reconduis à l'école. Allez, viens. Tu vas être en retard ».

Elle répondait pas ni rien. J'ai essayé de lui

prendre la main mais elle a pas voulu. Elle continuait à me tourner le dos.

J'ai demandé « T'as déjeuné ? T'as mangé quelque
chose ? »

Elle voulait pas répondre. Tout ce qu'elle a fait,
elle a attrapé la casquette qu'elle avait sur la tête
— la mienne, que je lui avais donnée — et elle me
l'a pratiquement jetée à la figure. Puis elle m'a
encore tourné le dos. Ça m'a tué ou presque, mais
j'ai rien dit. J'ai juste ramassé la casquette et je l'ai
fourrée dans la poche de mon manteau.

J'ai dit « Hey, viens. Je te raccompagne à l'école.

— Je retourne pas à l'école. »

Quand elle m'a lancé ça, j'ai pas su quoi répondre.
Je suis resté là sans savoir quoi répondre pendant
une ou deux minutes.

« Mais il *faut* que tu retournes à l'école. Tu veux
jouer la pièce, non ? Tu veux être Benedict Arnold,
non ?

— Non, justement.

— Mais si, bien sûr, j'ai dit. Certainement que tu
veux. Bon. Allons-y. D'abord, écoute, je pars pas. Je
rentre à la maison. Dès que tu seras à l'école, je
rentre à la maison. Je vais à la gare, je récupère
mes bagages et puis je rentre tout droit à... »

Elle a répété « Je retourne pas à l'école. Tu peux
faire tout ce que tu veux mais moi je retourne pas
à l'école. Alors ferme-la ». C'était bien la première
fois qu'elle me disait ça, « ferme-la ». C'était terrible
à entendre. C'était terrible, bon Dieu, c'était pire
que des gros mots. Et elle voulait toujours pas me
regarder et chaque fois que j'essayais de mettre ma
main sur son épaule elle s'écartait.

J'ai demandé « Écoute. Veux-tu qu'on fasse un
tour ? Veux-tu qu'on aille au zoo ? Si je te laisse
manquer l'école cet après-midi et qu'on parte se
balader, tu arrêtes cette comédie ? »

Elle répondait toujours pas, alors j'ai recommencé. « Si je te laisse manquer l'école cet après-midi et qu'on se balade tu arrêtes ta comédie ? Tu retournes à l'école demain comme une bonne fille ?

— Peut-être. Ou peut-être pas », elle a dit. Et subitement elle a traversé la rue en courant, sans même prendre garde aux voitures. Parfois elle est barjot.

J'ai pas galopé derrière elle. Je savais bien qu'elle me suivrait aussi je me suis dirigé vers le zoo, sur le trottoir côté parc et elle a pris la même direction sur le trottoir opposé. Elle avait pas l'air de se soucier de moi mais elle me surveillait probablement du coin de l'œil pour voir où j'allais et tout. Bon, on a continué comme ça jusqu'au zoo. Le seul moment où j'ai été ennuyé, c'est quand est passé un bus à impériale parce que je pouvais plus voir l'autre côté de la rue où elle était. Mais quand je suis arrivé au zoo j'ai gueulé « Phoebé, j'entre au zoo. Viens, maintenant ! » Elle a pas levé les yeux mais je savais qu'elle m'avait entendu et quand j'ai descendu les marches du zoo je me suis retourné et je l'ai vue qui traversait la rue et me suivait et tout.

Y avait guère de monde au zoo parce que c'était un jour plutôt moche mais y en avait tout de même un peu près du bassin des otaries. Comme je continuais ma route, Phoebé s'est arrêtée et elle a fait semblant de regarder le repas des otaries — un type leur jetait des poissons — aussi je suis revenu sur mes pas. J'ai pensé que c'était une bonne occasion de la rejoindre, je me suis arrêté derrière elle et j'ai mis mes mains sur ses épaules mais elle a plié les genoux et s'est dégagée — je vous l'ai dit qu'elle peut être une vraie chipie quand ça la prend. Elle est restée plantée là tout le temps que le type nourrissait les otaries et moi je suis resté juste derrière elle. J'ai pas remis mes mains sur ses épaules parce que si je l'avais fait elle aurait pris sa revanche. C'est marrant, les mômes. Avec eux, faut drôlement faire gaffe.

Quand on en a eu fini avec les otaries, elle a pas marché à côté de moi mais tout de même pas très loin. Elle était d'un côté du trottoir et moi de l'autre. C'était pas encore gagné mais ça valait mieux que de la voir filer au diable comme avant. On est montés sur la petite colline pour voir les ours. Mais y avait pas grand-chose à voir. Un seul, l'ours polaire, était dehors. L'autre, l'ours brun, voulait pas se décaniller de sa foutue grotte. On voyait que son arrière-train. A côté de moi y avait un petit mioche avec un chapeau de cow-boy enfoncé jusqu'aux oreilles et il arrêtait pas de dire à son père « Fais-le sortir, papa. Fais-le sortir ». J'ai jeté un coup d'œil à la môme Phoebé mais elle a pas ri. Les mômes, quand ils vous en veulent, vous savez ce que c'est. Rien ne les fera rire.

Après avoir quitté les ours on est sortis du zoo et on a traversé l'allée du parc et alors on a emprunté un de ces petits tunnels qui sentent toujours la pisse. On se dirigeait vers le manège. Phoebé me parlait toujours pas mais maintenant elle marchait près de moi. J'ai attrapé la martingale de son manteau, juste pour blaguer, mais elle s'est pas laissé faire. Elle a dit « Pas touche, s'il te plaît ». Elle m'en voulait encore. Mais plus autant que tout à l'heure. Bon, on s'approchait du manège et on commençait à entendre cet air idiot qu'il joue toujours, *Oh, Marie*. Il jouait déjà ça il y a au moins cinquante ans, quand j'étais môme. Les manèges, c'est ce qui est chouette, ils jouent toujours la même chose.

« Je croyais que le manège marchait pas pendant l'hiver », a dit Phoebé. Elle rouvrait la bouche pratiquement pour la première fois. Elle avait l'air d'oublier qu'elle était fâchée contre moi.

J'ai dit « Ça doit être parce que c'est bientôt Noël ».

Elle a pas répondu. Elle a dû brusquement se souvenir qu'elle était fâchée.

J'ai demandé « Tu veux faire un tour de manège ? » Je savais que sûrement elle en avait envie. Quand elle était toute petite et qu'on l'emmenait au parc, Allie et D.B. et moi, elle raffolait du manège. On pouvait pas l'en faire descendre.

J'avais cru qu'elle me répondrait pas. Mais elle a dit « Je suis trop grande.

— Sûrement pas. Vas-y. Je t'attends. Allez, va. » On était arrivés au manège. Y avait quelques gamins grimpés dessus, des petits mômes pour la plupart et quelques parents qui attendaient autour, assis sur les bancs et tout. Ce que j'ai fait, je suis allé au guichet où on vend les billets et j'en ai acheté un pour Phoebé. Et puis je le lui ai donné. Elle était là, tout près de moi. « Tiens », j'ai dit. Et puis « Attends une seconde, prends aussi le reste de ton fric ». J'ai voulu lui refiler le reste du fric qu'elle m'avait prêté. Elle a dit « Garde-le. Garde-le-moi ». Et tout de suite après « ... Je t'en prie ».

Quand quelqu'un vous dit « Je t'en prie » ça vous flanque le cafard. Je veux dire, si c'est Phoebé ou quoi. Ça m'a flanqué le cafard. Mais j'ai remis l'argent dans ma poche.

« Et toi, tu montes pas ? » Elle me regardait avec un drôle d'air. On voyait bien qu'elle était plus *trop* fâchée.

« Peut-être au prochain tour, j'ai dit. Je vais te regarder tourner. Tu as ton billet ?

— Oui.

— Alors vas-y. Je reste là sur le banc. Je te regarde. » Je suis allé m'asseoir sur le banc et elle est montée sur le manège. Elle en a fait le tour. Je veux dire qu'elle a marché le long du bord et fait le tour complet. Puis elle s'est assise sur un gros vieux cheval brun qui paraissait plutôt fourbu. Le manège s'est mis en marche et j'ai regardé Phoebé tourner, tourner. Y avait seulement cinq ou six autres gosses et la musique c'était l'air de *Smoke gets in your eyes*, joué très biscornu, très jazz. Tous les gosses s'efforçaient d'attraper l'anneau doré, Phoebé comme les autres, et j'avais un peu la trouille qu'elle tombe de son cheval, mais j'ai rien dit. Avec les mômes c'est comme ça. S'ils veulent attraper l'anneau il faut les laisser faire sans rien dire. S'ils tombent ils tombent mais c'est pas bon de les tanner.

Quand le manège s'est arrêté, elle est descendue de son cheval et elle est venue me retrouver. Elle a dit « Cette fois tu montes aussi.

— Non, je te regarde. Je crois que j'aime autant te regarder. » Je lui ai donné encore un peu de son argent. « Tiens. Achète des billets. »

Elle a pris l'argent. Elle a dit « Je suis plus en colère contre toi.

— Je sais. Grouille-toi. Ça va repartir. »

Tout d'un coup, elle m'a embrassé. Puis elle a allongé la main et elle a dit « Il pleut. Il commence à pleuvoir.

— Je sais. »

Alors ce qu'elle a fait — ça m'a tué ou presque — elle a fouillé dans la poche de mon manteau, elle en a sorti ma casquette et elle me l'a mise sur la tête.

J'ai dit « T'en veux plus ?

— Tu peux l'avoir un petit moment.

— Okay. Maintenant grouille. Ça va démarrer sans toi. Ton cheval sera pris. »

Mais elle se pressait pas. Elle a demandé « C'est bien vrai ce que tu as dit ? Que tu vas pas t'en aller. Que tu vas rentrer à la maison, après ?

— Ouais », j'ai dit. Et c'était vrai. Je lui ai pas

menti. Après, je suis rentré à la maison. « Et maintenant grouille-toi, j'ai dit. Ça démarre. »

Elle a couru acheter son billet et elle est revenue juste à temps sur le foutu manège. Puis elle a fait tout le tour pour retrouver son cheval. Elle est montée. Elle a agité la main vers moi. Et j'ai agité la main.

Ouah. Ça s'est mis à pleuvoir. A seaux. Je vous jure. Les parents, les mères, tout le monde est allé s'abriter sous le toit du manège pour pas être trempé jusqu'aux os mais moi je suis resté un moment sur le banc. J'étais vachement mouillé, spécialement dans le cou et puis mon pantalon. Ma casquette c'était pas mal comme protection, mais quand même j'étais traversé. Je m'en foutais. Subitement, je me sentais si formidablement heureux, à regarder la môme Phoebé qui arrêtait pas de tourner. J'ai cru que j'allais chialer tellement j'étais heureux, si vous voulez savoir. Pourquoi, moi je sais pas. C'était juste qu'elle était tellement mignonne et tout, à tourner sur le manège, dans son manteau bleu et tout. Bon Dieu j'aurais vraiment aimé que vous soyez là.

CHAPITRE 26

JE vous en dirai pas plus. Sans doute je pourrais vous raconter ce que j'ai fait une fois rentré à la maison et comment je suis tombé malade et tout, et à quel collège je suis censé aller l'automne prochain, quand je serai sorti d'ici mais j'ai pas envie. Sincèrement. Tout ça m'intéresse pas trop pour l'instant.

Y a un tas de gens, comme ce type, le psychanalyste qu'ils ont ici, ils arrêtent pas de me demander si je vais m'appliquer en classe quand j'y retournerai en septembre. A mon avis c'est une question idiote. Je veux dire, comment peut-on savoir ce qu'on va faire jusqu'à l'instant où on le fait ? La réponse est qu'on peut pas. Je vous jure, c'est une question idiote.

D.B., lui, est moins chiant que les autres mais il me pose aussi des questions. Samedi dernier, il est venu avec une Anglaise qui joue dans le film qu'il est en train d'écrire. Elle était plutôt maniérée mais elle avait une sacrée allure. Bon, à un moment elle est allée aux toilettes ; celles des dames c'est là-bas au diable et D.B. en a profité pour me demander ce que je pensais de tous ces trucs que je viens de vous raconter. Je savais vraiment pas quoi dire. La vérité c'est que je *ne sais pas* quoi en penser. Je regrette d'en avoir tellement parlé. Les gens dont j'ai parlé, ça fait comme s'ils me manquaient à présent, c'est tout ce que je sais. Même le gars Stradlater par exemple, et Ackley. Et même, je crois bien, ce foutu Maurice. C'est drôle. Faut jamais rien raconter à personne. Si on le fait, tout le monde se met à vous manquer.

Composition réalisée par C.M.L., Montrouge.

IMPRIMÉ EN FRANCE PAR BRODARD ET TAUPIN
Usine de La Flèche (Sarthe).
LIBRAIRIE GÉNÉRALE FRANÇAISE - 6, rue Pierre-Sarrazin - 75006 Paris.

ISBN : 2 - 253 - 00978 - 4 ✠ 30/2108/6

PENGUIN CRIME FICTION

Editor: Julian Symons

RAFFLES

Ernest William Hornung was born in Middlesbrough on 7 June 1866. He was educated at Uppingham School, and at the age of eighteen he went to Australia, where he spent two years. On his return he took up journalism, and spent the rest of his life writing. His first book, *A Bride from the Bush*, was published in 1890, *Raffles* in 1899, *Mr Justice Raffles* in 1909, and his last book, *Notes of a Camp-Follower*, in 1919. Stingaree, a character very like Raffles, but operating in Australia, appeared in 1905 in *Stingaree, A Thief in the Night*. Hornung wrote a large number of other novels, and a book of verse, *The Young Guard*. He lived at Partridge Green, in Sussex, and died on 22 March 1921.

RAFFLES

E. W. HORNUNG

PENGUIN BOOKS

Penguin Books Ltd, Harmondsworth, Middlesex, England
Penguin Books, 625 Madison Avenue, New York, New York 10022, U.S.A.
Penguin Books Australia Ltd, Ringwood, Victoria, Australia
Penguin Books Canada Ltd, 2801 John Street, Markham, Ontario, Canada L3R 1B4
Penguin Books (N.Z.) Ltd, 182–190 Wairau Road, Auckland 10, New Zealand

—

First published 1899
Published in Penguin Books 1936
Reprinted 1948, 1950, 1952, 1960, 1976, 1977

—

Made and printed in Great Britain by
Hazell Watson & Viney Ltd,
Aylesbury, Bucks
Set in Linotype Times

CONTENTS

THE IDES OF MARCH

I T was about half-past twelve when I returned to the Albany as a last desperate resort. The scene of my disaster was much as I had left it. The baccarat-counters still strewed the table, with the empty glasses and the loaded ash-trays. A window had been opened to let the smoke out, and was letting in the fog instead. Raffles himself had merely discarded his dining-jacket for one of his innumerable blazers. Yet he arched his eyebrows as though I had dragged him from his bed.

'Forgotten something?' said he, when he saw me on the mat.

'No,' said I, pushing past him without ceremony. And I led the way into his room with an impudence amazing to myself.

'Not come back for your revenge, have you? Because I'm afraid I can't give it you single-handed. I was sorry myself that the others – – '

We were face to face by his fireside, and I cut him short.

'Raffles,' said I, 'you may well be surprised at my coming back in this way and at this hour. I hardly know you. I was never in your rooms before to-night. But I fagged for you at school, and you said you remembered me. Of course that's no excuse; but will you listen to me – for two minutes?'

In my emotion I had at first to struggle for every word; but his face reassured me as I went on, and I was not mistaken in its expression.

'Certainly, my dear fellow,' said he, 'as many minutes as you like. Have a Sullivan and sit down.' And he handed me his silver cigarette-case.

'No,' said I, finding a full voice as I shook my head; 'no, I won't smoke, and I won't sit down, thank you. Nor will you ask me to do either when you've heard what I have to say.'

'Really?' said he, lighting his own cigarette with one clear blue eye upon me. 'How do you know?'

'Because you will probably show me the door,' I cried bitterly; 'and you'll be justified in doing it! But it's no good beat-

9

ing about the bush. You know I dropped over two hundred just now?'

He nodded.

'I hadn't the money in my pocket.'

'I remember.'

'But I had my cheque-book, and I wrote each of you a cheque at that desk.'

'Well?'

'Not one of them was worth the paper it was written on, Raffles. I am overdrawn already at my bank!'

'Surely only for the moment?'

'No. I have spent everything.'

'But somebody told me you were so well off. I heard you had come in for money?'

'So I did. Three years ago. It has been my curse; now it's all gone – every penny! Yes, I've been a fool; there never was nor will be such a fool as I've been ... Isn't this enough for you? Why don't you turn me out?' He was walking up and down with a very long face instead.

'Couldn't your people do anything?' he asked at length.

'Thank God,' I cried, 'I have no people! I was an only child. I came in for everything there was. My one comfort is that they're gone, and will never know.'

I cast myself into a chair and hid my face. Raffles continued to pace the rich carpet that was of a piece with everything else in his rooms. There was no variation in his soft and even footfalls.

'You used to be a literary little cuss,' he said at length; 'didn't you edit the mag. before you left? Anyway I recollect fagging you to do my verses; and literature of sorts is the very thing nowadays; any fool can make a living at it.'

I shook my head. 'Any fool couldn't write off my debts,' said I.

'You have a flat somewhere?' he went on.

'Yes, in Mount Street.'

'Well, what about the furniture?'

I laughed aloud in my misery 'There's been a bill of sale on every stick for months!' And at that Raffles stood still, with raised eyebrows and stern eyes that I could meet the better now that he knew the worst; then, with a shrug, he resumed his walk, and for some minutes neither of us spoke. But in his handsome unmoved face I read my fate and death warrant; and with every breath I cursed my folly and my cowardice in coming to him at all. Because he had been kind to me at school, when he was captain of the eleven, and I his fag, I had dared to look for kindness from him now; because I was ruined, and he rich enough to play cricket all the summer, and do nothing for the rest of the year, I had fatuously counted on his mercy, his sympathy, his help! Yes, I had relied on him in my heart, for all my outward diffidence and humility; and I was rightly served. There was as little of mercy as of sympathy in that curling nostril, that rigid jaw, that cold blue eye which never glanced my way. I caught up my hat. I blundered to my feet. I would have gone without a word, but Raffles stood between me and the door.

'Where are you going?' said he.

'That's my business,' I replied. 'I won't trouble you any more.'

'Then how am I to help you?'

'I didn't ask your help.'

'Then why come to me?'

'Why, indeed!' I echoed. 'Will you let me pass?'

'Not until you tell me where you are going and what you mean to do.'

'Can't you guess?' I cried. And for many seconds we stood staring in each other's eyes.

'Have you got the pluck?' said he, breaking the spell in a tone so cynical that it brought my last drop of blood to the boil.

'You shall see,' said I, as I stepped back and whipped the pistol from my overcoat pocket. 'Now, will you let me pass or shall I do it here?'

The barrel touched my temple, and my thumb the trigger. Mad with excitement as I was, ruined, dishonoured, and now finally determined to make an end of my misspent life, my only surprise to this day is that I did not do so then and there. The despicable satisfaction of involving another in one's destruction added its miserable appeal to my baser egoism; and had fear or horror flown to my companion's face, I shudder to think I might have died diabolically happy with that look for my last impious consolation. It was the look that came instead which held my hand. Neither fear nor horror was in it; only wonder, admiration, and such a measure of pleased expectancy as caused me after all to pocket my revolver with an oath.

'You devil!' I said. 'I believe you wanted me to do it!'

'Not quite,' was the reply, made with a little start, and a change of colour that came too late. 'To tell you the truth, though, I half thought you meant it, and I was never more fascinated in my life. I never dreamt you had such stuff in you, Bunny! No, I'm hanged if I let you go now. And you'd better not try that game again, for you won't catch me stand and look on a second time. We must think of some way out of the mess. I had no idea you were a chap of that sort! There, let me have the gun.'

One of his hands fell kindly on my shoulder, while the other slipped into my overcoat pocket, and I suffered him to deprive me of my weapon without a murmur. Nor was this simply because Raffles had the power of making himself irresistible at will. He was beyond comparison the most masterful man whom I have ever known; yet my acquiescence was due to more than the mere subjection of the weaker nature to the stronger. The forlorn hope which had brought me to the Albany was turned as by magic into an almost staggering sense of safety. Raffles would help me after all! A. J. Raffles would be my friend! It was as though all the world had come round suddenly to my side; so far, therefore, from resisting his action, I caught and clasped his hand with a fervour as uncontrollable as the frenzy which had preceded it.

'God bless you!' I cried. 'Forgive me for everything. I will tell you the truth. I did think you might help me in my extremity, though I well knew that I had no claim upon you. Still – for the old school's sake – the sake of old times – I thought you might give me another chance. If you wouldn't, I meant to blow out my brains – and will still if you change your mind.'

In truth I fear that it was changing, with his expression, even as I spoke, and in spite of his kindly tone and kindlier use of my old school nickname. His next words showed me my mistake.

'What a boy it is for jumping to conclusions! I have my vices, Bunny, but backing and filling is not one of them. Sit down, my good fellow, and have a cigarette to soothe your nerves. I insist. Whisky? The worst thing for you; here's some coffee that I was brewing when you came in. Now listen to me. You speak of "another chance." What do you mean? Another chance at baccarat? Not if I know it! You think the luck must turn; suppose it didn't? We should only have made bad worse. No, my dear chap, you've plunged enough. Do you put yourself in my hands or do you not? Very well then, you plunge no more, and I undertake not to present my cheque. Unfortunately, there are the other men; and still more unfortunately, Bunny, I'm as hard up at this moment as you are yourself!'

It was my turn to stare at Raffles. 'You?' I vociferated. 'You hard up? How am I to sit here and believe that?'

'Did I refuse to believe it of you?' he returned, smiling. 'And, with your own experience, do you think that because a fellow has rooms in this place, and belongs to a club or two, and plays a little cricket, he must necessarily have a balance at the bank? I tell you, my dear man, that at this moment I'm as hard up as ever you were. I have nothing but my wits to live on – absolutely nothing else. It was as necessary for me to win some money this evening as it was for you. We're in the same boat, Bunny, we'd better pull together.'

'Together!' I jumped at it. 'I'll do anything in this world for you, Raffles,' I said, 'if you really mean that you won't give me away. Think of anything you like and I'll do it! I was a desperate man when I came here, and I'm just as desperate now. I don't mind what I do if only I can get out of this without a scandal.'

Again I see him, leaning back in one of the luxurious chairs with which his room was furnished. I see his indolent, athletic figure; his pale, sharp, clean-shaven features; his curly black hair; his strong unscrupulous mouth. And again I feel the clear beam of his wonderful eye, cold and luminous as a star, shining into my brain – sifting the very secrets of my heart.

'I wonder if you mean all that!' he said at length. 'You do in your present mood; but who can back his mood to last? Still, there's hope when a chap takes that tone. Now I think of it, too,

you were a plucky little devil at school; you once did me rather
a good turn, I recollect. Remember it, Bunny? Well, wait a bit,
and perhaps I'll be able to do you a better one. Give me time to
think.'

He got up, lit a fresh cigarette, and fell to pacing the room
once more, but with a slower and more thoughtful step, and for
a much longer period than before. Twice he stopped at my
chair as though on the point of speaking, but each time he
checked himself and resumed his stride in silence. Once he
threw up the window, which he had shut some time since, and
stood for some moments leaning out into the fog which filled
the Albany courtyard. Meanwhile a clock on the chimney-piece
struck one, and one again for the half-hour, without a word
between us.

Yet I not only kept my chair with patience, but I acquired an
incongruous equanimity in that half-hour. Insensibly I had
shifted my burden to the broad shoulders of this splendid
friend, and my thoughts wandered with my eyes as the minutes
passed. The room was the good-sized, square one, with the folding doors, the marble mantelpiece, and the gloomy, old-fashioned distinction peculiar to the Albany. It was charmingly
furnished and arranged with the right amount of negligence
and the right amount of taste. What struck me most, however,
was the absence of the usual insignia of a cricketer's den. Instead of the conventional rack of war-worn bats, a carved oak
bookcase, with every shelf in a litter, filled the better part of
one wall; and where I looked for cricketing groups, I found
reproductions of such words as 'Love and Death' and 'The
Blessed Damozel,' in dusty frames and different parallels. The
man might have been a minor poet instead of an athlete of the
first water. But there had always been a fine streak of æstheti-
cism in his complex composition; some of these very pictures I
had myself dusted in his study at school; and they set me thinking of yet another of his many sides – and of the little incident
to which he had just referred.

Everybody knows how largely the tone of a public school depends on that of the eleven, and on the character of the captain
of cricket in particular; and I have never heard it denied that in
A. J. Raffles's time our tone was good, or that such influence as

he troubled to exert was on the side of the angels. Yet it was whispered in the school that he was in the habit of parading the town at night in loud checks and a false beard. It was whispered, and disbelieved. I alone knew it for a fact; for night after night had I pulled the rope up after him when the rest of the dormitory was asleep, and kept awake by the hour to let it down again on a given signal. Well, one night he was over-bold, and within an ace of ignominious expulsion in the hey-day of his fame. Consummate daring and extraordinary nerve on his part, aided, doubtless, by some little presence of mind on mine, averted that untoward result; and no more need be said of a discreditable incident. But I cannot pretend to have forgotten it in throwing myself on this man's mercy in my desperation. And I was wondering how much of his leniency was owing to the fact that Raffles had not forgotten it either, when he stopped and stood over my chair once more.

'I've been thinking of that night we had the narrow squeak,' he began. 'Why do you start?'

'I was thinking of it too.'

He smiled, as though he had read my thoughts.

'Well, you were the right sort of little beggar then, Bunny; you didn't talk and you didn't flinch. You asked no questions and you told no tales. I wonder if you're like that now?'

'I don't know,' said I, slightly puzzled by his tone. 'I've made such a mess of my own affairs that I trust myself about as little as I'm likely to be trusted by anybody else. Yet I never in my life went back on a friend. I will say that; otherwise perhaps I mightn't be in such a hole to-night.'

'Exactly,' said Raffles, nodding to himself, as though in assent to some hidden train of thought; 'exactly what I remember of you, and I'll bet it's as true now as it was ten years ago. We don't alter, Bunny. We only develop. I suppose neither you nor I are really altered since you used to let down that rope and I used to come up it hand over hand. You would stick at nothing for a pal – what?'

'At nothing in this world,' I was pleased to cry.

'Not even at a crime?' said Raffles, smiling.

I stopped to think, for his tone had changed, and I felt sure he was chaffing me. Yet his eye seemed as much in earnest as

15

ever, and for my part I was in no mood for reservations.

'No, not even at that,' I declared; 'name your crime, and I'm your man.'

He looked at me one moment in wonder, and another moment in doubt; then turned the matter off with a shake of his head, and the little cynical laugh that was all his own.

'You're a nice chap, Bunny! A real desperate character — what? Suicide one moment, and any crime I like the next! What you want is a drag, my boy, and you did well to come to a decent law-abiding citizen with a reputation to lose. None the less we must have that money to-night – by hook or crook.'

'To-night, Raffles?'

'The sooner the better. Every hour after ten o'clock to-morrow morning is an hour of risk. Let one of those cheques get round to your own bank, and you and it are dishonoured together. No, we must raise the wind to-night and re-open your account first thing to-morrow. And I rather think I know where the wind can be raised.'

'At two o'clock in the morning?'

'Yes.'

'But how – but where – at such an hour?'

'From a friend of mine here in Bond Street.'

'He must be a very intimate friend.'

'Intimate's not the word. I have the run of his place and a latchkey all to myself.'

'You would knock him up at this hour of the night?'

'If he's in bed.'

'And it's essential that I should go with you?'

'Absolutely.'

'Then I must; but I'm bound to say I don't like the idea, Raffles.'

'Do you prefer the alternative?' asked my companion, with a sneer. 'No, hang it, that's unfair!' he cried apologetically in the same breath. 'I quite understand. It's a beastly ordeal. But it would never do for you to stay outside. I tell you what, you shall have a peg before we start – just one. There's the whisky, there's the siphon, and I'll be putting on an overcoat while you help yourself.'

Well, I dare say I did so with some freedom, for this plan of his was not the less distasteful to me from its apparent inevitability. I must own, however, that it possessed fewer terrors before my glass was empty. Meanwhile Raffles rejoined me, with a covert coat over his blazer, and a soft felt hat set carelessly on the curly head he shook with a smile as I passed him the decanter.

'When we come back,' said he. 'Work first, play afterwards. Do you see what day it is?' he added, tearing a leaflet from a Shakespearean calendar as I drained my glass. 'March 15th. "The Ides of March, the Ides of March, remember." Eh, Bunny, my boy? You won't forget them, will you?'

And, with a laugh, he threw some coals on the fire before turning down the gas like a careful householder. So we went out together as the clock on the chimney-piece was striking two.

II

Piccadilly was a trench of raw white fog, rimmed with blurred street-lamps, and lined with a thin coating of adhesive mud. We met no other wayfarers on the deserted flagstones, and were ourselves favoured with a very hard stare from the constable of the beat, who, however, touched his helmet on recognising my companion.

'You see, I'm known to the police,' laughed Raffles as we passed on. 'Poor devils, they've got to keep their weather eye open on a night like this! A fog may be a bore to you and me, Bunny, but it's a perfect godsend to the criminal classes, especially so late in their season. Here we are, though – and I'm hanged if the beggar isn't in bed and asleep after all!'

We had turned into Bond Street, and had halted on the kerb a few yards down on the right. Raffles was gazing up at some windows across the road, windows barely discernible through the mist, and without the glimmer of a light to throw them out. They were over a jeweller's shop, as I could see by the peep-hole in the shop door, and the bright light burning within. But the entire 'upper part', with the private street door next to the shop, was black and blank as the sky itself.

'Better give it up for to-night,' I urged. 'Surely the morning will be time enough!'

'Not a bit of it,' said Raffles. 'I have his key. We'll surprise him. Come along.'

And seizing my right arm, he hurried me across the road, opened the door with his latchkey, and in another moment had shut it swiftly but softly behind us. We stood together in the dark. Outside, a measured step was approaching; we had heard it through the fog as we crossed the street; now, as it drew nearer, my companion's fingers tightened on my arm.

'It may be the chap himself,' he whispered. 'He's the devil of a night-bird. Not a sound, Bunny! We'll startle the life out of him. Ah!'

The measured step had passed without a pause. Raffles drew a deep breath, and his singular grip of me slowly relaxed.

'But still, not a sound,' he continued in the same whisper; 'we'll take a rise out of him, wherever he is! Slip off your shoes and follow me '

Well, you may wonder at my doing so, but you can never have met A. J. Raffles Half his power lay in a conciliating trick of sinking the commander in the leader. And it was impossible not to follow one who led with such a zest. You might question, but you followed first. So now, when I heard him kick off his own shoes, I did the same, and was on the stairs at his heels before I realised what an extraordinary way was this of approaching a stranger for money in the dead of night. But obviously Raffles and he were on exceptional terms of intimacy, and I could not but infer that they were in the habit of playing practical jokes on each other.

We groped our way so slowly upstairs that I had time to make more than one note before we reached the top. The stair was uncarpeted. The spread fingers of my right hand encountered nothing on the damp wall: those of my left trailed through a dust that could be felt on the banisters. An eerie sensation had been upon me since we entered the house. It increased with every step we climbed. What hermit were we going to startle in his cell?

We came to a landing. The banisters led us to the left, and to the left again. Four steps more, and we were on another and a longer landing, and suddenly a match blazed from the back. I never heard it struck. Its flash was blinding. When my eyes became accustomed to the light, there was Raffles holding up the match with one hand, and shading it with the other, between bare boards, stripped walls, and the open doors of empty rooms.

'Where have you brought me?' I cried. 'The house is unoccupied?'

'Hush! Wait!' he whispered, and he led the way into one of the empty rooms. His match went out as we crossed the threshold, and he struck another without the slightest noise. Then he stood with his back to me, fumbling with something that I could not see. But, when he threw the second match away, there was some other light in its stead, and a slight smell of oil. I stepped forward to look over his shoulder, but before I could do so he had turned and flashed a tiny lantern in my face.

'What's this?' I gasped. 'What rotten trick are you going to play?'

'It's played,' he answered, with his quiet laugh.

'On me?'

'I'm afraid so, Bunny.'

'Is there no one in the house, then?'

'No one but ourselves.'

'So it was mere chaff about your friend in Bond Street who could let us have that money?'

'Not altogether. It's quite true that Danby is a friend of mine.'

'Danby?'

'The jeweller underneath.'

'What do you mean?' I whispered, trembling like a leaf as his meaning dawned upon me. 'Are you going to get the money from the jeweller?'

'Well, not exactly.'

'What then?'

'The equivalent – from his shop.'

There was no need for another question. I understood everything but my own density. He had given me a dozen hints, and I had taken none. And there I stood staring at him, in that empty room; and there he stood with his dark lantern laughing at me.

'A burglar!' I gasped. 'You – you!'

'I told you I lived by my wits.'

'Why couldn't you tell me what you were going to do? Why couldn't you trust me? Why must you lie?' I demanded, piqued to the quick for all my horror.

'I wanted to tell you,' said he. 'I was on the point of telling you more than once. You may remember how I sounded you about crime, though you have probably forgotten what you said yourself. I didn't think you meant it at the time, but I thought I'd put you to the test. Now I see you didn't, and I don't blame you. I only am to blame. Get out of it, my dear boy, as quick as you can; leave it to me. You won't give me away, whatever else you do!'

Oh, his cleverness! His fiendish cleverness! Had he fallen back on threats, coercion, sneers, all might have been different even then. But he set me free to leave him in the lurch. He would not blame me. He did not even bind me to secrecy; he trusted me. He knew my weakness and my strength, and was playing on both with his master's touch.

'Not so fast,' said I. 'Did I put this into your head, or were you going to do it in any case?'

'Not in any case,' said Raffles. 'It's true I've had the key for days, but when I won to-night I thought of chucking it; for, as a matter of fact, it's not a one-man job.'

'That settles it. I'm your man.'

'You mean it?'

'Yes – for to-night.'

'Good old Bunny,' he murmured, holding the lantern for one moment to my face; the next he was explaining his plans, and I was nodding, as though we had been fellow-cracksmen all our days.

'I know the shop,' he whispered, 'because I've got a few things there. I know this upper part too; it's been to let for a month, and I got an order to view, and took a cast of the key before using it. The one thing I don't know is how to make a connection between the two; at present there's none. We may make it up here, though I rather fancy the basement myself. If you wait a minute I'll tell you.'

He set his lantern on the floor, and crept to a back window, and opened it with scarcely a sound; only to return shaking his head, after shutting the window with the same care.

'That was our one chance,' said he, 'a back window above a back window; but it's too dark to see anything, and we daren't show an outside light. Come down after me to the basement; and remember, though there's not a soul on the premises, you can't make too little noise. There – there – listen to that!'

It was the measured tread that we had heard before on the flagstones outside. Raffles darkened his lantern, and again we stood motionless till it had passed

'Either a policeman,' he muttered, 'or a watchman that all these jewellers run between them. The watchman's the man for us to watch; he's simply paid to spot this kind of thing.'

We crept very gingerly down the stairs, which creaked a bit in spite of us, and we picked up our shoes in the passage; then down some narrow stone steps, at the foot of which Raffles showed his light, and put on his shoes once more, bidding me do the same in rather a louder tone than he had permitted himself to employ overhead. We were now considerably below the level of the street, in a small space with as many doors as it had sides. Three were ajar, and we saw through them into empty cellars; but in the fourth a key was turned and a bolt drawn; and this one presently let us out into the bottom of a deep square well of fog. A similar door faced it across this area, and Raffles had the lantern close against it, and was hiding the light with his body, when a short and sudden crash made my heart stand still. Next moment I saw the door wide open, and Raffles standing within and beckoning me with a jemmy.

'Door number one,' he whispered. 'Deuce knows how many more there'll be, but I know of two at least. We won't have to make much noise over them, either; down here there's less risk.'

We were now at the bottom of the exact fellow to the narrow stone stair which we had just descended; the yard, or well, being the one part common to both the private and the business premises. But this flight led to no open passage; instead, a singularly solid mahogany door confronted us at the top.

'I thought so,' muttered Raffles, handing me the lantern, and pocketing a bunch of skeleton keys, after tampering for a few minutes with the lock. 'It'll be an hour's work to get through that!'

'Can't you pick it?'

'No. I know these locks. It's no use trying. We must cut it out, and it'll take us an hour.'

It took us forty-seven minutes by my watch; or rather it took Raffles, and never in my life have I seen anything more deliberately done. My part was simply to stand by with the dark lantern in one hand, and a small bottle of rock-oil in the other. Raffles had produced a pretty embroidered case, intended obviously for his razors, but filled instead with the tools of his secret trade, including the rock-oil. From this case he selected a bit, capable of drilling a hole an inch in diameter, and fitted it to a small but very strong steel brace. Then he took off his covert coat and his blazer, spread them neatly on the top step – knelt on them – turned up his shirt-cuffs – and went to work with brace-and-bit near the keyhole. But first he oiled the bit to minimise the noise, and this he did invariably before beginning a fresh hole, and often in the middle of one. It took thirty-two separate borings to cut round that lock.

I noticed that through the first circular orifice Raffles thrust a forefinger; then, as the circle became an ever-lengthening oval, he got his hand through up to the thumb, and I heard him swear softly to himself.

'I was afraid so!'

'What is it?'

'An iron gate on the other side!'

'How on earth are we to get through that?' I asked in dismay.

'Pick the lock. But there may be two. In that case they'll be top and bottom, and we shall have two fresh holes to make, as the door opens inwards. It won't open two inches as it is.'

I confess I did not feel sanguine about the lock-picking, seeing that one lock had baffled us already; and my disappointment and impatience must have been a revelation to me had I stopped to think. The truth is that I was entering into our nefarious undertaking with an involuntary zeal of which I was myself quite unconscious at the time. The romance and the peril of the whole proceeding held me spellbound and entranced. My moral sense and my sense of fear were stricken by a common paralysis. And there I stood, shining my light and holding my phial with a keener interest than I had ever brought to any honest avocation. And there knelt A. J. Raffles, with his black hair tumbled, and the same watchful, quiet, determined half-smile with which I have seen him send down over after over in a county match!

At last the chain of holes was complete, the lock wrenched out bodily, and a splendid bare arm plunged up to the shoulder through the aperture, and through the bars of the iron gate beyond.

'Now,' whispered Raffles, 'if there's only one lock it'll be in the middle. Joy! Here it is! Only let me pick it, and we're through at last.'

He withdrew his arm, a skeleton key was selected from the bunch, and then back went his arm to the shoulder. It was a breathless moment. I heard the heart throbbing in my body the very watch ticking in my pocket, and ever and anon the tinkle-tinkle of the skeleton key. Then – at last – there came a single unmistakable click. In another minute the mahogany door and the iron gate yawned behind us, and Raffles was sitting on an office table, wiping his face, with the lantern throwing a steady beam by his side.

We were now in a bare and roomy lobby behind the shop, but separated therefrom by an iron curtain, the very sight of which filled me with despair. Raffles, however, did not appear in the least depressed, but hung up his coat and hat on some pegs in the lobby before examining this curtain with his lantern.

'That's nothing,' said he, after a minute's inspection; 'we'll be through that in no time, but there's a door on the other side which may give us trouble.'

'Another door!' I groaned. 'And how do you mean to tackle this thing?'

'Prise it up with the jointed jemmy. The weak point of these iron curtains is the leverage you can get from below. But it makes a noise, and this is where you're coming in, Bunny; this is where I couldn't do without you. I must have you overhead to knock through when the street's clear. I'll come with you and show a light.'

Well, you may imagine how little I liked the prospect of this

23

lonely vigil; and yet there was something very stimulating in the vital responsibility which it involved. Hitherto I had been a mere spectator. Now I was to take part in the game. And the fresh excitement made me more than ever insensible to those considerations of conscience and of safety which were already as dead nerves in my breast.

So I took my post without a murmur in the front room above the shop. The fixtures had been left for the refusal of the incoming tenant, and fortunately for us they included Venetian blinds, which were already down. It was the simplest matter in the world to stand peeping through the laths into the street, to beat twice with my foot when anybody was approaching, and once when all was clear again. The noises that even I could hear below, with the exception of one metallic crash at the beginning, were indeed incredibly slight; but they ceased altogether at each double rap from my toe, and a policeman passed quite half a dozen times beneath my eyes, and the man whom I took to be the jeweller's watchman oftener still, during the better part of an hour that I spent at the window. Once, indeed, my heart was in my mouth, but only once. It was when the watchman stopped and peered through the peep-hole into the lighted shop. I waited for his whistle. I waited for the gallows or the gaol! But my signals had been studiously obeyed, and the man passed on in undisturbed serenity. In the end I had a signal in my turn, and retraced my steps with lighted matches down the broad stairs, down the narrow ones, across the area, and up into the lobby where Raffles awaited me with an outstretched hand.

'Well done, my boy!' said he. 'You're the same good man in a pinch, and you shall have your reward. I've got a thousand pounds' worth if I've got a penn'orth. It's all in my pockets. And here's something else I found in this locker; very decent port and some cigars, meant for poor dear Danby's business friends. Take a pull, and you shall light up presently. I've found a lavatory, too, and we must have a wash-and-brush-up before we go, for I'm as black as your boot.'

The iron curtain was down, but he insisted on raising it until I could peep through the glass door on the other side and see his handiwork in the shop beyond. Here two electric lights were left burning all night long, and in their cold white rays I could at first see nothing amiss. I looked along an orderly lane, an empty glass counter on my left, glass cupboards of untouched silver on my right, and facing me the filmy black-eye of the peep-hole that shone like a stage moon on the street. The counter had not been emptied by Raffles; its contents were in the Chubb's safe, which he had given up at a glance; nor had he looked at the silver, except to choose a cigarette-case for me. He had confined himself entirely to the shop window. This was in three compartments, each secured for the night by removable panels with separate locks. Raffles had removed them a few hours before their time, and the electric light shone on a corrugated shutter bare as the ribs of an empty carcase. Every article of value was gone from the one place which was invisible from the little window in the door; elsewhere all was as it had been left overnight. And but for a train of mangled doors behind the iron curtain, a bottle of wine and a cigar-box with which liberties had been taken, a rather black towel in the lavatory, a burnt match here and there, and our finger-marks on the dusty banisters, not a trace of our visit did we leave.

'Had it in my head for long?' said Raffles, as we strolled through the streets towards dawn, for all the world as though we were returning from a dance. 'No, Bunny, I never thought of it till I saw that upper part empty about a month ago, and bought a few things in the shop to get the lie of the land. That reminds me that I never paid for them; but, by Jove, I will to-morrow, and if that isn't poetic justice, what is? One visit showed me the possibilities of the place, but a second convinced me of its impossibilities without a pal. So I had practically given up the idea, when you came along on the very night and in the very plight for it! But here we are at the Albany, and I hope there's some fire left; for I don't know how you feel, Bunny, but for my part I'm as cold as Keats' owl.'

He could think of Keats on his way from a felony! He could hanker for his fireside like another. Flood-gates were loosened within me, and the plain English of our adventure rushed over me as cold as ice. Raffles was a burglar. I had helped to commit one burglary, therefore I was a burglar too. Yet I could stand and warm myself by his fire and watch him empty his pockets, as though we had done nothing wonderful or wicked!

My blood froze. My heart sickened. My brain whirled. How I had liked this villain! How I had admired him! Now my liking and admiration must turn to loathing disgust. I waited for the change. I longed to feel it in my heart. But – I longed and waited in vain!

I saw he was emptying his pockets; the table sparkled with their hoard. Rings by the dozen, diamonds by the score; bracelets, pendants, aigrettes, necklaces; pearls, rubies, amethysts, sapphires; and diamonds always, diamonds in everything, flashing bayonets of light, dazzling me – blinding me – making me disbelieve because I could no longer forget. Last of all came no gem, indeed, but my own revolver from an inner pocket. And that struck a chord. I suppose I said something – my hand flew out. I can see Raffles now, as he looked at me once more with a high arch over each clear eye. I can see him pick out the cartridges with his quiet cynical smile, before he would give me my pistol back again.

'You mayn't believe it, Bunny,' said he, 'but I never carried a loaded one before. On the whole I think it gives one confidence. Yet it would be very awkward if anything went wrong; one might use it, and that's not the game at all, though I have often thought that the murderer who has just done the trick must have great sensations before things get too hot for him. Don't look so distressed, my dear chap. I've never had those sensations, and I don't suppose I ever shall.'

'But this much you have done before?' said I hoarsely.

'Before? My dear Bunny, you offend me! Did it look like a first attempt? Of course I have done it before.'

'Often?'

'Well – no. Not often enough to destroy the charm, at all events; never, as a matter of fact, unless I'm cursedly hard up. Did you hear about the Thimbleby diamonds? Well, that was the last time – and a poor lot of paste they were. Then there was the little business of the Dormer house-boat at Henley last year. That was mine also – such as it was. I've never brought off a really big *coup* yet; when I do I shall chuck it up.'

Yes, I remember both cases very well. To think that he was

their author! It was incredible, outrageous, inconceivable. Then my eyes would fall upon the table, twinkling and glittering in a hundred places, and incredulity was at an end.

'How came you to begin? I asked, as curiosity overcame mere wonder, and a fascination for his career gradually wove itself into my fascination for the man.

'Ah! that's a long story, said Raffles. 'It was in the Colonies, when I was out there playing cricket. It's too long a story to tell you now, but I was in much the same fix that you were in to-night, and it was my only way out. I never meant it for anything more; but I'd tasted blood, and it was all over with me. Why should I work when I could steal? Why settle down to some humdrum uncongenial billet, when excitement, romance, danger, and a decent living were all going begging together? Of course, it s very wrong, but we can't all be moralists, and the distribution of wealth is very wrong to begin with. Besides, you're not at it all the time. I'm sick of quoting Gilbert's lines to myself, but they re profoundly true. I only wonder if you'll like the life as much as I do!'

'Like it?' I cried. 'Not I! It's no life for me. Once is enough!'

'You wouldn't give me a hand another time?'

'Don't ask me, Raffles. Don't ask me, for God's sake!'

'Yet you said you would do anything for me! You asked me to name my crime! But I knew at the time you didn't mean it; you didn't go back on me to-night, and that ought to satisfy me, goodness knows! I suppose I'm ungrateful, and unreasonable, and all that. I ought to let it end at this. But you're the very man for me, Bunny, the – very – man! Just think how we got through to-night. Not a scratch – not a hitch! There's nothing very terrible in it, you see; there never would be, while we worked together.'

He was standing in front of me with a hand on either shoulder; he was smiling as he knew so well how to smile. I turned on my heel, planted my elbows on the chimney-piece, and my burning head between my hands Next instant a still heartier hand had fallen on my back.

'All right, my boy! You are quite right and I'm worse than wrong. I'll never ask it again. Go, if you want to, and come again about midday for the cash. There was no bargain; but, of course, I'll get you out of your scrape – especially after the way you've stood by me to-night.'

I was round again with my blood on fire.

'I'll do it again,' I said through my teeth.

He shook his head. 'Not you,' he said, smiling quite good-humouredly at my insane enthusiasm.

'I will,' I cried with an oath. 'I'll lend you a hand as often as you like! What does it matter now? I've been in it once. I'll be in it again. I've gone to the devil anyhow. I can't go back, and wouldn't if I could. Nothing matters another rap! When you want me I'm your man.'

And that is how Raffles and I joined felonious forces on the Ides of March.

A COSTUME PIECE

LONDON was just then talking of one whose name is already a name and nothing more. Reuben Rosenthall had made his millions on the diamond fields of South Africa, and had come home to enjoy them according to his lights; how he went to work will scarcely be forgotten by any reader of the halfpenny evening papers, which revelled in endless anecdotes of his original indigence and present prodigality, varied with interesting particulars of the extraordinary establishment which the millionaire set up in St John's Wood. Here he kept a retinue of Kaffirs, who were literally his slaves; and hence he would sally with enormous diamonds in his shirt and on his finger, in the convoy of a prize-fighter of heinous repute, who was not, however, by any means the worst element in the Rosenthall *ménage*. So said common gossip; but the fact was sufficiently established by the interference of the police on at least one occasion, followed by certain magisterial proceedings which were reported with justifiable gusto and huge headlines in the newspapers aforesaid. And this was all one knew of Reuben Rosenthall up to the time when the Old Bohemian Club, having fallen on evil days, found it worth its while to organise a great dinner in honour of so wealthy an exponent of the club's principles. I was not at the banquet myself, but a member took Raffles, who told me all about it that very night.

'Most extraordinary show I ever went to in my life,' said he. 'As for the man himself – well, I was prepared for something grotesque, but the fellow fairly took my breath away. To begin with, he's the most astounding brute to look at, well over six feet, with a chest like a barrel and a great hook-nose, and the reddest hair and whiskers you ever saw. Drank like a fire-engine, but only got drunk enough to make us a speech that I wouldn't have missed for ten pounds. I'm only sorry you weren't there too, Bunny, old chap.'

I began to be sorry myself, for Raffles was anything but an excitable person, and never had I seen him so excited before.

Had he been following Rosenthall's example? His coming to my rooms at midnight, merely to tell me about his dinner, was in itself enough to excuse a suspicion which was certainly at variance with my knowledge of A. J. Raffles.

'What did he say?' I inquired mechanically, divining some subtler explanation of this visit, and wondering what on earth it could be.

'Say?' cried Raffles. 'What did he not say? He boasted of his race, he bragged of his riches, and he blackguarded society for taking him up for his money and dropping him out of sheer pique and jealousy, because he had so much. He mentioned names, too, with the most charming freedom, and swore he was as good a man as the Old Country had to show – *pace* the Old Bohemians. To prove it he pointed to a great diamond in the middle of his shirt-front with a little finger loaded with another just like it; which of our bloated princes could show a pair like that? As a matter of fact, they seemed quite wonderful stones, with a curious purple gleam to them that must mean a pot of money. But old Rosenthall swore he wouldn't take fifty thousand pounds for the two, and wanted to know where the other man was who went about with twenty-five thousand in his shirt-front, and the other twenty-five on his little finger. He didn't exist. If he did, he wouldn't have the pluck to wear them. But he had – he'd tell us why. And before you could say Jack Robinson he had whipped out a whacking great revolver!'

'Not at the table?'

'At the table! In the middle of his speech! But it was nothing to what he wanted to do. He actually wanted us to let him write his name in bullets on the opposite wall to show us why he wasn't afraid to go about in all his diamonds! That brute Purvis, the prize-fighter who is his paid bully, had to bully his master before he could be persuaded out of it. There was quite a panic for the moment; one fellow was saying his prayers under the table, and the waiters bolted to a man.'

'What a grotesque scene!'

'Grotesque enough, but I rather wish they had let him go the whole hog and blaze away. He was as keen as knives to show us how he could take care of his purple diamonds; and, do you know, Bunny, I was as keen as knives to see.'

And Raffles leant towards me with a sly, slow smile that made the hidden meaning of his visit only too plain to me at last.

'So you think of having a try for his diamonds yourself?'

He shrugged his shoulders.

'It is horribly obvious, I admit. But – yes, I have set my heart upon them! To be quite frank, I have had them on my conscience for some time; one couldn't hear so much of the man, and his prize-fighter, and his diamonds, without feeling it a kind of duty to have a go for them; but when it comes to brandishing a revolver and practically challenging the world, the thing becomes inevitable. It is simply thrust upon one. I was fated to hear that challenge, Bunny, and I, for one, must take it up. I was only sorry I couldn't get on my hind legs and say so then and there.'

'Well,' I said, 'I don't see the necessity as things are with us; but, of course, I'm your man.'

My tone may have been half-hearted. I did my best to make it otherwise. But it was barely a month since our Bond Street exploit, and we certainly could have afforded to behave ourselves for some time to come. We had been getting along so nicely; by his advice I had scribbled a thing or two; inspired by Raffles, I had even done an article on our own jewel robbery; and for the moment I was quite satisfied with this sort of adventure. I thought we ought to know when we were well off and could see no point in our running fresh risks before we were obliged. On the other hand, I was anxious not to show the least disposition to break the pledge that I had given a month ago. But it was not on my manifest disinclination that Raffles fastened.

'Necessity, my dear Bunny? Does the writer only write when the wolf is at the door? Does the painter paint for bread alone? Must you and I be driven to crime like Tom of Bow and Dick of Whitechapel? You pain me, my dear chap; you needn't laugh, because you do. Art for art's sake is a vile catchword, but I confess it appeals to me. In this case my motives are absolutely pure, for I doubt if we shall ever be able to dispose of such peculiar stones. But if I don't have a try for them – after to-night, I shall never be able to hold up my head again.'

His eye twinkled, but it glittered too.

'We shall have our work cut out,' was all I said.

'And do you suppose I should be keen on it if we hadn't?' cried Raffles. 'My dear fellow, I would rob St Paul's Cathedral if I could, but I could no more scoop a till when the shop-walker wasn't looking than I could bag apples out of an old woman's basket. Even that little business last month was a sordid affair, but it was necessary, and I think its strategy redeemed it to some extent. Now there's some credit, and more sport, in going where they boast they're on their guard against you. The Bank of England, for example, is the ideal crib; but that would need half a dozen of us with years to give to the job; and meanwhile Reuben Rosenthall is high enough game for you and me. We know he's armed. We know how Billy Purvis can fight. It'll be no soft thing, I grant you. But what of that, my good Bunny – what of that? A man's reach must exceed his grasp, dear boy, or what the dickens is a heaven for?'

'I would rather we didn't exceed ours just yet,' I answered, laughing, for his spirit was irresistible, and the plan was growing upon me, despite my qualms.

'Trust me for that,' was his reply; 'I'll see you through. After all, I expect to find that the difficulties are nearly all on the surface. These fellows both drink like the devil, and that should simplify matters considerably. But we shall see, and we must take our time. There will probably turn out to be a dozen different ways in which the thing might be done, and we shall have to choose between them. It will mean watching the house for at least a week in any case; it may mean lots of other things that will take much longer; but give me a week, and I will tell you more. That's to say if you're really on?'

'Of course I am,' I replied indignantly. 'But why should I give you a week? Why shouldn't we watch the house together?'

'Because two eyes are as good as four, and take up less room. Never hunt in couples unless you're obliged. But don't look offended, Bunny; there'll be plenty for you to do when the time comes, that I promise you. You shall have your share of the fun, never fear, and a purple diamond all to yourself – if we're lucky.'

On the whole, however, this conversation left me less than lukewarm, and I still remember the depression which came over me when Raffles was gone. I saw the folly of the enterprise to which I had committed myself – the sheer, gratuitous, unnecessary folly of it. And the paradoxes in which Raffles revelled, and the frivolous casuistry which was nevertheless half sincere, and which his mere personality rendered wholly plausible at the moment of utterance, appealed very little to me when recalled in cold blood. I admired the spirit of pure mischief in which he seemed prepared to risk his liberty and his life, but I did not find it an infectious spirit on calm reflection. Yet the thought of withdrawal was not to be entertained for a moment. On the contrary, I was impatient of the delay ordained by Raffles; and, perhaps, no small part of my secret disaffection came of his galling determination to do without me until the last moment.

It made it no better that this was characteristic of the man and of his attitude towards me. For a month we had been, I suppose, the thickest thieves in all London, and yet our intimacy was curiously incomplete. With all his charming frankness, there was in Raffles a vein of capricious reserve which was perceptible enough to be very irritating. He had the instinctive secretiveness of the inveterate criminal. He would make mysteries of matters of common concern; for example, I never knew how or where he disposed of the Bond Street jewels, on the proceeds of which we were both still leading the outward lives of hundreds of other young fellows about town. He was consistently mysterious about that and other details, of which it seemed to me that I had already earned the right to know everything. I could not but remember how he had led me into my first felony, by means of a trick, while yet uncertain whether he could trust me or not. That I could no longer afford to resent, but I did resent his want of confidence in me now. I said nothing about it, but it rankled every day, and never more than in the week that succeeded the Rosenthall dinner. When I met Raffles at the club he would tell me nothing; when I went to his rooms he was out, or pretended to be. One day he told me he was getting on well, but slowly; it was a more ticklish game that he had thought; but when I began to ask questions he would say no more. Then and there, in my annoyance, I took my own decision. Since he would tell me nothing of the result of his vigils, I determined to keep one on my own account, and that very evening found my way to the millionaire's front gates.

The house he was occupying is, I believe, quite the largest in the St John's Wood district. It stands in the angle formed by two broad thoroughfares, neither of which, as it happens, is a bus route, and I doubt if many quieter spots exist within the four-mile radius. Quiet also was the great square house, in its garden of grass-plots and shrubs; the lights were low, the millionaire and his friends obviously spending their evening elsewhere. The garden walls were only a few feet high. In one there was a side door opening into a glass passage; in the other two five-barred grained-and-varnished gates, one at either end of the little semi-circular drive, and both wide open. So still was the place that I had a great mind to walk boldly in and learn something of the premises; in fact, I was on the point of doing so, when I heard a quick, shuffling step on the pavement behind me. I turned round and faced the dark scowl and the dirty clenched fists of a dilapidated tramp.

'You fool!' said he. 'You utter idiot!'

'Raffles!'

'That's it,' he whispered savagely; 'tell all the neighbourhood – give me away at the top of your voice!'

With that he turned his back upon me, and shambled down the road, shrugging his shoulders, and muttering to himself as though I had refused him alms. A few moments I stood astounded, indignant, at a loss; then I followed him. His feet trailed, his knees gave, his back was bowed, his head kept nodding; it was the gait of a man eighty years of age. Presently he waited for me midway between two lamp-posts. As I came up he was lighting rank tobacco, in a cutty pipe, with an evil-smelling match, and the flame showed me the suspicion of a smile.

'You must forgive my heat, Bunny, but it really was very foolish of you. Here am I trying every dodge – begging at the door one night – hiding in the shrubs the next – doing every mortal thing but stand and stare at the house as you went and did. It's a costume piece, and in you rush in your ordinary clothes. I tell you they're on the look-out for us night and day. It's the toughest nut I ever tackled!'

'Well,' said I, 'if you had told me so before I shouldn't have come. You told me nothing.'

He looked hard at me from under the broken rim of a battered billycock.

'You're right,' he said at length. 'I've been too close. It's become second nature with me, when I've anything on. But there's an end of it, Bunny, so far as you're concerned. I'm going home now, and I want you to follow me; but for Heaven's sake keep your distance, and don't speak to me again till I speak to you. There – give me a start.' And he was off again, a decrepit vagabond, with his hands in his pockets, his elbows squared, and frayed coat-tails swinging raggedly from side to side.

I followed him to the Finchley Road. There he took an omnibus, and I sat some rows behind him on the top, but not far enough to escape the pest of his vile tobacco. That he could carry his character-sketch to such a pitch – he would only smoke one brand of cigarettes! It was the last, least touch of the insatiable artist, and it charmed away what mortification there still remained in me. Once more I felt the fascination of a comrade who was for ever dazzling one with a fresh and unsuspected facet of his character.

As we neared Piccadilly I wondered what he would do. Surely he was not going into the Albany like that? No, he took another omnibus to Sloane Street, I sitting behind him as before. At Sloane Street we changed again, and were presently in the long lean artery of the King's Road. I was now all agog to know our destination, nor was I kept many more minutes in doubt. Raffles got down. I followed. He crossed the road and disappeared up a dark turning. I pressed after him, and was in time to see his coat-tails as he plunged into a still darker flagged alley to the right. He was holding himself up and stepping out like a young man once more; also, in some subtle way, he already looked less disreputable. But I alone was there to see him, the alley was absolutely deserted, and desperately dark. At the farther end he opened a door with a latchkey, and it was darker yet within.

Instinctively I drew back and heard him chuckle. We could no longer see each other.

'All right, Bunny! There's no hanky-panky this time. These are studios, my friend, and I'm one of the lawful tenants.'

Indeed, in another minute we were in a lofty room with skylight, easels, dressing-cupboard, platform, and every other adjunct save the signs of actual labour. The first thing I saw, as Raffles lit the gas, was its reflection in his silk hat on the pegs beside the rest of his normal garments.

'Looking for the works of art?' continued Raffles, lighting a cigarette and beginning to divest himself of his rags. 'I'm afraid you won't find any, but there's the canvas I'm always going to make a start upon. I tell them I'm looking high and low for my ideal model. I have the stove lit on principle twice a week, and look in and leave a newspaper and a smell of Sullivans – how good they are after shag! Meanwhile I pay my rent and am a good tenant in every way; and it's a very useful little *pied-à-terre* – there's no saying how useful it might be at a pinch. As it is, the billycock comes in and the topper goes out, and nobody takes the slightest notice of either; at this time of night the chances are that there's not a soul in the building except ourselves.'

'You never told me you went in for disguises,' said I, watching him as he cleansed the grime from his face and hands.

'No, Bunny, I've treated you very shabbily all round. There was really no reason why I shouldn't have shown you this place a month ago, and yet there was no point in my doing so, and circumstances are just conceivable in which it would have suited us both for you to be in genuine ignorance of my whereabouts. I have something to sleep on, as you perceive, in case of need, and, of course, my name is not Raffles in the King's Road. So you will see that one might bolt farther and fare worse.'

'Meanwhile you use the place as a dressing-room?'

'It's my private pavilion,' said Raffles. 'Disguises? In some cases they're half the battle, and it's always pleasant to feel that, if the worst comes to the worst, you needn't necessarily be convicted under your own name. Then they're indispensable in dealing with the fences. I drive all my bargains in the tongue and raiment of Shoreditch. If I didn't there'd be the very devil to pay in blackmail. Now, this cupboard's full of all sorts of toggery. I tell the woman who cleans the room that it's for my models when I find 'em. By the way, I only hope I've got something that'll fit you, for you'll want a rig for to-morrow night.'

'To-morrow night!' I exclaimed. 'Why, what do you mean to do?'

'The trick,' said Raffles. 'I intended writing to you as soon as I got back to my rooms, to ask you to look me up to-morrow afternoon; then I was going to unfold my plan of campaign, and take you straight into action then and there. There's nothing like putting the nervous players in first; it's the sitting with their pads on that upsets their apple cart; that was another of my reasons for being so confoundedly close. You must try to forgive me. I couldn't help remembering how well you played up last trip, without any time to weaken on it beforehand. All I want is for you to be as cool and smart to-morrow night as you were then; though, by Jove, there's no comparison between the two cases!'

'I thought you would find it so.'

'You were right. I have. Mind you, I don't say this will be the tougher job all round; we shall probably get in without any difficulty at all; it's the getting out again that may flummux us. That's the worst of an irregular household!' cried Raffles, with quite a burst of virtuous indignation. 'I assure you, Bunny, I spent the whole of Monday night in the shrubbery of the garden next door looking over the wall, and, if you'll believe me, somebody was about all night long! I don't mean the Kaffirs. I don't believe they ever get to bed at all, poor devils! No, I mean Rosenthall himself, and that pasty-faced beast Purvis. They were up and drinking from midnight when they came in, to broad daylight, when I cleared out. Even then I left them sober enough to slang each other. By the way, they very nearly came to blows in the garden, within a few yards of me, and I heard something that might come in useful and make Rosenthall shoot crooked at a critical moment. You know what an I.D.B. is?'

'Illicit Diamond Buyer?'

'Exactly. Well, it seems that Rosenthall was one. He must

have let it out to Purvis in his cups. Anyhow, I heard Purvis taunting him with it, and threatening him with the breakwater at Cape Town; and I begin to think our friends are friend and foe. But about to-morrow night: there's nothing subtle in my plan. It's simply to get in while these fellows are out on the loose, and to lie low till they come back, and longer. If possible we must doctor the whisky. That would simplify the whole thing, though it's not a very sporting game to play; still, we must remember Rosenthall's revolver; we don't want him to sign his name on us. With all those Kaffirs about, however, it's ten to one on the whisky, and a hundred to one against us if we go looking for it. A brush with the heathen would spoil everything, if it did no more. Besides, there are the ladies – –'

'The deuce there are!'

'Ladies with an "i", and the very voices for raising Cain. I fear, I fear the clamour! It would be fatal to us. *Au contraire,* if we can manage to stow ourselves away unbeknownst, half the battle will be won. If Rosenthall turns in drunk, it's a purple diamond apiece. If he sits up sober, it may be a bullet instead. We will hope not, Bunny; and all the firing wouldn't be on one side; but it's on the knees of the gods.'

And so we left it when we shook hands in Piccadilly – not by any means as much later as I could have wished. Raffles would not ask me to his rooms that night. He said he made it a rule to have a long night before playing cricket and – other games. His final word to me was framed on the same principle.

'Mind, only one drink to-night, Bunny. Two at the outside – as you value your life – and mine!'

I remember my abject obedience, and the endless, sleepless night it gave me; and the roofs of the houses opposite standing out at last against the blue-grey London dawn. I wondered whether I should ever see another, and was very hard on myself for that little expedition which I had made on my own wilful account.

It was between eight and nine o'clock in the evening when we took up our position in the garden adjoining that of Reuben Rosenthall; the house itself was shut up, thanks to the outrageous libertine next door, who, by driving away the neighbours, had gone far towards delivering himself into our hands.

Practically secure from surprise on that side, we could watch our house under cover of a wall just high enough to see over, while a fair margin of shrubs in either garden afforded us additional protection. Thus entrenched we had stood an hour, watching a pair of lighted bow-windows with vague shadows flitting continually across the blinds, and listening to the drawing of corks, the clink of glasses, and a gradual crescendo of coarse voices within. Our luck seemed to have deserted us; the owner of the purple diamonds was dining at home and dining at undue length. I thought it was a dinner-party. Raffles differed; in the end he proved right. Wheels grated in the drive, a carriage and pair stood at the steps; there was a stampede from the dining-room, and the loud voices died away, to burst forth presently from the porch.

Let me make our position perfectly clear. We were over the wall, at the side of the house, but a few feet from the dining-room windows. On our right, one angle of the building cut the back lawn in two, diagonally; on our left, another angle just permitted us to see the jutting steps and the waiting carriage. We saw Rosenthall come out – saw the glimmer of his diamonds before anything. Then came the pugilist; then a lady with a head of hair like a bath sponge; then another, and the party was complete.

Raffles ducked and pulled me down in great excitement.

'The ladies are going with them,' he whispered. 'This is great!'

'That's better still.'

'The Gardenia!' the millionaire had bawled.

'And that's best of all,' said Raffles, standing upright as hoofs and wheels crunched through the gates and rattled off at a fine speed.

'Now what?' I whispered, trembling with excitement.

'They'll be clearing away. Yes, here come their shadows. The drawing-room windows open on the lawn. Bunny, it's the psychological moment. Where's that mask?'

I produced it with a hand whose trembling I tried in vain to still, and could have died for Raffles when he made no comment on what he could not fail to notice. His own hands were firm and cool as he adjusted my mask for me, and then his own.

'By Jove, old boy,' he whispered cheerily, 'you look about the greatest ruffian I ever saw! These masks alone will down a nigger, if we meet one. But I'm glad I remembered to tell you not to shave. You'll pass for Whitechapel if the worst comes to the worst and you don't forget to talk the lingo. Better sulk like a mule if you're not sure of it, and leave the dialogue to me; but, please our stars, there will be no need. Now, are you ready?'

'Quite.'

'Got your gag?'

'Yes.'

'Shooter?'

'Yes.'

'Then follow me.'

In an instant we were over the wall, in another on the lawn behind the house. There was no moon. The very stars in their courses had veiled themselves for our benefit. I crept at my leader's heels to some french windows opening upon a shallow verandah. He pushed. They yielded.

'Luck again,' he whispered; 'nothing but luck! Now for a light.'

And the light came!

A good score of electric burners glowed red for the fraction of a second, then rained merciless white beams into our blinded eyes. When we found our sight, four revolvers covered us, and between two of them the colossal frame of Reuben Rosenthall shook with a wheezy laughter from head to foot.

'Good evening, boys,' he hiccoughed. 'Glad to see ye at last! Shift foot or finger, you on the left, though, and you're a dead boy. I mean you, you greaser!' he roared out at Raffles. 'I know you. I've been waitin' for you. I've been watching you all this week! Plucky smart you thought yerself, didn't you? One day beggin', next time shammin' tight, and next one o' them old pals from Kimberley who never come when I'm in. But you left the same tracks every day, you buggins, an' the same tracks every night, all round the blessed premises.'

'All right, guv'nor,' drawled Raffles; 'don't excite. It's a fair cop. We don't sweat to know 'ow you brung it orf. On'y don't you go for to shoot, 'cos we ain't awmed, s'help me Gord!'

'Ah, you're a knowin' one,' said Rosenthall, fingering his triggers. 'But you've struck a knowin'er.'

'Ho, yuss, we know all abaht thet! Set a thief to catch a thief – ho, yuss.'

My eyes had torn themselves from the round black muzzles, from the accursed diamonds that had been our snare, the pasty pig-face of the over-fed pugilist, and the flaming cheeks and hook-nose of Rosenthall himself. I was looking beyond them at the doorway filled with quivering silk and plush, black faces, white eyeballs, woolly pates. But a sudden silence recalled my attention to the millionaire. And only his nose retained its colour.

'What d'ye mean?' he whispered with a hoarse oath. 'Spit it out, or, by Christmas, I'll drill you!'

'Whort price thet brikewater?' drawled Raffles coolly.

'Eh?'

Rosenthall's revolvers were describing widening orbits.

'What price thet brikewater – old I.D.B.?'

'Where in hell did you get hold o' that?' asked Rosenthall, with a rattle in his thick neck meant for mirth.

'You may well arst,' says Raffles. 'It's all over the plice w'ere I come from.'

'Who can have spread such rot?'

'I dunno,' says Raffles; 'arst the gen'leman on yer left; p'raps 'e knows.'

The gentleman on his left had turned livid with emotion. Guilty conscience never declared itself in plainer terms. For a moment his small eyes bulged like currants in the suet of his face; the next, he had pocketed his pistols on a professional instinct, and was upon us with his fists.

'Out o' the light – out o' the light!' yelled Rosenthall in a frenzy.

He was too late. No sooner had the burly pugilist obstructed his fire than Raffles was through the window at a bound; while I, for standing still and saying nothing, was scientifically felled to the floor.

I cannot have been many moments without my senses. When I recovered them there was a great to-do in the garden, but I had the drawing-room to myself. I sat up. Rosenthall and

Purvis were rushing about outside, cursing the Kaffirs and nagging at each other.

'Over that wall, I tell yer!'

'I tell you it was this one. Can't you whistle for the police?'

'Police be damned! I've had enough of the blessed police.'

'Then we'd better get back and make sure of the other rotter.'

'Oh, make sure o' yer skin. That's what you'd better do. Jala, you black hog, if I catch you skulkin' ...'

I never heard the threat. I was creeping from the drawing-room on my hands and knees, my own revolver swinging by its steel ring from my teeth.

For an instant I thought that the hall also was deserted. I was wrong, and I crept upon a Kaffir on all-fours. Poor devil, I could not bring myself to deal him a base blow, but I threatened him most hideously with my revolver, and left the white teeth chattering in his black head as I took the stairs three at a time. Why I went upstairs in that decisive fashion, as though it were my only course, I cannot explain. But garden and ground floor seemed alive with men, and I might have done worse.

I turned into the first room I came to. It was a bedroom – empty, though lit up; and never shall I forget how I started as I entered, on encountering the awful villain that was myself at full length in a pier-glass! Masked, armed, and ragged, I was indeed fit carrion for a bullet or the hangman, and to one or the other I made up my mind. Nevertheless, I hid myself in the wardrobe behind the mirror, and there I stood shivering and cursing my fate, my folly, and Raffles most of all – Raffles first and last – for I dare say half an hour. Then the wardrobe door was flung suddenly open; they had stolen into the room without a sound; and I was hauled downstairs, an ignominious captive.

Gross scenes followed in the hall. The ladies were now upon the stage, and at sight of the desperate criminal they screamed with one accord. In truth I must have given them fair cause, though my mask was now torn away and hid nothing but my left ear. Rosenthall answered their shrieks with a roar for silence; the woman with the bath-sponge hair swore at him shrilly in return; the place became a Babel impossible to describe. I remember wondering how long it would be before the police appeared. Purvis and the ladies were for calling them in and giving me in charge without delay. Rosenthall would not hear of it. He swore that he would shoot man or woman who left his sight. He had had enough of the police. He was not going to have them coming there to spoil sport; he was going to deal with me in his own way. With that he dragged me from all other hands, flung me against a door, and sent a bullet crashing through the wood within an inch of my ear.

'You drunken fool! It'll be murder!' shouted Purvis, getting in the way a second time.

'Wha' do I care? He's armed, isn't he? I shot him in self-defence. It'll be a warning to others. Will you stand aside, or d'ye want it yourself?'

'You're drunk,' said Purvis, still between us. 'I saw you take a neat tumblerful since you came in, and it's made you drunk as a fool. Pull yourself together, old man. You ain't a-going to do what you'll be sorry for.'

'Then I won't shoot at him, I'll only shoot roun' an' roun' the beggar. You're quite right, ole feller. Wouldn't hurt him. Great mishtake. Roun' an' roun'. There – like that!'

His freckled paw shot up over Purvis's shoulder, mauve lightning came from his ring, a red flash from his revolver, and shrieks from the women as the reverberations died away. Some splinters lodged in my hair.

Next instant the prize-fighter disarmed him; and I was safe from the devil, but finally doomed to the deep sea. A policeman was in our midst. He had entered through the drawing-room window; he was an officer of few words and creditable promptitude. In a twinkling he had the handcuffs on my wrists, while the pugilist explained the situation, and his patron reviled the force and its representative with impotent malignity. A fine watch they kept; a lot of good they did; coming in when all was over and the whole household might have been murdered in their sleep. The officer only deigned to notice him as he marched me off.

'We know all about you, sir,' said he contemptuously, and he refused the sovereign Purvis proffered. 'You will be seeing me again, sir, at Marylebone.'

'Shall I come now?'

'As you please, sir. I rather think the other gentleman requires you more, and I don't fancy this young man means to
give much trouble.'

'Oh, I'm coming quietly,' I said.

And I went.

In silence we traversed perhaps a hundred yards. It must
have been midnight. We did not meet a soul. At last I whispered:

'How on earth did you manage it?'

'Purely by luck,' said Raffles. 'I had the luck to get clear away
through knowing every brick of those back-garden walls, and
the double luck to have these togs with the rest over at Chelsea.
The helmet is one of a collection I made up at Oxford; here it
goes over this wall, and we'd better carry the coat and belt before we meet a real officer. I got them once for a fancy ball –
ostensibly – and thereby hangs a yarn. I always thought they
might come in useful a second time. My chief crux to-night was
getting rid of the cab that brought me back. I sent him off to
Scotland Yard with ten bob and a special message to good old
Mackenzie. The whole detective department will be at Rosenthall's in about half an hour. Of course I speculated on our gentleman's hatred of the police – another huge slice of luck. If
you'd got away, well and good; if not, I felt he was the man to
play with his mouse as long as possible. Yes, Bunny, it's been
more of a costume piece than I intended, and we've come out of
it with a good deal less credit. But, by Jove, we're jolly lucky to
have come out of it at all!'

GENTLEMEN AND PLAYERS

OLD Raffles may or may not have been an exceptional criminal, but as a cricketer I dare swear he was unique. Himself a dangerous bat, a brilliant field, and perhaps the very finest slow bowler of his decade, he took incredibly little interest in the game at large. He never went up to Lord's without his cricket-bag, or showed the slightest interest in the result of a match in which he was not himself engaged. Nor was this mere hateful egotism on his part. He professed to have lost all enthusiasm for the game, and to keep it up only from the very lowest motives.

'Cricket,' said Raffles, 'like everything else, is good enough sport until you discover a better. As a source of excitement it isn't in it with other things you wot of, Bunny, and the involuntary comparison becomes a bore. What's the satisfaction of taking a man's wicket when you want his spoons? Still, if you can bowl a bit your low cunning won't get rusty, and always looking for the weak spot's just the kind of mental exercise one wants. Yes, perhaps there's some affinity between the two things after all. But I'd chuck up cricket to-morrow, Bunny, if it wasn't for the glorious protection it affords a person of my proclivities.'

'How so?' said I. 'It brings you before the public, I should have thought, far more than is either safe or wise.'

'My dear Bunny, that's exactly where you make a mistake. To follow crime with reasonable impunity you simply must have a parallel ostensible career – the more public the better. The principle is obvious. Mr Peace, of pious memory, disarmed suspicion by acquiring a local reputation for playing the fiddle and taming animals, and it's my profound conviction that Jack the Ripper was a really eminent public man, whose speeches were very likely reported alongside his atrocities. Fill the bill in some prominent part, and you'll never be suspected of doubling it with another of equal prominence. That's why I want you to cultivate journalism, my boy, and sign all you can. And it's the one and only reason why I don't burn my bats for firewood.'

Nevertheless, when he did play there was no keener performer on the field, nor one more anxious to do well for his side. I remember how he went to the nets, before the first match of the season, with his pocket full of sovereigns which he put on the stumps instead of bails. It was a sight to see the professionals bowling like demons for the hard cash, for whenever a stump was hit a pound was tossed to the bowler and another balanced in its stead, while one man took £3 with a ball that spread-eagled the wicket. Raffles's practice cost him either eight or nine sovereigns; he had absolutely first-class bowling all the time, and he made fifty-seven runs next day.

It became my pleasure to accompany him to all his matches, to watch every ball he bowled, or played, or fielded, and to sit chatting with him in the pavilion when he was doing none of these three things. You might have seen us there, side by side, during the greater part of the Gentlemen's first innings against the Players (who had lost the toss) on the second Monday in July. We were to be seen, but not heard, for Raffles had failed to score, and was uncommonly cross for a player who cared so little for the game. Merely taciturn with me, he was positively rude to more than one member who wanted to know how it had happened, or who ventured to commiserate him on his luck; there he sat, with a straw hat tilted over his nose and a cigarette stuck between lips that curled disagreeably at every advance. I was, therefore, much surprised when a young fellow of the exquisite type came and squeezed himself in between us, and met with a perfectly civil reception despite the liberty. I did not know the boy by sight, nor did Raffles introduce us; but their conversation proclaimed at once the slightness of acquaintanceship and a licence on the lad's part which combined to puzzle me. Mystification reached its height when Raffles was informed that the other's father was anxious to meet him, and he instantly consented to gratify that whim.

'He's in the Ladies' Enclosure. Will you come round now?'

'With pleasure,' said Raffles. 'Keep a place for me, Bunny.' And they were gone.

'Young Crowley,' said some voice farther back. 'Last year's Harrow Eleven.'

'I remember him. Worst man in the team.'

'Keen cricketer, however. Stopped till he was twenty to get his colours. Governor made him. Keen breed. Oh, pretty, sir! Very pretty!'

The game was boring me. I only came to see old Raffles perform. Soon I was looking wistfully for his return, and at length I saw him beckoning me from the palings to the right.

'Want to introduce you to old Amersteth,' he whispered, when I joined him. 'They've a cricket week next month, when this boy Crowley comes of age, and we've both got to go down and play.'

'Both!' I echoed. 'But I'm no cricketer!'

'Shut up,' says Raffles. 'Leave that to me. I've been lying for all I'm worth,' he added sepulchrally, as we reached the bottom of the steps. 'I trust to you not to give the show away.'

There was the gleam in his eye that I knew well enough elsewhere, but was unprepared for in those healthy, sane surroundings; and it was with very definite misgivings and surmises that I followed the Zingari blazer through the vast flower-bed of hats that bloomed beneath the ladies' awning.

Lord Amersteth was a fine-looking man with a short moustache and a double chin. He received me with much dry courtesy, through which, however, it was not difficult to read a less flattering tale. I was accepted as the inevitable appendage of the invaluable Raffles, with whom I felt deeply incensed as I made my bow.

'I have been bold enough,' said Lord Amersteth, 'to ask one of the Gentlemen of England to come down and play some rustic cricket for us next month. He is kind enough to say that he would have liked nothing better, but for this little fishing expedition of yours, Mr –, Mr –,' and Lord Amersteth succeeded in remembering my name.

It was, of course, the first I had ever heard of that fishing expedition, but I made haste to say that it could easily, and should certainly, be put off. Raffles gleamed approval through his eyelashes. Lord Amersteth bowed and shrugged.

'You're very good, I'm sure,' said he. 'But I understand you're a cricketer yourself?'

'He was one at school,' said Raffles, with infamous readiness.

'Not a real cricketer,' I was stammering meanwhile.

'In the eleven?' said Lord Amersteth.

'I'm afraid not,' said I.

'But only just out of it,' declared Raffles, to my horror.

'Well, well, we can't all play for the Gentlemen,' said Lord Amersteth slyly. 'My son Crowley only just scraped into the eleven at Harrow, and he's going to play. I may even come in myself at a pinch; so you won't be the only duffer, if you are one, and I shall be very glad if you will come down and help us too. You shall flog a stream before breakfast and after dinner, if you like.'

'I should be very proud,' I was beginning, as the mere prelude to resolute excuses; but the eye of Raffles opened wide upon me; and I hesitated weakly, to be duly lost.

'Then that's settled,' said Lord Amersteth, with the slightest suspicion of grimness. 'It's to be a little week, you know, when my son comes of age. We play the Free Foresters, the Dorsetshire Gentlemen, and probably some local lot as well. But Mr Raffles will tell you all about it, and Crowley shall write. Another wicket! By Jove, they're all out! Then I rely on you both.' And, with a little nod, Lord Amersteth rose and sidled to the gangway.

Raffles rose also, but I caught the sleeve of his blazer.

'What are you thinking of?' I whispered savagely. 'I was nowhere near the eleven. I'm no sort of cricketer. I shall have to get out of this!'

'Not you,' he whispered back. 'You needn't play, but come you must. If you wait for me after half-past six, I'll tell you why.'

But I could guess the reason; and I am ashamed to say that it revolted me much less than did the notion of making a public fool of myself on a cricket-field. My gorge rose at this as it no longer rose at crime, and it was in no tranquil humour that I strolled about the ground while Raffles disappeared in the pavilion. Nor was my annoyance lessened by a little meeting I witnessed between young Crowley and his father, who shrugged as he stopped and stooped to convey some information which made the young man look a little blank. It may have been pure self-consciousness on my part, but I could have sworn that the trouble was their inability to secure the great Raffles without his insignificant friend.

Then the bell rang, and I climbed to the top of the pavilion to watch Raffles bowl. No subtleties are lost up there; and if ever a bowler was full of them, it was A. J. Raffles on this day, as, indeed, all the cricket world remembers. One had not to be a cricketer oneself to appreciate his perfect command of pitch and break, his beautifully easy action, which never varied with the varying pace, his great ball on the leg-stump – his dropping head-ball – in a word, the infinite ingenuity of that versatile attack. It was no mere exhibition of athletic prowess, it was an intellectual treat, and one with a special significance in my eyes. I saw the 'affinity between the two things,' saw it in that afternoon's tireless warfare against the flower of professional cricket. It was not that Raffles took many wickets for a few runs; he was too fine a bowler to mind being hit; and time was short, and the wicket good. What I admired, and what I remember, was the combination of resource and cunning, of patience and precision, of hard work and handiwork, which made every over an artistic whole. It was all so characteristic of that other Raffles whom I alone knew!

'I felt like bowling this afternoon,' he told me later – in the cab. 'With a pitch to help me, I'd have done something big; as it is, three for forty-one, out of the four that fell, isn't bad for a slow bowler on a plumb wicket against those fellows. But I felt venomous! Nothing riles me more than being asked about for my cricket as though I were a pro myself.'

'Then why on earth go?'

'To punish them, and – because we shall be jolly hard up, Bunny, before the season's over!'

'Ah!' said I. 'I thought it was that.'

'Of course it was! It seems they're going to have the very devil of a week of it – balls – dinner-parties – swagger house-party – general junketings – and, obviously, a houseful of diamonds as well. Diamonds galore! As a general rule nothing would induce me to abuse my position as a guest. I've never done it, Bunny. But in this case we're engaged like the waiters and the band, and by heaven we'll take our toll! Let's have a quiet dinner somewhere and talk it over.'

'It seems rather a vulgar sort of theft,' I could not help saying; and to this, my single protest, Raffles instantly assented.

'It is a vulgar sort,' said he; 'but I can't help that. We're getting vulgarly hard up again, and there's an end on't. Besides, these people deserve it and can afford it. And don't you run away with the idea that all will be plain sailing; nothing will be easier than getting some stuff, and nothing harder than avoiding all suspicion, as, of course, we must. We may come away with no more than a good working plan of the premises. Who knows? In any case, there's weeks of thinking in it for you and me.'

But with those weeks I will not weary you further than by remarking that the 'thinking' was done entirely by Raffles, who did not always trouble to communicate his thoughts to me. His reticence, however, was no longer an irritant. I began to accept it as a necessary convention of these little enterprises. And, after our last adventure of the kind, more especially after its *dénouement*, my trust in Raffles was much too solid to be shaken by a want of trust in me, which I still believe to have been more the instinct of the criminal than the judgment of the man.

It was on Monday, August 10, that we were due at Milchester Abbey, Dorset; and the beginning of the month found us cruising about that very county, with fly-rods actually in our hands. The idea was that we should acquire at once a local reputation as decent fishermen, and some knowledge of the countryside, with a view to further and more deliberate operations in the event of an unprofitable week. There was another idea which Raffles kept to himself until he had got me down there. Then one day he produced a cricket-ball in a meadow we were crossing, and threw me catches for an hour together. More hours he spent in bowling to me on the nearest green; and, if I was never a cricketer, at least I came nearer to being one, by the end of that week, than ever before or since.

Incident began early on the Monday. We had sallied forth from a desolate little junction within quite a few miles of Milchester, had been caught in a shower, had run for shelter to a wayside inn. A florid, overdressed man was drinking in the parlour, and I could have sworn it was at the sight of him that

Raffles recoiled on the threshold, and afterwards insisted on returning to the station through the rain. He assured me, however, that the odour of stale ale had almost knocked him down. And I had to make what I could of his speculative, downcast eyes and knitted brows.

Milchester Abbey is a grey, quadrangular pile, deep-set in rich woody country, and twinkling with triple rows of quaint windows, every one of which seemed alight as we drove up just in time to dress for dinner. The carriage had whirled us under I know not how many triumphal arches in process of construction, and past the tents and flag-poles of a juicy-looking cricket-field, on which Raffles undertook to bowl up to his reputation. But the chief signs of festival were within, where we found an enormous house-party assembled, including more persons of pomp, majesty, and dominion than I had ever encountered in one room before. I confess I felt overpowered. Our errand and my own pretences combined to rob me of an address upon which I had sometimes plumed myself; and I have a grim recollection of my nervous relief when dinner was at last announced. I little knew what an ordeal it was to prove.

I had taken in a much less formidable young lady than might have fallen to my lot. Indeed, I began by blessing my good fortune in this respect. Miss Melhuish was merely the rector's daughter, and she had only been asked to make an even number. She informed me of both facts before the soup reached us, and her subsequent conversation was characterised by the same engaging candour. It exposed what was little short of a mania for imparting information. I had simply to listen, to nod, and be thankful. When I confessed to knowing very few of those present, even by sight, my entertaining companion proceeded to tell me who everybody was, beginning on my left and working conscientiously round to her right. This lasted quite a long time, and really interested me; but a great deal that followed did not: and, obviously to recapture my unworthy attention, Miss Melhuish suddenly asked me, in a sensational whisper, whether I could keep a secret.

I said I thought I might, whereupon another question followed, in still lower and more thrilling accents:

'Are you afraid of burglars?'

Burglars! I was roused at last. The word stabbed me. I repeated it in horrified query.

'So I've found something to interest you at last!' said Miss Melhuish in naïve triumph. 'Yes – burglars! But don't speak so loud. It's supposed to be kept a great secret. I really oughtn't to tell you at all!'

'But what is there to tell?' I whispered, with satisfactory impatience.

'You promise not to speak of it?'

'Of course!'

'Well, then, there are burglars in the neighbourhood.'

'Have they committed any robberies?'

'Not yet.'

'Then how do you know?'

'They've been seen. In the district. Two well-known London thieves!'

Two! I looked at Raffles. I had done so often during the evening, envying him his high spirits, his iron nerve, his buoyant wit, his perfect ease, and his self-possession. But now I pitied him; through all my own terror and consternation I pitied him as he sat eating and drinking, and laughing, and talking, without a cloud of fear or of embarrassment on his handsome, taking, dare-devil face. I caught up my champagne and emptied the glass.

'Who has seen them?' I then asked calmly.

'A detective. They were traced down from town a few days ago. They are believed to have designs on the Abbey!'

'But why aren't they run in?'

'Exactly what I asked papa on the way here this evening; he says there is no warrant out against the men at present, and all that can be done is to watch their movements.'

'Oh! so they are being watched?'

'Yes, by a detective who is down here on purpose. And I heard Lord Amersteth tell papa that they had been seen this afternoon at Warbeck Junction.'

The very place where Raffles and I had been caught in the rain! Our stampede from the inn was now explained; on the other hand, I was no longer to be taken by surprise by anything that my companion might have to tell me; and I succeeded in looking her in the face with a smile.

'This is really quite exciting, Miss Melhuish,' said I. 'May I ask how you come to know so much about it?'

'It's papa,' was the confidential reply. 'Lord Amersteth consulted him, and he consulted me. But for goodness' sake don't let it get about! I can't think what tempted me to tell you!'

'You may trust me, Miss Melhuish. But – aren't you frightened?'

Miss Melhuish giggled.

'Not a bit! They won't come to the rectory. There's nothing for them there. But look round the table; look at the diamonds. Look at old Lady Melrose's necklace alone!'

The Dowager Marchioness of Melrose was one of the few persons whom it had been unnecessary to point out to me. She sat on Lord Amersteth's right, flourishing her ear-trumpet, and drinking champagne with her usual notorious freedom, as dissipated and kindly a dame as the world has ever seen. It was a necklace of diamonds and sapphires that rose and fell about her ample neck.

'They say it's worth five thousand pounds at least,' continued my companion. 'Lady Margaret told me so this morning (that's Lady Margaret next your Mr Raffles, you know); and the old dear will wear them every night. Think what a haul they would be! No; we don't feel in immediate danger at the rectory.'

When the ladies rose, Miss Melhuish bound me to fresh vows of secrecy; and left me, I should think, with some remorse for her indiscretion, but more satisfaction at the importance which it had undoubtedly given her in my eyes. The opinion may smack of vanity, though, in reality, the very springs of conversation reside in that same human universal itch to thrill the auditor. The peculiarity of Miss Melhuish was that she must be thrilling at all costs. And thrilling she had surely been.

I spare you my feelings of the next two hours. I tried hard to get a word with Raffles, but again and again I failed. In the dining-room he and Crowley lit their cigarettes with the same match, and had their heads together all the time. In the drawing-room I had the mortification of hearing him talk interminable nonsense into the ear-trumpet of Lady Melrose, whom he knew in town. Lastly, in the billiard-room, they had a great and lengthy pool, while I sat aloof and chafed more than ever in the company of a very serious Scotsman, who had arrived since dinner, and who would talk of nothing but the recent improvements in instantaneous photography. He had not come to play in the matches (he told me), but to obtain for Lord Amersteth such a series of cricket photographs as had never been taken before; whether as an amateur or a professional photographer I was unable to determine. I remember, however, seeking distraction in little bursts of resolute attention to the conversation of this bore. And so at last the long ordeal ended : glasses were emptied, men said good night, and I followed Raffles to his room.

'It's all up!' I gasped, as he turned up the gas and I shut the door. 'We're being watched. We've been followed down from town. There's a detective here on the spot!'

'How do you know?' asked Raffles, turning upon me quite sharply, but without the least dismay. And I told him how I knew.

'Of course,' I added, 'it was the fellow we saw in the inn this afternoon.'

'The detective?' said Raffles. 'Do you mean to say you don't know a detective when you see one, Bunny?'

'If that wasn't the fellow, which is?'

Raffles shook his head.

'To think that you've been talking to him for the last hour in the billiard-room, and couldn't spot what he was!'

'The Scotch photographer – '

I paused aghast.

'Scotch he is,' said Raffles, 'and photographer he may be. He is also Inspector Mackenzie of Scotland Yard – the very man I sent the message to that night last April. And you couldn't spot who he was in a whole hour! Oh, Bunny, Bunny, you were never built for crime!'

'But,' said I, 'if that was Mackenzie, who was the fellow you bolted from at Warbeck?'

'The man he's watching.'

'But he's watching us!'

Raffles looked at me with a pitying eye, and shook his head again before handing me his open cigarette-case.

'I don't know whether smoking's forbidden in one's bed-room, but you'd better take one of these and stand tight, Bunny, because I'm going to say something offensive.'

I helped myself with a laugh.

'Say what you like, my dear fellow, if it really isn't you and me that Mackenzie's after.'

'Well, then, it isn't, and it couldn't be, and nobody but a born Bunny would suppose for a moment that it was! Do you seriously think he would sit there and knowingly watch his man playing pool under his nose? Well, he might; he's a cool hand, Mackenzie; but I'm not cool enough to win a pool under such conditions. At least, I don't think I am; it would be interesting to see. The situation wasn't free from strain as it was, though I knew he wasn't thinking of us. Crowley told me all about it after dinner, you see, and then I'd seen one of the men for myself this afternoon. You thought it was a detective who made me turn tail at that inn. I really don't know why I didn't tell you at the time, but it was just the opposite. That loud, red-faced brute is one of the cleverest thieves in London, and I once had a drink with him and our mutual fence. I was an East-ender from tongue to toe at the moment, but you will understand that I don't run unnecessary risks of recognition by a brute like that.'

'He's not alone, I hear.'

'By no means; there's at least one other man with him; and it's suggested that there may be an accomplice here in the house.'

'Did Lord Crowley tell you so?'

'Crowley and the champagne between them. In confidence, of course, just as your girl told you; but even in confidence he never let on about Mackenzie. He told me there was a detective in the background, but that was all. Putting him up as a guest is evidently their big secret, to be kept from the other guests because it might offend them, but more particularly from the servants whom he's here to watch. That's my reading of the situation. Bunny, and you will agree with me that it's infinitely more interesting than we could have imagined it would prove.

'But infinitely more difficult for us,' said I, with a sigh of pusillanimous relief. 'Our hands are tied for this week, at all events.'

'Not necessarily, my dear Bunny, though I admit that the chances are against us. Yet I'm not so sure of that either. There are all sorts of possibilities in these three-cornered combinations. Set A to watch B, and he won't have an eye left for C. That's the obvious theory, but then Mackenzie's a very big A. I should be sorry to have any boodle about me with that man in the house. Yet it would be great to nip in between A and B and score off them both at once! It would be worth a risk, Bunny, to do that; it would be worth risking something merely to take on old hands like B and his men at their old game! Eh, Bunny? That would be something like a match. Gentlemen and Players at single wicket, by Jove!'

His eyes were brighter than I had known them for many a day. They shone with the perverted enthusiasm which was roused in him only by the contemplation of some new audacity. He kicked off his shoes and began pacing his room with noiseless rapidity; not since the night of the Old Bohemian dinner to Reuben Rosenthall had Raffles exhibited such excitement in my presence; and I was not sorry at the moment to be reminded of the fiasco to which that banquet had been the prelude.

'My dear A. J.,' said I in his very own tone, 'you're far too fond of the uphill game; you will eventually fall a victim to the sporting spirit and nothing else. Take a lesson from our last escape, and fly lower as you value our skins. Study the house as much as you like but do – not – go and shove your head into Mackenzie's mouth!'

My wealth of metaphor brought him to a standstill, with his cigarette between his fingers and a grin beneath his shining eyes.

'You're quite right, Bunny. I won't. I really won't. Yet – you saw old Lady Melrose's necklace? I've been wanting it for years! But I'm not going to play the fool, honour bright, I'm not; yet – by Jove! – to get to windward of the professors and Mackenzie too! It would be a great game, Bunny, it would be a great game!'

'Well, you mustn't play it this week.'

'No, no, I won't. But I wonder how the professors think of going to work? That's what one wants to know. I wonder if they've really got an accomplice in the house? How I wish I knew their game! But it's all right, Bunny; don't you be jealous; it shall be as you wish."

And with that assurance I went off to my own room and so to bed with an incredibly light heart. I had still enough of the honest man in me to welcome the postponement of our actual felonies, to dread their performance, and to deplore their necessity; which is merely another way of stating the too patent fact that I was an incomparably weaker man than Raffles, while every whit as wicked. I had, however, one rather strong point. I possessed the gift of dismissing unpleasant considerations, not intimately connected with the passing moment, entirely from my mind. Through the exercise of this faculty I had lately been living my frivolous life in town with as much ignoble enjoyment as I had derived from it the year before; and similarly, here at Milchester, in the long-dreaded cricket-week, I had after all a quite excellent time.

It is true that there were other factors in this pleasing disappointment. In the first place, *mirabile dictu,* there were one or two even greater duffers than I on the Abbey cricket-field. Indeed, quite early in the week, when it was of most value to me, I gained considerable kudos for a lucky catch; a ball, of which I had merely heard the hum, stuck fast in my hand, which Lord Amersteth himself grasped in public congratulation. This happy accident was not to be undone even by me, and, as nothing succeeds like success, and the constant encouragement of the one great cricketer on the field was in itself an immense stimulus, I actually made a run or two in my very next innings. Miss Melhuish said pretty things to me that night at the great ball in honour of Viscount Crowley's majority; she also told me that was the night on which the robbers would assuredly make their raid, and was full of arch tremors when we sat out in the garden, though the entire premises were illuminated all night long. Meanwhile, the quiet Scotsman took countless photographs by day, which he developed by night in a dark room admirably situated in the servants' part of the house; and it is my firm belief that only two of his fellow-guests knew Mr

Clephane of Dundee for Inspector Mackenzie of Scotland Yard.

The week was to end with a trumpery match on the Saturday, which two or three of us intended abandoning early in order to return to town that night. The match, however, was never played. In the small hours of the Saturday morning a tragedy took place at Milchester Abbey

Let me tell of the thing as I saw and heard it. My room opened upon the central gallery, and was not even on the same floor as that on which Raffles – and I think all the other men – were quartered. I had been put, in fact, into the dressing-room of one of the grand suites, and my two near neighbours were old Lady Melrose and my host and hostess. Now, by the Friday evening the actual festivities were at an end, and, for the first time that week, I must have been sound asleep since midnight, when all at once I found myself sitting up breathless. A heavy thud had come against my door, and now I heard hard breathing and the dull stamp of muffled feet.

'I've got ye,' muttered a voice. 'It's no use struggling.'

It was the Scotch detective, and a new fear turned me cold. There was no reply, but the hard breathing grew harder still, and the muffled feet beat the floor to a quicker measure. In sudden panic I sprang out of bed and flung open my door. A light burnt low on the landing, and by it I could see Mackenzie swaying and staggering in a silent tussle with some powerful adversary.

'Hold this man!' he cried, as I appeared. 'Hold the rascal!'

But I stood like a fool until the pair of them backed into me, when, with a deep breath, I flung myself on the fellow, whose face I had seen at last. He was one of the footmen who waited at table; and no sooner had I pinned him than the detective loosed his hold.

'Hang on to him,' he cried. 'There's more of 'em below.'

And he went leaping down the stairs, as other doors opened, and Lord Amersteth and his son appeared simultaneously in their pyjamas. At that my man ceased struggling, but I was still holding him when Crowley turned up the gas.

'What the devil's all this?' asked Lord Amersteth, blinking. 'Who was that ran downstairs?'

'Clephane!' said I hastily.

'Aha!' said he, turning to the footman. 'So you're the scoundrel, are you? Well done! Well done! Where was he caught?'

I had no idea.

'Here's Lady Melrose's door open,' said Crowley. 'Lady Melrose! Lady Melrose!'

'You forget she is deaf,' said Lord Amersteth. 'Ah! that'll be her maid.'

An inner door had opened; next instant there was a little shriek, and a white figure gesticulated on the threshold.

'Où donc est l'écrin de Madame la Marquise? La fenêtre est ouverte. Il a disparu!'

'Window open and jewel-case gone, by Jove!' exclaimed Lord Amersteth. 'Mais comment est Madame la Marquise? Est-elle bien?'

'Oui, milord. Elle dort.'

'Sleeps through it all,' said my lord. 'She's the only one, then!'

'What made Mackenzie – Clephane – bolt?' young Crowley asked me.

'Said there were more of them below.'

'Why the devil couldn't you tell us so before?' he cried, and went leaping downstairs in his turn.

He was followed by nearly all the cricketers, who now burst upon the scene in a body, only to desert it for the chase. Raffles was one of them, and I would gladly have been another, had not the footman chosen this moment to hurl me from him, and to make a dash in the direction from which they had come. Lord Amersteth had him in an instant; but the fellow fought desperately, and it took the two of us to drag him downstairs, amid a terrified chorus from half-open doors. Eventually we handed him over to two other footmen who appeared with their night-shirts tucked into their trousers, and my host was good enough to compliment me as he led the way outside.

'I thought I heard a shot,' he added. 'Didn't you?'

'I thought I heard three.'

And out we dashed into the darkness.

I remember how the gravel pricked my feet, how the wet grass numbed them as we made for the sound of voices on an outlying lawn. So dark was the night that we were in the cricketers' midst before we saw the shimmer of their pyjamas, and then Lord Amersteth almost trod on Mackenzie as he lay prostrate in the dew.

'Who's this?' he cried. 'What on earth's happened?'

'It's Clephane,' said a man who knelt over him. 'He's got a bullet in him somewhere.'

'Is he alive?'

'Barely.'

'Good God! Where's Crowley?'

'Here I am,' called a breathless voice. 'It's no good, you fellows. There's nothing to show which way they've gone. Here's Raffles; he's chucked it, too.' And they ran up panting.

'Well, we've got one of them, at all events,' muttered Lord Amersteth. 'The next thing is to get this poor fellow indoors. Take his shoulders, somebody. Now his middle. Join hands under him. Altogether, now; that's the way. Poor fellow! Poor fellow! His name isn't Clephane at all. He's a Scotland Yard detective, down here for these very villains!'

Raffles was the first to express surprise; but he had also been the first to raise the wounded man. Nor had any of them a stronger or more tender hand in the slow procession to the house. In a little we had the senseless man stretched on a sofa in the library. And there, with ice on his wound and brandy in his throat, his eyes opened and his lips moved.

Lord Amersteth bent down to catch the words.

'Yes, yes,' said he, 'we've got one of them safe and sound. The brute you collared upstairs.' Lord Amersteth bent lower. 'By Jove! Lowered the jewel-case out of the window, did he? And they've got clean away with it! Well, well! I only hope we'll be able to pull this good fellow through. He's off again.'

An hour passed; the sun was rising.

It found a dozen young fellows on the settees in the billiard-room, drinking whisky and soda-water in their overcoats and pyjamas, and still talking excitedly in one breath. A time-table was being passed from hand to hand: the doctor was still in the library. At last the door opened, and Lord Amersteth put in his head.

'It isn't hopeless,' said he, 'but it's bad enough. There'll be no cricket to-day.'

Another hour, and most of us were on our way to catch the early train; between us we filled a compartment almost to suffocation. And still we talked all together of the night's event; and still I was a little hero in my way, for having kept my hold of the one ruffian who had been taken; and my gratification was subtle and intense. Raffles watched me under lowered lids. Not a word had we had together; not a word did we have until we had left the others at Paddington, and were swimming through the streets in a hansom with noiseless tyres and a tinkling bell.

'Well, Bunny,' said Raffles, 'so the professors have it, eh?'

'Yes,' said I. 'And I'm jolly glad!'

'That poor Mackenzie has a ball in his chest?'

'That you and I have been on the decent side for once.'

He shrugged his shoulders.

'You're hopeless, Bunny, quite hopeless! I take it you wouldn't have refused your share if the boodle had fallen to us? Yet you positively enjoy coming off second best – for the second time running! I confess, however, that the professors' methods were full of interest to me. I, for one, have probably gained as much in experience as I have lost in other things. That lowering the jewel-case out of the window was a very simple and effective expedient; two of them had been waiting below for it for hours.'

'How did you know?' I asked.

'I saw them from my own window, which was just above the dear old lady's. I was fretting for that necklace in particular, when I went up to turn in for our last night – and I happened to look out of the window. In point of fact, I wanted to see whether the one below was open, and whether there was the slightest chance of working the oracle with my sheet for a rope. Of course, I took the precaution of turning my light off first, and it was a lucky thing I did. I saw the pros right down below, and they never saw me. I saw a little tiny luminous disc just for an instant, and then again for an instant a few minutes later. Of course, I knew what it was, for I have my own watch-dial daubed with luminous paint; it makes a lantern of sorts when you can get no better. But these fellows were not using theirs as a lantern. They were under the old lady's window. They were watching the time. The whole thing was arranged with their accomplice inside. Set a thief to catch a thief; in a minute I had guessed what the whole thing proved to be.'

'And you did nothing!' I exclaimed.

'On the contrary, I went downstairs and straight into Lady Melrose's room – –'

'You did?'

'Without a moment's hesitation. To save her jewels. And I was prepared to yell as much into her ear-trumpet for all the house to hear. But the dear lady is too deaf and too fond of her dinner to wake easily.'

'Well?'

'She didn't stir.'

'And yet you allowed the professors, as you call them, to take her jewels, case and all!'

'All but this,' said Raffles, thrusting his fist into my lap. 'I would have shown it you before, but really, old fellow, your face all day has been worth a fortune to the firm!'

And he opened his fist, to shut it next instant on the bunch of diamonds and of sapphires that I had last seen encircling the neck of Lady Melrose.

LE PREMIER PAS

THAT night he told me the story of his earliest crime. Not since the fateful morning of the Ides of March, when he had just mentioned it as an unreported incident of a certain cricket tour, had I succeeded in getting a word out of Raffles on the subject. It was not for want of trying; he would shake his head, and watch his cigarette smoke thoughtfully; a subtle look in his eyes, half cynical, half wistful, as though the decent honest days that were no more had had their merits after all. Raffles would plan a fresh enormity, or glory in the last, with the unmitigated enthusiasm of the artist. It was impossible to imagine one throb or twitter of compunction beneath those frankly egoistic and infectious transports. And yet the ghost of a dead remorse seemed still to visit him with the memory of his first felony, so that I had given the story up long before the night of our return from Milchester. Cricket, however, was in the air, and Raffles's cricket-bag back where he sometimes kept it, in the fender, with the remains of an old Orient label still adhering to the leather. My eyes had been on this label for some time, and I suppose his eyes had been on mine, for all at once he asked me if I still burned to hear that yarn.

'It's no use,' I replied. 'You won't spin it. I must imagine it for myself.'

'How can you?'

'Oh, I begin to know your methods.'

'You take it I went with my eyes open, as I do now, eh?'

'I can't imagine your doing otherwise.'

'My dear Bunny, it was the most unpremeditated thing I ever did in my life!'

His chair wheeled back into the books as he sprang up with sudden energy. There was quite an indignant glitter in his eyes.

'I can't believe that,' said I craftily. 'I can't pay you such a poor compliment.'

'Then you must be a fool – –'

He broke off, stared hard at me, and in a trice stood smiling in his own despite.

'Or a better knave than I thought you, Bunny, and by Jove, it's the knave! Well – I suppose I'm fairly drawn; I give you best, as they say out here. As a matter of fact, I've been thinking of the thing myself; last night's racket reminds me of it in one or two respects. I tell you what, though, this is an occasion in any case, and I'm going to celebrate it by breaking the one good rule of my life. I'm going to have a second drink!'

The whisky tinkled, the siphon fizzed, and ice plopped home; and seated there in his pyjamas, with the inevitable cigarette, Raffles told me the story that I had given up hoping to hear. The windows were wide open; the sounds of Piccadilly floated in at first. Long before he finished, the last wheels had rattled, the last brawler was removed, we alone broke the quiet of the summer night.

'... No, they do you very well indeed. You pay for nothing but drinks, so to speak, but I'm afraid mine were of a comprehensive character. I had started in a hole, I ought really to have refused the invitation; then we all went to the Melbourne Cup, and I had the certain winner that didn't win, and that's not the only way you can play the fool in Melbourne. I wasn't the steady old stager I am now, Bunny; my analysis was a confession in itself. But the others didn't know how hard up I was, and I swore they shouldn't. I tried the Jews, but they're extra fly out there. Then I thought of a kinsman of sorts, a second cousin of my father's whom none of us knew anything about, except that he was supposed to be in one or other of the Colonies. If he were a rich man, well and good, I would work him; if not there would be no harm done. I tried to get on his tracks, and, as luck would have it, I succeeded (or thought I had) at the very moment when I happened to have a few days to myself. I was cut on the hand, just before the big Christmas match, and couldn't have bowled a ball if they had played me.

'The surgeon who fixed me up happened to ask me if I was any relation of Raffles of the National Bank, and the pure luck of it almost took my breath away. A relation who was a high official in one of the banks, who would finance me on my mere name – could anything be better? I made up my mind that this Raffles was the man I wanted, and was awfully sold to find next moment that he wasn't a high official at all. Nor had the doctor so much as met him, but had merely read of him in connection with a small sensation at the suburban branch which my namesake managed; an armed robber had been rather pluckily beaten off, with a bullet in him, by this Raffles; and the sort of thing was so common out there that this was the first I had heard of it! A suburban branch – my financier had faded into some excellent fellow with a billet to lose if he called his soul his own. Still a manager was a manager, and I said I would soon see whether this was the relative I was looking for, if he would be good enough to give me the name of that branch.

' "I'll do more," said the doctor. "I'll give you the name of the branch he's been promoted to, for I think I heard they'd moved him up one already." And the next day he brought me the name of the township of Yea, some fifty miles north of Melbourne; but, with the vagueness which characterised all his information, he was unable to say whether I should find my relative there or not.

' "He's a single man, and his initials are W. F.," said the doctor, who was certain enough of the immaterial points. "He left his old post several days ago, but it appears he's not due at the new one till the New Year. No doubt he'll go before then to take things over and settle in. You might find him up there and you might not. If I were you I should write."

' "That'll lose two days," said I, "and more if he isn't there," for I'd grown quite keen on this up-country manager, and I felt that if I could get at him while the holidays were still on, a little conviviality might help matters considerably.

' "Then," said the doctor, "I should get a quiet horse and ride. You needn't use that hand."

' "Can't I go by train?"

' "You can and you can't. You would still have to ride. I suppose you're a horseman?"

' "Yes."

' "Then I should certainly ride all the way. It's a delightful road, through Whittlesea and over the Plenty Ranges. It'll give you some idea of the bush, Mr Raffles, and you'll see the sources of the water-supply of this city, sir. You'll see where every drop of it comes from, the pure Yan Yean! I wish I had time to ride with you."

' "But where can I get a horse?"

'The doctor thought a moment.

' "I've a mare of my own that's as fat as butter for want of work," said he. "It would be a charity to me to sit on her back for a hundred miles or so, and then I should know you'd have no temptation to use that hand."

' "You're far too good," I protested.

' "You're A. J. Raffles," he said.

'And if ever there was a prettier compliment or a finer instance of even Colonial hospitality, I can only say, Bunny, that I never heard of either.'

He sipped his whisky, threw away the stump of his cigarette, and lit another before continuing.

'Well, I managed to write a line to W. F. with my own hand, which, as you will gather, was not very badly wounded; it was simply this third finger that was split and in splints; the next morning the doctor packed me off on a bovine beast that would have done for an ambulance. Half the team came up to see me start; the rest were rather sick with me for not stopping to see the match out, as if I could help them to win by watching them. They little knew the game I'd got on myself, but still less did I know the game I was going to play.

'It was an interesting ride enough, especially after passing the place called Whittlesea, a real wild township on the lower slopes of the ranges, where I recollect having a deadly meal of hot mutton and tea with the thermometer at three figures in the shade. The first thirty miles or so was a good metal road, too good to go half round the world to ride on, but after Whittlesea it was a mere track over the ranges, a track I often couldn't see and left entirely to the mare. Now it dipped into a gully and ran through a creek, and all the time the local colour was inches thick: gum trees galore and parrots all colours of the rainbow. In one place a whole forest of gums had been ringbarked, and were just as though they had been painted white, without a leaf or a living thing for miles. And the first living thing I did meet was the sort to give you the creeps; it was a riderless horse coming full tilt through the bush, with the saddle twisted round and the stirrup-irons ringing. Without thinking, I had a shot at heading him with the doctor's mare, and blocked him just enough to allow a man who came galloping after to do the rest.

' "Thank ye, mister," growled the man, a huge chap in a red checked shirt, with a beard like W. G. Grace, but the very devil of an expression.

' "Been an accident?" said I, reining up.

' "Yes," said he, scowling as though he defied me to ask any more.

' "And a nasty one," I said, "if that's blood on the saddle!"

'Well, Bunny, I may be a blackguard myself, but I don't think I ever looked at a fellow as that chap looked at me. But I stared him out, and forced him to admit that it was blood on the twisted saddle, and after that he became quite tame. He told me exactly what had happened. A mate of his had been dragged under a branch, and had his nose smashed, but that was all; had sat tight after it till he dropped from loss of blood, another mate was with him back in the bush.

'As I've said already, Bunny, I wasn't the old stager that I am now – in any respect – and we parted good enough friends. He asked me which way I was going, and when I told him, he said I should save seven miles, and get a good hour earlier to Yea, by striking off the track and making for a peak that we could see through the trees and following a creek that I should see from the peak. Don't smile, Bunny! I began by saying I was a child in those days. Of course, the short cut was the long way round; and it was nearly dark when that unlucky mare and I saw the single street of Yea.

'I was looking for the bank when a fellow in a white suit ran down from the verandah.

' "Mr Raffles?" said he.

' "Mr Raffles!" said I, laughing, as I shook his hand.

' "You're late."

' "I was misdirected."

' "That all? I'm relieved," he said. "Do you know what they

are saying? There are some brand-new bushrangers on the road between Whittlesea and this – a second Kelly gang! They'd have caught a Tartar in you, eh?"

' "They would in you," I retorted, and my *tu quoque* shut him up and seemed to puzzle him. Yet there was much more sense in it than in his compliment to me, which was absolutely pointless.

' "I'm afraid you'll find things pretty rough," he resumed, when he had unstrapped my valise, and handed my reins to his man. "It's lucky you're a bachelor like myself."

'I could not quite see the point of this remark either, since, had I been married, I should hardly have sprung my wife upon him in this free-and-easy fashion. I muttered the conventional sort of thing, and then he said I should find it all right when I settled, as though I had come to graze upon him for weeks! "Well," thought I, "these Colonials do take the cake for hospitality!" And, still marvelling, I let him lead me into the private part of the bank.

' "Dinner will be ready in a quarter of an hour," said he, as we entered. "I thought you might like a tub first, and you'll find all ready in the room at the end of the passage. Sing out if there's anything you want. Your luggage hasn't turned up yet, by the way, but here's a letter that came this morning."

' "Not for me?"

' "Yes; didn't you expect one?"

' "I certainly did not!"

' "Well, here it is."

'And, as he lit me to my room, I read my own superscription of the previous day – to W. F. Raffles!

'Bunny, you've had your wind bagged at footer, I dare say; you know what that's like? All I can say is that my moral wind was bagged by that letter as I hope, old chap, I have never yet bagged yours. I couldn't speak. I could only stand with my own letter in my hands until he had the good taste to leave me by myself.

'W. F. Raffles! We had mistaken each other for W. F. Raffles – for the new manager who had not yet arrived! Small wonder we had conversed at cross-purposes; the only wonder was that we had not discovered our mutual mistake. How the other man would have laughed! But I – I could not laugh. By Jove, no, it was no laughing matter for me! I saw the whole thing in a flash, without a tremor, but with the direct depression from my own single point of view. Call it callous if you like, Bunny, but remember that I was in much the same hole as you've since been in yourself, and that I had counted on W. F. Raffles even as you counted on A. J. I thought of the man with the W. G. beard – the riderless horse with the bloody saddle – the deliberate misdirection that had put me off the track and out of the way – and now the missing manager and the report of bushrangers at this end. But I simply don't pretend to have felt any personal pity for a man whom I had never seen; that kind of pity's usually cant; and besides, all mine was needed for myself.

'I was in as big a hole as ever. What the devil was I to do? I doubt if I have sufficiently impressed upon you the absolute necessity of my returning to Melbourne in funds. As a matter of fact, it was less the necessity than my own determination which I can truthfully describe as absolute.

'Money I would have – but how – but how? Would this stranger be open to persuasion – if I told him the truth? No; that would set us all scouring the country for the rest of the night. Why should I tell him? Suppose I left him to find out his mistake ... would anything be gained? Bunny, I give you my word that I went to dinner without a definite intention in my head, or one premeditated lie upon my lips. I might do the decent, natural thing, and explain matters without loss of time; on the other hand, there was no hurry. I had not opened the letter, and could always pretend I had not noticed the initials; meanwhile something might turn up. I could wait a little and see. Tempted I already was, but as yet the temptation was vague, and its very vagueness made me tremble.

' "Bad news, I'm afraid," said the manager, when at last I sat down at his table.

' "A mere annoyance," I answered – I do assure you – on the spur of the moment and nothing else. But my lie was told; my position was taken; from that moment onward there was no retreat. By implication, without realising what I was doing, I had already declared myself W. F. Raffles. Therefore, W. F.

Raffles I would be, in that bank, for that night. And the devil teach me how to use my life!'

Again he raised his glass to his lips – I had forgotten mine. His cigarette-case caught the gaslight as he handed it to me. I shook my head without taking my eyes from his.

'The devil played up,' continued Raffles, with a laugh. 'Before I tasted my soup I had decided what to do. I had determined to rob that bank instead of going to bed, and be back in Melbourne for breakfast if the doctor's mare could do it. I would tell the old fellow that I had missed my way and been bushed for hours, as I easily might have been, and had never got to Yea at all. At Yea, on the other hand, the personation and robbery would ever after be attributed to a member of the gang that had waylaid and murdered the new manager with that very object. You are acquiring some experience in such matters, Bunny. I ask you, was there ever a better get-out? Last night's was something like it, only never such a certainty. And I saw it from the beginning – saw to the end before I had finished my soup!

'To increase my chances, the cashier, who also lived in the bank, was away over the holidays, had actually gone down to Melbourne to see us play; and the man who had taken my horse also waited at table; for he and his wife were the only servants, and they slept in a separate building. You may depend I ascertained this before we had finished dinner. Indeed, I was by way of asking too many questions (the most oblique and delicate was that which elicited my host's name, Ewbank) nor was I careful enough to conceal their drift.

' "Do you know," said this fellow Ewbank, who was one of the downright sort, "if it wasn't you, I should say you were in a funk of robbers? Have you lost your nerve?"

' "I hope not," said I, turning jolly hot, I can tell you; "but – well, it's not a pleasant thing to have to put a bullet through a fellow!"

' "No?" said he coolly. "I should enjoy nothing better myself; besides, yours didn't go through."

' "I wish it had!" I was smart enough to cry.

' "Amen!" said he.

'And I emptied my glass: actually I did not know whether

70

my wounded bank-robber was in prison, dead, or at large!'

'But now that I had had more than enough of it, Ewbank would come back to the subject. He admitted that the staff was small; but as for himself, he had a loaded revolver under his pillow all night, under the counter all day, and he was only waiting for his chance.

' "Under the counter, eh?" I was ass enough to say.

' "Yes; so had you!"

'He was looking at me in surprise, and something told me that to say "of course – I had forgotten!" would have been quite fatal, considering what I was supposed to have done. So I looked down my nose and shook my head.

' "But the papers said you had!" he cried.

' "Not under the counter," said I.

' " But it's the regulation!"

'For the moment, Bunny, I felt stumped, though I trust I only looked more superior than before, and I think I justified my look.

' "The regulation!" I said at length, in the most offensive tone at my command. "Yes, the regulation would have us all dead men! My dear sir, do you expect your bank-robber to let you reach for your gun in the place where he knows it's kept? I had mine in my pocket, and I got my chance by retreating from the counter with all visible reluctance."

'Ewbank stared at me with open eyes and a five-barred forehead, then down came his fist on the table.

' "By God, that was smart! Still," he added, like a man who would not be in the wrong, "the papers said the other thing, you know!"

' "Of course," I replied, "because they said what I told them. You wouldn't have had me advertise the fact that I improved upon the bank's regulations, would you?"

'So that cloud rolled over, and by Jove it was a cloud with a golden lining! Not silver – real good Australian gold! For old Ewbank hadn't quite appreciated me till then; he was a hard nut, a much older man than myself, and I felt pretty sure he thought me young for the place, and my supposed feat a fluke. But I never saw a man change his mind more openly. He got out his best brandy, he made me throw away the cigar I was smoking, and opened a fresh box. He was a convivial-looking party, with a red moustache, and a very humorous face (not unlike Tom Emmett's), and from that moment I laid myself out to attack him on his convivial flank. But he wasn't a Rosenthall, Bunny; he had a treble-seamed, hand-sewn head, and could have drunk me under the table ten times over.

' "All right," I thought, "you may go to bed sober, but you'll sleep like a timber yard!" And I threw half he gave me through the open window when he wasn't looking.

'But he was a good chap, Ewbank, and don't you imagine he was at all intemperate. Convivial I called him, and I only wish he had been something more. He did, however, become more and more genial as the evening advanced, and I had not much difficulty in getting him to show me round the bank at what was really an unearthly hour for such a proceeding. It was when he went to fetch the revolver before turning in. I kept him out of his bed another twenty minutes, and I knew every inch of the business premises before I shook hands with Ewbank in my room.

'You won't guess what I did with myself for the next hour. I undressed and went to bed. The incessant strain involved in even the most deliberate impersonation is the most wearing thing I know; then how much more so when the impersonation is impromptu! There's no getting your eye in; the next word may bowl you out; it's batting in a bad light all through. I haven't told you half the tight places I was in during the conversation that ran into hours and became dangerously intimate towards the end, you can imagine them for yourself, and then picture me spread out on my bed, getting my second wind for the big deed of the night.

'Once more I was in luck, for I had not been lying there long before I heard my dear Ewbank snoring like a harmonium, and the music never ceased for a moment; it was as loud as ever when I crept out and closed my door behind me, as regular as ever when I stopped to listen at his. And I have still to hear the concert that I shall enjoy much more. The good fellow snored me out of the bank, and was still snoring when I again stood and listened under his open window.

'Why did I leave the bank first? To catch and saddle the mare and tether her in a clump of trees close by: to have the means of escape nice and handy before I went to work. I have often wondered at the instinctive wisdom of the precaution; unconsciously I was acting on what has been one of my guiding principles ever since. Pains and patience were required; I had to get my saddle without waking the man, and I was not used to catching horses in a horse-paddock. Then I distrusted the poor mare, and I went back to the stables for a hatful of oats, which I left with her in the clump, hat and all. There was a dog, too, to reckon with (our very worst enemy, Bunny); but I had been cute enough to make immense friends with him during the evening; and he wagged his tail, not only when I came downstairs, but when I reappeared at the back door.

'As the *soi-disant* new manager, I had been able, in the most ordinary course, to pump poor Ewbank about anything and everything connected with the working of the bank, especially in those twenty last invaluable minutes before turning in. And I had made a very natural point of asking him where he kept, and would recommend me to keep, the keys at night. Of course, I thought he would take them with him to his room; but no such thing; he had a dodge worth two of that. What it was doesn't much matter, but no outsider would have found those keys in a month of Sundays.

'I, of course, had them in a few seconds, and in a few more I was in the strong-room itself. I forgot to say that the moon had risen and was letting quite a lot of light into the bank. I had, however, brought a bit of candle with me from my room; and in the strong-room, which was down some narrow stairs behind the counter in the banking chamber, I had no hesitation in lighting it. There was no window down there, and though I could no longer hear old Ewbank snoring, I had not the slightest reason to anticipate disturbance from that quarter. I did think of locking myself in while I was at work, but, thank goodness, the iron door had no keyhole on the inside.

'Well, there was heaps of gold in the safe, but I only took what I needed and could comfortably carry, not much more

than a couple of hundred altogether. Not a note would I touch,
and my native caution came out also in the way I divided the
sovereigns between all my pockets, and packed them up so
that I shouldn't be like the old woman of Banbury Cross. Well,
you think me too cautious still, but I was insanely cautious
then. And so it was that, just as I was ready to go, whereas I
might have been gone ten minutes, there came a violent knocking at the outer door.

'Bunny, it was the outer door of the banking chamber! My
candle must have been seen! And there I stood, with the grease
running hot over my fingers, in that brick grave of a strong-
room!

'There was only one thing to be done. I must trust to the
sound sleeping of Ewbank upstairs, open the door myself,
knock the visitor down, or shoot him with the revolver I had
been new chum enough to buy before leaving Melbourne, and
make a dash for that clump of trees and the doctor's mare. My
mind was made up in an instant, and I was at the top of the
strong-room stairs, the knocking still continuing, when a
second sound drove me back. It was the sound of bare feet
coming along a corridor.

'My narrow stair was stone. I tumbled down it with little
noise, and had only to push open the iron door, for I had left
the keys in the safe. As I did so I heard a handle turn overhead,
and thanked my gods that I had shut every single door behind
me. You see, old chap, one's caution doesn't always let one
in!

'"Who's that knocking?" said Ewbank, up above.

'I could not make out the answer, but it sounded to me like
the irrelevant supplication of a spent man. What I did hear
plainly, was the cocking of the bank revolver before the bolts
were shot back. Then, a tottering step, a hard, short, shallow
breathing, and Ewbank's voice in horror:

'"Good Lord! What's happened to you? You're bleeding
like a pig!'

'"Not now," came a grateful sort of sigh.

'"But you have been! What's done it?"

'"Bushrangers."

'"Down the road?"

' "This and Whittlesea – tied to tree – pot-shots – left me –
bleed to death. ...'

'The weak voice failed, and the bare feet bolted. Now was
my time – if the poor devil had fainted. But I could not be sure,
and there I crouched down below in the dark, at the half-shut
iron door, not less spell-bound than imprisoned. It was just as
well, for Ewbank wasn't gone a minute.

' "Drink this," I heard him say, and when the other spoke
again his voice was stronger.

' "Now I begin to feel alive."

' "Don't talk!"

' "It does me good. You don't know what it was, all those
miles alone, one an hour at the outside! I never thought I
should come through. You must let me tell you – in case I
don't!"

' "Well, have another sip."

' "Thank you. ... I said bushrangers; of course there are no
such things nowadays."

' "What were they, then?"

' "Bank thieves; the one that had the pot-shots was the very
brute I drove out of the bank at Coburg, with a bullet in
him!" '

'I knew it!'

'Of course you did, Bunny; so did I, down in that strong-
room; but old Ewbank didn't, and I thought he was never going to speak again.

' "You're delirious," he said at last. "Who in blazes do you
think you are?"

' "The new manager."

' "The new manager's in bed and asleep upstairs!"

' "When did he arrive?"

' "This evening."

' "Call himself Raffles?"

' "Yes."

' "Well, I'm damned!" whispered the real man. "I thought it
was just revenge, but now I see what it was. My dear sir, the
man upstairs is an impostor – if he's upstairs still! He must be
one of the gang. He's going to rob the bank – if he hasn't done
so already!"

' "If he hasn't done so already," muttered Ewbank after him; "if he's upstairs still! By God, if he is I'm sorry for him!"

'His tone was quiet enough, but about the nastiest I ever heard. I tell you, Bunny, I was glad I'd brought that revolver. It looked as though it must be mine against his, muzzle to muzzle.

' "Better have a look down here, first," said the new manager.

' "While he gets through his window? No, no, he's not down here."

' "It's easy to have a look."

'Bunny, if you ask me what was the most thrilling moment of my infamous career, I say it was that moment. There I stood at the bottom of those narrow stone stairs, inside the strong-room, with the door a good foot open, and I didn't know whether it would creak or not. The light was coming nearer – and I didn't know! I had to chance it. And it didn't creak a bit; it was far too solid and well-hung; and I couldn't have banged it if I'd tried. It was too heavy; and it fitted so close that I felt and heard the air squeeze out in my face. Every shred of light went out, except the streak underneath, and it brightened. How I blessed that door!

' "No, he's not down there," I heard, as though through cotton-wool; then the streak went out too, and in a few seconds I ventured to open once more, and was in time to hear them creeping to my room.

'Well, now, there was not a fifth of a second to be lost; but I'm proud to say I came up those stairs on my toes and fingers, and out of that bank (they'd gone and left the door open) just as gingerly as though my time had been my own. I didn't even forget to put on the hat that the doctor's mare was eating her oats out of, as well as she could with a bit, or it alone would have landed me. I didn't even gallop away, but just jogged off quietly in the thick dust at the side of the road (though I own my heart was galloping), and thanked my stars the bank was at the end of the township, in which I really hadn't set foot. The very last thing I heard was the two managers raising Cain and the coachman. And now, Bunny – –'

He stood up and stretched himself, with a smile that ended in a yawn. The black windows had faded through every shade of indigo; they now framed their opposite neighbours, stark and livid in the dawn; and the gas seemed turned to nothing in the globes.

'But that's not all?' I cried.

'I'm sorry to say it is,' said Raffles apologetically. 'The thing should have ended with an exciting chase, I know, but somehow it didn't. I suppose they thought I had got no end of a start; then they had made up their minds that I belonged to the gang, which was not so many miles away; and one of them had got as much as he could carry from that gang as it was. But I wasn't to know all that, and I'm bound to say that there was plenty of excitement left for me. Lord, how I made that poor brute travel when I got among the trees! Though we must have been well over fifty miles from Melbourne, we had done it at a snail's pace; and those stolen oats had brisked the old girl up to such a pitch that she fairly bolted when she felt her nose turned south. By Jove, it was no joke, in and out among those trees, and under branches with your face in the mane! I told you about the forest of dead gums? It looked perfectly ghostly in the moonlight. And I found it as still as I had left it – so still that I pulled up there, my first halt, and lay with my ear to the ground for two or three minutes. But I heard nothing – not a thing but the mare's bellows and my own heart. I'm sorry, Bunny; but if ever you write my memoirs, you won't have any difficulty in working up that chase. Play those dead gum trees for all they're worth, and let the bullets fly like hail. I'll turn round in my saddle to see Ewbank coming up hell-for-leather in his white suit, and I'll duly paint it red. Do it in the third person, and they won't know how it's going to end.'

'But I don't know myself,' I complained. 'Did the mare carry you all the way back to Melbourne?'

'Every rod, pole, or perch! I had her well seen to at our hotel, and returned her to the doctor in the evening. He was tremendously tickled to hear I had been bushed; next morning he brought me the paper to show me what I had escaped at Yea!'

'Without suspecting anything?'

'Ah!' said Raffles, as he put out the gas; 'that's a point on which I've never made up my mind. The mare and her colour was a coincidence – luckily she was only a bay – and I fancy

77

the condition of the beast must have told a tale. The doctor's manner was certainly different. I'm inclined to think he suspected something, though not the right thing. I wasn't expecting him, and I fear my appearance may have increased his suspicions.'

I asked him why.

'I used to have rather a heavy moustache,' said Raffles, 'but I lost it the day after I lost my innocence.'

WILFUL MURDER

OF the various robberies in which we were both concerned, it is but the few, I find, that will bear telling at any length. Not that the others contained details which even I would hesitate to recount; it is, rather, the very absence of untoward incident which renders them useless for my present purpose. In point of fact, our plans were so craftily laid (by Raffles) that the chances of a hitch were invariably reduced to a minimum before we went to work. We might be disappointed in the market value of our haul; but it was quite the exception for us to find ourselves confronted by unforeseen impediments, or involved in a really dramatic dilemma. There was a sameness, even in our spoil; for, of course, only the most precious stones are worth the trouble we took and the risks we ran. In short, our most successful escapades would prove the greatest weariness of all in narrative form; and none more so than the dull affair of the Ardagh emeralds, some eight or nine weeks after the Milchester cricket week. The former, however, had a sequel that I would rather forget than all our burglaries put together.

It was the evening after our return from Ireland, and I was waiting at my rooms for Raffles, who had gone off as usual to dispose of the plunder. Raffles had his own method of conducting this very vital branch of our business, which I was well content to leave entirely in his hands. He drove the bargains, I believe, in a thin but subtle disguise of the flashy-seedy order, and always in the Cockney dialect, of which he had made himself a master. Moreover, he invariably employed the same 'fence', who was ostensibly a money-lender in a small (but yet notorious) way, and in reality a rascal as remarkable as Raffles himself. Only lately I also had been to the man, but in my proper person. We had needed capital for the getting of these very emeralds, and I had raised a hundred pounds, on the terms you would expect from a soft-spoken greybeard with an ingratiating smile, an incessant bow, and the shiftiest old eyes that ever flew from rim to rim of a pair of spectacles. So the original sinews and the final spoils of war came in this case from the self-same source – a circumstance which appealed to us both.

But these same final spoils I was still to see, and I waited and waited with an impatience that grew upon me with the growing dusk. At my open window I had played Sister Ann until the faces in the street below were no longer distinguishable. And now I was tearing to and fro in the grip of horrible hypothesis – a grip that tightened when at last the lift-gates opened with a clatter outside – that held me breathless until a well-known tattoo followed on my door.

'In the dark!' said Raffles, as I dragged him in. 'Why, Bunny, what's wrong?'

'Nothing – now you've come,' said I, shutting the door behind him in a fever of relief and anxiety. 'Well? Well? What did they fetch?'

'Five hundred.'

'Down?'

'Got it in my pocket.'

'Good man!' I cried. 'You don't know what a stew I've been in. I'll switch on the light. I've been thinking of you and nothing else for the last hour. I – I was ass enough to think something had gone wrong!'

Raffles was smiling when the white light filled the room, but for the moment I did not perceive the peculiarity of his smile. I was fatuously full of my own late tremors and present relief, and my first idiotic act was to spill some whisky and squirt the soda-water all over in my anxiety to do justice to the occasion.

'So you thought something had happened?' said Raffles, leaning back in my chair as he lit a cigarette, and looking much amused. 'What should you say if something had? Sit tight, my dear chap! It was nothing of the slightest consequence, and it's all over now. A stern chase and a long one, Bunny, but I think I'm well to windward this time.'

And suddenly I saw that his collar was limp, his hair matted, his boots thick with dust.

'The police?' I whispered, aghast.

'Oh dear, no; only old Baird.'

'Baird! But wasn't it Baird who took the emeralds?'

'It was.'

'Then how came he to chase you?'

'My dear fellow, I'll tell you if you give me a chance, it's really nothing to get in the least excited about. Old Baird has at last spotted that I'm not quite the common cracksman I would have him think me. So he's been doing his best to run me to my burrow.'

'And you call that nothing!'

'It would be something if he had succeeded; but he has still to do that. I admit, however, that he made me sit up for the time being. It all comes of going on the job so far from home. There was the old brute with the whole thing in his morning paper. He knew it must have been done by some fellow who could pass himself off for a gentleman, and I saw his eyebrows go up the moment I told him I was the man, with the same old twang that you could cut with a paper knife. I did my best to get out of it – swore I had a pal who was a real swell – but I saw very plainly that I had given myself away. He gave up haggling. He paid my price as though he enjoyed doing it. But I felt him following me when I made tracks – though, of course, I didn't turn round to see.'

'Why not?'

'My dear Bunny, it's the very worst thing you can do. As long as you look unsuspecting they'll keep their distance, and so long as they keep their distance you stand a chance. Once show that you know you're being followed, and it's flight or fight for all you're worth. I never even looked round; and mind you never do in the same hole. I just hurried up to Blackfriars and booked for High Street, Kensington, at the top of my voice; and as the train was leaving Sloane Square out I hopped, and up all those stairs like a lamp-lighter, and round to the studio by the back streets. Well, to be on the safe side, I lay low there all the afternoon, hearing nothing in the least suspicious, and only wishing I had a window to look through instead of that beastly skylight. However, the coast seemed clear enough, and thus far it was my mere idea that he would follow me; there was nothing to show he had. So at last I marched out in my proper rig – almost straight into old Baird's arms!'

'What on earth did you do?'

'Walked past him as though I had never set eyes on him in my life, and didn't then; took a cab in the King's Road, and drove like the deuce to Clapham Junction; rushed on to the nearest platform, without a ticket, jumped into the first train I saw, got out at Twickenham, walked full tilt back to Richmond, took the District to Charing Cross, and here I am! Ready for a tub and a change, and the best dinner the club can give us. I came to you first, because I thought you might be getting anxious. Come round with me, and I won't keep you long.'

'You're certain you've given him the slip?' I said, as we put on our hats.

'Certain enough; but we can make assurance doubly sure,' said Raffles, and went to my window, where he stood for a minute or two looking down into the street.

'All right?' I asked him.

'All right,' said he; and we went downstairs forthwith, and so to the Albany arm-in-arm.

But we were both rather silent on the way. I, for my part, was wondering what Raffles would do about the studio in Chelsea, whither, at all events, he had been successfully dogged. To me the point seemed one of immediate importance, but when I mentioned it he said there was time enough to think about that. His other remark was made after we had nodded (in Bond Street) to a young blood of our acquaintance who happened to be getting himself a bad name.

'Poor Jack Rutter!' said Raffles, with a sigh. 'Nothing's sadder than to see a fellow going to the bad like that. He's about mad with drink and debt; did you see his eye? Odd that we should have met him to-night, by the way; it's old Baird who's said to have skinned him. I've a jolly good mind to skin old Baird!'

And his tone took a sudden low fury, made the more noticeable by another long silence, which lasted, indeed, throughout an admirable dinner at the club, and for some time after we had settled down in a quiet corner of the smoking-room with our coffee and cigars. Then at last I saw Raffles looking at me with his lazy smile, and I knew that the morose fit was at an end.

'I dare say you wonder what I've been thinking about all this time?' said he. 'I've been thinking what rot it is to go doing things by halves!'

'Well,' said I, returning his smile, 'that's not a charge that you can bring against yourself, is it?'

'I'm not so sure,' said Raffles, blowing a meditative puff; 'as a matter of fact, I was thinking less of myself than of that poor devil of a Jack Rutter. There's a fellow who does things by halves; he's only half gone to the bad; and look at the difference between him and us! He's under the thumb of a villainous money-lender; we are solvent citizens. He's taken to drink; we're as sober as we are solvent. His pals are beginning to cut him; our difficulty is to keep the pal from the door. *Enfin,* he begs or borrows, which is stealing by halves; and we steal outright and are done with it. Obviously, ours is the more honest course. Yet I'm not sure, Bunny, but we're doing the thing by halves ourselves!'

'Why? What more could we do?' I exclaimed in soft derision, looking round, however, to make sure that we were not overheard.

'What more?' said Raffles. 'Well, murder – for one thing.'

'Rot!'

'A matter of opinion, my dear Bunny; I don't mean it for rot. I've told you before that the biggest man alive is the man who's committed a murder, and not yet been found out; at least he ought to be, but he so very seldom has the soul to appreciate himself. Just think of it! Think of coming here and talking to the men, very likely about the murder itself; and knowing you've done it; and wondering how they'd look if they knew! Oh, it would be great, simply great! But, besides all that, when you were caught, there'd be a merciful and dramatic end of you. You'd fill the bill for a few weeks and then snuff out with a flourish of extra-specials; you wouldn't rust with a vile repose for seven or fourteen years.'

'Good old Raffles!' I chuckled. 'I begin to forgive you for being in bad form at dinner.'

'But I was never more earnest in my life.'

'Go on!'

'I mean it.'

'You know very well that you wouldn't commit a murder, whatever else you might do.'

'I know very well I'm going to commit one to-night!'

He had been leaning back in the saddle-bag chair, watching me with keen eyes sheathed by languid lids; now he started forward, and his eyes leapt to mine like cold steel from the scabbard. They struck home to my slow wits; their meaning was no longer in doubt. I, who knew the man, read murder in his clenched hands, and murder in his locked lips, but a hundred murders in those hard blue eyes.

'Baird?' I faltered, moistening my lips with my tongue.

'Of course.'

'But you said it didn't matter about the room in Chelsea?'

'I told a lie.'

'Anyway, you gave him the slip afterwards!'

'That was another. I didn't. I thought I had when I came up to you this evening; but when I looked out of your window – you remember? – to make assurance doubly sure – there he was on the opposite pavement down below.'

'And you never said a word about it!'

'I wasn't going to spoil your dinner, Bunny, and I wasn't going to let you spoil mine. But there he was as large as life, and, of course, he followed us to the Albany. A fine game for him to play, a game after his mean old heart; blackmail for me, bribes from the police, the one bidding against the other; but he shan't play it with me, he shan't live to, and the world will have an extortioner the less. Waiter! Two Scotch whiskies and sodas. I'm off at eleven, Bunny; it's the only thing to be done.'

'You know where he lives, then?'

'Yes, out Willesden way, and alone; the fellow's a miser among other things. I long ago found out all about him.'

Again I looked around the room; it was a young man's club, and young men were laughing, chatting, smoking, drinking, on every hand. One nodded to me through the smoke. Like a machine I nodded to him, and turned back to Raffles with a groan.

'Surely you will give him a chance!' I urged. 'The very sight of your pistol should bring him to terms.'

'It wouldn't make him keep them.'

'But you might try the effect?'

'I probably shall. Here's a drink for you, Bunny. Wish me luck.'

'I'm coming too.'

'I don't want you.'

'But I must come!'

An ugly gleam shot from the steel-blue eyes.

'To interfere?' said Raffles.

'Not I.'

'You give me your word?'

'I do.'

'Bunny, if you break it – –'

'You may shoot me too!'

'I most certainly should,' said Raffles solemnly. 'So you come at your own peril, my dear man; but if you are coming – well, the sooner the better, for I must stop at my rooms on the way.'

Five minutes later I was waiting for him at the Piccadilly entrance to the Albany. I had a reason for remaining outside. It was the feeling – half hope, half fear – that Angus Baird might still be on our trail – that some more immediate and less cold-blooded way of dealing with him might result from a sudden encounter between the money-lender and myself. I would not warn him of his danger; but I would avert tragedy at all costs. And when no such encounter had taken place, and Raffles and I were fairly on our way to Willesden, that, I think, was still my honest resolve. I would not break my word if I could help it, but it was a comfort to feel that I could break it if I liked, on an understood penalty. Alas! I fear my good intentions were tainted with a devouring curiosity, and overlaid by the fascination which goes hand in hand with horror.

I have a poignant recollection of the hour it took us to reach the house. We walked across St James's Park (I can see the lights now, bright on the bridge and blurred on the water), and we had some minutes to wait for the last train to Willesden. It left at 11.21, I remember, and Raffles was put out to find it did not go on to Kensal Rise. We had to get out at Willesden Junction and walk on through the streets into fairly open country that happened to be quite new to me. I could never find the house again. I remember, however, that we were on a dark footpath between the woods and fields when the clocks began striking twelve.

'Surely,' said I, 'we shall find him in bed and asleep?'

'I hope we do,' said Raffles grimly.

'Then you mean to break in?'

'What else did you think?'

I had not thought about it at all; the ultimate crime had monopolised my mind. Beside it burglary was a bagatelle, but one to deprecate none the less. I saw obvious objections; the man was *au fait* with cracksmen and their ways, he would certainly have firearms, and might be the first to use them.

'I could wish nothing better,' said Raffles. 'Then it will be man to man, and devil take the worst shot. You don't suppose I prefer foul play to fair, do you? But die he must by one or the other, or it's a long stretch for you and me."

'Better that than this!'

'Then stay where you are, my good fellow. I told you I didn't want you; and this is the house. So good-night.'

I could see no house at all, only the angle of a high wall rising solitary in the night, with the starlight glittering on battlements of broken glass and in the wall a tall green gate, bristling with spikes, and showing a front for battering-rams in the feeble rays of an outlying lamp-post cast across the new-made road. It seemed to me a road of building sites, with but this one house built, all by itself, at one end; but the night was too dark for more than a mere impression.

Raffles, however, had seen the place by daylight, and had come prepared for the special obstacles; already he was reaching up and putting champagne corks on the spikes, and in another moment he had his folded covert coat across the corks. I stepped back as he raised himself, and saw a little pyramid of slates snip the sky above the gate; as he squirmed over I ran forward, and had my own weight on the spikes and corks and covert coat when he gave the latter a tug.

'Coming after all?'

'Rather!'

'Take care, then; the place is all bell-wires and springs. It's

no soft spring this! There – stand still while I take off the
corks.'

The garden was very small and new, with a grass-plot still
in separate sods, but a quantity of full-grown laurels stuck into
the raw clay beds. 'Bells in themselves,' Raffles whispered;
'there's nothing else rustles so – cunning old beast!' And we
gave them a wide berth as we crept across the grass.

'He's gone to bed!'

'I don't think so, Bunny. I believe he's seen us.'

'Why?'

'I saw a light.'

'Where?'

'Downstairs, for an instant, when I – –'

His whisper died away; he had seen the light again, and so
had I.

It lay like a golden rod under the front door – and vanished.
It reappeared like a gold thread under the lintel – and vanished
for good. We heard the stairs creak, creak, and cease, also
for good. We neither saw nor heard any more, though we
stood waiting on the grass till our feet were soaked with the
dew.

'I'm going in,' said Raffles at last. 'I don't believe he saw us
at all. I wish he had. This way.'

We trod gingerly on the path, but the gravel stuck to our
wet soles, and grated horribly in a little tiled verandah with a
glass door leading within. It was through this glass that Raffles
had first seen the light; and he now proceeded to take out a
pane, with the diamond, the pot of treacle, and the sheet of
brown paper which were seldom omitted from his impedi-
menta. Nor did he dispense with my own assistance, though
he may have accepted it as instinctively as it was proffered. In
any case it was these fingers that helped to spread the treacle
on the brown paper, and pressed the latter to the glass until
the diamond had completed its circuit and the pane fell gently
back into our hands.

Raffles now inserted his hand, turned the key in the lock,
and, by making a long arm, succeeded in drawing the bolt at
the bottom of the door; it proved to be the only one, and the
door opened, though not very wide.

'What's that?' said Raffles, as something crunched beneath his feet on the very theshold.

'A pair of spectacles,' I whispered, picking them up. I was still fingering the broken lenses and the bent rims when Raffles tripped and almost fell, with a gasping cry that he made no effort to restrain.

'Hush, man, hush!' I entreated under my breath. 'He'll hear you!'

For answer his teeth chattered – even his – and I heard him fumbling with his matches.

'No, Bunny; he won't hear us,' whispered Raffles presently, and he rose from his knees and lit a gas as the match burnt down.

Angus Baird was lying on his own floor, dead, with his grey hairs glued together by his blood; near him a poker with the black end glistening; in the corner his desk, ransacked, littered. A clock ticked noisily on the chimney-piece; for perhaps a hundred seconds there was no other sound.

Raffles stood very still, staring down at the dead, as a man might stare into an abyss after striding blindly to its brink. His breath came audibly through wide nostrils; he made no other sign, and his lips seemed sealed.

'That light!' said I hoarsely; 'the light we saw under the door!'

With a start he turned to me.

'It's true. I had forgotten it. It was in here I saw it first!'

'He must be upstairs still!'

'If he is we'll soon rout him out. Come on!'

Instead I laid a hand upon his arm, imploring him to reflect – that his enemy was dead now – that we should certainly be involved – that now or never was our own time to escape. He shook me off in a sudden fury of impatience, a reckless contempt in his eyes, and, bidding me save my own skin if I liked, he once more turned his back upon me, and this time left me half resolved to take him at his word. Had he forgotten on what errand he himself was here? Was he determined that this night should end in black disaster? As I asked myself these questions his match flared in the hall; in another moment the stairs were creaking under his feet, even as they had creaked under those of the murderer; and the humane instinct that inspired him in defiance of his risk was borne in also upon my slower sensibilities. Could we let the murderer go? My answer was to bound up the creaking stairs and to overhaul Raffles on the landing.

But three doors presented themselves; the first opened into a bedroom with the bed turned down but undisturbed; the second room was empty in every sense; the third door was locked.

Raffles lit the landing gas.

'He's in there,' said he, cocking his revolver. 'Do you remember how we used to break into the studies at school? Here goes!'

His flat foot crashed over the keyhole, the lock gave, the door flew open, and in the sudden draught the landing gas heeled over like a coble in a squall; as the flame righted itself I saw a fixed bath, two bath-towels knotted together – an open window – a cowering figure – and Raffles struck aghast on the threshold.

'Jack – Rutter?'

The words came thick and slow with horror, and in horror I heard myself repeating them, while the cowering figure by the bath-room window rose gradually erect.

'It's you!' he whispered, in amazement no less than our own; 'it's you two! What's it mean, Raffles? I saw you get over the gate; a bell rang, the place is full of them. Then you broke in! What's it all mean?'

'We may tell you that, when you tell us what in God's name you've done, Rutter!'

'Done? What have I done?' The unhappy wretch came out into the light with bloodshot, blinking eyes, and a bloody shirt-front. 'You know – you've seen – but I'll tell you if you like. I've killed a robber; that's all. I've killed a robber, a usurer, a jackal, a blackmailer, the cleverest and the cruellest villain unhung. I'm ready to hang for him. I'd kill him again!'

And he looked us fiercely in the face, a fine defiance in his dissipated eyes; his breast heaving, his jaw like a rock.

'Shall I tell you how it happened?' he went on passionately. 'He's made my life a hell these weeks and months past. You

may know that. A perfect hell. Well, to-night I met him in
Bond Street. Do you remember when I met you fellows? He
wasn't twenty yards behind you; he was on your tracks,
Raffles; he saw me nod to you, and stopped me and asked me
who you were. He seemed as keen as knives to know. I couldn't
think why, and didn't care either, for I saw my chance. I said
I'd tell him all about you if he'd give me a private interview.
He said he wouldn't. I said he should, and held him by the
coat; by the time I let him go you were out of sight, and I
waited where I was till he came back in despair. I had the
whip-hand of him then. I could dictate where the interview
should be, and I made him take me home with him, still
swearing to tell him all about you when we'd had our talk.
Well, when we got here I made him give me something to eat,
putting him off and off; and about ten o'clock I heard the gate
shut. I waited a bit, and then asked him if he lived alone.

' " Not at all," says he; "did you not see the servant?"

'I said I'd seen her, but I thought I heard her go; if I was
mistaken, no doubt she would come when she was called; and I
yelled three times at the top of my voice. Of course there was
no servant to come. I knew that, because I came to see him
one night last week, and he interviewed me himself through the
gate, but wouldn't open it. Well, when I had done yelling, and
not a soul had come near us, he was as white as that ceiling.
Then I told him we could have our chat at last; and I picked
the poker out of the fender, and told him how he'd robbed
me, but by God he shouldn't rob me any more. I gave him
three minutes to write and sign a settlement of all his iniqui-
tous claims against me, or have his brains beaten out over his
own carpet. He thought a minute and then went to his desk for
pen and paper. In two seconds he was round like lightning
with a revolver, and I went for him bald-headed. He fired two
or three times and missed – you can find the holes if you like;
but I hit him every time – by God! I was like a savage till the
thing was done. And then I didn't care. I went through his desk
looking for my own bills, and was coming away when you
turned up. I said I didn't care, nor do I; but I was going to give
myself up to-night, and shall still; so you see I shan't give you
fellows much trouble!'

He was done; and there we stood on the landing of the lonely house, the low, thick, eager voice still racing and ringing through our ears; the dead man below, and in front of us his impenitent slayer. I knew to whom the impenitence would appeal when he had heard the story, and I was not mistaken.

'That's all rot,' said Raffles, speaking after a pause; 'we shan't let you give yourself up.'

'You shan't stop me! What would be the good? The woman saw me; it would only be a question of time; and I can't face waiting to be taken. Think of it: waiting for them to touch you on the shoulder! No, no, no; I'll give myself up and get it over.'

His speech was changed; he faltered, floundered. It was as though a clearer perception of his position had come with the bare idea of escape from it.

'But listen to me,' urged Raffles. 'We're here at our peril ourselves. We broke in like thieves to enforce redress for a grievance like your own. But don't you see? We took out a pane — did the thing like regular burglars. We shall get the credit of all the rest!'

'You mean that I shan't be suspected?'

'I do.'

'But I don't want to get off scot-free,' cried Rutter hysterically. 'I've killed him. I know that. But it was in self-defence; it wasn't murder. I must own up and take the consequences. I shall go mad if I don't.'

His hands twitched; his lips quivered; the tears were in his eyes. Raffles took him roughly by the shoulder.

'Look here, you fool! If the three of us are caught here now, do you know what the consequences would be? We should swing in a row in six weeks' time! You talk as though we were sitting in a club; don't you know it's one o'clock in the morning, and the lights on, and a dead man down below? For God's sake pull yourself together, and do what I tell you, or you're a dead man yourself.'

'I wish I was one!' Rutter sobbed. 'I wish I had his revolver, I'd blow my own brains out. It's somewhere under him! O my God, my God!'

His knees knocked together; the frenzy of reaction was at its height. We had to take him downstairs between us, and so through the front door out into the open air.

All was still outside – all but the smothered weeping of the unstrung wretch upon our hands. Raffles returned for a moment to the house; then all was dark as well. The gate opened from within; we closed it carefully behind us; and so left the starlight shining on broken glass and polished spikes, one and all as we had found them.

We escaped; no need to dwell on our escape. Our murderer seemed set upon the scaffold: drunk with his deed, he was more trouble than six men drunk with wine. Again and again we threatened to leave him to his fate, to wash our hands of him. But incredible and unmerited luck was with the three of us. Not a soul did we meet between that and Willesden; and of those who saw us later, did one think of the two young men with crooked white ties, supporting a third in a seemingly unmistakable condition, when the evening papers apprised the town of a terrible tragedy at Kensal Rise?

We walked to Maida Vale, and thence drove openly to my rooms. But I alone went upstairs; the other two proceeded to the Albany, and I saw no more of Raffles for forty-eight hours. He was not at his rooms when I called in the morning, he had left no word. When he reappeared the papers were full of the murder; and the man who had committed it was on the wide Atlantic, a steerage passenger from Liverpool to New York.

'There was no arguing with him,' so Raffles told me; 'either he must make a clean breast of it or flee the country. So I rigged him up at the studio, and we took the first train to Liverpool. Nothing would induce him to sit tight and enjoy the situation as I should have endeavoured to do in his place; and it's just as well! I went to his diggings to destroy some papers, and what do you think I found? The police in possession; there's a warrant out against him already! The idiots think that window wasn't genuine, and the warrant's out. It won't be my fault if it's ever served!'

Nor, after all these years, can I think it will be mine.

'WELL,' said Raffles, 'what do you make of it?'

I read the advertisement once more before replying. It was in the last column of the *Daily Telegraph*, and it ran:

'TWO THOUSAND POUNDS REWARD. – The above sum may be earned by any one qualified to undertake delicate mission and prepared to run certain risk. – Apply by telegram, Security, London.'

'I think,' said I, 'it's the most extraordinary advertisement that ever got into print!'

Raffles smiled.

'Not quite all that, Bunny; still, extraordinary enough, I grant you.'

'Look at the figure.'

'It is certainly large.'

'And the mission – and the risk!'

'Yes, the combination is frank, to say the least of it. But the really original point is requiring applications by telegram to a telegraphic address! There's something in the fellow who thought of that, and something in his game; with one word he chokes off the million who answer an advertisement every day – when they can raise the stamp. My answer cost me five bob; but then I prepaid another.'

'You don't mean to say that you've applied?'

'Rather,' said Raffles. 'I want two thousand pounds as much as any man.'

'Put your own name?'

'Well – no, Bunny, I didn't. In point of fact, I smell something interesting and illegal, and you know what a cautious chap I am. I signed myself Glasspool, care of Hickey, 38 Conduit Street; that's my tailor, and after sending the wire I went round and told him what to expect. He promised to send the reply along the moment it came. I shouldn't be surprised if that's it!'

And he was gone before a double knock on the outer door had done ringing through the rooms, to return next minute with an open telegram and a face full of news.

'What do you think?' said he. 'Security's that fellow Addenbrooke, the police court lawyer, and he wants to see me *instanter*!'

'Do you know him, then?'

'Merely by repute. I only hope he doesn't know me. He's the chap who got six weeks for sailing too close to the wind in the Sutton-Wilmer case; everybody wondered why he wasn't struck off the rolls. Instead of that he's got a first-rate practice on the seamy side, and every blackguard with half a case takes it straight to Bennett Addenbrooke. He's probably the one man who would have the cheek to put in an advertisement like that, and the one man who could do it without exciting suspicion. It's simply in his line; but you may be sure there's something shady at the bottom of it. The odd thing is that I have long made up my mind to go to Addenbrooke myself if accidents should happen.'

'And you're going to him now?'

'This minute,' said Raffles, brushing his hat; 'and so are you.'

'But I came in to drag you out to lunch.'

'You shall lunch with me when we've seen this fellow. Come on, Bunny, and we'll choose your name on the way. Mine's Glasspool, and don't you forget it.'

Mr Bennett Addenbrooke occupied substantial offices in Wellington Street, Strand, and was out when we arrived; but he had only just gone 'over the way to the court'; and five minutes sufficed to produce a brisk, fresh-coloured, resolute-looking man, with a very confident, rather festive air, and black eyes that opened wide at the sight of Raffles.

'Mr – Glasspool?' exclaimed the lawyer.

'My name,' said Raffles, with dry effrontery.

'Not up at Lord's, however!' said the other slyly. 'My dear sir, I have seen you take far too many wickets to make any mistake.'

For a single moment Raffles looked venomous; then he shrugged and smiled, and the smile grew into a little cynical chuckle.

'So you have bowled me out in my turn?' said he. 'Well, I don't think there's anything to explain. I am harder up than I wished to admit under my own name, that's all, and I want that thousand pounds reward.'

'Two thousand,' said the solicitor. 'And the man who is not above an alias happens to be just the sort of man I want; so don't let that worry you, my dear sir. The matter, however, is of a strictly private and confidential character," and he looked very hard at me.

'Quite so,' said Raffles. 'But there was something about a risk?'

'A certain risk is involved.'

'Then surely three heads will be better than two. I said I wanted that thousand pounds; my friend here wants the other. We are both cursedly hard up. and we go into this thing together or not at all. Must you have his name too? I should give him my real one, Bunny.'

Mr Addenbrooke raised his eyebrows over the card I found for him; then he drummed upon it with his finger-nail, and his embarrassment expressed itself in a puzzled smile.

'The fact is, I find myself in a difficulty,' he confessed at last. 'Yours is the first reply I have received; people who can afford to send long telegrams don't rush to the advertisements in the *Daily Telegraph*; but on the other hand, I was not quite prepared to hear from men like yourselves. Candidly, and on consideration, I am not sure that you are the stamp of men for me – men who belong to good clubs! I rather intended to appeal to the – er – adventurous classes.'

'We are adventurers,' said Raffles gravely.

'But you respect the law?'

The black eyes gleamed shrewdly.

'We are not professional rogues, if that's what you mean,' said Raffles, smiling. 'But on our beam-ends we are; we would do a good deal for a thousand pounds apiece, eh, Bunny?'

'Anything,' I murmured.

The solicitor rapped his desk.

'I'll tell you what I want you to do. You can but refuse. It's illegal, but it's illegality in a good cause; that's the risk, and my client is prepared to pay for it. He will pay for the attempt, in case of failure; the money is as good as yours once you consent to run the risk. My client is Sir Bernhard Debenham, of Broom Hall, Esher.'

'I know his son,' I remarked.

Raffles knew him too, but said nothing, and his eye drooped disapproval in my direction. Bennett Addenbrooke turned to me.

'Then,' said he, 'you have the privilege of knowing one of the most complete young blackguards about town, and the *fons et origo* of the whole trouble. As you know the son, you may know the father too, at all events by reputation; and in that case I needn't tell you that he is a very peculiar man. He lives alone in a storehouse of treasures which no eye but his ever beheld. He is said to have the finest collection of pictures in the south of England, though nobody ever sees them to judge; pictures, fiddles, and furniture are his hobby, and he is undoubtedly very eccentric. Nor can one deny that there has been considerable eccentricity in his treatment of his son. For years Sir Bernard paid his debts, and the other day, without the slightest warning, not only refused to do so any more, but absolutely stopped the lad's allowance. Well, I'll tell you what has happened; but first of all you must know, or you may remember, that I appeared for young Debenham in a little scrape he got into a year or two ago. I got him off all right, and Sir Bernard paid me handsomely on the nail. And no more did I hear or see of either of them until one day last week.'

The lawyer drew his chair nearer ours, and leant forward with a hand on either knee.

'On Tuesday of last week I had a telegram from Sir Bernard; I was to go to him at once. I found him waiting for me in the drive; without a word he led me to the picture-gallery, which was locked and darkened, drew up a blind, and stood simply pointing to an empty picture-frame. It was a long time before I could get a word out of him. Then at last he told me that that frame had contained one of the rarest and most valuable pictures in England – in the world – an original Velasquez. I have checked this,' said the lawyer, 'and it seems literally true; the picture was a portrait of the Infanta Maria Teresa, said to be one of the artist's greatest works, second only to another portrait of one of the Popes of Rome – so they told me at the National Gallery, where they had its history by heart. They say there that the picture is practically priceless. And young Debenham has sold it for five thousand pounds!'

'The deuce he has,' said Raffles.

I inquired who had bought it.

'A Queensland legislator of the name of Craggs – the Hon. John Montague Craggs, M.L.C., to give him his full title. Not that we knew anything about him on Tuesday last; we didn't even know for certain that young Debenham had stolen the picture. But he had gone down for money on the Monday evening, had been refused, and it was plain enough that he had helped himself in this way; he had threatened revenge, and this was it. Indeed, when I hunted him up in town on the Tuesday night, he confessed as much in the most brazen manner imaginable. But he wouldn't tell me who was the purchaser, and finding out took the rest of the week; but I did find out, and a nice time I've had of it ever since! Backwards and forwards between Esher and the Metropole, where the Queenslander is staying, sometimes twice a day; threats, offers, prayers, entreaties, not one of them a bit of good!'

'But,' said Raffles, 'surely it's a clear case? The sale was illegal; you can pay him back his money and force him to give the picture up.'

'Exactly; but not without an action and a public scandal, and that my client declines to face. He would rather lose even his picture than have the whole thing get into the papers; he has disowned his son, but he will not disgrace him; yet his picture he must have by hook or crook, and there's the rub! I am to get it back by fair means or foul. He gives me *carte blanche* in the matter, and, I verily believe, would throw in a blank cheque if asked. He offered one to the Queenslander, but Craggs simply tore it in two; the one old boy is as much a character as the other, and between the two of them I'm at my wits' end.'

'So you put that advertisement in the paper?' said Raffles, in the dry tones he had adopted throughout the interview.

'As a last resort, I did.'

'And you wish us to steal this picture?'

It was magnificently said; the lawyer flushed from his hair to his collar.

'I knew you were not the men!' he groaned. 'I never thought of men of your stamp! But it's not stealing,' he exclaimed heatedly; 'it's recovering stolen property. Besides, Sir Bernard will pay him his five thousand as soon as he has the picture; and, you'll see, old Craggs will be just as loath to let it come out as Sir Bernard himself. No, no – it's an enterprise, and adventure, if you like – but not stealing.'

'You yourself mentioned the law,' murmured Raffles.

'And the risk,' I added.

'We pay for that,' he said once more.

'But not enough,' said Raffles, shaking his head. 'My good sir, consider what it means to us. You spoke of those clubs; we should not only get kicked out of them but put in prison like common burglars! It's true we're hard up, but it simply isn't worth it at the price. Double your stakes, and I for one am your man.'

Addenbrooke wavered.

'Do you think you could bring it off?'

'We could try.'

'But you have no – –'

'Experience? Well, hardly!'

'And you would really run the risk for four thousand pounds?'

Raffles looked at me. I nodded.

'We would,' said he, 'and blow the odds!'

'It's more than I can ask my client to pay,' said Addenbrooke, growing firm.

'Then it's more than you can expect us to risk.'

'You are in earnest?'

'Yes!'

'Say three thousand if you succeed!'

'Four is our figure, Mr Addenbrooke.'

'Then I think it should be nothing if you fail.'

'Double or quits?' cried Raffles. 'Well, that's sporting. Done!'

Addenbrooke opened his lips, half rose, then sat back in his chair, and looked long and shrewdly at Raffles – never once at me.

'I know your bowling,' said he reflectively. 'I go up to Lord's whenever I want an hour's real rest, and I've seen you bowl again and again – yes, and take the best wickets in England on a plumb pitch. I don't forget the last Gentlemen and Players; I was there. You're up to every trick – every one .. I'm inclined to think that if anybody could bowl out this old Australian ... Damme, I believe you're my very man!'

The bargain was clenched at the Café Royal, where Bennett Addenbrooke insisted on playing host at an extravagant luncheon. I remember that he took his whack of champagne with the nervous freedom of a man at high pressure, and have no doubt I kept him in countenance by an equal indulgence; but Raffles, ever an exemplar in such matters, was more abstemious even than his wont, and very poor company to boot. I can see him now, his eyes on his plate – thinking – thinking. I can see the solicitor glancing from him to me in an apprehension of which I did my best to disabuse him by reassuring looks. At the close Raffles apologised for his preoccupation, called for an A.B.C. time-table, and announced his intention of catching the 3.2 to Esher.

'You must excuse me, Mr Addenbrooke,' said he, 'but I have my own idea, and, for the moment I would much prefer to keep it to myself. It may end in fizzle, so I would rather not speak about it to either of you just yet. But speak to Sir Bernard I must, so will you write me one line to him on your card? Of course, if you wish you must come down with me and hear what I say; but I really don't see much point in it.'

And as usual Raffles had his way, though Bennett Addenbrooke showed some temper when he was gone, and I myself shared his annoyance to no small extent. I could only tell him that it was in the nature of Raffles to be self-willed and secretive, but that no man of my acquaintance had half his audacity and determination; that I for my part would trust him through and through and let him gang his own gait every time. More I dared not say, even to remove those chill misgivings with which I knew that the lawyer went his way.

That day I saw no more of Raffles, but a telegram reached me when I was dressing for dinner:

'Be in your rooms to-morrow from noon and keep rest of day clear. – RAFFLES.'

It had been sent from Waterloo at 6.42.

So Raffles was back in town; at an earlier stage of our relations I should have hunted him up then and there, but now I knew better. His telegram meant that he had no desire for my society that night or the following forenoon; that when he wanted me I should see him soon enough.

And see him I did, towards one o'clock next day. I was watching for him from my window in Mount Street, when he drove up furiously in a cab, and jumped out without a word to the man. I met him next minute at the lift gates, and he fairly pushed me back into my rooms.

'Five minutes, Bunny!' he cried. 'Not a moment more.'

And he tore off his coat, flinging himself into the nearest chair.

'I'm fairly on the rush,' he panted; 'having the very devil of a time! Not a word till I've told you all I've done. I settled my plan of campaign yesterday at lunch. The first thing was to get in with this man Craggs; you can't break into a place like the Metropole, it's got to be done from the inside. Problem one, how to get at the fellow. Only one sort of pretext would do – it must be something to do with this blessed picture, so that I might see where he'd got it and all that. Well, I couldn't go and ask to see it out of curiosity, and I couldn't go as a second representative of the old chap, and it was thinking how I could go that made me such a bear at lunch. But I saw my way before we got up. If I could only lay hold of a copy of the picture I might ask leave to go and compare it with the original. So down I went to Esher to find out if there was a copy in existence, and was at Broom Hall for one hour and a half yesterday afternoon. There was no copy there, but they must exist, for Sir Bernard himself (there's "copy" there!) has allowed a couple to be made since the picture has been in his possession. He hunted up the painters' addresses, and the rest of the evening I spent in hunting up the painters themselves; but their work had been done on commission; one copy had gone out of the country, and I'm still on the track of the other.'

'Then you haven't seen Craggs yet?'

'Seen him and made friends with him, and if possible he's the funnier old cuss of the two; but you should study 'em both. I took the bull by the horns this morning, went in and lied like Ananias, and it was just as well I did – the old ruffian sails for Australia by to-morrow's boat. I told him a man wanted to sell me a copy of the celebrated Infanta Maria Teresa of Velasquez, that I'd been down to the supposed owner of the picture, only to find that he had just sold it to him. You should have seen his face when I told him that! He grinned all round his wicked old head. "Did old Debenham admit the sale?" says he; and when I said he had, he chuckled to himself for about five minutes. He was so pleased that he did just what I hoped he would do; he showed me the great picture – luckily it isn't by any means a large one – also the case he's got it in. It's an iron map-case in which he brought over the plans of his land in Brisbane; he wants to know who would suspect it of containing an Old Master too? But he's had it fitted with a new Chubb's lock, and I managed to take an interest in the key while he was gloating over the canvas. I had the wax in the palm of my hand, and I shall make my duplicate this afternoon.'

Raffles looked at his watch and jumped up, saying he had given me a minute too much.

'By the way,' he added, 'you've got to dine with him at the Metropole to-night!'

'I?'

'Yes; don't look so scared. Both of us are invited – I swore you were dining with me. I accepted for us both; but I shan't be there.'

His clear eye was upon me, bright with meaning and with mischief. I implored him to tell me what his meaning was.

'You will dine in his private sitting-room,' said Raffles; 'it adjoins his bedroom. You must keep him sitting as long as possible, Bunny, and talking all the time!'

In a flash I saw his plan.

'You're going for the picture while we're at dinner?'

'I am.'

'If he hears you!'

'He shan't.'

'But if he does!'

And I fairly trembled at the thought.

'If he does,' said Raffles, 'there will be a collision, that's all. Revolvers would be out of place in the Metropole, but I shall certainly take a life-preserver.'

'But it's ghastly!' I cried. 'To sit and talk to an utter stranger and to know that you're at work in the next room!'

'Two thousand apiece,' said Raffles quietly.

'Upon my soul I believe I shall give it away!'

'Not you, Bunny. I know you better than you know yourself.' He put on his coat and his hat.

'What time have I to be there?' I asked him, with a groan.

'Quarter to eight. There will be a telegram from me saying I can't turn up. He's a terror to talk, you'll have no difficulty to keep the ball rolling; but head him off his picture for all you're worth. If he offers to show it you, say you must go. He locked up the case elaborately this afternoon, and there's no earthly reason why he should unlock it again in this hemisphere.'

'Where shall I find you when I get away?'

'I shall be down at Esher. I hope to catch the 9.55.'

'But surely I can see you again this afternoon?' I cried in a ferment, for his hand was on the door. 'I'm not half-coached up yet! I know I shall make a mess of it!'

'Not you,' he said again, 'but I shall if I waste any more time. I've got a deuce of a lot of rushing about to do yet. You won't find me at my rooms. Why not come down to Esher yourself by the last train? That's it – down you come with the latest news! I'll tell old Debenham to expect you : he shall give us both a bed. By Jove! he won't be able to do us too well if he's got his picture.'

'If!' I groaned as he nodded his adieu; and he left me limp with apprehension, sick with fear, in a perfectly pitiable condition of pure stage-fright.

For, after all, I had only to act my part; unless Raffles failed where he never did fail, unless Raffles the neat and noiseless was for once clumsy and inept, all I had to do was indeed to 'smile and smile and be a villain.' I practised that smile half the afternoon. I rehearsed putative parts in hypothetical conversations. I got up stories. I dipped in a book on Queensland at the club. And at last it was 7.45, and I was making my bow to a somewhat elderly man with a small bald head and a retreating brow.

'So you're Mr Raffles's friend?' said he, overhauling me rather rudely with his light small eyes. 'Seen anything of him? Expected him early to show me something, but he's never come.'

No more, evidently, had his telegram, and my troubles were beginning early. I said I had not seen Raffles since one o'clock, telling the truth with unction while I could; even as we spoke there came a knock at the door; it was the telegram at last, and, after reading it himself, the Queenslander handed it to me.

'Called out of town!' he grumbled. 'Sudden illness of near relative! What near relatives has he got?'

I knew of none, and for an instant I quailed before the perils of invention; then I replied that I had never met any of his people, and again felt fortified by my veracity.

'Thought you were bosom pals?' said he, with (as I imagined) a gleam of suspicion in his crafty little eyes.

'Only in town,' said I. 'I've never been to his place.'

'Well,' he growled, 'I suppose it can't be helped. Don't know why he couldn't come and have his dinner first. Like to see the deathbed I'd go to without my dinner; it's a full-skin billet, if you ask me. Well, must just dine without him, and he'll have to buy his pig in a poke after all. Mind touching that bell? Suppose you know what he came to see me about. Sorry I shan't see him again, for his own sake. I like Raffles – took to him amazingly. He's a cynic. Like cynics. One myself. Rank bad form of his mother, or his aunt, and I hope she will kick the bucket.'

I connect these specimens of his conversation, though they were doubtless detached at the time, and interspersed with remarks of mine here and there. They filled the intervals until dinner was served, and they gave me an impression of the man which his every subsequent utterance confirmed. It was an impression which did away with all remorse for my treacherous presence at his table. He was that terrible type, the Silly Cynic, his aim a caustic commentary on all things and all men, his achievement mere vulgar irreverence, and unintelligent scorn. Ill-bred and ill-informed, he had (on his own showing) fluked into fortune on a rise in land; yet cunning he possessed, as well as malice, and he chuckled till he choked over the misfortunes of less astute speculators in the same boom. Even now I cannot feel much compunction for my behaviour to the Hon. J. M. Craggs, M.L.C.

But never shall I forget the private agonies of the situation, the listening to my host with one ear and for Raffles with the other! Once I heard him – though the rooms were not divided by the old-fashioned folding-doors, and though the door that did divide them was not only shut but richly curtained, I could have sworn I heard him once. I spilt my wine and laughed at the top of my voice at some coarse sally of my host's. And I heard nothing more, though my ears were on the strain. But later, to my horror, when the waiter had finally withdrawn, Craggs himself sprang up and rushed to his bedroom without a word. I sat like stone till he returned.

'Thought I heard a door go,' he said. 'Must have been mistaken ... imagination ... gave me quite a turn. Raffles tell you of the priceless treasure I've got in there?'

It was the picture at last; up to this point I had kept him to Queensland and the making of his pile. I tried to get him back there now, but in vain. He was reminded of his great ill-gotten possession. I said that Raffles had just mentioned it, and that set him off. With the confidential garrulity of a man who has dined too well, he plunged into his darling topic, and I looked past him at the clock. It was only a quarter to ten.

In common decency I could not go yet. So there I sat (we were still at port) and learnt what had originally fired my host's ambition to possess what he was pleased to call 'a real, genuine, twin-screw, double-funnelled, copper-bottomed Old Master'; it was to 'go one better' than some rival legislator of pictorial proclivities. But even an epitome of his monologue would be so much weariness; suffice it that it ended inevitably in the invitation I had dreaded all the evening.

'But you must see it. Next room. This way.'

'Isn't it packed up?' I inquired hastily.

'Lock and key. That's all.'

'Pray don't trouble,' I urged.

'Trouble be hanged!' said he. 'Come along.'

And all at once I saw that to resist him further would be to heap suspicion upon myself against the moment of impending discovery. I therefore followed him into his bedroom without further protest, and suffered him first to show me the iron map-case which stood in one corner; he took a crafty pride in this receptacle, and I thought he would never cease descanting on its innocent appearance and its Chubb's lock. It seemed an in-terminable age before the key was in the latter. Then the ward clicked, and my pulse stood still.

'By Jove!' I cried the next instant.

The canvas was in its place among the maps!

'Thought it would knock you,' said Craggs, drawing it out and unfolding it for my benefit. 'Grand thing, ain't it? Wouldn't think it had been painted two hundred and thirty years? It has, though, my word! Old Johnson's face will be a treat when he sees it; won't go bragging about his pictures much more. Why, this one's worth all the pictures in Colony o' Queensland put together. Worth fifty thousand pounds, my boy – and I got it for five!'

He dug me in the ribs, and seemed in the mood for further confidences. My appearance checked him, and he rubbed his hands.

'If you take it like that,' he chuckled, 'how will old Johnson take it? Go out and hang himself to his own picture-rods, I hope!'

Heaven knows what I contrived to say at last. Struck speech-less first by my relief, I continued silent from a very different cause. A new tangle of emotions tied my tongue. Raffles had failed – could I not succeed? Was it too late? Was there no way?

'So long,' he said, taking a last look at the canvas before he rolled it up – 'so long till we get to Brisbane.'

The flutter I was in as he closed the case!

'For the last time,' he went on, as his keys jingled back into his pocket. 'It goes straight into the strong-room on board.'

For the last time! If I could but send him out to Australia with only its legitimate contents in his precious map-case! I could but succeed where Raffles had failed!

We returned to the other room. I have no notion how long he talked, or what about. Whisky and soda-water became the order of the hour. I scarcely touched it, but he drank copiously, and before eleven I left him incoherent. And the last train for Esher was the 11.50 out of Waterloo.

I took a cab to my rooms. I was back at the hotel in thirteen minutes. I walked upstairs. The corridor was empty; I stood an instant on the sitting-room threshold, heard a snore within, and admitted myself softly with my gentleman's own key, which it had been a very simple matter to take away with me.

Craggs never moved; he was stretched on the sofa fast asleep. But not fast enough for me. I saturated my handkerchief with the chloroform I had brought, and I laid it gently over his mouth. Two or three stertorous breaths, and the man was a log.

I removed the handkerchief; I extracted the keys from his pocket. In less than five minutes I put them back, after winding the picture about my body beneath my Inverness cape. I took some whisky and soda-water before I went.

The train was easily caught – so easily that I trembled for ten minutes in my first-class smoking carriage, in terror of every footstep on the platform – in unreasonable terror till the end. Then at last I sat back and lit a cigarette, and the lights of Waterloo reeled out behind.

Some men were returning from the theatre. I can recall their conversation even now. They were disappointed with the piece they had seen. It was one of the later Savoy operas, and they spoke wistfully of the days of *Pinafore* and *Patience*. One of them hummed a stave, and there was an argument as to whether the air was out of *Patience* or the *Mikado*. They all got out at Surbiton, and I was alone with my triumph for a few intoxicating minutes. To think that I had succeeded where Raffles had failed! Of all our adventures this was the first in which I had played a commanding part; and, of them all, this was infinitely the least discreditable. It left me without a conscientious qualm; I had but robbed a robber, when all was said.

And I had done it myself, single-handed – *ipse egomet!*

I pictured Raffles, his surprise, his delight. He would think a little more of me in future. And that future, it should be different. We had two thousand pounds apiece – surely enough to start afresh as honest men – and all through me.

In a glow I sprang out at Esher, and took the one belated cab that was waiting under the bridge. In a perfect fever I beheld Broom Hall, with the lower story still lit up, and saw the front door open as I climbed the steps.

'Thought it was you,' said Raffles cheerily. 'It's all right. There's a bed for you. Sir Bernard's sitting up to shake your hand.'

His good spirits disappointed me. But I knew the man; he was one of those who wear their brightest smile in the blackest hour. I knew him too well by this time to be deceived.

'I've got it!' I cried in his ear. 'I've got it!'

'Got what?' he asked, stepping back.

'The picture!'

'What?'

'The picture. He showed it me. You had to go without it; I saw that. So I determined to have it. And here it is.'

'Let's see,' said Raffles grimly.

I threw off my cape and unwound the canvas from about my body. While I was doing so an untidy old gentleman made his appearance in the hall, and stood looking on with raised eyebrows.

'Looks pretty fresh for an Old Master, doesn't she?' said Raffles.

His tone was strange. I could only suppose that he was jealous of my success.

'So Craggs said. I hardly looked at it myself.'

'Well, look now – look closely. By Jove, I must have faked her better than I thought!'

'It's a copy!' I cried.

'It's the copy,' he answered. 'It's the copy I've been tearing all over the country to procure. It's the copy I faked back and front, so that, on your own showing, it imposed upon Craggs, and might have made him happy for life. And you go and rob him of that!'

I could not speak.

'How did you manage it?' inquired Sir Bernard Debenham.

'Have you killed him?' asked Raffles sardonically.

I did not look at him: I turned to Sir Bernard Debenham, and to him I told my story, hoarsely, excitedly, for it was all that I could do to keep from breaking down. But as I spoke I became calmer, and I finished in mere bitterness, with the remark that another time Raffles might tell me what he meant to do.

'Another time!' he cried instantly. 'My dear Bunny, you speak as though we were going to turn burglars for a living!'

'I trust you won't,' said Sir Bernard, smiling, 'for you are certainly two very daring young men. Let us hope our friend from Queensland will do as he said, and not open his map-case till he gets back there. He will find my cheque awaiting him, and I shall be very much surprised if he troubles any of us again.'

Raffles and I did not speak till I was in the room which had been prepared for me. Nor was I anxious to do so then. But he followed me and took my hand.

'Bunny,' said he, 'don't you be hard on a fellow! I was in the deuce of a hurry, and didn't know that I should get what I wanted in time, and that's a fact. But it serves me right that you should have gone and undone one of the best things I ever did. As for your handiwork, old chap, you won't mind my saying that I didn't think you had it in you. In future – '

'Don't talk to me about the future!' I cried. 'I hate the whole thing! I'm going to chuck it up!'

'So am I,' said Raffles, 'when I've made my pile.'

THE RETURN MATCH

I HAD turned into Piccadilly, one thick evening in the following November, when my guilty heart stood still at the sudden grip of a hand upon my arm. I thought – I was always thinking – that my inevitable hour was come at last. It was only Raffles, however, who stood smiling at me through the fog.

'Well met!' said he; 'I've been looking for you at the club.'

'I was just on my way there,' I returned, with an attempt to hide my tremors. It was an ineffectual attempt, as I saw from his broader smile, and by the indulgent shake of his head.

'Come up to my place instead,' said he. 'I've something amusing to tell you.'

I made excuses, for his tone foretold the kind of amusement, and it was a kind against which I had successfully set my face for months. I have stated before, however, and I can but reiterate, that to me, at all events, there was never anybody in the world so irresistible as Raffles when his mind was made up. That we had both been independent of crime since our little service to Sir Bernard Debenham – that there had been no occasion for that masterful mind to be made up in any such direction for many a day – was the undeniable basis of a longer spell of honesty than I had hitherto enjoyed during the term of our mutual intimacy. Be sure I would deny it if I could; the very thing I am to tell you would discredit such a boast. I made my excuses, as I have said. But his arm slid through mine, with his little laugh of light-hearted mastery. And even while I argued we were on his staircase in the Albany.

His fire had fallen low. He poked and replenished it after turning on the lights. As for me, I stood by sullenly in my overcoat until he dragged it off my back.

'What a chap you are!' said Raffles playfully. 'One would really think I had proposed to crack another crib, this blessed night! Well, it isn't that, Bunny; so get into that chair and take one of these Sullivans, and sit tight.'

He held the match to my cigarette; he brought me a whisky and soda. Then he went out in the lobby, and, just as I was beginning to feel happy, I heard the bolt shot home. It cost me an effort to remain in that chair; next moment he was straddling another and gloating over my discomfiture across his folded arms.

'You remember Milchester, Bunny, old boy?'

His tone was as bland as mine was grim when I answered that I did.

'We had a little match there that wasn't down on the card. Gentlemen and Players, if you recollect?'

'I don't forget it.'

'Seeing that you never got an innings, so to speak, I thought you might. Well, the Gentlemen scored pretty freely, but the Players were all caught – '

'Poor devils!'

'Don't be too sure. You remember the fellow we saw in the inn? The florid, over-dressed chap who I told you was one of the cleverest thieves in town?'

'I remember him. Crawshay his name turned out to be.'

'Well, it was certainly the name he was convicted under, so Crawshay let it be. You needn't waste any pity on him, old chap; he escaped from Dartmoor yesterday afternoon.'

'Well done!'

Raffles smiled, but his eyebrows had gone up and his shoulders followed suit.

'You are perfectly right; it was very well done indeed. I wonder you didn't see it in the paper. In a dense fog on the moor yesterday good old Crawshay made a bolt for it, and got away without a scratch under heavy fire. All honour to him, I agree; a fellow with that much grit deserves his liberty. But Crawshay has a good deal more. They hunted him all night long; couldn't find him for nuts; and that was all you missed in the morning papers.'

He unfolded a *Pall Mall*, which he had brought in with him.

'But listen to this; here's an account of the escape, with just the addition which puts the thing on a higher level. "The fugitive has been traced to Totnes, where he appears to have committed a peculiarly daring outrage in the early hours of this morning. He is reported to have entered the lodgings of the Rev. A. H. Ellingworth, curate of the parish, who missed his clothes on rising at the usual hour; later in the morning those of the convict were discovered neatly folded at the bottom of a drawer. Meanwhile Crawshay had made good his second escape, though it is believed that so distinctive a guise will lead to his recapture during the day." What do you think of that, Bunny?'

'He is certainly a sportsman,' said I, reaching for the paper.

'He's more,' said Raffles; 'he's an artist, and I envy him. The curate, of all men! Beautiful – beautiful! But that's not all. I saw just now on the board at the club that there's been an outrage on the line near Dawlish. Parson found insensible in the six-foot way. Our friend again. The telegram doesn't say so, but it's obvious; he's simply knocked some other fellow out, changed clothes again, and come on gaily to town. Isn't it great? I do believe it's the best thing of the kind that's ever been done!'

'But why should he come to town?'

In an instant the enthusiasm faded from Raffles's face. Clearly I had reminded him of some prime anxiety, forgotten in his impersonal joy over the exploit of a fellow-criminal. He looked over his shoulder towards the lobby before replying.

'I believe,' said he, 'that the beggar's on my tracks!'

And as he spoke he was himself again – quietly amused – cynically unperturbed – characteristically enjoying the situation and my surprise.

'But look here, what do you mean?' said I. 'What does Crawshay know about you?'

'Not much; but he suspects.'

'Why should he?'

'Because, in his way, he's very nearly as good a man as I am; because, my dear Bunny, with eyes in his head and brains behind them, he couldn't help suspecting. He saw me once in town with old Baird. He must have seen me that day in the pub, on the way to Milchester, as well as afterwards on the cricket-field. As a matter of fact, I know he did, for he wrote and told me so before his trial.'

'He wrote to you! And you never told me!'

The old shrug answered the old grievance.

'What was the good, my dear fellow? It would only have worried you.'

'Well, what did he say?'

'That he was sorry he had been run in before getting back to town, as he had proposed doing himself the honour of paying me a call; however, he trusted it was only a pleasure deferred, and he begged me not to go and get lagged myself before he came out. Of course he knew the Melrose necklace was gone, though he hadn't got it; and he said that the man who could take that and leave the rest was a man after his own heart. And so on, with certain little proposals for the far future, which I fear may be the very near future indeed! I'm only surprised he hasn't turned up yet.'

He looked again towards the lobby, which he had left in darkness, with the inner door shut as carefully as the outer one. I asked him what he meant to do.

'Let him knock – if he gets so far. The porter is to say I'm out of town; it will be true, too, in another hour or so.'

'You're going off to-night?'

'By the 7.15 from Liverpool Street. I don't say much about my people, Bunny, but I have the best of sisters married to a country parson in the eastern counties. They always make me welcome, and let me read the lessons for the sake of getting me to church. I'm sorry you won't be there to hear me on Sunday, Bunny. I've figured out some of my best schemes in that parish, and I know of no better port in a storm. But I must pack. I thought I'd just let you know where I was going, and why, in case you cared to follow my example.'

He flung the stump of his cigarette into the fire, stretched himself as he rose, and remained so long in the inelegant attitude that my eyes mounted from his body to his face; a second later they had followed his eyes across the room, and I also was on my legs. On the threshold of the folding doors that divided bedroom and sitting-room, a well-built man stood in ill-fitting broadcloth, and bowed to us until his bullet head presented an unbroken disc of short red hair.

Brief as was my survey of this astounding apparition, the interval was long enough for Raffles to recover his composure;

his hands were in his pockets, and a smile upon his face, when my eyes flew back to him.

'Let me introduce you, Bunny,' said he, 'to our distinguished colleague, Mr Reginald Crawshay.'

The bullet head bobbed up, and there was a wrinkled brow above the coarse, shaven face, crimson, also I remember, from the grip of a collar several sizes too small. But I noted nothing consciously at the time. I had jumped to my own conclusion, and I turned on Raffles with an oath.

'It's a trick!' I cried. 'It's another of your cursed tricks. You got him here, and then you got me. You want me to join you, I suppose? I'll see you damned!'

So cold was the stare which met this outburst that I became ashamed of my words while they were yet upon my lips.

'Really, Bunny!' said Raffles, and turned his shoulder with a shrug.

'Lord love yer,' cried Crawshay, ' 'e knew nothin'. 'E didn't expect me; 'e's all right. And you're the cool canary, you are,' he went on to Raffles. 'I knoo you were, but, do me proud, you're one after my own kidney.' And he thrust out a shaggy hand.

'After that,' said Raffles, taking it, 'what am I to say? But you must have heard my opinion of you. I am proud to make your acquaintance. How the deuce did you get in?'

'Never you mind,' said Crawshay, loosening his collar; 'let's talk about how I'm to get out. Lord love yer, but that's better!' There was a livid ring round his bull-neck, that he fingered tenderly. 'Didn't know how much longer I might have to play the gent,' he explained, 'didn't know who you'd bring in.'

'Drink whisky and soda?' inquired Raffles, when the convict was in the chair from which I had leapt.

'No, I drink it neat,' replied Crawshay, 'but I talk business first. You don't get over me like that, Lor' love yer!'

'Well, then, what can I do for you?'

'You know without me tellin' you.'

'Give it a name.'

'Clean heels, then; that's what I want to show, and I leaves the way to you. We're brothers in arms, though I ain't armed this time. It ain't necessary. You've too much sense. But brothers we are, and you'll see a brother through. Let's put it at that. You'll see me through in your own way. I leaves it all to you.'

His tone was rich with conciliation and concession; he bent over and tore a pair of button boots from his bare feet, which he stretched towards the fire, painfully uncurling his toes.

'I hope you take a larger size than them,' said he. 'I'd have had a see if you'd given me time. I wasn't in long afore you.'

'And you won't tell me how you got in?'

'Wot's the use? I can't teach you nothin'. Besides, I want out. I want out of London, an' England, an' bloomin' Europe too. That's all I want of you, mister. I don't arst how you got on the job. You know w'ere I come from, 'cos I heard you say; you know w'ere I want to 'ead for, 'cos I've just told yer; the details I leaves entirely to you.'

'Well,' said Raffles, 'we must see what can be done.'

'We must,' said Mr Crawshay, and leaned back comfortably, and began twirling his stubby thumbs.

Raffles turned to me with a twinkle in his eye; but his forehead was scored with thought, and resolve mingled with resignation in the lines of his mouth. And he spoke exactly as though he and I were alone in the room.

'You seize the situation, Bunny? If our friend here is "copped," to speak his language, he means to "blow the gaff" on you and me. He is considerate enough not to say so in so many words, but it's plain enough, and natural enough for that matter. I would do the same in his place. We had the bulge before; he has it now; it's perfectly fair. We must take on this job; we aren't in a position to refuse it; even if we were, I should take it on. Our friend is a great sportsman; he has got clear away from Dartmoor; it would be a thousand pities to let him go back. Nor shall he; not if I can think of a way of getting him abroad.'

'Any way you like,' murmured Crawshay, with his eyes shut. 'I leaves the 'ole thing to you.'

'But you'll have to wake up and tell us things.'

'All right, mister; but I'm fair on the rocks for a sleep!'

And he stood up blinking.

'Think you were traced to town?'

114

'Must have been.'

'And here?'

'Not in this fog – not with any luck.'

Raffles went into the bedroom, lit the gas there, and returned next minute.

'So you got in by the window?'

'That's about it.'

'It was devilish smart of you to know which one; it beats me how you brought it off in daylight, fog or no fog! But let that pass. Don't you think you were seen?'

'I don't think it, sir.'

'Well, let's hope you are right. I shall reconnoitre and soon find out. And you'd better come too, Bunny, and have something to eat and talk it over.'

As Raffles looked at me, I looked at Crawshay, anticipating trouble; and trouble brewed in his blank, fierce face, in the glitter of his startled eyes, in the sudden closing of his fists.

'And what's to become of me?' he cried out with an oath.

'You wait here.'

'No, you don't,' he roared, and at a bound had his back to the door. 'You don't get round me like that, you cuckoos!'

Raffles turned to me with a twitch of the shoulders.

'That's the worst of these professors,' said he; 'they never will use their heads. They see the pegs, and they mean to hit 'em; but that's all they do see and mean, and they think we're the same. No wonder we licked them last time!'

'Don't talk through yer neck,' snarled the convict. 'Talk out straight, curse you!'

'Right,' said Raffles. 'I'll talk as straight as you like. You say you put yourself in my hands – you leave it all to me – yet you don't trust me an inch! I know what's to happen if I fail. I accept the risk. I take this thing on. Yet you think I'm going straight out to give you away and make you give me away in my turn. You're a fool, Mr Crawshay, though you have broken Dartmoor; you've got to listen to a better man, and obey him. I see you through in my own way, or not at all. I come and go as I like, and with whom I like, without your interference; you stay here and lie just as low as you know how, be as wise as your word, and leave the whole thing to me. If you won't – if

you're fool enough not to trust me – there's the door. Go out
and say what you like, and be damned to you!'

Crawshay slapped his thigh.

'That's talking!' said he. 'Lord love yer, I know where I am
when you talk like that. I'll trust yer. I know a man when he
gets his tongue between his teeth; you're all right. I don't say
so much about this other gent, though I saw him along with
you on the job that time in the provinces; but, if he's a pal of
yours, Mr Raffles, he'll be all right too. I only hope you gents
ain't too stony – –'

And he touched his pockets with a rueful face.

'I only went for their togs,' said he. 'You never struck two
such stony-broke cusses in yer life.'

'That's all right,' said Raffles. 'We'll see you through properly.
Leave it to us, and you sit tight.'

'Rightum!' said Crawshay. 'And I'll have a sleep time you're
gone. But no sperrits – no thank'ee – not yet! Once let me loose
on lush, and, Lord love yer, I'm a gone coon!'

Raffles got his overcoat, a long, light driving coat, I remember, and even as he put it on our fugitive was dozing in the
chair; we left him murmuring incoherently, with the lights out,
and his bare feet toasting.

'Not such a bad chap, that professor,' said Raffles on the
stairs; 'a real genius in his way, too, though his methods are a
little elementary for my taste. But technique isn't everything;
to get out of Dartmoor and into the Albany in the same
twenty-four hours is the whole that justifies its parts. Good
Lord!'

We had passed a man in the foggy courtyard, and Raffles had
nipped my arm.

'Who was it?'

'The last man we want to see! I hope to Heaven he didn't
hear me! Our old friend Mackenzie, from the Yard!'

I stood still with horror.

'Do you think he's on Crawshay's track?'

'I don't know. I'll find out.'

And before I could remonstrate he had wheeled me round;
when I found my voice he merely laughed, and whispered that
the bold course was the safe one every time.

'But it's madness – –'

'Not it. Shut up! Is that you, Mr Mackenzie?'

The detective turned about and scrutinised us keenly; and through the gaslit mist I noticed that his hair was grizzled at the temples, and his face still cadaverous from the wound that had nearly been his death.

'Ye have the advantage o' me, sirs,' said he.

'I hope you're fit again,' said my companion. 'My name is Raffles, and we met at Milchester last year.'

'Is that a fact?' cried the Scotsman, with quite a start. 'Yes, now I remember your face, and yours too, sir, Ay, yon was a bad business, but it ended vera well, an' that's the main thing.'

His native caution had returned to him. Raffles pinched my arm.

'Yes, it ended splendidly, but for you,' said he. 'But what about this escape of the leader of the gang, that fellow Crawshay? What do you think of that, eh?'

'I havena the parteeculars,' replied the Scot.

'Good!' cried Raffles. 'I was only afraid you might be on his tracks once more!'

Mackenzie shook his head with a dry smile, and wished us good evening, as an invisible window was thrown up and a whistle blown softly through the fog.

'We must see this out,' whispered Raffles. 'Nothing more natural than a little curiosity on our part. After him, quick!'

And he followed the detective into another entrance on the same side as that from which we had emerged, the left-hand side on one's way to Piccadilly; quite openly we followed him, and at the foot of the stairs met one of the porters of the place. Raffles asked him what was wrong.

'Nothing, sir,' said the fellow glibly.

'Rot!' said Raffles. 'That was Mackenzie, the detective. I've just been speaking to him. What's he here for? Come on, my good fellow; we won't give you away, if you've instructions not to tell.'

The man looked quaintly wistful, the temptation of an audience hot upon him; a door shut upstairs, and he fell.

'It's like this,' he whispered. 'This afternoon a gen'leman comes arfter rooms, and I sent him to the orfice; one of the

clurks, 'e goes round with 'im an' shows 'im the empties, an'
the gen'leman's partic'ly struck on the set the coppers is up in
now. So he sends the clurk to fetch the manager, as there was
one or two things he wished to speak about; an' when they
come back, blowed if the gent isn't gone! Beg your pardon, sir,
but he's clean disappeared off the face of the premises!' And
the porter looked at us with shining eyes.

'Well?' said Raffles.

'Well, sir, they looked about, an' at larst they give him up for
a bad job; thought he'd changed his mind an' didn't want to
tip the clurk; so they shut up the place and come away. An'
that's all till about 'alf an hour ago, when I takes the manager
his extry-speshul *Star*; in about ten minutes he comes running
out with a note an' sends me with it to Scotland Yard in a
hansom. An' that's all I know, sir – straight. The coppers is up
there now, and the tec and the manager, and they think their
gent is about the place somewhere still. Least, I reckon that's
their idea; but who he is, or what they want him for, I dunno.'

'Jolly interesting!' said Raffles. 'I'm going up to inquire.
Come on, Bunny; there should be some fun.'

'Beg yer pardon, Mr Raffles, but you won't say nothing
about me?'

'Not I; you're a good fellow. I won't forget it if this leads to
sport. Sport!' he whispered, as we reached the landing. 'It looks
like precious poor sport for you and me, Bunny!'

'What are you going to do?'

'I don't know. There's no time to think. This, to start with.'

And he thundered on the shut door; a policeman opened it.
Raffles strode past him with the air of a chief commissioner,
and I followed before the man had recovered from his astonishment. The bare boards rang under us; in the bedroom we found
a knot of officers stooping over the window-ledge with a constable's lantern. Mackenzie was the first to stand upright, and
he greeted us with a glare.

'May I ask what you gentlemen want?' said he.

'We want to lend a hand,' said Raffles briskly. 'We lent
one once before, and it was my friend here who took
over from you the fellow who split on all the rest and
held him tight. Surely that entitles him, at all events, to see any

fun that's going? As for myself, well, it's true I only helped to carry you to the house; but for old acquaintance I do hope, my dear Mr Mackenzie, that you will permit us to share such sport as there may be. I myself can only stop a few minutes, in any case.'

'Then ye'll not see much,' growled the detective, 'for he's not up here. Constable, go you and stand at the foot o' the stairs, and let no other body come up on any consideration; these gentlemen may be able to help us after all.'

'That's kind of you, Mackenzie!' cried Raffles warmly. 'But what is it all? I questioned a porter I met coming down, but could get nothing out of him, except that somebody had been to see these rooms and not since been seen himself.'

'He's a man we want,' said Mackenzie. 'He's concealed himself somewhere about these premises, or I'm vera much mistaken. D'ye reside in the Albany, Mr Raffles?'

'I do.'

'Will your rooms be near these?'

'On the next staircase but one.'

'Ye'll just have left them?'

'Just.'

'Been in all the afternoon, likely?'

'Not all.'

'Then I may have to search your rooms, sir. I am prepared to search every room in the Albany! Our man seems to have gone for the leads; but unless he's left more marks outside than in, or we find him up there, I shall have the entire building to ransack.'

'I will leave you my key,' said Raffles at once. 'I am dining out, but I'll leave it with the officer down below.'

I caught my breath in mute amazement. What was the meaning of this insane promise? It was wilful, gratuitous, suicidal; it made me catch at his sleeve in open horror and disgust; but, with a word of thanks, Mackenzie had returned to his window-sill, and we sauntered unwatched through the folding doors in the adjoining room. Here the window looked down into the courtyard; it was still open; and as we gazed out in apparent idleness, Raffles reassured me.

'It's all right, Bunny; you do what I tell you and leave the

119

rest to me. It's a tight corner, but I don't despair. What you've got to do is to stick to these chaps, especially if they search my rooms; they mustn't poke about more than necessary, and they won't if you're there.'

'But where will you be? You're never going to leave me to be landed alone?'

'If I do, it will be to turn up trumps at the right moment. Besides, there are such things as windows, and Crawshay's the man to take his risks. You must trust me, Bunny; you've known me long enough.'

'And you're going now?'

'There's no time to lose. Stick to them, old chap, don't let them suspect you, whatever else you do.' His hand lay an instant on my shoulder; then he left me at the window, and recrossed the room.

'I've got to go now,' I heard him say; 'but my friend will stay and see this through, and I'll leave the light on in my rooms – and my key with the constable downstairs. Good luck, Mackenzie; only wish I could stay.'

'Good-bye, sir,' came in a preoccupied voice, 'and many thanks.'

Mackenzie was still busy at his window, and I remained at mine, a prey to mingled fear and wrath, for all my knowledge of Raffles and of his infinite resource. By this time I felt that I knew more or less what he would do in any given emergency; at least I could conjecture a characteristic course of equal cunning and audacity. He would return to his rooms, put Crawshay on his guard, and – stow him away? No – there were such things as windows. Then why was Raffles going to desert us all? I thought of many things – lastly of a cab. These bedroom windows looked into a narrow side-street; they were not very high; from them a man might drop on to the roof of a cab – even as it passed – and be driven away – even under the noses of the police! I pictured Raffles driving that cab, unrecognisable in the foggy night; the vision came to me as he passed under the window, tucking up the collar of his great driving-coat on the way to his rooms; it was still with me when he passed again on his way back, and stopped to hand the constable his key.

'We're on his track,' said a voice behind me. 'He's got up on the leads, sure enough, though how he managed it from yon window is a myst'ry to me. We're going to lock up here and try what it is like from the attics. So you'd better come with us if you've a mind.'

The top floor at the Albany, as elsewhere, is devoted to the servants – a congeries of little kitchens and cubicles, used by many as lumber-rooms – by Raffles among the many. The annexe in this case was, of course, empty as the rooms below; and that was lucky, for we filled it, what with the manager, who now joined us, and another tenant whom he brought with him, to Mackenzie's undisguised annoyance.

'Better let in all Piccadilly at a crown a head,' said he. 'Here, my man, out you go on to the roof to make one less, and have your truncheon handy.'

We crowded to the little window, which Mackenzie took care to fill; and a minute yielded no sound but the crunch and slither of constabulary boots upon sooty slates. Then came a shout.

'What now?' cried Mackenzie.

'A rope,' we heard, 'hanging from the spout by a hook!'

'Sirs,' purred Mackenzie, 'yon's how he got up from below! He would do it with one o' they telescope sticks, an' I never thocht o't! How long a rope, my lad?'

'Quite short. I've got it.'

'Did it hang over a window? Ask him that!' cried the manager. 'He can see by leaning over the parapet.'

The question was repeated by Mackenzie; a pause then, 'Yes, it did.'

'Ask him how many windows along!' shouted the manager in high excitement.

'Six, he says,' said Mackenzie the next minute; and he drew in his head and shoulders. 'I should just like to see those rooms, six windows along.'

'Mr Raffles's,' announced the manager after a mental calculation.

'Is that a fact?' cried Mackenzie. 'Then we shall have no difficulty at all. He's left me his key down below.'

The words had a dry, speculative intonation, which even

then I found time to dislike; it was as though the coincidence had already struck the Scotsman as something more.

'Where is Mr. Raffles?' asked the manager, as we all filed downstairs.

'He's gone out to his dinner,' said Mackenzie.

'Are you sure?'

'I saw him go,' said I. My heart was beating horribly. I would not trust myself to speak again. But I wormed my way to a front place in the little procession, and was, in fact, the second man to cross the threshold that had been the Rubicon of my life. As I did so I uttered a cry of pain, for Mackenzie had trod back heavily on my toes; in another second I saw the reason, and saw it with another and a louder cry.

A man was lying at full length before the fire, on his back, with a little wound in the white forehead, and the blood draining into his eyes. And the man was Raffles himself!

'Suicide,' said Mackenzie calmly. 'No – here's the poker – looks more like murder.' He went on his knees and shook his head quite cheerfully. 'An' it's not even murder,' said he, with a shade of disgust in his matter-of-fact voice; 'yon's no more than a flesh-wound, and I have my doubts whether it felled him; but, sirs, he just stinks o' chloryform!'

He got up and fixed his keen grey eyes upon me; my own were full of tears, but they faced him unashamed.

'I understood ye to say ye saw him go out?' said he sternly.

'I saw that long driving-coat; of course I thought he was inside it.'

'And I could ha' sworn it was the same gent when he gave me the key!'

It was the disconsolate voice of the constable in the background; on him turned Mackenzie, white to the lips.

'You'd think anything, some of you damned policemen,' said he. 'What's your number, you rotter? P 34? You'll be hearing more of this, Mr P 34! If that gentleman were dead – instead of coming to himself while I'm talking – do you know what you'd be? Guilty of his manslaughter, you stuck pig in buttons! Do you know who you've let slip, butterfingers? Crawshay – no less – him that broke Dartmoor yesterday. By the God that made ye, P 34, if I lose him I'll hound ye from the forrce!'

Working face – shaking fist – a calm man on fire. It was a new side of Mackenzie, and one to mark and to digest. Next moment he had flounced from our midst.

'Difficult thing to break your own head,' said Raffles later; 'infinitely easier to cut your own throat. Chloroform's another matter; when you've used it on others, you know the dose to a nicety. So you thought I was really gone? Poor old Bunny! But I hope Mackenzie saw your face?'

'He did,' said I. I would not tell him all Mackenzie must have seen, however.

'That's all right. I wouldn't have had him miss it for worlds; and you mustn't think me a brute, old boy, for I fear that man; and, you know, we sink or swim together.'

'And now we sink or swim with Crawshay too,' said I dolefully.

'Not we!' cried Raffles with conviction. 'Old Crawshay's a true sportsman, and he'll do by us as we've done by him; besides, this makes us quits; and I don't think, Bunny, that we'll take on the professors again!'

THE GIFT OF THE EMPEROR

I

WHEN the King of the Cannibal Islands made faces at Queen Victoria, and a European monarch set the cables tingling with his compliments on the exploit, the indignation in England was not less than the surprise, for the thing was not so common as it has since become. But when it transpired that a gift of peculiar significance was to follow the congratulations, to give them weight, the inference prevailed that the white potentate and the black had taken simultaneous leave of their fourteen senses. For the gift was a pearl of price unparalleled, picked aforetime by British cutlasses from a Polynesian setting, and presented by British royalty to the sovereign who seized this opportunity of restoring it to its orginal possessor.

The incident would have been a godsend to the Press a few weeks later. Even in June there were leaders, letters, large headlines, leaded type; the *Daily Chronicle* devoted half its literary page to a charming drawing of the island capital which the new *Pall Mall,* in a leading article headed by a pun, advised the Government to blow to˙flinders. I was myself driving a poor but not dishonest quill at the time, and the topic of the hour goaded me into satiric verse which obtained a better place than anything I had yet turned out. I had let my flat in town, and taken inexpensive quarters at Thames Ditton, on a plea of a disinterested passion for the river.

'First-rate, old boy,' said Raffles (who must needs come and see me there), lying back in the boat while I sculled and steered. 'I suppose they pay you pretty well for these, eh?'

'Not a penny.'

'Nonsense, Bunny! I thought they paid so well? Give them time, and you'll get your cheque.'

'Oh no, I shan't,' said I gloomily. 'I've got to be content with the honour of getting in; the editor wrote to say so, in so many words,' I added. But I gave the gentleman his distinguished name.

'You don't mean to say you've written for payment already?'

No; it was the last thing I had intended to admit. But I had done it. The murder was out; there was no sense in further concealment. I had written for my money because I really needed it; if he must know, I was cursedly hard up. Raffles nodded as though he knew already. I warmed to my woes. It was no easy matter to keep your end up as a raw free-lance of letters; for my part, I was afraid I wrote neither well enough nor ill enough for success. I suffered from a persistent ineffectual feeling after style. Verse I could manage; but it did not pay. To personal paragraphs or to baser journalism I could not and I would not stoop.

Raffles nodded again, this time with a smile that stayed in his eyes as he leant back watching me. I knew that he was thinking of other things I had stooped to, and I thought I knew what he was going to say. He had said it before so often; he was sure to say it again. I had my answer ready, but evidently he was tired of asking the same question. His lids fell, he took up the paper he had dropped, and I sculled the length of the old red wall of Hampton Court before he spoke again.

'And they gave you nothing for these! My dear Bunny, they're capital, not only *qua* verses, but for crystallising your subject and putting it in a nutshell. Certainly you've taught me more about it than I knew before. But is it really worth fifty thousand pounds – a single pearl?'

'A hundred, I believe; but that wouldn't scan.'

'A hundred thousand pounds!' said Raffles, with his eyes shut. And again I made certain what was coming, but again I was mistaken. 'If it's worth all that,' he cried at last, 'there would be no getting rid of it at all; it's not like a diamond that you can sub-divide. But I beg your pardon, Bunny. I was forgetting!'

And we said no more about the emperor's gift; for pride thrives on an empty pocket, and no privation would have drawn from me the proposal which I had expected Raffles to make. My expectation had been half a hope, though I only knew it now. But neither did we touch again on what Raffles professed to have forgotten – my 'apostasy,' 'my lapse into virtue,' as he had been pleased to call it. We were both a little silent, a little constrained, each preoccupied with his own thoughts. It was months since we had met, and, as I saw him off towards eleven o'clock that Sunday night, I fancied it was for more months that we were saying good-bye.

But as we waited for the train I saw those clear eyes peering at me under the station lamps, and when I met their glance Raffles shook his head.

'You don't look well on it, Bunny,' said he. 'I never did believe in this Thames Valley. You want a change of air.'

I wished I might get it.

'What you really want is a sea voyage.'

'And a winter at St. Moritz, or do you recommend Cannes or Cairo? It's all very well, A. J., but you forget what I told you about my funds."

'I forget nothing. I merely don't want to hurt your feelings. But, look here, a sea voyage you shall have. I want a change myself, and you shall come with me as my guest. We'll spend July in the Mediterranean.'

'But you're playing cricket – –'

'Hang the cricket!'

'Well, if I thought you meant it – –'

'Of course I mean it. Will you come?'

'Like a shot – if you go.'

And I shook his hand, and waved mine in farewell with the perfectly good-humoured conviction that I should hear no more of the matter. It was a passing thought, no more, no less. I soon wished it were more; that week found me wishing myself out of England for good and all. I was making nothing. I could but subsist on the difference between the rent I paid for my flat and the rent at which I had sublet it, furnished, for the season. And the season was near its end, and creditors awaited me in town. Was it possible to be entirely honest? I had run no bills when I had money in my pocket, and the more downright dishonesty seemed to me the less ignoble.

But from Raffles, of course, I heard nothing more; a week went by, and half another week; then, late on the second Wednesday night, I found a telegram from him at my lodgings, after seeking him vainly in town, and dining with desperation at the solitary club to which I still belonged.

'Arranged to leave Waterloo by North German Lloyd special,' he wired, '9.25 a.m. Monday next, will meet you Southampton aboard *Uhlan* with tickets, am writing.'

And write he did, a light-hearted letter enough, but full of serious solicitude for me and for my health and prospects; a letter almost touching in the light of our past relations, in the twilight of their complete rupture. He said that he had booked two berths to Naples, that we were bound for Capri, which was clearly the Island of the Lotos-eaters, that we would bask there together, 'and for a while forget'. It was a charming letter. I had never seen Italy; the privilege of initiation should be his. No mistake was greater than to deem it an impossible country for the summer. The Bay of Naples was never so divine, and he wrote of 'faery lands forlorn', as though the poetry sprang unbidden to his pen. To come back to earth and prose, I might think it unpatriotic of him to choose a German boat, but on no other line did you receive such attention and accommodation for your money. There was a hint of better reasons. Raffles wrote, as he had telegraphed, from Bremen; and I gathered that the personal use of some little influence with the authorities there had resulted in a material reduction in our fares.

Imagine my excitement and delight! I managed to pay what I owed at Thames Ditton, to squeeze a small editor for a very small cheque, and my tailors for one more flannel suit. I remember that I broke my last sovereign to get a box of Sullivan's cigarettes for Raffles to smoke on the voyage. But my heart was as light as my purse on the Monday morning, the fairest morning of an unfair summer, when the special whirled me through the sunshine to the sea.

A tender awaited us at Southampton. Raffles was not on board, nor did I really look for him till we reached the liner's side. And then I looked in vain. His face was not among the many that fringed the rail; his hand was not one of the few that waved to friends. I climbed aboard in a sudden heaviness. I had no ticket, nor the money to pay for one. I did not even know the number of my room. My heart was in my mouth as I waylaid a steward and asked if a Mr. Raffles was on board. Thank Heaven – he was! But where? The man did not know;

he was plainly on some other errand, and a-hunting I must go. But there was no sign of him on the promenade deck, and none below in the saloon; the smoking-room was empty but for a little German with a red moustache twisted into his eyes; nor was Raffles in his own cabin, whither I inquired my way in desperation, but where the sight of his own name on the baggage was certainly a further reassurance. Why he kept himself in the background, however, I could not conceive, and only sinister reasons would suggest themselves in explanation.

'So there you are! I've been looking for you all over the ship!'

Despite the graven prohibition, I had tried the bridge as a last resort; and there, indeed, was A. J. Raffles, seated on a skylight, and leaning over one of the officers' long chairs, in which reclined a girl in a white drill coat and skirt – a slip of a girl with a pale skin, dark hair, and rather remarkable eyes. So much I noted as he rose and quickly turned; thereupon I could think of nothing but the swift grimace which preceded a start of well-feigned astonishment.

'Why – Bunny?' cried Raffles. 'Where have you sprung from?'

I stammered something as he pinched my hand.

'And you are coming in this ship? And to Naples too? Well, upon my word! Miss Werner, may I introduce my friend?'

And he did so without a blush, describing me as an old schoolfellow whom he had not seen for months, with wilful circumstance and gratuitous detail that filled me at once with confusion, suspicion, and revolt. I felt myself blushing for us both, and I did not care. My address utterly deserted me, and I made no effort to recover it, to carry the thing off. All I would do was to mumble such words as Raffles actually put into my mouth, and that I doubt not with a thoroughly evil grace.

'So you saw my name in the list of passengers, and came in search of me? Good old Bunny! I say, though, I wish you'd share my cabin! I've got a beauty on the promenade deck, but they wouldn't promise to keep me by myself. We ought to see about it before they shove in some alien. In any case we shall have to get out of this.'

For a quartermaster had entered the wheel-house, and even

while we had been speaking, the pilot had taken possession of the bridge; as we descended, the tender left us with flying handkerchiefs and shrill good-byes; and as we bowed to Miss Werner on the promenade deck there came a deep, slow throbbing underfoot, and our voyage had begun.

It did not begin pleasantly between Raffles and me. On deck he had overborne my stubborn perplexity by dint of a forced though forceful joviality; in his cabin the gloves were off.

'You idiot,' he snarled, 'you've given me away again!'

'How have I given you away?'

I ignored the separate insult in his last word.

'How? I should have thought any clod could see that I meant us to meet by chance!'

'After taking both tickets yourself?'

'They know nothing about that on board; besides, I hadn't decided when I took the tickets.'

'Then you should have let me know when you did decide. You lay your plans and never say a word, and expect me to tumble to them by the light of nature. How was I to know you had anything on?'

I had turned the tables with some effect. Raffles almost hung his head.

'The fact is, Bunny, I didn't mean you to know. You – you've grown such a pious rabbit in your old age!'

My nickname and his tone went far to mollify me; other things went further, but I had to forgive him still.

'If you were afraid of writing,' I pursued, 'it was your business to give me the tip the moment I set foot on board. I would have taken it all right. I am not so virtuous as all that.'

Was it my imagination, or did Raffles look slightly ashamed? If so, it was the first and last time in all the years I knew him; nor can I swear to it even now.

'That,' said he, 'was the very thing I meant to do – to lie in wait in my room and get you as you passed, but – –'

'You were better engaged?'

'Say otherwise.'

'The charming Miss Werner?'

'She is quite charming.'

'Most Australian girls are,' said I.

'How did you know she was one?' he cried.

'I heard her speak.'

'Brute!' said Raffles, laughing; 'she has no more twang than you have. Her people are German, she has been to school in Dresden, and is on her way out alone.'

'Money?' I inquired.

'Confound you!' he said, and, though he was laughing, I thought it was a point at which the subject might be changed.

'Well,' I said, 'it wasn't for Miss Werner you wanted us to play strangers, was it? You have some deeper game than that, eh?'

'I suppose I have.'

'Then hadn't you better tell me what it is?'

Raffles treated me to the old cautious scrutiny that I knew so well; the familiarity of it, after all these months, set me smiling in a way that might have reassured him; for dimly already I divined his enterprise.

'It won't send you off in the pilot's boat, Bunny?'

'Not quite.'

'Then – you remember the pearl you wrote the – –'

I did not wait for him to finish his sentence.

'You've got it!' I cried, my face on fire, for I caught sight of it that moment in the state-room mirror.

Raffles seemed taken aback.

'Not yet,' said he; 'but I mean to have it before we get to Naples.'

'Is it on board?'

'Yes.'

'But how – where – who's got it?'

'A little German officer, a whipper-snapper with perpendicular moustaches.'

'I saw him in the smoke-room.'

'That's the chap; he's always there. Herr Captain Wilhelm von Heumann, if you look in the list. Well, he's the special envoy of the emperor, and he's taking the pearl out with him.'

'You found this out in Bremen?'

'No, in Berlin, from a newspaper man I know there. I'm ashamed to tell you, Bunny, that I went there on purpose!'

I burst out laughing.

'You needn't be ashamed. You are doing the very thing I was rather hoping you were going to propose the other day on the river.'

'You were hoping it?' said Raffles, with his eyes wide open. Indeed, it was his turn to show surprise, and mine to be much more ashamed than I felt.

'Yes,' I answered, 'I was quite keen on the idea; but I wasn't going to propose it.'

'Yet you would have listened to me the other day?'

Certainly I would, and I told him so without reserve; not brazenly, you understand; not even now with the gusto of a man who savours such an adventure for its own sake, but doggedly, defiantly, through my teeth, as one who had tried to live honestly and had failed. And, while I was about it, I told him much more. Eloquently enough, I dare say, I gave him chapter and verse of my hopeless struggle, my inevitable defeat; for hopeless and inevitable they were to a man with my record, even though that record was written only in one's own soul. It was the old story of the thief trying to turn honest man; the thing was against nature, and there was an end of it.

Raffles entirely disagreed with me. He shook his head over my conventional view. Human nature was a board of chequers; why not reconcile one's self to alternate black and white? Why desire to be all one thing or all the other, like our forefathers on the stage or in the old-fashioned fiction? For his part, he enjoyed himself on all squares of the board, and liked the light the better for the shade. My conclusion he considered absurd.

'But you err in good company, Bunny, for all the cheap moralists who preach the same twaddle; old Virgil was the first and worst offender of you all. I back myself to climb out of Avernus any day I like, and sooner or later I shall climb out for good. I suppose I can't very well turn myself into a Limited Liability Company. But I could retire and settle down and live blamelessly ever after. I'm not sure that it couldn't be done on this pearl alone!'

'Then you don't still think it too remarkable to sell?'

'We might take a fishery and haul it up with smaller fry. It would come after months of ill-luck, just as we were going to

131

sell the schooner; by Jove, it would be the talk of the Pacific!'

'Well, we've got to get it first. Is this von What's-his-name a formidable cuss?'

'More so than he looks; and he has the cheek of the devil!'

As he spoke, a white drill skirt fluttered past the open stateroom door, and I caught a glimpse of an upturned moustache beyond. 'But is he the chap we have to deal with? Won't the pearl be in the purser's keeping?'

Raffles stood at the door, frowning out upon the Solent, but for an instant he turned to me with a sniff.

'My good fellow, do you suppose the whole ship's company knows there's a gem like that aboard? You said that it was worth a hundred thousand pounds; in Berlin they say it's priceless. I doubt if the skipper himself knows that von Heumann has it on him.'

'And he has?'

'Must have.'

'Then we have only him to deal with?'

He answered me without a word. Something white was fluttering past once more, and Raffles, stepping forth, made the promenaders three.

II

I do not ask to set foot aboard a finer steamship than the *Uhlan* of the Norddeutscher Lloyd, to meet a kindlier man than her then commander or better fellows than his officers. This much at least let me have the grace to admit. I hated the voyage. It was no fault of anybody connected with the ship; it was no fault of the weather, which was monotonously ideal. Not even in my own heart did the reason reside; conscience and I were divorced at last, and the decree made absolute. With my scruples had fled all fear, and I was ready to revel between bright skies and sparkling sea with the light-hearted detachment of Raffles himself. It was Raffles himself who prevented me, but not Raffles alone. It was Raffles and that Colonial minx on her way home from school.

What he could see in her – but that begs the question. Of course he saw no more than I did, but to annoy me, or perhaps to punish me for my long defection, he must turn his back on me and devote himself to this chit from Southampton to the Mediterranean. They were always together. It was too absurd. After breakfast they would begin, and go on until eleven or twelve at night; there was no intervening hour at which you might not hear her nasal laugh, or his quiet voice talking soft nonsense into her ear. Of course it was nonsense! Is it conceivable that a man like Raffles, with his knowledge of the world, and his experience of women (a side of his character upon which I have purposely never touched, for it deserves another volume); is it credible, I ask, that such a man could find anything but nonsense to talk by the day together to a giddy young schoolgirl? I would not be unfair for the world. I think I have admitted that the young person had points. Her eyes, I suppose, were really fine, and certainly the shape of the little brown face was charming, so far as mere contour can charm. I admit also more audacity than I cared about, with enviable health, mettle, and vitality. I may not have occasion to report any of this young lady's speeches (they would scarcely bear it), and am therefore the more anxious to describe her without injustice. I confess to some little prejudice against her. I resented her success with Raffles of whom, in consequence, I saw less and less each day. It is a mean thing to have to confess, but there must have been something not unlike jealousy rankling within me.

Jealousy there was in another quarter – crude, rampant, undignified jealousy. Captain von Heumann would twirl his moustaches into twin spires, shoot his white cuffs over his rings, and stare at me insolently through his rimless eyeglasses; we ought to have consoled each other, but we never exchanged a syllable. The captain had a murderous scar across one of his cheeks, a present from Heidelberg, and I used to think how he must long to have Raffles there to serve the same. It was not as though von Heumann never had his innings. Raffles let him go in several times a day, for the malicious pleasure of bowling him out as he was 'getting set'; those were his words when I taxed him disingenuously with obnoxious conduct towards a German on a German boat.

'You'll make yourself disliked on board!'

'By von Heumann merely.'

'But is that wise when he's the man we've got to diddle?'

'The wisest thing I ever did. To have chummed up with him would have been fatal – the common dodge.'

I was consoled, encouraged, almost content. I had feared Raffles was neglecting things, and I told him so in a burst. Here we were near Gibraltar, and not a word since the Solent. He shook his head with a smile.

'Plenty of time, Bunny, plenty of time. We can do nothing before we get to Genoa, and that won't be till Sunday night. The voyage is still young, and so are we; let's make the most of things while we can.'

It was after dinner on the promenade deck, and as Raffles spoke he glanced sharply fore and aft, leaving me next moment with a step full of purpose. I retired to the smoking-room, to smoke and read in a corner, and to watch von Heumann, who very soon came to drink beer and to sulk in another.

Few travellers tempt the Red Sea at midsummer; the *Uhlan* was very empty indeed. She had, however, but a limited supply of cabins on the promenade deck, and there was just that excuse for my sharing Raffles's room. I could have had one to myself downstairs, but I must be up above. Raffles had insisted that I should insist on that point. So we were together, I think, without suspicion, though also without any object that I could see.

On the Sunday afternoon I was asleep in my berth, the lower one, when the curtains were shaken by Raffles, who was in his shirt-sleeves on the settee.

'Achilles sulking in his bunk!'

'What else is there to do?' I asked him as I stretched and yawned. I noted, however, the good-humour of his tone, and did my best to catch it.

'I have found something else, Bunny.'

'I dare say!'

'You understand me. The whipper-snapper's making his century this afternoon. I've had other fish to fry.'

I swung my legs over the side of my berth and sat forward, as he was sitting, all attention The inner door, a grating, was shut and bolted, and curtained like the open port-hole.

'We shall be at Genoa before sunset,' continued Raffles. 'It's the place where the deed's got to be done.'

'So you still mean to do it!'

'Did I ever say I didn't?'

'You have said so little either way.'

'Advisedly so, my dear Bunny; why spoil a pleasure trip by talking unnecessary shop? But now the time has come. It must be done at Genoa or not at all.'

'On land?'

'No, on board, to-morrow night. To-night would do, but to-morrow is better, in case of mishap. If we were forced to use violence we could get away by the earliest train, and nothing be known till the ship was sailing and von Heumann found dead or drugged – –'

'Not dead!' I exclaimed.

'Of course not,' assented Raffles, 'or there would be no need for us to bolt; but if we should have to bolt, Tuesday morning is our time when the ship has got to sail, whatever happens. But I don't anticipate any violence. Violence is a confession of terrible incompetence. In all these years how many blows have you known me strike? Not one, I believe; but I have been quite ready to kill my man every time, if the worst came to the worst.'

I asked him how he proposed to enter von Heumann's state-room unobserved, and even through the curtained gloom of ours his face lighted up.

'Climb into my bunk, Bunny, and you shall see.'

I did so, but could see nothing. Raffles reached across me and tapped the ventilator, a sort of trap-door in the wall above his bed, some eighteen inches long and half that height. It opened outwards into the ventilating shaft.

'That,' said he, 'is our door to fortune. Open it if you like; you won't see much, because it doesn't open far; but loosening a couple of screws will set that all right. The shaft, as you may see, is more or less bottomless; you pass under it whenever you go to your bath, and the top is a skylight on the bridge. That's why this thing has to be done while we're at Genoa, because they keep no watch on the bridge in port. The ventilator opposite ours is von Heumann's. It again will only mean a couple

135

of screws and there's a beam to stand on while you work.'

'But if anybody should look from below?'

'It's extremely unlikely that anybody will be astir below, so unlikely that we can afford to chance it. No, I can't have you there to make sure. The great point is that neither of us should be seen from the time we turn in. A couple of ship's boys do sentry-go on these decks; and they shall be our witnesses; by Jove, it'll be the biggest mystery that ever was made!'

'If von Heumann doesn't resist.'

'Resist! He won't get the chance. He drinks too much beer to sleep light, and nothing is so easy as to chloroform a heavy sleeper; you've even done it yourself on an occasion of which it's perhaps unfair to remind you. Von Heumann will be past sensation almost as soon as I get my hand through his ventilator. I shall crawl in over his body, Bunny, my boy!'

'And I?'

'You will hand me what I want, and hold the fort in case of accidents, and generally lend me the moral support you've made me require. It's a luxury, Bunny, but I found it devilish difficult to do without it after you turned pi!'

He said that von Heumann was certain to sleep with a bolted door, which he, of course, would leave unbolted, and spoke of other ways of laying a false scent while rifling the cabin. Not that Raffles anticipated a tiresome search. The pearl would be about von Heumann's person; in fact, Raffles knew exactly where and in what he kept it. Naturally, I asked how he could have come by such knowledge, and his answer led up to a momentary unpleasantness.

'It's a very old story, Bunny. I really forget in what book it comes; I'm only sure of the Testament. But Samson was the unlucky hero, and one Delilah the heroine.'

And he looked so knowing that I could not be in a moment's doubt as to his meaning.

'So the fair Australian has been playing Delilah?' said I.

'In a very harmless, innocent sort of way.'

'She got his mission out of him?'

'Yes; I've forced him to score all the points he could, and that was his great stroke, as I hoped it would be. He has even shown Amy the pearl.'

'Amy, eh! and she promptly told you?'

'Nothing of the kind. What makes you think so? I had the greatest trouble in getting it out of her.'

His tone should have been a sufficient warning to me. I had not the tact to take it as such. At last I knew the meaning of his furious flirtation, and stood wagging my head and shaking my finger, blinded to his frowns by my own enlightenment.

'Wily worm!' said I. 'Now I see through it all; how dense I've been!'

'Sure you're not still?'

'No; now I understand what has beaten me all the week. I simply couldn't fathom what you saw in that little girl. I never dreamt it was part of the game.'

'So you think it was that and nothing more?'

'You deep old dog – of course I do!'

'You didn't know she was the daughter of a wealthy squatter?'

'There are wealthy women by the dozen who would marry you to-morrow.'

'It doesn't occur to you that I might like to draw stumps, start clean, and live happily ever after – in the bush?'

'With that voice? It certainly does not!'

'Bunny!' he cried so fiercely that I braced myself for a blow. But no more followed.

'Do you think you would live happily?' I made bold to ask him.

'God knows!' he answered. And with that he left me, to marvel at his look and tone, and, more than ever, at the insufficiently exciting cause.

III

Of all the mere feats of cracksmanship which I have seen Raffles perform, at once the most delicate and most difficult was that which he accomplished between one and two o'clock on the Tuesday morning, aboard the North German steamer *Uhlan*, lying at anchor in Genoa harbour.

Not a hitch occurred. Everything had been foreseen; everything happened as I had been assured everything must. Nobody was about below, only the ship's boys on deck, and nobody on the bridge. It was twenty-five minutes past one when Raffles, without a stitch of clothing on his body, but with a glass phial, corked with cotton-wool, between his teeth, and a tiny screwdriver behind his ear, squirmed feet first through the ventilator over his berth; and it was nineteen minutes to two when he returned, head first, with the phial still between his teeth, and the cotton-wool rammed home to still the rattling of that which lay like a great grey bean within. He had taken screws out and put them in again; he had unfastened von Heumann's ventilator and had left it fast as he had found it – fast as he instantly proceeded to make his own. As for von Heumann, it had been enough to place the drenched wad first on his moustache, and then to hold it between his gaping lips; thereafter the intruder had climbed both ways across his shins without eliciting a groan. And here was the prize – this pearl as large as a filbert – with a pale pink tinge like a lady's finger-nail – this spoil of the filibustering age – this gift from a European emperor to a South Sea chief. We gloated over it when all was snug. We toasted it in whisky and soda-water, laid in overnight in view of the great moment. But the moment was greater, more triumphant, than our most sanguine dreams. All we had now to do was to secrete the gem (which Raffles had prised from its setting, replacing the latter), so that we could stand the strictest search and yet take it ashore with us at Naples; and this Raffles was doing when I turned in. I myself would have landed incontinently, that night, at Genoa, and bolted with the spoil; he would not hear of it, for a dozen good reasons which will be obvious.

On the whole I do not think that anything was discovered or suspected before we weighed anchor; but I cannot be sure. It is difficult to believe that a man could be chloroformed in his sleep and feel no tell-tale effects, sniff no suspicious odour, in the morning. Nevertheless, von Heumann reappeared as though nothing had happened to him, his German cap over his eyes and his moustaches brushing the peak. And by ten o'clock we were quit of Genoa; the last lean, blue-chinned official had left our decks; the last fruitseller had been beaten off with bucketsful of water and left cursing us from his boat; the last passenger had come aboard at the last moment – a fussy greybeard who kept the big ship waiting while he haggled with his boatman over half a lira. But at length we were off, the tug was shed, the lighthouse passed, and Raffles and I leaned together over the rail, watching our shadows on the pale green, liquid, veined marble that again washed the vessel's side.

Von Heumann was having his innings once more; it was part of the design that he should remain in all day, and so postpone the inevitable hour; and, though the lady looked bored, and was for ever glancing in our direction, he seemed only too willing to avail himself of his opportunities. But Raffles was moody and ill at ease. He had not the air of a successful man. I could but opine that the impending parting at Naples sat heavily on his spirit. He would neither talk to me, nor would he let me go.

'Stop where you are, Bunny. I've things to tell you. Can you swim?'

'A bit.'

'Ten miles?'

'Ten?' I burst out laughing. 'Not one! Why do you ask?'

'We shall be within a ten miles' swim of the shore most of the day.'

'What on earth are you driving at, Raffles?'

'Nothing; only I shall swim for it if the worst comes to the worst. I suppose you can't swim under water at all?'

I did not answer his question. I scarcely heard it; cold beads were bursting through my skin.

'Why should the worst come to the worst?' I whispered. 'We aren't found out, are we?'

'No.'

'Then why speak as though we were?'

'We may be; an old enemy of ours is on board.'

'An old enemy?'

'Mackenzie.'

'Never.'

'The man with the beard who came aboard last.'

'Are you sure?'

'Sure! I was only sorry to see you didn't recognise him too.'

I took my handkerchief to my face; now that I thought of it, there had been something familiar in the old man's gait, as well as something rather youthful for his apparent years; his very beard seemed unconvincing, now that I recalled it in the light of this horrible revelation. I looked up and down the deck, but the old man was nowhere to be seen.

'That's the worst of it,' said Raffles. 'I saw him go into the captain's cabin twenty minutes ago.'

'But what can have brought him?' I cried miserably. 'Can it be a coincidence – is it somebody else he's after?'

Raffles shook his head.

'Hardly, this time.'

'Then you think he's after you?'

'I've been afraid of it for some weeks.'

'Yet there you stand!'

'What am I to do? I don't want to swim for it before I must. I begin to wish I'd taken your advice, Bunny, and left the ship at Genoa. But I've not the smallest doubt that Mac was watching both ship and station till the last moment. That's why he ran it so fine.'

He took a cigarette and handed me the case, but I shook my head impatiently.

'I still don't understand,' said I. 'Why should he be after you? He couldn't come all this way about a jewel which was perfectly safe for all he knew. What's your own theory?'

'Simply that he's been on my track for some time, probably ever since friend Crawshay slipped clean through his fingers last November. There have been other indications. I am really not unprepared for this. But it can only be pure suspicion. I'll defy him to bring anything home, and I'll defy him to find the pearl! Theory, my dear Bunny! I know how he's got here as well as though I'd been inside that Scotsman's skin, and I know what he'll do next. He found out I'd gone abroad, and looked for a motive; he found out about von Heumann and his mission, and here was his motive cut and dried. Great chance – to nab me on a new job altogether. But he won't do it, Bunny; mark my words, he'll search the ship and search us all, when the loss is known; but he'll search in vain. And there's skipper beckoning the whipper-snapper to his cabin; the fat will be in the fire in five minutes!'

Yet there was no conflagration, no fuss, no searching of the passengers, no whisper of what had happened in the air; instead of a stir there was portentous peace; and it was clear to me that Raffles was not a little disturbed at the falsification of all his predictions. There was something sinister in silence under such a loss, and the silence was sustained for hours, during which Mackenzie never reappeared. But he was abroad during the luncheon-hour – he was in our cabin! I had left my book in Raffles's berth, and in taking it after lunch I touched the quilt. It was warm from the recent pressure of flesh and blood, and on an instinct I sprang to the ventilator; as I opened it the ventilator opposite was closed with a snap.

I waylaid Raffles. 'All right. Let him find the pearl.'

'Have you dumped it overboard?'

'That's a question I shan't condescend to answer.'

He turned on his heel, and at subsequent intervals I saw him making the most of his last afternoon with the inevitable Miss Werner. I remember that she looked both cool and smart in quite a simple affair of brown holland, which toned well with her complexion, and was cleverly relieved with touches of scarlet. I quite admired her that afternoon, for her eyes were really very good, and so were her teeth, yet I had never admired her more directly in my own despite. For I passed them again and again in order to get a word with Raffles, to tell him I knew there was danger in the wind; but he would not so much as catch my eye. So at last I gave it up. And I saw him next in the captain's cabin.

They had summoned him first; he had gone in smiling; and smiling I found him when they summoned me. The stateroom was spacious, as befitted that of a commander. Mackenzie sat on the settee, his beard in front of him on the polished table; but a revolver lay in front of the captain; and, when I had entered, the chief officer, who had summoned me, shut the door and put his back to it. Von Heumann completed the party, his fingers busy with his moustache.

Raffles greeted me.

'This is a great joke!' he cried. 'You remember the pearl you were so keen about, Bunny, the emperor's pearl, the pearl money wouldn't buy? It seems it was entrusted to our little friend here, to take out to Canoodle Dum, and the poor little chap's gone and lost it; *ergo,* as we're Britishers, they think we've got it!'

'But I know ye have,' put in Mackenzie, nodding to his beard.

'You will recognise that loyal and patriotic voice,' said Raffles. 'Mon, 'tis our auld acquaintance Mackenzie, o' Scoteland Yarrd an' Scoteland itsel'!'

'Dat is enought,' cried the captain. 'Have you submid to be searge, or do I vorce you?'

'What you will,' said Raffles, 'but it will do you no harm to give us fair play first. You accuse us of breaking into Captain von Heumann's stateroom during the small hours of this morning, and abstracting from it this confounded pearl. Well, I can prove that I was in my own room all night long, and I have no doubt my friend can prove the same.'

'Most certainly I can,' said I indignantly. 'The ship's boys can bear witness to that.'

Mackenzie laughed, and shook his head at his reflection in the polished mahogany.

'That was vera clever,' said he, 'and like enough it would ha' served ye had I not stepped aboard. But I've just had a look at they ventilators, and I think I know how ye worrked it. Anyway, captain, it makes no matter. I'll just be clappin' the darbies on these young sparks, an' then – –'

'By what right?' roared Raffles in a ringing voice, and I never saw his face in such a blaze. 'Search us if you like; search every scrap and stitch we possess; but you dare to lay a finger on us without a warrant!'

'I wouldna dare,' said Mackenzie gravely, as he fumbled in his breast-pocket, and Raffles dived his hand into his own. 'Haud his wrist!' shouted the Scotsman; and the huge Colt that had been with us many a night, but had never been fired in my hearing, clattered on the table and was raked in by the captain.

'All right,' said Raffles savagely to the mate. 'You can let go now. I won't try it again. Now, Mackenzie, let's see your warrant!'

'Ye'll no mishandle it?'

'What good would that do me? Let me see it,' said Raffles

peremptorily, and the detective obeyed. Raffles raised his eye-brows as he perused the document; his mouth hardened, but suddenly relaxed; and it was with a smile and a shrug that he returned the paper.

'Wull that do for ye?' inquired Mackenzie.

'It may. I congratulate you, Mackenzie; it's a strong hand, at any rate. Two burglaries and the Melrose necklace, Bunny!' And he turned to me with a rueful smile.

'An' all easy to prove,' said the Scotsman, pocketing the warrant. 'I've one o' these for you,' he added, nodding to me, 'only not such a long one.'

'To thingk,' said the captain reproachfully, 'that my shib should be made a den of thiefs! It shall be a very disagreeable madder. I have been obliged to pud you both in irons until we ged to Nables.'

'Surely not!' exclaimed Raffles. 'Mackenzie, intercede with him; don't give your countrymen away before all hands! Captain, we can't escape; surely you could hush it up for the night? Look here, here's everything I have in my pockets; you empty yours too, Bunny, and they shall strip us stark if they suspect we've weapons up our sleeves. All I ask is that we are allowed to get out of this without gyves upon our wrists!'

'Webbons you may not have,' said the captain, 'bud wad about der bearl dat you were sdealing?'

'You shall have it!' cried Raffles. 'You shall have it this minute if you guarantee no public indignity on board!'

'That I'll see to,' said Mackenzie, 'as long as you behave yourselves. There now, where is't?'

'On the table under your nose '

My eyes fell with the rest, but no pearl was there; only the contents of our pockets – our watches, pocket-books, pencils, penknives, cigarette-cases – lay on the shiny table along with the revolvers already mentioned.

'Ye're humbuggin' us,' said Mackenzie. 'What's the use?'

'I'm doing nothing of the sort,' laughed Raffles. 'I'm testing you. Where's the harm?'

'It's here, joke apart?'

'On that table, by all my gods.'

Mackenzie opened the cigarette-case and shook each particular cigarette. Thereupon Raffles prayed to be allowed to smoke one, and, when his prayer was heard, observed that the pearl had been on the table much longer than the cigarettes. Mackenzie promptly caught up the Colt and opened the chamber in the butt.

'Not there, not there,' said Raffles; 'but you're getting hot. Try the cartridges.'

Mackenzie emptied them into his palm, and shook each one at his ear without result.

'Oh, give them to me!'

And, in an instant, Raffles had found the right one, had bitten out the bullet, and placed the emperor's pearl with a flourish in the centre of the table.

'After that you will perhaps show me such little consideration as is in your power. Captain, I have been a bit of a villain, as you see, and as such I am ready and willing to lie in irons all night if you deem it requisite for the safety of the ship. All I ask is that you do me one favour first.'

'That shall debend on wad der vafour has been.'

'Captain, I've done a worse thing aboard your ship than any of you know. I have become engaged to be married, and I want to say good-bye!'

I suppose we were all equally amazed; but the only one to express his amazement was von Heumann, whose deep-chested German oath was almost his first contribution to the proceedings. He was not slow to follow it, however, with a vigorous protest against the proposed farewell; but he was overruled, and the masterful prisoner had his way. He was to have five minutes with the girl, while the captain and Mackenzie stood within range (but not earshot), with their revolvers behind their backs. As we were moving from the cabin in a body, he stopped and gripped my hand.

'So I've let you in at last, Bunny – at last and after all! If you knew how sorry I am ... But you won't get much – I don't see why you should get anything at all. Can you forgive me? This may be for years, and it may be for ever, you know! You were a good pal always when it came to the scratch; some day or other you mayn't be so sorry to remember you were a good pal at the last!'

There was a meaning in his eye that I understood; and my teeth were set, and my nerves strung ready, as I wrung that strong and cunning hand for the last time in my life.

How that last scene stays with me, and will stay to my death! How I see every detail, every shadow on the sunlit deck! We were among the islands that dot the course from Genoa to Naples; that was Elba falling back on our starboard quarter, that purple patch with the hot sun setting over it. The captain's cabin opened to starboard, and the starboard promenade deck, sheeted with sunshine and scored with shadow, was deserted but for the group of which I was one, and for the pale, slim, brown figure farther aft with Raffles. Engaged? I could not believe it, cannot to this day. Yet there they stood together, and we did not hear a word; there they stood out against the sunset, and the long, dazzling highway of sunlit sea that sparkled from Elba to the *Uhlan's* plates; and their shadows reached almost to our feet.

Suddenly – an instant – and the thing was done – a thing I have never known whether to admire or to detest. He caught her – he kissed her before us all – then flung her from him so that she almost fell. It was that action which foretold the next. The mate sprang after him, and I sprang after the mate.

Raffles was on the rail, but only just.

'Hold him, Bunny!' he cried. 'Hold him tight!'

And, as I obeyed that last behest with all my might, without a thought of what I was doing, save that he bade me do it, I saw his hands shoot up and his head bob down, and his lithe, spare body cut the sunset as cleanly and precisely as though he had plunged at his leisure from a diver's board!

.   .   .   .   .   .

Of what followed on deck I can tell you nothing, for I was not there. Nor can my final punishment, my long imprisonment, my everlasting disgrace, concern or profit you, beyond the interest and advantage to be gleaned from the knowledge that I at least had my deserts. But one thing I must set down, believe it who will – one more thing only and I am done.

It was into a second-class cabin, on the starboard side, that I was promptly thrust in irons, and the door locked upon me as though I were another Raffles. Meanwhile, a boat was lowered, and the seas scoured to no purpose, as is doubtless on record elsewhere. But either the setting sun, flashing over the waves, must have blinded all eyes, or else mine were victims of a strange illusion.

For the boat was back, the screw throbbing, and the prisoner peering through his port-hole across the sunlit waters that he believed had closed for ever over his comrade's head. Suddenly the sun sank behind the Island of Elba, the lane of dancing sunlight was instantaneously quenched and swallowed in the trackless waste, and in the middle distance, already miles astern, either my sight deceived me or a black speck bobbed amid the grey. The bugle had blown for dinner; it may well be that all save myself had ceased to strain an eye. And now I lost what I had found, now it rose, now sank, and now I gave it up utterly. Yet anon it would rise again, a mere mote dancing in the dim grey distance, drifting towards a purple island, beneath a fading western sky, streaked with dead gold and cerise. And night fell before I knew whether it was a human head or not.

NO SINECURE

I

I AM still uncertain which surprised me more, the telegram calling my attention to the advertisement or the advertisement itself. The telegram is before me as I write. It would appear to have been handed in at Vere Street at eight o'clock in the morning of May 11, 1897, and received before half-past at Holloway B.O. And in that drab region it duly found me unwashed but at work before the day grew hot and my attic insupportable.

'See Mr Maturin's advertisement *Daily Mail* might suit you earnestly beg try will speak if necessary ... '

I transcribe the thing as I see it before me, all in one breath that took away mine; but I leave out the initials at the end, which completed the surprise. They stood very obviously for the knighted specialist whose consulting-room is within a cab-whistle of Vere Street, and who once called me kinsman for his sins. More recently he had called me other names. I was a disgrace, qualified by an adjective which seemed to me another. I had made my bed, and I could go and lie and die in it. If I ever again had the insolence to show my nose in that house, I should go out quicker than I came in. All this, and more, my least distant relative could tell a poor devil to his face; could ring for his man, and give him his brutal instructions on the spot; and then relent to the tune of this telegram! I have no phrase for my amazement. I literally could not believe my eyes. Yet their evidence was more and more conclusive; a very epistle could not have been more characteristic of its sender. Meanly elliptical, ludicrously precise, saving half-pence at the expense of sense, yet paying like a man for 'Mr' Maturin, that was my distinguished relative from his bald patch to his corns. Nor was all the rest unlike him, upon second thoughts. He had a reputation

147

for charity; he was going to live up to it after all. Either that, or it was the sudden impulse of which the most calculating are capable at times; the morning papers with the early cup of tea, this advertisement seen by chance, and the rest upon the spur of a guilty conscience.

Well, I must see it for myself, and the sooner the better, though work pressed. I was writing a series of articles upon prison life, and had my nib into the whole system; a literary and philanthropic daily was parading my 'charges', the graver ones with the more gusto; and the terms, if unhandsome for creative work, were temporary wealth to me. It so happened that my first cheque had just arrived by the eight o'clock post; and my position should be appreciated when I say that I had to cash it to obtain a *Daily Mail*.

Of the advertisement itself, what is to be said? It should speak for itself if I could find it, but I cannot, and only remember that it was a 'male nurse and constant attendant' that was 'wanted for an elderly gentleman in feeble health'. A male nurse! An absurd tag was appended, offering 'liberal salary to University or public-school man'; and of a sudden I saw that I should get this thing if I applied for it. What other 'University or public-school man' would dream of doing so? Was any other in such straits as I? And then my relenting relative; he not only promised to speak for me, but was the very man to do so. Could any recommendation compete with his in the matter of a male nurse? And need the duties of such be necessarily loathsome and repellent? Certainly the surroundings would be better than those of my common lodging-house and own particular garret; and the food; and every other condition of life that I could think of on my way back to that unsavoury asylum. So I dived into a pawnbroker's shop, where I was a stranger only upon my present errand, and within the hour was airing a decent if antiquated suit, but little corrupted by the pawnbroker's moth, and a new straw hat, on the top of a tram.

The address given in the advertisement was that of a flat at Earls Court, which cost me a cross-country journey, finishing with the District Railway and a seven minutes' walk. It was now past midday, and the tarry wood-pavement was good to

smell as I strode up the Earls Court Road. It was great to walk
the civilised world again. Here were men with coats on their
backs, and ladies in gloves. My only fear was lest I might run
up against one or other whom I had known of old. But it was
my lucky day. I felt it in my bones. I was going to get this
berth; and sometimes I should be able to smell the wood-pavement on the old boy's errands; perhaps he would insist on
skimming over it in his bath-chair with me behind.

I felt quite nervous when I reached the flats. They were a
small pile in a side-street, and I pitied the doctor whose plate
I saw upon the palings before the ground-floor windows; he
must be in a very small way, I thought. I rather pitied myself
as well. I had indulged in visions of better flats than these.
There were no balconies. The porter was out of livery. There
was no lift, and my invalid on the third floor! I trudged up,
wishing I had never lived in Mount Street, and brushed against
a dejected individual coming down. A full-blooded young
fellow in a frock-coat flung the right door open at my sum-
mons.

'Does Mr Maturin live here?' I inquired.

'That's right,' said the full-blooded young man, grinning all
over a convivial countenance.

'I – I've come about his advertisement in the *Daily Mail*.'

'You're the thirty-ninth,' cried the blood; 'that was the thirty-
eighth you met upon the stairs, and the day's still young. Excuse my staring at you. Yes, you pass your prelim., and can
come inside; you're one of the few. We had most just after
breakfast, but now the porter's heading off the worst cases, and
that last chap was the first for twenty minutes. Come in here.'

And I was ushered into an empty room with a good bay-
window, which enabled my full-blooded friend to inspect me
yet more critically in a good light; this he did without the least
false delicacy; then his questions began.

' 'Varsity man?'

'No.'

'Public School?'

'Yes.'

'Which one?'

I told him, and he sighed relief.

'At last! You're the very first I've not had to argue with as to what is and what is not a public school. Expelled?'

'No,' I said, after a moment's hesitation; 'no, I was not expelled. And I hope you won't expel me if I ask a question in my turn?'

'Certainly not.'

'Are you Mr Maturin's son?'

'No, my name's Theobald. You may have seen it down below.'

'The doctor?' I said

'His doctor,' said Theobald, with a satisfied eye. 'Mr Maturin's doctor. He is having a male nurse and attendant if he can get one. I rather think he'll see you, though he's only seen two or three all day. There are certain questions which he prefers to ask himself, and it's no good going over the same ground twice. So perhaps I had better tell him about you before we get any further.'

And he withdrew to a room still nearer the entrance, as I could hear, for it was a very small flat indeed. But now two doors were shut between us, and I had to rest content with murmurs through the wall until the doctor returned to summon me.

'I have persuaded my patient to see you,' he whispered, 'but I confess I am not sanguine of the result. He is very difficult to please. You must prepare yourself for a querulous invalid, and for no sinecure if you get the billet.'

'May I ask what's the matter with him?'

'By all means – when you've got the billet.'

Dr Theobald then led the way, his professional dignity so thoroughly intact that I could not but smile as I followed his swinging coat-tails to the sick-room. I carried no smile across the threshold of a darkened chamber which reeked of drugs and twinkled with medicine bottles, and in the middle of which a gaunt figure lay abed in the half-light.

'Take him to the window, take him to the window,' a thin voice snapped, 'and let's have a look at him. Open the blind a bit. Not as much as that, damn you, not as much as that!'

The doctor took the oath as though it had been a fee. I no longer pitied him. It was now very clear to me that he had one

patient who was a little practice in himself. I determined there
and then that he should prove a little profession to me, if we
could but keep him alive between us. Mr Maturin, however,
had the whitest face that I have ever seen, and his teeth gleamed
out through the dusk as though the withered lips no longer met
about them; nor did they except in speech; and anything
ghastlier than the perpetual grin of his repose I defy you to
imagine. It was with this grin that he lay regarding me while
the doctor held the blind.

'So you think you could look after me, do you?'

'I'm certain I could, sir.'

'Single-handed, mind! I don't keep another soul. You would
have to cook your own grub and my slops. Do you think you
could do all that?'

'Yes, sir, I think so.'

'Why do you? Have you any experience of the kind?'

'No, sir, none.'

'Then why do you pretend you have?'

'I only meant that I would do my best.'

'Only meant, only meant! Have you done your best at everything else, then?'

I hung my head. This was a facer. And there was something
in my invalid which thrust the unspoken lie down my throat.

'No, sir, I have not,' I told him plainly.

'He, he, he!' the old wretch tittered; 'and you do well to own
it; you do well, sir, very well indeed. If you hadn't owned up,
out you would have gone, out neck and crop! You've saved
your bacon. You may do more. So you are a public-school
boy, and a very good school yours is, but you weren't at either
University. Is that correct?'

'Absolutely.'

'What did you do when you left school?'

'I came in for money.'

'And then?'

'I spent my money.'

'And since then?'

I stood like a mule.

'And since then, I say!'

'A relative of mine will tell you if you ask him. He is an

eminent man, and he has promised to speak for me. I would rather say no more myself.'

'But you shall, sir, but you shall! Do you suppose that I suppose a public-school boy would apply for a berth like this if something or other hadn't happened? What I want is a gentleman of sorts, and I don't much care what sort; but you've got to tell me what did happen, if you don't tell anybody else. Dr Theobald, sir, you can go to the devil if you won't take a hint. This man may do or he may not. You have no more to say to it till I send him down to tell you one thing or the other. Clear out, sir, clear out; and if you think you've anything to complain of, you stick it down in the bill!'

In the mild excitement of our interview the thin voice had gathered strength, and the last shrill insult was screamed after the devoted medico, as he retired in such order that I felt certain he was going to take this trying patient at his word. The bedroom door closed, then the outer one, and the doctor's heels went drumming down the common stair. I was alone in the flat with this highly singular and rather terrible old man.

'And a damned good riddance!' croaked the invalid, raising himself on one elbow without delay. 'I may not have much body left to boast about, but at least I've got a lost old soul to call my own. That's why I want a gentleman of sorts about me. I've been too dependent on that chap. He won't even let me smoke, and he's been in the flat all day to see I didn't. You'll find the cigarettes behind the *Madonna of the Chair*.'

It was a steel engraving of the great Raffaele, and the frame was tilted from the wall; at a touch a packet of cigarettes tumbled down from behind.

'Thanks; and now a light.'

I struck the match and held it, while the invalid inhaled with normal lips; and suddenly I sighed. I was irresistibly reminded of my poor dear old Raffles. A smoke-ring worthy of the great A. J. was floating upward from the sick man's lips.

'And now take one yourself. I have smoked more poisonous cigarettes. But even these are not Sullivans!'

I cannot repeat what I said. I have no idea what I did. I only know – I only knew – that it was A. J. Raffles in the flesh.

'Yes, Bunny, it was the very devil of a swim; but I defy you to sink in the Mediterranean. That sunset saved me. The sea was on fire. I hardly swam under water at all, but went all I knew for the sun itself; when it set I must have been a mile away; until it did I was the invisible man. I figured on that, and only hope it wasn't set down as a case of suicide. I shall get outed quite soon enough, Bunny, but I'd rather be dropped by the hangman than throw my own wicket away.'

'Oh, my dear old chap, to think of having you by the hand again! I feel as though we were both aboard that German liner, and all that's happened since a nightmare. I thought that time was the last!'

'It looked rather like it, Bunny. It was taking all the risks, and hitting at everything. But the game came off, and some day I'll tell you how.'

'Oh, I'm in no hurry to hear. It's enough for me to see you lying there. I don't want to know how you came here, or why, though I fear you must be pretty bad. I must have a good look at you before I let you speak another word!'

I raised one of the blinds, I sat upon the bed, and I had that look. It left me all unable to conjecture his true state of health, but quite certain in my own mind that my dear Raffles was not and never would be the man that he had been. He had aged twenty years; he looked fifty at the very least. His hair was white; there was no trick about that; and his face was another white. The lines about the corners of the eyes and mouth were both many and deep. On the other hand, the eyes themselves were alight and alert as ever; they were still keen and grey and gleaming like finely tempered steel. Even the mouth, with a cigarette to close it, was the mouth of Raffles and no other: strong and unscrupulous as the man himself. It was only the physical strength which appeared to have departed; but that was quite sufficient to make my heart bleed for the dear rascal who had cost me every tie I valued but the tie between us two.

'Think I look much older?' he asked at length.

'A bit,' I admitted. 'But it is chiefly your hair.'

'Whereby hangs a tale for when we've talked ourselves out, though I have often thought it was that long swim that started it. Still, the Island of Elba is a rummy show, I can assure you. And Naples is a rummier.'

'You went there after all?'

'Rather! It's the European paradise for such as our noble selves. But there's no place that's a patch on little London as a non-conductor of heat; it never need get too hot for a fellow here; if it does it's his own fault. It's the kind of wicket you don't get out on, unless you get yourself out. So here I am again, and have been for the last six weeks. And I mean to have another knock.'

'But surely, old fellow, you're not awfully fit, are you?'

'Fit? My dear Bunny, I'm dead – I'm at the bottom of the sea – and don't you forget it for a minute.'

'But are you all right, or are you not?'

'No; I'm half poisoned by Theobald's prescriptions and putrid cigarettes, and as weak as a cat from lying in bed.'

'Then why on earth lie in bed, Raffles?'

'Because it's better than lying in gaol, as I am afraid *you* know, my poor dear fellow. I tell you I am dead; and my one terror is of coming to life again by accident. Can't you see? I simply dare not show my nose out of doors – by day. You have no idea of the number of perfectly innocent things a dead man daren't do. I can't even smoke Sullivans, because no one man was ever so partial to them as I was in my lifetime, and you never know when you may start a clue.'

'What brought you to these mansions?'

'I fancied a flat, and a man recommended these on the boat; such a good chap, Bunny; he was my reference when it came to signing the lease. You see, I landed on a stretcher – most pathetic case – old Australian without a friend in old country – ordered Engadine as last chance – no go – not an earthly – sentimental wish to die in London – that's the history of Mr. Maturin. If it doesn't hit you hard, Bunny, you're the first. But it hit friend Theobald hardest of all. I'm an income to him. I believe he's going to marry on me.'

'Does he guess there's nothing wrong?'

'Knows, bless you! But he doesn't know I know he knows, and there isn't a disease in the dictionary that he hasn't treated me for since he's had me in hand. To do him justice, I believe he thinks me a hypochondriac of the first water; but that young man will go far if he keeps on the wicket. He has spent half his nights up here, at guineas apiece.'

'Guineas must be plentiful, old chap!'

'They have been, Bunny. I can't say more. But I don't see why they should be again.'

I was not going to inquire where the guineas came from. As if I cared! But I did ask old Raffles how in the world he had got upon my tracks; and thereby drew the sort of smile with which old gentlemen rub their hands, and old ladies nod their noses. Raffles merely produced a perfect oval of blue smoke before replying.

'I was waiting for you to ask that, Bunny; it's a long time since I did anything upon which I plume myself more. Of course, in the first place, I spotted you at once by these prison articles; they were not signed, but the fist was the fist of my sitting rabbit!'

'But who gave you my address?'

'I wheedled it out of your excellent editor; called on him at dead of night, when I occasionally go afield like other ghosts, and wept it out of him in five minutes. I was your only relative; your name was not your own name; if he insisted I would give him mine. He didn't insist, Bunny, and I danced down his stairs with your address in my pocket.'

'Last night?'

'No, last week.'

'And so the advertisement was yours, as well as the telegram!'

I had, of course, forgotten both in the high excitement of the hour, or I should scarcely have announced my belated discovery with such an air. As it was, I made Raffles look at me as I had known him look before, and the droop of his eyelids began to sting.

'Why all this subtlety?' I petulantly exclaimed. 'Why couldn't you come straight away to me in a cab?'

He did not inform me that I was hopeless as ever. He did

not address me as his good rabbit. He was silent for a time, and then spoke in a tone which made me ashamed of mine.

'You see, there are two or three of me now, Bunny: one's at the bottom of the Mediterranean, and one's an old Australian desirous of dying in the old country, but in no immediate danger of dying anywhere. The old Australian doesn't know a soul in town; he's got to be consistent, or he's done. This sitter Theobald is his only friend, and has seen rather too much of him; ordinary dust won't do for his eyes. Begin to see? To pick you out of a crowd, that was the game; to let old Theobald help to pick you, better still! To start with, he was dead against my having anybody at all; wanted me all to himself, naturally; but anything rather than kill the goose! So he is to have a fiver a week, while he keeps me alive, and he's going to be married next month. That's a pity in some ways, but a good thing in others; he will want more money than he foresees, and he may always be of use to us at a pinch. Meanwhile he eats out of my hand.'

I complimented Raffles on the mere composition of his telegram, with half the characteristics of my distinguished kinsman squeezed into a dozen odd words; and let him know how the old ruffian had really treated me. Raffles was not surprised; we had dined together at my relative's in the old days and filed for reference a professional valuation of his household goods. I now learnt that the telegram had been posted, with the hour marked for its dispatch, at the pillar nearest Vere Street, on the night before the advertisement was due to appear in the *Daily Mail*. This also had been carefully pre-arranged; and Raffles's only fear had been lest it might be held over despite his explicit instructions, and so drive me to the doctor for an explanation of his telegram. But the adverse chances had been weeded out, and weeded out to the irreducible minimum of risk.

His greatest risk, according to Raffles, lay nearest home: bedridden invalid that he was supposed to be, his nightly terror was of running into Theobald's arms in the immediate neighbourhood of the flat. But Raffles had characteristic methods of minimising even that danger, of which something

anon; meanwhile he recounted more than one of his nocturnal
adventures, all, however, of a singularly innocent type; and
one thing I noticed while he talked. His room was the first as
you entered the flat. The long inner wall divided the room not
merely from the passage but from the outer landing as well.
Thus every step upon the bare stone stairs could be heard by
Raffles where he lay; and he would never speak while one was
ascending, until it had passed his door. The afternoon brought
more than one applicant for the post that it was my duty to
tell them I had already obtained. Between three and four,
however, Raffles suddenly looking at his watch, packed me off
in a hurry to the other end of London for my things.

'I'm afraid you must be famishing, Bunny. It's a fact that I
eat very little, and that at odd hours, but I ought not to have
forgotten you. Get yourself a snack outside, but not a square
meal if you can resist one. We've got to celebrate this day this
night!'

'To-night?' I cried.

'To-night at eleven, and Kellner's the place. You may well
open your eyes, but we didn't go there much, if you remember, and the staff seems changed. Anyway, we'll risk it for
once. I was in last night, talking like a stage American, and
supper's ordered for eleven sharp.'

'You made as sure of me as all that!'

'There was no harm in ordering supper. We shall have it in
a private room, but you may as well dress if you've got the
duds.'

'They're at my only forgiving relative's.'

'How much will get them out, and square you up, and bring
you back bag and baggage in good time?'

I had to calculate.

'A tenner, easily.'

'I had one ready for you. Here it is, and I wouldn't lose any
time if I were you. On the way you might look up Theobald,
tell him you've got it and how long you'll be gone, and that I
can't be left alone all the time. And, by Jove, yes! You get me
a stall for the Lyceum at the nearest agent's; there are two or
three in High Street; and say it was given you when you come
in. That young man shall be out of the way to-night.'

I found our doctor in a minute consulting-room and in his shirt-sleeves, a tall tumbler at his elbow; at least, I caught sight of the tumbler on entering; thereafter he stood in front of it, with a futility which had my sympathy.

'So you've got the billet,' said Dr. Theobald. 'Well, as I told you before, and as you have since probably discovered for yourself, you won't find it exactly a sinecure. My own part of the business is by no means that; indeed, there are those who would throw up the case, after the kind of treatment that you have seen for yourself. But professional considerations are not the only ones, and one cannot make too many allowances in such a case.'

'But what is the case?' I asked him. 'You said you would tell me if I were successful.'

Dr. Theobald's shrug was worthy of the profession he seemed destined to adorn; it was not incompatible with any construction which one chose to put upon it. Next moment he had stiffened. I suppose I still spoke more or less like a gentleman. Yet, after all, I was only a male nurse. He seemed to remember this suddenly, and he took occasion to remind me of the fact.

'Ah,' said he, 'that was before I knew you were altogether without experience; and I must say that I was surprised even at Mr. Maturin's engaging you after that; but it will depend upon yourself how long I allow him to persist in so curious an experiment. As for what is the matter with him, my good fellow, it is no use my giving you an answer which would be double Dutch to you; moreover, I have still to test your discretionary powers. I may say, however, that that poor gentleman presents at once the most complex and most troublesome case, which is responsibility enough without certain features which make it all but insupportable. Beyond this I must refuse to discuss my patient for the present; but I shall certainly go up if I can find time.'

He went up within five minutes. I found him there on my return at dusk. But he did not refuse my stall for the Lyceum, which Raffles would not allow me to use myself, and presented to him off-hand without my leave.

'And don't you bother any more about me till to-morrow,'

snapped the high thin voice as he was off. 'I can send for you now when I want you, and I'm hoping to have a decent night for once.'

III

It was half-past ten when we left the flat, in an interval of silence on the noisy stairs. The silence was unbroken by our wary feet. Yet for me a surprise was in store upon the very landing. Instead of going downstairs, Raffles led me up two flights, and so out upon a perfectly flat roof.

'There are two entrances to these mansions,' he explained between stars and chimney-stacks: 'one to our staircase, and another round the corner. But there's only one porter, and he lives in the basement underneath us, and affects the door nearest home. We miss him by using the wrong stairs, and we run less risk of old Theobald. I got the tip from the postmen, who come up one way and down the other. Now follow me, and look out!'

There was indeed some necessity for caution, for each half of the building had its L-shaped well dropping sheer to the base, the parapets so low that one might easily have tripped over them into eternity. However, we were soon upon the second staircase, which opened on the roof like the first. And twenty minutes of the next twenty-five we spent in an admirable hansom, skimming east.

'Not much change in the old hole, Bunny. More of these magic-lantern advertisements ... and absolutely the worst bit of taste in town, though it's saying something, is that equestrian statue with the gilt stirrups and fixings: why don't they black the buffer's boots and his horse's hoofs while they are about it? ... More bicyclists, of course. That was just beginning, if you remember. It might have been useful to us ... And there's the old club, getting put into a crate for the Jubilee; by Jove, Bunny, we ought to be there. I wouldn't lean forward in Piccadilly, old chap. If you're seen I'm thought of, and we shall have to be jolly careful at Kellner's ... Ah, there it is! Did I tell you I was a low-down stage Yankee at Kellner's? You'd better be another, while the waiter's in the room.'

We had the little room upstairs; and on the very threshold I, even I, who knew my Raffles of old, was taken horribly aback. The table was laid for three. I called his attention to it in a whisper.

'Why, yep!' came through his nose. 'Say, boy, the lady, she's not com'n', but you leave that tackle where 'tis. If I'm liable to pay, I guess I'll have all there is to it.'

I have never been in America, and the American public is the last on earth that I desire to insult; but idiom and intonation alike would have imposed upon my inexperience. I had to look at Raffles to make sure that it was he who spoke, and I had my own reasons for looking hard.

'Who on earth was the lady?' I inquired, aghast, at the first opportunity.

'She isn't on earth. They don't like wasting this room on two, that's all. Bunny – my Bunny – here's to us both!'

And we clinked glasses swimming with the liquid gold of Steinberg, 1868; but of the rare delights of that supper I can scarcely trust myself to write. It was no mere meal, it was no coarse orgy, but a little feast for the fastidious gods, not unworthy of Lucullus at his worst. And I who had bolted my skilly at Wormwood Scrubs, and tightened my belt in a Holloway attic, it was I who sat down to this ineffable repast! Where the courses were few, but each a triumph of its kind, it would be invidious to single out any one dish; but the *jambon de Westphalie au champagne* tempts me sorely. And then the champagne that we drank, not the quantity but the quality! Well, it was Pol Roger, '84, and quite good enough for me; but even so it was not more dry, nor did it sparkle more, than the merry rascal who had dragged me thus far to the devil, but should lead me dancing the rest of the way. I was beginning to tell him so. I had done my honest best since my reappearance in the world; but the world had done its worst by me. A further antithesis and my final intention were both upon my tongue when the waiter with the Château Margaux cut me short; for he was the bearer of more than that great wine; bringing also a card upon a silver tray.

'Show him up,' said Raffles laconically.

'And who is this?' I cried, when the man was gone. Raffles

reached across the table and gripped my arm in his vice. His eyes were steel points fixed on mine.

'Bunny, stand by me,' said he in the old irresistible voice, a voice both stern and winning. 'Stand by me, Bunny – if there's a row!'

And there was time for nothing more, the door flying open, and a dapper person entering with a bow; a frock-coat on his back, gold *pince-nez* on his nose; a shiny hat in one hand, and a black bag in the other.

'Good-evening, gentlemen,' said he, at home and smiling.

'Sit down,' drawled Raffles in casual response. 'Say, let me introduce you to Mr Ezra B. Martin, of Shicawgo. Mr Martin is my future brother-in-law. This is Mr Robinson, Ezra, manager to Sparks and Company, the celebrated joolers on Regent Street.'

I pricked up my ears, but contented myself with a nod. I altogether distrusted my ability to live up to my new name and address.

'I figured on Miss Martin bein' right here, too,' continued Raffles, 'but I regret to say she's not feelin' so good. We light out for Parrus on the 9 a.m. train to-morrer mornin', and she guessed she'd be too dead. Sorry to disappoint you, Mr Robinson; but you'll see I'm advertisin' your wares.'

Raffles held his right hand under the electric light, and a diamond ring flashed upon his little finger. I could have sworn it was not there five minutes before.

The tradesman had a disappointed face, but for a moment it brightened as he expatiated on the value of the ring and on the price his people had accepted for it. I was invited to guess the figure, but I shook a discreet head. I have seldom been more taciturn in my life.

'Forty-five pounds,' cried the jeweller; 'and it would be cheap at fifty guineas.'

'That's right,' assented Raffles. 'That'd be dead cheap, I allow. But then, my boy, you gotten ready cash, and don't you forget it.'

I do not dwell upon my own mystification in all this. I merely pause to state that I was keenly enjoying that very element. Nothing could have been more typical of Raffles and the past. It was only my own attitude that was changed.

It appeared that the mythical lady, my sister, had just become engaged to Raffles, who seemed all anxiety to pin her down with gifts of price. I could not quite gather whose gift to whom was the diamond ring; but it had evidently been paid for; and I voyaged to the moon, wondering when and how. I was recalled to this planet by a deluge of gems from the jeweller's bag. They lay alight in their cases like the electric lamps above. We all three put our heads together over them, myself without the slightest clue as to what was coming, but not unprepared for violent crime. One does not do eighteen months for nothing.

'Right away,' Raffles was saying. 'We'll choose for her, and you'll change anything she don't like. Is that the idea?'

'That was my suggestion, sir.'

'Then come on, Ezra. I guess you know Sadie's taste. You help me choose.'

And we chose – Lord! What did we not choose? There was her ring, a diamond half-hoop. It cost £95, and there was no attempt to get it for £90. Then there was a diamond necklet – two hundred guineas, but pounds accepted. That was to be the gift of the bridegroom. The wedding was evidently imminent. It behoved me to play a brotherly part. I therefore rose to the occasion; calculated she would like a diamond star (£116), but reckoned it was more than I could afford; and sustained a vicious kick under the table for either verb. I was afraid to open my mouth on finally obtaining the star for the round hundred. And then the fat fell in the fire; for pay we could not; though a remittance (said Raffles) was 'overdoo from Noo York.'

'But I don't know you, gentlemen,' the jeweller exclaimed. 'I haven't even the name of your hotel!'

'I told you we was stoppin' with friends,' said Raffles, who was not angry, though thwarted and crushed. 'But that's right, sir! Oh, that's dead right, and I'm the last man to ask you to take Quixotic risks. I'm tryin' to figure a way out. Yes, *sir*, that's what I'm tryin' to do.'

'I wish you could, sir,' the jeweller said, with feeling. 'It isn't as if we hadn't seen the colour of your money. But certain rules I am sworn to observe; it isn't as if I were in business for myself; and – you say you start for Paris in the morning!'

'On the 9 a.m. train,' mused Raffles; 'and I've heard no-end yarns about the joolers' stores in Parrus. But that ain't fair; don't you take no notice o' that. I'm tryin' to figure a way out. Yes, *sir!*"

He was smoking cigarettes out of a twenty-five box; the tradesman and I had cigars. Raffles sat frowning with a pregnant eye, and it was only too clear to me that his plans had miscarried. I could not help thinking, however, that they deserved to do so, if he had counted upon buying credit for all but £400 by a single payment of some 10 per cent. That again seemed unworthy of Raffles, and I, for my part, still sat prepared to spring any moment at our visitor's throat.

'We could mail you the money from Parrus,' drawled Raffles at length. 'But how should we know you'd hold up your end of the string, and mail us the same articles we've selected tonight?'

The visitor stiffened in his chair. The name of his firm should be sufficient guarantee for that.

'I guess I'm no better acquainted with their name than they are with mine,' remarked Raffles, laughing. 'See here, though! I got a scheme. You pack 'em in this!'

He turned the cigarettes out of the tin box, while the jeweller and I joined wondering eyes.

'Pack 'em in this,' repeated Raffles, 'the three things we want, and never mind the boxes; you can pack 'em in cotton-wool. Then we'll ring for string and sealing-wax, seal up the lot right here, and you can take 'em away in your grip. Within three days we'll have our remittance, and mail you the money, and you'll mail us this darned box with my seal unbroken! It's no use you lookin' so sick, Mr Jooler; you won't trust us any, and yet we're goin' to trust you some. Ring the bell, Ezra, and we'll see if they've gotten any sealing-wax and string.'

They had; and the thing was done. The tradesman did not like it; the precaution was absolutely unnecessary; but since he was taking all his goods away with him, the sold with the unsold, his sentimental objections soon fell to the ground. He packed necklet, ring, and star, with his own hands, in cotton-wool; and the cigarette-box held them so easily that at the last moment, when the box was closed, and the string ready, Raffles very nearly added a diamond bee-brooch at £51 10s. This temptation, however, he ultimately overcame, to the other's chagrin. The cigarette-box was tied up, and the string sealed, oddly enough, with the diamond of the ring that had been bought and paid for.

'I'll chance your having another ring in the store the dead spit of mine,' laughed Raffles, as he relinquished the box, and it disappeared into the tradesman's bag. 'And now, Mr Robinson, I hope you'll appreciate my true hospitality in not offering you anything to drink while business was in progress. That's Château Margaux, sir, and I should judge it's what you'd call an eighteen-carat article.'

In the cab which we took to the vicinity of the flat, I was instantly snubbed for asking questions which the driver might easily overhear, and I took the repulse just a little to heart. I could make neither head nor tail of Raffles's dealings with the man from Regent Street, and was naturally inquisitive as to the meaning of it all. But I held my tongue until we had re-gained the flat in the cautious manner of our exit, and even there until Raffles rallied me with a hand on either shoulder and the old smile upon his face.

'You rabbit!' said he. 'Why couldn't you wait till we got home?'

'Why couldn't you tell me what you were going to do?' I retorted as of yore.

'Because your dear old phiz is still worth its weight in inno-cence, and because you never could act for nuts! You looked as puzzled as the other poor devil; but you wouldn't if you had known what my game really was.'

'And pray what was it?'

'That,' said Raffles, and he smacked the cigarette-box down upon the mantelpiece. It was not tied. It was not sealed. It flew open from the force of the impact. And the diamond ring that cost £95, the necklet for £200, and my flaming star at another £100, all three lay safe and snug in the jeweller's own cotton-wool!

'Duplicate boxes!' I cried.

'Duplicate boxes, my brainy Bunny. One was already packed, and weighted, and in my pocket. I don't know whether you noticed me weighing the three things together in my hand? I know that neither of you saw me change the boxes, for I did it when I was nearest buying the bee-brooch at the end, and you were too puzzled, and the other Johnny too keen. It was the cheapest shot in the game; the dear ones were sending old Theobald to Southampton on a fool's errand yesterday afternoon, and showing one's own nose down Regent Street in broad daylight while he was gone; but some things are worth paying for and certain risks one must always take. Nice boxes, aren't they? I only wished they contained a better cigarette; but a notorious brand was essential; a box of Sullivans would have brought me to life to-morrow.'

'But they oughtn't to open it to-morrow.'

'Nor will they, as a matter of fact. Meanwhile, Bunny, I may call upon you to dispose of the boodle.'

'I'm on for any mortal thing!'

My voice rang true, I swear, but it was the way of Raffles to take the evidence of as many senses as possible. I felt the cold steel of his eye through mine and through my brain. But what he saw seemed to satisfy him no less than what he heard, for his hand found my hand, and pressed it with a fervour foreign to the man.

'I know you are, and I knew you would be. Only remember, Bunny, it's my turn to pay the shot!'

You shall hear how he paid it when the time came.

A JUBILEE PRESENT

THE room of gold, in the British Museum, is probably well enough known to the inquiring alien and the travelled American. A true Londoner, however, I myself had never heard of it until Raffles casually proposed a raid.

'Is the Room of Gold a roomful of sovereigns?'

Raffles laughed softly at my scorn.

'No, Bunny, it's principally in the shape of archaic ornaments, whose value, I admit, is largely extrinsic. But gold is gold, from Phœnicia to Klondike, and if we cleared the room we should eventually do very well.'

'How?'

'I should melt it down into a nugget, and bring it home from the U.S.A. to-morrow.'

'And then?'

'Make them pay up in hard cash across the counter of the Bank of England. And you *can* make them.'

That I knew, and so said nothing for a time, remaining a hostile though a silent critic, while we paced the cool black leads with our bare feet, softly as cats.

'And how do you propose to get enough away,' at length I asked, 'to make it worth while?'

'Ah, there you have it,' said Raffles. 'I only propose to reconnoitre the ground, to see what we can see. We might find some hiding-place for a night; that, I am afraid, would be our only chance.'

'Have you ever been there before?'

'Not since they got the one good, portable piece which I believe that they exhibit now. It's a long time since I read of it – I can't remember where – but I know they have got a gold cup of sorts worth several thousands. A number of the immorally rich clubbed together and presented it to the nation; and two of the richly immoral intend to snaffle it for themselves. At any rate, we might go and have a look at it, Bunny, don't you think?'

Think! I seized his arm.

'When? When? When?' I asked, like a quick-firing gun.

'The sooner the better.'

'Well, then, when – when?' I began to repeat.

'To-morrow, if you like.'

'Only to look?'

The limitation was my one regret.

'We must do so, Bunny, before we leap.'

'Very well,' I sighed. 'But to-morrow it is!'

And the morrow it really was.

I saw the porter that night and, I still think bought his absolute allegiance for the second coin of the realm. My story, however, invented by Raffles, was sufficiently specious in itself. Would the porter help me in so innocent and meritorious an intrigue? The man hesitated. I produced my half-sovereign. The man was lost. And at half-past eight next morning – before the heat of the day – Raffles and I drove to Kew Gardens in a hired landau which was to call for us at midday and wait until we came. The porter had assisted me to carry my invalid downstairs, in a carrying-chair hired (like the landau) from Harrod's Stores for the occasion.

It was little after nine when we crawled together into the gardens; by half-past my invalid had had enough, and out he tottered on my arm; a cab, a message to our coachman, a timely train to Baker Street, another cab, and we were at the British Museum – brisk pedestrians now – not very many minutes after the opening hour of 10 a.m.

It was one of those glowing days which will not be forgotten by many who were in town at the time. The Diamond Jubilee was upon us, and Queen's weather had already set in. Raffles, indeed, declared it was hot as Italy and Australia put together; and certainly the short summer nights gave the channels of wood and asphalt and the continents of brick and mortar but little time to cool. At the British Museum the pigeons were crooning among the shadows of the grimy colonnade, and the stalwart janitors looked less stalwart than usual, as though their medals were too heavy for them. I recognised some habitual readers going to their labour underneath the dome; of mere visitors we seemed among the first.

'That's the room,' said Raffles, who had bought the two-penny guide, as we studied it openly on the nearest bench; 'Number 43, upstairs and sharp round to the right. Come on, Bunny!'

And he led the way in silence, but with a long methodical stride which I could not understand until we came to the corridor leading to the Room of Gold, when he turned to me for a moment.

'A hundred and thirty-nine yards from this to the open street,' said Raffles, 'not counting the stairs. I suppose we *could* do it in twenty seconds, but if we did we should have to jump the gates. No, you must remember to loaf out at slow march, Bunny, whether you like it or not.'

'But you talked about a hiding-place for a night?'

'Quite so – for all night. We should have to get back, go on lying low, and saunter out with the crowd next day – after doing the whole show thoroughly.'

'What! With gold in our pockets – –'

'And gold in our boots, and gold up the sleeves and legs of our suits! You leave that to me, Bunny, and wait till you've tried two pair of trousers sewn together at the foot! This is only a preliminary reconnoitre. And here we are.'

It is none of my business to describe the so-called Room of Gold, with which I, for one, was not a little disappointed. The glass cases, which both fill and line it, may contain unique examples of the goldsmith's art in times and places of which one heard quite enough in the course of one's classical education; but, from a professional point of view, I would as lief have the ransacking of a single window in the West End as the pick of all those spoils of Etruria and of Ancient Greece. The gold may not be so soft as it appears, but it certainly looks as though you could bite off the business ends of the spoons, and stop your own teeth in doing so. Nor should I care to be seen wearing one of the rings; but the greatest fraud of all (from the aforesaid standpoint) is assuredly that very cup of which Raffles had spoken. Moreover, he felt this himself.

'Why, it's as thin as paper,' said he, 'and enamelled like a middle-aged lady of quality! But, by Jove, it's one of the most beautiful things I ever saw in my life, Bunny. I should like to have it for its own sake, by all my gods!'

The thing had a little square case of plate-glass all to itself at one end of the room. It may have been the thing of beauty that Raffles affected to consider it, but I for my part was in no mood to look at it in that light. Underneath were the names of the plutocrats who had subscribed for this national gewgaw, and I fell to wondering where their £8,000 came in, while Raffles devoured his twopenny guide-book as greedily as a schoolgirl with a zeal for culture.

'Those are scenes from the martyrdom of St Agnes,' said he ... ' "translucent on relief ... one of the finest specimens of its kind." I should think it was! Bunny, you Philistine, why can't you admire the thing for its own sake? It would be worth having only to live up to! There never was such rich enamelling on such thin gold; and what a good scheme to hang the lid up over it, so that you can see how thin it is. I wonder if we could lift it, Bunny, by hook or crook?'

'You'd better try, sir,' said a dry voice at his elbow.

The madman seemed to think we had the room to ourselves. I knew better, but like another madman, had let him ramble on unchecked. And here was a stolid constable confronting us, in the short tunic that they wear in summer, his whistle on its chain, but no truncheon at his side. Heavens! how I see him now; a man of medium size, with a broad, good-humoured, perspiring face, and a limp moustache. He looked sternly at Raffles, and Raffles looked merrily at him.

'Going to run me in, officer?' said he. 'That *would* be a joke – my hat!'

'I didn't say as I was, sir,' replied the policeman. 'But that's queer talk for a gentleman like you, sir, in the British Museum!' And he wagged his helmet at my invalid, who had taken his airing in coat-frock and top-hat, the more readily to assume his present part.

'What!' cried Raffles, 'simply saying to my friend that I'd like to lift the gold cup? Why, so I should, officer, so I should! I don't mind who hears me say so. It's one of the most beautiful things I ever saw in all my life.'

The constable's face had already relaxed, and now a grin

peeped under the limp moustache. 'I dare say there's many as feels like that, sir,' said he.

'Exactly; and I say what I feel, that's all,' said Raffles airily. 'But, seriously, officer, is a valuable thing like this quite safe in a case like that?'

'Safe enough as long as I'm here,' replied the other between grim jest and stout earnest. Raffles studied his face; he was still watching Raffles; and I kept an eye on them both without putting in my word.

'You appear to be single-handed,' observed Raffles. 'Is that wise?'

The note of anxiety was capitally caught; it was at once personal and public-spirited, that of the enthusiastic savant, afraid for a national treasure which few appreciated as he did himself. And, to be sure, the three of us now had this treasury to ourselves; one or two others had been there when we entered; but now they were gone.

'I'm not single-handed,' said the officer comfortably. 'See that seat by the door? One of the attendants sits there all day long.'

'Then where is he now?'

'Talking to another attendant just outside. If you listen you'll hear them for yourself.'

We listened, and we did hear them, but not just outside. In my own mind I even questioned whether they were in the corridor through which we had come; to me it sounded as though they were just outside the corridor.

'You mean the fellow with the billiard-cue who was here when we came in?' pursued Raffles.

'That wasn't a billiard-cue! It was a pointer,' the intelligent officer explained.

'It ought to be a javelin,' said Raffles nervously. 'It ought to be a pole-axe! The public treasure ought to be better guarded than this. I shall write to *The Times* about it – you see if I don't!'

All at once, yet somehow not so suddenly as to excite suspicion, Raffles had become the elderly busybody with nerves; why, I could not for the life of me imagine; and the policeman seemed equally at sea.

'Lor' bless you, sir,' said he, 'I'm all right; don't you bother your head about *me*.'

'But you haven't even got a truncheon!'

'Not likely to want one either. You see, sir, it's early as yet; in a few minutes these here rooms will fill up; and there's safety in numbers, as they say.'

'Oh, it will fill up soon, will it?'

'Any minute now, sir.'

'Ah!'

'It isn't often empty as long as this, sir. It's the Jubilee, I suppose.'

'Meanwhile, what if my friend and I had been professional thieves? Why, we could have overpowered you in an instant, my good fellow!'

'That you couldn't; leastways, not without bringing the whole place about your ears.'

'Well, I shall write to *The Times* all the same. I'm a connoisseur in all this sort of thing, and I won't have unnecessary risks run with the nation's property. You said there was an attendant just outside, but he sounds to me as though he were at the other end of the corridor. I shall write to-day!'

For an instant we all three listened; and Raffles was right. Then I saw two things in one glance. Raffles had stepped a few inches backward, and stood poised upon the ball of each foot, his arms half raised, a light in his eyes. And another kind of light was breaking over the crass features of our friend the constable.

'Then shall I tell you what *I'll* do?' he cried, with a sudden clutch at the whistle-chain on his chest. The whistle flew out, but it never reached his lips. There were a couple of sharp smacks, like double barrels discharged all but simultaneously, and the man reeled against me so that I could not help catching him as he fell.

'Well done, Bunny! I've knocked him out – I've knocked him out! Run you to the door and see if the attendants have heard anything, and take them on if they have.'

Mechanically I did as I was told. There was no time for thought, still less for remonstrance or reproach, though my surprise must have been even more complete than that of the

constable before Raffles knocked the sense out of him. Even in
my utter bewilderment, however, the instinctive caution of the
real criminal did not desert me. I ran to the door, but I sauntered through it, to plant myself before a Pompeian fresco in
the corridor; and there were the two attendants still gossiping
outside the farther door; nor did they hear the dull crash
which I heard even as I watched them out of the corner of
each eye.

It was hot weather, as I have said, but the perspiration on
my body seemed already to have turned into a skin of ice.
Then I caught the faint reflection of my own face in the casing
of the fresco, and it frightened me into some semblance of
myself as Raffles joined me with his hands in his pockets. But
my fear and indignation were redoubled at the sight of him,
when a single glance convinced me that his pockets were as
empty as his hands, and his mad outrage the most wanton and
reckless of his whole career.

'Ah, very interesting, very interesting, but nothing to what
they have in the museum at Naples or in Pompeii itself. You
must go there some day, Bunny. I've a good mind to take you
myself. Meanwhile – slow march! The beggar hasn't moved
an eyelid. We may swing for him if you show indecent
haste!'

'We!' I whispered. 'We!'

And my knees knocked together as we came up to the chatting attendants. But Raffles must needs interrupt them to ask
the way to the Prehistoric Saloon.

'At the top of the stairs.'

'Thank you. Then we'll work round that way to the Egyptian
part.'

And we left them resuming their providential chat.

'I believe you're mad,' I said bitterly as we went.

'I believe I *was*,' admitted Raffles; 'but I'm not now, and I'll
see you through. A hundred and thirty-nine yards, wasn't it?
Then it can't be more than a hundred and twenty now – not
as much. Steady, Bunny, for God's sake! It's *slow* march –
for our lives.'

There was this much management. The rest was our colossal
luck. A hansom was being paid off at the foot of the steps out-

side, and in we jumped, Raffles shouting 'Charing Cross!' for
all Bloomsbury to hear.

We had turned into Bloomsbury Street without exchanging
a syllable when he struck the trapdoor with his fist.

'Where the devil are you driving us?'

'Charing Cross, sir.'

'I said King's Cross! Round you spin, and drive like blazes,
or we miss our train! There's one to York at 10.35,' added
Raffles as the trapdoor slammed; 'we'll book there, Bunny, and
then we'll slope through the subway to the Metropolitan, and
so to ground *via* Baker Street and Earl's Court.'

And actually in half an hour he was seated once more in
the hired carrying-chair. Then, and not until then, when we
were alone at last, did I tell Raffles, in the most nervous English at my command, frankly and exactly what I thought of
him and of his latest deed. Once started, moreover, I spoke as
I have seldom spoken to living man; and Raffles, of all men,
stood my abuse without a murmur, or rather he sat it out, too
astounded even to take off his hat, though I thought his eyebrows would have lifted it from his head.

'But it always was your infernal way,' I was savagely concluding. 'You make one plan, and you tell me another – –'

'Not to-day, Bunny, I swear!'

'You mean to tell me you really did start with the bare idea
of finding a place to hide in for a night?'

'Of course I did.'

'It was to be the mere reconnoitre you pretended?'

'There was no pretence about it, Bunny.'

'Then why on earth go and do what you did?'

'The reason would be obvious to any one but you,' said
Raffles, still with no unkindly scorn. 'It was the temptation of
a minute – the final impulse of the fraction of a second, when
Roberto saw that I was tempted, and let me see that he saw it.
It's not a thing I care to do, and I shan't be happy till the
papers tell me the poor devil is alive. But a knock-out shot
was the only chance for us then.'

'Why? You don't get run in for being tempted, nor yet for
showing that you are!'

'But I should have deserved running in if I hadn't yielded

to such a temptation as that, Bunny. It was a chance in a hundred thousand! We might go there every day of our lives, and never again be the only outsiders in the room, with the billiard-marking Johnnie practically out of earshot at one and the same time. It was a gift from the gods; not to have taken it would have been flying in the face of Providence.'

'But you didn't take it,' said I. 'You went and left it behind.'

I wish I had had a Kodak for the little smile with which Raffles shook his head; for it was one that he kept for those great moments of which our vocation is not devoid. All this time he had been wearing his hat, tilted a little over eyebrows no longer raised. And now at last I knew where the gold cup was.

It stood for days upon his chimney-piece, this costly trophy whose ancient history and final fate filled newspaper columns even in these days of Jubilee, and for which the flower of Scotland Yard was said to be seeking high and low. Our constable, we learnt, had been stunned only, and, from the moment that I brought him an evening paper with the news, Raffles's spirits rose to a height inconsistent with his equable temperament, and as unusual in him as the sudden impulse upon which he had acted with such effect. The cup itself appealed to me no more than it had done before. Exquisite it might be, handsome it was, but so light in the hand that the mere gold of it would scarcely have poured three figures out of the melting-pot. And what said Raffles but that he would never melt it at all!

'Taking it was an offence against the laws of the land, Bunny. That is nothing. But destroying it would be a crime against God and Art, and may I be spitted on the vane of St. Mary Abbots if I commit it!'

Talk such as this was unanswerable; indeed, the whole affair had passed the pale of useful comment; and the one course left to a practical person was to shrug his shoulders and enjoy the joke. This was not a little enhanced by the newspaper reports, which described Raffles as a handsome youth, and his unwilling accomplice as an older man of blackguardly appearance and low type.

'Hits us both off rather neatly, Bunny,' said he. 'But what they none of them do justice to is my dear cup. Look at it; only look at it, man! Was ever anything so rich and yet so chaste? St Agnes must have had a pretty bad time, but it would be almost worth it to go down to posterity in such enamel upon such gold. And then the history of the thing. Do you realise that it's five hundred years old and has belonged to Henry the Eighth and to Elizabeth among others? Bunny, when you have me cremated, you can put my ashes in yonder cup, and lay us in the deep-delvèd earth together!'

'And meanwhile?'

'It is the joy of my heart, the light of my life, the delight of mine eye.'

'And suppose other eyes catch sight of it?'

'They never must; they never shall.'

Raffles would have been too absurd had he not been thoroughly alive to his own absurdity; there was, nevertheless, an underlying sincerity in his appreciation of any and every form of beauty, which all his nonsense could not conceal. And his infatuation for the cup was, as he declared, a very pure passion, since the circumstances debarred him from the chief joy of the average collector, that of showing his treasure to his friends. At last, however, and at the height of his craze, Raffles and reason seemed to come together again as suddenly as they had parted company in the Room of Gold.

'Bunny,' he cried, flinging his newspaper across the room, 'I've got an idea after your own heart. I know where I can place it after all!'

'Do you mean the cup?'

'I do.'

'Then I congratulate you.'

'Thanks.'

'Upon the recovery of your senses.'

'Thanks galore. But you've been confoundedly unsympathetic about this thing, Bunny, and I don't think I shall tell you my scheme till I've carried it out.'

'Quite time enough,' said I.

'It will mean your letting me loose for an hour or two under cloud of this very night. To-morrow's Sunday, the Jubilee's on Tuesday, and old Theobald's coming back for it.'

'It doesn't much matter whether he's back or not if you go late enough.'

'I mustn't be late. They don't keep open. No, it's no use your asking any questions. Go out and buy me a big box of Huntley & Palmer's biscuits; any sort you like, only they must be theirs, and absolutely the biggest box they sell.'

'My dear man!'

'No questions, Bunny; you do your part and I'll do mine.'

Subtlety and success were in his face. It was enough for me, and I had done his extraordinary bidding within a quarter of an hour. In another minute Raffles had opened the box and tumbled all the biscuits into the nearest chair.

'Now newspapers!'

I fetched a pile. He bid the cup of gold a ridiculous farewell, wrapped it up in newspaper after newspaper, and finally packed it in the empty biscuit-box.

'Now some brown paper. I don't want to be taken for the grocer's young man.'

A neat enough parcel it made, when the string had been tied and the ends cut close; what was more difficult was to wrap up Raffles himself in such a way that even the porter should not recognise him if they came face to face at the corner. And the sun was still up. But Raffles would go, and when he did I should not have known him myself.

He may have been an hour away. It was barely dusk when he returned, and my first question referred to our dangerous ally, the porter. Raffles had passed him unsuspected in going, but had managed to avoid him altogether on the return journey, which he had completed by way of the other entrance and of the roof. I breathed again.

'And what have you done with the cup?'

'Placed it!'

'How much for? How much for?'

'Let me think. I had a couple of cabs, and the postage was a tanner, with another twopence for registration. Yes, it cost me exactly five-and-eight.'

'*It* cost *you*? But what did you *get* for it, Raffles?'

'Nothing, my boy.'

'Nothing!'

'Not a crimson cent.'

'I am not surprised. I never thought it had a market value. I told you so in the beginning,' I said irritably. 'But what on earth have you done with the thing?'

'Sent it to the Queen.'

'You haven't!'

Rogue is a word with various meanings, and Raffles had been one sort of rogue ever since I had known him; but now, for once, he was the innocent variety, a great grey-haired child, running over with merriment and mischief.

'Well, I've sent it to Sir Arthur Bigge, to present to Her Majesty, with the loyal respects of the thief, if that will do for you,' said Raffles. 'I thought they might take too much stock of me at the G.P.O. if I addressed it to the Sovereign herself. Yes, I drove over to St. Martin's-le-Grand with it, and I registered the box into the bargain. Do a thing properly if you do it at all.'

'But why on earth,' I groaned, 'do such a thing at all?'

'My dear Bunny, we have been reigned over for sixty years by infinitely the finest monarch the world has ever seen. The world is taking the present opportunity of signifying the fact for all it is worth. Every nation is laying of its best at her royal feet; every class in the community is doing its little level – except ours. All I have done is to remove one reproach from our fraternity.'

At this I came round, was infected with his spirit, called him the sportsman he always was and would be, and shook his dare-devil hand in mine; but, at the same time, I still had my qualms.

'Supposing they trace it to us?' said I.

'There's not much to catch hold of in a biscuit-box by Huntley & Palmer,' replied Raffles; 'that was why I sent you for one. And I didn't write a word upon a sheet of paper which could possibly be traced. I simply printed two or three on a virginal post card – another halfpenny to the bad – which might have been bought at any post office in the kingdom. No, old chap, the G.P.O. was the one real danger; there was one detective I spotted for myself; and the sight of him has left me with a thirst. Whisky and Sullivans for two, Bunny, if you please.'

Raffles was soon clinking his glass against mine.

'The Queen,' said he. 'God bless her!'

THE FATE OF FAUSTINA

"Mar – ga – rì,
　　e perzo a Salvatore!
Mar – ga – rì,
　　Ma l'ommo è cacciatore!
Mar – ga – rì,
　　Nun ce aje corpa tu!
Chello ch' è fatto, è fatto, un ne parlammo cchieù!"

A PIANO-ORGAN was pouring the metallic music through our open windows, while a voice of brass brayed the words, which I have since obtained, and print above for identification by such as know their Italy better than I. They will not thank me for reminding them of a tune so lately epidemic in that land of aloes and blue skies; but at least it is unlikely to run in their heads as the ribald accompaniment to a tragedy; and it does in mine.

It was in the early heat of August, and the hour that of the lawful and necessary siesta for such as turn night into day. I was therefore shutting my window in a rage, and wondering whether I should not do the same for Raffles, when he appeared in the silk pyjamas to which the chronic solicitude of Dr Theobald confined him from morning to night.

'Don't do that, Bunny,' said he. 'I rather like that thing, and want to listen. What sort of fellows are they to look at, by the way?'

I put my head out to see, it being a primary rule of our quaint establishment that Raffles must never show himself at any of the windows. I remember now how hot the sill was to my elbows, as I leant upon it and looked down, in order to satisfy a curiosity in which I cóuld see no point.

'Dirty-looking beggars,' said I over my shoulder: 'dark as dark; blue chins, oleaginous curls and earrings; ragged as they make them, but nothing picturesque in their rags.'

'Neapolitans all over,' murmured Raffles behind me; 'and

179

that's a characteristic touch, the one fellow singing while the other grinds; they always have that out there.'

'He's rather a fine chap, the singer,' said I, as the song ended. 'My hat, what teeth! He's looking up here, and grinning all round his head; shall I chuck them anything?'

'Well, I have no reason to love the Neapolitans; but it takes me back – it takes me back! Yes, here you are, one each.'

It was a couple of half-crowns that Raffles put into my hand, but I had thrown them into the street for pennies before I saw what they were. Thereupon I left the Italians bowing to the mud, as well they might, and I turned to protest against such wanton waste. But Raffles was walking up and down, his head bent, his eyes troubled; and his one excuse disarmed remonstrance.

'They took me back,' he repeated. 'My God, how they took me back!'

Suddenly he stopped in his stride.

'You don't understand, Bunny, old chap; but if you like you shall. I always meant to tell you some day, but never felt worked up to it before, and it's not the kind of thing one talks about for talking's sake. It isn't a nursery story, Bunny, and there isn't a laugh in it from start to finish; on the contrary, you have often asked me what turned my hair grey, and now you are going to hear.'

This was promising, but Raffles's manner was something more. It was unique in my memory of the man. His fine face softened and set hard by turns. I never knew it so hard. I never knew it so soft. And the same might be said of his voice, now tender as any woman's, now flying to the other extreme of equally unwonted ferocity. But this was toward the end of his tale; the beginning he treated characteristically enough, though I could have wished for a less cavalier account of the Island of Elba, where, upon his own showing, he had met with much humanity.

'Deadly, my dear Bunny, is not the word for that glorified snag, or for the molluscs its inhabitants. But they started by wounding my vanity, so perhaps I am prejudiced after all. I sprung myself upon them as a shipwrecked sailor – a sole survivor – stripped in the sea and landed without a stitch – yet they took no more interest in me than you do in Italian organ-grinders. They were decent enough. I didn't have to pick and steal for a square meal and a pair of trousers – it would have been more exciting if I had. But what a place! Napoleon couldn't stand it, you remember, but he held on longer than I did. I put in a few weeks in their infernal mines, simply to pick up a smattering of Italian; then got across to the mainland in a little wooden timber-tramp; and ungratefully glad I was to leave Elba blazing in just such another sunset as the one you won't forget.

'The tramp was bound for Naples, but first it touched at Baiæ, where I carefully deserted in the night. There are too many English in Naples itself, though I thought it would make a first happy hunting-ground when I knew the language better and had altered myself a bit more. Meanwhile I got a billet of several sorts on one of the loveliest spots that ever I struck on all my travels. The place was a vineyard, but it overhung the sea, and I got taken on as tame sailor-man and emergency bottle-washer. The wages were the noble figure of a lira and a half, which is just over a bob, a day, but there were lashings of sound wine for one and all, and better wine to bathe in. And for eight whole months, my boy, I was an absolutely honest man. The luxury of it, Bunny! I outheroded Herod, wouldn't touch a grape, and went in the most delicious danger of being knifed for my principles by the thieving crew I had joined.

'It was the kind of place where every prospect pleases – and all the rest of it – especially all the rest. But may I see it in my dreams till I die – as it was in the beginning – before anything began to happen. It was a wedge of rock sticking out into the bay, thatched with vines, and with the rummiest old house on the very edge of all, a devil of a height above the sea; you might have sat at the windows and dropped your Sullivan-ends plumb into blue water a hundred and fifty feet below.

'From the garden behind the house – such a garden, Bunny – oleanders and mimosa, myrtles, rosemary, and red tangles of fiery untamed flowers – in a corner of this garden was the top of a subterranean stair down to the sea; at least, there were nearly two hundred steps tunnelled through the solid rock; then an iron gate, and another eighty steps in the open air; and last of all a cave fit for pirates a-penny-plain-and-twopence-coloured. This cave gave upon the sweetest little thing in coves, all deep blue water and honest rocks; and here I looked after the vineyard shipping, a pot-bellied tub with a brown sail, and a sort of dinghy. The tub took the wine to Naples, and the dinghy was the tub's tender.

'The house above was said to be on the identical site of a suburban retreat of the admirable Tiberius; there was the old sinner's private theatre with the tiers cut clean to this day, the well where he used to fatten his lampreys on his slaves and a ruined temple of those ripping old Roman bricks, shallow as dominoes and ruddier than the cherry. I never was much of an antiquary, but I could have become one there if I'd had nothing else to do; but I had lots. When I wasn't busy with the boats I had to trim the vines, or gather the grapes, or even help make the wine itself in a cool, dark, musty vault underneath the temple, that I can see and smell as I jaw. And can't I hear it and feel it too! Squish, squash, bubble; squash, squish, guggle; and your feet as though you had been wading through slaughter to a throne. Yes, Bunny, you mightn't think it, but this good right foot, that never was on the wrong side of the crease when the ball left my hand, has also been known to

> ... crush the lees of pleasure
> From sanguine grapes of pain.'

He made a sudden pause, as though he had stumbled on a truth in jest. His face filled with lines. We were sitting in the room that had been bare when first I saw it; there were basket-chairs and a table in it now, all meant ostensibly for me; and hence Raffles would slip to his bed, with schoolboy relish, at every tinkle of the bell. This afternoon we felt fairly safe, for Dr. Theobald had called in the morning, and Mrs Theobald still took up much of his time. Through the open window we could hear the piano-organ and 'Mar – ga – rì' a few hundred yards farther on. I fancied Raffles was listening to it while he paused. He shook his head abstractedly when I handed him the cigarettes; and his tone hereafter was never just what it had been.

'I don't know, Bunny, whether you're a believer in trans-migration of souls. I have often thought it easier to believe than lots of other things, and I have been pretty near believing in it myself since I had my being on that villa of Tiberius. The brute who had it in my day, if he isn't still running it with a whole skin, was or is as cold-blooded a blackguard as the worst of the emperors, but I have often thought he had a lot in common with Tiberius. He had the great high sensual Roman nose, eyes that were sinks of iniquity in themselves, and that swelled with fatness, like the rest of him, so that he wheezed if he walked a yard; otherwise rather a fine beast to look at, with a huge grey moustache, like a flying gull, and the most courteous manners even to his men; but one of the worst, Bunny, one of the worst that ever was. It was said that the vineyard was only his hobby; if so, he did his best to make his hobby pay. He used to come out from Naples for the week-ends – in the tub when it wasn't too rough for his nerves – and he didn't always come alone. His very name sounded un-healthy – Corbucci. I suppose I ought to add that he was a Count, though Counts are two-a-penny in Naples, and in sea-son all the year round.

'He had a little English, and liked to air it upon me, much to my disgust; if I could not hope to conceal my nationality as yet, I at least did not want to have it advertised; and the swine had English friends. When he heard that I was bathing in November, when the bay is still as warm as new milk, he would shake his wicked old head, and say, "You are very audashuss – you are very audashuss!" and put on no end of side before his Italians. By God, he had pitched upon the right word unawares, and I let him know it in the end!

'But that bathing, Bunny; it was absolutely the best I ever had anywhere. I said just now the water was like wine; in my own mind I used to call it blue champagne, and was rather annoyed that I had no one to admire the phrase. Otherwise I assure you that I missed my own particular kind very little in-deed, though I often wished that *you* were there, old chap; particularly when I went for my lonesome swim; first thing in the morning, when the bay was all rose-leaves, and last thing at night, when your body caught phosphorescent fire!

Ah, yes, it was a good enough life for a change; a perfect paradise to lie low in; another Eden until –

'My poor Eve!'

And he fetched a sigh that took away his words; then his jaws snapped together, and his eyes spoke terribly while he conquered his emotion. I pen the last word advisedly. I fancy it is one which I have never used before in writing of A. J. Raffles, for I cannot at the moment recall any other occasion upon which its use would have been justified. On resuming, however, he was not only calm, but cold; and this flying for safety to the other extreme is the single instance of self-distrust which the present Achates can record to the credit of his impious Æneas.

'I called the girl Eve,' said he. 'Her real name was Faustina, and she was one of a vast family who hung out in a hovel on the inland border of the vineyard. And Aphrodite rising from the sea was less wonderful and not more beautiful than Aphrodite emerging from that hole!

'It was the most exquisite face I ever saw or shall see in this life. Absolutely perfect features; a skin that reminded you of old gold, so delicate was its bronze; magnificent hair, not black but nearly; and such eyes and teeth as would have made the fortune of a face without another point. I tell you, Bunny, London would go mad about a girl like that. But I don't believe there's such another in the world. And there she was wasting her sweetness upon that lovely but desolate little corner of it! Well, she did not waste it upon me. I would have married her, and lived happily ever after in such a hovel as her people's – with her. Only to look at her – only to look at her for the rest of my days – I could have lain low and remained dead even to you! And that's all I'm going to tell you about that, Bunny; cursed be he who tells more! Yet don't you run away with the idea that this poor Faustina was the only woman I ever cared about. I don't believe in all that "only" rot; nevertheless, I tell you that she *was* the one being who ever entirely satisfied my sense of beauty; and I honestly believe I could have chucked the world and been true to Faustina for that alone.

'We met sometimes in the little temple I told you about,

sometimes among the vines; now by honest accident, now by flagrant design; and found a ready-made rendezvous, romantic as one could wish, in the cave down all those subterranean steps. Then the sea would call us – my blue champagne – my sparkling cobalt -- and there was the dinghy ready to our hand. Oh, those nights! I never knew which I liked best, the moonlit ones when you sculled through silver and could see for miles, or the dark nights when the fisherman's torches stood for the sea, and a red zigzag in the sky for old Vesuvius. We were happy. I don't mind owning it. We seemed not to have a care between us. My mates took no interest in my affairs, and Faustina's family did not appear to bother about her. The Count was in Naples five nights of the seven; the other two we sighed apart.

'At first it was the oldest story in literature – Eden *plus* Eve. The place had been a heaven on earth before, but now it was heaven itself. So for a little; then one night, a Monday night, Faustina burst out crying in the boat; and sobbed her story as we drifted without mishap by the mercy of the Lord. And that was almost as old a story as the other.

'She was engaged – what! Had I never heard of it? Did I mean to upset the boat? What was her engagement beside our love? 'Niente, niente,' crooned Faustina, sighing yet smiling through her tears. No, but what did matter was that the man had threatened to stab her to the heart – and would do it as soon as look at her – that I knew.

'I knew it merely from my knowledge of the Neapolitans, for I had no idea who the man might be. I knew it, and yet I took this detail better than the fact of the engagement, though now I began to laugh at both. As if I were going to let her marry anybody else! As if a hair of her lovely head should be touched while I lived to protect her! I had a great mind to row away to blazes with her that very night, and never go near the vineyard again, or let her either. But we had not a lira between us at the time, and only the rags in which we sat barefoot in the boat. Besides, I had to know the name of the animal who had threatened a woman, and such a woman as this.

'For a long time she refused to tell me, with splendid obduracy; but I was as determined as she; so at last she made conditions. I was not to go and get put in prison for sticking a knife into him – he wasn't worth it – and I did promise not to stab him in the back. Faustina seemed quite satisfied, though a little puzzled by my manner, having herself the racial tolerance for cold steel; and next moment she had taken away my breath. 'It is Stefano,' she whispered, and hung her head.

'And well she might, poor thing! Stefano, of all creatures on God's earth – for her!

'Bunny, he was a miserable little undersized wretch – ill-favoured – servile – surely – and second only to his master in bestial cunning and hypocrisy. His face was enough for me; that was what I read in it, and I don't often make mistakes. He was Corbucci's own confidential body-servant, and that alone was enough to damn him in decent eyes; always came out first on the Saturday with the *spese,* to have all ready for his master and current mistress, and stayed behind on the Monday to clear and lock up. Stefano! That worm! I could well understand *his* threatening a woman with a knife; what beat me was how any woman could ever have listened to him; above all, that Faustina should be the one! It passed my comprehension. But I questioned her as gently as I could; and her explanation was largely the threadbare one you would expect. Her parents were so poor. They were so many in family. Some of them begged – would I promise never to tell? Then some of them stole – sometimes – and all knew the pains of actual want. She looked after the cows, but there were only two of them, and brought the milk to the vineyard and elsewhere; but that was not employment for more than one; and there were countless sisters waiting to take her place. Then he was so rich, Stefano.

' "Rich?" I echoed. "Stefano?"

' "Si, Arturo mio."

'Yes, I played the game on that vineyard, Bunny, even to going by my own first name.

' "And how comes he to be rich?" I asked suspiciously.

'She did not know; but he had given her such beautiful jewels; the family had lived on them for months, she pretending an *avocat* had taken charge of them for her against her marriage. But I cared nothing about all that.

' "Jewels! Stefano!" I could only mutter.

' "Perhaps the Count has paid for some of them. He is very kind."

' "To you, is he?"

' "Oh yes, very kind."

' "And you would live in his house afterwards?"

' "Not now, cara mia – not now!"

' "No, by God you don't!" said I in English. "But you would have done so, eh?"

' "Of course. That was arranged. The Count is really very kind."

' "Do you see anything of him when he comes here?"

'Yes, he had sometimes brought her little presents, sweetmeats, ribbons, and the like; but the offering had always been made through this toad of a Stefano. Knowing the men, I now knew all. But Faustina, she had the pure and simple heart, and the white soul, by the God who made it, and for all her kindness to a tattered scapegrace who made love to her in broken Italian between the ripples and the stars. She was not to know what I was, remember; and beside Corbucci and his henchmen I was the Archangel Gabriel come down to earth.

'Well, as I lay awake that night, two more lines of Swinburne came into my head, and came to stay:

> God said, "Let him who wins her take
> And keep Faustine."

'On that couplet I slept at last, and it was my text and watchword when I awoke in the morning. I forget how well you know your Swinburne, Bunny; but don't you run away with the idea that there was anything else in common between his Faustine and mine. For the last time let me tell you that poor Faustina was the whitest and the best I ever knew.

'Well, I was strung up for trouble when the next Saturday came, and I'll tell you what I had done. I had broken the pledge and burgled Corbucci's villa in my best manner during his absence in Naples. Not that it gave me the slightest trouble; but no human being could have told that I had been in, when I came out. And I had stolen nothing, mark you, but only bor-

rowed a revolver from a drawer in the Count's desk, with one
or two trifling accessories; for by this time I had the measure
of these damned Neapolitans. They were spry enough with a
knife, but you show them the business end of a shooting-iron,
and they'll streak like rabbits for the nearest hole. But the revolver wasn't for my own use. It was for Faustina, and I taught
her how to use it in the cave down there by the sea, shooting at
candles stuck upon the rock. The noise in the cave was something frightful, but high up above it couldn't be heard at all,
as we proved to each other's satisfaction pretty early in the
proceedings. So now Faustina was armed with munitions of
self-defence; and I knew enough of her character to entertain
no doubt as to their spirited use upon occasion. Between the
two of us, in fact, our friend Stefano seemed tolerably certain
of a warm week-end.

'But the Saturday brought word that the Count was not
coming this week, being in Rome on business, and unable to
return in time; so for a whole Sunday we were promised peace;
and made bold plans accordingly. There was no further merit
in hushing this thing up. "Let him who wins her take and keep
Faustine." Yes, but let him win her openly, or lose her and
be damned to him! So on the Sunday I was going to have it
out with her people – with the Count and Stefano as soon as
they showed their noses. I had no inducement, remember, ever
to return to surreptitious life within a cab-fare of Wormwood
Scrubs. Faustina and the Bay of Naples were quite good
enough for me. And the prehistoric man in me rather exulted
in the idea of fighting for my desire.

'On the Saturday, however, we were to meet for the last time
as heretofore – just once more in secret – down there in the
cave – as soon as might be after dark. Neither of us minded if
we were kept for hours; each knew that in the end the other
would come; and there was a charm of its own even in waiting
with such knowledge. But that night I did lose patience; not in
the cave but up above, where first on one pretext and then on
another the *direttore* kept me going until I smelt a rat. He was
not given to exacting overtime, this *direttore*, whose only fault
was his servile subjection to our common boss. It seemed
pretty obvious, therefore, that he was acting upon some secret

instructions from Corbucci himself, and, the moment I suspected this, I asked him to his face if it were not the case. And it was; he admitted it with many shrugs, being a conveniently weak person, whom one felt almost ashamed of bullying as the occasion demanded.

'The fact was, however, that the Count had sent for him on finding he had to go to Rome, and had said he was very sorry to go just then, as among other things he intended to speak to me about Faustina. Stefano had told him all about his row with her, and moreover that it was on my account, which Faustina had never told me, though I had guessed as much for myself. Well, the Count was going to take his jackal's part for all he was worth, which was just exactly what I expected him to do. He intended going for me on his return, but meanwhile I was not to make hay in his absence, and so this tool of a *direttore* had orders to keep me at it night and day. I undertook not to give the poor beast away, but at the same time told him I had not the faintest intention of doing another stroke of work that night.

'It was very dark, and I remember knocking my head against the oranges as I ran up the long, shallow steps which ended the journey between the *direttore's* lodge and the villa itself. But at the back of the villa was the garden I spoke about, and also a bare chunk of the cliff where it was bored by that subterranean stair. So I saw the stars close overhead, and the fisherman's torches far below, the coastwise lights and the crimson hieroglyph that spelt Vesuvius, before I plunged into the darkness of the shaft. And that was the last time I appreciated the unique and peaceful charm of this outlandish spot.

'The stair was in two long flights, with an airhole or two at the top of the upper one, but not another pinprick till you came to the iron gate at the bottom of the lower. As you may read of an infinitely lighter place, in a finer work of fiction than you are ever likely to write, Bunny, it was "gloomy at noon, dark as midnight at dusk, and black as the ninth plague of Egypt at midnight." I won't swear to my quotation, but I will to those stairs. They were as black that night as the inside of the safest safe in the strongest strong-room in the Chancery Lane Deposit. Yet I had not got far down them with my bare

189

feet before I heard somebody else coming up in boots. You may imagine what a turn that gave me! It could not be Faustina, who went barefoot three seasons of the four, and yet there was Faustina waiting for me down below. What a fright she must have had! And all at once my own blood ran cold; for the man sang like a kettle as he plodded up and up. It was, it must be, the short-winded Count himself, whom we all supposed to be in Rome!

'Higher he came and nearer, nearer, slowly yet hurriedly, now stopping to cough and gasp, now taking a few steps by elephantine assault. I should have enjoyed the situation if it had not been for poor Faustina in the cave; as it was, I was filled with nameless fears. But I could not resist giving that grampus Corbucci one bad moment on account. A crazy hand-rail ran up one wall, so I carefully flattened myself against the other, and he passed within six inches of me, puffing and wheezing like a brass band. I let him go a few steps higher, and then I let him have it with both lungs.

' "Buona sera, eccellente signore!" I roared after him. And a scream came down in answer – such a scream! A dozen different terrors were in it; and the wheezing had stopped, with the old scoundrel's heart.

' "Chi sta la?' he squeaked at last, gibbering and whimpering like a whipped monkey, so that I could not bear to miss his face, and got a match all ready to strike.

' "Arturo, signore."

'He didn't repeat my name, nor did he damn me in heaps. He did nothing but wheeze for a good minute, and when he spoke it was with insinuating civility, in his best English.

' "Come nearer, Arturo. You are in the lower regions down there. I want to speak with you."

' "No thanks. I'm in a hurry," I said, and dropped that match back into my pocket. He might be armed, and I was not.

' "So you are in a 'urry!' and he wheezed amusement. 'And you thought I was still in Rome, no doubt; and so I was until this afternoon, when I caught train at the eleventh moment and then another train from Naples to Pozzuoli. I have been rowed here now by a fisherman of Pozzuoli. I had not time to stop anywhere in Naples, but only to drive from station to

station. So I am without Stefano, Arturo, I am without
Stefano."

'His sly voice sounded preternaturally sly in the absolute
darkness, but even through that impenetrable veil I knew it for
a sham. I had laid hold of the hand-rail. It shook violently in
my hand; he also was holding it where he stood. And these
suppressed tremors, or rather their detection in this way, struck
a strange chill to my heart, just as I was beginning to pluck
it up.

' "It is lucky for Stefano," said I, grim as death.

' "Ah, but you must not be too 'ard on 'im," remonstrated
the Count. "You have stole his girl, he speak with me about it,
and I wish to speak with you. It is very audashuss, Arturo, very
audashuss! Perhaps you are even going to meet her now,
eh?'

'I told him straight that I was.

' "Then there is no 'urry, for she is not there."

' "You didn't see her in the cave?" I cried, too delighted at
the thought to keep it to myself.

' "I had no such fortune," the old devil said.

' "She is there, all the same."

' "I only wish I 'ad known "

' "And I've kept her long enough!"

In fact, I threw this over my shoulder as I turned and went
running down.

' "I 'ope you will find her!" his malicious voice came croak-
ing after me. "I 'ope you will – I 'ope so."

'And find her I did.'

Raffles had been on his feet some time, unable to sit still or
to stand, moving excitedly about the room. But now he stood
still enough, his elbows on the cast-iron mantelpiece, his head
between his hands.

'Dead?' I whispered.

And he nodded to the wall.

'There was not a sound in the cave. There was no answer to
my voice. Then I went in, and my foot touched hers, and it was
colder than the rock ... Bunny, they had stabbed her to the
heart. She had fought them, and they stabbed her to the
heart!'

191

'You say "they",' I said gently, as he stood in heavy silence, his back still turned. 'I thought Stefano had been left behind?'

Raffles was round in a flash, his face white-hot, his eyes dancing death.

'He was in the cave!' he shouted. 'I saw him – I spotted him – it was broad twilight after those stairs – and I went for him with my bare hands. Not fists, Bunny; not fists for a thing like that; I meant getting my fingers into his vile little heart and tearing it out by the roots. I was stark mad. But he had the revolver – hers. He blazed it at arm's length, and missed. And that steadied me. I had smashed his funny-bone against the rock before he could blaze again; the revolver fell with a rattle, but without going off; in an instant I had it tight, and the little swine at my mercy at last.'

'You didn't show him any?'

'Mercy? With Faustina dead at my feet? I should have deserved none in the next world if I had shown him any in this! No, I just stood over him, with the revolver in both hands, feeling the chambers with my thumb; and as I stood he stabbed at me; but I stepped back to that one, and brought him down with a bullet in his guts.

' "And I can spare you two or three more," I said, for my poor girl could not have fired a shot. "Take that one to hell with you – and that – and that!"

'Then I started coughing and wheezing like the Count himself, for the place was full of smoke. When it cleared my man was very dead, and I tipped him into the sea, to defile that rather than Faustina's cave. And then – and then – we were alone for the last time, she and I, in our own pet haunt; and I could scarcely see her, yet I would not strike a match, for I knew she would not have me see her as she was. I could say good-bye to her without that. I said it; and I left her like a man, and up the first open-air steps with my head in the air and the stars all sharp in the sky; then suddenly they swam, and back I went like a lunatic, to see if she were really dead, to bring her back to life ... Bunny, I can't tell you any more.'

'Not of the Count?' I murmured at last.

'Not even of the Count,' said Raffles, turning round with a sigh. 'I left him pretty sorry for himself; but what was the good of that? I had taken blood for blood, and it was not Corbucci who had killed Faustina. No, the plan was his, but that was not part of the plan. They had found out about our meetings in the cave: nothing simpler than to have me kept hard at it overhead and to carry off Faustina by brute force in the boat. It was their only chance, for she had said more to Stefano than she had admitted to me, and more than I am going to repeat about myself. No persuasion would have induced her to listen to him again; so they tried force; and she drew Corbucci's revolver on them, but they had taken her by surprise, and Stefano stabbed her before she could fire.'

'But how do you know all that?' I asked Raffles, for his tale was going to pieces in the telling, and the tragic end of poor Faustina was no ending for me.

'Oh,' said he, 'I had it from Corbucci at his own revolver's point. He was waiting at his window, and I could have potted him at my ease where he stood against the light listening hard enough but not seeing a thing. So he asked whether it was Stefano, and I whispered, "Si, signore"; and then whether he had finished Arturo, and I brought the same shot off again. He had let me in before he knew who was finished and who was not.'

'And did you finish him?'

'No; that was too good for Corbucci. But I bound and gagged him about as tight as man was ever gagged or bound, and I left him in his room with the shutters shut and the house locked up. The shutters of that old place were six inches thick, and the walls nearly six feet; that was on the Saturday night, and the Count wasn't expected at the vineyard before the following Saturday. Meanwhile he was supposed to be in Rome. But the dead would doubtless be discovered next day, and I am afraid this would lead to his own discovery with the life still in him. I believe he figured on that himself, for he sat threatening me gamely till the last. You never saw such a sight as he was, with his head split in two by a ruler tied at the back of it, and his great moustache pushed up into his bulging eyes. But I locked him up in the dark without a qualm, and I wished and still wish him every torment of the damned.'

'And then?'

'The night was still young, and within ten miles there was the best of ports in a storm, and hundreds of holds for the humble stowaway to choose from. But I didn't want to go farther than Genoa, for by this time my Italian would wash, so I chose the old Norddeutscher Lloyd, and had an excellent voyage in one of the boats slung inboard over the bridge. That's better than any hold, Bunny, and I did splendidly on oranges brought from the vineyard.'

'And at Genoa?'

'At Genoa I took to my wits once more, and have been living on nothing else ever since. But there I had to begin all over again, and at the very bottom of the ladder. I slept in the streets. I begged. I did all manner of terrible things, rather hoping for a bad end, but never coming to one. Then one day I saw a white-headed old chap looking at me through a shop window – a window I had designs upon – and when I stared at him he stared at me – and we wore the same rags. So I had come to that! But one reflection makes many. I had not recognised myself; who on earth would recognise me? London called me – and here I am. Italy had broken my heart – and there it stays.'

Flippant as a schoolboy one moment, playful even in the bitterness of the next, and now no longer giving way to the feeling which had spoilt the climax of his tale, Raffles needed knowing as I alone knew him for a right appreciation of those last words. That they were no mere words I know full well. That, but for the tragedy of his Italian life, that life would have sufficed him for years, if not for ever, I did and do still believe. But I alone see him as I saw him then, the lines upon his face, and the pain behind the lines; how they came to disappear, and what removed them, you will never guess. It was the one thing you would have expected to have the opposite effect, the thing indeed that had forced his confidence, the organ and the voice once more beneath our very windows:

'Margarita de Parete,
    era a' sarta d' e' signore;
    se pugneva sempe e ddete
    pe penzare a Salvatore!

Mar – ga – rì,
  e perzo a Salvatore!
Mar – ga – rì,
  Ma l' ommo è cacciatore!
Mar – ga – rì,
  Nun ce aje corpa tu!
Chello ch' è fatto, è fatto, un ne parlammo cchieù!'

I simply stared at Raffles. Instead of deepening, his lines had vanished. He looked years younger, mischievous, and merry and alert as I remembered him of old in the breathless crisis of some madcap escapade. He was holding up his finger; he was stealing to the window; he was peeping through the blind as though our side street were Scotland Yard itself; he was stealing back again, all revelry, excitement, and suspense.

'I half thought they were after me before,' said he. 'That was why I made you look. I daren't take a proper look myself, but what a jest if they were! What a jest!'

'Do you mean the police?' said I.

'The police! Bunny, do you know them and me so little that you can look me in the face and ask such a question? My boy, I'm dead to them – off their books – a good deal deader than being off the hooks! Why, if I went to Scotland Yard this minute, to give myself up, they'd chuck me out for a harmless lunatic. No, I fear an enemy nowadays, and I go in terror of the sometime friend; but I have the utmost confidence in the dear police.'

'Then whom do you mean?'

'The Camorra!'

I repeated the word with a different intonation. Not that I had never heard of that most powerful and sinister of secret societies; but I failed to see on what grounds Raffles should jump to the conclusion that these everyday organ-grinders belonged to it.

'It was one of Corbucci's threats,' said he. 'If I killed him the Camorra would certainly kill me; he kept on telling me so; it was like his cunning not to say that he would put them on my tracks whether or no.'

'He is probably a member himself!'

'Obviously, from what he said.'

'But why on earth should you think that these fellows are?'
I demanded, as that brazen voice came rasping through a
second verse.

'I don't think. It was only an idea. That this is so thoroughly
Neapolitan, and I never heard it on a London organ before.
Then, again, what should bring them back here?'

I peeped through the blind in my turn; and, to be sure, there
was the fellow with the blue chin and the white teeth watching
our windows, and ours only, as he bawled.

'And why?' cried Raffles, his eyes dancing when I told him.
'Why should they come sneaking back to *us*? Doesn't that look
suspicious, Bunny; doesn't that promise a lark?'

'Not to me,' I said, having the smile for once. 'How many
people, should you imagine, toss them five shillings for as
many minutes of their infernal row? You seem to forget that
that's what you did an hour ago!'

Raffles had forgotten. His blank face confessed the fact.
Then suddenly he burst out laughing at himself.

'Bunny,' said he, 'you've no imagination, and I never knew
I had so much! Of course you're right. I only wish you were
not, for there's nothing I should enjoy more than taking on
another Neapolitan or two. You see, I owe them something
still! I didn't settle in full. I owe them more than ever I shall
pay them on this side Styx!'

He had hardened even as he spoke: the lines and the years
had come again, and his eyes were flint and steel, with an
honest grief behind the glitter.

THE LAST LAUGH

A s I have had occasion to remark elsewhere, the pick of our exploits from a frankly criminal point of view are of least use for the comparatively pure purposes of these papers. They might be appreciated in a trade journal (if only that want could be supplied) by skilled manipulators of the jemmy and the large light bunch; but, as records of unbroken yet insignificant success, they would be found at once too trivial and too technical, if not sordid and unprofitable into the bargain. The latter epithets, and worse, have indeed already been applied, if not to Raffles and all his works, at least to mine upon Raffles, by more than one worthy wielder of a virtuous pen. I need not say how heartily I disagree with that truly pious opinion. So far from admitting a single word of it, I maintain it is the liveliest warning that I am giving to the world. Raffles was a genius, and he could not make it pay! Raffles had invention, resource, incomparable audacity, and a nerve in ten thousand. He was both strategist and tactician, and we all now know the difference between the two. Yet for months he had been hiding like a rat in a hole, unable to show even his altered face by night or day without risk, unless another risk were courted by three inches of conspicuous crape. Then thus far our rewards had oftener than not been no reward at all. Altogether it was a very different story from the old festive, unsuspected, club and cricket days, with their *noctes ambrosianæ* at the Albany.

And now, in addition to the eternal peril of recognition, there was yet another menace of which I knew nothing. I thought no more of our Neapolitan organ-grinders, though I did often think of the moving page that they had torn for me out of my friend's strange life in Italy. Raffles never alluded to the subject again, and for my part I had entirely forgotten his wild ideas connecting the organ-grinders with the Camorra, and imagining them upon his own tracks. I heard no more of it, and thought as little, as I say. Then one night in the autumn – I shrink from shocking the susceptible for nothing – but there was a certain house in Palace Gardens, and when we got there Raffles would pass on. I could see no soul in sight, no glimmer in the windows. But Raffles had my arm, and on we went without talking about it. Sharp to the left on the Notting Hill side, sharper still up Silver Street, a little tacking west and south, a plunge across High Street, and presently we were home.

'Pyjamas first,' said Raffles, with as much authority as though it mattered. It was a warm night, however, though September, and I did not mind until I came in clad as he commanded to find the autocrat himself still booted and capped. He was peeping through the blind and the gas was still turned down. But he said that I could turn it up, as he helped himself to a cigarette and nothing with it.

'May I mix you one?' said I.

'No, thanks.'

'What's the trouble?'

'We were followed.'

'Never!'

'You never saw it.'

'But *you* never looked round.'

'I have an eye at the back of each ear, Bunny.'

I helped myself, and I feared with less moderation than might have been the case a minute before.

'So that was why – –'

'That was why,' said Raffles, nodding; but he did not smile, and I put down my glass untouched.

'They were following us then!'

'All up Palace Gardens.'

'I thought you wound about coming back over the hill.'

'Nevertheless, one of them's in the street below at this moment.'

No, he was not fooling me. He was very grim. And he had not taken off a thing; perhaps he did not think it worth while.

'Plain clothes?' I sighed, following the sartorial train of thought, even to the loathly arrows that had decorated my person once already for a little æon. Next time they would give me double. The skilly was in my stomach when I saw Raffles's face.

'Who said it was the police, Bunny?' said he. 'It's the Italians. They're only after me; they won't hurt a hair of *your* head, let alone cropping it! Have a drink, and don't mind me. I shall score them off before I'm done.'

'And I'll help you!'

'No, old chap, you won't. This is my own little show. I've known about it for weeks. I first tumbled to it the day those Neapolitans came back with their organs, though I didn't seriously suspect things then; they never came again, those two, they had done their part. That's the Camorra all over, from all accounts. The Count I told you about is pretty high up in it, by the way he spoke, but there will be grades and grades between him and the organ-grinders. I shouldn't be surprised if he had every low-down Neapolitan ice-creamer in the town upon my tracks! The organisation's incredible. Then do you remember the superior foreigner who came to the door a few days afterwards? You said he had velvet eyes.'

'I never connected him with those two!'

'Of course you didn't, Bunny, so you threatened to kick the fellow downstairs, and only made them keener on the scent. It was too late to say anything when you told me. But the very next time I showed my nose outside I heard a camera click as I passed, and the fiend was a person with velvet eyes. Then there was a lull – that happened weeks ago. They had sent me to Italy for identification by Count Corbucci.'

'But this is all theory,' I exclaimed. 'How on earth can you know?'

'I don't know,' said Raffles, 'but I should like to bet. Our friend the bloodhound is hanging about the corner near the pillar-box; look through my window, it's dark in there, and tell me who he is.'

The man was too far away for me to swear to his face, but he wore a covert-coat of un-English length, and the lamp across the road played steadily on his boots; they were very yellow, and they made no noise when he took a turn. I strained my eyes, and all at once I remembered the thin-soled, low-heeled, splay yellow boots of the insidious foreigner, with the soft eyes and the brown-paper face, whom I had turned from the door as a palpable fraud. The ring at the bell was the first I had heard of him, there had been no warning step upon the stairs, and my suspicious eye had searched his feet for rubber soles.

'It's the fellow,' I said, returning to Raffles, and I described his boots.

Raffles was delighted.

'Well done, Bunny; you're coming on,' said he. 'Now I wonder if he's been over here all the time, or if they sent him over expressly? You did better than you think in spotting those boots, for they can only have been made in Italy, and that looks like the special envoy. But it's no use speculating. I must find out.'

'How can you?'

'He won't stay there all night.'

'Well?'

'When he gets tired of it I shall return the compliment and follow *him*.'

'Not alone,' said I firmly.

'Well, we'll see. We'll see at once,' said Raffles, rising. 'Out with the gas, Bunny, while I take a look. Thank you. Now wait a bit ... yes! He's chucked it; he's off already; and so am I!'

But I slipped to our outer door, and held the passage.

'I don't let you go alone, you know.'

'You can't come with me in pyjamas.'

'Now I see why you made me put them on!'

'Bunny, if you don't shift I shall have to shift you. This is my very own private one-man show. But I'll be back in an hour – there!'

'You swear?'

'By all my gods.'

I gave in. How could I help giving in? He did not look the man that he had been, but you never knew with Raffles, and I could not have him lay a hand on me. I let him go with a shrug and my blessing, then ran into his room to see the last of him from the window.

The creature in the coat and boots had reached the end of our little street, where he appeared to have hesitated, so that Raffles was just in time to see which way he turned. And Raffles was after him at an easy pace, and had himself almost reached the corner when my attention was distracted from the alert nonchalance of his gait. I was marvelling that it alone had not long ago betrayed him, for nothing about him was so unconsciously characteristic, when suddenly I realised that Raffles was not the only person in the little lonely street. Another pedestrian had entered from the other end, a man heavily built and clad, with an astrakhan collar to his coat on this warm night, and a black slouch hat that hid his features from my bird's-eye view. His steps were the short and shuffling ones of a man advanced in years and in fatty degeneration, but of a sudden they stopped beneath my very eyes. I could have dropped a marble into the dinted crown of the black felt hat. Then, at the same moment, Raffles turned the corner without looking round, and the big man below raised both his hands and his face. Of the latter I saw only the huge white moustache, like a flying gull, as Raffles had described it; for at a glance I divined that this was his arch-enemy, the Count Corbucci himself.

I did not stop to consider the subtleties of the system by which the real hunter lagged behind while his subordinate pointed the quarry like a sporting dog. I left the Count shuffling onwards faster than before, and I jumped into some clothes as though the flats were on fire. If the Count was going to follow Raffles in his turn, then I would follow the Count in mine, and there would be a midnight procession of us through the town. But I found no sign of him in the empty street, and no sign in the Earl's Court Road, that looked as empty for all its length, save for a natural enemy standing like a waxwork with a glimmer at his belt.

'Officer,' I gasped, 'have you seen anything of an old gentleman with a big white moustache?'

The unlicked cub of a common constable seemed to eye me the more suspiciously for the flattering form of my address.

'Took a hansom,' said he at length.

A hansom! Then he was not following the others on foot; there was no guessing his game. But something must be said or done.

'He's a friend of mine,' I explained, 'and I want to overtake him. Did you hear where he told the fellow to drive?'

A curt negative was the policeman's reply to that; and if

ever I take part in a night assault-at-arms, revolver *versus* baton in the back kitchen, I know which member of the Metropolitan Police Force I should like for my opponent.

If there was no overtaking the Count, however, it should be a comparatively simple matter in the case of the couple on foot, and I wildly hailed the first hansom that crawled into my ken. I must tell Raffles who it was that I had seen; the Earl's Court Road was long, and the time since he vanished in it but a few short minutes. I drove down the length of that useful thoroughfare, with an eye apiece on either pavement, sweeping each as with a brush, but never a Raffles came into the pan. Then I tried the Fulham Road, first to the west, then to the east, and in the end drove home to the flat as bold as brass. I did not realise my indiscretion until I had paid the man and was on the stairs. Raffles never dreamt of driving all the way back; but I was hoping now to find him waiting up above. He had said an hour. I had remembered it suddenly. And now the hour was more than up. But the flat was as empty as I had left it; the very light that had encouraged me, pale though it was, as I turned the corner in my hansom, was but the light that I myself had left burning in the desolate passage.

I can give you no conception of the night that I spent. Most of it I hung across the sill, throwing a wide net with my ears, catching every footstep afar off, every hansom bell farther still, only to gather in some alien whom I seldom even landed in our street. Then I would listen at the door. He might come over the roof; and eventually someone did; but now it was broad daylight, and I flung the door open in the milkman's face, which whitened at the shock as though I had ducked him in his own pail.

'You're late,' I thundered as the first excuse for my excitement.

'Beg your pardon,' said he indignantly, 'but I'm half an hour before my usual time.'

'Then I beg yours,' said I; 'but the fact is, Mr. Maturin has had one of his bad nights, and I seem to have been waiting hours for milk to make him a cup of tea.'

This little fib (ready enough for a Raffles, though I say it) earned me not only forgiveness but that obliging sympathy which is a branch of the business of the man at the door. The good fellow said that he could see I had been sitting up all night, and he left me pluming myself upon the accidental art with which I had told my very necessary tarradiddle. On reflection I gave the credit to instinct, not accident, and then sighed afresh as I realised how the influence of the master was sinking into me, and he Heaven knew where. But my punishment was swift to follow, for within the hour the bell rang imperiously twice, and there was Dr Theobald on our mat, in a yellow Jaeger suit, with a chin as yellow jutting over the flaps that he had turned up to hide his pyjamas.

'What's this about a bad night?' said he.

'He couldn't sleep, and he wouldn't let me,' I whispered, never loosening my grasp of the door, and standing tight against the outer wall. 'But he's sleeping like a baby now.'

'I must see him.'

'He gave strict orders that you should not.'

'I'm his medical man, and I – –'

'You know what he is,' I said, shrugging; 'the least thing wakes him, and you will if you insist on seeing him now. It will be the last time, I warn you! I know what he said, and you don't.'

The doctor cursed me under his fiery moustache.

'I shall come up during the course of the morning,' he snarled.

'And I shall tie up the bell,' I said, 'and if it doesn't ring he'll be sleeping still, but I will not risk waking him by coming to the door again.'

And with that I shut it in his face. I was improving, as Raffles had said; but what would it profit me if some evil had befallen him? And now I was prepared for the worst. A boy came up whistling and leaving papers on the mats; it was getting on for eight o'clock, and the whisky and soda of half-past twelve stood untouched and stagnant in the tumbler. If the worst had happened to Raffles, I felt that I would either never drink again, or else seldom do anything else.

Meanwhile I could not even break my fast, but roamed the flat in a misery not to be described, my very linen still unchanged, my cheeks and chin now tawny from the unwholesome night. How long would it go on? I wondered for a time. Then I changed my tune: how long could I endure it?

It went on actually until the forenoon only, but my endurance cannot be measured by the time, for to me every hour of it was an arctic night. Yet it cannot have been much after eleven when the ring came at the bell, which I had forgotten to tie up after all. But this was not the doctor; neither, too well I knew, was it the wanderer returned. Our bell was the pneumatic one that tells you if the touch be light or heavy; the hand upon it now was tentative and shy.

The owner of the hand I had never seen before. He was young and ragged, with one eye blank, but the other ablaze with some fell excitement. And straightway he burst into a low torrent of words, of which all I knew was that they were Italian, and therefore news of Raffles, if only I had known the language! But dumb-show might help us somewhat, and in I dragged him, though against his will, a new alarm in his one wild eye.

'Non capite?' he cried when I had him inside and had withstood the torrent.

'No, I'm bothered if I do!' I answered, guessing his question from his tone.

'Vostro amico,' he repeated over and over again; and then, 'Poco tempo, poco tempo, poco tempo!'

For once in my life the classical education of my public-school days was of real value. 'My pal, my pal, and no time to be lost!' I translated freely, and flew for my hat.

'Ecco, signore!' cried the fellow, snatching the watch from my waistcoat pocket, and putting one black thumb-nail on the long hand, the other on the numeral twelve. 'Mezzogiorno – poco tempo – poco tempo!' And again I seized his meaning, that it was twenty past eleven, and we must be there by twelve. But where, but where? It was maddening to be summoned like this, and not to know what had happened, or to have any means of finding out. But my presence of mind stood by me still, I was improving by seven-league strides, and I crammed my handkerchief between the drum and hammer of the bell before leaving. The doctor could ring now till he was black in the face, but I was not coming, and he need not think it.

I half expected to find a hansom waiting, but there was none, and we had gone some distance down the Earl's Court Road before we got one; in fact, we had to run to the stand. Opposite is the church with the clock upon it as everybody knows, and at the sight of the dial my companion had wrung his hands; it was close upon the half-hour.

'Poco tempo – pochissimo!' he wailed. 'Bloomburee Ske-warr,' he then cried to the cabman – 'numero trentotto!'

'Bloomsbury Square,' I roared on my own account. 'I'll show you the house when we get there, only drive like be-damned!'

My companion lay back gasping in his corner. The small glass told me that my own face was pretty red.

'A nice show!' I cried; 'and not a word can you tell me. Didn't you bring me a note?'

I might have known by this time that he had not, still I went through the pantomime of writing with my finger on my cuff. But he shrugged and shook his head.

'Niente,' said he. 'Una questione di vita, di vita!'

'What's that?' I snapped, my early training coming in again. 'Say it slowly – andante – rallentando.'

Thank Italy for the stage instructions in the songs one used to murder! The fellow actually understood!

'Una – questione – di – vita.'

'Or mors, eh?' I shouted, and up went the trapdoor over our heads.

'Avanti, avanti, avanti!' cried the Italian, turning up his one-eyed face.

'Hell-for-leather,' I translated, 'and double fare if you do it by twelve o'clock.'

But in the streets of London how is one to know the time? In the Earl's Court Road it had not been half-past, and at Barker's in High Street it was but a minute later. A long half-mile a minute, that was going like the wind, and indeed we had done much of it at a gallop. But the next hundred yards took us five minutes by the next clock, and which was one to believe? I fell back upon my own old watch (it was my own), which made it eighteen minutes to the hour as we swung across the Serpentine bridge, and by the quarter we were in the Bayswater Road – not up for once.

'Presto, presto,' my pale guide murmured. 'Affrettatevi — avanti!'

'Ten bob if you do it,' I cried through the trap, without the slightest notion of what we were to do. But it was 'una questione di vita', and 'vostro amico' must and could only be my miserable Raffles.

What a very godsend is the perfect hansom to the man or woman in a hurry! It had been our great good fortune to jump into a perfect hansom; there was no choice, we had to take the first upon the rank, but it must have deserved its place, with the rest nowhere. New tyres, superb springs, a horse in a thousand, and a driver up to every trick of his trade! In and out we went like a fast half-back at the Rugby game, yet where the traffic was thinnest, there were we. And how he knew his way! At the Marble Arch he slipped out of the main stream, and so into Wigmore Street, then up and in and out and on until I saw the gold tips of the Museum palisade gleaming between the horses' ears in the sun. Plop, plop, plop; ting, ling, ling; bell and horseshoes, horseshoes and bell, until the colossal figure of C. J. Fox in a grimy toga spelt Bloomsbury Square, with my watch still wanting three minutes to the hour.

'What number?' cried the good fellow overhead.

'Trentotto, trentotto,' said my guide, but he was looking to the right, and I bundled him out to show the house on foot. I had not half a sovereign after all, but I flung our dear driver a whole one instead, and only wished that it had been a hundred.

Already the Italian had his latchkey in the door of 38, and in another moment we were rushing up the narrow stairs of as dingy a London House as prejudiced countryman can conceive. It was panelled, but it was dark and evil-smelling, and how we should have found our way even to the stairs but for an unwholesome jet of yellow gas in the hall, I cannot myself imagine. However, up we went pell-mell, to the right-out on the half-landing, and so like a whirlwind into the drawing-room a few steps higher. There the gas was also burning behind closed shutters, and the scene is photographed upon my brain, though I cannot have looked upon it for a whole instant as I sprang in at my leader's heels.

This room also was panelled, and in the middle of the wall on our left, his hands lashed to a ring-bolt high above his head, his toes barely touching the floor, his neck pinioned by a strap passing through smaller ring-bolts under either ear, and every inch of him secured on the same principle, stood, or rather hung, all that was left of Raffles, for at the first glance I believed him dead. A black ruler gagged him, the ends lashed behind his neck, the blood upon it caked to bronze in the gaslight. And in front of him, ticking like a sledge-hammer, its only hand upon the stroke of twelve, stood a simple, old-fashioned, grandfathers' clock – but not for half an instant longer – only until my guide could hurl himself upon it and send the whole thing crashing into the corner. An ear-splitting report accompanied the crash, a white cloud lifted from the fallen clock, and I saw a revolver smoking in a vice screwed below the dial, an arrangement of wires sprouting from the dial itself, and the single hand at once at its zenith and in contact with these.

'Tumble to it, Bunny?'

He was alive; these were his first words; the Italian had the blood-caked ruler in his hand, and with his knife was reaching up to cut the thongs that lashed the hands. He was not tall enough. I seized him and lifted him up, then fell to work with my own knife upon the straps. And Raffles smiled faintly upon us through his bloodstains.

'I want you to tumble to it,' he whispered; 'the neatest thing in revenge I ever knew, and another minute would have fixed it. I've been waiting for it twelve hours, watching the clock round, death at the end of the lap! Electric connection. Simple enough. Hour-hand only – O Lord!'

We had cut the last strap. He could not stand. We supported him between us to a horse-hair sofa, for the room was furnished, and I begged him not to speak, while his one-eyed deliverer was at the door before Raffles recalled him with a sharp word in Italian.

'He wants to get me a drink, but that can wait,' said he in a firmer voice; 'I shall enjoy it the more when I've told you what happened. Don't let him go, Bunny; put your back against the door. He's a decent soul, and it's lucky for me I got word with

207

him before they trussed me up. I've promised to set him up in life, and I will, but I don't want him out of my sight for the moment.'

'If you squared him last night,' I exclaimed, 'why the blazes didn't he come to me till the eleventh hour?'

'Ah, I knew he'd have cut it fine, though I hoped not quite so fine as all that. But all's well that ends well, and I declare I don't feel so much the worse. I shall be sore about the gills for a bit – and what do you think?'

He pointed to the long black ruler with the bronze stain; it lay upon the floor; he held out his hand for it, and I gave it to him.

'The same one I gagged him with,' said Raffles, with his still ghastly smile; 'he was a bit of an artist, old Corbucci, after all!'

'Now let's hear how you fell into his clutches,' said I briskly, for I was as anxious to hear as he seemed to tell me, only for my part I could have waited until we were safe in the flat.

'I do want to get it off my chest, Bunny,' old Raffles admitted, 'and yet I hardly can tell you after all. I followed your friend with the velvet eyes. I followed him all the way here. Of course I came up to have a good look at the house when he'd let himself in, and damme if he hadn't left the door ajar! Who could resist that? I had pushed it half open and had just one foot on the mat when I got such a crack on the head as I hope never to get again. When I came to my wits they were hauling me up to that ring-bolt by the hands, and old Corbucci himself was bowing to me, but how *he* got there I don't know yet.'

'I can tell you that,' said I, and told how I had seen the Count for myself on the pavement underneath our windows. 'Moreover,' I continued, 'I saw him spot you, and five minutes after in Earl's Court Road I was told he'd driven off in a cab. He would see you following his man, drive home ahead, and catch you by having the door left open in the way you describe.'

'Well,' said Raffles, 'he deserved to catch me somehow, for he'd come from Naples on purpose, ruler and all, and the ring-bolts were ready fixed, and even this house taken furnished for nothing else! He meant catching me before he'd done, and scoring off me in exactly the same way that I scored off him, only going one better of course. He told me so himself, sitting where I am sitting now, at three o'clock this morning, and smoking a most abominable cigar that I've smelt ever since. It appears he sat twenty-four hours when I left *him* trussed up, but he said twelve would content him in my case, as there was certain death at the end of them, and I mightn't have life enough left to appreciate my end if he made it longer. But I wouldn't have trusted him if he could have got the clock to go *twice* round without firing off the pistol. He explained the whole mechanism of that to me; he had thought it all out in the vineyard I told you about; and then he asked if I remembered what he had promised me in the name of the Camorra. I only remembered some vague threats, but he was good enough to give me so many particulars of that institution that I could make a European reputation by exposing the whole show if it wasn't for my unfortunate resemblance to that infernal rascal Raffles. Do you think they would know me at the Yard, Bunny, after all this time? Upon my soul I've a good mind to risk it!'

I offered no opinion on the point. How could it interest me then? But interested I was in Raffles, never more so in my life. He had been tortured all night and half a day, yet he could sit and talk like this the moment we cut him down; he had been within a minute of his death, yet he was as full of life as ever; ill-treated and defeated at the best, he could still smile through his blood as though the boot were on the other leg. I had imagined that I knew my Raffles at last. I was not likely so to flatter myself again.

'But what has happened to these villains?' I burst out, and my indignation was not only against them for their cruelty, but also against their victim for his phlegmatic attitude towards them. It was difficult to believe that this was Raffles.

'Oh,' said he, 'they were to go off to Italy *instanter*; they should be crossing now. But do listen to what I am telling you; it's interesting, my dear man. This old sinner Corbucci turns out to have been no end of a boss in the Camorra – says so himself. One of the *capi paranze*, my boy, no less; and the velvety Johnny a *giovane onorato*, Anglicé, fresher. This fellow here was also in it, and I've sworn to protect him from them ever more; and it's just as I said, half the organ-grinders in London belong, and the whole lot of them were put on my tracks by secret instructions. This excellent youth manufactures iced poison on Saffron Hill when he's at home.'

'And why on earth didn't he come to me quicker?'

'Because he couldn't talk to you, he could only fetch you, and it was as much as his life was worth to do that before our friends had departed. They were going by the eleven o'clock from Victoria, and that didn't leave much chance, but he certainly oughtn't to have run it as fine as he did. Still you must remember that I had to fix things up with him in the fewest possible words, in a single minute that the other two were indiscreet enough to leave us alone together.'

The ragamuffin in question was watching us with all his solitary eye, as though he knew that we were discussing him. Suddenly he broke out in agonised accents, his hands clasped, and a face so full of fear that every moment I expected to see him on his knees. But Raffles answered kindly, reassuringly, I could tell from his tone, and then turned to me with a compassionate shrug.

'He says he couldn't find the mansions, Bunny, and really it's not to be wondered at. I had only time to tell him to hunt you up and bring you here by hook or crook before twelve to-day, and after all he has done that. But now the poor devil thinks you're riled with him, and that we'll give him away to the Camorra.'

'Oh, it's not with him I'm riled,' I said frankly, 'but with those other blackguards, and – and with you, old chap, for taking it all as you do, while such infamous scoundrels have the last laugh, and are safely on their way to France!'

Raffles looked up at me with a curiously open eye, an eye that I never saw when he was not in earnest. I fancied he did not like my last expression but one. After all, it was no laughing matter to him.

'But are they?' said he. 'I'm not so sure.'

'You said they were!'

'I said they should be.'

'Didn't you hear them go?'

'I heard nothing but the clock all night. It was like Big Ben striking at the last – striking nine to the fellow on the drop.'

And in that open eye I saw at last a deep glimmer of the ordeal through which he had passed.

'But, my dear old Raffles, if they're still on the premises – '

The thought was too thrilling for a finished sentence.

'I hope they are,' he said grimly, going to the door. 'There's a gas on! Was that burning when you came in?'

Now that I thought of it, yes, it had been.

'And there's a frightfully foul smell,' I added, as I followed Raffles down the stairs. He turned to me gravely with his hand upon the front-room door and at the same moment I saw a coat with an astrakhan collar hanging on the pegs.

'They are in here, Bunny,' he said, and turned the handle.

The door would only open a few inches. But a detestable odour came out, with a broad bar of yellow gas-light. Raffles put his handkerchief to his nose. I followed his example, signing to our ally to do the same, and in another minute we had all three squeezed into the room.

The man with the yellow boots was lying against the door, the Count's great carcase sprawled upon the table, and at a glance it was evident that both men had been dead some hours. The old Camorrist had the stem of a liqueur-glass between his swollen blue fingers, one of which had been cut in the breakage, and the livid flesh was brown with the last blood that it would ever shed. His face was on the table, the huge moustache projecting from under either leaden cheek, yet looking itself strangely alive. Broken bread and scraps of frozen macaroni lay upon the cloth and at the bottom of two soup-plates and a tureen; the macaroni had a tinge of tomato; and there was a crimson dram left in the tumblers, with an empty *fiasco* to show whence it came. But near the great grey head upon the table another liqueur-glass stood, unbroken, and still full of some white and stinking liquid; and near that a tiny silver flask, which made me recoil from Raffles as I had not from the dead; for I knew it to be his.

'Come out of this poisonous air,' he said sternly, 'and I will tell you how it has happened.'

So we all three gathered together in the hall. But it was Raffles who stood nearest the street-door, his back to it, his

eyes upon us two. And though it was to me only that he spoke
at first, he would pause from point to point, and translate into
Italian for the benefit of the one-eyed alien to whom he owed
his life.

'You probably don't even know the name, Bunny,' he began,
'of the deadliest poison yet known to science. It is cyanide of
cacodyl, and I have carried that small flask of it about with
me for months. Where I got it matters nothing; the whole point
is that a mere sniff reduces flesh to clay. I have never had any
opinion of suicide, as you know, but I always felt it worth
while to be forearmed against the very worst. Well, a bottle of
this stuff is calculated to stiffen an ordinary roomful of ordinary
people within five minutes; and I remembered my flask when
they had me as good as crucified in the small hours of this
morning. I asked them to take it out of my pocket. I begged
them to give me a drink before they left me. And what do you
suppose they did?'

I thought of many things but suggested none, while Raffles
turned this much of his statement into sufficiently fluent Italian.
But when he faced me again his face was still flaming.

'That beast Corbucci!' said he – 'how can I pity him? He
took the flask; he would give me none; he flicked me in the
face instead. My idea was that he, at least, should go with me
– to sell my life as dearly as that – and a sniff would have
settled us both. But no, he must tantalise and torment me; he
thought it brandy; he must take it downstairs to drink to my
destruction! Can you have any pity for a hound like that?'

'Let us go,' I at last said hoarsely, as Raffles finished speaking in Italian, and his second listener stood open-mouthed.

'We will go,' said Raffles, 'and we will chance being seen; if
the worst comes to the worst this good chap will prove that I
have been tied up since one o'clock this morning, and the
medical evidence will decide how long those dogs have been
dead.'

But the worst did not come to the worst, more power to my
unforgotten friend the cabman, who never came forward to
say what manner of men he had driven to Bloomsbury Square
at top speed on the very day upon which the tragedy was discovered there, or whence he had driven them. To be sure, they

had not behaved like murderers, whereas the evidence at the inquest all went to show that the defunct Corbucci was little better. His reputation, which transpired with his identity, was that of a libertine and a renegade, while the infernal apparatus upstairs revealed the fiendish arts of the anarchist to boot. The inquiry resulted eventually in an open verdict, and was chiefly instrumental in killing such compassion as is usually felt for the dead who die in their sins.

But Raffles would not have passed this title for this tale.

TO CATCH A THIEF

I

SOCIETY persons are not likely to have forgotten the series of audacious robberies by which so many of themselves suffered in turn during the brief course of a recent season. Raid after raid was made upon the smartest houses in town, and within a few weeks more than one exalted head had been shorn of its priceless tiara. The Duke and Duchess of Dorchester lost half the portable pieces of their historic plate on the very night of their Graces' almost equally historic costume ball. The Kenworthy diamonds were taken in broad daylight, during the excitement of a charitable meeting on the ground floor, and the gifts of her belted bridegroom to Lady May Paulton while the outer air was thick with a prismatic shower of confetti. It was obvious that all this was the work of no ordinary thief, and perhaps inevitable that the name of Raffles should have been dragged from oblivion by callous disrespecters of the departed and unreasoning apologists for the police. These wiseacres did not hesitate to bring a dead man back to life because they knew of no one living capable of such feats; it is their heedless and inconsequent calumnies that the present paper is partly intended to refute. As a matter of fact, our joint innocence in this matter was only exceeded by our common envy, and for a long time, like the rest of the world, neither of us had the slightest clue to the identity of the person who was following in our steps with such irritating results.

'I should mind less,' said Raffles, 'if the fellow were really playing the game. But abuse of hospitality was never one of my strokes, and it seems to be the only shot he's got. When we took old Lady Melrose's necklace, Bunny, we were not staying with the Melroses if you recollect.'

We were discussing the robberies for the hundredth time, but for once under conditions more favourable to animated conversation than our unique circumstances permitted in the

flat. We did not often dine out. Dr Theobald was one impedi-
ment, the risk of recognition was another. But there were ex-
ceptions, when the doctor was away or the patient defiant, and
on these rare occasions we frequented a certain unpretentious
restaurant in the Fulham quarter, where the cooking was plain
but excellent, and the cellar a surprise. Our bottle of '89 champagne was empty to the label when the subject arose, to be
touched by Raffles in the reminiscent manner indicated above.
I can see his clear eye upon me now, reading me, weighing me.
But I was not so sensitive to his scrutiny at the time. His tone
was deliberate, calculating, preparatory; not as I heard it then,
through a head full of wine, but as it floats back to me across
the gulf between that moment and this.

'Excellent fillet!' said I grossly. 'So you think this chap is as
much in society as we were, do you?'

I preferred not to think so myself. We had cause enough for
jealousy without that. But Raffles raised his eyebrows an elo-
quent half-inch.

'As much, my dear Bunny? He is not only in it, but of it;
there's no comparison between us there. Society is in rings like
a target, and we never were in the bull's-eye, however thick
you may lay on the ink! I was asked for my cricket. I haven't
forgotten it yet. But this fellow's one of themselves, with the
right of *entrée* into houses which we could only "enter" in a
professional sense. That's obvious unless all these little exploits
are the work of different hands, which they as obviously are
not. And it's why I'd give five hundred pounds to put salt on
him to-night!'

'Not you,' said I, as I drained my glass in festive incredulity.

'But I would, my dear Bunny. Waiter! another half-bottle of
this,' and Raffles leant across the table as the empty one was
taken away. 'I never was more serious in my life,' he continued
below his breath. 'Whatever else our successor may be, he's
not a dead man like me, or a marked man like you. If there's
any truth in my theory he's one of the last people upon whom
suspicion is ever likely to rest; and oh, Bunny, what a partner
he would make for you and me.'

Under less genial influences the very idea of a third partner
would have filled my soul with offence; but Raffles had chosen

his moment unerringly, and his arguments lost nothing by the flowing accompaniment of the extra pint. They were, however, quite strong in themselves. The gist of them was that thus far we had remarkably little to show for what Raffles would call 'our second innings'. This even I could not deny. We had scored a few 'long singles', but our 'best shots' had gone 'straight to hand', and we were 'playing a deuced slow game'. Therefore we needed a new partner – and the metaphor failed Raffles. It had served its turn. I already agreed with him. In truth I was tired of my false position as hireling attendant, and had long fancied myself an object of suspicion to that other impostor the doctor. A fresh, untrammelled start was a fascinating idea to me, though two were company, and three in our case might be worse than none. But I did not see how we could hope, with our respective handicaps, to solve a problem which was already the despair of Scotland Yard.

'Suppose I have solved it,' observed Raffles, cracking a walnut in his palm.

'How could you?' I asked, without believing for an instant that he had.

'I have been taking the *Morning Post* for some time now.'

'Well?'

'You have got me a good many odd numbers of the less base society papers.'

'I can't for the life of me see what you're driving at.'

Raffles smiled indulgently as he cracked another nut.

'That's because you've neither observation nor imagination, Bunny – and yet you try to write! Well, you wouldn't think it, but I have a fairly complete list of the people who were at the various functions under cover of which these different little *coups* were brought off.'

I said very stolidly that I did not see how that could help him. It was the only answer to his good-humoured but self-satisfied contempt; it happened also to be true.

'Think,' said Raffles, in a patient voice.

'When thieves break in and steal,' said I, 'upstairs, I don't see much point in discovering who was downstairs at the time.'

'Quite,' said Raffles – 'when they do break in.'

'But that's what they have done in all these cases. An upstairs door found screwed up, when things were at their height below; thief gone and jewels with him before alarm could be raised. Why, the trick's so old that I never knew you condescend to play it '

'Not so old as it looks,' said Raffles, choosing the cigars and handing me mine. 'Cognac or Benedictine, Bunny?'

'Brandy,' I said coarsely.

'Besides,' he went on, 'the rooms were not screwed up; at Dorchester House, at any rate, the door was only locked; and the key missing, so that it might have been done on either side.'

'But that was where he left his rope-ladder behind him!' I exclaimed in trimph; but Raffles only shook his head.

'I don't believe in that rope-ladder, Bunny, except as a blind.'

'Then what on earth do you believe?'

'That every one of these so-called burglaries has been done from the inside, by one of the guests; and what's more, I'm very much mistaken if I haven't spotted the right sportsman.'

I began to believe that he really had, there was such a wicked gravity in the eyes that twinkled faintly into mine. I raised my glass in convivial congratulation, and still remember the somewhat anxious eye with which Raffles saw it emptied.

'I can only find one likely name,' he continued, 'that figures in all these lists, and it is anything but a likely one at first sight. Lord Ernest Belville was at all those functions. Know anything about him, Bunny?'

'Not the Rational Drink fanatic?'

'Yes.'

'That's all I want to know.'

'Quite,' said Raffles; 'and yet what could be more promising? A man whose views are so broad and moderate, and so widely held already (saving your presence, Bunny), does not bore the world with them without ulterior motives. So far so good. What are this chap's motives? Does he want to advertise himself? No, he's somebody already. But is he rich? On the contrary, he's as poor as a rat for his position, and apparently without the least ambition to be anything else; certainly he won't enrich himself by making a public fad of what all sensible people are agreed upon as it is. Then suddenly one gets one's own old idea

– the alternative profession! My cricket – his Rational Drink! But it is no use jumping to conclusions. I must know more than the newspapers can tell me. Our aristocratic friend is forty, and unmarried. What has he been doing all these years? How the devil was I to find out?'

'How did you?' I asked, declining to spoil my digestion with a conundrum, as it was his evident intention that I should.

'Interviewed him!' said Raffles, smiling slowly on my amazement.

'You – interviewed him?' I echoed. 'When – and where?'

'Last Thursday night, when, if you remember, we kept early hours, because I felt done. What was the use of telling you what I had up my sleeve, Bunny? It might have ended in fizzle, as it still may. But Lord Ernest Belville was addressing the meeting at Exeter Hall; I waited for him when the show was over, dogged him home to King John's Mansions, and interviewed him in his own rooms there before he turned in.'

My journalistic jealousy was piqued to the quick. Affecting a scepticism I did not feel (for no outrage was beyond the pale of his impudence), I inquired dryly which journal Raffles had pretended to represent. It is unnecessary to report his answer. I could not believe him without further explanation.

'I should have thought,' he said, 'that even you would have spotted a practice I never omit upon certain occasions. I always pay a visit to the drawing-room and fill my waistcoat pocket from the card-tray. It is an immense help in any little temporary impersonation. On Thursday night I sent up the card of a powerful writer connected with a powerful paper; if Lord Ernest had known him in the flesh I should have been obliged to confess to a journalistic ruse; luckily he didn't – and I had been sent by my editor to get the interview for next morning. What could be better for the alternative profession?'

I inquired what the interview had brought forth.

'Everything,' said Raffles. 'Lord Ernest has been a wanderer these twenty years. Texas, Fiji, Australia. I suspect him of wives and families in all three. But his manners are a liberal education. He gave me some beautiful whisky, and forgot all about his fad. He is strong and subtle, but I talked him off his guard. He is going to the Kirkleathams' to-night – I saw the

218

card stuck up. I stuck some wax into his keyhole as he was switching off the lights.'

And, with an eye upon the waiters, Raffles showed me a skeleton key, newly twisted and filed; but my share of the extra pint (I am afraid no fair share) had made me dense. I looked from the key to Raffles with puckered forehead – for I happened to catch sight of it in the mirror behind him.

'The Dowager Lady Kirkleatham,' he whispered, 'has diamonds as big as beans, and likes to have 'em all on – and goes to bed early – and happens to be in town!'

And now I saw.

'The villain means to get them from her!'

'And I mean to get them from the villain,' said Raffles; 'or, rather, your share and mine.'

'Will he consent to a partnership?'

'We shall have him at our mercy. He daren't refuse.'

Raffles's plan was to gain access to Lord Ernest's rooms before midnight; there we were to lie in wait for the aristocratic rascal, and if I left all details to Raffles, and simply stood by in case of a rumpus, I should be playing my part and earning my share. It was a part that I had played before, not always with a good grace, though there had never been any question about the share. But to-night I was nothing loath. I had had just champagne enough – how Raffles knew my measure! – and I was ready and eager for anything. Indeed, I did not wish to wait for the coffee, which was to be specially strong by order of Raffles. But on that he insisted, and it was between ten and eleven when at last we were in our cab.

'It would be fatal to be too early,' he said as we drove; 'on the other hand, it would be dangerous to leave it too late. One must risk something. How I should love to drive down Piccadilly and see the lights! But unnecessary risks are another story.'

II

King John's Mansions, as everybody knows, are the oldest, the ugliest, and the tallest block of flats in all London. But they are built upon a more generous scale than has since become the rule, and with a less studious regard for the economy of space.

We were about to drive into the spacious courtyard when the gatekeeper checked us in order to let another hansom drive out. It contained a middle-aged man of the military type, like ourselves in evening dress. That much I saw as his hansom crossed our bows, because I could not help seeing it, but I should not have given the incident a second thought if it had not been for its extraordinary effect upon Raffles. In an instant he was out upon the kerb, paying the cabby, and in another he was leading me across the street, away from the mansions.

'Where on earth are you going?' I naturally exclaimed.

'Into the park,' said he. 'We are too early.'

His voice told me more than his words. It was strangely stern.

'Was that him – in the hansom?'

'It was.'

'Well, then, the coast's clear,' said I comfortably. I was for turning back then and there, but Raffles forced me on with a hand that hardened on my arm.

'It was a nearer thing than I care about,' said he. 'This seat will do; no, the next one's farther from a lamp-post. We will give him a good half-hour, and I don't want to talk.'

We had been seated some minutes when Big Ben sent a languid chime over our heads to the stars. It was half-past ten, and a sultry night. Eleven had struck before Raffles awoke from his sullen reverie, and recalled me from mine with a slap on the back. In a couple of minutes we were in the lightest vestibule at the inner end of the courtyard of King John's Mansions.

'Just left Lord Ernest at Lady Kirkleatham's,' said Raffles. 'Gave me his key and asked us to wait for him in his rooms. Will you send us up in the lift?'

In a small way, I never knew old Raffles do anything better. There was not an instant's demur. Lord Ernest Belville's rooms were at the top of the building, but we were in them as quickly as lift could carry and page-boy conduct us. And there was no need for the skeleton key after all; the boy opened the outer door with one of his own, and switched on the lights before leaving us.

'Now that's interesting,' said Raffles, as soon as we were alone; 'they can come in and clean when he is out. What if he keeps his swag at the bank? By Jove, that's an idea for him! I don't believe he's getting rid of it; it's all lying low somewhere, if I'm not mistaken, and he's not a fool.'

While he spoke he was moving about the sitting-room, which was charmingly furnished in the antique style, and making as many remarks as though he were an auctioneer's clerk with an inventory to prepare and a day to do it in, instead of a cracksman who might be surprised in his crib at any moment.

'Chippendale of sorts, eh, Bunny? Not genuine, of course; but where can you get genuine Chippendale now, and who knows it when they see it? There's no merit in mere antiquity. Yet the way people pose on the subject! If a thing's handsome and useful, and good cabinet-making, it's good enough for me.'

'Hadn't we better explore the whole place?' I suggested nervously. He had not even bolted the outer door. Nor would he when I called his attention to the omission.

'If Lord Ernest finds his rooms locked up he'll raise Cain,' said Raffles. 'We must let him come in and lock up for himself before we corner him. But he won't come yet; if he did it might be awkward, for they'll tell him down below what I told them. A new staff comes on at midnight. I discovered that the other night.'

'Supposing he does come in before?'

'Well, he can't have us turned out without first seeing who we are, and he won't try it on when I've had one word with him. Unless my suspicions are unfounded, I mean.'

'Isn't it about time to test them?'

'My good Bunny, what do you suppose I've been doing all this while? He keeps nothing in here. There isn't a lock to the Chippendale that you couldn't pick with a penknife, and not a loose board in the floor, for I was treading for one before the boy left us. Chimneys no use in a place like this where they keep them swept for you. Yes, I'm quite ready to try his bedroom.'

There was but a bathroom besides; no kitchen, no servant's room; neither is necessary in King John's Mansions. I thought it as well to put my head inside the bathroom while Raffles went into the bedroom, for I was tormented by the horrible idea that the man might all this time be concealed somewhere in the flat. But the bathroom blazed void in the electric light. I found Raffles hanging out of the starry square which was the bedroom window, for the room was still in darkness. I felt for the switch at the door.

'Put it out again!' said Raffles fiercely. He rose from the sill, drew blinds and curtains carefully, then switched on the light himself. It fell upon a face creased more in pity than in anger, and Raffles only shook his head as I hung mine.

'It's all right, old boy,' said he; 'but corridors have windows too, and servants have eyes; and you and I are supposed to be in the other room, not in this. But cheer up, Bunny! This is *the* room; look at the extra bolt on the door; he's had that put on, and there's an iron ladder to his window in case of fire! Way of escape ready against the hour of need; he's a better man than I thought him, Bunny, after all. But you may bet your bottom dollar that if there's any boodle in the flat it's in this room.'

Yet the room was very lightly furnished; and nothing was locked. We looked everywhere, but we looked in vain. The wardrobe was filled with hanging coats and trousers in a press, the drawers with the softest silk and finest linen. There was a camp bedstead that would not have unsettled an anchorite; there was no place for treasure there. I looked up the chimney, but Raffles told me not to be a fool, and asked if I ever listened to what he said. There was no question about his temper now. I never knew him in a worse.

'Then he's got it in the bank,' he growled. 'I'll swear I'm not mistaken in my man!'

I had the tact not to differ with him there. But I could not help suggesting that now was our time to remedy any mistake we might have made. We were on the right side of midnight still.

'Then we'll stultify ourselves downstairs,' said Raffles. 'No, I'll be shot if I do! He may come in with the Kirkleatham diamonds! You do what you like, Bunny, but I don't budge.'

'I certainly shan't leave you,' I retorted, 'to be knocked into the middle of next week by a better man than yourself.'

I had borrowed his own tone, and he did not like it. They never do. I thought for a moment that Raffles was going to strike me – for the first and last time in his life. He could if he liked. My blood was up. I was ready to send him to the devil. And I emphasised my offence by nodding and shrugging towards a pair of very large Indian clubs that stood in the fender, on either side of the chimney up which I had presumed to glance.

In an instant Raffles had seized the clubs, and was whirling them about his grey head in a mixture of childish pique and puerile bravado which I should have thought him altogether above. And suddenly as I watched him his face changed, softened, lit up, and he swung the clubs gently down upon the bed.

'They're not heavy enough for their size,' said he rapidly; 'and I'll take my oath they're not the same weight!'

He shook one club after the other, with both hands, close to his ear; then he examined their butt-ends under the electric light. I saw what he suspected now, and caught the contagion of his suppressed excitement. Neither of us spoke. But Raffles had taken out the portable tool-box that he called a knife, and always carried, and as he opened the gimlet he handed me the club he held. Instinctively I tucked the small end under my arm, and presented the other to Raffles.

'Hold him tight,' he whispered, smiling. 'He's not only a better man than I thought him, Bunny, he's hit upon a better dodge than ever I did, of its kind. Only I should have weighted them evenly – to a hair.'

He had screwed the gimlet into the circular butt, close to the edge, and now we were wrenching in opposite directions. For a moment or more nothing happened. Then all at once something gave, and Raffles swore an oath as soft as any prayer. And for the minute after that his hand went round and round with the gimlet, as though he were grinding a piano-organ, while the end wormed slowly out on its delicate thread of fine hard wood.

The clubs were as hollow as drinking-horns, the pair of them, for we went from one to the other without pausing to undo the padded packets that poured out upon the bed. These were deliciously heavy to the hand, yet thickly swathed in cotton-wool, so that some stuck together, retaining the shape of the cavity, as though they had been run out of a mould. And when we did open them – but let Raffles speak.

He had deputed me to screw in the ends of the clubs and to replace the latter in the fender where we had found them. When I had done, the counterpane was glittering with diamonds where it was not shimmering with pearls.

'If this isn't the tiara that Lady Mary was married in,' said Raffles, 'and that disappeared out of the room she changed in, while it rained confetti on the steps, I'll present it to her instead of the one she lost ... It was stupid to keep these old gold spoons, valuable as they are; they made the difference in the weight. ... Here we have probably the Kenworthy diamonds ... I don't know the history of these pearls ... This looks like one family of rings – left on the basin-stand, perhaps – alas! poor lady! And that's the lot.'

Our eyes met across the bed.

'What's it all worth?' I asked hoarsely.

'Impossible to say. But more than all we ever took in all our lives. That I'll swear to.'

'More than all – –'

My tongue swelled with the thought.

'But it'll take some turning into cash, old chap!'

'And – must it be a partnership?' I asked, finding a lugubrious voice at length.

'Partnership be damned!' cried Raffles heartily. 'Let's get out quicker than we came in.'

We pocketed the things between us, cotton-wool and all, not because we wanted the latter, but to remove all immediate traces of our really meritorious deed.

'The sinner won't dare to say a word when he does find out,' remarked Raffles of Lord Ernest; 'but that's no reason why he should find out before he must. Everything's straight in here, I think; no, better leave the window open as it was, and the blind up. Now out with the light. One peep at the other room. That's all right, too. Out with the passage light, Bunny, while I open – –'

His words died away in a whisper. A key was fumbling at the lock outside.

'Out with it – out with it!' whispered Raffles in an agony; and as I obeyed he picked me off my feet and swung me bodily but silently into the bedroom, just as the outer door opened, and a masterful step strode in.

The next five were horrible minutes. We heard the apostle of Rational Drink unlock one of the deep drawers in his antique sideboard, and sounds followed suspiciously like the splash of spirits and the steady stream from a siphon. Never before or since did I experience such a thirst as assailed me at that moment, nor do I believe that many tropical explorers have known its equal. But I had Raffles with me, and his hand was as steady and as cool as the hand of a trained nurse. That I know because he turned up the collar of my overcoat for me, for some reason, and buttoned it at the throat. I afterwards found that he had done the same to his own, but I did not hear him doing it. The one thing I heard in the bedroom was a tiny metallic click, muffled and deadened in his overcoat pocket, and it not only removed my last tremor, but strung me to a higher pitch of excitement than ever. Yet I had then no conception of the game that Raffles was deciding to play, and that I was to play with him in another minute.

It cannot have been longer before Lord Ernest came into his bedroom. Heavens, but my heart had not forgotten how to thump! We were standing near the door, and I could swear he touched me; then his boots creaked, there was a rattle in the fender – and Raffles switched on the light.

Lord Ernest Belville crouched in its glare with one Indian club held by the end, like a footman with a stolen bottle. A good-looking, well-built, iron-grey, iron-jawed man; but a fool and a weakling at that moment, if he had never been either before.

'Lord Ernest Belville,' said Raffles, 'it's no use. This is a loaded revolver, and if you force me I shall use it on you as I would on any other desperate criminal. I am here to arrest you for a series of robberies at the Duke of Dorchester's, Sir John Kenworthy's, and other noblemen's and gentlemen's houses during the present season. You'd better drop what you've got in your hand. It's empty.'

Lord Ernest lifted the club an inch or two, and with it his eyebrows – and after it his stalwart frame as the club crashed back into the fender. And as he stood at his full height, a courteous but ironic smile under the cropped moustache, he looked what he was, criminal or not.

'Scotland Yard?' said he.

'That's our affair, my lord.'

'I didn't think they'd got it in them,' said Lord Ernest. 'Now I recognise you. You're my interviewer. No, I didn't think any of you fellows had got all that in you. Come into the other room, and I'll show you something else. Oh, keep me covered by all means. But look at this!'

On the antique sideboard, their size doubled by reflection in the polished mahogany, lay a coruscating cluster of precious stones, that fell in festoons about Lord Ernest's fingers as he handed them to Raffles with scarcely a shrug.

'The Kirkleatham diamonds,' said he. 'Better add 'em to the bag.'

Raffles did so without a smile; with his overcoat buttoned up to the chin, his tall hat pressed down to his eyes, and between the two his incisive features and his keen, stern glance, he looked the ideal detective of fiction and the stage. What *I* looked God knows, but I did my best to glower and show my teeth at his side. I had thrown myself into the game, and it was obviously a winning one.

'Wouldn't take a share, I suppose?' Lord Ernest said casually.

Raffles did not condescend to reply. I rolled back my lips like a bull-pup.

'Then a drink, at least!'

My mouth watered, but Raffles shook his head impatiently.

'We must be going, my lord, and you will have to come with us.'

I wondered what in the world we should do with him when we had got him.

'Give me time to put some things together? Pair of pyjamas and toothbrush, don't you know?'

'I cannot give you many minutes, my lord, but I don't want to cause a disturbance here, so I'll tell them to call a cab if you like. But I shall be back in a minute, and you must be ready in five. Here, Inspector, you'd better keep this while I am gone.'

And I was left alone with that dangerous criminal! Raffles

nipped my arm as he handed me the revolver, but I got small comfort out of that.

' "Sea-green Incorruptible?" ' inquired Lord Ernest, as we stood face to face.

'You don't corrupt me,' I replied through naked teeth.

'Then come into my room. I'll lead the way. Think you can hit me if I misbehave?'

I put the bed between us without a second's delay. My prisoner flung a suit-case upon it, and tossed things into it with a dejected air; suddenly, as he was fitting them in, without raising his head (which I was watching), his right hand closed over the barrel with which I covered him.

'You'd better not shoot,' he said, a knee upon his side of the bed; 'if you do it may be as bad for you as it will be for me!'

I tried to wrest the revolver from him.

'I will if you force me,' I hissed.

'You'd better not,' he repeated, smiling; and now I saw that if I did I should only shoot into either the bed or my own legs. His hand was on the top of mine, bending it down, and the revolver with it. The strength of it was as the strength of ten of mine; and now both his knees were on the bed; and sudden y I saw his other hand, doubled into a fist, coming up slowly over the suit-case.

'Help!' I called feebly.

'Help, forsooth! I begin to believe *you are* from the Yard,' he said – and his upper-cut came with the 'Yard'. It caught me under the chin. It lifted me off my legs. I have a dim recollection of the crash that I made in falling.

III

Raffles was standing over me when I recovered consciousness. I lay stretched upon the bed across which the blackguard Belville had struck his knavish blow. The suit-case was on the floor, but its dastardly owner had disappeared.

'Is he gone?' was my first faint question.

'Thank God you're not, anyway!' replied Raffles, with what struck me then as mere flippancy. I managed to raise myself upon one elbow.

'I meant Lord Ernest Belville,' said I with dignity. 'Are you quite sure that he's cleared out?'

Raffles waved a hand towards the window, which stood wide open to the summer stars.

'Of course,' said he, 'and by the route I intended him to take; he's gone by the iron ladder, as I hoped he would. What on earth should we have done with him? My poor dear Bunny, I thought you'd take a bribe! But it's really more convincing as it is, and just as well for Lord Ernest to be convinced for the time being.'

'Are you sure he is?' I questioned, as I found a rather shaky pair of legs.

'Of course!' cried Raffles again, in the tone to make one blush for the least misgiving on the point. 'Not that it matters one bit,' he added airily, 'for we have him either way; and when he does tumble to it, as he may any minute, he won't dare to open his mouth.'

'Then the sooner we clear out the better,' said I, but I looked askance at the open window, for my head was spinning still.

'When you feel up to it,' returned Raffles, 'we shall *stroll* out, and I shall do myself the honour of ringing for the lift. The force of habit is too strong in you, Bunny. I shall shut the window and leave everything exactly as we found it. Lord Ernest will probably tumble before he is badly missed; and then he may come back to put salt on us; but I should like to know what he can do even if he succeeds! Come, Bunny, pull yourself together, and you'll be a different man when you're in the open air.'

And for a while I felt one, such was my relief at getting out of those infernal mansions with unfettered wrists; this we managed easily enough; but once more Raffles's performance of a small part was no less perfect than his more ambitious work upstairs, and something of the successful artist's elation possessed him as we walked arm in arm across St. James's Park. It was long since I had known him so pleased with himself, and only too long since he had had such reason.

'I don't think I ever had a brighter idea in my life,' he said; 'never thought of it till he was in the next room; never dreamt of its coming off so ideally even then, and didn't much care, because we had him all ways up. I'm only sorry you let him knock you out. I was waiting outside the door all the time, and it made me sick to hear it. But I once broke my own head, Bunny, if you remember, and not in half such an excellent cause!'

Raffles touched all his pockets in his turn, the pockets that contained a small fortune apiece, and he smiled in my face as we crossed the lighted avenues of the Mall. Next moment he was hailing a cab – for I suppose I was still pretty pale – and not a word would he let me speak until we had alighted as near as was prudent to the flat.

'What a brute I've been, Bunny!' he whispered then; 'but you take half the swag, old boy, and right well you've earned it. No, we'll go in by the wrong door and over the roof; it's too late for old Theobald to be still at the play, and too early for him to be safely in his cups.'

So we climbed the many stairs with cat-like stealth, and like cats crept out upon the grimy leads. But to-night they were no blacker than their canopy of sky; not a chimney-stack stood out against the starless night; one had to feel one's way in order to avoid tipping over the low parapets of the L-shaped wells that ran from roof to basement to light the inner rooms. One of these walls was spanned by a flimsy bridge with iron hand-rails that felt warm to the touch as Raffles led the way across, a hotter and a closer night I have ever known.

'The flat will be like an oven,' I grumbled, at the head of our own staircase.

'Then we won't go down,' said Raffles promptly; 'we'll slack it up here for a bit instead. No, Bunny, you stay where you are! I'll fetch you a drink and a deck-chair, and you shan't come down till you feel more fit.'

And I let him have his way, I will not say as usual, for I had even less than my normal power of resistance that night. That villainous upper-cut! My head still sang and throbbed, as I seated myself on one of the aforesaid parapets, and buried it in my hot hands. Nor was the night one to dispel a headache; there was distinct thunder in the air. Thus I sat in a heap, and brooded over my misadventure, a pretty figure of a subordinate villain, until the step came for which I waited; and it never struck me that it came from the wrong direction.

'You have been quick,' said I simply.

'Yes,' hissed a voice I recognised; 'and you've got to be quicker still! Here, out with your wrists; no, one at a time; and if you utter a syllable you're a dead man.'

It was Lord Ernest Belville; his close-cropped, iron-grey moustache gleamed through the darkness, drawn up over his set teeth. In his hand glittered a pair of handcuffs, and before I knew it one had snapped its jaws about my wrist.

'Now come this way,' said Lord Ernest, showing me a revolver also, 'and wait for your friend. And, recollect, a single syllable of warning will be your death!'

With that the ruffian led me to the very bridge I had just crossed at Raffles's heels, and handcuffed me to the iron rail midway across the chasm. It no longer felt warm to my touch, but icy as the blood in all my veins.

So this high-born hypocrite had beaten us at our game and his, and Raffles had met his match at last! That was the most intolerable thought, that Raffles should be down in the flat on my account, and that I could not warn him of his impending fate; for how was it possible without making such an outcry as should bring the mansions about our ears? And there I shivered on that wretched plank, chained like Andromeda to the rock, with a black infinity above and below; and before my eyes, now grown familiar with the peculiar darkness, stood Lord Ernest Belville, waiting for Raffles to emerge with full hands and unsuspecting heart! Taken so horribly unawares, even Raffles must fall an easy prey to a desperado in resource and courage scarcely second to himself, but one whom he had fatally underrated from the beginning. Not that I paused to think how the thing had happened; my one concern was for what was to happen next.

And what did happen was worse than my worst foreboding, for first a light came flickering into the sort of companion-hatch at the head of the stairs, and finally Raffles – in his shirt-sleeves! He was not only carrying a candle to put the finishing touch to him as a target; he had dispensed with coat and waistcoat downstairs, and was at once full-handed and unarmed.

'Where are you, old chap?' he cried softly, himself blinded by the light he carried; and he advanced a couple of steps towards Belville. 'This isn't you, is it?'

And Raffles stopped, his candle held on high, a folding-chair under the other arm.

'No, I am not your friend,' replied Lord Ernest easily; 'but kindly remain standing exactly where you are, and don't lower that candle an inch, unless you want your brains blown into the street.'

Raffles said never a word, but for a moment did as he was bid; and the unshaken flame of the candle was testimony alike to the stillness of the night and to the finest set of nerves in Europe. Then, to my horror, he coolly stooped, placing candle and chair on the leads, and his hands in his pockets, as though it were but a pop-gun that covered him.

'Why didn't you shoot?' he asked insolently as he rose. 'Frightened of the noise? I should be, too, with an old-pattern machine like that. All very well for service in the field – but on the housetops at dead of night!'

'I shall shoot, however,' replied Lord Ernest, as quietly in his turn, and with less insolence, 'and chance the noise, unless you instantly restore my property. I am glad you don't dispute the last word,' he continued after a slight pause. 'There is no keener honour than that which subsists, or ought to subsist, among thieves; and I need hardly say that I soon spotted you as one of the fraternity. Not in the beginning, mind you! For the moment I did think you were one of these smart detectives jumped to life from some sixpenny magazine; but to preserve the illusion you ought to provide yourself with a worthier lieutenant. It was he who gave your show away,' chuckled the wretch, dropping for a moment the affected style of speech which seemed intended to enhance our humiliation; 'smart detectives don't go about with little innocents to assist them. You needn't be anxious about him, by the way; it wasn't necessary to pitch him into the street; he is to be seen though not heard, if you look in the right direction. Nor must you put all the blame upon your friend; it was not he, but you, who made so sure that I had got out by the window. You see, I was in my bathroom all the time – with the door open.'

'The bathroom, eh?' Raffles echoed with professional interest. 'And you followed us on foot across the park?'

'Of course.'

'And then in a cab?'

'And afterwards on foot once more.'

'The simplest skeleton would let you in down below.'

I saw the lower half of Lord Ernest's face grinning in the light of the candle set between them on the ground.

'You follow every move,' said he; 'there can be no doubt you are one of the fraternity; and I shouldn't wonder if we had formed our style upon the same model. Ever know A. J. Raffles?'

The abrupt question took my breath away; but Raffles himself did not lose an instant over his answer.

'Intimately,' said he.

'That accounts for you, then,' laughed Lord Ernest, 'as it does for me, though I never had the honour of the master's acquaintance. Nor is it for me to say which is the worthier disciple. Perhaps, however, now that your friend is handcuffed in mid-air, and you yourself are at my mercy, you will concede me some little temporary advantage?'

And his face split in another grin from the cropped moustache downward, as I saw no longer by candlelight, but by a flash of lightning which tore the sky in two before Raffles could reply.

'You have the bulge at present,' admitted Raffles; 'but you have still to lay hands upon your, or our, ill-gotten goods. To shoot me is not necessarily to do so; to bring either one of us to a violent end is only to court a yet more violent and infinitely more disgraceful one for yourself. Family considerations alone should rule that risk out of your game. Now, an hour or two ago, when the exact opposite – –'

The remainder of Raffles's speech was drowned from my ears by the belated crash of thunder which the lightning had foretold. So loud, however, was the crash when it came, that the storm was evidently approaching us at a high velocity; yet as the last echo rumbled away, I heard Raffles talking as though he had never stopped.

'You offered us a share,' he was saying; 'unless you mean to murder us both in cold blood, it will be worth your while to repeat that offer. We should be dangerous enemies; you had far better make the best of us as friends.'

'Lead the way down to your flat,' said Lord Ernest, with a flourish of his service revolver, 'and perhaps we may talk about it. It is for me to make the terms, I imagine, and in the first place I am not going to get wet to the skin up here.'

The rain was beginning in great drops, even as he spoke, and by a second flash of lightning I saw Raffles pointing to me.

'But what about my friend?' said he.

And then came the second peal.

'Oh, *he's* all right,' the great brute replied; 'do him good! You don't catch me letting myself in for two to one!'

'You will find it equally difficult,' rejoined Raffles, 'to induce me to leave my friend to the mercy of a night like this. He has not recovered from the blow you struck him in your own rooms. I am not such a fool as to blame you for that, but you are a worse sportsman than I take you for if you think of leaving him where he is. If he stays, however, so do I.'

And, just as it ceased, Raffles's voice seemed distinctly nearer me; but in the darkness and the rain, which was now as heavy as hail, I could see nothing clearly. The rain had already extinguished the candle I heard an oath from Belville, a laugh from Raffles, and for a second that was all. Raffles was coming to me, and the other could not even see to fire; that was all I knew in the pitchy interval of invisible rain before the next crash and the next flash.

And then!

This time they came together, and not till my dying hour shall I forget the sight that the lightning lit and the thunder applauded. Raffles was on one of the parapets of the gulf that my footbridge spanned, and in the sudden illumination he stepped across it as one might across a garden path. The width was scarcely greater, but the depth! In the sudden flare I saw to the concrete bottom of the well, and it looked no larger than the hollow of my hand. Raffles was laughing in my ear; he had the iron railing fast; it was between us, but his foothold was as secure as mine. Lord Ernest Belville, on the contrary, was the fifth of a second late for the light, and half a foot short in his spring. Something struck our plank bridge so hard as to set it quivering like a harp-string; there was half a gasp and half a sob in mid-air beneath our feet; and then a sound far below that I prefer not to describe. I am not sure that I could hit upon the perfect simile; it is more than enough for me that I can hear it still. And with that sickening sound came the loudest clap of thunder yet, and a great white glare that showed us our enemy's body far below, with one white hand spread like a starfish, but the head of him mercifully twisted underneath.

'It was his own fault, Bunny. Poor devil! May he and all of us be forgiven; but pull yourself together for your own sake. Well, you can't fall; stay where you are a minute.'

I remember the uproar of the elements while Raffles was gone; no other sound mingled with it; not the opening of a single window, not the uplifting of a single voice. Then came Raffles with soap and water and gyve was wheedled from one wrist, as you withdraw a ring for which the finger has grown too large. Of the rest, I only remember shivering till morning in a pitch-dark flat, whose invalid occupier was for once the nurse, and I his patient.

And that is the true ending of the episode in which we two set ourselves to catch one of our own kidney, albeit in another place I have shirked the whole truth. It is not a grateful task to show Raffles as completely at fault as he really was on that occasion; nor do I derive any subtle satisfaction from recounting my own twofold humiliation, or from having assisted never so indirectly in the death of a not uncongenial sinner. The truth, however, has after all a merit of its own, and the great kinsfolk of poor Lord Ernest have but little to lose by its divulgence. It would seem that they knew more of the real character of the apostle of Rational Drink than was known at Exeter Hall. The tragedy was indeed hushed up, as tragedies only are when they occur in such circles. But the rumour that did get abroad, as to the class of enterprise which the poor scamp was pursuing when he met his death, cannot be too soon exploded, since it breathed upon the fair fame of some of the most respectable flats in Kensington.

AN OLD FLAME

I

THE square shall be nameless, but if you drive due west from Piccadilly the cabman will eventually find it on his left, and he ought to thank you for half a crown. It is not a fashionable square, but there are few with a finer garden, while the studios on the south side lend distinction of another sort. The houses, however, are small and dingy and about the last to attract the expert practitioner in search of a crib. Heaven knows it was with no such thought I trailed Raffles thither, one unlucky evening at the latter end of that same season when Dr. Theobald had at last insisted upon the bath-chair which I had foreseen in the beginning. Trees whispered in the green garden aforesaid, and the cool smooth lawns looked so inviting that I wondered whether some philanthropic resident could not be induced to lend us the key. But Raffles would not listen to the suggestion, when I stopped to make it, and what was worse, I found him looking wistfully at the little houses instead.

'Such balconies, Bunny! A leg up, and there you would be!'

I expressed a conviction that there would be nothing worth taking in the square, but took care to have him under way again as I spoke.

'I dare say you're right,' sighed Raffles. 'Rings and watches, I suppose, but it would be hard luck to take them from people who live in houses like these. I don't know, though. Here's one with an extra story. Stop, Bunny; if you don't stop I'll hold on to the railings! This is a good house; look at the knocker and the electric bell. They've had that put in. There's some money here, my rabbit! I dare bet there's a silver-table in the drawing-room; and the windows are wide open. Electric light, too, by Jove!'

Since stop I must, I had done so on the other side of the road, in the shadow of the leafy palings, and as Raffles spoke the ground-floor windows opposite had shown a light, show-

235

ing as pretty a little dinner-table as one could wish to see with a man at his wine at the far end, and the back of a lady in evening dress towards us. It was like a lantern-picture thrown upon a screen. There was only the pair of them, but the table was brilliant with silver and gay with flowers, and the maid waited with the indefinable air of a good servant. It certainly seemed a good house.

'She's going to let down the blind!' whispered Raffles, in high excitement. 'No, confound them, they've told her not to. Mark down her necklace, Bunny, and invoice his stud. What a brute he looks! But I like the table, and that's her show. She has the taste; but he must have money. See the festive picture over the sideboard? Looks to me like a Jacques Saillard. But that silver-table would be good enough for me.'

'Get on,' said I. 'You're in a bath-chair.'

'But the whole square's at dinner! We should have the ball at our feet. It wouldn't take two twos!'

'With those blinds up, and the cook in the kitchen underneath?'

He nodded, leaning forward in the chair, his hands upon the wraps about his legs.

'You must be mad,' said I, and got back to my handles with the word, but when I tugged the chair ran light.

'Keep an eye on the rug,' came in a whisper from the middle of the road; and there stood my invalid, his pale face in a quiver of pure mischief, yet set with his insane resolve. 'I'm only going to see whether that woman has a silver-table – –'

'We don't want it – –'

'It won't take a minute – –'

'It's madness, madness – –'

'Then don't you wait!'

It was like him to leave me with that, and this time I had taken him at his last word, had not my own given me an idea. Mad I had called him, and mad I could declare him upon oath if necessary. It was not as though the thing had happened far from home. They could learn all about us at the nearest mansions. I referred them to Dr Theobald; this was a Mr Maturin, one of his patients, and I was his keeper, and he had never given me the slip before. I heard myself making these explanations on the doorstep, and pointing to the deserted bath-chair as the proof, while the pretty parlourmaid ran for the police. It would be a more serious matter for me than for my charge. I should lose my place. No, he had never done such a thing before, and I would answer for it that he never should again.

I saw myself conducting Raffles back to his chair, with a firm hand and a stern tongue. I heard him thanking me in whispers on the way home. It would be the first tight place I had ever got him out of, and I was quite anxious for him to get into it, so sure was I of every move. My whole position had altered in the few seconds that it took me to follow this illuminating train of ideas; it was now so strong that I could watch Raffles without much anxiety. And he was worth watching.

He had stepped boldly but softly to the front door, and there he was still waiting, ready to ring if the door opened or a face appeared in the area, and doubtless to pretend that he had rung already. But he had not to ring at all; and suddenly I saw his foot in the letter-box, his left hand on the lintel overhead. It was thrilling even to a hardened accomplice with an explanation up his sleeve! A tight grip with that left hand of his, as he leant backward with all his weight upon those five fingers; a right arm stretched outward and upward to its last inch; and the base of the low, projecting balcony was safely caught.

I looked down and took breath. The maid was removing the crumbs in the lighted room, and the square was empty as before. What a blessing it was the end of the season! Many of the houses remained in darkness. I looked up again, and Raffles was drawing his left leg over the balcony railing. In another moment he had disappeared through one of the french windows which opened upon the balcony, and in yet another he had switched on the electric light within. This was bad enough; but the crowning folly was still to come. There was no point in it; the mad thing was done for my benefit, as I knew at once and he afterwards confessed; but the lunatic reappeared on the balcony bowing like a mountebank – in his crape mask!

I set off with the empty chair, but I came back. *I* could not desert old Raffles, even when I would, but must try to explain away his mask as well, if he had not the sense to take it off in time. It would be difficult, but burglaries are not usually committed from a bath-chair, and for the rest I put my faith in Dr. Theobald. Meanwhile Raffles had at least withdrawn from the balcony, and now I could see his head as he peered into a cabinet at the other side of the room. It was like the opera of *Aïda*, in which two scenes are enacted simultaneously, one in the dungeon below, the other in the temple above. In the same fashion my attention now became divided between the picture of Raffles moving stealthily about the upper room and that of the husband and wife at table underneath. And all at once, as the man replenished his glass with a shrug of the shoulders, the woman pushed back her chair and sailed to the door.

Raffles was standing before the fireplace upstairs. He had taken one of the framed photographs from the chimney-piece, and was scanning it at suicidal length through the eye-holes in the hideous mask which he still wore. He would need it after all. The lady had left the room below, opening and shutting the door for herself; the man was filling his glass once more. I would have shrieked my warning to Raffles, so fatally engrossed overhead, but at this moment (of all others) a constable (of all men) was marching sedately down our side of the square. There was nothing for it but to turn a melancholy eye upon the bath-chair, and to ask the constable the time. I was evidently to be kept there all night, I remarked, and only realised with the words that they disposed of my other explanations before they were uttered. It was a horrible moment for such a discovery. Fortunately the enemy was on the pavement, from which he could scarcely have seen more than the drawing-room ceiling, had he looked; but he was not many houses distant when a door opened and a woman gasped so that I heard both across the road. And never shall I forget the subsequent tableaux in the lighted room behind the low balcony and the french windows.

Raffles stood confronted by a dark and handsome woman whose profile, as I saw it first in the electric light, is cut like a cameo in my memory. It had the undeviating line of brow and nose, the short upper lip, the perfect chin, that are united in marble oftener than in the flesh; and like marble she stood, or rather like some beautiful pale bronze; for that was her colouring, and she lost none of it that I could see, neither trembled; but her bosom rose and fell, and that was all. So she stood without flinching before a masked ruffian, who, I felt, would be the first to appreciate her courage! To me it was so superb that I could think of it in this way even then, and marvel how Raffles himself could stand unabashed before so brave a figure. He had not to do so long. The woman scorned him, and he stood unmoved, a framed photograph still in his hand. Then, with a quick, determined movement she turned, not to the door or to the bell, but to the open window by which Raffles had entered; and this with that accursed policeman still in view. So far no word had passed between the pair. But at this point Raffles said something, I could not hear what, but at the sound of his voice the woman wheeled. And Raffles was looking humbly in her face, the crape mask snatched from his own.

'Arthur!' she cried; and that might have been heard in the middle of the square garden.

Then they stood gazing at each other, neither unmoved any more, and while they stood the street-door opened and banged. It was the husband leaving the house, a fine figure of a man, but a dissipated face, and a step even now distinguished by the extreme caution which precedes unsteadiness. He broke the spell. His wife came to the balcony, then looked back into the room, and yet again along the road, and this time I saw her face. It was the face of one glancing indeed from Hyperion to a satyr. And then I saw the rings flash, as her hand fell gently upon Raffles's arm.

They disappeared from that window. Their heads showed for an instant in the next. Then they dipped out of sight, and an inner ceiling flashed out under a new light; they had gone into the back drawing-room beyond my ken. The maid came up with coffee, her mistress hastily met her at the door, and once more disappeared. The square was as quiet as ever. I remained some minutes where I was. Now and then I thought I heard voices in the back drawing-room. I was seldom sure.

My state of mind may be imagined by those readers who take an interest in my personal psychology. It does not amuse me to put myself in Raffles's place. He had been recognised at last, he had come to life. Only one person knew as yet, but that person was a woman, and a woman who had once been fond of him, if the human face could speak. Would she keep his secret? Would he tell her where he lived? It was terrible to think we were such neighbours, and with the thought that it was terrible came a little enlightenment as to what could still be done for the best. He would not tell her where he lived. I knew him too well for that. He would run for it when he could, and the bath-chair and I must not be there to give him away. I dragged the infernal vehicle round the nearer corner. Then I waited – there could be no harm in that – and at last he came.

He was walking briskly, so I was right, and he had not played the invalid to her; yet I heard him cry out with pleasure as he turned the corner, and he flung himself into the chair with a long-drawn sigh that did me good.

'Well done, Bunny – well done! I am on my way to Earl's Court; she's capable of following me, but she won't look for me in a bath-chair. Home, home, home, and not another word till we get there!'

Capable of following him? She overtook us before we were past the studios on the south side of the square, the woman herself, in a hooded opera-cloak. But she never gave us a glance, and we saw her turn safely in the right direction for Earl's Court, and the wrong one for our humble mansions. Raffles thanked his gods in a voice that trembled, and five minutes later we were in the flat. Then for once it was Raffles who filled the tumblers and found the cigarettes, and for once (and once only in all my knowledge of him) did he drain his glass at a draught.

'You didn't see the balcony scene?' he asked at length; and they were his first words since the woman passed us on his track.

'Do you mean when she came in?'

'No, when I came down.'

'I didn't.'

'I hope nobody else saw it,' said Raffles devoutly. 'I don't say that Romeo and Juliet were brother and sister to us. But you might have said so, Bunny!'

He was staring at the carpet with as wry a face as lover ever wore.

'An old flame?' said I gently.

'A married woman,' he groaned.

'So I gathered.'

'But she always was one, Bunny,' said he ruefully. 'That's the trouble. It makes all the difference in the world!'

I saw the difference, but said I did not see how it could make any now. He had eluded the lady, after all; had we not seen her off upon a scent as false as scent could be? There was occasion for redoubled caution in the future, but none for immediate anxiety. I quoted the bedside Theobald, but Raffles did not smile. His eyes had been downcast all this time, and now, when he raised them, I perceived that my comfort had been administered to deaf ears.

'Do you know who she is?' said he.

'Not from Eve.'

'Jacques Saillard,' he said, as though now I must know.

But the name left me cold and stolid. I had heard it, but that was all. It was lamentable ignorance, I am aware, but I had specialised in Letters at the expense of Art.

'You must know her pictures,' said Raffles patiently; 'but I suppose you thought she was a man. They would appeal to you, Bunny; that festive piece over the sideboard was her work. Sometimes they risk her at the Academy, sometimes they fight shy. She has one of those studios in the same square; they used to live up near Lord's.'

My mind was busy brightening a dim memory of nymphs reflected in woody pools. 'Of course!' I exclaimed, and added something about 'a clever woman.' Raffles rose at the phrase.

'A clever woman!' echoed he scornfully; 'if she were only that I should feel safe as houses. Clever women can't forget their cleverness, they carry it as badly as a boy does his wine, and are about as dangerous. I don't call Jacques Saillard clever outside her art, but neither do I call her a woman at all. She does man's work over a man's name, has the will of any ten men I ever knew, and I don't mind telling you that I fear her more than any person on God's earth. I broke with her once,' said Raffles grimly, 'but I know her. If I had been asked to name the one person in London by whom I was keenest *not* to be bowled out, I should have named Jacques Saillard.'

That he had never before named her to me was as characteristic as the reticence with which Raffles spoke of their past relations, and even of their conversation in the back drawing-room that evening; it was a question of principle with him, and one that I like to remember. 'Never give a woman away, Bunny,' he used to say; and he said it again to-night, but with a heavy cloud upon him, as though his chivalry was sorely tried.

'That's all right,' said I, 'if you're not going to be given away yourself.'

'That's just it, Bunny! That's just – –'

The words were out of him, it was too late to recall them. I had hit the nail upon the head.

'So she threatened you,' I said, 'did she?'

'I didn't say so,' he replied coldly.

'And she is mated with a clown!' I pursued.

'How she ever married him,' he admitted, 'is a mystery to me.'

'It always is,' said I, the wise man for once, and rather enjoying the *rôle*. 'Southern blood?'

'Spanish.'

'She'll be pestering you to run off with her, old chap,' said I. Raffles was pacing the room. He stopped in his stride for half a second. So she had begun pestering him already! It is wonderful how acute any fool can be in the affairs of his friend. But Raffles resumed his walk without a syllable, and I retreated to safer ground.

'So you sent her to Earl's Court,' I mused aloud; and at last he smiled.

'You'll be interested to hear, Bunny,' said he, 'that I'm now living in Seven Dials, and Bill Sikes couldn't hold a farthing dip to me. Bless you, she had my old police record at her fingers' ends, but it was fit to frame compared with the one I gave her. I had sunk as low as they dig. I divided my nights between the open parks and a thieves' kitchen in Seven Dials. If I were decently dressed it was because I had stolen the suit down the Thames Valley beat the night before last. I was on my way back when first that sleepy square and then her open window proved too much for me. You should have heard me beg her to let me push on to the devil in my own way; there I spread myself, for I meant every word; but I swore the final stage would be a six-foot drop.'

'You did lay it on,' said I.

'It was necessary, and that had its effect. She let me go. But at the last moment she said she didn't believe I was so black as I painted myself, and then there was the balcony scene you missed.'

So that was all. I could not help telling him that he had got out of it better than he deserved for ever getting in. Next moment I regretted the remark.

'If I have got out of it,' said Raffles doubtfully. 'We are dreadfully near neighbours, and I can't move in a minute, with old Theobald taking a grave view of my case. I suppose I had better lie low, and thank the gods again for putting her off the scent for the time being.'

No doubt our conversation was carried beyond this point, but it certainly was not many minutes later, nor had we left the subject, when the electric bell thrilled us both to a sudden silence.

'The doctor?' I queried, hope fighting with my horror.

'It was a single ring.'

'The last post?'

'You know he knocks, and it's long past his time.'

The electric bell rang again, but now as though it never would stop.

'You go, Bunny,' said Raffles, with decision. His eyes were sparkling. His smile was firm.

'What am I to say?'

'If it's the lady let her in.'

It was the lady, still in her evening cloak, with her fine dark head half hidden by the hood, and an engaging contempt of appearances upon her angry face. She was even handsomer than I had thought, and her beauty of a bolder type, but she was also angrier than I had anticipated when I came so readily to the door. The passage into which it opened was an exceedingly narrow one, as I have often said, but I never dreamt of barring this woman's way, though not a word did she stoop to say to me. I was only too glad to flatten myself against the wall, as the rustling fury strode past me into the lighted room with the open door.

'So this is your thieves' kitchen!' she cried, in high-pitched scorn.

I was on the threshold myself, and Raffles glanced towards me with raised eyebrows.

'I have certainly had better quarters in my day,' said he, 'but you need not call them absurd names before my man.'

'Then send your "man" about his business,' said Jacques Saillard, with an unpleasant stress upon the word indicated.

But when the door was shut I heard Raffles assuring her that I knew nothing, that he was a real invalid overcome by a sudden mad temptation, and all he had told her of his life a lie to hide his whereabouts, but all he was telling her now she could prove for herself without leaving that building. It seemed, however, that she had proved it already by going first to the porter below stairs. Yet I do not think she cared one atom which story was the truth.

'So you thought I could pass you in your chair,' she said, 'or ever in this world again, without hearing from my heart that it was you!'

II

'Bunny,' said Raffles, 'I'm awfully sorry, old chap, but you've got to go.'

It was some weeks since the first untimely visitation of Jacques Saillard, but there had been many others at all hours of the day, while Raffles had been induced to pay at least one to her studio in the neighbouring square. These intrusions he had endured at first with an air of humorous resignation which imposed upon me less than he imagined. The woman meant well, he said, after all, and could be trusted to keep his secret loyally. It was plain to me, however, that Raffles did not trust her, and that his pretence upon the point was a deliberate pose to conceal the extent to which she had him in her power. Otherwise there would have been little point in hiding anything from the one person in possession of the cardinal secret of his identity. But Raffles thought it worth his while to hoodwink Jacques Saillard in the subsidiary matter of his health, in which Dr Theobald lent him unwitting assistance, and, as we have seen, to impress upon her that I was actually his attendant, and as ignorant of his past as the doctor himself. 'So you're all right, Bunny,' he had assured me; 'she thinks you knew nothing the other night. I told you she wasn't a clever woman outside her work. But hasn't she a will!' I told Raffles it was very considerate of him to keep me out of it, but that it seemed to me like tying up the bag when the cat had escaped. His reply was an admission that one must be on the defensive with such a woman and in such a case. Soon after this, Raffles, looking far from well, fell back upon his own last line of defence, namely, his bed; and now, as always in the end, I could see some sense in his subtleties, since it was comparatively easy for me to turn even Jacques Saillard from the door, with Dr Theobald's explicit injunctions, and with my own honesty unquestioned. So for a day we had peace once more. Then came letters, then the doctor again and again, and finally my dismissal in the incredible words which have necessitated these explanations.

'Go?' I echoed. 'Go where?'

'It's that ass Theobald,' said Raffles. 'He insists.'

'On my going altogether?'

He nodded.

'And you mean to let him have his way?'

I had no language for my mortification and disgust, though neither was as yet quite so great as my surprise. I had foreseen almost every conceivable consequence of the mad act which brought all this trouble to pass, but a voluntary division between Raffles and me had certainly never entered my calculations. Nor could I think that it had occurred to him before our egregious doctor's last visit this very morning. Raffles had looked irritated as he broke the news to me from his pillow, and now there was some sympathy in the way he sat up in bed, as though he felt the thing himself.

'I am obliged to give in to the fellow,' said he. 'He's saving me from my friend, and I'm bound to humour him. But I can tell you that we've been arguing about you for the last half-hour, Bunny. It was no use; the idiot has had his knife in you from the first; and he wouldn't see me through on any other conditions.'

'So he is going to see you through, is he?'

'It tots up to that,' said Raffles, looking at me rather hard. 'At all events he has come to my rescue for the time being, and it's for me to manage the rest. You don't know what it has been, Bunny, these last few weeks; and gallantry forbids that I should tell you even now. But would you rather elope against your will, or have your continued existence made known to the world in general and the police in particular? That is practically the problem which I have had to solve, and the temporary solution was to fall ill. As a matter of fact I am ill; and now what do you think? I owe it to you to tell you, Bunny, though it goes against the grain. She would take me "to the dear, warm underworld, where the sun really shines," and she would "nurse me back to life and love!' The artistic temperament is a fearsome thing. Bunny, in a woman with the devil's own will!'

Raffles tore up the letter from which he had read these piquant extracts, and lay back on the pillow, with the tired air of the veritable invalid which he seemed able to assume at will. But for once he did look as though bed were the best place for him; and I used the fact as an argument for my own retention in defiance of Dr Theobald. The town was full of typhoid, I said, and certainly that autumnal scourge was in the air. Did he want me to leave him at the very moment when he might be sickening for a serious illness?

'You know I don't, my good fellow,' said Raffles wearily; 'but Theobald does, and I can't afford to go against him now. Not that I really care what happens to me now that that woman knows I'm in the land of the living; she'll let it out, to a dead certainty, and at the best there'll be a hue and cry, which is the very thing I have escaped all these years. Now, what I want you to do is to go and take some quiet place somewhere, and then let me know, so that I may have a port in the storm when it breaks.'

'Now you're talking!' I cried, recovering my spirits. 'I thought you meant to go and drop a fellow altogether.'

'Exactly the sort of thing you would think,' rejoined Raffles, with a contempt that was welcome enough after my late alarm. 'No, my dear rabbit, what you've got to do is to make a new burrow for us both. Try down the Thames, in some quiet nook that a literary man would naturally select. I've often thought that more use might be made of a boat, while the family are at dinner, than there ever has been yet. If Raffles is to come to life, old chap, he shall go a-Raffling for all he's worth! There's something to be done with a bicycle, too. Try Ham Common or Roehampton, or some such sleepy hollow a trifle off the line; and say you're expecting your brother from the Colonies.'

Into this arrangement I entered without the slightest hesitation, for we had funds enough to carry it out on a comfortable scale, and Raffles placed a sufficient share at my disposal for the nonce. Moreover, I for one was only too glad to seek fresh fields and pastures new – a phrase which I determined to interpret literally in my choice of fresh surroundings. I was tired of our submerged life in the poky little flat, especially now that we had money enough for better things. I myself had of late had dark dealings with the receivers, with the result that poor Lord Ernest Belville's successes were now indeed ours. Subsequent complications had been the more galling on that account, while the wanton way in which they had been created was the most irritating reflection of all. But it had brought its own punishment upon Raffles, and I fancied the lesson would prove salutary when we again settled down.

'If ever we do, Bunny!' said he, as I took his hand and told him how I was already looking forward to the time.

'But of course we will,' I cried, concealing the resentment at leaving him which his tone and appearance renewed in my breast.

'I'm not so sure of it,' he said gloomily. 'I'm in somebody's clutches, and I've got to get out of them first.'

'I'll sit tight until you do.'

'Well,' he said, 'if you don't see me in ten days you never will.'

'Only ten days?' I echoed. 'That's nothing at all.'

'A lot may happen in ten days,' replied Raffles, in the same depressing tone, so very depressing in him; and with that he held out his hand a second time, and dropped mine suddenly after as sudden a pressure for farewell.

I left the flat in considerable dejection after all, unable to decide whether Raffles was really ill, or only worried as I knew him to be. And at the foot of the stairs the author of my dismissal, that confounded Theobald, flung open his door and waylaid me.

'Are you going?' he demanded.

The traps in my hands proclaimed that I was, but I dropped them at his feet to have it out with him then and there.

'Yes,' I answered fiercely, 'thanks to you!'

'Well, my good fellow,' he said, his full-blooded face lightening and softening at the same time as though a load were off his mind, 'it's no pleasure to me to deprive any man of his billet, but you never were a nurse, and you know that as well as I do.'

I began to wonder what he meant, and how much he did know, and my speculations kept me silent. 'But come in here a moment,' he continued, just as I decided that he knew nothing at all. And leading me into his minute consulting-room, Dr Theobald solemnly presented me with a sovereign by way of compensation which I pocketed as solemnly, and with as much gratitude as if I had not fifty of them distributed over my person as it was. The good fellow had quite forgotten my social status, about which he himself had been so particular at our earliest interview; but he had never accustomed himself to treat me as a gentleman, and I do not suppose he had been improving his memory by the tall tumbler which I saw him poke behind a photograph-frame as we entered.

'There's one thing I should like to know before I go,' said I, turning suddenly on the doctor's mat, 'and that is whether Mr Maturin is really ill or not!'

I meant, of course, at the present moment, but Dr Theobald braced himself like a recruit at the drill-sergeant's voice.

'Of course he is,' he snapped – 'so ill as to need a nurse who can nurse, by way of a change.'

With that his door shut in my face, and I had to go my way, in the dark as to whether he had mistaken my meaning, and was telling me a lie, or not.

But for my misgivings upon this point I might have extracted some very genuine enjoyment out of the next few days. I had decent clothes to my back, with money, as I say, in most of the pockets, and more freedom to spend it than was possible in the constant society of a man whose personal liberty depended on a universal supposition that he was dead. Raffles was as bold as ever, and I as fond of him, but whereas he would run any risk in a professional exploit, there were many innocent recreations still open to me which would have been sheer madness in him. He could not even watch a match, from the sixpenny seats, at Lord's Cricket-ground, where the Gentlemen were every year in a worse way without him. He never travelled by train, and dining out was a risk only to be run with some ulterior object in view. In fact, much as it had changed, Raffles could no longer show his face with perfect impunity in any quarter or at any hour. Moreover, after the lesson he had now learnt, I foresaw increased caution on his part in this respect. But I myself was under no such perpetual disadvantage, and, while what was good enough for Raffles was quite good enough for me, so long as we were together, I saw no harm in profiting by the present opportunity of 'doing myself well'.

Such were my reflections on the way to Richmond in a hansom cab. Richmond had struck us both as the best centre of operations in search of the suburban retreat which Raffles wanted, and by road, in a well-appointed, well-selected hansom, was certainly the most agreeable way of getting there. In a week or ten days Raffles was to write to me at the Richmond post office, but for at least a week I should be 'on my own'.

It was not an unpleasant sensation as I leant back in the comfortable hansom, and rather to one side, in order to have a good look at myself in the bevelled mirror that is almost as great an improvement in these vehicles as the rubber tyres. Really I was not an ill-looking youth, if one may call oneself such at the age of thirty. I could lay no claim either to the striking cast of countenance or to the peculiar charm of expression which made the face of Raffles like no other in the world. But this very distinction was in itself a danger, for its impression was indelible, whereas I might still have been mistaken for a hundred other young fellows at large in London. Incredible as it may appear to the moralists, I had sustained no external hall-mark by my term of imprisonment, and I am vain enough to believe that the evil which I did had not a separate existence in my face. This afternoon, indeed, I was struck by the purity of my fresh complexion and rather depressed by the general innocence of the visage which peered into mine from the little mirror. My straw-coloured moustache, grown in the flat after a protracted holiday, preserved the most disappointing dimensions, and was still invisible in certain lights without wax. So far from discerning the desperate criminal who has 'done time' once, and deserved it over and over again, the superior but superficial observer might have imagined that he detected a certain element of folly in my face.

At all events, it was not the face to shut the doors of a first-class hotel against me, without accidental evidence of a more explicit kind, and it was with no little satisfaction that I directed the man to drive to the Star and Garter. I also told him to go through Richmond Park, though he warned me that it would add considerably to the distance and to his fare. It was autumn, and it struck me that the tints would be fine. And I had learnt from Raffles to appreciate such things, even amid the excitement of an audacious enterprise.

If I dwell upon my appreciation of this occasion it is because, like most pleasures, it was exceedingly short-lived. I was very comfortable at the Star and Garter, which was so empty that I had a room worthy of a prince, where I could enjoy the finest of all views (in patriotic opinion) every morning while I shaved. I walked many miles through the noble park, over the commons of Ham and Wimbledon, and one day as far as that of Esher, where I was forcibly reminded of a service we once rendered to a distinguished resident in this delightful locality. But it was on Ham Common, one of the places which Raffles had mentioned as especially desirable, that I actually found an almost ideal retreat. This was a cottage where I heard, on inquiry, that rooms were to be let in the summer. The landlady, a motherly body, of visible excellence, was surprised indeed at receiving an application for the winter months; but I have generally found that the title of 'author', claimed with an air, explains every little innocent irregularity of conduct or appear-

ance, and even requires something of the kind to carry conviction to the lay intelligence. The present case was one in point,
and when I said that I could only write in a room facing north,
on mutton chops and milk, with a cold ham in the wardrobe in
case of nocturnal inspiration to which I was liable, my literary
character was established beyond dispute. I secured the rooms,
paid a month's rent in advance at my own request, and moped
in them dreadfully until the week was up and Raffles due any
day. I explained that the inspiration would not come, and asked
abruptly if the mutton was New Zealand.

Thrice had I made fruitless inquiries at the Richmond post
office; but on the tenth day I was in and out almost every hour.
Not a word was there for me up to the last post at night. Home
I trudged to Ham with horrible forebodings, and back again
to Richmond after breakfast next morning. Still there was
nothing. I could bear it no more. At ten minutes to eleven I
was climbing the station stairs at Earl's Court.

It was a wretched morning there, a weeping mist shrouding
the long straight street, and clinging to one's face in clammy
caresses. I felt how much better it was down at Ham, as I
turned into our side street, and saw the flats looming like mountains, the chimney-pots hidden in the mist. At our entrance
stood a nebulous conveyance that I took at first for a tradesman's van; to my horror it proved to be a hearse; and all at
once the white breath ceased upon my lips.

I had looked up at our windows and the blinds were down!

I rushed within. The doctor's door stood open. I neither
knocked nor rang, but found him in his consulting-room with
red eyes and a blotchy face. Otherwise he was in solemn black
from head to heel.

'Who is dead?' I burst out. 'Who is dead?'

The red eyes looked redder than ever as Dr Theobald opened
them at the unwarrantable sight of me; and he was terribly
slow in answering. But in the end he did answer, and did not
kick me out as he evidently had a mind.

'Mr Maturin,' he said, and sighed like a beaten man.

I said nothing. It was no surprise to me. I had known it all
these minutes. Nay, I had dreaded this from the first, had
divined it at the last, though to the last also I had refused to

entertain my own conviction. Raffles dead! A real invalid after all! Raffles dead, and on the point of burial!

'What did he die of?' I asked, unconsciously drawing on that fund of grim self-control which the weakest of us seem to hold in reserve for real calamity.

'Typhoid,' he answered. 'Kensington is full of it.'

'He was sickening for it when I left, and you knew it, and could get rid of me then!'

'My good fellow, I was obliged to have a more experienced nurse for that very reason.'

The doctor's tone was so conciliatory that I remembered in an instant what a humbug the man was, and became suddenly possessed with the vague conviction that he was imposing upon me now.

'Are you sure it was typhoid at all?' I cried fiercely to his face. 'Are you sure it wasn't suicide – or murder?'

I confess that I can see little point in this speech as I write it down, but it was what I said in a burst of grief and of wild suspicion; nor was it without effect upon Dr Theobald, who turned bright scarlet from his well-brushed hair to his immaculate collar.

'Do you want me to throw you out into the street?' he cried; and all at once I remembered that I had come to Raffles as a perfect stranger, and for his sake might as well preserve that character to the last.

'I beg your pardon,' I said brokenly. 'He was so good to me – I became so attached to him. You forget I am originally of his class.'

'I did forget it,' replied Theobald, looking relieved at my new tone, 'and I beg *your* pardon for doing so. Hush! They are bringing him down. I must have a drink before we start, and you'd better join me.'

There was no pretence about his drink this time, and a pretty stiff one it was, but I fancy my own must have run it hard. In my case it cast a merciful haze over much of the next hour, which I can truthfully describe as one of the most painful of my whole existence. I can have known very little of what I was doing. I only remember finding myself in a hansom, suddenly wondering why it was going so slowly, and once more awaking to the truth. But it was to the truth itself more than to the liquor that I must have owed my dazed condition. My next recollection is of looking down into the open grave, in a sudden passionate anxiety to see the name for myself. It was not the name of my friend, of course, but it was the one under which he had passed for many months.

I was still stupefied by a sense of inconceivable loss, and had not raised my eyes from that which was slowly forcing me to realise what had happened, when there was a rustle at my elbow, and a shower of hothouse flowers passed before them, falling like huge snowflakes where my gaze had rested. I looked up, and at my side stood a majestic figure in deep mourning. The face was carefully veiled, but I was too close not to recognise the masterful beauty whom the world knew as Jacques Saillard. I had no sympathy with her; on the contrary, my blood boiled with the vague conviction that in some way she was responsible for this death. Yet she was the only woman present – there were not half a dozen of us altogether – and her flowers were the only flowers.

The melancholy ceremony was over, and Jacques Saillard had departed in a funeral brougham, evidently hired for the occasion. I had watched her drive away, and the sight of my own cabman, making signs to me through the fog, had suddenly reminded me that I had bidden him to wait. I was the last to leave, and had turned my back upon the grave-diggers already at their final task, when a hand fell lightly but firmly upon my shoulder.

'I don't want to make a scene in a cemetery," said a voice, in a not unkindly, almost confidential whisper. 'Will you get into your own cab and come quietly?'

'Who on earth are you?' I exclaimed.

I now remembered having seen the fellow hovering about during the funeral, and subconsciously taking him for the undertaker's head man. He had certainly that appearance, and even now I could scarcely believe that he was anything else.

'My name won't help you,' he said pityingly. 'But you will guess where I come from when I tell you I have a warrant for your arrest.'

My sensations at this announcement may not be believed,

but I solemnly declare that I have seldom experienced so fierce a satisfaction. Here was a new excitement in which to drown my grief; here was something to think about; and I should be spared the intolerable experience of a solitary return to the little place at Ham. It was as though I had lost a limb and someone had struck me so hard in the face that the greater agony was forgotten. I got into the hansom without a word, my captor following at my heels, and giving his own directions to the cabman before taking his seat. The word 'station' was the only one I caught, and I wondered whether it was to be Bow Street again. My companion's next words, however, or rather the tone in which he uttered them, destroyed my capacity for idle speculation.

'Mr Maturin!' said he. 'Mr Maturin, indeed!'

'Well,' said I, 'what about him?'

'Do you think we don't know who he was?'

'Who was he?' I asked defiantly.

'You ought to know,' said he. 'You got locked up through him the other time, too. His favourite name was Raffles, then.'

'It was his real name,' I said indignantly. 'And he has been dead for years.'

My captor simply chuckled.

'He's at the bottom of the sea, I tell you!'

But I do not know why I should have told him with such spirit, for what could it matter to Raffles now? I did not think; instinct was still stronger than reason, and, fresh from his funeral, I had taken up the cudgels for my dead friend as though he were still alive. Next moment I saw this for myself, and my tears came nearer the surface than they had been yet; but the fellow at my side laughed outright.

'Shall I tell you something else?' said he.

'As you like.'

'He's not even at the bottom of that grave! He's no more dead than you or I, and a sham burial is his latest piece of villainy!'

I doubt whether I could have spoken if I had tried. I did not try. I had no use for speech. I did not even ask him if he were sure, I was so sure myself. It was all as plain to me as riddles usually are when one has the answer. The doctor's alarms, his unscrupulous venality, the simulated illness, my own dismissal, each fitted in its obvious place, and not even the last had power as yet to mar my joy in the one central fact to which all the rest were as tapers to the sun.

'He is alive!' I cried. 'Nothing else matters – he is alive!'

At last I did ask whether they had got him too; but thankful as I was for the greater knowledge, I confess that I did not much care what answer I received. Already I was figuring out how much we might each get, and how old we should be when we came out. But my companion tilted his hat to the back of his head, at the same time putting his face close to mine, and compelling my scrutiny. And my answer, as you have already guessed, was the face of Raffles himself, superbly disguised (but less superbly than his voice), and yet so thinly that I should have known him in a trice had I not been too miserable in the beginning to give him a second glance.

Jacques Saillard had made his life impossible, and this was the one escape. Raffles had bought the doctor for a thousand pounds, and the doctor had bought a 'nurse' of his own kidney, on his own account; me, for some reason, he would not trust; he had insisted upon my dismissal as an essential preliminary to his part in the conspiracy. Here the details were half humorous, half gruesome, each in turn as Raffles told me the story. At one period he had been very daringly drugged indeed, and, in his own words, 'as dead as a man need be'; but he had left strict instructions that nobody but the nurse and 'my devoted physician' should 'lay a finger on me' afterwards; and by virtue of this proviso a library of books (largely acquired for the occasion) had been impiously interred at Kensal Green. Raffles had definitely undertaken not to trust me with the secret, and, but for my untoward appearance at the funeral (which he had attended for his own final satisfaction), I was assured and am convinced that he would have kept his promise to the letter. In explaining this he gave me the one explanation I desired, and in another moment we turned into Praed Street, Paddington.

'And I thought you said Bow Street!' said I. 'Are you coming straight down to Richmond with me?'

'I may as well,' said Raffles, 'though I did mean to get my kit first, so as to start in fair and square as the long-lost brother from the bush. That's why I hadn't written. The function was a day later than I calculated. I was going to write to-night.'

'But what are we to do?' said I, hesitating when he had paid the cab. 'I have been playing the Colonies for all they are worth!'

'Oh, I've lost my luggage,' said he, 'or a wave came into my cabin and spoilt every stitch, or I had nothing fit to bring ashore. We'll settle that in the train.'

AN UNEXPECTED POTENTIAL

Rheinallt saw the faint gleam peeping from the outer edge of Wirtellin's boot, a starlit reflection straight as a knife edge.

The haywire was under Rheinallt's arm, his big hand wrapped around the trigger guard. It was pointing negligently between the two of them, and he waggled the barrel slightly in a gesture universally understood.

Wirtellin leaped forward, with arms flung up to protect his helmet—the only mortally vulnerable target for a haywire dart.

Rheinallt didn't try for the helmet.

As Wirtellin was in his second stride, Rheinallt shot him in the torso with a dart and, with a sigh of bioelectrical release, pumped five thousand volts down the wire.

Wirtellin stiffened convulsively, and a bright white arc flashed from his trailing foot down to the ground where he collapsed in a heap.

Glenavet knelt by this new corpse added to this dead world. He peered into the helmet, felt through the thin airsuit at neck and wrist, and finally stood up.

He stared at Rheinallt, then said slowly, "Are you human?"

THE SHADOW OF THE SHIP

Robert Wilfred Franson

A Del Rey Book

BALLANTINE BOOKS • NEW YORK

A Del Rey Book
Published by Ballantine Books

Copyright © 1983 by Robert Wilfred Franson

The Shadow of the Ship was first published as a novella in 1976;
Copyright © 1976 by Franson Publications.

Translation of Parmenides is by John Mansley Robinson, in his
An Introduction to Early Greek Philosophy, reprinted by permission of Houghton Mifflin Company; Copyright © 1968 by John
Mansley Robinson.

The included poems first appeared in *The Oasiad: Waysong of a
Pilgrim Mind*; Copyright © 1980 by Robert Wilfred Franson.

Library of Congress Catalog Card Number: 82-90920

ISBN 0-345-30688-0

Manufactured in the United States of America

First Edition: May 1983

Cover art by David B. Mattingly

For Dean M. Sandin
—since March 1959—

Contents

The moving Moon went up the sky,
And nowhere did abide;
Softly she was going up,
And a star or two beside—

Her beams bemocked the sultry main,
Like April hoar-frost spread;
But where the ship's huge shadow lay,
The charmed water burnt alway
A still and awful red.

Beyond the shadow of the ship
I watched the water-snakes:
They moved in tracks of shining white,
And when they reared, the elfish light
Fell off in hoary flakes.

Within the shadow of the ship
I watched their rich attire:
Blue, glossy green, and velvet black,
They coiled and swam; and every track
Was a flash of golden fire.

—SAMUEL TAYLOR COLERIDGE

It is necessary to speak and to think what is; for being is, but nothing is not. These things I bid you consider. For I hold you back from this first way of inquiry; but also from that way on which mortals knowing nothing wander, of two minds. For helplessness guides the wandering thought in their breasts; they are carried along deaf and blind alike, dazed, beasts without judgment, convinced that to be and not to be are the same and not the same, and that the road of all things is a backward-turning one.

—PARMENIDES

1. Caravaneers

SEEING SOMEONE ABOARD WHOM HE DID NOT RECOGNIZE SUR-
prised Rheinallt. After all these clockdays spent traversing the
flat and endless night of subspace, there hardly could be anyone
new.

"Where've *you* been hiding?" he asked her. "Snaking along
the Blue Trail with us like an invisible sprite?"

Rheinallt's questions sounded casual, almost bantering, as
he thudded into a leather seat in the lounge car of the caravan.
The young woman had been sitting there quietly, alone, when
he had entered; she looked out of place. Why couldn't he
remember seeing her before? He had by now not only a mental
picture, but a rough characterization also of each passenger,
but this one he had somehow missed.

She took a while to gather a reply. "Here and there," she
answered with a shrug. "I'm not invisible."

Purposefully he let his attention wander to the nearby low
bartop, as if he had forgotten her already. A groundside handbill
had been pressed to the counter and varnished over thickly,
and Rheinallt pretended to study this. From a glassy depth big
glowing letters spoke the slogan:

Come with Eiverdein!
Extend the Accessible Galaxy!
Scientists and Adventurers
wanted for a
Special Caravan.

Rheinallt had half turned away from this young woman who should not be a stranger, when her outlines seemed to blur slightly, and he blinked to clear his eyes. The blur remained. He glanced to his own hands, to the ornate carved-wood ceiling, to a neatly dressed oldster passing by. All these appeared normal. Then back to his companion.

She was visibly wavering. Squinting did not sharpen the focus.

The black pseudosurface of the subspatial meadow was smoother under the caravan's runners than it had been in several days' traveling. No side effect of the caravan's motion could affect only her.

There was a barely perceptible vibration passing all through her, skin rippling like breeze-ruffled water, a girlish blush in motion rather than in color. As if she were trying to hold down a pneumatic drill meant to be operated by a man with twice her mass. That cloud of dark hair might develop a blurred outline from the ventilator currents, but surely not her face? Or slim arms? It couldn't be his own vision, for nothing else had blurred or wavered.

And then, after only twenty seconds at most, the effect stopped.

There are no unconnected monads: no chance, randomness, or events which merely occur, floating in isolated splendor. And certainly not here, not aboard the Special Caravan where Rheinallt liked to think that all was carefully foreseen.

Rheinallt frowned heavily. "By your accent, you're not from the Nation," he probed, not gently.

His statement was a fabrication, as he could not identify dialects from a couple of sentences in a language not his native one. In the last couple of years he had worked hard to minimize his own accent. Fortunately the habitual quirks of gesture and interpersonal distance, so important for intimacy and offense, had all the usual variations among the Trail worlds.

She was even slower to respond this time. In the distance

2

came a faint sound of someone sobbing, an edgy, lonely appeal. Passengers and crew alike were all under the steady tension of their over-prolonged journeying. So he shouldn't contribute to it himself. Rheinallt visualized his bushy eyebrows, so heavily frowning a moment before, floating lightly up his forehead and blending guerillalike into the upper waves of hair. This image, although a little foolhardy for a bloodsweater to dwell upon, was silly enough that his mood lightened sufficiently for a smile.

The young woman was mollified. "No, I'm from Fleurage," she said finally. "A forest world on the Yellow Trail."

Her mouth was red, relaxed now and pretty; almost smiling, but hovering somewhere short of warmth. That same off-balance repose in her eyes showed only far distances, empty dawn sky without horizon.

Rheinallt nodded. "Galactic Northwest, right? I've heard of it."

Her lips tightened slightly. "Oh, I don't know any astronomy. But certainly it's out of the way."

"Out of the way of general trade, at least," he agreed.

"Yes!" she said too abruptly. With more control she returned, "And you?"

She watched Rheinallt now with an elaborate coolness as she took a sip of her wine. Definitely quite young, or an innocent; not his type, or not for some while yet, anyway, he thought.

"From Blueholm," he temporized. "In the Blue Free Nation."

"Blueholm Station. Our jumping-off point, I remember, but I was there only briefly. A busy city." She paused, then asked with a show of indifference, "Won't you have some refreshment?"

"Might as well." The caravan's bar was not crowded; he turned to Haderun, the bartender; lifted a finger. "What's your name?" he asked her.

"Susannilar."

The bartender unobtrusively slid a drink to Rheinallt's place, withdrew.

"I'm Eiverdein," he told her.

In full, Hendrik Eiverdein Rheinallt, but the rest of the name went with a different territory. Someday he might again get to

3

use it all, and not just the euphonious part. The Earth where he had been given those names was immensely far away.

Rheinallt had been told on occasion that he wielded a heavy hand, but he managed not to crush the mug as he wrapped his hand around it, sipped, and set it down again. Tart and sweet together: two contrasting fruit flavors, one fermented, and not totally mixed.

Susannilar's eyes flicked to the mug and back to his face. "So this is *your* expedition."

"My initiative," he conceded.

Her face appeared a little less thin, a little less of tautness emulating relaxation and a little more actual ease. He revised an opinion: she had not been on the verge of a smile earlier but of a moue of nervous exhaustion. Her fingers trembled, not an optical effect this time but simply strained nerves. Could she really have been hiding?

Most of the hopeful researchers had spent many days on Blueholm, assembling odd collections of instruments. An interesting and sophisticated planet, but Susannilar had intimated that she hadn't had the time or attention to enjoy it. Possibly she had been a late arrival to some larger, established group aboard: an apprentice to some salesman of celebrity science. A supernumerary, even; certainly there were a few of the decorative and entertaining on the caravan, helping to leaven and lighten the long journey.

"When did you first hear of the Ship?" she asked.

He snorted. "The shadow, you mean. The shadow of a ship. We don't know yet what's really out there."

Deliberately she scanned him, and he felt her gaze pass over his face, shoulders, thick hands. It was a childlike analysis from a person new to such processes, but in a strange way this seemed not only an innocent look but a bitter one.

Rheinallt had the feeling then, for the first time since childhood, that someone was *looking* at him; actually seeing not just the publicized trail explorer called Eiverdein, but all of himself at once, as a person. Like the difference in seeing binocularly after one has gone through life with one eye closed or blind, except that this was reversed, this was *being seen* binocularly. He did not like it.

"Whatever Trigotha found out here," she asked after this

4

scrutiny, "it has to be a ship before it can be a shadow, doesn't it?"

"I should think so," he said dryly.

"I mean, I understand Trigotha mentioned a shadow, but there had to be the Ship for there to be a shadow."

His fingers strummed a slow rhythm on the wet-slick wood of the bartop. If this was ingenuousness, he didn't feel drawn by it. Not after that demonstration of binocularity or whatever. The more he mulled that, the more disturbing it seemed. Related to her apparent vibration a few minutes earlier? He ran a quick check on his intraocular muscles and the relevant nerves, but everything seemed fine.

"Our meager data claim there's something there," he told her. "Who knows what it is?"

"Something in the semblance of a vehicle, I hope," Susannilar said slowly. "Did Trigotha say definitely that it was artificial, at least, whatever he found? An artifact?"

Rheinallt stroked his beard. "From the reports I managed to gather, Trigotha's crew had no doubt about that. In fact, I don't think it occurred to any of them that it might be only a natural phenomenon."

She pondered during another sip of wine. "That's not quite as good."

"As if it *had* occurred to them, and they'd analyzed the thing? No."

"But of course if they'd had the airtime and equipment, and had been able to analyze it, our trip wouldn't be an adventure. Just a dangerously long vacation tour."

Susannilar might be more youthfully curious than informed, but she was no fool. She must have kept herself secreted away during the long stretches that had taken the caravan to increasingly less-visited planets, sliding away from the populous centers of humanity's self-defined civilization and the sunlit worlds. Was it belated curiosity that now had drawn her out of her shell?

"So share with me," she persisted. "When did you first hear of it?"

"Well, about a year ago, trans-Blue calendar. Trigotha was the man who found it, of course, and sent back the word before he died."

5

His words brought back his joy at hearing that first vast hint: a starship, an abandoned starship! A real ship to use, freedom from the slow drag along the trails. A way home, for him, insofar as he still had a home in the unwelcoming air of Earth.

"Fifty-four worlds," he mused. "Humanity here travels between stars only where the trails lead, and we only may touch upon those worlds that the trails touch. Enough of infinity to be maddening. All these worlds trapped like beads on a string, on a few colored fragments of string lost by a god and never found."

"More worlds than that," she said. "Hundreds, aren't there?"

"If you count the uninhabitable ones. Poison atmosphere or heavy gravity or airless rock. The caravan'll be passing another of those dubious semiplaces soon. Starved Rock by name: I'm not looking forward to it." He shook his head. "So many places to be, and so few that are worth being at."

"So we need the Ship to expand," she said as if by rote.

"To explore, to grow!" Rheinallt said forcefully. To demaroon himself.

Susannilar made an elaborate shrug, flipping her hands open; then smiled to take any sting out of her failure to empathize. As she gestured, Rheinallt caught a whiff of a perfume like a spring night full of flowers, a multiflora scent full of happy garden memories.

Sensing his interest she said, "The perfume is kind of rare, isn't it? I walk down to hydroponics a lot, but flowering fruit and vegetables can't match it."

"Without exaggeration, it's lovely. Complex, too."

"It ought to be." Her thoughts were far away for a moment. "It's a patent blend invented by the botanist Ytrenath. My grandfather. Using it's a memory splurge as well as a money one."

Rheinallt smiled to encourage her.

"I suppose it's a little funny. My grandfather used to call me a hog in armor when I dressed up in my mother's clothes. You know, awkwardness armed in steel, like a bumpkin in evening clothes. All shined up on the outside. He said I wouldn't learn to grow into Alalortern's clothes just by slipping into them. I'd need to learn to slip out of myself into a bigger, shinier me to be like my mother.

6

"I didn't understand," Susannilar went on, "and got upset. He gave me a sample-size bottle of the eau de millefleurs. I didn't know then how unique it was, or how valuable. He was heir to some traditions, techniques of structure and function. The perfume was only one of his distillations from those techniques. Anyway, the scent's like a childhood reminder to keep learning and growing."

"And did you learn to slip?" Rheinallt asked.

She suddenly was reticent again. "Slip? Ah, yes, to shift."

Ah. But that half-answer was all she would tag onto her anecdote of the perfume. Her expression altered a couple of times, then she turned to gaze absorbedly at the woodwork, her vision calmly tracing the curves of the paneling and molding.

Rheinallt knew only a little of Fleurage, her planet. Persuasively smooth-tongued tradesmen called it the gourd of perfume on the vine of worlds.

Out of place, yes. Restless, idle, bored? Rheinallt had not tried to winnow these adventurers of science, nor even found time before leaving the Nation to know everyone personally. Yet no one came so far as this, and abandoned their worldbeads of knowledge and warmth, without a reason. Perhaps not without many reasons. The meadow could swallow a good billion reasons of a billion people and yet still be neutrally empty, still be dark, still be reasonless and unhuman.

Rheinallt couldn't kid himself that the "Come with Eiverdein!" slogan was anything but bait. The Ship was the hook on the line.

Susannilar was wrapped in her insistent repose. Rheinallt swiveled to look outward, toward the object of his thoughts — as if calling the pseudosurface an object made an easier mental footing, or the homely label of "meadow" could pin the concept of subspace to a tolerant ground.

The caravan's bar ran lengthwise along one of the sectioncars. Facing the bartender—so the patrons could keep their backs to it if they chose—was a window of reinforced glass which swept along one entire wall for the length of the car.

Out there was the meadow, the bottomlands of nothingness. Hard vacuum it was, and else, and other. The black emptiness beneath the universe, the dead medium for the gossamer trails. One scholar of the philosophy of mind had deemed the meadow

7

to be the Significant Other to life itself, as though it were outside the light which a conscious mind could cast.

A motion within the car caught Rheinallt's eye. From the forward door Arahant padded noiselessly into the room, his muscles bunching and rolling under the fleecy white fur. The catadrome was built rather like a lynx and walked like one, with the feline quality of ignoring anything unworthy of his attention. His gaze passed Rheinallt without acknowledgment, but lingered briefly on Susannilar. Did he notice something strange about her too?

Arahant jumped gracefully to a high shelf behind the bar, barely touching a barstool on the way up. There he settled and coolly surveyed the rest of the room.

"Is that the aircat?" Susannilar asked hesitantly.

"Yes. Arahant is his name."

"From very far away? I never heard of aircats until this caravan."

"Very. 'Catadrome' is part of the technical name, meaning down-running. Perhaps I could get him to show you some time."

Rheinallt didn't try to tell her *Catadromous dermaptera*, in a language of which she had never heard. Certainly he wouldn't explain all of Arahant's talents any more than he would his own. Some things are best kept in reserve. Arahant and he had been marooned in exile together, and both were far from home.

"A number of passengers prefer to avoid sight of the meadow altogether," Susannilar offered, dropping her attention from the aircat to the various people sitting below Arahant's shelf. "Even among us adventurers and investigators."

"No wonder." The wonder that was there wasn't in the avoidance.

"Don't you worry about people getting drunk to hide from meadow-fear? I've only been on a few caravans before, short-run rurals on the Yellow Trail. None of them had anything like this lounge."

"The bar *is* elaborate: did that deliberately. Designed it myself, in fact."

She twisted her mouth in a faint show of disgust. "How could you take such a risk? You're the captain-of-caravan. One drunken fool could endanger us all."

"Is that why you've been hiding in your compartment?"

"What? I haven't been hiding." She seemed surprised. "I've seen you, Eiverdein, lots of times. I even talked with you for a minute on Blueholm. I didn't know who you were, but I remember seeing *you*."

Rheinallt let that drop. "The lounge car performs several functions for me. One is that advertising the bar beforehand minimized how much alcohol came aboard among the luggage and scientific equipment. Prohibition isn't something I could or would do. Another function is to not let anyone's consumption get out of hand, without being too officious. Haderun there knows everyone aboard by now and has a fair idea of their tolerances."

Susannilar laughed. "That's great. Those rural caravaneers out Fleurage way are deathly afraid that someone would get drunk and broach the air."

"Justified, too. Get half seas over and snatch at an airhose to keep upright, we'd start feeling short of breath. To say nothing of fights poured out of a bottle."

She inclined her head toward a surly man sitting by himself in the corner almost under Arahant's high shelf. "That one could make a fight without being liquored up."

Rheinallt glanced that way. "That's Wirtellin; doesn't even need an antagonist to make a tussle. A natural hothead. I've exchanged words with him a couple of times, and once when he tried to slug me, I decked him."

Alarmed, she asked, "Are you armed?"

"Of course," he said mildly.

"Maybe you should have eliminated weapons instead of intoxicants."

"Hah. Impossible, and I wouldn't even if I could. I'm sure there're more knives and machetes aboard than people, to say nothing of bullet guns for indoors and haywires for the meadow. Those weapons are the crew's insurance against *me* doing something weird. Besides, I haven't eliminated alcohol."

"Well, at least you lock up this place periodically, don't you? But all that tubing looks like a mess. Surely cutting into it wouldn't be hard." She stared at the paraphernalia disapprovingly.

"Locking's just to break the routine. All those tubes you see coming down through the tantalus to the spigots can be shut off, and the cabinet tanks sealed. No one's likely to break

9

in, though. Drinking that much will just cause diarrhea. The proof is so low that what you're drinking is mostly fruit juice."

"Oh. It seemed strong enough to me." She sounded disappointed.

"Don't let it worry you. The virtue in what you're drinking is the vitamins to prevent you from getting scurvy."

"I guess I'm still a hick. What's a vitamins?"

"Vitamins, plural. Qualities in fruit your body needs to stay healthy. It's a new theory."

She shook her head. "Developed in the Nation? I never heard of them."

Only a thread of truth here: "Yes. Lots of meadow-interested folks in the Nation are starting to talk about it. Other societies have known about the effects of diet on health over long periods of isolation from natural environments. I'm sure it's valid, and I want everyone staying as well as possible."

Wirtellin had stood up in the far corner and was looking fixedly in Rheinallt's direction. From above Arahant was looking down with his idle whether-to-pounce expression.

"Will you excuse me a moment?" Susannilar said suddenly. "I'll be right back. I'd really like to hear more."

"Surely," Rheinallt said, leaning back in his chair. He meditated on the meadow as an exercise in relaxation, while a corner of his awareness waited for Wirtellin to make his move.

The meadow was a blackened heath, gentle curves and valleys scorched and twisted, as by a universal breath with here and there an old, cold volcanic upheaval. Harsh ashy stubble, dry and curdled black lava, the embodiment of emptiness. For its entire breadth the meadow supported only hard vacuum on its pseudosurface. Fixed ashiness that no breeze would ever stir, twisted with the ancient gravitational gradients. Space below the space where things of nature or things of man could exist naturally, unattended. Subspace that could be moved across, but not resided in except as on the lip of a grave.

Each trail was a royal road, beneath no light of stars, which ran from planet to occasional planet: a deathly trap baited with commerce.

Even these knowledgeable caravaneers aboard had no idea of the exotic geometries of Earth which tried to map four dimensions of "normal" star-strewn spacetime onto the darkly twisted two-dimensional subspatial plane of the meadow. Travel

10

could plod along without geometry if there were marked traversable routes.

No stars shone. But the trail was here, and *it* shone.

"Say, Eiverdein!"

Without moving his head Rheinallt glanced aside at the speaker, saying nothing.

Wirtellin's eyes narrowed. "You are a man of peace?"

"Usually." Rheinallt readied his electrotoned muscles, in case this wasn't a philosophical gambit but a warning.

Wirtellin shifted his feet apart. "It's been my observation that peaceful men often come from violent lands, where a snow ax or machete always is visible as the final arbiter."

"And violent men?"

"Men exploiting the appearance of violent strength come from safe lands, where a shove or a punch is the worst of physical results; so violent gestures and attitudes are meaningless except as intimidation or insults."

Rheinallt grinned. "You wish to apply this dichotomy to me rather than to yourself? Remember that not all weapons are as visible as an ax."

"Correct. There is also organization. Come, Eiverdein: from what sort of place do you hail?"

"A cloud-soft land, but there were violent elements."

"You see, you taunt me and my purposes. The men I represent have not grouped together for any ordinary reasons. I weary of asking permission for my activities."

"What have I refused you that's within my gift, Wirtellin? If any caravaneers want to join the Federated Trailmen, that's their business."

Wirtellin snorted. "This isn't a political choice, or a matter of simple personal preference. It's a spiritual commitment, of which you should set the example. The crew are stubborn, and resist banding together for an ideal."

Rheinallt's grin hardened. "Whose ideal? We talked about this before we left the Nation. Who wears the ring in his nose, and who tugs on the rope?"

"It's not a matter for humor, Eiverdein! Nor for sarcasm. The men need spiritual leadership."

Rheinallt shrugged, looking up at him. "Free men are usually too busy *doing* to worry about who's leading. These are hardworking caravaneers, not worshipers of any person or or-

11

ganization. They sure won't take any guff from me about their celestial mission. Their mission is to keep this caravan intact while it moves, and they do it well."

Wirtellin's fists clenched at his sides. "You're stifling their higher faculties."

"I am? Anybody with guts enough to take a walk on the meadow is a pretty substantial person on my list. And anybody who tries that without all his or her higher faculties in high gear is a gone gosling. As you well know."

"You mock me, Captain. Worse, you balk the legitimate urges to spiritual wholeness of those in your care, even if they are intransigent Bluebacks like yourself."

Rheinallt laughed. "No wonder you haven't had success recruiting in the Nation. Coming way out here isn't going to help. Wirtellin, get out of here. I won't stop your talking, but you sure need a better line. I'm a leader, not a master."

Wirtellin held his right arm stiffly, made as though to shake something out of his sleeve.

With a look that glittered like a cold blade, Rheinallt shook his head slightly. He remained seated but he looked coiled. In a very soft tone he said, "Don't do it. I've had to hurt you once before; I shouldn't need to again, and I'll give you a last warning." Without changing expression he spat a small gob of blood onto Wirtellin's shirtfront.

After a moment of shock and disgust, and another of obvious internal debate, Wirtellin turned and stalked off to the door leading to the rear of the caravan, and left the car.

Rheinallt let out a long slow breath, and let his mood lift again by running his glance affectionately along the trail.

2. On the Trail of Light

AT THIS POINT IN THE VENTURE THE TRAIL WAS AN EERIE, MISTY blue with an elfin inner glow, its gentle curve revealing the forward cars of the Special Caravan. Small in the distance ahead were the forty teams of giant squeakers, the plodding draft behemoths which drew uncomplainingly a few men and their works between places where there are worlds. In the lonesome illumination of the forward gas spotlight, these waybeasts were huge clots of golden hair, thick legs pumping slowly, with here and there a gleam of ivory tusk.

The squeakers' individual strides, their jerks and pulls, averaged to a smooth rhythm for the caravan. To the passengers, after initial nausea in a few cases, the sense of motion had been integrated into the sense of place and no longer was in conscious awareness. To the crew, the rhythm was normal and soothing, a life-pulse whose beat they could feel.

Outside, a narrow handcar-sized sled was being winched forward on the trail, alongside and parallel to the caravan. The cable drawing it stretched tautly to a side-jutting joist in the lead car. The motive winch mounted at the bow of the sled was hand-cranked by the airsuited sled rider, the sled gaining in relative position to the caravan at about a human's walking pace. Friction from the trail wasn't high for an object in contact with a man or a squeaker, and the crewman precisely cranking kept the handcar sliding smoothly forward.

Turning the winch was a young rifleman named Bremolando. A long-barreled haywire, harpoonlike but distinctive with its reel of microwire mounted below the stock next to the bandolier, was slung across his back. A gas lantern, fed air through a tiny tube from his own suit, was clipped to his chest and lit his immediate vicinity. The glistening of sweat visible on his face within the helmet came from the repetitive exercise of crank, relax, crank, relax, rather than any real strenuousness of the activity.

Rheinallt was reminded of the twist and cramp of the crank in his own gloved hand as he worked similar mechanisms himself on various meadow outings. In the lounge his fingers spread and flexed in sympathy.

Behind Bremolando and occupying the entire rest of the sled was a yard-thick, four-yard-long metallic cylinder of compressed oxygen. For some reason, perhaps of balance, the caravan's cargomaster had ordered it shifted forward. The air in the ventilation system was cycled throughout all the cars in the caravan, but there were a number of such reserve tanks carried unconnected to the system. With luck those tanks all would return home unbroached, but in case of catastrophe or some extreme perversity in the automatic controls, quite a lot of air would be left.

A donkey engine would have been nice, thought Rheinallt, even one of the pre-electric types the Trails culture used groundside. On the meadow, though, the standard was muscle power, human or waybestial. The gas lighting aboard was risky enough. Combustion engines were rarely ventured in vacuum.

As the people in the lounge idly watched Bremolando's steady cranking, on one turning the cable snapped off clean at the winch and whipped itself forward out of sight.

With a short, sharp whistled note of annoyance, Rheinallt cast off his cloak of repose and stepped quickly to the window, but already too late. Bremolando had immediately stepped off the sled and was sprinting ahead along the trail, his feet outlined by the glowing blue in that one-foot-always-touching-down gait peculiar to travelers on the meadow.

Susannilar had returned quietly and stood beside Rheinallt

14

at the lounge window, fingertips pressed to the insulated glass. Glancing aside, Rheinallt hesitated a moment recognizing her face: it was incredibly hard to hold in the memory.

Rheinallt unclenched his big hands from the railing in front of the glass, pulled on the overhead cord, two sharp tugs. On the second tug the cord broke, and with a flick of thick fingers the remnant was cast into a corner. In moments the caravan began slowing to a halt with jerks of couplers and creaks of air fittings.

"What's happening?" Susannilar asked.

"Too late. He's gone after the cable." Rheinallt moderated his pulse. The damage was done.

Susannilar pointed outside in astonishment. "Look at the sled! It's breaking up!"

"It's reverting to starspace, without the help of a squeaker. Which means it's disintegrating. Unguarded metal can't take the strain here."

There was a gigantic green flash from the forward end of the caravan, gone in an instant.

"Uh-oh. Something upset one of Whitnadys' beasties," Rheinallt explained. "I'll bet the cable end hit one of them like a snapping whip. If so, I'm sure it was surprised and annoyed."

Susannilar craned her head to see forward better, uselessly. The flash itself had lasted longer on the retina, in afterimage, than on the meadow.

"I hope that was all," Rheinallt added. "A really angry squeaker could be a lot more trouble than a lost hand sled and a lost container of oxygen."

While they were talking the sled and cylinder continued disintegrating. Shortly there were only a few big shards of the thin hull of the sled itself. A breach opened in the tougher cylinder and a puff of misty air appeared, to vanish instantly. Then the shards were gone and the now-broken airtank followed quickly. The whole process extended so many seconds only because the accident had been on the trail; if the sled had been abandoned a few yards more to the side, on the black vastness, a wink would have missed its going.

Everyone in the lounge had swiveled to watch the outside scene. Some now slipped out to other cars and quietude, others watched Rheinallt. From his high shelf Arahant gazed down with cat-lidded eyes.

"So the squeakers are dangerous after all?" Susannilar asked.

She was staring fascinatedly at the spot of trail where the sled had rested so heavily just moments before. The gently blue trail was quiescent underneath instead of sliding by, but there was no evidence now that the sled had ever existed. Except that the squeaker teams had ceased to pull the caravan forward.

Susannilar went on in a rush, "Everyone among the passengers has been reassuring everyone else that waybeasts are calm and docile. And that the caravan is solid as a rock." She waved at nothingness where tank and sled had been. "Could *we* go like that?"

"It's happened," Rheinallt admitted. "But if no one panics, we're a lot less likely to go off the deep end."

Her eyes were wide. "It's really happened? A whole caravan?"

"Yes. For instance, the *Blue Signjack*, a mail express. They tried to turn on a bad patch for some reason—no one ever knew why. They turned too sharply and broke the back of the caravan. In the ensuing panic and confusion the whole thing was lost. There was an unconnected witness trailing way behind on a tramp sled or we would not know even that much."

"He didn't panic." She indicated where the rifleman had legged it hastily out of sight toward the caravan head.

"Haste. Thoughtlessness."

"It wasn't his fault," she pleaded.

"The accident, probably not. The loss was."

Another minute or two passed beside the empty trailside, which glowed with its elfin glow upon the blackly frowning meadow.

Only some of the big natural-gas spotlights on each caravan car's roof were lit. They didn't have energy to waste trying to illumine the endless empty leagues of pseudosurface. Several spotlights, clustered on the roof of the leading car, probed the general area ahead. One or two others were always watching backward from the caboose: a post of boredom for card-playing crewmen, this far from civilized or barbarous sources of traffic. From a middle car two more spotlights stabbed into the darkness on either side of the route.

Right behind the leading brace of squeakers, quiet now in their traces, was another light pointing between the waybeasts

16

directly onto the trail, adding extra illumination to the next hundred yards to be traversed. The squeakers didn't need the light, but it made the beast handlers' worries of guiding the caravan bearable. Gravitic irregularities often could be predicted by seeing the pseudosurface's malformations ahead with an experienced eye. In case of extreme fluctuations, the caravan could be slowed, or even segmented temporarily to cross.

Like constant-level pedestrian routes everywhere, the glowing Blue Trail followed smooth graviclines, staying within quite tolerable gravitic ranges. Only veteran trailmen noticed the subtle fluctuations, but even so, small side lights along the caravan flanks were kept lit to aid their footing outside whether the whole shebang was moving or still.

Sometimes subspace was dull as a grave to a gravedigger. Other times "trailman's luck" or competence ran thin and the grave ate.

Two human figures appeared, walking back down the trail alongside the motionless cars. One slouched along dejectedly, clearly Bremolando in the glare of the roof spotlights. The shorter one was Whitnadys, waving a fist and apparently shouting, though with meadow-vacuum between the two this was patently useless.

The sign language woven by the luminous-painted fingertips of her gloves was a flashing dance of disapproval. Intersign, the language grown up for vacuum usage among the Trail worlds, had as much potential for invective as speech and body language combined, and she was using a lot of it.

Bremolando became even more hangdog as they reached the empty site beside the lounge car: no sled, no oxygen tank.

"Who's the angry one?" Susannilar asked from within the window. "Her signing is too fast for me to follow."

"Whitnadys," Rheinallt identified. "She's the beast handler." Her function as lead teamster actually was a biological analogue for chief engineer. Rheinallt would have been surprised if Susannilar could follow any of the signing outside. "It's also trailsign she's using, technicalese and specialized cusswords."

Rheinallt tried to lip-read Whitnadys' torrent of spoken commentary, but her intervening gestures and half-facing toward Bremolando as she strode made this too difficult. He could guess, though. Bremolando avoided looking at her.

17

Rheinallt waved to get the attention of the two outside, then beckoned them in. As they walked into the lounge from the intercar airlock, still in suits except for helmets, all the onlookers fell quiet.

"Eiverdein—" Whitnadys began.

"Cool it down," he said, palm upraised. "The sled is wasted. That's not a fatal loss. But next time, Bremolando, unsling your haywire and zip a dart across to the caravan, then crossfasten the sled's mooring cable to keep a solid contact. *Then* go after your towing cable."

"Right, Captain." Bremolando shifted his haywire sling. "The cable didn't have any defective or Use-Last tag on it. Looked good to me."

"Just tell the cargomaster about it when you ask him if he still needs an oxygen tank forward. Is anything left of the fore part of the cable?"

"Nothing," Whitnadys stated. "It slapped one of my squeakers and then its momentum broke it right off at the stanchion. Poof!" She chopped one hand down. "And then Dort flashed green; almost blinded me."

Turning to the rifleman, Whitnadys added, "Lucky it was Dort who got hit, and not one of the more excitable ones. I like to put Dort last, next to the cars, because he's so stolid."

Rheinallt said to her, "You're lucky it wasn't you that got hit. The cable would have sliced you in two."

"Yes!" Whitnadys agreed. "The end snapped forward must have been like a scimitar before it broke."

"Take care on your end, too," Rheinallt told Whitnadys. "Check over the cables, capstans, and whatnot at the caravan head; and make sure your drovers are really into living according to the safest procedures."

"I don't—" Whitnadys began, then recalled the listening bystanders in the lounge. "Well, we've got plenty of margin, but no sense throwing any away. Bremolando, I'm sorry I got mad, but we're beyond the reach of help out here."

Bremolando spread tired hands. "No problem. I understand. Take care, that's the word."

"Good," Rheinallt concluded, gesturing a genial dismissal. "No major harm done." He signaled the bartender to hand him the speaking tube from behind the bar, said clearly into it,

18

"This is Eiverdein. Proceed. I say again, proceed.

"We'll have to schedule some mobility training next time the caravan stops," Rheinallt mentioned to Whitnadys, loudly enough for bystanders to take note. "Airlock and airsuit procedures; how to walk safely on the meadow; maybe some useful words of trailsign. We're all deaf, dumb, and crippled out there on the meadow. The pseudosurface is entirely treacherous enough to change those handicaps into death, if what we do on that terrain so close to death isn't second nature."

Whitnadys grinned. "Crew, too?"

"Sure. They'll teach; they shouldn't mind too much. Refresh their own reflexes while they help the passengers."

"I'll enter it in the tickler file," Whitnadys promised. "Man, I'm tired. I'll make sure the waybeasts are settled down to slogging again, and then I'm turning in. See you soon?"

"Not directly, but not too long," he answered.

Later, when the lounge was nearly deserted, Rheinallt slipped into a sleepy contemplation of the slow-passing panorama of the meadow.

He estimated that the light-minutes dropped behind at a man's good marching pace, at the steady lumbering of the squeakers. A light-minute every half-second, a light-year every three days; a trail speed.

The squeakers would not leave the trails, but no means other than the squeakers could pull a train of cars on the meadow. The great creatures projected a mentational field, as yet unanalyzable in the Nation, that buoyed the merely material. An unenhanced man or woman in an airsuit could carry or drag over the rough stubble a mass several times his or her own, but multiweek supplies required waybeasts.

Rocketry alone wouldn't suffice in subspace. More societies than this one had launched rockets from a trail or directly from a sled, and seen them disappear. The darkness "above" the meadow was not what men thought of as space: it could not be traveled in.

Rheinallt felt a tremor working its way down the articulated caravan. The leading cars were crossing a rough stretch. Weak tremors raced through intercar cables and tubes, the non-load-bearing connectors, then heavier ripples through the solid couplers from car frame to frame set the gas jets wavering and

19

their cast shadows to swaying gently. Then those heavier ripples from ahead were subsumed in the direct vibration as the lounge car's own runners encountered the tiny gravitic variations in the pseudosurface.

Despite such homely traits, transportation on the meadow was not entirely physical: it required a mind. But not even the philosophers had yet fathomed the minds of the silently amenable squeakers, or defined their strange similarity to the minds of men. Mental processes of even the most open of humans in the most natural of settings remained rather mystery than science. Out here they sometimes seemed all mystery; and squeakers' consciousness glowed but opaquely.

Assuming one could strike out boldly across the meadow, and in the vastness find the gravity well of a nontrail world—how then leave the infinitely planed meadow and pass into the cheerful starspace which actually held that world in the warmth of its mother star? Only the waybeasts, squeaking casually in atmosphere, could tug a sled or caravan through breakpoint from hospitable air to vacuum, from planetary surface to subspatial pseudosurface, from good solid dirt to textured nothing. And back again.

Naturally, sometimes worlds the trails touched held only vacuum themselves. These had as many caravans pass, but few stop.

Rheinallt's own origins lay in another part of the field. Ironic, he thought, that in a hugely strung-out culture of fifty-four inhabited worlds he was marooned. Like a continental castaway rafting along an island chain, he longed for the home coastal waters and the sight of Earthly landfalls.

Well, flukes you can't repeat, luck is her own mistress. But rationality helps those who help themselves, so here he was, a caravaneer.

The vibrations in floor and lamp flame had diminished now toward the rear as they had minutes before increased from the head of the caravan. The rough spot was passed.

Haderun the bartender came over to Rheinallt, holding out a folded piece of paper. "A message was left with me for you. There didn't seem to be any hurry, so I decided to wait until you were alone."

"Thanks." Rheinallt unfolded the stiff paper. On ornately flower-bordered stationery he read:

Captain-of-Caravan Eiverdein:

A witch from Fleurage is aboard the caravan.

Do not fear unduly, as she is harmless most of the time, and when she becomes dangerous she also will become vulnerable. At such time I shall act to put an end to the menace.

I will endeavor not to disturb the caravan unnecessarily, but I believe the time for action draws near, and wish you as official in charge to be properly informed.

Nollinsae,
of the Guard of Fleurage

What the hell was this? He put the note in his pocket, feeling the heavy folded paper like a block of wood.

A witch? He hadn't heard that concept used seriously in many years or parsecs.

With wide-open eyes but narrowed pupils he leisurely examined the nearest gaslight fixture, burning steadily with its glass-hooded yellow flame. He could feel the wakeup rhythms in his body clamoring to be let loose, to return him to full readiness. However curious the note might be, though, it really was something to look into rather than react to, and round-the-clock wakefulness he preferred to save for emergencies. He could do without sleep physically, but found it more than cosmetic for mental reknitting.

So far there had been nothing about traveling beyond End-of-Blue that he had not faced before, except perhaps this young woman Susannilar; they were simply farther out on this trail than regular commerce had ever come, passed into unknown subspatial territory where, as far as he knew, only one previous bunch had managed to reach. Yet Rheinallt could feel the mental tension of the caravan's need for life, health, and forward motion, although it was the waybeasts that pulled the Special Caravan and not he.

He stood, agreeing with the capricious caravan clocks that it was time for sleep, and damped down his internal wakeup impulses. It already was late on this watch; Haderun had shut down the bar itself and gone to his bed. Rheinallt decided to assign someone discreet to keep an eye on Wirtellin and his two friends of the Federated Trailmen. There already had been several private disputes on the expedition, one fatal. After

Rheinallt had intervened to stop Wirtellin's manhandling a crewman, the organizer had confined his bullying to the verbal. He would hate to have a genuine donnybrook instigated in the name of a fictitious dispute about spiritual leadership. If Wirtellin were genuinely concerned there might be a complaint based on the snapped cable as a safety violation, but so far Wirtellin had been oblivious to such issues.

The Guardsman Nollinsae and the organizer Wirtellin must have this much in common, he thought, that officials liked to deal with other officials. When there was no corresponding titleholder, they'd try to fasten the burden on some leader of a wholly different kind.

Two other members of the investigating parties which made up the passenger list, both men clad in long coats of crimson fur, strolled through the emptying bar heading for the forward observation car. One carefully carried a large detached telescope lens, an item rare enough to be quite expensive. They were discussing theories of the Ship, and Rheinallt lingered to listen to a few phrases:

"In an ordinary solid," one of the redcoats declaimed to his companion, "the monads or atomic loci are fixed in a framework. But the entire framework is not fixed in space. For instance, a cannonball in trajectory. Now suppose we postulate an absolute solid which is fixed to the fabric of the universe."

The second man, nearly a twin, began speaking immediately the other paused, but his interpretation was altogether different. "The key is time, not space. As we move through time we leave images behind us. A train of husks, a wake. Everyone drags a cometary trail of images after him in the timestream . . ."

They passed out of Rheinallt's hearing. He was left with an odd amalgam of pictures in his mind: an old-fashioned witch on a broomstick, candlelit in the rushes before her, and a whole succession of witch-shadows of the same shape but less substance strung out in the night air behind her.

Time to go to bed, definitely. He walked to the door, looking up at a favorite sign above the bar, which read:

The thread draws the cable, the cable draws the bridge.

He should meet Whitnadys soon, and it was late. The rhythm of motion had been broken and rehealed. He was tired, not with physical effort but with the awareness that held it all together and in forward progression. As he reached the door to the between-cars airlock, he looked at Arahant on the high shelf above the bar. The aircat was still there, and winked at him.

3. Down into Gravity

THE NEXT MORNING, BY GUESS AND BY DEFINITION, FOUND
Rheinallt studying. He had the gaslight turned up to read the
irregularly inked printing.

He thumbed his worn copy of *The Meadow Trails Pilot*. As
an adventure book it was great fun to read while lolling in a
sunny backyard hammock. As a practical guide it had draw-
backs. There were striking examples of inaccuracy, such as
the location of one world on the wrong trail altogether. Other
planets were listed with radically wrong trail lengths; or inhabitants of trailside were lauded as peaceable and friendly
when in fact they had permanent ambushes which were hastily
manned whenever a caravan appeared; or the atmosphere of
another place was less perfumed than it was noxious.

There were no striking examples of accuracy.

The gravitational well into which the Special Caravan had
been winding down since early this clockmorn ought to lead
to the resort of Starved Rock: inhabitants zero, oxygen none,
attractions skimpy, amenities scarcely imaginable. It was a true
landmark, an obstacle rather than an objective. Since it was in
the way they would visit it.

Rheinallt wished it were a landmark already passed. For days he had expected it daily, but without a reliable clock one had to be patient. If such a mechanism could be had in the Blue Free Nation he would have traded a brace of squeakers for it. Nonfunctioning physiological timekeepers were among his injuries when he'd been dumped on Rainstone; but still his gut time-reckoning was as accurate as the wayclock. Of course, when Trigotha himself had found Starved Rock, he'd had no decent clock either to help estimate its location.

Day and night on the caravan were for human convenience only, meadow and waybeasts being uncaring of measured time. Navigation was by the trails and dead reckoning. The measurement of speed relative to starspace depended on whatever mapping algorithm one thought more useful than a wild guess. The charting of distance in yards by counting squeaker strides was laughable.

Even assuming a navigator had a full and capable crew to keep track of niceties—as Trigotha definitely had *not* on his disaster-prone way back—the clockless or semiclocked estimate could only be approximate. Rheinallt wasn't too sure about Trigotha's outward leg either.

He turned thick pages to Ortelius' foreword to *The Meadow Trails Pilot* and read again the claim "All descriptions and distances are by actual survey," and chuckled. He flipped to the end of the long section on the Blue Trail, where on one of several blank pages had been handwritten the thin knowledge on Starved Rock. Ortelius himself had written the short paragraph in this copy; Rheinallt had made a trip to see the great mapmaker, back in the Nation, when being beyond the pale was chafing and he was contemplating various long shots such as this Special Caravan.

The handwritten information was meager:

STARVED ROCK. 18 DAYS BEYOND PREVIOUS END-OF-BLUE AT FARLOST. NO AIR. DIM—NO CHARTABLE STARS VERIFIED. NO SIGNS EVER INHABITED. TRAIL LENGTH ON SURFACE 20–30 YARDS. GOOD LUCK.

Rheinallt smiled at the last phrase in the careful handwriting. In his years Ortelius had seen more men hit the trail than ever would come back, and the expeditionist was warmed by the mapmaker's good wishes: the sentiment was sincere, more than just an apology for the paucity of the information. Or misinformation. Already, with the barren planet not yet attained, the distance cited was short by at least a third.

Lacking a decent clockwork escapement that would move through constant intervals when in dubious and changeable gravity, times and distances given in times were speculative. On the established trade routes there were so many estimates that a brute-force average could be taken as actual. In a few cases astronomical observations could be coordinated and a ratio between calendars established, usually by a solar flare somewhere in starspace where two trail worlds could see it. For more venturesome subspatial routes, compilers like Ortelius were glad when explorers came back with news that a route existed, let alone having enough energy to spare for tinkering with chronometers or tabulating their squeakers strolling along.

The Trails culture was a pleasant group of people to live with. However, if Rheinallt's state of maroonment among them began looking more like a century than a few years, he would have to buckle down seriously to inventing—or reinventing. Electricity certainly was called for, electronics. He had forgotten a lot of rudiments and primitivisms necessary to start that particular industry from scratch. Still, the discipline of electric potential was second nature to him.

Rheinallt looked out the window of his compartment to the great bowl of black outside. A few caravan spotlights probed out and across, revealing little. It looked like a monstrous open-pit mine, dug by the Prince of Darkness for meadow-coal wherewith to stoke eternal fires. The broad gossamer ribbon of trail led down at a long blue slant toward the unseeable bottom, where lay the transition to the whistlestop planet or planetoid.

Oh, yes, size; *mass*. He reread the memorized description. Trigotha, or whoever had passed on Trigotha's words, had neglected to say. Rheinallt was sure that the compiler had written all he knew. He had himself been pumped by Ortelius, sitting in the dark study with the glittering spider web of the master map.

Rheinallt knew a lot more about what lay beyond the edge of that map than Ortelius could possibly guess, but he couldn't

27

say how to get from here to there, so ought he share knowledge of the unattainable? Contact between cultures is a street with two sides and a lot of potholes, a moral question he felt little need to prejudge until he had solved the physical question. Without transportation the next contact besides him might be a very long time, and Rheinallt had lived long partly by being circumspect when necessary. And Arahant even more so.

The meadow obviously could not be merely a two-dimensional map of four-dimensional spacetime. It was properly known as subspatial, following its own esoteric geography. Planetary orbit, solar and galactic movement in starspace were only tangentially significant to the meadow and the trails.

The blurred and binocular girl, Susannilar, had mentioned her grandfather Ytrenath. Now Rheinallt remembered the name: not just a botanist, but a theorist about trails and their possible motions relative to planets. Could that explain why Trigotha's find of the Ship had not been reported before? That the Blue Trail in these obscure parts had shifted enough to bring the Ship within sight of passersby on the trail? Unfortunately that would increase the chances of the Ship's being an old derelict rather than a recent stranding. Of course, the more modern the explorers, the better the airtime they would have in their caravan's tanks, and hence a longer range beyond the last known oxygen planet on any trail.

Whitnadys rang through on the speaking tube. Her voice came out tinnily: "Boss man, we're about there. Do you want me to take a scout before we shoot the works?"

"Definitely. Two squeakers, one to lag. Make the second your quickest responder."

"Least slow, you mean?" she answered with a tinny chuckle.

"Yeah. And pack a standard mortar as well as rifles."

"Gotcha."

"And I'll be along too," he told her. "No saddles this time."

"Dibs on first through."

Rheinallt hesitated. Neither personally nor as a caravaneer did he relish any risk to Whitnadys. Still, it wasn't an excursion, and certainly if anyone was best qualified to sit in a squeaker's howdah and ensure the survival of creature and riders, that person was Whitnadys.

"All right," he said.

"You sound reluctant. Worried about irreplaceable me?"

"Irrepressible you? No, actually more worried about my being on any squeaker other than the one you're riding."

Instantly she dropped the tease. "I'll give you Seebanone as drover. My best apprentice: she's quite good."

"Thanks," he said. She had not questioned that they would not ride together.

She was silent for a few moments, leaving only the faint pressure-sigh of the speaking tube. He imagined fingers pressed lightly to her chin as she thought.

"Do you want me to give the stop order at a likely place? We're close enough for you to suit up," she added.

"Fine. Not too far outside, though." A howdah trip was like wearing a suit of armor in an earthquake, inside a fortieth-floor closet.

"Right. I'll have trail flares set out when we stop, although I'm sure no other caravan's going to be hauling along way out here."

"Be with you shortly. Take care, darling."

She murmured wordlessly in return, then closed the tube.

Unfortunate, Rheinallt thought, that he couldn't simply return to where Whitnadys' caravan had rescued Arahant and himself, marooned on the wet planet he had named Rainstone on the Green Trail. But that was not a stop Earth's starships were likely to be making again, or obstreperous undesirables would not have been dropped there. North of Rainstone, galactically speaking, if one went far enough the Green Trail was stopped cold by the so-called Whitecloud phenomenon, a huge and effective barrier to trail travel.

Rheinallt idly tapped his pen on the edge of the desk. Outside, the huge bowl of blackness seemed even huger: the optical penalty for trying to return, no matter how briefly, to groundside back in starspace.

The caravan moved cautiously downward, feeling its way down the gravitically inclined pseudosurface like a snake in a funnel. At the head were the chryselephantine waybeasts, plodding coarse gold with ivory flashing in the spotlights. Whitnadys would be devoting extra care to them on this downward slope, for psychological reasons. Friction on the meadow was a source of disputation among infraphysicists; at any rate there was enough for traction. The slope here was not so steep that the caravan needed to be reversed, with the squeakers pulling rearward to brake it; but the squeakers' knowledge of the weight of caravan at their backs understandably tended to make them nervous.

Grasping the speaking tube again, with the other hand Rheinallt turned the selector dial to All Hands, then one more notch past that to All Compartments. He turned up the pneumatic booster.

"Let me have your attention, please; this is Eiverdein. Let me have your attention, please." He hunched forward over the desk as he felt the projective urge to move closer to the unseen audience.

"We are about to halt near the bottom of the gravitational well of a planet or planetoid called Starved Rock. Most of you have noticed it on our big wall map in the corridor by the chartroom; it's the last landmark before reaching the Ship. When we're past Starved Rock we ought to be on the last stretch of our outward journey.

"Now, Trigotha was here before us but he didn't pass on any souvenirs. So we're going to stick our nose in first to check it out. I suspect his name for the place describes it well enough, so don't expect dancers and gourmet chefs to cheer us on our way.

"The length of trail on surface is supposed to be only twenty or thirty yards. This is far too short to park the caravan without disassembling it and pulling off the trail. I'm reluctant to do that so far from home, and on a world apparently without air.

"So while a few of us crew go through breakpoint, the caravan will be halted on the meadow. I intend this to be our last stop until the near vicinity of the Ship, and this would be a good time to make a final check of your equipment. If you haven't reproved your airsuit recently, do so.

"Remember, though, this stop will be just long enough to scout the trail through Starved Rock. Do *not* set up any equipment that blocks the corridors, or outside. The auxiliary tent will *not* be set up. If you go outside, *don't* go out of sight.

"Those passengers who would like mobility training to upgrade their meadow-walking skills, report in your airsuits to Car Two, right behind the head of the caravan. And, folks— if you want to be sure of living until your vacuum training starts—even though we're parked, walk up there *inside* the caravan, all right?

"Thank you."

After replacing the speaker tube, he got his airsuit from a locker, unclipped his personal haywire from its wall stand, and pulled a powerful portable light from a bottom desk drawer. He lit the lantern—a process vastly easier while he was still in atmosphere—and suited up. Grabbing the equipment, he went forward to join the other scouts.

Once he actually was in the howdah on a squeaker moving down toward Starved Rock, he felt pleased at how much progress had been made. At least progress of journey: progress of application was yet to be seen. The secrets of the Ship might turn out to be undecipherable, or unusable; the whole expedition a wild goose chase.

He suddenly had a real longing to see again a vee of wild geese slipping past a cloud with a cold wind blowing. Grasses waving on a marsh far below, and the only sound the faintest of honks as an echo from the highest cloud. If a homeward glance could undo the exile, could lift him out of this maze of trails on abstract wing back to fleecy skies where the goose honks high—well, he would be home already.

The well here was tremendously steep as the trail wound down to the surface of the planet. Like a funnel, the upper part was broad, the equivalent of perhaps a hundred planetary diameters. Looking around he could, just barely, distinguish the shape of the well, caravan lights a sparkling string high and to the rear. Toward the bottom the glowing trail defined the funnel tip of the gravitational depths, where the other detached waybeast was a moving spot on the blue thread.

On the far side the trail came up and out again, its light thin but not diminished by intervening distance. In between the well went down and down. The steady rhythm of the squeaker's motion, dampened and softened while on the caravan, was ragged and jouncy in the howdah as though he were trying to breathe but only could cough.

Fortunately the waybeasts weren't built for cavorting, for an all-feet-off-the-meadow leap upward into nothingness would be a one-way jump. We all tend to act as though we're immortal in safety, Rheinallt thought, and avoid believing that immortality comes only through disciplining our own ongoing death.

Yet the meadow's pure pseudosurface, with nothing above and nothing below, will make the nondisciplined into nonexisters quicker than a wink.

The long and powerfully flexible trunk of their waybeast curled around through the open struts of the howdah to slobber briefly against Rheinallt's helmet. A few high-pitched squeaks came down the temporarily air-filled fleshy tube to resound inside the helmet. He reached his gloved hand to squeeze the golden trunk where it was narrow near the tip; after a moment it withdrew from his hand with a slither like rough leather.

He leaned forward and touched his helmet to that of the woman sitting cross-legged in front. "Seebanone, what's this squeaker's name?"

The mahout leaned back to ensure a solid contact, while keeping her eyes on the trail in front. "Deasy."

"Ah, yes. Reliable. Breakout soon?"

"Transition's coming up." Seebanone chuckled. "Deasy's more reliable out of harness than in, according to Whitnadys. He's been good on the slope, but we'll have to see how he'll do reentering starspace and groundside simultaneously without his mates."

She leaned forward, tapping the waybeast's broad shoulder twice lightly with her ankus. The pace slowed slightly, maintaining the interval with Whitnadys' leading squeaker. She straightened but did not make contact again, pointing instead to a side-mounted mirror reflecting her hands, and switched to sign language.

"Breakout very soon," she warned in trailsign. "Ready?"

"Slow down more."

Rheinallt wished that he could handle a subspace breakout himself: without either the waybeast-generated aura or an Earth starship's mind-bending mentation enhancement. Moving in and out of subspace was too strait a gate for the unaided human mind. The Earth culture's enhancement technology which allowed people to pilot starships over the meadow required tremendous portable power. And who could reproduce the unknown, cryptic neuropaths and unobservable techniques within a massive waybestial brain?

He rechecked his safety harness, fingers passing over buckles and quick-release snaps. There had been no indications that

Starved Rock had a sun, so the planet ought to be reasonably stable, cold and solid all the way through. They might break out onto the surface of some gravel pile, although trails and complex multibodies rarely made connection. Emerging into a volcano or triggering a landslide were likelier risks, although still unlikely. Still, Trigotha had had big problems on his way back, some of which might have happened here. In some situation Rheinallt had not been able to pin down, Trigotha must have blundered.

Reckoning that Whitnadys had an adequate lead, Rheinallt was about to give an affirmative to the Ready question, when Seebanone jerked in front of him, rapidly twisting her shoulders to look up their back trail toward the parked caravan.

Seebanone made the quick finger-twirl signifying a twirly, meadow-mad state of affairs. "We're being followed," danced her fingers. "Deasy gave a sort of signal, a body tremor, in reaction to something behind us."

Rheinallt turned for a long look himself, straining a little against the safety harness, scanning carefully up the long slope of the back trail. At a great distance he could see the caravan; nothing else.

"Can you see anything yourself?" he asked her.

"No, but I'm sure there's someone."

"Someone—who?"

"A squeaker," Seebanone amplified. "Either one's wandered off by itself, or more people decided to come ahead of the caravan." With her knees she nudged the waybeast into greater speed forward.

"Deasy reacted to some other squeaker on the trail this side of the caravan?" He glanced back once more.

"I suppose it would have to be. I don't think he could know about something beyond all the confusion where we parked the caravan." She spread her hands in a gesture of uncertainty, then chopped one hand forward suddenly in the most unmistakable motion of caravaneers' technicalese that could be expressed in trailsign: "Breakpoint! Do it?"

"Go!" he told her.

Before he could take another whole breath the squeaker lumbered through the breakpoint from the pseudosurface of the meadow to a relatively normal patch of starspace on the surface

33

of the planet. There was a rainbow coruscation in his mind, a subjective explosion of colors as deeper levels below consciousness reoriented themselves. Solid ground with freckled starspace overhead. Good to be back, sort of.

4. Starved Rock

WHITNADYS STOOD ON GROUNDSIDE A YARD OFF THE TRAIL. She was already dismounted, leaning on her rifle. Her squeaker with its drover still mounted loomed golden above her, its eyes banked down to huge green slits.

Rheinallt grabbed his haywire from clips on the inner wall of the howdah and jumped down. A slight shifting of the rough gravel under his feet reminded him that he was in vacuum nearly as hard as that upon the meadow, and quite as dangerous. He signed to Seebanone to move her waybeast off the trail, and to Whitnadys for voice contact. Unlike the neutral meadow, the rocks were cold under his boots as he walked to Whitnadys.

"Squeakers hate to leave the trail until they're sure we've touched down for a stay," Whitnadys said as soon as they made helmet contact. "I think they consider us unpredictable."

"So do I," he said. "We're being followed."

"What? From the caravan?"

"Apparently. I couldn't see it behind us, but Deasy sensed company. We've a little time yet." He looked around as he gave Whitnadys a moment to digest this.

Starved Rock was dark: a stray without a sun of its own.

The sky was brightly spangled with pinpoint stars, and compared with the meadow the lonely place was bright enough. His night vision was recovering from the transitional dazzling of the inner eye at breakthrough. A few streaks still danced and writhed on his visual field, but the distant mountains were blackly outlined by starlight on the horizon. A rugged world.

Closer to hand were jagged boulders, a giant field of them beginning a couple of hundred yards to one side of the trail and extending until he could no longer discern them from their own shadows. The basic ground was gritty sand and gravel. Not much color, outside of Whitnadys' face and the waiting waybeasts; and in this light any color would have given up the ghost ages ago.

The two giant squeakers glowed like elongated pale boulders among the native rocks, coarse hair and shiny tusks gleaming in gold and ivory, as they ambled aimlessly alongside the trail's thin blue glow.

He leaned again into contact with Whitnadys, noting her puzzled frown. "Could that be a runaway squeaker on the trail behind us?"

"I doubt it," she replied aloud. "No others should have been unharnessed at all. You announced a short stop for a quick scout, and I passed that on to everybody in the beast gang. Besides, squeakers rarely panic; they're the slow-but-sure type."

"Nobody would have released one, then."

"No. I was already out and aground, apparently, before you folks noticed the follower, or our squeaker would have picked it up too. I haven't any ideas. Let's get out of sight of the trail until we see what's going on."

"Right. Good you've got a rifle." Rheinallt looked around at the starlit rubble. "You and I will stay just inside the edge of the jumble over there. We'll send the squeakers farther away so if they're spotted, whoever's coming can assume we're all off exploring mounted."

As they started a fast walk toward the squeakers, though, Rheinallt stumbled. He grabbed Whitnadys' gloved hand and kept his balance.

"Thanks," she signed. "Almost did a nosedive." The starlight was faint on her luminescent-painted glove fingertips.

"You're thanking me? Did you stumble too?"

36

She stared briefly. "Sure. Didn't you see me trip? Or did you just grab me for old times' sake?"

He had to grin, but said, "Forget old times. We both tripped. That was an earthquake."

"Huh. Groundside foolishness. Short and sweet, anyway." Her expression was sour.

"Sure, but we just got here. If the planet's gravitically unstable, I wonder if the trail could be shifting, or the planet drifting beyond the elasticity of the trail to stay in contact."

"Trail elasticity? I bet you just made that up. Say, why don't you get going! I'll look for a hidey-hole."

Rheinallt felt an urge to wipe his face where some sweat was running under his beard; he took a few seconds to reabsorb it. Then a multitude of itches suddenly woke, under the skin-tight suit, and clamored for attention. Suit paranoia: his body wanted *out*, to go home and be safe.

"Those rocks look kind of broken up," he signed. "Don't get caught under anything unstable."

"Hey, thanks for the warning."

He waved her away and, grinning, set off at a cautious lope to tell the two mahouts the plan of action. They had managed to stroll the waybeasts many yards from trailside without getting out of sight. Fine, except he wanted them to be wary, and not come tripping back merrily until called for.

As he went, Rheinallt stole long sweeping glances at the sky, trying without much hope to recognize constellations or any unusual stellar features. Starved Rock was even farther from Earth than the planet of his initial exile, Rainstone; there was nothing he could relate to any landmark from his own neck of the woods.

In newer editions of *The Meadow Trails Pilot*, Ortelius had begun including night-sky star charts as seen from trailside aground on the major commercial worlds. As yet he hadn't covered all even of the standard trade routes within the Blue Free Nation, but the fledgling charts were helping Rheinallt refine his sense of place. Along some routes the locals were so rapacious, or physical conditions so violent, that no useful observations existed.

Ortelius was farsighted enough to see the potential value of knowing the locations of worlds in starspace as well as meadowspace, and slowly was laying foundation blocks for an astronomy which someday could prove immensely useful.

Some traditional old caravaneers had complained bitterly about Ortelius' wasting space and making their handbook thicker. Star charts in a meadow navigation manual, they said, were worse than useless; because however ornamental to armchair browsers, for hardworking caravaneers star charts were a distraction and a nuisance.

This common attitude had amused Rheinallt since the star charts had first appeared in the *Pilot* last year and provoked the first growls. Rheinallt himself could take some of the credit for the innovation, but then he too was a practical man with his own goals.

Reaching the two squeakers, with a few quick signs Rheinallt informed their human riders of his intentions. He heightened his oxygen flow from his backpack, and his metabolic rate to match, and began loping back toward Whitnadys.

Scanning the hard and unwinking stars from this opposite direction, Rheinallt found himself wishing that the Ship somehow could be visible from here. But if it was in starspace, floating among the stars, he would not be able to get at it.

A ferryboat drawn up and left on the far side of a river was a tolerable groundside analogy. It was moored to land, and you're on land, so it is in the same spatial medium you are; but you can't get at it. In contrast, even a *sunken* ferryboat, so long as it is in the shallows on your own side of the river, *is* attainable despite being in a different medium. It can be grappled, hauled out and repaired, and used to reach the far bank.

Only the fact that the Ship seemed to have been stranded or abandoned in subspace made it attainable at all to the Trails culture. If the dubious medium of the meadow had to be traversed beyond previous explorations, that was acceptable. To have a ship again, and slide it on home!

Shortly Rheinallt and Whitnadys were crouched behind a boulder, waiting impatiently for the squeaker which had followed them down into the gravity well. The darkness here among the larger rocks couldn't approach that of the meadow as long as any of the overhead starfield was visible, but it did offer good concealment. Rheinallt wanted to be the one to decide if any encounter would take place.

"Interesting magnetostratification here," he signed to Whitnadys, using for the technical term a rare word from intersign and a common one from trailsign. "I feel more pressures than there ought to be in such a castaway place."

Whitnadys had propped her long-barreled haywire against a small stone to keep the mechanism a few inches off the grit and gravel. She rolled her eyes, signing briefly, "Someday tell me what lodestones have to do with landforms."

With wide-lensed meadow binoculars she watched the point where the trail appeared on the surface, hoping to catch a glimpse in the few unguarded moments which necessarily followed breakout.

To anyone who didn't know that the trail spent most of its length in subspace—and only deigned to touch a planetary surface when the quirks in the gravitational structure of the universe caught the trail like the bottommost droop of a loop of kite string—this groundside snippet of trail would have seemed strange enough.

A god with two paintbrushes must have passed this way: the first stroke had made a bluish roadway twenty-some yards long, and wide enough that a couple of caravans could have passed abreast. A two-dimensional and softened sapphire, stretched into pavement. Then with the brush in his other hand the god swiped the still-wet roadway again, and left an inner aura along those twenty-plus yards, an unworldly radiance within the sapphire mist. The trail glowed with its own light, and was beautiful.

To a traveler, however, the trail segment that was visible would be inseparable in his mind's eye from its vast length in both directions.

Waiting, Rheinallt thought nostalgically of the long familiar vistas where the trail—in his memory—was a blue so intense that it was hypnotic, back where the worlds of the Nation touched the trail and thereby visited with each other at only a few clockdays' distance. Less hypnotic to the eye than the memory, though: he had not even reached the Ship yet, his goal and probable turnaround point, and already he was hankering to go back even to an adopted home and recent memories.

At the end of the visible trail a squeaker suddenly appeared, striding ponderously along without a care in the world. Three men were on its back, in safety harness but without a howdah structure.

Whitnadys flicked the binoculars' focal point from the first to the second to the third of the riders, delaying only a couple of seconds on each. Then she shrugged and handed the binoculars to Rheinallt.

"I'm not sure if I recognize them or not," she said. "They all look sort of familiar, but I can't name them. Sure cold here."

"My job, knowing passengers." He scanned the three on the swaying golden back as quickly as had Whitnadys, nodded, then retraversed them leisurely. "The nearest one is Glenavet; the other two are his henchmen. Wirtellin, for one, and I'm pretty sure Tadako's the drover."

"Well, space them for bringing Duurs down here against my orders," Whitnadys said vehemently, striking the boulder with a fist. "Duurs needs the rest."

Rheinallt grinned inwardly, but not unsympathetically, at her concern for her cherished beastie. He was more curious about the men who had caused a squeaker to be broken out of traces to bring them here.

If Duurs felt disappointment at not being able to fill up his aircells with fresh planetary oxygen, he didn't show it. The extra trek meant nothing special to him.

"Why do you call them henchmen?" Whitnadys asked aloud so suddenly that her helmet made a sharp click striking the side of his.

"Because I think they're all with the Federated Trailmen. Assistants? Glenavet isn't the only one on the caravan who brought along some personal muscle."

His attention remained directed through the lenses.

"Hmm, really? I remember Glenavet now: kind of swarthy guy, looks like he's been around." She paused. "He gave our gang up front a kind of pitch once, garbled economics. But he didn't strike me as a bad type."

"Didn't say he was bad; but he might be dangerous."

"And you knew about him? Oh, Hendrikal. Couldn't you have left him to cool his heels on Blueholm while we were still safe in the Nation? Or quietly dropped him off somewhere along trailside with ten light-years to walk to nowhere?"

"They've dismounted, and now one of them has found something," he reported. "Something small on the ground—I can't make it out. They're handing it around, so it's not just a sample rock."

He looked aside at her briefly. "Darling, we have a whole caravan full of dangerous people. If we had winnowed the tough, the foolhardy, the armed, and the however otherwise dangerous types back on Blueholm, we wouldn't have any adventurers left to be paying passengers. And we couldn't have afforded this expedition, even with my invention royalties."

After a few moments she said quietly, "I follow you."

"Glenavet is interesting. I haven't quite made him out yet. But one of his associates, Wirtellin, dropped some words once in my hearing, about how the anarchic conditions in the Nation would be tremendously improved if all the routes were licensed and policed by the Federated Trailmen. They've already got a chokehold on a few of the outlying branch trails, he intimated."

"Damned monopolists."

"Yes, I think they're trying to set themselves up as the core of a state. Representing working folk is such a low priority for them that when they were nosing around among the people aboard from the Nation itself, they were asking about the Blue Army." Rheinallt still held the lenses glued to his helmet.

"Whatever for?" Whitnadys asked. "That's just the people armed, so to speak. It's not something that could be taken over by outsiders."

"Get up! A couple of them are coming this way."

Quickly they edged away from visibility, back around another giant rock.

Whitnadys waved excitedly. Rheinallt turned to examine where she was pointing. There was a man—a body, he amended. Before he even squatted alongside he could see the desiccation. Obviously a human body, in an ordinary trail airsuit; it had received some kind of fireblast at close range directly into the faceplate. The wearer certainly had died instantly.

A few feet away Whitnadys was examining curiously a high-quality telescope on a portable tripod: a rarity in the Nation, the kind an astronomer might use, rather than a surveyor or military man. An excellent, beautiful instrument that would have been expensive in a more mechanically advanced human culture.

Rheinallt tapped Whitnadys on the shoulder, and again they

41

moved farther into the jumble of gray-black masses, putting more rocks between them and the presumed Federated explorers.

How had the dead man gotten here? Why the telescope? Was he one of Trigotha's decimated crew? As far as Rheinallt knew, and it matched what Ortelius had told him, never before Trigotha had human foot set upon Starved Rock. His own expedition was the second.

Trigotha's much smaller expedition had been first, and that had been strictly a shot in the dark into unexplored and dubious territory. Trigotha had taken his long shot, apparently hit a jackpot, and then died before he could follow up his find or even spread the word as to exactly what it was. But the magical word *starship* had been whispered around: hence the Special Caravan.

Rheinallt had hunted for Trigotha's scattered cohort in half a dozen worlds on the Blue, but all had dropped from sight. He didn't even know how many companions of that ill-fated venture had come back alive. It made sense that one of those companions had fallen here. Yet the tuber's body was not buried, the telescope not salvaged. What had happened?

Their route slanted deliberately through the rocks relative to the trail segment. After a few minutes he found what he wanted: a rock with enough loose rubble flanking it so he could climb, and positioned so he could see, from its top, the gap where the dead telescopist lay. If, Rheinallt thought, the dead man had indeed been the user of the telescope.

Rheinallt lay down across the top of the boulder, haywire convenient to hand. He beckoned Whitnadys up and appropriated her binoculars. He felt the icy cold of the boulder thrusting through his thin airsuit. He raised his body temperature, signing to Whitnadys to lie as much as possible on top of him rather than on the rock directly.

She scrunched over, letting their helmets touch also, but said nothing. He could hear her breathing softly.

After a moment of observation he told her, "They're heading right for the telescope fellow."

"Looks like it. *We* found it by coincidence."

"Yeah."

"It's *possible* that they're going to stumble over the body

42

by coincidence too. How could they possibly know that tuber's there? He's not sitting on a beacon."

"Don't know. Don't like it." Slowly a revised opinion was growing in Rheinallt. "I'm afraid we're getting a hint what kind of people took the trouble to follow us down. What remains is to find out what they're planning to do right now. Maybe I can joggle their elbows."

He handed the binoculars back to Whitnadys. "Can you see the body and the telescope clearly?"

She slid off him, twisted the focus. "Yes. The men are just arriving. One's pointing. You're right—they don't act as surprised as we were."

"Fine. I'll confront them there."

"What are you going to do? Be careful."

"I'll play it by ear. You cover me from here and I'll be all right."

She slid her haywire up and slipped her arm through the sling for the prone firing position. "Stay out of my line of fire."

Rheinallt bumped and slid down the rough back of the boulder and walked the short distance toward the little hollow where the fireblasted man and the telescope lay. It was a dark pocket, for being so near the trail.

Suddenly he realized that the telescope had been set upon its tripod in that particular patch of gravel because the man needed shielding from the trail glow if he was to see the stars at all clearly. Any place along the edge of the field of boulders would have done for watching the groundside trail, and the spot where Whitnadys and he had first stopped was far better for that. But for an undimmed starfield, the extra shadow behind the giant rock was likely the closest good viewpoint.

So why look at the stars from Starved Rock? Charting: a remote possibility, considering Trigotha's circumstances. Could Trigotha's man on the way back have been looking for the Ship in starspace? Did they have reason to expect to see it among stars? Or effects of its presence?

The silence was beginning to feel oppressive. Rheinallt resolved to ask the old singer Lhudesin for a public antidote back at the caravan, some cheerful airs.

Glenavet was startled to see Rheinallt emerge from behind a shadowed boulder. His attention had been on the telescope, his companion Wirtellin's on the dead man; they both straightened abruptly when they saw Rheinallt.

With a minute shake of his head Rheinallt saw the faint gleam peeping from the outer edge of Wirtellin's boot, a starlit reflection straight as a knife edge.

The haywire was under Rheinallt's arm, his big hand wrapped around the trigger guard. It was pointing negligently between the two of them, and he waggled the barrel slightly in a gesture universally understood.

Unfortunately, Wirtellin took a chance. The delegate must really have been longing to attack him, Rheinallt thought, on more or less equal terms. Wirtellin leaped forward, with arms flung up to protect his helmet—the only mortally vulnerable target for a haywire dart. A dart in the body, especially in vacuum, might leave a nasty flesh wound but wouldn't necessarily bleed all your air.

Rheinallt didn't try for the helmet. As Wirtellin was in his second stride Rheinallt shot him in the torso with a dart, and with a sigh of bioelectrical release pumped five thousand volts down the wire.

Wirtellin stiffened convulsively, and a bright white arc flashed from his trailing foot down to the ground. He collapsed forward in a heap, but even most of his momentum had been neutralized by the total muscular contraction that had killed him.

Glenavet stood stock still. After a minute he asked in intersign, with fingers stumbling almost unreadably, "Is he dead?"

Rheinallt signed with his free hand, "I'm sure. Feel free to check."

Glenavet moved forward, eyeing Rheinallt, and knelt by this new corpse added to this dead world. He peered into the helmet, felt through the thin airsuit at neck and wrist, and finally stood up.

"I see you're not a fanatic," Rheinallt signed.

Glenavet's hands stayed visible, but motionless. He shrugged.

"I notice you not only kept your hands away from the knife on his belt," Rheinallt explained, "but you also avoided coming close to that retractile blade in his boot. I think it's melted anyway."

Startled again, Glenavet's eyes flicked to the fallen man's feet. When he raised his look he stared at Rheinallt, then said slowly, "Are you human?"

It was a question he ought to have expected, but he had been more occupied with survival just then than with implication of how he survived. He was tempted to joke that he was more human than Glenavet, but that was not true, although in a philosophical discussion of human potential he might have claimed that.

Although difficult and dangerous, the advantage of electricity as a chosen subject for internal control is its intimacy to normal human functioning. Neural storage and pathways are basically electrical, as are many of the more mechanical processes. Rheinallt's skill was extremely rare even among blood-sweaters.

"Certainly," Rheinallt said with easy gestures. "Did you know that Whitnadys and I have a young son, back on Blueholm?"

"What did you do to Wirtellin, then?"

"It's called electric shock. Perhaps now, Glenavet, you'll tell me what you were doing here." Rheinallt had tweaked off the wire at the rifle's breech, and snapped it around the next dart in the clip.

Glenavet paused, considering. "Never heard of it."

"Nor will you now. Go on."

The other shuddered visibly in his airsuit. "Ah—did you know that Wirtellin actually was my superior in the Federated Trailmen? Not in an administrative sense, but in a sort of ideological way. He was cadre, and I wasn't, although I've had charge of more people." Glenavet looked uncertain at whether this would be understood, or believed; his hands dropped from their signing. "Do you follow me?"

Sure. Church and State, Party and State; cadre and cannon fodder. There were lots of setups like that. "I've run into such before."

"You have?" Glenavet seemed to exchange one uncertainty for another. Probably he thought his organization pioneering not only in virtue but in structure.

"Yes," Rheinallt emphasized. That was part of the cause of his exile, but he wasn't about to explain. "So Wirtellin *was* the fanatic then; truly."

Glenavet was about to assert his own dedication with some bluff and hearty statement of commitment, but thought better of it.

45

Rheinallt's feet were growing colder, and he didn't want to prolong this. "Bury them," he signed, pointing to the older corpse and the new. "Gravel's all right. Drag them together and make a mound. I'm sorry we can't have a farewell now; we'll try it on the return trip. And be straight—you're also covered at a distance."

"I know. I saw a glint of starlight on metal, right after you came up. Another reason not to have jumped."

While the other was burying, Rheinallt dismantled the telescope into its major components: main tube, small area-spotting scope, tripod, and universal mount between tube and tripod. Whitnadys had come down at his wave; she and Rheinallt each fastened one of the smaller pieces to their belts, then she shouldered the tripod and he the telescope. It wasn't as heavy as it looked.

The three of them walked back to the trail segment, Glenavet in the lead.

Waiting for the squeakers to regather, Whitnadys signed, "They came for that telescope; they knew just about where it was. Could the Federated Trailmen have been gathering information back on Blueholm when you were?"

"Don't know," Rheinallt said thoughtfully. "Take your squeaker and briefly check out the opposite breakpoint, then come back here. I don't think Starved Rock itself is a problem."

"And the people on it?" she demanded.

"If all the people on the planet return aboard the caravan simultaneously, we'll worry about them on the caravan. Glenavet hasn't yet shown any homicidal inclinations, and I don't think he will."

Glenavet's drover, Tadako, took in the changed situation stolidly, offering no comment as Rheinallt checked him for weapons. None: they hadn't been expecting a conflict.

Whitnadys climbed onto the waybeast patiently awaiting her. The squeaker wheeled ponderously about, and trudged in a few long strides to the opposite breakpoint, and through.

"Your compartment is in Car Nine, isn't it?" Rheinallt asked Glenavet.

"Yes," he signed readily enough. "I take it you want more information?"

"You got it; I want it."

"Are you putting me under arrest?"

"Not unless you offer violence yourself. I'm not a jailer. I'll come and talk after we've got the whole works clear on the other side of this rock."

"I'll be there," Glenavet promised.

Tadako was uninterested in the whole proceeding. Patently he was the one of the trio who was along mostly as muscle.

After a few minutes Whitnadys and her assistant reappeared on their waybeast. She halted briefly, waved, and sent the squeaker trundling back toward the nearer end of the trail segment and the breakpoint that led to the parked caravan. Rheinallt signaled to her that Glenavet's squeaker would follow her, and that Seebanone and he would bring up the rear.

Before Rheinallt mounted to leave the relatively safe vacuum of the starspatial, ordinary graveled surface of Starved Rock, he took a few giant leaps right off the ground for the sheer joy of that unconfined action. He came down on his feet, yanked a deep breath out of the suit's airtank, and jumped again. He couldn't do that on the meadow's pseudosurface— at least, no more than once, an absolutely final act. Here it felt good, refreshing.

Still, he was looking forward to being out of sight of this sad groundside. When they brought the caravan through they would not halt at all. Not a rest stop he could recommend to Ortelius to flag in the handbook.

5. Federated Trailmen

GUIDING THE WHOLE CARAVAN DOWN INTO THE WELL AND spiraling up was taxing, if not unusual. As manager of a good crew, Rheinallt had little to do once the go command was given. Deliberately he had brought no novice trailmen along, having carefully paid more for those who knew what they might be getting into, could avoid disaster if it was avoidable, and if disaster struck had already a good idea of what to do to get out of it.

There was one bad moment when a minor earthquake occurred, with parts of the fourteenth and fifteenth cars on the groundside stretch of trail. Starved Rock, though lacking tidal forces of a solar primary or of significant satellites of its own, was none too stable. A few people were jerked around or fell, but there were no injuries beyond bruises.

Slightly more material damage resulted. The main intercar speaking tube snapped when the cars rocked. A couple of gas lamps popped their chimneys and threatened to toast all and sundry, but a little scurrying soon had them capped. No fires developed, although one lamp made a scarily flaming torch in a corridor for a few minutes.

The speaking tube was even less trouble to fix. Rheinallt couldn't quite see how it had taken up all its slack and popped, while the comparatively inflexible metal couplers had just shrugged and grated their knuckles and kept their grip. Rheinallt had been on the tube, talking forward, when the sudden clutch at his gullet with wind whistling past his face toward the vacuum at the tube's break made him gulp and gasp. The simple mechanical safety valves justified their existence before he had suffered more than a dry-chilled tongue. For some moments thereafter, though, he was champing for extra saliva and swallowing excessively.

Everyone on the caravan managed to get a glimpse of Starved Rock as that world of starlit rocks and violent death streamed past outside the insulated windows. A glimpse only, for the twenty-odd yards of trail was traversed by each car in a period of a few breaths. Passengers regretted that the caravan was too long to stop in such a restricted space without first being laboriously dismantled and then carefully reassembled. As much as they might have enjoyed diversionary sightseeing, no careful caravaneer would do it. The strains the two starspace breakpoints imposed on the articulated structure of the caravan were not to be risked any longer than necessary.

At least a transit of Starved Rock was vacuum to vacuum. On an inhabited world it was vacuum to air to vacuum, which put more strain on all the little joints and flexible seals that kept the caravan alive. In those cases normal procedure was to disassemble on the meadow and make a commercial stop, with local squeakers coming out like tugs to bring the caravan's components down to groundside. In the Blue Free Nation, where groundside trail segments were luxuriously long blue runways that an entire caravan could stop on, travel and trade boomed.

Pulling the leading cars off a trail, groundside, while the trailing cars were still the other side of breakpoint, on the meadow, usually led to infraphysical problems. The physical outcome was that the trailing part of the caravan still on the meadow telescoped into the breakpoint and did not emerge into normal starspace. Presumably going off the trail, groundside, meant one more energy-level difference than the trail could accommodate, or the waybeasts compensate for.

So they chugged through Starved Rock as a unit, and stayed

on the trail. Being on solid ground for a few moments was nice, but the vision of unknown stars whetted the impatience to be on to the Ship.

When the rearmost car was safely back upon the meadow, and the whole caravan was slowly moving up the trail on the other slope of the gravity well, Rheinallt went to see Glenavet.

On the way he stopped by his own stateroom and woke Arahant.

The aircat was curled up in his favorite armchair like a fluffy white lynx. As the door closed behind the man on entering, Arahant's eyes snapped open, his nose wrinkling. "Gas! I smell gas, Hendrik!"

"It's okay. Already capped, and the leak wasn't in this car anyway."

Arahant eyed the man askance, nose still wrinkling. "I'll take your word for it, but you know I've a sensitive nose. Besides, the gravity's changed again."

"Yes, we're past the planet, going up and out."

The catadrome yawned. "That's nice. So what's the drift?"

"Going to see Glenavet, like I told you. Come along?"

"Sure." He stood up, stretched, and leaped lightly down to the floor. "Am I supposed to do anything besides decorate the occasion?"

Rheinallt shrugged. "Back me up, if I need it. And keep your trap shut."

"Can do. But playing dumb can be tiresome, you know. Not that you and Whitnadys aren't fascinating company—"

"I do know that none of these people have ever run into nonhuman sentience, and while we're stranded among them isn't the time to be the great enlighteners. They don't even know anything, really, about squeakers."

"Whitnadys is a member of this culture."

"She rescued us. She knows damn well we're outsiders."

Arahant laughed, a low musical purr. "Just pulling your tail. Let's swoop." He walked on all fours to the door, reached up one paw and twisted the doorknob, then dropped quickly back down as the door swung open. He sauntered into the corridor, where Rheinallt couldn't remonstrate with him without breaking his own rule.

In the ninth-car corridor they encountered Whitnadys.

"Hi, sweetheart," she called out. "Going to hear Lhudesin?"

Rheinallt kissed her quickly. "Can't right now. Is he set up to sing already?"

"Starts pretty soon. Can't you come?" She looked at him appealingly, swung her honey-brown hair in a swishing semi-circle like an invitation to a dance.

He hooked a thumb at a nearby door. "Got to see Glenavet."

She nodded slowly. "Right. Did you tell Bremolando where you'll be?"

"Yes. And Arahant will be with me."

Whitnadys looked down at the aircat, who winked at her. "Be careful, and come down as soon as you can. We'll be jammed into the lounge car again."

"Don't let them hold up the proceedings for me."

Whitnadys laughed. "No way. But I'll wait for you there."

Inside his compartment, Glenavet rose from behind a small desk to offer a handshake. "Hello, Eiverdein. Glad we finally have a chance to talk."

"And I," Rheinallt replied rather dryly.

Calmly Glenavet asked, "I don't understand how you killed Wirtellin, but I'd like to know. Then I'd like to know why."

"When attacked with deadly force, I tend to respond with deadly force."

Arahant, whose lower-level stalk into the compartment had gone unnoticed by Glenavet, now padded softly over to a position right beside the desk. His ears were white cones pointed upward as he listened.

"Please say on," Glenavet said.

"I'm not trying to provoke you. But let me ask: did you know about that blade in Wirtellin's boot?"

Glenavet hesitated. "Yes."

Crossing his arms, Rheinallt leaned forward, still standing. "Point one: the attack was Wirtellin's choice. Two: we were in a situation where even horseplay could kill accidentally. Three: if Wirtellin's intent had been to immobilize me, to secure some purpose of his own, he wouldn't have triggered the spring of that concealed blade. I doubt you'd have done otherwise in my place."

Glenavet settled back in his chair with a half-smile and let his eyes close for a few moments. The lines on his face smoothed and he looked relaxed. Relieved.

Arahant turned to Rheinallt and nodded. Muscles rippled under the white fur as the catadrome relaxed in his turn. Then he began taking deep breaths in succession without breathing out, and his airsacs ballooned out from his belly like water wings. After a few more breaths he floated gently upward toward the ceiling. He reached out a paw and snagged the bracket of a gas lamp and floated there, the picture of ease.

Glenavet opened his eyes as he heard the humming. "What's that? Oh, that thing—I've seen it around. What is it?"

"An aircat. His name's Arahant."

"Never saw one before this trip. A floater, huh? Most unusual. Where do they originate?" Glenavet was talking to let his own thoughts coalesce.

Rheinallt hesitated. "Way the hell-and-gone out somewhere."

"Guess so." Glenavet turned back to the other man. "Frankly, I'm relieved by what you say. I agree with your analysis. And that means I have no quarrel to pick with you myself."

On those grounds, anyway, Rheinallt thought. And it's lucky for him, another part of his mind couldn't resist adding. But he was glad of it.

"Won't you sit down?" Glenavet asked, gesturing toward a chair.

"Now, yes, thanks." He sat, but stayed alert.

"You *aren't* going to tell me what you did to Wirtellin."

"Sorry. You wouldn't understand the half of it."

Glenavet nodded. "Perhaps not." He steepled callused fingers. "I'm along on this expedition partly as an observer for the Council of Federated Trailmen. You knew this already."

"I'm surprised at three. Perhaps I ought to be flattered."

"Well you might be. We Federated Trailmen tend to be practical fellows, not dabblers in astronomy or chasers after so-called star-traveling vehicles. Three passages on your Special Caravan were fiendishly expensive, to pay for this first-rate crew and team of squeakers, and that young mountain of supplies you've got in the storage cars. But you set a good table, Captain, so I guess it's worth it."

Glenavet grinned reminiscently as he went on. "You should have seen the Council when they heard your prices! They nearly choked. They'd already put down deposits for three reservations, so they figured they were committed. That's when they

53

decided to send Wirtellin along to get their money's worth. I can't say I've been glad of the help."

"Well, the food wouldn't justify a gourmet's ticket," Rheinallt said, "but it's good and simple, and as you say, I brought a lot of it. Plenty of margin for a good diet." Let Glenavet choose the topics, he thought.

"I can see by the menu you're following the new theories."

Glenavet also seemed in no real hurry to press things now. For that matter, hadn't he successfully avoided Rheinallt's attention almost perfectly prior to Starved Rock?

"I'm a caravaneer myself, Eiverdein. I've been on a few long ones where we all got cramps and sore gums, and on a couple where crewmen died. Scurvy is bad news. I'm glad you know what you're doing!" he added in a burst of apparent sincerity.

"And the air, man!" Glenavet went on in the same vein. "The air is so good! Coming out of that airsuit, the caravan air was heavenly. Your hydroponics is the best I've ever traveled with."

Rheinallt leaned back. "Well, thanks. Part of the freshness owes to extra species for nutrition. They flavor the air as well."

"You do impress me as knowing what you're doing. Would you let me have a list of your live plants, with ratios and schedules and such?"

"I'll have a copy made up. Still, half the passengers have complained about the air. Good you appreciate it."

Glenavet snorted. "They just haven't been out enough. They want a groundside spring breeze in vacuum. Wait till they spend some time in an airsuit. Me, I once spent eight days in a suit inside a busted car, waiting for another caravan to come along."

"It came eventually?"

"Sure. But by that time I was having delusions—I was going to take a hike off onto the meadow to look for a water hole. That pool I was imagining wasn't for dunking, it was for breathing, to cool my lungs. I was about at my limit."

The chair was comfortable, and as Rheinallt listened to Arahant humming arias in the background, he found himself warming to a fellow meadow hand, talking shop. People who lived only in their workaday worlds and never brushed death in vacuum couldn't appreciate how gloriously fine were simple breaths of oxygen.

54

"I've been in some tight spots myself," Rheinallt admitted. "For a while I thought I was in one down on Starved Rock."

"I think you were," Glenavet agreed simply. "I hadn't wanted to barge down on you like that, but both your exploring squeakers were away down the trail already when we got up to the front of the caravan. So we sneaked out one and came along anyway. Wirtellin's idea."

"You might have told me ahead of time."

"To what point? Would you have let us? Passengers?"

"Probably not. But in the case of something to do with Trigotha's expedition—" for now Rheinallt avoided probing just what—"I could have made an exception."

Scrunching around in his chair, Glenavet laid empty hands palm up on the desk. "I didn't know myself."

"Entirely on Wirtellin's initiative? I wish I'd known his intentions. I might have headed him off somehow."

"He was secretive by nature. He enjoyed it."

That was a definite statement. Perhaps because Rheinallt wasn't even traveling under his own full cognomen, he decided to go along with that.

"The orders were not shared," Glenavet went on. Fingers drummed on the desk in what must have been a long-smoldering frustration. "That's worse than silly, but the Council's a little paranoid. Why we waited for the last minute and then went down to Starved Rock by ourselves, *I* can't tell you."

"So the Federated's Council was aware that there was something salvageable of Trigotha's on the planet."

"Yes, of course."

"And you knew exactly where to look?"

"Certainly. The dead tuber wasn't too far from the trail, but I doubt we'd have just stumbled over him."

Rheinallt grinned. "Curious. Whitnadys and I *did*, a few minutes before you and your pal got there."

"You did? Well, I'd have told you anyway. The Council may be as secretive as they like while they play their politics, but that's not my way. They told me to cover what I was along for. Not my style at all. I said I'd keep a low profile while I kept my eyes peeled, answer no questions until asked; but they could keep their falsehoods for the exploiters." He blinked. "Meaning the likes of you, Eiverdein. No offense."

"Did you manage to talk with any of Trigotha's people?"

"Huh? Why, no, I haven't."

"Did you know that as far as I could discover they're all dead?"

Glenevat straightened with a jerk, looking genuinely surprised. "No! Is that the truth?"

"Like I said."

"I'm sorry to hear that. Good trailmen all, so I heard. Wouldn't have minded pulling with any of them someday." His eyes pierced into Rheinallt's. "How'd you find out?"

"After I heard the first rumors about the Ship, I started looking for returnees. They had scattered to their homes and haunts, naturally. By the time I traced them down, one after another, it was too late. So all I got were more rumors and some secondhand information through people like Ortelius."

"The mapmaker? He's a magnet for news." Glenavet frowned thoughtfully. "From what I heard, Trigotha died on the way back. But obviously, rumors did spread from the others before they died. Or"—he waved his hand fore and aft—"none of this would be in motion now. Strange."

They sat in silence for a couple of minutes.

"By the way," Glenavet said, "the telescope's a valuable instrument. I ought to return it to the Council."

"Really? Our late observer, some unknown tuber found dead on Starved Rock, was a member of your Federation?"

Glenavet flushed slightly. "Not explicitly."

"I don't care for implicit commitments made after the subject has breathed vacuum."

"He died a true trailman," Glenavet asserted stoutly.

"Very likely. He did not, however, die a Federated Trailman."

"You state that for a fact."

"Trigotha did leave records of his proposed journey, made before he left on the outward trip and not taken with him. Intentions, route, material, crew. No crewmen were listed as belonging. Trigotha's preference; but also few of us working the Nation or based there do belong."

"The Nation is proving slow, yes."

"So unless one of them experienced spontaneous conversion when they discovered the Ship, there wasn't a single Federated member aboard. So now we come down to ground: Isn't it unwarranted arrogance that your Council has information about

56

this doubtful stretch of trail which they won't share with trail-men traversing it for only the second time known? And if the telescope belongs to anyone, it's Trigotha's heirs and his crew's."

Glenavet squirmed. "Are you more concerned with trail information or the telescope?"

"As far as the Special Caravan goes, the telescope doesn't matter. That can be settled judicially when we're home in the Nation. *Do* you know anything about the rest of the trail?"

"Sorry."

Would the dead Wirtellin have shared information about some impending general danger with his colleagues? Impossible to tell now.

"Do you know how the tuber died?" Rheinallt asked.

The earlier death looked like the result of a blast from an energy weapon such as this culture did not possess, but which Rheinallt was as used to as a spacesuit glove. He heard a faint hiss from Arahant as the aircat adjusted the lower-than-atmosphere pressure in the flat sacs under his skin. Rheinallt glanced up at him and saw the vertically slit pupils fixed intently on Glenavet.

"Why yes," Glenavet answered readily, "I suppose he died by looking through the telescope at the Ship."

That didn't make sense at all. Rheinallt looked up at Arahant after a moment; the aircat shrugged his white-furred shoulders as if to say: You're the blaster expert, not me.

After a pause that must have lasted several minutes, Rheinallt asked, "What do you intend to do on the rest of the journey?"

Glenavet jumped up, paced the small floor a couple of times. "I don't know, damm it! I feel like a babe in the dark! Crawling along the meadow with all the excitement everyone else feels, but also I'm supposed to observe and report, sneak around and spy. There's nothing to spy on! Just another caravan."

"Looking for a starship."

"Yes, yes."

"An enhancement, or a transport," Rheinallt pointed out, "that might totally change the economies of the Trail worlds, remake the balances of power. Certain quarters might be upset if we find a usable starship."

Glenavet dropped into his chair heavily. "I'm not a saboteur." He hunched forward, awkwardly forceful in the small

57

chair. "Let me tell you what I'm doing. I'm an observer. The Federated Trailmen would like to know what's going on beyond the known End-of-Blue. What your expedition might mean for them. Which leads to what actions of mine you can expect once we do reach the Ship."

He enumerated on his fingers:

"The Council needs a Federated report rather than somebody else's propaganda.

"They don't want the point of view of a big director of their spiritual-guidance thing, but of a caravaneer; like me.

"And they want an up-front, in-the-thick analysis of this Ship or whatever it is. So when we get there I'll be poking my nose into everything, underfoot for all the scientific types.

"That's the extent of my commission."

Rheinallt considered. "And if the circumstances seem to require you to do more, what then?"

"Then I'll do that, too. But look, Eiverdein: the Council didn't tell me to blow up the caravan or something stupid like that. And I wouldn't anyway. That's not my style, and I'm no one's toady. What Wirtellin was told I don't know; and since I don't, I'm not going to worry about it. I haven't any sealed orders. I'm not going to clog my mind with things I don't know, and there's no point in your doing so either. Understand?"

"All right, Glenavet. We'll continue on that basis."

Rheinallt wasn't perfectly pleased with this situation, but he felt he could live with it.

This whole aspect of totally divergent motives for being on his caravan had not been anticipated adequately. Oh, sure, he knew that people might want to get in his way, want the starship all for themselves. Harder to accept were those desiring to block the caravan for the benefit of conflicting economic concerns. He got up to leave.

"That's all I ask," Glenavet said. "The privilege of an ordinary paying passenger. With"—he grinned infectiously—"a little allowance for a headstrong fellow trailman."

"Try not to do anything rash," Rheinallt told him.

Out in the corridor Arahant stood beside Rheinallt as the latter slid aside heavy curtains for a look at the meadow. The blackly congealed ash of the well-slope plodded by satisfactorily. The gentle curve of the trail allowed them to see back down into the pit of the huge funnel, and up to the scarcely discernible break in the blackness which indicated the meadow horizon at the rim. The leagues continued to slide by underfoot.

How could anyone not share his dream about the Ship? No, wait, that was ridiculous. Most people were not lost, nor in exile. The majority on the Trail worlds hadn't even thought about it yet, and probably had never thought about such a thing as a starship. If someday subspace travel by ship, sliding independently on the black pseudosurface, became their most natural activity on the meadow—would that practicality leave anything of the caravaneer dream? Elsewhere—but no point raking up his own embers.

As he turned from the window he became aware of a faint tapping or knocking from within the compartment next to Glenavet's. Arahant sprang to listen outside the door. Rheinallt crossed the corridor and turned the handle with a polite caution.

From a crouching or crawling position a man tumbled out into the corridor and sprawled face down across the doorsill. Arahant took a light leap backward to avoid being fallen on. Rheinallt jerked his hand from the door handle as though it were red-hot, then quickly knelt to examine the man.

"Smells bad," Arahant whispered.

"Poison?"

"Maybe."

Gently Rheinallt turned the man's head to see the face. It was Tadako, the third of the Federated Trailmen retinue; on Starved Rock, the stolid one who had stayed with their squeaker.

Eyelids fluttered without opening.

Arahant laid a thumbpad on the man's wrist. "Still staggering along."

Carefully Rheinallt laid Tadako's head back on the carpet, tongue free and face to the side so he could breathe.

A few strides took him back to Glenavet's room, where he knocked and opened simultaneously. "Your man Tadako's collapsed. Right here," he announced with a jerk of his thumb toward the corridor.

In the corridor a couple of yards forward of the window was a speaking-tube station. Rheinallt went to this, whistled for attention, and said sharply, "This is Eiverdein. Will the healer and the surgeon please come at once to Car Nine. I say again: the healer and the surgeon at once to Car Nine."

From the floor Glenavet announced, "He's got a pulse."

Rheinallt racked the mouthpiece. "Yes, he seems just on the fringe of consciousness. Any idea what's wrong with him?"

"Do I?" Glenavet answered with unnecessary loudness. "I just got here! What do *you* know about it?"

Rheinallt rocked back a little in the kneeling position he had resumed on the carpet. "There was a feeble tapping from his door. I opened it, out he fell. When did you last see him?"

Glenavet shook his head worriedly. "Right before the last general meal."

"After we passed through Starved Rock?"

"Yeah, sure. The last one."

"You didn't eat with him?"

Glenavet looked squarely at Rheinallt. "No. We weren't close friends, like. He worked for me, a good guy and all that, but we weren't that close. I skipped that last meal, myself; too much to think about. Sometimes we might eat together, but not too often."

"So he was all right before the meal?"

"Far as I noticed."

Vibrations from pounding feet were transmitted through the flooring from the next car. Rheinallt stood and motioned Glenavet back to give the newcomers room. The healer and the surgeon of the caravan's crew came up then, breathing a little hard.

"You haven't moved him?" the surgeon snapped.

"Only his head, so he could breathe."

"Did he show any symptoms prior to this collapse?" the healer asked, kneeling.

"Not that we know of." Swiftly the scraps of information were shared, and then all were brusquely motioned away. After a swift conference a mattress was dragged out of the fallen man's room and he was carefully lifted onto it.

"Will you leave him in his room or take him to sick bay?" Rheinallt asked. At a twitch of Arahant's tailtip he added, "I would prefer the latter."

The medical men traded glances. The healer shrugged. "Sick bay, then," the surgeon said, and stepped to the speaking tube to call for a stretcher.

Rheinallt tugged Glenavet's elbow slightly. "Let's get out of their way," he said quietly.

"Yeah, sure." Glenavet transferred a rigid stare from the man on the mattress to Rheinallt. "Yeah, sure," he repeated hoarsely, and stumped off toward the front of the caravan, brushing past the surgeon. He didn't look back.

Rheinallt took two deep breaths, caught Arahant's eye, and turned away aft.

6. All Substance Forfeit

AT THE DOOR OF THE LOUNGE CAR RHEINALLT HAD TO STOP FOR the press of people, but Arahant managed to wend his way into the room at knee level. Lhudesin wasn't singing at the moment, but the crowd showed no signs of breaking up.

A crewman named Miranel sidled over to Rheinallt. "Captain Eiverdein, a few of the boys are maybe working up a complaint."

Rheinallt grinned. "Maybe, huh?"

"Well, you know how it is. Some hemming and hawing and thising and thating. Then maybe somebody will say something."

"Since you seem to be first in line, suppose you do the saying."

"It's about the food," Miranel said reluctantly.

"Yes: too much. The cooks'll have to cut back." Damn. He hoped no one else had gotten sick. "The only other cure for too much food is more exercise outside."

"Ho! Sounds great. Seriously, Captain, I'd probably not be putting in a bad word, but some of the boys kind of deputized me to put a bug in your ear."

"Other people's problems are mine too, whenever they want to share."

"Well, if you put it that way, that's real oxygen; yes, sir, real breeze." Miranel relaxed, planted a hand against the cloth-cushioned wall, and leaned. "The meal was short, last time. Skimpy, you know? Well, I was there right after the serving started—I like to be up front because I'm always ready. There was some ruckus behind the counter and a few kettles and pans hit the deck wrong side down. So most all of us got a hearty snack instead of a dinner. To me it's just one of those things. No squeak. But some of the gang who came in later after the mess was cleaned up just outright assumed they'd been shorted."

Rheinallt reflected. Presumably these didn't include any with whom he had trudged the meadow before, or they would have picked someone who knew him better to pass on their complaint. Shorting crew food to save money wasn't a silly notion, either; some caravans did it systematically. It was a false economy that Ortelius hammered as a chief cause of the debilitating scurvy. Besides, shorting was simply cheating people out of part of their pay.

"Did they go for seconds?" Rheinallt asked reasonably. "Usually there's a little extra."

"Yeah, but this time there wasn't. The cooks just told them to tighten their belts till next time, or breathe vacuum if that tasted better."

Not good. "Sounds like they were upset too."

"No doubt about it. Like I said, I saw some of that earlier ruckus. I can see why the cooks were grumped out, to see their work go to waste."

"It'll go through hydroponics, so you'll get to eat it eventually. Do you know what started the trouble?"

"It was settled down by the time I got a peek behind the serving counter," Miranel said. "No more action to see, just mess."

"Your friends didn't realize this was an unusual case?"

The crewman shrugged. "I tried to tell them, but some of the guys were too mad to listen. If you ask me, they're just restless and antsy. Want to see the Ship, see some action."

Rheinallt nodded emphatically. "You can bet your *next* meal I can sympathize with that. I'm ready for the Ship, too."

"Now, aside from a chance at prize money if we find that

64

Ship and bring it back, I signed on this Special Caravan because I heard you were a good caravaneer. Didn't stint the food. No martinet malarkey. I'm tired of risking my teeth falling out or my hide flogged off by some ass's excuse for a trailman. Well, anyway, when my mates started complaining I tried to lay it down. But when they began talking about short weights I knew it was getting serious and it'd have to be talked out."

"Whew," Rheinallt snorted. "False weights? Really?"

"Not my idea, Eiverdein." Miranel conveyed the attitude of one trying to maintain empathy in all directions.

Rheinallt chopped the air with his hand. "Tell you what to do. Round up your buddies, and have the one with the most mechanical savvy examine the quartermaster's weights. If none of you know how to calibrate the scale for meadow variations, get some unbiased passenger to show you. It isn't hard."

"Then compare the food. I follow you."

"And ask them to remember how many times there was *plenty* to eat. If I were paring the fruit to slight them, I'd make each slice thin, not all fat but one."

Miranel nodded vigorously. "Will do. And, well, thanks, Captain."

After the crewman left Rheinallt again took stock of the lounge car. There was a thick line of folk pressed against the bar, mostly standing. On the opposite side of the car they were packed against the window rail, contemplating nothingness and the whichness of what. Rheinallt decided that the latter group had been absorbing the music as though it were a phenomenon of the meadow rather than mere entertainment in a brightly lit room. A central clot occupied the middle of the car, clustered around Lhudesin.

Rheinallt liked the idea of fitting surges of music to rolls and dips of the meadow, and it helped that Lhudesin was among the best. He had signed on the singer as supernumerary: the arrangement was an outstanding bargain for the caravan, and Rheinallt would have to devise some appropriate "singer's bonus" when they returned to Blueholm. Perhaps he could publicize this morale prescription, to include song in the spiritual diet of far wayfarers. Ortelius would be tickled by the diet analogy, and likely include it in the next edition of the *Pilot*.

By the time he had threaded his way through the throng to arm's reach of the bar, Haderun had his favorite concoction sliding across the slick wood countertop. The flavor was good but it wasn't as cool as usual. The car was overcrowded, and in the middle it was obvious that air circulation had fallen woefully behind. He borrowed the bartender's towel to blot up some of his sweat, not wishing to appear too overtly self-cooled.

Behind Rheinallt's left shoulder the feminine voice of a physicist passenger said, "I think we must be almost there."

"Certainly," asserted another woman jammed close at his back. "Isn't that why you're celebrating?"

"Not really; I'm saving that."

"No? Say, there's the captain. We *are* close, aren't we, Eiverdein?"

Rheinallt twisted around briefly. "Fairly close, I imagine. But don't hold your breath just yet."

"If our air gets much fouler, I'll have to," she said, laughing. To her friend she rephrased herself, "Then what is it you're celebrating, if not the imminence of the Ship?"

"I've just finished a series of spectra analyses of an un-reachable world back in the Nation, but not of it—not on the Blue Trail. I commissioned the detail observations last year, and the observatory delivered the raw data just before we left. I've been working on it the whole trip."

"So that's why you've been so closeted. Observatory—where they look at stars through telescopes?"

There was amusement in the physicist's voice. "Sure. Haven't you ever looked through a telescope yourself?"

"Why, not really, not at stars and planets. Never seemed any use. Although I'm sure with the Ship all that will change. By the way," she added conspiratorily, "there's a telescope over in the aft corner by the window. Eiverdein found it on that dreadful dark planet."

Rheinallt's ears perked at this. Fragments of other nearby conversations faded into background noise. He had collared Bremolando on returning from Starved Rock, telling that young man to have the machinists in the repair shop check over the instrument for anything unusual and then, if the instrument was ordinary and harmless brass and glass, to set it up here in the lounge car. Would this bait provoke more than curiosity in anyone other than Glenavet?

"Really?" the physicist said to her friend. "We ought to have a look. Maybe we can spot the Ship."

"Suits me," the nonastronomer said. "Just a minute while I finish my drink." She took a last swallow of her juice, elbowing Rheinallt gently in the back as she did so, then reached past to deposit her glass on the bar. "You haven't told me why these spectra are so important."

"Looking at stars is only one thing an observatory does. Looking at planets in a solar system with one Trail world in it is a lot more interesting, and soon may be a lot more useful."

"So enlighten me." Pause. "I can't get out this way. Try pushing somebody on your side."

"Here's an opening," the physicist said. "I've got a couple of compressed-air and chemical companies interested in mining the atmosphere of a planet we can't get at now, but which ought to be accessible through starspace. It's in an inhabited system—as close as the back of your head, as stellar distances go. If only we could get at it, it might be tremendously lucrative."

"If we had ships, yes, the planets really near each trail world would be so convenient. Very clever. All sorts of valuable building materials, chemically speaking. Say, let's get moving. I want to see the Ship through the telescope, if we're close enough yet." She pushed at a man next to her. "It's too beastly crowded all the way to the corner. Hey, what's that?"

In the small faceted mirrors high above the bar Rheinallt too had seen the flash somewhere back in the car. Near the telescope? The reversed and multiplied images confused the direction. A bomb? There was no explosion, nor rush of air. Some sort of energy weapon? It was definitely *within* this car, and everyone was babbling loudly now.

Rheinallt plopped down on the bar both his half-finished drink and the bartender's towel he had borrowed to wipe his face and neck. Getting the corners straight in his mind with an instant of irritation at his own need to decode the reflections, he twisted to look directly, but could see nothing. The two women who had been talking just behind him had made almost no progress. Another way? The press of bodies and the hubbub had, if possible, increased.

He vaulted onto the bar top, carefully establishing footing

on the slick wood. The air near the ceiling was so thick he had to work to breathe, and his sweating increased. He beckoned to Haderun, who had quickly positioned himself near his feet, making a few guarding sweeps with another towel.

"The megaphone!" Rheinallt shouted down to him. "Have you still got it?"

Haderun nodded wordlessly, passed his hand over his face, and rummaged under the bar. After a few moments of tumbling miscellaneous glassware out to bounce or shatter on the floor, he came up with the megaphone.

Rheinallt snatched it up. "Thanks." He hadn't used it since leaving Blueholm when he had coordinated a gaggle of stevedores, but there were several stashed in the caravan awaiting a needful occasion. To Haderun he added quickly, "Get the fans going faster. Bleed air to vacuum to increase the draft. Hurry."

Rheinallt started what would have been a bellow into the megaphone but changed the tone instinctively into a loud but firmly controlled shout: *"Hold it all!"*

Heads spun, torsos twisted to look back up at him. Was there a fire in the corner by the telescope? Smoky in that direction. A fire would be a first-rate disaster.

"Calm down! That's right: take it easy, please!" The megaphone handle slipped in his sweaty palm, and he surreptitiously reabsorbed the moisture so fast his palm ached. His free arm he waved in a slow steady arc, a visibly bracing gesture which would have a subconsciously soothing influence. Agitation in the car began subsiding.

"Thank you," he said more quietly after a few moments. A full panic in a bottleneck-doored car with vacuum outside and fire inside was something he had heard terror-tales of but never witnessed. Living witnesses to meadow panics were rare.

"There's no fire here," a voice called from the corner. "A little explosion—caused some smoke, but no fire at all." Arahant's voice, the first time he had spoken in public on the Special Caravan. And if Rheinallt knew him, the aircat had arranged adequate misdirection before calling out. The anonymous assertion was another calming influence.

"What's going on?" someone called.

"Spaced if I know," he replied through the megaphone, eyes sweeping the crowd. "Tell you what. If any of you people

68

immediately in front of the doors, either fore or aft, feel like leaving, please do so. You've seen the flash. I think that's all you're going to see. You'll all hear the whole gossip soon enough, probably over and over until you're sick of it."

Amid laughter, a few drifted through the locks. He could feel fresh air coming now, curling under his hair and cooling his neck where he stood near the ceiling.

Sharp of Arahant to head for the disturbance; he could travel routes that Rheinallt, like the two women conversing behind him earlier, couldn't use. Had Arahant gotten to the scene of the explosion, as he had called it, soon enough to pick up any evidence? Vital clues might be missing by the time Rheinallt himself got there.

By now several more had left. Rheinallt still couldn't see anything out of the way from the bartop. Time to go and look. He held out his arm straight toward the far corner.

"Now if you folks along this line will sidle one way or another and clear a lane for me, I'd like to see if we can find out what's been going on." He swayed his arm slightly back and forth, and was gratified to see an irregular gap open, a devil's lane leading more or less crookedly toward the site of the mysterious flash.

Rheinallt jumped down into the crowd, taking the megaphone with him. When he got to the aft window corner he found the telescope, clamped upon its tripod as he had seen it on Starved Rock. This time the instrument faced a blackness devoid of stars, darkly rolling meadowland. The caravan had finished its long climb out of the planetary gravity well and was again on the illimitable harsh plain. The trail undulated into the distance, appearing and reappearing until it became a bright thread and was swallowed in vast subspatial darkness.

Was the Ship out there? He looked, saw nothing, and returned to the business at hand.

On the floor, almost hidden by a shuffling eddy of feet and legs, was a man with a blast-burned face. The crew, like all professional trailmen who traveled the Blue Trail of the Nation, wore no uniform. He couldn't even tell if the dead man was one of his own, and felt an extra pang of regret that whoever had died here might be a friend.

Arahant sat on his haunches nearby, eyes half closed but ears pricked to full alertness.

Rheinallt knelt, then gently touched the charred front of the head. Hardly a face anymore. "Does anyone know who this is?"

Silence with scuffling feet. Finally someone answered, "Don't know for sure. I mean, don't know him myself, but he was one of the cooks. He was chief souper last time."

"In charge of the last general meal?"

"Yeah."

Another tragedy for which there was no obvious cause. Rheinallt felt he was being dogged, all in the last clockday, with events of deadly import but whose meanings escaped him individually. One dead uselessly on Starved Rock, one badly sick in the ninth car, one blasted in the lounge car. And of course the first observer, the telescopist blasted on Starved Rock; that tuber's death, removed in time, seemed somehow to impinge on the other three.

The poor cook was quite dead. Out of long habit Rheinallt had reached for the pulse, and his fingertips on the wrist found none. The skin was still warm there, if not as warm as the face. Definitely a burn, on the face.

Close by the floor here the smell was bad too. Arahant's nose was wrinkled almost shut and he was probably breathing stored air. Fortunately the fans already were doing their extra work.

"Who was close by when that flash happened?" Rheinallt asked.

"It came from the meadow," a voice muttered surprisingly.

"Yes!" stated another.

"Not true," a third chimed in. "Came out of that telescope thing. Hit him right in the face."

"Didn't have a chance."

"No, no. That first man was right, too. It came right out of the meadow and down through the telescope."

"Right, the magnification killed him."

"What a pity."

"But still—what caused it?"

Rheinallt held up a hand to sustain the silence which followed this last question. He could see apprehensive glances stolen at the meadow only a few feet beyond the window. This time the vast emptiness spoke to his years of experience in subspatial travel. "Nothing's out there," he tried to reassure them.

But among this melee of eyewitnesses were there none who could give a coherent account? The muttering showed only the residual excitement from an almost-panic caused by the red flash. Had they all mazed each other? Great observers of the Ship they were going to make, he thought sardonically, great theoreticians and practical engineers!

"Who—" he began.

"A deodand!" someone shouted.

"Yes, yes. Of course!" came immediate agreement in a similar voice.

"What's that?" a voice asked from the rear.

"Claim the deodand!"

"Heard you the first time," the inquirer said. Bremolando, the young crewman who accidentally had lost the air storage tank earlier. "What in blazes *is* that?"

"A forfeit. The telescope is forfeit. It killed a man."

Rheinallt stood up. The reaction to the death was becoming as weird as the death itself. "Wait a minute, folks. I never heard of this deodand thing, myself."

"Me neither," the nearby Bremolando backed him up. "Forfeit? We've nothing like that in the Nation."

A chunky man wormed his way out of the press of people to stand in the small clearing near the body. "I'm Nollinsae," he announced, more to the crowd than to Rheinallt. "I'm a Guard officer. Those of you who claim the deodand are correct. The telescope is the proximate instrument of this man's death, and is forfeit to the government."

Bremolando pushed forward, honestly puzzled. "But there *is* no government in the Blue Free Nation. Who's supposed to claim whatever it is?"

"Quite true," Nollinsae agreed crisply. "I therefore will undertake to convey it to the proper officials of my own government."

"So who's that?" someone asked, querulous rather than disputing the right.

"Fleurage," Nollinsae said with deliberate patience. "Yellow Trail."

71

Rheinallt didn't like the turn of this. "We're nowhere near any Yellow territory."

Inwardly he asked himself what was the point of the fuss over the telescope itself. He had gone over the instrument closely enough when it had been brought aboard the caravan. Glass lenses and a metal tube didn't flashburn a man.

Nollinsae was ready for this. "Of course not, Captain Eiverdein. But surely we are in no other sovereignty. As a credentialed officer of the Fleurage Guard, I am the best qualified of the many worthy people present to convey the deodand. Harm has been done by unknown forces, acting through this instrument, to our late companion here. It is only natural that the human collectivity should take responsibility for the instrument of harm to itself. In due course the initiator of this attack upon humankind will be found and battled with."

Suddenly Rheinallt realized that this person was the author of the strange note he had received before the descent to Starved Rock. Nollinsae, of the Guard. He remembered the face now, and the name came to life.

"I need to talk to you on another matter," he said softly to Nollinsae.

The Guard officer smiled. "Certainly." He laid a hand on the tripod. "I'll take this now. In the meantime, I suggest your crew see to the burial. Our air has become rather foul."

"That's right, Captain," Bremolando said. "We got to put this body out pretty quick."

Events were not happening so quickly that Rheinallt had not had his chance to peek into the telescope tube and verify that it was indeed empty. They were right about burial. What more could be learned from studying the corpse with primitive medical facilities? Powder burns? That he had not seen any meant only that a coarse powder was not the blasting agent. Absence of small fragments or shards meant only that there was no conventional grenade involved.

Quite possibly, the man had been murdered in some subtle fashion by an energy weapon; but by whom, toward what end? Where could such an advanced weapon come from in the Trails culture? That charred face already had told its only fact: death by flashburn.

Volunteers had taken grips on the demised's limbs and were lifting him. Rheinallt found the corpse blocking him from Nollinsae and the telescope. The Guardsman was forging into the crowd with that instrument held before him as an effective prow, tripod folded and all held aimed for streamlining his exit.

"Nollinsae," Rheinallt called, "wait. How do you know the telescope killed him?"

Did Nollinsae think that there had been a bomb concealed inside, or know it? Wait yourself, he thought. Remember Trigotha's tuber on Starved Rock: he looked blasted, too. What did they have in common except the cursed telescope? The inside of the tube didn't even contain a spotlight or such that could blow up in a user's face; and in fact the instrument itself still didn't look damaged.

Nollinsae was almost out of sight. "Isn't it obvious, Captain Eiverdein?" he called back loudly over people's heads. "He saw the Ship through the telescope, and its awful light was concentrated through the lenses and killed him."

This revelation set off such a hubbub that Rheinallt resolutely closed his ears to it. If the Ship had indeed been briefly visible when the caravan topped the rim of the gravity well, then the caravan would come to it in due time.

Since it hadn't killed Trigotha or his men—except maybe one back on Starved Rock?—he would have to assume it wasn't necessarily fatal. His working hypothesis was that it was only fatal when a person with a weapon was involved, but this had yet to be demonstrated. Added caution for the whole caravan wouldn't hurt. He felt he could let go the evidence at hand, the body of the cook and the telescope, with nothing more to be learned from them. The body had to go anyway, either to vacuum or to hydroponics, and he could always pry the telescope away from Nollinsae if other developments pointed back that way.

Of much more interest was Nollinsae himself, who had tipped his hand—but what had he shown?

The subspatial equivalent of burial took place from the intercar airlock while the caravan was still moving. Bremolando and the three handiest crewmen carried out the body and walked out a few yards. The caravan's continued motion shortly brought the grand side window of the lounge car opposite the burial party. Then, with reverent deliberateness, the four placed the body gently on the bluely glowing trail. At Bremolando's nod they released their grips simultaneously and straightened up.

73

Before they could regain a standing posture the dead man had vanished without a trace. The meadow, the pure surface and bottom boundary of existence, had claimed him.

Bremolando and the others clumped back into the lounge car, unfastening helmets and stripping off skintight airsuits. Some of the passengers very likely never had seen a burial on the meadow, and the solemnity of the simple procedure without ceremony had quieted them as the mysterious death had excited them.

Rheinallt lifted the almost-forgotten megaphone to his lips and without force said the name "Lhudesin."

He felt sure that the singer had not left the car, and when he glanced down at the aircat, Arahant nodded. There might be dark vacuum outside, but in here were people who could use a dirge to reestablish contact with each other. He hoped whatever song was chosen would have some bite to it, a hard touch.

Across the big room Lhudesin toyed with the strings of his instrument for a few minutes, striking random chords. After a while the notes resolved themselves into premonitions of the old dirge, "Black Meadow Music"; then the song began itself properly and his voice caught up the tune. Rather high and definitely quavering, the old man's tone still had the sincerity and mellow roundness of projection which had brought him fame long before.

The words drifted, lost, without punctuation to nail them to the ear. The room now was totally quiet, and in the stillness the music did not seem an accompaniment because it was lost too, separately.

> "Whistle down the darkened plain
>   Where the silent vacuum shrieks
>   Like time's hungry wind alone
>
> "Some are sinking all the same
>   Where the meadow has no floor
>   To shatter out to all their fragments
>   And scatter loose among the stars
>   A silent song like rain
>
> "Some are leaping up to vanish
>   Where a fear of edge of death

74

Can't flatter life to bribe a foothold
To matter where there is none
So long the chord is gone

"Some are rushing home to nothing
Where they're turning off their mind
To chatter brightly like a person
And batter down their echoed soul
An empty hiss like steam

"Some are floundering back and forth
Where the meadow called them out
To tatter home and rock to longing
And latter nights of saints are grazing
A grassy hymn to doom

"Whistle down the darkened plain
Where the silent vacuum shrieks
Like some hungry mind alone."

7. From the Waterflower Pool

LATE ON THE NEXT CLOCKDAY RHEINALLT WAS SITTING AT HIS desk, feeling bewebbed in the hassles of administering a caravan en route. Glenavet, he thought, was more or less neutralized by the death of his active associate, the delegate Wirtellin. Rheinallt did not expect him to cease his advocacy among the caravaneers, but tentatively had pegged him as a basic trailhand: honest enough, not imaginative, and not unnecessarily violent. Trying to sell the idea of the Federated Trailmen might even give the crew something professionally exciting to discuss, and Rheinallt saw no reason why it should be more exciting than that.

The Fleurage Guardsman, Nollinsae, was coming to the fore as a potential problem. Like Wirtellin, Nollinsae might be happiest when the people around him were standing on their knees; not for ideological reasons, though, but for more personal, slipperier motives.

Conceivably Nollinsae just happened to rub Rheinallt the wrong way, as officious types often did without being consciously immoral. What in the abysmal hell, though, had been that business with the telescope? As a scientist he doubted

Nollinsae could tell a star from a candle. Yet if he was along as a beast of prey, so far Rheinallt could not make hide nor hair of him.

That telescope was a worrier. Not who possessed it, but the antics of those around it. Like the king's ankus in the old story, one could follow its progress down the jungle trail by the bodies it left behind. But only bodies of those who held certain values, who considered the jewel-encrusted ankus a treasure in itself as well as a goad.

His thoughts were interrupted as Susannilar, the unfocused girl-woman, snatched open the door and slipped in, closing it carefully behind her. Her face was sharp like that of a hunted fox, but her breathing seemed normal; she was not actually being pursued.

"You've got to help me!" she blurted out.

"About Nollinsae?" Rheinallt was deliberately calm.

She stared. "You know—yes, of course you do."

Permitting himself a mild smile, he said, "I know lots of things, and I've known lots of different kinds of people."

Her laugh was jerked out of her, half finished: "Ha, you're in for some surprises."

"No doubt," he said equably. "I've known personally perhaps a hundred thousand people in my life, and been acquainted with many more. Being surprised by people is nothing new to me."

Now he indeed had her attention outside herself. "A hundred thousand, Eiverdein? No one can possibly know so many. It would be hard to even *meet* that many."

"Some of them were hard to meet," he agreed, waving her toward a comfortable chair. "Like to sit down?"

"Why, yes. I need your help," she repeated, with less tremolo in her voice.

"I'll be glad to if I can. Didn't you mention that you were Ytrenath's granddaughter? The botanist and genius perfumer?"

"Right, that's him. Ah—did you know he was also a member of the political underground on Fleurage?"

"I've heard his name in strange contexts, but I don't really have a picture of him."

Rheinallt was glad he had been able to steady her. At least Susannilar's face was becoming easier for him to remember

78

now. Why had he found that so difficult? It was no quirk in his own memory; it was something about her.

"Are you helping Nollinsae?" she asked, studying her hands.

"Right now both of you seem determined to spark off each other. Maybe you're willing to tell me why. But as of now, I'm warning you not to get in my way and not to get in the caravan's way."

"That's pretty blunt."

"I'm trying to be fair. I've assigned a man, Bremolando, to watch Nollinsae because I know he's brought arms with him."

"And me?"

Rheinallt looked into those distant eyes. "Well, it's more than just a professional caravaneer's curiosity about the people sharing a journey. You bother me, and I want to find out why." Grinning at her with a slight effort, he asked, "Do you have a predilection to violence? Or a history of it? Nollinsae seems to think you're a witch—whatever he means by that."

Susannilar had quickly tilted her head forward to shield her reaction. "I might be very valuable to you and the other researchers when we reach the Ship. If I can prove that I'm useful, can you protect me from Nollinsae?"

He thought about this. The crew would have Rheinallt's head if he outraged caravaneer tradition by trying to impose restrictions on travelers without some godawfully stark provocation. Keeping watch was expected of him; handling caravaneers preemptively was definitely not. If he locked up Nollinsae for threats, with or without similarly maltreating Susannilar, the crew would challenge his right to lead the caravan—before that wretched primitive clock staggered through another artificial day. Too bad; he rather liked her.

"I'd like to help—" he began.

"But you won't?" she rasped out, bitterly.

"Well, let's talk it out. Nollinsae sent me a note implying that I automatically would give him some official sanction to act aboard the Special Caravan. He assumed me to have more authority than I in fact possess, or want, or would be allowed by the crew to wield. I'm not a lawgiver for these people."

"But you killed a man back on Starved Rock! That union organizer, wasn't it? What do you call that?"

79

"He attacked me with a weapon," he told her patiently. "While I thought he was an agitator, and perhaps dangerous to the smooth functioning of the caravan to have along, there was nothing I could do about Wirtellin in that capacity. Unfortunately for him, he was also a fanatic, and decided to stab me on Starved Rock. I killed him while he was trying to kill me. Now *that* was expected of me; I mean, that kind of response. As a simple troublemaker, though, I couldn't have touched him."

"Convenient for you?" she asked with sarcasm, stuttering a little as if she were not used to sarcasm.

"No, sad rather. I hold that each person is unique, and uniquely valuable in ways that others may not see or appreciate. If their individuality brings them to a bad pass, that's a tragedy, not a convenience. I would happily have gone the whole journey without laying a hand on him."

"Just how did you kill him, anyway? I didn't quite get that straight." A hostile curiosity from her now; with almost a professional interest. Strange.

"My business."

"Ah. Well, still you showed that you're capable of taking that kind of responsibility when necessary."

Rheinallt rubbed his bearded face with his palm. "Certainly: as an individual. If justice requires some action, it's not the man the crew calls Captain who gets to act gratuitously, but the man they call Eiverdein whom they'll hold accountable. Don't you see? I can't convict before the fact, or punish on suspicion. Among Bremolando's numerous duties is now the extra one of forestalling violence around Nollinsae, should it come to that. He's on the lookout to protect the caravan."

"And how about me then?" she demanded. "If you assigned someone to protect the caravan from *me*, that protector would be handy for keeping me safe, too. Right?" Then she giggled, a childishly incongruous reaction. Was she becoming hysterical from her tension, or was her mind oscillating between two unmerged and irreconcilable states?

"I can have Seebanone keep tabs on you. She's in Whitnadys' gang, and all-around competent."

She blinked at him, surprised. "Fine!"

He felt relief. Enough sparring. "That's good, then. As we find time on this home stretch toward our problematical starship, we'll get together again. I'll try to draw out your story, and you can try to draw out more of my sympathy."

"You aren't going to listen now?" she cried.

"Remember: as I said, I'm not a lawgiver—"

She was on her feet now, storming at him. "You think I'm too young to have anything interesting to say! That I'm hardly a woman yet, and that I must have too little experience of human worlds to have anything special to tell at all! That I probably don't know anyway what might be important to relate, important to the caravan; and what are just bitsy personal anecdotes. Right?"

Rheinallt jumped up and took her hands in his. "My smile is of empathy, not mockery. But you credit me with too much ability toward setting your affairs aright for you."

Her hands squeezed his convulsively. "It really wouldn't take long, just to *explain*."

"Well, let's make a start, at least." He drew her down to sit again. "Let's see what I think I know so far. You come from Fleurage, a world on the Yellow Trail a long way from its intersection with the Blue. Your grandfather is a famous botanist—"

"He was an infraphysicist, too! He was accused of trying to move Fleurage off the trail, but they got it all backwards, the stupids."

"Well, I've been a dissident myself, and I'm predisposed to listen about someone 'accused' of anything. More to the point, any scraps of theory about worlds and trails may help us shortly when we have to deal with the Ship."

"Really? How? If I could help instead of just dragging along, it'd be great."

"I don't know." He grinned. "Right now you're simply pure research, so go ahead."

Susannilar settled back into her chair, looking at him with a fixed dreamy stare. Almost a hypnotic stare, he thought, before her narrative drew him into itself, and subsumed his rational faculties into those of pure observation. She was compelling, incredibly compelling.

Apparently unready to analyze her current affairs, she steered firmly back into random thoughts of her childhood, memorable no doubt but irrelevant. Yet her soft narrative was disconcertingly vivid. Rheinallt closed his eyes, and in his mind as she talked, he built up a picture of a quiet district on Fleurage. She painted details and more details with her soft words, and then the picture flowed of itself into color and motion and imagined life:

The trees were huge, with creamy white the sole color in trunks, branches, and leaves. They were spaced well apart on the savannah sloping down to the lake, and the shaded ground beneath the trees and the sunny ground between encouraged several varieties of summery grasses. The trees were white plumes on the long smooth stretches of slanting green.

Little Susannilar had snapped her fingers in exasperation at a squirrelish creature which had scampered into hiding among the waving grass, and which obstinately refused not only to play with her but even to reappear at all. She continued walking, angling back down toward the shore of the lake. The deep water was an achingly sharp blue, a blue of blues.

She had loved the colors and reveled in their beauty.

Her route that day had been a long arc, up from her family's vacation cottage, into the parklike quietude of the great white trees and slopes of grass. Now she was again approaching the lake, and she hoped she remembered correctly where Grandfather Ytrenath's place was. In spite of diversions after small native wildlife, she felt confident that she was heading rightly. On these slopes, though, the puffed crowns of the trees obscured the near shoreline below her, so she thought it was quite a fair test of her dead-reckoning ability. Her sandals scuffed and skipped through the grasses, staining greener with every step.

After a few more minutes the nearer lakeshore was in view again, and Ytrenath's house was almost directly in front of her. But her attention was preempted by the flowers. There were four broad swathes of them, reaching like fingers into the lake from the shore by the big white house. Red, yellow, green, and white, the flowered stripes stood out sharply against the blue water. Beyond, dotting the surface of the lake, were random swirls and curls and blobs of color, some pure like the stripes and some mixed. These were wildflowers, the lovely strays.

Even in her small experience she knew this was a florist's paradise. The red powderpuff flower was a feature of her mother's home. A flower developed by her grandfather, Susannilar knew, it was in demand on Lorann and was starting to win fans on the neighboring worlds on the Yellow Trail. The powderpuff was easily dried and transported.

Susannilar had experimented with powderpuffs herself, although her mother said she was too young to use rouge. So what? Some compliment on her botanical abilities! It was fun, though, and she could pretend she was two people: a grownup on the outside who never had to cry or do something she didn't want to, or even pay attention to other people. On the inside, underneath the gentle blush of the natural rouge, she stayed herself, out of touch and out of reach of the world. If she didn't feel like reaching out, she didn't have to. She could play inwardly while the outer Susannilar, rouged and grown up, did whatever relating and accommodating was necessary.

Yes, the red powderpuff was lots of fun. Her mother, Alalortern, had bushels of them. Her mother often worked the stage when they were visiting a big enough town. Apparently rouge was a big help when you were entertaining: the people in the theater could see you easier.

Her pace had slowed with her absorption in the flowery lake surface until she was hardly moving forward at all. The rippling lake was so beautiful that words in her mind came fewer and more slowly. Now she drifted forward without deliberate intent, and yet without inertia, but rather as a bee is drawn by instinctive affinity to what it requires.

The powderpuffs were *more* than nice to look at, she thought, focusing on the most familiar blossoms. The puff's niceness rubbed off on you. Rub it on your face and you were prettier, nicer. That allowed you to share the flower's niceness with other people. She skipped a couple of steps as the slope flattened and she drew near the house.

Certainly her friends said that Susannilar looked very grown-up indeed when she rouged her cheeks into a powderpuff glow. That was great. Her mother was doubtful, but it was all right. The outer Susannilar could be as sophisticated as necessary.

Ytrenath's house had been built long ago from the wood of the great white trees. Its walls had never been painted, and the tiers of wood forming each side now looked like a rack of aged deep-yellow ivory from some elephants' burying ground. The walls cradled the sunlight and caressed it before letting the enriched light slip lovingly onto the faces of occasional passersby.

Susannilar could hear angry voices, and she scuffed slowly through the grass until she could see the strip of yard between house and shore. In a slow voice a man was saying, "Madam, the matter is too ridiculous to consider. Good day."

Susannilar recognized the thin but erect shape of her grandfather, white-haired and tanned. A tall woman in an ornate uniform turned on her heel and strode off, her sharp eyes sparing a piercing glance for Susannilar as she left.

"Hello, Grandfather!" Susannilar cried, running down to him.

"Why, hello!" Ytrenath said, picking her up under the shoulders and swinging her in a half-circle. "You're just in time to see my flowers." As he set her down he added breathlessly, "And you're getting too big now for me to swing you."

"It's *always* time to see the flowers, though," she said, laughing.

"Of course. It's fair: they'll always find time for you if you can find time for them." Hand in hand they walked the few steps to the thin margin of clean sand which marked the shore. "Can you see the progress I've made?"

"Sure. You've got lots more flowers."

"That's right. Anything else?"

"Well—you've got a dock. Sort of a dock, anyway."

This was a yard-wide plank which butted against the shore at their feet and stretched about fifty yards out into the lake, lying flat and steady upon the water. Wavelets, ripples really, skated along its edges but were too small to rinse its top, a dry yellow-brown in the sun.

He laughed. "Yes, of course. I hardly need the little boat any more. I save it for looking over the wild, stray ones. But about the specials, my custom flowers. I've added another brand-new kind. Can you tell which it is?"

She looked over at the other flower-fingers that reached across the laketop. There were the four strips of flowers: red, yellow, green, and white. These might have been longer than she remembered. Altogether there were not one but three new docks, one between each pair of flower strips, and she was mildly surprised that she had not noticed the planking as she

84

came down the hill. Only narrow ribbons of free water lapped unused between the long edges of the docks and the parallel rows of bobbing flowers.

As on her previous visits, the white planting was most thickly covered with blooms, while in the red stripe the plants were larger, more generously spaced, with the various red and pink-red flowers showcased against intervening blue water and not just thickly packed green stalks. Among the reds she saw whole rows of powderpuffs, their feathery balls nodding gently in the breeze. Even that little breeze was enough to cause the faintest fog of red pollen to dust the air downwind. She blinked to make sure she saw it, but the cloud was truly there, drifting daintily.

"Grandfather, can I take some powderpuffs home for Mother and me?"

"So it's both you and Alalortern who are using them now? You certainly are getting toward being a big girl. Sure you can. A half-bushel if you want."

"Oh, thank you. They're such fun, and very grown-up," she confided.

"That they are," Ytrenath said slowly.

Susannilar glanced away from him, wanting to change the subject. She spotted something in the next moment, and forgot that she had wanted to manufacture a topic.

She tugged at his flowing sleeve. "Hey, Grandfather," she exclaimed, pointing. "Those waves. They aren't moving!"

Six of the little wavelets that nestled up to the planking did not rub along at all but were content to lie still. Other, ordinary waves rolled under the six or washed around their tapered edges, but these six stood fast, firm as tiny anchored boats. Each was only an inch tall and a few inches long.

Ytrenath nodded. "That's right. They're standing waves."

"They stand still?"

"Yes. They're a by-product of my research into growing standard dirt-rooted species in a holding net here on the surface of the lake. Over the years I've been gradually improving my nets, down even to the molecular level. A net, after all, is really nothing more than an imposed pattern on the water."

Susannilar frowned. "Water doesn't have a pattern. If it did, it wouldn't be water anymore. Water has to flow. It'd be ice or something."

He beamed at her. "Exactly right. What I've been doing is experimenting with other theoretical forms of water. Artificially imposed patterns which are effectively new phases of the substance. These other phases have been hypothesized for years, but I believe I am the first to achieve one."

"Artificial, though? Not like ice and vapor?"

"Well, not entirely. Artificial in the sense that my standing waves by your toes there don't occur naturally in any lake on Fleurage, or anywhere else that was convenient to check. I've heard tales but they were vague and hintful only."

"Trail tales! Oh, do tell me!"

"Another time, perhaps. Yes, another time: you can practice your patience! Now let me go on about these wavelets."

She tapped a toe on the planking to feel the vibration. "I don't understand it at all."

"That's all right. I can't show off my special creations to very many people, so you'll have to be my audience today." He winked winningly at her.

She bent to examine the six miniature standing waves more closely. "These are just patterns? Like the rows the flowers grow in are arrangements of flowers? The nets make the rows, don't they?"

"You're on the trail of it. I've managed to modify the structural chemistry of water very slightly. Water does have a structure, its own internal pattern which gives it a shape, just like everything else. I'm sure you've heard that the human body is mostly moisture, for instance. As in the other natural elements, the structure of water is too small to see. But it is there, and it can be changed. Ice is an example of water with its internal structure changed a bit."

"I guess it can change back, then."

"If the conditions are reversed."

Susannilar looked up at him. "Could you make one do it? Change a regular wave to a standstill wave and change it back for me?"

Shaking his head ruefully, Ytrenath replied, "No. The process is too elaborate to demonstrate off the cuff." He paused. "But there is something I can show you now."

"With the waves?"

He indicated the nearest tiny ridge of water which swayed

gently on the laketop by the dock, but refused to move before the breeze. "Reach out and touch it."

Kneeling on the planking, Susannilar reached a small hand to the steady wavelet. She missed: her hand went right past it. Puzzled, she reached again. It didn't seem to be where she saw it. She blinked. Her eyes were in focus; she saw it clearly in the round right where it ought to be. Slowly she reached out her hand and with palm flat to the water, she skimmed it above the surface to and fro in increasing arcs.

Using this method, she found the wavelet quickly; when she touched it, it broke. Her fingers were wet and the wavelet slumped down into the lake, ordinary water again.

"I've upset it," she apologized, flicking droplets off her fingers to sparkle in the warm sunlight.

"No problem," Ytrenath said abstractedly. "You upset its structure, which is rather delicate. Eventually I'll have bigger and more stable ones. These are only prototypes." He was staring at her eyes. "Tell me, Susannilar, has your mother ever hypnotized you?"

"I don't know what that is," she said simply.

Ytrenath carefully let himself down so that he was seated cross-legged on the dock, facing the girl. The dock did some slow heaves on the water in spite of his exaggerated slowness. "Sit like I'm sitting."

She scrambled quickly into the position, causing further heaves. "I think I've got a splinter in my knee."

"Don't worry about it. I think you're developing a doubled viewpoint. A dual stance."

"Is that good or bad?"

"I don't know. I think my daughter, your mother Alalortern, has been developing that queer trick of yours farther than she's told me. Not that she has to tell me—but if I know her she probably didn't want me to worry." He snorted. "I don't see that she inherited it from me anyway."

"What queer trick?" Susannilar demanded. "Do you mean her shift? That's not queer."

"It's not? I'll bet she ordered you never to talk about it in front of strangers."

"How did you know that?"

"A little flower told me."

87

"That's funny. Anyway, you're not a stranger."

Ytrenath smiled sympathetically. "Certainly not. In any case, it's not for you to worry over. Tell you what. Suppose I tell you some more about flowers, and then you can tell me what you and your folks have been up to since last I saw you. That's called a contract trade."

"Sure."

"Let's see. Look at that cloth your clothes are made of, Susannilar. The cloth itself is made out of fiber from the seeds of those red flowers growing in the far waterstrip."

"I thought those were all powderpuffs."

"They are. It's those fibers which are so good for weaving cloth, after the flowers form their seeds. The red fibers, whose powder such young people of fashion as yourself dust and smear over their faces, are wonderful material. Cortian fibers, the botanists call them."

She blushed at the allusion to face-smearing. "So the fibers are braided together. Like this?" She interlaced her fingers at right angles.

"Rather like that. Braiding creates a rope, weaving a flat sheet. Speaking of ropes, properly cured cortian fibers are used in all sorts of rope and cord, too. Each piece of natural fiber is only about half the length of your little finger, but when they're put all together they can make a cord as long as you want and as strong as you want."

Susannilar was doubtful. "Ever so long? Could we wrap one around the world?"

"Like a meadow trail in the gravity well? Undoubtedly, if we had the patience to make one." Ytrenath hesitated, scratching his chin. "When you're older, you'll see how all channels of binding energy have much in common."

She was still trying to visualize a cord wrapped around all of Fleurage. "Sounds like an awful lot of fibers."

"Each powderpuff has ten thousand of them."

"Wow! I guess you've got enough flowers on the lake to make a cord as long as the Yellow Trail!"

"Perhaps not quite so long as that. The trails are longer than you can imagine."

She twisted around to see better the red powderpuffs, growing row on row in the gentle water. "How come they don't get wet?"

"The same reason a plant on land doesn't get wet in your garden when you water its roots. It sucks up the moisture internally."

"I know, Grandfather, but look at this: if I dip just the teensiest corner of my sleeve in the water, the water climbs up it. Watch." She demonstrated. "If these whatchamacallit cortian fibers are the same in the plants over there, how come the tops of the plants are dusty instead of soaking wet?" She yanked her sleeve out of the water and squeezed the end of it to mere dampness.

"Ah, I see what you mean. That's a good question. The answer lies in the internal structure of the plant. Remember, the whole plant is called a powderpuff, not just its flower. It needs that water because it's thirsty, so it drinks it up. It doesn't send much up to the flower, because it doesn't need much there until the seed is being made, and then only a little more."

Suddenly he reached to tweak her ear. "Just like you don't send much water up here no matter how much you drink."

She laughed happily.

"The fibers are hydrophilic," he went on. "They've an affinity for water, as your sleeve testifies. They're hollow. That's where the water moves."

Her eyes widened. "Really? They're so tiny."

"The tube inside them, the lumen, is tinier still. But it's there, and that helps to make the cloth, when that's woven, easy to dye. The cloth absorbs water and along with it, the dye that's already dissolved in the water. So we can have pretty clothes with bright colors."

"I can hardly see one fiber all alone, if it's fallen off a powderpuff. The lumen is the tube inside? It goes all the way through?"

"End to end," he told her solemnly, eyes twinkling.

"That's neat. Does the pollen come out of the tubes?"

He nodded, shifting to a more comfortable position on the wood. The dock rocked gently under them. "Comes out of, and goes into. The stamen, which makes the pollen, and the pistil, which helps the pollen grow into a seed, are very small, so tiny that you need a magnifying lens to see them. But these are really important parts of the flower."

"Not the fibers." She realized her sleeve was still damp and began waving her arm rhythmically in the sunshine to speed its drying.

"No. What the fibers do is help convey the pollen which is released into the air—if it's not dusted onto someone's face—to regather the pollen and slide it down its inside corridor for the pistil. Insects help in this, as I think you know. The lumen, with some roundabouting, is the corridor between the fertile parts of the flower, and between flowers."

"I get it, Grandfather," she asserted matter-of-factly. "The flowers make the contact."

"Correct. Contact, whether internal or external, is all-important. It's an old spinners' joke that cordage binds our civilization together. I suspect that they're right."

Ytrenath was silent for a long time, gnarled fingers dabbling in the water, his head turned toward the grassy green slope that swooped gracefully down to his house and around it to the sandy lakefront.

"Tell me some more," she implored finally.

He turned back to her. "Not now," he said gently. "Another time. Now it's your turn: tell me what you've been doing and how you've managed to grow so fast your hair can hardly stay on top of your head!"

She giggled.

He reached behind him to the yellow stripe of ranked flowers growing in the water. He plucked a blossom off a long stem with a twist of his fingers. "Besides, I'm getting cramped sitting here. My bones are creaky."

"Hmm." She rested chin on fist. "What should I tell you?"

He dangled the yellow flower by its stem. "What I've always been interested in, as your mother may have mentioned, is philosophy of mind. Your mother, Alalortern, possesses a very unusual mind, and I've speculated about what makes her tick when everyone else tocks."

She smiled at the thought, made as if to speak, but he distracted her.

Ytrenath placed his elbow on his knee to provide a steady fulcrum, and the yellow flower swung back and forth as his thumb and forefinger evenly twitched the green stalk. He made it swing in a broad, slow arc, a constant period.

"This is an experiment," he told her. "Try to keep your eyes on the flower. Follow it back and forth. Back and forth. Now

90

I'll chant you a little song. A ticktock song that goes like the strokes of a clock, like ringing a bell, and the flower is the pendulum of the clock as it goes back and forth:

"One!
O man, take care!

Two!
What says the meadow so dark?

Three!
'I am asleep—

Four!
From a sleep of death I look and mark:

Five!
Man is new light,

Six!
Brighter than light had been shone,

Seven!
Gloried his trails,

Eight!
Light—lighter yet than falling;

Nine!
Death commands: Fall!

Ten!
But all light makes not alone,

Eleven!
Wants light, lives floating lightness.'

Twelve!"

Susannilar blinked. Ytrenath was bending over her, painfully snapping his old fingers unrhythmically. She stretched and decided to get up, as she felt rather cramped too.

Ytrenath repeated an earlier statement: "I've added a brand-new kind of flower, Susannilar. Can you find it?" He watched her carefully as she peered around her.

Unsuccessfully she studied the flowers standing in their watery beds on both sides of the dock. She took a pace forward, feeling the continuing firmness of the wood, and walked slowly away from the shore. Ytrenath followed. Finally, at the end of the long plank, she had to admit defeat.

"No. I don't see any that's really a new kind. All these, even the pink ones, I think you had before, only hardly so many or so happy-looking. Show me?" she pleaded.

Leaning past her, he pointed to a small and unobtrusive flower of a translucent blue, barely two inches tall. It was naturally camouflaged, a match for the water. Like a watery curl standing above the water, it stood firmly among the passing wavelets.

"I didn't see that at all!" She leaned awkwardly out to examine it. "Doesn't look much like a flower. I mean, it looks like one, but it doesn't *act* like it's made the same way flowers are, sort of. More like one of your bitsy standing waves, back there."

Ytrenath smiled with creative pride. "Rather, it is the true waterflower, growing *out* of the lake rather than *on* it. All of these other flowers have roots and require ordinary nutrients, food, from the water. Their land cousins, by my house there, are rooted in a more solid medium, but live the same kind of lives for the same kind of goals. This little one is different."

"It's so pretty. Are you going to have lots of them?" She tried to imagine whole fields of these translucent blue water-flowers lying upon the blue lake, waving easily to her as the ripples passed beneath them.

"Well, I don't know." He paused, deliberating. "Would you like this one?"

She looked up at him. "Yes! But can you get more?"

"Make more? Now that I know how, yes. Go ahead. Pull it up." The old man tensed into stillness as he watched her. His hands were at his waist, and he bent forward with fixed attention.

She reached out her small arm. Finding it too short for the second time that day, she got down on her knees on the hard planking. With a careful lunge she managed to pull the water-flower loose at the base, uncertain of whether she liked the gelled feeling in her hand.

"I'll call it 'Bluest,' and replant it at home." But her hand was wet, and she saw that the waterflower had no proper base. Its substance was trickling out across her hand.

"Oh, I've killed it!" she cried miserably.

A grave expression passed across Ytrenath's face. "So it cannot be moved," he said slowly, more to himself than to her. "I should have anticipated it. Again the goal recedes," he added in a tone so funereal as to be comic.

The little girl was too downcast to notice this feeble attempt to cheer her. "What shall I *do*?" she asked.

Drops of water plopped on the dock in front of her as she knelt clutching the waterflower. Its blue translucence, its lovely watery curl of stem and petals, were rapidly draining away through its severed tube.

Then in one swift motion she answered her own question, out of her own need. She pressed her clutching hand to her mouth and ate the waterflower in a swift gulp. Inside her, she felt it burst, cool and quenching and flowing down her throat to the innermost Susannilar. As her grandfather stared at her in astonishment, she knew that she had preserved it in the only way she could.

8. The Detenebrator

RHEINALLT CLOSED HIS COMPARTMENT DOOR BEHIND HIM AND placed his flickering lamp on the stand by the door. The session with Susannilar had tired him, and he felt groggy. He could not have predicted her intensity, nor that absorbing a fragment of her history would exhaust him. And there would have to be more, until he understood her. Obviously he already felt empathy; if that had been the purpose of her narration, certainly she had succeeded.

The wavering gas flame from the hand lamp threw grotesque, leaping shadows across the otherwise darkened room. He must have set it down fairly hard, in his weariness, for the mantle to jig so annoyingly and pass on its flickering to his furniture. The canopied bed, the wardrobe, the desk: wooden all, but all seemed to glow obscurely from some light within themselves, drowsing in half-dream.

He looked around for Arahant, but did not see him.

The furniture took its animation from the mantle of the lamp, which took its animation from his prior motion. So what? he asked himself. He felt too tired to try to analyze how furniture should look in the dark.

Whitnadys had not yet come tonight. Or perhaps she had been by, grew tired of waiting, and left already for sleep of her own.

The only sound in the room was the faintly rasping whirr of the ventilator, dispensing fresh air from one of the caravan's tank cars. The air felt stuffy, the pressure too high. He took a step toward the desk to light the other lamp there, then stopped. He thought he heard his heartbeat, then lost the sound.

There was a vague rumbling from behind the thick curtain that shut away the view of the meadow. This rumbling revived last-year memories of thunder within the confines of a small trail sled, deep heavy bass notes more felt than heard. His muscles vibrated to the thrumming note.

The sound from behind the curtain was the sonic equivalent of a distant lamp passing before closed eyelids: stringy tone values flickering yellow and orange and red. Sonically, the yellow pierced, the orange bathed, the red heated.

Rheinallt had heard these vibratos before, and felt this fear that accompanied the bass rumbling. He could block a sonic attack—but he was so tired. His teeth clenched involuntarily. Harsh memories hammered into his still-groggy mind, further blurring thoughts and weakening muscles.

Being kicked while he was down from Susannilar, he thought uncertainly. To cast off this tinge of self-pity, he reminded himself that fear was a mental phenomenon, that the effects of fear were internally caused. With an effort, he asserted more control over his minute bodily processes. That helped brace him for what came next.

Across the room came a shouted thunderclap, rocking his whole body. It had started like this before. He gasped, stumbling backward, throwing his arm in front of his face as the whipping sound virtually burned the air of the room. The lampstand rocked, brushed by his outflung arm, and the room optically shook in the feedback of the moving flame—much more violently than when he had entered and joggled the lampstand. The afterecho in his ears brought sympathetic spots to his eyes to chase the tears around.

The Detenebrator, he subvocalized. The Detenebrator is here. He forced open his eyes, not until that moment realizing that he had closed them.

In the center of the most open, furniture-free part of the

room, between the soft cloth canopy of the bed and the closed insulating curtains of the window, in midair, was a pearly-white globe, looking like a fuzzy basketball on the rebound, or a jellyfish with its tentacles drifting finely around it. The tiniest of strands seemed to hook to a few projections on walls and ceilings, to suspend it. This was the visible aspect of the Detenebrator.

"The greetings of light to you, Eiverdein!" it boomed cheerfully.

Rheinallt's fingernails bit into his palms within clenched fists. "And to you, Detenebrator," he ground out as evenly as he could.

How had it gotten into his compartment? Or for that matter, how had it managed to board the Special Caravan? Or could the cursed thing have been hidden somewhere the whole duration of the journey? It was not very big. Dwelling on such practical considerations helped calm the man, pegging down the weird entity so his emotions could get a handle on it, and themselves.

"You make much progress, Eiverdein!"

"How so?" he asked warily.

"Why, you are here instead of there. And you have kept your mind intact. Truly, Eiverdein, you are doing superbly. I have great hopes for you." The booming mouthless voice rolled out laughter in great tides.

"While I can, I will," Rheinallt said, referring to intactness.

"Are you still worrying about that little incident?" The Detenebrator conveyed wounded feelings, the tone of let's-put-the-past-behind-us.

Rheinallt stared at the alien thing, trying to evaluate, trying to think through his sense of renewed disaster. Did this apparition have a purpose? Was it here for observation, capricious meddling, shaping of what it considered lesser beings? Or just a random catalyst of arbitrariness and madness?

Steady, steady.

It had called itself Detenebrator before, and answered to that name now. Before, that self-naming had been the only one of its shrieks his tortured ears could decode. Obviously it had progressed substantially in its ability to communicate. Unanswered questions from the previous year came boiling up.

"Why did you stop our sled, that time on the Green Trail

97

out toward Whitecloud?" he asked it, as he had wanted to then.

Rheinallt's surprise at that previous encounter, on one of his first trail ventures away from Blueholm, was clear in his mind, now that the first quick lash of fear was manhandled into submission. The surprise, and the anger, that something could interfere maliciously with his attempt to find a way out of his exile. The fear of its alienness had come afterward.

"Why not?" it asked.

"That's not enough answer." A part of him wondered why he stood there, defying the thing. Likely though there was little point in running away. Arahant and he, though they had survived, had felt that too.

"Well," the globe boomed thoughtfully, "that is what the Detenebrator does."

"Stop sleds."

"More or less."

"And one man dead of sonic shock. And another with an addled mind, who suicided with a jump above the meadow?" Rheinallt felt a cold trickle on his neck, and realized he was sweating.

"That is what they did, not I."

"To themselves?" At least he was learning something now.

"Yes," said the Detenebrator imperturbably, steady in mid-air, supported by its thinly thrumming filaments.

"I don't understand that. How?"

"I tried to explain at the time. The tendrils I extruded into their ears created too many decibels. Perhaps your brain is a tougher nexus, or your heightened electrical flows constituted some sort of defense."

"That's no more explanation than we got on that sled, that people *died* for! Why are you here?"

"*Why*, you ask?" The Detenebrator affected overwhelming amazement. "You brought me yourself. The Ship, of course!"

Of course, Rheinallt thought. That's why we're all here. The Ship had drawn all manner of seekers, crew as well as paying passenger-adventurers—why should it not attract this thing too?

What was quite clear was that this blithe destroyer would yield some of its secrets, even if Rheinallt had to rend that booming nonchalant voice into its component squeals, bass string by bass string. There must be no repetition of last year's tragedy.

At least Whitnadys had not been along then, and the crew had been tiny, on only a single sled. But now she was aboard, and there was a caravan of vulnerable people. There might be wholesale carnage if one had to be a bloodsweater to stand against the Detenebrator.

How to start now? "How did you hear about the Ship?" Rheinallt asked.

"By following you around," the Detenebrator replied.

"Following me? But—why? What did you expect me to lead you to? Surely not the Ship, if you found out about that only after you were tailing me. Besides, I never heard a sound out of you."

The sphere tensed its supporting strands and bobbed once in midair. "To answer the latter question first, I am capable of learning finesse; and silence conserves my energy. You haven't noticed my distinctive voice heretofore on your current expedition, have you? I became attracted to you initially because you were an inventor of unusual prowess concerning trail transportation. Money was starting to flow to you for all sorts of useful gadgets and procedures that you introduced into the Nation. I was curious about a man who, out of nowhere, suddenly was displaying an original grasp of vacuum engineering that could generate such royalties."

Rheinallt schooled his face to show a reasonable disbelief. He didn't want questions of *his* origin to get into the discussion. Wait—*could* it see him? Yes, of course, or perceive anyhow. Had it really sprung, as it had appeared to, through the thick window from the meadow? If it had needed to ride, at least that was a distinct limitation of its powers.

Unabashedly changing the subject, he asked, "Have you been on the caravan all along?"

"Accompanying the caravan," the Detenebrator amended. "Not exactly in the living quarters."

"Not in, not on?" He felt like a straight man for a particularly gruesome comic.

"Anchored underneath. I use very little oxygen, when I'm only passively feeling the rhythm of waybestial strides vibrating through the car runners. The squeakers make travel convenient,

99

but their trailboundedness limits them. Really, Eiverdein, you've no idea how restricting their channeled minds are."

Rheinallt felt the devilish urge to tell it that he was a pilot, and if he possessed the enhancement equipment of any meadow-traversing vehicle made on Earth, he could happily dispense with the plodding trailbound squeakers and leave them free to rove. Lovable though waybeasts might be, he would almost-jump for joy at something familiar that he could operate to take him home.

Given the speed, the mind-directed power that did not need a trail to make full use of the subspatial meadow, given a real *ship* under his hands and mind again—then he could whistle at exile! But if he had to create a brick sidewalk to get home, he would do it, brick by golden brick; and trip the light fantastic as he went.

A correlation with last year's sled disaster struck him then. "Wait a minute. If you've been riding along since the Special Caravan broke out from Blueholm, then were you along all the time with our sled, while we were trudging down the Green toward Whitecloud? Were you lying low then, too?"

"My dear fellow, perhaps because you are always alert, you do have glimmerings of sense. I'm proud that my patient faith in you is rewarded."

In a turnabout of feeling that surprised himself, Rheinallt decided that the floating fuzzball was all too human in the worst way. Its fibrous, alien aspects were disquieting, yet it did display a distinct personality.

Rheinallt hoped Whitnadys would not walk into the middle of this discussion. As for being in the middle of the situation, they all were in that together: whatever the Detenebrator might be intending, he did not think it would have happy results. Maybe he could spike the creature's plans, or even—too bad it was so well grounded against electricity.

Personality. Why did the Detenebrator choose to speak in such a pettily provocative manner? Was this unpleasant conversation the best it could do? This was far better than the previous contact. On that smaller-scale trip there had been almost no communication from it. He had understood the creature's name for itself. The rest had been a deafening torrent of confusion and pain. Perhaps it had learned better how to make contact with people, or perhaps it was behaving differently merely because it wanted something different this time.

Rheinallt had no trouble recalling his earlier conjectures. "We thought you'd come aboard at Whitecloud. That you belonged to, or emanated from, the Whitecloud barrier which we had almost reached. Or that you somehow were resident in that part of the meadow."

"Not at all, Captain Eiverdein. I stowed away on your little Whitecloud exploration because I wanted to examine what you call a barrier. Alas, I could not make use of it."

"You couldn't *use* it? How——"

"No. Others may have better luck eventually. Yourself, for instance."

The callous smugness of the thing was infuriating. Another insight into parallels between then and now came to him. "Do you hope to make the same use of the Ship as you had hoped to of the Whitecloud?"

It rolled out a laugh, revealing nothing. "Certainly. In the sense that I suspect you, Eiverdein, intend the same use."

"Do you know what use you hope for?"

"I know. For that *you* have a lesser priority, and will have to wait."

Rheinallt stood solidly with feet apart and arms folded, feeling that he had extracted a concession of sorts. This was only intuition, and for a few moments he groped in silence toward whatever it was that he had achieved. He had not teetered near mental jellification, which had loomed as a real threat on the previous encounter. He had learned some miscellaneous and not visibly useful facts about the Detenebrator's actions.

With a slow grin, he realized that the Detenebrator had put off telling him something. Why? Because that information might be useful to the man in some not too obscure way. At the least, the bouncehead assumed that Rheinallt might act differently if the man knew more, and did not want him to know whatever that more might be.

If not exactly thrilling, this was grounds for the first solid confidence he had felt since the Detenebrator had appeared in this room and on the caravan, and had begun this strange conversation. Whatever needed to be found out he would discover.

Maybe he could even make up for last year.

The Detenebrator broke into this study. "Have you more

101

questions?" It actually sounded disappointed. "So far you've been a fountain of questions. A means of conquering fear, or suppressing it."

Rheinallt laughed at this dig; he definitely felt better now. "Would you like more questions? Are you lonely?"

"While I am here, you may as well ask away—if you possess further curiosities. I am too busy to be lonely."

Many curiosities indeed. If only Arahant were here. His hunger for explanations, after last year's havoc on the sled, had been as great as Rheinallt's. And his anger could flow like a jet stream.

Trying a sly probe, Rheinallt said, "It must be nice to be so sure of yourself that you can invite open questioning. No inadmissible mistakes?"

The Detenebrator made a noise like a small steam whistle, or an ultra-high-pressure basketball being squeezed like a pip. It modulated the whistle into words with an audible effort.

"As you may have guessed," it said, "your Whitecloud expedition was a failure for me as well as for you and your associates. What I was looking for there was some means of transmission or propagation of certain elements dear to my being. Of course we found that we could make no use at all of the Whitecloud. Whatever it is, it's not tractable to our present designs. It's just a barrier on the Green Trail.

"When I tried to communicate with you, Eiverdein, and with the other two humans aboard, I compounded the error. The chaos I created inadvertently destroyed your companions and gave yourself a severe trial." The sphere gave forth a sound resembling a delicate cough.

"In fact, it was because of your managing to survive my primitive communications attempts that I determined to break contact but to follow your endeavors afterward.

"Thus when you were redirected outward again so soon by the rumors that Trigotha had found a subspace-traversing starship out beyond the known End-of-Blue, clearly I would be at your side. The Ship does seem a hopeful omen for our various dreamings, does it not?"

Rheinallt walked slowly to his desk. He turned on the gas of the desk lamp, rasped the attached flint as he always did in front of doubtful company, and watched this cheerful yellow ally glow into its latest reincarnation. The lamp was one of his favorite furnishings: it had accompanied him from his first trail voyage in this part of the galaxy, the voyage when Whitnadys had found him.

Staring at the lamp, he collected his thoughts. The yellow flame reached through the glass chimney to highlight the green ceramic base, and when the flame flickered because of room air currents strong enough to eddy within the chimney, the base seemed to deintegrate by one order: the reflected highlights dancing like sunlit leaves of a tiny green bush.

This Detenebrator, as the creature called itself, hardly acted like the same thing he had encountered on the sled. Whether provocative or contrite, it now communicated in deliberative words of a vocal hurricane. Practice in language, or practice in self-control?

"I hope the Ship is more than an omen for dreams," Rheinallt answered eventually. He blew gently across the top of the glass chimney and watched green leaf-shapes stir to his breath.

Then he felt a cold draft on his ankles, a short puff which died away immediately. This was repeated twice more.

So Arahant *was* in the room! The catadrome must be hiding somewhere, his big lynx-shape likely jammed under an armchair or the bed. The draft had not come from the desk, the closest hiding place; but Arahant's bellowslike breathing and inflating apparatus could easily send a puff of air all the way across the room.

The Detenebrator waxed still more rhetorical. "Dreams are night's autumnal seeds cast upon day's springtime soil. If they sprout, new-colored flowers spring up."

"You speak in human words this time, but your newfound coherence conveys scarcely more than your cataract of noise-pain did at Whitecloud. My patience is slightly short of infinite, and I'm not on this caravan to keep you company."

Rheinallt wished he could scoop up traillight and shine it into the fibrous basketball innards until he could see an inkling of what it was and what it wanted. The additional lamp was not much help, and he was reluctant to use lightning in a confined gaslit space.

Nettled, the Detenebrator repeated, "I am not lonely. When the time comes, I will demonstrate. I'll neither tell nor show, but will embody. It will then be up to you, and certain others. You and I may try your self and see its strength, Eiverdein.

103

We may melt your soul and draw it out like fine wire, tune the strands of your mind. It will be great fun."

"Great," Rheinallt said sardonically. Was that an articulate description of what it had tried, so inarticulately, on his late companions of the sled?

The Detenebrator's tone grew almost friendly. "I approve of you, Eiverdein. You're a survivor. Among all three men aboard that sled, there were none with whom I was able to communicate at all. Ah, I sense you understand. Of those whose brains I touched directly with my garbled fiber-talk, one kept functioning: yours. The cortians carry sound all too well.

"Perhaps I ought not to have tried at all after I saw that the Whitecloud obstacle was useless. As I suppose you know, some barriers engender bridges in the way that some poisons engender curatives; but that didn't seem to be the case there.

"Needlessly, I took the risk of communicating anyway. The result was not an absolute disaster, since I gained further appreciation of your unusual abilities, Eiverdein. That did cause me to delay longer than was prudent, waiting for some better situation: this trip has dragged with a slowness to try the patience of a squeaker.

"The aircat, of course," the Detenebrator boomed out as an afterthought, "I could not contact in sound symbols at all: he simply close-reefed his ears. Now I imagine he's becoming quite cramped under that armchair."

Maybe it could hear Arahant breathing. Rheinallt ignored this sally. "What capabilities of mine?"

"Allow me to be the expert on capabilities, my dear Eiverdein. After all, I only am a potential entity myself. This chance is the culmination of much work and much suffering. More than you know, more—if I seem to say it who shouldn't— more than I hope you ever will have to bear." The Detenebrator shifted its fuzzy sphere back and forth, touching no surfaces. "I honestly hope and expect you will survive, or else half of my hopes will have gone for naught. In the meantime, keep air in your lungs!"

There was a thin, piercing whistle, hissingly drawn out, and the Detenebrator pulled itself along by extruded fibers like a jellyfish to the door. A rope of fibers twisted the handle, and it vanished into the corridor.

Rheinallt took a deep breath, let it out. His ears ached. The door drifted shut in the draft, and the latch clicked.

Arahant crawled out from under the armchair. He elaborately stretched all four legs, one at a time, then shook himself to refluff the fur that had been compressed by the constricted space under the chair.

"Couldn't outbluster it, huh?" Arahant said.

"That wasn't quite my intention."

"So what was?"

"To find out what it wants, you catadupe."

With a claw tip Arahant scratched in the tight fur beneath his ear. "Do you think it's true, about the Detenebrator wanting to explain before? When it accosted us on the sled?"

Moving around the desk, Rheinallt dropped into the lighterweight but upholstered chair and stared at the leaf-motion within the decorated lamp. "Could be."

"It sure has changed. Are you positive it's the same creature?"

"I'm going to assume so. The, ah, quality of the screeching on the sled, and its talk just now, feels similar. Like an incoherent shout and a conversational sentence spoken with the same voice."

"A voice I almost managed not to hear at all, on the sled," Arahant said thoughtfully. "I was ready again to shut it out if its voice went wild."

"Are you complaining?"

The aircat smiled his feline grin. "Certainly not. I appreciate the superb functioning of my mind as it is. I don't care to be soniferously killed or addled, and if I also happen to be hearing on partially wrong wavelengths for the Detenebrator, that's fine with me. Hmph."

"It's voice is on a wavelength more accessible to the human ear and brain than to the catadromic?"

"Basically, yes. Apparently its darling little sensory filaments could touch my presence, but not get at my delicate ears." Arahant flicked his pointed ears to illustrate their delicacy. His eyes sparkled. "Perhaps you are more kin to it than I am."

"Great."

"Perhaps that lack of kinship is what saved my aural channels from overload at Whitecloud. A selective deafness to overbearing shrillness is scarcely vulgar. It's essential to be able to close one's ears to high-altitude winds; all the Luftmenschen know that. Besides, I wouldn't be able to appreciate the structural nuances of my own operas if—"

"Get back on the track, please," Rheinallt interrupted.

"In any case, another puzzle. I'll take care not to have my tail trodden upon. Do you the same." Arahant switched his thick tail forward and studied the fluffy white tailtip as if he were studying upon a safe place to hide it. "Personally I'm more concerned with how it manages to hide so well."

Rheinallt hesitated, shook his head. "I confess that I've been thinking of its mobility as almost a miraculous phenomenon. Although of course it wasn't."

"Define 'miraculous.'"

"Scary, dangerous, and unfathomable with present data. Like its sudden appearance from the window."

Arahant twitched the tailtip a few times in tiny arcs. "I see. Well, not having felt the baneful sonic influence as strongly as you have, I've been paying more attention to its physical aspects. Mind you, I don't know just what manner of thing it is. I do think it definitely is material, and capable of movement using those darling fibers to push and pull when necessary. Or maybe exclusively."

"It couldn't move in vacuum without something to cling to? That could be a help. Confidence, Arahant."

"Caution, my dear Hendrik Eiverdein Rheinallt."

"It was confidence that got us off the rain planet, out of the first stage of our exile after being marooned by those low-lifes and abandoned to die."

"To this Trails culture where we're still in exile."

Rheinallt nudged the lamp to make the green leaves flicker. "At least we're making progress."

"Yes, but the direction is questionable. I only mean to suggest that if we're near another turning point in our fortunes, let's not blow it."

"I'm with you there." Rheinallt slapped the table lightly. "And now, if you'll kindly vacate the premises, I'd like to be alone with Whitnadys."

"Whitnadys isn't here yet."

"I'd like some time alone with myself first."

"Good idea," Arahant said. "You could use a bath."

"It's been a long day for some of us. Take your nose with you when you go."

Arahant clapped the end of his tail over his nose like an ostrich plume. "Ah, one more item, Hendrik, if you please. When did you notice I was here in the room with you?"

"You were puffing on my ankles."

The aircat scowled comically. "You knew I was under the armchair?"

"No; I suppose you dove there when the Detenebrator showed up. Still, that can't be right. You must have already been there, snoozing or something."

"Hendrik, I—"

"You could have slipped me a warning."

Arahant maintained his scowl. "I did. The reason I was under the armchair was that you were acting unpredictably. You were in here an hour, I estimate, before the Detenebrator pushed the door open and wandered around the wall to behind the curtain."

"Huh?"

"When you walked in that door you were in a virtual trance. I started off chatting with you, and you scarcely were able to respond. When you did begin talking, your sentences were sort of coherent but the conversation wasn't. I suspect the Detenebrator might have told you more if you hadn't been so under the weather."

"Lord! It seemed like I heard the Detenebrator—well, essentially the same minute I came in. I remember its advent was pretty strange emotionally. How long was I like that?"

Arahant considered. "Maybe half a clockhour like talking to an idiot. Then the Detenebrator came in, started talking, and shocked you out of it. Did the surgeon try a practice lobotomy on you?"

"Was I really that bad?" What could have happened?

"Definitely. I told you fourteen choice anecdotes about my sisters, and you didn't complain once." Arahant blinked slowly.

"Amazing." Rheinallt thought in silence for several minutes. He reconstructed his day, came finally down to the conversation with Susannilar. She really had witched him! But how? And was it deliberate?

"It was Susannilar," he said, and relayed as much of her

107

tale of childhood as he could remember. And he found he remembered vast gobs of it, in vivid detail, as if she had carried him back psychically to glimpse her childhood.

"She has a strong mind, that one," Arahant said when Rheinallt finally wound down. "Best you keep clear of her for a while. When we undertook the bloodsweater discipline, we gained awesome powers of self-healing, but your mind needs to be working clearly. Else the next time you do one of those electrical tricks that only you can do, you'll kill yourself."

Rheinallt held his hand under his chin and a single hair from his beard fell onto his palm. Taking the hair between thumb and forefinger, he held it upright on the line of sight between himself and Arahant, and with the slightest, most controlled trickle of electricity flowing from fingertip, he split the hair from base to top. When the split hair had ceased smoking he tossed it on the rug.

With a small bow, Arahant said, "My apologies. Even weirded half out of your mind, you've got such strength that I can only admire, not emulate."

"Let me know when you want lessons."

"Ho, ho. Choosing to master the processes of one's blood is risky enough."

"But you did that long ago," Rheinallt said with a chafing tone. "Look at the benefits: gaining power over the cellular triggers of disease containment, controlled growth, refreshment and regeneration. As you well know, sickness, indigestion, poison, and wounds are all conditions diminishing in harmfulness as skill increases. Being able to spit blood, piss blood, and sweat blood are corollary features: any of these would indicate grave, possibly fatal organic malfunctions in a mammal of less mind-body integration, or less control."

"Quite true," Arahant agreed. "Next you'll tell me that neither of us has abilities outside the range of any self-aware mammal. Bioelectricity is an entirely different skill."

"Sure. You've managed not to poison yourself, so far. What makes you think you'd necessarily electrocute yourself?"

"The friends of our youth who did electrocute themselves."

More soberly, Rheinallt said, "I was very lucky."

"That's why I say you should be careful of encounters that fog your clarity."

"No. I appreciate your warning, but it's even more important now that I figure out who and what Susannilar is. She's got something unique. She even told me she could get into the Ship if no one else could."

Squinting at his tailtip, Arahant asked, "Do you believe that?"

"I'm not sure. Not yet."

The aircat sniffed disdainfully. "Maybe she plans to hypnotize everyone into thinking that she's gone in and that it's full of boogie-woogies."

"That's bogeymen."

"Whatever."

"Thus reserving the Ship all for herself? A number of the expeditionaries may have that in mind, but they won't get away with it. The rest are too watchful."

"Well, stay watchful yourself." Arahant nodded abruptly, and with a low purring chuckle of dubious import, opened the door and left.

What a series of ordeals, Rheinallt thought. He was glad Arahant had hung around to help jolly him back to a relaxed state of mind.

Later, sponged and refreshed, Rheinallt considered that the Detenebrator, almost as much as the Ship itself, had been for him like an unseen companion this last year. A mystery customized for him, the knowledge of the thing was borne along in his mind like that Ship, or the image of a ship. He did not relish the comparison. One monkey on one's mental back at a time ought to be enough.

Susannilar? He would need to deal with her again later, definitely. She was a powerful force on this expedition—another sleeper who turned out to be a porcupine when you stumbled over it. But useful and valuable if her talents could be channeled helpfully.

Later, but not tonight, he would ask Whitnadys for help with Susannilar. She would have some ideas. It was hard to believe that Susannilar's girlish recital had affected his mind, but he couldn't doubt Arahant's testimony; he had known him too long not to trust the aircat perfectly. Next time he talked with that budding hypnotist, he might take an escort, though.

This second encounter with the Detenebrator was another factor in this caravan-equation that held too many unknowns already. The Detenebrator was dangerous, and did its capri-

109

ciousness intensify the risk, or ameliorate it? The memory of the hotly twisted eyes of his two friends, of the cooling skin of the one corpse that remained on the sled—

Arahant was right, of course: caution was required here. Was his Special Caravan marked for the same fate as the sled? And its passengers? How tough were the rest of them? For that matter, how tough was he if the Detenebrator's sonic powers had escalated as much as its ability to communicate, and the entity's aims had not softened?

Meditating, relaxing, he continued gently pushing the clotted extraordinary sensations from the forefront of his mind, shelving the worries.

Despite a leader's worry and a survivor's recall, he still retained a capacity for wonder. Of what nature was the Detenebrator? Was it really proper to consider it an alien, a creature? From whence, and why?

Rheinallt had heard persistent rumors that out beyond the last starveling planet on the far end of the Green Trail toward Galactic South, the trail did not merely vanish into illimitable distance but rather was actively barred against the caravans. If there was a trail nation beyond End-of-Green, possibly it was alien, and no guessing its size. Sometimes even he, the much-traveled, forgot for a while that planets accessible on the trails known to humans were infinitesimal against the size of the rest of the galaxy. The word "accessible" had a sharp-edged handle.

But the Detenebrator? It seemed unique. He felt a wrongness in trying to assign the being to some particular galactic location. Even a home unknown, no matter how distant and rumor-shrouded, seemed too prosaic. The Detenebrator was above geography, or beyond it.

There was a knock and Whitnadys slipped into the room, happy feminine contrast with what had gone before. Good that she had not arrived earlier.

She propped her ankus in the corner, gave out an exaggerated sigh. "I'm glad I don't work as long hours as the squeakers," she said. Seeing his expression, she demanded, "What's with you?"

"The Detenebrator was here. Arahant and I met it once before, on our little four-squeaker sled foray. I told you about that."

"I remember," she said soberly. "Two guys died. Bad news, huh?"

"One more imponderable, anyway."

"Sounds like disaster in a small package. Luckily, I was home on Blueholm finishing the pregnancy when you ran into that. Our baby came just at the right time, since I couldn't deliver him by proxy like I've been mothering him by proxy all these weeks. No way I was going to miss your Special Caravan, no matter what oddities we turn up."

She laughed, a soprano ripple, and batted at him playfully. "Hey, no need to be so gloomy. So it's a strange trip. We expected that. Maybe all the imponderables will gang up on each other and leave us be. Knock each other out. Or if not, we'll just throw them overboard."

Rheinallt grinned faintly. "But suppose we are among the imponderables?"

She laughed again, eyes bright, and he drew her to him for a long hug.

"We could decree a new fashion in earplugs," Whitnadys said after a few minutes.

"Screening would be nice," he told her seriously. "The Detenebrator's generated voice was powerful last year, and now he's got it under fine control. What addled brains last year might be able to structurally warp them this time around."

"Can you counter it with your—what do you call them—electric waves?"

"Perhaps. My heightened bioelectricity might just make me more vulnerable than most."

She shook her head emphatically, hair a honeyed swirl. "No. You did fine at Whitecloud. If the necessity arises, you'll do fine again."

They talked desultorily for a while, letting the problems of their day seep out of them and away. After a while he rose, carefully shut off the lamps one by one, and with a heavy tug on a pullcord, swept back the curtains from the thickly glassed window. Into the room, faintly reflected from the ceiling, crept the elfin blue glow of the trail beneath the plodding caravan.

"Feeling better?" Whitnadys asked, warm and sympathetic.

"Much."

She stood too, and they came together in front of the win-

111

dow, feeling the strong reality of bodily contact and the contrast with the unreality of the meadow. Or rather, with the deadline of real things, the bottom, that absolute zero of existence which they dared and defied.

"Oh, your touch is so good," she whispered as they slowly undressed each other.

They both knew what she meant by those words, spoken on a soft carpet with the black dead meadow outside: That in this expression of each other through touch, through feeling, was not only the standard idea of affection and lovemaking but a basic, primevally human defiance of the meadow and its neutrally empty nothingness. And this idea itself was not only a thought but a feeling.

Later, among minor caresses, Whitnadys propped herself on one elbow and said, "I hate to change the subject, Hendrikal, but I forgot to mention it earlier; I heard a story today that Trigotha was assassinated. That it wasn't just an accident on his way back from finding the Ship."

He smiled lazily at her. "No trouble to change it back again," and he ran a fingertip along her arm, enjoying the soft warmth.

"Your electrotoned muscles are too much for me! But is that true, have you heard that story?"

"Well, I was told by someone that he was killed by a fanatic of some sort. Whether the assassin just found the news intolerable, or also thought he could squelch it by killing Trigotha, I don't know. I understand the assassin didn't survive Trigotha by long enough to explain."

"We are all so full of fear," she mused.

"Ah, then let's return to the main subject," he said, laughing, and took his turn to tease her, tickling her until she laughed too.

"When did you find time to learn so much?" she asked.

"A long life among the fleshpots," he answered sleepily.

After a moment she asked, "How long?" Deliberately casual.

He yawned. "Talk about it later?"

"Well, all right."

They kissed gently.

All that was human here was theirs. There was nothing alive outside, and nothing that ever had been alive. Inside was Whitnadys, the friend and lady lately so special to him, and her

112

touch, her contact and communication and sharing. The caravan, their minuscule glowworm crammed with humanity, seemed so tiny and alone. He repressed a shiver, not wanting her to feel that now, but he suspected she already had felt such a shiver more than once. He would not have liked to make this trip without her humorous competence and loving support. He kissed her again, softly, as she slept.

So empty all around.

Still there was the Ship, somewhere ahead. That sustained him, and could perhaps if all else failed out here. As when a wounded soldier left for dead wakes from thirst on the now deserted battlefield, sees the glowing radiance of a campfire far away in the darkness where some friend of light rests upon the meadow.

The trodden ways were so few and so difficult of passage, the conveyances so limited. Trigotha had made the great discovery: a towering, legendary event of this age and this culture. The only starship yet known to these fifty-four worlds of the accessible galaxy. The new medium of interpersonal contact. The friend not merely by presence, but by existence.

9. A Cry of Crimson

THE NEXT DAY DRAGGED ON WITH A MISCELLANY OF SLOW PAS-times—until the caravan topped a small rise in the gravitic pseudosurface.

"The Ship!" someone cried, and quickly the caravan's cars from head to tail were ablaze with lights, filled with wild hopeful words, strained peerings engendering hot speculations in heads that had thought themselves all speculated out. This was the call, finally puncturing the long clockdays of the caravan.

"We've found it!"

A drop of blood with a flame behind it, the Ship glinted on the horizon of the meadow.

"At last!"

"Will the trail pass near it?" a voice asked from the milling crowd.

"We'll see pretty soon, for sure," someone stated with anonymous confidence.

"About time."

"Damn right."

All jostled for good positions at the view windows, or for positions in the lounge car close enough to the bar to order a celebratory drink. Sets of binoculars passed from hand to hand, wide eyes widened by the huge meadow-lenses.

"Hey! How about a name?"

"Yeah!" Various throats took up the cry. "What'll we call it?"

"Can't go on calling it 'the Ship' no more."

"Didn't Trigotha give it a name?"

"Naw."

"Any ideas?"

Finally one of the two men who perpetually sweltered in red fur coats clambered up to stand on a chair and roared out, *"Falling Angel!"* and stepped down again to stand with his look-alike partner.

"What'd he say?" came voices amid the babble.

The excitement reached everyone, even those who Rheinallt felt sure were along mainly to shine up their credentials for the lecture circuit back home.

"What?"

"Stop hogging those lenses."

"Fallen Angel."

"No, no. *Falling Angel."*

"That's right."

"Sounds good to me."

"Falling Angel it is, then."

"A toast!"

"Good."

Step by step the Special Caravan drew nearer to the Ship. Now that the Ship was visible, a reddish blob in the distance, many of the passengers found to their surprise that they scarcely had believed in its reality; that they had come all this long way mentally holding their breaths.

The relief was immense. A pressure that had been suppressed from consciousness was lifted, and the whole complement aboard acted more than a little hyperventilated. Rheinallt was tempted to reduce the oxygen ratio in the supplier system.

"I had no idea it would be so big!"

"Hand back those glasses. You look like a big-eyed bug."

Soon now they would get down to the real business. The sophisticated languor of never-say-quit was replaced by the scurrying bumptiousness of gosh-wow-we-made-it. Everywhere plans were being reviewed and equipment lists checked.

A woman caught at Rheinallt's arm to ask, "Captain Eiverdein! When we get up to the Ship, what airlock do we use?"

"Any one you want," he told her genially.

"I mean, from which end of the caravan ought we to disembark?"

"Either end, madam—both ends stop."

Rheinallt hooked out a few of the more patient of the crew and started them circulating with renewed offers of mobility training for whoever wanted it. The woman who was the best signjack aboard, her hand signals sharply formed and clear, agreed to concentrate on brushing up the passengers' intersign and pounding some trailsign into them. Gestures which had been too bothersome to learn in an airy, gaslit car would seem well worth the effort when in the isolation of an airsuit in vacuum.

The next time Rheinallt saw Susannilar in the corridors of the caravan, he stopped her. "Getting ready to debark?"

"Sure!"

"Is Nollinsae actively pursuing you, aboard the caravan? You seem to run hot and cold on whether you're worried about him or not."

The beginning smile on her face was dashed. She began instead to tremble. "Nollinsae?" she said, as if she could hardly remember the name. "Of the Guard of Fleurage?" The pink hydroponics flower in her hair waggled with her agitation.

"Yes, of course." Rheinallt had not shown her the note.

"No, he can't harass me here!" Her eyes were pits. "Can he? No, certainly not."

"Well—"

"This is the Blue Trail! He has no authority, no jurisdiction—wait. He hasn't bothered me so far since—" Biting her lip, she added, "You must—" Her torrent of thoughts overtook her words, and she fell silent.

Earlier, before the sighting of the Ship, Rheinallt had rechecked the names on the passenger lists, found both names present, as if neither was avoiding the other. He had not yet looked up the man in person about this; prior to the note he had only met Nollinsae passingly a few times, and then during the telescope affair in the lounge car. If Nollinsae was important to Susannilar, why hadn't she mentioned him in that long hypnotic recital?

117

With a mind full of the imminence of the Ship and the unpleasant shock of the Detenebrator's presence aboard, Rheinallt had not concluded what attitude he ought to take toward a planetary military officer traveling with the expedition. Or—as a caravaneer with a potential treasure trove almost at hand now—what ought to be his policy toward the Guard itself. Was Nollinsae its representative aboard, its tentacle? Or simply riding as a private speculator-adventurer, like the others? Conceivably, even, in official pursuit of Susannilar herself all this long way?

"We're no longer in the Blue Free Nation," he said slowly.

"I know that!" she snapped.

In this moment she reminded Rheinallt of a long-ago lover, all flash and fire, full of vast power and rent with devastating self-contradiction. Heady starfire.

"In fact," he added, trying to calm her, "the trail along here seems almost a frosty blue. Our societal support system is attenuated, too. Of legal authority none at all remains. We're out of the Nation's jurisdiction—"

"But we've got to be outside Fleurage's too! It's northwest, on the other side of the Nation. Right?"

"Legal authority is cooperative by definition. We're beyond the reach of free law, except what we've brought with us. We're not beyond the reach of force," he added simply.

"I see," she said quietly. "What should I do? Run? Fight?"

Again, as at their first real meeting in the lounge car, Rheinallt had the strong sensation of twoness, that the girl was shifting back and forth; as while standing, one's weight is subtly rebalanced from one foot to the other without actually lifting the feet.

"I'm responsible for the Special Caravan. Everyone aboard who wants it has my protection. Do you want that?"

She shivered. "I—I'm not sure."

He decided to reask his original question. "You *did* know this Nollinsae before? Are you really fleeing him?"

"I fear I—I hate him!" she gasped out. She took a deep breath, then added, "He burned my mother," with a cold flatness. And then, blinded with quick tears, she turned and walked shakily down the corridor, brushing unseeingly past bustling passengers.

He did not follow her. Burned, she said.

Her desperation might well become Rheinallt's problem. Nollinsae's doggedness might well be a complementary problem, since it seemed beyond coincidence now that the self-labeled Guardsman was aboard the same caravan as Susannilar.

Yet Susannilar acted too unstable for Rheinallt to press her strongly. And in what direction could he press her? He wanted to help her, but in the absence of a direct threat that he could counter, force against force, what could he do that would not eliminate her own freedom? Or violate Nollinsae's without any overt action on the fellow's part? Rheinallt despised preventive custody, on either side of some unknowable act that had not yet happened. And the crew, in any case, used to breathing the libertarian air of the Nation, would not tolerate his standing less strong for freedom than they. He had chosen them well.

What he could do was start sharing his information and analysis of the Susannilar-Nollinsae affair with the whole crew, adding more information as he learned it himself. If a time of action came, they all would be ready, and capable of judgment as well as action. They were a rough gang, but he was proud of them.

Most odd that she could not settle within herself whether she wanted help. What could he do without that?

Presumably Nollinsae, in his turn, would have something to say about Susannilar beyond the simplistic accusation in his note.

Thoughtfully, Rheinallt turned toward a window as he felt the caravan come slowly to a stop with clankings of couplers and hissings of air hoses. The gravity had felt smooth, hardly variant on the approach; the meadow roundabout should present no roughness in the way of setting up camp in the vicinity of the Ship.

The thing was massive. He stared at it in awe.

The *Falling Angel* loomed redly over the tiny men and women peeping up out of caravan windows, loomed over the sturdy cars of the caravan and the huge resting golden squeakers, dwarfed the misty breadth of the trail. Rheinallt had wanted the caravan halted wherever the trail curved closest to the side of the Ship, and this was the place. For convenience's sake, until they learned better, they had agreed to call the bow that end of the Ship pointing outward, farther along the trail.

Assuming it was a ship.

119

This unwelcome thought almost got by Rheinallt's blood-sweater discipline into the realm of nausea, but he reshelved that recurring doubt until the evidence would be in. He also would continue to keep this possibility to himself, for regardless of marvels the ghostly red object might be or contain, what the people wanted was a starship. They all knew that it might not be what they wanted, but he doubted that many *felt* that it might not be. Disappointment of such emotionally high hopes might be disastrous, here beyond the frontier.

Cigar-shaped, the Ship stretched for perhaps ten times the length of the caravan: ten times the whole length from the golden-trunk nose tip of the lead waybeast to the waiting muzzle of the wired-cannon in the caboose turret that watched their back trail.

The newly named *Falling Angel* seemed to rest heavily on the black meadow, but without penetrating the pseudosurface. Rather it rested in a long depression, presumably of its own making, to a depth of a quarter or perhaps a fifth of its own width. This alone was unique. While everywhere the meadow had its own undulations and locally characteristic features, Rheinallt could not recall hearing of any artificial influencing of its topography. This was a hint of power or properties of the Ship to make its value more than match its size.

The glowing red bulk looked like nothing ever seen before by the Trails culture, he was sure. But it bothered him that neither did it look like anything that he was familiar with. Of the whole complement of the caravan, passengers and crew, only he and Arahant had ever seen a true starship before, a vehicle which could traverse the meadow without benefit of trails, or of squeakers to pull it through breakpoint. That knowledge Rheinallt had kept to himself; and he had long ago warned the aircat to keep his sentience to himself, as the Trails culture had never encountered aliens and he did not want Arahant to be their guinea pig.

Was this Ship an alien craft? Likely so, he had to admit, with some disappointment for the ancillary hope he had held that it might be a starship from his own neck of the woods. Some meadow-slider gone hard aground, out of communication and beyond help, with its crew unable to repair it themselves.

The fifty-four worlds on the accessible trails could not build such a vehicle, and in spite of his knowlege Rheinallt could not build one from scratch with however much help he might coax from people who did not have electricity yet. However, given a moderately malfunctioning ship; the resources of the Trails culture, particularly of the burgeoning engineers of the Nation; and himself to mate them properly—this combination might do wonders for his and Arahant's stranded situation, and then the trailmen could take the mentational technology of the propulsion and run with it themselves.

And yet no one had seen the *Falling Angel* before Trigotha and his crew. The trail that ran along in silence here was utterly deserted and led to no known planets. Some few explorers, though, ought to have ventured out at least this far before Trigotha. Could they have missed something this size? Maybe it arrived after those first utmost-reach probings? That was possible, but that dent in the meadow spoke of great age. Perhaps they suppressed their findings, or were not believed.

That it had not been found before argued that it was newly in place, contrary to the mysterious indentation in which it lay. That indentation, plus its strange glow, argued that it had not come from any shipyard Rheinallt had heard of before his exile: no, not from among the planets and the swathe of meadow Earth knew, human *or* alien.

What had Trigotha thought about it? He wished again he could have met the earlier pioneer leader. A brave man, and without Rheinallt's motivations. Among scraps of information about that trip, he had found nothing so complete as a diary.

An apparently calm Susannilar joined Rheinallt at the window and stared up at the Ship. Her face took on a ruddy tinge in the glow from outside.

"Doesn't it seem—kind of ephemeral, to you?" she asked.

Surprised, he said, "No. Quite the opposite. Old, very old, perhaps. Look at that dent in the meadow. That's solidity verging on the unliftable."

"Well, ghostly, then."

"Is that how it looks to you?"

"I'm—not sure." She bit her lip lightly. "To me, it doesn't quite belong. As though it weren't altogether here."

He considered this. It did look ghostly at this distance, luminescent. The red was less a colored surface than a bulky glow. Yet, through collision or weight or whatever, it *had* made quite a dent.

Near the caravan some workmen, suited against the vacuum, were beginning to set up a large air-bubble dome for the convenience of the members of the expedition while they explored their find. He assumed that all would continue to sleep aboard the caravan, but the airtent bubble would furnish workspace for examining portable or detachable items from the Ship. Some scientists also had portable labs to assemble.

Normally dense air could carry the extended mentational field necessary to keep itself on the meadow, as long as the air was itself in contact with a person. Without the skin of the airtent or of a suit it would disperse: attenuate quickly toward vacuum and so disappear. The tent was ribbed and double-walled for safety against a blowout, and the material itself was quite strong. Not even a coal mine protected by planetary air and rock was so safe against flying objects as even the flimsiest structure on the meadow: no meteorite punctures here. Heavy tubing led to that car of the caravan which contained the major air-recycling equipment. The tent itself would open onto Car Fourteen directly.

Susannilar, apparently still with the same thoughts, was murmuring to herself in a childish singsong:

"You have to be here, before you can be anything; you have to be here before you can be anywhere. Here before there, here before there, here and there before everywhere." Her eyes were closed as she swayed to the beat of her chant.

Rheinallt could not make sense of these whispered scraps.

"Ah, Susannilar. And Captain Eiverdein."

Susannilar spun around. Rheinallt turned more slowly. A chunky man with a cool square-mouthed smile stood there at ease, hands in pockets: the Guardsman.

"We have arrived at our goal, I see," the newcomer said cheerfully.

"Nollinsae," the girl named him flatly. Her facial muscles twitched. She began edging away.

Nollinsae looked directly at Rheinallt. "How soon will we be allowed to visit the Ship? *Falling Angel* I believe is the consensus choice for its name, assuming we cannot decipher any it bears."

"Anytime you wish. Some are suiting up already; but no equipment can be unpacked until the bubble tent is erected."

"Good. I am very curious, of course—but then curiosity is the magnet that has drawn us all so far from home."

Indeed, Rheinallt thought.

Nollinsae's gaze moved to the looming Ship. "I believe I saw a flicker of movement. You are certain the Ship is abandoned?"

With a pulse of excitement Rheinallt turned back to the window. "Where?"

Then he saw it, a gliding moonlet above the curve of the Ship, tiny in the distance, looping easily along like a white tick exploring a great red dog. Rheinallt snatched up binoculars racked next to the adjoining window. The apparent moonlet, seen through the lenses, was slightly fuzzy, like a dandelion puffball, and the thinnest of filaments strung out behind it and down, to keep it in contact with the meadow pseudosurface.

"That's the Detenebrator," Rheinallt said reluctantly.

"So? A thing of yours?" Nollinsae glanced at him shrewdly.

"Not at all. Whatever it is, it's all its own thing."

Nollinsae shrugged, but regarded Rheinallt with an added wariness. Spontaneously they looked around, and saw that Susannilar had slipped away.

"Do not be misled by her side of charm," Nollinsae said without raising his voice. "Susannilar is a floozy and a scofflaw, a child of flowers; and worse. She is not one of your peaceful Bluebacks from the Nation, with eyes only for what they call science. I am not joking, I assure you, Captain. Believe me—for the sake of your caravan, if not for your own self."

"I'm always ready to take any needful precautions—" Rheinallt began.

"Good."

"—but do you know this for a fact? She is a killer?" The last word came out strangely.

Rheinallt knew well enough that he had here a personal problem, and a problem of justice, of administration, perhaps of safety. But damn it, the Ship was the true problem for Rheinallt and for them all. Did they have to bring their personal conflicts along? When the caravan had brought him to his destination, couldn't he cease being concerned with the caravan?

No, if he could bring them all through safely to their dreams, he would. But, oh, how the Ship called to him!

Nollinsae nodded easily. "Certainly. She is a death-bringer. I've seen her in action."

"How so? What did she do?"

Rheinallt tried to imagine her doing violence, but it was difficult. In that long trancelike monologue, her self-portrayal had been of a happy, sensitive child. Hardly grown now, she ought not to have changed that much.

Rheinallt noticed that outside the workers had finished spreading the tent floor, and were now erecting the arching struts that would hold up the dome of the airtent. Self-contained lanterns already hung from interior poles, flaming hospitably.

Just as soon as the big bubble workshop was safely completed, Rheinallt would head up to the Ship himself. Some of the more determined or foolhardy were already in their color-tagged or transparent airsuits and struggling up the long gentle slope toward the *Falling Angel*, bits of color like sparks in ashes. All carried lanterns, either self-contained or the kind that leeched off a suit's air supply. Drawn toward the fire? he wondered fancifully.

"Listen to me, blast it, sir! She is dangerous, deadly dangerous!" The Guardsman's heavy hand on Rheinallt's shoulder jerked him hard around.

Letting his face go hard to match the motion, Rheinallt pulled himself from the other's grasp. You fool, he thought contemptuously, stormtrooper manners don't win friends among trailmen.

"You play with force, Nollinsae. I hold that blade by its handle."

Nollinsae's surprise at the other's reaction set him back only a moment, "Forgive me, Captain. But please! I myself have seen her mortally stab three soldiers assigned to guard her. Three big men, and armed. She uses some craft or trick of witches to confuse men's senses until they are but stumbling clowns for her easy murdering. She seems to rush upon you from in front and then she slits your throat from behind. I brought up a platoon on the run, but by then she had escaped in the crowd."

"Crowd? What was the occasion for all this violence?"

"Her mother was in the final stages of cleansing, and I

124

ordered Susannilar brought out to witness the moment of purification."

Rheinallt just looked at him.

"Of death, that is," Nollinsae explained. "The only true purification is at the stake." Nollinsae did not look at all defensive; he sketched what patently was not justification but simple explanation.

"Captain Eiverdein, we of Fleurage do not have the riches, the margin for living, that you have in the Nation. We cannot tolerate attacks on the fabric of our society and our way of life. We cannot tolerate poison in our system; we must root it out, burn it out before our society rots from within."

So they *had* burned Alalortern. No wonder Susannilar was shaky!

Rheinallt said very slowly and evenly, "Need I remind you that neither you nor she is in that society now?"

Was Susannilar as innocent—in contrast with Nollinsae— as Rheinallt wanted to assume? Conscious of his responsibility for the safety of the whole caravan, he was loathe to bring or allow force to be brought by others, if the parties possibly could be kept at arm's length until all were safely back in the Nation.

Nollinsae gave the impression that he realized that he had overreached himself, perhaps that he had bet too heavily on an emotional fellow-officer approach, and lost the round. Maybe the idea that his society had limits had never been proposed to his face before. Whatever the reason, he cooled suddenly.

"Perhaps we can continue this discussion another time," Nollinsae said.

"Surely."

Nollinsae nodded, turned abruptly, and left.

Yes, no wonder that Susannilar was shaky, strung out into weirdness. Rheinallt turned gratefully back to the window, wanting to take a few minutes to saturate his cells with oxygen before he went out.

A lone figure in an airsuit straggled up the slope after the first wavelet of impatient explorers. From the curious blurring of its outlines he knew it must be Susannilar, and the binoculars verified his impression.

The empty meadow allowed light to carry all details faithfully, and the singleton figure was the only thing visible which was difficult for his eyes to outline. Even the hugely glowing Ship was clearly demarcated, red against black, and all the manmade paraphernalia of the caravan could not have seemed clearer to the imagination of their creators than now to his eye.

Only Susannilar, of all the bustling caravaneers' camp, on all that plain of darkness: it was only she who was shaky, who apparently blurred, vibrated, oscillated, or whatever it was that she did. Rheinallt wondered how clearly she saw the death that was whole hog after her, the relentless pursuit of the Guardsman. If she could not elude him on her home world, what could she hope to do here? The surroundings were so limiting.

Had she hid from Nollinsae, or avoided him, on the journey out? Certainly it had taken a long time for Rheinallt to notice her adequately; but neither had he known her previously. More likely Nollinsae had watched her like cat with mouse, biding until he could catch her outside the caravan. The Guardsman did seem fastidious in his own way.

Yet what weapon did Nollinsae have now that he could not bring to bear when she first escaped him? What was his confidence, that the Guardsman thought he now could succeed alone at what before he could not handle with platoons of troops at his back?

Nollinsae was not really a fool: the man showed too much careful determination. And if Nollinsae was merely a fanatic, how could he bear to take so long about his appointed task? Less pressure than that had been too much for poor Wirtellin, the delegate. Foolish but purposeful, fanatical but patient? What the hell kind of a combination was that?

In many different situations Rheinallt had become used to managing diverse teams of people, but how could he keep the peace without understanding what these two were, let alone were up to? How to make better contact with them?

Rheinallt took a last look from within the caravan, from a human space looking out at a vista which was not, at the glowing red Ship and the starkly black meadow. Whistling randomly, he racked the binoculars and went along to his compartment to don his airsuit.

His tuneless notes stumbled in his mouth as he remembered the telescopic death in the lounge car. Rheinallt had just now examined the *Falling Angel* himself through fairly powerful

126

lenses without any harm whatsoever. The glowing red of the ship was pervasive, but not all that bright in absolute magnitude. The telescope was stronger than those hand-held lenses, but surely not that much stronger.

If the telescopic deaths were superstition on the part of Nollinsae and the others, how had the men died? And why? The same questions applied even if Nollinsae merely battened on some presumed superstitions of others aboard. Were the two deaths less unsettling for *not* being caused by mysterious fiery magnifications?

10. Within the Shadow

THE HUGE HULL OF THE *FALLING ANGEL* CURVED UP IN FRONT of Rheinallt, a gentle curve rising to such a height above the meadow that it leaned far out over him. Like an ant encountering a lawn roller in the pinched angle where the roller met the ground. Red wall curving up above, black plane dipping here to meet it. Maybe the size would be the worst of it.

He put out his hand to touch the wall of the Ship. Nothing. No texture, no movement, no resistance to gloved fingertips tentatively probing. He might as well have been waving his hand in a bank of red fog, but with no air resistance and no displacement of the fog.

Involuntarily dragging a deep breath from the measuring dispenser in his helmet, he stepped forward into the side of the Ship.

It was a faery maze of red shadows. Floors, ceilings, walls were insubstantial. Symmetries pleasing to the mind's eye but insensible to all else. He wandered over the interior curve of the hull where it fit snugly into the depression in the meadow, but there was no hull, just smoothed meadow in which the subspatial flooring was cloaked in red. He was immersed, a hundred fathoms deep in a red shadow-pool of hull. His body felt less impact from stepping through what must be thick bulkheads than it would from smoke rings.

In many of the compartments were what once might have been consoles, engines, or other items of equipment. But in contrast with the walls these outlines were quite hazy and conveyed only blurs which were blocky, narrow, longish, or whatever. Guesses at function were pure speculation.

An impression of immense age stole over him. His mouth quirked, not liking the taste of crumbling hopes and presentiments. Sure, hopes were still there, he thought, but they were all of a sudden getting kind of chewed around the edges.

Falling Angel was not a wreck. In all its lineaments it seemed perfectly intact. The dimly visible machinery might well be functional if only Rheinallt could get at it, if he could force a full and normal materiality, or else join the great vessel on its own terms.

Nor, perhaps, was the Ship necessarily even a derelict. He might be surrounded, here in this great outer curve of hull, with the owners of the Ship. Owners? What kind of owners? Who had, perhaps, merely parked here for a while for a picnic? If so, it must be a geologically long picnic to allow the Ship to settle so imperturbably into the meadow as to bend the very subsurface of space itself.

The upper or interior reaches of the *Falling Angel* would be unreachable without a platform, or extensible ladders, set up within this fog of corridors. Somewhere within would be a control room presumably. An engine room, an astrogation room, crew's quarters. Aggravating that he might be standing in the grand ballroom and not recognize it. No, actually, the walls so faintly suggested here were too close together for dancing. Assuming again, always assuming, that the builders of the Ship had been capable or desirous of anything like dancing.

What fabulous machinery must the glorious vessel have, to have brought it to this bleak resting place. For long minutes he tried to imagine the technology of the unguessable.

Finally Rheinallt put one harsh possible conclusion in words: there was no ship. Nothing but shadows, red shadows. Useless. His throat felt clogged, as if the subvocalization of such damning words could choke.

His friends: Arahant's sadness would match his own. Whit-nadys—she was more complicated, or rather, her motives were mixed, forming only an aggregate and not an alloy. She would be angry and relieved both.

In the midst of his goal, of this vast red-shadowed depression, Rheinallt could lighten his discouragement only by thinking that his depression at least was not heavy enough to make a dent in the meadow. Graveyard humor, suitable for the grave of a starship.

Without conscious aim he wandered about in the *Falling Angel*, the ethereal texture of the giant shadow so misty a red that it was minutes before he realized that he was seeing it through tears. With a movement unnecessary since his youth he reached a hand to wipe them away, only to be blocked by the helmet. Calmly he reabsorbed the tears, keeping articulate thoughts out of his mind. He passed through partitions like planed tendrils of fog.

After a while he saw that he had meandered again toward the side of the Ship facing the trail and the parked caravan. As he climbed up toward the lip of the dent full of ship-fog, he came to a height where, while still within the shadow of the Ship, he could see a long vista beyond the shadow. For the first time he looked at objects outside the Ship from an interior vantage.

There was a salty residue on his cheeks as Rheinallt began enhancing his interior electric field like spinning an electromagnet, more current, more spin, more field. Feeding on itself, faster and faster. If the *Falling Angel* had possessed the reciprocity of a stone he would have moved it in that instant, piloting and propelling it over the meadow, sliding free as the wind under the enhancing hurricane lash of his brain.

The Ship, of course, did not move. As his vision focused outside the Ship, though, the trail *writhed*. From within the perspective of the red fog, the great Blue Trail shimmied like an overflowing river that had forgotten its bed.

It had been long since Rheinallt had been in a house of illusion, and long since he had been in free fall in starspace, three-dimensional space without gravity. His internal balancers had grown lazy, his unconscious grown rigid in its determinations of what was solid and still, and irrefutably ought to be solid and still. He felt a quiver in his inner ear from trying to order his eyes to compensate for the motion of the trail, for trails did not move, could not move.

Beyond the shadow of the Ship he could now recognize the simple, stark surroundings only by an effort of will. Of the caravan he caught only glimpses, could not focus on it. And the trail that he knew so well, knew by its elfin blue color and ribbonlike proportions, now writhed and humped and coiled and straightened, randomly undulating.

What was happening? Had the fabric of subspace gone mad?

Rheinallt tried to damp down his enhancement, to still the ecstatic field intensities that could feed into a starship to move it across subspace, yet now bit into nothing and turned on themselves, whirling dizzily. His anguished concentration in setting up the mentational field had been so strong that now when he tried to turn it off he could not.

And beyond, far beyond, were other threads of colors, green and yellow and red, and all of these moved too. His look went far, far. He knew those distant stripes for trails too, could see the nearby one's happy blue curves shifting to meet the other trails, where the breakpoints to the Blue Free Nation and the human trail worlds would be.

Rheinallt tried to close his eyes and could not muster the strength. As carefully as he could, he let himself sink to his knees. Air—he must have more air.

The meadow beyond the red shadow was black and stark as always. Veins in ashes. Did they demarcate some meteoritic way to die, space decaying into subspace with an energy that made the trails twist and turn and coil upon themselves? Why would they seem to move under his heightened perception?

Somehow he slammed the valve that released air into his suit, and the freshness poured into his helmet, his lungs, and the blood which carried it to his brain. Here and there he still saw a flake or sparkle of light, tiny, as a natural eye will discover against even the blankest wall or sky. Levering his eyelids down, he squeezed his eyes shut to ease and moisten them, stopping the effect of dry burning from the blast of oxygen that had rasped across them.

Still with eyes closed he stumbled up the last few steps out of the shadowy hull. Outside the hull, on the clear blackness of the meadow, he felt calm and ventilated enough to look around. The only things that moved were people in suits, and a couple of restless squeakers rocking back and forth in their traces before being unhitched by Whitnadys' crew.

Out here the Blue Trail was as still as in the planet-thick Nation, lying sedately upon the meadow as it had for so many analogous light-years behind the caravan. None of the more distant trails were visible. The Special Caravan, windows streaming yellow gaslight onto the meadow, rested reassuringly where it had been parked, and he had no difficulty focusing on it. The mentational enhancement was lapsing gently as his mind cleared.

Not thinking now, just resting, Rheinallt stood there in the darkness next to that glowing red wall curving up and over, letting his visual center regain its equipoise in the clear infinity of meadow vacuum.

Hmm. So the Ship—wait, wait, he told himself, no need to try conclusions right now. Give yourself a little time to breathe. Let the head clear a bit.

Well, he thought cautiously after a few minutes, he certainly wouldn't be a pilot without a functioning starship. The *Falling Angel* patently was not at the moment a working vehicle; and whatever he had just done to himself by using the enhancement process without the corresponding technology was not something he would care to risk again.

As a pilot he needed a starship. He could not be a simple waybeast.

Rheinallt stepped slowly back into the red shadow, then turned and faced beyond the hull again. There were no effects this time, no moving Blue Trail. A few pumped strides brought him out onto the meadow once more, his perceptions still reporting everything normal.

Something had been learned. Or perceived anyway.

Dimly within the Ship, as he now looked back in from outside, he could see other people from the caravan exploring the interior, figures in a mist. Although their motions were blurred and indistinct with the shadow-substance intervening, it was apparent that most walked slowly and aimlessly. As puzzled as Rheinallt was, and probably as discouraged.

Without a source of light, and clearly there was none sufficient on the meadow, what could cast such a shadow, and upon what medium? The gas lamps and spotlights of the caravan

133

could light up a person and throw his shadow against the solid hull of a car, but there was never yet a shadow outlined above the pseudosurface of the meadow, blackness itself.

Rheinallt sat on the lip of the meadow depression, then lay back with head supported by hands and stared up at that great curving wall, red as brick in fog, and thought.

What kinds of shadows were there? Sound, wind, rain, heat? All these were directional forces; all interruptible by some object capable of creating a lack downstream, down-direction, where that force was blocked. None of these applied to the subspace meadow at all, let alone the ghostly Ship. Was he on the right track at all, with this "shadow" concept?

Standing up, he dusted the seat of his airsuit as a small joke, and went back into the *Falling Angel*. A mirage of some esoteric kind, a projection from somewhere else on the meadow? This hypothesis was tempting, because insubstantiality here might be a clue to hands-on reality elsewhere, maybe just a few days down the trail...? To his senses, the huge starship, derelict and empty as a wrecker could ask for, was a purely optical phenomenon; to the dark universal floor, however, the wraithlike Ship lay as ponderously heavy as a metal-ore planetoid. Mirages don't make dents.

When he climbed eventually up the gentle opposite slope of the hull-dent, out to the pure night of the meadow, the black vacuum outside the Ship was cheerful by contrast: as even the backyard outside the neighborhood haunted house, overgrown with vines and owls, is moonlit safety to the panting, surviving young spirit-hunters. Could a body be taken from its grave and yet occupy the hollowed ground with its soul's ghost?

Rheinallt decided to walk around the end of the Ship back to the caravan, the rearward end that they were arbitrarily calling the stern. Shortly he recognized Nollinsae and Susannilar.

Nollinsae was slowly walking toward Susannilar, and she was backing up at about the same speed: hands raised defensively, although the Guardsman was not that close to her. Was she afraid to turn her back on him? Nollinsae moved forward in slow even strides, while Susannilar made little mincing skips backward.

Nollinsae's hands and arms hung relaxed at his sides, but that might be for convenience to some unobtrusive belt weapon.

But he too had adopted an odd motion. As he paced in Susannilar's direction, he was almost continually snapping his helmeted head this way and that, to scan as completely as he could
the meadow at his sides and back. Watching Susannilar, but
nervously covering the rest of his surroundings.

Yet what could approach without being seen a long way
off? Bremolando, whom Rheinallt had deputed to watch, was
nowhere around. The two of them were alone and more or less
isolated by distance and silence.

Susannilar was wary of Nollinsae, watching him fixedly;
and Nollinsae was wary of Susannilar and of—what?

Each had helmet lanterns on, so they were not striving for
concealment, although the Ship was between them and the
caravan. Shielding his own suit light to a minimum, Rheinallt
began walking over the dark meadow, trying not to stumble
on small pseudosurface irregularities.

Shortly both the others moved suddenly, and Rheinallt
couldn't tell who had begun this new phase. Nollinsae had a
handweapon out—a short-range haywire, it must be, for any
kind of bullet or free-trajectory weapon was useless here—and
was drawing a quick but careful bead on Susannilar. Even at
this distance there were enough reflected glints on the man's
suit that Rheinallt could detect the stance of a marksman by
the two-handed grip on the weapon.

It was immediately obvious that he was having difficulty.
There seemed to be two Susannilars.

Like a juggler keeping two balls in motion between his
hands, shifting them so quickly that they seem to blur, Susannilar was shifting herself. The two places where she appeared
were endpoints of some quickly truncated trajectories. And
after a few moments one of these split Susannilars would disappear, to spring up again almost immediately at an odd angle
or a new distance.

Both of these images—no, both of these Susannilars—were
in constant motion by more normal means too, by whatever
dartings, duckings, and random sidesteps which are a part of
anybody's attempts at dodging.

Nollinsae could not hit her.

Moving forward as quickly as he could with safety, Rheinallt
continued watching closely. Susannilar's main tactic in these
gyrations was to keep one of her split selves always behind the

135

Guardsman. Nollinsae dared not take time for cool accuracy at the dodging apparition in front of him, lest the one ever shifting behind him should dart up and yank an airhose, or knock him off his feet. Without either air or meadow contact he would be a goner, and the jerkiness of his double-gunhand swings showed his apprehension.

Every few moments a wire would spring forth, trailed from a dart launched by the small haywire in Nollinsae's hand. The dart would zip through a place where one of the shifting Susannilars had just been, and fall to the meadow harmlessly. Nollinsae would quickly twist the wire through the cutter on the grip of the haywire and loop the end from the spool around the notched tail of the next dart fed from the magazine. The wasted dart and its few yards of thin, shining wire, unable to exist unsupported in subspace, would disappear.

Then Susannilar would reappear like a juggler's ball at a new endpoint of her oscillatory arc with another feint. But she seemed unable or unwilling to connect, to strike a blow in her own behalf.

All so far had occupied a very short time. Already the movements of the fighters had begun to slow, however, the strain and effort quickly undermining them both. Remembering *never* to run or jump, never to have both feet out of meadow contact at once, was itself a tremendous source of nervous strain on anyone acting in haste on the meadow. They now began disengaging, separating, with Nollinsae's shots and Susannilar's feints coming less often.

Finally they were too far apart for useful action. Susannilar recoalesced into one body, one location, and stepped into the foggy slab side of the Ship. Nollinsae turned and headed down around the far end, still occasionally looking this way and that. It was over; a draw.

Rheinallt contemplated briefly imprisoning both of them somehow. Practically it didn't look too good. Nollinsae apparently had brought his own small arsenal; and how pen up someone who could shift herself through space? And morally, more important—if they were set on killing each other, Rheinallt didn't see by what right he could stop them. He had hinted at protection for the young woman if attacked, but she had not been eager to take it up, only to ascertain if Fleurage and its Guard held any rights over her here.

The two of them shouldn't be in any hurry to cross again after this short but obviously draining episode, until they had rebuilt their energies. Before then Rheinallt might be able to have another reconstructive talk with Susannilar, to discover some more of her past. What was Nollinsae's fanaticism, that his need would propel him so far? Did the determination come from a desperately felt threat to Nollinsae's own self-preservation? Nollinsae's inner motivations would be better armored, harder to approach, in the mature and hardened man than in the young Susannilt, but maybe Rheinallt could find entree.

Gazing at the *Falling Angel* abstractedly while thinking about the aftermath of the strange combat, he had another idea. Presume that the shadow of the Ship was a phenomenon of the meadow, as was the softly glowing curve of the trail. Was there any way he could apply what was known about the trail to increase what they knew about the Ship?

People knew more or less where trails went, and how, with waybeasts, to use them; but of how the trails came to snake easily across the meadow, or of what their natures were, humanity knew nothing. The geometers and infraphysicists of Earth knew less about trails than did the commercial travelers of the Blue Free Nation.

Through the Ship's shadow as a lens, in his attempt at enhancement, he had seen the faraway trails—or something—writhe and twist colorfully, but they had not approached more closely except in vision. Nor did he think they could be made close physically. Where was the visionary division between optics and hallucination, anyway?

Rheinallt would like to try the experiment of bringing the Blue Trail to the *Falling Angel*, so to speak. Not just for the day-to-day convenience of the expedition, as had occurred to him on first parking the caravan here, but mentally, in terms of understanding. Yet those few hundred yards of sloping meadow could not be bridged by him physically, and he was at an equal loss as to bringing them together conceptually. Damnation.

Then he thought of the squeakers.

Walking, while he thought, sidewise along the slope on the flank of the Ship opposite to the waiting caravan, he came level with the bow. Yes, the waybeasts. That would be a confrontation that he would have to see.

137

Back in the vicinity of the caravan, he went to the puffed airtent, entering through an airlock in the transparent tent wall. Through a babble of voices he called out, "Whitnadys!"

There was no direct answer. A number of passengers began stalking toward the airlock, shaking their heads angrily.

"The expedition's not over yet!" Rheinallt said loudly. "Now the real work begins. Sure, it's a puzzle. That's why you came. Start using your heads."

Taking care not to appear hurried, he backed out the airlock and walked to a 'tween-cars lock to reenter the caravan itself.

Whitnadys was in the foremost car, sitting at her desk, looking over some charts. Many handwritten extensions and corrections made a colorful rat's-nest of the indifferently printed charts.

Rheinallt nodded to Arahant, drowsing on a large cushion in the corner by the window. He took off his helmet and dropped it onto a chair. "Hello, honey."

"Well, back so soon. Any progress?" Her eyes sparkled as she looked up.

"Nothing substantial. Literally."

"It's about the weirdest thing I've ever seen. At least since we rescued you and Arahant off that awful wet place where your own people marooned you."

He rubbed the base of his neck where the helmet had rested. "Have you been over to see it yet?"

"Just for a minute. Like a valley full of fog, with yeast in it. Didn't get any useful ideas right off, so I scooted back here to make sure the menage is buttoned up for our stay."

"Don't believe that," Arahant interrupted. "She's as nervous as a cat, if you'll pardon an unlikely simile. All she's done since she got back from checking out that bloody great Ship is slide charts back and forth like playing solitaire."

"At least I've scraped the dust off the charts," she retorted. "All you've done is snooze."

"Different metabolism, my dear Whitnadys," the catadrome returned archly.

"It's his life cycle," Rheinallt explained to Whitnadys. "I think he's taken a hundred-year vow of torpidity."

"Hmph," snorted Arahant. "At least I'm willing to talk back to a human, which is more than you can say for our preciously squeaking *Viatherium chryselephantine*. Maybe a squeaker has

138

the right idea at that: power-squeaks are all the signal that gets through to you."

"Returning to matters of substance," Rheinallt said briskly to Whitnadys, "I would like to bring the squeakers to bear on our problem of the Ship. Can you do something along that line?"

Whitnadys' thumb riffled the edge of her stack of charts. "Can you move the Ship?"

Rheinallt began to pace, scuffing the carpet in the confined space in front of her desk. "I don't think so. We can't get a grip on it: there's nothing to grasp. If it is as heavy as it seems from that valley-sized dent in the meadow, we couldn't even make it wobble unless we figure out its own power system and fire it up. And from our viewpoint, it's lighter than air: so much of nothingness that we can't even touch it."

"Make up your mind," growled Arahant.

"Either as heavy as a star, or a mountain of nothing?" Whitnadys smiled. She riffled the charts again, fanning them higher and harder. The minute breeze was refreshing. "I'll never get a squeaker to leave the trail."

Rheinallt's hand chopped the air. "I've heard that a thousand times. Is it really true? Have you tried yourself?"

"With different waybeasts on different trails. Coax or threaten: they don't care. They will not move off the trail in subspace. The ordinary meadowland might as well not exist for them. They can't walk on it."

"Can't or won't?" Rheinallt had gone into these questions on the versatility of squeakers when he had first encountered the Trails culture, and had been forced to conclude that they would not be helpful in breaking out of the pattern in which they were stranded. Although Arahant had not agreed fully on that. She spread her hands. "I don't know. Within the range of treatment that a squeaker will tolerate, they can't be budged."

"Hmm. Has anyone exceeded that 'range' somehow?"

"Ethics aside"—Whitnadys grinned—"I've never heard of anyone who radically maltreated a squeaker and lived to tell the tale."

"After all," Arahant reminded, "they've meadow-quality minds also."

"I know that," Rheinallt said. "I assume that they're not only conscious but more aware of human purposes than their own actions show. If they weren't conscious of death, the squeakers couldn't maintain themselves on the meadow. Why they associate with humanity we don't really know—"

"Hardly a unique question," Arahant murmured.

"—but I'm sure they've reasons, however obscure and untranslatable to us," Rheinallt finished.

After a silence, Whitnadys asked, "So you think proximity may demonstrate something even though we can't communicate our desire or understand the response?"

Arahant snorted, and began grooming carefully a select patch of fur.

"Well, I don't know," Rheinallt admitted. "It's just a chance. How about your lead squeaker, Whitnadys? Haven't you said that the one you use to lead the rest, who walks point for the caravan, is the one in whom you see the most personality?"

She shook her head. "I have two good leaders, but neither would leave the trail himself, let alone bring others with him to have a sniff at the Ship. To us, the trail is a road; to them, it's more like a canal. We can step off a road and back on again. Water creatures pulling canal barges wouldn't be able to just hop right out of the water."

Rheinallt considered this.

Whitnadys went on, "I don't know whether the trails follow lines of least stress, or least friction, or if they're some kind of magnetic bridge or watershed break, but none of those ideas works for squeakers as simply as my canal analogy."

"Where we come from," Arahant said, "subspace is defined as a gravitational sheer. The meadow itself is deemed to be only our subjective experience of a boundary phenomenon."

Whitnadys whistled. "A mightily powerful experience it is, too."

"I think they've got it backwards," Rheinallt said softly. "But that's neither here nor there. A canal barge between the stars, huh? I rather like that."

"But?" she invited.

"If our trail here had depth like a canal, we could move it," he pointed out. "Dig a cross-canal. But we can't. And another thing: in your canal analogy, why can any of the self-conscious species follow a trail over the meadow, but only the squeakers can follow it through breakpoint to a world and back again?

Human or catadromic caravaneers can't make that vital transit alone."

Arahant blinked. "You don't have to follow the king's highway to get into a city."

"Ho," Whitnadys chortled. "If the city's got a moat you'd better use the ferry."

"Depends on what lurks in the waters," Arahant countered.

"Precisely," Whitnadys said. "The squeakers—"

Rheinallt held up a hand. "Just a minute, folks. Are we agreed that we can't bring a waybeast to the *Falling Angel*, and vice versa?"

They both nodded.

"All right. It was an idea. Now listen to this: while I was making my first snoop around the Ship, I ran into our sweetest pair of passengers."

Whitnadys frowned, twined her fingers, and let the knuckles crack. "Well?"

Rheinallt told them about the confrontation he had witnessed between Susannilar and Nollinsae. "There'll be another time, some kind of conclusion. It's just been postponed."

"Why didn't you share this bit of theater when you first came in?" Arahant inquired caustically.

"Wanted a technical opinion before I got an emotional one."

Arahant hissed. Whitnadys cracked a couple more knuckles.

"Suggestions?" Rheinallt asked.

Several emotions contested on Whitnadys' face. After a pause, she said slowly, "I don't know what to do about their fighting. I guess as long as they do their duelling in private, it's no concern of the caravan."

"That's how I feel," Rheinallt said.

"However—" she pointed a pixieish finger at him "—maybe our oscillating girl can help with the Ship."

He smiled. "How? Jump out of her skin and dance around in her bones?"

"Be bones soon enough, the way they're going at it," Arahant said darkly.

"No bones on the meadow, mister aircat," Whitnadys returned. "I'm serious. Maybe she can shift herself, or half of herself, into the Ship, or wherever and however the Ship is. I don't know how she does what you saw, but maybe she can

141

do it to get into the Ship. Or at least see into it."

Arahant stared at her. "Out of the mouths of babes!" he exclaimed. "Hendrik, you're luckier than you thought you were. This woman is awake. Profit from her example."

"Thanks," he said dryly. "I take it you think Susannilar could help?"

"Don't know," Arahant admitted soberly. "It's a chance."

"A sort of phasing, or synchronizing?" he hazarded.

"Yeah." Arahant gained enthusiasm. "If the shadow of the Ship out there is a mirage, projected from somewhere else on the meadow, could be that Susannilar will be able to sense that. Find out where it is."

"And if it's slightly out of phase here," Rheinallt added, "by shifting into it she might be able to take control of it and bring it to proper phase with us."

"Doubtful about her taking control." The aircat shook his head violently enough to make white whiskers quiver. "Unless she's had the technical training for it—equivalent to yours or mine—she'd be more likely to blow it up if she experimented with controls. Besides, if it is a projection, all she has to do is tell us where away. Then we can go play with the real thing."

"If it's as trail-accessible as the shadow ship." Rheinallt resumed pacing. "I was so intensely disappointed at not having a solid starship under my hand and mind again that I tried enhancement without one."

"You're fortunate you aren't dead," Arahant said quickly. "Old friend, if you decide to kill yourself, at least try not to make an ass of yourself while you're doing it. *Don't* do that again."

"You're going to wear a trail in my carpet," Whitnadys said.

Rheinallt stopped. "Would you like to ask her, Whitnadys? It's your idea."

She leaned forward eagerly. "Sure. Maybe she herself doesn't know what she's capable of. That oscillating sounds neat; I wish I'd seen it. You said she hasn't talked about that at all?"

"Not yet."

"I disagree," Arahant put in. He stood up on his cushion and stretched all four limbs. "Hendrik should talk to Susannilar again."

Whitnadys looked wary. "Why?"

Arahant looked at her quizzically. "First, because he already has her confidence. Second, because a request for help coming from the captain-of-caravan, our glorious Eiverdein here, will carry more weight with her than you would, my dear."

Not altogether humorously, Whitnadys said, "I'm kind of sorry that Hendrikal didn't extend his gag rule for you, to keep you quiet all the time."

"No need for jealousy yet," Arahant said mildly.

Calmly Rheinallt said, "I'll talk to Susannilar again. Don't worry about it, honey. She's easy to listen to, but that long session with her left me with such a headache that I'm not looking forward to it."

"Subsonic oscillations?" Arahant suggested. "Vocal modulations she doesn't herself realize she has?"

"Could be."

"Tell her," Arahant said. "Ask her to keep it down, shut it off if she can."

"All right. Whitnadys, do you want to come along?"

Relieved, she said, "No. You handle it. I bet she'd be willing to help."

"Maybe." Rheinallt snagged his helmet and made for the corridor door.

Whitnadys asked irrelevantly, "Hendrikal, my darling— how old are you?"

Arahant snickered.

Rheinallt turned a glare on the aircat, then hesitated. That question had not come up so directly since he had met Whitnadys, and in the short couple of years they had lived and loved together he had avoided the topic. It would have been nice to keep on avoiding it until a more relaxed time: either back on Blueholm or with a functioning starship thrumming under their feet.

A compromise, he thought. Tell her, but make a game out of her acquiring the information, let that soften it. He held up his hands in front of her, dropping the suit helmet again. Eyeing the thick knuckles and the backs of his hands, he flashed both hands open twice before her.

"Twenty?" Whitnadys said unbelievingly. "You're older than twenty. That can't be right. But—twenty years older than I am? That can't be right either: you're *about* my generation, anyway."

143

Arahant snickered again.. "She wants to know if you're beyond the age of folly."

"Never," Rheinallt said, opening the door.

"You're twenty years older than I am, though?" She looked sorry she had asked.

"That's closer," he admitted, and headed out to find Susannilar.

11. Too Quickly the Garden

SUSANNILAR WAS NOT IN HER ROOM. RHEINALLT WALKED ALL the way to the end of the caravan, checking all the public areas down to the caboose. From the tail he worked his way back forward, this time knocking on locked doors and sticking his head into every corner he could think of. She could not be still outside, as her stored air would have run out by now and she had not been by the tank car for a refill.

Then, outside a locked door to a small closet that he would have skipped even on this second pass, he heard a faint sound of sobbing. Rheinallt studied the narrow door. This was not a proper room, just a leftover wedge between two bulkheads, one of dozens of such places throughout the caravan, most common in cars a few years older than average. The newer ones had slightly more efficient designs. Now what was in this one? He had to think for a minute, and meanwhile the hint of a feminine voice crying came softly from beyond the door.

Hoses: that was it, spare air and water lines available for repairs or for such extra needs as setting up the air-bubble tent outside. Rapidly Rheinallt fingered his collection of master keys until he came to one marked "Hoses—19," which opened the narrow door with some tugging and creaking.

It was dark in there; when assembling the caravan Rheinallt had rented only cars that had no live gas connections to dead-storage rooms. He learned which builders had been lavish on atmospheric integrity and parsimonious with structure-weakening luxuries and fire hazards. Fire on the meadow was an occasional caravaneer's horror.

Holding out his hands to the dark doorway, Rheinallt spread his fingers into fans, letting a natural soft brush discharge crackle with cold light. The flickers, as of ten matches, were fitful but sufficient.

Susannilar was there all right, like a larva in a cocoon. Face down in the dark tangle, so totally surrounded by coils of rubbery hoses that obviously she could not move more than inches in any direction. She couldn't have gotten in there by herself, he thought; she's really buried.

Rheinallt quenched the brush discharge to free his hands for some heavy work. She was invisible again in the interior dimness. Not much light at all penetrated into that tangle from the lamps in the corridor, and he could not enter the closet himself, could not even get one foot all the way across the threshold.

Gingerly he pulled on the nearest coil. It was heavy and resistant to his hand, and he did not want to shift any more weight onto her than she probably already had pressing her down.

"Who—?" she cried out in alarm. She twisted frantically to try to see the door from within her coarse cocoon.

"Eiverdein," he said soothingly. "Hold still. It'll take me a few minutes to get you out of there, so just relax while I'm moving hoses."

"I—all right."

He stacked a second coil in the corridor. "Did Nollinsae put you in here?"

Surprised, Susannilar said, "Nollinsae? Why, no. I—just needed to be alone. How did you find me, anyway?"

"You were crying," he told her gently. "You still are."

"Crying? Oh!" All at once the faint crying stopped entirely.

Rheinallt laid down the third coil of hose and listened, but could hear nothing except her breathing. Had that crying been louder after he unlocked and opened the door than it had been in the corridor with the door closed? No.

"That *was* you crying, Susannilar, wasn't it?"

"Ah—yes." She paused. "Wait. Don't move any more of those heavy old hoses. I can get out by myself."

"You can?"

"I got *in* here by myself. I'll be right out."

A ghostly projection of Susannilar appeared, standing in the corridor next to him. Rapidly this projection solidified until the young woman physically stood there, and had vanished from among the coils in the narrow closet. She had transferred herself, hived off an insubstantial fraction of herself first, and then—moved across.

"See?" she said brightly. She smoothed at crumpled clothes, rubbing at some grimy streaks left by the hoses.

"Guess so." With an amused groan, Rheinallt began heaving the removed coils back into the storage closet. When the door was shouldered shut once more he asked, "Did you go in right through the door?"

She hesitated, then nodded.

"Was that you crying?" he asked.

"Sort of."

He eyed her. "Do you always do things piecemeal?"

"Not exactly. I was feeling sorry for myself, and a little fraction of me kind of slipped away to do some crying. I wasn't even aware of it, until you mentioned it."

"Hmm." Now he remembered something similar, an unfocused distant sobbing, during his first effective encounter with her in the lounge car. At the time he had dismissed it, but that phenomenon must be another aspect of whatever Susannilar was.

"I'm all right now," she assured him.

He couldn't see any streaks of tears on her face. "Like to talk some more?"

"Sure. I've been talking to Glenavet, a little, and I think he's beginning to understand too."

"Glenavet?" It seemed like a long time since he had talked to the Federated Trailmen's representative. A couple of days? Did Glenavet also sense some sort of resource in this girl on the run?

147

"Yeah. You know him? I'm pretty hard to understand, I think. Sometimes it's kind of lonely." She paused, added honestly, "*Usually* lately it's real lonely. The last few days have been better."

Glenavet might be harder hit by the death of his comrade Wirtellin than the fellow let on. The bluff trailman might not be introspective enough to feel that death diminishes us all, but Rheinallt was sure he would feel some of that loneliness that can be endemic on the meadow.

The mention of Glenavet sidetracked Rheinallt, made him reluctant to hit her up immediately for a contribution from her special talent, or whatever it was she did. He wished he knew more about her.

Also, he was being cautious about the Ship. Protectiveness toward that cigar-shaped mountain of red fog outside bore more than a tinge of the ridiculous. Still, he wanted to know more before he helped get her any closer to the heart of his own plans.

Rheinallt took Susannilar's arm and they began walking forward to the car which contained her room. "Can we go more slowly this time, or more easily? I came out of your big flashback recitation with a terrible headache."

"I'll try." She was contrite. "I think that's something I get from my grandfather. I didn't know I was hurting you."

"Your grandfather, Ytrenath—was that the same person who was trying to shift the Yellow Trail in subspace?"

"That's not true at all! The whole business about him interfering with the trail on Fleurage was just a trumped-up charge."

Her previous recitation of her history had a dreamlike quality in his memory. He would have to get farther with it, and doubts he had aplenty. The success of the Special Caravan's mission, with all that it meant to him personally too, might hang on how well he managed Susannilar's cooperation. Not the fact of her helping, of which he was fairly confident, but the way she approached the problem of the Ship. Could be dangerous, and not just for her.

Once they were comfortably ensconced in her room, he encouraged her to talk, to reminisce. He tried to brace himself for the disorientation that the intense recital had brought before;

148

but it was worth the chance. If none of them among the expedition could show any progress at all in dealing with the Ship, there might be a mutiny among the disaffected.

So again Susannilar talked of the past, and again Rheinallt closed his eyes and let her paint a picture with her words. The picture grew more easily this time, as if he were more used to empathizing with her, to this alienness of seeing from another's viewpoint.

Absorb, evaluate, and respond. He had assumed that this was what he had always done when talking with people, but now he was not so sure. So she talked, and he was sucked in:

The lake was so blue she sometimes wondered if it wasn't the bluest blue in the world. Young Susannilar seriously thought for a long while that the people who worked in factories and cloth mills far away, all those who made things, must have sent agents and representatives to the lake to try to copy the color. She assumed they all meant well, and tried hard, but even the best ceramics and cloth and painted metal were only feeble imitation hues.

The happy deep blue of the lake was the true color, and no one could copy it quite correctly. All of the other colors, and things which had to be painted or woven or just grown those colors, were envious of the lake blue. Of course they couldn't change: they had to be what they were. Sometimes she felt sorry for them and tried to make it up to them, especially the trees.

One day her grandfather Ytrenath took her by the hand and they walked out onto the lake. It was a soft, lovely day, clear and warm with the faintest of breezes that stroked the water like a cat. The plank docks were gone, no longer needed. The water felt cushiony under her feet, and dry as if the lake had grown a skin.

It made her think of playing on a waterbed, and she wondered if Ytrenath would mind if she jumped up and down a little, which was great fun on a waterbed if you didn't get caught. Of course she was rather mature and dignified for such things now, almost grown.

So she didn't ask if she could play, but rather said diffidently, "May I dance here?"

"I'm afraid not. This isn't a place where you can play around until you have enough control of your own."

With dignity Susannilar said, "I said dance, not play. This is a place for artistry."

Ytrenath managed a smile. "Thank you." He held her hand more tightly. "In fact, however, do *not* let go, or pull away from me. Without this contact you would sink."

This frightened her, although she tried not to show it. She had been very light-headed, grand as a frog on a lily pad, and he had made her suddenly realize that she had no lily pad under her. Only water and more water down to the bottom of the lake. She looked down now, saw currents flowing, bearing tiny bubbles and smaller unidentifiable motes.

It was incredibly clear. She had never seen the lake bluer than when she looked straight down into it that day. There were strange shapes down there, too, but they were very deep and she couldn't tell if they were fish or bottom markings or what. Looking down while they walked along had ensnared her so easily into the enjoyment of seeing that she soon had forgotten all about sinking. When she did remember, she gleefully thought that what she had was a transparent lily pad which moved in front of her wherever she went.

"Did you make this lily pad, Grandfather? This skin on the water?"

"Why, yes. Patterns, my dear. It's not really a skin; merely rearranged water. A boundary phenomenon, like surface tension itself, but a vastly greater magnitude."

"I know about boundary phenomena," she told him proudly.

Ytrenath was pleased. "Well, good. That school your mother found for you must be decent after all."

"Yes, but now I've graduated, and she says there isn't money enough to send me off-planet where I could get real scientific training."

He frowned. "You should go to the Nation. They seem to have the most open minds, and that would probably be the best place for you to learn. We're rather a backwater here." And then he sputtered at his own unintentional pun, there on the softly quivering water surface. "I'll talk with Alalortern about the money situation."

They glided among the wildflowers and water grasses of the lake. Soon Ytrenath asked her, "Can you see the bottom?"

She shook her head, dark hair flying.

"I think you'll see a hint of red, way down deep," he told her, "if you look with care."

"I'm not sure—"

He smiled down at her. "No doubt it will come with time. You are still young yet, although you may be finished with growing taller. We'll see."

They came to a small rise in the water. It was about eight feet tall above the general surface of the lake. Maybe thirty yards long, parallel with the near shore. The slopes of the rise were very gentle on the long side facing the beach and house, and on the ends; but she was surprised to find as they skirted it that it was very abrupt on the far side. Like a sand dune, it was perfectly stationary, and while she had seen swells before they were always moving at a fair clip, pushed by the wind and the lake tides. This wave was perfectly still, although one could see ripples from the ordinary little waves and from their footsteps pass right through it.

Another pattern. Her grandfather was a master of form. But she rather missed the old, low plank docks made from the ivoried wood of the great white trees.

Beyond the standing wave was the garden! There were flowers, it was all flowers, standing upright and colorful in the blue water. The masses of color waved like a shaken carpet as the ripples and wavelets passed through the water.

Susannilar fell on her knees, not letting go her grandfather's hand, and gently touched the nearest flower. It was golden-yellow, with deep-green leaves and stem, about a foot high. Very pretty, growing out of the blue water.

She was glad she was older and better able to appreciate the garden. Even though for technical reasons she had to hold Ytrenath's hand, she felt the maturity of insight and deliberation within her. Now the pleasure ran even deeper in her, she felt entranced. She stroked the leaves and petals gently, letting her hand make sure it was real on that level.

"Just a flower, an ordinary flower," Ytrenath said, laughing.

"But it isn't growing in an ordinary place!" She reached out to touch another, then another, as though the lake were a giant window box. Where was the soil to be added? Looking around, she spotted a small wooden raft with a basket on top of it floating a few yards away.

"You may add some dirt if you wish," Ytrenath said. "I'm

151

glad to see your interest extend to contributory aspects of my gardening," he added dryly. "Usually when you've come here you're all a-goggle, but then on to something else."

"I was younger then," she told him stiffly.

"Ah, yes."

"Now I know lots about botany. Nutrients as well as looks. I've even learned some geometry and physics."

"And I'll bet you want me to start teaching you about manipulating boundary layers."

"Anytime!"

"There is much to learn about yourself, also," he cautioned her. "Discipline, self-knowledge, self-management. These are all difficult, and all essential."

"Sure," she said, pulling him toward the floating basket, then dragged the basket on its raft to some rows that Ytrenath indicated. With her free hand Susannilar scooped dirt from the basket, and let it drift dustily between her cupped fingers near the base of one bobbing plant. Fine loam already, it dispersed in the water around the roots. She did the same for several dozen of the nearer plants.

"Do you have any real waterflowers out here? Like the one when I was small?"

"One at present, less unstable than its predecessors. They're not exactly the most important experiment, except to me personally. A demicarnation, I'm tempted to call it." With an amusement that seemed forced to her, he added, "This one may survive away from the pool."

She blushed. "I'd like very much to see it. This time I'll be careful."

They threaded their way among the flowers. Like the little one she had swallowed precipitately years ago, the waterflower was the blue of the lake. In size it was much bigger, in form more involved, and to Susannilar it even surpassed that first miniature in grace. Serenely it stood forth from the base water in which it grew, and its curves and convolutions hinted at depths and lobed capacities more important than its mere volume.

"Demicarnation. Why do you call it that?"

"Hmm, well. Because this is a way that I may myself participate in creation. There is a good deal of me in the waterflower."

"Of you?" Suddenly it flashed on her that this really was important to her grandfather, and that this importance spilled over into her. "I don't understand," she said with a new seriousness. "Can you please explain some more?"

He looked at her squarely. "Yes, I'll be happy to." Together they sat on the billowing water, as comfortably as on a waterbed mattress. He held her smooth hand in his wrinkled hand, and with his other he tapped idly on the lake surface and watched tiny ripples speed away.

"For a long time," he began, "I've worked on a project to preserve the future of Fleurage. Recently I've convinced your parents to help. The two brief arrests of your father for political reasons shocked them awake. To you these arrests were sudden storms that passed quickly. To your parents they were evidence that their lives were changing sharply for the worse.

"Unfortunately, the government of Fleurage has interdicted their freedom to travel off-planet. Our little stretch of the Yellow Trail is so hedged about with Guardsmen, with weapons and prohibitions, that the chances of any of us contacting off-world help have collapsed—at least through any conventional means.

"Briefly, Fleurage is faced by two problems. One is cultural: our political stability is a thin veneer over violent forces. In a few years we'll be living under a full-blown dictatorship. For you, Susannilar, that means you'll be dead, or a slave, or a fugitive. The same for your parents and myself. The chief counterinfluence on Fleurage is the greater culture of the other Trail worlds, whose public opinion of events here is the greatest restraint on our future dictators. Not preventing, only making its arrival slow and furtive.

"The second problem is a physical one, inherent in the nature of starspace, subspace, and the trails. Fleurage is losing contact with the Yellow Trail. Whether the planet is drifting in starspace away from the trail or the trail is drifting in subspace away from Fleurage, we lack the sophistication in astronomy and infraphysics to tell. In a few years we'll be exiles from the rest of humanity. Now, in stable and self-contained people, a period of exile might not be harmful, but Fleurage's culture is sick: persons like you and me won't survive our fellows during such a period."

After a long unhappy silence while Susannilar tried to digest this disaster, or twin disaster, she asked slowly, "How could Fleurage slip from, be away from, the trail? I thought it was sort of glued to the planet."

Ytrenath shook his head. "The trail is no more glued down than a river is glued to its bed. A change in the gravitational vector, or a counterforce like an earthquake, can shift a river that's been constant throughout recorded history. The change will be coming soon. The isolation period could be brief, or millennia."

"That's awful."

"Yes. I had two plans. One was to convince someone trustworthy, and more spry than myself, to travel to the Blue Free Nation, and stimulate research there in ways to keep Fleurage in touch with humanity—after our portion of the trail has slipped too far on the meadow for us to touch. Perhaps means of transportation other than the trails, or even a way to redirect and reroute the trail back here where we need it. Stopping the slippage would be quite good enough if achieved before our trailside shrinks to nothingness."

"You wanted Mom and Dad to do that? Wouldn't it cost a lot of money?"

From a pocket Ytrenath withdrew a small bottle. "Today's output of eau de millefleurs," he said with his first smile in many minutes. "The best perfume found on fifty-four worlds, and the most expensive, drop by drop. This little bottle easily would pay for a ticket for you to the Nation."

"Wow!" she said, impressed more by the boosting of something she already knew about than by abstract disasters. "Oh— do you mean *me* to go?"

"I'm not enamored of the idea. Do you know intersign yet, the meadow travelers' sign language? No? Well, that's another item for you to add to your education. We have a family warehouse in the Nation from which a factor doles out millefleurs depending on the state of the market. The income from that will outlast Fleurage's being cut off—in fact, would increase with the source cut off—and ought to finance a great deal of the research I mentioned. However, you're too young to handle such things yet."

"But I'll study hard, and I'll be ready when you want me to go!"

He smiled at her, but his eyes remained sad. "It's not a

154

question of me wanting you to go, or when, but of being forced to it."

Feeling the springiness of the controlled lake surface under her, she tried to recall the fun of bouncing on a waterbed, but it seemed very long ago. "You said you had two plans, though?"

"The other involves the waterflowers, and myself. I'm trying to design a tool, a research tool to help me unlock the secrets of breaking through from starspace to subspace and back. All research is rather a gamble; this too, as much as what I'd hoped for your parents to do in the Nation, among their physicists. My project here has had many vicissitudes, and I may not live to see it completed properly. Or it may be less than I hope for, when the crisis comes. By then I hope to have you off-planet."

The complex vistas which these last few statements opened for Susannilar in the realms of mortality and loss were too much for her to dwell upon. She stared at the tiny bottle of millefleurs, and the breeze over the lake was cool on her face.

"Remember," Ytrenath said, "our enemies look forward to the isolation of Fleurage. The Guard will then be a large frog in a small pond. But they also hate and fear their means of triumph, although they are powerless to stop it or hasten it. When Fleurage is alone so they will be, alone in the dark."

Those words, the climax of that initiatory day, stayed vividly in her memory during the ensuing year as she plugged ahead in the education program her elders laid down for her. The responsibilities were harder than the study, so she worked hard, preparing for the time when she might be on the outside of Fleurage, looking in; and then not even being able to look in anymore. Unless she could guide the millefleurs fortune in the Blue Free Nation into some successful recontact program.

It wasn't infraphysics she studied in that year, for she could learn science more freely in the Nation. Rather her parents' circle tried to teach her about human nature; about her own special talents and how they fit into the scheme of things; about the philosophy of mind; about the geography of the meadow; and about how not to make a stink in the wholesale perfume business.

On an afternoon late in the following year, when men in uniform first came in force to their house, Susannilar was taking a break from studying. She was wading along the lakeshore idly, ostensibly weeding shoots of the wild lake grasses from

155

among the flowers. She answered their questions frankly, as her parents had warned her she must to postpone violence, but worriedly.

"Hello, girl," said the chunky one in the fanciest uniform, the leader. "My name is Nollinsae; we are officers of the Guard. Do you live here?" He smiled at her.

"Yes, since my father died, my mother and I live here with my grandfather."

He consulted a notebook. "What are their names?"

"Ytrenath and Alalortern."

"And your father died last summer? Yes, that matches. Your name?"

"Susannilar." Was this the crisis? Somehow she had thought it would be more obviously villainous.

"Grandfather is home. Mother is away in Siasntown, working."

"Excellent," Nollinsae said, making a couple of marks in his notebook. "Her we have already. And now Ytrenath. He, too, has been allowed to undermine the state of our secure world for much too long."

He gestured, and a couple of the nearer Guardsmen grabbed Susannilar. Beach sand scattered from her feet as she went up to her toes to keep from losing her balance in their grip.

"A clean sweep of these," Nollinsae said softly to himself. "The old man here on the lake, his daughter gypsying from town to town."

"Yes, both of them subversive and destructive," one of his men murmured in support. "A true danger to Fleurage—ending."

"And this young one, a wrecker in training," said one of those holding Susannilar, giving her a shake.

Suddenly she took a deep breath to cry out, but a hand was clapped over her mouth. Nollinsae waved toward the house, and several Guardsmen moved forward, unlimbering what she realized must be flamethrowers. Trickles and spurts of fire flickered from the snouts of the weapons as they were started up. Then one burst forth with a roar, flame leaping to the yellowed-ivory walls of the house. The others followed, and the old wood began to blacken.

She saw her grandfather running in old but long strides down to the water's edge. The Guardsman, having the house covered on the landward side, had not entirely cordoned the lake side.

"There are no boats. We'll get him," Nollinsae said confidently. More men went forward, fanning out around either side of the house and moving toward Ytrenath. Still more appeared from among the trees.

Carefully, because of his age, Ytrenath stepped from the sandy shore over some wavelets and onto the surface of the lake. Quickly but not hastily he walked straight out across the water, heading for the water-swell ridge marking the most secluded part of the lake gardens. Susannilar wondered anxiously if he would be safe behind that little ridge of water. Could he get there in time?

Nollinsae's men, in spite of a new and superstitious nervousness about their quarry, had by now set the house fully alight. She could feel the heat on her face. The wood was old and dry, but also massively dense, and would be a long time burning. The Guardsmen walked down to the shore, scorching grass, sending bushes bursting into flame. Gusts of heated air beat at the people. Great swathes of flame jetted from the muzzles onto the nearer fields of lake flowers. The clear pool of the lake began to look sullied and burned along the closer edge.

Ytrenath had disappeared behind the swell of water. Was he trying to save his newest and most special waterflower? In spite of her other concerns, and anguish for him, she hoped so.

Men with searing flame in their hands moved along the shore, looking for an angle which would reveal the old man. As they walked they continued to burn.

Susannilar struggled, but she couldn't get free. Were all their plans hopeless of fulfillment?

In a short time the Guardsmen reached positions far enough around the curving shore to flank the standing wave. Flames reached across the lake, beyond updrafts of steam. Their hot punch fell on the area concealed from her sight, but the effects were not hard to imagine. Susannilar was crying. It hadn't worked, it hadn't worked!

There was a shout from those further Guardsmen, and Susannilar shook her head to clear tear-damp hair from her eyes. Beyond the watery ridge was rising a whitish globe like a melon-sized puffball of a plant gone to seed. It floated leisurely upward, borne along by the breeze and updrafts from smoldering vegetation. Why it had not itself been burned she didn't know; yet in the air it had a knack of riding updrafts just beyond the tongues of flame.

The flamethrowers slacked off, their wielders looking on uncertainly. Nollinsae waved his arm peremptorily. A couple of jets of fire searched upward belatedly for the white sphere, but it was beyond their reach. The Guardsmen probed the sky with flames for a while to show their diligence, but they soon gave it up as obviously useless. The escaped puffball was followed by Susannilar's gaze into soft blue distances of sky.

Nearer, she noticed that the white-plumed trees were smudged and spotted.

She looked back at the lake. The waters were no longer her loveliest blue of blues, but an ashy blue-black. Scraps of charred plants floated on the waves or washed up on the beach below the still-flickering house. Farther out, the ridge of water was slumping back to level, and when it had subsided completely it revealed only more of the same: floating ashes, charred stems, and soggy flakes of leaves.

Her pets, she knew, were dead or fled. She tried not to think of her grandfather, the things that were his, the waterflower. Had his plan worked? The fuzzy puffball had wafted away free, but had the rest of his hopes worked out? He had tried to bring together the subtle topology of the lobed waterflower, and his theories of the philosophy of mind. Had he succeeded? She was very glad at least that she hadn't had to look at his body.

And her mother! Her mother was caught too, somewhere; but if they were brought together the two women might think of a way to escape. She trembled, shivered with thoughts of death and transfiguration, and of her own mission and responsibility.

"Goodbye," she had whispered, for everything.

12. A Hog in Armor

FOR SOME REASON WHITNADYS WAS SCREAMING AT HIM, AND Rheinallt couldn't make out why, or what she was saying. He had his hands over his ears. He blinked, shook his head, and stared at Whitnadys. Suddenly she snapped into focus.

"What have you done with that witch girl? What's happened to you?"

"Shut up," he ground out, taking his hands from his ears. Maybe she hadn't been screaming after all, but the sound of her voice had rattled him as much as a well-sharpened shriek.

"What—" Whitnadys began.

"Give him a break," he heard Arahant saying, very softly.

"So what do you know about it?" she demanded of the aircat.

"Not much more than you, except that he's been in a strange place mentally but ought to come out of it shortly. The same happened the other time he talked with Susannilar."

Rheinallt grew aware they were in the lounge car, and the handful of passengers and crew present were frankly staring.

"One of her marathon sessions again," Arahant was continuing quietly. "She's a spellbinder, all right."

"Is that why Nollinsae's after her?" Whitnadys asked.

"Could be." The catadromic whiskers barely quivered with his unobtrusive conversing.

"Did you find me here?" Rheinallt asked Whitnadys.

She heaved a theatrical sigh of relief and threw her arms around him for a clinging hug. "Yes—now," she whispered.

Rheinallt squeezed her, breathing the scent of her hair.

Over her shoulder he saw Arahant frowning. "You blew it, Hendrik."

"Failure of control in public?"

"That's right." Arahant glanced around at the sprinkling of avid onlookers. "You may be tougher than they can imagine, but all they can see is how shook you've just been. When they spread the word it'll erode your ability to lead."

Still holding Whitnadys, he disagreed. "I'll have plenty of chances to tell them what was going on."

Arahant shrugged fluff-coated shoulders. "Keep your voice low while you're talking to me, remember. No, you won't have those chances. They'd much rather condemn you in silence. Brave explorers they may be, but a fair hearing . . . You're far too old to delude yourself about human nature; you just haven't quite recovered from Susannilar yet. If your reputation aboard is hurt, you'll have to work around it and compensate. They can dress you in their thoughts but they can't make you wear them."

Rheinallt put a little static charge into Whitnadys' hair, and watched it stand out in a huge honeyed cloud as each hair became an electric pathway and tried to create its own territory of air far from each other strand of hair. She pulled away to arm's length, looking at him and laughing with the tingle. She spun to look at herself in the mirror behind the bar.

"I look like my head's exploding, Eiverdein!" she said delightedly. "You haven't done this in a long time."

Rheinallt grinned. "The life of the party."

Arahant nodded slightly in approval.

Casually Rheinallt scanned the faces of the people in the lounge. If anything they were staring more open-mouthed than before. Some at Whitnadys' charged hair with expressions approximating horror; others switched their attention between Rheinallt and Whitnadys with a more, subtle, exquisite awareness that he had pulled another devilish attribute out of his hat. As for noticing Arahant talking, the aircat was sitting on the floor as though he were hibernating, and the human watchers saw nothing unusual. Their attention was on Rheinallt's doings with Whitnadys, and her screaming while he was comatose would now be inextricably bound up with the charged hair. He did not think he would be lessened by this episode, taken as a whole.

Whitnadys' hair began descending into limpness, so he pushed his fingers into the frothy mass again and gave it a booster charge. Again the hairs jumped to perpendicularity from her scalp.

"I'm so glad you're all right," Whitnadys said softly.

"Come to my room and I'll tell you about it," he said to Whitnadys, but including Arahant. As he led the way to the forward door, passengers shrank from Whitnadys, fascinated by the swaying and crackling honey-cloud of her hair.

Once in Rheinallt's compartment, he and Whitnadys collapsed into chairs, feeling the letdown from the emotions in the lounge car, and he in addition the hangover from Susannilar.

"Whatever cross-fertilization there might have been in the past between the Earth-centered culture and the Trails culture," Rheinallt said, "I'm glad for once that electricity is still only in the 'natural philosophy' stage of development along the trails."

Arahant yawned. "Let's hear what Susannilar's going to do for us."

"I think I forgot to ask."

Whitnadys did not seem too unhappy about that. "About cultures: if they have starships on Earth, how come no one in the Nation's been able to make one?"

"A starship depends on an absolutely huge technology backing it up. The best metallurgists in the Nation couldn't even make the door of the ship that marooned us on Rainstone. As for motive power, they hardly understand it themselves."

She frowned. "Does it have to do with electricity? That power of yours, that you used to light the lamp with just now and that you used to spring my hair all out? It still tingles."

Where to begin with electricity—and what had he already told her? "Everything in a starship depends in some way or another on electricity, but the motive power is an enhanced field which is a by-product of a conscious brain. The enhancing is done by electricity, yes, but I couldn't build a fraction of the necessary equipment myself to drive a starship. Takes a vast amount of specialized knowledge. I wasn't sneering at the Nation's metallurgists, either: I couldn't build one of those doors myself. Nor could I build the tools to build the machinery to build the door."

"Human technology is top-heavy," Arahant put in, tacitly accepting a moratorium on Susannilar. "Bunch of ratchet-brains."

Whitnadys glanced at him puzzledly. "You know so much, though, Eiverdein. You know more than any ten people I've ever met."

Rheinallt said seriously, "I do know a great deal. Still I believe I lack organizing principles adequate to the quantity of individual facts I have."

"Lacks sense!" Arahant murmured.

"Principles? Surely you're smart enough."

"The brain and mind have far more capabilities than anyone has ever employed. Arahant and I have gained considerable control over our physiological processes, and we're both mentational pilots, and of course there's my bioelectric skill. This is only scratching the surface of what we could do. Anyway, I'll save database theory and hierarchies of knowledge for the long haul back to Blueholm, or some rainy afternoons in front of a fire back home on your Azuline. Suffice it for now that the Earth-centered culture is absolutely glutted with facts, a tremendously complicated technological base. A lot of that I've never learned, and a lot of what I once knew I've forgotten, because of the weakness of organizational principles I mentioned. A price of maturity."

"I guess I understand." Whitnadys said. "If the squeakers all decided to scamper off to some squeakers' burying ground, I couldn't make a new one."

"Better keep a good grip on the traces," Rheinallt said. "Waybeasts dying and disintegrating on the meadow is not what the caravan needs right now, even if they'll reappear as hydrogen atoms in starspace."

"Another metaphor," Arahant said, looking abstractedly out the window at the dark meadow and the few hopeful beams of spotlights that slashed across it.

"Which?" Whitnadys asked both of them. "Nobody's ever

seen an atom. And starspace isn't a place you can live on, like the surface of a world, or space you can travel a trail on, like the meadow. I think they're both fictions. Theoretical things to make up for observational confusions."

There was a knock at the door. "Come in!" Rheinallt called.

Glenavet stuck his head in, then entered diffidently. "Talk to you, Eiverdein?"

"Sure."

Glenavet gestured, then sidled into a corner. He leaned against a cloth wall hanging and waited until Rheinallt had moved next to him before he spoke. "About that girl, Susannilar." His voice was barely audible.

"Is she all right?" Rheinallt asked sharply.

"Yeah, I guess so."

"I just spent some time with her. She was telling me her life story—second installment. A strong, strange person."

"She sure is. The little of her I've seen, I mean. Say, how come the only times I can find her, she's got someone hanging around, a chaperon? Course, no one can stick to Susannilar if she wants to give them the slip."

"Some of the crew have been alerted to keep a friendly eye on Susannilar. Not to chaperon. She *is* a handful, as far as the caravan's concerned."

Glenavet smiled, glancing sidelong at Whitnadys. "Not especially your handful, though, Eiverdein. Is that right?"

"If more people spent time with Susannilar it'd be all to the good. Give her some cushion."

"Is somebody bothering her?"

"She and Nollinsae have some critical disagreements. Ask Susannilar, why don't you? She'll give you an earful." Rheinallt felt sorry for the state of Glenavet's head after Susannilar got through overdosing him with her memories, but another friend for her would be nice.

"You know, Eiverdein, it's funny, but I didn't notice her all this time on the trip until just a few days ago. She must have been around, out of her cabin sometimes, but I don't remember ever seeing her."

"Protective coloration?"

"Huh?"

"She's hard to focus on when she doesn't want to be seen.

I'm not sure if it's a fully conscious process or not. I didn't notice her until recently, myself." Had he encouraged Glenavet sufficiently?

Glenavet smiled again, out of words.

Surely the man didn't really need Rheinallt's permission. Probably just bubbling with his discovery, and wanting to share it. Rheinallt signed a casual dismissal, and ambled to rejoin Whitnadys and Arahant.

"Well, thanks a lot, Eiverdein!" Glenavet moved awkwardly to the door and left.

"What was that all about?" Whitnadys asked.

"Lovesick," he answered shortly.

"Uh-oh," she said. "Deep water."

Arahant made puffing sounds from the air sphincters under his armpits. They sounded like a chorus of dubious sniffs, which Rheinallt supposed was the intention. Sometimes it's hard to tell with a catadrome, even one he had known as long as Arahant. For instance, if Glenavet's love life somehow turned out tragically, and Rheinallt upbraided Arahant on his callous sniffs, the aircat would claim they were gasps of dismay given in great sympathy for all concerned. Arahant was a high flyer, but not above playing them close to the fluff and then sandbagging you.

"Well," Rheinallt said heavily, "I don't know what Susannilar's going to do, but I think it's time to force a couple more confrontations."

"Recovered from Susannilar, I trust?" Arahant asked.

"Well enough." Rheinallt rubbed his face between hairline and beard.

"Who are you going to see?" Whitnadys wanted to know.

"Nollinsae, for starters."

Whitnadys frowned. "I think he's avoiding you. He made as if to let you in on his big plans, with that note he passed to you. But he didn't."

He regarded her thoughtfully. "Could be." He steepled his hands, one finger at a time. "Do you think he's added me to the official enemies list, along with Susannilar?"

"As an enemy of Fleurage? How could you be?" She looked worried, though.

"As an obstacle to Nollinsae," Arahant interjected.

"I wouldn't want to be an obstacle all unknowing."

"And be removed, all unknowing," Arahant agreed sarcastically.

Rheinallt shrugged. "I think I can handle Nollinsae, if it becomes absolutely necessary."

Arahant gave the man the look that meant he thought Rheinallt was beyond rational redemption.

After some minutes of mutual silence, Whitnadys said, "I hope you aren't forgetting that Detenebrator thing."

"It's not a thing, it's a creature. That name it calls itself just means 'dispeller of shadows,' or some such. Like a light source, although physically at least it's not much of one."

"But it's not human—" Whitnadys began.

"On the contrary," Rheinallt said, slashing the air with his hand, "it's all too human to suit me. I don't think it's an alien at all, a member of an alien race."

Arahant simultaneously twitched his ears toward each other, while swinging his tail up and over his back in a swift arc. The tips of his ears caught the tip of his tail in a neat pinch, then released it. The ears snapped back into verticality, while the fluffy tail descended slowly back to the floor.

"'Too human,' is it now, that you don't like?" Arahant said, widening the slits in his pupils. "I'll remember that the next time my activities seem tainted by unnecessary humanness."

"We didn't mean you," Whitnadys told him in her best beastmaster voice.

"Can't vamp *me*, Whitnadys," Arahant said, chuckling. "Save it for the big and slow."

"Anyway," Rheinallt said, "I'd like to get Nollinsae to show more of his hand."

"I'm far more distressed about the Detenebrator," Whitnadys maintained. "Remember what happened on that sled trip. You two were lucky. Suppose it pulls something like that again? What would you do with a whole caravan full of madmen? You two might come through all right: Hendrik because you're tough, and Arahant because your mind's not speaking the same signs, or something. Can you take a risk like that for all the other caravaneers?"

It took Rheinallt a while to figure out an answer to this. Mostly because he had no answer yet. Did his friends, though?

"Let's take a poll," Rheinallt suggested. "The easier one first. Do you think I ought to kill Nollinsae?" He paused. "Arahant?"

The aircat let out his breath slowly. "No grounds yet."

"Whitnadys?"

"There are other—"

"Other choices later. Yes or no?"

She was less stoical about the possibility than Arahant. "You can't! He hasn't *done* anything yet. Right, I know he's dangerous, I've said so myself. But then so am I. All you really have against him so far is that tale of Susannilar's, which you said yourself was more hypnotic than rational."

"What about the telescope business?"

"Research," Arahant grunted.

Whitnadys took it up. "Sure. All these scientific types are hugging little theories to their chests, on the best way to crack the secrets of the Ship. They've been like that since before we left Blueholm. I'm sure you're aware, Hendrikal, that the adventurers are as secretive as the scientists. They've got schemes too. Now, don't look at me like that! My point is that those schemes are harmless: research sort of things. Not guileful tricks to wrest the Ship from the rest of us and hightail it."

"You mean," Rheinallt said agreeably, "that we can't rightfully prejudge our companions, in accuracy any more than in principle. Which I've maintained all along."

A faint blush appeared on her face. "Have I been overadvising?"

Arahant laughed. "Of course not. He needs it. I always remind him not to trust too much in his admittedly high-class mind and skills. Time and chance wait for us all."

Rheinallt smiled at Whitnadys. "I'll bet Arahant doesn't even remember the first time he gave me advice."

Arahant's slit pupils opened wide for an instant, then snapped to slits again. "Good Lord of the Air, how could I? The wind has blown away worlds since we were young!"

"I do."

"Really? Well then, out with it."

Rheinallt drew out a pause. "You told me not to catch the lightning."

"The devil in a dream!" Arahant exclaimed. "You're right. But so long ago."

"And did he do it anyway?" Whitnadys asked, her eyes sparkling.

"Of course, my child," Arahant told her, still looking at Rheinallt. "It accounts for his electric personality."

"Is that a joke?"

"Not really," Rheinallt said. "I've told you a little about 'mastering the blood,' the group of psychobiological processes that Arahant and I use as a discipline to maintain our health. 'Mastering the lightning' covers the related processes of electroneuronic and electromuscular nature."

"Is that another discipline? You don't do that, Arahant, do you?" She moved to sit on the arm of Rheinallt's chair, needing the physical contact.

"I value my life," Arahant said.

Whitnadys leaned her cheek gently against Rheinallt's. "Does that mean that you don't, Hendrikal?"

"Becoming a bloodsweater was a necessity obvious to us in our youth. The other was thrust on me through my own innocent bravado."

"Tell me!"

"There was a legendary challenge, old tales about the exquisite sensations available to a person with electrotoned nerves, about the thrill of having the power of the lightning at your beck and call. This was pretty heady to young people who didn't know better, who didn't realize that there were no living 'masters of lightning' not because no one had ever thought to try for it, but because those who had tried had died."

Rheinallt slipped his arm around her waist and squeezed her. "It was a discipline," he went on, "like bloodsweating. We thought if we could master passing blood, with all that means for internal control, we could master anything. So once, in a high place, I took the challenge."

"You don't mean you actually tried to catch a lightning bolt!"

"I mean exactly that. When my friends saw that I hadn't been killed immediately, some of them tried too. Nature's airy dare, to stand in front of the lightning and make it your own. They were equally brave, equally foolhardy. I was too stunned to warn them, still struggling internally with the awful shock. I suffered through a mad, painful juggling of high-energy potentials for a few terribly sizzling minutes, an internal blitz-

167

krieg, but I was lucky enough to survive. I lived through the internal burns and the neural overload."

"Oh," she said very quietly after a moment. She brushed a few tears from her lashes. "I'm sorry, Hendrikal. I thought this was another funny story between you and Arahant. I didn't mean you to bring up old hurts."

"It was a long time ago, and being a bloodsweater I could block a lot of the pain."

"I meant your friends," she explained, still more quietly.

He smiled affectionately at her. "I knew what you meant. Thank you. The memories, like the discipline, are old clothes now that fit me comfortably enough."

Whitnadys blotted her eyes. "So Eiverdein's consort is not totally in the dark now as to the springs of his character," she observed with satisfaction. "Sometimes I wonder if I'll ever catch up."

"In Rheinallt's house are many mansions," Arahant commented cryptically.

Rheinallt stood, gently disengaging Whitnadys. He hooked his airsuit out of its locker and headed for the door. "I'm leaving," he said over his shoulder. "Later."

As the door was closing behind him, he heard Whitnadys saying to Arahant, "He has a well-ballasted soul. That may save him."

With this thought echoing in his mind, Rheinallt headed down the linked corridor toward Car Fourteen, where the airtent was attached. He passed a few people on the way but managed to avoid conversation. The expedition's healer was calming a woman who had let herself get overly frustrated about the inherent secretiveness of the shadow hulk. A bad sign, but her flash of anger was already on the ebb.

He passed through the open hatchway which from Car Fourteen gave on the big airtent. The tent was crowded, with people fussing over their equipment, overhauling suits, eating, and arguing about the Ship. There was a portable latrine in one corner, but no facilities for sleeping. That they would have to do in their relatively cramped compartments on the caravan; it was too noisy in here anyway.

Some passengers had suggested breaking up the caravan into segments, or drawing the cars into a circle with the tent bridging the middle, or other schemes they thought would be

convenient. But he had vetoed all these, as being too immo-
bilizing. They were not, after all, breathing warm air and treading solid ground where they could fix the little problems that
such gratuitous hassling with the caravan would cause. The
airtent he had planned all along: that was standard practice.
Even short-haulers carried them in case they needed elbowroom
in an emergency.

Rheinallt was running his fingers up the pressure seal on
the front of his suit when the Detenebrator whipped up to him.
Through the outer lock of the airtent it had come, humming
compactly like a bee swarm. Rheinallt held still, but the effort
to suppress the impulse to snap his head back and away from
the Detenebrator made his neck muscles ache. It came within
a yard, and he could have felt its breath if it had had any.

The hubbub in the tent, after an intermission of shocked
silence, resumed in whispers and exclamations. He caught the
word "corposant" a couple of times.

Rheinallt was quick enough this time to take the initiative.
"You're not helping my reputation," he told the Detenebrator
thing quietly. "They think you're some kind of spirit, and I'm
a spirit-monger."

"That's all right, Eiverdein," the Detenebrator boomed out
in its fibrous, mouthless joviality. "Such little worries as that
ought only to stimulate you to a greater concentration on your
real problem."

After a moment the man said, "I'll bite. What is it?"

"Ho, ho. You, of course."

"Your comments are the usual jagged blades, Detenebrator.
Have they barbs to break off in my flesh, to keep their poisoned
wounds open? Come on, give."

"Very well, my dear Eiverdein," it boomed. "Your concept
of yourself is too confining. You are all dressed up in con-
ventions, but what is your *core* doing? Have you no internal
compass, that you need help to see the route you need to travel?
Are you determined to be unworthy of your mind, unworthy
of your body? Now, scarcely anyone wears his self easily, but
that isn't much excuse: certainly not for someone like yourself,
who I suspect has lived long enough to almost have come into
your maturity."

Rheinallt glanced aside and around at the fascinated, though
fearful, researchers and adventurers. They all were silent now,

listening carefully, gathering material for wonder. And for what else?

He studied the fuzzy spheroid of the Detenebrator. "Go on."

"You are no fool," it said with admiration in the great voice. "I wish I could have had the time you've had—but never mind; that's neither here nor there."

In a way Rheinallt felt they were both glad of that previous encounter near Whitecloud on the Green Trail. It had tried to twist and re-mind him, and couldn't; he had tried to shoot and electrocute it, and done it no damage. That cleared the air for the current series of encounters. Made talking easier by eliminating more extreme alternatives.

If he had had an energy weapon, though, it might have been different.

"Have *you* done anything worthwhile yet, Detenebrator?" he asked it. "Or are you all words, a bag of bluster?"

"Leave goading to the herdsman." It sounded offended. Good.

"I am no herd."

"In a way you are, Eiverdein," it said surprisingly. "You are a bundle of force vectors and creative urges, with an inadequate governor."

"So I need a herdsman? No thanks."

"No, no! *You* need to be a herdsman, *as well*."

"Interesting," he conceded. "I thought you had yourself slated for that job."

"I have, and have had, no such intention," it boomed almost sadly.

Among the restless movements at the open doorway into Car Fourteen, Rheinallt suddenly noticed one man moving less furtively, more assertively; actually daring to come into the airtent. A bright uniform: it was Nollinsae. He slipped down onto the tent floor and stepped sideways into a group of the watchers. Great.

The Detenebrator seemed to be having trouble making up its mind what to say next. He felt a flash of sympathy for it, because a conjecture had come to him, that it was dying. The Detenebrator was alone; it had so far failed in what it was trying or it would not be around talking to Rheinallt; and whatever internal flows held it together were coming unglued. Its appearance had mottled since he had seen it first on this expedition; and, thinking back to the Whitecloud trip, then it had looked crisper.

"Your time is running out?" he prodded it speculatively.

"I am a bundle of potentialities," it rumbled.

"When do you become actual, or shall you? Not only me, but the others here"—Rheinallt waved his arm toward the onlookers—"would like to know what in space you're doing."

"In good time. It remains to be seen whether any of you can profit by what you see before you, or if all your thoughts will remain in the darkness of your skull. I'm not speaking metaphorically; I'm describing the structure of your mind, the terribly real landscape in which you live. You walk in the land of death, Eiverdein, and only you can find the way you need to go."

"Why me?"

"Not just you. Of course not. All of you, particularly Susannilar, because she was the first I worked with."

Ah, Rheinallt thought, but he said harshly, "The first people you worked with you killed."

"Not so. Actually I'd worked with her mother first, but on a simpler plane; she was murdered before she could realize her full potential. Susannilar, though, has great things in store for her. The difficulties of reaching her mind from this kerneled form of myself have proved far more than I anticipated. I am still trying.

"Every communication must have a beginning, Eiverdein, and before Whitecloud I'd observed that you, of anyone among the Trail worlds, had a good chance of making a breakthrough out of our shiny net-with-floats."

Rheinallt wanted now to ask if it knew he was from outside this skein of worlds, but not with all those people in earshot. His image here was already perceived as strange enough without hassles about whence and whither.

The Detenebrator rumbled on, "If these others can profit from your explorations, or from Susannilar's double-mindedness, no one would be more pleased than I. Even so, I don't expect to see it myself.

"And that is not my prime mission. I'm trying to save a world, Eiverdein, to save a world from slipping into the darkness and silence where only mad thoughts rule. Not for a small goal would I risk hurting people. Please believe this. I am a

171

lover of things that grow, that glow with their own light or develop their own strengths, their own structured sweetness. If I had been born to this form, instead of creating it and energizing it briefly like a vehicle, doubtless I would know better how to handle myself. But this is the best I can do, and I have little time."

"And Susannilar is your star pupil."

"Yes. Or so I had hoped. Her hypnotic powers are now stronger than mine are in this form, and I have great difficulty reaching her."

Rheinallt was reviewing what Susannilar had told him, turning over the force-fed impressions as quickly as possible. "You hope to raise her to a higher level of adeptness?"

"Correct. As I suspect you have guessed, this form is unstable and I haven't long to live. Susannilar must carry on in my place." It paused. "I've lately discovered a method of— of transport, a technique of passage. Ironically, this is what I set out to find elsewhere, and also sent Susannilar out to find. A world's peace depends upon it."

"Why are you telling me this? Why wait a clockyear or two to do so?" A method of transport? A *new* method? Could it be talking about breakin/breakout? Rheinallt might be able to perform a single transition without a starship, by burning out Arahant's mind. Or Arahant, as a pilot, might do the same for Rheinallt. Such boosting was not an acceptable solution.

"I tried to begin on your sled trip, but I hadn't the technique then, only the hope. Also, my mastery of this fibro-spherical form was pitiful. I did far more harm than good. On this caravan I was less eager to come forward, but for two reasons I felt I must. One is that there are forces aboard which could stymie my plans: nothing must interfere with Susannilar before I can complete her training."

"Nollinsae could interfere," Rheinallt said softly. "I don't think any of the other passengers or crew have shown much concern about her; they're too wrapped up in their own experimental affairs."

"You omit yourself."

"Huh? I have no intention of harming Susannilar. I've tried to help her, in fact, as much as she'll allow."

"Ah, but you are so powerful an individual, Eiverdein, a

172

wildlight, that you may be an obstacle without being aware of it."

"Your illumination is the only true one?"

There was a sound like a booming sigh. "I am not a luminary. Your gang of explorers has only the faintest idea of what a sun really is; and I am only the ghost of a luminary, the satellite of a source, the reflector of light. I generate nothing. I can only pass on what my earlier nature set in motion.

"In any case, my other reason: I haven't much more time to exist upon the meadow, for the energy drain of the meadow causes me to wane rapidly. In the meantime, I will do as much damage as I must."

Its booming voice thinned. "I hope I can call on you to help me educate Susannilar," it added surprisingly. "Because of her vibrato, I can't achieve the requisite fullness of contact. Neurosonically, she automatically tunes me out."

Now the weakness in the huge voice abruptly steepened its descent, became hoarse and ragged like tattered reeds. "Now I must rest, Eiverdein, and try to reknit. Later!"

The Detenebrator whirled erratically half around the tent, self-tugged by thin filaments, and then flashed away through the open airlock into the caravan too quickly for anyone to react.

Rheinallt breathed deeply a few times, distributed extra oxygen to tense muscles. Whew, what a conversation; each encounter was an ordeal. But this time he felt he had learned far more. To save a world, it had said. Fleurage?

How was he supposed to assist Susannilar to learn something that she was resisting? She obviously had difficulties coming to an internal consensus, and besides, the girl was slippery as an eel.

The bystanders began milling around the tent, murmuring to each other. Rheinallt did not care much for all this fascinated attention, and he hoped they would tire of it naturally.

"Catalpa!" one was saying.

"Like a winged head? Yes, I suppose so."

"I didn't understand at all."

"A fuzzball, like a dandelion seed group."

"But what did it want?"

"You're asking *me*? Ask the captain!"

"Course I'm not asking you, bozo. Who would?"

"Does what it wants have anything to do with the Ship?"

"Didn't see no wings, anyway."

"Looked a lot like that aircat creature, if you ask me."

"I think it was a spirit entity. You know, a corposant, a ship's spirit."

"Ridiculous. Those are just ball lightning."

"But—"

"Besides, corposants only show up on a caravan during a storm. In atmosphere, get me? And we've seen this thing in vacuum."

"I'm scared of corposants. They're weirdly."

"I *told* you—"

"What's Eiverdein doing talking with it, anyway?"

"Did you hear about the corposant that acted like a headlight once, leading up to breakpoint after sunset, with the trailside awash with mud?"

"Don't forget that aircat. It's white too, and sort of fuzzy—"

"Fluffy, not fuzzy. We see it perfectly clearly. The aircat's just an unusual mammal. That floating threadball is something altogether strange. Besides, the aircat can't talk."

As he heard that bit Rheinallt relaxed, relieved that Arahant and he had agreed to play so many things close, out of prudence. It was hard on him, being cut off from his usual garrulity except in private, but it might save his life.

Even the Detenebrator the caravaneers were trying to fit into their understanding as some physical-psychic manifestation rather than as an intelligent alien, but of course conceivably they were right about that. At least Arahant's silence had just saved him from some possible guilt by similar strangeness.

A moment later Nollinsae walked over to Rheinallt. "You cavort with creatures beyond your capabilities to handle," the Guardsman said.

Rheinallt turned sharply, said, "So do you."

Nollinsae puffed himself up a little, squared his shoulders. He had changed his previous garb for what must be the full dress uniform of the Guard of Fleurage: a glaring yellow draped suit with a purple sash crossing from the shoulder down to a peppermint-striped belt. A sidearm and appurtenances were attached to the belt. A spectacle: comfortable enough as uni-

174

forms go, probably, but it certainly would stand out on a parade ground.

Despite the garishness Rheinallt noted that there were no loosely hanging cords, medals, or other doodads which could interfere with efficient action. Nollinsae was as scintillating as the Ship was, and as hard to grasp.

Rheinallt's mind was still roiled by the strain of dealing with the Detenebrator, and in no mood for kid gloves. "A clever panoply," he said with deliberate insolence. "If you don't overawe your opponent visually, you can still run."

Although clearly annoyed by this unwarranted attack on a doubtless beloved uniform, Nollinsae kept his temper well. He replied in kind, "A long tongue wants cutting."

Grudgingly Rheinallt raised his opinion of the Guardsman slightly from the possibly tainted picture he had been shown. The man was clad in better armor than his clothes, and would not be drawn so easily. And Nollinsae, also, deserved to be heard.

"Have your plans for Susannilar been firmed yet?" Rheinallt asked, more conversationally.

"No, not yet. In our present situation there is really no hurry. I'll keep watch on her; there's no need for you to worry overmuch. Have you experienced her spell at close quarters yet?"

"Yes, I have. It wasn't pleasant. Her mind is like a suction."

"Awful." Nollinsae shook his head sadly. "At least one of her interrogators on Fleurage had to be confined."

Had Rheinallt resisted better than he had thought? "What happened to him?"

"Inside? I don't know. I experienced the fringes of the disorientation she causes, but I wasn't the main focus. Fortunately she had another target, and he took the brunt of it."

Rheinallt remembered a critical point. "How much of what you think about Susannilar is a result of personal observation, and how much is hearsay?"

"I've encountered her myself," he said stiffly. "Several times. I don't believe I am fabricating anything, Captain. You've said that you've already been too close to her yourself. You know there's far more to her than a casual observer would note. In fact, she's almost immune from casual observation."

"Why is that? Do you know?"

"Only that she makes herself extraordinarily difficult to focus upon. Her features are often blurred, as though seen through a mist. It's part of her protective coloration. I've never seen the like among people."

Rheinallt moved his shoulders uneasily. "Are you saying she's not altogether human?" Being fully human himself, but also with a few charmingly uncommon characteristics, this was a point on which he was sensitive.

"No, not at all. She's human, all right, as much as you or me."

Nice. "Is this certainty, or only think-so?"

"Her family's perfectly normal, except for her mother, who was a shifter too. Her father and grandfather were involved with some radical ideas and subversions, but otherwise ordinary as far as we could discover."

"Are the ideologies and the strange abilities connected?"

"How could they be?" Nollinsae looked genuinely puzzled.

"Perhaps their ways of thinking encouraged them in enhancing seeds of abilities they might otherwise have ignored."

"I suppose I follow you. Lots of good folk might have it in them to become witchlike, but have got the good sense not to try."

"Right," Rheinallt said, smiling.

"Look you, Eiverdein," he said earnestly, "I'm no professional witch-finder. I know there're plenty of theories by those who make such distasteful things a matter of enjoyment. For me this is just part of my job, which is to protect Fleurage from whoever might harm it. That Susannilar's left the planet doesn't mean she's given up her evil intentions. Her relatives on Fleurage mostly have been caught and eliminated, so now she's looking for off-planet allies. Then she'll be back in force."

Rheinallt admitted to himself that Nollinsae did project a certain sincerity. A negative force, but not a rotten one? "Are you going to force an action with Susannilar, or are you waiting for her activities to develop something?"

Nollinsae did not give. "I'll keep you posted. I've got some plans maturing, but there's plenty of time yet."

"You don't need my active help?"

"Thank you, but I think not." Nollinsae grew philosophical. "It is a shame, no doubt about it, but sometimes a little blood must be shed as an adhesive of social order and conformity."

Rheinallt tried to appear thoughtful. "Perhaps I have looked on blood as only a physical thing—"

"Yes, yes! It is a spiritual thing; you are right, you're coming to see the light. A drop of blood is a lens to magnify a pinprick. Bloodshed, a proper purifying and necessary bloodshed, shows up injuries and at the same time washes, cleanses, the body of society. It is a physical and social necessity that bad blood be leeched to preserve the pure spirit of the remainder." Nollinsae's eyes were alight with his enthusiasm.

Real information on Nollinsae's activities would come only from watching him. Rheinallt decided to put some more men to watching the Guardsman, in rotation, whenever the latter emerged from his compartment into any public place.

"A sublime theory," Rheinallt murmured. "Cleansing bloodshed." Another thought, on a less deadly subject—or was it: "The telescope, Nollinsae? You claimed it as a deodand. What have you done with it?"

"I took it apart," he answered simply.

"Looking for what?"

"For some mechanism that could have killed the two men, the tuber from Trigotha's expedition and the cook from yours."

"Find anything?"

"No, I'm afraid not. Come examine it if you wish. I'll soon be putting it back together." He grinned suddenly. "Perhaps we may find some harmless uses for it before I deliver it to Fleurage."

"I'm sure we could. Nothing but brass and wood, huh? I'll admit I would have disassembled it all the way myself." Looking for an energy weapon, just on the off chance. Rheinallt really thought, though, that both deaths had been by rather ordinary bombs and had nothing specifically to do with the telescope at all. Trail flares, for instance, were easily convertible into explosives, and left minimal residue.

"What do you think did them in, then?" Rheinallt asked, not very hopefully.

Nollinsae shrugged in his brilliant suit. After the rest of them became used to that uniform, Rheinallt realized, the Guardsman would be far less noticeable if he slipped out of it. Something to tell Bremolando.

"The tuber on Starved Rock I of course know nothing about,"

177

Nollinsae said. "The cook in the lounge car—well, I know as much as you, which is very little. I'll be careful if I decide to use the telescope myself, you can be sure. Perhaps I shall test its death-focusing powers on some small animal from the garden cars before I risk my face next to it."

"Good idea," Rheinallt said, losing interest in the conversation. Whatever Nollinsae might know, he would not share anything of practical value. Or anything detrimental to himself. Could Nollinsae have set off a small bomb in the face of the cook while the crewman was near the telescope, some little shaped charge or self-contained flare? But for what?

Rheinallt nodded solemnly at the Guardsman. "I'll have to think more upon all these things." He checked by feel his suit's oxygen-tank indicators. "And now, if you'll excuse me, I'm going up to the *Falling Angel* again."

First, though, if Susannilar had gotten his message, he had an appointment to meet that young woman; in protective vacuum, to try out Whitnadys' idea that Susannilar shift into the Ship, or the area occupied by the Ship.

The hubbub in the airtent caused by the Detenebrator had died down, although Rheinallt caught some strange looks. Thrusting his way through a knot of people near the tent's airlock which most directly faced the Ship, Rheinallt put on his helmet and went out onto the meadow. He felt as if he were casting off dirty clothes.

All at once he was back in the darkness and the silence.

13. Riding Double-Jaded

RHEINALLT BEGAN THE SHORT TREK UP THE SLOPE TO THE looming Ship. He wondered what the *Falling Angel* would look like if he could see its features beneath the fog. There were faint contours, but he felt their definition was more clear in his mind than in that eternally still fog. He imagined long rows of portholes, and giant shielded view windows and airlocks. Turrets with heavy plating, perhaps, armor for war or corrosive atmosphere. Fins for aid in landing the behemoth in a planetary atmosphere. Miniships, the size of the caravan's cars, or even of the caravan itself, passing through a huge freight port to load or unload within the *Falling Angel*'s massive protecting walls. Everything bustling with life.

As he came to the Ship the great red wall towered above him. Slowly he moved into the shadow redness.

Would those builders, faraway or ancient, be amused at his picture of their great Ship in action? Embarrassed at his primitive embellishment? Perhaps they always had intended it to be stark, haughty, unapproachable.

Or even, horrors, a work of art, as idle as a painted ship and intended for nothing except contemplation? Perhaps this shadow of the *Falling Angel* was all there had ever been, and he ought to be glad to see it thus, pure in its natural beauty like a rainbow. Still, something in him would not accept this idea: that beauty, purified to intangibility, was therefore of no value in reality. He would assume serious engineering.

The Ship was stripped down, perhaps, to its basic principle, the meadow's equivalent of a pile of rust in a rainy-planet forest. Yet to an expert with an imaginative eye that pile of rust would tell much about the soaring vehicle it once had been. But could all the years of Rheinallt-experience divine anything from a glowing shadow?

He dwelt on the image of the rusted hulk, formless in the rain. A savage with a rude scientific inclination might learn more from the rust than from the smooth and closed steel of that ship when it had been intact. The savage might be enabled to take a few first steps toward metallurgy, instead of worshiping the shiny and unbroachable mountain-sized egg. The mountainous egg would have been a dead end, but from the action of the rust he might create some first concepts of metallic change.

When he found Susannilar, she waved. Her face and posture, red-lit, showed both eagerness and a quivering strain. He lip-read her words.

"I've done it!" she was saying. Too excited apparently to use sign language, she beckoned him closer. "Come here, come on, listen!" she yelled across the vacuum.

Quickly he strode the few yards between them and touched his helmet to hers.

"Oh, Eiverdein!" Her voice was faint, fainter than it should be. "It's so lovely!"

"Yes, yes," he agreed soothingly. Her eyes were on his, through the glass, but she seemed detached at the same time. What was wrong? Something about the proximity of the Ship?

Susannilar—had she split? He had a hunch she had jumped the gun, had shifted somehow, attuned part of herself with the *Falling Angel*. At least the Ship was not a hypnotizable subject.

She talked, faintly, of what she was seeing with her other eyes of that other Ship, one perhaps more real or more tangible than the hulking red shadow which lay upon the dark meadow. Rheinallt could not make out half her words nor guess where away in space or time her other viewpoint lay. All she could do was describe what she saw, and he listened. He forced a firm contact, and strained to hear her whispered words.

"The Ship is solid now," the near-Susannilar said, eyes unfocused. No, not a whisper, only distant, though he was only inches away from her face. He tried to stare over the horizon in her eyes.

"It's big, big, big," she said. "Not a mountain of shadow but a mountain of metal. I think it's metal. Nothing misty at all. Hard, sharp, bright colors everywhere, more artistic than a fountain. And the energy! It's vibrant, I can feel it flowing through me and all around, piercing and flowing and weaving like channeled lightning.

"There are long corridors running fore and aft, long and empty but very brightly lit. Always too much light. There are no people that I can see. Nothing moving at all. But the Ship feels so alive, it's as though they just went around a corner or ducked into their rooms a moment ago.

"I've been walking along what I think is a transverse corridor, and now I'm turning up one of the fore-and-aft ones. This is empty, too. There are rooms off this corridor, but the first ones along here at least are bare. The doorways are more or less human-type; the rooms are rectangular. No furnishings.

"Everything is so incredibly bright! My eyes are watering. I'm trying to shade my eyes but I can't."

Rheinallt tore his attention away from the scene she was describing, and looked closely at the eyes of this Susannilar next to him. He wished he had been here when she had begun to oscillate, splitting into the woman who was here and the woman who was not; he wished he knew more about how she had gone and by what route. Her eyes were moist from the transferred, or doubly felt, sensation of brightness. Moist and unfocused. All her attention was for the bright solidity of the faraway Ship.

"So bright," she went on whispering, faint and hoarse. "A suit of armor, bright but empty. The people burned away long ago, sad ashes and all gone. The Ship outshines its contents as though they never had been at all. I know it was built but I can't see anybody, any sign of builders except the Ship itself. Like a mirror, like a lens, so bright, brighter than stars, brighter than the stars could shine themselves!

"The fires of hell," she went on in a worsening voice, her

mouth obviously dry but eyes tightly shut now and streaming. Her face was flushed an angry red. "The fires of stars, of galaxies, of creation, the old strong vessel."

Worried now, Rheinallt debated shaking her gently. This was a physical ordeal, and she was buckling visibly.

Then her voice strengthened slightly, her mouth set. She said clearly, "I've had enough. This is too much, I can't take any more. I'm coming back."

Tensely, he waited, gripping her suited arm tightly now in case by some accident of her returning state she lost consciousness. The hungrily disintegrating meadow would not care what she had seen if she lost consciousness on the way back. At least he was here to support her now.

At first, nothing happened. She was silent. Would she make it? Then, ever so gradually, he detected a kind of thickening in Susannilar, a growing in weight and substantiality. By imperceptible degrees, something was being put back that had been missing so subtly that in her heated narration he had not really been aware of her lack. He had not realized how much of her had been—elsewhere.

After a few minutes of labored breathing he could feel through her suit, she opened her eyes and there was recognition in them. She smiled briefly, then closed her eyes again. Presumably she needed to keep concentrating on her reintegration.

Later, after she had recovered somewhat and they were walking slowly back down toward the parked caravan and the airtent, he asked her in intersign where she had been. But she only shook her head. He decided that, considering the health of her equilibrium after her venture, there was no urgency to press her. Certainly, though, this was a great breakthrough. The restless expedition members would have a progress report to chew on.

It was only when they were entirely away from the reddening shadow, off the meadow and into the well-lit airtent, that he saw the blisters forming on her skin where Susannilar's face was freshly, rudely sunburned.

After salving her face, he took her to her room and let her stumble into her bed. Tiredly he went to his own compartment.

After the caravan's crude clock had turned around a little further to what it claimed was night back on faraway Blueholm, Rheinallt had a fitful sleep, full of dreams of bifurcation, os-

cillation, and great red ghosts. The damned clock even got into
one dream, wherein it was vital that he know the precise time
for navigational purposes, but the clock's pitiful ratchet-brain
only clanked and chuckled inanely, and its hands always pointed
in opposite directions. In his dream he pitched it overboard
and tried to construct an hourglass out of black meadow-sand.
But the sand turned to ashes and blew away in the vacuum
when he tried to pick it up; while the clock, instead of disintegrating, thinned and faded into a reddish glow in which he
could no longer discern even its feeble-minded approximations
of the time.

"Bad sleep, huh?" Whitnadys said when he awoke puffy-
eyed.

"Yeah," he grunted

"Well, don't go outside until you're awake. It's too dangerous."

Rheinallt splashed some water onto his face from the cupboard basin Whitnadys had opened up already for her own use.
"I'm going to be walking up and down in the caravan for most
of the day, I expect. Talk to the expeditionaries, share the
news, buck them up, and all that."

"Good idea. A lot of them are depressed. Going to tell them
what Susannilar did yesterday, that she seems to have penetrated the Ship?"

"Sure. It's a breakthrough. Unless some of the others are
hoarding information, it's the first one. Our investigation isn't
exactly a team effort, but everybody can use some encouragement that progress is being made."

Whitnadys' eyes twinkled as she threw back her hair and
began to brush it out, a deep golden brown like sage honey.
"No one will ever think the trip's a waste after they get home,
and they can dine out for years on the story of the Special
Caravan and the shadow of the Ship. They'll lap it up."

"Maybe then they will. Now they're frustrated."

"Seriously, though, you might try to step on that corposant
business. Your public conversation with the Detenebrator in
the airtent spread like wildfire. Explanations run all the way
from your carrying on a hallucinatory dialogue with a locus of
ball lightning, down to your cavorting with a demon."

He frowned. "What do I tell them?"

"You don't have to make up anything, but do reassure them

183

that it's all right. You may have seen scads of aliens, but they're naturally freaky to us. Arahant's a dear friend, but it was a good idea to keep him under wraps."

"Didn't do that for the *caravan's* sake, although it only takes one percent xenophobia, as it only takes one percent criminality, to make a society uncomfortable to live in. A long shot into the dark on a caravan creates tensions enough of its own without adding to them before it's necessary."

"The Detenebrator, though?" she persisted.

Rheinallt began pulling on a loose white shirt and pants. Fortunately, fifty-four worlds held so many variations of clothing styles that the fact that his own set of preferences never quite coincided with any fancied norm was never a cause for comment. Same with other little cultural peculiarities, like the proper personal distance preferred for conversations, privacy demands, and so on.

The Trail societies were mostly pretty loose, and the Blue Free Nation was the loosest and most tolerant of all, which was a significant factor in his choosing it for a base. That it was Whitnadys' home turf was another.

Of course, professional traveling people like trailmen would never hassle someone on a point of individuality, considering it rather part of the universal entertainment for their benefit if they did not actually like it. Alienness was an untried stimulant, though.

"I can't guarantee anybody's response to an alien when they've never met one," Rheinallt admitted. "But I don't assume the Detenebrator is alien."

She looked at him skeptically. "It's human, then? Or was, or will be?"

"Was. At least according to what I've heard: fitting together the halves of the story it gave me, and Susannilar gave me."

"Well, if you talk about it, don't drag Susannilar in to get blamed for that, too," Whitnadys warned. "The girl's got enough troubles of her very own."

"Agreed, for now, anyway. And I'll also take your suggestion about calming incipient fears about the Detenebrator."

"Time to make my rounds of the squeakers," Whitnadys said. "See you later."

He blew a kiss at her, finished pulling on his soft boots, and folded the basin back into the cupboard. Then he headed

184

out too, with no particular destinations. He just wanted to talk to people, as and where he found them, being himself one of the unifying forces that kept the caravan's individualities from scooting off in all directions.

As Rheinallt buttonholed people and explained Susannilar's new information about the Ship, he let on that she had used instruments rather than direct perception, and that her instrumentation was proprietary. That kept anyone from inquiring too closely about Susannilar's actual method of penetrating Ship secrets, while encouraging them to try new lines of endeavor themselves.

Much later, when he entered the lounge car for the third or fourth time, but intending on this occasion to take a break, he saw Glenavet at a table near the big window.

"How're you doing, Eiverdein? Pull up a chair."

"Thanks." Rheinallt picked one so that he, like Glenavet, could see outside: see the edge of the Blue Trail in the foreground, the long black slope with one or two suited figures moving on it, and the glowing red *Falling Angel* hulking above it all.

Rheinallt signed to the waiter to bring him a mixed salad. Since salads only had to come from a few dozen yards away, and were only picked to order, they were as fresh as could be.

The representative of the Federated Trailmen was flushed and grinning. "I hear Susannilar told you about her walking tour of the Ship," he said happily. "You know, I'm really amazed that someone like that could exist. And I don't mind telling you that I'm just as amazed that I've come across her. I never expected to meet anybody who was, well, unique. Don't know how I took so long to notice her, must have been blind. Let alone that heavenly smell! I've never been much for perfumery, but what Susannilar daubs on herself packs a wallop."

"It is beautiful," Rheinallt agreed sincerely.

"Goes with her, or something. Like the glow goes with the Ship, I guess. Although Susannilar got a bit burned yesterday, sort of a glow herself: she wouldn't tell me how." Glenavet's attention drifted to the *Falling Angel* outside. "Too bad we can't use it, after all this trouble."

What had gotten into him? No, that wasn't quite fair: he had come along as organizer, not adventurer. "How's the Federated's recruiting?" Rheinallt countered.

185

Glenavet looked a little disconcerted. "Oh, fine. Haven't given much thought to it the last few days. Susannilar, naturally. She takes up a lot of my time, even when I'm not with her, if you know what I mean."

"I can guess." The guy fell hard.

"Say, Eiverdein, Susannilar's a really great person, and I know you're kind of a friend of hers, so I figured you wouldn't mind me talking about it. Right? She's a wonder and no mistake! Pretty—well, anyone can see that, although I'm slow, took me a long time to notice her." He slowed down, laughed indulgently. "And more than exciting, because we'll be able to bring her back, which is a lot more than we'll be able to do with your *Falling Angel* obsession."

"So you're going to bring Susannilar back with you?" Rheinallt asked quietly.

Glenavet's face went through some subtle changes. "Sure! Sure I am."

"Otherwise she'll just have to ride back with the caravan?" he asked, because Glenavet had answered more than Rheinallt had inquired.

"Oh, hell, Eiverdein. You know we'll both be on the caravan." Glenavet was grinning helplessly with a mixture of adoration and embarrassment for his subject. "What I mean is, we'll be together."

"I take it you've been together already?"

Glenavet blushed. He leaned forward, glancing around to assure that no one was near. "That girl is unimaginable," he asserted in a soft but intense tone. "She's a wonder. Like making love with two women at once."

"She's a doppelganger."

"Yeah, she said she tried to explain all that to you, but she wasn't sure how much you picked up. But you're sharp, you probably understood it all right away. Me, I'm still trying to soak it all in."

"I confess I hadn't thought about what it would be like making love to a doppelganger," Rheinallt said, smiling. The salad arrived, and he began digging into it.

"Sometimes it's like there's two of her just an eighth of an inch offset, like vibrating faster than your eye can follow. And other times she's all the way separated, with her totally apart as if they were twins, with me in the middle.

"Hard on her," Glenavet continued, "to be so innocent and so sad at the same time. I've sworn to do whatever I can to make things better for her. I think she knows I'm sincere. Now I have to figure out what to do. Not even deciding to join the Federated was as heavy a situation."

"Well, Glenavet, I hope the liaison will help both of you."

"I suppose it will," he said ruefully. "I feel so different from the fellow I was before I met her. I guess I'm changing already, but that's supposed to happen when you fall in love, right?"

Rheinallt wondered if Susannilar had told him about Nollinsae's pursuit. Her method of sharing confidences was staggering. "When did you meet her first?"

"I heard this sobbing: it was a young woman's voice, but distant. There was nobody in sight. I thought, too bad; but I wasn't barging in on somebody's private troubles. Still, the crying kept on and on, and I was getting edgy. What was all that heartrending? None of my business, but maybe I could help."

Glenavet reminisced in a hushed solemnity. "So there I went nosing down the corridor. In this alcove I found her, nestled behind a stubby potted tree. She was scrunched into the corner and hanging on to the tree for dear life.

"It was her that was sobbing, no question about the source. But she was dry-eyed! Nobody else nearby, so I looked closer at this lady, a girl really. I was starting some soothing-type noises but when I got closer, I saw that she was quivering. More than just a sob-quiver, she was really vibrating.

"So she wasn't just fooling around with that tree. She really was hanging on. As she was vibrating away, I saw a couple of leaves flutter down. She was in trouble, even if I didn't understand it.

"I gathered her into my arms and hugged her gently like she was real fragile. I didn't say anything at all. I mean, I'm good at organizing people, getting them all fired to stand together. This was something I hadn't practiced much."

Glenavet stopped. "Don't know as I want to go any further," he said gruffly. "Hope you don't mind. Gets more personal, both of Susannilar and me."

"Sure. That's fine," Rheinallt said. The burst of new emotions that had overreached the barrier of shyness was subsiding.

Yet Glenavet was not quite talked out. "Guess I ought to

grab some more ears and work on the organization. But you know, it all seems different now. Have to start thinking about my own goals here. Like the real point of my being on this expedition turns out to have been meeting Susannilar. My old purposes feel threadbare, but if meeting Susannilar has set me a new way, what is it? Got some heavy figuring to do."

Glenavet stood, looked out upon the black starkness outside for a moment, then lifted a hand in casual goodbye and walked off.

"Later," Rheinallt said cordially, and turned to polishing off the salad.

Yes, Glenavet had been dropped into a crucible. He hoped the man would recognize himself when he found those new purposes, and like what he found. The vital encounter had not even been with their so-glorious Ship but with an oscillating and pursued refugee girl.

After he finished lunch Rheinallt resumed his floor-walking, conversing with whoever felt like it, and with whoever looked in need of cheer.

Rheinallt's face must have shown more strain than he realized. He was just about to pass out of a car down in the tail of the caravan when a passenger nudged him. He turned in the narrow corridor, recognizing a self-touted metallurgy expert.

"Say, Captain! Don't look so worried! Don't dwell on your problems," the passenger said earnestly. "Put them behind you and live in the present."

"Oh? How can I do that?"

"Just don't let the past get to you. So what if we've used more than half our supplies? We've got to enjoy each day as it comes, get rid of old thoughts."

Rheinallt slouched against the wall. Who would start such an outrageous rumor? He hadn't heard it before today. In a dryly innocent tone he asked, "You mean, suppress my thoughts?"

The passenger threw up his hands. "No, no. You can't do that. You have to live through all your old feelings. It's when you haven't lived through them that you're carrying all the dead weight around with you. That's suppression: very bad for you."

"How do I tell when I've lived through my old problems? By running out of food?"

"You'll know," the metallurgist assured him. "You'll be altogether in the present. Everything will feel right. And that Guardsman fellow said not to worry about the food."

Rheinallt rubbed his shoulder blade on a seam in the wall, alleviating a sudden itch to be elsewhere, and deep-six someone. "But some of my past concerns are still alive and kicking now, in the present. Like the Ship there, for instance, and that deadly telescope. So I worry some."

"But that's what's holding you back. Don't you see?"

"No," Rheinallt said. The other's mentioning the Guardsman and food together had gotten Rheinallt thinking about the cook the telescope allegedly killed.

"You must live in the now." The metallurgist stamped his foot on the thinly carpeted decking.

"Of course, we live in the now," Rheinallt said patiently; although Susannilar had him wondering. "Part of the definition of life is its currency. But a man whose present includes none of his past and none of his future is scarcely a man. I grant you, certainly such a present-bound thing wouldn't be capable of introspection, wouldn't be conscious in any meaningful sense, and certainly couldn't exist unsupported on the meadow."

He shuffled his feet. "I don't follow."

"Your present is where you live," Rheinallt said slowly. "If you let go of your past, or of your future, you simply won't be alive in *any* present. You can't maintain a mind without a past. Try to live solely in the present, if you're sure you really want to: take a little leap out on the meadow with both feet off the surface. That'll be your very last instant of presence."

"No, that's death you're talking about," the metallurgist said brightly.

"You can live in a present that doesn't have death in it? Did the Guardsman Nollinsae, when he was talking about food, tell you that salt is the only food that never was alive?"

"Why, no. He just said that the trailman in sick bay, Tadako I think, probably just ate some tainted food, and that the cooks had to dump a lot of it."

Rheinallt tried to fit morale-sapping by Nollinsae into the Guardsman's campaign against Susannilar, but he couldn't.

"You're trying to confuse me," the passenger went on. "Take that tuber, now, who was blasted by the telescope. He was trying to borrow against the future, see what he couldn't see

189

from where he was. Awful. Captain, I'm just trying to *help* you. You don't know how much your refusal to let go of your past is holding you up."

Rheinallt had to laugh; this fellow was superb. "Exactly. You've got it *exactly* right."

"Huh?"

Suddenly two different past events came together in Rheinallt's mind: he was sure that the whole telescope business was just a shuck. "Two men were murdered—referring to your illustration. The one of Trigotha's expedition happened to be caught off guard, near his telescope, when a bomb or something went off in his face. Then, *imitatively*, another man was murdered in our own lounge car. The involvement of the telescope in the first death was almost certainly fortuitous, don't you see; and in the second death a diversion. And when we know who did that second murder, we'll make sure someone pays for it."

The metallurgist still looked puzzled; in fact, he had the look of someone who manages the difficult feat of being puzzled on several discrete levels of consciousness simultaneously.

"I think I'll make your conversation a problem in the past," Rheinallt said cheerfully, shoving off from the supporting wall he had been leaning on. "I do know how much my refusal to let go of my mind, with all its history, is what's *holding me up*. And the same for you. Luckily the subconscious strata of your own mind have been impervious to your philosophy. But if I were you, until we're safely groundside in oxygen again, I'd think twice about going outside."

He stuttered in amazement. "Captain—you're talking about dying?"

Rheinallt continued sharply, "You hear? Once more—for the present—*don't* go out on the meadow. You can't get any closer to death than subspace, and a micro-instant of presentness isn't enough to protect you. I can't take responsibility for your state of mind. But you will. See you around."

Rheinallt strolled off, whistling runs from a tune of long ago.

Near Nollinsae's compartment, he found Bremolando on watch in the corridor. "Don't let Nollinsae close to any food storage or preparation," he told the rifleman. "Air storage, too, come to think of it."

"You finally get something on him, Captain?"

"Don't quite see his game yet. Just give him room enough to stumble, without endangering the caravan. I think he may be trying to create a riot situation, some violent confusion that he can drag Susannilar into as a help to doing away with her. No proof yet."

"Sounds weird, but if he can't do it any other way—I'll tell the others watching him."

"Thanks."

Moving up the caravan, whistling again, Rheinallt did not hear Whitnadys' soft footfalls on the corridor carpet until she had almost caught up with him.

"Ah ha, there you are," she said, and linked her arm with his as they walked.

"Hello, darling."

She glanced back to see if anyone was close behind. "You know, Hendrikal, there's something we were going to talk about."

He looked into her mischievous face. "What?"

"How old are you?" she asked softly. "You promised to tell me."

"Remember the little puzzle, the number twenty?" He gave her a moment to think. Past time she knew, anyway. "It's twenty times."

Whitnadys stared. "Oh, vacuum eat me," she whispered. "Wow, you aren't kidding, are you? *Twenty times* older than I am?"

"About that. Your chronometry in the Nation is so casual—"

"Don't fool with the decimals," she interrupted tensely; her pacing had stiffened. "You know I'm not so much for arithmetic as for symbolic logic, but I have absolutely no trouble adding. You were marooned with Arahant on that rain planet for a couple of years, and it's been several more since I found you there. No problem. But hints you've dropped of your life on Earth or whatever it is, and zooming over faraway tracts of meadowspace in your fancy starships—well, that's a lot of adventures! So I knew you'd been around, even more than I have. With that many years, though, you were probably being modestly selective when I thought you were multiplying stories!"

Placating her, folding both her hands within his as they

walked, Rheinallt said, "I knew we'd get around to it, although I'd rather have postponed major issues between us until after we acquired control of the Ship. You're so busy now, but if we demoted you to *Falling Angel* passenger for a while, you'd have some mentational energy left over, and a lot fewer distractions."

"Why? So I could concentrate on your bragging about your longevity?"

He laughed, and she was offended. "No, no, Whitnadys. You should know my character better than that by now, even if you don't know all my history."

Whitnadys sighed wearily. "I don't think you're lying. Neither do I question your right to tell me in your own sweet time. Lover, what scares me is the *difference* between us. This is too much for me, it's unbridgeable."

"Never jump to conclusions on the meadow."

"What, then?" She did not sneer but obviously was close to it. "Teach me how?"

"Yes."

Her eyes opened so wide that Rheinallt thought he would see the back of her skull. She snatched her hands out of his light grasp and covered her face, stopping dead still in the middle of the corridor. A few tears escaped under her fingers to plop soundlessly on the carpet.

Rheinallt stopped too, glad that so many passengers and crew were outside: the corridor was otherwise empty in this car. For this had gone too far, too hurtfully, for him not to share the truth with her this minute.

"Hendrikal—"

"I'm here."

"You've never lied to me yet."

"Nor am I now. Whitnadys, I said that I dole out my history. That's because my throat would give out before I finished telling it. But the procedures of longevity are teachable. The bloodsweater discipline is a matter of structural mind-body integration, certain specific techniques. I suspect you're capable of learning them."

She still would not look at him. "You learned how not to *age*?"

"Your ageing right now is the result of mental control over

particular physical processes. Some, like adrenaline, come easier out of the vasty deep when you call for them."

"When you said you were a bloodsweater, I didn't know you meant that too."

"It's much more powerful than we usually let on to others. All the processes are there within you, potentially at your command, and the guidance of them can be mastered. It takes a lot of strength of mind to furnish the discipline. That's harder of attainment than the specific ageing processes themselves."

"You frighten me."

"Think about this, then," Rheinallt said quietly. "I would never have told you this if I didn't think you were capable of it. Without mastering the blood during one's first, 'given' lifespan, the natural chances of growth and decay lead to cancer or ageing; the inexorable house percentages that no mere tenant of a body could long hold out against."

He felt bad for her. Even his little joke about the age ratio upset her. But this was no easy news to break, although still he would have wished to share it in a quieter time.

"Hey, Whitnadys, if Arahant could get the techniques past all those operatic cascades he's always juggling mentally— why, I'm sure you can handle it. As you said, you're no slouch at symbolic logic."

"Arahant, too?" she whispered. She removed her hands from her face, and her liquid eyes appealed to him. "You don't understand." She started to say more but choked on the next word. "Do I deserve something like that?"

"Sure. And Arahant deserves long life all right, in spite of that warped tongue of his. If I could put up with him all these years, surely you don't think a little raspiness on your part would make me disown you." He groped again for words to restore her lightheartedness. "After all, Arahant's musical sensibility has to put up with my whistling."

"Oh, Hendrikal!" She threw herself into his arms. "How dare you make me laugh when I'm crying?" she said happily. "I don't know how to believe this."

Rheinallt hugged her. "Later," he said softly into her ear. "Later, we'll talk more about it. It really will be easier when we haven't so many other cares."

"Oh!" Her hand flew to her mouth. "That reminds me! I

was due up at Squeakerville—must have been half a clockhour ago!"

"Blame it on the clock," he suggested. "The squeakers love you, and they'll wait. And so will I."

"Love you too," she said, gave a quick kiss, and raced lightly up the corridor.

What a woman. He wasn't at all sorry he had let their lifelines become entangled with each other. What a joy.

Feeling all talked out, and wanting some quiet time, he got his airsuit out of his room and took a walk outside beyond the front of the caravan. Whitnadys waved to him from her ministrations in what she had called Squeakerville, the golden cluster of waybeasts near the head of the parked caravan. Rheinallt waved back encouragingly and continued.

After a few hundred yards of the glowing blueness of the trail beneath his feet, he veered to one side onto the unrelieved blackness of the meadow.

It was so quiet out here. No talk, no hustle and bustle. There was the sound of his own flows, of air through all its roundabout passages in his suit and in him. There was the subsonic neural tingle of the trickling electrical fields that any human body maintained, and that he was more aware of than most. There was a circular roll and surge of blood sent to the periphery of flesh and regathered. These rhythms and textures were natural, calm, and quieting: the simple sounds of him being him.

He lay down on the textured pseudosurface. The meadow was not hard in the sense of brittle, but neither was it soft and bouncy. A firm demarcation.

Rheinallt felt sleepy. Considering carefully the level of consciousness he would have to maintain, or subconsciousness, would he be safe in taking a nap? It was so peaceful out here. He was sleepy, but clear: he decided he could get away with it. Putting his hands under the back of his helmet, he let his eyes close.

When he awoke he estimated that several hours had passed. He felt buoyant and bouncy. It was not a pastime he could recommend generally, though; it more than bordered on the risky.

Heading back to the caravan his step was lighter and he felt entirely refreshed, ready even to continue his survey of the caravan. But did anything more need to be done? Everyone seemed happily industrious, barring false rumors. If the *Falling Angel* was proving hard to grasp, that proved their need for subtlety in gripping techniques. There were lots of grumbles, but they were technical gripes rather than existential ones.

No sooner had he returned to his compartment and stripped off his airsuit than Glenavet came barging in. The latter was agitated and full of a myriad tiny movements, which Rheinallt noted vividly in contrast to his own post-meadow-nap quietude.

"What's on your mind, Glenavet?"

"Remember that rougher path of meadow we crossed a few clockdays before Starved Rock? Before we started noticing Susannilar? I think that may have brought her out of herself. See, I figure she's got a subliminal, minor vibration going all the time. Natural as breathing to her by now, poor kid. But when the caravan itself is creaking and jiggling under her, she has to settle down a notch her own self. Else she gets dizzy, she tells me."

Rheinallt turned on the gas jet for his desk lamp, lit it using the flint. "So it was where we were, not when, that made the difference."

Glenavet smiled broadly. "But that scent of hers! Now, that's a wonder and a half. The millefleurs, you know? It's like the breath of spring hitting my lungs all at once. So sweet. Her grandfather must have been a genius."

Was Glenavet burbling with a purpose? Before, he had only wanted to talk about trailmen and trail adventures. Today, it was Susannilar all the way: or at least Susannilar and Glenavet. An order of magnitude loopier than that morning: perhaps he had gone through another heavy-duty session—or was that uncharitable?

"Have the Detenebrator or Nollinsae been bothering Susannilar lately?" Rheinallt asked.

"Not really. That Detenebrator thing stuck like a burr for a while, always hanging around, she said. But about the time she and I started getting together, it's been scarce. I think she thought it was dying, because she didn't want to talk about it; everything else just poured out of her."

Interesting. "And the Guardsman from Fleurage?"

"Oh, that stiffy fellow Nollinsae was complaining about

some of the publications along. There's been a regular flood lately of astrological stuff: so-called learned treatises, popular pamphlets, and so on. Stupid to worry about it."

Rheinallt nodded. "Astronomy's finally making some headway, particularly in the Nation." He wondered if Glenavet was still uninterested. "Has Susannilar talked about Fleurage's trail-drift with you?"

"Yeah, in fact the idea got Nollinsae really riled, I heard: someone aboard was reading in one of those new almanacs how the Yellow trailside on Fleurage is shrinking."

"That set him off?"

"Angry beyond words. His own steam like to have snapped him through breakout right then and there, and left him breathing interstellar vacuum to cool himself off. He was really fried; wish I could have seen it myself."

Rheinallt chuckled. "Me, too. Not to mention Susannilar."

Glenavet's voice lowered. "Why, that was almost the worst of it. Seems Susannilar's parents were among the ones on Fleurage who did the mapping of its trailpoint movements, and her parents wrote up their findings for that almanac."

"Whew."

"No vacuum about that. Nollinsae must have a grudge as long as a trail. But we're not worrying. He can't touch us."

"Hope so, for your sakes."

With a fleeting expression that struck Rheinallt as crafty, Glenavet said, "She's really a boggler and no mistake. It's like being in bed with two people at once, sometimes. One on either side, the two of her in total rapport, like twins, doing every little thing in harmony. Neuromeshed—is that the word? Anyway, it's a perfect dance, but with two partners. Other times it's like making it with a woman while a ghost is behind you. Present just enough, on that other side of the split, to give you a creepy tickle. Weird, but sexy too."

Rheinallt recalled the other man shyly mentioning this private topic that morning; now he was lathering it on thick. Why? A distraction?

"And even when she's all together," Glenavet gushed on, "her vibrato's like a whole body massage right in the middle of it all. Turns my brain to jelly!"

Trying to appear entranced, Rheinallt said, "Guess that makes up for being looked at binocularly," remembering his own first experience of Susannilar.

That must have been the wrong thing to say, though, for Glenavet suddenly sobered and changed subjects again. The romantic spell was broken, and he went on in a practical political vein.

"Confidentially, Eiverdein, I've been suspicious it must have been the Federated Trailmen that put the squeeze on the survivors of Trigotha's old crew. Maybe bumped off some of them."

Rheinallt hoped Glenavet's actual romancing would not fly so quickly as the man's accounting of it. What was the game here, though? "Were they that afraid of a nontrail conveyance, even one that was likely a derelict?"

"Just shortsighted, I guess. Kind of thing Wirtellin would have thought was clever."

"Really?" Rheinallt stroked his beard. "If so, I'm glad he gave me the opportunity to kill him."

"No great loss." Glenavet laughed harshly. "Here's an opportunity for the common man to get a grasp on history and remake it. How far did Wirtellin's vision extend? He only saw a threat to his petty power structure. I don't think anymore that it was an accident that I survived on Starved Rock when Wirtellin didn't. I was being saved, and the Ship's been the means that brought Susannilar and me together. It's like a prophecy, you know? A sign that there's no stopping the two of us now.

"Messing around with the Federated Trailmen was in a good cause. Before Susannilar, though, that hunger in me for a wider sphere of action was just being wasted. I mean I knew that hunger was there, but I had no way to fill it."

"I see," Rheinallt said. More than he wanted to see, he had to conclude. Susannilar's outpourings to Rheinallt had rocked *him* pretty hard; Glenavet was sounding like he had gone off his rocker altogether. However, Rheinallt had managed to throw off her hypnotic influence. Glenavet, being in love with her, would take longer.

Glenavet did not seem able to stay on one subject for more than a few sentences running. Where was the careful, stolid trailman Rheinallt had talked to on Starved Rock and after? Even in the course of this very day, Glenavet's character seemed

197

to have wobbled down some strange direction, or been pulled.

A quick experiment. "Too bad the Blue Army isn't something a fellow can *wield*," Rheinallt said as if to himself.

"Yeah, there's too many masterless men and women in the galaxy," Glenavet said intensely.

"You speak for the whole galaxy?" Rheinallt tried to make the question sound reasonable.

"I—of course not. But see here, Eiverdein: think how much easier this Special Caravan would have been for Susannilar if you'd made Nollinsae take the deep jump the first hour out of Blueholm."

Along with several Federated Trailmen, Rheinallt thought sourly.

"Well, got to get back to that double-sweetness of mine," Glenavet said abruptly, and left.

Rheinallt sank back in his chair, feeling rather less refreshed than after his meadow-nap.

Had Glenavet been trying to feel out Rheinallt cautiously? Distracting him from considering Fleurage with talk about sex, and then from debating destiny with a jab at Nollinsae, so as to touch those subjects but not too closely? It was the kind of oscillatory conversation an overdose with Susannilar might just inspire. The sooner Glenavet got over it, the better.

What would happen if Susannilar managed to hail Nollinsae before a court of law elsewhere than on paranoid, superstitious Fleurage? Where Susannilar could deliver her hypnotic spiel directly to a judge? She might be entirely in the right, but would the resulting *process* be justice?

How much of Rheinallt's own sympathy for Susannilar was a natural feeling, and how much was due to her particular talent for press-ganging emotions? Turning rudimentary favorable feelings into strong support? Already there had been times when his concern for Susannilar's problems had caused him to be with her, when he might have delegated that task and spent more time managing the caravan as a whole.

Rheinallt did not like to think that Nollinsae's blatant hatred was the best defense against being caught between dual charms of scent and looks, presence and recalled childhood, and being sucked in like bee into flower.

He had been sitting and thinking for a long time when

Whitnadys knocked quietly and slipped into the room. "Hendrikal?"

"I'm here." He looked up. "I need to talk to you."

"Anytime," she said softly.

14. Exhaustion to Vacuum

THE NEXT MORNING RHEINALLT SPENT AT A PORTABLE DESK in the airtent, carrying out promises made the previous clockday to give technological advice to various investigators. A lot of them had balky equipment; even though he had never heard of some of the instruments, or indeed of what they purported to measure, often he was able to delve into his dustiest memory files and recall some analogous device. Sometimes he was unhelpful, other times he suggested improvements along lines so radical that he was forced to spend a lot of time explaining physical principles in analogies the investigators could understand. As some of them were trained scientists, with opinions well buttressed by the certification of other alleged experts, he ran into strong personality intransigence as well as paradigm confusions.

The other side of the equipment problem was the Ship problem: that the equipment might be working perfectly well for what it was intended, but simply not finding anything about the *Falling Angel* to bite into. Prima facie, there often was no way to tell which kind of problem an investigator had. Rheinallt's theories about the Ship so far had been as infertile as anyone's. With this class of problems he could only reboost yesterday's encouragements, and try to send each adventurer away in a renewedly adventurous frame of mind. Some did not look very happy.

Rheinallt was glad for the break when Whitnadys came, plopping herself into the folding chair where the supplicant adventurers had been sitting one after another.

"Whew!" she said. "Hard day, already."

"I agree. How so for you?"

She slumped further into the chair. "Oh, the beasties are restless. I know you think I have a large crew, and we get to ride along and loaf a lot. Well, so do your airhose fitters, runner and suspension mechanics, and such. It's the same for us with the waybeasts. Nothing to do and then too much."

"What set them off?"

"Don't know." She frowned unhappily. "We're all depressed: squeakers' moods are infectious. A squeaker may not let on that she's thinking about anything at all. One of my crew will be changing harness or whatever, not worrying, and some snaky trunk will press its moist tip against a helmet and throw in a few squeaks. Not quite random, of course. Then that beast handler will find herself drifting off into daydream, snarling the harness or simply forgetting it for a while.

"Usually it doesn't matter. Sometimes, though, there seem to be general moods. Today has been a downer among the handlers, and we attribute it to the squeakers." She flicked at helmet-crimped hair.

"So the squeakers are restless, and your handlers are worried. How about you, honey?"

"Well—how old *are* you, anyway?" Whitnadys laughed at his expression. "No, not again: we had enough of that last night. Actually, I've been thinking about home. The Azuline tidewater farms. Little sinks of swamp, what the little animals did with their lives. Green smells and tastes."

"Susannilar's childhood helped her to become a doppelganger."

"And me to become a beast master," Whitnadys said. Her eyes glinted. "At least I'm all in one piece."

"I'm glad you're intact," Rheinallt said with a smile. "Arahant is, too."

202

"Nice to be appreciated by such renowned travelers." Examining the clutter in the airtent, she asked, "Is he around? Oh, I see him: over there."

Rheinallt turned, spotted the catadrome asleep, drifting in midair near the side wall of Car Fourteen. Rheinallt whistled softly; again. Arahant opened one eye, blinked at the man expressionlessly, then closed it again.

"See?" Rheinallt said to Whitnadys. "The very picture of adoration."

"Perfect. Next time we're on Azuline, I want to stop to visit, make myself unbusy. Even though I've not yet been responsible for a whole caravan, you've seen what I have to do. All preparations that involve waybeasts. Commercial arrangements. Hiring replacement crew, and giving bonuses to the regulars. Research on biology, and on theory of interspecies communication. Which is a laugh."

"In the meantime it's nice to relax." He waved airily around the airtent.

"The chairs are too hard. Anyway, in the meantime we have the meadow. Empty, empty, empty. I get to feeling empty myself, don't you?"

"Yes," he said slowly, "but we're not quite dead yet. We still can go back."

"Even if we have to walk, I suppose. Don't be mad, Eiverdein. It's just a bad day, and a slow clock for it."

"I'm not mad; but you're brash, babe, even when you're down. I expect to get back all right."

Whitnadys sniffed doubtfully. "Back to sensation, and everything?" she said wistfully. "Don't you sometimes feel like you're walking a tightrope, out here? And one bad step can send you plunging into the abyss."

"Not—"

"And you wouldn't have time to scream," she continued inexorably. "Nothingness would reclaim you. There wouldn't be a trace. Couldn't even send your bones home. As if you never—"

"Enough!" he said. "You paint it awfully dark."

"It is dark. Look." She pointed at the plain beyond the tent. "It'll drain you down to nothing if you don't watch out. I might not be able to reach you in time. Get tired, make a misstep,

203

and you're gone. That damned meadow is waiting to suck us into the abyss, and it'll do it, too. Time is on the side of nothing."

"You're only three shades less bleak than the meadow yourself, today. Is all this brought on by a skittish squeaker?"

She shrugged, a nervous jerk. "I feel trouble coming. It's not—well, with the meadow always there, any tiny thing could be a disaster. And from what you've said, Susannilar's found some other side to the *Falling Angel*, somewhere. We're operating on quintessential thin ice and quicksand."

Rheinallt realized that merely waiting in his helmetless airsuit was making him restless now. He decided he would have to cheer up Whitnadys. He did not want her circulating around the crew in her present mood, and among the sensitive waybeasts her gloom would echo and reinforce, as much as her normal steadiness usually helped. Besides, he liked her happy.

"How'd your people ever venture onto the meadow if it was so obviously scary?" he asked her.

Whitnadys stirred in her chair, draping her slim-muscled, suited legs over one arm of the chair and lolling her head over the other. "Are you thinking about that guy long ago who first rode a squeaker?"

"Before my time." Maybe.

She grinned with an effort.

"Don't know much about him," Rheinallt said. "The first of your profession, Whitnadys; and really the first of all trailmen."

"The first beast handler. I'll claim him."

"A lot of guts," Rheinallt whistled an empathetic note.

She tilted her head straight up at the puffed ceiling of the tent, bowed out by air pressure from the caravan. "Yeah, imagine that. The fascination of the coarse golden hair, tusks of ivory. A hero's mount! The first man to ride a squeaker. He must have caught the great elephantine thing standing still, or just lazing along the groundside; then he ran alongside, jumped to grab some hide, and scrambled aboard. Then the squeaker put his trunk up and pounded down the trail hell for leather; our brave jumper-on was scared stiff, hanging on for dear life."

"Repenting frantically as his friends watched him carried off?"

"Maybe." She half straightened. "Maybe he was devising the first draft of the first clause of the beast handlers' credo, which is never to abandon a squeaker in trouble."

"I think our human pioneer of that long-ago ride was in more trouble than the squeaker."

"Sure, but he didn't know that. Because he was only an apprentice, you see, if it was his first trip out."

Rheinallt laughed, but insisted, "He must have been more than just professionally excited."

"So was the squeaker," Whitnadys pointed out. "Probably panicked. I suppose often enough they'd been attacked by big groundside carnivores on various worlds. Carnivores desperately hungry to try to pull down a creature so big. They wouldn't care if its flesh was luminescent in subspace; they'd just sniff a banquet on the hoof. Anyway, on Blueholm way back when, that first-ridden squeaker would have reacted from a normal fear, and run for safety in vacuum."

"Yes, a big carnivore could harm a waybeast."

"Oh, yes. If for some metabolic reason some species couldn't eat it, even those could maul it and destroy its energy balance, or simply injure it badly enough to bleed to death. The energy disruption could kill an injured squeaker that tried to shift into subspace from groundside, if disruption went far enough.

"But think, lover, what a rainbow must have exploded in that rider's untrained mind as he transited into subspace. How beautiful it must have been, all those colors inside and all that dark outside."

"Not much time to enjoy," Rheinallt demurred. "That first breath is short on nutrition, and he didn't get a second one."

"Enough time," she said positively. "Enough to realize the beauty and the starkness. I know the pioneer would have had air in his lungs for the moment of entering subspace: he definitely would have experienced the subjective breakthrough rainbow.

"And beyond that moment, I believe he saw the meadow from the squeaker's back. I believe he saw the Blue Trail like a burning line on the meadow, and the infinite black without stars. He didn't know where he was, except that he quickly would have realized that he was facing a strange but clean death in those next few moments. Of subspatial travel to other worlds he had of course not an inkling."

Rheinallt said, "I'll bet with the meadow so bleak the trail seemed like a bright line to heaven."

"I suppose so. He would have had no time to analyze. The old legend is that afterward the other tribesmen said they could see a blue line, vertical, in each of his dead, open eyes. That's a nice touch."

"The sight of the trail imprinted on his eyeballs? The other side of the miraculous coin was that the squeaker brought him back."

"Surely. After all, he *was* the first beast handler."

"Speaking as a squeaker expert, my lovely beast handler, do you think the squeaker was sorry the man had died of chewing vacuum? Wanted to make amends?"

"Speaking as an expert, I don't know." She waggled her booted feet in the air. "It's quite possible. We don't know if the first deliberate human encounter with squeakers was also the first consciousness that waybeasts had of humans. I would guess that it wasn't mutual initial contact. Naturally at this distance in time we'll never know, unless the squeakers open some ethereal racial archives they've kept hidden all these years. I think the squeakers, or some of them at least, were already aware of humanity.

"Anyway, the legend says that when the Blueholmian tribesmen saw their late companion stone-dead on the back of the returning squeaker they panicked themselves. But the squeaker waited, and eventually a few of the hardier ones got up nerve enough to sidle up to the creature and placate it, while others pried the pioneer's fingers loose from their deathgrip on the squeaker's hair."

"Pallbearers?" Rheinallt asked.

"No, the squeaker was really the pallbearer. The legend claims it felt sorry. Certainly it brought back the man deliberately."

"The body, you mean. Did the squeaker realize the man was dead?"

Whitnadys hesitated a long time, playing with the fastenings of her helmet. "I think so. It wouldn't have done the same for some big carnivore. One of those it could have carried out on the trail until the claws relaxed in vacuum or the squeaker could shake loose, and then let the body tumble off its back to vanish on the meadow.

"That first squeaker was a pioneer, too. Bright enough to realize that the man on its back had been an entity not totally unlike itself, and sympathetic enough to bring his body back to his relatives."

Rheinallt reflected on the tale. Likely enough, at least as concerned the beginnings of the Blue Free Nation. But humanity had a long history to date, sprinkled already with many strange encounters, of which he was sure many had never been noted or recorded sufficiently well to be remembered.

Susannilar came into the tent from an airlock opening onto the meadow. Rheinallt tapped on the table with a fingertip, sharply, and made a gesture in intersign to Whitnadys.

Whitnadys casually glanced in the indicated direction. She signed back, "Looks thin."

"Not all here?" he responded silently.

"Perhaps avoiding Nollinsae."

"Yes. Keeping a foothold elsewhere, for escape."

"I suppose she's been doing that fairly often, right along," Whitnadys signed, looking at Susannilar.

Rheinallt made an affirmative sign. Aloud he said, "I've given out enough scientific advice for today. Let's go up to the Ship. Yes, why not? Maybe you'll be struck with a new angle about squeakers and the Ship. After all, it was through watching waybeasts in planetary skies that some men first discovered the trails and began connecting worlds."

"Not in the skies, but along groundside trails," Whitnadys objected, getting up. "I just told you the legend. Weren't you listening?"

"Ah, sure," he said agreeably. "But space is deep."

Whitnadys frowned, rubbing her booted toes on the floor of the airtent and fiddling with her helmet fastenings. "Yes, but we, our ancestors, had only to observe and harness the waybeasts. So they'd spare a little energy to pull us along while they kept on going their natural way. But the Ship is different; going off the trail is different."

Susannilar had moved indecisively toward Whitnadys and Rheinallt, but now stood uncertainly. Then she shook her head slightly and walked away, negligently dropping her helmet on the tent floor.

"She looks petulant," Whitnadys signed.

"Yes," Rheinallt said, drawing Whitnadys with him toward

an outer airlock. "Yet on those worlds where one can glimpse a squeaker on a portion of trail in the upper atmosphere, the trail is often invisible and it's the squeaker that appears as a glow. If men on such worlds had assumed that there was no waybeast behind the glow, and never checked it out, they would still be planetbound, never have discovered the higher connections."

"I understand you now," she said, smiling. "You're speaking from experience. At least one, anyway: Rainstone. Well, I'll think about it."

They refastened their helmets just inside the airlock. Since they had not removed their airsuits, that was all that was necessary.

Before they entered the lock, though, Whitnadys noticed Nollinsae entering the airtent, striding through the open door from Car Fourteen. She tapped Rheinallt's shoulder and pointed. He nodded, and signed to her to wait a moment.

Rheinallt glanced out the transparent sections of the tent wall at the meadow, then looked within again. Nollinsae had brought the telescope, the instrument that he had deemed an instrument of death and claimed as a deodand. A few in the tent stood up from their own equipment or shifted in their chairs to get another look at the telescope. One of the riflemen watching Nollinsae came out of Car Fourteen and stood casually by the door.

Nollinsae moved toward the center of the airtent, moving a little awkwardly with the big telescope in his arms. His glance moved around the tent in long jerky sweeps as he walked, but whether he noticed anyone in particular Rheinallt couldn't tell. Nollinsae stopped in the central area of the tent and began setting up the brass tube and tripod, and passengers clustered thickly around.

Whitnadys nudged Rheinallt's arm. "Helmet!" she signed. "He's got his helmet on!"

The Guardsman had come from the air-filled caravan, and was now setting up within the air-filled tent. Everyone went from air to vacuum often enough that it was no more odd to have a helmet on indoors than to be carrying it in one's hand, yet breathing canned air unleavened by hydroponics was not thrilling.

Now Nollinsae had the telescope on its tripod, and he stood

back briefly with an attitude of satisfaction. But the telescope was aiming straight up at the roof of the dome. Not out at the red bulk of the Ship, but up into empty blackness.

Suddenly Rheinallt knew what Nollinsae was going to do. Could he strike at the Guardsman? No, too crowded. He ripped open his helmet fastenings and shouted, "*Air break!*"

Nollinsae was already leaning forward, touching something at the base of the telescope. A few people looked around for the source of the yell, doubtful of any emergency. Nollinsae made several twisting motions, taking pains that the sections of the tube had a precise alignment. Then he stood at arm's length and pressed some recessed lever.

A few people in the tent had left off gawking and gaping to hunt for their helmets; fewer still were putting them on.

Rheinallt shouted again, "*Air break!*" and began putting on his own helmet again, hampered by the slight destruction he had wrought in taking it off so quickly.

All of this, since he had opened the helmet to shout, took only seconds.

Out of the telescope's tube, as Nollinsae's hand now touched it, a smaller cylindrical object leaped toward the zenith of the domed tent. A yard-long pencil of rocket blast blackened Nollinsae's heavy glove, thrusting the cylinder vertically to the arching tent almost instantly, yet the rocket did not reach there.

The slim rocket exploded a few feet short of the ballooned fabric and tore gaping rents in the dome. The fragments of rocket vanished as their momentum carried them outside the field. The shock of massive punctures rippled in slow motion through the rubbery fabric, with long tears opening up as the air rushed out to nothingness. Big, heavy swatches wrenched themselves loose of the base ring and as they did so, vanished. A ripple moved, a slow solid whip-snap, down an arching wedge of tentcloth and ripped it raggedly at its base, but in the next blink that wedge was gone.

Everyone who was suitless within the dome when it burst died quickly of explosive decompression. If they died very quickly with blood shock to the brain, their bodies vanished before they could hit the floor of the dome. The floor itself remained only because it was attached through its base ring to the caravan with its squeaker-produced field of safety, and to those people who were still standing.

One of the caravan's cars, Fourteen, had been fully open to the dome without benefit of airlock, and any occupants in the corridor or open rooms would also be dead of decompression. Otherwise the car was visibly unchanged, light streaming from the open door nakedly onto the meadow and the twisting shards of tent.

In the chaos of the explosion, roaring air and debris, Rheinallt lost sight of the saboteur himself. A number of others had managed to don their helmets in time: mostly those who had just entered or were just leaving, still suited except for helmets which they had near to hand.

At least one person had grabbed up a helmet and placed it over his head with the air turned on full, although he was otherwise not suited for vacuum. This might have worked, leaving him with relatively minor decompression bruises. As Rheinallt started to help, though, one of the valves in the man's helmet burst from the too unequal pressure, flushed all his air down about his shoulders at once, and let him die. Other unclaimed helmets in the tent had all been destroyed, or had no fitted booster chambers charged with air.

Arahant! Where was the aircat? Rheinallt looked in vain among the still-whipping, still-snapping loose rags of tent, among the disintegrating pieces of the heavier furniture and solid equipment on the tent floor. The floor itself was developing cracks where it should not and becoming only meadow, piecemeal. The flimsier folding chairs and the like were already gone: knocked down and vanished. The heavier equipment and the human corpses which were still anchored to someone living, and too weighty to be blown away in the blast, would be disintegrating soon if the survivors kept wandering around. Clearly, though, Arahant was gone.

There must have been a backwash from the rocket to carve up the tent floor so. Perhaps its flame had slithered around momentarily as the rocket was exploding.

Rheinallt felt sick, the extra personal pain at not seeing Arahant anywhere. The aircat had considerable natural protection against low pressure, even against vacuum, but once blown out of the popped bubble of air there would be no returning from the nothingness "above" the meadow.

If the massacre was a quick, fresh spear in his guts, Arahant's death was a slow, bitter poison on that spear. His size, mostly fluff and hollow bones, was deceptive. The aircat's actual mass was small. He must not have stood a chance.

In words as close as he was ever likely to come to prayer, Rheinallt muttered tensely inside his helmet, "God rot Nollinsae!"

Nollinsae had made his move, and not against Susannilar only. He had struck at the caravaneers in wanton and wholesale murder.

Rheinallt saw out of the corner of his eye that Whitnadys was hurrying carefully through the wrack toward someone who might still be able to profit from help. The person was suited, shaky but all right. It was Susannilar.

In the distance were a couple of squeakers mildly surprised, and these moved restlessly in their traces for some minutes. As soon as those disastrous few seconds were over, Rheinallt detached Whitnadys and sent her speeding to the front of the caravan to ensure the safety of their transportation, and to make sure that neither the surviving passengers nor the squeakers did anything rash.

Most of those standing among the diminishing confusion of the tent site probably were crewmen, who did not have to stop to think when their air supply was threatened by anything unforeseen.

Frustratingly, Rheinallt realized that even if he had ignored bystanders and struck at Nollinsae electrically, the bolt would only have detonated the explosive rocket immediately, with no warning time. He might have gotten Nollinsae, though.

The telescope was gone, disintegrated. Where was the Guardsman? Likely he had slipped between the cars to the other side of the caravan, away from the Ship, and could be anywhere. Nollinsae must have a backup plan to finish the job, and Susannilar was still alive—she was standing by herself, shaky but upright—and so after all were most of the crew and passengers of the caravan.

Had Nollinsae noticed that Whitnadys and Rheinallt, standing within the tent wall, had just rehelmeted? Perhaps not, or perhaps he could not risk changing his scenario once he had begun. His timing had been good, certainly; maybe he had been watching from within the now sucked-clean Car Fourteen corridor for a worthy combination of victims helmetless within the tent. Susannilar, Whitnadys, and Rheinallt all had come too close to becoming his victims for the timing to be accidental.

And even Arahant, poor Arahant.

What fears fueled those hates? Whatever they were, Rheinallt had underestimated those fears and hates, and the man.

Grimly Rheinallt scanned the remains of the airtent. A few riflemen had happened to be in a protected stage of suiting or desuiting for their normal tasks, and had reacted quickly enough when they saw the rocket go up. Now they all looked limp, standing there.

Rheinallt waved, got the attention of the nearest, and signed to him, "Find Nollinsae. Search parties to go through the whole caravan, and check the other side. A quick dash through, and then a careful combing if you don't find him right off: spread the word. Warn everybody who isn't already aware of what happened and who did it. Don't bring him to me living."

"Right, Captain," he signed quickly, and turned to gather up his fellows.

One, Rheinallt noted, somehow held two haywires, a long barrel clutched pathetically in each hand as if he felt they had let him down in time of need. Rheinallt strode over, plucked one from his grasp, and shooed him after the others.

Hands on hips, with haywire tucked under his arm, Rheinallt looked again at the wreckage, more coolly now. Could Nollinsae have been hoist with his own petard? If the Guardsman was the martyr type he might welcome that. Likely, though, efficiency was more important; Nollinsae would need to know if the job had been done right. In which case he would have ducked into hiding to gauge the disaster he had made, and observe the reaction.

A group of suited figures were clustered around Susannilar, and Rheinallt walked over there, picking his way over the tent floor now cluttered not only with equipment but with bodies. All these would have to be cast off, or interred in the hydroponics. Whatever had disconnected totally in those first few seconds already had disintegrated.

Suited figures swung shut the outer airlock door of Car Fourteen. The cars were far tougher than the allegedly safe tent, and would not have been damaged structurally. You could be in subspace where no meteorite could puncture your air, Rheinallt reflected, but still not be safe from people.

212

Susannilar looked ghastly. Rheinallt was surprised at the way she drew the attention of other survivors. They ought to be either running around like chickens, or if they were unfazeable perhaps trying to rescue the abandoned equipment. She drew his own concern, too, interfering with the rising tide of his mourning for Arahant?

Rheinallt stopped just outside the circle around Susannilar. She was attenuated. Split, yes, and oscillating—but this Susannilar was a ghost, a wraith of the person. Her mouth was open gasping, and a trickle of blood ran from her nose. What had happened to her?

He remembered her entering the tent. She had taken off her helmet, and spurned it. Maybe she had not retrieved and dogged it down quite quickly enough. Now two in suits, one man and one woman, stood at her sides fumbling with her helmet fastenings. Susannilar herself was almost limp between them, although she seemed to be standing with her own strength.

Her lips moved within the helmet. "Air," he thought he could lip-read her saying. "Air."

"She's fighting us," a third helper signed to Rheinallt. "See—there, she's twisting her head again. Doesn't she know she needs air, Eiverdein? And why the hell does she look so faded?"

"Sick from shock?"

"Somebody clapped that helmet on her while she was in convulsions," the man volunteered. "We thought we'd saved her, but now she's thrashing around like she's dying."

"The helmet's functioning?" Rheinallt asked.

"Sure," he signed back. "Checked that right away, as soon as she started trying to get it off. Does that have anything to do with her looking sort of see-through, transparent almost?"

"Probably." Would oxygen starvation have crippled her brain's ability to recoalesce?

Susannilar's lips were moving again. If her twitching arms were capable of making sign, she was not using it, but instinctively trying to speak. "Dying," Rheinallt lip-read. "Hurt—can't take back. Dying here."

"Can I help?" Rheinallt signed slowly, his hands held high, directly in front of her helmet.

"Dying here," she repeated painfully. "Help—help the other."

Without warning she twisted awkwardly free of the two

213

people next to her, and took a few stumbling steps outside the circle of would-be helpers. She fumbled blindly at the helmet, half-undogged already, and the air within puffed out.

Then a flash of almost happy realization lit her pain-contorted face. She bent her knees slightly and made a tiny jump upward. In that complete vacuum, in that nothingness that was the apparent-above of the meadow, she vanished instantly.

After a dumbfounded long moment, the little circle of helpers turned slowly away from the place of meadow where she had just been, to face Rheinallt. None made a sign, just waited for some shred of enlightenment.

For a minute Rheinallt could not think what had happened; and then he could not think how to explain it. It must have been a ninety-ten split this time, maybe a ninety-nine-to-one. Susannilar must already have been split when she entered the airtent: wary, if not quite wary enough. The decompression had caught her by surprise and injured her badly enough so that she couldn't, or didn't dare, complete the reunification. Was it like lopping off a gangrenous limb? Susannilar may not have even fully understood why the doppelganging faculty was failing, any more than most people have the subtle processes of chemical usage of oxygen under the same control as they do their grosser breathing.

Anyway, this part of her was simply gone away to absence. She was a shadow in the wind, and the wind had gone.

The suited people in front of Rheinallt moved restlessly. Lights from the caravan's windows, and brighter ones from the cartops, cast chiaroscuro ripples on their arms and legs, and within their helmets.

Still, Rheinallt was saved from an immediate sharing of his deductions.

Susannilar arrived, walking slowly off the dark meadow and onto the ruined floor. She looked blankly at the group of would-be rescuers. If they had questions to ask her in person, no doubt a bevy of conflicting emotions got in their way.

Rheinallt took Susannilar by the arm and gently led her toward the nearest airlock, the ill-fated door of Car Fourteen. He tried to indicate to the helpers that they were appreciated, but he doubted if any saw his signs. Their eyes were all for her. At least she was solid under his grip.

The thought of wind that he had entertained moments before

214

now crept back into his mind by a hidden chink, and penetrated deeper. There was no wind on the meadow. And yet, any sailor who has maneuvered sailboats on blue water, any kid with a duck pond who has played with several woodchip-and-rag rafts simultaneously, has seen the working of wind and the effects of a shadow cast by the wind. What kind of wind could exist on the meadow?

There was no sign of Nollinsae, or of those on the search.

Rheinallt urged Susannilar to a faster pace, but she did not respond. She now was missing so little, that if he had not seen part of her go into absence forever he could not guess that a part of her had died. If he could get her, this whole-minus-wraith almost-all of her, inside amid human surroundings, surely that would help her.

Perhaps her disinterest and unresponsiveness, behind that fixed smile, was not entirely the result of her fractional death, but quite normal shock at the mass murder and sabotage. Also at being the recipient of a full to-the-death attack aimed at her personally, whoever else it happened to include.

If her detachment was deliberate, or instinctive, might such a tourniquet have helped her survive part of her being sliced off into nothingness? If she pinched herself away too tightly, though, strangled all her veins conveying reality, she would never recover.

What is lacking in a shadow? he wondered tiredly. Within one, that is? Simply constant input, compared with the surroundings.

Rheinallt needed a strategy to help Susannilar become, not together again, but healed and whole. Whatever that meant to a doppelganger. She needed help quickly. Rheinallt felt stretched among a multitude of necessities, tired and dizzy from trying to hold too many disparate threads in his hands at once.

With a slow detached stateliness they entered together the airlock of Car Fourteen. It occurred to him that within a shadow one could not be dazzled.

15. The Cables Between Faces

INSIDE THE CARAVAN THERE WAS A LOT OF CONFUSION, people scurrying between cars with little reason. Most were suited against further emergencies. All the traffic ought to make it harder for Nollinsae to maneuver without bumping into someone.

Rheinallt decided to take Susannilar to Glenavet's room in Car Nine, and passed the word that messages could come to him there. Holding the stricken young woman firmly by the arm, he piloted her unresisting in that direction.

Susannilar had shifted into being one of the most useful members of the Special Caravan, the only one who had made any real progress for them. She obviously needed some particularly good help to come out of the shock from her semi-death in the tent, and Rheinallt meant to make sure she got it. Her bravery alone deserved no less.

"She's hurt!" Glenavet said on the instant he saw Susannilar. He jumped up to help guide her to a chair, but she seemed not to notice his presence any more than she had Rheinallt's. She sat down willingly enough under their gentle pressure, as if it did not matter. They removed her helmet.

"Part of her was in the airtent, split, when Nollinsae blew it open," Rheinallt told Glenavet quickly. "She suffered explosive decompression while trying to transfer away that portion of her. But it was too injured, and she either couldn't rejoin, or sacrificed the lesser part rather than bring the injuries back within the rest of her."

"I understand," Glenavet said somberly. "Did—did she suffer long?"

"After she realized it was hopeless, she jumped."

"Ah." The trailman understood perfectly. Glenavet had not taken his eyes from Susannilar's disassociated smile, and he held one of her hands. Now he knelt alongside her chair. "Susannilar," he said softly. "Can you hear me? It's Glenavet."

Susannilar made no response. She sat neither firmly nor limply, but indifferently.

Deep lines had grown into Glenavet's face since Rheinallt had had the long talk with him after Starved Rock. All those lines had not come in the last couple of minutes, Rheinallt thought. One supposes that love lightens the spirit, not weights it with new cares.

Why wasn't Arahant here? For a desolate moment he couldn't remember; and when he did, his concern for Susannilar was somehow stronger.

"Keep talking," Rheinallt encouraged him. "She needs human contact. She hears us, all right, but doesn't care." Behind her back he added in intersign, "We've got to reintegrate her—as much as she can be again."

So Glenavet talked. Endearments, little things they had done together in the short clockdays they had known each other, tidbits of history from Glenavet's own past and from what she must have shared semihypnotically of her past. He talked until he grew hoarse.

It puzzled Rheinallt that Glenavet omitted any mention of a future the two of them might have together. Was this so ephemeral they had made no mutual plans, or were their plans too intimate to be brought out before one not a member of the love pair? Hopes for a happy future ought to be the best antidote to a depressive withdrawal. Finally he told Glenavet, "Let me take over for a while." Talk and massage might not be the best way to bring someone out of a catatonic trance, but any other approach was like using a club to treat a wound.

Rheinallt slid a chair next to Susannilar's. Glenavet continued to hold her hand, moving to her side to make room. Rheinallt picked up her other hand in both of his, the millefleurs scent strong in his nostrils.

As Susannilar gazed unseeingly at him, Rheinallt was chilled by how thin a look it was, yet there must be some infinitesimal response on her side. Glenavet had done enough in the way of personal pleading; Rheinallt decided to talk about contact itself.

"I'm going to talk for a while now," he told her. "Glenavet's said how much he loves you. Well, I'll try to throw a different kind of thread across the gap. You see, Susannilar, that we try to communicate at all is a substantial part of our being human. I feel that a cortian fiber, a thread of true contact, has been established between us. We've already shared thoughts, made contact. A micron-wide channel has been lit across the dark, through the distance which separates our existences.

"Each time eyes meet in a glance, a further thread is tossed across the gulf. Distance *can* be bridged; it happens every day, every second. Each time a word is spoken and heard, a rope is shot over the silent stretches and made fast to another's spiritual deck, that the ship of her spirit need not sail alone.

"The heaviest rope is woven from the minutest strands of fiber; the solidest cable is molded from the tiniest wire. The fiber enjoys holding the weight and load of contact, the wire delights in speeding the energy and signal.

"Alike to these are the threads between faces, the cables between faces. They bear the weight of human difference and the burden of human contact. A glance, a word, or a touch may be gossamer, thinner than a spider's strand, and stronger than a girder. And yes, more electric than the lightning."

With these words Rheinallt sent the faintest tingle of electric current from his hands to hers. There seemed to be an answering flicker down deep in her eyes. He knew the current went *through* her, at least, because Glenavet was still holding her other hand and he jumped, startled and puzzled.

Rheinallt hoped she was improving. If she went any further, if she broke her last emotional threads or let them attenuate to nothingless, she would be gone. Pulling her back would have to be accomplished soon. He increased the trickle of current.

"It's all right," Rheinallt said forcefully. "We all oscillate, but only some can profit by it. This is your life, and it's all

219

one. Think of having two different viewpoints when you need them, two perspectives. Most of us are trapped by our fears into immobility, and think that our inability to change viewpoints is a sign of strength or wholeness. But this is wrong; certainly wrong for you. Your ability is good.

"Now, a stone, on the other hand, is our opposite. A stone doesn't worry about integration, it only has one form, monolithic. All it has to do is be a stone. No alternatives to reconcile, perspectives to analyze, or views to bring into focus.

"Most of us try to imitate stones. A stone's thoughts are simple. Its self-maintaining statement to the universe is just 'stone . . . stone . . . stone . . .' Imitating such a minimal existence seems so safe.

"There's barely more than that left of the minds that once drove the Ship. The *Falling Angel* must contain consciousness of a sort to remain upon the meadow, but it's no longer active: only the pattern or momentum of consciousness is left. Those originating minds who launched the Ship have faded to a shadowy living monument.

"We mustn't do the same. Imitating the existential pattern of the stone is a false refuge. It seems so steady, yet this is our deepest and most dangerous self-deception. No stone can lie upon the meadow.

"You're split by the conflict within you, between aspects of your own essential nature. Creation and will, thought and passion, idea and impulse—these are partial labels for great opposites. They are not irreconcilable antagonists, they're aspects of a whole consisting of tensions, but also of necessary connections between tensions."

Rheinallt felt Susannilar's hand stir in his, an uncertain motion. An expression hinting at self-confidence formed on her face.

"Yes," she whispered. "Please go on."

"Whew!" Rheinallt said, damping the flow of current. "You're right, Susannilar: come on back. Most people keep their vision narrowed down to a monochromatic slot. Yet the colors are so bright, and there's lots for you to see and do."

She nodded. Her eyes held a waking depth now, and she took a long breath experimentally.

The door opened, and Susannilar was present enough to

want to see who came in, and to care. She smiled with warmth, Rheinallt was glad to note.

It was Whitnadys, towing the white-haired Lhudesin. Rheinallt signaled them that he was almost done. There was only one more point he could think of; might as well wrap it up.

"Without an internal richness and diversity," Rheinallt said to her, "there's no need for integration. A stone does not consider its soul, the state of its being: it has room only for its stone-thought. But if the human body is the mind's hand, then you are ambidextrous. And that is quite all right."

Susannilar by now really did look present, and he felt free to release her hand. He reabsorbed in his palms the sweat he had used to improve the contact.

Glenavet still pressed Susannilar's other hand, inexpressibly happy. There was something else in his face, also: relief at a possession restored? That was not too unreasonable in a lover.

"There's a lot of minor messages for you," Whitnadys said to Rheinallt. "The caravan's organization wasn't really disrupted. Found two small spring bombs well concealed in Nollinsae's room: like the rocket, small enough to fit in that jinxed telescope, and he launched from it. There's eight dead from the tent explosion, which is better than it looked at the time."

With quick fingers he signed to her, "Don't want to talk about death now. Can you help draw her into conversation?"

Whitnadys' sympathy came easily. "Sure. But when I heard you were here I guessed what you were doing. That's why I brought Lhudesin along."

The old gentleman bowed slightly. "With your permission, Captain."

Lhudesin checked the tune of his instrument with a few quick strums across the strings. To Susannilar he said quietly, "Young lady, I've been brought to entertain you with a song. I hope that meets with your approval?" The words of the request were brusque, as if it was a question he did not normally bother to ask, but the tone was soft and gently inviting.

Susannilar smiled with a grateful warmth. "Yes, please. Choose one for me?"

Rheinallt caught Whitnadys' eye and winked. Good medicine. Each in his own way, they were helping.

"Well," Lhudesin drawled, "observing that sweet smile has

decided me that only the old welcoming song 'A Smile Is Your Banner' will do for you." His playing of the piece matched his voice: soft, gentling, no harmonics but only a simple hummable melody.

"A smile is the banner of your ship
As you sail upon the gentle sea,
A banner bright like a joyous wave
Of the current that rocks you so softly.

"The colors are friendship and love
Where you raise your banner to the sky,
A trade wind blowing the values you hold
On the vastness that rocks you so softly.

"Those passing will hoist their copied best
To show that they sail in peace,
And even colors of war will dip
To what happiness rocks you so softly.

"When storms come and the banner is down,
The sea seems cold and all is dark,
And the winds are trying to tear your heart
From the ocean that rocked you so softly.

"Yet here's a port in which you may rest
And shake out your banner again,
Because ripples don't move the sea from its bed
Where it always will rock you so softly.

"A smile is the banner of your ship
As you sail upon my gentle sea,
A banner bright like a joyous wave
Of the current that rocks you so softly."

With a shy, calm smile of his own, Lhudesin tucked his instrument under his arm, gave a short, stiff bow, and left as quietly as he had come.

After a minute Glenavet said, "Sure couldn't have said that as well myself. But I agree with it, every word."

Susannilar kissed him. "I know you do." She looked around at Whitnadys and Rheinallt. "I was a long ways away, wasn't I? Thank you for pulling me back."

Whitnadys followed Rheinallt's line. "Susannilar, you can

walk the tightrope, but now you've made it across and back again, here with us. Now you're back on the ground—"

"Thanks, Whitnadys," Susannilar brushed off this effort. "I think I'll be all right. You needn't be so intense. I'm as returned now as I'm going to be, so why don't we all just relax."

"Fine with me," Whitnadys said immediately, but Rheinallt could tell she was miffed.

Rheinallt agreed it was time to let the therapeutic efforts lapse into regular conversation. The talking had helped him too, helped him forget about Arahant for a while. He had picked up sympathetic glances from Whitnadys. Right now he felt lonelier than when he was first exiled—with Arahant.

Whitnadys said, "You're from Fleurage, I understand. Kind of a refugee? What's so bad there?"

"Physically, it's simple," Susannilar said. "Fleurage is slowly sliding out of contact with the Yellow Trail. In less than a decade, supposedly, we'll be cut off. *They'll* be cut off. And that's really scary."

"You mean Fleurage won't be a Trail world any more? Wow! I never heard of that before, anywhere."

"Well, you couldn't," Glenavet put in. "Not unless it happened pretty recently. There'd be no way for the news to get out."

"Some surveyors noticed it," Susannilar said. "When they told the government there, it was hushed up. A couple of years after that, the customs building at one end of the groundside segment had to be moved. It was being bypassed. Then everybody got worried, and a few panicked."

She frowned, remembering. "My mother caused a riot. You understand, it was obvious that nobody knew why the trail was shifting or what to do about it. In spite of the official propaganda, we all knew the planet was helpless, and that's a heavy lot of pressure to live under. I was young when the troubles began, but they reached right into my family."

"Scapegoats?" Whitnadys asked.

"Yes. Alalortern, my mother, was one of the first, I think. You have to realize all this came about in the last few years. She traveled a lot, moving her nightclub act from town to town—"

"Act?"

"Or carnival act. She described it differently depending on

223

what kind of place she was angling to play. The name of her show was always 'Night Shift,' but she varied the subtitle on the promotion boards. Sometimes 'Sleight-of-Mind by the Spectacular Alalortern,' or maybe 'Alalortern: The Stripper Too Fast to Follow.' It never paid very much, so she needed to hit a club one night, a carnival the next, and a school in between. Then we'd head on down the road. Most of Fleurage's towns aren't very big."

Rheinallt was intrigued away from some now-relaxed thoughts on the Yellow Trail's subspatial drift. "Stripping for a school? I wouldn't have thought Fleurage had that kind of school."

Susannilar shook her head. Only her cloud of dark hair now looked blurred. "For the schools she did it as part of a lecture-demonstration on applied optics. No hootchy-kootchy frills, or taking her clothes off. She unnerved the school adminstrators enough as it was."

Rheinallt sat back in his chair. "That must have been some lesson, to explain doppelganging. That's a thing out of legend, and not only on Fleurage." Convergent legends were less likely than parallel bases in fact.

"Oh, but she couldn't explain *herself*," Susannilar said animatedly. "If she could have, she would; but she never figured it out and never met anyone else who could say what her oscillating meant, or why she was able to do it—except my grandfather, and she was feuding with him until the last couple of years. Able?" She grimaced briefly. "My mother always considered it as much curse as ability."

"And you, love?" Glenavet asked intensely.

She thought a moment. "All curse. Or almost, anyway." She flashed a smile at Glenavet.

Whitnadys looked at her somberly, with unfeigned sympathy. "So you, too, are out of phase with the people around you. You follow in your mother's footsteps."

"Obviously." Susannilar was silent awhile, added, "Even while my mother was still alive, this was my recurring vision: that the best life I could hope for in society was the same as hers. 'The Young Alalortern.' Shifting in and out of my clothes on a trick-lighted stage. Being a sexy performer until I scared someone in authority, and then being condemned as a witch. Fun before the fall. Ugh!"

"And she never knew how she did it," Rheinallt mused.

"No. My grandfather Ytrenath hassled her about it sometimes. I think my mother thought his ideas were too abstract; after all, she was the one who had to live with it. Several times she mentioned to me that maybe someday one of those schoolchildren would grow up to be a great researcher on optics, and explain it to her. But there aren't too many great researchers on Fleurage."

"I had heard of Ytrenath before," Whitnadys said.

"His specialty was planets, though," Susannilar maintained.

Not entirely true, Rheinallt thought, stretching shoulder and arm muscles. "Yet your shifting isn't really an optical phenomenon," he reminded her, "any more than the Detenebrator is."

She looked startled. "Well, no," she said lamely. "Maybe it's not entirely optical. But then what else is it?"

"You're evading my point," Rheinallt told her casually. "Your oscillation isn't optical at all, any more than your seeing Whitnadys over there makes Whitnadys an optical phenomenon. Your oscillation is a really powerful tool, do you know that?"

She shrugged, trying to make it appear doubtful.

To her side, Rheinallt could see Glenavet holding himself so very still that his stillness and retained breath were clearer than a shout. What was going on with him?

"Your grandfather Ytrenath was not so much expert in plants as expert in fibers," Rheinallt stated. "Through his mastery of fibers he bred certain plants for perfume as though he was designing a distillery. I'm sure it was proceeds from his fabulous perfume blend that paid your way on the Special Caravan. I wish you would tell us why you came."

But Whitnadys cut in excitedly. "That's clear. First, she was hoping to develop something out of the Ship discovery that might rescue Fleurage from isolation. Right?" she demanded of Susannilar.

Susannilar nodded.

"And second," Whitnadys went on, "she could put off the confrontation with Nollinsae until she worked out a certain way to beat him."

"At first I had hoped to escape him altogether for the duration of the trip," Susannilar amended. "When he signed up

225

after me, I knew there'd be no escape until one of us was dead." Her face hardened. "I—I'm still pretty young, you realize. Even with what the Guard did to my family, it took me a long time to work myself up to where I thought I could strike back."

She laughed harshly, scanning the rest of them challengingly. "And it's so funny! Nollinsae helped me so much! I think he sort of sliced away part of me today, part of my inhibitions. I know now I can kill him. I've decided how to do it, and it's really no problem at all anymore."

"I hope you'll rest first, at least," Glenavet said.

"Oh, I will. He's hiding somewhere, and it'll take a while to find him. And I need the rest for two reasons. It'll be a strain on me again; maybe as bad as today. I need to be strong enough." She laughed again. "Also, I want to be exquisitely alert, so I can watch his reactions as he dies."

Rheinallt and Whitnadys exchanged glances. This certainly wasn't the same Susannilar they had begun to know in these last few clockdays. Her ordeal had indeed changed her.

Glenavet seemed rather pleased. The way the owner of a prizefighter might be pleased? What was his stake in her? Rheinallt had the impression that he was playing a deeper game than he had ever played for the Federated Trailmen. Susannilar's semihypnotic technique of reminiscence, one on one, had hit Rheinallt hard; had she hit Glenavet even harder? Rheinallt wondered if either Susannilar or Glenavet was clear on what was happening to them.

"To revert to optics," Rheinallt said, not wanting to dwell on Nollinsae with Susannilar still in her weird emotional state, "there is also the mind that sees and interprets, that sees where we are and where another person is. Your interaction with your physical environment is a mental phenomenon."

Rheinallt yawned, realizing the weariness of the day was demanding rest. He needed to bring out a couple more key points, though. "As your control and confidence increase you'll be more relaxed using it. For you it oughtn't be any stranger than using your two eyes for binocular vision."

Susannilar smiled, grateful for someone's acknowledging that she was not a freak. She gripped Glenavet's hand a little tighter.

226

"So now we can understand what Ytrenath was able to do," Rheinallt went on. "He created a fibrous bundle that was similar enough to the network of neural pathways to sustain his personality for a while. From what you told me, Susannilar, his keenest interest was in osmosis. Damned if I can see how he transferred his nervous energy into a cottony ball, but he managed it. I suppose the secret will die with him."

Without being too ostentatious about it, he watched Glenavet and Susannilar from under heavy lids for their reactions. Both, he thought, looked acutely unhappy. For the same reason? Neither said anything.

"How'd you figure that out?" Whitnadys asked, surprised.

"Yeah, how?" Glenavet reinforced gruffly.

Rheinallt chuckled. "Everybody stuffed me so full of half-truths I was able to assemble a few truths. That's all."

Whitnadys broke in. "Time you got some rest, Eiverdein. You too, Susannilar. And we all could use something to eat. If Nollinsae is turned up, we'll find out soon enough."

"Yes," Susannilar said. "After I rest I will kill him."

Rheinallt stood, feeling his exhaustion. "The squeakers were all right?" he asked Whitnadys.

"Sure. Also, I've placed a strong guard to make sure that Nollinsae can't make off with one, either to escape or to try doing something else weird to the caravan."

"Good," Rheinallt said. "He won't hurt the caravan while he's in it."

"Are you sure he's inside?" Susannilar asked. A cool voice.

"No," Whitnadys told her. "But if he's out on the meadow he won't be able to get back aboard. We've got riflemen watching the whole length of the caravan on the outside, and it's well lit. I've rousted out every spotlight I could find aboard. And if he is inside, he must be in some cramped place where he won't be able to get into mischief. Everybody is armed, and I've enlisted most of the passengers into Bremolando's patrols and guard posts."

"Great," Rheinallt commended.

"Say, Whitnadys," Glenavet asked, "do you mean Nollinsae could make off with a squeaker, just like that? I thought only you expert beast-handler folks could do that. I'm glad you've got a good guard on them."

"The squeakers are really pretty helpful to a rider," Whitnadys said. "It's the harnessing and coordination of pull that takes so much training. We'll be pulling the guards off as soon as we nail Nollinsae."

Glenavet nodded, satisfied. "I see."

Whitnadys took Rheinallt by the arm and gently steered him to the door and down the corridor. Outside his compartment door she asked, "How did you get so tired?"

"I put a lot of energy into drawing Susannilar back into the land of the living. More than I should have, maybe."

"Why, Hendrikal! That's a mean thing to say."

"Sure?" He leaned on the doorjamb. "Glenavet wants to steal a squeaker. Why do you think he wants to do that?"

Her eyes widened. "I'm sure I don't know. What gave you the idea?"

"Glenavet's an old trail hand. He knows as well as I do how squeakers are employed on caravan hauls. He didn't want information on squeakers. He wanted to hear about the plans for guarding them."

"You think so? There's an easy solution—the guards can stay on after we catch Nollinsae. Now, you get some good rest," Whitnadys repeated, and left.

Rheinallt entered the room, nodding a goodnight to the rifleman on duty at the far end of the car. That had been a good idea, too; Whitnadys', probably. There was a light on inside already.

Heading toward the canopied bed, he stopped short. The catadrome was sprawled on the softest armchair, snoring raggedly and loudly.

"Arahant!" he shouted. Rheinallt ran to the chair, picked up the aircat, and tossed him.

Arahant woke in midair, stretching his float sac and complaining. "That hurts," he said gustily, floating chairward again.

"What? How could it? And how is it you're alive for anything to hurt?"

"What're you talking about, Hendrik?"

"I thought you were dead."

Arahant settled back onto the cushion of the chair, closed his eyes, opened one eye again to look at the man. "That's nice. How'd you get that idea?"

228

"The airtent explosion!" He threw up his hands. "You were in midair when the tent blew. How did you escape?" He dropped to the rug in front of the armchair, letting the pile absorb some tiredness. He felt he had been snapped wide awake, but that could not last.

Arahant closed the open eye. "Many brave men lie asleep in the deep," he intoned solemnly.

"Come on, give. I'm tired."

He twitched his tailtip. "Well, Hendrik, when that fiendish passenger of yours set off his rocket, I was asleep, but the noise of the rocket whooshing up blew into my dreams. It sounded rather like one of my sisters; at least in the dream. I was jerked awake by the explosion, but because of the dream I already was in a mood to flee the premises, if you see what I mean."

"Your beloved sisters. Sure."

"So I was in motion from the second the rocket hit the tent top, and instinctively I headed for the open airlock door to Car Fourteen. I haven't got thrust in my sac to fly upwind against explosive decompression, but I was in the car before the suction in the airlock door got really fierce."

Rheinallt lay back on the rug. "Go on."

Arahant stuck his nose over the edge of the chair to peer down at the man. "You'll fall asleep there, and regret it when you wake up. Anyway, some quick-thinking fellow on your crew took a moment from dogging down his own helmet to shove me into an open airsuit cabinet by the airlock, and slammed it shut. That held air well enough for the couple of minutes until the outer door was shut and air restored to the car's corridor. Then I opened the cabinet and drifted up here."

"Great." Rheinallt gestured sleepily. "Come on down *here*."

Arahant floated gently down and Rheinallt gave him a hug. After a minute the aircat disengaged himself and floated back up to the chair, knowing Rheinallt would not be off that rug soon.

But Rheinallt did not fall asleep. The searching riflemen would be keen for vengeance, so he wasn't worried about Nollinsae's getting a few clockhours' slack. He was much more revved up from finding Arahant all right.

Blessedly at ease now, he waited for that excitement to

229

recede. He lay on the rug, letting his relaxed mind wander. He thought about the trails, and about the human society growing in their necklaced environment.

The trail was the measure of wealth: a world with only a few hundred yards of trail on its surface had almost more frustration than trade, sparks instead of light. All the known worlds had, necessarily, at least a short section of a trail lying across them, like the quayside of a river town. With half a mile of trail upon a planet, folks could trap and cajole wild squeakers and begin a commerce, or build an aisle of shops and warehouses and caravanserais to encourage what already passed.

Or set up ambuscades and other piratical traps, but those weren't popular long.

Fleurage needn't turn outlaw to keep other cultures at bay. Instead it was being turned hermit forcibly by the natural shifting of its trail. A whole world inexorably exiled, and they could watch it happening.

Blueholm was doubly fortunate in a luxuriously long contact with the Blue Trail where its worlds were thickest, a shiny bead in the midst of the shiniest strand of beads. The Yellow Trail, too, emerged out of subspace to share a segment of itself with the human surface of Blueholm.

From time immemorial squeakers had passed through Blueholm on the Blue or Yellow, trudging sometimes cross-country to the other. Blueholmians were the first to cast off superstitions of "moving lights in the sky"—which is what the waybeasts had looked like when the section of Yellow was long ago suspended in midair—and to divine that these elephantine lumberers were capable of human association, could be communicated with for mutual benefit. Hence the traffic between worlds.

No one like Nollinsae ever would befriend a squeaker, whether the latter was sauntering and sweltering in its golden hide on some fair planet, or trickling air among compartmented lungs as it helped drag a caravan through vacuum. Waybeasts and xenophobia didn't go together. No squeaker could hold its breath longer than a man like Nollinsae could avoid the notion of worthy minds different from his own.

Mustn't underestimate the force of envy; the Nation was rich, and some hated it for that reason.

The Nation owned two hundred thousand yards of the Blue Trail at groundside—and thereby was rich beyond the dreams of avarice. Blueholm, Azuline, and the rest of the Blue Free Nation had the best quayside on the vast meadow: like the combined river frontage of riverine cities.

Groundside trail length meant caravans stopping to feed and breathe their draft waybeasts. Poor diminishing Fleurage kept prices low lest travelers drag through without stopping.

Rheinallt knew of one rock somewhere on the Red where trail frontage was under two yards. Too small for a squeaker to stop; hardly enough for a glimpse. A couple of times men had succeeded in disembarking, but no one ever had reembarked.

That was what Fleurage was heading for, as surely as any riverine city with its lifeblood river drying up. Soon the whole planet full of people would be in that unenviable position, and then beyond it. Detachment, and silence. No wonder that Fleurage could breed up people with strong and strange passions.

Yet the strength of the Nation lay not only in accessibility to commerce, but in its libertarian hinterland whose people generated values worth trading, and in people who insisted on the freedom to enjoy values.

Could that be explained to someone like Nollinsae? Wealth was not just superb communications, nor hothouse flowers. The very happy formlessness of the Nation threatened his structured universe.

16. An Explosion of Moonbeams

RHEINALLT WOKE FEELING STIFF, STILL ON THE RUG. ARAHANT was sitting up in the chair, using tongue and claws to make his fluff even fluffier.

Bremolando had stuck his head in the doorway. "Excuse me. Captain Eiverdein, we've found Nollinsae."

"Oh? Great." Rheinallt got up slowly, went to the retractable basin, and splashed some water on his face. "Where?"

Arahant listened alertly. He as well as some others now had a personal grudge against Nollinsae.

"On the meadow. You can see it from your window, I think." Bremolando strode to the sash and pulled open the heavy curtain. He leaned to look forward along the parked caravan. "See that oxygen tank? He's in that." Bremolando pointed triumphantly.

"What happened, Captain, was that a couple of the fellows were checking a storage room that already had been checked. But we hadn't found him, and intended to keep looking until we did. These guys heard a scratching or scraping coming from inside one of the oxygen tanks.

"Just like that, they had him! They put their ears to the

airtank and listened, just to be sure. It sounded like somebody shifting position—those tanks are big when you're moving one, but there's not enough room to stand inside. The finders shooed the passengers out of that car, evacuated the air, and hauled the tank out onto the meadow."

Rheinallt nodded. "That it sits on the meadow unattended is proof that *someone's* in it."

Bremolando flushed, remembering the airtank he had been dragging on a sled and lost, a few clockdays before.

"That was good thinking," Rheinallt said. "I'll commend you all. If he had a bomb in the tank for sabotage, it's no use now."

"Thank you, Captain," Bremolando said, smiling again. "We all did think right out on the meadow was the safest place for it."

Rheinallt could see out the window that a crowd of airsuited figures had gathered around the oxygen tank, keeping a safe distance. Spotlights from several of the nearer caravan cars played upon the tank. It looked forlorn and stillborn.

"Go on out," Rheinallt said. "I'll be with you in a few minutes."

After Bremolando had left jauntily, Arahant said, "Damn. I'd like to see this close up, too."

"Why not? Go on up to the head of the caravan." Rheinallt looked for his helmet, found it in a corner. He had slept in his airsuit, but he was used to that and it had given him no more discomfort than sleeping on the floor had. "You know that observation bubble on the roof of the lead car? Climb up there; you ought to be able to see over the heads of the crowd outside. Whitnadys will be around there. Anything weird, she makes a beeline for the squeakers."

"I'm glad I'm not a waybeast," Arahant said, lingering by the door. "Don't know when I'd find the solitude to work on my operas."

"*I'll* be glad when we can scare up an orchestra or a synthesizer and you can get the music out of your system for a while. If you were a waybeast you'd just have plodding music instead of soaring music. Let's roll!"

Arahant grinned and scooted soft-footed up the corridor. Rheinallt dogged down his helmet, picked up his haywire, and headed for the nearest airlock.

Outside, the crowd seemed to have stopped growing, except for a few stragglers. Many remained inside to ogle the miscreant tank from the Shipside windows of the caravan.

In the middle of the crowd was the oxygen tank. Rheinallt did not like all these people hanging around, showing up for a potential battle as if it were a picnic. These were probably ones who had missed the gasping terror in the airtent but still wanted a quick thrill to offset frustration over the unbendable Ship.

Rheinallt pulled a few riflemen out of the crowd and harangued them in intersign. "You're supposed to protect the passengers, not be ushers at a carnival! I want you all to start collaring people and getting them inside the caravan, or away from that tank. If any go in, tell them to keep their helmets on, and pass that word to the others inside."

"Say, Captain, if they want to stay out and watch, how far back is all right?"

He picked a figure. "Two hundred yards. They can use binoculars, or squint. Now jump!" They moved quickly away, and cut into the crowd like sheep dogs. Of course none of them jumped.

With the people backing and filing and drifting away from the putative container of Nollinsae, Rheinallt felt better.

Did Nollinsae have a way to see out? He must have, to keep a minimal peace of mind while self-incarcerated.

There was motion at the top of the airtank. Looking around, he saw only a few people besides himself still standing dangerously close. Susannilar was one. Bremolando, his haywire cradled ready in his arm, was pointing at the tank from where he stood with a couple of other riflemen.

Rheinallt gestured to those still too near to move off, and began slowly backing away himself.

The upper third of the tank swung back on hinges that no real storage tank would have. Some sort of mechanism now unfolded and stretched upward about two yards. Rheinallt could not see what it was intended to do. Above the lower portion of the split tank, on thin struts, was a shiny paddlewheel. There were lights or lenses as well, though these were not turned on and only shiny from the caravan's spotlights.

No one had taken Rheinallt's further suggestion to move away; all eyes had been on the tank.

235

It hit Rheinallt with an ill feeling that Nollinsae's intention all along had been to have the tank brought out here on the meadow. But for what? A clear field of fire?

Nollinsae's helmeted head appeared above the truncated airtank, shielded by struts of his mechanism—which also would ground into the metal any electrical attack Rheinallt might make.

Rheinallt tried a snap shot with the haywire, but the dart did not make it between the struts. He snapped off the wire and readied another.

Bremolando had his own haywire fully unlimbered and at his shoulder now, carefully sighting from his closer distance and possibly better angle. Before he could fire, though, Susannilar walked over to him in a few swift steps and knocked the barrel up. Bremolando looked around angrily.

The girl was signing, "He's mine!"

Rheinallt was close enough to see Nollinsae's lips move inside his helmet. He didn't know if the words were actually intended to reach those afoot on the meadow, or if they were more of a private incantation, thoughts spoken aloud.

"A maroon and visible death," Nollinsae was saying across the gap of vacuum. "Blood is only the sign of death. Your lovely ghost-blood Ship will be the eternal tombstone for you all forever."

Susannilar made a slight movement.

After taking a few more cautious steps backward, Rheinallt knelt and tried another haywire shot, with no better results. Was there a fine mesh in the way, between those struts?

Nollinsae's gloved hand flicked a lever. The wheel began to turn, and simultaneously some enclosed lamps, as powerful as the caravan's searchlights, flared into life. The axis of the now-spinning wheel was aimed directly at Susannilar.

What the devil was his power source? Must be a miniature oxygen torch, magnified and reflected through those lenses on the wheel. If so, it couldn't last long; there couldn't be much oxygen, even supercompressed into a miniature inner tank, within Nollinsae's contraption.

In spite of his caution Rheinallt was caught close enough to be dazzled. What kind of machine was that? Almost blindly he moved away, stumbling. After a few seconds he had suppressed the colored pain in his eyes, filtering them as well as he could, and glanced back. This time it was not so terribly bright; his eyes were compensating. He identified the generating device: a stroboscope.

Rheinallt had never heard of one among the Trail worlds before. This one had a tremendous potency: the untethered light created an acute physical pain, a lance stabbing through the eyeballs into the brain. Was it a witch-killing device, developed by paranoid or Guard-commanded scientists on Fleurage? Schizophrenics were notoriously vulnerable to harsh vibrations, because their own internal processes were so easily heterodyned.

In spite of filtering his vision, Rheinallt could not see the glittering airtank quite well enough to try another shot. The strobe was a weapon designed to attack Susannilar, and all too likely designed properly for its target. But it also hurt Rheinallt's eyes, and moving over the bespotted meadow where a misstep could be fatal had become very difficult.

Where were all the cretins with weapons? Could nothing be brought to bear?

Some well-meaning nincompoop was turning out the closest of the caravan's roof spotlights, undoubtedly thinking that to douse the friendly lights would diminish the effect of the unfriendly one. Any firefighter experienced with backfires in a forest district could have told the helpful crewman better, but there was no way to undo that now. The reverting pitch of the background pseudosurface only enhanced the strobe.

In his next hurried and shielded backward glance, Rheinallt saw that through a system of small mirrors the Guardsman was maintaining a moving, broken circle of stroboscopic light all around himself and the tank. The pulsating beam, multiplied, raked colorfully along the length of the parked caravan. The meadow sloping down from the Ship toward the caravan seemed to erupt with smallpox of light, making its roughened surface appear to writhe heavily under the stings of the strobe.

Some haywire darts zapped through the vacuum toward Nollinsae, but the aims were spoiled just enough by the erratic lighting to miss him. The wires draped themselves over the strobe like so many spent strands of cobweb, and were about as useful. Segments of color seemed to run up and down the webbing with the turning of the strobe system.

Did Nollinsae have a haywire of his own there? Probably.

Now he was cutting and casting loose the ineffectual but entangling microwire.

Anyone who tried to move—and that was all of them—even if facing away from the strobe toward the vast dark meadow had to pick his or her way through a mottled dazzle underfoot. A few figures moved down by the cars of the caravan: the ones caught in the open were crawling carefully toward cover, and others who had been nearer the cars were opening airlock doors or stepping back behind something.

Aside from the discomfort, it was obvious that there was total disorganization on the meadow between the Special Caravan and the *Falling Angel*. No doubt this would pass, but for those few minutes all but the wielder of the strobe were sitting ducks. Or not entirely: Nollinsae's own vision must surely be less than perfect right now, and he was by the nature of the meadow limited to the strobe tank or to contact with it, lest he lose it. Still, those few minutes might be too long.

A separate green flash from beyond the head of the caravan showed that the squeakers were aroused, and not pleased. Rheinallt strove to see into the confusion of their goldenly milling forms, but between the distance and the strobe light he could discern nothing in particular.

The thing was hellishly bright. Rheinallt kept edging away. Fleurage had sent Nollinsae out loaded for trouble, all right. Perhaps the rocket in the airtent had been a general improvisation, as he had come more to hate the very idea of the Special Caravan. But the strobe was a specifically designed attack mechanism that must have been made on Fleurage and transferred aboard at Blueholm.

The wretched device displayed ingenuity, and perhaps the dark meadow as background was prechosen to enhance the effect on anyone not trained or accustomed to standing fast in the face of weird and unpredictable optics. Objectively Rheinallt could not tell if the lightpox on the meadow was in front of his eyes or within them.

He stumbled again, dangerously. When was the low-life going to run out of power?

Between pulses Rheinallt caught a glimpse of Nollinsae crouched down, outside the hinged dummy tank, below the direct line of the beams. It was hard for Rheinallt to hold his face in that direction long enough to see anything besides the stabbing pulses from the strobe and its mirrors, but he thought Nollinsae had put on a protective overhelmet of some kind. Maybe darkened or polarized. More than that he could not make out.

Kneeling again, Rheinallt squeezed off another shot, but he could not even see where it went. He snapped off the near end of the wire disgustedly.

Where was Susannilar? Was it working on her? Rheinallt searched the area with eyes narrowed and smarting until he saw her.

Already she had covered more distance away from the strobe than Rheinallt had. She also was peering this way and that as she moved, trying to assimilate the eerily changed scene. She seemed thin.

Rheinallt wanted to signal her, talk to her, but communication was impossible. It took him a long dizzy moment to realize that Susannilar looked thin because she had split. The *strobe* must be doing it, he thought, forcing her into vibration, oscillation, and the split. Had those on Fleurage calculated that enough pressure from the strobe could kill her? Or just render her so helpless that any conventional means would suffice?

Off in the distance he now saw the other Susannilar, receding, almost-running over the stubbled meadow. He wanted to cry out, Don't run! Keep your contact with the meadow surface—but she could not hear.

Nollinsae was shoving or dragging his strobe-tank outfit slowly up the slope. He was moving it onto the direct line between the split Susannilars, and correcting his pull as necessary to keep it centered on that line.

Some smart witch-haters on Fleurage, if not Nollinsae himself, had divined the inherent weakness in the girl's strength and enabled Nollinsae to use her own unlucky talent against her. If Rheinallt found it hard to think or act under the influence of the stroboscope, how much harder now for Susannilar to get her bearings.

Salty tears ran down Rheinallt's face to his mouth, and his breathing, echoing off the interior of the helmet, was harsh and distracting. He wanted neither to turn his back on Nollinsae nor to face the light directly, so he followed a mixed strategy; this gave his stumbling walk a kind of slow twirling effect which might have been hilarious in other circumstances.

Rheinallt wished he could have trained the riflemen how to act in emergencies on the meadow when one can't quite see what one is doing, but he had not thought of it. He could dimly make out the trailing lines of several haywire darts that had been lofted toward Nollinsae and the strobe. They showed up as ultrafine linear flickers lying on the dark surface. So far none had done any good at all.

There were more flashes of violent green from the direction of the squeakers. Strobes obviously disagreed with the waybestial equipoise.

Rheinallt had an idea. Was Whitnadys down there among her charges, and could she see him amid this visual havoc? She probably was out calming them down; if they got too excited they might wreck the caravan. Whitnadys would have anticipated that from the first flashes of the strobe and, he hoped, had made her way through the cars to the front by now.

But that was precisely the trouble. She would be too busy petting and soothing restless masses of chryselephantine flesh to be scanning in his direction right now. Certainly she would not be staring into the strobe, or across the dark stretch it speckled and dominated.

A few lights had been added from the caravan, additional spotlights trained on the meadow slope. Not everyone aboard was dimwitted; the extra spots would reduce the strobe's contrast, and therefore its confusion. Only a few extra spotlights so far, though, and Rheinallt needed something quicker.

Who aboard the caravan, then, would be most likely to have an eye on him? And understand a signal that he might give? Certainly any use of intersign or trailsign was out of the question; finger-twitches could never be perceived across that flicker-filled gap.

Arahant? Rheinallt squinted, trying to see if the aircat was in the observation bubble on top of the first caravan car. There might be a white blur there, but he couldn't tell for sure.

Rheinallt raised his arm, gave a nice long whole-arm wave. Would Arahant see it? Yes—there was definitely a white motion in the observation bubble. Arahant had seen, and waved back.

He hoped Arahant could see him better than he could see the aircat. He began waving one arm in a wide, slow circle over his head. Would Arahant understand?

Again and again Rheinallt made the slow circle, trying to pantomime the idea of a whip or flail. Another giant green flash cut through the strobe pattern. Golden-haired waybeasts milled irritably near the head of the caravan. Rheinallt made a few quick up-and-down motions so that Arahant might make some connection with that flashing from the squeakers, then went back to the slow circlings.

A lesser problem was that if Arahant did understand the signal, then he would have to give the order. Going into an empty room and calling up someone on a speaking tube could take care of that.

By now Rheinallt's eyes were producing so many after-images of their own that he could hardly make out the articulated line of the caravan. The strobe seemed less important than the welter of its own afterimages, like a repeated sound drowning in its own echoes. Smaller forms danced all over the landscape, impossible to identify or locate properly. Rheinallt could not tell if Arahant was still at his domed window.

Perhaps one of Nollinsae's extra purposes was indeed to goad the squeakers into running amok and smashing up the caravan. Then the awkwardly probing expedition and the oscillating girl would be eliminated together. But they might not have known as much about waybeasts on sad Fleurage as they did about witches.

Rheinallt's arm was beginning to ache, so he switched to the other, maintaining the flailing motion. Then, foggily, he saw something pass overhead in a huge arc.

Immediately he threw himself flat, taking care not to break contact with the meadow, and rolling into the nearest small dip in the pseudosurface.

Overhead a shiny line passed again, faster and slightly lower. He twisted around on his belly so he could see Nollinsae and the apparatus. Their outlines seemed scattered, for his eyes were stung afresh by the strobe, but he was able to decipher what was happening.

Rheinallt's idea had gotten through his obscure line of communication: him to Arahant to Whitnadys, and then to one of her more stable squeakers.

As the shining cable swung by the squeaker passed overhead

again, the topmost lattice of mirrors was clipped off without a quiver from the cable. Separated, the lattice and mirrors vanished from the conflict on the meadow.

The strobe equipment seemed suddenly to have shrunk, because there was no debris from the disconnected portions. Vibrating light ceased to pour out of the mutilated stroboscope.

At once the meadow was almost calm again. There were still a myriad afterimages, and his eyes still hurt, so it remained hard to see people and things in detail. Yet the improvement was genuine, and the spotlights with their clear light reasserted their authority.

The squeaker holding the cable end apparently thought that the improved visibility simply allowed it to take more painstaking aim. It kept the cable revolving in its great circle, only lowering it slightly as it came around again.

While the cable, taut as a giant wheelspoke, passed over the huddled figures toward the front of the caravan, Nollinsae jumped from his equipment and strode off at a near run. But he was linked, still, to the strobe and airtank by some cords: a bundle of control pull-wires, Rheinallt guessed. It was clear from his grasping and yanking motions as he fled that the cord bundle must have been clipped to Nollinsae's suit to ensure against the accidental loss of the strobe. Now it was a hindrance.

Once more the cable came around, and Rheinallt ducked his head. Nollinsae threw himself flat. The cable hit the strobe right about the level of the opened tank, shattering the mechanism and carrying away all the lights, mirrors, and struts remaining. These disappeared. The oxygen tank, caught at its farther edge, was flipped up and tumbled along the meadow, revolving slowly as it jerked and snapped the control cord, and disintegrated. It lasted a few seconds only, unattended.

Nollinsae finally released his useless length of cord, and it, like a snake in the grass, also disappeared.

The heavy cable from the caravan was released by the squeaker on that portion of its arc on the far side of the caravan, and it went the way of the cord.

The strobe was utterly destroyed.

After a few long moments filled largely with gasps of relief, Rheinallt stood up and began checking on the others.

Susannilar was on the point of entering into the great curving

242

wall of red shadow; he saw her glance back, then step into the nonsubstantial Ship.

Nollinsae was up and out of his own hidey-hole already, following quickly after Susannilar. His special equipment was overcome but not his determination. Probably he still had a sidearm. Legs pumping solidly, the Guardsman almost-ran up the long slope leading to the *Falling Angel*.

Then the Detenebrator appeared. From within the caravan? The fuzzy basketball shape was moving above the meadow, trailing a long and nearly invisible stem down to the black pseudosurface.

Before Rheinallt could do more than blink, the Detenebrator rushed over to him, and another extremely thin fiber whipped out of it and wrapped around the man's neck. He jerked back instinctively, but it did not contract. Immediately he heard the voice of the Detenebrator booming inside the helmet, conduction so loud that it might as well have been inside his head. Certainly Ytrenath was a master of fibers.

"Wake up, Eiverdein!" the big voice boomed at him. But there was a wobble in that voice, a tremor that Rheinallt had not heard before, like a steam boiler pushed beyond its maximum pressure. He looked up at it searchingly; it was hovering and bobbing unsteadily overhead, linked by one thread to the meadow and by another to the man.

"Where've you been, Detenebrator?" Rheinallt asked inside his helmet.

"Dying, Eiverdein. There's only one thing I have left to do, and I've been gathering my energy for it. This long, fool expedition of yours took a lot out of me, more than I expected, and I've suffered for it."

"I'm sorry to hear that—"

"So has Susannilar. Suffered, I mean. I came along to help her and guide her, and give her my last discovery before— But I'm coming apart; I have been for clockdays. Ever been in a mind, Eiverdein, whose brain was progressively unraveling in a physical sense? I daresay not. Take my word that it's not fun, nor even edifying at this stage."

Rheinallt stole a glance around. Nollinsae had disappeared into the *Falling Angel* in search of Susannilar. But now here came Susannilar herself, walking very slowly back down the slope toward him and the Detenebrator. Was another segment of her still within the *Falling Angel*, decoying Nollinsae away?

"What happens now?" he asked the Detenebrator.

"Right now you're just a convenient anchor. I don't mean to disparage. I enjoy talking to you, but it's imperative for Fleurage's sake that I pass on to Susannilar now . . . I'd hoped to wait until she and I could communicate more easily, but I've just temporarily halted a stuporous decline that's gripped me for days. I can't wait any longer."

"What brought you out of it?" Maybe he could put it back into its decline.

There was a monstrous chuckle from the fiber contact at the base of the helmet. "Mostly regathering my energies along simplified pathways; reknitting myself, as it were. But our mutual friend the Guardsman, and his infernal machine, helped give me a few stings to get moving again."

How weak was it? "What is it you're going to tell Susannilar?"

"As she may have told you, I sent her out to try to find some way of keeping Fleurage open to subspatial commerce even after the world becomes trailless. The irony, though, is that after I wove this temporary container for my own personality, I rode several caravans in and out of subspace, finally including yours. And I realized that I had found the solution."

Coolly, Rheinallt masked his amazement. "You have?"

"Yes," it confirmed simply, the wobble in the great voice increasing. "The structure of the trails is not dissimilar to the microstructure of the human brain. I'd speculated on this before, but my experiences of breakin and breakout in this fiber-bundle form confirmed one of my many infraphysical hypotheses. Breakthrough is a teachable discipline I can share with Susannilar."

Teachable? Yes, Rheinallt of all people could believe that. "Why then," he growled within his helmet, "in the name of all who've traveled the meadow, why haven't you shared it? That ability is priceless—why do you think we value the squeakers so? Because although they're trailbound, that's the one thing they can do that the unenhanced human can't. Impressing them as draft animals is wholly secondary."

The Detenebrator sounded sad now. "I haven't the energy to teach everyone, but I thought you would be happy to know that such a process really is attainable. I have to reserve my germinant help for Susannilar. The preservation of Fleurage must come first."

"Don't you know she's unstable? You couldn't get past her vibrato before, and the airtent disaster's unhinged her. You can't give a power discipline to someone in her condition." If it killed her, the discovery would be lost.

"Oh, but I must. What disaster do you mean? It's a great responsibility for Susannilar, I agree. But she's always been a good, steady girl, and I have no alternative. She'll be here in a moment, I see, and that is good, for I am very weary."

Rheinallt could easily visualize a shaky Susannilar attempting breakout without enhancement, and merely disappearing. He was thinking frantically for a way to salvage this mess before the Detenebrator and Susannilar both wound up dead, and the subspatial breakout processes with them.

"Why did you wait until we got all the way out to the Ship to share this?" Rheinallt finally asked for lack of a better question.

"Because of that Ship. I'd hoped Susannilar might gather strength from it, or clarity from studying it, that would damp her vibrato and better enable her to handle the control procedures I'm about to give her. I'm sure she'll manage, though. The qualities needed are a disciplined mind, and a reservoir of natural energy to employ the techniques."

"A tremendous energy?" Rheinallt asked almost absently. If anyone had such a natural reservoir, that person was he. He looked for Susannilar; she was moving almost randomly, her attention elsewhere. Her other self must have her hands quite full dodging Nollinsae inside the *Falling Angel*.

"Yes, indeed," the Detenebrator wavered. "You were almighty slow eliminating the strobe. The stimulation revived me, but at the cost of an accelerated deterioration. *Your* mind probably feels as if it's been slept in. As for *mine*—well, I can no longer retain my integrity as an entity. I am coming apart, and I can scarcely move. I do wish that girl would get here quickly!" it finished petulantly.

"She's coming," Rheinallt shook his head to clear it, to roll out the multicolored marbles the strobe had left rattling in his skull and knocking his eyeballs from behind. "I'm sorry for you, but I recall my dead companions on the sled, and I doubt they're sorry."

245

"Yes," it said sorrowfully, "my first experiments in communication, and in the transfer of the control procedures. You understand that I couldn't experiment to the limit on my own granddaughter."

Rheinallt looked back up at the Ship, but nothing was visible inside, and outside in that direction there was only the dilatory split-Susannilar vaguely wending her way. He would like to go in there, and see this final hand-to-hand confrontation between Susannilar and Nollinsae, but the desire was more powerful to see the Detenebrator through to whatever conclusion it hinted was imminent within minutes. He was not quite rooted to the spot, in spite of the Detenebrator's communication filament, but as surely as he breathed oxygen he wanted what it called control procedures for transferring in and out of subspace.

"What then can you offer?" he suggested.

"Nothing. I regret it, but Susannilar must be my heir in this. Fleurage must not be pinched off the vine of worlds like a rotten gourd. I know you've suffered through my actions, and I acknowledge the fault. But that's the way—it is too late for me to think of sharing with two. I'll barely be able to manage one."

The Detenebrator's voice was vibrating strongly, setting up a secondary resonance in Rheinallt's helmet glass. It added a few more words in a vibrato screech, underlaid with what he thought to be genuine regret: "Forgive a dead hand this dead torch, Eiverdein! I make no offers. Take what you can, learn wherever you can!"

Susannilar had wandered close now, her eyes wide and not comprehending, but she must know this was a vital moment. Perhaps Ytrenath, or his later form the Detenebrator, had warned her to expect some such lesson. But she was weakened now, damaged from the airtent loss, further split and distracted for Nollinsae's sake right now, and probably generally confused.

The Detenebrator whipped out another filament and wrapped it around Susannilar's neck at the base of her helmet.

Rheinallt reached up a gloved hand to grip the filament touching him, and held it strongly. He sensed the Detenebrator's neuroelectric potential, and shifted his own energies to make of himself a ground, to draw any impulses that it sent out. Susannilar was weak and not focused. Rheinallt was nei-

246

ther. When the Detenebrator sent down the coded impulses that comprised those control procedures—or a summarized seed-prototype from which they could be constructed—they began flowing Rheinallt's way.

But the impulses were more than electric, they were sub-sonic, the Detenebrator using his subtlest skill. Rheinallt's head began to ache, and he gritted his teeth to hold them still against the vibrations that were just the crude shell of the subtler neurosonic knives.

Susannilar stood dumbfounded, obviously hurting too, but with too much attention elsewhere to grasp what was going on, and unable to discipline and encourage the brain-twisting process. Her faculty for duality was not a help: any bifurcation necessarily weakened in the implicit tug-of-war between her and Rheinallt. It also meant, Rheinallt had to assume, that part of the physical structure of her brain could not be accessed by the Detenebrator's probing and altering sonics.

Behind Rheinallt's eyes the pain rose to the intense, as if a physical arrow had penetrated his head. He staggered, then slumped to a sitting position. Fortunately the pain at this level did not last, for he was afraid he would foul the sonosurgical process if he tried to block that pain. Visions of multipetaled flowers danced in his mind, colored highlights of softly curved petal edges opening and unfolding in slow time, lineaments of color attracting and contracting in slow motion.

Rheinallt had tried to keep looking at the Detenebrator as it developed this filamental firework. As that arrow of intricate sonic impulses came down the fiber, drawn deliberately by Rheinallt's own potential, the arrow had seemed to pierce his brain and paradoxically blind him, so that for a moment he thought the meadow was everywhere.

Like the black meadow-blindness, the pain receded quickly. The blackness was replaced with the unfolding image of the flower, his mind's attempt to heal its brain's sutures. It was too late to duck for cover. He knew that the transfer of knowledge, in the form of neural microstructure, had been completed by that master of fibrous sounds.

A key inserted in a lock is more than a transfer, more than a material change-of-place of the key. The action implies an openable door. A visible flower is only an image, of which a botanist perceives the intricacy within. What structural change in his brain had the Detenebrator's sonic key made possible of utilization?

What have I let myself in for? Rheinallt thought raggedly.

Susannilar collapsed to the meadow, then thinned measuredly to nothingness, withdrawing to her other half within the Ship. So many blows for her talent, so few rewards. Had she profited from the Detenebrator's dying burst of information through structural change, or not? Was too much of her away?

For that matter, Rheinallt wondered, had he profited? He could not tell, so far at least. He was dizzily aware that this discipline, like the others he employed, could easily kill him if fumbled.

The Detenebrator began pushing itself into an upward arc which would bring it to a zenith above the encamped caravan. The filament connecting it to Rheinallt attenuated still further, keeping its contact. Within a few seconds it was a fuzzy dot in the immense blackness.

Rheinallt sensed people watching from the neighborhood of the caravan, though probably all were further rattled by these events. This arching upward would have to be the booming puffball's last journey. It continued to rise like a full moon climbing.

Suddenly the Detenebrator exploded. Its constituent fibers flew in all directions, bright streaks of light vanishing quickly. As a fluffy seed clump scatters its myraid seeds while the wind puff strikes it, the Detenebrator broke up. Hundreds of bright shafts streaked in all directions.

People around the caravan headed for cover momentarily, remembering the stroboscope, but it was not needful. As the fibers stretched and broke, the bright streaks winked out. None reached down as far as the meadow.

Some of the shafts of light had gone in the direction of the Ship: the largest if the most elusive target. Strange streaks or tracks cut right through the *Falling Angel* for several seconds, chords of white light.

The passengers and crew who had slid away came back out of hiding. There was nothing left. Dully, Rheinallt broke off the trailing dead fiber from his own helmet and watched it disappear.

Rheinallt was ready to let black asbestos fall in safe folds across this scene in his memory, but it had to be faced. Letting

248

himself sweat within the airsuit, he struggled with the patterns the Detenebrator had passed. Its end upon the meadow, restored and broken apart by the strobe near the ungraspable shadow by the lonely trail, had come down to those patterns.

Feeling that he had gained a realization of something he had always known dimly and without words, Rheinallt began walking carefully toward the Ship.

In his mental afterimage of the Detenebrator's web-flash of light, the vast interstellar network of trails connected human worlds with a gossamer touch, and the trails moved. Slow majestic turning in ethereal glory, galactic coilings and stretchings. Snakelike stars writhed in two dimensions, infinite light reflected through darkness in infinite beams.

This light was cool: these were not luminaries but reflections only, gentle moonlight on dull ashes. Visible history in retrospect, like tree rings which can only be counted when the tree is dead.

Rheinallt noticed that the row of squeakers in front of the caravan was turned toward him. Each squeaker stared at the man with its huge green eyes. He shivered in his suit, feeling the clammy touch of cooling sweat. What did they see? What dead torch had the Detenebrator passed?

Ahead was the redly curving hulk of the Ship. Somehow he would have to experiment. A vision by itself brought no help. The rewards of time went to the embodiers of visions.

Rheinallt took several deep and slow breaths, there under the slab side of red fog. Another deep breath, and then he brought enough calm to his mind to keep functioning on the currently necessary plane. He stepped into the red shadow.

§§§§§§§§§§§§§§§§§§§§§§§§§§§§§

17. The Bloom of Death

WHERE WAS THE ORIGINAL SHIP THAT CAST THIS RED DESERT of shadow? When had it been a solid entity accessible to the universe of substantial solids and clear spaces? That original *Falling Angel* had cast a huge, permanent shadow which was constant in direction—that is, location and orientation—regardless apparently of stars, trails, or any lesser sources of light.

The ancient starship might have been too close to a long-ago supernova in starspace, or some catastrophic energy burst in meadowspace. Or stayed in enhancement too long and become, through the operation of its stardrive field, part of the fabric of the universe. Had the Ship left a wake when it traversed subspace long ago, great colored trails as meadow-petrified wakes left in the immeasurable past?

What infraphysics could describe and what it could explain satisfactorily were no closer than law and justice.

An explosion of merely stellar magnitude would not have been enough. The *Falling Angel*'s faded ghost was all that was left of what once was a whole and self-contained existence. A universe, perhaps, antedating the monobloc; a universe before that deluge of fire swept it clean.

Susannilar's earlier description of her penetration or perception of a more solid *Falling Angel* supported this. Her semi-related tale was filled with impressions of intolerable heat and light. Rheinallt could almost hear a wail of sadness keening down the years, the wail of the lost forever.

Rheinallt saw blurred figures ahead, and he slowed to a pace appropriate to a fog-shrouded dueling ground.

One of the human outlines was closer: Susannilar, out of focus and barely less shadowy than the Ship itself. She seemed to have picked up some of the reddish cast, but that was probably the effect of the Ship's glowing through and around her.

Rheinallt made some interrogatory gestures in intersign. He could not tell whether she was unwilling to answer or too preoccupied elsewhere. After a few moments she waved and disappeared.

He came up to the other, far more solid figure. It was Glenavet, with an expression of suspenseful satisfaction.

"Do you know where Susannilar is?" Rheinallt asked him with his fingers.

"She should be right back," Glenavet replied. "Wait."

After a few minutes a blood-red Susannilar returned and beckoned the two men forward. They moved forward a couple of hundred yards deeper into the Ship. The hazy red girl stopped and pointed.

Away ahead came another Susannilar, circling, followed by Nollinsae, who drew steadily closer. That other Susannilar looked perfectly solid from their vantage, as solid as the Guardsman. All was in pantomime.

It was evident that those two had followed a long arc within the Ship, and Rheinallt realized that Susannilar had arranged her finale so that he and Glenavet could witness it. The hazy Susannilar moved closer to Glenavet, but did not try to touch him. She stood, hands on hips, as a matter-of-fact spectator, although this Susannilar held scarcely more substance than the Ship.

This staged resolution happened deceptively quickly. The solid Susannilar who was baiting Nollinsae slowly had let the Guardsman gain on her. Now he was close enough to reach out and grab her, and he did, jerking her to a stop. With his

252

other hand he drew a knife, and, clearly enjoying the finesse of his stroke and this long-awaited termination, Nollinsae swiftly brought the blade forward and down.

Yet things changed: the universe, or Nollinsae. *Together*, Susannilar and Nollinsae were thinning, so rapidly thinning that while Rheinallt blinked in astonishment, their density, or opaqueness, had been halved. Physically, it must have been intolerable for Nollinsae. The now-red knife had fallen from the stunned Guardsman's hand, and it was now Susannilar who was gripping Nollinsae with both hands.

The two of them were shadows within the shadow, red within the red. And then Susannilar let go her grip, and disappeared.

Rheinallt had been aware with a corner of his mind that the split-Susannilar beside him had been solidifying rapidly in the last few seconds, and now she was back, solid, normal; but leaning almost collapsed into Glenavet's supporting arms. She had pulled back together again across whatever gulf she had been astride.

Glenavet's attention was all for her, while she slumped with eyes closed. She was violently sunburned on her face: blisters had flared up on her skin in a dozen places under her helmet.

Walking forward, with some effort Rheinallt could barely make out a shape: Nollinsae's form, his shadow embedded in the shadow of the Ship.

Rheinallt stood looking at it for long moments.

Moving back to Susannilar, whose eyes were resolutely closed, Rheinallt touched helmets, but asked nothing.

"I took him back," she said softly, "and left him there."

Rheinallt took a couple of deep breaths, glancing once more at the foglike statue within the wider hulk of fog. "Dead."

"I imagine so. By now."

"By now? How far——?"

"A long way back. A very long way. Maybe half the age of the universe."

Half the age . . . Nollinsae was now a passenger in the shadow of the Ship, borne along effortlessly, a part of the fabric of space. Buried alive in the past.

And his awareness? How long had wispy threads of that lasted? How clearly had he seen what was happening to him? Great eternity, what a way to die.

253

Glenavet led Susannilar away, half carrying her and half dragging. Rheinallt did not follow them. *Falling Angel* surrounded them, imperturbable.

Susannilar had come of age, had mastered the talent which was her birthright, and had avenged her family. Had she found in the Ship a fault in the continuum which enabled her to shift in time's dimension? Whatever secrets the Ship held, she had found one she could use.

Rheinallt did not think she would or could do that again. With her shifting she had sidled very close to death within the Ship. He was sure she was radiant-burned within, in addition to the blisters and sunburn on her skin. But she had struck, and had her revenge. Rheinallt was also sure she had guessed the probable price beforehand, that she would be deeply injured if she survived at all.

At his feet was the knife so recently held by Nollinsae, and dropped by him in his first startled realization that the hunter had been trapped in his turn. The knife, lost in transit, had also come aboard. The *Falling Angel*, in that nearer but far-distant time, had still retained enough of a field to keep the knife and not let it fall to nothingness, but acted as a lens passing to the knife light from the light beyond the Ship. So the knife joined the Ship in the latter's shadowy, infinitesimally attenuating journey down eternity.

Rheinallt bent and studied the insubstantial knife. It was a little more dense than its lost owner, perhaps itself now only a billion or two years old, aged and leached toward nothingness.

The tenuous Ship had once conveyed the consciousness whose faintest remnant had held the knife from the subspatial disintegration of random matter. What could be seen now was its feeblest aura, the last imprint of minds who had built the *Falling Angel* and launched it on the space beneath the universe. The last reflection of a guttered candle, the Ship was now only warmth where there had been fire, a red shadow where once had wrought active and creating minds.

Rheinallt imagined a planetside equivalent: an entire civilization reduced to the primal nothingness, dead and blown away except for a glazed pot, or a hard wooden boat buried in the river sand. Or a countryside, take Blueholm or far Earth itself, with fields and trees, streams and hills and prickly-burred grasses, reduced to one dry corpse of a flower and all else gone

254

where there's no retrieving. Could you explore a civilization from a last pot, or perceive a landscape in a dead flower?

That remnant aura, that reflection through a lens of those minds of long ago, had still possessed in its ever-fading grasp enough field of mentation to retain that knife. How long? A billion, two? A shadow still held on.

And Nollinsae, and Nollinsae, half an age away.

Rheinallt turned and headed through the reddish fog back to the caravan. It was the drag end of the day, and he was exhausted; for the dragging out had taken a lot out of everyone. Maybe his physiological clock was sick again, but it was not the clocks on the walls within the caravan that had burned so many hours.

Very late that night, according to the variable whim of the wayclock, Rheinallt was awakened from a deep sleep by Whitnadys.

"Hendrikal, come quick!" she cired. "Susannilar and Glenavet are gone!"

"Huh? Gone where?"

"Back down the trail!" She was dancing with excitement. "Toward the Nation."

He was awake now, up and pulling on clothes. "How'd they go?"

"They took the last car, the caboose." She rolled her eyes. "The one with the wired-cannon."

"Figures. Harder to chase after them without taking our only other wired-cannon from the nose-car. And without either of those, the remainder of the caravan's too vulnerable for the trip back." Rheinallt stood. "How many squeakers?"

"Two. It won't cripple us. I don't think Glenavet wanted to try reharnessing more than two. If a person isn't trained as a beast handler, the complexity of the traces goes up geometrically with the number of squeakers."

Rheinallt was about to head for the rear of the parked caravan when Arahant thrust open the door to the compartment and burst in, panting in great billows of white fur. The catadrome vaulted into the armchair and sat.

"What have you been up to?" Rheinallt asked him.

"Thought you were too groggy to ask," he said promptly, jumping down again although he was still breathing heavily.

"Come on. It's too late to do anything more, but you might get a last glimpse of the former rattle on your tail."

"Fine." The three of them left, striding rapidly rearward down the long carpeted, car-segmented corridors.

After a minute Rheinallt asked, "What do you mean, do anything more?"

"Yes. Well, I was ambling around, keeping an eye on Glenavet. Most of the people aboard were worn out, of course. Been a hectic day. You know, that man's personality has really upgraded since he's been hanging out with that young witch of yours."

"She's no witch," Rheinallt said irritably.

"Get on with it," Whitnadys demanded. "At least tell him what you told me by speaking tube. About following that millefleurs scent, and all."

They went through another intercar airlock on their way back through the caravan. The corridors were empty and they kept their voices low, not wanting to wake the passengers unnecessarily. Whitnadys seemed to feel no need to wake any others of the crew, so Rheinallt thought they could put that off. Already he had made up his mind not to go chasing after Glenavet and Susannilar. What would be the use?

"Your caboose crew had deserted for the downy fields of sleep, Hendrik," Arahant said. "You might lean on them for that. Anyway, not too long ago I was drifting toward the tail of the caravan, following a trace of a certain exotic perfume. When I got to the last car but one, I saw Glenavet in the airlock detaching the couplers between the cars."

"Casting them off or capping them?" Whitnadys asked.

"Capping them. No, he wasn't doing any kind of sabotage. Besides, that isn't easy: any old trailman knows about air-safety interlocks. As soon as I realized what he was doing, I gave him the evil eye and my best expression of disapproval. But I realized that he didn't know an aircat's expressions from a hump on the meadow, so that wouldn't do the caravan much good. So I fluffed up as large as I could, but dug my claws into the carpet so if there was a blowout, I wouldn't be at the mercy of the air currents as I'd been when the airtent blew."

"Good idea," Rheinallt said briefly.

"Then I saw a length of pipe that had been left in a corner, and I grabbed that, and very slowly I brought it to bear on the airlock door as though it were some esoteric weapon." Arahant chuckled. "Really spooked him. Between my sudden fluff-up which he'd never seen before, and my pointing a strange pipe-like gizmo at him, he was ready to run for it.

"Glenavet slammed the airlock door on the caboose side. I ran and propped the piece of pipe in the airlock so it was pointing outward, and jumped back within the next-to-last car.

"I slammed *that* airlock door, and turned off all the airlocks leading back to the connections with the caboose. I was afraid Glenavet might just order the squeakers to haul down the trail and wrench loose anything he hadn't already detached. And that's what he did, but apparently everything vital had been detached already. Pulled out the speaking tube, maybe; little things of that order."

"Is everything sealed off now?" Rheinallt needed to know.

"Right as rain," the aircat said.

"Don't bring that up now. So he already had the squeakers hitched, and pulled the caboose away?"

"Yes. They didn't stop, either. When they looked back, they must have seen that pipe pointing at them like a gun barrel." Arahant sounded pleased with himself.

"I see," Whitnadys said. "The wired-cannon mounted in the caboose faces *forward* for them, if the two squeakers they hijacked were pulling the car directly away from the rest of the caravan. They couldn't stop for a parting shot without turning and stopping, and you had them too scared to try that."

"Correct, my dear lady," Arahant said.

"You didn't mention Susannilar," Rheinallt said. "Are you positive she's with Glenavet?"

"Definitely. She at least *did* look back at the caravan. I recognized her by her glowing red face through the caboose airlock's porthole. The red was no ordinary sunburn."

"Here we are," Rheinallt said. They had arrived at what was now the last car. He went to the utility porthole in the rear airlock door.

"They're almost out of sight," he reported. A tiny hint of yellow lamplight was visible for a few moments, then it disappeared, drawn down behind some intervening rise in the meadow. "They're gone now."

"They can't have much in the way of supplies," Whitnadys said sympathetically. "I don't know if they'll make it."

"Well, you're the expert, Whitnadys," Arahant said. "If not to escape, why else would they have tried it?"

Rheinallt put in, "Arahant may have foiled an attempt to take over the caravan, using the wired-cannon as a weapon. His pipe trick may have scared them off from that. Glenavet seemed to think lately that the spirit of the Ship had entered into him with Susannilar's esoteric help, or some such."

Whitnadys laughed. "Sounds like a simpleminded, twisted version of you, almost."

"Thanks," Rheinallt said dryly. "What happened to Tadako?"

"Never saw him tonight," Arahant confirmed.

"This bodes no good at all," Rheinallt said with a yawn.

"Why?" Whitnadys asked. "Assuming they never really meant to try to capture the caravan, and did stock up on supplies, I think it's sort of romantic. Like an elopement."

Arahant shook his head, twitching pointed ears. "Remember how they've both been changing. That's not been too good for them. And what Hendrik means is that there are two people with newfound power out for a spree. Wherever they alight there's going to be trouble. I could see Glenavet's increasing effect on other people aboard. He's far more dangerous than when he was content to be a minor organizer of trailmen. Now he's going to want to organize worlds."

"Oh," Whitnadys said faintly. "I see what you mean."

"Fortunately," Arahant went on, "not being human myself, I was immune to blandishments of a human on the make, or I might have 'eloped' with them."

Whitnadys knelt down and hugged Arahant.

"I'll have to roust out some of the crew to keep watch," Rheinallt said. "I don't think they'll be back, though."

"I can do that," Whitnadys said, straightening. "I also need to talk to some overly sleepy, or witch-susceptible, beast handlers."

Arahant's slitted eyes sparkled. "I wish I could have signed our late Detenebrator for an orchestra. You know I've a huge vocal range myself, thanks to species adaptations, that allows me to write unusual but entirely live-performable effects into my operas. The Detenebrator would have been as good a shrieker as a couple of my sisters together. Incredible sonics. A real blateroon it was."

18. A Track of Golden Fire

THE FOLLOWING DAY THEY HAD A CELEBRATION. SOME AT least of their ends had been achieved. The caravaneers all drifted outside, except for a few delegated to hold down the caravan's presence. As they went out Seebanone handed each a gas torch. They gathered like fireflies on the gentle slopes of a hollow a third of the way up toward the Ship.

The very bottom of this depression was the size of a sunken bathtub. The water in it had been brought from the caravan's tanks. The surplus had better go back afterward, too, or the cargomaster would make the revelers spit up whatever they had swallowed.

Meadow-tea was another arcane detail of the subspace traveler's life in this culture that Rheinallt was supposed to know all about. Whitnadys was leading the uncommon ceremony, but the captain-of-caravan would have to play a major part. She had promised to cover any lapse of his.

Dozens were gathered in a circle around the hollow in the pseudosurface, and more were ambling over. Not even all the crew had drunk the tea before, so there was plenty of trailsign going back and forth as the procedure was explained to the newer trailmen as well as to most of the passengers.

A crewman brought up a last bucket of water and poured it into the hollow with a flourish. The water came down in an unbroken stream, glittering transparently, and merged with a silent splash and rippling into the little pool. Droplets that edged away from the bucket's stream vanished without fuss, so the column of poured water was clean-sided as polished metal. Droplets splashed up from the black vanished too, but left a tiny peak of separation behind them for an instant, like a golf tee after the golf ball is knocked galley-west.

At one end of the hollow, Whitnadys lay on her belly with her ungloved hands in the water, keeping a human contact with the pool lest the whole mass disappear. The meadow itself would not leak water any more than it would leak consciousness.

"Are your hands cold?" Rheinallt asked Whitnadys.

She shook her head no.

The crewman returned the last empty bucket to the always-manned caravan. Another, who had been standing by with a waterproof as well as vacuum-proof lantern, hunkered down next to Whitnadys and shined the beam on her hands where they were thrust into the water. The ring of people edged closer to see, with the ones in front kneeling or squatting.

The dark surface of the water twinkled in the lantern light as Whitnadys' hands moved gently with her breathing. Slowly, with beautiful hulalike dancing motions, her hands moved into the gestures which invited all present to partake of meadow-tea.

Sharing of water in vacuum. But no one moved yet.

Slowly Rheinallt unsnapped his glove and drew it off. Taking a utility knife from a belt sheath, he pantomimed cutting a small incision in the vein at his wrist. Although the knife did not actually cut him, Rheinallt caused the blood to well up anyway. Then more quickly, but still striving for clearly differentiated motions as though he were on stage, he knelt by the edge of the basin and thrust his bleeding wrist into the dark water.

In the lantern light, Whitnadys' fingers flashed and sparkled. In trailsign she said, "In our captain's blood is the strength which keeps breath within us, waters of life within us, freely supporting minds within us, will to press on within us, taste of home within us."

Subtle currents in the dark pool spread tinted streamers of his blood away from his wrist. They wended down to the end of the basin and began to curl back toward the lantern. Rheinallt could not tell if Whitnadys was affecting this motion yet; it seemed natural so far. He kept his wrist low, and his heart obligingly leaned on the pump handle and tried to fill the void it felt, not knowing this gap was immense and unfillable.

Rheinallt presumed he would not get dizzy from loss of blood before Whitnadys gave the sign for the next stage. If he did, he would just have to grit it out.

With quick motions underwater, Whitnadys began finger-painting, swirling the blood into bold arcs. Before exiting the caravan earlier she had coated her fingertips with various mixtures chosen to alter the microstructure of her skin: a vertical patch of skin will adhere more water than will a vertical patch of glass. Her unguents had enhanced this effect like hook-and-eye cloth, except that she was fastening to the heavier and more cohesive blood cells among the slipperier molecules of water.

Also, her fingers were webbed with small wedges of a transparent plastic sheeting, so that when her pale fingers gestured languidly toward a streamlet of blood, the blood was scooped by the semiporous membranes and deposited where she wished.

The unguents on the fingers represented an older tradition; the membrane was a technological improvement which the tea makers had snapped up. Whitnadys used both means.

She nodded to Rheinallt that he had bled enough for the cause. He pulled his wrist from the water, refusing a bandage readied beforehand and caused the cut to close. His wrist throbbed a little. He drew his glove over the aching hand and massaged it gently with the other.

Whitnadys now sketched a flower, the petals taking form in three dimensions, highlighted by the rays of the lantern, as her fingers fluttered gracefully in the gleaming pool. Now and then the hands formed a word or two in trailsign, then drew out a reddish curve of petal, then went on to more words. Occasionally, in fantastically planned gestures which the audience could only appreciate when one was completed, she both sketched and signed simultaneously.

As she completed these extraordinary flourishes, indrawn breaths in dozens of helmets made flickers of light as those who held gas lanterns that leached air from their suits changed their breathing abruptly enough to force-feed or starve their gas flames. As Whitnadys' efforts developed, these appreciative flickers increased.

As a work of art it was wholly plastic and ephemeral, but it held them all so spellbound Rheinallt wished he could have recorded her shapings. But electronic recorders were not so easy to contrive as fruit juice in the diet.

Whitnadys went on making her swirls live and writhe in the black-cupped pool. The flower she drew in silence became more and more complex, yet at the same time more abstract and arabesque: a mandala.

A jerking movement among the ranks of watchers caught Rheinallt's attention. He looked up reluctantly, then saw the weakened Tadako standing close, recovering now from the poison he said Nollinsae had slipped him. Could Nollinsae also have goaded the late Wirtellin into the foolhardy attack, back on Starved Rock? He would have to ask Tadako if he had noticed any such activity. Tadako rubbed his sleeve thoughtlessly on the outside of his helmet; the stolid, loyal trailman was crying.

When Rheinallt looked down into the pool again, Whitnadys had begun drawing his own face. A caricature, naturally, without much shading. But it definitely was his image forming, metamorphosing from the flower she had drawn. His heavy eyebrows could not be mistaken for pistils, stamen, or anything else.

He glanced at Whitnadys' expression, fully expecting to see her impish guess-what-Hendrikal! look, but her face was smooth, eyes intent and wholly serious. She had not told him beforehand about the subjects of the designs.

Already now Whitnadys was blurring the smiling face, smearing the floating streaks of brows and cheekbones into a featureless ovoid. He was sorry to see his likeness go so quickly. The new mass of red rested on the black meadow-bottom of the pool, as though it were flattened there, or dug in like the Ship.

Yes, a model of the *Falling Angel* as it appeared on the meadow, as it now loomed in the middle distance above them. A miniature of the shadowy red form, imbedded intangibly in the meadow. Involuntarily Rheinallt glanced toward the real thing, and saw others do likewise. Then he grinned at his own label, for the realness of the Ship was the most debatable part of this whole caravan-quest. Had they settled that reality to anyone's entire satisfaction? Already the watery model was blurring and diffusing.

There was some elbow-pushing, stares, and a flurry of intersign among the spectators. The final stage of the ceremony was to begin.

Rheinallt wished the old mapmaker Ortelius could have been there to see it. He would have to hunt him up as soon as they got back to Blueholm. His trip narrative would be garnished with some hard navigational records, and sweetened vastly for the patient dreamer with hints of travel breakthroughs. Ortelius would love it. Also he would be pleased to hear that, so far at least, no one had died from vacuum-related accidents, or from lifting one foot too many off the pseudosurface. Only by hostile action: the betrayal by other consciousnesses than one's own.

Whitnadys pulled a long tube from her belt, stretching one arm to uncoil the long rubbery length while she kept her other hand firmly in the water. Without looking up she reached above her head with one end of the tube; as it was accepted by the nearest crewman she plunged the other end in the water.

One by one the whole crowd of watchers circulated alongside Whitnadys, and each in turn took a sip of the meadow-tea through the tube. As each who was running a firebrand came by, he or she removed that feeder tube from the air valve in the helmet, inserted Whitnadys' hose, and sucked. Then the crewmember or expeditionary would hand the sipping tube to another, replace the firebrand, and puff it alight again. There was a continuing lantern-flicker in the vicinity.

As the tube was first proffered, Rheinallt had put one hand back into the pool, and allowed a faint electric charge to pass from his fingers through the tube to tingle the palate of each sharer. Even the most bemusedly nonceremonious had their eyes snapped wide by the sensation.

Next-to-last, Rheinallt took a sip himself. It seemed cold to the palate, but that was imagination. It had an undefinable taste which had not quite the warm saltiness of blood licked from a fresh cut, but savored of it.

Whitnadys finished the tasting, then recoiled the tube one-handed and clamped it again to her belt. In the earliest days the tea makers had used swamp reeds. Before her time.

Now, at last, he caught an impish glance from her; but it was only visible an instant before she turned to look off across the meadow at the huge hull of the *Falling Angel*. She looked for a long minute, and many of the rest saw the direction of her gaze and imitated her, thoughtfully.

Suddenly she snapped her head back to face the pool in front of which she still lay. Startled, the watchers who had become participants did too. In spite of knowing what must come next, and despite various cramps and odd tastes in their mouths, few were ready for it to end.

As they focused again, along with Whitnadys, on the pool of meadow-tea, she dallied no more with ornate passes of the hands, but pulled them out with a rush, droplets shaken off her fingers and vanishing. Instinctively Rheinallt, and the other meadow hands in the closer rows, made a motion toward the pool to preserve it. Yet it was clear that the pool would have to go its own way. The tea-maker's action was too quick to counter: before another of them could touch the water, it had vanished like a popped bubble.

Rheinallt blinked. Whitnadys stood briskly; the ceremony was over.

Some while later, after Rheinallt and Arahant had shared a meal in his compartment, they discussed the probable fortunes of their breakaways, Glenavet and Susannilar.

"I wonder what their reception will be," Arahant said, "when they arrive back in the Nation minus the rest of the Special Caravan."

"They'll have some explaining to do." Rheinallt ran a brush over his hair and beard, enjoying the sensuous feel. He tossed it to Arahant, who instead of plucking it out of the air batted it into a corner.

"That's what a certain new vibrant partnership is going to be doing to whole worlds pretty soon," Arahant said. "Figuratively, anyway. Trailwise, I won't hazard a guess yet. The two of them have suffered a ship-change, and I fear a lot of heads will roll in atonement."

Rheinallt dredged up a sentiment from distant memory. "A godless woman is a good match for a lawless husband."

"Look who's talking," Arahant said with an affectionate

sneer. "You, who fear neither God nor man nor beast, deriding a match that scarcely can fail to help both people."

"I'm not deriding what their match may do for them," he said mildly. "It's the combining of their mutual lacks that makes me worry for the rest of us. We'll have to follow them now."

"At least for a while, to see the results of their mutual powers," Arahant agreed. "What mutual lacks?"

"In a way, they're now musclebound. Susannilar is like two halves of a critical mass looking for each other. Glenavet is the barrel down which her force has started to speed. They may not be whole people, but in the paring away of some qualities we liked, they've shaped themselves into very powerful forces."

"Hendrik, do you recall the time I inflated, when you were interrogating Glenavet right after Starved Rock?"

"Sure. In Glenavet's compartment."

"I had it in mind then to test a couple of things. One, his knowledge: if Glenavet had encountered a catadrome previously, that made it more likely that he also could have encountered an energy weapon."

He nodded. "And used it for the telescope deaths."

"Two," Arahant continued, "his imagination. I was curious if he would realize that I wasn't a product of any of the worlds of the Trails society. Without giving away my advantage of presumed animal dumbness."

"So he failed both tests."

"Right, but there's a ringer." Arahant twitched his whiskers. "He still knows nothing about energy weapons. That part of the test conveyed no new information. The imaginative part is bearing slow fruit: after Susannilar binocularized his mind and gave him introspection, or whatever she did, he's been *thinking*."

"I don't think she—"

"Well then, poured perfume on his brain to grease the ratchets. Whatever she did to or for him, Hendrik, you know he's no longer a second-string union organizer. He's loaded for bear, and he knows there are new worlds to conquer."

"You don't think they'll head for Fleurage? Surely that's what Susannilar wants most. It's what her grandfather sent her out for, to find help for Fleurage before it's too late."

Arahant shook his head. "Susannilar and anyone would make a powerful pair. Susannilar's been hurt, though, psychically

265

and emotionally, and she's not quite the same girl who barely escaped from Fleurage. Glenavet never had an interest in Fleurage except for any he's picked up from her. The two together mean that Glenavet's going to use the power he now holds as her partner.

"That's where I let the cat out of the bag: he now can surmise the existence of the Earth-based society—between my demonstrated alienness and your fixation about wanting a starship."

Rheinallt let out a long breath, "Yeah. He won't be satisfied with Fleurage. He's a trail-oriented person, accustomed to thinking in terms of as many planets as are reachable. Besides, Fleurage is an agricultural world: not helpful as a base."

"No way. I doubt he'll even visit it, lest he be sucked into a struggle with the local fascists." Arahant paused. "At least he'll be confined to the Trails society, and maybe the Nation will be too tough for them."

"So they'll just hassle less-defensible places? Arahant, that's no solace to the worlds that get hassled."

"Still it gives us time to get back to the Nation, rub their noses in the danger we've helped set up. Before our vibrant pair builds an organization which allows them to take on the Nation itself."

"Sounds like the least damaging scenario," Rheinallt agreed.

"We'll see. Did you think about what I just said about their being confined to the fifty-four worlds along the trails? Is that a safe assumption?"

"I think it is. I don't believe Susannilar got anywhere near as much as I did from the Detenebrator's final attempt at structural transfer. After all, we're not planaria, and luckily enough I have experiential and structural advantages over her."

"You mean you had more, so you gained more?"

"That's right. At the lowest level, transfer of knowledge is virtually transfer of infrastructure." He grinned. "Haven't had much chance to check it out yet, but I will shortly."

Arahant looked at him with slitted eyes. "Mentation is more than just an analogy of potential, it's an activated structure of potential?"

"Yes." Rheinallt stood, looked around for his airsuit.

"You're going out now? To experiment?" Arahant couldn't keep the worry out of his voice.

"To meditate awhile, at least."

"Now, Hendrik, you just said that was almost the same thing."

Rheinallt's grin was slightly strained. "Well, isn't this what we came for? If not quite what we expected. So infraphysics is dangerous, down to the bottom line. We've known that for a long time."

"We've been together a long time, too." Arahant sighed so heavily that he deflated where he sat. "Be careful?"

"Sure." He began pulling on the airsuit.

Once outside again with the Blue Trail under his feet, Rheinallt rambled up alongside the caravan's stretched-out cars toward its head. He felt a heightened calm: whatever was going to happen would be something he made happen himself.

Whitnadys waved from among the squeakers, a happy wave easily recognizable. With a warm feeling he waved back and moved on, away from the trail and into even purer darkness. Out he walked, farther and farther.

Was he ready yet to try the channeling techniques for interspatial movement that had fallen to him from the dying Detenebrator?

In a sense, one could say that all of matter and energy, lizards and flowers, starspace and subspace, were projections from the universal creation down the depths of time to their creature present. If the steady-state theory was correct, then the projection was local, and continuous.

What did the *Falling Angel* have in common with that elusive infrastructure passed by the Detenebrator? A lens for a projection? Now the Ship was only a ghost: the flower of consciousness still recognizable but eternally fading, the flower forever blown. Rheinallt did not want to become a shadow, glowing or not.

Could he make the energy flows in his brain match the complexities that Ytrenath had discovered while in the fibrous complexity of the Detenebrator—but had not had the energy to use? The Detenebrator's neurosonics had affected Rheinallt like the insertion of a key. To realize the potential of this structural change he had to turn the key, open the door.

Trying to back up to that door metaphorically, Rheinallt used his conceptions of the *Falling Angel* to tighten his grip on his own mentational functioning. He could not quite hear the key clicking, but he could feel the Ship glowing, in his mind. How many pins could one stick in the head of an angel?

If the Ship ever had flowered, it was essentially dead now, the desert detritus of generative energy. As a faded bloom the *Falling Angel* was useless. One might find value in a tombstone, historic or nostalgic according to one's purposes, but Rheinallt had not risked his life for such. A few members of the expedition could go home satisfied with the experience as adventure, and let it go at that. But for Rheinallt, as for most of them, traveling long and dangerously to reach a Ship that one could not touch, a tombstone that one could not read . . . a gravestone rubbing was a gold mine by comparison.

Susannilar and Glenavet had found each other, or each had found more of themselves in the other, for good or ill. They had left to wreak whatever their mutually strengthened natures now allowed and encouraged.

Rheinallt needed more. He felt strengthened too, and not compensatingly diminished.

Soon it would be time to turn the caravan around, to head back to Blueholm and the Nation. There he could warn whoever wanted to hear that Susannilar and Glenavet made a dangerous combination. Also, he could consider outfitting another, smaller expedition, to convey Arahant and himself back toward realms they knew better, along with a few from the Trails culture who were dearest to them: Whitnadys, and their infant son, and whoever felt like another adventure. And he would use the Detenebrator's breakout technique, to escape the trails' limitations—if he could make it work.

He stopped walking to look back through the darkness at the tiny investigators with sparks of headlamps moving in and around the Ship. As he watched, one or two entered hopefully, another emerged again on the black plain. The distant person standing there probably was looking upward into that bulging curve, studying the red wraith awesome in its passionate loneliness.

Rheinallt knew what he had to try to give them, the only reason they would accept for concluding the expedition. What Susannilar had found, in her draining, once-in-a-lifetime effort, could neither be repeated nor shared.

He looked among the far, still ranks of Squeakerville, seeking Whitnadys. He could not spot her. Human sparks moved

268

restlessly only toward the long towering sides of red glow, the merging of Ship and meadow in violent repose.

Wait—one of those sparks was moving in a peculiar pattern. It had to be Whitnadys, with her long-distance lamp, and she was aiming it into the darkness where she knew he must be. It was a signal not of particular content, but just of acknowledgment, of presence. She was thinking of him, and signaling, and he flushed with the love he felt across the distance.

Idly Rheinallt held out both gloved hands in front of him, fingertips touching, and let a tiny electrical flow trickle from right fingers to left. He reversed it, and the darting sparks leaped back. He let this go on for the benefit of the distant Whitnadys until the tingle in his fingers slacked to numbness with the effort of discharge and reception. The golden-yellow flicker was bright between the gloves.

What was energy, anyway? A movement, not necessarily of a material substance, along a route.

He felt a tingle of excitement deep within, and he knew he was moving toward the decision. He began walking outward again, hammering at the dividing line where concepts became infraphysics.

How much does an artifact stand out in the wilderness, or a living being in the desert? Like a beacon. In a city among crowds we notice neither artifacts nor lives: trappings and decorations and counterfeits cover natures and functions. The *Falling Angel* was visible *here* precisely because this was the meadow; evidence not of death but of life, but such ephemeral evidence as was visible only against a background as harsh as death itself—this flattening deep upon which a mind might move, precariously. He had come to the Ship and learned, from it and from other pathfinders. All that remained of that challenge was movement along the route he had seen. That was what he had come for, if he could grasp the energic infrastructure and live through it.

The Detenebrator had given him new patterns, in those dying pulses. It had illumined nooks of his own inner structure which previously he had not been able to explore. The cortian fibers were within him, with their potential patterns, and a few of them he had used all his life.

Was this the place? No. He continued walking.

The *Falling Angel* was stripped clean, the glowing minimum anything could be reduced to and still be something.

Be reduced to, or begin with?

What was in the mind of that first baby who could be called human, when that baby took its first steps? What a blinding sensation, in those first human eyes, in that first terrible conscious grasping at the tree of life. The black sink of gravity defied: the fear, the gamble, the exultant step; the fall and the pain. But the memory remained of that momentary elevation, that height of vision. And now a little bit of the bound earth had partaken of a viewpoint that had belonged only to the sky.

What terrible spark burned red in that infant mind? How could anyone label a spark so kindling harsh as to make flesh get up and walk? Along what paths must one move to face that spark within oneself?

So dark is death by falling, what could prevail against it?

Rheinallt crossed a random tiny billow of darkness, and began the pilot's enhancement of his mentational field. He could feel that he was descending into a very small gravity well. Twisting, over his shoulder he saw the tiny pseudohorizon blocking the glowing Ship from view.

And then he saw something new. There were footprints behind him, golden soft footprints on the meadow, trailing back to where he had begun enhancement. The footprints were obviously his, as if he had debarked with wet feet from the Ship like a honeybee converting its own pollen. The footprints trailed lesser glimmers between, wet-honey drippings as feet wet from a pool will cast little rivulets before and behind the greater squish and splat of the wet footfalls themselves.

He could feel the energy drain of enhancement, faint tingles within his body like circulation returning to cramped muscles. His reserves were draining into footprints in vacuum, footprints on the pure pseudosurface.

Tracks, the definitive sign of conscious motion. Their color was golden, the mellowness with depth of fine spun gold.

Rheinallt spiraled slowly down the small but steepening cone of the tiny gravity well until he spread solid legs on the single flat square yard, a truncated apex, wondering what an ant feels like in an ant-lion trap. The ant's discovery of the Schwarzchild radius was usually fatal.

So far Rheinallt had been too integrated to age to death,

and as a pilot he had done meadowspace breakthrough only with machine enhancement: Orpheus with water wings. Calmly he faced the prospect of kicking death's dark fence in a new way, here in this black cone of nothing. He turned up his oxygen valve, took a few deep breaths to ventilate previously stale corridors of his brain.

He pushed his own energy down the newly learned paths of mind, watching dry channels flood into vibrant color. Like an oxygen-starved muscle blooded and reviving, his head ached with new strength.

Flexing muscularly, his mind *reached* for a different grip.

Barely did he have time to notice the coruscation in his mind, did *not* have time to mark the resemblance to the coruscation of breakout, before he found himself in free fall. The stars pricked his vision from all directions, the beautiful, distantly hard lamp points of starspace.

He drank in the sight of the skyful of yellow and white stars like the faces of old friends. The band of the galaxy was a smear of milk beyond his shoulder. By any man's measure, civilization was a long way off, but this was the way.

Grinning with the joy of breakthrough, he found himself floating near a small rugged boulder, a few cubic yards of temperature-fractured granite. Affectionately he ran a gloved palm over the coarse, lonely surface, then broke off a thumb-sized outcropping which he tucked in an outside pocket.

A heated ache in his head was increasing rapidly, along with an inner-ear pounding. He had not toned down the enhancement, the new flows of blood, oxygen, and energy; obviously this high level was not sustainable indefinitely. Before restoring his normal levels he wanted to break into subspace again, lest he should prove to be exhausted—beyond recharging to this pitch again—and float here forever.

Again, his mind *reached* for the grip on meadowspace.

Another rainbow in his mind, and he was back in the dark conical hollow. Quickly, smoothly, he throttled back the rush of internal energies. Manually, he turned the suit oxygen valve to only slightly above normal, so he would not hyperventilate just walking back to the caravan.

His facial muscles felt strained too, which puzzled him until he realized he had been grinning continuously so hard it hurt.

In sheer happiness, he climbed up out of the cone and looked

271

down into it. New footprints had appeared where he had touched the meadow. They were of the same golden quality as the first. Not bright in the sense of shiny or glossy, neither did they show signs of a quick fading, the very first he had made continuing to glow serenely.

Rheinallt began walking outward again, faster, until he was in an easy near-lope as fast as a man could move on the meadow. The glowing golden track stretched behind him. The footprints a little way back appeared as small fiery points, and farther back seemed to merge as a thin but solid golden trail.

He stretched his legs and lengthened his pace, and the Ship receded. He sped over a low rise in the meadow, down into the suggestion of a gravitically shallow valley, and then up another rise.

Halting, he breathed deeply, panting with the physical side of his exertion, and having to pull hard with his lungs to snatch the air at a higher rate through the regulator valve. He spun slowly on his heel, looking all around.

Beautiful. A reserve of oxygen, advanced neurological discipline for channeling his own energy flows, and he could *be* his own starship. His helmet echoed with laughter at the wonder of being able to touch the deathly nothingness, pass into and along it and safely out again. And neither a lumbering squeaker nor a steel cacophony of screaming electronics would be needed for his song to flower.

He exulted. Ah, Whitnadys, I love you so; and I know where the flower is.

A starship, or a flower, might be constrained in time, but yet there were means and ways of sharing and propagation. Rheinallt licked sweat from almost-running off his lips and it was sweet as honey.

Yes, he thought, we of the Nation own two hundred thousand yards of the Blue Trail, and thereby we are rich beyond the dreams of avarice. Or so the idea went. He could not deny that it was a pleasant thought. How safe, how cozy and homelike, to have a sure safe route wherewith to skirt death profitably.

With hands on hips Rheinallt surveyed the lamp sparks in the middle distance signifying life. He had little doubt now that in remembrance of Ytrenath he would be able to find some way to maintain communications with Fleurage. That scented

272

world might eventually lose its trail frontage, but it need not be a gourd pinched off from the vine to rot.

However, there were established routes for seekers; and then there were horizons, for makers. He gazed back happily at that first thin and intermittent golden trail. This phase was done, and the Special Caravan was ready to head back to Blueholm. He was sure the other adventurers would follow him back.

Oh, there would be other trips out here later, and even Rheinallt might come here again sometime. No future trip could benefit from a Susannilar or a Detenebrator, but there would be determined investigators and they would continue to probe and to learn.

This expedition was complete. He had a way home. He knew the route of honey, and its source. His very body image felt golden to him.

Away stretched a golden track, over the black from and toward the Ship and the Special Caravan. The caravan was all alight, and there near it loomed the Ship with the tiniest of human sparks moving between. Yes, there, a drop of blood with a flame behind it, the Ship glinted on the horizon of the meadow.

About the Author

Robert Wilfred Franson was born in Eugene, Oregon, and now lives in San Diego, where it rains less. Among fellow visionaries his appearance is usually likened to that of the Russian anarchist, Mikhail Bakunin. Although addicted to the printed word he dislikes desks, preferring to read and write outdoors. In breaks from writing science fiction he's a computer-software consultant. He plants evergreens and onions successfully, enjoys exploring city streets and country roads, and hiking in the desert in the summertime.